I0766951

THE CHRONICLES OF

JEGRA

THE COMPLETE SAGA

VOL. 1

GLADIATRIX OF THE GALAXY

THE CHRONICLES OF

THE COMPLETE SAGA

VOL. 1

BOOKS 1-3

TRISTAN VICK

A REGOLITH PUBLICATIONS BOOK

The Chronicles of Jegra: Gladiatrix of the Galaxy
The Complete Saga Books 1-3 Vol. 1
DEXLUXE HARDCOVER EDITION
By Tristan Vick ©2018. All Rights Reserved

Published by Regolith Publications
First Edition, copyright © September 8, 2020

The Chronicles of Jegra: Origins of the Gladiatrix
A Cosmic Alliance Prequel Novella
By Tristan Vick ©2018. All Rights Reserved
First Edition, copyright © March 30, 2018.

Edited by Sheila Shedd
Box Set cover art by Tum Dechakamphu
Additional art by Jackson Tjota
Opening graphic by Jackson Tjota
Interior book design by Tristan Vick
www.tristanvick.com

ISBN-13: 978-1-950106-08-0
ISBN-10: 1-950106-08-0

CONTENTS

THE CHRONICLES OF

JEGRA

ORIGINS OF THE GLADIATRIX

PROLOGUE

Hushed whispers filled the dimly lit room. Jessica Hemsworth stirred awake to find herself trapped in a cold, dank kennel, the kind meant for keeping and transporting large animals. As the realization that she hadn't merely dreamed it all set in, she seized with fear. She truly had been abducted by aliens.

Eyes wide open, she awoke to a nightmare–trapped inside a cage like common livestock. Half blind without her eyeglasses, she felt around the floor of the kennel and searched for them and let out a sigh of relief when she found them nearby.

Quickly, she put her glasses on and took in a deep breath and practically choked on the myriad of foul odors that assaulted her sense of smell.

The air was musky and hung thick. It stung the insides of her nostrils, making breathing a chore, and caused her eyes to water. So much so, in fact, that she had to take off her glasses just to wipe away the tears streaming from her eyes.

Hands trembling as she fumbled to place her glasses back on, she tried to calm her racing heart before she suffered a panic attack.

Just keep breathing, she told herself. She put her rectangular, black-framed glasses back on and tried to steady herself. After a minute, the tightness in her chest relinquished and she was able to resume breathing normally again.

Once she had centered herself as best she could, she scanned her surroundings and tried to get a better fix on her current situation.

The bad news was that she didn't recognize anything. Even the cacophony of whispers were spoken on foreign tongues and in alien languages unfamiliar to her.

The worse news was she couldn't make out a single thing being said but she most certainly recognized the fear and anxiety in the voices of people who were just as terrified as she was.

The room that she and her fellow captives occupied was fairly large, and obviously for storying livestock. It was so large, in fact, that she couldn't see the outer walls beyond the rows of cages. The kennels merely faded into darkness, which didn't bode well for her, in her estimation.

If not for a series of running lights that stretched around the perimeter of the caged area, she wouldn't have been able to make anything out at all.

As her eyes slowly adjusted to the dim lighting, an alien face, reminiscent of a bat, abruptly pressed itself up against the adjacent bars and startled her.

"Holy crap!" Jessica yelped at the unexpected intruder, shock strangling her voice. She scurried to the corner of her kennel, away from the strange, alien face that stared back at her from between the thick iron bars.

That's when she realized it was just a child. The poor thing scrambled back as she did, obviously startled by her overreaction to it, and scurried into its mother's arms. A child? *Who abducts a child?* she wondered, *other than lowlifes and scumbags?*

Gradually, a litany of alien faces came into view. Sentient beings not of Earth, also trapped in cages just as she was. Jessica pushed her glasses up and looked at them as they, in turn, gazed back at her with a cautious sort of curiosity. All of them seemed just as confused and frightened as she was.

Among the group of outlandish creatures, there were a variety of species with unique physical features. Some were hairless, while others were completely covered in fur. Some were mammalian in appearance; others resembled reptiles, while still others looked much like human beings, but had light green or dark blue skin.

Regardless of their physical differences, however, they all had one thing in common. They were all prisoners, all afraid.

Without a doubt, Jessica's day was already turning out to be one of the absolute worst Mondays of her life.

"Jessica?" a familiar voice called out. It sounded alarmed and relieved at the same time.

She looked around the open spaces between the cages, scanning the faces of those within her scope, trying to pinpoint where the voice had emanated. She heard it call her name again.

"*Pssst.* Jessica! Over here."

Finally, she spotted her boss, Donald Bloom, trapped in a neighboring cage a short distance away from her. Although she found him to be a loathsome, sexist, and generally revolting person, seeing a familiar face just now gave her a huge sense of relief. At least she wasn't alone.

"Donald? Where are we?"

"I don't know," he replied. "Some kind of alien ship, I think. All I remember is being in the parking lot with you and then there was a bright light that came down from the sky. The next thing I know, I was sucked up here and placed in this miserable cage."

"The bright light!" Jessica gasped, the recollection coming back to her. She remembered the light, too, but everything else seemed foggy for some reason, as though she'd been roofied. "I remember it now. It took us up."

"But up to where?"

The gravity of Donald's question did not escape her. But what would aliens want with her? For that matter, what did they want with all the others they'd taken? It didn't make any sense.

"Grem-lek dah-gra, tutti ven grogdon," a voice said.

Jessica looked up from the inside of her cage. Outside, a giant lizard-man stood peering down at her. He gazed at her with light green reptilian eyes and blinked with nictitating eyelids. She shot him a puzzled look, as she hadn't the faintest clue as to what he'd just said.

"Grem-lek dah-gra!" he hissed, repeating the same set of words. He sounded annoyed by the fact that she couldn't understand him. Showing his frustration, he banged her cage with a baton and then stormed off.

Jessica waited for him to leave before deciding it was safe to resume her conversation with Donald.

Once the lizard-man was out of earshot, she gripped the bars to her cage and, pressing her face between them, whispered across the divide of the walkway. "Donald, how long have you been awake?"

"About an hour, I suppose."

"The aliens didn't…" she looked around the room then back at her boss, "probe us or anything while we were unconscious, did they?"

Donald shook his head. "Not that I'm aware of. The only anal pain I'm experiencing is an acute case of hemorrhoids."

That was more information than Jessica cared to know. She shook her head and shoved the off-putting mental image out of her mind.

Without warning, there was a resounding clunk and all the cages opened at the same time. All sorts of strange-looking creatures emerged from their pens, all of them as timorous as she was and looking to each other for answers, although none seemed to have any.

"Grem-dar lagran! Grem-dar largran!" the lizard-man shouted above the din of bewildered whispers. He waved his baton in the air, beckoning them to follow him toward the large doors that stood directly behind him.

From what Jessica could gather, they were in a cargo hold of some kind. And this vessel, if that's really what it was, was some sort of alien trafficking ring. But what kind of beings would kidnap other species, she wondered? And for what purpose? Were they going to be ground up as hamburger and turned into feed or was there some other nefarious reason for their abduction?

The lizard-man tapped his foot and huffed impatiently as he slapped his open palm with the baton and nodded his head, gesturing for everyone to hurry up and move it. Naturally, the other beings all did as requested, forming a long line and then slowly shuffling toward the exit.

For all Jessica knew, they could be sheep being led to slaughter. But seeing as there wasn't any other way out of the room, she didn't feel she had much choice, other than to comply.

The moment an opening appeared in the crowd, she felt a strong nudge at her elbow and looked back to find Donald gesturing for her to keep quiet with one stout finger pressed to his lips. Then he nodded his head at the back of the room, away from where they were headed.

"I'm getting the heck out of here. You'd be wise to do the same."

"I don't think that's such a good idea, Don," Jessica cautioned, eyeing him sternly over the rims of her glasses. But it was too late. He was already turning to make a break for it.

Donald took off down the corridor without a second's hesitation, running in the opposite direction of the double doors. The crowd of aliens swiftly parted, making way for Donald to flee, simply letting him go without so much as a sign of protest. It was clear by their body language that they wanted nothing to do with him or his desperate escape attempt.

"JOGOTH!" lizard-man shouted. "JOGOTH!"

Jessica intuitively knew that it meant stop. The tone of the message was quite clear even if the words were baffling. But Donald's fright-and-flight response was already dialed up to full and there was no way he was going to listen.

Oh, Donald, Jessica thought. *Big mistake.*

The lizard-man let out a perturbed sigh and then pulled out a gun. At least, Jessica assumed it was a gun. In actuality, it resembled a type of ray gun from the old science fiction shows her father used to love watching. Decked out in muted silver, it had all the indications of being a weapon, including a thin line that ran down its side and glowed a menacing red.

With a zap, a red, energy beam blasted out of the device. A crimson streak of light crossed the distance of the room in the blink of an eye and hit Donald squarely in his back.

Donald cried out in agony as his body lit up bright orange, literally glowing with an infusion of energy. Then, his scream suddenly dissipated into the thin air as his body exploded, burning up from the inside out. It was as though he'd internally combusted.

The scattered fragments of his flesh burst into flame before they could make any sort of mess, and dry, gray ash rained down onto the metallic surface of the floor. His body had evaporated right before Jessica's very own two eyes. Nothing remaining of Donald except for the scorch marks of where his boots had been standing when he was shot.

Donald had been vaporized.

Hyperventilating, Jessica tried to pull herself together as she rejoined the line with the other aliens. The line merely reformed, as though this were a common occurrence, and everyone began their previous march toward the large doors at the other end of the room.

Oh, my god. Oh, my god, Jessica thought, her mind racing a million miles a second. *I've been kidnapped by aliens and they just disintegrated my boss.*

1

Soaked to the bone, rain and looked both ways before scurrying across the street. She adjusted her glasses which had started to slide down her nose due to the slickness of the raindrops cascading down her skin, and then rubbed her thumb under her eyes and across both cheeks as she brushed the residue away. It was pouring cats and dogs outside and she'd forgotten her umbrella at home, so she used a newspaper to try and block the fat droplets from drenching her headscarf.

Almost forgetting to lock her car door, she skidded to a stop in the middle of the wet street and pulled out her keys. She clicked the button on the smart-key-chain; her car bleeped from a distance and a sense of deep relief washed over her. At least she didn't have to run all the way back to the parking area to lock her car.

Honk! Honk! An angry driver bleated his horn at her to get out of the road, having been stopped by her diddle-daddling in the street. Fumbling with her free hand to get her keys back into her purse, which hung from her left shoulder, she apologized profusely and turned to leave when a different car, in the opposite lane, whisked by without even slowing down.

The vehicle kicked up a spray of water as it sloshed through a puddle and Jessica took the brunt of the splash.

Dirty water infused with grime from the street and oil from years of heavy traffic flew into Jessica's mouth. She spit and coughed it back out. Finally making it to the other side, she hacked the remaining water up and wiped the excess from her chin. Not that it mattered, since she was drenched through and though.

Jessica pulled out a lens cloth from the inside breast pocket of her jacket and wiped the water from her eyeglasses. It did little good, though, since the cloth was also sopping wet. She sighed, ringed out the cloth, and tucked it back into her inside breast pocket.

Of course! If it weren't for bad luck, I'd have none at all, she thought, as she always did. Although her colleagues said it was all in her mind, she wasn't so sure. It seemed that Murphy's Law was working overtime just for her.

The climb up the stairs of the W. Dale Clark public library in downtown Omaha was a perilous one in the rain. The polished granite concrete stairs grew slick with rainwater as the downpour picked up. To Jessica's dismay, however, the moment she reached the doors, the rain slowed to a gentle trickle.

She turned and looked up at the dark and dusky sky, now breaking with traces of white light that cast angelic beams of radiance down into a patchwork of bright and dark areas across the surrounding cityscape. She frowned. She'd never really had all that much good luck, and this was just another reminder of it. It was as though Mother Nature was rubbing in her face.

As she was entering the building, another guest was leaving, who announced in the way of friendly conversation, "Looks like it's clearing up."

Jessica sighed again. Puffing out her remaining stress, she pushed her glasses up and nodded politely as the man fetched his large, dry umbrella from the umbrella rack then headed outside without so much as having to open it.

After spending ten minutes in the ladies' restroom, trying to blow-dry her mud-stained white blouse using the hand dryer so her floral bra would stop showing through, she headed to the sink and, pulling a hair brush out from her purse, she washed and combed the remaining street filth out of her hair.

The sink gradually filled with a film of dirty brown water, and, although she rinsed her hair using the fresh water several times, she couldn't get the stench of oil out of it. She smelled like an auto mechanic, earthy and greasy on top of being sweaty.

Although it was out of her control, she knew that her boss, Donald Bloom, would make a mountain out of a molehill. And she really didn't want another chastising. Not after the last one he'd given her, when she'd accidentally left the coffee maker on all night.

Even though she had apologized profusely, it didn't seem to matter. He just kept on saying it was an "Unforgivable thing to do." He went on and on about the risk of potential fires in a building full of books and threatened to let her go if it ever happened again.

The way he had drilled into her for the coffee incident made it seem as though she'd almost caused the end of the world.

Now she had to go out there and take her post, looking like a drenched rat. Needless to say, she was not looking forward to Donald's negativity. Especially not after the morning she'd had.

Donald was already waiting for her outside the women's restroom, which wasn't weird at all, and scowled at her as she emerged. He had on a yellow flannel shirt and brown slacks and dark rimmed glasses that made him look like a hipster, although he was a couple decades too old and a bit too stout to pull off the "look."

"You're late," he said, folding his arms and tapping his foot anxiously as though he had nothing better to do than hurry up and wait around to torment her.

"I'm sorry, Mr. Bloom. I've just been having the worst morning."

"Honestly, Jessica, I don't care to hear it. Nancy's shift ended fifteen minutes ago and now I have to pay her over-time. And you know what the city can't afford right now?"

"To pay overtime?"

"To pay overtime!" he exclaimed, without so much as acknowledging she had said it first. It was as though she didn't exist.

"It won't happen again, sir," she apologized.

"It had better not," he grumbled, pushing his glasses back up the bridge of his nose. He shot her a disapproving look, an unnecessary reminder of how pathetic he found her, and then turned and stormed off.

Jessica was on the verge of tears by the time she got to the front counter. She raised her eyeglasses to rub her eyes and wiped away the budding drops with her thumb. Nancy was leaning back in her chair, filing her finger nails. With Nancy, it was a never-ending ritual of grooming and self-pampering. The only reason she took this job was because her husband refused to pay for any more of her spa treatments, so now she had to work to treat herself.

Nancy glanced up and saw how wretched Jessica looked and gasped. "Oh, you poor thing."

"I know, right? Thanks. Finally, somebody who shows an ounce of sympathy."

"No," Nancy said, "I mean, Donald…he fired you. Right?"

"No," Jessica replied, a puzzled look coming over her face.

"Oh, well…*oopsie!* I guess I let that cat out of the bag."

"What are you talking about, Nance?"

"Oh, sweetie. Donald is planning on letting you go. I suppose he's being a gentleman about it though, allowing you to clock in a final days' worth of work before giving you the bad news." Nancy stopped her grooming, tossed her fingernail file back into her bag, and stood up. "Please don't tell him I mentioned it. I could get into big trouble."

Jessica had so many questions, but before she could say a single word, Nancy slung her bag over her shoulder and headed off to yet another afternoon of fancy seaweed treatments and heavenly massages.

Jessica found herself gazing enviously at Nancy as she sauntered off. She loved the fact that Nancy was bold, courageous; she couldn't help but feel in awe at her confidence.

How could she not admire that woman? She was willing to do anything it took to have her way and Jessica knew that if she ever wanted to get anywhere in life, she'd have to strive to be more like Nancy.

The day inched by at a snail's pace, but finally closing-time came. Jessica filed all the library cards and double checked to see if she'd mistyped any of the books. Although most cards were digital these days, some of the older guests still had their original library cards, which meant doing things the old-fashioned way.

Squaring things away, she headed out at 10 PM, just as the security officer was closing up. As she passed him, he gave her an eerie look–as though she wasn't supposed to be in the building, even though it was clear that she worked there.

She hurried down the steps of the library, feeling his eyes chase her away, and ran across the empty street. Arriving at the parking area, she quickly located her car–a modest Toyota Corolla hybrid in unassuming lavender. Upon getting to her car door, however, she was startled to find Donald leaning against the rear end of her vehicle, folded arms, waiting for her.

Dammit, she thought. *He really is going to fire me.*

2

"Donald?" she gasped, surprised to have her boss ambush her at her car after work. A nervous lump formed in Jessica's throat and she choked it down. "Is everything all right?" she asked, pushing up her black frames. She held her arms awkwardly as he turned to greet her, and she looked timidly at him, wondering what this was all about.

"Yes," he said, clearing his throat. A faint smile formed on his paper-thin lips. "Why wouldn't things be all right?"

"Well, because you're waiting for me out here in the middle of the night. I just assumed that—"

"See, that's the problem with you, Jessica Hemsworth," he said, using her full name, which was never a good sign. "You assume too much."

"I guess it's something else I need to work on," she hastily replied. "I didn't mean to come off as sounding presumptuous. It's just that—"

"That's fine, Jessica" he interrupted, not caring about what she had to say. "But I think we need to discuss your future here at the library."

"My future? What is that supposed to mean?" *I knew it,* she thought, growing defensive. Her job was everything to her. Library science was the one thing she was good at and she sure as hell didn't go to graduate school to flip burgers.

"Jessica, how do I say this? It just seems that things with you, in the workplace, just aren't working out."

"But I've been here for over eight years," she stated quite emphatically, hoping that her seniority would persuade him to reconsider.

"Indeed. And in those eight years, six of which have been under my purview, I just feel your mediocrity is not the kind of message we want to be sending."

"Mediocrity?" she balked. The least he could do was attempt to veil the insult, but no. Angry, she snapped, "I work at a library, Donald. Library science isn't exactly a trending social fad at the moment, not as *hip* as you seem to think. But it's necessary, and I take my job quite seriously."

Surprised by her talking back, he raised an eyebrow at her. After a brief pause, he took a step toward her.

She immediately regretted losing her temper and apologized. "I'm so sorry, Donald. I shouldn't have snapped. It's just been…well…it's just been one of those days."

"And I hate to do this to you, really, I do. But…"

There it was. The big, fat, drawn out *but.* "Donald. Don. Please. I need this job."

He took another step closer. "I know, and I'm sorry. But my hands are tied. There's nothing I can do."

"Wait! I can do better. Just give me one more chance," she pleaded, throwing up her hands frantically. She was seconds away from dropping to her knees and begging for her job.

"Well," he said, scratching his chin, as though he were mulling over other possibilities. He took another step closer to her; they were now standing nose to nose. "There may be one thing."

"Anything," she said, her spirits perking up at the chance to redeem herself. "Anything at all. Just name it."

Donald threw his arm out and pressed it against the driver's side window of her car, boxing her in tight. Pressing his body into hers, a lascivious grin spread across his thin lips as he pushed his bulky glasses up his pudgy nose. "Anything?"

She blinked at him twice but did not reply. She didn't have the words. She knew exactly where this was going and had pretty good idea of what was on his mind. It made her sick to her stomach just thinking about it.

Donald puckered his lips and moved in to steal a kiss, which caused every muscle in Jessica's wiry body to tense up. As he came within centimeters of making contact, she suddenly reeled back.

"Don, please. This isn't appropriate," she said.

Indecent as he was being, Jessica didn't know what to do. Should she run? Should she close her eyes and pretend it wasn't happening? No. She knew that if she fled, he'd merely hand her a pink slip the next day and that would be the end of it.

Part of her told her she should just go through with it. Save her job at any cost. Pull a Nancy. Another part of her grew furious at the fact that she found herself in this situation at all.

For him, it was just a business transaction. He'd get what he wanted, and she'd get what she wanted. For her, though, it was her life. Her body. She knew that if she went through with it she'd have to live with the deluge of never-ending regret and self-loathing that would inevitably follow.

Jessica couldn't possibly imagine how this Monday could get any worse, seeing as it was already shaping up to be one of the worst of her entire existence.

Donald forced himself on her; he reached his hand under her blouse and began groping at her padded bra in search of her breasts. She squirmed with equal parts anxiety and disgust, but she didn't shove him away. After all, she desperately wanted to keep her job. And if all he wanted was to fondle her barely-existent breasts, well, she supposed that she could live with that.

A fine film of sweat glistened on his bald forehead as he heated up rather quickly and tore open Jessica's blouse-top, sending buttons careening off into the night. Her collarbone exposed, he began plastering her chest with lustful kisses.

"Donald, I don't think we should be..." Jessica began, but he merely ignored her and groped her breast so hard she thought she'd scream. She clinched her jaw and fought off the urge to yelp from the intense discomfort. "No," she insisted. "This isn't right."

"You turn me away now," warned Donald, "and I'll see to it you don't work in this town again. I'm the only one who cares enough to keep someone like you on his payroll."

"Well, technically I'm on the city's payroll," she corrected.

"Nobody likes a smarty-pants, Jessica," he fired back. With that he pulled down her shirt around her shoulders, tearing it even more, and clawed at her bra.

Before he could free a nipple, however, a bright light came down from the sky and landed on both of them. It lit them up like a spotlight.

Startled by the sudden brilliance, Donald abruptly stopped what he was doing and looked up, shielding his eyes with the palm of his hand. At the same time, Jessica quickly did up her bra and wrapped her torn blouse around her.

Embarrassment quickly turned to anger and Donald shouted up at the bright light and shook his fist. "Hey, up there! This ain't no peepshow! Mind your own damn business!"

"I don't think they can hear you, Don."

Donald shot Jessica a disgruntled look. She ignored his sour face, adjusted her glasses, and squinted into the strange light. Although it was kind of a nuisance, she was grateful for the interruption.

"It's probably just some teenage twerps messing about with a drone," she said. "The moment they realize the show is over they'll get bored and leave." She felt it necessary to add that the show was, indeed, over. And if the dejected look on his face was any sign, he'd got her message loud and clear.

It appeared that Donald wanted to give her a piece of his mind, but before he could even open his mouth, the most peculiar thing happened. His body starting to break into small, hexagonal fragments of light. Each light packet, to call it that, carried a piece of him up into the sky.

She'd never seen anything like it. After a few moments of Donald being systematically disassembled and taken into the sky, she looked down at her hands to find that the same thing was happening to her, too. "Oh, my," she gasped.

Perhaps the strangest thing was that, she knew she should feel terrified, but she wasn't. Not in the slightest. In fact, it didn't even bother her one bit. It was all rather quite painless.

Actually, whatever it was that was happening to her felt kind of nice. Like basking in the warm glow of sunlight on a wooden floor on a nice summer day.

As her hand glittered away on the small packets of light, she closed her eyes and thought to herself, *this isn't such a bad way to go out. At least now I won't have to suffer being sexually molested by this asshole*, she thought.

3

An hour after her abduction, Jessica sobbed lightly to herself as she sat beside her cage and gazed at the blackened remains of Donald, now singed into the floor like a permanent shadow. Small wisps of white smoke rose from the smoldering remains and spiraled upward until they faded into nothingness. Though seeing Donald evaporate was beyond shocking, she had to pull herself together. Now was not the time to lose her shit. Donald lost his shit and look at where that got him.

With a deep breath she sank to her knees, perched on her heels in the middle of the aisle, and gathered her thoughts. The past twenty-four hours had been a blur. One moment she'd was getting groped by her perverted boss in the parking lot, the next they'd been caged like lab rats to be experimented on or worse, and now...now Donald was dead.

Although it was in poor taste to think ill of the recently deceased, it wasn't like Donald had been aiming to win any popularity contests. Hell, he'd barely avoided being a rapist. If it wasn't for the alien intervention, to call it that, Jessica knew that she'd have had a much stickier, not to mention more demoralizing, problem on her hands than being kidnapped by extraterrestrials.

In the end, her only regret was not having told him what a scumbag she thought he was before he'd been inconveniently vaporized. But, then again, she supposed that this turn of events was, perhaps, the only real silver lining in all this. As cruel as it sounded, at least now she had one less problem to contend with. He was out of her hair. For good. And she wouldn't have to keep looking over her shoulder all the time dreading his lingering presence as he watched her with an obsessive, lecherous gaze that betrayed his depraved intentions.

"Le'Dagra!" an angry voice called out from behind her.

She looked over her shoulder to see a giant fury creature with red eyes looking down at her. He hadn't any mouth or snout, just a flat, almost cute face with a couple of oversized eyes and gray fur as soft as a hamster. He was about a foot taller than her. He looked down and repeated his words.

"Le'Dagra!"

"I'm sorry," she said. "I don't know what that means."

Irritated by her inability to grasp his meaning, the creature reached past her head and pointed toward the line with a long finger, drawing her attention to the fact that it had already begun moving along and she was holding everyone else up.

"Oh, right." Jessica felt embarrassed and quickly turned and rejoined the procession of aliens.

Together, they shuffled in the direction of the lizard-man who waved his baton in the air and grunted more commands at them. Although she didn't understand a single word he was saying, she figured she'd merely follow suit. *When in Rome*, after all.

Besides, drawing too much attention to herself was the last thing she wanted right now. Especially after the whole ordeal that Donald had sparked. She didn't want to be grouped in with any rabble-rousers or lowlifes, so she did her best to keep her head down and not step on any toes.

The line moved up again and the fuzzy alien urged her along with a gentle nudge. "Gradack!" he said impatiently. "Gradack!"

She didn't need to be told twice to realize he wanted her to speed it up. "All right, all right. I'm going," she said defensively, raising her hands and easing forward with the rest of the line.

As she made her way up queue, the creature continued to complain to his comrade behind her back. She didn't understand the words that he uttered, but she could tell by his tone he wasn't at all happy. She was amazed that even other species had their share of troubles and that a bad day was a bad day, regardless of where you were from.

Once they had all amassed in front of the large cargo bay doors, they were ordered to stand in two rows that faced the exit. The lizard-man shouted something indiscernible and then slammed his fist on the control panel.

The giant metal doors lurched and then slowly slid apart. Standing at the center was a handsome man who looked like a mix between Johnny Depp and a Smurf. He had the most luxuriant blue skin and the whitest hair she'd ever seen.

His outfit appeared to be created from a mixture of different eras and styles. He had a fancy Baroque styled shirt with plumed scarf tucked into a fancy vest; he wore a long leather trench coat and sported a weathered pirate's hat to top it off.

"Antor de'Gralli, eptu sven Mardok," the green lizard thing shouted, gesturing with a wave of his hand in the man's general direction by way of introduction.

"Ladies and gentlemen," the man said in perfectly spoken English. "My name is Antor de'Gralli, and I'm but a humble merchant, purveyor of talent, and renowned smuggler. As many of you know, my business is trade, and business is good. It's what makes the galaxy go 'round, you know." He took a deep bow.

Rising back up, he paced up and down the row of aliens, inspecting all their weary faces. He examined the whole lot of them at least twice until, finally, his eyes settled on Jessica. "You've abducted a human, I see."

"Igdar belerian muck dash!" the lizard-man growled.

Antor waved his hand dismissively. "Don't worry, friend. I won't be reporting you for illegal poaching. But I will be taking her off your hands. And those two over there," he added at the last minute, pointing to a scrawny reptilian and one of the furry creatures.

"If you'll come this way," Antor said to Jessica, extending his hand and offering it to her, "we'll get you cleaned up and presentable."

"Presentable?" Jessica asked, reluctantly taking his hand.

"For the auction, of course!" he gladly announced. "The Intergalactic Gladiatorial Syndicate is looking for some exciting new faces for this season's matches. And I think you'll be just the thing they're looking for."

"Did you just say gladiatorial matches?" she asked, her voice cutting off as her throat clinched with dread.

"It's the hottest thing this side of the Empire, my dear. Reality televid at its finest."

"Great. Just great," Jessica lamented. Not only had she been fired from her job, sexually assaulted by her boss, and abducted by aliens, but now she was being sold into slavery and forced into some kind of twisted reality TV death-sport.

Needless to say, this was, without a doubt, the absolute worst Monday in the whole history of Mondays.

"If you'll come this way, my dear. We'll take my ship," Antor said. "It's faster than this old heap of space junk."

Jessica accompanied Antor onto his shuttle craft, just the right size for all four occupants, and they decoupled from the large smuggling vessel.

As they pulled away, Jessica could see that, from outside, it looked like a car engine floating in space. She turned her head and looked out the starboard window as they moved away from the Earth at a blistering speed. In a matter of minutes, they passed the moon, and that's when she heard a strange murmuring sound emanating from the engines. Antor hit a few switches on the control dash and suddenly, the stars outside stretched into long white streaks that seemed to trail on forever.

"Are we...?"

"Traveling though hyperspace? Yes, my dear," Antor replied, swiveling around in his chair. He pulled out a small device and held it up for her to see. "The trip is rather long, so I'm giving you a sedative."

"No, wait!" Jessica said, throwing up a hand in protest. But she wasn't fast enough. Antor pressed the device to her neck and there was an abrupt hiss of air followed by what felt like a bee sting. "Ow!" Jessica yelped, reaching up and touching the welt on her neck.

Unable to fight it, she quickly grew weary and slumped over in her seat. That injection was the last thing she remembered before waking up in a new cage. This time, inside a massive gladiatorial arena.

4

A thunderous boom shook the inhabitants of Arena City, down on the desert moon of Thessalonica, as the Dagon royal battle cruiser, *The Dreadnaught*, jumped into the system.

Thessalonica, an oasis mottled, sand-laden moon with only a crab-grass like cactus plant with seasonal lavender blossoms as indigenous flora was roughly the size of Mars. The dusty ball was the only habitable moon of a three-moon system that orbited the Dagon homeworld, called Dagon Prime—a beautiful blue-green orb that hung in a remote sector of space, approximately three hundred light years from Earth.

The massive Dagon vessel, which contained a crew compliment of over a thousand, looked like a double-pronged blade floating in the sky, but it wasn't at all sleek or slender. The slit down the center traveled halfway up the length of the ship and ended at the bridge, which sat just above the wedge.

The cruiser was fatter at the aft section than at its front, shaped as though two isosceles triangles had been mashed together. The ugly geometric monstrosity was covered with hundreds of disrupter canons, laser turrets, and missile bays. It wasn't pretty by any stretch of the imagination, but it sure as hell was domineering.

Emperor Rhadamanthus Dakroth linked his cobalt blue hands behind his back as he strode across the deck of his bridge in his white military uniform. His long, silvery hair flowed behind him as his metal-toed boots clanked across the cold, metallic surface until he came to a standstill in front of a large view portal. Pausing to take in the vista, he looked out at the sand-laden sphere which sat directly ahead of his massive vessel.

Although there was little-to-no green on the medium sized moon, there were areas where spring water allowed sage plants, violet fountain grasses, purple thistle, and other desert flora to grow. In the spring on Thessalonica, vast swaths of light purple spread across the desert landscape. It was a stunning sight to behold, which is why the emperor had always felt a certain fondness for his unassuming little moon.

More importantly, however, Thessalonica was the home to Arena City, the number-one ranked planetary member of the Intergalactic Gladiatorial Syndicate.

The popular blood-sport was endlessly lucrative for the emperor, so, he had expanded his barbaric death matches to other systems across the Dagon empire. This season would mark the hundred and seventy-fifth year anniversary of the galactic gladiatorial games.

Now, beamed into every home via televid, over seventy-million viewers tuned in each week as combatants from countless worlds went at each other for a chance to become the reigning champion supreme.

The fame, honor, and wealth of becoming a well-liked champion meant one could retire with an amassed fortune that rivaled even the emperor's. And it was this sport which kept the people's mind off the war Dakroth currently waged against the malevolent Nyctan Empire.

The Nyctans were a hyper-religious species that had a long-standing feud with the Dagon Empire, and now the two giants battled over who had control over the Golden Trade Route between the Seyfferian Republic, Nyctan, and Dagon Prime. Whoever controlled the trade routes had influence in all nine-systems of the Commonwealth. And Dakroth already controlled seven of the systems.

Just back from his latest campaign, Emperor Dakroth decided to make an appearance at this week's match. He had been informed that several fresh faces would be going up against the current standing champion and that one of these newcomers was a Human.

It was extremely rare for Humans to ever get caught up in galactic affairs, seeing as how their planet was still quite primitive. It was rarer still to find one this deep into the territories of the Commonwealth. But every once in a while, one showed up and made a scene. Humans, he thought, were always quite entertaining.

The Commonwealth was simply the name given to all nine major systems and the charted territories thus far. It wasn't an entity so much as a collegian of independent systems; systems which Emperor Dakroth plotted to overtake in the near future.

It was his hope that once he locked down the trade route, he could begin expanding the empire into the outer rim territories. First, he'd take the Seyfferian Republic. After which only his enemy, the Nyctan Empire, would remain.

Until then, however, he knew he had to keep the morale of his crew up. So, with that in mind, he treated those in his service to the best seats in the amphitheater in Arena City. They could enjoy the spectacle and he could make his appearance for all the systems to see.

Being emperor had its perks. And showing up in the stands and being beamed directly into the homes of over seventy-million televid watchers meant the entire empire would see his face and marvel at his graciousness as he gave them what they craved. Mindless violence, in the form of entertainment.

At the same time, he solidified himself as an ever-present figure. He was everywhere all at once. He was fighting a war on the front line. He was sitting in the front row at the gladiatorial games, smiling and waving at the crowd. He was inside everyone's homes on their televid screens. There was no escaping his presence. It was for good reason the emperor of Dagon was appropriately referred to as the Emperor of the Galaxy.

Right now, however, he shelved his ambitions for a later time and allowed himself the small pleasure of enjoying the show. Looking forward to the match, he tapped his data bracelet and set the coordinates to beam down to his personal booth.

Bright yellow light whisked him away on small hexagonal packets of energy, disassembling him piece by piece. Moments later, he rematerialized again, the same hexagonal blocks of energy rebuilding him from the ground up. And there he was, standing in the royal balcony of the stadium.

The crowd roared with applause at his arrival and, raising his blue hand to great them, he threw back his cape and stepped up to the edge of his viewing gallery. Televid drones swooped down and got a closeup of his blue face, and he smiled. Raising both arms, he signaled that he was about to speak and the crowd fell silent.

He waited for the hush to fall across the whole arena, then, in a commanding voice, the emperor shouted, "Let the games begin!"

The crowd erupted into a fever pitch as they screamed out in elation. A couple of attractive green-skinned women lifted up their shirts, flashing their forest-green nipples at him. He smiled at them and beckoned them to come join him. At the same time, a servant appeared by his side and offered him a blue ale. He took the glass and held it out, sloshing the bright blue liquid around as though it were a find wine.

In the distance, someone started chanting, "Long live the emperor! Long live the emperor!" Soon enough, the whole arena was doing the same and Dakroth smiled and waved again. Looking toward a televid drone which hovered near his balcony, he raised his glass to the audiences at home, downed the drink in one go, then tossed it down into the arena. The moment the glass broke the warriors circled around and made ready to fight to the death.

5

"KaLaar the magnificent!" blared the two-headed serpentine announcer who watched from a special booth high up in the stands of the gladiatorial arena. The crowd went wild.

Dead bodies lay strewn out across the blood-soaked sands of the arena—over half of them missing their heads—as a massive, six-armed lizard creature with a red fin on top of his bald head stepped into the center of the hushed battleground.

KaLaar, a veteran warrior of the Intergalactic Gladiator Syndicate, had remained victorious for seventeen bouts and was this season's preferred favorite throughout most of the sector.

High above the open roof of the arena hovered Emperor Dakroth's royal battlecruiser. A quaint reminder to the inhabitants of the various planets in attendance that his dominion throughout the Dagon empire was absolute.

Fresh in from a new conquest, Dakroth was attending the games for the first time in five Keks. He now stood upon his personal balcony and watched the games with half-hearted interest.

The games paled in comparison to the thrill of real combat. These were just a mundane facsimile. Nothing of much excitement ever happened. *I suppose I must make these appearances,* he thought dully, *if only to keep my glowing presence in the minds of the rabble.*

KaLaar raised a battle axe and a longsword high above his head, crossing them with a resounding clangor as battle worn steel scraped steel. He boomed, "I salute you!" His voice rose above the white noise of the roaring crowd like a hero of old.

Emperor Dakroth batted his heavily kohl painted eyes and tossed his long silvery hair across his blue-skinned shoulder. He tugged at his white tunic and then raised his arm high into the air. The crowd fell silent and waited with baited breath for the emperor's final arbitration.

In the sand, scurrying back on all fours, was a rather scrawny cat-person. He had the appearance of a human in almost every respect but for his fur coat, yellow eyes, pointy-tipped ears, and obvious tail.

The poor thing looked half-starved and was little more than a bag of bones. The cat-man was dressed in oversized battle armor that was badly gouged and dented and barely fit his undernourished form. He stared up at KaLaar with fearful, yellow, cat eyes and hissed. *"Hssssk!"*

KaLaar ignored the puny thing groveling in the sand and continued showing off for the spectators. Raising his arms into the sky, he turned slowly, scanning all the faces of the roaring crowd. Finally, he came full circle and looked up at the emperor's blue, poker-face.

Emperor Dakroth held out his arm out and gave a decisive thumbs down, signaling for KaLaar to finish off his less than worthy opponent. The crowd erupted with bloodthirsty applause.

Jessica peered through the bars of her cell, which was tucked away in what appeared to be the entrance to the arena by way of an underground hypogeum, and watched the spectacle with wide-eyed wonder.

She gazed past the row of guards standing just beyond the gate and looked out at the events of the arena with profound curiosity.

Several green female aliens in the stands, the same species which doted on the emperor in his balcony, hollered lustful cat-calls at KaLaar and pulled their shirts up, exposing their breasts along with their forest green nipples for all to leer at. They looked mostly human but for their *eau de nil* skin and luxuriant hair which shone viridescent under the twin suns of this strange new world.

Jessica turned her attention back toward the action in the arena in time to see KaLaar spin around and, with one swift swipe of his battle ax, lop off the cat-man's head. The wretched creature's noggin hit the ground and rolled right up to Jessica's cage. She gasped and recoiled, scurrying back from the prison crate's bars. Gazing down at the yellow eyes that stared vacantly up at her, she whispered, "Poor kitty."

"Don't worry," a nearby voice said to her. "You'll get used to it. Eventually, we all get used to it. The violence. The blood. The stench of it all."

Jessica looked to either side of her; there were two additional cages besides hers. On her right was a large rhinoceros type man-beast who merely grunted at her. He obviously wasn't the chatty type. To her left, however, was a satyr.

The satyr looked at her with his yellow goat eyes and smiled. "The name's Grendok. A pleasure to make your acquaintance, miss…?"

"I'm Jessica Hemsworth."

"Nice to meet you, Jegra," Grendok said, muddling her name.

"Jessica," she corrected. But he didn't seem to take notice of his mistake. After a moment, she asked, "Where am I?"

"You're in the slave pits of Emperor Dakroth's gladiatorial arena—the Jewel of the Dagon empire, as they fondly call it." Grendok eyed Jessica up and down and ran his fingers through the orange goatee on his chin. "If you don't mind my saying so, you seem to be a little out of place for a gladiatrix."

"Out of place?"

Grendok bowed his head apologetically. "What I meant was, you seem too young to be conscripted into the games."

"I'm twenty," Jessica said, pushing her thick framed glasses back up her nose.

"Twenty what?" Grendok asked.

"Twenty years old," Jessica replied.

"If that's anything like twenty cycles, then you're extremely young. Tell me, girl. How'd you come to find yourself in the gladiatorial matches, anyway?"

"I was abducted by aliens," she answered.

"Ah, yes," Grendok said knowingly. "Poachers."

"Poachers?" asked Jessica.

"Basically, a group of greedy asshole hunter-types who poach the far-off regions of the outer rim, beyond the jurisdiction of the Dagon empire. They snatch beings from their worlds to sell to the slavers for a handsome profit."

"So, what? I'm a slave, then?"

"You and everyone else thrown down into the pit. The slavers maintain a steady business by handing fresh blood over to the Intergalactic Gladiator Syndicate. It's all quite illegal, I assure you. But nobody seems to care about enforcing the law these days. All they care about is their entertainment and having a good 'ole time at the arena."

"I can relate," Jessica replied. "Back home we have something similar. It's called *Keeping Up with the Kardashians*."

"It sounds barbaric," Grendok said. "Oh, it is," informed Jessica. "It most certainly is."

Suddenly, a massive, muscle bound guard with bright blue skin came over and rattled the cages. "You there!" he said, pointing his blue finger at Jessica. "What are you called?"

"I'm—"

"Jegra the Merciless," Grendok interrupted.

Although he'd hand-picked her gladiator name for her without even asking, she deferred to his wisdom, seeing as he sounded quite knowledgeable about everything so far.

"Fine. Jegra the Merciless, you're up next," the guard grumbled.

"Up next? What do you mean I'm next? You mean I have to fight?" Jessica snorted and laughed at the absurdity of the very notion of it. But when she realized he wasn't kidding, her smirk melted from her face and turned to dazed disbelief. "Oh," she said, her voice fading to a meek whisper. *"Shit."*

6

Before she had time to process the direness of her situation, the guard returned and pulled out a high-tech cylindrical tube that had a blue light on one end and a spray nozzle on the other.

Without warning, he reached through her bars and jammed the device into the side of her neck. A harsh sounding hiss was followed by a sharp pain as it injected her with something.

"Ouch!" Jessica yelped, reaching up and touching her neck. This time the sting left a swollen lump, but apparently the guard didn't care as he was already off to the next cage.

"Don't fret, Jegra. It's just some medication to ensure your health is maximally optimized. They don't want unfit warriors now, do they?" Grendok laughed to himself and then leaned back in his cage.

"I feel sick," Jessica said, her complexion draining of all color until she was as pale as a sheet.

"It'll pass," Grendok assured her.

Without warning, Jessica threw up all over her own feet.

"Then, again, I could be wrong," Grendok added, correcting himself.

Jessica stumbled back in her cage and fell onto her butt, knocking her eyeglasses off in the process. "I'm so dizzy," she informed her strange friend. Grendok merely raised an eyebrow and watched Jegra with a keen interest.

Unexpectedly, Jessica's body started to grow larger. It was just like the story of *Alice in Wonderland* when Alice had eaten the sweets and grew into a giant girl. Like Alice from the storybook, Jessica's arms grew large and powerful.

At the same time, her legs became strong and defined, her every muscle swelling with raw strength. Her abs were a six-pack to envy, and she even increased in height by over a foot, going from five-feet four inches to six-foot five inches. She grew so much her clothes began to stretch and tear as her body rippled with the musculature of a body builder.

"Odd," Grendok said as he stared at his transformed prison mate.

"What is?" she asked, still feeling a bit disoriented. She shook her head and tried to regain her focus.

"I've never seen anyone react that way to getting the shot. Anyway, I suppose it doesn't matter." He leaned back in his cage and started chewing on a piece of straw he had plucked off the ground.

Hunched over, Jessica shuffled around under her new weight, trying to get comfortable in her cramped cage and, in the process, accidentally crushed her glasses under her own foot. "Oops," she said picking up her shattered glasses and watching as the broken shards of the lenses fell out of the frames.

"Hope you didn't need those," Grendok said.

"Under ordinary circumstances, I would," Jessica said, squinting at the satyr with one eye and then switching to the next as she checked both. "But it seems my vision has completely cleared up." Continuing her self examination, she looked down at the rest of her body to find something quite unexpected. "Holy shitballs!"

"What is it?" Grendok asked, anxiously leaning in to see what it was that had so excited his cellmate.

Unable to believe her own eyes, Jessica grabbed her breasts in both hands and squeezed them tightly. Her cleavage mashed up like two inflated beach balls and she laughed. It was unbelievable. In a matter of second, she'd gone from a meager C-cup to an astonishing 42 J bust size. "My tits are huuuge!" she exclaimed.

Grendok rolled his eyes. "Yes. It would appear they are. You must be very proud."

Struggling just to fit inside the confines of her cage, Jessica kicked out a foot and inadvertently burst the door wide open. The steel lock on the hinge broke clean off, snapping like a brittle twig.

Embarrassed by her clumsiness and inability to gauge her nascent strength, she quickly reached over and pulled the prison bars shut. Jessica looked around nervously to see if anyone had noticed her mishap, but it was only her and Grendok–and rhino-man–who just sat in his cage drooling like an idiot.

"Is he all right?" Jessica asked, jutting a thumb over toward the other prisoner.

"He'll be fine," Grendok said, flicking his hand as though he were brushing away a pesky insect. "Don't pay him any mind."

Just then, the guard returned with burlap sack full of body armor and an assortment of other protective gear. Stepping up to their cages, he dumped the contents of the bag onto the ground and said, "Put this on."

With that he unlocked Grendok's cage, but when he came to Jessica's cage he looked down to find the lock already unhinged. He shrugged and turned and walked off.

"Wait," Jessica called out. "What about him?" She opened her cage door and stepped out next to Grendok, who was trying on different leather breast plates. Realizing that the guard wasn't coming back any time soon, Jessica turned and smashed her fist down on the lock to the rhino's cage. It popped off and fell to the ground in three pieces. Jessica gasped and then started laughing as she examined her hand. There wasn't a scratch on her. She was strong. *Really* strong. Like She-Hulk level strong.

"Here," Grendok said, handing Jessica a leather breastplate. "This seems like it will fit you."

Jessica slipped the armor on over her shredded shirt and massive chest and strapped it down tight. Her cleavage swelled, filling the top of the breastplate, but she didn't mind. Glancing down at her legs, which were as bare as the day she was born, she noticed her pants were all but torn to ribbons.

She doubted her tightly stretched underpants would last a gladiatorial match and so bent down and rummaged through the pile of armor until she found what appeared to be steel bikini bottoms. "What in the world is this?" she asked, fishing them out from the pile and holding them out in front of her to better inspect them.

Grendok looked over and chuckled. "It seems to be the chastity belt of a KreeZok woman. They tend to be on the larger side of species, in general. It's rather extraordinary, though. They release a pheromone so potent that every known species of male in the galaxy goes mad with lust and instantly tries to mate with them."

"Which would explain the need for armored underpants, I presume."

"Precisely," Grendok answered, shooting her a wink. "It makes the competition rather one-sided."

Jessica shrugged and slipped them on over her thinly stretched underpants. To her surprise, they fit her like a glove. Grabbing some leather belts, she strapped three to her left leg.

"What are you doing?" Grendok asked.

"I assume that there will be plenty of discarded weapons on the battle field. This way I can arm myself to the teeth if need be."

"Good thinking," Grendok said, finding a large belt and throwing it across his shoulder like a sash.

When the guard returned, he wasn't alone. There were three other soldiers dressed in black armor with long, flowing purple capes. They had on helmets that concealed their faces and carried spears with brass plated tips that shone gold in the light of the arena.

"Rise," the blue skinned guard said, gesturing for the next fighters to stand up and form a line, and they did as requested of them. "You will step out onto the sands of the arena. There you will gather at the center and pay your respects to the emperor. Only after he has given his blessing, may you select a weapon and take your positions. Should you fall out of line or disrespect the emperor in anyway, you will be summarily executed. Do you understand what I have relayed to you?"

Jessica nodded along with Grendok and then looked over at the rhino dude, who continued to drool.

The guard turned and threw open the gates to the holding area, and the black armored guards escorted the three warriors out onto the field.

Up in the stands, Emperor Dakroth smiled and then took his seat. The two green women who joined him in his private gallery pressed their bikini-clad bodies into his back and shoulders and rubbed against him like a couple of horny teenagers. Tossing his silvery hair over his shoulder, Dakroth leaned back in his oversized chair, a replica of his throne in the Royal Palace down on Dagon Prime, and let his gaze settle on the first few contestants.

An Earth woman stepped out onto the sands of the arena and, looking like a fish out of water, caught his eye. Taken by her beauty, he raised an eyebrow and a subtle grin crept across his lips. *Well, this ought to be interesting,* he thought.

It wasn't every day a Human turned up in the heart of the empire. Especially not one as stunning as this. Crossing his legs, he kicked back and prepared to enjoy the show.

7

"**We who are** about to die, salute you!" Grendok shouted up toward Emperor Dakroth. The blue skinned emperor nodded, but before he could raise his hand to signal the start of the games, the rhino-man to Jessica's right roared out.

Startled, Jessica jumped in fright and managed to step aside just as the rhino-man smashed two of the black guards together, incapacitating them. He quickly grabbed one of their spears and launched it at the emperor.

The spear whistled viciously as it sailed through the air, traveling right for the emperor's head. Dakroth, however, merely tilted his head to the side just the right amount to narrowly escape the spear's piercing flight.

Although, to Jessica, his movements seemed too calculated for the miss to have been a mere coincidence. Rather, it seemed Dakroth had had some expert training in the art of war.

One of the green skin women screamed as the spear had nearly taken her head off, and her friend fainted. Dakroth ignored both women's skittishness and kept his gaze fixed on the enchanting Earth woman who gazed back up at him with her brown eyes.

"Jegra," Grendok said, touching Jessica's arm. She looked back and the satyr nodded towards the weapons. "Come, it has begun."

"But the emperor hasn't..." Jessica looked over to see the rhino rushing the wall of the arena.

The large creature aimed his solitary horn at the wall and smashed into it with a resounding force that shook the ground. The wall cracked and chipped and shocked gasps broke out in waves across the crowd.

Up in the stands, the green skinned women screamed in fangirl fright, yet the emperor didn't exhibit an ounce of concern. He merely watched with, perhaps, a slightly higher-piqued interest.

"Jegra," Grendok called out again. When Jessica turned, he tossed her a giant, double sided axe. Although he had to use both arms and swing with all his might just to toss it to her, she reached out and caught it by one hand.

Amazed by her new abilities, Jessica laughed and swung the battle axe about as though it weighed nothing. When she turned back toward the action, the rhino-man had leaped up and was climbing the wall to try and get to the emperor. She wondered if her strength might even equal his as she watched as his fingers pierce the rockface as easily as the beak of a crow pierces stale bread.

The rhino-man ascended to the booth where the emperor stood waiting, and clambered over the railing. To Jessica's amazement, Emperor Dakroth didn't show an ounce of fear. The rhino rose up before the emperor, an obvious display of intimidation with his bulky mass, and raised its two large fists high above its head. Frothing at the mouth with bloodthirsty rage, the rhinoceros roared, "I KILL YOU NOW!"

The entire arena fell silent in anticipation of what would happen next.

Emperor Dakroth casually reached up and brushed away the strands of saliva which plastered his regal tunic, then lifted a single finger and pointed it at the rhino's chest. A hot beam of red light shot out of his blue fingertip and passed directly through the rhino-man's torso. The neon flash of the laser beam happened so quickly that if you had blinked you would have missed it.

Gray smoke rose into the air. The rhino-man gulped hard and looked down at his torso only to find a hole in his chest the size of a wagon wheel. The edges of the gaping crater still glowed orange-hot. There was no blood, however, as everything had been instantly cauterized by the intense heat of the laser blast.

Wide-eyed with shock, the rhino-man tottered on wobbly feet and then tripped over the balcony railing and toppled over the edge.

The massive beast plummeted back into the arena and hit the ground with a resounding thud. But he didn't feel the crushing blow of the unforgiving ground racing up to him, for he was dead before he even hit the ground—his heart vaporized. He'd never had a chance to realize what had happened.

The crowd went wild and the entire stadium erupted with cheers. "Long live Dakroth!" they chanted in admiration of their mighty emperor–the man with silver hair and blue skin who could fell his enemies with but one finger.

"And that's why he's the emperor," Grendok said through clinched teeth.

It seemed to Jessica that maybe Grendok nurtured a bit of a grudge against the emperor. Perhaps it was jealously, perhaps something else. Whatever it was, she recognized the general sense of resentment of not being able to do anything about it, the anger of being powerless against a tyrant who exhibited near omnipotence. She recognized it because powerless is exactly how she had felt her entire life.

"Ladies and gentlemen," the two-headed serpent announcer bellowed over the intercom. "Once again entering the arena is the one and only...KaLaar the Magnificient!"

Another uproarious round of applause erupted from the crowd. KaLaar sauntered into the arena, and brushed his red fin back. It snapped back into place as soon as he removed his hand, creating quite the effect. He then turned toward the emperor, threw a fist over his heart as a show of respect, and took a deep, reverent bow.

"Begin!" the emperor boomed, giving his blessing.

Jessica looked at Grendok, who'd slunk back to the edge of the arena and picked up some chains with spiked balls at the end. He'd also found a shield.

When Jessica turned back around, KaLaar was standing before her. He looked down at her and sneered. Jessica slowly took a step backward. Even at her new height of six-eight, KaLaar stood more than two feet over her.

Throwing out all six of his arms, he leaned in and roared in her face.

"That's just rude," Jessica fired back, although KaLaar didn't seem to care.

In fact, KaLaar wasn't impressed with her at all. Throwing out three of his arms, he swatted her away as though she were a pesky insect. The impact of his blow picked her up off her feet and flung her halfway across the arena. She crashed to the ground with a thud and rolled a few times before skidding to a halt in the dirt.

Down on all fours, Jessica spit out the sand that had gathered in her mouth, then did a quick mental check of how she faired. KaLaar's hit, although powerful, barely registered as a tickle to her. Jessica laughed to herself and looked up just in time to see KaLaar leap into the air and land on top of Grendok.

"No!" Jessica shouted, stretching her hand out toward her only friend.

KaLaar landed on top of the satyr and began pummeling him with all six arms. Each blow sounded like rolling thunder. She couldn't imagine how a creature so small could take such a beating. But to her surprise, halfway through his abuse, Grendok reached up and caught KaLaar's punches—stopping his fists in mid-air as if they were nothing.

"ENOUGH!" the satyr growled. Grendok pushed KaLaar off of him and stood up. KaLaar rolled away and then scrambled to his feet, looking up just in time to see Grendok begin to grow. In the breadth of a single moment, the satyr had grown thirty feet tall. He was gigantic.

Jessica rubbed her eyes. She could scarcely believe it, but sure enough, Grendok was huge. He literally towered over the six-armed lizard man who looked more like a common skink in comparison and was about as much of a threat to the monstrous satyr. The tables had turned.

Grendok picked up KaLaar, tossed him into the air, and opened his mouth wide. KaLaar landed in his gaping mouth and Jessica cringed as a spray of blood shot out from Grendok's chomping teeth. Some of it spilled across her face and chest.

She watched in a dreadful grimace as Grendok tore the bottom half of KaLaar's body from his chomping jowls and tossed his legs to the ground. The bones of KaLaar's upper body crunched in between the satyr's teeth and the crowd erupted with the loudest applause Jessica had heard yet.

"GRENDOK THE UNDEFEATED!" the announcer boomed over the speaker system.

Jessica looked up at Grendok. "Undefeated?" *Just my luck*, she thought. *Not only do I have to fight my very first match against an undefeated goat monster, but he lied to me by pretending to be my friend.*

8

Grendok smiled sinisterly, wiping his red stained maw with the back of his bloody hand. "What can I say?" he shrugged. "The crowd loves me. They really do love me."

"You must be so proud of yourself," Jessica fired back sarcastically, echoing the satyr's words from earlier.

Grendok tapped his brow in a quaint salute and grinned. "Touché!"

"You have any last words of wisdom for me?" Jessica asked.

He cocked his head to the side and stroked his chin as he mulled over the question for a moment. "Nope. But I will promise you a swift and painless death." With that, he leaped into the air.

All Jessica could see was a flash of white and orange fur. Then, before she knew it, his giant hoof came crashing down on her chest. Grendok stood over her, pressing her firmly to the ground—not enough to fracture her bones, but enough to make it impossible for her to escape. Even so, she struggled beneath his foot, writhing to try to free herself. But it was no use. His weight was too much and she was pinned to the ground.

"I'm going to have a lot of fun breaking every bone in your puny body, Jegra."

Anger flooded into Jessica's veins. An anger so deeply repressed she never knew she possessed it as years of bullying and being picked on at school came flooding back to her memory. Being taken advantage of at work. Of being used by people pretending to be her friend only to drop her when they could no longer get what they wanted out of her. Then came the rage for being taken by the poachers and her helplessness to do anything about it. Well. She wasn't helpless anymore. Not by a longshot.

As her glands pumped super-charged adrenaline into her system (thanks to the shot she'd been given), Jessica grabbed Grendok's hoof and heaved as hard as she could. She screamed so fiercely her voice carried to the highest echelons of the arena. And the crowd cheered.

It seemed her strength was still growing; how strong she'd become was anyone's guess. But the moment she threw Grendok into the air, he practically flew to the heights of the arena, nearly passing beyond the open topped dome. While he was airborne, Jessica even managed to climb back to her feet.

Jessica stepped aside and watched Grendok topple back to the ground. He crashed down with a force so devastating it shook the entire arena. It was as if a bomb had gone off. Sand and dust shot out in every direction and engulfed the first couple of tiers of the stadium.

The crowd fell quiet as they watched in stunned awe. As the dust settled, Jessica brushed herself off and then scanned the faces of the crowd. Raising her first into the air, she roared, "You want blood!? I'll give you blood!"

"JEGRA THE MERCILESS!" the announcer shouted over the speakers. The crowd went wild, and for whatever reason, the rush of their energy spilled over and energized her. She'd never felt so great in her entire life.

If it's Jegra the Merciless they want, then it's Jegra the Merciless they'll get, she mused. Bending down, she grabbed a nearby spear and heaved it at the satyr, who was only starting to get up. The spear lodged itself in his shoulder and he snorted in anger and plucked it out.

Furious, Grendok launched the spear, sending it back at her. She watched it sail through the air only for it to strike her abdomen. The pole snapped and splintered and its remains fell to the ground in disarray. The metal spear tip ricocheted off her body and spiraled to the ground. Her skin wasn't only strong, it was virtually impenetrable.

Jegra looked up at Grendok and grinned. He raised an eyebrow as he attempted to assess her peculiar reaction. Jegra knew that he was accustomed to warriors more experienced than she screaming out in terror before the almighty satyr. But not her. Never again would she fear anyone or anything.

Exhilarated, Jegra sprinted forward and leaped into the air. She effortlessly rose fifty feet and flew forward as fast and straight as a dart. Thrusting her right knee forward, she hit Grendok squarely on his chin with the force of a hundred cannon balls impacting all at once.

Blood sprayed out as Grendok's head snapped back and the satyr stumbled backward. Losing his footing, he fell into the lower rung of spectators, crushing about a dozen people and wounding at least a dozen more. But it didn't seem to phase the spectators one bit. Even the nearest to the fallen beast's crippled body roared out in excitement, their eyes wild with the hunger for more blood, they chanted, "Jegra! Jegra! Jegra!"

"Hey, Jegra!" a feminine voice called out, cutting through the noise of the crowd. Jegra looked toward the sound of the voice and saw one of the green skinned women staring back at her from the stands. Rising to her feet, the woman blew Jegra a kiss and then pulled up her shirt up and shook her breasts. Her forest green nipples stood erect as she jiggled her melon-sized tits in the cool breeze of the arena and the onlookers all bellowed with ribald laughter.

Jegra blushed and then looked up at emperor Dakroth who leaned back in his chair and rested his chin on a ring encrusted finger. He watched with an amused expression on his face and Jegra smiled. Then, motioning with his hand, he gestured for her to carry on. This tickled Jegra, and she nodded in dutiful compliance.

"I'll kill you…you greasy pink-skin!" Grendok shouted, rising back up to his hooves.

Jegra turned and looked up just in time to see Grendok's two large fists come crashing down on her. She barely had time to raise her arms in defense.

There was a thunderous rumbling as Grendok pounded Jegra's armor into the dirt amidst a fog of dust. Bleating out in rage, he didn't stop pounding, nor would he stop until she was nothing but a dead pile of mush.

Again, the crowd fell silent. "Grendok the Undefeated!" the announcer called out. But the cheers didn't come so readily this time, for there was something that Grendok failed to see. Standing in the haze of the dust, was the figure of a woman, a mere Human, pink skinned and large-breasted, one whose eyesight was perfect and whose temper was unleashed. As the dust slowly settled, Jegra stepped out from the lingering dimness and wiped the blood from her cracked bottom lip.

"Oohs" and "ahhs" flooded the arena as the stadium's countless eyes beheld Jegra the Merciless, barely a scratch on her, take center stage.

Jegra grinned and cracked her neck across her shoulders. "My turn," she said, without so much as looking at her opponent.

Unable to see her gaze, he wouldn't be able to predict what her next move would be. It also had the added benefit of pissing him off by withholding from him the attention he so craved.

Instead of attacking head on, as would be expected, she raced to a toppled chariot left over from a previous bout. She grabbed it by the hitch, swiveled around, pivoting on one foot, and launched it as hard as she could at Grendok. The chariot shot through the air then shattered against Grendok's chest. Its impact was so harsh it sent the giant satyr staggering back several massive steps.

Determined not to lose to a mere Human woman, he kicked back his thick leg and braced himself. Bleating in his terrible goat voice, amplified to deafening tones by his massive size, he leapt forward. His large yellow eyes and unnerving slatted pupils homed in on Jegra.

To Jegra, the satyr seemed to be sailing through the air in slow motion. She had time to survey the faces in the crowd; she even saw Emperor Dakroth slowly rise to his feet in restrained anticipation of the last act of the match.

Jegra kicked off the ground and flew up into the air like a real-life superhero. She moved so fast that she turned into a blur. Unable to anticipate her speed and trajectory, Grendok was struck directly in his sternum.

The wind flew out of him as the thirty-foot tall satyr slammed into the concrete wall of the arena. Large chunks of rubble rained down all around him. Glancing over at Jegra, who was already crouching in the dirt, getting ready to spring again, he smirked. *Perhaps today is a good day to die*, he thought.

In a flash, Jegra was above him—her impossibly powerful fist bearing down on him in a conjoined blow. The impact of her hit sent out a blast of air in every direction, causing the audience to momentarily divert their gaze. When they turned their eyes back to the arena, they found a battered and bleeding Grendok slowly, painfully, climbing out of an impact crater in the center of the arena.

Barely able to breathe due to a collapsed lung and several broken ribs, he dragged himself out of the pit, coughing up blood. Raising his head, he found her standing stoically in front of him, just beyond a stone's toss.

Her every muscle glistened with sweat and her hair flowed epically in the breeze. She tossed her dark tresses over her shoulder and then bent down and picked up her battle axe.

"Grah!" Jegra roared, swinging the axe as hard as she could. Letting go, it spiraled through the air and logged itself right in the center of Grendok's brow.

The satyr's eyes went wide with the realization of his demise, and whispered, "Bitch," with his last breath. Then the beast collapsed face-first into the dirt. Grendok the Undefeated was now thoroughly, unmistakably, defeated.

"We have a new victor!" the announcer cried out. "JEGRA THE MERCILESS!"

The crowd went ballistic. Jegra slowly spun around and looked up at all the strange faces from countless alien worlds starring back at her from the stands.

Back on Earth she had been an unassuming nobody, a Library Sciences major with a government job. Always kept to herself. Too shy to even ask a guy on a date. But here, she was practically a goddess—worshipped by thousands of adoring fans. She even had the admiration of an intergalactic space emperor.

Jegra looked up at Emperor Dakroth and he nodded his head signaling his pleasure. Satisfied by his acknowledgement of her minor feat, she bowed reverently then turned and sauntered off the sands of the arena.

9

When Jegra finally returned to the waiting area, the blue skinned guard was waiting for her there. He smiled at her and said, "Pretty good for a first-time."

She smiled in return and asked, "When's the next bout?" She was eager to test out her newborn abilities. She wanted to see how strong she'd truly become. Like, could she punch through another person's chest and tear out their beating heart? She was sure she'd have many more opportunities to try. *I used to abhor violence*, she thought. Now it excited her.

"Patience," the guard replied. "First, the emperor would like to see you in his private chambers."

Private chambers? She hadn't a clue what the emperor wanted to see her about, but the scandalous thought of alien lovemaking had crossed her mind. She bit her bottom lip and smiled to herself.

The thought of being with the emperor in that way titillated her greatly. Whatever was in that shot they'd given her had changed her in every way. Not only had it made her stronger physically, but it boosted her confidence and made her fiercer. More virile even. Her libido was practically shooting off the charts.

A pair of the black-armored guards in their purple capes appeared from behind a corner and motioned for her to follow. She did. They escorted her to the emperor's chambers. The guards stepped aside, taking their posts on either side of the door. Jegra knocked on the large wooden doorway and waited.

"Enter," a voice called out.

Jegra opened the door and stepped inside the lavish room. To her surprise, she was greeted by the two green women from earlier—the emperor's groupies. They were already naked and lying in Dakroth's bed, lusting for his return.

The emperor, who stood off to the side, poured himself a glass of glowing green liquid. He had on a tunic that hung open and did little to conceal his naked form. Upon noticing Jegra standing in the doorway, he turned to her and raised his glass.

"To the victor!" he said in her honor, and took a large swig of glowing ale.

Jegra blushed. Not only was she not accustomed to being flattered by royalty, she also couldn't help but glance down at the emperor's dual penises. She looked back up in time to catch him smiling at her and her cheeks flushed even more.

Dakroth finished his drink and then tossed the glass to the floor in front of her. It shattered into a thousand tiny pieces, jagged shards glittering like sparkling sand in the moonlight.

With a warm smile, he held out his hand and welcomed Jegra over to them. "Come, join us, won't you?" He nodded at the two naked women lounging in his bed, his robe slipping down his shoulder.

She hesitated and murmured an indecisive "Um."

"Is something the matter?" he asked, pulling his robe back up and repositioning it.

Embarrassed by her lack of resolve, the old Jessica threatening to make a prude of her in front of the emperor, but the new Jegra took a deep breath and replied, "No. Nothing, your grace."

To prove she meant it, she quickly unfastened her many straps and buckles and shed her armor and clothes. She walked across the broken glass on the floor without so much as a twinge; with her new enhancements, she didn't feel any pain. In fact, the glass couldn't even penetrate her skin. It crackled and popped beneath her feet like freshly fallen snow.

The green women giggled with libidinous excitement as the new champion of the games came over to the bed. *I am really doing this*, she thought. It was so unlike her. But, at the same time, it felt right.

Opening his arms wide, Emperor Dakroth embraced Jegra and kissed her on both cheeks and then her lips. His forked tongue slipped into her mouth and their tongues danced sensually about. She let out a carnal moan and reached around the emperor and squeezed his tight blue buttocks in her powerful hands.

Dakroth placed his hands on either side of Jegra's face and brushed her lower lip with his blue thumb. Looking deep into her brown eyes with his red ones, he smiled wantonly.

"In all my years, I've never tasted a female's lips as sweet as yours. Tell me, Jessica Hemsworth of Earth, is the rest of you just as sweet tasting?"

"Why don't you find out?" Jegra teased. Grabbing the emperor by his shoulders, she shoved him backward and he toppled onto the bed. He laughed with equal parts excitement and lustful anticipation as he watched her saunter over to him.

Jegra climbed onto the bed and situated herself on top of him, straddling his pelvis with her powerful thighs. Unfastening her loincloth, she let it fall to the wayside and settled down onto him, tossing her hair across her powerful shoulders.

"It's just Jegra now, my lord," she said, leaning over him, letting her watermelon sized breasts settle onto his chest as they compressed into taught ovals.

When their two bodies met, Dakroth smiled and took her in his arms. His Prussian blue lips found her soft pink ones and an electric excitement crackled between them.

As they kissed, the green women's hands slid across their skin and petted them with sensual strokes of their delicate fingers, enhancing the pleasure of both parties and acting as guides who ushered them to the gates of tantric bliss and beyond.

Before Jegra knew it, liquid fire was gushing down the tender insides of her thighs as she gave into the passion that erupted between them. The old Jessica would have never been so adventurous. So promiscuous. But, then again, the old Jessica Hemsworth would have been too timid to climb into bed with a strange man, let alone an emperor.

As Jegra, champion of the arena, she relinquished such Human fears and took control of her own destiny. The weak Earth woman who couldn't even muster up enough courage to say no to being molested by her boss in the parking lot was but a distant memory fading with each new moment.

Being abducted by aliens may have turned out to be the best thing that had ever happened to her. It caused her to re-evaluate her life. It forced her to take a good hard look at who she was; what she saw didn't sit well with her. It was time for a change.

It was time to discard her old persona just as the serpent discards its molted skin. Like she'd been cocooned by self-doubt and timidity, she was free to emerge a much more glorious creature, unburdened by the traumas of the past.

Being reborn as Jegra–champion of the arena–was a second chance at life. A chance to be the brave and courageous woman she always knew she could be. A chance to become a great warrioress. A sensual lover. And a woman who feared no man or beast.

She was free at last.

But this wasn't the end of her story. No. Not by a long shot. Jegra's story was just beginning. And this moment, here and now, caught in a tangle of blue and green arms, feeling an ecstasy she had never imagined possible, was but the first chapter in an entirely new life.

10

Somewhere in the Zargora system, a fissure of radiant golden light opened up in space and time. The tear, but a small crack in the expanse of the entire cosmos, suddenly widened as though it were being pried open by some mysterious power. Emerging from the glowing fissure came lambent tentacles like those of a squid—a starship-sized squid.

A sleek vessel with a dark chrome hull which seemingly blended into the distant stars slowed to a stop and took position just beyond the tear in space. The vessel was no trivial spacecraft, but a state-of-the-art battlecruiser carrying the elite Knights of Caelum. Warriors of an ancient order devoted to keeping the Nyctan Empire safe at any and all cost.

Along with a formidable array of disruptor cannons, the ship, called the *Oath Bringer*, also boasted being the fastest and toughest ship in the Nyctan fleet. But perhaps the best tool in its arsenal was the reputation of the Knights themselves. Known as unstoppable forces of righteous vindication, they were feared across all nine systems.

Nobody dared go up against the Knights of Caelum. Not unless they had a death wish. Space pirates avoided them. Smugglers and bandits ran from them. And allied species grew extremely cordial and cooperative when in their presence. They were both guardians and defenders of their realm. But if one thing was certain, they were not to be trifled with.

As the vessel slowly passed under the glowing object and took its scans, a lone warrior stood on the bridge and gazed out of the observation window at the strange special anomaly.

The Knight, dressed in high-tech battle armor, turned to one of the officers and cleared his throat. "Inform the Nyctan High Command that we've made contact with the celestial entity."

"Yes, sir," replied the crewman. He was a young looking man with porcelain white skin and large, oversized black eyes which gave him an eerily demonic appearance, a hallmark of his species.

A man of few words, the Knight turned back around and watched as the space-squid slowly squeezed its way out of the glowing fissure and into Nyctan space.

This would be the third sighting this month. The first two vessels, one cargo ship and one imperial frigate, were both destroyed by an entity meeting this creature's exact description. Now, the military was involved and it was Galahad's mission to assess the threat level this thing posed. If it was deemed dangerous, he had orders to destroy it.

Without warning, the ship's collision alarm went off. The floor jolted and went out from under him as the artificial grav-plating cut out. Galahad, replete with his bulky armor, floated up into the zero-g atmosphere of the command center of the ship. He glanced over at the rest of the crew members, who were swimming in place as they wafted about, suspended in the air like a bloom of jellyfish.

All of a sudden, the gravity kicked back on and everyone crashed to the harsh, metallic floor of the ship. Pushing himself up to his hands and knees, Galahad looked up in time to see one of the squid's tentacles coiling itself around the ship.

The officer he'd previously spoken with scrambled back up into his chair and gave him an update. "The creature has attached itself to the hull of the ship."

Galahad struggled to his feet and grunted, "Fire everything we have at it."

"Yes, sir," the tactical officer said, just past his soldier. Of the bridge crew, she was the only female.

A volley of green disruptor blasts erupted from the heavy canons, each one trained on the massive body of the creature. After a furious barrage, the canons stopped and whined as they cooled in the cold vacuum of space.

"Ensign…report."

"Direct hits, sir," he announced triumphantly.

Just then, the ship shuddered violently as it was wrenched out of its flight path. The structural integrity alarm went off and sparks rained down from the ceiling as bulkheads buckled and electrical panels burst.

"Sir, the creature seems to be unfazed by our weapons. In fact, we're reading an energy spike in its vital signs. It's off the scale!"

Galahad's instinct told him they were thirty seconds away from losing the ship. Tapping the side of his armor, a retractable helmet unfolded from his suit and formed over his face. Using the comm inside his environmental power suit, he issued the order to abandon ship.

"All hands, abandon ship! I repeat, all hands abandon…"

Before he could even finish the call to abandon ship, the hull of the *Oath Bringer* tore open and everyone was jettisoned out into space. Luckily, Galahad had actuated his EVP just moments prior. Even so, he cried out inside his helmet as he watched his crew get sucked out into the void.

Their faces were wide eyed with terror as they gasped their last breaths and then slowly froze in the frigid vacuum of space, floating away from him like lifeless dolls. Galahad used his suit's thrusters to turn and look up at the glowing space-squid that unfurled before him. The debris of the ship hung about him like a ship graveyard.

Satisfied at the destruction it had wrought, the squid began to glow bright gold then turned hot white. It became so bright that Galahad had to look away, even with the polarization on his visor turned up to full.

There was a loud bang and then darkness. Galahad opened his eyes and felt a sunburn forming across his face, which suffered light UV burns. The creature, however, was nowhere in sight. It had jumped away. *What kind of entity could enter hyperspace? Was it a starship or a living organism? Or was it some kind of hybrid?* Galahad couldn't answer.

Even though the deaths of his entire crew weighed heavily on his mind, the good news was that Galahad hadn't been vaporized by a core breach, which meant that the ship's fusion core was still intact somewhere in the debris field. Which meant junkers would pick it up on their scanners and come to salvage it. If he hung out long enough, he might just survive this ordeal.

Galahad tapped his touch-panel arm display. "Scan system for vessels and send an SOS."

The computer chimed and a feminine voice informed him, "There is currently one vessel within communications range."

"Designation and class?" he asked.

"The freighter *Reventón,*" replied the computer.

With his SOS sent, all he could do was wait for help to arrive, assuming they were the generous type. If not, then he'd just have to show them exactly why the Knights of Caelum were the most feared warriors in all the Commonwealth.

TO BE CONTINUED IN...

THE CHRONICLES OF JEGRA: BOOK 1
GLADIATRIX OF THE GALAXY

BOOK 1

THE CHRONICLES OF

JEGRA

GLADIATRIX OF THE GALAXY

1

Jegra stepped out of her chambers and tossed her long, brown hair over her shoulder. The wooden soles of her leather wrapped sandals clapped against the sandstone floor as trumpets bleated a level above her announcing to the whole amphitheater her pending arrival.

She nodded at the two guards who stood at either side of her entrance, spears in hand, as they stoically protected the reigning champion from overzealous fans and other unwanted visitors. So they said. It was clear to Jegra that their real duty was to safeguard the Intergalactic Gladiatorial Syndicate's prized possession at all costs.

Jegra's matches always drew the largest crowds from all corners of the empire, and she garnered the most televid downloads in the system. All this meant more credits to the empire and more funding for the war effort; credits, of which she herself only ever saw a small fraction.

The guards nodded their heads ever so slightly at her passing and then, without saying a word, she turned from them and headed up the long corridor that led to the mouth of the arena.

As she walked up the darkened hall that led to the waiting area beneath the amphitheater, she took in the smell of the sweat and blood of fallen heroes that came rushing into her nostrils. In the stadium above, the roar of the crowd flooded into the narrow antechamber, becoming a cacophony that washed over her.

Other gladiators sat in the darkness, waiting for their turn to run out onto the field to try to claim some ounce of glory. When Jegra appeared, the other alien faces looked up at her to catch a glimpse of the famous Earther who had been a slave and then who, against all odds, became Gladiatrix of the Galaxy. Maybe, if they were lucky, they'd one day go up against her, perchance to claim the title of reigning champion.

As she walked past them they shifted their eyes away; they were simultaneously in awe of her and frightened by her. It was her curse to be loved and feared, adored, yet marked for death, all at the same time.

She ignored their fleeting glances and stood before the gate to the arena. She cracked her neck, rotating her head across her shoulders. She hopped up and down to get her blood flowing and listened to the uproarious noise of the crowd. It filled her with excitement and she made two fists and took a deep breath as she tried to bring herself back to a calm focus.

Once in control, Jegra adjusted her metal fish-scale bikini and threw her royal blue tunic over her shoulders.

Other than the tunic and chain mail, she wore a broad leather belt clad with feathers and other trinkets—souvenirs of matches she'd won, and a pair of armor bracers for deflecting lancing blades and arrows.

She fought most of her gladiatorial battles wearing the bare minimum; whatever armor she wore got so banged up it typically hindered her movement or fell off anyway. One of the downsides of being endowed with super-strength.

Besides, fighting half naked seemed to please the crowd. And in this sport, pleasing the crowd was everything.

When she was back on Earth, she'd never been the exhibitionist type. Hell, back then, she was so modest she wouldn't have been caught dead wearing a two-piece, much less a bikini. Now, though...now, things were different.

It had been a year and a half since her former self, Jessica Hemsworth, had been abducted by extraterrestrial poachers and sold off to slavers and then to the Gladiatorial Syndicate. It was here where she'd been given a strange injection—some sort of super-human growth serum and vaccination steroid blend all-in-one cocktail; it had quite literally transformed her into the She Hulk.

She was amazed by her transformation; her arms had grown thick and powerful, her legs became strong and muscular, and her every ab swelled with raw strength. Even her scant C-cup bra size ballooned to a full 42 J, and they weren't just ornaments; her breasts could now literally deflect steel-tipped arrows.

She even increased in height by a full foot, going from five-foot five to six-foot five.

In fact, the strange substance had transformed her small, wiry frame into that of a voluptuous Greek goddess, something between Aphrodite and Hercules—sensual, yet, at the same time, as powerful as they came. She hadn't gone up against a creature or being yet over whom she hadn't prevailed.

With her new body and heightened abilities, she had quickly risen to the status of reigning champion in the gladiatorial games and garnered the favor of the crowd.

Not only that, but Emperor Dakroth of the Dagon Empire, and ruler of most of the known galaxy, had also taken a liking to her.

Captivated by her beauty and her fierceness in the arena, he had paid her numerous visits over the course of the year, treating her as his consort. She suspected, however, he secretly came to enjoy her company—for although he had sixteen wives from all over the system, none were quite like her.

In her mind, that was a good thing. The prudish, timid, cowering Jessica Hemsworth was no more. Only Jegra the Masterful, Jegra the Merciless, as they called her, remained. She smiled to herself and then rolled her head back across her shoulders, cracking her neck again as she limbered up for the upcoming match.

Golden light shone in through the mouth of the corridor. She strolled confidently up to the arena entrance. Pausing in the shadows, just beyond the cusp of light, she put her hand on the wall and closed her eyes as she listened for the announcer to call her name.

"Ladies and Gentlemen, Lifeforms and Beings from every sector of the Dagon Empire, the moment you've all been waiting for, the undefeated, reigning champion of the 75th annual Gladiatorial Games...*Jegra the Masterful, Jegra the Merciless!*"

Cheers and applause erupted throughout the stadium. Jegra stepped forward onto the sand covered arena and raised her arms to the crowd. As she appeared to all viewers, their cheers grew even louder until the din sounded like the thrusters of a royal battle cruiser breaking orbit.

Over the arena, ships hung in the sky as the richest purveyors of the sport watched the barbaric blood sport from their lofty, high priced, commercial space-yachts. They slowly circled Arena City, aptly named for its monumental size. It lay outside the largest populated area of the desert moon Thessalonica, the fifth and largest moon of Dagon Prime–the emperor's homeworld.

Jegra dramatically swirled the silken blue fabric of her tunic, throwing it off to the side in an exhibitionist display of her warrior's physique. She slowly spun around, arms still raised high, and smiled up at all the outlandish alien faces that stared back at her from the stands with fanatic interest.

A flying televid recorder drone, a black ball with several cameras for eyes, swooped down and zoomed in on her enormous chest. As the hovering camera ball panned up to her face, she winked at the crowd—which appeared on the giant amphitheater monitors—as well as the millions of televids across the empire.

The din of the crowd showered her with praise and adoration, and the applause continued with a renewed vigor as she stretched and flexed her muscles for them.

Jegra couldn't help but smile. She had them eating out of the palms of her hands.

"Typical Terran," a voice jeered just over her shoulder.

Jegra turned around to see who it was that dared mock her. When she spun, she found a glamorous, Bre'lal woman wearing purple shoulder armor, a metallic bra, and a matching purple loincloth.

In addition to the stylish outfit, which only champions were given, she had on knee high, leather wrapped sandals. Most glorious of all was her beautiful, forest green hair; it complimented her emerald skin.

That's when Jegra realized that, somehow, she knew this woman. She squinted hard, and finally it dawned on her.

"Abethca Agnar?" Jegra gasped. Agnar had been the reigning champion of the arena, but she'd retired two cycles ago. "What in God's name are you doing here?"

The crowd's roar quickly died down to a low, bubbling simmer as they strained to hear the unexpected exchange.

"I've come to seek my revenge and reclaim my title," Abethca announced, addressing both Jegra and the crowd, "by claiming your life!"

Her boast was met with raucous, displeased "boos" and catcalls from the crowd. Jegra raised her hand and silenced the audience.

"What in Helios are you talking about, Abethca?"

"Don't play the fool, Jegra!" Abethca growled through clenched teeth. She shook with a broiling anger as she gazed menacingly at Jegra. "You killed my lover, the Angorian named Kel'Zellion, you vagina-toothed whore!"

Jegra gasped in shock. For the life of her, she couldn't remember having fought any Angorians lately, and, she didn't recollect anyone by the name of Kel'Zellion, a rather unique and unforgettable name, in her estimation. Yet clearly Abethca blamed her for his death, and either way, she genuinely felt sorry, and decided to act remorseful. At least playing the sympathy card would track well with the audience. "Kel...is dead? I'm so sorry."

"Don't act like you don't know! You killed him! He died in the hospital due to the wounds you inflicted."

"Enough! I've never fought an Angorian named Kel'Zellion," Jegra fired back, her patience growing thin.

"You didn't fight him," Abethca snarled. "You slept with him. He had a heart attack and died before the doctors could do anything to save him." A lecherous chuckle and murmur went through the crowd. This was better than they could have hoped for.

"A tragic story," Jegra admitted, "if true." And, sure, she felt bad that she had accidentally fucked someone to death, but that didn't change the fact that she didn't recollect bedding any Angorian, nor could she understand why Abethca was so hellbent on blaming her for something she clearly had no control over.

"I'll kill you here, Jegra. You'll see that for truth."

"I see. If it makes you feel any better," she continued, trying to smooth things over the best she could, "I don't remember this Kel'Zellion you speak of, in bed, or otherwise."

"What?! No! That doesn't make things better. What's the matter with you? *I loved him,*" she said, thumping her chest. "We were planning on starting a family together, getting out of this. But that's all gone because of *you.*"

"I'm terribly sorry," Jegra apologized for the umpteenth time. It was, without a doubt, possibly the strangest, most absurd conversation she'd ever had. And even as she was genuine in her apology, Abethca was so filled with green-eyed envy and rage that it wasn't going to make a difference either way.

"Sorry doesn't cut it," Abethca barked angrily. "You ruined my life. Now, I'm going to ruin yours."

The televid drone zoomed in on Jegra's steady, brown eyes then panned over to Abethca's azure eyes, which smoldered with unbridled hatred. The audience fell silent as they watched the drama unfold on live televid streams upon the giant monitors and across the system.

Abethca reached behind her back and pulled out two curved daggers. Smiling at Jegra with sinister intent, she informed her, "These are made of the finest korridium alloy. Call it a hunch, but I'm guessing they're sharp enough to even cut through your thick hide, Jegra."

"So, your plan is to exact revenge on me because your boyfriend cheated on you? That doesn't make any sense."

"*How dare you!* You'll pay for your insolence!" Abethca lunged forward, slashing wildly with her korridium blades.

Sure enough, just as she had explained, they crackled on the air with a raw, untapped energy that was, in some strange way, exhilarating to Jegra. The fact that she faced a real challenger who was capable of hurting her raised the stakes and aroused her carnal nature.

A woman scorned fought for the honor of her murdered lover. This made excellent drama and Jegra was certain that tonight's ratings would go through the roof.

Jegra shuffled back, evading each of Abethca's swipes. As she parried, she asked, "Answer me one thing. If revenge is what you seek, why did you sleep with me?"

"Because," Abethca replied, "I didn't believe him when he said you were the best. I had to prove him wrong."

"So, let me get this straight. You slept with me to prove to your boyfriend, who was cheating on you, that I was the inferior lover?"

"Exactly!" she said, taking another furious swipe.

"This is by far the weirdest conversation I've ever had," Jegra said, leaping to the side. Abethca, stretching out her blade in a reverse rotation, barely grazed Jegra's right cheek in a backhanded swipe.

A small, red cut opened up on Jegra's cheek and a trace of glistening blood began to dribble down her face. She leapt back in shock and touched her cheek. Glancing down at the smattering of blood that dappled her fingers, she gasped.

The audience fell silent as they slid to the edges of their seats. In over a year, no one had drawn blood from the champion. Jegra, wondering if it was a fluke, kicked up a spear from a previous battle, broke the shaft across her knee, and pointing it at her own abdomen, brought the spear into herself seppuku style.

The blade broke off the wooden spear and the pole splintered as it rebounded off her virtually invulnerable abs.

Abethca cackled wildly as the camera orb floated down and zoomed in on her. "This is your champion?" she balked, unimpressed. "This pink-bellied Terran swine?" She cackled some more then spun around to face her opponent.

Jegra, who was weaponless, widened her stance and put out her hands in a grappling formation. If a year of knocks and bruises had taught her anything, it was how to fight.

Sure, she had learned it all the hard way, getting beat to a pulp by almost every contestant she went up against almost every single damned time. But, in the end, she always prevailed.

Perhaps it was this underdog charm that made her so appealing to the audience. Perhaps it was her desperate kills which revealed that every single fight was a fight for her very life. Either way, she had become the most watched gladiator in the past hundred revolutions.

But she knew her ability to win her bouts had more to do with her stamina and her imperviousness than it did any honed skill. The truth was, she could take a beating and outlast her opponents in the arena; their bones broke, whereas hers did not. Eventually they each went down and she was all that was left. The last woman standing.

The rules of the match were simple. Fight to the death. Last contender standing wins. And Jegra wasn't about to let some random jealous girlfriend steal her thunder.

"Alright, sweet-pea," Jegra taunted. "That does it. Why don't you shut up and show me what you got?" Throwing up a hand, she waved at Abethca to come at her.

"My pleasure, you massive chested space-cow."

Abethca licked her dark green lips and a crooked smiled crawled onto her face. Running a pink tongue across her white teeth, to Jegra's surprise, the green skinned woman slowly faded into her surroundings, becoming invisible before her very eyes. Her vicious smile was the last thing to fade.

"Balls," Jegra cursed as her deadliest enemy just one-upped her in the awesome abilities department.

"I'm going to gut you like a Targaedian fish," Abethca spoke, as if out from thin air.

Jegra felt a lacerating pain tearing across her left thigh. She yelped as a bloody gash unexpectedly opened up on her leg, and, taking a couple of wild, aimless swipes with her fists, she tried to locate her opponent. All she met was the vapid air.

"Show yourself!" she demanded, hoping to goad her opponent into revealing her position.

But Abethca was smarter than that, and Jegra was met with a soft spoken, "I think not."

Out of the blue, another cut opened up across Jegra's back, right across her shoulder blades. She shrieked out in pain and staggered forward. Spinning on her heels, she took another haphazard swipe of the air around her but her fists came up empty. For all intents and purposes, Abethca was a ghost.

Jegra knew that if she didn't figure out a way to beat her opponent in the next few seconds, she was done for.

2

"**The returning champion**, Abethca Agnar, ladies and gentlemen," the two-headed serpentine broadcaster announced from his special booth way up high in the stands of the amphitheater.

Jegra scanned every inch of the arena with her eyes as she studied every little detail. "The keywords being *former champion*," Jegra sneered.

"I took my licks, just like you," Abethca said after a short pause. Then, after another, longer pause her voice broke out from a different location. "I won three hundred and fifty consecutive matches. Far more than you need to gain your freedom. But I had a certain, how shall I say? Fondness for the sport."

"You liked the power, didn't you?"

"You'd only be lying to yourself if you said you didn't."

Jegra sauntered in a circle, searching for any sound–no matter how minuscule–that might help to give away Abethca's location. But Abethca was well trained, and she didn't make any sound. Another cut opened up across Jegra's right bicep and she grunted as she grappled with the scoring pain of the korridium blades.

"I'm going to give you my special finishing move, Jegra, darling. A thousand kisses of death."

The throng of onlookers erupted with cheers and applause and Jegra, for the first time in over seventy-two consecutive matches, had lost the favor of the crowd. An exasperated expression came across her face as she watched the spectators' loyalties shift as idly as the afternoon breeze.

This pleased Abethca to no end, and she couldn't help but let out a faint chortle. It was just near enough to Jegra's neck that she could guess exactly where

Abethca was.

With a thrust of her elbow, she threw her arm back and made contact with something. She turned in time to see the far wall of the amphitheater crumple as Abethca's invisible body collided with it.

Chunks of rock and debris rained onto the dry dirt of the arena, kicking up a small cloud of dust. Peering into the dust cloud, Jegra could make out the silhouette of a rather fit body.

"Gotcha," Jegra whispered. Leaping into the air, Jegra shot high up into the hollow of the amphitheater and then came straight down. Landing on her knee and hammering the ground with both fists, she impacted with such a force it kicked up a fearsome sandstorm.

Abethca's shadow figure stopped mid-run to catch her bearings, but Jegra had already disappeared into the plume of sand. Even the televid orb flew blindly through the thick haze. That is, until a hand reached out and grabbed it.

Jegra chucked the drone at Abethca's head; the woman barely had time to raise her knife. The televid drone instantly split in half as Abethca's blade sliced through it. A spray of sparks flew out and she quickly regained a defensive stance, desperately searching for Jegra.

"Looking for me?"

Startled, Abethca spun around, swinging her blade recklessly. The sand gnawed at the blades as she cut through the silica-filled air. Soon enough the korridium blades no longer crackled. They had been dulled.

At the same time, Abethca's invisibility had begun to wear off. Whether from fatigue, the sandstorm, or some combination of both, she gradually grew more and more opaque, steadily transforming from a phantasmic, transparent green to a translucent, waxy green, and finally, to a mostly-solid green woman.

Abethca was rendered vulnerable and, wasting no time, Jegra bent down and snatched the discarded spearhead from earlier. Charging Abethca, Jegra flanked her from the south side of the oval arena.

As expected, Abethca shifted her footing to counter Jegra's attack, but Jegra flung the arrow head with a flick of her wrist and it cut across the distance between them like a dart.

Abethca yelped out in pain as the arrowhead pierced her right shoulder. She quickly pried the spearhead from her flesh with a tormented grunt and a healthy spray of blue blood. Luckily, Jegra's distraction had worked. Abethca no longer held the upper hand; the crowd was noisy, their loyalties split.

Abethca's draining wound caused her to lose her grip on one of her knives and she dropped it to the ground. This opened her up to a gut-wrenching punch from Jegra, who smiled manically for the televid drone as she doled out a punishing blow to her opponent's taut stomach.

Jegra roared out like a fierce lioness as her knuckles embedded themselves in Abethca's gut. The green woman's entire body rose off the ground as she crumpled around Jegra's mighty fist and relinquished her other blade.

Jegra held Abethca up with one arm, pandering to the audience to show them that this green woman was way out of her weight class. As Abethca lay slumped across Jegra's arm, she unexpectedly hurled her stomach contents all over the arena.

Jegra pulled her fist back and stepped away, narrowly avoiding the vomit shower. Abethca collapsed to the ground and then, defiantly, pushed herself up to her knees. She kneeled prostrate before Jegra and clutched her bruised ribs.

Jegra threw her arms into the air as she circled her foe and addressed the audience. "You dare doubt me? You dare turn on your undefeated champion?! I'm gravely disappointed in you all. Yet, here I stand. Victorious!"

The crowd grew silent. The only sound was that of Abethca's pathetic whimpering. Jegra looked down at the defeated woman and deliberated as to what to do with her. Cowering like a wounded dog, Abethca raised two fingers into the air and called for mercy. The crowd erupted with boos and hisses.

"Silence!" Jegra roared. Her voice rattled the upper echelons of the amphitheater and the ruckus quickly died down.

She reached over and grabbed Abethca by her right wrist and dragged her lethargic body to its feet. Holding her wrist, Jegra shouted out, "Your returning champion! Abethca Agnar!"

There was an awkward murmuring as the crowd didn't quite know how to respond. Even the televid drone hovered anxiously above the scene as it panned from Jegra's face to Abethca's. Breaking the long silence, the sport broadcaster came onto the comm system and announced, "Ladies and gentlemen, we have just witnessed something unprecedented! Two champions, going head to head, battling fiercely and ending in the first ever draw!"

The crowd erupted with another wave of applause and cheers. Jegra ignored their hollow praise. She turned and marched across the arena, dragging Abethca behind her, still clutching her opponent's wrist tightly in her hand.

"Wait, where are you taking me?" Abethca asked.

"Don't forget, Abethca Agnar of Bre'lal, I spared your life. Now you owe me a debt of servitude until you can either repay me in kind or until I release you of your obligation."

She shot Jegra a wide-eyed glance. "You're claiming me as your *spoils?*"

Jegra pulled Abethca into the dim tunnel that led to her bedroom chambers. "You're damn right I'm claiming you."

"But why? Why would you want me?"

Once inside the tunnel, Jegra stopped, spun around, and clutched Abethca's neck with her hand, squeezing tightly. She shoved Abethca forcefully into the cold stone wall. Abethca let out a huff of air and wheezed to take another breath. Jegra let up on her grip enough to let the Bre'lal woman breathe.

Jegra leaned in and pressed her chest into Abethca's. Then, raising Abethca's arm over her head and firmly pressing her wrist into the rock wall of the corridor, Jegra glanced at Abethca's fingers and then looked down into the green woman's shallow blue eyes. "These fingers will better suit me in other ways than lying cold and dead upon the sands of the arena."

"It would have been a fitting death. An honorable death."

"Perhaps," Jegra said with a deviant grin. Slowly, she slid Abethca's wrist down along the wall, guiding her arm down until it came to a rest on her thigh. She leaned in and, standing a full head above the green woman, she lowered her gaze and whispered into her ear, "But right now I want you right here."

Jegra slid Abethca's hands between her sweat laden thighs and pressed her fingers into the scaled bikini bottoms she wore. Abethca's eyes grew wide when she realized what Jegra wanted of her, but she remained hesitant.

Abethca found it rather difficult to gather her thoughts let alone articulate them. "I...I'm not...I know...it's just..." Not knowing what to say next, she trailed off without saying anything. A heavy sigh gave proof to her complete surrender.

Jegra smiled and then leaned in and kissed Abethca on her dark green lips. Abethca drew back, resisting the kiss of her sworn enemy.

Although Abethca detested Jegra, she knew that she'd lost the bout. And instead of killing her, Jegra had shown mercy. By the laws of the arena, whether she liked it or not, she belonged to Jegra now as her servant–to do with as she saw fit.

This, after all, was the punishment for surrendering the bout. Disgraced, you were destined to become the slave of a slave. There was no lower position in society than that.

Jegra felt a raw animal like attraction to Abethca, even though she had tried to kill her just minutes ago in the arena. There was nothing like the submission of an enemy that could enliven Jegra's carnal instincts. Pressing her chest into Abethca, Jegra wove her fingers through the woman's forest green hair and grabbed her firmly by the back of her head, forcing her lips back to hers.

Soon her tongue found Abethca's and what had begun as a feathery dance of tongue-play turned into a sultry tango between open mouths. Abethca's resistance gradually faded and she let out a prurient moan and fell into Jegra's arms.

"Does the champion of the arena always get what she wants?" Abethca asked in a sultry voice.

The Bre'lal woman's crystal-water blue eyes peered up at Jegra's inviting brown ones, and Jegra grabbed the green woman around her waist, their muscular thighs pressing into one another. Leaning into Abethca, she whispered into her ear, "When it fancies me."

Out of the blue, a thunderous explosion shook the amphitheater and interrupted their little make out session. Startled out of their lustful entanglement, both women looked at one another with staggered expressions. Perhaps even more startling than the ear rattling sound of the sonic disturbance in the sky was the realization of what accompanied it.

"Is that what I think it is?" Abethca asked.

Jegra relinquished her hold of Abethca and, fixing her bikini, hurried up the corridor, Abethca close behind her.

They stepped out into the stadium grounds, looked up into the sky and fixed their eyes on the object hanging low in the atmosphere. Its endless shadow cast dimness over the entire stadium.

Dakroth's Royale Battle Cruiser loomed over the colosseum. It had a double-forked hull that looked like a two-pronged blade; the huge curving fins along the top and the smooth, broad bottom made it look like a predatory shark.

Jegra had once asked a star-pilot why ships jumping in or out of hyperspace made the sound of a thunderclap; the pilot had explained to her that it had something to do with the terminal wave shock of entering or exiting FTL travel. The ships, dropping out of FTL, actually broke the sound barrier every time they entered or exited hyperspace. This shockwave crashed into you, and whether you were on a ship or a planet, depending on your distance from the source of the wave, it would sound like a resounding clap of thunder.

Abethca limped up to Jegra and took her place by her side. "Your boyfriend's back. A booty call?" she jested.

Jegra raised an eyebrow. "I doubt it. Dakroth is supposed to be at the front lines until next month. There's only one thing that could make him return before the allotted time."

"And, pray tell, what might that be?" asked Abethca.

"The war isn't going as planned and he's come to conscript any and all fighters he can find into his army."

Abethca gulped hard. Being a gladiator is one thing, but being made into a soldier, that's entirely another.

Jegra turned to Abethca and, with a stern expression, said, "No matter what, stay by my side and follow my lead–if you want to live."

"What?" Abethca asked. But before she could inquire as to what Jegra meant by her ominous demand, a beam of golden light appeared before them.

Inside the beam of light, sparks danced about as though they were caught in a firestorm. They flurried about rapidly, then, to their astonishment, a blue-skinned man appeared standing before them.

Jegra kneeled on one knee before the handsome, cobalt blue colored, platinum-haired figure. He wore a custom-tailored Imperial uniform and a flowing white cape. Abethca copied Jegra and knelt before the great warrior.

"My Lord," Jegra said, bowing her head.

Abethca gulped down the nervous lump in her throat. She had never met the Emperor before. She quickly followed suit and bowed her head, too.

Emperor Dakroth laughed and tossed his long, straight, silvery hair across his shoulder. It fell in a cascade down to his lower back. His blood-red eyes looked animated behind his blue, poker-faced expression. "My dear Daughter of Sol," he began, a smile slowly spreading across his face, "how many times have I asked you to simply call me Rhadamanthus?"

Lord Dakroth reached down, took Jegra by her hand, and bid her to rise. She did so, and Abethca was about to follow her up, but Jegra shook her head ever so slightly and waved her hand to warn her green skinned Bre'lal girl to stay down.

Dakroth is what Jegra considered a dedicated Sadist. He loved to cause pain; he lived for it. That is why he loved to fight in the campaigns himself. But he was also highly unpredictable. If she had to describe him in a word, it would be psychotic.

Regardless, he'd taken a liking to her. Especially since she could take it as well as he could dish it out. And there still wasn't a single thing he could do to her that would hurt her any more than it hurt him.

Sure, it wasn't an ideal relationship. He was as abusive as a Dragonian slaver. But by keeping him close, she enjoyed a certain privilege nobody else had. He confided in her, trusted her; she would always have that edge over him.

She knew his every dark little secret, and subsequently, the secrets of the entire galaxy. It was a position of power she wasn't willing to give up. And, besides, the sex wasn't half bad. Rough. But not bad at all.

"Rhadamanthus," Jegra said with a smile. "What brings you to my humble amphitheater?"

"I need to speak with you," he said, pausing long enough to lean to the side and glance warily down at the green-skinned girl groveling at his feet.

Jegra did a nervous double take between them and was about to introduce Abethca when Lord Dakroth beat her to it.

"And who might this lovely creature be?" he asked.

The televid drone hovered noisily above them. Growing annoyed, Dakroth raised his finger, aimed it like a pistol at the drone, and let off a powerful red laser beam. The blast took out the drone; its burning husk crashed to the arena floor.

"My apologies," he said, returning to their conversation. "I've been too easily distracted as of late.

"This is Abethca Agnar," Jegra said, nodding at the Bre'lal girl.

"And who is she to you?" Dakroth asked, taking Abethca's hand and having her rise up so he could better inspect her.

"She was my rival, now my prize," Jegra said. Of course, even if Jegra claimed ownership, meaning Dakroth could not claim her for his own, she knew he still might should he take a liking to the girl. After all, he was known to break the rules on more than one occasion.

"I see," he said, smiling warmly at Abethca.

"My Lord," Abethca said, bowing her head reverently.

Dakroth reached out and touched her chin and gently raised her blue eyes up so that they met his. His smile only grew wider. "Jegra, you'll have to inform me if it's true what they say. Bre'lal women make the best lovers."

"I will," Jegra answered, lowering her gaze.

"Until then, I formally invite you both aboard my cruiser for dinner. There is a lot we must discuss."

Dakroth stepped back and bowed ever so slightly. Then, in a flamboyant manner, he tossed his silvery hair across his shoulder, threw back his cape, and blew kisses at the crowd. The entire colosseum went wild at the gesture.

In a flash of the yellow, sparkling light of a particle beam, he was whisked back up to his ship.

When Jegra looked over at Abethca, she stood frozen, staring at the spot Dakroth had just dematerialized from. That's when Jegra recognized the symptoms. The woman was petrified.

"It's all right," Jegra said, placing a warm hand on Abethca's shoulder.

Abethca was shivering. "All I could feel was fear."

"Don't worry, it wears off after a while."

Abethca slowly turned her head and looked into Jegra's eyes. "Wears off? What the bloody hell *was* that?"

"He broadcasts the manifestation of your worst fears into your subconscious when you are in close proximity to him. He can cause you to see things that would make you go insane, even gouge out your own eyes. It's how he keeps everyone in submission. It's one of his many powers."

"And you've slept with that guy?"

Jegra shrugged. "What can I say? He's a good lay."

Abethca shuddered. "Forgive me, but I think I'll just have to take your word on that."

"Don't worry. As long as he believes that you're my concubine, he won't lay a finger on you. Probably."

"Probably?" Abethca said, catching Jegra's aside.

Jegra shrugged. He was the emperor, after all. He pretty much could do whatever he wanted. But she also knew him to be a man of discipline and self-control.

After a long pause, Abethca asked, "Why would you stick your neck out to protect me like this? I tried to kill you today. Earlier, back in the corridor, I was just playing along. Biding my time until you fell asleep. Then, I was going slit your throat and escape."

Jegra smiled at her green skinned companion. "I had a contingency plan for tonight, Abethca. If I stopped to worry about when or how I was going to die, I wouldn't have time to enjoy the present. Before my life in the arena, as far back as I can remember, I was a fearful weakling. A timid girl, always afraid of her own shadow. I can't go back to being that pathetic little weakling. Never again. So, now I choose to live in the moment, taking it a day at a time." Jegra slid off her bracer and showed Abethca her tattoo.

"*Carpe diem?*" Abethca read aloud. She looked up and gave Jegra a mystified look.

"It's an old Earth saying. It means, 'seize the day,'" she replied, sliding her bracer back into place. "Don't waste your time worrying about tomorrow. Just live today to its fullest."

Just then a new televid drone manifested above them and began recording.

Annoyed by the pesky eye in the sky, Jegra turned and marched back toward the corridor and her chambers. "Come," she called out over her shoulder. "Let's get you cleaned up. We have a dinner date with royalty."

Abethca let out a deep sigh then trailed after her new mistress. It wasn't every day you got invited to dine with the emperor of the entire galaxy.

3

 out into the hallway and drew the attention of the guards outside her door who looked at each other with stupid grins on their faces.

Upon her bed, she lay face down and topless, with Abethca perched on Jegra's buttocks while she gave her the deepest, most penetrating back massage of her life.

Abethca was also scantily clothed, wearing only a white gossamer loincloth and a matching white lehenga top that doubled as a sports bra. Jamming her thumb under Jegra's shoulder blade as hard as she could, she forced another moan from Jegra's lips.

"That's the spot," Jegra said, her voice muffled as she spoke into her pillow.

Abethca picked up a glass decanter filled with birtchkum oil, made from small, edible seeds that smell like almonds, and poured a large amount into the center of Jegra's back so it pooled between her shoulder blades. Rubbing her hands across Jegra's skin, she spread the oil with her palms.

Once Jegra's body was copper toned and glistening, Abethca gently stroked the scar on Jegra's back. "I can't believe you've already fully healed from our battle just hours ago," Abethca said in amazement, still tracing the contours of the scar with her fingers.

"Just another one of the many strange side effects of being amped up on alien steroids," Jegra laughed, turning her head to the side so she could see Abethca's soft green face and lovely blue eyes.

Abethca reached down and touched her own ribs. There was black and blue bruising all around and her abdomen had a nasty, yellow and purple bruise. "It'll take me at least a month to heal from this."

"Sorry about that," Jegra said remorsefully, rolling onto her side.

Abethca slid down from Jegra's slick thigh and stretched out next to her on the bed. Jegra brushed Abethca's hair away from her face and smiled at her affectionately. Noticing that Jegra was staring, she grew self-conscious and asked, "What?"

"Nothing," Jegra said, turning her face away. She was blushing slightly, but she didn't want Abethca to know that she was sort of "into her."

Abethca held up the bottle of oil and said, "Tell me, or I dump this entire thing onto your chest."

Jegra laughed. "You wouldn't dare!"

"Too late," Abethca teased, and she poured out the remaining oil all over Jegra's bare chest.

They both began laughing but Jegra grabbed Abethca and reeled her in close. Abethca's chest glided across Jegra's well-oiled breasts and then, once again, their lips were locked.

After a long, sultry kiss, Abethca pulled away slightly and asked, "Can I finish your massage for you?"

Jegra rolled onto her back and stared up at the stone ceiling and let out a deep sigh. "I supposed we should get ourselves ready for our fancy dinner party this evening."

She sounded less than enthused. But Abethca was starving, so she leapt out of bed and hopped up and down with excitement. "In that case, I'll prepare you a bubble bath."

Jegra chortled softly and nodded in agreement. With that settled, Abethca cheerfully scurried off to get things ready.

Jegra sat up in bed and, reaching over to a pile of disheveled clothes, fished for her top. Getting out of bed, she stretched, cracked her neck to either side, and then slipped her top back on.

Before she had even finished pulling her top over her head, she sauntered across the room to where there was a desk with a large video monitor built into the wall. Although the technology was somewhat dated, it still worked.

She fastened the strap on the back of her top and then adjusted her large breasts, making sure they were in their proper place. Taking a deep breath, she tossed her brown hair over her shoulder and flicked the display on. Then, her voice cool and calculated, she said, "Dial Emperor Dakroth."

The screen flickered and a beautiful, blue skinned woman in Imperial armor and wearing a tight ponytail that pulled the skin of her face tight appeared on the monitor. "This is Vice Admiral Cassera Van Danica Amelorak, who is this and how did you get this number?"

"Vice Admiral, it's me. Jegra."

The Vice Admiral squinted at her vidscreen and made a sour face, as if to let Jegra know she was disgusted by her. "And what do you want?"

"The Emperor extended an invitation for an evening dinner with him aboard his ship."

"Of course, he did," Cassera sighed in a vexed tone.

"I was wondering if the meal was going to be formal or informal."

Cassera eyeballed Jegra and laughed. "My dear," she said in a condescending fashion, "The only thing you'll ever be is an informal preoccupation. But don't worry, I'll have some proper clothes sent down."

"Please send for two," Jegra said. This caused Cassera to raise an eyebrow. "A friend will be accompanying me."

Cassera hit a button off screen and there was a chirp followed by a violet light that came through Jegra's chamber walls. She took a step back as it scanned the room and her. "I take it it's the Bre'lal woman bathing in your chambers?"

"That would be correct," Jegra said.

Cassera rolled her eyes and said, "Fine." Then the monitor went black as she abruptly ended the call.

"What a bitch," Jegra said in a hushed tone. When she turned around, a golden particle beam appeared on her bed and two elegant dresses manifested out of thin air, then the particles dissipated again.

Jegra walked over and held up the white dress, which was hers. She smiled. Even though Cassera was a royal pain in the ass, she did have good taste.

Abethca's dress was a form-fitting tube top with green zebra print on black. In fact, the green seemed to be color matched to her exact gradient of skin so that it would look as though the black dress was shredded and her skin was peeking out from beneath. Sexy and stylish.

Jegra laid her dress back onto the bed and then turned to head to the bathroom; she noticed water running out from under the door. "What in the world?"

She rushed to the door and practically broke it down as she burst onto the scene. Entering the bathroom chambers, Jegra found a bald, red-skinned female of an unknown alien race strangling Abethca in the rectangular stone tub. The tub was built into the wall, and water was sloshing over the edges of the bath as it overflowed onto the floor.

The mysterious woman had intricate, circuitry-like black tattoos running from the top of her smooth head down either side of her neck and to her sternum. They disappeared beneath her thick, black armor, which Jegra could only describe as techno-gothic. It looked like something right out of the middle ages, but with veins of red light pulsing through it–definitely technology she hadn't seen before.

Not waiting around for introductions, Jegra grabbed the towel hanger bolted to the wall and tore the metal rod off. The screws shot out and ricocheted against the side wall with a resounding ping. This caught the assassin's attention, but by the time she had spotted Jegra bearing down upon her, it was already too late.

The assassin barely had time to grab the rod with both hands as Jegra forced it down across her neck. Colliding with the red-skinned assassin, they skidded back on the wet floor, a spray of water shooting up around them. With bone shattering force, the assassin slammed into the rock wall. Some of the stones cracked from the strength of the impact.

Through a clenched jaw, Jegra leaned forward and growled, "You chose the wrong gladiator's bedroom to pick a fight in. Now. Tell me what you're doing here and who sent you."

The red-skinned woman had yellow eyes that flared bright, as though they coursed with raw energy, and her armor began to hum. Then, unexpectedly, she shoved Jegra off her–matching Jegra's incredible strength. This surprised Jegra, since there weren't many who could equal her in power.

With great force, Jegra slid back, kicking up another spray of water. She stuck her right leg back and dug her heel in, slowing herself and quickly coming to a halt in the center of the room.

She glanced to the side to see Abethca's naked body laying at the bottom of the tub, her bright blue eyes staring vacantly up at Jegra from beneath the water. A shocked expression on her face. It was obvious the assassin had caught her off guard.

Jegra knew that she needed to get Abethca out of the water as soon as possible. Abethca's heart had stopped and the clock was ticking.

Ready to get her revenge, Jegra popped her knuckles and then, balling up her fists, asked, "Now, where were we?"

The red-skinned assassin shot her a jeering grin and, without breaking eye contact, slowly reached down and tapped a touch-button pad on her forearm. A computer beeped with a transmission and almost instantly, a yellow beam of light came down and whisked the red-skinned woman away.

Her opponent gone, Jegra rushed over to the bath, scooped Abethca up in both arms, and brought her out. Laying her naked body down onto the bathroom floor, she knelt down next to her and began administering CPR.

After tilting Abethca's head back to open the air passage of her throat and blowing air into her mouth, Jegra pumped on her chest ten times. She repeated the process several more times and whispered, "Don't die on me. You're stronger than this."

As she worked desperately to save her friend, Jegra realized that she was crying. It was the first time she'd cried since the slavers abducted her from Earth; she'd been trapped in a cage in a cold and frightening place aboard an old cargo frigate, leaving her solar system.

She had watched Earth fade away into the distance until it was a pale blue dot. That's when they jumped into faster than light travel; she broke down in her cage, weeping as though a loved one had died.

Of course, being powerful didn't mean she no longer had feelings. She still had feelings. But she had learned to suppress them. She had to; feelings led to weakness, vulnerability. Killing helpless creatures much weaker than herself for sport had become her profession. She couldn't afford to be compassionate. That would only cause her to question her actions, to hesitate in the arena. And that would spell certain doom for her.

It was kill or be killed. And it wasn't like she had any choice in the matter. She had tried to escape only once, when she had first been forced into the arena. She had made it only as far as Riverion, a moon edging on the outer rim, before the Intergalactic Gladiatorial Syndicate's goons caught up to her.

She was out of her depth and they easily subdued her and brought her back to Thessalonica, desert moon to the planet Dagon Prime–home of Emperor Dakroth.

Jegra stopped compressing Abethca's chest and laid her head down onto her bosom. She sobbed until she felt numb. She had failed.

Very gently, Jegra scooped Abethca's still warm body off the floor and carried her out into the main bedroom and laid her down on her bed. She gathered herself and wiped a tear from her cheek.

"Rest peacefully, my strange and wonderful friend."

Jegra walked over to the wall and touched an orange button next to a metal panel. The panel slid open and she reached in and opened up a false bottom to the cubby. Inside was a laser pistol.

She took out the pistol and set it to vaporize, then aimed it at Abethca's deceased body. "I wish we could have had more time together," she said. Taking a deep breath, she pulled the trigger.

A steady beam of red light shot out of the laser pistol and disintegrated Abethca's body, which burned away like paper set aflame.

As the last pieces of her body dissolved into thin air, Jegra let up on the trigger and ceased firing. She watched as a couple of flakes of ash, all that remained of her friend, fluttered down onto her bed. She returned the pistol to the cubby and sealed it up.

Technically, she wasn't supposed to be in possession of such a weapon, but it was given to her by Lord Dakroth, who felt it might come in handy in her new, hostile environment. "Just in case," he'd told her.

Once Jegra had changed out of her work clothes and into the evening dress, she marched out of her chambers and headed up the hall toward the silent arena. It was mostly empty, nothing but drunkards sleeping in the tiered bleachers and several homeless children scavenging beneath the seats for discarded food scraps– any decent sized morsels to eat.

Because of her dour mood, Jegra felt it awfully sad for the street urchins. But soon enough, the colosseum's security detail, two Dragonian security guards with their menacing lizard faces, chased the vagabonds and loiterers out.

At the same time, a clean-up crew began tidying things up for tomorrow's match, to be held in honor of Emperor Dakroth's return.

Jegra sauntered out into the center of the arena in her nearly see-through gossamer dress. Although her dark nipples shone through the fabric, her white silk panties prevented her nether region from being revealed. It wasn't at all a modest dress, which surprised her since Cassera typically derided the idea of the Emperor's dalliances with a common gladiatrix.

Regardless, when she got to the center of the arena, she looked up at the battle cruiser hanging low in the sky and said in her normal tone of voice, "I'm ready."

A yellow beam of light came down from the ship and engulfed her. In the blink of an eye, she was transported to Dakroth's ship.

4

Rematerialized and reassembled, Jegra staggered off the transporter pad. Her head spun uncontrollably and her stomach felt as though it had been turned inside out. *Teleportation sucks,* she thought.

Even as she said the words to herself, alarm bells started ringing in her head, and she knew an emergency was brewing in the depths of her gut. Lurching forward, Jegra collapsed onto her hands and knees and spewed the contents of her stomach onto the finely polished floor.

If puking all over the place wasn't embarrassing enough, some of her vomit splashed onto a pair of shiny black boots which stood directly in front of her. Gulping nervously, she slowly raised her head to find the vice admiral, Cassera Van Danica Amelorak, scowling down at her in disgust.

"Oh, God. I'm so sorry," Jegra apologized. "I'm still not used to the dematerializing process."

"I could hardly tell," Cassera quipped sarcastically, her disdainful gaze drilling into the top of Jegra's scull and making her humiliation that much worse.

Cassera pulled out a black handkerchief from a back pocket and held it out for Jegra. She took it without hesitation and began to wipe the excess vomit from her chin.

As she cleaned herself off, the transporter room officer scurried over and waited impatiently until she had finished. Helping her to her feet, he took the handkerchief from her and promptly got down on all fours and began cleaning the vice admiral's boots.

Nervous that she may have sullied her dress with her own sick, Jegra checked to make sure she didn't accidentally splash any vomit on her borrowed gown. Groping her large chest, she mashed her breasts from side to side, and even hoisted them up briefly to check underneath, as she searched for any excess spillage.

Satisfied that she was in the clear, she readjusted her chest, and made sure her girls were presenting themselves well–since it was, after all, a transparent gown. The last thing she wanted was to be seen on her way to meet the emperor with mashed up areolas and wonky nipples pointing in opposite directions. Running her hands down her sides and over her hips, she chased away the creases and smoothed out her dress.

Not waiting for the officer to finish buffing her boots to their former luster, Cassera spun on her heel, whipping her long, white ponytail behind her like a horse tail chasing away pesky flies, and then marched out of the double sliding doors and exited the transporter room.

Without looking back, she beckoned Jegra, and said, "This way, if you please."

Straight forward and to the point. That was Cassera's way. And even though she had the emotional warmth of an icicle, Jegra could at least respect Cassera's no-nonsense personality.

Over the course of a year, if there's anything that Jegra had learned, it's that ninety-nine percent of the alien species she'd met lied without reservation. It was refreshing to meet someone like Cassera, who simply didn't have time for conjuring up falsehoods. The truth was much more economic. And Cassera was as pragmatic as they came.

Complying with the vice admiral's wishes, she followed Cassera out of the transporter room. Along the way, she passed the officer cleaning up her vomit and glanced down at him as she went, but said nothing, out of embarrassment.

When she entered the corridor of the battle cruiser, she glanced back and caught him starring at her ass. The moment she caught him watching her, however, he quickly diverted his gaze and went back to his begrudging task of cleaning up after her.

Normally, she would have shot him a nasty look, but seeing as he was currently cleaning up her disgusting mess, she figured the least she could do was allow him the privilege of having a little look-see. No harm in that.

When she turned back around, she saw Vice Admiral Cassera impatiently tapping her foot as she waited for her in the middle of the open corridor. "Coming?" she griped, her arms folded across her white uniform, her yellow eyes staring at Jegra with immense irritation.

"Apologies, Vice Admiral," Jegra answered as she caught up to Cassera.

As she moved up the corridor at a brisk pace, the long tail of Cassera's platinum hair swayed behind her shoulder blades, her hips seductively swiveling side-to-side as she went. She swaggered across the deck like a veritable supermodel who was strutting her stuff on the catwalk. As a Dagon woman, she always presented herself as the most formal and appealing version of herself she could.

Personally, Jegra felt the Dagon people were, perhaps, a bit too vain for their own good. But, even she had to confess, they all looked stunning. Like Asians back on her homeworld, they all shared certain homogenous traits. Every Dagon man and woman had blue skin and white hair. Meanwhile, the men had red eyes, the women typically had yellow, but she'd seen children with orange eyes.

At the same time, Dagons were larger than standard Earth humans, standing an average of six feet five inches. Even the women. Many of them had tall, pointy-tipped ears, like real-life elves; while others had diminished features, like a subtle crest.

During her time on Thessalonica, Jegra had noticed that all of the Dagon women who had made personal visits to her chambers after her bouts had an aristocratic air about them. Dagon women were notoriously well groomed. Their skin tended to be a slightly lighter hue of blue than their darker male counterparts. And, unlike the males, Dagon women were all hermaphrodites. A strange, vestigial trait of their evolutionary past. But unlike the males, who had two penises, the females only had one, which somehow retracted up into the cervix when it wasn't needed.

It was rumored that the Dagon people had been maintaining their empire for so long that the numerous wars had taken their toll on the males of the species and had decimated their gender's numbers so severely that females had begun to adapt by first parthenogenesis and then by taking on male characteristics, including developing their own male organs.

But, still, it was all just rumor. Whether or not this trait really was the byproduct of three thousand years of imperialistic warmongering or if some other factor had spurred their strange reproductive evolution, Jegra did not know. Not that it mattered to her, either way. Both the Dagon men and women made excellent lovers, regardless of their appearance.

It was no secret; Jegra was fond of the blue-bloods, as the other races called them. Dagon women had insatiably carnal appetites. And Jegra enjoyed helping them quench their thirst, so to speak, after a bloody bout in the arena.

Besides, as champion, she was allowed all the sex and alcohol she could desire. And she kept it flowing freely as it helped her to take her mind off the horrors of her kills.

If she was being honest with herself, although she excelled at fighting, the killing came far too easily for her lately. And not in the good kind of way, either. If not for the inebriated orgies she partook in almost every night, she was positive that visions of the dead, conjured up from her guilty subconscious, would drive her to madness. So, she soaked her guilt in booze and kept her inner demons at bay.

After a long silence, Vice Admiral Cassera finally glanced over at Jegra and asked, "Where's your friend? The one you told me you'd be bringing this evening."

A lump formed in Jegra's throat and she swallowed hard. "There was a complication," she replied, doing her best to keep a poker face and her emotions in check.

She knew that grand displays of emotion were viewed by the Dagon people as a kind of mental illness. The calmer and more collected you were, the better standing you had with them. Although, they did display hints of emotion, but it was extremely subtle.

"She couldn't make it," Jegra said in a cool voice.

"I'll be sure to inform the cook," Cassera said.

Jegra continued following the vice admiral up one corridor and down another until she was thoroughly lost. The *Dreadnaught* was the largest ship in the fleet and it was a veritable labyrinth. She couldn't have found her way out in a year, she'd been turned around more times than she could count.

She suspected the labyrinthine interior of the ship was a deliberate architectural choice. It was much like the roads leading to and from Japanese castles back on Earth, which always twisted and bent around backwards to confound invading enemies and led them away from the main castle.

"Are you sure we haven't passed this exact same corridor?" Jegra asked aloud. "Because it seems we've been past this point before."

"No," Cassera answered. "This is a different section of the ship."

"Are you sure? Because I can't make heads or tails of this place."

Without looking back, Cassera replied, "Unlike your species, my people have a superior memory."

Jegra raised an eyebrow. Considering that she was probably the only human Cassera had ever met, it was highly unlikely she knew all that much about human physiology. It rather seemed like a personal put down, if you asked her.

"May I ask you something, Vice Admiral?" Jegra asked.

Cassera nodded. "Go ahead."

"Why don't you like me? Have I done something to offend you in some way?"

Cassera stopped in the middle of the passage and turned to face Jegra. "It's not that I don't like you; in fact, I respect your prowess as a warrior. But I don't trust you."

"You mean you don't trust me with *him*."

"Lord Dakroth can take care of himself. But when he's with you, he is vulnerable. And that makes you dangerous."

"I'm not going to hurt your precious blue-skinned leader," Jegra said, brushing her hair out of her eyes.

"I know," Cassera replied, a hint of a smile turning up the corners of her mouth. "I'll see to that."

"By doing what?"

"By watching your every move," Cassera asserted, her jaw tightening.

"You're free to watch us fuck, if you like!" Jegra fired back.

"I already do," Cassera answered.

"Oh," Jegra said, rubbing the back of her neck as she took in the information. She thought about the numerous times she and the emperor had shared one another's company, thinking they were alone, but, apparently, were being watched by Cassera.

"So, let me get this straight. You've been watching me, in the privacy of my own chambers, for over a year?" Jegra asked, feeling the back of her neck starting to get warm as her temper began to heat up.

"It was a necessary precaution," Cassera stated, as a matter of fact. "Besides," she continued, "I only allowed it to go on as long as it has because you seem to bring, how shall I say...a certain joy to the emperor."

"Really?" Jegra asked, thinking she might mean something more to the emperor than just the gladiator slave girl he occasionally fucked during his furlough.

"Yes. You bring him an unparalleled physical enjoyment."

Jegra bit her lip and squinted at Cassera. "Do you think maybe there's something more, perhaps? I mean, to the emperor's liking me?"

"No," Cassera staunchly replied, her truth crushing Jegra's hopes of finding anything resembling love this side of the galaxy. "It's purely physical."

"Fine," Jegra answered, scowling at Cassera. She appreciated honestly, but there was such a thing as being *too honest*. "At least now we're on the same page."

Cassera turned and continued up the length of the corridor and Jegra followed, her posture slumped slightly as a harsh sense of dejection set in.

Soon enough they came to a large oval doorway with two guards posted outside. Cassera gestured for Jegra to go ahead and enter the room with a wave of her hand. "He's waiting for you inside."

Without so much as waiting for a reply, Vice Admiral Cassera marched back the way they'd come and disappeared around the corner of the bending corridor. Off to bust some balls, no doubt. And maybe crush a few hearts just for funsies while she was at it, Jegra mused.

Nervous, she stood outside the emperor's personal quarters and took a deep breath. *It's just the emperor of the whole friggin' galaxy,* she told herself. Facing the large entrance, she fidgeted with her breasts one more time out of nervous anticipation and a keen desire to make a good impression. She took another deep breath, exhaled, and brushed down her dress, chasing out any wrinkles. Satisfied that she was as good as she could get, at least without a full team of stylists, she boldly stepped up to the entrance and tapped the door panel. She heard the chime from within. It played a melodic ditty that she'd heard a couple times before as she'd stalked the corridors of the ship.

"Enter," a voice commanded.

The doors parted with a whisk and the pleasant aroma of wine and salad with a vinaigrette dressing wafted out of the emperor's quarters and into the corridor. Jegra smiled and then confidently strode inside to find a large chamber unlike any she'd ever seen before. Especially aboard a starship. Although, to be fair, to date, her starship excursions had been rather limited.

Even so, she was astonished to find a fountain in the middle of room. It had two mermaid-like aliens, bare-breasted and each holding up a large chalice that poured out water from its spout onto a center figure. The center figure was the very effigy of the emperor himself, and like the mermaids he was fully nude. In addition to the emperor's sculpted likeness, along with the mermaids that sensually bathed his Adonis form, there were three Japanese-like koi fish, the size of great white sharks, jumping up mid-air and which spat little streams that crisscrossed one another in pulsating squirts.

Jegra almost laughed out loud at the sight of a fountain in a starship, but she knew that Lord Dakroth was a somewhat decadent type. The seemingly Greek styled sculptures complimented the rest of the ship rather nicely with its strange techno-gothic aesthetic that was both sleek and menacing. Just like the emperor.

As she scanned her surroundings, she found that the room was unusually large, even for an emperor's suite. It reminded her of her old high school's auditorium. There was even a raised level, a platform, that wrapped around the entire circumference of the room with curved stairs to either side of her. Beneath the platform was an open bar that looked out at the fountain.

Above her, hanging from the ceiling, was a magnificent crystal chandelier that provided a warm candlelight to the room. Running along the brushed metal of the space-gray walls were a series of matching wall lights, meant to look like candelabrums.

"Over here," a voice called out to her. Jegra looked up to find the emperor standing next to a round table set for three. She smiled and waved and then started up the stairs to meet him.

When she arrived at the top of the stairs, she found him waiting there for her. She curtseyed deeply and held her slight bow, then slowly rose when he took her hand.

He immediately placed his hand on the small of her back and pulled her into him, kissing her lips. Jegra didn't know what to do but accept the kiss. She smiled when he'd had his fill of her and then waited for him to speak.

"Please, take a seat, my dear Jessica."

She hated it when he called her by her Earth name. She was Jegra the Merciless. The undefeated champion of the galaxy. Jessica was just a ghost. A fleeting memory of the woman she had been. But she dared not correct him. He was the emperor of the Dagon Empire and seven star systems.

Only the Nyctan Empire rivaled his power. The Nyctan ruled five systems and managed to hold Emperor Dakroth's imperial fleet at bay–a topic that was a rather sore spot for him.

"I hear the Nyctan fleet is putting up an impressive fight at the front," she said as Dakroth slid out her chair and gestured for her to sit.

She smiled and took her seat at the dining table. He sat down opposite her and unfolded his napkin and pressed it to his lap. She followed suit and did likewise.

A waiter promptly appeared out of nowhere and took away the third set of plates and silverware meant for Abethca. Jegra watched him rush off and then turned to face Dakroth.

"Yes, the Nyctans boast superior shield technology which allows them to hold out in a fight longer. But our laser canons are far more powerful which levels the playing field considerably."

Jegra nodded as though she were interested in the specs of the large battle cruisers. She wasn't. But she humored him as she waited to learn why she was here. Was it just a booty call, or did he have something specific to discuss with her?

"My Lord," she began, but they had begun to speak at the same time. Catching herself, she gave a diminutive laugh and apologized. "I'm sorry, you go ahead."

"No, you go on. I insist."

"I was just wondering," she said, batting her lovely brown eyes at him, "if you called me here for something other than my physical charms and riveting company."

Lord Dakroth laughed and tossed his silver hair over his shoulder. "My dear Jessica," he said, his narrow smile widening into a full grin. "I've invited you here because I want to ask you something. Something of utmost importance."

"Yes?" she asked.

Dakroth slid his chair back and rose to his feet. Walking around the table to her, he got down on one knee, and pulled out a Seyfferian Sapphire, the largest and brightest sapphires in the whole star system. "Will you, Jessica Hemsworth, do me the honor of becoming my seventeenth wife?"

Jegra's jaw fell open and she mumbled senseless sounds as she searched for the proper response. After a moment of her being tongue-tied, Dakroth scratched his chin and looked down at the sapphire.

"Did I do it wrong? My research said that the males of your species get down on one knee when they ask a woman to marry them."

"Oh, you did fine," Jegra said.

She could see this news relieved the emperor greatly. "Excellent!" he said, holding up the ring for her to slip onto her finger.

Jegra wasn't in love with the emperor. They had chemistry, though. A raw, sexual attraction existed between them for sure. But she wasn't expecting him to make her into one of his many wives, adding her to his already robust harem. Quite frankly, she suspected that he had ulterior motives.

"Before I accept," she said, holding out her fingers, but pulling back just enough to delay the inevitable. "Why, may I ask, the sudden urge to marry me? Do you need me to fight in the campaigns? Or do you just desire my body?"

"By the almighty Hastur, I swear to you, it is because you've stolen my heart that I so desire you. There isn't a moment that goes by that I can't stop thinking of you. The sound of your voice. The smell of your hair. And, yes, even I admit the sex is great. But you're more than just a trophy wife to me. I want you by my side, Jegra. I swear it."

She felt he hammed his speech up far too much for any of it to be sincere, but she knew that he'd likely reveal all in due time. So, she let out a deep sigh and then slid her finger into the ring.

"Yes!" she answered enthusiastically. "I will marry you."

Although the words had slipped out of her mouth without the slightest inkling of forethought, she was committed. After all, it wasn't every day the emperor of the entire friggin' galaxy asked you to marry him.

5

Out of wind, Jegra rolled off Dakroth's waist and fell back onto the silky, golden sheets of his gilded bed, her sweat dappled chest heaving with the aftershocks of salacious delight.

Jegra fanned her glistening chest and reached across the smooth sheets that were made from the finest silk of the Angorian weaving spider which populates Dagon Prime. They also infest the darker regions of the catacombs beneath the arena, but although they were a pretty, iridescent teal, to her they were just ordinary spiders. She looked over at Dakroth, who gazed up at the ceiling, still in a daze of euphoria and said, "That was…"

"Invigorating!" Dakroth interrupted, finishing her sentence for her.

"You spoke my mind, your majesty."

"Please, you are my bride-to-be. You can dispense with the formalities and refer to me by my name when in private. In public, Emperor Dakroth will suffice."

"Yes, my lovely Rhadamanthus." Jegra sat up and swung her legs over the bed, slid to the cold floor, and then sauntered over to a small mini-bar at the edge of the room. "Would you like something to drink?"

Dakroth licked his lips, the taste of her essence still lingering there. "I'm more than satisfied, for the time being."

Jegra chortled as she poured herself a Tragellion ale and mixed it with a Dragonian elixir that tasted like raspberry flavored tequila, except that it glowed bright green. When the two combined, they turned into a luminescent blue drink. She raised the glass and examined the contents with keen interest.

"Suit yourself," she replied, and downed the entire drink before pouring herself another. When she turned around, the emperor had drifted off to sleep.

Jegra smiled and then, remembering what Cassera had said earlier, about keeping an eye on her at all times, she sauntered drunkenly around the room inspecting the walls and behind furniture for hidden cameras or concealed mics.

Tipsy, she took another sip of her blue liquor and then, looking up at the ceiling, called out to Cassera. "I know you're eavesdropping, Vice Admiral Snoopy-pants. Why don't you come over for a visit? Our boy-toy is passed out with exhaustion, but I still have a deep thirst that needs to be quenched. Come play with me Cassera. *Please?!'*

Jegra shrugged when there was no immediate reply and tossed back her drink. It slid down her throat slicker than vodka; she wiped her mouth with the back of her hand and let out a delicious sounding sigh.

Still horny, she looked over at the emperor sleeping on the bed and studied his naked, blue form, sprawled out for all the world to see. She smiled and bit her bottom lip as she contemplated what to do. But she didn't want to disturb the emperor's slumber, so, instead, she plopped down on the bed and admired her engagement ring.

She didn't know the value of the sapphire, but it looked like an enormous blue diamond set inside a wide, korridium wedding band. Etched along the circumference of the ring was what she recognized to be Dagoni. The only part she could make out, however, was *"Dakroth Ne Dekwe'gon"* which meant "Dakroth's beloved one," in the Dagoni language. Pulling up the covers, Jegra tucked in her sleeping emperor and then rose up to make the long walk back around to her side of the bed. But before she could sink back into the silky sheets, the door chimed.

She stopped and turned to see the doors slide open. To her pleasant surprise, Cassera stood in the entrance, tottering on a pair of long sexy blue legs that ran up the length of her short, oriental styled nightgown, and almost seemed to go on forever after disappearing inside.

Cassera tilted her hips and rested her shoulder on the door frame as she gazed across the room at Jegra with maudlin eyes that sparkled golden. Like her eyes, her oriental gown glittered with a medallionesque sheen in the soft light streaming in from the hallway. Her gown's sash had slackened and her cleavage was spilling out in generous amounts. It was also the first time Jegra had seen her wear her hair down.

As Cassera tipsily swayed in the doorway, Jegra noticed that she had a bottle of something orange in her hands. She raised it to her lips, tipped her head back, and took a deep gulp, and then slowly lowered her gaze until it met Jegra's. They held one another's gazes and an ebrious grin slowly spread across Cassera's beautiful Prussian blue lips.

"Watching you two made me...*hic*" she stopped herself, putting a fist to her mouth to prevent another hiccup from escaping, and then raised a finger, as if to say, hold on for just a moment and forced the subsequent hiccup back down. Having defeated a bout of hiccups, she looked up and said, "Wetter than a Brilaxian eel!"

"I'll take your word for it," Jegra laughed. She had no clue what a Brilaxian eel was.

Cassera stumbled across the room and, tripping on her own feet, fell into Jegra's arms. Stabilizing them both, Jegra set her back on her feet and smiled at her. She never expected that the vice admiral was even capable of letting down her hair like this. Yet, here she was.

Propped up against Jegra's body, Cassera leaned in, deliberately rubbing herself against Jegra's soft flesh and nestling in to her, and kicked back her head and guzzled the orange stuff straight from the bottle. It smelled of mead and carrot juice, but with a significantly higher alcohol content.

Everything in the Dagon Empire had to be the best; the strongest, the rarest, the most desired, which meant, consequently, the alcohol was always the finest money could buy, and there was always plenty to be had. Dagons were intemperate, to say the least. And they liked their alcohol just as they liked their sex—rich and fulfilling.

Cassera pulled down her evening gown's spaghetti straps and let it slip off her body. The navy blue of her erect nipples stood upon her cobalt skin in the cool air. She then pushed Jegra back onto the bed. Luckily, the emperor was out like a light and remained undisturbed.

"You want girl on girl or guy on girl?" Cassera asked, slowly crawling onto the bed.

Jegra smiled and brushed back her hair as she watched the Cassera climb onto her, straddling her waist with her blue thighs.

Cassera discarded the bottle and it rattled when it hit the floor. She slowly slid down the length of Jegra's body, dappling her sunbaked bosom with a spread of feathery light kisses. By the time Cassera reached Jegra's neck, Jegra was just starting to get turned on. But then she heard the light sound of snoring coming from Cassera's half open mouth.

"Cassera?" Jegra asked, craning her neck to find Cassera fast asleep and breathing warm breath into her neck. "Honey?" She gave the vice admiral a nudge, hoping to rouse her, but it was no use. She was out cold.

Unable to make love to Cassera, Jegra sighed disappointedly and then slowly pushed Cassera off of her. The Dagon slipped onto her side and drearily threw her right arm across Jegra's chest and went back to snoring.

Jegra stroked the blue woman's hair and admired her Prussian blue lips. Unable to resist stealing a kiss, Jegra leaned in and touched her lips to Cassera's lips. They tasted of the orange tonic that she'd finished off earlier. "Sweet dreams," Jegra said in a soft voice, being sure not to wake the blue sleeping beauty next to her.

Apparently, when it came to Cassera, who seemed to be wound up tighter than most, a little alcohol went a long way with her. Jegra made a mental note of it.

Although she didn't get the second round of love making she'd hoped for, for some reason she felt satisfied just holding the sleeping Dagon woman in her arms and letting Cassera nestle up beside her as she fell away into an even deeper slumber. The poor woman was exhausted. As for Jegra, she was finally feeling an ounce of affection from a woman she wanted desperately to impress. Which is why she didn't want to let a single moment go to waste.

Jegra curled up on the bed between the two sleeping Dagons, wrapped her arms around Cassera's perfectly cobalt-blue body, placed her cheek on the top of Cassera's silver head, and then dozed off to sleep.

In the morning, Jegra was aroused by the chatter of a large gaggle of women. She opened her eyes to find about a dozen women scurrying about.

Jegra shot up in bed and covered her private bits the best she could. "Who are you?" she asked. Noticing that both the emperor and Cassera were gone, she added, "Where's Cassera and Rhadamanthus?"

"Oh, isn't that sweet?" one of the green-skinned Bre'lal women said. "She thinks because he lets her use his first name that she's somehow special."

"Knock it off, Gaela. You were once in her shoes. And if you recall, you were the one who passed out before the Rhadamanthus could finish."

"Besides," a purple skinned woman with an orange mohawk chimed in, "She managed to bed Cassera. None of us had ever had that pleasure."

"You must be the emperor's wives," Jegra said.

A fourth woman, with ivory skin, black eyes, and short, cropped black hair brought Jegra her clothes. She didn't say anything, but Jegra nodded in thanks and began to dress herself.

"So, is it true what they say about you Terrans?" Gaela began, her eyes narrowing as she judged Jegra silently. "You like to wear the stink of your own sweat-laden ravishment as a perfume? I've heard you will go days on end without bathing?!"

"No. I mean...sometimes. Wait. That's not..." Jegra didn't know how to reply to such a mean-spirited attack.

"Ignore her," another woman said. Jegra turned to see a woman knitting in the corner of the room. She had three eyes and a large green head, but looked very pretty. "She's just jealous."

"Jealous? Of me?"

Gaela folded her arms and huffed angrily. "I'm not jealous. I just don't know what he sees in her. I mean, she's a slave girl, for crying out loud!"

"She's Lord Dakroth's bride to be!" a voice boomed.

All the women grew silent and turned to gaze upon the head mistress. Lady Dakroth, the first of the wives. She was, of course, Dagoni. Her skin was pale blue, like that of a gorgeous lagoon. "She'll be one of our sisters, soon enough. So, you will respect her as you respect me. Do I make myself clear?"

"Yes, mum," Gaela replied, lowering her eyes in shame.

"Come dear," Lady Dakroth said, taking Jegra's hand in hers and guiding her to her side. "Let me introduce you to the rest of Lord Dakroth's harem. First, let me inform you that Rhadamanthus picks a favorite woman almost every cycle to add to his harem. Although you're special, you're only as special as the next woman he chooses. Some people would do well to remember that." She shot an indignant look at Gaela, who diverted her eyes and, being shunned by the head mistress, scurried out of the bedroom.

"What do I call you, mistress?"

"My name is Jennica."

"It's a pleasure to meet you, Jennica. I'm…"

"I know who you are, Jegra. Everyone who has ever turned on a televid knows who you are. In fact, I'd be surprised if there wasn't a single soul in this entire system who didn't know who you are."

"You flatter me," Jegra said, bowing.

Jennica reached down and pulled up Jegra's chin. "No, my dear. You flatter me by showing undeserved reverence. Although you are rough around the edges, you have a good heart. I can see that. But I should warn you. Some of these women are less like you and I and more like Lord Dakroth."

"Ambitious?" asked Jegra.

"I was going to say ruthless," Jennica replied.

Both women leaned into one another and laughed.

"Well, he is that too, I suppose," Jegra said.

Just then the doors swooshed open and Emperor Dakroth entered. About half the women squealed with glee, ran up to him, and immediately began stroking him and rubbing their hands all over him like a bunch of sex-starved nymphs.

"Ladies, ladies, all in due time! There's plenty of me to go around. But first, I should probably inform you that I have a special day planned for you all.

"Oh, do tell!" the purple skinned woman pleaded.

"My dear wives," he said, his tone jovial. "It has come to my attention that there are just far too many of you. As much fun as we have had together, and the memories we've shared, I'm afraid that the time has come to pick one–and only one wife to inherit the title of Imperatrix."

Gasps broke out all across the room and a couple of women began sobbing.

Although Jegra wasn't quite sure what Dakroth was on about, she could see that his words had caught even the attention of Jennica.

"I knew this day would come," Jennica whispered from behind clenched teeth. She shot Jegra a sad look and then began to inch away, toward the back of the room.

That's when Jegra knew something was gravely wrong.

"But don't be disheartened my loves. If anything, I'm a fair man. Which is why I've designed a little contest for you all to compete in to win the coveted position as my one true empress!"

"What is it?" Gaela asked, falling to her knees at Dakroth's feet. "Tell me—and I'll do it. I'll do anything for you!"

"It's simple," he said, looking down into her eyes. And as he answered her, he issued the rules of the contest to all the wives in his harem. "All you have to do is fight to the death. The last one standing wins everything!"

Dakroth let out a hardy chuckle and then excused himself from the room. Once the doors had shut behind him, one of his more overzealous wives ran after him.

"My Lord, don't leave me!" she cried out, but when she came to the door she found it was locked.

"We're sealed in," she said in complete dismay. As she turned around, something struck her in the head. She reached up and touched the large gash with her hand. Gaela stood in front of her, eyes wild, her body shaking as she held a thick crystal vase in her trembling hands.

"No! Please, don't do this," the other wife pleaded. But Gaela didn't wait for her to finish her sentence before she struck her again. The woman yelped like an ill-fated animal and fell to her knees. This only spurred Gaela on further. She was determined, and she struck a final, lethal blow to the poor woman's head.

Gaela turned around, blood dripping off the vase, and grinned at the rest of the women maniacally.

The entire harem of women shared stunned glances as the room fell deathly silent. Jegra knew that Jennica had foreseen this terrible outcome minutes earlier, knowing Dakroth's penchant for cruelty. Likely, this wasn't the first time this had happened. And if so, Jegra knew that Jennica was a contender.

Pandemonium broke loose as the gaggle of women began attacking one another, clawing and biting with a barbaric viciousness that shocked even Jegra.

Red laser beams flickered across the room and Jegra ducked, tucked, and rolled. She looked over her shoulder to see two wives drop. Their headless necks smoldered from where Jennica's lasers had cut them.

"Jegra!" Gaela shouted, pointing the bloodied vase at her opponent. "You're next, you filth-ridden land cow!"

Gaela dashed forward, shoving everyone out of the way to get to Jegra. Although she had spunk, Gaela was no match for Jegra. Just to prove that point, Jegra let Gaela smash the vase across her jaw.

Gaela watched in dismay as the thick crystal shattered against Jegra's unflinching jaw.

Shards of crystal rained to the ground, making a pleasant tinkling noise as they reverberated off the cold, hard surface. Popping her knuckles, Jegra grinned down at Gaela. "My turn."

Frightened, Gaela tried to turn and flee, but Jegra swiftly caught her by her shoulder and, in one fluid twist of the hips, flung Gaela across the room–directly at Jennica.

Jennica's lasers sawed Gaela's body in half. Her torso and legs hit at the same time but skidded off in different directions.

Jennica and Jegra made eye contact and Jegra whispered, "Oh, shit!"

Leaping behind a couple of women who were busy wrestling and pulling each other's hair, Jegra slid to the banister of the second floor in which the royal rumble had spilled out onto.

Not wasting a second, she leapt up and over the railing and crashed down in the fountain. Looking up, she saw two orange, glowing holes appear in both women's heads and watched them fall away.

Above her, a flurry of laser blasts danced about in such a way that it reminded her of a light show. She heard screams as women were sliced and diced by Jennica's lasers. Knowing she'd be next if she didn't act fast, she quickly grabbed the marble statue of Dakroth that stood at the center of the fountain and tore it off its pedestal.

"Let's see you dodge this, *sister*," Jegra growled, lobbing the hunk of rock toward the second floor.

The marble shot through the floor like a battle cruiser's missile tearing into the hull of an enemy ship and then impacted against the back wall.

The statue shattered upon impact and broke into smaller chunks which ricocheted off the wall and flew back in a debris storm. Jegra listened intently as the screams turned to whimpers and then faded to silence.

"Nice try, but you'll need to do better if you hope to defeat me," Jennica said, emerging from the haze of dust and debris.

Jegra took a step back as Jennica aimed a red glowing fingertip at her as though it were a blaster.

"This isn't the first melee I've survived, little one. There's a reason I'm the alpha of this harem."

"What harem?" Jegra said. "All I see is blood and dead bodies."

"Exactly," Jennica said, a vicious grin curling onto her luxurious lips. "And I'm afraid you're next.

A blast of light flew from Jennica's fingertip and penetrated Jegra's right shoulder. Jegra screamed out in pain and fell backward. She landed hard on the ground and began backpedaling as Jennica eased up on her.

"That was just the low setting. Shall we try the high setting, luv?"

Jegra's back found the wall and she grunted from the surge of pain that shot through her body like a thousand red hot needles. The hole was still smoldering when her healing factor kicked in, but a blast like that between the eyes would, in all likelihood, end her.

Stuck with nowhere to go, she gripped her shoulder and stared back at Jennica with a look as sharp as daggers.

6

Emperor Dakroth peered out across steepled fingers and watched the activity beyond the view portal of his royal battle cruise, the *Dreadnaught*.

Shuttles and other small space craft zoomed in and out of Thessalonica's shimmering blue atmosphere as commerce continued on as usual. It was almost as though he wasn't anxiously awaiting the news of which woman would emerge victorious from his sick and twisted little game of "last wife standing," tearing apart his harem with no holds barred. A barbaric game which he never got tired of playing.

Oh, well, he thought to himself. *It was about time to start fresh anyway.*

The bridge doors slid open and Dakroth swiveled around in his throne chair at the center of a colossal oval room to see who'd entered. Display panels all around him blinked and flashed as a dozen bridge crewmen manned their stations.

The throne was raised above the officers who sat below in a relief. A long walkway stretched from the main door all the way to the throne. The throne itself sat before a large glass viewing portal that allowed Dakroth to see everything beyond the bow of his ship. And everything was his for the taking.

"You summoned me, my lord?" Vice Admiral Cassera Van Danica Amelorak asked, taking a deep bow.

"Yes, it's about time to check on our victor. And I wanted to ask you about that other thing as well." The emperor stood up and beckoned Cassera with a nod to walk with him.

Once they left the busy work of the bridge and stepped out into the wide corridors of the cruiser, Dakroth locked his arms behind his back and asked, "Did you run the tests?"

Cassera looked at him with a profound expression. "It was as you predicted. When I got the analysis back, I found that my DNA had been rewritten by thirteen percent."

"And you're positive it was being with her that caused the alteration?"

"I ran the test before and after as you commanded. It's definitive. Jegra's body is overriding our genetic code and rewriting it."

"Rewriting it to be what, exactly?" asked Dakroth, his left eyebrow rising inquisitively on his face.

"To be human," Cassera answered.

"And how much of a threat is she to me?"

"At this stage, if you continue your gene therapy sessions with me, I say you can safely copulate with Jegra a dozen more times. But our physical therapy can only curtail the effects. This isn't some simple interplanetary transspecies pansexual disease we're talking about here. This is a full rewiring of what constitutes Dagon DNA."

They rounded a corner and walked in contemplative silence for a few klicks and then Dakroth stopped and looked at Cassera with a grin.

"If she should be the one to survive today, I want you to study this more. In detail. There may be a way to reverse engineer whatever she is doing to our DNA and weaponize it."

"Anything for you, my lord," Cassera said, throwing her right arm across her chest and bowing.

"Of course," Lord Dakroth continued, tossing his silver hair over his shoulder. "If she is dead, I'll need you to gather her remains so we can study them in other ways."

Cassera nodded. Just then they arrived at Dakroth's quarters. He motioned for Cassera to open the door and go in ahead of him. She swiped her hand over the door censor and the red lamp switched to green. A pleasant chime accompanied it and the doors opened wide.

"You son of a bitch," Jegra said, hunched over in the doorway. She was panting heavily and was soaked head to toe in fresh blood. Blood rained down from the ceiling and walls and she was bleeding profusely from numerous laser wounds. Jegra held her gut tightly, applying pressure to what appeared to be a severe laceration across the middle of her abdomen.

"My dear Jessica! I'm so pleased to see that it is you who emerged victorious. Congratulations, my bride. You have earned your place upon a throne, by my side!"

"Go to hell, you bastard," Jegra barked.

With a wild punch, she clocked the emperor in his jaw and sent him flying. He soared through the wall on the opposite side of the corridor with a resounding crash, sending a shudder through the entire deck. Loose wires hissed and sparked while paneling fell to the floor with metallic clanks. In the distance, a second crash could be heard as he passed through another wall.

"And the name is Jegra from now on."

Cassera stood looking at Jegra, unamused.

"Weren't you supposed to protect your precious emperor or something?" Jegra jeered, thumbing toward the gaping hole in the wall.

"Indeed," Cassera answered, manifesting a baton from her belt. She squeezed the trigger and it sparked to life with a blue arc of crackling electricity. Before Jegra could react to Cassera, however, the vice admiral merely touched Jegra's arm with the baton and tazed her.

"*You bitch! I'll...*" Jegra said, her words cutting out and her eyes rolling back as she lost consciousness. Jegra fell face first into the metal plating of the floor beneath the open archway and landed at the feet of Vice Admiral Cassera Danica.

"She's coming to," a voice said. It came dimly from beyond the darkness that shrouded Jegra's consciousness. But as she crawled back out of the insentient void that had pulled her under, she slowly grew aware of the voices in the room with her.

Jegra slowly opened her eyes and looked around at her surroundings. She was lying in her own bed, in her gladiatorial chambers back on Thessalonica. Standing at the foot of her bed were the emperor and vice admiral.

Dakroth rubbed his chin, which had a slight bruise from where she'd clocked him, and grinned down at her. "That's quite a right hook you have, my dear. Consider me impressed."

Jegra looked at Cassera and then back at Dakroth. Sitting up, she rubbed her head and asked, "Why did you bring me back here?"

"I thought you'd feel more comfortable in your own room," Dakroth relayed. He tossed his white hair and then smiled at her again. "You stay here and get your rest. I'll announce the wedding to the crowd. After all, we'll make an empress of you yet."

With that he turned and exited her room.

Jegra looked back at Cassera who stared down at her with a blank expression that she couldn't see through. "What?" Jegra snapped, glowering at the vice admiral.

"I'm supposed to accompany you out once he makes the announcement. You'll appear before the audience, kiss Emperor Dakroth, and then, in his honor, you will fight and kill a Nogrossian Razor Boar."

"Are those the big ones with actual razors or the tiny ones with the hard, spiny shells and poison-tipped quill darts that give you temporary paralysis?"

"The big kind, I believe. Why do you ask?"

"I was sort of hoping it was the small ones, because I was going to take a handful of those pointy little needles, make a special bouquet for you, and then shove it where the sun doesn't shine."

"Charming."

Jegra stood up and got in Cassera's face. She was taller by almost a foot so her chest bumped Cassera's chin. Cassera merely turned her face, avoiding eye contact, and let out a sigh that revealed her disgust with Jegra's crude behavior.

"You think you're better than me, don't you?"

"Think?" Cassera balked. "No, Terran pink-skin. I don't just think it. I know it."

Jegra balled up her fist and snarled, "Is that so?"

Cassera merely glanced down at Jegra's fist and then looked back up at Jegra's face. After a moment her eyes softened as did her voice and she changed her tune.

"Listen," she said, glancing side to side. "I don't actually hate you, Jegra. It's all a ruse. But the walls have ears, and I have to put on a good show." She smirked and turned her back on the gladiatrix. "You didn't hear that from me."

The complete 180-degree turn threw Jegra for a loop. She wasn't sure what Cassera was playing at. But, whatever it was that had prompted the brief break in her façade, the urge to knock the smirk from Cassera's face was slowly fading.

"Why are you telling me this?" Jegra asked in a hushed tone, leaning in to hear what Cassera had to say.

Cassera spoke from the corner of her mouth, over her shoulder at Jegra. "Once you and Lord Dakroth are married, you'll live aboard the *Dreadnaught* for a year. I'm hoping that, in that time, we might become friends."

Jegra pulled back and turned the vice admiral to face her, looking long and hard at Cassera's eyes. "You really mean that? You're not just pulling my leg?"

"I haven't touched your leg," Cassera replied, not understanding the Earth idiom. "But I could if you want." She moved in so that her thigh brushed up against Jegra's and her eyes slowly settled on Jegra's lips.

A loud knock at the door sent them scurrying apart, and a guard entered. "Your majesty," he said reverently, alerting them to the fact that the announcement had been made, "It's time." He bowed before his future empress.

Jegra looked at Cassera and bit her lip as she mulled over whether Cassera was being genuine. She'd never known her to lie, at least, not like the emperor, but she couldn't be certain. She decided the best she could do was to go along with it and see where it led them. Smiling at Cassera, she teased, "Admit it. You like me."

"You're Jegra the Masterful! Of course I like you. Everyone likes you."

"But, I mean, you *really* like me," Jegra stressed.

"I'm fond of you, yes."

Jegra made a sour face and folded her arms. This gesture confused Cassera and the guard.

"My mistresses," the guard repeated, growing nervous by their delay of the emperor's grand announcement. "It's time."

She stared at Cassera for a moment, one eye narrowing with annoyance at her obstinance, and then huffed. "I'm not going anywhere until you admit that you like me," she said, placing a finger on Cassera's chest.

Cassera looked down at Jegra's finger, then over at the guard, and then back at Jegra. "We don't have time for this."

"Oh, I have all the time in the world," Jegra replied, folding her arms and stubbornly planting her feet. "I'm the next Imperatrix of the Dagon Empire."

"Not yet you're not," Cassera said, grabbing Jegra's hand. She tried to guide Jegra to the door but Jegra didn't budge.

"Come on, Jegra!" Cassera pleaded. "End this childish protest. You're keeping the emperor waiting."

"Say it!"

"No!" she said with a laugh.

"Then I'm staying right where I am." Jegra folded her arms and turned her back to Cassera just to drive the point home.

"Fine!" Cassera finally admitted, relenting to Jegra's persistent stubbornness. "I *like* you."

"Yeah, you do." Jegra smiled, and slapped the vice admiral's ass as she walked past her and out into the corridor.

Cassera let out a pent-up sigh and then laughed quietly to herself, amused by Jegra's pig-headedness.

Jogging up the dim passage, Jegra made her way toward the light and the roar of the crowd. When she emerged, Dakroth extended his arm to her and she walked up and took it. Standing by his side, he waved to the crowd and the millions watching on their televid displays at home.

"Ladies and gentlemen, and all intergalactic transspecies of the Dagon Empire, I am proud to announce that I have taken Jegra's hand in marriage!"

The crowd erupted with an applause like never before. An additional four televid drones swooped down and buzzed noisily overhead as they broadcast the happy news clear across the galaxy.

Jegra smiled and waved to the crowd.

As she smiled, she spoke discretely through her teeth. "I don't know what you're scheming, but just know that I'm watching you."

Matching her grin with one of his own, he replied, "That's all part of the fun, my dear."

The vice admiral stepped up to them and ushered Jegra off to the side. The emperor pandered to the audience a bit more, then shouted, "Long live the Dagon Empire!"

His words were echoed back to him in waves and with that, he tossed his cape, spun, and blew Jegra a kiss just as a yellow beam of light came down from his ship.

"You're not returning back to the ship?" Jegra asked, watching with great interest as Vice Admiral Cassera Danica took off her over jacket and tossed it aside.

"My orders are to remain by your side, day and night, until the wedding."

"Is that so?" Jegra said with a grin.

Cassera glanced at her and smiled. "Stop it! We have a giant razorback to kill."

She wasn't kidding, either. Nogrossian razorbacks were twice as large as Earth elephants and twice as mean as any razorback warthog back on her planet.

Also, to make things even more interesting, they had real razors all along their backs, right to the ends of their tails, similar to the extinct stegosaurus. This creature was difficult to best and downright lethal.

As the gate at the end of the arena opened and Jegra could smell the beast, she cracked her neck and popped her knuckles then said, "Follow my lead."

An enraged snort came from the beast as it shook off its chains from the handlers who then scurried away in fright. The giant, razor-backed warthog burst out of its cage, bending the iron bars as it pushed through and charged tusk first into the arena. When it made eye contact with Jegra, it swung its head side to side, snorted, and stomped its back hoof, kicking up dirt in a grand display of dominance.

Nogrossian boars were extremely territorial, and they are always ready to fight. And Jegra was happy to oblige.

She rushed forward and the razorback met her in the middle of the arena, its giant tusks plowing through the sand with little resistance. Attempting to spear the smaller female biped with one of its tusks, the giant hog was surprised when its whole body lurched to a stop.

"I've got it!" Jegra shouted, holding onto the creature's tusk with two hands.

Standing just behind her, Cassera said, "What do you want me to do about it?"

"Zap it with your laser fingers!"

"I don't have that skill," Cassera replied.

"What are you talking about?" Jegra asked, holding the pig at bay.

The warthog thrashed wildly in a desperate attempt to get away, but Jegra held on.

"My people have developed different skill sets. Some can produce energy discharges. Others can create forcefields."

"So, you're telling me you can create a protective bubble?"

"It's how I got the rank of vice admiral."

"Let me guess, to protect the emperor."

She nodded in the affirmative and then placed her hand on Jegra's shoulder. "I have an idea."

"I'm all ears," Jegra replied, struggling to hold the panicked animal that was two elephants tall and twice as long.

"Let him go."

"What?"

"Do you trust me?" Cassera asked.

Jegra looked over her shoulder at Cassera. The truth was, she didn't trust her motives, but in this moment, here and now, she trusted her instincts as a fighter. "Yes," Jegra answered, and let go, flinging the stunned animal back away from them.

Cassera threw up a shield by extending the palms of her hands and focusing. It looked like a disk of blue and green energy and when she separated her hands, fanning them apart, the shield responded to her motion and grew larger, wide enough to deflect the charge of an angered razorback warthog the size of a space barge.

The warthog deflected off the shield and tumbled to the ground. It whined as it rolled in the dirt and fought frantically to get back up to its feet.

Not wasting another moment, Jegra leapt high into the air. Cassera created a shield about three meters up for Jegra to leap off of. She created another three meters above that.

Just as the beast had gotten back up on all fours, Jegra came crashing down on the warthog's forehead like a meteorite.

It groaned out as its head smashed into the ground of the arena. The entire stadium shook with the crash of the armored beast.

A large dust cloud shot up when the beast's body finally collapsed to the ground, and Jegra emerged from the cloud, dusting off her hands.

"We make a good team, you and I," she said.

"Jegra, watch out!" Cassera said, throwing up a hand in alarm.

Jegra felt a lacerating pain and looked down in alarm. The spiked end of the beast's tail had penetrated her torso and a large spine was protruding from the middle of her chest.

"Fuck me," she said, and then collapsed to her knees.

At the same time, the beast gasped its last breath and let out a death rattle. Its mucus coated tongue slid out of its mouth and flopped onto the sand signaling that it was, without a doubt, dead.

Cassera rushed forward and caught Jegra in her arms. "Don't worry. We beat it," she said. "Just stay with me."

Jegra began to feel dizzy; she wanted to thank Cassera for fighting with her even though she didn't have to make such a grand gesture, but the blackness came before she could form the words.

7

"No!" Jegra shouted, sitting up in bed. She immediately regretted the sudden jolt to consciousness and gripped her aching side. Bandages held her together but her entire body throbbed with a lingering pain that wouldn't soon go away.

"You're finally awake," a voice said. She looked over to see Cassera walking over to her bedside, silver tray in hand. On the tray was a steaming cup of fresh herbal tea along with an ointment she recognized by the scent; a root that had numbing properties, something she used a lot these days.

Although she healed fast and was exceptionally strong, her body took its fair share of beatings. And she wasn't immune to the pain. She just grew a tolerance to it because it was so constant. But every once in a while, it was nice to not have to feel all the thousand aches and pains the body was heir to. Even she had her limitations.

"Thanks," Jegra said, taking the tea from Cassera who seated herself on the side of Jegra's bed as she cared for her.

"How long was I out for?"

"About twelve hours."

"Twelve hours?" Jegra gasped. "But that means it's a whole new day."

"It's the middle of a whole new day, actually. But you looked as though you needed the rest."

"You know," Jegra said, holding the cup in both hands in front of her face and letting the soothing aroma flood into her nostrils, "a year ago they wouldn't even have let me have time to fully recuperate. I'd have been in the arena the very next day, fighting to survive. Every day just like the one before."

"You are a survivor, Jegra," Cassera replied. "It's one of the things that I find so fascinating about you. Your ability to push past all the pain and just keep going. No matter what."

Jegra smiled. "And what about you?" she asked, reaching over and brushing a strand of Cassera's white hair to the side of her face and tucking it behind her blue ear, "what kind of woman are you?"

"For years I've been whatever kind of woman the emperor needed me to be. Now? Well, that remains to be seen," Cassera replied, looking away.

Jegra gently pulled her face back to hers and leaned in and kissed Cassera on her lips. It was partly because Jegra wanted to thank her for tending to her wounds and taking care of her, but also it was to see if she could break through that icy-cold exterior of hers and get to know the real woman underneath it all.

Cassera kissed her back, but it was short and awkward. She pulled away and said, "I'm on duty. I'm supposed to help you mend for your wedding day, and I've failed."

"Nonsense," Jegra said. "I'll be as good as new in no time. But since we have some time to kill, why don't we make the best of it?"

Cassera smiled and then stood up. Her face and skin still had dirt stains from their bout against the Nogrossian razorback hog as she hadn't even left Jegra's side for one moment. But Jegra didn't care if Cassera was sweaty and a bit salty. Sometimes the added flavor made it all the better. Right now, though, she just wanted to feel good. And Cassera could help with that.

"Right now?" Cassera asked, looking around the room as though she searched for some distraction to use as an excuse. But there wasn't any.

Jegra reached across the bed and grabbed Cassera's hand and pulled her back down onto the bed with her. "There's no better time," she answered.

She climbed on top of Jegra, who lay back. They gazed into one another's eyes for a long while, then Cassera sniffed her armpit and cringed. "But I'm filthy."

"The filthier the better," Jegra teased. Reaching up, she grabbed Cassera by her neck and reeled her in for another kiss. This time Cassera's Prussian blue lips met Jegra's pink ones with an equal thirst and their tongues danced a sultry tango inside one another's mouths.

"I want you," Jegra said, frantically trying to peel Cassera's clothes off. "All of you."

But just as she had gotten her half-undressed a loud boom sounded from above. Then another. And another.

"What in the world?"

Cassera leapt up off the bed, pulling her clothes back on as she went. "Come on!" she shouted, making her way to the door. "We have to go. Now!"

Jegra didn't know what was going on, but before she'd even climbed out of bed there was a large explosion. The wooden door of Jegra's chambers blew off its hinges and smashed into Cassera, knocking her to the floor.

Jegra leapt out of bed and rushed over to her friend. "Are you all right?"

Cassera was already pushing herself up. "I think so," she replied.

"What's going on?" Jegra asked, helping Cassera the rest of the way to her feet.

"Come on," Cassera said, dragging Jegra by her hand. "We have to get up to the *Dreadnaught*.

The two women ran out into the arena. Half the stadium was on fire, the other half demolished. "What could have done this?" Jegra asked, looking at the destruction in horror. When there was no reply, she looked back over at Cassera who was staring up at the sky. Jegra slowly looked up, shielding her eyes from the mid-day sun with the palm of her hand. There were five giant ships, each at least as big as the *Dreadnaught*, and all of them were firing on the ship.

"It's the Nyctan fleet," Cassera said, her voice growing hard and angry.

"What do we do?" Jegra asked.

Cassera tapped the underside of her wrist and Jegra noticed a little, orange glowing dot just under her blue skin. "Emergency transport," she said. "Bring us up." But there was no response. Agitated, she mashed the dot with her thumb and growled, "This is Vice Admiral Cassera Danica of the Imperial fleet. Bring us up now. That's an order."

Unexpectedly, a beam of yellow light hit the ground, but it missed its mark and appeared several feet away. Jegra shot Cassera a puzzled look and then they both turned to see Emperor Dakroth materialize. He was badly injured and his uniform was charred from a disrupter blast. Blood trickled down from his mouth and he gripped his left arm which hung limply at his side.

"My Lord!" Cassera gasped, rushing up to him to offer support. To Jegra's surprise, he accepted it.

"It was a surprise attack. They hit the *Dreadnaught* with everything they had.

She's dead in the water."

They all looked up and watched as the Nyctan fleet continued bombarding the flag ship of the Dagon Empire with everything they had. Pieces of the ship broke off and re-entered the atmosphere of Thessalonica, burning up as they came. It looked like a thousand shooting stars, but in broad daylight. Soon enough there was a deafening boom and the *Dreadnaught* split in two, its severed halves sailing away from one another as a series of explosions went off.

"Come on," Jegra said, ushering Cassera and the emperor back to her chambers, which provided better cover than just standing out in the open. "We'll be safer inside."

Once back in her chambers, she helped Cassera lay Dakroth down onto her bed.

"How could have I been so stupid?" he grumbled, chastising himself for his strategic mistake. "I should have never left the front line. The Nyctans knew that the *Dreadnaught* was without the protection of the royal fleet. They ambushed me above my own homeworld!"

"I should have been up there with you," Cassera said.

"No," Dakroth replied, raising a hand to stop her from taking the blame for his mistake. "You had your orders. Keeping my bride safe was your top priority. Keeping the fleet safe was mine. I'm the one who has failed, not you."

Another boom shook the room and Jegra looked at them both with worried eyes. "Is this an invasion?"

"No," Dakroth grunted, re-situating himself as Cassera took his dislocated arm and jammed it back into place. "Argh! *Ahhh...*that's better," he said with a relieved sigh, rotating his arm and reorienting it. Watching his hand, he made a fist and opened it again, then relayed their situation without ever diverting his gaze. "The Nyctans don't have the manpower to carry out a full-fledged invasion. This is just a blitz attack to try and declaw the Dagon fleet's main asset."

"The *Dreadnaught*."

"They'll likely tuck tail and retreat like the cowards they are once the Imperial fleet jumps back to the system."

"How long will that take?"

"Depending on their current positions, anywhere from five to ten hours," Cassera replied.

"Then we'll regroup and take the fight back to them."

Jegra scratched her chin and murmured something to herself.

"What is it?" Dakroth asked, noticing she was busy unraveling something.

"It seems that's what they want you to do. They attack here, then feign their escape once the fleet arrive. Seeking revenge, you chase after them, leaving the back door open…"

"It is an invasion!" Cassera gasped.

The emperor's face grew deathly serious. "Remind me to kill Vice Admiral Akkatan when the fleet gets here," he growled. "Not only has his intel been wrong this whole time, but the two-faced coward insisted we were winning the war."

"I'll kill him myself," Cassera said, punching a fist into her palm and grinding it in as though she were mashing Admiral Akkatan's bones.

"No. The message needs to come from me."

Another large boom shook the arena, but it felt different somehow.

"That wasn't debris from the ship," Jegra said.

"It was a disrupter blast," Cassera said, her voice growing apprehensive for the first time since Jegra had known her. Turning to the emperor, she said, "They must have traced the coordinates of your last transport."

"Which means," Dakroth said with a grunt as he rose to his feet. "We can't stay here. They'll be bombarding this place until nothing is left but a smoldering crater."

"We can't go out that way," said Jegra, thumbing over her shoulder at her broken entrance. A blast shook the entire complex of the arena, shaking dust from the ceiling. Several slaves ran past her entrance, making a desperate escape to get out of the hypogeum before it came collapsing down on their heads, but she felt that maybe it was safer down here than up there.

Another blast shook the entire underground complex, and the slaves that had just run past a moment earlier came flying back in pieces.

Jegra cringed. "See?" she said, her point proved for her.

"Right," Dakroth said, and he walked over to Jegra's vanity table and mirror which she never used. Being a dirty, bloody, sweaty gladiator never gave her the opportunity to glam herself up. She'd always found the vanity a huge waste of space.

Emperor Dakroth shoved the table out of the way and then searched the rockface of the wall with his fingers. Finding what he was looking for, he pressed a seemingly arbitrary rock and an entire portion of the wall opened up, revealing a secret passageway.

"How Come I didn't know about this?" Jegra asked, both hands on her hips as she stood by and watched in disbelief as a secret passage was revealed to her. An escape route had been right under her nose this whole time.

"Every emperor likes to have his fun," Dakroth said with a wink. Then he tossed his white hair across his shoulders and marched into the dark mouth of the newly revealed exit. "Follow me," his voice came floating back to them.

Cassera and Jegra shared a glance and Jegra smiled. "After you," she said, gesturing for Cassera to go on ahead of her. Cassera went forward, but as she passed Jegra something swatted her ass. This caused Cassera to jump and tense up.

"You won't be doing that the entire way, will you?"

"Oh, I don't know," Jegra said, shifting her hips and placing a finger on her chin and she ogled Cassera's butt. "It's such a fine ass."

Cassera let out an exasperated sigh and then followed after the emperor. Jegra looked back at what had become home to her for the past year and a half. It felt weird to be leaving it like this. But another rumble and more debris falling from the ceiling reminded her why she needed to go.

After what seemed the longest, darkest, trek of her life, she finally emerged in the brilliant light of the desert day. She shielded her eyes and gave them time to adjust to the unrestricted radiance of the surface.

When her eyes finally adjusted, she found Cassera tying her jacket around her waist. Sweat stains soaked through her light gray, military issue tank top and she pulled on her collar to let what little breeze there was lap at her chest, perchance to cool her.

Dakroth stood a ways off, staring up at the sky as he watched the Nyctan fleet lay waste to his ship.

Jegra turned and looked back at Arena City, as it was known to the inhabitants of the moon, and the colosseum, which was little more than burning rubble at this point. Occasionally, disrupter blasts of green energy came down from the sky and bombarded the flattened arena merely to add insult to injury.

The Nyctan battle cruisers had already done their worst, wiping out a city of roughly three thousand souls, but Jegra knew their continued barrage was just a reminder for Emperor Dakroth that they were still here and that there was nothing he could do about it.

Jegra didn't hear or see any signs of survivors in the town, which meant the Nyctans had probably vaporized everyone above ground.

If there were survivors, she hoped they were dug in tightly. Most likely, they were trapped beneath the surface, just as she would have been, had it not been for the secret passageway out that only the emperor knew about. Knowing there was nothing she could do for the lost citizens, however, she turned and faced her two blue-skinned Dagon guardians. Her fate was in their hands now.

"Where to now?" Jegra asked, glancing at Dakroth and then Cassera.

"There's a small oasis about twelve klicks from here. A trading hub for the black market," Emperor Dakroth replied.

"Mardok," Jegra said, less than enthused.

"You've heard of it?" he asked.

"I couldn't forget it even if I wanted to," Jegra lamented. "The slaver who purchased me and sold me into the arena is from Mardok."

Jegra found herself unable to hold back the flood of emotions. Mardok was the first place, other than Earth, she'd ever set foot and it was the last place she expected to see again anytime soon. She took a deep breath and composed herself.

"What's in Mardok that's so important?"

"I've an old acquaintance there who can hook us up with passage off this desolate rock," Dakroth said waving his hand across the panoramic scenery of Thessalonica's endless array of sand dunes.

Jegra liked how they always reflected bright orange at this time of day, just before the twin suns of Dagon began to set.

"And go where, exactly?" Jegra asked. "The Nyctan fleet is currently blockading anything from entering or leaving the Dagon homeworld and Thessalonica has nothing of worth on it–except for the arena which now lays in ruin."

"We won't be going to the Dagon homeworld, my dear," the emperor informed her with a sly grin. "We'll be headed to the Zargora system."

"Your majesty," Cassera interrupted, glancing at Jegra and then to the emperor. "This is classified information."

"It's fine, Cassera," he said, waving his hand as though he were brushing aside her concerns. "It's on a need-to-know basis and, right now, she needs to know."

Jegra looked at the vice admiral with a puzzled expression on her face. She'd heard that the Zargora system was unclaimed space. Much of it was uncharted, which made for the perfect environment for smugglers and space pirates who wanted to avoid confrontation with the Nyctans and Dagons. But she had never heard of anything of value to the empire there, which is why it had been largely ignored. "What's in the Zargora system?"

"You mean other than marauders and space pirates and the scum and villainy of seven star systems?"

"Of course," Jegra jested, "Other than that, obviously."

"The asteroid MK-29-388-XP3 is there."

Jegra shot Emperor Dakroth a puzzled look.

"It's a secret military base," he informed her, settling any further confusion. "The new flagship of the fleet is being built there. A type-three Nova class destroyer."

"Then, allow me to act as your personal bodyguard for this mission. And I swear to you, I will get you to your ship."

"Splendid!" Dakroth chirped. Then, pulling out a tracker from his jacket, he followed a little blip on his screen. Turning up the sandy hill, he began heading in the direction of Mardok. "Now that we're all up to speed, let's get a move on."

"Are you alright?" Cassera asked, noticing Jegra's forlorn expression.

It was the first time Cassera had showed anything in the way of genuine sympathy toward her, and she smiled. "You know something?" Cassera's eyes widened in anticipation of Jegra's reply. "I think I'm going to be just fine."

Cassera smiled and turned to follow after the emperor when she felt a smack across her buttocks. Sighing out, she asked in a less than tolerant tone of voice, "Must you?"

Jegra marched past her with zest in her step but deliberately ignored Cassera's lamentation and continued onward.

Amused by Jegra's undying persistence to try to get a rise out of her, she laughed to herself. In the short few days she'd spent with the Earth woman, she'd felt a strong connection form between them. It was a shame that, after all was said and done, she'd have to be the one to kill her.

8

A scorching sun beat down on Jegra's bronzed skin as she squatted at the foot of the dune, one of the many they'd traversed over the past three hours. Unable to hold it in any longer, she pulled down her bikini bottoms and released the flood gates.

Jegra let out a deep sigh of relief as a gleaming puddle formed beneath her, and Emperor Dakroth, who stood at the top of the dune, watched with an amused grin while Vice Admiral Cassera Danica made a sour face and looked away.

"Must you always act so primitively?" Cassera carped, repulsed by Jegra's lewd and uncensored behavior.

She breathed out a deep sigh of relief as she finished her business and replied, "When you gotta go, you gotta go. And, besides, I've been holding it in since the tea you gave me. So, in a way, this is all your fault."

Cassera smacked her teeth in displeasure and folded her arms across her chest, turning her body away to better show her deep-felt disgust.

"Do Earth women always leave their scent wherever they please?" Dakroth asked.

"No," Jegra replied. "Most would never allow you to be in their presence when they did so. But there aren't a lot of facilities nearby, are there?"

"Fascinating," he said, watching her pull up her undergarments and kick sand onto the damp area she'd made.

Much rejuvenated, Jegra stretched her arms over her head, bending her elbows near her head, and cracked her neck. Sweat streamed down her face, neck, and chest, and she was on the verge of dehydration. "How much further till Mardok?" she inquired.

Dakroth pulled out his scanner and scanned the horizon in a north-westerly direction. "About five klicks," he replied.

Jegra estimated that a klick was about a kilometer, just shy of a mile. So that meant they could probably make it there in the next hour and forty minutes. She wiped some sweat off her chest and let out another long sigh.

Another hour or so of walking across the scorching deadlands of Thessalonica was not her idea of a leisurely outing, but it sure beat getting pulverized by the Nyctan disrupter canons, which continued to bombard Arena City from space.

With a bit of trouble, Jegra hiked up the shifting sands. When she neared the cusp of the dune, she saw a blue hand extend toward her and looked up to find Cassera offering assistance.

Pleased by the unexpected gesture of kindness, Jegra took Cassera's hand and let her hoist her up to the top of the dune. Jegra hopped up beside Cassera and made sure to press her sweaty chest into her.

"Thanks," she said in a parched voice, her chest heaving as she tried to catch her breath.

"You would have done the same for me," Cassera replied.

"Yes, I would have," Jegra said with a smile. Jegra leaned close and whispered in Cassera's ear. "I guess I'm beginning to rub off on you. Be careful, Cassera, you may just be in danger of becoming more human."

Cassera recoiled and shot Jegra a perturbed look. "There's no reason to be insulting," she scoffed.

"What?" Jegra said, throwing up her hands and feigning ignorance. "It was a compliment."

"Being compared to your kind is degrading. Dagons are the supreme species in the galaxy. Saying that I'm becoming more human is like saying you are becoming more like the primitive reptiles of your world."

"Reptiles are fierce predators on my homeworld," Jegra informed Cassera. "It wouldn't be much of an insult."

"I meant to say it implied you are simple minded."

"Is that really how you see me?" Jegra asked, although she was simply pushing Cassera's buttons for the fun of it. Even so, discovering how Cassera truly viewed her hurt her feelings. If she really thought Jegra was nothing but a dumb, bumbling oaf, then why had she taken any interest in her to begin with?

"Ladies, please. Enough chin wagging. We must get to Mardok before nightfall. Once the sun goes down, the sand worms hunt using their infrared heat vision. You don't want to be caught on the open dunes without protection come nightfall."

Cassera began following after the emperor, but when the customary swat on the buttocks didn't come, she looked back to find Jegra gazing off at the blue sky with a sad look on her face. She then regretted being so harsh about the matter.

Little did Jegra know, however, that Cassera wasn't just upset by the awful notion of a Dagon being compared to a human, she was actually more concerned with the fact that Jegra's DNA was somehow rewriting the DNA of anyone who engaged in sexual intercourse with her. This included both her and the emperor.

Once Cassera had confirmed the emperor's worst suspicions, however, he'd rushed back to Thessalonica to investigate personally and had begun to lay the ground work for making Jegra the legend she was to become.

At the same time, the emperor had assigned Cassera the task to study how far the effects went. So, it was up to her to continue her intimate relations with Jegra until her DNA was so scrambled she could no longer be considered a pure-blood.

Once her DNA was rendered human, she was to research a cure that would reverse the damage. Then, with any luck, they would find a way to weaponize the effect.

It was the emperor's idea to use the DNA rewriting sequence on all non-Dagon species and render them more like the inferior humans. That way they'd be easier to subjugate.

In the meantime, Emperor Dakroth would build up Jegra as a legend. A human slave who rose up from the arena to win his heart and become his empress—ruling alongside him as Imperatrix of the Dagon Empire.

The truth was much more insidious, however. Jegra was simply a means to an end. By making an inferior creature such as her his empress, it would give all species hope that they, too, could aspire to such greatness. It would give them a myth to believe in.

This fabricated myth, however, would allow him to maintain their loyalty while he continued to break and subjugate them without his oppressive measures ever coming into question. As long as they believed they could one day rise to Jegra's status, they'd blindly follow.

Cassera felt it was a genius plan, but in order for it to work, she had to sacrifice the thing she held most dear, her Dagon purity. She had to give herself over to Jegra and allow her very genetic superiority to be degraded by an oily pink-skin from a world so unimportant that it hadn't even been a blip on the radar.

The sun was already setting by the time they reached the city limits of Mardok. The three rested under some palm trees and watched as the hot orange sunset gradually faded to pink before their very eyes. Soon, the slender band of radiant color would be snuffed out by the encroaching purple of night.

"This way," Dakroth said, cautiously stepping over an inverse electric field consisting of an electrified net which went twenty feet down into the sand and spanned the entire circumference of the town.

The electric net prevented the sand worms from getting into the oasis at night. "Watch your step," warned Jegra, seeing as she knew the terrain well. "There are worm traps for the next several meters."

Once all of them had safely passed the electrified field, the emperor led them into town and took them down a series of winding alleyways where, after several sharp hooks and turns, they emerged before the dim glow of a tavern.

Although Mardok was only half the size of Arena City, it boasted a thriving night life. An entire street running through the center of town was lit up with small taverns, gambling establishments, strip clubs, and a host of slattern women soliciting anyone who had an itch for interspecies sex.

"You won't find a more wretched den of scumbags and villains," Cassera warned her travel companions as the three of them cut briskly across the street to the pub on the other side.

"Or loose women wanting to show you a good time," the Emperor added as he looked an orange-skinned Salamandarian girl working the corner up and down.

Her face was pretty enough, and she had two different colored eyes—one light green and the other light blue. She had a plump tail and she batted her kohl painted eyes and flashed her fetching purple lashes at him.

"This way, lover boy," Jegra said, clearing her throat and pointing him in the right direction.

The sign above the pub, which flickered in neon green and orange, read *Scarback's.* Although the building looked rather dilapidated, the sounds of drunkards having an uproariously good time seeped out into the evening.

As they approached the entrance, Jegra reached out and grabbed the emperor's sleeve and cautiously guided him toward the side alley. "This way," she beckoned, dragging him along behind her. "The streets have eyes and ears. Best to keep a low profile."

"How can you tell?" he asked, scanning their surroundings for anything out of the ordinary.

"Maybe because you're the emperor and I'm a celebrity," she said. "And maybe because the moment we stepped out into the street the business and chatter died down half fold."

"She's right," Cassera added. "We have multiple eyes on us. It serves our interests best to be a bit more discrete."

"I think you're both being overly cautious," the emperor said, tossing his hair nonchalantly over his shoulder. "Nobody would dare defy me on my own moon."

"There are more than just smugglers and loose women in Mardok, your majesty," Jegra informed. "There are spies and assassins. And not all of them work for you."

"Are you saying the Nyctans have planted agents against me?!" His eyes flared bright red with a crimson energy that surged inside him as he became agitated.

"It's not a risk I'm willing to take," Jegra said.

"Nor I," Cassera added. "Not with the Nyctan fleet overhead. Who knows how many assassins they could have planted across the moon in the time it took us to get here?"

"Well, as it seems you're both in agreement, I highly doubt I'll win this argument." Agreeing with their plan of erring on the side of caution, the emperor followed Jegra into the alley behind Scarback's which would take them to the back entrance.

As they cut through the narrow alley, they passed a clothesline full of freshly dried clothes. Jegra reached up and pulled down a woman's cloak and immediately flung it over the emperor's shoulders. "Here," she said, pulling the hood up for him. "Use this."

Jegra grabbed a janitor's overalls and quickly slipped into them. Zipping up the zipper, it got stuck at her bosom. Unable to traverse the mound of her breasts, she left it wedged halfway. She supposed a stimulating service worker wasn't the worst possible disguise and shrugged it off.

The moment Emperor Dakroth and Jegra's eyes met, it seemed as though they had read each other's minds. They both slowly turned toward Cassera and began staring at her intensely.

Cassera, wearing only her military issue tank top and white slacks, stuck out like a sore thumb. She looked the very image of a military officer. The exact opposite of what they needed to be to blend in.

"What to do with you?" Jegra contemplated aloud, scratching her chin as she studied Cassera's figure. "Ah!" she exclaimed with a snap of her fingers, a salacious grin spreading across her lips. "Take off your pants."

"I beg your pardon?" Cassera gulped in horror. Getting drunk and being with Jegra was one thing. But she wouldn't be caught dead prancing around half naked anywhere in the entire system. She was the kind of woman who felt it perfectly natural to wear turtle necks to the beach. There was no way she was going to strip down. "I certainly will not," she grumbled, folding her arms across her chest.

Without hesitation, Jegra bent down, grabbed Cassera's waistband, and gave a mighty tug. In one rapid jerk, she tore Cassera's pants right off her body.

Cassera gasped out and promptly covered her exposed bits. Cassera's knees clamped together and she placed her hand over her black lace panties. "You're out of your mind," she said, giving Jegra the good ole stink-eye.

"That's a nifty trick," Dakroth said, impressed by Jegra's dressing down of Cassera. "You'll have to teach me that one sometime."

"Naturally," Jegra replied. Looking around she found a hot orange miniskirt on a separate clothesline and snatched it down from the hanger. It was made of a shiny pleather and probably belonged to any number of Mardok's women of the night.

"I'm so not wearing that," Cassera protested.

"Would you rather go inside wearing a sweat drenched tank top that shows precisely how blue your nipples are and lace panties which cover you about as well as a see-through screen door?"

Cassera looked down at herself and realized Jegra had a point. Her dark blue nipples appeared through the wet fabric of her gray tank top and the black lace panties did little to give her the bare minimum security she required to feel at ease.

Unable to come up with a better alternative, she let out a defeated sigh and took the miniskirt from Jegra. "Fine," she said angrily. "Have it your way."

Once she'd finished zipping up the waist, she twisted the skirt around so the zipper would be at the back and tugged down on the hemline. Even with all the fine-tuning, it was still far too short for her liking.

"Turn around," Jegra demanded. Cassera shot her a suspicious look but did as requested. No sooner had she turned her back to Jegra when she felt a sudden jerk on her collar. Looking down in dismay, she watched as her tank top tore off her. Again, she instantly covered her breasts and turned around. "What the bloody Helios do you think you're doing?" she raged, cupping her breasts with both hands.

Jegra thrust out her jaw toward a white tube top next to Dakroth and gestured for him to fetch it for her. He gladly did so and, accepting the garment from the emperor, Jegra handed it over to Cassera. "Here."

Cassera quickly covered both breasts with her right arm and reached out and took the tube top from Jegra. Turing back around, she quickly put it on. "There," she said, spinning in place as she showed off her rather revealing outfit. "Satisfied?"

"I am," Dakroth answered, grinning at Cassera who looked indistinguishable from an upscale call-girl.

"I'm not," Jegra said, mulling over what could possibly be missing. "Wait a minute. I've got it," she said, and reached up and ran her fingers through Cassera's hair. Ruffling her hair up until her it was frazzled and messy, she finally stepped back to inspect her handiwork. Jegra let out a whistle. "Now that's what I'm talking about."

Cassera turned toward the glass window of the pub's back entrance and inspected her reflection. "For the love of Hastur!" she gasped. "You've turned me into a whore!"

"A very lovely whore," teased Jegra. And, with that, she swatted Cassera on her ass. Cassera shot her a cold glare with narrow eyes that flickered with yellow energy, then went back to looking in the glass at her ghastly reflection.

"You'll blend right in," Dakroth said in a serious manner that revealed that it was time to get back to business. Then, opening the back door, he stepped inside.

Not wasting a second, Jegra shoved Cassera inside after him, as she was still preoccupied with her reflection in the glass.

With both of them safely inside, Jegra looked back and double checked to see if anyone had followed them. After determining that the coast was clear, she quickly disappeared through the entrance and let the door shut behind her.

9

His arms draped around both women's waists, Dakroth leaned over the counter and asked the barkeep, "Do you have any booths available for the evening?"

Without looking up from drying a beer mug, the bartender asked, "The whole evening?"

Unamused by the dodge, the emperor's blood red eyes flashed with crimson energy from beneath his hood, signaling that he was of Dagon lineage.

The bartender, a mere Mee'lak from a dead system that had gone up with its star when it went supernova, gulped down the nervous lump in his throat and cut the chitchat. Promptly setting the glass down and coming around the bar to greet them, he personally showed them to their booth. "Right this way, if you please."

The bartender led them across the bar to a corner booth that was secluded but still had a good view of the room. Dakroth sat on the inside next to the wall, Jegra sat next to the emperor, while Cassera sat across from them.

"What can I get for ya'll?" the bartender asked, waiting by the table for their order.

"Six Dagoni ales, three Buldorvian vodkas, and three glasses of ice water," Dakroth said.

"And a platter of cheese-fries," Jegra added.

The bartender nodded and scurried off to get their orders. When Jegra turned around, she found Dakroth and Cassera starring at her with stunned expressions.

"What? I'm hungry," she said.

"You're lucky you are immune to the effects of cheese," Cassera said. "It makes me ill."

"What effects?" Jegra asked.

"Most Dagons have allergies that prevent them from eating cheese. We don't even make it on our homeworld. You only find it among the more primitive species, those that live with domesticated animals," Dakroth informed, a hint of disgust lingering on his voice.

"I love cheese," Jegra chirped. "But if it bothers you both so much, I'll try to be discrete with my consumption of it and will always be sure to brush my teeth afterward."

After their order had arrived, Dakroth waited for the bartender to leave and then pulled back his hood. He scanned the room looking for his contact but huffed in annoyance when he couldn't find him. "He said he would be here after sundown, but I don't see him anywhere."

"Are you sure you should be out in the open like this?" Jegra asked, nodding at Dakroth's exposed face.

"We're perfectly secluded here," he answered. "Besides, it's not like anyone here would even believe it was me, even if they did make me out."

"Right," Jegra said with a wink. "We'll just say you're the emperor's lookalike."

Jegra pulled the steaming appetizer towards her, picked up three gooey wedges of potato, ran them through the creamy yellow cheese that had pooled at the edge of the plate, and shoved them in her mouth.

"I think I'm going to be sick," Cassera said looking away.

"If so," Jegra mumbled, jamming another helping of cheese fries into her face, "feel free to hurl on my shoes."

"It would be fair play, wouldn't it?" Cassera chuckled.

Dakroth raised an eyebrow and Cassera folded her arms over her chest and grew stern again. "It's a long story."

"Maybe you'll share with me some time," Dakroth said. "But right now, I think we have more urgent matters."

"Like what?" Jegra asked.

"Like the fact that the bartender is talking to what looks like a bounty hunter.

Jegra looked over and squinted at the woman talking to the barkeep. She looked rugged, for sure, but she wasn't sure whether or not she constituted a threat. "If you want, I'll go over and snap her neck for you."

"No, that won't be necessary," Dakroth said. "We'll play it cool for now."

"Good plan," Jegra replied. In the middle of bringing another serving of fries to her mouth, some cheese dripped off and landed right in the middle of her cleavage. "Oh, shit," she said, taking the fry and dipping it into the lake of cheese that had pooled in the crevice between her breasts.

A sudden wave of disgust overcame Cassera and caused her to choke down her own gag reflex. Looking rather ill, she quickly excused herself from the table. "Pardon me, but I need to go to the restroom and hurl."

"Have fun!" Jegra said, waving to Cassera as she went. She smiled, cramming more cheese fries into her mouth.

"Here," Dakroth said, waving a napkin in front of Jegra's face. She took it from him and dabbed the corners of her mouth. "At least you blend in well," he said.

"You're too wound up. Just drink your beer and relax," she said, chewing with her mouth open.

Downing his beer in one long guzzle, Dakroth slammed the mug down and belched. "You mean like that?"

Jegra smiled and slid another beer over to him. "That's more like it. Try not to worry so much. You'll get the hang of it."

He downed the second one too, just as quickly, and Jegra slid a third over to him. This time he took a couple breaths in between swigs, but managed to finish it off in no time. Wiping some froth from his lips he let out a satisfied belch.

When Cassera returned, she quietly sat down and didn't say a word. Taking a sip of her water, she forced herself to act cool.

"Why do I get the feeling your hiding something?" Jegra said, pointing a cheesy finger at Cassera and taking a gulp from her water.

Nervous, Cassera glanced around, scanning the faces in the room, and then leaned across the table. "A girl came on to me in the restroom. She wanted to take me back to her place."

"You should have taken her up on the offer," Dakroth said, releasing another belch. Jegra subtly slid a fourth beer over to him and he happily picked it up. "Why not let your hair down for once? Have a little fun!"

"Drink your beer, sweetie," Jegra said, patting Dakroth's forearm which rested on the table next to her. He grinned at her and then began downing his fourth Dagon ale.

"That's not why I'm upset," Cassera replied. "When I was exiting the washroom, I glimpsed her reflection in the mirror as she stood behind me. She scanned me with something. Some kind of device. I would have confronted her but I didn't want to alert her to the fact that I was on to her. But odds are, we're going to have company any minute."

"Bring it on," Dakroth said, finishing his fourth drink. Jegra slid the fifth over to him to keep him busy.

"Drink these," Jegra said, passing all three Buldorvian vodkas across the table to Cassera.

"All of them?" she asked.

"You need to look a whole lot drunker than you currently are if you're going to fool anybody this evening." Rising to her feet, she said, "Now, you watch him while I go take care of this mysterious woman who seems to be stalking us."

"Good luck," Cassera said, and then she kicked back her head and downed the whole glass in one amazing, long gulp.

Jegra glanced around the room as she headed toward the women's restroom. There were three suspicious looking figures, all of them trying to act inconspicuous by sticking out like sore thumbs.

Inside the women's bathroom was exactly what she expected. Plain. Dirty. All metallic. Four toilet stalls sat along the back wall. The first one was missing a door, so she skipped it. Then she pushed open the second. Nothing but an empty stall on the other side.

She proceeded to open the remaining two doors in the same way, but just as with the prior stalls, they too, were empty.

"Where did you go?" Jegra asked.

"I'm right here," a voice said, startling the living bejesus out of Jegra.

Jegra spun around to see a woman materialize from thin air. Rather, she was wearing cloaking technology. She appeared to be a Dagon but was heavily modified by all kinds of tech. Not quite a cyborg, but definitely an enhanced alien. "Who are you?" Jegra asked. But the woman didn't answer.

"I need you to come with me, Jessica Hemsworth." Noticing the shocked look on her face, a subtle smile formed on the woman's lips, and she added, "Yes, I know who you are."

"I don't know who you're talking about," Jegra replied, playing it dumb.

"Look, I was paid to bring you to Grendok. He said you knew him."

"Grendok?" Jegra echoed, her curiosity piqued. The last time she'd seen the satyr was when she'd cut his head clean off in the arena. There was no way he was still alive. "I'm afraid you're mistaken. Grendok is dead. I mean, I heard he was killed in the arena."

The woman sighed impatiently and said, "Suit yourself." Raising her hand, she brushed Jegra's arm and sent an intense electrical shock into her. Jegra's entire body seized and then she fell over.

Half conscious, she watched through blurry vision as the woman bent down and grabbed her by the ankles and began dragging her away. But the harder she tried to focus the more impossible it seemed. Add her heat stroke, dehydration, and too many cheese fries into the mix and she was bound to pass out.

"Gwahfff!" Jegra rushed back to consciousness as a cold bucket of water was tossed onto her. She found herself seated on a bench in the alley with her hands bound behind her back. She tried to tear free of the bonds, but they were a korridium alloy and magnetically sealed.

These were state of the art, military issue, restraints. Either this woman was with secret ops, or she was an overpaid bounty hunter. Jegra assumed the latter.

"I won't ask again," Jegra growled through her teeth. "Who are you?"

"Who I am is unimportant," the woman replied. She crouched down so she could look into Jegra's eyes. That's when Jegra noticed that the woman's eyes weren't yellow, like most Dagons, but purple. Looking closer, she saw that they were prosthetic eyes. "All that matters is that I always get the job done. *Always.*"

The woman rose up and walked past Jegra. Unable to see where she went made Jegra nervous, and she struggled against her restraints some more. "Wait, where you going?" she called out. But there was no answer.

After a moment of silence, she heard the clap of hoof steps behind her. *It can't be,* she thought. *He's dead.*

To her surprise, however, Grendok strode past her, his arms behind his back. He wore a fancy burgundy vest and, as typical, no pants. The white bearded satyr turned and smiled at her. "Long time, no see, Jegra the Merciless."

"Impossible," she gasped. "I...I killed you."

"That's where you're wrong, my dear. You merely destroyed one copy of me." Brushing his hand across his body as if he were proudly displaying himself, he added, "Just as this vessel is also a copy."

"You mean clones?"

"Yes, clones," he replied.

Although cloning was banned in the Commonwealth due to slave labor disputes, Jegra knew that black market cloning facilities still operated under the radar and fetched a pretty penny. A single clone with full memory implants could cost upward of fifty billion credits, equivalent of a single blue-collar worker's entire lifetime salary. Only the extremely wealthy could even afford to own their own clones let alone multiple copies.

"But why?" she asked.

He smiled at her and stroked his beard. "Let's just say my line of business is rather hazardous for my health."

"And what kind of business would that be?"

"Arms dealing, of course. But, more than that, I trade in technology and information."

"Of course, you do," Jegra quipped.

"No need to get prickly with me," Grendok said. "We're on the same side."

"Oh, yeah? Then why am I tied up?"

"Because you refused to meet with me."

"That's because I thought you were dead."

"Yes, well, we've already been over this. So, I'll just cut to the chase. About a week ago I happened to come into possession of a highly encrypted data stick."

"A data stick?" Jegra repeated. "What was on it?"

"That's just the thing I wanted to meet with you about. You see, as one who deals in the sale of highly sensitive information, I was curious as to what datum it contained. I immediately put my best people on it and three days ago they finally cracked it."

"Congratulations," Jegra said, not trying in the slightest to mask her sarcasm.

"Yes, well, the whole reason for this clandestine meeting is that the information on that data stick was about you."

"Me?" Jegra asked, her head perking up as she gained a newfound interest in what Grendok version 2.0 had to say. "What did it say, precisely?"

"It had your genome, completely encoded. I don't know what they want your genome for, but my best guess would be plans to make super soldiers for an unstoppable army of Jegra clones."

"But who would conceive such a cruel plan?"

"I think you already know the answer to that."

"You telling me this is Emperor Dakroth's doing?"

"Would you have me believe you actually trust him? No, dear. I think you know, like I do, that he's as corrupt as they come. He just happens to be infatuated with you for the moment. But when that ends, so does any semblance of kindness."

"And why should I believe you?" Jegra asked.

Grendok pulled a small data stick from his breast pocket and held it out for her to see. "Don't take my word for it. See for yourself." Placing the data stick between her tightly pressed breasts, he smiled at her one last time and then bid her adieu.

"I'm glad we could have this chat. It was nice catching up." Then, without saying another word, Grendok disappeared the way he'd come.

Once he was safely away, Jegra's restraints automatically unlocked and fell to the ground. She jumped up to her feet and plucked the data stick out from her cleavage. Although she didn't have time to inspect it right now, she'd be sure to do so the first chance she got.

Jegra hurried back inside and quickly seated herself at the booth. She'd tucked the data stick in the waistband of her underwear to keep it concealed and out of sight.

"What took you so long?" Cassera said, her cheeks flushing purple as the third drink gave her that buzz Jegra hoped would make "stick-up-the-butt" Cassera loosen up to become the fun "want to have a threesome" Cassera.

"It was the cheese fries," Jegra lied. "Clogged me up good."

"Ew, gross!" Cassera said. "Too much information."

"You asked," Jegra fired back with a bit of snark. She scanned all the faces in the room one more time and figured that Dakroth's contact was a no-show. Grabbing the emperor by his arm, she said, "Come on. We're getting a room for the evening."

"You read my mind," he said drunkenly, half his face twisting into a scandalous smile.

Cassera followed after them and, wobbling drunkenly, called out, "Wait for me."

Jegra paid the tab by using the barcode tattoo under her wrist that she got once her credits for winning matches started rolling in. The bartender looked down at his tablet then up at Jegra then down at his tablet again, as he pieced together who she really was.

"Keep your lips zipped if you don't want me tearing them off and shoving them up your ass. Are we clear?"

"Crystal," the bartender whimpered.

"Good. Now point me in the direction of the nearest hotel."

"I'm afraid the only vacancy is a love hotel a block from here," he said, pointing in the direction of the hotel. "It's called Neon Pussies. You'll recognize it by the giant fluorescent kitten atop of the building."

"Give yourself a tip," Jegra said, waving her wrist over the scanner once more. "Eighty credits."

"Eighty credits?" the man gasped. "That's awfully generous."

"If you hear of anything regarding me or my travel companions, you'll let me know, yeah?"

"Y-yes, of course!" he agreed, nodding enthusiastically.

Intimidation was only a last resort. She didn't like threatening people, but right now they didn't have anyone they could trust.

Jegra eyeballed him hard, letting him know that any slip of the tongue would mean unpleasantries for him, then grabbed her two drunken Dagon companions and yanked them out of the bar.

Linking arms, the three of them swayed drunkenly as they headed down the street toward the giant neon kitten.

10

A shameless moan escaped Jegra's lips as she kissed the Emperor Rhadamanthus Dakroth's mouth and then rolled off of him. Falling onto her back on the bed beside Cassera, who lay panting, Jegra gasped, "That was…fucking phenomenal."

"Indeed, it was," Dakroth said, rising out of the bed. His skin prickled in the cool of the evening air as he walked over to the window. Standing unabashedly in front of the large glass pane, he peered out and lost himself in his thoughts.

Cassera slid up against Jegra and kissed her on her shoulder. "Truly, you must be blessed by the Gilded God, Hastur," Cassera said, dabbling Jegra's body with several more delicate kisses.

"Hastur?" asked Jegra. "I know he's the deity most species in the Dagon Empire worship, but I only know what I've heard in passing on the lips of those praying to Hastur before a match. More than that, I'm afraid that I'm at a loss."

"None is mightier than the Gilded Master. Even Emperor Dakroth recognizes Hastur's true power."

Dakroth waved his hand as if to suggest he wasn't interested in getting into a religious debate. But Jegra was curious. "Tell me more," she insisted.

"Hastur is the beginning and the end of all things. He is the golden filament that sparked the universe into being, and he is the golden flame which will snuff it out again."

"I've heard rumors that the Nyctans also believe in Hastur. Is this true?"

"The Nyctans have perverted the sacred teachings of Dagon with fabrications and delusional fantasies based on their subjective understanding of our people's most ancient sacred texts. Don't let them fool you, they worship a false god."

"It's all so fascinating," Jegra said, brushing Cassera's white hair behind her ear and looking deep into her eyes. "You know something? When I look into your golden eyes, I think maybe your god forged you from that same awesome fire."

"You flatter me unnecessarily," Cassera said, diverting her gaze. Her blue cheeks flushed and turned violet with embarrassment. Although Jegra didn't see why she should be embarrassed. When Cassera let her silver hair down, she was quite stunning indeed.

Jegra wrapped her arms around Cassera and drew her in tight, basking in her warmth. "My words are sincere."

"Enough talk," Cassera said, snuggling up to Jegra and resting her head on her shoulder. Closing her eyes, she yawned, and in a sleepy voice said, "Let's sleep."

Jegra looked over at Dakroth and, with her free arm, patted the vacant side of the bed. "Are you coming to bed, my love? It's cold. And I miss your warmth."

"In a moment," he said, locking his hands behind his back. He fixed his eyes on the sky and stared up at the stars.

Up there, somewhere, the Nyctan ships loitered, mocking his sovereignty. For that, they would surely pay.

"They're not going anywhere," Jegra informed him. "You'll have your revenge soon enough, my lord. Now, come to bed. You've had a long day and tomorrow promises to be even longer."

Dakroth turned and smiled at her. He nodded in agreement and then returned to bed. Slipping beneath the covers, he spooned Jegra, who lay wedged between two blue-skins.

As she dozed off, she couldn't help but think that these past few days had been the most interesting of her life. Allowing the embrace of sleep to fully engulf her, Jegra closed her eyes and drifted off.

Several hours later, the sound of secretive whispers aroused Jegra from her peaceful slumber. She pretended to remain asleep as she strained her ears to listen to their faint voices. She didn't stir for fear of dissuading anyone from sharing what needed to be shared.

"If you keep manipulating her like this, she'll do more than just resent you,"

Cassera chastised. "She might rebel. And we don't even know what her limits are yet. She went head-to-head with Jennica for crying out loud. Nobody's ever gone up against a Dagon of that magnitude and survived. And don't even get me started on that psychotic red-skin you employ."

"The assassin was necessary. The green-skin's interference would have thrown a wrench into my plans. Now, with her out of the way, Jegra's focus is right where it ought to be."

"My lord, I rarely ever question your authority on these matters, but I feel there is another way to go about it. One that is less barbaric."

"Your feelings betray you, Cassera" Dakroth replied. "But what is done is done. We have no choice but to move forward with the plan or else risk losing the trade-war with the Nyctans."

"Right now, I'm more concerned about Abethca's immediate family. Her eldest sister has a powerful voice in the Commonwealth senate. If she finds out that we assassinated her beloved sibling in cold blood—"

"She won't," growled Dakroth with his standard level of impatient obstinance.

"*If she finds out,*" Cassera stressed, ignoring his impolite interruption, "we can't afford to have the Seyfferians and Nyctans unite against us."

"All together, the Commonwealth is only three systems, vice admiral. And, even if they did join forces with the Nyctans, it wouldn't be enough to overthrow the Dagon Empire. We are seven systems strong and growing."

"But our fleet is stretched thin as it is. We are waging too many campaigns and the shipyards can't keep up with the demand for new ships. There's simply not enough ore in the system."

"We'll mine the outer rim if we have to."

"And while we do that, against the Trade Federation rules and against the Commonwealth's interests, the Nyctans would jump at the opportunity to launch a full-fledged attack, and you know it. If they didn't take out our ship building facilities while we mined ore, they'd attack the fleet protecting our ore mining operations. Either way, it's a boon to them and a detriment to us. It could set us back for decades, your majesty."

"Which is why using Jegra in this way is part of my long-term plan. She's the key to everything."

Jegra slowly sat up in bed and looked over to find Cassera and the Emperor standing off in the corner by the dim light of a single lamp that hung on the cheaply painted lavender walls. Both of them stood fully dressed, which caused Jegra to suspect more was going on than just a heated conversation. They were discussing the very strategy that would keep the Dagon Empire the superpower that it was.

She watched them for a while without their knowledge and then cautiously rose out of bed.

"You had Abethca killed?" she asked, one eye squinting at Dakroth as she grilled him on the details of the conversation she had just overheard.

Both Dagons spun around with startled expressions on their faces. Dakroth immediately said in an uncommonly polite voice, "My dear, you're awake!" Immediately afterward he gave Cassera an icy look and snarled out of the corner of his mouth, "I told you this this wasn't the time or place to discuss such matters."

Cassera stepped in between Jegra and the emperor, hoping to intervene before things got out of hand, and put up both hands. "Jegra, wait. I can explain."

"She meant something to me," Jegra said, her voice flexing in her throat as her neck tightened with intense anger. The veins in her neck began to bulge as she pointed over Cassera's shoulder and aimed her finger at Dakroth. "You had no right!"

"*Right?*" Dakroth balked. "I'm the Dagon Emperor! And bride or not, you'll learn your place." He raised a glowing finger as a deterrent to Jegra's aggressiveness and a reminder that he had the power to end her if need be.

Cassera shot the emperor a sharp glance over her shoulder. "Not helping!"

Jegra balled up her fists and grinned. "It seems somebody needs to be knocked off his high horse."

"Jegra…" Cassera cautioned, "this won't end well…for any of us."

"No, it won't," she said popping her knuckles. Each crack a vicious reminder of the merciless power she was about to unleash.

"I'm warning you, Jegra," the emperor said, his voice wavering with apprehension. Even he wasn't aware of Jegra's full abilities and wasn't so sure a direct blast would take her out before she leapt across the room and snapped his neck. "Stay back."

Jegra pulled back her right arm and let loose a tremendous punch. Cassera immediately used her powers to throw up an energy shield and Jegra's fist smashed into it with a resounding crash.

The shield rippled with waves as the energy field displaced Jegra's kinetic force. A deep reverberation echoed throughout the third story room and, consequently, the entire building. The walls and furniture shuddered all around them.

"Big mistake," Jegra said with a grin.

"Oh, shit!" Cassera said, doing a quick mental calculation of the physics that had just transpired. Throwing back her other arm she used a shield to shatter the glass window behind them. "Brace yourself, my lord."

Dakroth didn't understand what had happened, but suddenly a fracture opened up in the floor, walls, and ceiling. It was as though an earthquake was tearing right through the building as it cut its way through the landscape and, consequently, everything in its path.

Jegra had split the building in half by using Cassera's forcefield against her. The pressure of the impact created a blast of air which deflected off the shield and, in turn, acted like a high-pressure air gun, slicing right through the building as though it were a Swiss roll cake.

"Impressive. She literally used our powers against us. This is why we have her with us," the emperor spoke aloud, admiring Jegra's ability to think on her feet.

Jegra pulled back and smiled at him. "A compliment from the emperor? I'm flattered. Thank you, sweetie." Naturally, she said it with an artificial graciousness which was lost on him.

"You're welcome," he replied, unaware that she didn't actually mean it, especially not after what she had just learned about his manipulation of her and what he had done to Abethca.

Actions spoke louder than words with Dakroth, which is why she didn't wait for him to figure out she wasn't being sincere. Without another word, she clapped her hands together with as much strength as she had and a mighty gush of air pushed the emperor's half of the building the rest of the way over.

Rubble rained down on the ground as half of the building tore away and collapsed into a heap. Jegra stood in the exposed room on the third story floor as she watched them go down in what looked like a controlled demolition.

A chill shooting down her spine reminded her of how cold it was at night on a desert world and, rubbing her arms to stay warm, Jegra turned and fetched her things.

Once she had finished putting on her metal bikini, she leapt down to the street below, landing on a pile of rubble and skidding off of it to solid ground.

Out of the top of a large mound of debris came a laser beam. It blasted out of the rubble and cut its way through the empty sky. This was followed by an explosive blast as Cassera used a shield to expand a bubble and throw the debris off of them.

Covered in ashen filth, Emperor Dakroth stood in the open street and dusted himself off. "Jegra, this extreme moodiness isn't becoming of a woman of your stature. Tsk, tsk," he groused. "Are we seriously going to do this?"

His words fell on deaf ears, however. Jegra picked up a large chunk of concrete the size of a bolder and chucked it at the emperor's head.

Before the slab of rock could decapitate him, though, he used a precisely timed finger-laser blast to cut it in two. The divided pieces flew by him without so much as leaving a scratch and then crashed to the ground and trundled away.

"I guess that answers my question," he said, letting out a disappointed sigh.

"My, my, my...what do we have here, boys?" a stranger's voice unexpectedly called out.

Jegra, Cassera, and Dakroth all stopped what they were doing and turned to see three ornery looking mercenaries standing out in the open street. All three of them looked like a blend of space pirate and special ops.

"Private contractors," Cassera sneered.

The middleman, and ringleader, took a bow. He was an enhanced humanoid with a grizzly beard. He had a giant, high-powered rail gun slung across his shoulders and stood with a casual tilt as he leaned to the side to offset the oversized weapon.

On his right was a huge Dragonian lizard man, with spiked shoulder armor and a broad, two-pronged, double-edged long sword right out of a *Dungeons and Dragons* campaign. Although Dragonians were a warlike species to begin with, this particular one looked as though he could level a tank.

The last member of the team was an orange-skinned woman with small round spots of red traced by black outlines, like that of a salamander back on Earth.

The Salamandarian girl had fine features and pretty eyes, one blue, one green. She licked her lips and grinned. The woman raised her hands; electricity arced between her fingertips with a menacing crackle and pop.

"I recognize you three. You're the bounty hunters from the bar," Jegra said, recognizing the two men and the girl from the street corner.

The humanoid bounty hunter stroked his beard as a manic grin gradually spread across his face. "Seems we have ourselves a bit of a domestic dispute," he chuckled.

"A lover's spat," the Salamandarian added with a snicker.

"It's none of your business," Jegra snapped, eyeing them both with an icy glare.

"Wait, don't I know you form somewhere?" the Salamandarian girl asked, eyeing Jegra up and down. After a brief moment of thought, her eyes lit up as she pieced it together. "Hey, ain't you that champion? From the gladiatorial matches."

"Hey, yeah!" the bearded mercenary said as the revelation sunk it. "You're that Jegra, babe, ain't yah?"

Dakroth raised a blue finger and pointed it at the man in the middle. As it lit up with red energy, he said, "I'm afraid I don't have time for this nonsense."

A laser blast shot out of his finger with a zap and everyone tensed and looked to the mercenary bounty hunter in the center. His eyes were wide with shock as a glowing red hole tunneled through his forehead. Small wisps of white smoke rose out as it continued to smolder.

His brains completely melted by the blast, he mumbled a nonsensical sound and then fell flat on his face.

"You'll pay for that," the lizard man roared. Swinging his blade, he lunged at the emperor and hissed.

Before he could cut the emperor down, however, Cassera stepped in between them and deflected his attack with an energy shield.

There was a twang and the Dragonian bounced off the shield. He did a back handspring to help divert the kickback and landed in a crouching position on the ground.

Almost as soon as the reptile skidded to a halt, the Salamandarian leaped over him, her fingers crackling with energy. Mid-air, she tossed spheres of crackling energy down like softballs. Resembling plasma globes, her projectiles glowed hot pink as blue strands of electricity branched across the orbs of super-charged energy.

Cassera widened the girth of her shield, but the Salamandarian grabbed the energy shield with her electric fingers and began pulling it apart as though it were made of saltwater taffy. The shield stretched and tore and soon enough the Salamandarian had broken through.

"Impossible!" Cassera gasped.

Grunting loudly, the Salamandarian finished shredding Cassera's shield and the lizard man charged forward, swinging his blade in one large swooping arc.

"My lord, get behind me," Cassera said, using her body as a shield. The lizard's blade came careening down, but stopped abruptly just centimeters above Cassera's nose. Looking over to her right, she saw Jegra holding the Dragonian's forearm with one hand, preventing him from cutting them down.

With a flick of her wrist, Jegra snapped the reptile's arm.

He reeled back and roared out in pain. A sudden laser blast from the emperor sheared off his head and put the beast out of his misery. The lizard's dead body collapsed where it stood and hit the ground with a thud.

Outnumbered, the Salamandarian slowly backed away. "You'll regret this," she growled.

"Not as much as you will," Jegra replied.

The girl raised her crackling fingers and let loose a wide discharge of electricity. Jegra threw up her arm bracers, made of korridium alloy, and crossed them. She managed to draw the electricity to her forearms, absorbing the energy. Her bracers started to glow red-orange and she shrieked with a mix of anger and pain and threw her arm out to the side, breaking the link with the charge.

Redirected through her korridium bracers, the electric current shot off to either side. One beam drilled a hole into the dirt while the other crashed into a fancy hoverbike sitting off to the side of the street. The bike exploded, going up in a yellow fireball that curled into the sky and blackened as flame evaporated into smoke.

Jegra rubbed her wrists, both singed with electric burns. Thanks to her rapid healing factor, however, they were already beginning to heal.

The emperor raised a finger to take out the Salamandarian, but Jegra deliberately stepped directly into his line of sight and prevented him from killing the girl.

Jegra looked over at the girl and scowled. "Who sent you? Why are you hunting us?"

"Her Grace, the Administratrix, has put a handsome bounty on all three of your heads. If one were to take any of you down they could buy their own moon and retire in peace."

"Anaïs Nin," Dakroth growled. "That treacherous white-skinned hag will pay for this."

"In that case," Jegra said, sauntering up to the girl who, although terrified of the domineering gladiatrix, held her ground. "Please pass along this message for me." Jegra reached up and lightly slapped the girl across her face.

The Salamandarian immediately touched the welt on her cheek and glanced up at Jegra, eyes wide with shock. Of course, Jegra had only used a fraction of her strength to slap the girl. Just enough to make it smart.

The girl wasn't entirely sure what to make of it, as Jegra slowly drew back. Not waiting around to find out, however, she glanced at everyone hesitantly, then turned and ran for dear life.

She was about a block down the street when, out of the dark, a red laser shot whizzed past Jegra's head and hit the girl squarely in her back just below her left shoulder blade. A shot through the heart. Mid-stride, the girl crashed to the ground, her face grinding into the dirt road. Her body slumped to the side and she flopped over, her heterochromatic eyes gazing up vacantly at the flickering neon-sign of a nearby tavern.

Jegra turned around, her eyes electric with rage. "Now, why'd you have to go and do that?"

The emperor blew on his finger and it cooled, turning from a hot orange to blue again. "I can't have our enemies catching wind of what we're up to. I'm sorry if that offends your sensibilities. But the days of honorable deaths in the arena are over, Jegra. Real wars, I'm afraid, are often fought without honor."

Jegra huffed angrily and then turned her back to the emperor. After a short silence, she said, "Follow me," and marched off into the night.

"Where are we going?" Cassera asked, following after her.

"Like I said," Jegra answered. "I know the slaver of this wasteland of a town."

11

At the far edge of town, Jegra led Emperor Dakroth and Cassera to a large domed structure the size of a warehouse. It looked like a giant mud igloo with yellow glowing lights for windows, perched on a bluff at the farthest edge of town.

The building was made out of Thessalonica red clay and was about eight stories high. Port-like windows three rows up glowed with a warm, inviting light that told them someone was home.

"Where are you taking us?" Cassera asked, making a disgusted face as she looked around at the slum-like conditions that surrounded the structure.

"Antor Tamoran, the man who bought and sold me, resides here," Jegra said.

"I didn't know you were on talking terms with your slaver," Dakroth said.

"I'm not," Jegra answered. "So, watch your backs. Antor can be…somewhat erratic in his temperament."

"I'm sure it's nothing you can't handle," Cassera added.

"You're probably right," Jegra replied. "But I think there's been enough bloodshed for one night," she added, shooting the emperor a nasty look. He shrugged it off as if to say it couldn't be helped and then turned away from her smoldering gaze.

The three of them strolled right up to the front doors of the complex. They were giant, iron doors with a humongous ring knocker at the center of each, like something out of the middle ages. Jegra reached up with a fist and banged on the door three times, rattling the knockers. Soon, a slat on the impervious door slid open and a bloodshot eye peeked out at them. "Who is it?" a gruff voice demanded to know.

"It's Jegra, champion of The Arena," Jegra answered. "I demand a sit-down with Antor."

The narrow slat slammed shut without so much as an utterance and, confused, they each looked to the other to see if anyone had an inkling of a clue as to what they should expect.

A couple of voices began squabbling on the other side of the door and then soon died down. Almost immediately after that, the door opened and a small toad-like man with bulging eyes looked up at them from his four-foot five stature.

"This way, if you please," he croaked.

They did as asked and entered the domicile, following the toad to a spiral staircase that wound around the inside wall of the dome, a design similar to the Guggenheim Museum in Manhattan, New York, back on Earth.

Halfway up the flight of stairs, Cassera couldn't help but show her displeasure at the aggravatingly long climb, and griped, "You'd think with as wealthy as Antor is, he could afford to install a decent elevator."

"There is an elevator, ma'am," the toad-man replied, his slatted pupils settling on Cassera's blue face.

"Then why in bloody Helios are you making us use the stairs?" Cassera nagged. As usual, she didn't try to soften her discontentment toward their less than gracious host or his dimwitted servant. Cassera knew her station and it was above most of those beings she encountered. Her tongue was always sharp and ready to wage war.

"I'm afraid the elevator is only reserved for the master, ma'am."

"Of course, it is," she sighed, blowing a strand of silver hair out of her golden eyes.

Atop the stairs, the toad creature scrambled on ahead and went over to a man half asleep on a large, burgundy sofa.

Sprawled out all around him were beautiful women, food, and golden trinkets of all kinds. The toad eased up to the man, who looked unconscious, and whispered something into his ear. There was a momentary pause, then the man abruptly sat up. Eyes as large as saucers, he looked around and, slurring his words like the drunk he was, mumbled, "Jegra?! Here? What on this scorching moon are you on about?"

Antor tried to stand up, but one of the groupies' arms was slung over him, and he collapsed back onto the sofa before trying again. Ever so careful not to wake one of his many sleeping beauties, he gently grabbed her wrist and untangled himself, setting her arm down across the bare chest of the fetching Bre'lal woman sleeping directly behind him.

He staggered to his feet, looked over to the elevator, only to realize nobody was there, then spun around, swaying like a tippling, gin-soaked fool, and spotted his guests. Reeling back, his arms shot out to stabilize him, and he staggered sideways and then back again, ending up in his original spot.

He waved them over to him, a maudlin grin forming on his chapped lips. As they approached him he bowed reverently, righting himself with a bit of effort. Immediately he placed his hands over Jegra's powerful arms, and leaned in. "A kiss for old time's sake," he said, his breath rancid with booze.

Jegra gently stopped him with a finger pressed to his chin and then slowly redirected his kiss toward the empty air.

"Still playing hard to get, I see," he said with a sozzled slur.

"It's been a long time, Antor," Jegra said.

"Indeed. It has. When I last saw you, my dear, you were as scrawny as a space-rat and so terrified you had pissed yourself in your own cage. Now look at you! The champion of the arena! The infamous Jegra the Merciless, Gladiatrix of the motherfucking galaxy." Turning his attention to her companions, his eyes instantly honed in on Cassera.

One eyebrow raised, a salacious grin slowly spread across his sunbaked lips as he studied her tight tube top and her perky nipples which jutted out from beneath the delicate fabric. "And who is this lovely femme fatale?" he asked.

"I am Vice Admiral Cassera Van Danica Amelorak, of the Dagon Imperial Fleet." The entire time she spoke, Antor's gaze never left her breasts, which compelled her to add, "And if you don't stop staring at my chest, I'll knock that stupid grin off your face and crush your testicles with my boot."

Antor laughed and turned to Jegra. "She's a spicy one. I like her already." Turning to the other Dagon, he paused and stared for the longest time as his sloshed mind tried to piece the images together. "Your majesty," Antor gasped, finally recognizing Emperor Dakroth for who he was.

Embarrassed for his less than gracious behavior, Antor immediately dropped to one knee and bowed his head. "Forgive this drunken old fool for not recognizing you sooner, your majesty."

"Rise," Dakroth said in a stately manner, waving his hand impatiently for Antor to get up.

In the blink of an eye, Antor had turned from a disinterested prick into a kiss-ass. He promptly reached out and took Dakroth's hand in his and kissed the golden ring upon the emperor's finger. Rising to his feet, he turned to the vice admiral and bowed reverently. She nodded in kind.

He drew back and waved his arm across his table of food and the scantily clad women sprawled out before them. "What's mine is yours," he said, bowing humbly.

"Enlighten me, Antor," Emperor Dakroth said, scratching his chin as he eyed Antor's lounging girls. "Do you own a ship?"

"I have a shuttlecraft capable of scuttling between Thessalonica and Dagon Prime, but if you need something with a bit more get up and go, I'm afraid there's currently nothing available. Not with the Nyctans raining disruptor fire down on anything that moves."

Dakroth shot him a sharp glance, forcing the sniveling drunk to gulp the nervous lump in his throat, and Antor quickly amended his words.

"If I had such a luxurious spacecraft in my possession," he began, "the Nyctans would have certainly obliterated it by now, seeing as they are targeting anything with faster than light travel. Presumably, to prevent you from leaving this moon."

"Come now, Antor," Jegra interjected. "We both know you didn't get to be the richest man on Thessalonica by simply scuttling about in a crammed shuttlecraft. Where's that type-three cruiser you were always bragging about?"

Antor shot Jegra a betrayed look then immediately melted into a smile and turned back to the emperor. Changing his tune, he said, "Yes, yes. It's true. I do *technically* own a type-three mid-sized cruiser. But it's currently in the employ of one Raven Nightguard. Amusingly enough, she quite literally thinks the ship is hers."

Jegra shot him a harsh glance. "May I remind you, Antor, that you are in the presence of the High Lord of Dagon."

He hemmed and hawed and then grinned sheepishly. "Alright, alright, it's not my ship. Not anymore. I lost it in a bet to that treacherous, back-stabbing, no-good pirate," he groused.

The emperor's eyes flashed red as he grew fed up with Antor's nonsense. "Any further stalling," growled Dakroth, "and I shall make a fried omelet out of your befuddled brains."

This compelled Antor to throw up his hands in complete surrender. "But I know where it is," he added, saving his neck.

"Tell me," the emperor said, throwing his arm around Antor's neck and grinning large. "Where is this ship?"

"It-it's...um ...," he fumbled over the words as Dakroth squeezed his neck so hard he winced. "It's currently parked in the pasture on the other side of town. There's a cloak, so you'll need to know its exact location if you're going to ask for passage. And even then, Raven isn't the kind of woman to do any favors. She comes at a premium. But she's the best freelancer this side of the system."

"Excellent, so you'll take us there."

Even Antor, in the inebriated state he was in, knew it wasn't a request. It was an order. Antor gulped as the emperor practically breathed down his neck, pretending to be all chummy like. "Um...there's just one problem, your grace."

"And what would that be, exactly?" asked Dakroth through his teeth.

"Raven wants me more or less dead."

"That sounds like a personal problem, if you ask me."

"Ah, yes. I see your point," said Antor, agreeing to the emperor's demands—even though it was under duress. "I'll take you to Raven as soon as you're ready."

"Antor," the emperor said, relinquishing his grip on the man's neck, "I must admit, I'm very impressed by your hospitality."

"Really?" he asked.

Jegra rolled her eyes and gave him a nudge on the shoulder to get him going. He staggered forward and glanced back at her only to see her nod her head in the direction of the elevator, urging him to get moving.

Moments later, the doors to the giant mud palace creaked open and Antor led the three cloaked figures into the night. They made haste and briskly stode over to a large hover skiff.

"This was made for moving heavy cargo, but it will get us there much quicker," Antor said, helping his guests onto the broad, square hover platform.

"Are you sure it's safe?" Jegra asked. "Because it doesn't look safe." Antor only responded with a wily grin.

The hover skiff had what appeared to be hoverbike handlebars welded onto one end. Antor jammed the ignition button starting up the magnetic coils, and the skiff rose up. Hovering only twenty inches above the ground, Antor looked back at his passengers and said, "Hold on to your butts!"

With a pulsing whirr of the mag-coils, the skiff shot off.

Minus any safety railings, Jegra had to steady herself as they sped off. It was a lot like trying to manage a surf board. Looking over her shoulder, she saw the Emperor and Cassera struggling to do the same, latching onto one another for support.

"How long till we arrive?" Jegra asked, shouting against the rush of oncoming air and the droning noise of the mag-coils.

"About five minutes," he replied. Glancing over his shoulder he shot Jegra a wink and then went back to piloting the skiff.

They flew up the street, kicking up a dust trail behind them as they went. Banking around a sharp bend, Antor took the skiff up so as to not throw his passengers. Then he swooped down again and raced up a different street.

Several pedestrians had to jump out of the way as they shot past, kicking up a whirlwind as they went.

"Are you trying to get us killed?" Cassera asked.

"No," their less than trustworthy guide answered. Shouting over his shoulder, he added, "Just hold tight. We're almost there."

The skiff shot out into an open area at the center of town and they flew into a large fenced-off area. It was a pen for swine. Or what appeared to be pigs; they had small trunks like those of a baby elephant where their snouts should be.

Out of the darkness came high-powered laser blasts. Not from any simple handheld blaster, but full on, wide-beam disrupter canons from a nearby ship. Though Jegra couldn't see any ship, it didn't matter; sure enough, as the dirt exploding around them from the warning blasts proved, it was out there.

Antor steered the skiff hard to the right, trying to pull away from the canon fire, but a warning shot into the dirt directly in their path caused it to lurch up into the air. Catching air, the skiff flipped over, tossing its occupants to the ground.

Everybody tumbled to a halt in the dirt. Clothes and hair a dusty mess, Jegra pushed herself to her hands and knees only to find the end of a blaster barrel pointed at her temple.

The muzzle of the gun pressed tightly against her head, and a most serious voice said, "Don't move."

Jegra slowly raised her eyes to find a familiar face looking down at her. "It's you!" she gasped, recognizing the blue-skinned woman from yesterday's encounter in the bar.

"What part of 'don't move' did you not understand?" the blue skinned woman with purple eyes asked in an obviously vexed tone.

"Hey'yah, Raven," Antor said shamefacedly, as two of Raven's four-member crew cuffed him and set him on his knees before their fearless captain. "Long time no see."

Raven pulled out a second blaster from the back of her waist and aimed it at Antor's grinning face. "Give me one good reason why I shouldn't just put a hole through that dumb-grinning face of yours, Antor?"

"Maybe because I brought you the most lucrative deal this side of the galaxy?"

"What are you talking about?" Raven barked. Her trigger finger itched like a son-of-a-bitch and she wanted ever so badly to blow that smirk right off his face, but she held back. She was ruthless, but she wasn't a cold-blooded killer, especially if there was profit in patience.

Antor nodded at the two hooded figures in their company, as if to say these are the gifts I speak of.

"Take their hoods off," she ordered.

A large Kree'alek fish-man stepped forward. He wore a custom-tailored aquatic-to-dry land respiration suit made from a copper colored alloy; it fit over his upper torso like a retro astronaut suit. It was filled with constantly filtering seawater for him to breathe through. He obeyed Raven's orders and pulled back the hoods of the captors to reveal the emperor of Dagon and the vice admiral of the fleet.

"Holieeey schizoid," a giant, green and blue striped Dragonian said, holding a much too heavy rifle in both clawed hands. His skin was like that of an alligator's, thick and rubbery with a patch work of scale patterns.

The lizard man's face was pleasant in a way. His greenish-yellow eyes had a depth to them. Almost a hypnotic quality. It felt like gazing into a beautiful marble and getting lost in the moment. And he was totally jacked. Muscles on top of muscles, which made him the hottest lizard man Jegra had ever seen. If this wasn't enough, his face consisted of a slight hump for a snout that blended nicely into his broad jawline, making him quite the handsome specimen.

Over to the right, a smaller, slender figure with a wrapped face and goggles guarded the loading ramp that revealed the entrance to the ship. The ship itself was cloaked, so all one could see was the ramp leading up into the cargo hold. The masked figure let out an awestruck whistle.

"Bloody Helios!" Raven gasped. "This is great, just fucking great. And here we were trying to keep a low profile, what with the Nyctan fleet shooting at everything in sight. Luckily, the *Skywend* has a cloaking device, so they haven't caught onto us yet. But chances are, if you're here, Nyctan spies already know about it."

"Will you help us or not?" Cassera asked.

Raven scowled at her and then looked over at the emperor with a more sympathetic expression. "I can't say no to the emperor of the whole bloody galaxy, can I?"

"I sense sarcasm in that," Dakroth said, raising an eyebrow.

"Do you?" Raven quipped, even more sarcastically than before. Turning on her heels, she holstered her blasters and headed toward the loading ramp of her ship. "Well, what are you all standing around for. Bring our guests aboard the *Skywend*."

"Yes, Raven," the Dragonian said, sounding genuinely apologetic. Then he ushered everyone on board, all but for one.

"Not you," he said, stopping Antor with the butt of his gun. Nudging the drunk back, he glared at the sniveling man and hissed in his baritone, reptilian tone, one that sent Antor scurrying back.

"Oh, and Antor," Jegra said, pausing halfway up the ramp and turning around to address him. "Unless you want me to pay you a visit late one night to play a little game I like to call 'let's see how many bones I can break in your body before you pass out', I wouldn't whisper a word of this to anyone. Savvy?"

"No problem," Antor said. "My lips are sealed." He pretended to twist an imaginary key above his pursed lips and tossed it aside. "Mum's the word," he mumbled through his pursed lips, like a complete idiot.

Jegra glared at him with distrust until, finally, he caved in to the intensity of it and slowly slunk backward. That's when the large, reptilian guard grunted and feigned a lunge toward Antor.

Startled, Antor yelped and turned and scurried away, tripping over his own feet numerous times as he struggled to hightail it out of there. Without stopping to look back, he ran into the night as fast as his two legs would carry him.

The Dragonian looked up at Jegra and winked. She smiled at him and then boarded the *Skywend*. He followed her up just as the ramp began to close.

12

 across the bow of the *Skywend* as she darted out of Thessalonica's atmosphere and into open space.

The 600-foot-long vessel, as big and sleek as a mega-yacht back on Earth, streaked across the sky as the much larger Nyctan cruisers, three times bigger than the biggest warships Jegra had ever seen, slowly brought their bows around and began pursuit of the small frigate.

"Bloody Helios!" Raven growled, jamming the throttle forward and opening up the thrusters to their maximum burn. "They were expecting us."

"Can you outrun them?" Cassera asked, leaning over Raven's seat. Raven shot her a sharp glance that said "Back off." Complying, Cassera took a step back and gave the captain her space.

"A bulky cruiser that size? You bet I can outrun it. We'll fly circles around them the entire time they try to pull away from the low orbit. It's like they say, the bulkier your hull, the harder you roll."

"This ship looks fresh out of spacedock," Emperor Dakroth said, running his hand along the sleek lines of the bulkhead. "Out of curiosity, how did you come by this vessel?"

"I thought you might ask, considering she was one of yours."

"Impossible," Cassera said. "As fleet's vice admiral, I would have heard about it."

"Not necessarily," Raven said. "Hold on," she interjected. Another blast shot across the bridge of the ship, and Raven pulled up on the joystick, rolled the *Skywend* onto its back, then dove back down, forcing the cruiser to have to readjust its cannons before getting off another round.

Continuing on where she'd left off, she informed them about how she came across the *Skywend.*

"The *Skywend* is a prototype ship I commandeered on a smuggling run. It was adrift in the Zargora system. When I came aboard, I found nothing but an empty vessel. Its entire crew having mysteriously vanished without a trace. And since nobody had laid claim to the missing vessel, I commandeered her under the official rules of the intergalactic trade commission."

"I heard you won it in a bet," stated Jegra, recalling what Antor had told them. Although he was most certainly a habitual liar, this seemed as though it would be a rather strange thing for him to lie about.

"I won her *back* in a bet," Raven said. "That scumbag Antor and his goons hijacked us when we stopped off at Plenar station to pick up a shipment of korridium alloy for another client. It took me three weeks and every resource I had to get her back. Ultimately, I caught up with him at the casino aboard Lilly's Lucky Star Station over the moon Rivelon. I paid a sweet million creds to buy into the game and then cleaned him out. Hurt him where it counts–his wallet. Got ten mill and the ship out of it."

"He's lucky you let him off the hook," Jegra said.

"I would love nothing more than to blot that terrible stain out of existence, but he's too well connected with the type of disreputable folks we tend to do business with."

Jegra folded her arms across her chest. "So, what you're saying is, he's a necessary evil."

"That's one way of putting it," Raven replied. "Hold on!" Raven jerked on the joystick and the ship veered hard to port. As the gravity of the small moon out the *Skywend's* window pulled on them, everyone braced themselves.

The masked figure Jegra remembered from earlier poked her head in and announced, "The FTL is primed, captain."

"Good work, Gyllek. Let me know if there's any hiccups in the engines."

"Wilco, boss-lady!" Gyllek said saluting. With that she ducked back out of the cabin and disappeared down a nearby hatch.

"Just give me your coordinates or destination and we'll split like a beam of light."

"We need to go to the Zargora system. Sector B-13. Asteroid MK-29-388-

XP3," relayed Dakroth.

Raven looked back and shot him a shocked look.

"I know, I know," he said.

"Bloody Helios," Raven said. Swiveling back around into her chair, she got on the comm. "Everyone sit down and strap in. We're jumping to an asteroid that orbits a black hole."

"We're what?" gasped Jegra in shock.

"This takes some precision flying, ladies and gents. So, please sit down and shut up. Thanks."

Everyone found themselves a seat in the oval bridge and strapped in.

"Engaging FTL drive in, three, two, one…"

With a flash of light, the ship blasted away from the system, leaving the Nyctan battle cruisers in its stardust.

Lines of starlight streaked by the windows as they traveled beyond the light barrier. After about fifteen minutes, Raven pulled back on the throttle of the FTL drive and dropped out of hyperspace.

The ship started shuddering, rattling violently.

"What's that?" Jegra asked, gripping her harness tight. She wasn't used to space travel. She'd spent most of her time with her feet firmly planted on the ground. Space travel didn't suit her.

"It's a meteor shower," Raven growled as she leaned across her controls and flicked numerous switches and twisted dials. There was a pulsating murmur and then the sound of a generator came on. "Front deflectors increased to full output."

A voice came on the intercom. "Boss-lady, I just wanted to say that those hiccups weren't me. I swear."

"I know," Raven replied. "It's a meteor shower."

"There shouldn't be a meteor cloud out this far," Cassera said. "Not unless…"

"I'm sorry to break it to you, Emperor Dakroth," Raven said swiveling around in her captain's chair. "But your asteroid has been obliterated."

Dakroth stepped forward and peered out the window. In the distance a massive black hole slowly gobbled up a string of rocks that slowly fell into it. Soon a ring, would form around it as the remaining debris found a steady, non-decaying orbit.

"What was out here this far?" Jegra asked.

"A secret shipyard," Dakroth informed. "It's where this vessel was made. And it's where my new cruiser was being built. Obviously the Nyctans found out about it and destroyed it before it could be completed."

"Actually," Raven cut in, "this damage is very recent."

"How recent?" Cassera asked.

Raven spun around and checked her display panel. She tapped a few touch sensitive buttons and then replied, "About three days."

"Raven," Jegra asked, placing her hand on Raven's shoulder. "Are there any pirates bold enough to attack an Imperial dry dock?"

"Not without fear of retaliation," Raven informed them.

"This has to be someone else. Someone new," said Dakroth, slamming his fist into an open palm out of frustration.

"Whoever is behind this, they're obviously trying to take advantage of the recent turmoil," Cassera said. "The only question is, how did they know about a top-secret facility that even I wasn't aware existed until a day ago?"

"That remains to be seen," the emperor said. "Until we have a shred of information to go on, however, we need to head to Cordova."

"Cordova?" Raven asked, a perplexed look coming over her. "What could you possibly need that's in Cordova?"

"It's not a what, but a who," Dakroth replied.

"Have it your way," Raven said, punching in the coordinates. "But you may all want to head back to the galley and make yourselves something to eat. This trip will be about three days at faster than light speed."

"Three days?" Jegra gasped.

"Cordova is at the very edge of the empire," Raven informed her. "And there's no straight route there. We have to pass through all seven systems. That means avoiding planets, stars, rogue asteroids, and any unfriendlies that might want to take us out." She looked over at her Dragonian co-pilot and added, "Kregor, take our guests to the galley and get them something to eat. Then help them settle into their guest quarters."

The Dragonian stood up and nodded. "Yes, ma'am. If you'll all follow me," he said, ducking under the low entrance of the bridge and out into the main corridor of the vessel.

Just as the emperor was about to leave the bridge, Raven cleared her throat.

Dakroth paused and, one arm on the doorway, he looked back.

"Is there something else?"

"As for the matter of payment…"

"Name your price."

"Two million credits."

"You'll have it the moment I set foot on Cordova. Is there anything else you'd like?"

"As a matter of fact, yes," Raven said pointing at a green display panel. "There's a special system I can't access. Gyllek has tried to hack it but it seems unbroachable. I was wondering…you wouldn't happen to have the access code or know what it does by any chance?"

"Strange, I wasn't aware of any hidden systems," Dakroth lied. "Anyway, I'm afraid that I'm not too familiar with these new systems."

"Well, thanks anyway." She could tell he was lying through his pearly white teeth, but she didn't want to push the matter any further for fear of getting on his bad side. Right now, she was a neutral agent, and that's exactly the way she intended to keep things. Amicable.

"No, problem," the emperor said. He smiled at Raven then left the bridge.

Raven slammed her fist on a button and shut the door to the bridge and shivered in disgust. "That guy gives me the creeps," she whispered to herself.

After Kregor treated everyone to a nice dehydrated pack of spicy Dragonian ramen with a side of Angorian wild turkey and some kind of sprout-like vegetable, the emperor and Cassera asked to be excused. The spice did not seem to sit well with them.

Gyllek offered to show them to the guest quarters, thinking they were a couple, and they followed after her.

As they headed off, Cassera paused and looked back at Jegra with dismay. "I do not see how you can stuff your face with that reptilian slag." She grimaced and then walked away.

"Don't listen to them," Jegra said, slurping up the noodles quite noisily. "This stuff is awesome!"

Kregor laughed and slapped Jegra across her bare back. His swat was so strong she actually felt it. The stun of it caused her to pause, and they shared a look and then both started bellowing with laughter.

A few moments later Kregor got up and opened a small pantry. He then brought out a bottle. "This is Dragonian shochu. Made from a rare, bitter red potato and sweetened with fermenting pill bugs."

"So, you're saying it's alcohol made from bug guts?"

"Only partially. It has that potato base," he said, offering her some of the wine-red drink. It was the consistency of stew.

She thought about it for a moment and then shrugged. "Why not? Fill me up!"

"Excellent!" he boomed. "None of the crew will drink it with me. They find Dragonian cuisine revolting."

"Well, I'm not any of them, am I?"

"No. You are Jegra the Magnificent!" he said filling her glass all the way to the brim. "I've watched nearly all of your bouts. You are the best warrior since La'Garren."

"La'Garren Bosch? I've heard of him. But I never had the privilege of meeting him. He was before my time."

"That's too bad. That would have made for an epic match. Old champion verses new."

"I did fight Abethca though," she said. "She was a returning champion."

"But not a reigning champion. She fought for her freedom and left. You easily obtained your freedom in, I believe your first month, correct? But chose to stay. You are a true warrior!"

Jegra looked up at him, mouth agape, noodles hanging out of her mouth. Biting the noodles away, she swallowed hard and asked, "What do you mean I gained my freedom in the first month? I hadn't won three hundred matches yet."

"It's not three hundred matches," Kregor chuckled. "It's three hundred kills. You easily racked that up in your first month."

Jegra sat, dumbfounded. She had been a free woman for over a year and hadn't even realized it. Funny that nobody, not even Emperor Dakroth, had the courtesy to inform her of it.

"Is something the matter?" Kregor asked.

"No," Jegra said, raising her cup. It wasn't as though she would have even known what to do with herself after a month anyway. So, she decided it was best to let bygones be. "To champions!"

"To you!" Kregor said and they clanked their glasses together.

Three Dragonian ales later, Jegra was quite buzzed. Staggering to her feet, she found her balance and then said, "I probably should turn in for the evening. Do you mind showing me to my quarters, kind sir?" She had a nice buzz and was feeling flirtatious, so she batted her eyes at him and held out her hand for him to take.

"I'd love to," Kregor said, rising slowly to his feet. He was a bit wobbly, too. He helped her up but staggered backward, almost toppling over.

Jegra clutched his hand in hers and reeled him back into her. His strong chest smashed into her voluptuous breast and they gazed at one another for longer than she intended. She finally broke their gaze and turned away, her cheeks blushing.

"This way," he said motioning toward a curved corridor.

They stumbled up the corridor together, swaying on tipsy legs. As they went, she tried her best to get a handle on the floorplan of the ship. As far as she could discern, the layout of the rooms was like that of an old-fashioned wagon wheel.

At the center of the ship's living quarters were the coed showers and restroom. The crew's quarters wrapped around the hub of the bathroom like a wheel, and the spokes were the corridors that led to the various areas of the ship.

Due to her crippling dizziness, Jegra paused to lean on the wall. "On second thought, I don't think we'll make it. Just leave me here."

"Nonsense," Kregor said, resting his hands on his knees as he tried not to teeter over and fall on his face. "I shall carry you!" he announced.

Jegra reached out for his hand and he tried to grab it but they missed one another. She laughed and they tried again, this time making a connection.

Reeling each other in, they met in the middle of the corridor and, swaying together as if caught up in some maudlin dance, their eyes locked.

Although reptiles didn't sweat, Jegra was sweating enough for the both of them. "Is it hot in here, or is it just me?" she inquired, fanning her glistening chest.

Kregor gulped. "Sorry," he apologized for no reason, seeing as it was no fault of his. "I'll see about the thermostat."

"Nah," she said, latching onto his arm for support. "I like it hot." She batted her eyes at him and said in a sensuous voice, "*Real hot.*"

She could tell he viewed her as a celebrity and so was reluctant to be brazenly smitten with her. However, this made him even more attractive in her eyes. And, besides, she wasn't going to lie. She wouldn't say no if he decided to man up and make a move.

13

Reeling from the Dragonian ale, they made their way up and down the corridors in what seemed like a slow-motion jaunt where gravity continually shifted about. Staggering up to a door, they both leaned on the wall to try and get their bearings. "Please tell me this is it," said Jegra.

"This is it," Kregor answered. "I think."

Jegra scrunched her nose up and gave him a coy look. "You think?"

Kregor scratched his chin. "I'm ninety-five percent sure."

"Good enough for me," she chortled. With that, she slapped the panel on the wall next to the door with the palm of her hand and the door swooshed open.

A pleasant, earthy scent greeted her as she poked her head inside and looked around. She took in a deep breath and smiled. It reminded her of the forests back home.

The inside was quaint, like a standard hotel room. Just a bed tucked into an inset wall, a small desk, and a vid-screen.

A green, leafy plant in the corner of the room added a bit of warmth; its genuine soil added a nice, earthy scent. Other than that, it was as spartan as it gets. But she wasn't complaining. A bed was a bed, and she was aching to fall into one and drift off to sleep.

Still light-headed, Jegra shuffled into the room and opened a slide away panel that revealed a closet full of clothes, most of which she was sure were far too tight to fit her athletic and busty build. Sliding the first panel shut she opened another and found a personal toilet. "Where's the shower?" she asked.

"There are shared, coed stalls down the hallway at the center of the living area," Kregor said, thumbing over his shoulder. "I could stand guard if you want to take a rinse in private."

"I appreciate the offer, but I'm exhausted," Jegra said. She yawned loudly, placing her hands on her hips and arching her back as she stretched. A habit she'd formed from endless nights of sore muscles. "I'll shower tomorrow. Right now, I think I'll turn in for the evening."

Kregor smiled and tottered back on his heels, his large boots clunking on the floor. "Well, in that case, I suppose this is where I ought to bid you goodnight."

Without warning, Jegra leaned forward and kissed Kregor on his forest green lips. The kiss apparently startled him and he drew back and gave her a surprised look.

"I'm sorry," she said, brushing a strand of brown hair behind her ear. She looked up at him, her cheeks glowing bright pink, and batted her eyelashes. "I don't know why I did that," she laughed.

"It's the alcohol," Kregor replied. "Dragonian ale has that effect on people."

"It makes them horny?" Jegra teased.

"No, drunk," Kregor chuckled.

"I know what you mean," she said, biting her lower lip. "Hey, you maybe want to stay the night?"

"I can't," Kregor replied, diverting his gaze as though he were ashamed of something.

"Why not?" Jegra asked. "Who knows? It might be kind of fun."

"As much as I appreciate the offer, I doubt it would be pleasant for you."

"What do you mean?" she asked.

"You've obviously never been with a Dragonian before," he said with a drunken lisp.

"Was it that obvious?" she asked, twirling a strand of hair around her finger as she gazed into his eau-de Nil-colored eyes.

"Dragonians have barbed genitals," he confessed.

Jegra squinted at him and tried to figure out if he was pulling her leg or not. She'd never been with a Dragonian so she didn't know much about the anatomy of the lizard people.

"Are you messing with me?"

"I'm afraid not," he said, sounding remorseful.

Her eyes fell to his crotch and she stared long and hard. "Screw it. Now I *have* to see," she said, a grin spreading across her face. Reaching up, she grabbed Kregor by his neck and pulled him into her lips.

Unprepared for her extreme sexual aggression, Kregor stumbled into her and, together, they staggered back and fell onto the bed.

Kregor kicked off his boots and hastily began unbuttoning his uniform while Jegra already had her bikini top off and was vigorously wriggling out of her bottoms.

Eager to get it on with the Dragonian, which she figured might be an evolved dragon, if dragons had ever existed, she helped him peel off his uniform. She yanked at his shirt, pulling it down around his shoulders, then she sat up. His knees straddling her thighs, she wrapped her arms around his waist and squeezed hard to let him feel her strength and began fondling his dark green nipples with her teeth.

As she felt him grow more excited by her vigorous foreplay, she reached down and helped him slip out of his pants, taking everything off in one fell swoop. Tossing their garments aside, she looked down at him in all his glory; she studied him with keen interest. "Oh my God!" she cried out excitedly.

"I told you," he said.

Out in the hallway, Skuld and Gyllek were heading back to their sleeping quarters after their shifts.

"I've always enjoyed the long, leisurely cruises," Skuld said to her. "It gives me time to catch up on the latest scientific journals from seven different systems."

"Not me," Gyllek said, letting out a sigh. "I get stir crazy on these deep space voyages." She paused in the middle of the corridor. Skuld paused along with her and listened, alerted by the expression on her face and the fact that she put her hand to her ear. "Did you hear that?"

Skuld cocked his fish-head in his aquatic helmet and listened. "If I'm not mistaken, it sounds like...giggling."

"It's coming from over here," Gyllek said, sneaking up to the door and putting her ear against it.

"I don't think we should be listening in on someone else's private affairs," Skuld said.

"It sounds like Kregor and Jegra are about to bump uglies," she said, a slight grin forming on her face.

"Bumping uglies is actually an extremely apt description of intergalactic multispecies pansexual activity," he informed her. "It's not always pretty and in about thirteen percent of the cases it can even prove fatal."

Gyllek nodded as though she were listening to him when, in actuality, she was listening to what was going on behind the closed door. After a moment, she peeled her ear away from the door. A confused expression fell across her face and she asked, "Skuld?"

"Yes?"

"What's leafy artichoke plant?"

"I believe it is an edible plant that resembles a Terran pinecone and is rather prickly, if I'm not mistaken."

A smile spread from one ear to another and she pressed her ear up against the door again. "And what's a cucumber?"

"It's another edible plant about yay long." He held his hands apart at about twenty inches.

Gyllek's eyes grew impossibly large, as though she'd just seen a ghost, and she gulped. It dawned on her what was prickly like an artichoke but as long as a cucumber.

"Are they making a salad?" Skuld asked, rather perplexed by all the produce questions.

"Something like that," Gyllek said.

A loud moan erupted from inside the bedroom and they turned to each other, surprised expressions plastered on their faces as all the pieces of the puzzle came together.

Another series of moans broke out and was promptly followed by a loud orgasmic gasp and Jegra's voice screaming out, "Yes, yes, yes!"

"Ah, I see. It all becomes clear to me," Skuld said, raising a finger. "An interesting fact about Dragonian genitalia," he began, but before he could finish his sentence Gyllek grabbed his webbed hand and towed him away from Jegra's room.

Inside Jegra's guest quarters, she clutched the bedspread with sweaty palms and strained her neck as her face turned beat red. Pausing momentarily, Jegra raised up to her elbows and gave Kregor a mystified look.

He stopped mid stroke and asked, "Am I hurting you?"

"No," she replied. "I thought I heard something."

He listened for a bit and then shrugged.

"Never mind," she said.

"Do you want me to stop?" he asked, still nervous about the anatomical differences between their species.

"God, no!" Jegra gasped. "Don't ever stop."

But just as soon as he resumed, the door chimed quite unexpectedly, forcing a premature end to their fun.

"Oh, shit," Jegra said, covering her mouth with her hand. It felt as though one of their parents had unexpectedly returned home from work only to catch them in the act.

"Maybe it is for the best," he said, climbing off her.

"Wait," Jegra whispered. "We could just ignore it."

"As tempting as that offer sounds," he informed her, "there's a strict policy against fraternizing aboard this ship; I believe this qualifies." He quickly dressed and then looked down at her one last time. "It has been a pleasure, Jegra."

"The pleasure was all mine," she insisted.

Kregor opened the door and rushed out of Jegra's quarters, almost crashing into his captain, Raven Nightguard.

"Kregor?" she asked in an amused yet somewhat puzzled tone. Strange, she thought. He looked flustered. But he never got flustered.

"Pardon me, captain," he said, shuffling past her. "I was just...Jegra wanted to...I need to fix the..." Unable to find right excuse to adequately explain himself, he stared awkwardly at his captain, who stared back at him. "So, yeah," he said, clearing his throat. Then, without so much as waiting to be dismissed, he raced off down the corridor.

Raven laughed, not quite knowing what had gotten into him. Entering Jegra's quarters, still looking over her shoulder at Kregor, she said, "In all my years, I've never seen that man blush. Until now."

With a swish of air, the door slid shut behind Raven. Coming around the corner of the inlet, she looked down to find Jegra sprawled out on her side, her head propped up on one arm, her other arm resting on the cusp of her hip, and not a trace of modesty on her. "And you're naked," she said, abruptly looking away.

"Is there something I can do for you, Captain?"

"Yes. Do you mind putting on some clothes, perhaps?"

Jegra held up her metal bikini and sighed. "Space isn't exactly made for barbarian girls' sport's attire, if you catch my meaning. You wouldn't happen to have anything a bit more space worthy, would you?"

"I think there may be a stretch suit in here that might fit you," Raven said, sliding open the wall panel. Ruffling through some outfits, she found one and pulled it out.

"Oh, that'll do nicely," Jegra said, taking the black outfit from Raven. It was a futuristic black spandex suit with a yellow stripe trailing down both sides of it.

It looked like something right out of the movie *Tron*. Squeezing into it, Jegra stretched out any creases and then zipped up. To her pleasant surprise, the zipper went up and over the massif that was her chest without a hiccup.

"Now, tap that little blinking green LED on the cuff just under your wrist," Raven informed her.

Jegra did as instructed and the suit refitted itself to her dimensions. Precisely. She was astonished by how easily she could move in it.

In the arena, she wore whatever they gave her. Most of it uncomfortable armor which was more for show than for utility, in fact, most of the outfits hindered her movement, which is why she chose to go with the stripped-down chainmail bikini. At least *it* was comfortable. But nothing compared to this space-age spandex suit.

"This is so freaking awesome! And stretchy," she chirped.

"Glad you approve," replied Raven.

"I doubt you came here to try on clothes and braid each other's hair." Still a little frustrated that Raven had interrupted her coitus, Jegra placed her hands on her spandex clad hips and shot the blue-skinned, purple-eyed vixen a scrutinizing look. "So, what do you want?"

"I know you have a reputation for being able to take care of yourself. Even so, I feel I should warn you to be careful around Emperor Dakroth. He isn't the benevolent ruler everyone thinks he is. He's a cruel, bloodthirsty, dictator that would kill you in a heartbeat if it served his best interest."

"You don't need to tell me," Jegra said, her voice growing serious. "I'm fully aware of Dakroth's double faced, scheming nature."

And without meaning to, Jegra's memory flashed back to that terrible, awful, bloody day.

Jennica stood above her, her finger glowing bright red as she was about to deal Jegra a lethal laser blast to the skull. But she was in luck. Lying within arm's reach was a shard of a broken mirror.

She grabbed the fragment of reflective glass just in time to deflect the blast away from herself. The laser beam refracted off the broken mirror and cut Jennica's left arm clean off.

Jennica drew back and screamed out in agony. Naturally, this gave Jegra the opening she needed, and she kicked Jennica's knee out from under her, snapping her leg like a twig. She toppled to the ground beside Jegra.

Not waiting for Jennica to get off another shot, Jegra grabbed Jennica's free hand before she could retaliate and locked it up in a relentless grip. Slowly, she twisted Jennica's arm back onto itself, holding her wrist tight. Jennica resisted, but Jegra overpowered her and, with a brutal crunch, Jennica's arm snapped.

Her opponent immobilized, Jegra threw herself onto Jennica and began to beat her to a bloody pulp. Jennica gurgled through a blood filled mouth, begging for Jegra to stop, but she knew Dagons; they often lied to save their own skins. And she wasn't about to risk a laser blast through the skull.

It wasn't her proudest moment, that was for sure. And it was this final vision of Jennica's battered and broken face, one eye popped out of its socket, her dislocated jaw hanging slack with all its front teeth broken out, that so haunted Jegra.

It was one of the reasons she couldn't help but fuck everything in sight. As long as she was fucking, she ain't sleeping. She ain't dreaming. And she's sure as hell ain't remembering.

When I fuck, I can live in the moment, she reasoned. *I can focus on just the raw, sensual ecstasy of it. The titillating sensations, the smell of it. And I can tune everything else out.*

Jegra didn't know how long she could go on like this. She wouldn't even venture to offer a guess.

"Probably as long as I need to," she said softly.

Perhaps the worst part, though, she thought, is that being forced to kill Jennica in cold blood wasn't even in the top three of my biggest regrets.

"Then you should know that he killed my parents," Raven shared, interrupting Jegra's regretful thoughts. The expression on Raven's face turned somber.

Jegra's eyes grew wide with shock. "I'm sorry. I didn't know."

"It's something I usually don't talk about, especially with strangers. But I wanted you to know that the only thing preventing me from jettisoning that piece of blue-skinned filth right out the nearest airlock is you."

"Me?" Jegra, gasped. She was utterly confused.

"There's only one person on Cordova that Emperor Dakroth would care about seeing. The High Priest of Hastur, Zira Ha'ppek. As such, I'm betting a wedding is in your near future." Raven kneeled down on one knee, and took Jegra's hand and kissed it, "Your majesty."

Jegra quickly reached down and grabbed Raven by her arm and brought her back to her feet. Embarrassed by Raven's grand display of veneration, her cheeks flushed bright pink.

"Don't do that," Jegra whispered apprehensively. "I'm not his wife. Not yet, anyway."

"Don't you see, though?" Raven asked, grabbing Jegra's arms and giving them a firm squeeze. "You will give a newfound hope to the entire galaxy. Once you are made the Empress of the Dagon Empire, you will rule with equal authority. It is the Dagon way."

"I am a little puzzled. Why would Dakroth bestow a lowly alien like me with so much power?" Jegra wondered.

"My best guess," Raven said, scratching her neck. "Is he is using you as a means to an end."

"But what end?" Jegra asked.

"You'd know better than I. But, let's not kid ourselves, it's not likely to be pleasant, whatever it is. Which is why you need to be careful. And why you need an ally. I can be that ally for you, if you want."

"Thank you," Jegra replied. "I appreciate that. And I'll be careful. Promise."

"I would wish to you the utmost happiness in your upcoming marriage, but seeing as he's the most miserable person in the galaxy, I'll just wish you the best of luck."

With that Raven turned and exited Jegra's quarters.

Jegra turned and looked at the wall. "Activate mirror," she said aloud and a display formed on the wall projecting her image back at her in high definition. She looked spiffy in her new outfit, even if she did say so herself.

Jegra lay back down on the bed and grabbed a pillow and curled up. Letting out a sigh, she closed her eyes and drifted off to sleep.

14

Steam filled the coed showers and a voice sang a pleasant tune. Jegra couldn't make out who it was, so she just tiptoed up to an available stall and turned on the hot water. Throwing her towel onto a peg on the wall, she stepped into the stream of hot water and let it massage the back of her neck.

An accidental release of tension led to a slight moan escaping Jegra's lips and the voice singing in the nearby stall suddenly stopped. "Who's there?" it called out.

"It's me."

"Who's me?"

"Me, Jegra."

The voice fell quiet.

"Hello?" Jegra asked. Looking up, she tossed her wet hair back and came face to face with the wide, perpetually shocked gaze of a fish face set atop a six-foot-three frame.

"Ah, yes," Jegra said, recognizing the familiar face. "I'd almost forgotten about you."

"Pleasure to meet you. My name is Skuld," he said, extending a webbed hand.

She gave his hand a firm shake and smiled. "Nice to meet you too, Skuld. I'm Jegra."

"Oh, everyone knows who you are," he said, returning to his stall. "You're quite famous around here."

"I'm beginning to think there isn't anyone in the galaxy who doesn't know me by now."

"There may be a few," Skuld jested.

"If you don't mind my asking, how do you breathe in the open air without your suit?" Jegra asked, after wracking her brain to no avail.

"It's the steam," said Skuld. He waved his hand through the humid air. "As long as I keep my gills saturated with moisture, I can retain enough salinity to breathe without my suit for extended periods of time."

"That's amazing," Jegra replied. She enjoyed being sociable, something that her alter ego, Jessica Hemsworth, could never manage. Jegra was good at finding reasons to engage in idle chit chat.

What's more, allowing her curiosity to get the better of her, she snuck a peek at the Skuld's aquatic gear below the waist. It wasn't entirely deliberate; her gaze just sort of involuntarily slipped.

By the time she realized what she was doing and looked back up, it was too late. He blinked at her with his big fish eyes and she blushed. She was about to apologize for her invasive gaze when, to her surprise, she caught him doing the same. She chalked it up to something people do when meeting at the crossroads of the coed showers.

After he'd scanned her body from head to toe, she placed a hand on her hip and struck a pose. "So, what do you think?"

"I take it your species evolved from primates, is that correct?"

"How'd you know?"

"Well, at first glance, you are obviously a mammalian with a large cranium, suggesting a high capacity for intelligence that's common among most primates in the galaxy. The number of lenses over your eyes suggest your vision is stereoscopic. Your face is flat, suggesting prognathism, a trait familiar to all apes, including the giant gorillas of Satorix 9."

Glancing down at her ass, he continued on with his science lesson. "You lack a tail, which rules out all mammals but primates. By the width of your pelvic bone, I'd assume your species' females have particularly large uteruses for long term gestation of your young; anywhere from six to nine months by my estimation. You're a heterodont, meaning you have many types of teeth, a trait you likely evolved to suit the needs of an omnivorous diet. Oh, and you're a pentadactyl with opposable thumbs."

"You got all that with just one glance?"

"I would hope so," he chortled, his giant fish eyes blinking twice. "I wouldn't make a very good science officer, otherwise."

"At least now I know why I didn't understand half of what you said," Jegra laughed.

"You are very attractive for an ape, mistress Jegra," he said, paying her a compliment.

"Why thank you."

He nodded his head with a reverent dip of the chin. She smiled at him and then turned and started washing her body.

While she worked up a good lather with a bar of soap, she thought about the past couple of days and how it had brought her into the company of this eccentric group of galactic wayfarers and how much being aboard the *Skywend* already felt like home away from home.

Raven's quirky crew wasn't at all what Jegra had expected. She was expecting cut-throat mercenaries. But everyone had been overly pleasant and always accommodating. They made her feel right at home and that pleased her to no end.

"Morning," a third voice called out to them.

They both looked over to find Kregor standing in the entrance of the shower, a towel draped over his forearm.

"Good morning, ole chap!" Skuld said, turning off his water and sauntering out of the stall. Glancing over at Jegra then at Kregor, he smiled at them, his fish lips stretching wide. "Well, I guess I'll leave you two lovebirds alone."

Leaving them to it, Skuld exited the showers and headed into the changing room.

"We're roommates," Kregor explained, in case Jegra got the wrong idea about him. "And, also, he's really, really smart. He kind of pieced events together."

"Ah," Jegra said with a subtle grin. "That would explain how he knew about last night."

"Yeah," Kregor said, nervously rubbing the back of his neck. Hanging his towel on a wall hook, he climbed into the showers opposite Jegra and turned on the hot water.

"I'm sorry we didn't get to finish what we had started last night. The interruption was quite unexpected."

"That's alright," he said, lathering his body with a bar of soap. "Like I said, it was probably for the best, seeing as when male Dragonians ejaculate they shoot out fiber sized needles that paralyze the female for up to three days while the sperm imbed themselves into the thick uterine lining of the womb with drill-like tendrils."

It took Jegra all of five seconds to realize that, this time, he really was messing with her. "Oh, you little shit!" she laughed. "You almost had me there for a moment."

The two of them stood there staring at one another in silence for what seemed like ages. As piping hot water dripped down Jegra's neck and chest, she heated up to the point she could no longer help herself. She had to finish what they had started. Besides, deep space was boring her to death, and it wasn't like they had anything better to do.

Just as they were about to take it to the next level, however, the ship dropped out of hyperspace. Since it was far too early for them to be arriving at Cordova, something else had caused them to stop. Kregor immediately shut off the nozzles and the hot water drizzled to a halt.

Raven's voice came over the comm. "Ladies and gentlemen, it seems we're picking up a distress call. Please report to your stations in five."

Duty called. "We'd better get going," he said.

"I know," she answered, feeling let down that they were interrupted a second time by the same aggravating woman. Edging past him in the narrow stall, she intentionally pressed her breasts up against his thick chest and slowly slid her wet body across his.

After she'd slipped past, Kregor let out a deep sigh and watched her saunter out of the shower, her hips swiveling seductively as she went.

Jegra reached over and grabbed her towel from the hook and wrapped it around her body. Looking over her shoulder, she blew him a parting kiss and then exited the showers.

By the time Kregor had caught up to her in the changing room, she had already dressed and was zipping up her snug fitting spandex smart-suit.

"You headed to the bridge?" she asked.

"As soon as I'm dressed."

"Meet you there?"

"Sure thing," he replied.

Dressed and ready to go, Jegra rushed out of the coed changing area and headed for straight for the bridge. At least she thought she was, before the spunky engineer Gyllek appeared from around a corner.

"The other way," she said, pointing up the corridor.

"Right," Jegra replied, swiveling on the spot and making a course correction.

Accompanying Gyllek to the bridge, the doors opened with a swish, and Jegra entered to find Emperor Dakroth and Cassera already there.

"I still think we should ignore it," Cassera said, glancing at Jegra as she came into the room. "It could be a trap."

"It's an imperial SOS," Dakroth said. "We can't ignore it. Protocol dictates…"

"I know what the protocol dictates," Cassera said in an agitated voice, "I'm the bloody vice admiral of the fleet."

"Remind me again, what does the protocol dictate?" Jegra asked. The moment she'd stepped foot onto the bridge she could feel the tension between Dakroth and Cassera. They must have had a row. Probably something about her. Lately, it always seemed to be about her, for some reason.

"Standard distress calls require that we scan their ship and try to determine what the problem is. If, for whatever reason, they're hostile, we blow them out of the sky. No questions asked. If they're friendly, we offer to assist."

"I see," Jegra replied. It was pretty straight forward stuff, really. And even though she preferred the glare of the dessert sun beating down upon her back, she started to feel like she was actually getting the feel for all this space travel.

"What'd I miss?" Kregor asked, as he came aboard the bridge.

"There's a ship adrift," Raven said, pointing out the starboard window at a black object lingering in their view port.

Jegra placed her face up to the window and looked out. Sure enough, there was a ship drifting in the middle of nowhere. It had no power. No lights. Just a big, clunky ship about twice the size of the *Skywend*, rotating ever so slowly in the dead of space. It was kind of spooky, when she thought about it, so she tried not to.

"It looks like a freighter," Kregor said.

"Maybe," Raven said, unbuckling herself and getting out of her seat. "Kregor, you're with me."

"Wait. What's going on?" Jegra asked.

"We're boarding the ship."

"I thought we were just going to scan it."

"Under normal circumstances, yes. But the power is completely out so there's no ship-to-ship communications. Without an S2S link, our computers cannot read their computers, so, we have to go over there and reboot their entire system."

"I'm coming too," Dakroth insisted.

"No," Cassera immediately protested. "If it is a Nyctan trap, then they'll have you where they want you."

"I'm in agreement with her," Jegra said, poking her chin at Cassera. "It's too risky. Let me go instead." Jegra felt butterflies fluttering about in her stomach. She'd never been in space much before yesterday, and now here she was volunteering to go aboard a desolate ship that may or may not be a trap? She could hardly believe it herself. And yet, here she was.

"Fine," Dakroth said in an annoyed tone. "But take Cassera with you. She knows all the activation codes."

"Great. Now let's suit up." Raven gestured with a nod for them to follow her and they all left the bridge together.

Twenty minutes later, they finished suiting up and entered the airlock. Wearing stealthy black environmental spacesuits which were not only slim fitting but looked like the latest in military tech, Jegra turned around and handed her helmet to Kregor. "Could you help me with this?" she asked.

She was a complete rookie when it came to space related tasks. She was much more confident with both feet on the ground and a blue sky above her. At least on the ground, she knew which way "up" was. In space, every which way was up, or not, and it always made her dizzy just thinking about it.

"My pleasure," he said. Kregor placed her helmet over her head and locked it into place. A light came on signaling that the seal had been made.

"Now, where to?" Jegra asked, turning back toward Raven Nightguard.

Raven pointed out the portal window of the airlock and at the silent cargo freighter.

"You're not saying we're going *out there*...into space?" Jegra's voice dropped along with the pit of her stomach.

"Docking is too risky," Raven informed. "Pirates like to boobytrap drifting ships. Then they linger in the system until someone sets off one of their booby traps, then they jump in to ransack your ship, rape your crew, and gut your FTL drive."

"Trust her," Kregor said. "She knows exactly what she's talking about."

"Don't worry," Cassera said, taking Jegra's hand in hers. Jegra looked down, shocked by the unexpected contact. "Stick with me and just do your best to relax."

"I'll go, but I don't know if I can relax. My heart is racing."

"It's a lot like floating in a pool, but with less resistance. You'll get the hang of it in no time."

Raven looked back and sealed the main doors. "Depressurizing the airlock in three, two, one."

She hit a red button and it turned to orange. A hiss of air being sucked out of the room signaled that they were all ready to go.

"Ready?" she asked, looking back one last time and checking her crew.

"Ready," Jegra said. She totally wasn't, though, but she didn't want to let everyone down.

Kregor and Cassera merely replied with a nod. With that, Raven hit a round nob and two yellow lights above the outside door began to flash. The door slowly rolled open and Raven walked up to the edge.

"The artificial gravity ends at this red line," she informed them, pointing down at the red strip before the airlock doorway.

Jegra nodded. Then, looking up again, she watched Raven leap out into open space. Trembling, her heart raced in her chest and her breathing became sporadic as her nerves went haywire. "I can't do this," she whispered to herself.

"Take a deep breath," Cassera said, squeezing her hand.

"See you over there?" Kregor asked, smiling down at Jegra.

Fuck me, she thought to herself. But she put on a brave face. "You bet," she said, attempting her best to smile back at him.

She caught a glimpse of her own reflection in her helmet visor and was a little embarrassed to see that the grimace she was making was the same one she often made whenever she had to take a rather unpleasant dump.

Kregor leapt out into space too, and Jegra drew back. "Nope. Yep, I can't do this."

"Yes, you can," Cassera said, tugging gently on her arm to get her to come back to her side. "We'll do it together. On the count of three."

They both stepped up to the red line. Holding one another's hand, Cassera began the countdown. "Three, two..."

Before she even started on one, Cassera gave Jegra a strong tug on the elbow of her EV suit and pulled her out into space with her.

"You bitch!" Jegra shouted into her helmet and they floated away from the *Skywend* and into deep space.

Cassera tapped on the side of her helmet to let Jegra know she needed to turn her comm-link on first if she wanted to be heard.

Jegra tapped her helmet and screamed, "You crazy bitch!"

"Oh, stop being such a cry baby," Cassera replied. "You can charge head first into the arena to face down a giant Nogrossian razorback hog, but you pee your pants at the slightest little spacewalk?"

Jegra gulped. "How did you know I peed myself?"

Cassera laughed. "Because peeing, puking, and shitting all over the place is apparently what you do best."

Jegra laughed. "Bitch," she repeated in a playful tone, and she stuck her tongue out at Cassera.

Cassera smiled at her and then turned her face to the freighter. They'd be there in another couple of minutes.

"Don't worry, Jegra," reassured Cassera. "We'll be in and out of there before you know it."

Although she knew that Cassera was only trying to help, she couldn't shake the nagging feeling that something wasn't quite right. Her instincts were rarely wrong, although she hoped to God that this was one of the times she was mistaken.

15

 "Raven said over the comm, masterfully spinning herself around and rotating into the precise position that would allow her to land feet first on the hull of the ship.

A loud clank came over the comm and then a relieved sounding sigh. "We have touch-down, ladies and gentlemen."

Kregor followed suit and made a stiffer, albeit no less impressive, landing.

"Oh, shit," Jegra said, the hull of the derelict ship coming up on her fast.

"Just breathe," Cassera reminded her. "I'll help you through it."

As they came down, Cassera flipped them both right side up in orientation to the hull, and stuck her legs out. Jegra, however, wobbled about behind her like a stringer on a kite.

Cassera made contact, but Jegra smashed down onto her ass and rebounded off the hull. Letting out a yelp, she was certain she was going to drift off into space just as a hand reached up and caught her by the ankle.

"Got you," Kregor said, pulling Jegra back down and setting her upright.

"My hero," she said, her lips forming a smile when her eyes met his.

"Alright people, let's do this by the book. I want to be in and out in thirty. Keep the comms open at all times. If you see anything suspicious, report it. If you're uncertain, report it anyway. Are we clear?"

Everyone replied with a simultaneous, "Yes," and Raven tapped her helmet and then pointed at Kregor to hack into the hatch on the hull for her.

Kregor pulled out a small black a device of some kind, and knelt down near the hatch. Placing the box next to the digital locking mechanism, he tapped a button and a series of symbols started cycling through the box's display.

"Seyfferian tech," Cassera said.

"I keep hearing about the Seyfferians, but I've never met one."

"Raven is one," Cassera replied, contempt dripping from her words.

"But she's a blue-skin, like you."

"*Not* like me," Cassera snarled. She almost lost her composure. Taking a deep breath, she calmed herself. "That woman is a defector and a traitor as far as I'm concerned. She's a disgrace to the empire."

"You do realize the shared comm-link is still on, don't you?" Kregor asked, shooting Cassera a disdainful look.

"She heard me," Cassera said, scowling at Kregor and then turning away.

Just then the icons on the black box came up green, and with a hiss of stale air decompressing, the hatch opened.

Raven ignored Cassera's scornful dig and leapt through the opening and into the ship.

"What's gotten into you today?" Jegra asked, shooting Cassera a nasty look. "First you're at it with Dakroth over who knows what. And now you're having at Raven like she's your personal punching bag even though she's only doing her best to help us. If I didn't know any better, I'd say you were being overly emotional."

Cassera frowned. "It's nothing," she said. Her voice dropped and she looked away.

Jegra knew something was eating at her, and she glanced at Cassera one last time, hoping she might open up about it, but Cassera just shut herself down again and went back to being like a cold-hearted android. Jegra figured Cassera would tell her when she felt ready. She turned toward the hatch where Kregor was waiting for her. He already had his hand out for her and she gladly accepted it as he helped her down into the ship.

Cassera gazed up at the *Skywend*. Dakroth was right. It was the prototype that had been stolen three keks ago. But who in their right mind would steal from the Dagon Empire, let alone leave it abandoned the same week they hijacked it?

She turned and entered the ship, dropping into the dark opening as though it was second nature to her. She'd been looking to get away from Dakroth for a while. Not that she didn't enjoy the company of her emperor, but he was an eccentric person who, like a rich curry, was fine to sample once in a while. But to constantly be in his presence was overkill.

Kregor was the last to come through the hatch and he sealed it behind him. Tapping his helmet, he said, "Hatch secure."

Raven opened the inside door to the ship and then checked her arm scanner to determine if the environmental conditions were good. "There's breathable atmosphere," she said, unlatching her helmet and twisting it clockwise. It unsealed with a hiss and she popped it off and set it on the floor beside her.

Everyone followed her lead, so Jegra did too. After getting her helmet off, she asked, "But I thought you said there was no power. How can there be life support?"

"Not life support," Cassera corrected. "Breathable air. They must have an atrium or some kind of plant-based oxygen producing system."

Raven tapped her environmental suit's arm panel and a shoulder light flipped up. She also twisted her cuff, which lit up with a ring-type LED lamp. Holding up her wrist, she said, "I'll get to the bridge and run the reboot sequence. Kregor, you get to the engine room and make sure we can jump start this old girl."

"What do we do?" asked Jegra.

Arm straight out, her wrist lamp lighting up the unassuming gray panels of the deck, Raven stepped into the corridor. "You two head to the cargo area and see whether what they were carrying is still there."

"Don't you need my codes?" Cassera asked Raven.

Raven glanced back at Cassera and smiled. Jegra could tell it was feigned, but at least Raven was being the consummate professional. "I don't need them," Raven replied, tapping her temple. Just beneath her skin, a web of vein-like circuitry pulsed. The light traveled up her neck, into her cheeks, and then her purple eyes flashed a bright violet.

"You're enhanced," Cassera said. "Of course, *you* would be. Seyfferians don't care about polluting their bodies with unnecessary technology. And even though we're at war with the Nyctans, at least I can respect their vow of purity."

"Unlike you, Vice Admiral, I wasn't born with a silver spoon in my mouth. I had to get by anyway I could. The enhancements aren't a fashion choice. For me, they're a matter of survival in a cold and indifferent galaxy." Having spoken her mind, Raven took off down the corridor.

"Well, you heard the lady," Kregor said, and he followed after her.

Jegra looked back at Cassera who was turning on her wrist lamp. Realizing that it might be a good idea to do the same, Jegra copied what she did and managed to get hers working as well.

"Ow!" Jegra said as the light turned on right in her eyes. She held her arm out and gave her eyes time to adjust.

"You all right?" Cassera asked, placing a hand on Jegra's shoulder.

"I will be," she said, embarrassed that she was so clumsy around technology. "Let's go."

They headed down the long corridor together and then hooked a right at a T-junction. There they passed through another bulkhead and several more doors.

Cassera stopped in the middle of the hall and checked her EV suit's wrist panel.

"What is it?" asked Jegra, glancing down at the display on Cassera's arm. She didn't understand the symbols, but the readout seemed to be glowing in a soft green, and their path was lit up by a yellow line as the active sonar mapped out the deck for them.

"I thought I saw a strange reading, but then, just like that, it was gone."

"What kind of strange reading?"

"I don't know. It was probably nothing," Cassera said, starting up the corridor again. "Never mind."

As they walked along, there was a static crackle and Kregor's voice came over the comm. "I'm afraid the FTL has been stripped," he informed them.

Raven's voice replied. "See if you can get the backup generators online. At least that way we could get some power and check the systems logs."

"Wilco," Kregor replied. "Over and out."

Another junction came up and Cassera took a left. Then, all of a sudden, there was a loud electrical clunk, like a breaker switch being flipped on; dim red lights illuminated the room.

"I got the generators running, but they only have enough juice to last about twenty minutes, give or take."

"Understood," Raven replied over the comm. "Everyone, time is limited. So, let's do what we came here to do. I'm downloading the black box data now."

"Come on," Cassera said, pointing at a large double door area. "This is the main cargo hold.

They walked up to the door panel and Cassera tapped the button. But it buzzed at her, signaling it was locked. She hit the panel again but again it buzzed.

"Bloody Helios," she griped. Tapping her arm panel, she got on the comm. "Raven, this is Cassera. We're at the main cargo bay entrance but the doors seem to have been sealed. Is there any way you can unlock them from up there?"

"Let me see what I can do," Raven replied. After a long silence, her voice came back. "Try it now."

Cassera smashed the panel; the light above the doors switched to green and the doors pulled apart.

"Holy fuck!" Jegra gasped.

Cassera and Jegra stood before a cavernous cargo-hold filled with all kinds of glowing plants and particles that lingered in the air like fireflies. Green, leafy vines grew up along the walls and had buds that also glowed with the same turquoise-blue energy.

"What is it?" Jegra asked.

"I have no clue," Cassera said, checking her arm display. "But the readings suggest they're safe."

The two women slowly stepped into the cargo hold and looked around at the indescribable sight. Feeling a strange sensation beneath her feet, Jegra looked down. "The floor is squishy. It feels like moss."

A large series of fern-like plants stood at the center of the room. They were as tall as a row of corn, Jegra guessed, and these filled the main cargo hold. The glowing motes fluttered around on the air that they'd let in and the scene left Jegra in awe. "It's breathtaking," she said.

Cassera tapped her arm display. "There's that strange reading again." Making her way into the ferns, brushing giant leaves of flora out of her way, she disappeared into the bush.

Jegra gulped nervously as she realized she was alone. "Hey, wait up," she said, following after Cassera.

Jegra brushed aside the leaves as she slowly made her way through the thick growth. After a minute, she came out the other side; when a hand flew up and halted her.

"Why'd you turn off your lamp?" Jegra asked.

"*Shhh,*" Cassera replied, gesturing with her finger for Jegra to go silent.

Cassera reached down and grabbed Jegra's wrist and aimed it at the ground. Then, she slowly extended her finger out toward a dark object in the corner of the room.

"What's that?" Jegra whispered.

Still holding tight to Jegra's wrist, Cassera cautiously raised Jegra's arm until her lamp lit up a dark figure standing at the back wall. It was metallic, dark metallic–a space gray color with a glossy shine to it.

Jegra squinted as she tried to make out what she was looking at. "It appears to be some kind of armor."

"It's a Knight," Cassera whispered, her voice wavering with a hint of fear.

"A Knight?" Jegra repeated.

"A Knight of Caelum informed her in a hushed tone. "They're the most elite soldiers of the Nyctan Empire."

"It seems to be hibernating," Jegra said, inching forward. Cassera immediately jerked on her arm and reeled her back.

"We're in no position to take on one of these," Cassera said. "I suggest we slowly back out of here and reseal this door."

Just then, the thin, cross-styled visor on the Knight's helmet flashed red. The Knight's suit activated and its body rose up.

"Run!" Cassera said, turning and shoving Jegra ahead of her.

The two women raced through the flora, thrashing about like wild animals to try and escape the micro jungle of the cargo hold. Jegra was the first to make it to the corridor. When she turned around, she saw Cassera shoot out of the bush at a dead sprint. "Go, go!" she yelled, waving at Jegra to keep moving.

But Jegra was stubborn. She wasn't going to leave her friend. And as much as it pained her to say it, she considered Cassera a friend.

Cassera skidded out of the cargo hold and spun around. Just as she looked back, the Knight slowly emerged from the luminescent plants, his visor glowing menacingly.

Not waiting to find out what it would do next, Cassera smashed the button and the door slammed shut. Pulling out her blaster, she shot the panel and fried it.

Jegra threw her hands up as the panel spat sparks at them and hissed. "Are you going to tell me why you're so scared of that thing, or what?"

Before Cassera could relay to Jegra the severity of the situation, the comm crackled and Raven's voice came on.

"What's going on down there?" Raven asked. "Your comm-link cut out for a moment."

"We've got trouble, captain," Cassera replied. "We have company."

"I'm sure it's nothing Jegra can't handle," Raven replied.

"There's a Knight in here," Cassera stated, her voice filled with urgency and fear.

"Get to the bridge, asap," Raven said.

"I'll meet you all there," Kregor, informed them, coming onto the comm just as Raven cut out. "Just keep your distance from that thing and, whatever you do, don't engage it."

"You don't need to tell me twice," Cassera replied.

A flash of orange and red light appeared as a plasma blade shot through the cargo hold door. Jegra screamed.

"He's cutting through," Cassera said, easing away from the door. "Come on, we'd better be gone by the time he cuts through that."

Jegra and Cassera ran back down the corridor the way they had come. As they were about to pass the airlock, Jegra turned and went to fetch their helmets.

"Wait, where you going?" Cassera asked.

"To get our suits' helmets," she replied innocently.

Seeing as she was already halfway there, Cassera glanced down the hall and then sighed out anxiously. "Fine," she said. "I'll help you."

Jegra and Cassera put on their helmets and then grabbed the other two and returned to the T-junction of the corridor. They hooked a left at the corner and headed in the direction of the bridge. That's when they heard the low, pulsing hum.

"Do you hear that?" Jegra asked. Cassera and Jegra slowed to a halt in the middle of the corridor. Cautiously, they turned around to see the Knight at the very end of the corridor standing there, his plasma blade glowing as he held it at his side, the colors of the energy sword cascading across his lustrous armor.

There was a long silence and then the Knight tapped the floor with his blade, sending up sparks. He started marching forward, tapping the sword every few steps and sending up more sparks.

"Go, go," Cassera said, turning around and running alongside Jegra who was already racing up the corridor.

They tore around the final corner and met Kregor at the entrance of the bridge.

"It's right behind us," Jegra said.

"Quick, inside," he said.

Both women rushed onto the bridge to find Raven waiting for them. Kregor held back and waited. He'd never seen a Knight in person, and this might be his only chance.

Kregor tensed up when the Knight appeared from around the corner. When it turned to find a larger Dragonian staring at him, it paused momentarily to reassess the situation. Without waiting for it to come to a definitive conclusion, Kregor stepped onto the bridge and manually shut the doors. He then tapped something into the pad and the giant blast doors came crashing down.

"Doors are sealed," he said.

"It won't hold it for long," Cassera said. "Nothing ever does. It's why The Knights of Caelum are the most feared warriors in the system."

"For your people, maybe," Raven said. "The Seyfferians have a treaty with the Nyctans."

"Well, why don't you just open up the door and tell him that," Cassera snapped.

Raven shot her a less than amused look. Then, turning to the larger control panel, she brought up the ship-to-ship communications.

"*Skywend*, this is the freighter *Reventón*. Do you read me?"

"We read you," Skuld's voice answered.

"Is Gyllek there?"

"I'm here, Captain."

"I know it wasn't a top priority until now, but I need you to get that long-distance phase transporter up and running. And fast."

"I'm on it," she said. "One LPT coming right up!"

"I'll assist you," Skuld replied over the comm. The sound of the *Skywend's* bridge doors swishing open and closing again could be heard in the background.

"What's going on over there?" Emperor Dakroth inquired in a serious tone.

"We ran into a little trouble," Raven answered.

"A Knight of Caelum," Jegra said, wanting to add to the discussion.

"A Knight?" the emperor echoed. "What's it doing on a derelict freighter? Unless…" his voice cut off.

"Your majesty," Cassera said, leaning over the console. "If this is an ambush, we'll be getting company any minute now."

"I'm bringing the *Skywend* closer to you," the emperor, replied.

"You'll do no such thing!" Raven barked. "If a ship drops out of hyperspace and blows us out of the sky, you'll be taken out along with us. Stay your distance. The transport is our best shot."

"Um, about that…" Jegra said thumbing over her shoulder. "You might want to make it a rush order."

Everyone turned in time to see a glowing spot on the blast door. Soon enough, molten metal began dripping to the floor.

"He's cutting through," Kregor said in a stunned voice.

"That's what they do. They hunt and kill. And they don't stop. They never stop," Cassera said, shooting everyone a grave look.

16

Molten steel dripped onto the floor. A hiss of steam shot up as the hot tangerine-red glowing metal met the cool surface of the freighter's plating.

"He's still coming through," Jegra informed the group, even though everyone was standing right there with her, watching the door with equally timorous gazes.

"Raven to *Skywend*. How's it coming on that transporter?"

Gyllek responded with a mumble, as though she had a flashlight in her mouth. "I'm about to start up one pad."

"Only one?" said Cassera in a shocked tone.

"It was easier to bypass the power relays into just the primary unit. Otherwise it would take a week to build this thing back up to its proper working order."

"But that means you can only transport us off this boat one at a time," Cassera complained.

"It's better than nothing," Kregor said with a grunt, folding his arms across his chest. He was growing tired of Cassera always badmouthing his crew. Raven held up a hand and gestured for him to ease back and he huffed and turned and went to the corner where he perched on the edge of a dead navigation panel.

"The hole is getting bigger, you guys," Jegra said. She stood in front of the entrance and watched; that was all she could do for now. And if the Knight got through, she was the only one with the strength to subdue it, if only temporarily.

"Gyllek," Raven said, her voice wobbling. "Any day now would be just fine."

"I'm doing my best, Captain," she replied.

"On that you can rely," Skuld added. "I can vouch for the girl. She's working magic like you've never seen before."

"I can see him now," Jegra said.

Everyone looked over. The hole wasn't big enough for armor that size to pass, but big enough for a small child or animal to run through.

"Dragonian, hand me your blaster rifle," Cassera ordered, extending her hand toward Kregor.

He gave her a sharp glance and then looked over at Raven who shook her head in the negative and he went back to ignoring the Dagon.

"There's an open shot!" she said, turning to Raven.

"You can't take down a Knight with a hand blaster," Raven said. "Their armor is too strong."

"But we might be able to slow it down," she insisted.

"Or you might just piss him off more," Raven shot back.

Gyllek's voice came over the ship's comm. "Captain, we're ready to bring one of you aboard now."

"Cassera," Raven said. "You go first. It's better if a Dagon isn't here when he gets through." She nodded at the Knight, who was churning his sword as though he were mixing butter instead of steel.

"I'm not leaving Jegra alone," Cassera snapped.

"Fine," Raven replied, letting out an annoyed sigh. "Since there's no time to argue, Kregor, you get over to the *Skywend* and prep the ship to jump out of here at the slightest sign of trouble."

"Affirmative," he said with a nod. Then, stepping out into the middle of the room, he said, "Ready when you are, Gyllek."

Out of nowhere came a yellow beam of light with bright sparkles swirling about in it. It engulfed Kregor, and then his body broke up into a million small fragments and he disappeared in the swirling vortex of light. With that, the beam faded and he was gone.

"Captain," Kregor's voice came over the comm after a moment. "Made it back safe and clear. I'll be on the bridge if you need me."

"Gyllek, beam me over next," Raven said. With that the beam of light wrapped itself around her and she began to phase. She looked over at Jegra one last time before she disappeared.

"You go next," Jegra urged Cassera.

"There's no way I'm leaving you here alone with that thing," she said, nodding at the gaping hole in the doors and the gray metallic Knight peering at them through its narrow, menacing, visor.

"I'm not asking," Jegra said with a smile.

"Fine," Cassera replied, reluctantly agreeing to be the next to transport out of there. "But if he gets in here, don't engage him. Just, I don't know, try and stall him somehow."

"I'll see you soon," Jegra said with a warm smile. She then leaned over and swatted Cassera on her butt.

"You bitch," Cassera teased, smiling back at Jegra.

The beam of light surrounded Cassera and she dissipated in a flash of bright particles. The beam slowly faded again and she was gone.

Jegra turned to face the entrance. It was just her and the Knight now.

The Knight didn't even wait for the door to cool. He walked right under the molten steel and onto the bridge. As he passed under the doorway several drops of molten metal dripped on to his armor. But it slipped right off as though the armor was frictionless.

"My name is Jegra Alakandra," she said, inching back slowly. "You may be interested to know," she continued, trying to stall the Knight, "the name Alakandra was a present from my captor, Antor of Thessalonica. He'd made me a galactic passport for my travels and had asked me what I wanted for my name. Since I was still technically his slave at the time, getting to pick my own name was a big deal for me. Alakandra sounded powerful. Like a female Alexander. And it complimented Jegra nicely too. Jegra, as I later found out, was simply the Dagon translation of the Earth name, Jessica. That was my name before my life in the arena. Now, I just go by Jegra Alakandra. You can just call me Jegra, though. What's your name?"

The Knight, who had paused to listen to her, started toward her again. His boot clanking on the cold metal floor of the ship as he approached her.

Jegra stepped back, but her EV suit clanged against the cockpit's control panel. She was between a rock and a hard place, so to speak.

The Knight's visor flashed red as it came to a halt directly in front of her. She gazed up at it as it came to a stop directly before her. Their suits were practically touching, when a sparkling golden beam of light came over her.

"You're standing too close to it," Gyllek shouted into the comm. "I can't get a lock."

Jegra looked up at the Knight and said, "Sorry about this." She threw forward her palms and shoved the Knight as hard as she could.

The Knight's bulky armor flew back like a cannon ball. With a sudden impact, it tore off what remained of the blast doors as it burst through and crashed into the opposite wall. The back wall managed to catch him, but not before flexing and bending like a catcher's mitt.

Sparks rained down on the Knight from where the ceiling paneling had collapsed. As he got up, a bulkhead came crashing down.

Not letting a pesky thing like a gigantic support beam stand in his way, he raised his plasma sword and brought it down hard. A thin, orange line appeared on the steel beam as his sword passed through. Then it fell in two.

As metal clangored to the floor, Jegra spoke into the comm, "Now would be a good time."

The beam of light came down again and snatched her away from the freighter. She felt a dizzy spell, then her consciousness seemed to disappear for a moment. It felt strange, like being unconscious after a brutal K.O. but, somehow, she was still aware of her surroundings. The next thing she knew, she was standing aboard the *Skywend*.

"You made it!" Skuld cheerfully chirped as he reached up and helped Jegra step down off the platform.

"Thanks," Jegra said. Then, looking down at Gyllek, who had the floor panel off and was digging through wires and circuit boards, Jegra added, "The both of you. Thank you."

"It's our duty," Skuld replied, his optimism never fading for a moment. Gyllek, a woman of few words, merely nodded.

Jegra smiled at them as she pulled away and into the corridor. Dashing all the way to the bridge, she practically stumbled into the room. Everyone looked over at her.

"You can take that thing off now, if you'd like," Kregor said, glancing at Jegra still in her EV suit.

"Oh, right," she said, and she began unfastening her helmet.

"Here, let me help you with that," Cassera said, offering a helping hand.

"I'll do it," Kregor said, stepping in front of her and cutting her off.

She scoffed and stepped back, folding her arms in dissatisfaction. The emperor simply raised an eyebrow at the bit of drama.

Raven plopped down in the pilot's seat and hit some controls. "Shit," she growled.

"What is it?" Emperor Dakroth asked.

"The freighter just sent out a coded distress call."

Jegra finally stepped out of the spacesuit and helped Kregor tuck it away in a rear storage compartment. She had on her black stretch suit with yellow lines. As they bent over together, their eyes met.

Raven called out to the crew. "Buckle up, ladies and gents. We're about to have company."

A thunderous boom rattled the ship as a giant Nyctan frigate jumped into the system just above their starboard bow.

"That thing is huge," Cassera said.

"The *Dreadnaught* was bigger," Dakroth bragged, leaning in to see the Nyctan ship out the starboard window.

"Gyllek, Skuld, please tell me you have the FTL prepped and ready."

"Thought you might ask that," Skuld's voice came over the comm. "And the answer is—"

"Yes, Captain," Gyllek cut in. "It's the first thing I did the moment you all departed the ship."

"All right," Raven said taking the controls. "Making the jump now."

She jammed the throttle of the FTL all the way to maximum and the ship's FTL wined like a supercharged electric engine. Then everything seemed to momentarily slow down to a crawl, the stars stretched, and they snapped into hyperspace with a bang.

"What are the odds that they can track us?" Jegra asked.

"It's impossible to track a ship through hyperspace," Raven said. "But who knows what that Knight was doing the whole time we were exploring the freighter? He could have somehow hacked our coordinates."

"I don't want to take any chances," Dakroth said. "If we jump into the orbit of Cordova and minutes later the entire Nyctan fleet shows up, we're doomed."

"I'll personally send a subspace transmission on ahead to Zira Ha'ppek and have him meet us with his frigate in orbit of Cordova. If the Nyctans do jump in after us, I'd prefer to stack the odds in our favor and face them two to one."

Raven nodded and Emperor Dakroth headed off to his quarters to make the call in private.

"How long until we reach Cordova?" Jegra asked.

"Approximately, eighteen hours," Raven answered, after taking a quick glance at the readout of her navigation display.

She turned and smiled at Kregor, who looked at her with an inquisitive glance. She nodded toward the door, as if to suggest they get out of there. But just then, Raven cleared her throat and called out to her officer.

"Kregor, I need you to run a full weapons check."

"Yes, ma'am," he said. He turned to Jegra and mouthed the word, "Sorry."

She smiled and shrugged. Turning to leave, she grabbed Cassera's hand. "Come on," she said. "I'm thirsty."

Several minutes later, in Jegra's personal quarters, Cassera arched her back, her sweat dripping down her blue, naked body as she lay on Jegra's bed, and screamed out in ecstasy.

Jegra buried her face even deeper between Cassera's smoldering thighs. This caused Cassera to squirm uncontrollably. Another several minutes of bliss went by and, finally, Jegra came up for breath.

"Told you I was thirsty."

"When you said you were thirsty, I thought you wanted to hit the open bar and get some drinks with me. I didn't think you meant you wanted to do this."

"I needed the distraction," she said, sliding up Cassera's body. She kissed Cassera's stomach, and chest, and neck until she came to her lips. She paused and let her eyes linger for a moment, and then her mouth plummeted and crashed into Cassera's lush lips.

They shared mutual moans of sensuous delight and Cassera reached between Jegra's thighs and found just the right cadence to make her squirm. And she didn't stop until Jegra groaned with pleasure. Turn around was fair play, after all.

Jegra fell onto the bed next to her and then placed her cheek on her hand

and stared into the yellow eyes of her blue-skinned lover. "You realize this is the first time we've been together without him, right?"

"I can't believe I ever let that son of a bitch inside of me," Cassera lamented, letting out a deep sigh of regret.

Jegra raised an eyebrow. Something was up between Dakroth and Cassera, and she was curious to find out what it was. "You want to talk about it? About whatever that was between you and Dakroth this morning?"

Cassera looked at Jegra for a long time and then closed her eyes. "I can't," she said.

"Is it why you've been so bitchy lately?"

Cassera gave Jegra a bitter-sweet smile. She wanted to tell Jegra everything. Tell her what Dakroth was plotting, what he had in mind for her, but she couldn't. Worse than this, however, was that if they deemed her a threat to the Dagon way of life, Cassera would have no choice but to kill Jegra. And she didn't want to do that. Because, for the first time in her life, she was falling in love.

"Let's just say because he claimed you, we can't...what I'm trying to say is..."

"Yes?" Jegra probed.

"I can never be your...what I mean to say is...I think I'm falling for you."

"I love you too," Jegra replied without a second's hesitation. And she quickly silenced Cassera with a long, passionate, kiss.

A single tear seeped out of the corner of Cassera's eye as she fell into Jegra's warm embrace. There had to be an alternative, she thought. Jegra wasn't the inferior species she had believed. Crude, sure. Lacking in manners and social grace, yes. But at the genetic level, everything about her human DNA was so advanced. So evolved.

The real threat wasn't to the purity of the Dagon race. The real threat was the superiority of human genetics, specifically, a single gene that Cassera had found lying dormant in Jegra's genetic code. A gene that, if activated, would allow humans to procreate with sixty percent of the known species in the known galaxy.

That was the real threat to the Dagon empire. Human ascendancy and the rise of a mixed-race empire that stretched across every single system. A genetic code so proficient in its ability to rewrite other species' genetic makeups that it would take root like a pernicious weed.

As for Jegra's peculiar ability to rewrite a Dagon's DNA through physical contact, Cassera felt it was likely just a fluke of Jegra's strange transformation. Not all of her powers had fully manifested yet. It seemed to her that the growth serum Jegra had been injected with over a year ago was still affecting her. She was, for lack of a better term, a work in progress. But what she'd eventually turn out being was anybody's guess.

And that's why Cassera had been so upset. Emperor Dakroth wanted a progress report on her findings. But if she shared the truth with him, he'd order Jegra's extermination. And she didn't think she could live with herself if she was forced to kill Jegra. Not now. Not after all they'd been through.

17

"Shit," Jegra yelped, tumbling out of bed naked. She was rudely awoken by a loud blast and the ship shuddering violently. There was another blast and Cassera's naked body rolled out of bed and landed on her.

Cassera's eyes shot wide open as the ship jolted again. This time the ship's alarm started blaring. Looking down at Jegra's face, she asked, "Think we should get dressed?"

"You read my mind," Jegra replied.

Both women scrambled to their feet and dressed as fast as they could. Once they'd gotten themselves presentable, Cassera turned to head out. Before she got out the door, however, Jegra caught her arm and stopped her.

"Hey," Jegra said, drawing Cassera back to her. She gave her a quick peck on the lips. "I just wanted to say thanks for last night. Thanks for opening up your feelings to me."

Cassera blushed and brushed her platinum hair out of her golden eyes. "We really should get going," she said with a sense of urgency. When she tried to pull away, Jegra held her firm. She looked into Jegra's brown eyes and smiled. "What is it now?"

Jegra pulled Cassera into her by the back of her neck and kissed her with the sultriest kiss she'd ever given anyone in her whole life. It was so good, in fact, that Cassera, in an uncharacteristic move, grabbed Jegra's ass and kissed her back.

Another jolt shook the room and reminded them that they had other things they needed to be doing.

A chime came on over the comm and it was promptly followed by Raven's voice. "To battle stations, everyone! We have company."

It only took them a couple of minutes to arrive at the bridge. When they did, they saw the green and tan swirls of Cordova out the window. In the foreground, three Nyctan battlecruisers were concentrating all of their firepower onto Zira Ha'ppek's frigate. Yellow plumes exploded outward all along the hull as venting gas was ignited by the disrupter blasts.

"What's going on?" Cassera asked, as she strode onto the bridge.

"We jumped out of hyperspace to find three Nyctan battle cruisers waiting for us. Your friend's ship was already taking heavy fire when we arrived."

Emperor Dakroth stepped onto the bridge and peered out the window with a stern gaze but said nothing. His red eyes hung on a fixed point in the middle of empty space as he found himself deep in thought, his mind calculating every possible scenario they might encounter.

"We're getting a hail," Raven informed them.

"Put it through," Dakroth ordered.

The cockpit's heads up display switched to a live video feed. Ha'ppek stood on his bridge, wires dangling over him as sparks rained down onto his majestic religious garb.

"You were right, my lord," he said, bowing his head and showing his respect to the emperor. "The moment a Dagon ship entered orbit they de-cloaked and began their assault."

"Wait," Jegra said, puzzled. "You used Ha'ppek's ship as bait to lure them out?"

"I suspected the Nyctan's would be monitoring the outer rim. Ha'ppek agreed to draw them out."

"Can you get the *Skywend* close enough to transport him off that thing?" Cassera asked Raven.

"I'll try," she said, taking the ship in. More stray disrupter blasts grazed the bow of the *Skywend* and shook the ship.

"Come along, my dear," Cassera said, taking Jegra's hand in hers. "We have a wedding to prepare for."

"Right here and now?" Jegra asked. Admittedly, she knew she'd be married eventually. But not in the middle of a starship battle above the moon of a gas giant.

"I'll meet the high priest in the transporter room," the emperor informed. Raven merely nodded her head but kept her focus on evading the more dangerous laser blasts.

Kregor came onto the bridge and strapped himself into a chair. "All weapons are go, captain."

"Your timing couldn't be better, Kregor."

"Come," Cassera urged, leading Jegra by her hand.

Not more than ten minutes later Cassera was putting the final touches on Jegra's hair.

"Do you think I'll need makeup?" Jegra asked.

"Right," Cassera said, embarrassed that she'd almost forgot. She reached over and grabbed a long slender device that looked like a vape pen. But when she waved it in front of Jegra's face a spread of light imprinted makeup into Jegra's flesh. "That's better," she said, placing her hands on Jegra's shoulders and gently turning her toward the vanity mirror so she could see her reflection.

Jegra admired her glammed-up look, but somehow it didn't seem like her. Gazing at her face, she felt a strange disconnect. As if a different woman was staring back at her.

"Hide mirror," Jegra said, and the screen showing her reflection turned off.

"Are you ready?" Cassera asked.

"Ready as I'll ever be," Jegra answered with a sigh. Then looking down at herself, she said, "What about a dress?"

"I'm afraid there's not a single wedding dress aboard. I scoured everywhere, but nothing remotely formal."

"That's alright," she replied. "I found out this smart suit can change colors. Jegra tapped the green dot on her cuff and spoke into her wrist, "White."

Her black jumpsuit swiftly changed from black with yellow stripes to white with blue stripes. She held up her wrist and added, "No stripes."

Dressed in all white, Jegra unzipped the top of her suit a little to allow her cleavage to rise out, like a couple of loaves of baked bread.

"You look hot," Cassera teased.

"Maybe for my honeymoon I'll ditch Dakroth and bed you instead."

"No more threesomes?" Cassera asked.

"That last one ended in a street brawl, so…"

They both started laughing. After their fit of giggles died down, Jegra looked at Cassera and took a deep breath.

"You'll be fine. I'll see to it personally."

"I know," Jegra replied. "Well, I'd better not keep the emperor waiting."

As Jegra turned to leave, she felt a firm swat on her butt. She looked back at Cassera who, after all these weeks, had finally found the perfect time to get her back. Jegra laughed out loud and then marched out of her room and to the transporter.

When she entered the transporter room, she was surprised to see Skuld, Gyllek, Kregor, and Raven all standing along the wall in their formal clothes.

"What's all this?" Jegra asked, stunned to see everyone in one spot together.

"It wouldn't be a proper wedding without guests," Skuld informed her.

"Or a bridesmaid," Cassera said, stepping up beside her.

Jegra scanned all the smiling faces. "Thank you, everyone. Just one small question though…if you're all here, who is flying the ship?"

"It's on autopilot," Raven said.

"In the middle of a firefight?" gasped Jegra.

"Don't worry," Kregor chuckled. "We're cloaked."

Jegra paused. Then she repeated herself. "In the middle of a firefight?"

"I parked her the last place in the galaxy the Nyctans would ever suspect us."

The emperor raised an eyebrow.

"You should have seen it," Kregor said. "It was genius. She parked us right under their hull."

The emperor pointed a finger over at Raven and said, "Now."

Happy to oblige, Raven went over to the controls and with a push of a lever and the twisting of some nobs, the transporter hummed to life.

The room flooded with yellow light and then, standing on the pad, was Ha'ppek.

"Are you unharmed?" Dakroth asked.

"I'm a little shaken, but quite all right.

"Good, good. Then let the ceremony begin." The emperor turned to Jegra and took her hands in his. Then he waited for Ha'ppek to begin.

"We are gathered here, amongst friends, to witness the union of his royal majesty, Lord Rhadamanthus Dakroth of the Dagon Empire, son of Helios, and his betrothed, Jegra Alakandra, daughter of Sol."

Turning toward Jegra, Ha'ppek took her hand in his and then placed it on

Dakroth's. He repeated the procedure and stacked Dakroth's other hand on hers, so that her hand was sandwiched in between his.

"Do you, Jegra, daughter of Sol, take this man to be your lawfully wedded husband?"

"I do," replied Jegra.

"And do you, Emperor Rhadamanthus Dakroth, son of Helios, take Jegra to be your lawfully wedded wife?"

"I do," Dakroth replied with an enthusiastic grin.

"Then, with the power invested in me by the great lord Hastur, I pronounce you husband and wife. You may now kiss the bride."

Dakroth pulled Jegra into his chest, wrapped his arms around her, and kissed her. After that, he nodded at everyone and thanked them. "I appreciate you all being witness to this happy moment. I know it meant a lot to Jegra that you all came."

"It did," Jegra said, smiling at all the faces that smiled back at her in return. "I can't thank you enough."

Emperor Dakroth then dragged Jegra out of the room. "Come, my dear, we must consummate our union, otherwise you cannot carry the title of Empress of Dagon."

It wasn't that she didn't want to, but Jegra felt bad that Cassera and Kregor had to watch her paraded off like the emperor's trophy wife. His infatuation was nothing compared to their love and affection. But when she saw Raven giving her that look, she recalled her words and how imperative it was to have a just and compassionate empress on the throne that could balance Dakroth's cruelty and darkness.

That night, Jegra fucked emperor Dakroth into a veritable comma. As he lay asleep in his bed, she quietly dressed and returned to her quarters. When she got there, she was expecting to find Cassera waiting for her. Instead, to her surprise, she found Raven Nightguard.

Raven dropped to her knee and knelt before her empress. "Your majesty," she said.

"Raven?" Jegra asked, confounded. "What are you doing here?"

"I thought I would say my goodbyes. It seems that this is where we part ways."

"I don't blame you," Jegra said. "We've been bad luck since the get go."

"Let's just say that conducting business is much easier without having a target on your back."

They both laughed. Then fell silent again.

"Where will you go next?"

"I was thinking of cracking down on some sex traffickers. Blow off some steam. Then maybe head back to the Zargora system and collect on some old debts."

"I wish you the best of luck," Jegra said.

Raven, still kneeling, took Jegra's hand and kissed it. "If you should ever need me, your majesty."

Jegra gestured for Raven to rise, and she gave her a big hug. "Til we meet again."

Raven winked at her and then left her to her own thoughts. As the doors hissed shut, Jegra turned and walked over to her bedroom window. The *Skywend* was already making its final approach to Cordova. They'd be on the ground in no time.

Her thoughts shifted to Cassera. Where was her lover, she wondered? That's when she heard her door open again. Smiling, she turned around and said, "It's about time you got here."

Jegra's face dropped when she saw Abethca standing in the doorway. She slowly backed away.

The mysterious figure entered her room and the doors shut again.

"Stay back," Jegra said.

"You don't need to be afraid," the voice said. Then Abethca reached up and touched her forearm. Without provocation, her image flickered and dissolved, leaving only Gyllek. "It's only me."

"What the hell do you think you're doing?" Jegra barked angrily. If this was a prank, it wasn't the least bit amusing.

"Calm your tits, hot stuff," Gyllek said, sliding off her bracelet and handing it to Jegra.

"I made it for you. I think you'll find it will come in handy. Consider it a wedding gift."

Jegra took it from her and nodded thankfully. Gyllek then turned and left without so much as uttering a formal word goodbye. She actually found it kind of refreshing that Gyllek couldn't care less that she was the official empress.

As Jegra stood in the entrance to her room, Cassera appeared in the doorway. She looked back as Gyllek as she left Jegra's quarters. "What did she want?"

"Nothing," Jegra replied, her grin growing wide at the sight of Cassera. Then, unable to restrain herself any further, she reached out of her room, clutched Cassera by her collar, and pulled her inside.

"I missed you," Jegra said, nudging Cassera's shoulder with hers.

"Jegra, I just wanted to say…"

"Yes?" Jegra asked in a sensual voice, her brown eyes fixing themselves on Cassera's deep blue lips.

"Never mind. It's not important." She lied. Of course, it was important. It involved Jegra's very life. But if she told her what she knew, the emperor might have them both killed.

18

Clambering down the ramp of the Skywend, Jegra found Cassera, Emperor Dakroth, and Ha'ppek waiting for her outside the ship. Once she stepped onto the ground, she turned and looked up to find Raven and the rest of the crew standing in the cargo bay waiting to see her off. She smiled at them and they smiled back. "Thanks again. For everything."

Raven nodded, keeping her trademark stoic look, and then reached up and hit the red button on the side of the cargo hold. As the ramp slowly closed, Skuld waved at her like an excited child. She waved back and blew him a kiss. Before the ramp clamped shut completely, she shot a quick glance at Kregor. They stared into each other's eyes and just moments before the ramp slammed shut, he winked at her.

Dakroth cleared his throat, drawing her attention back to their current mission, and said, "Best not stay out in the open for too long. The Nyctans are bound to run frequent scans of the surface."

Although Cordova was a much lusher moon than Thessalonica, they happened to be in the most barren part. Giant rock formations, which resembled the Coyote Buttes of Utah and Arizona back home, surrounded them for several miles in every direction.

Although the orange and tan striated landscape was certainly pretty, Jegra was growing rather tired of seeing deserts. She just wanted a beautiful beach with a cool blue ocean and a nice palm tree with ample shade to lie under.

"I know the way to the temple from here," Ha'ppek said, gesturing for them to follow him in the direction of some nearby rock formations. "But it will be a two-hour hike yet, so we'd best be going if we want to make it there before nightfall."

Before they could get too far along, the *Skywend*'s thrusters turned on and the ship rose up, kicking up a sandstorm in the process.

Sand blasted, Jegra shielded her eyes and looked up, watching the ship climb into the sky. About a hundred and fifty feet up, the ship cloaked, fading away until all that was left was a vast swath of blue sky.

As soon as the ship had cloaked, an abrupt blast of hot wind ruffled everyone's clothes and hair as the *Skywend*'s main thrusters kicked on and the ship tore away from them as it left Cordova. A sonic boom signaled that it had breached the atmosphere and then everything settled back down.

"I'm going to miss them," Jegra said, wiping some sweat from her forehead.

"Time's a wasting," Dakroth urged, gesturing for Jegra to stop lingering about and hurry up with a wave of his hand.

She huffed at his impatience and reluctantly followed after him. She didn't like being second fiddle in any scenario let alone the one involving their honeymoon, if that is what one could even call it.

The emperor, enthusiastic to get the show on the road, marched on up ahead. Once he was out of earshot, Cassera shuffled up to Jegra and whispered to her. "You have to get out of here. It's a trap."

"What?" Jegra asked, shooting Cassera a bewildered look. It wasn't like Cassera to pull her leg. She wasn't the type. But her warning came out of nowhere and seemed so outlandish as not to be believable.

"You need to run," Cassera urged. "There's no time to explain. Just go."

But Jegra just laughed off her warning. Even if she wasn't joking, which she rarely ever did, where could Jegra go? She had no contacts on Cordova. No way to get off the planet. And nobody knew she was the Empress. No official announcements had been made and, besides all this, she half assumed that Dakroth's plot was to abandon her here.

"What are you trying to say?" Jegra asked. "Is there something I should know about?"

They emerged from the orange and tan striped rock bed and stepped into a large clearing. Only a few multicolored pillars of sandstone stood off in the distance when a faint warbling sound broke out into a shrill whine.

"What's that?" Ha'ppek asked, spinning around as he tried to locate where the peculiar sound was emanating from.

Several red beams of light fell from the sky and dotted the ground all around them like an army of laser pointers coming down from the heavens.

Jegra instantly recognized the bands of light as transporter beams. They resembled the yellow transporter beams the Dagons used except in color. And there were a lot of them. At first glance, she counted twelve. Maybe more.

"Shit," Cassera whispered. "It's too late."

Manifesting all around them were two rings of Nyctan soldiers, all of them wearing their high-tech, gothic styled armor. All black. All lavishly detailed. At the center of the squad was a single Knight of Caelum.

To Jegra's surprise, Emperor Dakroth casually strode up to the Knight and said, "You're just in time."

The Knight didn't respond verbally. He merely scanned the unfamiliar faces until his sights settled on Jegra.

Apparently, Ha'ppek wasn't the only one who Dakroth had sent a communique to. That's when Jegra realized that Dakroth had planned to double cross her. But why? Why marry her only to hand her over to the enemy? Did being the empress give her more clout as a ransom than just a warrior celebrity? Was it some kind of ploy to create an excuse to continue to war with the Nyctans? Something else perhaps? None of it made any sense.

"Hand over the human female," the Knight said in a low, gravelly voice. Its visor flared red as it kept its gaze fixed on her. Jegra stood frozen, not knowing what to do.

"Jegra, my love," the emperor said, gesturing for her to come closer to him. "Would you be so kind as to join me?"

Cassera shook her head subtly, warning Jegra not to do it. Jegra winked, letting her know she had no intention of listening to her back-stabbing husband. Emperor or not, she wasn't going to forfeit her life for him.

Jegra lunged at one of the Nyctan guards and rammed him with her shoulder. As he flew back into a fellow soldier, she stripped him of his blaster. Spinning around, she began firing at the dozen or so remaining Nyctan soldiers.

Obviously, they wanted her alive, otherwise they wouldn't have bothered coming all the way down to the surface of Cordova to collect her themselves. Not when a disrupter from space could have eliminated her and the emperor all the more easily.

Cassera whipped out her personal blaster and began to lay down cover fire for Jegra.

"What are you doing, Vice Admiral?" Dakroth roared in anger. "You'll ruin everything!"

"I won't let them take her," Cassera said, firing at will.

Before she could do too much damage, however, a laser blast struck her in the abdomen and Cassera collapsed to the ground. Clutching her gut, she screamed out, "Run, Jegra! Run!"

Emperor Dakroth raised a hot glowing finger, still smoking from the blast he'd dealt Cassera, and carefully trained it on Jegra.

As soon as Cassera fell out of the way, Jegra reached out and grabbed a Nyctan soldier by his arm, then spun him around and tossed him like a ragdoll into a line of fellow soldiers. Four men collapsed at once, giving Jegra the window of opportunity she needed to escape.

But just as she turned to run, a laser grazed the side of her arm. She yelped out and grabbed her singed flesh, shooting a menacing glare back at Dakroth, who aimed his glowing finger at her.

Just then, the Knight stepped in front of Dakroth, preventing him from firing another shot. Whether it was deliberate or not, she didn't know. But she didn't wait around to find out. Taking advantage of the opening, Jegra sprinted off toward the bigger rock formations in the distance.

As she went, she reached behind her back and blasted holes into three other soldiers. Their bodies dropped to the ground, armor smoldering as wisps of smoke rose from their blast wounds.

In truth, she was trying to hit Dakroth, but due to the fact that she'd never actually wielded a high-powered blaster before, her aim was sadly lacking. All she did was simply keep her finger on the trigger until the blaster's battery packs ran out. Still, she managed to hit enough targets to give herself a good head start to make a break for it.

The blaster coils overheated and the battery spent, Jegra tossed the weapon aside and sprinted as fast as she could. Having gained super strength gave her the ability to run quite well, although she'd never really opened up, having always been confined to the arena.

A cloud of dust shot up behind her as she raced faster and faster. She estimated she was running upwards of 80 kilometers per hour, but she was beginning to overheat and needed to stop. Skidding to a halt, a blast of sand shot by her from her own dust trail. She pressed her hands to her knees and panted, taking in as much air as she could.

She was certain that as long as she kept moving, their scans would have trouble pinpointing her exact location, so there was no way they could beam her away.

Although the Knight was, in all likelihood, already in pursuit, she had put enough distance between them to buy her some time. She tapped the cuff of her smart-suit and spoke into the bottom of her wrist. "Camo."

Swirls of colors danced about her suit and then settled on a series of red and tan topographical striations that matched the multicolored layers of the surrounding sandstone.

Jegra slowly turned to face the way she had come. She wanted to go back for Cassera. But with a Knight standing between her and saving Cassera, she knew it wasn't possible. She'd have to find another way to deal with this new threat. Once she found a way out of this mess, then she could go and rescue Cassera.

Back at the clearing, the Knight spun around and shot Dakroth a menacing look.

"This wasn't part of the deal," the Knight said, glaring at Dakroth as Jegra's dust trail faded into the foothills.

"I warned you she was a handful."

The Knight growled like an angered beast and then slowly turned. The hulking Knight, determined to catch his prey, headed off toward the rock formations and began his hunt.

"You cowardly bastard," Cassera growled, furious at Dakroth for his betrayal.

She had only known about his plan to hand Jegra over to the Nyctans since the space walk. That's why she had been so upset that day. She had adamantly disagreed with his strategy and questioned him on it. He reassured her it was necessary to test his theory, see if she could manipulate Nyctan DNA in the same way she had theirs.

If so, then Dakroth felt that weaponizing Jegra's biology would become the greatest weapon the Dagon Empire had ever yielded. Yet, at the same time, he had betrayed her in a way that was unworthy of a person of her stature.

After all, they had been through the ringer together. Although it had been only a week, they'd been together constantly, and under pressure. It was becoming harder and harder to pretend that she hadn't fallen madly in love with Jegra. Cassera couldn't bear to see her darling Earthling be abused in such a heinous and ungrateful manner. Although the emperor was infamously ruthless, this was crossing a line as far as she was concerned.

But as usual, Dakroth ignored her advice. He always ignored her advice. In fact, the only reason she felt he had kept her around for so long was that, before Jegra had arrived on the scene, cheating on his wife, Jennica, with her gave him a rise.

Those days were behind them now, though. And now Cassera had betrayed the emperor by being more loyal to Jegra, which was as good as a death sentence and explained why he hadn't hesitated to shoot her just now.

The blast wound in her side shot a sharp throbbing pain throughout her whole body and she clamped her hands down over the wound and let out an agonizing groan.

Dakroth sauntered up to her, wearing a roguish grin on his face. Coming up alongside her, he knelt down and brushed her white bangs away from her face and gently tucked them behind her ear.

"I brokered a ceasefire with the Nyctans," he explained to her. "All I needed to do was hand over Jegra. In return, they agreed to all my terms and conditions. Besides, Vice Admiral, as I recall, I specifically told you not to get attached."

"Your lordship, if I may," Ha'ppek interjected, trying to offer a fresh perspective on things. "Jegra is, after all, the rightful Empress of the Dagon Empire now. Wouldn't it better serve the Empire to continue to safeguard her from the Nyctans?"

"You see, Ha'ppek," the emperor began, fetching Cassera's blaster up off the ground. "There are only three people here who know that Jegra is officially the Empress." Rising back up, he aimed the blaster at Ha'ppek.

"Your majesty?" he asked, confounded.

Without any qualms, Dakroth pulled the trigger. The squeal of the disrupter blast rang out and Ha'ppek looked down at the smoldering hole in his stomach.

Then, he let out a gasp of air, smoke coming from his mouth. Tottering briefly, his legs gave out from under him and the weight of his dead body crashed to the ground in a heap of holy robes and blue skin. Ha'ppek's red eyes were as wide as a Nogrossian deer as he gazed up at the blue sky, his face frozen in a state of bewildered shock, a few wisps of white smoke still curling out of his gaping mouth.

Emperor Dakroth trained his laser pistol onto Cassera and pondered, "What to do with you, my dear vice admiral?"

"Wait," she said, holding up her hand.

"Are you begging for my mercy? My, oh my. How the mighty have fallen." A disgusted look came over his face and he sneered, "Disgraceful."

"Not a disgrace, my lord. I have sequenced Jegra's DNA and know everything there is to know about her. I know the truth of what she really is. But if you kill me, you'll have to wait until you can get back to Dagon Prime to begin your experiments all over again. Even then, who could you trust with this monumental secret? It seems to me, you have no choice but to spare me. For the time being. But, as always, it's your choice, my lord."

Dakroth glared at Cassera, resenting her cunning. Relinquishing his anger, he lowered the gun as a cruel smile curled onto his lips. "Well played, Vice Admiral. Well played, indeed."

19

Sparkling beads of sweat dappled Jegra's chest like a jewel encrusted necklace as she lingered under the blistering Cordova sun.

It was almost as hot out here as on Thessalonica. Almost. Unzipping her smart-suit down to her belly button, which was as far down as it would go without her spilling out, she leaned up against a pillar of orange striped sandstone and fanned herself. It did little to help cool her, let alone prevent the beads of perspiration from slipping in between her breasts as they trickled down her body.

The infernal Knight had been playing a game of cat and mouse with her for the past hour and a half and she was getting really fed up with it. Cassera was correct. Once a Knight begins pursuing you, they don't ever give up.

She knew that eventually she'd have to face the thing, but she wondered what she could do to get the edge up on a fully armored power suit. Getting the bright idea that her suit might be able to do more than just camouflage, she held her wrist up and spoke into the cuff. "Color change. Clear."

Her suit went transparent and she looked down to see her naked body fully on display. "Shit," she said, bringing the cufflink control unit to her mouth. "I meant, invisible."

The suit flickered, turned black, then white, then clear again. Again, she looked down to see her naked body. "No, no, no," she said, letting out an agitated sigh. "Cancel."

The suit turned back to its colorful pattern of orange and tan swirls which mimicked the landscape. She let out a sigh of relief when she was no longer in the nude.

That's when it dawned on her. She still had the hologram bracelet on that

Gyllek had given her. Twisting it, she spoked into the device and said, "Match terrain." Immediately she turned into part of the pillar of sand.

Naturally, it was just a hologram, but one which also happened to scramble scanners. She learned this rather quickly, because no sooner had she disappeared from sight than the Knight stepped into view.

She stood frozen as the Knight scanned the entire area. Not picking up her vitals, he clunked off toward the north end of the rock formations. Once he was out of sight, Jegra twisted the bracelet and reappeared.

"She wasn't kidding," Jegra said to herself. "This thing will come in handy."

With the tables turned, she decided to stalk the Knight for a while. See if there was anything she could learn about it. Her last encounter with a Knight was intense, to say the least.

Jegra sat perched on top of a tall pillar about twenty feet up and just watched the Knight roam about as he continued searching for her in vain. She waited at least another hour and was slowly going out of her mind due to the heat and the monotony of the landscape. Forty-five additional minutes crept by and, oddly enough, the Knight stopped searching and just stood there. Waiting.

He waited a good, long thirty minutes and then another thirty more. By now, the sun was beginning to go down and a sunset was forming on the horizon. Another half-hour passed and the sky began to turn purple as the orange sunset had compressed into a narrow pink band that stretched across the horizon.

Jegra was growing weary and her butt was sore from sitting on a rock for hours on end. She wanted to eat and take a shower. Also, she had to pee like a son of a bitch but knew that the moment she moved from her spot she'd give away her position.

Jegra covered her mouth and yawned. The slight noise of her yawning caused the Knight to look in her general direction. This, of course, made her nervous and she grew deathly silent as the Knight stared at her.

When it finally looked away again she carefully let out the breath she'd been holding the whole time and tried breathing through her nose so as to minimize the amount of sound. *That was a close one,* she thought.

That's when she heard the hum of a plasma blade igniting. Jegra scooted to the edge of her perch and looked down at the Knight who reached back with his flaming hot sword and then lobbed it like a boomerang. The sword spun through the air like a flaming helicopter blade, its plasma humming dangerously with each rotation, until finally it collided with the base of the pillar of rock that she sat on.

The pillar of stone toppled down like a domino and Jegra shouted, "Shit!"

She leapt off before it all came down around her and she hit the ground a few meters off. And she hit hard. So hard that it caused her holographic disguise to falter.

The hologram flickered as she tumbled to a stop. Unable to get the image to stabilize, she smacked the bracelet hoping to jar it back into work order, but instead it completely cut out.

The hologram that had mimicked the surrounding terrain disappeared and she was standing in the open. Vulnerable.

"Well, I can't say it was fun," she sighed, looking up at the Knight who marched toward her with a dogged relentlessness.

As was her ritual before a fight, she cracked her neck across her shoulders and then rotated her arms in large swooping circles out to her sides. Grabbing her elbows, she stretched her arms over her head, bending first to the left and then to the right. As the Knight was almost upon her, she hopped up and down a couple times to get the blood to her legs flowing.

"But it's about to get *real fun*," she added at the last moment just as the Knight came within grappling distance.

The Knight lunged at her and she dodged. It moved faster than a regular combatant.

They circled one another and held each other's gaze. Jegra had experience fighting on the sands, and tucked and rolled toward the Knight. She came up with a handful of sand and tossed it in his face.

The Knight was blinded by the cloud of sand, and Jegra punched him in his chest as hard as she could. The Knight flew into the air and crashed down onto a rock formation about half the size of the one she'd been sitting on. It broke in half as the hulking armored Knight impacted with it and it all came toppling down. An avalanche of rubble buried the Knight, but, unfazed by her punch, he pushed himself up. Debris poured off his armor like sand slipping out of an hourglass. Rising back up, he turned to her, his visor flashing red.

"What are you? A bloody robot?" she asked.

The question was rhetorical, however. She found a huge rock and chucked it at the Knight.

He batted it away from himself, and the boulder split in two, both halves rolling away from him like runaway tumbleweeds. Not that it was difficult to break sandstone, but the way he casually kept moving forward didn't fill her with very much optimism.

Not giving him a chance to get on the offensive, she dashed toward the Knight and leapt up into the air and kneed it in the chest. It staggered back, but caught himself and quickly regained his composure.

Grunting, she did a round house kick and hit the same spot on the Knight's chest. She was bound and determined to crack this thing open like a walnut.

The Knight staggered back but, again, caught its footing. Jegra leapt up and came down on him with her elbow. His head rocked back with a clang but it righted itself almost instantly.

Jegra rubbed her elbow and hopped up and down. "Ow," she complained. "That fucking hurt."

The Knight looked down at the ground and Jegra followed its gaze. Laying in the dirt just at its feet was the plasma sword. She surmised that it must have an automatic turn-off, since it wasn't melting through the planet at the moment. Bending down, the Knight retrieved the sword and ignited it.

"A girl just can't catch a break," Jegra groaned. She wiped the sweat from her brow, flicked it off her fingers, and then balled her fists up and raised them as she prepared for round two of their little tango.

She widened her stance, placing once foot slightly behind her body, keeping her center of gravity squarely over her feet, and took a defensive posture.

"Surrender," the Knight said in a booming voice.

She waited for him to say something else. Something like, *surrender and you won't be harmed.* Or, *surrender and I'll make your death painless.* Instead, all she got was *surrender.*

"Funny," she quipped. "I was about to tell you the same thing."

The Knight swung the plasma blade and Jegra bent over backwards as the blade scorched over her. When she sprang back up, she realized her suit was on fire.

"Shit, shit, shit," she said, falling to the ground and rolling in the dirt. She made sure to roll away from the Knight.

When she clambered back to her feet, a thin film of mud dappled her sweaty flesh. The Knight was already advancing on her.

He took another wide swing and Jegra jumped out of the way. She hit the ground and rolled; this time ensuring she smothered any fires before they could do any damage.

Even with all her ducking and dodging, she still noticed a large slice had been taken out across her back. Her skin was fine, but her suit, made mainly from rubber mesh of fiberoptic textile, was dissolving fast. Apparently, smart-suits weren't intended for intense heat.

Each slash of the Knight's blade melted more and more of her suit away until all that was left was a series of pleather strands that stretched tight across her curvaceous body, it could barely conceal all of her. She feared any further attacks would render her completely naked.

"Okay, this is starting to get ridiculous. Are you trying to see me naked or what? Because I could save you the trouble and just take it all off, if you'd like."

The Knight stopped dead in his tracks and flicked off the sword. "Apologies," he said. "It was not my intention to sin."

Jegra raised an eyebrow. *These Knights were pretty strange adversaries,* she thought. *Not my intention to sin?' What in the blazes was he yammering on about?*

"If I surrender to you, what then?"

"I am to bring you before the Administratrix, Anaïs Nin, where you will be judged accordingly."

"Judged?" Jegra asked, confused.

"Judged for your sins."

"Ah, I see. And as fun as that sounds, how about *no.*" Jegra took advantage of the fact that the Knight had turned off his blade and lunged forward. Throwing out her right leg she landed a solid kick right onto his chest. This time he did go down and lost hold of his sword in the process.

In a split second, Jegra landed on top of the Knight, her meaty thighs straddling his waist. Dialing it up to eleven, she attacked in full-on rage mode. Her fists pounded the Knight's armor with such fierceness they shot up sparks.

Her knuckles began to bleed under the severe force of each Herculean blow, but she kept on bashing the Knight's armor, regardless.

Determined to crack him open like a walnut so she could reach in and drag out the sniveling nosed weakling hiding inside and beat him to a pulp, she gritted her teeth and fought through the pain.

"My only sin today will be killing you!" she growled above the clang of her fists reverberating off bent steel.

Then, raising both arms high above her head, she clasped her hands together and brought them down with the force of an anvil dropping from a passing airplane. Then another. And another.

The Knight's armor finally cracked, and this only incentivized Jegra to hammer him even harder.

"Wait!" the Knight finally pleaded, raising his hand and extending his fingers in a request for clemency.

But Jegra wasn't going to simply give up. She was going to turn whoever was inside into bean paste and send the rest of the Knights of Caelum the message that you don't mess with Jegra, champion of the arena, the Jewel of Dagon, and Gladiatrix of the Galaxy.

She screamed out again as her hair picked up in a breeze and waved behind her. Her every muscle rippled with the full force of her raw energy. At last, the crack in the armor was big enough for her to cram her fingers into. And she did. Grunting out loud, she pried apart the armor.

The metal whined as it was sheered away from the body inside. Jegra ripped the chest plate off and tossed the two separate pieces aside.

Eyes filled with the frenzied look of a warrior who had reverted back to their basic instincts, she gazed down at the man inside with smoldering brown eyes. Her arms hung limp at her sides, blood drizzled from her battered knuckles, and her chest heaved as she wheezed to catch her breath. Amazingly enough, in all this furor, her shredded suit managed to stay on her body.

Jegra wanted to reach into the gaping opening she had made and grab the man by his scrawny neck and snap it, except her arms were too heavy to lift and her hands were too numb to feel. She'd overexerted herself.

Although she didn't have anything left to give, she knew she couldn't let the Knight know that, so she bluffed. "Any last words before I send you to meet your maker?" she asked with a snarl.

"Just one," the man inside replied. "Please, allow a Knight the honor of a merciful death."

"Mercy?!" Jegra scoffed. "Do you not know who I am? I'm Jegra! The Merciless!"

But the Knight wasn't asking for her mercy. Rather, it was a secret code. Knight. Honor. Mercy. Death. The moment he had uttered the words, beams of light lit up all around her.

Six Knights arrived in the teleport and took position around them, enclosing Jegra and her opponent in a tight circle. The middle Knight was decked out in all black armor and had a black cape with a red lining. As he stood looking down at her, his cape flapped gently on the breeze.

"You've got to be fucking kidding me." Jegra sighed.

Drained of all energy, she fell off the Knight and hit the ground with a thud. Exhausted, it took every ounce of strength she had just to roll onto her back. She grunted from the pain and looked up at the black Knight who, in turn, gazed down at her from behind the narrow slits of his visor. She couldn't tell what he was thinking behind that visor of his, but she could take a couple of good guesses.

Then Jegra did something she never thought she'd do and spoke the words she swore to herself she would never speak. "I surrender," she said, at last.

It hurt her pride terribly to admit it, but she was defeated. As much as she wanted to stand back up and show them her iron will, she couldn't. She wasn't fooling anyone. Not with her tits about to burst out of the strands of what was left of her outfit and bloody hands the consistency of applesauce. No. She was done for now. That much was for certain.

The black Knight raised his hand and the other Knights took a couple of steps back, giving her room. Just then, several red beams of energy came down from above to gather them all up and take them back to the ship. Including Jegra.

20

Scared, Jegra scrambled to her feet but immediately collapsed again. Kicking frantically, she scurried on her back to the corner of the teleporter room so as to have a better position to defend herself and kick wildly.

If she got lucky, she might nail one of the Knights right in their nut-sack. If they even had nut-sacks. For all she knew, as religious fanatics, they may have all become eunuchs.

But to Jegra's astonishment, the Knights ignored her entirely. Instead of coming for her, they tended to their friend. Two of them dragged away their wounded comrade by his arms, his armor scraping along the floor as they went. She watched the wounded Knight's feet slide out of the door and then turned to face the others, but they merely followed after them. Only the black Knight remained behind.

Alone in the room with a single Knight was bad enough. It took all her strength and fighting prowess to take down just one of them. There was no way she would be able to do it again and assuredly she had no desire to try.

The Knight reached up and flipped a couple of latches on his helmet. It was a power-suit, but also an environmental suit. A hiss of decompressed air shot out as he removed his mask.

Jegra let out a gasp of astonishment. Beneath the mask was a gorgeous, black haired man with porcelain skin that made him look more like a doll than a person. He had a broad jaw, was clean shaven, and had mysterious black eyes that lacked irises, pupils, or any amount of white, for that matter.

All but for the haunting eyes, however, he looked human. There was also a subtle speckling, like blue painted freckles, that ran down from his temples and neck and, she mused, perhaps the rest of his body as well.

With as many horror stories that she'd heard involving the nefarious, blood thirsty Nyctans, she half expected a monster. Not a gorgeous hunk that resembled one of the gallant vampires of an Anne Rice novel.

"My name is Galahad," he said, looking down at her with an expressionless face.

"Of course, it is," Jegra replied, a subtle smile forming on her face. Not only was he an actual space-knight, but this knight also had a knight's name. She wondered if there was any connection to Earth's own Arthurian legend or if it was just a strange coincidence.

Galahad took a step toward her and she tensed up.

"Don't worry," he said, cautiously raising his hand. "I will not hurt you."

"How do I know what you are or aren't willing to do?"

"As a Knight of Caelum, I've sworn to protect all possible candidates. You will not be harmed aboard this ship. You have my word."

"Candidate?" asked Jegra. She covered her breast, realizing that it was making him divert his gaze at an awkward angle so as not to be staring right into her nipple.

His eyes slowly came back to hers. "Every seven years, our oracle gives a list of two names. Each name is a possible match for the resurrected form of Hastur. This year, Sanakar, picked your name as one of the candidates."

"Sorry to disappoint you," Jegra said. "But if I were a god, I think I'd know it."

This seemed to amuse Galahad and he smiled. "No," he said. "You'd merely be the vessel of our Lord. You would undergo conditioning and then, in our most sacred ritual, your essence and his would be melded."

Although Jegra didn't too much like the sound of that, she was in no position to argue theology. She merely sat on the floor looking up at the fair skinned knight with black eyes, and blinked.

He reached out his hand and offered to help her up. She reluctantly took it, but as soon as she did he pulled her up to her feet. She was still weak from her fight and stumbled forward and he caught her. She still clutched her chest, so as not to be immodest, and he helped her wrap her other arm over his shoulder.

"This way," he said, guiding her out of the doors and into the corridor.

Unlike a Dagon ship, which was all brushed metal and blinking lights, the Nyctan ship was white with a black touch panel running the whole length of the corridor. The floor was a pleasant, tan carpet with a burgundy triangle pointing outwards from each door that led into the corridor.

The lighting was soft and atmospheric and reminded her of the church her mother used to drag her to when she was a little girl.

Luscious paintings with a baroque style that reminded her of Caravaggio, Rembrandt, and Ruben hung on the wall about every fifty meters or so. This surprised her.

"Are these scenes from your religious book?" she asked.

"Some are," Galahad replied. "Some are depictions of our holy wars. This one," he said, nodding at the painting nearest to them, "was the third crusade into the third star system, where the Knights first encountered the Dagons."

"I'm surprised you brokered a deal with Emperor Dakroth at all," Jegra said. "He's not the most pleasant man in the galaxy to deal with."

"And yet, you married him," the Knight said, giving her a peculiar look.

"It's complicated," she informed him, glancing away.

"Most relationships are," he said.

After another fifty meters, they came to a large doorway and paused. He tapped on the controls and the doors opened. Waiting inside were three women attendants. They were petite, and all had porcelain skin. They looked like china dolls with big, mysterious black eyes. No pupils. No irises. No color of any kind. Just glossy black alien eyes that stared back at her with an equal amount of curiosity.

All three women bowed as one as Jegra and Galahad entered. Glancing around the room, Jegra's jaw about hit the floor when she saw how lavish everything was. There was even a pool in the middle of the room which was fed by an artificial waterfall.

In addition to this there was a fireplace, a sofa, and a mini library with a book shelf that ran from the fireplace all the way along half the back wall. It was chock full of books that were probably all written in languages she couldn't comprehend.

Perhaps the most lavish aspect of the whole room was the bed, which had golden covers and golden sheets with matching pillows cases. The bed was topped by burgundy pillows that complimented the glistening gold. It looked like the royal suite of the most expensive five-star hotel she'd ever seen.

"What is this place?" she asked.

"This is your room," Galahad replied.

"Bullshit!" Jegra exclaimed.

Galahad stepped back and looked about his feet as though he actually had stepped in manure.

"No," Jegra said, laughing slightly. She touched his arm. "It's just an expression of excitement."

"That is a very strange expression," Galahad answered.

"I suppose it is." She laughed again. To settle any doubt in his mind as to her feelings on the matter, she added, "I think it's lovely. More than lovely. It's perfect."

"I'm glad you approve." Turning to the three women who had been quietly and patiently standing by, he said, "And these are your servants. Feel free to use them as you please."

Each of the women had a different color hair, all in bright colors. The first girl had claret colored hair, and the second had Byzantine blue, while the third had pitch black hair.

She didn't know if Nyctans dyed their hair or if their natural colors were this vibrant, but the bright hues of their hair really complimented their black eyes and white skin.

"I could use a bath," Jegra finally said, rolling her neck across her tired shoulders.

One of the women stepped forward and bowed slightly. "Mistress, my name is Estan, and I am a medically trained nurse. I can see to any wounds you may have."

The second woman standing in the row came forward and Estan stepped back into line. "Mistress," she said, "my name is Ellia, and I will handle all your fashion and beauty requirements. I am also a professional masseuse and stylist."

As Ellia stepped back the third woman came forward, she bowed her head. Rising back up, she blinked her black eyes and said, "I am Laquiea, and I am your cultural advisor and tutor. Consider me an ambassador to the Nyctan people and way of life. If you ever have any questions, do not hesitate to ask."

This was very much different from her treatment by the Dagons. The Dagon people seemed to tolerate her, but she always had the distinct feeling they were always looking down their noses at her and whispering snide remarks behind her back.

However, since the moment she arrived aboard the Nyctan vessel she hadn't been treated as anything other than a very important guest.

Galahad cleared his throat and she turned to him.

"I apologize, Mistress Alakandra, but I must return to my duties."

"I didn't tell you my last name was Alakandra," Jegra said. She was somewhat taken aback by the fact he knew her full name even though she hadn't divulged such information. Then it dawned on her. The derelict ship adrift in space.

"Wait," she murmured, the memory coming back to her. "It was you aboard that ship, wasn't it?"

Galahad smiled, and then without replying, he bowed and took his leave, his cape flowing behind him.

Jegra turned around and looked at the three women standing before her. "So, what does a girl have to do around here to get a hot bath?"

Estan gestured for Jegra to follow her. "First, I'm going to run a full biomed scan."

"How long with that take?" Jegra asked.

Estan ushered her to the corner of the room and she reached up and tapped a panel on the wall. It slid open and she took out a little handheld scanning device no bigger than your average smart-phone. As she waved it across Jegra's body, a little blue light was emitted from the scanner along with a faint beeping as it collected her vitals and other important details.

"You have three hairline fractures to your ribcage, a torn rotator cuff, and a broken collar bone."

"Scan me again," Jegra said with a smile. "Just to be sure."

Estan scanned her again and stared at the medical scanner. She tapped on its side, as if it were broken, and then looked up again. "I don't believe it. The wounds have miraculously healed themselves."

"It's not miraculous," Jegra replied. "I just heal fast."

"Amazing," Ellia gasped. "Glory be to Hastur."

"Glory be to Hastur," they all said in unison.

Jegra drew back, her neck flexing. This was the first strange thing she'd experience since being brought aboard. But they were a religious people, so she shrugged it off as one of the eccentric rituals of a highly devout people.

"Come," Ellia said, gently helping Jegra peel off her clothes. "Let's help make you presentable."

Nimble fingers stripped her bare, and taking her by the hands, they led her to the edge of the pool. Jegra sank down to her shoulders and then turned to watch what the three women would do next.

Laquiea set some black satin pajamas on a side bench and bowed. "These are your evening clothes, milady."

"Thank you," Jegra replied.

"You must be exhausted," Ellia said.

"We'll let you rest," Estan added.

"If there's anything you need," Laquiea added, "Do not hesitate to summon us. All you have to do is touch the green panel by the door and it will open a direct link to our quarters."

"I would love some food, if you don't mind," Jegra said.

"Of course, you must be starved," Ellia said. "I'll get you something. What would you like?"

"I would die for an Earth cheeseburger and Coke right about now," Jegra said. "But I doubt you have anything like that here."

"Let me see," Ellia said. She walked over to a small inlet in the wall that looked like a tray return booth. She touched a panel and said, "Earth cheeseburger with a Coke."

The computer chimed and asked, <<What style of burger do you prefer. Regular or deluxe.>>

She glanced over her shoulder and shot Jegra a confused look.

"Deluxe," Jegra blurted, her mouth beginning to water and her eyes widening with excitement.

"Deluxe," Ellia replied.

<<Would you like fries as a side order?>>

"Yes!" Jegra cried out, wading through the bath to the edge where she climbed out. Drying herself off with the towel that Estan handed her, she quickly threw on her pajamas and rushed over to Ellia who was pulling a tray out of the food synthesizer unit. Sure enough, it had a burger, a side of fries, and a bottle of Coke.

"It appears we do have some limited Earth cuisine on file," Ellia said. "You can search the data bank for anything else you may desire."

Eyes as big as saucers, Jegra didn't even wait for her to hand her the tray. She snatched the burger off of it and began scarfing it down like a starved animal.

Barely able to keep the food from flying out of her mouth, she grabbed the bottle of Coke, kicked back her head and guzzled it. Finishing it off in one go, she turned her head and belched loudly.

The three women watched her with amusement, but said nothing. She knew that Cassera would have balked, made a disgusted face, and called her a loathsome toad or some other degrading term. But the Nyctans just watched and studied her.

It made her feel a little self-conscious, but she was positive she could get used to the weirdness given enough time. After all, they were an entirely different culture and people, so culture shock was bound to be inevitable. She still had a lot to learn about them and they her.

"Anything else, milady?"

Her mouth full of synthesized burger, which tasted as real as the genuine thing, she pushed the wad of food into her right cheek and, with her mouth full, replied. "No. I'll be fine." She shoved fries into her mouth, took the tray from Ellia, and sat on the floor.

As she ate in the middle of the floor like a commoner or a very small child, the three women bowed and took their leave. Once they had exited the room, Jegra swallowed what was left in her mouth and leapt to her feet, rushed over to the door, and tried to open it, but it clicked angrily at her and refused her access.

"Locked," she sighed, realizing the restriction meant they either didn't trust her or else she really was their prisoner, after all. Neither possibility filled her with much optimism.

The silver lining in all this, however, was she had a nice comfortable bed that she could sink into and get some much needed rest. Space travel, as it turned out, wasn't for the weak willed. It was cold, dangerous, and above all completely exhausting. After being on the run non-stop for the past several days, she was looking forward to getting a good night's sleep.

21

Automated natural lighting gradually grew bright and mimicked the effect of the sun coming up at dawn. Jegra slowly opened her eyes at the radiance and took a moment to bask in its warmth. Spaceships were cold, space was dark, and she found that it was nice to have a warm luminescence to wake up to. That's when her door chimed.

Jegra sat up in bed and stared at the door. She didn't know what to do or say, so she just said, "Enter."

Her bedroom doors swished open and Ellia stood in the entrance wearing a cute blue dress that complimented her blue hair and speckled neck. She stepped in and bowed reverently.

Jegra slowly slid out of bed and got up to greet the young woman; Ellia walked into the center of the room and, unpredictably, unfastened her dress, letting her garments fall to the floor. She stood before Jegra, completely naked.

"It was deemed by the oracle that there should be balance between us. I am yours to do with as you please."

Not understanding exactly what all this was about, Jegra rushed over to the girl and bent down, picked up her things, and handed them to her. "That's not necessary," Jegra replied.

"But we witnessed you bathe yesterday. It is only fair that you should see one of us naked. That is the Nyctan way. An eye for an eye, a heart for a heart, an oath for an oath."

As fascinating as this little cultural lesson was, Jegra wasn't concerned with sexual matters right now. "It's fine," she reiterated. "Here, get dressed."

The girl blushed and then did as she was asked.

"Is it true," Ellia asked, "that you've slept with over two dozen species?"

"More or less," Jegra answered. Throwing a hand up on her hip, she looked down at Ellia, who stood about five feet six inches. "Why? Is that important somehow?"

"No," Ellia blushed. "Just a personal curiosity. In the Nyctan culture, prurience of that sort is strictly forbidden."

"Sex is illegal?"

"No, mistress," Ellia laughed. "Sex for procreation is perfectly allowed. But fornication for sport, for pleasure, is considered a sin."

"You can't fuck for fun?" Jegra gasped.

Ellia cringed. "We're not supposed to curse either."

Jegra stared at the girl for a moment. "What if you like someone and you want to express yourself physically. Do you just refrain?"

"No, mistress," she replied. "There are erotic dances you can learn. In our culture, we dance for one another. It is the closest to, um, actual sexual gratification we can get."

"Fascinating," Jegra said. After another short pause, Jegra asked, "What about me? Do your laws apply to guests as well?"

"I suppose not. But I'm no expert in this area, you'll need to consult with Laquiea."

"Ah, yes," Jegra responded, scratching her chin. "The one with the stick up her butt."

Ellia laughed. "Why would Laquiea keep a tree in her butt?"

"It's a figure of speech where I'm from," Jegra replied. "It means you're stiff, overly conservative, basically, no fun."

"Laquiea isn't all that bad once you get to know her," Ellia replied.

"I guess I am not great at first impressions," Jegra admitted. "I shouldn't have judged her prematurely."

"It's perfectly understandable. And, you're not entirely mistaken. There are many days where it seems Laquiea has, as you say, a tree in her ass."

Jegra smothered a laugh. She enjoyed the way Ellia kept saying tree instead of stick. But, then, in Nyctan speech, there may not be any distinction between the two. Even universal translators, it would seem, had their limitations, especially when it came to culturally specific idioms.

"Anyway," Jegra sighed. "What's on the docket for today?"

"I'm here to fit you," Ellia answered.

"Fit me? For what?"

"For numerous things. But today we'll be giving you a set of military issue clothes and some special armor."

"Armor?" Jegra repeated.

Ellia looked around the room and leaned in and whispered into Jegra's ear. "Knight's armor."

"You're shitting me?" Jegra gasped.

"I'm not supposed to tell you any of this, but the oracle, Sanakar Vesta, deemed it to be so."

"I'm going to be a Knight?" Jegra asked.

"Not only that, but her grace, Anaïs Nin, has deemed it you be the new Sub Commander of the Knights of Caelum."

"Commander?" Jegra laughed. "I'm no military leader."

"Like I said," Ellia replied, pulling out what looked like a digital pen from her pocket, "I'm not even supposed to be telling you all this. Now, please hold still."

A beam of green light came out of the pen-sized device as she waved it over and around Jegra's body. After a moment, she placed the pen in her pocket and looked at Jegra with a smile.

"That's it?" asked Jegra, thinking there would be more to it than that.

"That's it," Ellia chirped. "Now, if you'll come along with me, we'll get you into your armor."

"Um...okay," Jegra replied as she followed Ellia to the entrance. "But is it all right for me to go out looking like this?"

"It's just across the hall," Ellia laughed.

The doors slid open and they stepped out into the corridor. Jegra glanced to her right, then left, embarrassed to find two Nyctan officers passing by. They nodded politely and kept on their course. They didn't even so much as utter any gossip after having seen her.

Across the hall, Ellia pushed the door panel and the doors opened. Inside were Estan and Laquiea waiting for her.

"Good morning," they said in unison, "mistress, Jegra."

"Good morning," Jegra replied cheerfully. Peeling off her clothes, she let them slip to the floor where they landed in a heap next to her feet. "Where's the armor?"

Ellia cleared her throat and tilted her head toward the corner of the room, her eyebrow riding high on her brow as she gave Jegra a strict look.

Jegra turned to find Galahad, dressed in a standard officer's uniform, staring right at her naked form.

"Apologies, Sir Galahad," Ellia replied. "We did not know you were here."

Although she wasn't particularly bashful, Jegra was left feeling like quite the fool for having stripped before even checking the room and she quickly covered herself.

"Apologies, Galahad. If I would have known…"

Galahad turned his back, so as to allow her some privacy, and replied, "It was an honest mistake. No harm was done."

"This way," Estan said, nervously glancing back and forth between Jegra and Galahad. Men weren't supposed to see women they weren't married to in the nude. Especially since getting caught in the presence of another's nakedness was considered lewd and punishable by up to ten lashes.

But with Jegra, the rules were a little less clearly defined and, she supposed, exceptions would have to be made. At least, that's what everyone was thinking. Without the oracle or the administratrix to arbitrate, nobody had the authority to say. So, they all blushed and kept the incident to themselves. Of course, the only one wearing a grin in all of this was Galahad.

"Let me help you into the smart-suit," Estan said. She helped Jegra squeeze into a smart-suit that resembled the color changing one Raven had given her aboard the *Skywend*. This suit, however, was a charcoal gray and had what felt like a more nylon quality to it.

Once she zipped her suit all the way up to the Mandarin style collar, she turned to find Laquiea pulling out a mannequin with a slimmer and sleeker version of the Knight's armor. It looked almost the same, except it was clearly designed for a woman.

"This is amazing," Jegra said, as all three women helped her into the suit. Its black paneling opened up to allow her to more easily slip into it. Once inside, her maidservants all stepped back. Jegra's panels all automatically clamped shut and sealed themselves. A hiss of air shot out of the heels of her black, metallic boots and the suit shrank in around her as though she was being vacuum wrapped.

After dressing her, Laquiea cleared her throat and summoned Galahad. "It's quite alright now, Sir Galahad."

He turned around and smiled at Jegra who flexed her arm and opened and closed her fist. "Is this tension normal?" she asked.

"The suit takes a minute to calibrate to your physiology. It also will estimate what percentage strength boost it can safely add, given your tensile strength."

Without warning, the suit's right arm locked up straight.

"Now try and bend it," Galahad added.

Jegra struggled at first, but slowly she managed to bend her arm at the elbow. The suit's gears and motors whined as they fought against her strength.

[Simulation complete] a mechanical voice came from the armor. [Suit power assist set at forty-seven percent].

"Oh, my stars!" Ellia gasped. "That's even higher than yours, Galahad."

"Ellia!" Laquiea chastised the girl for speaking out of turn to a Knight. "Mind your manners around the Knight."

"Forgive me, Galahad," Ellia said, bowing her head in shame. "I didn't mean to imply weakness."

Galahad laughed. "It's quite all right, ladies. It was to be expected. Jegra, after all, is ranked as a class nine warrior. I'm only a class seven."

"Out of curiosity, what is your suit's power assist rating anyway?" Jegra asked.

Galahad smiled. "Twenty-six percent," he replied. But I have taken safety protocols off; I had it up to thirty-one percent a while back. Nothing to brag about, however, as I shredded my knees and had to have reconstructive surgery."

"So, you were able to squeeze about five percent extra power out of it? Good to know."

"You probably will be able to squeeze ten percent out of yours in a pinch," he said. "But it puts great strain on the body."

Jegra rotated her arms and swiveled her legs. The suit now felt well-primed and moved fluidly. It still felt bulky, but from what she had seen of the Knights, they didn't let it slow them down.

"Do I get a helmet, too?" Jegra asked.

"When we deploy," Galahad replied.

"What if I have an itch?" Jegra asked.

"The suit has comfort settings that can help with that."

"What if I need to pee?" she asked.

"You just go in the suit. It will take care of everything for you."

"Amazing," Jegra said, flexing her arm and hand again as she inspected the tech.

"Come," Galahad said, opening the door and looking back at her. "We will go meet Anaïs Nin and Azra'il Nun."

"I know Anaïs Nin is the administratrix, but who is Azra'il Nun?"

"She is Adjunct High Commander, second in command only to Anaïs Nin."

"What would your rank be?" Jegra inquired.

"I'm Knight, First Class."

"Will I get a rank too?"

"If you do, it will be Adjunct Commander."

"But how?" Jegra asked. "I've not been to any military academy. I've had no proper training."

"That is my duty," Galahad replied. "To train you and bring you up to speed. You're looking at a couple grueling months of the hardest training you've ever undergone."

"I could probably use it," Jegra said. "I may have had a cheeseburger or two last night. And then six more."

Ellia snickered and Jegra looked over and smiled at her just in time to see Laquiea elbow her in her rib.

"See, I told you," Jegra said, addressing Ellia. "A big stiff tree."

Ellia laughed out loud, so loud that everyone turned and looked at her. "Sorry," she said, covering her mouth.

Jegra laughed, too, and then followed Galahad, who was always so patient, out into the corridor.

Upon entering the bridge, Jegra gasped. It looked like the inside of a gorgeous Gothic cathedral back on Earth, only with much more tech built in.

At the center of the large chamber stood a woman gazing out of a three-meter-high observation window, her eyes fixed on a seemingly unimportant swath of star speckled space. The verdant moon, Cordova, lingered in the distance and orbited a red gas giant with a narrow ring around it called Gamidon.

The woman wore her hair tied up into a knot on her head. Her dress was backless, and it had many layers. So many in fact that, to Jegra, it resembled a bird's feathers.

The woman slowly turned around to reveal another set of black eyes. All Nyctans had the same, giant, squid-like black eyes. To Jegra, they looked demon-possessed, but she knew that it was just their natural evolution.

Anaïs Nin smiled at Jegra. "Welcome, my child. The oracle foresaw your coming."

Galahad took a knee before the administratrix and Jegra copied him.

"No need for such formalities," Anaïs Nin said, beckoning them to rise. "This is not a formal visit. Just a casual hello. How are things, Empress Alakandra? Do you find your quarters satisfactory?"

"More than satisfactory," she answered. "And, please, call me Jegra."

"Jegra it is, then. If you will," Anaïs Nin said, briskly gliding past her in her white feather-like gown. "Come with me."

They walked up to the observation window and gazed out together.

"What do you see?" asked Anaïs Nin as she folded her arms behind her back.

"I see the moon, Cordova."

"Look closer," the administratrix beckoned.

"I see empty space. Stars. Planets."

"You see light versus darkness, too, do you not?"

"I suppose," Jegra said, straightening her posture as Anaïs Nin looked at her. "That's one way of putting it."

"For eons, the heavens have been separated by vast swaths of empty blackness. But our god, Hastur, promises to bring light to the darkness and rebuild the universe in his image."

"The Dagons worship Hastur as the bringer of fire. The God of the final judgement, right?" inquired Jegra with a sincere curiosity. She pressed her finger to her chin and continued to listen with a keen interest.

"I presume that Dagons also told you that our religion is a perversion of their ancient faith. But what if I told you we had in our possession an artifact that proved the Nyctans were the original believers."

"It would not make much difference to me, ma'am. I am not the kind of person to think deeply on such matters. I live in the moment. That is where my life plays out."

"And this is the answer of a true warrior. I see I was correct in assigning you to the Knights of Caelum. They believe, as you do, in an honorable, yet always fleeting, existence. Their souls are best served as bright sparks that quickly fade— a contribution to the light worthy of their God."

"I apologize for my ignorance," Jegra said. "But if I'm not Nyctan, how can I be promoted to the head of the Knights?"

"Our oracle has deemed it so."

"So, let me get this straight, you go by the words of one oracle and then simply take it all on faith?"

"Hastur speaks through the oracle. And he has selected you as one of his candidates to become his avatar. It is a most sacred and coveted position. You are lucky to have been chosen."

Jegra nodded. It's not that she didn't believe the Nyctan's sincerity in the matter. It's just that she'd rather not have been hand-picked to be the chosen one; it seemed like an awful lot of responsibility.

"And what is it I'm supposed to do, exactly?"

"To start with," Anaïs Nin, said with a scheming grin, "you can show your allegiance by destroying the Dagon armada that has blockaded us from entering into the Zargora system."

"What's so important about that system?" Jegra asked.

A new voice arose from behind them. "It is the place where Hastur is destined to return."

They all turned around to see a woman in bright red armor. It looked very similar to Jegra's but with some extra flourishes and rectangular shoulder pads that stuck out like wings.

"Azra'il Nun," Anaïs Nin said, making the introductions. "This is Empress Jegra Alakandra of the Dagon Empire."

"Jegra, this is my second in command. Adjunct High Commander Azra'il Nun."

"Pleasure to finally meet you, empress," Azra'il Nun said, taking a knee before Jegra.

"There's no need for that," she said. "It's not like Emperor Dakroth even actually wanted me as his empress, seeing as he sold me off to you first chance he got."

"She doesn't know?" Azra'il asked, shooting a shocked look at Anaïs Nin.

"Forgive us," said Anaïs Nin. "We're not accustomed to revealing top secret information to strangers. But seeing as you are no longer a stranger to us, I feel comfortable in revealing the truth."

"What are you talking about?" Jegra asked, glancing at all their faces.

Azra'il blinked her dark eyes and said, "Emperor Dakroth announced yesterday that he had made you his empress but that you died in a horrible shuttle accident on Cordova. They are having the rite of passage this very evening in your honor."

The fumes practically began seeping up out of Jegra's collar. "That swine," she growled, clasping her fist. "If he thinks he can just erase me from his life that easily, he has a thing or two coming to him."

Azra'il Nun and Anaïs Nin shared a glance and smiled.

"Let me show you to your battlecruiser," Galahad said.

"What?!" Jegra gasped.

"The *Light Bringer*," he replied, pointing out the window at a sleek-looking battleship. "It's the pride of the fleet. The fastest, toughest, and best equipped ship in the galaxy. The ship of the Knights of Caelum."

Stunned, Jegra turned around. "You're giving me a starship?"

"You're the chosen one," Azra'il Nun, answered. "And we must obey the wishes of our lord, Hastur."

Jegra turned to Galahad. "Well, what are we waiting for? I hear my estranged husband has a fleet that needs destroying."

Galahad smiled. "As you wish, milady."

Jegra followed him through the arched doorway of the bridge, glancing back to see the two Nyctan women smiling at her. She pivoted and threw her right fist over her chest and bowed. It may not be their custom, but as a gladiator, it was hers.

Both women bowed in response and, satisfied, Jegra exited the bridge.

"What about the other?" Azra'il asked her partner.

"The other remains in her prison cell where she belongs." Her voice dripped with disdain.

"And if Hastur should choose the hybrid over the human? What then?"

"In 700,000 years, Hastur has never chosen a mongrel to be his vessel. Therefore, it seems a safe bet he won't. But keep her alive, just in case he should...surprise us."

"And the Empress of Dagon? If Hastur possesses her, both empires would submit to her rule. She wouldn't merely be Dagon's empress anymore. She'd be Nyctan's Empress as well."

"If it comes to that," Anaïs Nin said in a cold voice, "then so be it. Until that time, however, we can use her in our present campaign."

Both women smiled and turned back toward the window and looked out as the *Light Bringer* came fully into view.

22

Dropping out of hyperspace, the Nyctan battlecruiser, the *Light Bringer*, appeared in the Zargora system with a flash of light and a boom caused by the terminal shock wave that occurs exiting hyperspace.

The *Light Bringer* snapped into focus as it slowed to normal cruising speed and then cut between two binary stars as it headed toward an asteroid belt that orbited a super massive black hole.

The Dagon Imperial fleet was on the other side, blockading a supposed trade route. But Jegra knew that was a bunch of B.S. Emperor Dakroth was protecting something and she intended on finding out exactly what was so important that he devoted half of his fleet to safeguarding it.

In the meantime, her fleet would gather on the opposite side of the black hole, using the electromagnetic interference of the singularity to prevent long range scans from detecting their arrival.

It had been three months since Emperor Dakroth's betrayal of her at Cordova and she had spent every waking moment training with Galahad, three long, grueling months of training with the Knights. And although Jegra had become a member of the Nyctan military order, she still felt out of place. They were borderline obsessed with duty and honor, and they only cared about their mission. Nothing else.

Still, they had given her a starship and, what's more, promoted her to commander, second class, of an entire division of their fleet. All because some oracle had told them that's what their god, Hastur, wanted them to do.

Aboard the bridge, Jegra stood gazing out of the main viewscreen at the purple nebulae that hung before them. Her sleek space-gray armor that shimmered like liquid glass in the starlight and she locked her wrists behind her back as she admired the scenery.

Even though she knew it was only a vast collection of gas, ice, water, and space dust, it was still beautiful.

Galahad sauntered up to her side and gazed out at the cosmic vista with her. They shared a moment of silence, both in awe of the beauty displayed before them. After a moment, he cleared his throat.

"Commander, we've arrived at the coordinates you gave us. But where exactly are we? There's nothing of strategic value on any of our scanners and there are very few inhabitable systems in this area."

"This is where Dakroth said the secret shipyard was. He thought maybe the Nyctans had gotten some intel on it and had destroyed it."

"We did not know of this secret installation until you alerted us as to its presence. But it would explain how Emperor Dakroth was able to keep such a stronghold on the Zargora system without having laid claim to any of the planets or moons here."

"Remind me why nobody has colonized this system, again?"

Galahad turned toward Jegra. He was wearing his infamous black armor. "Many settlers have come out this far, seeking life away from the rule of the Nyctans and the tyranny of the Dagons, both of which they find to be oppressive regimes. But only smugglers, space pirates, and a host of intrepid frontier folk call this backwater place home."

"Sounds like the Wild West, if you ask me."

"Wild West?" asked Galahad.

"It was a time of lawlessness for my people; an entire region populated by survivalists and speculators. Everyone fought for survival and laid claim to their own space. They relied only on themselves to get by."

"Sounds very similar to the Zargora system and the few outcroppings of colonies that exist around the four quads."

Before Galahad managed to finish his explanation, an alarm sounded and one of the bridge officers looked up. "Sirs, we have another ship entering the system."

"Is it Dagon?" Jegra asked.

The officer glanced down at his panel. "No, it appears to be a freighter. But it's heavily modified."

Jegra shot Galahad a confused look.

"Space Pirates," he informed her. After a brief pause, he asked, "Your orders, Sub Commander?"

"Advise me. What is the standard protocol when dealing with space pirates?"

"Blow them out of the water, ma'am," the officer relayed.

She shot Galahad a startled look to which he merely shrugged. "He's not wrong."

Jegra scratched her chin. Then settled on what she wanted to do. "Jam their comms, I don't want them alerting the Dagon fleet of our presence. Then scan their ship."

"Ma'am?" the officer asked, puzzled.

"Are you questioning the commander?" Galahad growled.

"No, sir," the officer replied, swiveling back in his chair and running the scan as ordered. "Nothing out of the ordinary," the officer replied.

Without warning, although not entirely unexpectedly, the pirate vessel opened fire on the Nyctan battlecruiser. Even though it was no match for them, their disruptors were amped up enough to cause a small shuddering as they pinged off the electromagnetic shields.

"Is he an idiot?" Jegra asked.

"Most pirates are," Galahad answered. "They only care about their booty. He probably thinks we dropped into the system to plunder his trinkets."

Firing on a Nyctan destroyer unprovoked was a death sentence in and of itself. Only a fool would do such a thing.

"Hail them," she said.

"Comm channels are open, ma'am."

"This is Sub Commander Jegra Alakandra of the Nyctan battle cruiser *Light Bringer*. Cease firing immediately and state your business. This will be your first and final warning."

The bulky pirate ship slowly turned toward them and then began unloading everything it had. The *Light Bringer* shuddered briefly and Jegra rolled her eyes and let out a sigh.

Seeing as the pirates didn't want to play nice or respond to her attempts to open a dialog with them, she figured she had no real choice but to do it the Nyctan way. "If it's a death wish they have, then who are we to deny them it? Target that ship and fire."

"Yes, ma'am!" the officer said in a cheerful manner. He pushed a few red and orange buttons on his display and the ship's forward disruptor canons fired.

The pirate ship exploded off the port bow and dissolved into glistening space debris that gently arched across a black sky and would, eventually, join the asteroid belt.

Jegra put her arms behind her back and thought for a moment. "Galahad," she said, calling her Knight to her side.

"Yes, mistress?"

"Is the third wing of the Nyctan fleet still in orbit over Dagon?"

"Yes. But the cease fire brokered by Emperor Dakroth means they are merely a wasted resource. We cannot engage the enemy unless fired upon."

"I have an idea," Jegra said, her grin slowly curling into a vicious smile. "Order the third wing to jump to the Zargora system. I think it's time I blow the cover on my dear husband's little ploy."

Within the hour the third fleet arrived. Jegra smiled as ship after ship popped into view. She sauntered over to the large captain's chair and sat down.

"What now, commander?" Galahad asked.

"How long would it take to disguise our disrupters to look like Dagon disruptors?" She looked down at the officer.

"Let's see...some minor energy tweaks...removing the cooling dampeners...I'd say about two hours."

"Good. Get on it. I want our front canons firing red instead of green."

"Yes, ma'am," the officer said, leaping up and carrying out his orders.

"I think I see where you're going with this," Galahad said.

Jegra shot him a stern look. "There's a reason he wanted to call the cease fire. Obviously, he's losing the war on all fronts." She turned and looked out at the long line of ships under her command. "But he's dedicated half of his fleet to protecting something in the Zargora system and I intend to find out what that is."

Jegra rose out of her chair and gestured to Galahad to take a seat. "I'm headed to my quarters for a later supper. The bridge is yours."

He complied and she left the bridge and wandered down the hall to her personal quarters. They were smaller than her royal suite aboard the Nyctan flagship, the *Omikran*. But Jegra wasn't complaining.

She passed a Knight in the hall and nodded. The Knight nodded back. She paused briefly and looked back over her shoulder. "Wait," she called out.

The Knight stopped and turned around.

"You look familiar," she said.

"The name is Percival, ma'am. We've met once before."

Jegra squinted hard as she studied his face. "Oh, my God! You're the Knight I fought with on Cordova."

"Yes, ma'am," he said, bowing his head.

"I'm glad to see you're unharmed," she said.

"I appreciate that," Percival replied. "But you should know I've taken a lot of flak for being beaten by a woman without a power suit in single-handed combat."

"I'm sure you have," Jegra said, grinning ear to ear. "Just tell your buddies that if anyone of them had gone up against me, their outcome would have been the same."

"I'll do that," he replied, smiling back at her.

She nodded her head and then let him carry on with his duties.

When she finally got to her quarters she found Ellia waiting for her there. "Oh, you're here," Jegra said to her unexpected guest.

"Yes, mistress," Ellia replied. "I was assigned to be your personal servant aboard this ship."

"What about the others?" Jegra asked.

"They have other duties they must attend to aboard the *Omikran*. I, however, am rather low on the totem pole in both rank and social standing."

The doors slammed shut behind Jegra and she shuffled over to a large chair and sat herself down. "Help me get this armor off," she said.

Ellia did as requested and as soon as Jegra emerged from the armor she took a whiff of her armpits and made a sour face. "I'm going to go hit the showers," she said, thumbing over her shoulder.

Ellia simply nodded and watched Jegra saunter off. Before she left the main bedroom, Jegra leaned back and glanced over her shoulder at Ellia.

"You care to join me?" Jegra asked, tossing her brown hair across her shoulder as she started unzipping her smart-suit.

"Only if it is what you desire, mistress Jegra."

"You're good at massages, right?"

"I am a skilled masseuse, yes."

"Then get undressed and get your cute little butt over here," Jegra ordered, pointing at her heels as she ordered Ellia to come to her.

"Yes, mistress," Ellia replied. She began to strip her clothes off as she came and Jegra smiled.

Ellia's white skin glistened in the humidity of the shower, and the blue freckled pattern ran all the way down her neck, sides, and thighs right on down to her ankles. Jegra thought she looked rather fetching, but she also seemed on the young side.

Although, to be honest, Jegra hadn't a clue what her servant's age might be. Aliens all seemed to age at different rates on other worlds depending on how dense their planet was, how far out from their host star, and how long it took for the planet to do one revolution in a year.

After a fifteen-minute massage in the shower, Jegra let out a subtle, yet audible moan.

"I can stop, if I'm hurting you," Ellia said, rubbing her thumbs across Jegra's shoulder blades.

"No, keep going. That was a good moan. Harder, if you can."

"I can," Ellia said, jamming her fingers into Jegra's back as hard as she could as she worked out all the kinks.

Even though it was forbidden, Jegra knew it would be so easy to order Ellia to sleep with her. But she liked Ellia and she knew that using her position of authority over the girl would be wrong. So, she enjoyed the massage and tried to get to know the girl.

"Ellia," Jegra asked, "have you ever been in love?"

"I love my God, mistress."

"Sorry...I meant, like, a proper romantic interest."

"I am not allowed to socialize freely," she answered. "I lack the social standing to engage in normal social functions. My duties, my service, and my faith are all that I am."

"So, there's never been a boy or other girl you have taken a liking to?"

"If you mean, have I had impure thoughts about anyone, there was this one time…I dreamed about Sir Galahad."

"Oh, yeah?" Jegra asked, raising and eyebrow and cocking her head to better glimpse the embarrassed look on Ellia's face. Jegra was thirsty to know more. So, she prodded a bit. "By all means, do tell. I'd love to hear more about it."

Ellia shrugged. "I suppose I can tell you, seeing as you're my mistress. And, it was just a dream, after all."

Jegra nodded in silence and grinned.

"It was a couple of days before your arrival. I dreamed that Galahad and I were at the Vestian Falls on Nyctan, bathing together in the glowing pools below a foamy spray of water. The pools of Vestia glow iridescent blue from the unique algae that grows there. It's quite beautiful." She let out a sigh of longing and paused for a bit.

"And did you make love to him? In your dream, I mean."

"No. It was so much better. We held each other and gazed into one another's eyes the whole evening. Saying nothing but sharing our minds and souls. I felt his spirit touch mine. It was the most amazing dream I've ever had."

It didn't sound all that appealing to Jegra, just gazing at someone. All night. *But, to each their own,* she thought. Still, curiosity gripped her. There had to be some juicy detail that had been omitted. Something more scandalous than a staring contest and souls touching, or whatever. "I assume that, in your dream, you were naked together, right?"

"Yes," Ellia said bashfully. She looked away as though Jegra's attentive gaze was too much to bear and her typically porcelain white cheeks glowed bright pink from her embarrassment and the deep sense of shame she experienced for having had such impure thoughts about Galahad, even though it was no fault of her own.

"Well, there you go!" Jegra said.

"Please, don't tell him," Ellia pleaded, her face turning whiter than usual. She seemed on the verge of bursting into tears just at the mere thought of her secret getting out. "I would literally die if you told him anything of what I just said."

Jegra didn't quite know if what she had just said was simply a figure of speech or if her punishment would literally be death. She didn't press the girl any further, however, for fear it might be too stressful for her. "Don't worry, girl talk stays amongst the girls."

"But you are a woman, mistress."

Jegra sighed. "Yes. What I meant was, I'll keep your secrets if you keep mine."

"Oh, I see," Ellia replied, blushing again.

"By the way, if you don't mind my asking, how old are you, Ellia?"

"I'm twenty-one revolutions old."

"How many days is a revolution on Nyctan?"

"One revolution around our star takes 581 days."

"That's almost twice of what my planet is. So, you're like, 40 years old in Earth years or something?"

"I suppose," Ellia said, giving a shrug.

"But you look so young! I honestly thought you were a teenager. A mere child."

"I suppose that, in many ways, mistress, I am still a child. Regardless, we Nyctans have long lifespans. The oldest living Nyctan, you might like to know, is 183 revolutions old."

Jegra counted on her fingers as she tried to do that math. "You're shitting me?!" Jegra gasped, realizing that it was over 300 Earth years old.

Ellia was about to ask a question and, by the confused look on her face, Jegra knew that it was probably going to be about what shit had to do with any of it. To avoid having to explain yet another idiom to her, Jegra quickly got a word off before Ellia could ask her question.

"Nyctan women don't have vestigial penises, do they?" she asked, glancing at Ellia's naked body.

Ellia looked down at the blue tuft of hair between her slender white legs and then back up at Jegra. "Not that I'm aware of," she laughed.

"Dagon women do," Jegra said. It was true too. Apparently, the male sex organ, which could retract up into the vulva, was a vestigial trait from a bygone era. Jegra wasn't clear about the details. But it never had bothered her. People were people no matter what their anatomy might be. And if you enjoyed someone, it was because you enjoyed being with them. Not because they had a more or less complicated anatomy than you did.

"You're...shitting on me..." Ellia said, trying to copy Jegra's earlier use of the idiom. Jegra laughed.

"No. I shit on you not," she replied, deliberately using it in the way Ellia had so as to not make her feel bad. After all, she was still learning. "Their penises actually fold up into the cervix and only come out if you reach in and pry them out. But, sure enough, a fully functioning male organ tucked right alongside their women bits."

"Can one female impregnate another female?" she asked.

"You know," Jegra mused, scratching her chin. "I forgot to ask. They don't have testicles, however, so maybe they don't produce sperm. Although, I'm not entirely sure. But the moment I find out, I'll let you know."

By the look on Ellia's face, she was really beginning to get into the conversation. And that's exactly what Jegra had hoped for. She wanted Ellia to let her guard down just long enough to let her real personality out.

Jegra didn't care about the façade of the dutiful servant, she wanted to know the personality behind the mask.

"Please, forgive my boldness, mistress. But have you ever let any of the Dagon women mount you?" Ellia asked in a soft whisper, leaning in so as to keep their conversation as confidential as possible–even though they were completely alone in her private quarters aboard her very own starship.

"One," Jegra said, smiling as she recollected Cassera fondly. "She's kind of a stubborn Dagon. Really uptight, if you know what I mean, kind of a tree up her ass. And she's brutally honest with how she feels."

"I suppose brutal honesty in a culture dedicated to lying to one another as a form of social grace would be refreshing."

"It is," she replied. "I ought to know. Nobody lies more than my husband, Emperor Dakroth."

"The woman," Ellia continued. "Do you miss her?" Ellia continued rubbing Jegra's shoulders as they gossiped.

Jegra closed her eyes and let the water cascade down her chest. "I do miss her. And, if I wasn't married to that ass-hat Rhadamanthus Dakroth, I could easily see myself marrying Cassera Van Danica Amelorak."

All of a sudden Ellia stopped massaging Jegra's neck. Realizing something was the matter, Jegra turned around and looked over at the girl. She wore a startled look on her face and slowly drew back as though she were afraid of Jegra. If that wasn't bad enough, Jegra noticed tears gushing out of her eyes.

"What's wrong?" Jegra asked. "Is it something I said?"

"*That woman*, the one you just mentioned," Ellia hissed through clenched teeth, "destroyed my family's colony on the moon Novac when I was but a child."

"My God," Jegra gasped, appalled by Ellia's terrible news regarding Cassera's cruelty. "I had no idea."

"My parents and little brother were vaporized in an unwarranted attack on Nyctan's furthest moon. The official excuse was that they blew up a long-distance communications array that was supposedly tracking Dagon fleet deployments. But that was a lie. I grew up on Novac. There was nothing there but simple farmers and ore diggers. People trying to make a living the best they could in the harsh end of the system."

"I'm sorry," Jegra apologized. She didn't know what else to say. Cassera was her friend. But this...this merciless act of cruelty was unconscionable.

"How can you love a woman like that?" Ellia asked, her voice sounding awfully condemnatory. Her hands palpably shook with rage as her hard gaze burned with a smoldering fury that hadn't died down after all these years. The grudge she'd been harboring against the Dagons forced her emotional anger to come boiling to the surface.

"I..." Jegra's voice faded. She didn't have any answers that would appease Ellia or make her feel better about what had happened to her family. "Thanks for the massage," Jegra said in a firm, commanding tone. "You may be excused."

Ellia shot her a disapproving glance, bowed dutifully, and quickly scurried off. Her cheeks glowed with anger as she stormed out of the room, fists balled up tight.

Jegra let out an exasperated sigh and pressed her forehead against the glass shower wall and let the water beat down on her back.

The more she learned about the Dagons the more it seemed to her that they were the bad guys in this section of the galaxy. And here she was, married to their supreme leader, and in love with another who, as she had just learned, also so happened to be a cold-blooded killer and tyrant. A murderer of women and children.

What did this say about herself, she wondered. Ellia was not mistaken. If Jegra could so casually fall in love with a person like Cassera, then she had to have something seriously wrong with her. That much was clear to her by now. But could she be fixed? Or would she just continue down this dark path until she self-destructed?

Jegra chased the thought out of her mind and quickly set to task figuring out her next strategy.

She turned off the faucet and the water drizzled to a stop. Suddenly, it all became clear in her mind and she smiled at her own reflection in the glass wall of the shower stall.

She reached up with her finger and drew the letter "J" on the steamy glass of the shower wall. Then, wiping it away in one swipe of the palm of her hand, she smiled. Emperor Dakroth wouldn't even know what had hit him.

Ellia reappeared in the doorway and bowed. Jegra looked over at her with a blank gaze. "Mistress, Sir Galahad wishes me to inform you that the Dagon fleet has come into range of our scanners and he'll be awaiting your presence on the bridge."

"Excellent," Jegra replied. "Tell him that I'll be there shortly."

Ellia bowed deeply and then started to pull away when she stopped herself. "Mistress?"

Jegra looked up but said nothing.

"I just wanted to apologize for earlier. I was out of line."

"No, you weren't," Jegra said. "You were wronged. And I swear to you, Ellia, I will get vengeance for both you and your family. And for all the Nyctan families my malevolent war-mongering husband has ruined."

23

Effervescent fireballs plumed out of the Nyctan battlecruiser in the distance. Smashing both fists down onto the arms of his command chair, Emperor Dakroth leaned forward and growled. "Who fired that shot?"

"It wasn't us, sire," the officer below him stated, mashing frantically at the keys to keep up with the readings.

"I don't care who it *wasn't*. I want you to find out who it *was*," he snarled.

Dakroth stood up and paced back and forth in front of his chair. Turning back toward the viewscreen, he gazed out at the Nyctan fleet hanging against the backdrop of a purple nebula and a spackle of white stellar dots which spread out into a black void as far as the eye could see.

The second Nyctan ship from the middle was igniting on fire from a disrupter blast that supposedly came from one of Dakroth's ships. This enraged him since he hadn't given the order to fire. What's more, this unfortunate incident ended the ceasefire between the Dagon and Nyctan empires. Now it would devolve into a free-for-all fire fight. And his fleet was already stretched thin as it was.

"Sir, the lead enemy cruiser is hailing us," the officer said, touching an earpiece.

Emperor Dakroth's eyes flashed red and he growled, "Put them through."

Upon seeing Jegra's face appear on the viewscreen, Dakroth stumbled back and fell into his chair. His face when white as he watched with slack-jawed awe at the woman sitting before him.

As he stared, mouth gaping, it almost appeared to him as though Jegra seemed downright pleased by his complete shock and dismay. She flashed him a glimpse of an imperial yet unmistakably haughty smile and then casually uncrossed her legs and stood up to greet him.

"Hi, sweetie-pie. Did you miss me?" Jegra asked in her most playful and desirous manner.

"Wha—what's all this...wait...what? What's happening right now?" Dakroth was, perhaps for the first time in his life, utterly speechless. Rising back to his feet, he demanded to know what was going on. "I don't know what kind of twisted game the Nyctans are playing, but I demand you tell me right this instant. As your emperor, I command you!"

"And, as your empress, I'll tell you what's going on," Jegra said with a sneer. "Your fleet just fired on my fleet. I'm the Empress of Dagon, and rule 400 and 20 dash J makes it quite clear that should a Dagon vessel accidentally fire on another Dagon vessel in a time of war, the person who fired the shot shall forfeit his rank and title, hand over his vessel, and turn himself over to their Sub Commander to be officially court-martialed."

"You have actually read all 1700 codes of the Dagon intergalactic trade and citizenry laws and bylaws?"

"I was going to be the new empress, wasn't I? Seemed like something I should know."

Dakroth flew into a rage and pointed his finger at the officer in front of him and fired off a laser blast. The officer fell out of his chair, his uniform smoking from the blast. No sooner had he hit the ground, however, another officer came over to relieve him.

"I want to know who fired on that vessel and I want to know now!" he growled, pacing back and forth in front of the viewscreen.

"Um, sir..." the new officer said, his voice quivering with fear. "Our internals scans are now saying we were the ones who fired that shot."

"Impossible!" Dakroth roared.

"Sweetums!" Jegra called out in a trill voice from the monitor. "I believe you owe me your ship. And, also, your resignation as Emperor of the Dagon Empire."

"*You traitorous hag!*" Dakroth shouted, pointing his glowing finger at the view screen. "If you were here now I'd laser my way into that scheming, no good, two-faced skull of yours and turn your brains to soup!"

"So, is that a *yes,* then?" Jegra said, sighing out of the corner of her mouth and checking her nails out of boredom. Dakroth's tirades were often tiresome and this one was no exception. She'd lost interest the moment he resorted to petty threats.

At the same time, in her other hand, she fiddled with a black data stick which she'd been holding onto since she'd made the call to his ship. It was the same memory stick that Grendok had given her in the back alleys of Mardok. And, yes, she had read every single file twice over.

"Nice try. But you're not aboard any Dagon vessel and you're not a ranking officer in my fleet, my dear. No Dagon would ever get caught wearing that ridiculous Nyctan armor. You're a traitor, plain and simple. And the rules of the law, well, they don't apply to traitors." He was practically frothing at the mouth, his red eyes wild with rage.

"So, I'll take that as a no, then." Jegra sat back down in her chair, leaned back, and crossed her legs. She still fiddled with the data stick in her fingers, twiddling it between her forefinger and thumb, taunting him with the fact that she had all his secrets right in the palm of her hand.

"Do you know what this is?" she said, holding up the data stick for him to see.

"No, what is it?" he snarled.

"It's all your secrets, my love. It's the fact that you have sequenced my genome without my knowledge or consent. It's the blueprints for your new destroyer that's being built at the secret facility at Cordova that you didn't want anyone to know about. And it's the shield frequencies for all your ships."

Panicked, the emperor spun around and shouted, "Blow that back-stabbing whore out of the sky!"

Jegra blew him a kiss and, leaning forward in her chair, replied with a cold and cool, "See you in hell, darling."

With that, the screen went black.

No sooner had their viewscreens gone to black than a barrage of green and red disrupter blasts erupted between the vessels as both fleets began their relentless exchange of fire. A flamboyant reminded to all the galaxy that this was the lover's quarrel to end all lover's quarrels. But, it's as the saying went, Jegra felt. Truly, hell hath no fury like a woman scorned. Or, for that matter, a woman betrayed by her lover, given up to her enemies, and left for dead.

"Mistress," one of her officers called out to her. She turned her attention back to the matters at hand and shot him a look that urged him to come out with it. "They're already modulating their shield frequencies in an attempt to dampen our disruptor fire."

"That's quite all right," she said, sliding back into her chair. "I only wanted to rattle his cage." Jegra reclined in her chair, arched her back, and uncrossed then recrossed her legs again, repositioning the top onto the bottom and vice versa.

The look on Dakroth's face was worth the vid-call alone. The man didn't handle pressure well. Besides, if she had used the frequencies to decimate his fleet it would have given away the fact that her attack was pre-meditated. No. It had to look as though the blasts had come from him. It had to look like he was the one who'd started the war.

Still fuming aboard his ship, Dakroth paced some more before the view of the battle. "Get the vice admiral on the viewer," Dakroth ordered. He couldn't stop pacing as he waited for the return call.

Finally, the viewscreen came on and Cassera swiveled around in her chair to face him.

"Why have we engaged the Nyctans?" she asked, obviously upset by this turn of events.

"It was Jegra," he informed her. "Somehow she's finagled her way up to the top of the Nyctan chain of command and is leading the imperial fleet with her own invasion force."

"Impossible," she said, taken aback. Jegra was as tenacious as they came, but this was too fantastic to believe. Which meant, in all likelihood, it was true.

"That's what I said!" Dakroth balked.

"What about project Zeta?"

"For now, we'll bide our time. We'll engage the Nyctans with the full force of the Dagon armada, and when they are weakened, I'll be in position to crush them once and for all."

"Are you sure it's wise to take on the Nyctans now? We've lost our flagship and our secret shipyard in less than a month's time. A full assault on the Nyctans will be more damaging to us than to them. If our projections are accurate, our fleet will be diminished by thirty percent while they will only loose about eighteen percent. You'd be giving up the strategic advantage in the system."

"You just carry out my orders and let me worry about the casualties of war. With Zeta ready for launch, we'll make up the difference of that ten percent in no time."

"And if we should lose?"

"We won't," he reassured her. But the truth was, this was going to be the fight that changed the tide or broke the empire's back. Even so, he wasn't planning on going down as the emperor who saw the fall of Dagon. Dakroth had one more trick up his sleeve: Project Zeta.

But that was a last resort–an untested, experimental biological weapon. Something he was sure the Nyctans would appreciate. Something that would have them merrily singing their sacred religious hymns all the way to their destruction.

As thrilled as the thought of laying the Nyctan armada to waste made him, he knew that right now, at this very moment, they had the upper hand. And, perhaps worse still, his darling empress, Jegra Alakandra, had found a way to seize the entire military might of the Nyctans. Now she was coming for him. And that revelation didn't fill him with joy, seeing as he had practically abused her at every turn.

Control. That was his entire game with Jegra. Seeing who could control the other. She had her sex. Her strength. Her intoxicating methods of seduction. He had his cruelty and manipulation. But there was a lot she resented him for; he'd taken so much and given nothing back.

In his mind, that was the most dangerous kind of woman. One who had nothing to lose and everything to gain by his death. And like a fool, he went and married her.

If he would have waited, he could have seized the opportunity at Cordova without having made her his empress. But even trying to cover up the fact by leaking the fake news of her death backfired in his face the moment she came onto the viewscreen. Half his crew saw that broadcast. There was no getting the Vorgathian cat back into the bag, so to speak.

"You called for me, your majesty?"

Dakroth spun in his chair to find a woman with red skin kneeling before him, head bowed. She looked up at him and he smiled. It was his favorite assassin for hire. The same woman he'd hired to kill Abethca.

"Ishtar Bantu," he said cheerfully. "I have a highly classified mission for you. It appears my darling wife somehow managed to survive her shuttle crash. Now, she's aboard a Nyctan destroyer."

Bantu rose up and adjusted her black body armor then gave him a stern look. "You want me to infiltrate a Nyctan cruiser and kill the empress?" she asked.

"Yes," he snarled through his teeth. "Can you do it?"

"It won't be cheap."

"How much?"

"I want thirty million credits, unrestricted access through Dagon space, and I want my entire digital profile to be erased indefinitely."

"You want to be a ghost?"

"Only a ghost could pull off what you're asking for."

"Fine," Dakroth said with a wave of his hand. "Have it your way."

Ishtar Bantu nodded her chin in a subtle display of reverence and then spun and started to march away. As she went, he called out to her.

"Oh, and one more thing. I want you to make it excruciatingly painful."

A malicious grin spread across Ishtar's black painted lips and, without so much as a word, she left the bridge to carry out her wicked task.

Emperor Dakroth put his arms behind his back and turned to gaze back out at the firefight. Green and red lasers crisscrossed in the space between both fleets. The lead ships took the brunt of the disrupter blasts. It was only a matter of time before their shields began to fail and his ships began to burst in a daisy chain of epic explosions which would light up the sky like fireworks.

The Nyctans, after all, had superior shield technology. They'd outlast them in a head-on firefight. Jegra knew this; he was the one who had told her.

Emperor Dakroth's red eyes flashed. Full of fury, he had relished every moment that he tormented Jegra. Making her watch her friend and lover die. Forcing her to kill his useless wives. Making her empress only to take it back from her. Turning her over to his enemies. It was all one long game of ruthless manipulation.

He had even managed to get Cassera to denounce her now that Cassera now had over twenty percent of her DNA rewritten. She wasn't even pure enough to count as a Dagon anymore–a secret she'd rather take to the grave than be generally known.

All Dakroth really had left to do was take Jegra's life from her. Hopefully Ishtar Bantu would make Jegra's death long and painful. Because all he wanted, even more than cracking the secret of her mysterious genetic mysteries, was for his beloved Jegra to suffer. And suffer she would.

<h1 style="text-align:center">24</h1>

"Please, reconsider," Jegra pleaded. She stood before the viewscreen on the *Light Bringer* and stared up at Vice Admiral Cassera Van Danica Amelorak's blue, stoic face.

Cassera's golden eyes and platinum hair shone like the brightest star in the sky and her feminine beauty made Jegra miss her all the more. For the life of her, Jegra couldn't begin to imagine what thoughts might be racing through Cassera's mind right now.

The last time she'd seen Cassera, Jegra was being hunted down by a Knight. Then, three months later, they met upon the battlefield on opposing sides of the fight. Even Jegra had a hard time believing it.

"You, of all people, should know I can't and won't betray my Emperor, my fleet, or my people."

"I'm not asking you to join us," Jegra said, her mouth twisting as she mulled over how best to put it. "All I'm asking is for you not to die on Emperor Dakroth's hill. Not for a man like him. The empire would be better off without him, and I think you know it. Find your own hill to die on, Cassera. Find a leader that's worth dying for."

Cassera opened her mouth to speak, closed it, then opened it again. "I wish it were that simple."

Obviously, the tactic of playing it nice and breaking the news to her gently wasn't working. It was time to take off the padded gloves and talk like adults.

"Look, we both know that the Dagon fleet cannot hold out much longer. You've lost three of your ships already and more will fall if you persist in your prideful obstinance. If you surrender to me now, I will see to it that you and your crew are taken unharmed."

"You know that a Dagon would rather die than surrender to the enemy, Jegra, it's just not possible. Please, accept this for what it is...a mutual parting of ways. The next time we see each other, it will be as enemies."

Jegra's breath caught in her throat and she had trouble breathing. It felt as though her heart was breaking into a thousand pieces and there was nothing she could do to make it stop. "I hope you know what you are doing," she said, on the verge of tears.

"I was going to say the same thing to you." Cassera leaned back in her chair and gazed at Jegra with her naturally perfect resting bitch-face. It was the first time Jegra had felt that Cassera was truly working against her.

With a wave of her hand, the feed of Cassera went away and the display of the space battle came up.

"Galahad," she said, turning to her loyal Knight who stood by her right side.

"That woman is as stubborn as they come. But I know her. I know there is good inside her. If I could only get her to sit down with me face-to-face, I'm certain I could convince her of my plan."

"What would you have me do?"

"I need you to take your best men and go over to that ship and retrieve her for me. She's far too stubborn to leave her post of her own volition. I need someone to, how shall I say this, motivate her to come along."

"Yes, commander." Galahad bowed and then headed off to retrieve Cassera for the commander.

"Mistress, we're getting a hail from the *Omikran*. It's Adjunct High Commander Azra'il Nun."

"Put her through," Jegra responded.

"Why are our ships firing on the Dagons? What happened to the cease fire agreement?"

"I'm afraid Emperor Dakroth grew overly zealous in his desire for control over this sector. Our presence here must have pushed his buttons. He opened fire on us."

"I see," she said, leaning back in her chair and resting her chin on her clasped fingers.

"My orders, your grace?"

"Blow that insufferable deceiver out of the sky," she growled.

"As you wish," Jegra replied with an enthusiastic grin.

"We'll join you with reinforcements within the hour. It's time the Nyctans stop playing nice with the Dagons and put Emperor Dakroth in his place once and for all."

The screen went black and then Jegra swiped her hand and flipped the screen to the outside view of the battle.

As she watched the firefight, laser blast collided with energy shields that lit up each time they were struck, revealing a small portion of a much larger, hidden bubble that engulfed and protected the ships.

The hour was up and, as promised, Azra'il Nun and the first wing of the Nyctan fleet jumped into the fray. A dozen more ships immediately opened fire on the Dagon fleet, their green disruptors pounding the living hell out of Dakroth's soon to be obliterated armada.

"Focus all forward firepower on Dakroth's battlecruiser," Jegra yelled, aiming a finger at the imperial flagship of the Dagon empire. While Azra'il held the other ships at bay, Jegra's five ships, including the *Light Bringer*, all concentrated their fire power on Dakroth's vessel. If he was determined to act like an ass, then she'd pound him like one. Mercilessly and without remorse.

A daisy chain of explosions began erupting across the bow of Dakroth's ship as his shields failed. But to Jegra's surprise, the vice admiral's ship dropped down in front of Dakroth's flaming hunk of space junk and gave him cover.

"Cease your fire," she ordered.

"Ma'am?"

"I want her alive. We need to give Galahad time to extract her. Refocus our main disrupter canons on the remaining ships in the Dagon fleet." The officer did as commanded. Jegra leaned back and thought, now for the boring part of watching ships go down in fiery slow-motion as they leaked trails of flaming gas.

Two hours later, Galahad's shuttle returned to the *Light Bringer*. "Permission to dock," Galahad asked. Behind him, a blue-skinned woman sat with a black sack over her head.

"Permission granted," Jegra replied. As the feed cut out, Jegra got up and informed the bridge crew, "I'll meet them on the hangar deck. Alert me if there are any developments."

"Yes, ma'am," the bridge officer answered.

She hurried to the hangar, anxious to confront Cassera. She arrived just moments before they did and watched as the shuttle rose up through the rectangular opening on the deck.

With a waver, it passed through the blue energy shield that kept the atmosphere in, and then hovered for a moment as the hangar doors slammed shut beneath it.

The craft's landing skiffs extended just in time as it set down and it landed with a loud clunk. The hydraulics whined as the bulk of the ship settled onto its chicken-like legs and there was a loud hiss as air decompressed.

Jegra marched around to the landing ramp, which was slowly coming down. The ramp clanked on the deck of the landing bay and Jegra looked up to see Galahad in full armor, holding the blue-skinned woman's slender arm with his thick gauntlet. Her wrists were bound with korridium restraints.

"I extracted the prisoner as requested, Sub Commander Alakandra," he said, using her formal title.

"Good," Jegra said, smiling. "Leave her to me."

Galahad gave his prisoner a shove and she stumbled down the ramp. He then pulled off her hood to reveal Cassera's scowling face. The moment she saw Jegra standing in front of her she spat at her. "How dare you kidnap me!"

Cassera's spit landed on Jegra's cheek and she calmly reached up and wiped it away with her hand. "Nice to see you again, too," she sarcastically quipped, brushing her hand on her thigh and wiping off the spittle.

"You have no right to take me prisoner! You're breaking so many intergalactic regulations right now!"

"Galahad," Jegra said, turning to her Knight, "you're excused. Update me on anything vital to the mission at twenty-two hundred hours."

He nodded in affirmation of her request and promptly left the landing bay. Once he was gone, Jegra turned toward Cassera and reached down and unlocked her restraints. The korridium handcuffs fell to the floor with a harsh clank.

Cassera rubbed her wrists while Jegra reached out to touch her. "I'm sorry for any discomfort, but—"

Cassera pulled away and shot Jegra a hurt look. "You're sorry? *You're sorry?!* That's rich coming from you."

"Believe me or don't. But the truth is, I haven't lied to you. If anything, we've always been brutally honest with one another. Even when it hurt."

"How's this for brutally honest?" she growled. "I wish that I'd never met you."

"You don't mean that," Jegra replied, her voice catching in her throat.

"Sure, I mean it. So why don't you take me to your brig as your prisoner or send me back. Otherwise, I think we're done here."

Jegra's eyes welled up with tears and she preemptively brushed away a stray one before it had a chance to roll down her cheek.

From behind her, the shuttle bay entrance doors swooshed open and, to her surprise, Ellia entered. Jegra shot her a puzzled look as if to say, what are you doing here? There was no reason for her to be here.

"Ellia?" Jegra asked, confused.

"Mistress, forgive my intrusion, but Sir Galahad just called from his shuttle to inform you that he'll be here within the next half hour."

"But Galahad just arrived with the prisoner," Jegra informed Ellia, turning back toward Cassera.

When their eyes met Jegra's heart dropped. Cassera's eyes weren't the lovely gold she knew so well. They were a muddy yellow. A bad imitation. And that wasn't the only thing off about her. She seemed taller by several inches. And, the final giveaway, her scowl had turned into a smirk.

"Who are you?" Jegra asked.

Before she had time to react, the woman grasped Ellia and reeled her in, taking her hostage. Drawing a korridium blade, she held it to the girl's throat as she clasped her tight. "You fool," the woman laughed. Holding onto Ellia, she slid her hand down the girl's body and then reached across Ellia to touch a device strapped to her own belt.

Jegra glanced down at the device and recognized it. It looked almost identical to the device Gyllek had given her before her arrival at Cordova. A holographic masking device.

The blue skin of Cassera flicked and then dissolved to reveal a red skinned female with black tattoos. The same woman who had murdered Abethca.

"It's you," Jegra gasped.

"Surprise," Ishtar Bantu hissed. Then, without warning, she slit Ellia's throat.

"Nooo!" Jegra screamed as Ellia's blood splattered across her face.

The red-skinned assassin moved fast. Faster than Jegra could react in her bulky armor.

A lacerating pain tore into her abdomen and she looked down to see the korridium blade sticking out of her gut.

"Oops," Ishtar Bantu joked. But of course, her attempted murder was quite deliberate.

Ishtar tried to pry the knife out again, but it was snagged on Jegra's armor. This gave Jegra the opening she needed; she thrust her head forward and headbutted the bitch in front of her.

Their skulls cracked loudly and they both staggered backward. "You'll pay for this," Jegra growled. A sudden surge of pain, however, caused her to drop to one knee. She was already starting to feel lightheaded, too, but with the blade lodged inside her she wasn't bleeding out.

Unable to account for the sudden onset of dizziness, she snarled, "What did you do to me?"

"The blade is coated with the venom of a Kreelak needle spider. The venom is slow acting but extremely lethal, and the pain is said to cause its victims temporary insanity just before death. Oh, and, a little FYI for you, there's no known cure in the entire galaxy."

The red skin assassin walked over and grabbed the knife again. This time she jerked it out with such brutal force that Jegra's insides almost came out with it.

Jegra gripped her wound and sank to her knees, her knee-guards clanking on the deck as she collapsed. Vertigo seized her and she toppled over onto her side. Her vision blurred in and out as she watched Ishtar turn away.

Jegra's blood dripped off the dagger, leaving a dotted trail of crimson as Ishtar returned to the shuttle.

Soon enough, the shuttlecraft rose up as the launch sequence was initiated. Jegra groaned and rolled over the yellow perimeter line to Ellia, who lay a safe distance away from the shuttle bay doors. Exerting herself in this manner, however, caused her to begin to hemorrhage profusely.

With a painful grunt, Jegra turned her head and looked over at Ellia. The young woman's eyes were vacant, yet Jegra could see fearful shock as they stared back at her. And although she was dead, Ellia's blue blood continued gushing out of her neck, pooling a short distance from Jegra's body, which also bled heavily. The red and blue pools of their blood met in the middle and mingled to form a ghastly purple mess.

The shuttle exited the hangar and then darted away. As Jegra watched it leave, she thought to herself, *this sucks royal balls.* Not only had she been poisoned, but she just lost Ellia, a dutiful servant and someone she had begun to think of as a friend. And, to make things worse, the assassin had gotten away. For a second time.

"Dakroth," she snarled, as razorblades of pain surged throughout her entire body.

Even though she didn't have a shred of evidence to prove it, she knew in her gut that this was *his* doing. First, he took Abethca from her. Then, he took her home. Then he married her, betrayed her, and took her title from her all in the course of a week. He left her to his enemies and, now, he was doing it all over again.

"*Fuuuck!*" She screamed out as loud as she could muster, gripping her side. He had played her from the very beginning. And if she somehow survived this ordeal, she swore to whatever god was listening, she'd make him pay.

Just before she blacked-out from the intense pain of the Kreelack needle spider's venom, Ellia's words came back to her. *An eye for an eye, a heart for a heart, an oath for an oath.*

25

Chilled to a fraction above zero, Jegra awoke to find herself suspended inside a large glass cylinder filled with a thick cyan colored gel. A medical issue oxygen mask was strapped to her face with tubes running up and out of the tank as a respirator at the top kept her breathing.

"She's awake," a voice said. But Jegra couldn't make out who it was through the thick, blueish-green slime.

"Begin the thawing process and monitor her vitals."

An odd gurgling sound could be heard as the gel slowly drained from her glass tube and was promptly carried away by giant black hoses. Sinking gradually, her feet finally touched the cold metal bottom of the container.

Her legs were weak and her knees buckled under her weight. She leaned into the glass with her shoulder and pressed her forehead to it as a sharp pain abruptly shot through her frontal lobe and wrapped around to the back of her skull like a nasty migraine.

There was a hiss of air and then a pop which sounded as though a champagne cork was popped and, all of a sudden, the glass container opened.

Jegra spilled out onto the floor, her body smacking against the smooth surface with a sticky sound. The thickness of the gel was enough to break her fall as it oozed out from under her. As the gel warmed, it became the consistency of pudding and gradually dripped off her body, pooling all around her and forming a mottling of gooey islands.

When she tried to push herself up, she slipped on the gel and her cheek slapped the warm floor. It seemed that the ground had been heated to just the right temperature so as to provide her with some measure of comfort as she lay sprawled out on the tile.

She rolled onto her back, peeled off the oxygen mask, and took in a deep breath of fresh air. Wiping the slime from her eyes, she glanced around the room. Above her stood a woman in a fetching red dress. Her all-black eyes and porcelain skin gave away the fact that she was Nyctan.

"Who are you?" Jegra asked, her voice raspy and dry.

The woman settled down next to Jegra. Sitting on her heels and reaching under Jegra's neck, she gently helped her sit up. She cradled her in her arms; she didn't seem to be concerned about joining Jegra in the muck.

A servant soon arrived with a golden chalice and handed it to her. The woman took the cup from the servant, who quickly disappeared out of sight. She brought the chalice to Jegra's lips and said, "Drink."

Jegra craned her neck and her lips met the chalice. She took a long drink and swallowed. The moment she realized it was water, she started to guzzle it, but was too hasty in quenching her thirst and some of it went down the wrong pipe.

After a short bout of coughing, Jegra wiped her mouth and thanked the woman. "I appreciate your kindness." Looking up at the big black eyes that peered down at her, Jegra asked for the woman's name once more. "Who are you, again?"

"I'm Vesta Sanakar," she said, a coy smile spreading onto her face. "The Oracle of Nyctan and the holy seer of the things unseen."

"The oracle?" Jegra gasped. Sanakar smiled at her in reply but didn't say anything. Words weren't necessary.

Jegra looked around the room. It was an ornate sanctum with lots of inlet lighting; there were three women priests on either side of them chanting a kind of meditational hymn as they sat, legs crossed under them. They meditated in the nude, all but for the red paint they wore on their bodies.

The first woman had a red stripe running down her right shoulder and breast while another had an elaborate starburst painted on her. The other four had similar geometric designs painted across their bodies. And although it was strange to be surrounded by naked, chanting women, Jegra didn't feel the least bit disturbed by it. This place had a calming, almost serene atmosphere.

"Where are we? What happened to me?"

"What do you remember?" Sanakar asked in a soothing and sagely voice. She spoke like the Buddhist monks Jegra had met during a rejuvenation retreat she once took back on Earth. Always calm. Always mindful. And always pleasant.

"I remember fighting the red skinned assassin in the hangar. I remember watching her murder poor Ellia. I remember getting stabbed in the side. Then a searing pain so severe I blacked out."

"You were poisoned by Ishtar Bantu, the emperor's private assassin."

"Ishtar Bantu," Jegra repeated. It was the first time she'd heard the name of the woman in red. A name she burned into her memory.

Although Dakroth had been the one to pull the trigger, she was the willing tool. A sentient weapon that gleefully wreaked havoc and mayhem on others at the bidding of her cruel master. And who, Jegra suspected, enjoyed the sport of it as much as he did.

Jegra didn't care which order she killed them in, but each of their days were numbered as certainly as both were going to have the unique pleasure of experiencing her fists reach through their chests and tear out their beating hearts.

Her head finally began to clear up and she blinked, looked down at herself, and noticed that she had on what seemed to be a claret two-piece bathing suit. Her stab wound was almost healed, all except for the thin pink line that demarcated a trace of a scar. Although, her hyper-active healing factor–a lucky side effect of the mysterious injection which had turned her into a super-woman– would soon erase even that.

The scar was already healing nicely as it quickly faded from sight, which clued her in that she'd been under for quite some time.

"How many weeks have I been asleep?"

"Nearly three weeks," answered Sanakar.

"Why so long?" Jegra asked. "I tend to heal more quickly than that."

"The Kreelak needle spider's venom is usually lethal, as there is no known cure. But your unique hyper-immune system was your best bet to fight off the effects, if given adequate time to build enough antibodies to counteract the venom's effects. As such, we immediately had your body chilled to near freezing so that the venom would slow to a crawl, but your immunities would develop exponentially because of your hyper-immune system."

"Apparently, it worked."

"You are blessed," she said with a measured smile that was both wise and kind.

Jegra felt a raindrop, which was strange considering they were inside a large room. Then a gradual mist came down from the ceiling. As water drizzled down her face and body, she tasted what seemed like a saline solution. The slime on her body instantly dissolved and washed away in the runoff. Looking over at Sanakar, she saw the woman's dress getting soaked. "You're getting drenched," Jegra said.

Sanakar stood up and helped Jegra to her feet.

"It's all right," she assured her. "Come with me, my child."

It was weird, Jegra thought, to have someone roughly her same age call her *child*. But she knew it must be a religious thing. Either that or the universal translator was on the fritz again.

As they walked down the length of the room upon a red carpet that was laid out for ceremonial purposes, a series of rods rose from the ground, running the entire length of the chamber all the way to the large doors at the end.

Each rod, separated by about five feet, had a dozen tiny holes in it and as they passed by the rods, they shot warm air at them, gently drying them as they passed. By the time Jegra and Sanakar arrived at the doors they had been thoroughly dry-cleaned.

"Amazing," Jegra said as she studied her arms for any signs of leftover goo. But she was completely 'Spic and Span'.

When they got to the gigantic door at the end of the red carpet, the entrance parted in the middle and the doors pulled away to reveal towering windows looking out onto space. In the distance was another gigantic Nyctan battle cruiser flying in formation alongside them.

Dressed in red cloaks and waiting for them on either side of the entrance were two Nyctan priestesses who greeted them when they stepped out into the ship's corridor. Extending their arms with garments draped over them, they held out a long, gossamer robe of red with golden floral embroidery patterns for Jegra and bowed reverently as they presented her with it.

Sanakar gestured to them to help her slip into it and as quickly and silently as their orders they dutifully attended her, wrapping her up as though in a ceremonial kimono and tying off the broad, silken sash. Jegra spun once, taking a moment to admire the lavish dress.

Sanakar motioned for Jegra to walk beside her and they strolled down a long corridor with tall glass windows. Outside was the debris of a catastrophic space battle, and the remains of Dakroth's fleet glittered in the sky.

"What happened to Dakroth?" Jegra asked.

"Unfortunately, he managed to escape in a shuttle," Sanakar answered.

Of course he did, Jegra thought. He always had an out. And he probably sacrificed his entire crew just to save his own neck. For although Dakroth was undeniably a great warrior, he was without honor.

"This ship is too big to be the *Light Bringer*," Jegra observed.

"You're aboard the *Omikran*," Sanakar replied. "The *Light Bringer* is currently engaged with three Dagon battle-cruisers at the coordinates of the secret program, Project Zeta."

Jegra stopped in her tracks and grabbed Sanakar's arm. Sanakar glanced down at her hand, unaccustomed to being touched in such a casual manner, and then looked up at Jegra. "We have to call them back. Project Zeta is a ruse."

"A ruse for what, exactly?" asked Sanakar.

"I'm not sure. But there's nothing out here. Of that much I am certain."

"If so, why would Dakroth devote so much of the fleet to protect absolutely nothing?"

"My best bet is he was baiting us into a trap."

Sanakar raised an eyebrow as she mulled it over. But other than the slight pique in her curiosity, she remained unconvinced. "I'm sure Galahad has everything under control. Besides, once the doctors give you a clean bill of health, you will rejoin the Knights."

They hooked a right at the end of the corridor and got into a mag-lift elevator. Sanakar tapped the control panel and the elevator began to descend at a rapid, unnervingly frictionless speed. Jegra didn't even know how to explain the sensation of a magnetically guided elevator because it was entirely alien to her. In more ways than one.

"Wait," Jegra said, realizing they were headed the wrong way. "If I recall correctly, my quarters are on the upper deck."

"I'm not taking you to your quarters," Sanakar replied.

"You're not?" Jegra inquired, a puzzled expression stuck on her face.

"I'm taking you to see someone."

The elevator jolted to a stop, bobbing up and down ever so briefly before finding its equilibrium, and the doors slid open. They exited and went down a long passage. In the middle there was a door with two guards standing outside. When they saw Sanakar, their sacred oracle, they bowed their heads reverently and let her and Jegra enter the room.

"The brig?" Jegra asked, as they entered a large hexagonal shaped room with six cells. Each cell had one facing wall of glass so guards could see the prisoner at all times, but all the cells were empty, except for one. When Jegra saw who it was she cried out in joy. "Cassera!"

Cassera slowly rose to her feet and staggered to the glass, holding her side. She had a bruise on her forehead, a split-open lip, and looked terribly battered. Jegra went over to her cell and placed her hand on the glass divide. "What happened?"

"Apparently the Nyctans aren't above torture," she replied, shooting Sanakar a spiteful look.

Sanakar, in her perpetually sagely tone, informed them, "I shall leave you two alone." She bowed her head and slowly drew away from them, allowing them their privacy.

Before leaving, Sanakar hit a panel on the wall and the door to Cassera's glass cage slid open. With that, she excused herself from the room.

Once she was gone, Jegra rushed into the cell and embraced Cassera. But Cassera was so weak that she collapsed into Jegra's arms. Slowly, they both sank to the floor and sat together.

"I thought I was going to wilt and die," she said, breaking into sobs. "They never even asked me any questions."

"*Shhh*," Jegra consoled, hushing her and rocking her in her arms. "I won't let anything else bad happen to you."

Cassera placed her head on Jegra's chest and sobbed quietly as a child would with a mother. It was the first time Jegra had ever seen Cassera emotionally broken down. Although she didn't like to see her best friend in this condition, she knew that the only thing Cassera needed right now was a bit of love and warmth. And that, she could provide.

"Come, let's get you mended," Jegra said, hoisting Cassera up along with her. They went to the doors, which swished open, and headed out of the brig. As they limped out into the corridor, the two guards shared perplexed glances as they tried to figure out whether this was allowed.

"Ma'am," the guard on the right said, clearing his throat. "I don't think you have clearance for…"

Jegra shot him a sharp look that put him in his place. "It's Sub Commander Alakandra, ensign," she snapped. "Report me if you wish, but I'm taking this woman to my quarters. She'll be confined there until further notice. Do I make myself clear?"

The two guards glanced at one another a second time and, not wanting to challenge Jegra on the matter, stepped aside and allowed them to pass freely.

After arriving at her quarters, she promptly secured her door behind them ensuring they'd have privacy. Then, heading over to her bed, she gently set Cassera down.

Cautiously peeling off her clothes from her battered and bruised form one delicate layer at a time, Jegra stripped Cassera bare. When she saw the amount of damage that had been done to her lover's body she burst into tears.

"Jegra," Cassera said, putting her arm on Jegra's shoulder. "I'm alive. And here with you. That's all that matters now."

Jegra remembered when Estan gave her the medical scan and rushed to the corner of the room. Feeling along the wall, she fumbled for the release to the wall panel. She hit the buttons at random until the panel slid open; she took out the med-kit and hurried back to the bed.

Inside the kit were several ointments and a device that looked like a mix between a flashlight and a magic wand. Jegra turned it on. It emitted a soothing orange light which she ran across Cassera's wounds. After several passes, the wounds began to shrink away as her healing was stimulated.

An hour crept by and Jegra had done everything she could. Although she was able to heal most of the cosmetic damage, she knew that Cassera's insides must be bruised terribly. "Rest," she said, laying Cassera onto her bed.

Jegra pulled her comforter up and tucked Cassera in and then lay down on the bed beside her. She stroked Cassera's platinum hair until she drifted off to sleep.

The thought of Cassera's abuse aroused an anger from deep within Jegra, and she wanted to get an explanation for this terrible act of cruelty. Rising out of bed, she paced the room trying to figure out the best way to go about it. That's when she saw it; a light bulb went on in her head.

In the corner of her room, Jegra found her armor waiting for her. Even though it took her about three times as long to get into it without servants to help her, she managed to fully suit up. Twisting her arm bracer so it locked into place, the suit turned on and the servos and hydraulic assists came to life.

Jegra looked over at Cassera sleeping and then turned back toward her door. She wanted to march onto the *Omikran's* bridge and grab whichever cruel bitch was standing there and choke them until they begged for mercy.

Of course, she knew that wouldn't go over well, so she stopped in front of her door and let out a long sigh.

All anybody wanted to do in this godforsaken part of the galaxy, it seemed, was dominate one another. Although she had the strength to make them fear her, she knew that it would take a cool head and a fair bit of cunning to prevail.

Out of the blue her door chimed, bringing her back to the present. She had a visitor. Smacking the panel, she opened the door and Azra'il Nun drew back, startled by the unexpected sight of a fully armored Knight standing in the entrance.

"Sub Commander," she said, her voice a bit shaken by the sudden surprise. "You look well."

"As well as can be expected," Jegra replied. Her voice was emotionless. Just cold and to the point.

Glancing over her shoulder at Cassera sleeping in Jegra's bed, Azra'il Nun said, "I heard you released the prisoner into your custody."

Jegra stepped to the side, interrupting her line of sight. Forcing Azra'il to look her in the eyes, Jegra said, "You've already used the stick, to no avail. It's time we try the carrot."

"As you wish," she said with a coy smile.

Jegra took a step forward and forced Azra'il to step out of her way. The doors slid shut behind her and she glanced at the commander. "Brief me on what we know so far."

Azra'il began to fill her in on everything that had happened as they headed to the bridge. "We have five cruisers and three frigates left after the battle. Emperor Dakroth, however, is down to his last three ships, I'm pleased to inform. Our victory is imminent."

"What of the *Light Bringer?*" Jegra asked, inquiring as to the status of her ship.

"Sir Galahad is hunting down the last of Dakroth's fleet and investigating the celestial object's last known whereabouts."

"I know it's not my position to question your orders, High Commander, but it's my opinion that this creature poses a risk to us. I think we should regroup and investigate further."

"Investigate further?" Azra'il chortled. "I thought you were a woman of action, Sub Commander."

The bridge doors opened with a hiss and they stepped onto the bridge. All heads turned to them and bowed when they saw the high commander and sub commander enter.

"As you were," Azra'il said, gesturing the crew to return to their duties with a wave of her hand.

In the middle of the room stood Anaïs Nin , her back to them.

"Your grace," Azra'il Nun said, taking a knee before the administratrix. Jegra did the same.

Anaïs Nin turned to greet them. "Rise, my fierce and loyal warriors." Anaïs Nin beckoned them to rise and they did. "I'm pleased to see you up and about, Jegra," she said, smiling at Jegra.

Her black eyes were hard to read, Jegra felt, but she showed the proper etiquette and bowed respectfully. "It's good to be back," she answered, slowly rising again.

"I'm afraid your weasel of a husband tucked tale and fled, like the wretched dog he is. But no matter. After we destroy his beloved secret project, the Nyctan Empire will reign supreme."

"That's what I'm here to talk to you about," Jegra said. "Although I'd never question your judgement, I do ask we tread with caution. There's something not right here."

"My dear, you just came out of a most terrible ordeal and I fear you're not thinking as clearly as you would, given the proper amount of rest. All I ask is that you put your faith in me like you always have. In the meantime, I'm ordering you to take some leave. Not long, just a day or two, to better catch your bearings."

Anaïs Nin took Jegra's hand in hers and patted it. Jegra nodded, deferring to the administratrix's superiority.

"Good," Anaïs Nin said, the corners of her mouth curling into a manipulative smile. "Now, go get some rest. I want you ready for deployment as soon as the *Light Bringer* returns."

Jegra bowed and then stormed off the bridge. She was angry that nobody would listen to her. But, more than this, she had the strangest sensation, like a premonition, that Project Zeta was going to be something terrible.

26

"No! Get away from me!" Cassera shook herself awake and shot straight up in bed.

Sweat dappled her chest and trickled down her back as she trembled with the residue of fear left by the intensity of her nightmare. Her eyes watered with dread induced tears and her breathing was shallow from the anxiety laden distress of her rude awakening.

The nightmare played fresh in her mind. She was surrounded by black eyes and vicious smiling faces. Her Nyctan tormentors gleefully inflicted pain on her with electric batons with which they clubbed and shocked her repeatedly.

She pleaded for them to stop, but they yelled at her to be silent. Called her a "Dagon mongrel not worth spitting on." They stripped her bare. Doused her in water. And repeated the cruel act of beating and electrocution until she was curled up in a ball on the floor begging them to stop.

But they didn't stop. They continued to beat her until she blacked out. How long they continued to beat her after that, she didn't know. She only remembered waking up in the brig, having been denied any medical treatment to mend her wounds. It was barbaric, even by Dagon standards.

The worst thing about it, however, was that it wasn't a nightmare at all. It was a memory.

Jegra rolled over to find Cassera sitting up in bed, drenched in sweat, and panting for breath as her heart pounded frantically in her chest.

"It was just a bad dream," Jegra consoled, sitting up alongside her and gently placing a warm hand on Cassera's cool back. "That's all."

Cassera turned to Jegra, tears brimming, and threw her arms around her.

Sobbing into Jegra's neck, she whimpered, "What did they do to me?"

"I don't know," Jegra said. "But I promise you that I won't let them hurt you anymore. Not while I have anything to say about it."

"When the shuttle brought me here, I thought you would be the one to collect me when I arrived. But it was that cold-hearted witch Azra'il Nun and a full squad of soldiers. After she had me shackled, she informed me that you had been attacked and severely wounded. I felt terrible, but only half as terrible when she informed me that I was to blame for it all."

"Oh, honey," Jegra said, embracing Cassera. "It wasn't your fault."

"But, in a way, it was. I didn't listen to you when you asked me to come to you. I thought that by being loyal to the emperor, I was being loyal to the cause. I had no idea that Dakroth had sent an assassin to kill you until they informed me of it. I swear to you, Jegra. If I'd have known, I would have tried to warn you somehow."

"I know," Jegra said, stroking Cassera's hair. "I know."

Her hands found the sides of Cassera's beautiful blue face and she pulled her face close, leaned in, and kissed the Dagon's incredible Prussian blue lips.

A comm alert bleeped, signaling an incoming call, and a voice came on Jegra's personal intercom.

"Sorry for the early wake up call, commander," the voice on the other end said. She recognized the voice as one of the officer's, but couldn't put a face to him. "We're picking up a distress signal from the *Light Bringer*. I thought you might like to know."

Jegra shot out of bed, tossing her blankets and pillows aside, and immediately replied, "It's no problem. I was already awake. I'll be up shortly."

The comm chimed a melodic yet distinctly lower tone, signaling the end of the call, and cut out. Jegra quickly dressed and rushed to the exit to leave. Before heading out, however, she looked back at Cassera.

She sat up in bed, her arms outstretched above her head as she let out a dreary yawn. This brought a smile to Jegra's face. When she caught Jegra watching her, she blushed and smiled. "Be careful."

"I will. Now, go back to bed and get some rest. I'll be back as soon as I can. The food synthesizer will provide you with anything you might need. I think you'll find the Earth dish called a 'deluxe cheeseburger and a Coke' quite interesting." With that Jegra spun on her heel and raced to the bridge.

When she arrived on the bridge Anaïs Nin and Azra'il Nun were nowhere to be found. She was the only senior officer. "Where's the Administratrix and High Commander?"

"The Administratrix is off duty. But the High Commander will be here shortly," a handsome young ensign replied. Jegra gave him the good ole double take because she was surprised at how chiseled his jawline was. He was like the Henry Cavill of the Nyctan Empire.

Shaking her head and clearing her mind, she turned to the viewscreen. "Show me the *Light Bringer.*"

The picture came on to the monitor and Jegra squinted. "Is that a giant, gold glowing space squid?"

"We believe it's Project Zeta, commander," the officer answered.

"That's Project Zeta?" Jegra hadn't had any idea of what to expect but she didn't expect this. Whatever *this* was.

The monster squid, which, shockingly enough, rivaled even the size of the *Omikran,* the flagship of the Nyctan Empire, already had two of Dakroth's own ships wrapped up in its tentacles. The third ship hung back a safe distance, so as not to meet the same fate as its comrades.

Something about it didn't sit right with her. Why would Dakroth's own top-secret project be attacking his ships? Jegra had the nagging suspicion that, somehow, this wasn't Project Zeta. This was something else entirely.

The creature's tentacles pulsed with waves of energy as it coiled its appendages around the ships. It seemed to be somehow syphoning energy from the vessels.

A giant explosion erupted as one of the ships' fusion cores went critical. But instead of the typical supernova-styled explosion that accompanies a starship when its core breaches, the energy blast was quickly absorbed by the giant glowing squid-thing.

Not waiting around to become the monstrosity's next victim, the last remaining Dagon ship jumped out of the system with a crack of thunder.

Jegra watched in awe as the squid grew even larger before her very eyes. Obviously, it fed on energy, and starships were just little delicious nuclear treats to it.

If Dakroth was behind this, he'd succeeded in creating the ultimate weapon. A starship killer. And as fascinating as that may be, she knew this was no time to study it. She had to kill it before it headed off into space, wreaking havoc and destruction everywhere it went.

"Ensign," she said in a commanding tone. "Lock disrupters on that…thing. And fire."

"Yes, commander," he replied. Before he could target it and fire, however, Azra'il Nun stormed onto the bridge.

"Belay that order!" she huffed. Stepping up alongside Jegra, she gazed out at the entity along with her.

"We need to destroy it," Jegra insisted. "Before it gets too powerful and threatens to destroy all of us, if not half the system."

"I have orders to try and communicate with it."

"Communicate with it?" Jegra gasped. "Are you out of your mind? That thing just ate an entire starship. It's a weapon of mass destruction, plain and simple!"

"Weapon or not, we won't know if it's sentient until we try to communicate with it. And if it is, opening a dialog with the creature may serve us far better than pissing it off."

Although Jegra agreed with the impulse to try and communicate with it, she knew that monsters that size rarely ever had the kind of intelligence one saw in other advanced beings. Monsters were usually just monsters. And, like Ahab's great white whale, they rarely cared about what stood in their path of destruction.

Azra'il Nun ordered the officer to hail the *Light Bringer*. The viewscreen came on and Galahad was standing aboard the bridge, his gaze fixed offscreen as golden light fell onto his face.

"Update," Azra'il said.

"This thing is pure energy," he replied. "It's like nothing we've ever encountered before."

"What does it seem to want?"

"Only to feed, High Commander," he answered.

"Is there any way you can communicate with it?"

"It hasn't responded to any hails in any of the thirty-seven thousand known languages in the universal translator. We tried light patterns and sound waves. It was unresponsive to all."

"Have you tried low-yield disruptor bursts?"

"The ship it just crushed had tried that to no effect. The creature merely absorbed the blasts as though it were a sponge soaking up water. Our only resort may be to fire a missile at it, but even then, it may not do any good."

Azra'il turned to Jegra. "It seems we will be doing it your way, after all." Turning back toward the viewscreen, she addressed Galahad.

"Fire when ready. But keep your distance. Should you anger it, I don't want to lose the *Light Bringer*."

Galahad bowed and then strode offscreen. Once he had disappeared from view, Azra'il swiped the screen away with a flick of her wrist and then swiped again to bring up the current view. Holding her hand up, she spread her fingers, fanning them wide, and the motion sensor read her subtle gesture and zoomed in on the scene.

The giant squid was wrapping its glowing tentacles around the second ship. Each snake-like appendage slowly coiled around the ship like a boa constrictor wrapping up its prey and tightening.

After a while, the celestial space-squid tightened its grip and the tangled-up ship bent as its hull buckled. This was followed by a concussive explosion which burst from the crumpled section of the hull. The fiery blast began to plume outward but then quickly reversed course and was sucked back as the creature's body absorbed every ounce of energy.

With the final Dagon ship destroyed, only the Nyctan fleet remained; seven ships in total after the battle with the Dagons. Now, Jegra's worries turned to the Nyctan fleet. With the Dagons out of the way, they were next on the menu. And *squidy* looked hungry.

The creature began to radiate bright, golden light and the residual effects of consuming so much nuclear energy caused it to grow exponentially. Now it was large enough to arrest the *Omikran*, the largest ship in the fleet, if it so chose.

Jegra took a step forward and studied the creature closely. Its tentacles slowly uncoiled and spread open. They swayed and rippled as if they were in a vast ocean as they unfurled themselves. It was beautiful, she thought. But, at the same time, she knew it was the most dangerous thing she'd encountered in her brief time in space.

A barrage of missiles fired from the *Light Bringer* as it flew toward the creature. The warheads began pelting the space-squid in quick succession, setting off a daisy chain of a dozen neutron explosions.

Squidy jolted back but immediately course-corrected itself and moved into the radiation field. Absorbing the energy of the high yield explosions, it basked in the afterglow of the nuclear assault. It glowed softly and looked peaceful, as though it were enjoying a nice salt bath.

Galahad came back onto the viewscreen. "High Commander," he said, bowing his head. "The missiles had little effect. The creature seems able to absorb every form of energy thrown at it. Even the kinetic friction of the ship's hull buckling was absorbed by it. Perhaps the only thing capable of taking it out is an anti-matter warhead."

"Anti-matter?" Jegra asked. "Do we even have any of those?"

"No," Azra'il replied tersely. "The technology is still only theoretical. Nobody has been able to stabilize anti-matter before it bonds with ordinary matter and erases itself."

"What about the black hole?" Jegra inquired.

"What about it?" Azra'il Nun asked, looking over to the far right of the monitor at the black hole glowing in the distance with its split double-halo, a trail of debris from the space battle mingling with the asteroid belt that was forming around it.

"If we could use the *Omikran*'s mega-thrusters, it might be enough to push the creature into the black hole."

Azra'il shot Jegra a surprised look. "That might just work. The only question is, where would the crew evacuate to?"

"The remaining seven ships, including *Light Bringer*, could be modified to hold all the *Omikran*'s crew and personnel. Each ship's cargo hold and shuttle bay would need to be refitted to house the *Omikran*'s crew, but it's doable."

"It will take time. Something we may not have the luxury of. What's to say that thing won't attack us while we're just floating out here making preparations?"

"I don't have any guarantees, but I'm betting on the fact that it has just fed so it won't be requiring its next meal anytime soon."

"Sir, we're reading an energy surge," the handsome officer said.

"From the creature?" Azra'il asked.

An alert chimed and he double checked his console. "No, commander. It appears to be coming from hyperspace."

"Hyperspace?" she repeated, at a loss to explain the peculiar readings.

The *Omikran* shuddered as an enormous ship jumped into the system just in front of its starboard bow. The thunderous boom caused everyone to cover their ears.

The triangular, wedge-shaped ship was charcoal gray, and its many windows were lighted, causing it to blend in with the stars. It was Goliath, nearly three times larger than the *Omikran*. And by the stunned looks on the bridge crew's face, nobody had ever seen anything like it.

"What is that thing?"

Jegra stared out at the giant triangular ship floating out in space. It reminded her of Dakroth's old flagship, the *Dreadnaught*, and that's when it sunk in. The sheer vanity of it. The absurd size of it trying to compensate for an ego of equal mass but which was as fragile as an egg shell. It was most definitely Emperor Dakroth's.

"I have a bad feeling about this," Jegra said.

Without warning, the massive destroyer trained its cannons on the Nyctan fleet and began firing at will. A relentless barrage of red laser blasts hailed down from the ugly vessel as it opened with a volley of fire power that rivaled all the remaining Nyctan ships combined.

"Evasive action!" Azra'il shouted.

Jegra stepped in, "Open a fleet wide communiqué," she ordered. The officer nodded at her when she was live. "This is Sub Commander Jegra Alakandra. The fleet is under attack by an unknown enemy vessel. All ships, protect the *Omikran* at all costs."

"You heard the lady," Azra'il growled while the crew looked to her to override Jegra's orders. But to Jegra's surprise, the high commander fully backed her strategy.

The remaining seven ships repositioned themselves between the *Omikran* and the beast of a warship that had just appeared in front of them. Using their shields, they provided cover to protect the *Omikran* long enough for them to deal with the space-squid.

"The blockade won't hold that thing for long. Not at the rate that they're getting bombarded by that disruptor fire," Azra'il said.

"I know," Jegra sighed. She stood next to the high commander watching the onslaught.

That infernal ship had enough fire power to decimate a fleet twice their size. It would eat all seven of the remaining Nyctan ships for breakfast and leave nothing but the carcasses of their burning hulls.

She knew she'd need a new strategy if she hoped to go up against Dakroth's juggernaut of a war ship. The only thing Jegra knew right now was that she wasn't going to let Dakroth defeat her. Not this time. This time, she'd show him a thing or two. That was a promise.

27

The mammoth warship continued its relentless volley of firepower as it targeted the remaining Nyctan ships. Jegra frowned and turned to the handsome officer to her right. "Hail that ship," she said.

He looked at her and shook his head, informing her that it was no good. They weren't responding.

"Send my dear idiot husband this message," she replied. "Tell him, it's not the size of the starship that matters, it's how you use it. And signal the *Light Bringer* to pick me up," she said turning toward the exit.

The high commander nodded at Jegra, to inform her that she was free to go, and then shot the handsome officer a look that said get on it. He quickly set to his task and hailed the *Light Bringer*, calling them to pick up Jegra.

She rushed to her quarters and quickly began gathering her things and whatever else she might need. After a moment she realized that Cassera wasn't anywhere to be found. Then she heard a loud belch escape from the bathroom.

"Are you okay in there?" Jegra asked aloud. She waited for a response and watched amusedly as the bathroom door abruptly slid open.

Cassera, who was now dressed in a form fitting, light gray tank-top and matching yoga pants that accentuated her heavenly ass, held an empty Coke bottle in her hand and scowled at Jegra. "What in Dagon did you do to me?! This stuff is...*burp*...hideous. The bubbles, they...*burp*...are still going up into my nose. And I can't...*burp*... stop belching like a flame breathing Tagarian lizard. *Burp!*"

Jegra smothered a laugh. "I think you look cute when you're helpless against the wiles of a fizzy beverage."

"How do your people…*burp*…stomach this stuff? I was…*burp*…trying to get myself to gag it back up. But it seems to have…*burp*…evaporated from…*burp*…my stomach!"

Jegra sauntered over to Cassera, grabbed her waist, and pulled her in close. She kissed her on the lips long and hard and then the inevitable happened. Cassera burped into her mouth. Both women shot each other surprised glances and then, as if on cue, they burst out laughing.

The laughter between them felt good. Wiping away tears of joy, Jegra said, "You should be glad it only makes you burp."

"Don't think I'm not on to you," Cassera said in an accusing tone, wagging a finger at Jegra. At a loss, all Jegra could do was blink and wait for her to finish. "You're trying to make me more like you. Obnoxiously crude, bodily functions erupting all over the place, foul odors emanating from who knows where twenty-four-seven," she jested.

"Admit it," Jegra said. "You love it because you love me."

Cassera brushed her silver hair back behind her blue, pointy-tipped ear and squinted at Jegra with a faux menace. Then she laughed only to interrupt herself with another belch. "I'll admit no such thing."

Jegra pulled her in again and kissed her once more. "Admit it. You can't get enough of me," she insisted.

"Is that so?"

"Yeah," Jegra answered, playfully watching the minute movements of Cassera's lovely mouth.

Cassera bit her lower lip. "Jegra," she replied, her voice turning sultry as her gaze fell to Jegra's pink, fleshy, lips, "it seems you have that 'thirsty' look in your eyes."

"You know me, babe. Always thirsty. But *that* will have to wait," she said, pulling away. "Right now, the *Light Bringer* is on its way to rendezvous with us."

"Why? What's going on? *Hic*!"

"Our dear little emperor's pet project has escaped, and is now eating starships for breakfast."

"Eating?" Cassera asked, a confused look coming over her face. Jegra looked at her with a blank stare. Something wasn't adding up here. "What are you talking about?" Cassera asked. "Dakroth's top secret project was a new, super heavy battlecruiser. A feat of Dagon engineering like nothing the Galaxy has ever seen before." Rolling her eyes, she added in a snarky tone, "He calls it the *Subjugator.*"

"Right then," Jegra replied. After all, that did sound more like Dakroth. "So, the glowing space squid-thing isn't—?"

"No," Cassera said, placing her hands on her hips. "I'm afraid not. In fact, the entire blockade was a ruse. A diversion to allow him to launch the ship from his secret shipyard just beyond Cordova."

"So that's the real reason we went to Cordova."

"I'm afraid so. I should have been up front with you, but I had no idea he was going to betray you. When the Nyctans showed up and that Knight chased you into the desert, my heart broke for you."

"So, why do you still serve that ass-wipe?" Jegra gave Cassera a long hard look. Cassera looked down at her feet.

"I have devoted my entire life to serving the emperor. But now...now all I want is to remain by your side. If you'll have me."

Cassera didn't know whether these feelings came from the human side of her–the part of her which had gradually been transformed by Jegra's DNA–or if these were her own genuine feelings. But she shrugged it off as unimportant. Jegra was right. It was time to make a choice and take sides. And the emperor's side was a losing one.

Jegra reached over and raised Cassera's chin and grinned at her for a long time. So long that it became a little awkward.

"Why are you smiling at me like that?"

"Because," Jegra said with a laugh, "I think I love you."

"You do realize we're all totally fucked though, right?"

The door chimed and Jegra looked at Cassera with wide eyes. "Shit. It's time. Get dressed."

Jegra had her servants, Estan and Laquiea, create a special suit of armor for Cassera. It only took about thirty minutes for them to gather all their provisions and meet Sanakar on the hangar deck.

"The armor suits you," Sanakar said to Cassera.

"Jegra informs me that your regulations state a high priority prisoner must be protected at all times."

"This is true," Sanakar replied, blinking her black eyes at them as her lips formed a sly grin.

"Except when she's being tortured," Cassera added.

The two women glared at each other for a couple of seconds and then Sanakar gave a remorseful nod. "A regrettable tactic. But one which the administratrix believed necessary."

"And nobody ever questions your supreme leader?" Cassera's voice was filled with anger which she wore on top of the pain like a suit of armor.

"Does anyone ever question your beloved emperor?"

"I did," Cassera informed Sanakar.

"As did I," Jegra added, bolstering her claim.

Sanakar answered in a calm voice. "Like your emperor, she considered her council's advice. In the end, Anaïs Nin chose what she felt was best for the Nyctan Empire. Are you telling me your people wouldn't have done the same?"

"We don't torture prisoners," Cassera said.

"No, you don't," Sanakar agreed. "You merely execute them."

Both women stared at each other with faux smiles, each trying to act more civilized than the other. Jegra knew, however, that the reality of it all was much more complicated.

Both races had been at war for at least three hundred years, by what Jegra could gather. And there was no quick, easy fix for two neighboring cultures that couldn't seem to even agree to disagree.

When power and domination is all one cares about, then bloodshed is bound to follow. People, as it turned out, don't like being subjugated.

And, as a wise man once said, 'absolute power corrupts absolutely'. Which is why the only way to achieve lasting peace, Jegra thought, was to forego the desire for power and instead take up the desire to spread love and compassion. But even that was difficult to achieve in the cold, dark recesses of intergalactic space.

According to the computer data banks aboard the *Omikran*, the feud between the Nyctans and Dagons had begun when a Dagon and rogue prophet of Hastur, named Thygron Addorix, left Dagon to preach his people's sacred gospels to outer rim settlers. Five decades soon passed by and a new cult had formed around the itinerant holy man's teachings.

The original colony, of course, consisted of mostly Nyctans, who then took this new religion, along with Thygron's sacred holy book, the Enchiridion of Hastur, back to their world as missionaries. The religion spread from there.

Regardless of how it all started, the beliefs were quite similar in ways but, at the same time, quite distinct. From what Jegra could gather from her reading, the Nyctan have a robust faith in the illusive yet always aware Gilded Master. A being of pure radiance that would return and balance the darkness with his golden light.

The Dagons, believe the same, more or less. A Golden being of pure radiance, they call Hastur, shall return to them and like Shiva, will destroy and rebuild the universe, keeping only his chosen people.

The question then became, which of the alien races were the true chosen people? Nyctans or Dagons? A theological dispute arose over Thygron's teachings and whether he was a theologaster and a false prophet or the real deal. It was obvious which side believed which claim.

Accusations arose that the Nyctans had culturally appropriated the Dagon god to gain favor with the interplanetary trade federation, thereby managing to secure the key galactic trade routes which the Dagons had traditionally benefited from.

Now, what had begun as a theological dispute also became embroiled in a land dispute regarding which race had the right to trade along the Golden Vail, a region of space both groups believe to be sacred ground—as it was the prophesied location where Hastur would one day return.

But, as always seems to be the case, the tensions between the races grew to a boiling point and, soon enough, there were civil disputes all across the galaxy.

Zealous and quasi-religious protest groups formed. Rival factions clashed at every interplanetary hub in the galaxy and the opposing factions grew more and more violent.

Eventually, it all came to a head at the intergalactic peace talks where a suicide bomber killed half the delegation. Both sides blamed the other with no faction claiming responsibility and the Nyctans and Dagons went to war to settle their grievances.

Fast forward three hundred years later, and here they were. Still at it. Fighting over the same god and the same plot of interstellar land.

It was a never-ending song and dance, Jegra thought. War, after all, was easier than peace. And cruelty was easier to come by than compassion. This was the way it had always been, and Jegra didn't see it changing anytime soon.

The handsome bridge ensign Jegra had made note of earlier emerged from the shuttlecraft and addressed her. "The shuttle is prepped and ready for departure, Sub Commander."

"Thank you," she said. "Will you be joining us?"

Cassera raised an eyebrow, noticing Jegra's attraction to the young man.

"Yes, ma'am," he replied. Then, turning to the oracle, he bowed reverently. Sanakar bowed in return and then placed her hand on his head and gave him a blessing. He quickly helped her with her things and promptly loaded them onto the ship.

"Estriel is one of my most faithful followers," informed Sanakar.

"Estriel?" Jegra repeated.

Cassera leaned in and whispered into Jegra's ear. "You so have the hots for him."

"Hush, you," Jegra said out of the corner of her mouth. And elbowed Cassera lightly in her ribs. "The oracle will hear you."

"Oh, I'm sure she is well aware," Cassera said, jabbing Jegra's ribs to get her back. "The amount of drool coming down your chin is a dead giveaway."

"*Shhh*," Jegra shushed, holding a finger up to her lips.

"Ladies, if you'll kindly step aboard the shuttle," Estriel said from the arch of the shuttle's back entrance, gesturing for them to board.

"Why aren't we using the quantum transportation device?" Sanakar asked, as she headed up the ramp and into the shuttle.

"Ever since the presence of the creature, it was deemed all energy transference devices were unsafe. Therefore, we have to travel the old-fashioned way," Estriel replied.

Jegra motioned for Cassera to go on ahead. She smiled and stepped up into the shuttle. As she did, Jegra gave her a welt inducing slap to her ass. She stopped in her tracks, let out a sigh, and kicked herself for not having seen what was coming sooner.

Jegra turned to her servants, who waited on standby, should she need them. She nodded at them, and they responded in kind. With that, Jegra marched onto the shuttle and closed the ramp-door behind her.

Jegra took the co-pilot's seat next to Estriel. He turned and smiled at her. "I didn't realize that you knew how to fly one of these things."

"It was part of my three-month long crash course with Galahad. I guess he figured a dumb ole Terran like me could benefit from gaining a pair of space-wings."

"You're not dumb," Estriel said. He shot her a warm smile and a look of confidence that made her heart flutter. Damn. Cassera was right. She had the hots for him.

Estriel turned back to the controls and began flipping switches and hitting buttons as he prepared to take off. Jegra gazed upon him with a pleased look. He glimpsed her gazing at him and smiled. She looked away, so as not to offend his Nyctan puritan sensitivities.

This was the closest to flirting she'd ever gotten with a Nyctan. They were always so prudent and taciturn. Flirting was as alien a concept to them as was the notion of bisexuality or polyamorous love. Their relationships were very rigid and business like, and it didn't really seem as though love, or rather mutual happiness amongst marriage partners, was a concern.

Early on, aboard the *Omikran* and later the *Light Bringer,* Jegra learned to keep her amorphous pansexuality to herself. Although they technically did have sex, it was reserved to mates only. And even though she found the Nyctan people's level of self-discipline admirable, she had been horny for almost three months now and needed a release. Hopefully sooner, rather than later.

She replied to Estriel's compliment of her, in the hopes to get him to speak a little bit more. "Most people only see the warrior ape slave that conquered the arena. And when they're not watching me for the sheer bloodlust of the sport, they're watching my body and lusting after me as an object." She nodded down at her ridiculously oversized chest.

Estriel glanced down and smiled, then, looked back out the forward view port yet said nothing. She knew he held her in high esteem and did not want to offend his ranking officer by being too bold with his opinions of her.

"Out of curiosity," Jegra said, running a clearance check. "Do you have a girlfriend, Estriel?"

"We don't date casually in my culture," he informed her. "We meet with our future spouses whom our parents have arranged for us a few times during our childhoods, then, upon entering adulthood, a wedding date is set. Once the date is agreed upon by both families, we marry the person and begin our lives together."

"Many ancient cultures on my planet practice arranged marriages too," Jegra informed him. "But nowadays we marry those who we are fondest of out of a sense of mutual respect and love."

Estriel smiled at her, yet again refrained from offering his opinion. He then hit the button which turned on the magnetic coils. The shuttle slowly rose up off the deck and, looking over his shoulder he addressed the rest of their passengers. All two of them. "Hang on tight."

Sanakar and Cassera looked at each other and raced one another to see who could strap in the fastest. Although the *Light Bringer* was positioning itself aft of the *Omikran*, away from the firefight, it was still an active war zone and things could get bumpy. Finishing first, Cassera gave Sanakar a victorious grin. Sanakar smiled with her eyes and looked away.

"Those two don't seem to get along," Estriel whispered, turning to see what had caught Jegra's attention.

"You're telling me?" Jegra snickered.

The shuttle rose up and quickly positioned itself before the open shuttle bay doors. Estriel turned his head toward Jegra and pointed his chin at the controls. "Sub Commander, I insist you do the honors of taking us out."

Jegra nodded and took ahold of the joystick in her left hand and the throttle in her right. Slowly throttling up, the ship began gliding forward, magnetic coils whining as the rear thruster pushed them out of the hangar.

Once clear of the hangar bay, Jegra brought the shuttle about and aimed it toward the stern of the *Omikran*. A little farther off, hanging in the shadow of the gigantic ship, was the *Light Bringer*, the medium sized battle cruiser of the Knights.

When Cassera saw which ship they were headed for, she gasped. "That's the ship everyone in the system fears."

"That's because everyone fears the Knights. And for good reason. They're merciless in their missions. You'll never meet a more dedicated group of soldiers. Believe me, I know."

"I believe you," she said, not questioning Jegra's sincerity. Under other circumstances, Cassera would be downright terrified. But, as it turned out, Jegra was now a Knight herself. Not only that, she was appointed their fearless leader.

Strange, she thought, how in a matter of months the thing they had been running from had now become their greatest ally.

The shuttle sped toward the *Light Bringer* at a brisk pace, when all of a sudden, there was a flash of light and the space-squid appeared out of nowhere and placed itself between the *Omikran* and Light Bringer and, subsequently, directly in their path.

"Did you know it could jump like that?"

"No, ma'am," Estriel said, taking evasive action.

Right on schedule, the *Omikran* and the *Light Bringer* opened fire on the creature. Disruptor blasts shot out of their phaser cannons and lit up the giant space-squid with a volley of high charged laser blasts.

But, as predicted, the creature merely absorbed the energy, its body remained undamaged by the attack.

Estriel turned the shuttle around and headed away from the barrage of disruptor fire at full speed.

Jegra looked back in time to see one of the tentacles of the space-squid latch onto the *Light Bringer*. "No!" she shouted, slamming her fist down on the comm. Opening a channel, she hailed Galahad aboard her ship.

Galahad's stressed voice came onto the comm. "My deepest apologies. It seems we won't be able to make the rendezvous, after all, Sub Commander."

"Next time," Jegra said.

"Final orders, ma'am?"

"Get yourselves free of that thing. If you can't, your orders are to get to the escape pods and abandon ship."

"Yes, ma'am," Galahad replied. With that, the comm went silent and everyone scooted to the edge of their seats as they watched the intense exchange play out.

The *Omikran* positioned itself in front of the space-squid. The mega-thrusters ignited and the ship prepared for ramming speed.

As the *Omikran* approached the entity, escape pods jettisoned from the endangered cruiser. It reminded Jegra of a white dandelion losing all of its parachute seeds, as a flurry of escape pods filled the space behind them.

"Bring the shuttle around over there," Jegra said, pointing at a distant black patch. Turning the ship about, Estriel did as requested and brought the ship full about and positioned themselves so that their starboard bow was facing the two ongoing battles.

Off the lower right of starboard, the *Omikran* and Light Bringer were tangled up with the squid entity. Off the upper port bow was Dakroth's monster battle cruiser, the *Subjugator*, pounding the remaining Nyctan fleet with a ridiculous amount of disruptor fire. Even the Nyctan's superior shield technology wouldn't be able to withstand such a volley for long.

Helpless to do anything about either battle except watch the horror of it all play out in real time, Jegra was beginning to feel that they really were trapped in a no-win situation.

"What are your orders, ma'am?" Estriel asked.

"Are you a praying man, Estriel?" asked Jegra.

"Yes, ma'am," he replied, his face looking amused by the randomness of such a question.

"Then, by all means, Estriel. Pray."

28

Radiant golden tentacles coiled around the *Omikran*. First just a couple, then three more. The vessel was completely tangled up in squid.

A sudden flash of light blinded everyone as the *Omikran*'s mega-thrusters discharged and the ship began its collision course. It would carry out Jegra's plan and carry the squid to the looming black hole that hung approximately 200 million keks away. About the same distance as from the Earth as to the sun, Jegra surmised.

A chime rang as a call came in from the *Omikran* and Jegra hit the receive button. The HUD on the dash lit up, showing a hologram of Azra'il Nun. She was still aboard the *Omikran*, wearing her finest battle armor.

"High Commander, you haven't evacuated the ship?" Estriel asked, confused as to why Azra'il would still be aboard.

"The creature's intense radiation output has scrambled the navigation systems. I'm going to have to fly this one in manually, I'm afraid."

"But you'll be killed!" he gasped.

"I'm beginning to think you were right, Jegra," Azra'il Nun said, turning her attention to Jegra. "This creature poses a much bigger threat than I initially realized. It could disrupt intergalactic trade throughout the entire quadrant. And, if it becomes powerful enough, it may stop suckling on starships and begin eating entire stars. I should have never doubted your warrior's instinct."

"It's all right," Jegra said.

"I'm sending you all the scans we've taken of the creature so far along with a copy of my final ship log. Jegra, one more thing. Once I ignite the afterburners, it will take only thirty-eight minutes for us to collide with the black hole. I'm not entirely sure what will happen so keep your distance. Wish me luck, and may Hastur watch over you all."

"May Hastur be with you, always," Estriel and Sanakar said in unison, bowing their heads and crossing their right fists over their left breast.

Jegra smiled at the High Commander. She was, in the end, an honorable person. "May Hastur be with you, now and forever," Jegra said, crossing her breast in the same customary manner.

Azra'il smiled at her and then the feed abruptly cut out.

Jegra looked down at the data stream coming in. "Good," she said. "The administratrix has taken her private shuttle and jumped out of the system."

"She just left us here?" Cassera asked.

"She just lost her flagship and nearly all of her fleet and those mid-sized cruisers certainly aren't going to hold out much longer," Jegra replied. "Abandoning ship was all she could do at this point. At least, now she can bring reinforcements and help take down Dakroth."

Estriel cleared his throat and gave her a dour look.

"She's not coming back with reinforcements?"

He shook his head in the negative. "The High Council would never permit it after such a loss. Now, she must stand before the council and explain how she could have lost her entire fleet. If they accept her answer, she'll retain her position. If not, she'll be stripped of her rank, court-martialed, and thrown in prison for the rest of her life."

Another blinding flare of white light forced everyone to divert their gaze away from the window. Once the flash died down, they looked out to find that the *Omikran's* thrusters had ignited to full. It would be a hot, fast burn to the end of the line, but at least Azra'il Nun would go out a hero.

As the *Omikran* and space-squid, along with the *Light Bringer* in tow, pulled away from them, Sanakar cleared her throat and pointed out the side window. "Pardon me, Sub Commander. But what's your plan if Dakroth should destroy the rest of the fleet and come looking for us?"

Jegra turned and watched in dismay as the Nyctan ships went up in fiery balls of flame. Hot orange and yellow explosions plumed out of all seven remaining vessels as their shields started to fail them. Several intense minutes later, a series of rapid concussive blasts discharged as all seven remaining ship's cores went critical and detonated at the same time.

Jegra knew it was a coordinated self-destruct sequence meant to try and knock Dakroth's battlecruiser out of the sky. But all it seemed to do was make the *Subjugator* look all the more menacing.

"Keep our front deflector shields at full and point us into that shockwave," Jegra ordered. Estriel obeyed. "How long until his scanners can pinpoint our location?"

"After the radiation levels die down, approximately an hour. Maybe sooner."

That news didn't exactly fill her with hope. An hour wasn't long. Jegra reached up and took the controls. Throttling up the thrusters, she aimed the ship at a still flaming piece of wreckage. Not only would it give them additional shielding against the shockwave, it would mask their presence.

"What are you going to do?" Estriel asked.

"I'm buying us some time."

Parking the ship under the chunk of debris, Jegra hit a button and released magnetic tethers. The tethers shot out into zero-gravity, their carbon-fiber mesh cords dangling behind them like slithering snakes. With a clunk, they latched on to the wreckage and anchored the shuttle. Flicking a few switches, she powered down the ship.

"Powering everything down except life-support." Jegra swiveled around in her chair and looked right at Cassera. "Let that asshole try and find us now."

"You know he's the most stubborn person in the galaxy, right?" Cassera tossed her platinum hair over her shoulder and pointed out the window. "He'll just stay out there sniping at random debris until, eventually, he gets to us."

"At least we won't be made into particle dust before we can come up with a plan to get out of this mess."

Cassera folded her arms. "I hope you're right," she said peering out at the monstrous ship that hunted them.

Several more minutes crawled by and Jegra was positive that time was deliberately inching by at the most aggravating rate possible. All that could be heard was their collective breathing and the occasional sigh.

After what seemed like forever, a scrambled transmission came in. It was Azra'il Nun. But the holographic image was too garbled and distorted to make out.

"Is there any way we can clear up just the audio?" asked Jegra.

Estriel frantically pounded away as the controls but he couldn't get the message to materialize. "I'm sorry," he said, shaking his head. "There's nothing I can do. There's just too much interference."

They all looked toward the black hole when, all of a sudden, a bright flash–as bright as a supernova–lit up the dark sky.

"There goes the *Omikran* and the *Light Bringer*," Estriel said with a sigh of sadness.

They shared a moment of silence which, unfortunately, didn't last very long. A sudden explosion jolted them back to the threat at hand.

"What was that?" Sanakar asked.

Jegra looked out the window. Another loud blast shook their ship. "That lunatic is firing on the larger sections of debris."

"He really dislikes you, doesn't he?" Sanakar asked.

"You have no idea," Cassera said, answering on Jegra's behalf.

This piqued Jegra's curiosity. "Oh, really?" she asked. "And just how long have you known about his great disdain for me?"

Cassera gulped nervously, having been found out. "It's not like I didn't want to tell you," she said apologetically.

"That he was just playing me? Don't worry. I wasn't born yesterday. I knew he was scheming against me."

"You knew about that?" Cassera gasped.

All of a sudden Jegra wasn't quite sure they were talking about precisely the same thing.

"Of course, I knew," she said, acting like she had known whatever it was Cassera thought she had known about all along. The feign worked, because Cassera let out a deep sigh and revealed the truth of the matter.

"I was so worried that he was going to dissect you, or pickle you, or something. I kept telling him that weaponizing your DNA would never fly with you and so he decided to gain your trust and experiment on you in secret."

This was Jegra's worst nightmare come true. Being experimented on by a mad-scientist, that is. And all this time, she was unaware of the fact that she was trapped in this nightmare.

"Weaponize my DNA?" she asked.

Cassera glanced around at all the faces in the shuttle. That's when she realized that Jegra hadn't known.

"I mean, yeah, that's what Dakroth's obsession with you has all been about. It certainly wasn't out of his deep-felt love for you that he wanted to marry you. He needed you close by. More precisely, he needed your DNA."

"What's so important about her DNA?" Estriel asked.

Cassera looked to Jegra who merely nodded, urging Cassera to spill it all.

"Well, Jegra's unique genetic code has the ability to overwrite other species' genetic code and make them more human."

"Wait," Sanakar interrupted, "are you saying that Jegra has the power to create hybrid entities?"

"Something like that, yes," Cassera answered.

"It's the fulfillment of prophecy!" Sanakar announced. Clamoring out of their seats, the two Nyctans hastily got down onto their knees and placed their heads on the floor, kowtowing to Jegra.

"Um...what's going on...exactly?" Cassera asked.

Sanakar rose to her knees and scuttling forward, she took Jegra's hands in hers. "The prophecy speaks of a Daughter of Sol who has the power to bind the light and to miraculously create hybrid entities that would go on to gain their celestial forms. It is how Nyctans believe we will ascend into the golden nexus and join Hastur in the eternal realm of light."

"Dagons believe something similar," Cassera informed them. "But we don't think it's through gaining a new body. We believe that we will shed our bodies and the radiant light inside us will join Hastur. Unified with his creation, he will then destroy the Great Darkness so that his light is all that remains."

"You know," Sanakar said, turning her smiling face to Cassera. "Your people and mine aren't so different, after all."

Another sudden blast violently shook the ship.

"That was a close one," Estriel said, hopping back to his feet and sliding into his chair.

Jegra smiled at Sanakar and then slowly drew her hands back, sliding them out of Sanakar's grasp. She then swiveled back into position and dialed up the ship's engines.

"It wasn't just close," Jegra growled. "It was too close."

She hit the ignition switch and the thrusters came online. Retracting the tethers, she dialed the thrusters to full and quickly darted away from the debris.

Just as they were pulling away a large disrupter blast erupted behind them as the debris went up in flames.

Sanakar screamed from the shock of it and Jegra aimed the shuttle straight at the monstrosity of a ship that loomed over them.

"Wait, what are you doing?" Estriel asked, his voice flooding with anxiety. "You're heading right for them."

"I know," Jegra snapped, not having the time to explain. "Everyone, strap in! This may get bumpy."

A volley of red disruptor blasts streaked through the sky—all of them trying to knock the tiny vessel out of the sky. But the shuttle was too small to pinpoint accurately, especially as Jegra dodged and weaved, carving out a haphazard trail like that of a common housefly.

"We're not going to make it," Estriel shouted.

"We'll make it!" Jegra shouted back.

Just then, from left field, came the *Light Bringer*. The ship, which was already severely damaged, rammed into the *Subjugator* and broke through the hull. Metal scraped against metal as the two ships collided. The *Light Bringer* scraped to a halt, getting wedged about a quarter of the way in.

"We're being hailed," Estriel said.

"Who's hailing us?" asked Cassera.

"The *Light Bringer*!" he replied joyously.

Jegra flipped on the holovid. Galahad stood in full battle armor with five of his finest warriors. "Miss us?"

"How in blazes are you still alive?"

"Hastur must be watching out for us," Galahad replied. "The moment the entity hit that event horizon, it began to squirm with panic and relinquished its grip of the ship and we had just enough time to rocket out of there before the *Omikran* went up."

"Hastur is indeed watching out for you, brother," Estriel said. Galahad nodded, his face plate looking majestic in the glowing light.

A sudden explosion rattled the screen and two Knights ran to meet their enemies head on, igniting their plasma blades as they disappeared off camera.

Galahad leaned into the camera as sparks streamed down from the damaged vessel. "I'm paying your emperor a little visit. Figured we could do more damage from the inside than the out."

Jegra smiled. "Give him hell," she said. "That's an order."

"Yes, Sub Commander," Galahad replied. With that, his plasma sword ignited and the holovid went dark.

Before they even had time to rest, another hail came in.

"Um...I think it's him," Estriel said in a timid voice.

"Well, it's about time," Jegra said in a vexed tone. "Put the asshole on."

"My treacherous, cold hearted, wife!" Emperor Dakroth sneered. "Do you honestly think you can defeat me with a handful of Knights and puny little shuttlecraft?"

"Of course not," she replied with a wicked grin. Then, popping her knuckles, she added, "I plan to defeat you with my fists...as I bash your stupid grinning face in."

Dakroth leaned back in his chair amused by her idle threat and grinned sinisterly at her. Then he cut the feed.

"Dock there," Jegra said, pointing at the *Light Bringer*. "We'll board one ship in order to make it onto the other. As long as those shields reinforce the structural integrity of the *Light Bringer*, we'll be—"

A powerful blast rocked the shuttle hard astern and sent it whirling out into deep space. Fighting to regain the controls, Jegra managed to wrangle the ship in and get her steady.

When she peered out the window, the *Light Bringer* had gone up in smoke. Luckily, it took a large chunk out of the *Subjugator* when it went, knocking the *Subjugator*'s engines offline. But for how long, Jegra didn't know.

That was the good news. The bad news was that the shuttle had incurred far more damage than Dakroth's ship. And their engines were completely shot.

Cassera came over to Jegra's seat and placed her hand on her shoulder. "Now what?"

"I don't know," Jegra replied.

For the first time since she had joined this war, she was at a loss. They had no engines. Their power would eventually fail. And if that wasn't bad enough, Dakroth was a rock's throw away. They were sitting ducks.

"It's up to Galahad now. Everything is riding on whether he fails or succeeds."

By the expressions on their faces, she knew that they, like her, believed the odds were entirely against them. It would take a miracle for Galahad to storm a ship that size let alone win against an entire army.

Besides, Jegra knew that Dakroth had the ability to take down Knights with a single laser blast from his finger. So, basically, they were all royally screwed. Right now, about the only thing they had going for them was the fact that they all had, somehow, managed to beat the odds. But eventually every gambler's luck runs out. Jegra feared, now, so had hers.

29

THOOM! Vibrations wracked the small shuttle as another ship came out of FTL just above its bow. The ship was a mid-sized frigate roughly the size of an ocean frigate. It was sleek and slender and had a recognizable look to it that brightened up Jegra's eyes when she saw it.

"Holieeey shit!" Jegra exclaimed, leaning forward in her seat to get a better angle on it as she gazed out the window at the ship. "Ain't she a pretty sight for sore eyes."

"Do you recognize that vessel, Sub Commander?" Estriel asked as he ran a quick security scan just to err on the side of caution, what with it being a Dagon class cruiser and all.

"It's the *Skywend*!" Jegra announced, turning around and looking at Sanakar and Cassera.

Cassera closed her eyes and let out a deep sigh.

"Don't worry," Jegra said, flicking on their comm, "they're friends of ours."

"Looks like you could use a little help," Raven said over the comm.

"How in the bleedin' galaxy did you find us?" Jegra asked, bending down to speak into the mic on the dashboard.

Ravens voice came back on and answered, "We received an encrypted message from someone named Galahad. He used the subspace carrier code I slipped you before you left us. Figured you wouldn't have given it to him if it wasn't important. Gave us your exact coordinates and said you might be needing our help. And here we are."

"I appreciate it, Raven." A grin spreading across her face, Jegra turned to Estriel and said, "Remind me to thank Sir Galahad when we see him again."

He nodded and smiled, making a mental note of it.

The docking clamps of the *Skywend* came down and latched onto the small shuttle. Reeling them in, there was a clunk followed by some clanking as the docking ramps attached themselves and created a seal between the *Skywend* and the shuttle. This was followed by a hiss of decompressed air as the shuttle matched the *Skywend's* pressurization.

Jegra flicked a few switches and buttons and powered down the craft. Getting up, she walked to the shuttle door and looked back at the three faces staring at her. "You all coming or what?"

She knew they were exhausted and on edge. The last forty-eight hours had been a grudge match. It was perfectly natural for them to be skeptical of the *Skywend*. But Jegra knew that once they met Raven's quirky crew of mercenaries they'd understand and maybe even find some piece of mind.

Cassera was the first to jump up and meet Jegra by the door. Standing closest to the entrance she waited for the green light above the door to flip on, signaling it was safe to exit the shuttle.

With a swish the door rose up and opened. To everyone's surprise, a giant, green Dragonian was standing on the other side. He was fully geared up in battle armor and held a blaster rifle at his side just in case those in the shuttle weren't what they appeared to be.

Kregor poked his head into the doorway with a big grin, but upon seeing it was Cassera that he greeted, his grin quickly faded away. "Oh. It's *you*," he said, lamenting the fact that the first person he met was the blue-skinned Dagon bitch.

"It's me," she said in a sardonic tone. She smacked him in the junk with an unexpected ball-tap as she walked past him causing him to jolt and tense up. Jegra laughed out loud.

"Kregor!" she chirped excitedly, throwing her arms around his thick neck and giving him a great big hug and a peck on the cheek. "I'm so glad to see you!"

"The feeling is quite mutual." Setting her back down, he smiled and informed her, "The captain regrets that she couldn't be here to greet you. She's needed on the bridge, what with that ugly monstrosity of a ship blasting everything in sight." Turning to the Nyctans, he grinned, his thin lizard lips pulling tight across his face. "Who are your friends?"

"These are the people who've been taking care of me for the past three months. Please see to it they're treated in kind."

"Of course," Kregor said, motioning for them to follow him. "Any friend of Jegra Alakandra's is a friend of mine." Waving his green hand toward the corridor of the ship, he added, "Right this way, if you please."

Jegra ushered them off the shuttle and then followed them onto the *Skywend*. She shut the airlock doors behind her and then headed to the bridge.

"Evasive action!" Raven shouted, as laser blasts lit up the *Skywend*'s bow.

Jegra entered the bridge and looked up at the *Subjugator* as it blotted out the systems binary stars. "He's already got his canons online?"

"What did you do to piss Emperor Dakroth off so badly?" Raven chuckled.

"I blew up his whole fleet."

Raven's purple eyes seized Jegra's face. Her expression was grim and then melted away as she began to laugh. "You would, wouldn't you? I guess my next question is, what did he do to deserve it?"

"The son of a bitch turned me over to his enemies as a distraction so they wouldn't discover he was secretly making that ugly ass ship," she said nodding at the hulking beast of a vessel that sat outside their window, "and then he left me for dead on Cordova and told the Dagon people the Empress of the Galaxy was lost in a shuttle incident."

"Not cool," Raven said, swiveling back in her chair. "Take a seat." She nodded at the co-pilot's chair beside her.

"You certain?" Jegra asked.

"You're going to need to learn how to fly this thing someday," she said.

"I am?" Jegra gave Raven a perplexed look.

Raven smiled at her. "I'm offering you a position on my crew. I don't have a co-pilot and I think you'd make a great addition. Just think about it."

Jegra's lips grew tight as her smile stretched far and wide. "Are you serious? You want me on your crew?"

Raven nodded in the affirmative but before she'd even finished answering Jegra's question Jegra reached out and grabbed Raven and gave her a warm hug.

After the long embrace, Raven brushed the purple stripe in her hair behind her ear and looked Jegra up and down. "Why in the quad are you wearing Nyctan battle armor?"

"I was given a ship," she said, pointing out the window at the hole in the

Subjugator. "But I'm afraid that's all that remains of it."

Raven glanced up at the gaping wound of Dakroth's ship. "Bold move," she said.

"It was the Knights."

"But, of course, it was" she said, grinning to herself. "If I'm not mistaken, I do believe you out rank me now. So, what's the plan, Sub Commander?"

Jegra looked at her with her most down to brass tacks expression and said, "Get us the fuck out of here."

"Yes, ma'am." Raven hit the controls and turned the *Skywend* about. Taking ahold of the FTL throttle, she looked out at the stars and jammed it forward. In a flash and a crack like a whip the *Skywend* jumped into FTL.

Hyperspace whisked by in long streaks of light separated by equally long bands of black, empty space.

"So, where we headed?" Jegra asked, curious as to where Raven was taking them.

"Before I got Galahad's distress call, we were *en route* to The Cove."

"The Cove?" asked Jegra.

"It's an old mining asteroid since turned into a pirate's way station. It's where all the black-market goods are brought in and out of the system. If Dakroth knew about it, he'd have had it destroyed already."

"What's at this Cove place?"

"Not a what, but a who," she replied. "We're picking up a Bre'lal woman of some importance. Her family is wealthy and her sister wants her to get home safely after she finishes trading korridium ore for some item of importance. What it is, however, remains a mystery."

"I thought you didn't transport cargo you didn't know the contents of?"

"I don't," Raven said. "Unless you can meet my price. Like I said, her sister is rich. So, I made a cool two and a half mill."

"A million and a half credits to look the other way?"

"Basically," she said, a coy grin spreading across her face.

"Suckers," Jegra said.

Both women laughed.

"It'll be three hours yet. Why don't you go get cleaned up and slip into something a little more comfortable? I fitted your room with several outfits I think you'll find appealing."

"Don't you mean, your room?"

"Not anymore," Raven replied. Her amethyst eyes locked onto Jegra's and she smiled. Her smile spoke volumes and Jegra didn't know what to say.

Jegra slowly rose to her feet, picked up her jaw off the floor, and placed her hand on Raven's shoulder. Giving her a firm squeeze, their eyes met and they shared a look of mutual understanding. And, to Jegra, it felt as though she had found her sister from a different mother. "Thank you. For everything."

"You'll always have a place here, empress," Raven said, turning back to her controls.

After exiting the bridge, Jegra went back to her quarters. It felt strange actually being able to say that now; she had her own place aboard the *Skywend*.

When she entered the room, she found Cassera sitting in a chair stark naked except for her armored boots and the defeated expression she wore on her face. Upon seeing Jegra framed in the doorway, she looked up at her with a look of sheer embarrassed shock.

"I don't know how to get my boots off," she said. She sounded like a distraught child who'd given up on trying to figure out how to tie their shoes for the first time.

Jegra laughed. "There's a trick to them," she said, kneeling down in front of Cassera. Pressing a button on the side, a latch popped up and Jegra pulled on it. The boot opened up like a ski boot and she slid it off Cassera's dainty blue foot. She repeated the process with the other foot and set the heavy boots to the side, next to the pile of armor.

"We have three hours to kill," Jegra informed her blue-skinned companion, gently resting her hands on Cassera's knees. She looked up into Cassera's golden eyes and smiled.

"You don't say?" Cassera said, biting her lower lip.

Jegra's gaze settled on Cassera's Prussian blue lips and the enticing pink tongue that she used to lick her teeth with. Becoming aroused, she slowly spread Cassera's knees apart, opening her thighs and revealing a snowy patch of white hair nestled between her legs. Jegra's eyes slowly fell onto the patch of white and she licked her lips in mouth-watering anticipation.

Cassera slid to the edge of her chair, leaned back, and closed her eyes to take it all in. The moment she felt Jegra's wet mouth begin to tease her with feathery kisses and titillating licks, she let out a deep sigh. "Don't stop," Cassera said. "Don't stop till I'm gushing like the waterfalls of Theta Prime and my legs are quivering so badly I can't take it a second longer."

Coming up for breath, Jegra replied, "As you wish, my love."

Three hours later both women lay in bed panting, their chests heaving, and bodies drenched with the sweet residue of satisfaction. They stared up at the ceiling as they basked in the aftershocks of minute orgasms that rippled throughout their bodies.

Cassera reached over and took Jegra's hand in hers. "That was..." Cassera began, pausing to take in a deep breath, "absolutely fucking glorious."

"No kidding. It felt like the first time between us."

Jegra rolled over and, stroking her partner's blue arm, looked into the Dagon's sparkling amber eyes. "What's the policy on your world about the Empress taking on a hetaera?"

"Your majesty is allowed up to twelve concubines of your choosing. They may live in the guest quarters of your domicile but you can never have more in your service than the emperor has in his. So, if, say, he has only five, you can have no more than four."

"Would you be willing to be my hetaera, Cassera Van Danica Amelorak?" Jegra gave Cassera's arm a firm squeeze to let her know she was serious about the request and that it wasn't just any fleeting fancy. It was the closest thing to making Cassera her wife without actually breaking Dagon imperial law.

"As a defector, I'd be killed if anyone found out my true identity. I'm afraid it wouldn't be possible. And if Dakroth found you were harboring me as your secret lover, there's no telling what he'd do."

"I could disguise you. All you need is a new look and a new name. What the emperor doesn't know won't hurt him." Jegra shot Cassera a playful wink.

"Really, is that all?"

"Yes," Jegra said.

"Well, consider my curiosity piqued. What did you have in mind?"

"How about Dani? Short for Danica."

"Dani? You know something...I like it." She bopped Jegra on the nose with a blue finger. "Especially because it's coming from you, J."

"Alright, I'll be your J-bird and you can be my Dani-girl."

"But, you do realize, Dakroth knows my face all too well." She sighed disappointedly and looked away from Jegra. "If he should ever find me by your side, he'd have a nuclear meltdown and throw me into his dungeon. Or worse."

"Well, I was thinking about that. And I know you're against modification, but Raven underwent mods and now has purple eyes and lots of cool cyber implants that do God knows what. And she turned out fine."

"You want me to defile my body so I can be with you?"

"I know, it's asking a lot. It goes against everything you believe. It goes against the notion of Dagon purity. Of being the supreme race and all that. But, at least, this way we could be together."

"It does more than goes against my personal beliefs. It would essentially erase my Dagon purity. Permanently. Apologies, Jegra, but I cannot in good faith make such a decision." There was a long pause between them, and then Cassera added in a rather solemn tone, "But if my empress should command it of me..."

Jegra gasped and gave Cassera an exasperated look. "You know I can't do that. Besides, that would make me no different from Dakroth ordering you to subject yourself to my aggressive DNA assimilation just to see what it would do to you. It's not right."

"Dakroth knew that I would never willfully undergo such a procedure, which is why he ordered me to do so, as his loyal subject. I'm afraid you'll have to do the same if you want me to go through with enhancements. You must command me to do it, as my empress."

"That's not fair," Jegra said, frowning disapprovingly at Cassera, "and you know it. I would never ask you to sacrifice part of your soul to me knowing you could never get it back."

"Consider it a lesson, then," she replied, stroking Jegra's face gently with fingers as light as feathers. "A lesson in having to make hard decisions as the Empress of Dagon."

"I hate that you're putting me in this position," Jegra griped. She huffed out a puff of hot air and fluttered her bangs.

"You need to stop thinking like a human and start thinking like a Dagon. My people have been ruthless for centuries. You're compassion, your emotional hesitancy, will only appear to them as weak-willed. It will give Dakroth all the ammunition he needs to plot against you in the hopes of your downfall. Don't give him the satisfaction."

"So, what are you suggesting? I act like Supreme Bitch of the Galaxy?"

"Let me ask you this. When you're fighting in the arena, do you halt mid-bout to apologize to your opponent for bashing them a bit too vigorously or stop because you may have inflicted one too many wounds upon them? No, because gladiators are slaves. And as a slave, you were ordered to fight, and you had no choice but to do so. And I, as your loyal servant, have no choice but to obey your commands. So, for one moment, don't be my lover. Don't be my girlfriend. Don't even be my J-bird. Be my *fucking* empress."

"No," Jegra replied. "I can't do it."

"You must. You are the Empress of Dagon now, Jegra. *You.* Not me. Not anybody else in this whole bleeding galaxy, but *you.* And it's time you started acting like it."

After a long pause, Jegra's scowl tightened and her jaw flexed. She hated herself for what she had to do but, all things considered, what choice did she have? As Cassera had pointed out, compassion would only make her appear weak. Dakroth would certainly use any sign of weakness against her as a means to twist public opinion and turn the Dagon people against her. Show them that she was ill suited to lead. That she wasn't worth their veneration.

"Fine," Jegra reluctantly answered, acknowledging that Cassera was right. There was only the lesser of two evils. Even though she didn't like it, that's just how it had to be; it was the only way to be with Cassera, the only way to save her lover from being executed. So be it.

Also, she'd see Hell freeze over before she'd ever let Dakroth play her for a fool again.

With a hardened gaze, she looked over at the lovely blue face in front of her, and ordered, "Cassera Van Danica Amelorak, from this point on you will be Dani Valencia, my personal stylist and fashion coordinator. This will explain why you are always by my side. You will also modify yourself so that the emperor will not be able to recognize you, even should he come into direct contact with you."

"Good," Cassera replied, with an encouraging smile. "Now you are talking like a true leader, not a slave who waits for others to decide her fate." She batted her amber eyes and leaned in, touching her forehead to Jegra's. "Anything else, my grace?"

Jegra reached down and cupped Cassera's breast in her hand and stroked her dark blue nipple with her thumb. "Yes, see to it that you get these boobs enhanced. They're a little on the small side."

Dani laughed and slapped Jegra's hand away. "No need to be a bitch about it," she teased, laughing at Jegra's joke.

Jegra wrapped her arms around Dani and pulled her in tight. "And maybe some filler for these thin wispy lips of yours, while you're at it."

"Oh, hush, you." Dani laughed and then stopped Jegra's teasing with a sultry kiss.

After a long, passionate, kiss, Jegra cupped her hands around Dani's face. "You do realize I think you're perfect the way you are, right?"

"I know," Dani replied, gazing back into Jegra's brown eyes.

"You also realize that I can't live a life on Dagon Prime without you, right? Not alone. Not with *him*."

"I know," Dani replied in a consoling tone.

"And, you do realize that I love you with all my heart," Jegra asked, pressing her head into Dani's just as she had done earlier.

"I know," Dani answered in a soft whisper.

With one last peck on the lips, Jegra slipped out of bed. "I'm gonna hit the showers. You want to come?"

"Not right now," Dani replied. "I think I'll try to catch a bit of rest, if you don't mind."

Jegra shrugged and then pulled a towel out of the closet and wrapped up. "See you in a while," she said, waving over her shoulder as she exited the room.

Once she was gone, Danica leapt out of bed and rummaged through the heap of armor lying on the floor until she found what she was looking for. Pulling out the korridian dagger, she stood in front of the wall and said, "Mirror on."

Her image appeared on the closet door panel as the 4K reflection of her stared back. Slowly, grabbing her long, silvery hair, she took the knife and cut over half of it off, leaving only shoulder length locks.

Danica dropped her white hair onto the floor and then tossed the knife onto the floor next to it. It rattled to a standstill and she stared at her naked body until she couldn't anymore.

Tears brimming, she wiped the corners of her eyes with her thumb and turned away from her reflection. "Mirror off," she said. The image disappeared and she threw herself onto the bed and curled up into a tight ball.

She had never felt so lost and helpless in all her life. She had been the most powerful woman in the Dagon Empire and commanded the largest fleet in the galaxy. Now, she was a fugitive on the run and her only chance of survival was to become the very thing she detested. A freaking *mod*.

Danica clutched her knees to her chest and did the one thing she hadn't done since she was a little girl. She cried, her tears brought on from the overwhelming sense of hopelessness she felt. For having lost her way. And for the fact that these emotions weren't manifested by the Dagon part of her but, rather, by the human part of her. She was changing. Losing herself. And that terrified her.

30

An asteroid the size of a small moon sat in the middle of a vast asteroid belt not so unlike that of Earth's Kuiper Belt, an extensive ring of predominantly icy planetesimals held in place by the gravity of the system's blue giant. A little smaller than Pluto, it was called The Cove—the site of a secret smuggling ring and black market weigh stop for pirates, mercenaries, smugglers, and home to countless other shady business practices. If you needed something, you could probably find it here.

The *Skywend* approached a stadium-sized opening in the asteroid and slowly started into the dark mouth of the rocky body. Running lights lit up and the *Skywend* disappeared into the asteroid.

Jegra tossed her still damp hair over her shoulder and leaned over Raven's shoulder. She was wearing another smart-suit. However, this one was gray with an orange stripe that ran down the left breast all the way down her leg.

"You smell good," Raven said quite casually.

"I took a much needed shower."

Emerging into a large hollow in the asteroid, there was a flicker as they passed through an enormous atmospheric, magnetically variable shield like the type that kept the shuttle bay pressurized but let ships pass in and out. It was the same concept behind how one bubble can pass through the film of another bubble without damaging either sphere. Only instead of surface pressure, they used high-powered shields.

Of course, if your ship was old and didn't have magnetic shielding it would bounce off the encompassing blue film like a rock ricocheting off a concrete wall.

"Oh, wow!" Jegra gasped as she saw numerous shuttles flying about inside the moon-sized cave. Raven brought the *Skywend* down on one of the large landing pads attached to what seemed to be a giant casino built right into the inner wall of the asteroid.

Down below, and all around, was a labyrinth of shops and places of pleasure which could satisfy any numerous vices. Jegra saw sex parlors, drug dens, gambling establishments, food places, and all manner of junk dealers peddling their second-rate wares.

"Don't buy anything from anyone down here except for food. And even then, be sure it's not still alive."

"Roger that," Jegra said.

"Oh, mistress, Jegra," a familiar voice said, in a pleasantly surprised tone.

"Skuld?" Jegra said, the realization settling in before she even had time to turn around. Spinning around she found the skinny, fish-man in his aquatic breathing gear standing behind her. Leaping up, Jegra threw her arms around his neck and gave him a great big hug.

"Oh, how I've missed you." Noticing a couple of small dark eyes peering out from behind the arch of the bridge entrance, Jegra winked and whispered, "I missed you too, Gyllek."

The girl ignored Jegra and wrapped her face up in a shawl and then put on some reflective sunglasses with a ruby tint.

"Where you guys going?"

"We have to retrieve the package. Oh, and I'm going to try and find some power converters for the *Skywend's* transporter unit."

"It's out of commission again?" Jegra asked.

"Can't seem to get the darn thing running smoothly," he said, waving his webbed hand as if to brush the pesky business aside. "At any rate, I hope to see you again soon."

"Likewise," Jegra said, bowing her head and letting him and Gyllek head off to do their errands.

Raven got up to join them and, pausing in the doorway, looked back at Jegra. "I have three rules. Nothing and no one boards this ship without my express permission. Second, we consider each other family, so if you aren't willing to die for any member of this crew, you aren't going to fit in here. Third, if you betray me or anyone of my crew, I will personally hunt you down and kill you myself.

Am I being clear?"

"Crystal clear," Jegra replied.

Raven smiled at her and then turned and disappeared out the door.

A moment later, Danica showed up. She was wearing the exact same outfit as Jegra.

"Oh, bother," she said. Grabbing the wrist, she pressed the blue LED on the cuff and said, "Electric purple with hot pink stripe."

Her suit promptly changed into a bright neon outfit meeting her exact specifications.

Jegra couldn't help but stare. It was spectacular.

"What?" Danica asked, feeling self-conscious.

"I'm just burning your perfect image into my memory."

"I thought you did that last night."

"Last night?" Jegra laughed. "Last night I had my face buried so deeply between your thighs I couldn't see for shit."

"All right, all right," Danica laughed. "I get the point."

"The point is," Jegra said, sauntering up to Danica. "I think you're amazing."

"You're pretty amazing yourself," Dani replied.

Jegra smiled and turned to head out when Dani's hand abruptly caught her by the arm and reeled her back. "What? No kiss?"

"Oh, greedy, are we?"

"In case you haven't heard," Danica whispered, leaning in, "I'm a fugitive now. I have no more rules and regulations to abide by. And right now, all I want is a taste of these cotton-candy pink lips of yours."

Danica and Jegra shared a sultry kiss and then, holding hands, headed off to find a modification joint. The kind that does off-the-books mods.

Leaving Sanakar and Estriel behind with Kregor, they exited the ship and then strolled up and down the busy promenade taking in the sounds and sights of a bustling marketplace. All manner of aliens tried to sell them things they didn't need. Finally, they came upon a mod parlor that looked promising.

"I'm keeping my eyes," Danica whispered out of the corner of her mouth.

"Good," Jegra said. "That's your best feature." She turned to Danica and squeezed her hand. "I'll be here, right beside you the whole way."

They entered the mod parlor together and walked up to the counter. It felt like a spa but much dingier. The girl at the counter was a Bre'lal woman with *eau de nil* skin and bright cobalt blue hair and was busy burning different colors of ink onto her nails with a nail-polish-gun. Smacking on some gum, she asked, "What can I do you for?"

"Do you do skin pigment augmentation?" Jegra asked.

The girl looked up and scanned Jegra. "We sure do. What color do you fancy yourself?"

"Oh, it's not for me. It's for my friend here." She gave Danica's hand a firm tug and she staggered up to the desk alongside Jegra.

Nervous, she fidgeted about. "I was thinking a light purple hue added to my skin color. Nothing too wild. And I want blue, turquoise, and purple ombre for my hair."

"And larger tits," Jegra added.

The girl looked Danica up and down and then smiled. "We can do all that. Anything else you'd like? Eye color change or maybe and neurotransmitter fitted behind your ear so you both can telepathically communicate with each other."

"You can do that?" Jegra asked excitedly.

"Uh-huh," the girl replied, smacking on her gum and going back to paying more attention to her nails than her customers.

"Sweet!" Jegra turned to Danica and squeezed her hand. "We could be inside each other's heads! How intimate is that?!"

"I dunno, J," Danica hesitantly replied. "Some of my thoughts can get pretty dark. My people aren't built to be compassionate."

"We'll keep them off most of the time. But how amazing would it be to share each other's thought?"

Jegra turned toward the girl. "All right, we'll do everything we discussed, except the eyes. How much will this run us?"

"Eight million credits," the girl answered.

"Eight million credits?" Danica barked. Growing angry, she slammed her hand down on the counter, her eyes flashing bright yellow as her energy flared up. Small bubbles of electromagnetic energy began to form around her as her power began to manifest.

The Bre'lal girl simply looked up and smacked her gum. "Fine," she sighed. "Three million credits. Not a penny less."

"One point five million," Jegra said. "Not a penny more."

"No, dice, lady," the Bre'lal woman replied.

"Fine," Danica snarled. "We'll just find someplace else."

Jegra and Danica turned to leave. Just before they exited the parlor, the girl called out to them. "Wait!"

They turned back around and faced her and waited patiently for her to admit defeat.

"Fine, two million and a half. But that's my final offer."

"Deal," Jegra said. She excitedly nudged Danica's arm with her elbow and the two of them headed toward the waiting room to get ready.

The Bre'lal girl cleared her throat. "Forgetting something?" She pointed at the scanner on the table.

"Oh, right," Jegra said, reaching out to have her wrist implant scanned so she could pay.

Danica quickly stopped her, however. "Wait, he might be able to track your purchases."

The girl behind the counter raised her eyes, her curiosity piqued from listening in on the conversation, and looked at them both. "Mean ex?" she asked, her eyes probing their faces as she fished for the juicy details.

"The worst," Jegra said.

The girl flipped a switch and the red laser turned blue. "This will charge all funds into a dummy account which will then be dumped back into our establishment under a randomly generated name."

Jegra sighed and looked at Danica who signaled with a nod that it was okay to proceed.

"Thanks," Jegra said. "You saved this girl's ass."

"Whatever," the Bre'lal girl said going back to her nails.

"Come on!" Jegra said cheerfully, looping her arm under Danica's and linking elbows.

"What's gotten into you?" Danica asked. "You're acting so spry. It's a little off putting."

"Oh, don't be such a worry-wart," Jegra said as they entered the waiting area. "We're a million miles from nowhere and surrounded by nothing but crooks and scumbags. Nobody would ever think to look for us here. So, just relax and get modded already."

"Yes, your grace," Danica said, curtseying.

"Oh, you stop that," Jegra said, tugging on Danica's elbow and bringing her back up.

Jegra stopped in the middle of the room and stared off into the distance. "Oh, shiiit," she said after a while.

"What is it?" Danica asked in a startled tone.

"Oh, it's nothing. I'm just realizing, now, that if we're sharing each other's thoughts during...you know what...then having an orgasm is going to be like a fucking neutron bomb going off right inside my c—"

"Ladies!" a voice interrupted. It had a subtle gentlemanly southern twang to it which caught Jegra's ear.

They both turned to find a human man in his late forties to early fifties with a thick auburn goatee and an all-white Colonel Sanders-type suit. He wore a raggedy ole straw cowboy hat and had on purple shades, reminiscent of John Lennon's.

"The name's Homer. Homer Edgington."

"Oh my God!" Jegra practically screamed when she saw another human. "You're human!"

"So are you, my dear." Scoping Jegra out, he raised an eyebrow and tipped his hat back to allow himself a better look.

"I am totally human," Jegra said grabbing Homer's hand and squeezing it so hard his joints cracked. Shaking vigorously, she repeated, "I am."

"Good to know," he said, patting her hand and then prying his away. "Never hurts to be among your kind."

"How long have you been at The Cove?" Danica asked.

"Oh," Homer said, taking his mangled hand back and scratching his beard. "About seven years now, give or take."

"Abducted by alien poachers?" Jegra asked.

"I was sold to a wealthy merchant where I worked until I gained my freedom. After that, I found myself here, eking out a meager living. The Cove offers the best free-market in the entire galaxy! Anything you'd ever want or ever hoped to find can be found here." He raised his arms and fanned the entire room as he alluded to the goings on in The Cove.

"All right," he said, rubbing his hands together. "What can I do for you fine ladies?"

"I need a makeover," Danica informed him in her matter-of-fact tone. Obviously, it was hard for Danica to shake years of military training. The regimental soldier in her was still stiff and mechanical.

"Yeah," Jegra said, nudging Danica with her shoulder. "I want my girlfriend looking hot!" Jegra squeezed Danica's ass for show and forced a nervous laugh out of her.

She leaned into Jegra. "What are you doing, sweetie?"

"Putting on a good show for the nice man, here," Jegra replied through the corner of her mouth. When they caught Homer smiling at them they both laughed and batted their eyes at him and tossed their hair, acting like a couple of silly girls spending a night out on the town. Or, in this case, a secret cove inside an uncharted asteroid belt. *Ah,* Jegra thought to herself. *The Cove. I get it now.*

"Excellent," he said, ignoring their awkwardness. "Don't you ladies worry your pretty little heads. Most people get the jitters the first time around. But it's perfectly safe."

"'The jitters' is an understatement," Danica griped. Jegra shook her head as if to say, not here. Not now.

Guiding Danica over to a large, pod-like canister, Homer pulled it open and a hiss of steam shot out. Continuing on with his pitch, he motioned for her to take a look inside. "This is a Makeover Pod; 7,000 series. State of the art, top of the line. You just program in the specifications of what you want to have done, using this touch-panel here and *abracadabra, walla-walla, presto!* you're modified, beautified, and most of all, 100% guaranteed satisfied!"

"Awesome!" Jegra gave Danica a gentle nudge toward the machine. But she could only look at it with intense dread.

Homer clapped his hands and wriggled his fingers enthusiastically. "Well, ladies, I'll leave you to it."

He took a deep bow, tipped his hat to them, and disappeared out of the room.

"He seemed nice enough," Jegra said, looking over her shoulder to be certain he had given them their privacy.

"I suppose so," Danica replied. She wasn't familiar with human interactions so didn't really think her opinion would be of any help. Getting ready, she stripped her clothes off and handed them to Jegra. "Well, here goes nothing."

Typing her specifications into the panel, she set up all the modifications they'd discussed earlier. Finishing on an anatomically accurate 3D rendering of a blue skinned Dagon female, she tapped on the picture's chest. Each time she tapped the image of the woman its breasts grew slightly bigger. Satisfied with a slightly larger bust size she let out yet another pent-up sigh.

Jegra rubbed Danica's neck and said, "It will be perfectly fine. And when you come out of there, no matter what you look like, I'll still love you."

She grinned at Dani and reached down and gave the display an extra couple of taps, inflating the 3D representation of a female Dagon's chest to ludicrous proportions.

"Um...no," Danica replied, glaring at Jegra and pressing her two fingers on the 3D model's chest and holding them down as the breast slowly deflated back to an acceptable size.

Shooting Jegra a stern look, as if to say leave it alone, she climbed into the pod and shut the chamber door. From inside cylinder, she called out, "Wish me luck."

"Best of luck, babe," Jegra said. She reached down and tapped the picture of the Dagon woman's chest three times, inflating the 3D images chest to a comfortable 36C. Not too big, not too small. Just right.

Dani might be mad that she had played such a juvenile prank on her, but at the same time these were her orders, as empress, and Dani had no choice to submit to her will. It may not be right, but this abuse of power came from a good place. She wanted Dani to be unrecognizable. That way she could remain off Dakroth's radar. It was the only way Jegra could ensure Dani would stay safe.

The timer counted down from fifteen minutes. Jegra took in a deep breath and put her hands on the back of her hips and leaned back and stretched. No sooner had she finished stretching than Homer reappeared with a small handheld injector gun. It reminded Jegra of a glue gun.

"What's that?" she asked, nodding at the device.

"It's the nano-tech you ordered," he replied, looking at her from across the rims of his lavender sunglasses. "Just place it behind your ear like this," he said, demonstrating how it worked, "and pull the trigger." He handed it off to Jegra who gladly accepted it. "You'll likely feel a pinch followed by a bit of pressure. Don't worry, put some ice on it and the swelling will go down in an hour."

"Thank you so much," Jegra gushed, examining the device in her hands.

"You know," Homer added, before leaving. "You look awfully familiar. Have we met?"

"No," Jegra answered. "I would have remembered. You're the first human I've come across in nearly two years."

"I see," Homer said, lifting up his hat and brushing his long wispy hair back on his head. "Well, there are a few of us bopping around out here at the ass-end of the galaxy. But be careful, most humans are just trying their best to survive the harsh conditions of the galactic Commonwealth and keep a low profile what with the war between the Nyctans and Dagons dragging on. But they'd sooner stab you in the back than lend you a helping hand. Consider yourself warned."

"Right," Jegra answered. She didn't like the ominousness that lingered in his words. It almost seemed like a veiled threat. "I'll definitely make sure to be extra careful."

He smiled at her with his unnervingly wide, artificially white, manic smile. She returned his smile in kind with one of her own, but felt unnerved by how long she was forced to hold it. If that wasn't bad enough, she had the distinct feeling that Homer wasn't everything that he pretended to be.

He was being overly friendly, even though he had no need to be. His ominous warning about other humans seemed to come from the place of a guilty conscience, which meant he was probably trying to warn her. Atone for some grievous sin of his past. Something was most definitely amiss, she felt.

Homer made up some pretext about attending to some other customers, even though there hadn't been any when they'd come into the mod parlor, and excused himself from the room.

Jegra looked at the clock. Eight more minutes to go. Tapping her foot anxiously, she whispered, *"Come on, come on, come on."*

The eight minutes crawled by, but finally the pod chimed and then, with a hiss of steam, it opened.

Danica stepped out and examined her arms. She was a deep shade of indigo, somewhere between her former dark blue self and her new, pinker self.

Her hair was a majestic blue and purple ombre which was feathered down to her shoulders and her chest was now downright corpulent, which made her perfectly side-set breasts look truly stunning. Looking down at herself, she grabbed her boobs and squeezed. "You didn't?!"

"I did," Jegra said, grabbing her arm. "But there's no time to discuss it, we've gotta go."

"What are you talking about?" Danica said, easing back.

"I think Homer has sold us down the creek without a paddle."

"Down the what without a what?" Danica asked, looking completely baffled.

"I think he recognized me and has probably informed the authorities. Bounty hunters. Maybe even Dakroth himself."

"Shit," Danica said, grabbing her things.

"Get dressed, we've got to get back to the *Skywend* and warn everybody."

Danica raced to get her clothes on. Just as they were about to leave, Homer came in with a tray full of champagne in lovely tall crystalline glasses.

"Won't you ladies stay awhile and have a nice relaxing drink. It's not every day I see a fellow Earthling. Maybe you can catch me up on what's been going on back on the homeworld. Tell me how the Red Sox are doing." He smiled and then handed Jegra a glass of champagne.

Confused as what to do and, presuming the drink was most likely drugged, Jegra laughed and tossed her hair. Then, without a second's hesitation, she cold-cocked Homer without so much as spilling a drop of champagne.

Out cold, the man crumpled to the ground with a resounding thud and his lavender glasses went skidding across the floor.

Both women looked down at Homer and then each other. Not waiting for him to regain consciousness, Jegra grabbed Danica's arm and hastily towed her out of the room. She still held the glass of champagne in her other hand.

"What about the neuro-transmitter link?" Danica asked, looking back over her shoulder.

"Leave it. It's probably bugged anyway," Jegra said as she and Danica rushed into the lobby and passed the girl at the front desk.

As they scurried by, Jegra set the glass of champagne down on the edge of the counter next to the girl and said, "Thanks, again. It was amazing!"

"Pleasure was all ours," the girl replied in a less than enthused drawl. "Come again."

Jegra and Danica swiftly exited the shop, the bell above the entrance jangling. When the shop girl heard the door bells, she looked up to find the two customers had vanished without a trace.

She shrugged and then was about to go back to doing her nails when she eyed the drink sitting next to her. A smile came onto her face and, looking around to make sure nobody was watching, she took a long swig of the bubbly beverage and gulped it all down.

Placing the glass back on the counter, she smiled. Almost as soon as she'd finished the drink, however, her eyes turned blurry and her upturned lips sunk into a woozy grin, and she abruptly passed out and fell out of her chair, disappearing behind the counter.

"This way," Jegra said, hooking a sharp right around the corner of the shop and turning down an alleyway. She ducked under some oriental style lanterns and dodged some food vendor selling what looked like soba noodles, except for the fact that they were squirming about in the bowls of soup and hissing.

"I'm trying to keep up," Danica panted. "But it's a bit difficult to run with these things." She pointed at her oversized chest. "Did you really need to make them so awfully big?"

"Oh, come on, Dani. Look what I'm dealing with," she said, pressing an extended finger into her voluptuous chest. "You don't hear me whining about it. Anyway, the whole idea was to completely transform you and throw Dakroth off our scent. And nothing diverts a guy's gaze like a pair of righteous boobs."

"Yeah, but my back doesn't have super-serum enhanced muscles to stop from aching all day long because of my stupidly enormous chest like some people," she said, eyeballing Jegra's equally enormous chest.

"Stop your griping. You'll be fine."

"Easy for you to say," Danica whispered, getting the last word in edgewise.

They shot out of the narrow alley at the corner of a dry cleaners which sat in front of a large open square. Looking up, Jegra spotted the *Skywend* perched upon a landing platform directly above them–about sixty meters up.

"There it is," Jegra said, pointing up at the ship.

"Um, Jegra?" Danica said, looking around them as she scanned their surroundings. All of a sudden, they were no longer alone.

Several dark figures emerged from the shadows and were now making their way through the crowded street towards them. They all moved and walked just as rigidly as soldiers, tipping Danica off that they were mercenaries for hire.

"If we could somehow find an elevator or…"

"Jegra," Danica barked in a hushed tone.

"What is it?" she asked, finally paying attention to what Danica had to say.

"I'm afraid we have company. And not the friendly kind."

Jegra looked around to see several cloaked figures honing in on their position from all sides. "Oh, shit," Jegra said, realizing the precariousness of their situation.

Three of the figures gathered at the center of the square while three others held back and set up a perimeter, probably to cut them off if they should try to escape. It was all by-the-book military tactics.

The lead figure stepped forward and, taking ahold of its hood, slowly pulled it away, revealing itself. A red skinned woman stared back at Jegra with a malicious grin.

"You," Jegra growled. Her eyes smoldered with rage as she greeted the familiar face with an equally menacing glare.

"Long time, no see, Jegra," Ishtar Bantu said. Raising her blaster, she pointed it right at Jegra and her companion. "Now, if you don't mind coming with me, I have a rather handsome bounty to collect."

31

 the alleyway as red and green disruptor fire was exchanged. Just before Ishtar Bantu could apprehend her targets, Skuld and Gyllek appeared out of nowhere with the Bre'lal woman who had a striking dark, emerald skin. Taking cover behind some crates, they started laying down cover fire and helped draw Ishtar and her goon's attention away from Jegra and Danica, giving them time to find cover.

As the fire exchange heated up, Skuld shouted above the blasts. "Jegra! Take this." He tossed her a blaster and she caught it.

"What now?" Jegra asked, shooting Danica a worried look. Although she was willing to fight, she deferred to Danica's strategic experience to find them another way out.

Danica looked around. "Over there," she said, pointing at a possible exit that was through a jeweler's shop across the street from them.

"Right," Jegra said. "You go first, I'll cover you."

Without warning, a glass jar of candies exploded above their heads as a poorly aimed disruptor blast hit it. Jegra threw her arms up to deflect the spray of glass and pushed Danica toward the street.

Danica leapt up and flew across the street, laser blasts streaking behind her. Jegra stood up and laid down a spread of cover fire and quickly followed after her. They raced through the shop as the owner, a Brilaxian catfish-looking gentlemen, screamed at them as his merchandise got shot up behind them.

"Sorry!" Jegra called back.

Ducking out the back door, they ran up the street and hooked a sharp left where they practically ran into Skuld, Gyllek, and the girl, who were in full retreat.

"This way," Skuld said, pointing in the opposite direction Jegra and Danica were headed.

"Right," Jegra said, spinning on her heels and following after them.

As they raced up the street, Skuld handed his blaster off to Danica. "Keep them occupied," he said, whipping out a communicator, "while I call on ahead. We're going to need a quick dust off."

Danica looked back and started blasting away at the mercenaries who pursued them up and down the back alleys of the merchant district.

"Raven, this is Skuld. Do you read me?"

Raven's voice came in loud and clear. "I read you, Skuld. What's up?"

"We're being pursued by hostiles. If you could have the ship's engines primed and ready to get off this rock by the time we get there, it would be much appreciated."

"I would, but I'm currently not aboard the ship," she replied apologetically.

Jegra shot Skuld a WTF look and he shrugged. Just then another voice came onto the comm. "This is Kregor, I'll reach the ship in two minutes. I'll have her ready for a prompt departure."

"My hero!" Jegra said, leaning closer to Skuld and speaking into the comm as they scurried up the street.

Skuld flicked the comm off and tucked it back into his belt. "Righteo, people! Let's double time it."

By the time they got to the ship, its engines were already purring. But to their dismay, Ishtar Bantu was waiting for them.

She stood between them and the ship's loading platform and held out a glowing plasma sword, the kind Knights used. The sword glowed hot white with a purple halo and crackled viciously on the cool air. The corners of Ishtar's mouth curled upward into a sadistic smile.

"And you all came so very far."

Jegra threw her arm up and gestured for everyone to stay back. "I've got this," she said.

"You've got this?" Ishtar balked. "Just like you did in your quarters when I snapped your green-skinned lover's neck? Or, do you mean that time aboard your ship when I gutted you and slit your sweet little servant girl's throat?"

Jegra didn't dignify Ishtar with a response. She merely cracked her knuckles and grinned menacingly.

"What are you going to do?" Ishtar taunted. "Punch your way through a flaming sword?"

"Something like that," Jegra said. Spitting on her knuckles, she raced forward, feigning an attack.

Ishtar swung the humming blade in a large swooping arc, hoping to meet Jegra's charge and cut her in two. But Jegra skidded to a stop just beyond the swords reach and shot Ishtar a look that said big mistake.

Jegra brought her fists down onto the pavement with such fury it unleashed a sizable tremblor. The ground quaked and fracture lines spread across the pavement as it crumbled beneath her powerful fists. The broken fragments of concrete rocked violently beneath Ishtar's feet, causing her to lose her footing and stumble backward.

Being so close to the *Skywend*, however, Ishtar stumbled right into the ship, smacking her head against its korridium reinforced hull. She rebounded off the ship's underbelly and fell to the ground, the harsh blow to her head rendering her unconscious.

The plasma sword fell to the ground beside her and automatically turned off, a safety feature which all plasma swords had. Lying on the ground, unconscious, Ishtar was no longer a threat to them. But her hired goons would be arriving shortly.

"All aboard?" Jegra said, gesturing for her friends to board the ship.

As her friends boarded, Jegra bent down and picked up Ishtar's unconscious body and strolled over to the ledge of the landing platform.

"What are you going to do?" Danica asked.

"I'm going to throw out the trash," Jegra replied. And with a heave-ho, she tossed Ishtar's limp body over the edge.

Jegra dusted her hands off and returned to the loading ramp of the *Skywend*. Just as she arrived, so did Raven.

"What'd I miss?" Raven asked.

"Nothing much," Jegra replied.

Raven looked at Danica and said, "You look nice."

"Thanks," Danica replied.

Raven then slapped Jegra's arm, as if to say well done, and hurried aboard her ship. Jegra and Danica quickly followed after her, just as the ramp began to close.

"Everyone strap in," Raven shouted above the whine of the engines as she raced up the hallway toward the bridge.

Everybody found their seats and buckled up tight.

The *Skywend* rose off the platform, kicking up a maelstrom of garbage and loose debris and, using its guidance thrusters, slowly turned toward the mouth of the subterranean cave of the giant asteroid. Leaving The Cove, she exited the tunnel and came out just in time to find Dakroth's ship, the *Subjugator,* waiting for them.

"For fuck's sake," Raven growled. "Can't a girl get a break?" Slamming her fist down on the comm, she called Jegra to the bridge.

"Jegra, get your hot ass up here. We've got company."

By the time Jegra arrived on the bridge, Raven already had the emperor on the holovid. He gripped one arm, which was bleeding profusely, and turned toward Jegra and glared at her with his red eyes and all the hatred he could muster.

"I just wanted you to know, sweetheart, your Knights failed. You failed. And now, you will be punished."

The holovid pulled back to show a badly beaten Galahad sitting on his knees before the emperor. He was stripped of his armor and it looked as though Dakroth had taken out some of his frustration on Galahad.

Dakroth's finger started to glow and he pressed it against the temple of Galahad's head. "Say goodbye to your precious Knight," he snarled.

"Wait, no!" Jegra screamed. But it was too late. The emperor had already discharged the condensed energy blast.

Galahad's face exploded right before Jegra's eyes. His right eyeball flew one way and the lower half of his jaw and teeth careened off the opposite way. His body tottered momentarily and then fell forward, the stump of his neck landing at Dakroth's feet with a thud.

The emperor bent over the dead Knight and grinned maniacally into the holovid camera. "I'm coming for you, my dear wife. Run all you like. But you can never hide from me. I'll always find you. And, one more thing. If you so much as think you can—"

Raven flicked off the holovid and leaned back in her chair. After a second, she realized Kregor, who sat in the co-pilot's seat next to her, was staring at her with a stunned expression plastered across his face. It was clear that he was surprised by the fact that she'd just hung up on the blood thirstiest psychopath in the galaxy.

She shrugged. "It was a boring conversation anyway."

Kregor swiveled around in the chair and looked at Jegra who was doing her best to keep it together. "I'm sorry about your Knight," he said.

"He was my friend," she replied in a hushed voice full of sadness. She knew Dakroth was ruthless, but now he'd gone and made things personal.

The *Subjugator* opened fire on the *Skywend* and Raven took evasive action. Kregor spun back into position and helped bring up the deflector shields. It was just in time, too, as a disruptor blast from Dakroth's ship jolted the *Skywend*.

The bulkheads of the ship shuddered violently and Kregor huffed anxiously. "We won't be able to take many more of those," he said.

"We won't have to," Raven replied, flipping a switch. "Spooling up the FTL now. Let's see him try to out fly one of his fastest ships."

"I've put you all in danger," Jegra whispered. "It's all my fault that this is happening."

Unable to contain her emotions any longer, tears began to stream out of Jegra's eyes. Wiping her cheek with the back of her hand, she apologized and fled the bridge. "I'm sorry," Jegra said, ducking under the archway of the door and disappearing around the corner as she entered the corridor.

"Jegra!" Kregor beckoned after her, spinning around in his chair, preparing to go after her. But a hand quickly landed on his shoulder and firmly pressed him back into his seat.

Raven shook her head and then whispered, "Let her go."

As she ambled down the corridor, Jegra felt the ship jump to FTL. When she arrived at her quarters, Danica was already waiting for her, arms open wide. Embracing Jegra, they sank down to the edge of the bed and sat there together.

Danica stroked her partner's hair and consoled Jegra the best she could. "What'd he do this time?"

"He killed Galahad," she sniffled.

"You'll get your revenge," Danica said.

"But how long will it go on like this?" Jegra asked. "I take something important from him, then he takes something important from me. It's a game to him. A vicious, never ending game where he gets to torture me and I can never hurt him back as much as he hurts me."

"That's what he does," Danica said. "He revels in hurting others. In dominating them. Breaking them. Especially those he views as a threat."

"But he's right," Jegra lamented. "There isn't anywhere I can go or hide that he won't find me. That he won't find a way to bring me back into his manipulative grasp."

"There is one place," Danica replied.

Jegra shot her an intrigued look.

Danica took Jegra's hand and placed it over her right breast, just above her heart. "He can't get you here."

Leaning in, Danica kissed Jegra's soft pink lips and drew back just enough to gauge her reaction. Although Jegra's tears still trickled down her face, she gave an attempt at a smile.

"I need to ask you a favor," she said, looking deep into Danica's eyes.

"Anything for you," Danica replied.

"I want you to weaponize my DNA like Dakroth wanted."

"What?" Danica gasped. "Why would you have me do such a thing?"

"Because, it's my choice. And because, if he wants my genetic code so bad, I plan on giving it to him. All of it."

"You want to use it against him?" Danica said, finally getting in tune with what Jegra had in mind.

"Once he's rendered powerless, then he's no longer a threat. Not to you. Not to me. Not to anybody. He'll just be an impotent, sniveling, weakling."

Danica fell back onto the bed and pulled Jegra on top of her. "I think I can help you with that."

After a vigorous round of love making, Jegra went over to the window and stood looking out at the stars streak by. The sweat on her body cooled in the recycled air of the ship and she let out a lengthy sigh.

"What are you doing?" Danica asked in a sleepy voice as she raised her head off the pillow to try and see what her girlfriend was up to.

"Nothing. Just thinking," replied Jegra.

"Well, get your cute butt back to bed. I'm cold and I miss you." Danica held up her arm and showed Jegra the prickling of her skin. "Look, I have goosebumps."

Jegra turned and looked at Dani. She smiled and then complied with her request. Sinking into bed, she slipped under the sheets and wrapped her arms around Danica who was already trailing off to sleep in the warmth of her lover's arms.

Jegra leaned in and kissed the side of Dani's cheek and then laid her head down on the pillow close to hers and watched her sleep. She stared at Dani's beautiful complexion until she, too, drifted off.

The crack of the ship coming out of hyperspace roused Jegra from her sleep. As the ship lurched back into regular space, and the brief feeling of disorientation dissipated, she shot up in bed when she realized Dani wasn't lying next to her.

Danica appeared from the bathroom, and was fastening a thigh-high red armor over her boot in an outfit that was part dominatrix and part gladiator. In fact, like Jegra's old gladiatorial garb, it showed more skin than was necessary.

"What in the galaxy are you wearing?" Jegra asked.

"You like it?" she said, spinning around for Jegra to see every soft rolling curve of her exposed body.

"I do, but it's so unlike anything I'd ever expect you to wear."

"You said it yourself. I have to be convincing enough not to be recognized as Cassera Van Danica. So, I figured, why not go for broke?"

"You must feel so ridiculous right now," Jegra laughed, tossing her hair over her shoulder.

"I feel like a prostitute with a license to kill," she replied, a mischievous grin spreading across her lips. "And," she added at the last moment, rubbing her arms, "A freezing cold one, at that."

Jegra laughed again and slowly swung her legs over the edge of bed. Her feet hit the cold floor with a soft smack and she grimaced. "You're right. It's a bit chilly in here."

"Get dressed," Danica said, nodding at a pile of freshly folded clothes on the end of the bed. "There's something I want to show you."

Once Jegra had finished dressing, Danica led her to the observation deck of the *Skywend*. The semicircular room had a crescent-shaped sofa that was built right into the floor. It faced a large glass viewing portal and allowed you to relax as you took in the view. Walking around to the front of the sofa, Jegra looked out at the vista to see a glorious blue and green planet hanging against a star spackled swath of endless space.

"Welcome to the Nyctan homeworld," Danica said, sidling up beside Jegra who stood enthralled by the beauty of the verdant planet.

"It's beautiful," Jegra whispered.

Danica leaned into Jegra and rested her head on her girlfriend's shoulder.

"It pales in comparison to Dagon," Danica jested. "But who am I to judge? A lush planet is a lush planet."

"I haven't told you this yet," Jegra said, resting her cheek on Danica's head as they stood next to one another in a cozy embrace. "But, this new look of yours, is totally hot."

"I appreciate you saying that," Danica said. She tossed her blue and purple ombre hair over her shoulder and squinted at Jegra. "But you do realize you made my boobs too big, right?"

"It's nothing to what I'd planned," Jegra admitted, a slight laugh escaping from her lips. "But I didn't want you pissed at me for the next decade."

Danica ribbed Jegra with her elbow. "Bitch," she teased.

The sound of the doors opening drew their attention away from the glittering panorama of sparkling oceans and shining clouds. They turned to find Sanakar and Estriel standing in the doorway. Both of them gave Jegra a grave look, as if to say it was time to follow the Pied Piper and see where his haunting melodies took her.

"It's time," Sanakar said.

Jegra nodded in confirmation and turned to leave. When Danica moved with her, she stopped and looked at her inquisitively as if to ask what she was doing.

"I'm coming too," Danica said.

"It's too dangerous," Jegra said.

Sanakar stood off to the side nodding, as if to reaffirm what Jegra was saying.

Danica's glabella creased with determination and she shot Jegra a hard look that said she was coming whether Jegra liked it or not. End of debate.

"Fine," she said, caving in to Danica's obduracy.

"Consider this a test run. If the Administratrix cannot recognize me, then Dakroth certainly won't either."

"If she does?" Jegra asked.

"Then we're screwed. And I did all this for nothing." Danica struck a pose and waved her hands across her body as though she were about to do a striptease.

"Sub Commander," Estriel cut in, clearing his throat in a polite attempt to draw her attention back to the task at hand. "A shuttle is coming to pick us up. It will be here shortly."

Jegra looked over at Sanakar and Estriel. They stared at her with their oversized, black Nyctan eyes. Other than the strange demonic look they sported, they seemed like ordinary people to her. The more time Jegra spent among other extraterrestrials, the more she felt like she fit right in.

"I'm looking forward to seeing Nyctan for the first time," she said as they all exited the observation deck and headed down the corridor together.

"I'm sure you will love it," Sanakar replied.

After a short jaunt down several intersecting corridors, they came to an airlock and watched as the Nyctan craft docked with the *Skywend*.

With a hiss the airlock door rolled back and Jegra about had a heart attack and staggered back.

"Galahad?" she gasped.

The man standing before her was the spitting image of Galahad. He was even a Knight.

"Apologies, Sub Commander," the man said, taking a reverent bow. "But you mistake me for my brother."

"Brother?" Jegra repeated, jarred by the revelation that Galahad had an identical twin brother. She shot Danica a confounded look only to find the same shocked expression plastered across Danica's face.

"I'm sorry that my brother is dead, but at least he died with honor, defending the empire."

"That he did," Jegra said. "Sir?"

"I beg your pardon. The name is Lance Bishop. Knight fourth class."

"Well, Sir Lance," Jegra said, boarding the shuttle. "Best not keep the Administratrix waiting."

The crew aboard, the Nyctan shuttle broke away from the *Skywend* and turned about. The majestic blue and green orb of Nyctan loomed in the distance.

Jegra had read that it was an exoplanet one and a half times larger than Earth, but with roughly the same gravity, and had more green than blue. Although there was a fair amount of both beneath the swirling white clouds. And now she was able to see it with her own two eyes.

Sure enough, it lived up to all the hype. It may even have been a more beautiful planet than Earth, and she was dying to just spend a month on solid ground again. Maybe do some hiking. Do some sightseeing and touristy stuff before jumping back into the fray.

The shuttle entered the atmosphere and began its descent. After breaking through the cloud cover, a lush landscape opened up before them and in the distance a grand city–the capital city, Nyla'Tek of Nyctan.

Lance Bishop brought the shuttle down in front of the Imperial Military Headquarters. Powering down the craft, he gestured for everyone to step outside.

Jegra was the first to exit. But what she found waiting for her caught her entirely off guard.

Anaïs Nin, wearing her glossy black battle armor, stood in front of the shuttle, her sword drawn. At least two dozen armed guards stood alongside her. To either side of her were two Knights, plasma blades humming in the broad light of day. Every single one of Anaïs Nin's soldiers' blasters were trained on her.

"Sub Commander Jegra Alakandra," Anaïs Nin said, her voice as cold as icicles. "Under Code 14 of the Nyctan military charter, I hereby place you under arrest for treason."

32

Jegra stood in her cell looking out at a large cylindrical complex of prison cells stacked on top of one another like giant rings as far as the eye could see up or down. It had an organic feel, however, like the architectural designs of Zaha Hadid and reminded her of the Galaxy SOHO in Beijing, China, or the BMW headquarters in Munich, Germany, if those places had been transformed into prisons. It was the most extensive holding facility she'd ever seen.

There were no stairs or elevators, no way in or out, except via the wafer-like hover platform which shuttled guards up and down on their shifts.

"You think an oracle might have been able to see this coming," Jegra griped, tapping the shield that concealed her.

A blue glow rippled with hexagonally linked energy and then quickly faded. The shield sent a strong electrical shock through her body, but being as strong as she was, she merely absorbed it. Anyone else would have dropped to the ground as though they had been tazed.

"It doesn't work like that," Sanakar said, sighing disappointedly.

She sat on a large white sofa that was placed in the quite sizable cell. A televid monitor showing the gladiator fights was on the wall. Like Jegra, she had on only what appeared to be white boxers and a white T-shirt that showed a lot of midriff.

Apparently, the outfits were designed so that prisoners couldn't conceal anything, yet be as comfortable as possible at the same time. This theme ran through the entire aesthetic of the Nyctan penitentiary: practical minimalist design, comfort.

A guard, dressed all in black and wearing a smooth black mask which concealed his face, stepped into view and stared at Jegra for a moment. Then, in a disgruntled voice, he growled, "Step back."

Jegra turned to look at her two roommates. Both Sanakar and Danica were with her. On her world, you'd never get placed in a cell with your friends. They'd be too worried about collusion and the off chance of a prison break. But the Nyctans prided themselves in their state of the art security measures so much they weren't worried about it. The prison was, for the lack of a better word, inescapable. So, as odd as it seemed to her, it was allowed.

Their prison cell, decked out in all white, was quite roomy. Nothing like the prisons on Earth. In addition to their comfortable sofa and televid monitor, there was a small aluminum dining table with four matching aluminum chairs, one king sized bed, and a food replicator which allowed them each three meals a day.

In the far corner of the cell was an aluminum toilet, no doors or curtain, but there was a small concrete partition which separated it from the rest of the room and blocked the view of the outside cells, giving the user a modicum of privacy.

Danica sat at the table and sipped a cup of tea. Although meals were limited to only meal times, beverages were allowed all day long. Crossing her right leg over her left knee, she bopped her foot under the table as she read a book on an e-reader.

Sanakar reclined on the sofa watching B-ranked gladiators duke it out on some distant moon. Unlike Jegra's triple A rating, which she got from defeating the reigning champion in her very first match, these gladiators were ranked by number of wins.

Recently, Jegra had also learned that fights to the death were barred on most worlds. Luckily for her, however, she got stuck on the psychopath Rhadamanthus Dakroth's moon Thessalonica. The bloodiest moon in the galaxy, as it was known. Also called the Jewel of Dagon. Of course, she later learned that the official gem of Dagon was a blood red sapphire. The irony of the namesake had not escaped her.

One of the reasons Thessalonica had the highest views in the system was because Dakroth allowed for all the violence and gore that excited that carnal bloodlust in its viewers.

Even though death matches were outlawed on most worlds, a B-ranked or C-ranked gladiator could request a bout at Thessalonica against the reigning champion. Against Jegra.

But she had been out of the picture for several months now, and with the Thessalonica arena destroyed and out of commission while a new arena was being built, there was no dominant contender. The vid-feeds merely focused on the up and comers from other systems and generated a scoring system to rank them all.

Jegra frowned as the top ranked gladiator came onto the screen. He was a Zarkonian, armor plated, armadillo looking fellow who could turn into a ball. Although she knew that she could boot him into the sun, the other contestants seemed to have their hands tied with the creature.

"Are you just going to sit there and watch televid all day?" Jegra asked, glaring at Sanakar.

"They only give us three channels. A weather channel, which seems quite useless being in a place like this. A cooking channel, which only makes me hungry. And the gladiator fights."

"I thought oracles were supposed to meditate and stuff," Jegra said, hinting strongly at the fact that her roommate's televid watching habit was driving her up the wall.

"Only part of the day," Sanakar said, brushing her reddish colored hair across her shoulder.

Danica looked up from her book. "Honestly, I thought they'd treat their oracle with more reverence than this."

"I was the one who prophesied Jegra's coming. I'm the one who saw her standing beneath the golden halo of the Gilded Master. But oracles have been wrong before." She sighed a lengthy sigh as if to suggest it couldn't be helped. It wasn't rocket science, after all. It was faith.

"So, are they also among the prisoners of Nyctan's maximum prison facility?" asked Danica.

"I highly doubt it," Sanakar reported. "None of the previous oracles put a war criminal into power. For this mistake, I must share in Jegra's punishment."

"Dani, you didn't need to pretend to be my slave."

"It was the only way I could get on the inside with you. As a slave, I count as your property, and had no choice but to share in your fate."

"It's very sweet of you, but I feel you could have served me better on the outside."

"Don't worry about that," she said with a wry smile.

Both Sanakar and Jegra turned to Danica and stared at her. She went back to reading her book as though she hadn't just let on that things were already in motion to have them sprung.

"Why do I get the sneaking suspicion that you know something I don't?" Jegra asked.

She sighed and put down her book again. "If you must know, Raven felt that if the administratrix was going to save her own neck she'd need to offer up a scapegoat. Who better to pin the failure of the campaigns on than a falsely appointed emissary? The Dagon Empress who lost the battle at Sector B-13 against the dreaded emperor Dakroth? Don't be naïve, Jegra. Of course, it was going to be you. It was a set up from the start. Now, the cruel bitch gets to go free and you're paying for her crimes. Which is why Raven and I put together this little rescue plan early this morning."

Unable to help herself, Jegra rushed over to Danica, hoisted her up into her arms, and gave her a bear hug. Setting her down again, she placed her hands on either side of Dani's face and bent down and kissed her.

"Did I ever tell you that you're the best?"

"Only every night," Danica teased.

"Oh, getting feisty, are we?"

"I thought I'd try to let my hair down. Get rid of the stiff soldier persona. Play the part of the horny slave girl."

"I like the confidence," said Jegra, nudging Dani with her elbow. "It's sexy on you."

"I hate to be the bearer of bad news," Sanakar interrupted. "But I don't think we'll be getting out of here anytime soon."

"What makes you say that?" Danica asked.

She cleared her throat and then nodded at the entrance. To their surprise, there were five guards standing around Raven Nightguard, who was wearing the trademark, prison issued white boxers and T-shirt.

They turned off the shield to the cell and shoved her into the room with the other three women. Then they flipped back on the power and the blue energy of the shield rematerialized behind her with a flicker.

Jegra opened her mouth to speak, then shut it again rethinking what she needed to say, then opened it again. "Raven? What are you doing here?"

"It seems there's been a change of plans."

"No, shit," Jegra replied, feeling like things kept taking a turn for the worse.

"What happened?" Sanakar asked, offering Raven a seat next to her on the white sofa.

"Using a skeleton key decryption hack, Gyllek hacked into the prison's firewall via a back door and found a system flaw in the facility's design that can be exploited. All you need is a level eight hacker on the inside to pull it off."

"You're a level eight hacker?" Danica balked.

"Level ten," Raven said with a grin, tapping her temple as if to highlight the genius underneath. Her electronic implants lit up like veins and pulsed rhythmically until they faded again.

"Of course, you are." Danica rolled her eyes and looked away.

She didn't have a leg to stand on, however, because now she was a mod, too. She knew that allowing her prejudice to show only made her look petty and hypocritical. But she really couldn't stand Raven Nightguard. The woman was just so damn righteous that it was aggravating.

Raven went over to the toilet and took the lid off. Reaching into the tank of water, she jostled her hand around and then plucked out a small, plastic device.

"What on Nyctan are you doing?" Sanakar asked.

Raven cracked open the module, then, fiddling with its rather simplistic circuitry a bit, she snapped the plastic lid back into place and placed it back inside the tank.

"As it turns out," she informed them, "all the flushing mechanisms in this entire facility are digitally regulated. All I did was program the device to tell all the toilets to flush at the same time. This will cause a backup in the pipes and all the toilets in the entire complex will flood simultaneously."

"So, you're trying to drown us?" Danica huffed, folding her arms across her chest.

"Oh, wait. I think I get it now," Sanakar said, hopping up onto her knees and leaning into the back of the sofa as she addressed everyone. "You're going to short circuit all the shields by overpowering the power grid."

"That's right," Raven replied. "The shields are modulated so that when one cell requires more power the system automatically sends more power to it. But if all the shields request more power at the same time due to their contact with the water, then the system will overload and annihilate itself."

"You girls ready?" Raven asked, reaching over to press the flush button.

Once the water contacted the high-power energy field, the feedback would send enough volts through the liquid to fry anyone standing in it. Not enough to kill them, but enough to give them a good burn. Jegra and Danica climbed up onto the bed so as to avoid the impending electrical surge while Sanakar chose to remain on her own little island of the sofa.

"Here goes nothing," Raven said. She flushed the toilet and then ran and leapt onto the bed.

The sound of toilets flushing in one explosive outburst mimicked the roar of an enormous waterfall.

Voices cried out in dismay as people's cells flooded and then there were yelps as prisoners were zapped and stunned.

The lights in the cell flickered and then the shields dropped and everything went dark. The entire facility was offline. Red emergency lighting powered up, but it was battery run. The main power grid remained offline.

"Now!" Raven shouted.

All four women rushed out of the cell and onto the terrace that wrapped itself around the entire inside of the holding level that they were on. But the veranda just wrapped around and came back to them. One giant circle. There was no getting on or off the platform. Not without the central hover disc that acted as an elevator.

Before they could make their grand escape, a guard spotted them. Lighting them up with a flashlight, he pointed a stun-stick at them that spat angry blue arcs of electricity, and yelled, "You there, halt!"

"Shit," cursed Jegra. They hadn't even made it more than a couple of steps outside of their cell before they'd been made by one of the guards—and with her recent spout of bad-luck more were probably already on the way.

As hard as it was for her to admit it, Jegra was beginning to think that this place really was inescapable.

33

Before the guard could square in on them and contain them, a large, horned alien the size and look of a rhinoceros flew out of a nearby cell and tackled the guard.

Bones crunched and the guard immediately crumpled into a pile of pulp beneath the mass of the powerful creature. The rhino man stood up, looked over at Jegra, and then throwing his arms into the air, shouted, "Long live the Empress!"

Immediately after he had alerted the rest of the prison that Jegra Alakandra, Empress of Dagon, was making a grand escape, all pandemonium broke loose on every level of the prison. Papers, bedding, clothes, you name it–even some unfortunate security guards–were tossed over the edges of each level. One Wilhelm scream after another went whooshing by as guards plummeted down the empty center of the facility to their imminent demise.

Raven ran over to the barred railing and looked over. "The skiff is coming up now. We're going to have to jump."

"Jump?" Danica asked, nervously edging away from the railing. "Nobody said anything about having to jump."

"Are you scared of heights?" Jegra asked in an amused tone. She chortled lightly and smiled at Danica who scowled back at her.

"What? Like you're so perfect?" she fired back defensively. "Jegra the Almighty! But don't let your fans' endless praise blind you to the truth. You're broken, Jegra. You always place your unquestioning trust in others. You keep forgiving those who repeatedly hurt and walk all over you, giving them the benefit of the doubt that they'll somehow change. Grow, up, Jegra! The galaxy is a cruel place. It doesn't have any room for your naïve optimism. And you're so dangerously unaware of it you actually put others in danger. The only invulnerable one here is you, Jegra. And that's not fair to any of us!"

Taken aback by the sudden chastising, Jegra gulped down the urge to get into a row with Dani. She didn't know where all of this pent-up anger was coming from but she could tell that Danica was on the verge of tears.

And as painful as it was for Jegra to hear the cold hard truth about her character flaw, Danica had a penchant for speaking the truth. In fact, it was one of Danica's most endearing qualities. She always called it like it was.

As usual, she wasn't wrong about Jegra. She did tend to let people walk over her so that they might pay attention to her. A lingering insecurity of not ever having felt welcome in a crowd, or even wanted, for that matter. An insecurity she hadn't quite gotten over yet, having gone from an unassuming nobody to Gladiatrix of the Galaxy almost overnight.

Her rapid rise to prominence in the arena, however, had given her great power and fame, though she wasn't always responsible with them. And, yes. Sometimes, people got hurt along the way.

She fought back tears as each name of someone she'd lost came back to her. Abethca, Jennica, Ellia, and now Galahad. Even Azra'il Nun had died in a hail Mary plan that Jegra herself had devised. It seemed wherever she went, her friends paid the ultimate price. And this weighed heavily on her.

"I know I'm not perfect," she said in a sullen tone. "And, I'm sorry. It was insensitive of me to highlight your fears and laugh. We're all afraid of losing something. I've lost a lot over this past year. And, at this very moment, I'm afraid of losing you. I promise you this...I'll try to do better. I'll do my best to do right by you, Dani."

"I know you will," Danica apologized, looking down at the ground. "And I'm sorry, too. I didn't mean to snap. It's just that I really, really hate heights."

"We can continue this discussion later," Raven cut in. "But if you want to get your cute lady butts out of this place, the time to act is...right...now." With that, Raven hopped up onto the railing and leapt off.

"By Hastur!" Sanakar gasped. "She jumped."

"Go!" Jegra said, helping Sanakar over the railing. Hanging onto the railing, Sanakar looked down over her shoulder to see that Raven had landed safely on the platform. Taking in a deep breath, she closed her eyes and let go.

Jegra rushed to the railing and looked over. "She made it!" she exclaimed, informing the others.

Not wasting another moment, Jegra turned and stretched her hand out, offering it to Danica.

She vigorously shook her head in protest and backed up against the wall. Her chest grew tight as she grew more anxious and fresh beads of sweat bloomed across her balmy skin. The palms of her hands grew sweaty and cold simultaneously and a frightful shiver shot down her spine.

"Come on, Dani! We don't have any more time to lose."

She shook her head again and wheezed as she began to hyperventilate. Walking up to Danica with intimidating strides, Jegra picked her up and slung her over her shoulder.

"What are you doing?" Danica cried out, her voice in a tizzy.

"I'm saving your hot piece of ass," Jegra barked. She swatted Danica's ass, her hand leaving its imprint in the form of a rosy welt on Danica's perfectly round butt cheek. Danica yelped out in pain, but it helped to get her mind off the situation and get her breathing normally again.

Without another second to spare, Jegra took off running. Full speed, she leapt up onto the railing just as the elevator skiff was rising past them. Using her superior strength, she kicked off the bars and the railing bent under her foot from the force. Launching into the air, she and Danica flew across the expanse.

It seemed too close to call as the skiff climbed away from them but, suddenly, her fingers met the edge and Jegra clamped on with one hand. In her other arm, she held Danica close to her.

Gradually, Jegra's fingers began to lose their grip. "I'm slipping!" she called out, hoping Raven or Sanakar would hear her.

In the blink of an eye, Raven's dark blue hand reached down from above and clutched Jegra's wrist just as Jegra couldn't hold on any longer and relinquished her grip.

"I've got you!" she shouted. The vein-like circuitry in her arm pulsed bright pink as her nano-tech enhancements compensated for the exertion of pulling both women back up to the platform.

With Sanakar holding Raven's other arm, she helped Raven drag Jegra and

Danica onto the hover skiff.

Out of breath, Jegra rolled onto her back and panted heavily. Danica lay beside her, her chest heaving with equal vigor. "Don't ever go and pull a stunt like that again!" she growled.

"Sorry," Jegra apologized with a light chortle. "But I wasn't going to just leave you there."

Danica groaned and rolled onto her side. Pulling down the elastic waist of her shorts, she examined the bright pink welt on her lavender butt cheek. "Did you have to go and slap me so hard? That stung."

Raven helped Jegra up and Sanakar did the same for Danica who was still rubbing her sore buttocks.

"What now?" Jegra asked, turning her gaze to Raven.

"Now we get up into the air vents before the laser grid comes back on."

"What happens when the laser grid comes back on?" asked Jegra in a credulous manner, although she fully suspected that she already knew the answer.

"Let's just say if you want to keep your body in one piece, it's best to be clear of the air vents before the laser grid turns back on."

It only took a few minutes for them to reach the top of the facility. Once the skiff came to a halt, Raven walked over to the edge, reached out, and grabbed ahold of a maintenance walkway off to the side. She pulled herself on to it and then helped Sanakar and the others across. All four women clambered down the walkway until they found an access panel to the ventilation system. Raven tried to pull the panel off but it was stuck tight.

"Let me try," Jegra said. She pushed her fingers through the grate and yanked off the panel in one hefty jerk. The screws tore through the plating as if it were melted butter and she discarded the covering.

Raven pursed her lips in a pleased fashion and nodded her head approvingly. "Well done."

"I'll go first," Sanakar said.

Raven squatted and had Sanakar place her foot on her bent thigh and then gave her a boost up. She then helped Danica and Raven up too. Jegra was tall enough that she could simply pull herself up into the ventilation duct and motioned for Raven to go on ahead of her.

Once everybody was inside the ventilation duct, Raven said, "Make your way toward the roof. When you see the fan, that means we're almost there."

They inched their way through the ventilation system like a train of caterpillars. Going up was the hard part, but with some elbow skin and a bit of effort, they finally made it to the fan. Just then, there was a clunk and the power came back on.

Jegra looked down and the laser grid turned on at the bottom of the ventilation shaft and slowly began rising up toward them. It combed the ventilation duct, burning up anything inside with a tartan of deadly red lasers.

"Um, ladies," Jegra said. "We have a problem."

"We have a problem up here too," Sanakar added.

The giant fan above them began to spin. As it menacingly chopped the air, it seemed there was no way to stop it. At the same time the laser grid slowly closed in on them from below.

"Jegra!" Danika shouted. "We need you up here."

Jegra tried to squeeze past Raven, but it was no use. There wasn't enough wiggle room to get by. "I'm sort of stuck down here at the moment. Are you sure there's nothing you can do?"

Sanakar looked down at everyone. Realizing they were running out of time and there weren't any good options, she took a deep breath and then threw her arm up into the fan. She screamed out in pain as the fan cut into her arm, but her bone was enough to stop it.

"Go!" she growled through gritted teeth. "Go!"

Danica scurried through the opening, quickly followed by Raven. By the time Jegra got to Sanakar she was already feeling light headed. Blue blood trickled down her arm.

Jegra reached up and grabbed the blade and bent it in on itself, wedging it so it couldn't start spinning again. Then, reaching around Sanakar's waist, she looked at her arm. It was mangled and broken, and there was no way they could save it. Not in the limited amount of time they had.

"This is going to hurt," Jegra said.

Sanakar nodded and then looked away as Jegra took her trapped arm in her hands.

Jegra pulled hard and Sanakar's arm tore free from where it was pinched by the fan blade. She yelped out in agony as her mangled arm dropped down and dangled limply by her side. But the pain was too much and she quickly fell silent as the shock of it caused her to black out. Holding on tight to Sanakar, Jegra pulled them both up in time to avoid getting diced by the laser grid.

The vent of the air duct on the rooftop flew off and Danica clambered out. Soon enough, all four women had made their way onto the top of the prison complex. It was a soaring tower, as tall as anything on Earth, but set in the middle of Nyctan's largest ocean. There was nothing for miles in every direction except for sky and the pterodactyl like birds which circled the platform.

"I sure hope those things aren't carrion birds," Danica said, craning her neck and looking up toward the sky and eyeing the flying creatures with suspicion.

"I doubt they pose much of a threat," Raven said, reaching into her pants and fiddling with herself.

Danica looked over at her in shock. "What are you doing? We don't have time for that right now," she reprimanded.

Raven ignored Danica's upbraiding and pulled her hand out of her shorts and withdrew a glistening communication device. Wiping it off on her shirt, she held it to her lips and spoke into it. "*Skywend*, this is Raven, do you read me?"

A garbled reply came almost immediately. Jegra recognized Skuld's voice.

"We hear you, captain. We're already en route."

"Good," Raven said, glancing at everyone's faces. "Get us out of here."

Golden beams of light came down from the sky and all four women's bodies disassembled, piece by piece, in a swirl of hexagonal energy packets made of the same golden light. The whirlwind of hexagonal energy rose into the sky and, then, after another few seconds, they found themselves standing aboard the transporter platform of the *Skywend*. Whole again.

Skuld, Gyllek, and Estriel stood behind the transporter control panel which sat along the back wall and greeted them with a smile. At least Skuld and Estriel did. Gyllek, on the other hand, was her typical poker-faced, anti-social self.

"Glad you could make it," Skuld said.

"We almost didn't," Danica informed him.

"Get us out of here," Raven said, marching off to the bridge. Nodding her head at Sanakar's unconscious body, cradled in Jegra's arms like a newborn infant, she added, "And see to it that she gets medical treatment, ASAP."

"Yes, ma'am," Skuld replied.

Estriel rushed over to Jegra and helped hoist up Sanakar's sleeping body. "What happened to her?" he asked, slipping his arm under hers and propping her up on his shoulder while Jegra did the same with the other shoulder.

"She saved our lives," Jegra answered.

He gave her a sympathetic look that hit her emotional heart strings. Like Sanakar, she saw that Estriel still believed in her. Believed in the prophecy. He had faith and would continue to stand by her side, even if it meant becoming a fugitive.

"Come," Skuld said, leading the way out of the transport room and into the corridor. "The medical bay is this way."

"I'll be on the bridge if you need me," Danica said, addressing Jegra who followed after Skuld.

Jegra looked over her shoulder and nodded. They shared a short glance and seemingly read each other's minds. Then, they parted ways and headed in opposite directions to attend to their separate duties.

34

"**Two bogies on** our six," Kregor informed the captain.

"I see them. I see them." Raven mashed the controls and sent all available power to the rear deflector shields. The ship shook as lasers bent off the shields, jarring everyone inside.

Danica stumbled onto the bridge, bracing herself against a bulkhead as the ship shuddered and swayed beneath her feet, her new chest bouncing annoyingly in her face. Wrapping her arms under her new tits, she held them in place and looked out at the two Nyctan ships chasing them.

"Those are Seyfferian corvettes," she informed. "There's no way we'll outrun them in an atmosphere like this. We need to make a jump."

"Are you out of your pretty little blue head?" Kregor asked. He shot her a look that said, *no way sister.* "An FTL jump through a rich atmosphere would tear us apart. Only battle cruisers have enough shielding to pull off such a maneuver. And even then, it's not advisable."

"We'll discuss it later. Right now, let's just stay focused on getting out of this mess," Raven ordered. "Now, sit down and strap in. Things are going to get bumpy."

A thunderous crack shook the ship and Raven took evasive action and flipped the *Skywend* upside down and pulled back and to starboard with all her might to avoid the battle cruiser that had just appeared above them.

Raven immediately took evasive action, the *Skywend's* hull screeching as its bottom scraped along the hull of the enemy vessel.

Their brush with the cruiser spat up a trail of sparks that extended behind them like a jet stream and the screeching of metal grinding on metal rang throughout every deck of the ship. Finally breaking free of the near collision, Raven sent the *Skywend* into a nosedive and quickly distanced the ship from the Nyctan battle cruiser.

Elated to be alive, Kregor cheered on the captain's flying. "That's what I'm talking about!" Kregor shouted, as he brought the stabilizers back online.

"I appreciate your confidence, but that was close. Too close," Raven said, shaking her head in disbelief at the recklessness of the Nyctan cruiser. Obviously, they were desperate to catch them.

"Who the hell would be insane enough to jump a cruiser into low orbit?" Danica asked.

"Besides you, you mean?"

She shot Kregor an ice-cold look. "Yeah, besides me," she snapped. Her suggestion was meant to save their necks. She'd never jump into an atmosphere to claim a single ship. She'd set up a blockade in space and then send boots down to the ground to smoke the enemy out of hiding.

"I think you know the answer to that. It's clearly the Queen Bitch of the Galaxy, Annie."

Danica began to giggle and then caught herself and gulped down her amusement at Kregor calling Anaïs Nin by the Terran nickname, Annie.

"That Nyctan bitch slaughtered many Dragonians at the battle of Kalex 5. My seven brothers and three of my sisters were among the casualties." Kregor hissed after the mere mention of her name, as though the very thought of the Nyctan Administratrix was offensive to him.

"I'm sorry," Danica said.

He nodded his head, accepting her apology, and then turned his attention back to co-piloting the ship.

"Watch your twelve," Kregor said, pointing out the window. "That thing is going to drop like a lead weight and smash into the planet. And we don't want to be underneath it when it does."

"Not if it jumps away first," Raven said.

"That would tear us apart, though," he realized as soon as he'd said it and shook his head. Destroying them was the whole point, "Which would be bad. Very, very bad."

"That's why we'll just have to make the jump first."

"I see how it is," he said, glancing between both women. "You all team up on the poor ole lizard man."

"Don't worry, at least you'll die a hero." Danica's voice trailed off as the gravity of the situation hit her like, well, a starship falling out of the sky. That's when they noticed the shadow of the cruiser bearing down on them.

"Ship! Ship!" Kregor shouted.

"I see it!" Raven shouted back, punching the thrusters to full.

"We're so screwed," Kregor said.

"Not necessarily," Danica said, pointing at the aft thrusters of the ship.

Raven gave her a look of acknowledgement, letting her know that they were on the same page. "It's crazy, but it just might work. Besides, it's not like we have a lot of options right at the moment," Raven growled, pulling back on the stick.

The *Skywend*'s nose came full about and aimed itself right at the battle cruiser's aft thrusters.

"What are you doing, Captain?" Kregor asked, his voice flexing with nervousness. "You're heading straight for it. Don't we want to be, you know, going the opposite way?"

"I'm going to ride the shockwave by putting us right in the path of its gas tail."

"That's assuming we can survive the turbulence of an FTL jump in low atmosphere at all."

Raven's facial tech lit up, every circuit aglow, the bright white lines of the circuitry outlined in red where the lines met her blue skin. Her eyes turned from purple to bright white as she began processing all the possible trajectories. "I can do it," she said, her voice growing more computer-like.

Danica strapped in tight and, holding the edges of her chair, she screamed, "*Fuuuck!*" just as the Nyctan cruiser jumped away.

"Shit!" Kregor shouted as the *Skywend*'s collision alarm automatically started to blare annoyingly all around them.

[Incoming shockwave], the computer relayed in a soothing woman's voice. The soothing voice seemed a bit out of place against the sheer intensity of the situation.

There was a bang and a crash, and the *Skywend*'s structural integrity alarm joined the collision alarm in a terrible cacophony that foreshadowed their impending demise.

White hot sparks flew out of the control panel and rained down from the ceiling as paneling burst open with small electrical explosions. The computer wasn't helping any either, as it kept warning, [Systems critical].

"Kindly turn that fucking thing off!" Raven shouted.

Kregor kicked his leg out and booted the controls and the computer's voice died away.

Although the droning of the computer's alarms stopped, the amount of turbulence caused a rattling so loud it was jarring. Danica felt like she was going to throw up.

Finally, after an extremely rough ride through the shockwave, they came out the other side. Shortly after that, they breached the atmosphere.

The *Skywend* found a fixed orbit and Raven cut the engines.

"You did it!" Kregor cheered.

Danica let out a deep sigh of relief.

Raven flipped on the comm. "I realize we're falling apart at the seams up here, but there's no time for a ship wide maintenance check. It's best we be getting on before more cruisers show up," Raven said, and she spooled up the FTL drive. "Everyone, hold tight." With that, she hit the ignition button.

Instead of leaping into streaks of light stretching infinitely into the recesses of hyperspace, however, the drive gurgled and sputtered and then wound down with a whine.

Kregor looked at Raven and she groaned.

"What's happening?" Danica asked.

"Nothing. Absolutely nothing," Raven complained, her white eyes cooling back to a honeyed violet. Smashing the comm, she shouted, "Gyllek, where are my engines?"

"I'm working on it!" a frantic voice replied.

Off the starboard bow, three Nyctan battle cruisers appeared, all of them as big as the *Omikran*.

"Shit," Raven said. "They've already found us."

"What are we going to do?" asked Danica, as she stared out at the pack of angry looking ships. The looked like a pack of wolves, slowly closing in on their prey.

The *Skywend* slowly came about and then turned toward the rings of Nyctan's largest moon. "We'll try and lose them in there," Raven said, pointing at the rings.

"Are you crazy?" Danica gasped. "We'll be torn apart."

"But so will they," Raven added. "And we're smaller, so we'll have a better chance of not dying."

"I am really beginning to dislike this ship," Danica groaned.

"Don't worry, sister. The feeling is mutual." Raven looked over at Danica and smiled. But it was a harsh smile. Not hostile, but not friendly either.

"I'm sorry," Danica said. "I didn't mean to insult you or your ship. I've just had a stressful few days is all."

"You and me both," Raven replied.

Jegra appeared on the bridge and Danica swiftly unbuckled herself and flew into her arms.

"What's this now?" Jegra laughed, tickled by Danica's uncharacteristic display of affection.

"She thought we were going to die," Kregor said, answering on Danica's behalf. "But the captain got us through. She always does."

"How does Sanakar fare?" Raven asked.

"She's sedated and resting. But there's been too much nerve damage. Skuld will have to amputate her arm and fit her with a prosthetic. But she'll survive."

Raven nodded and then jammed the throttle full tilt. The *Skywend*'s thrusters grew hot as they blasted toward the moon with rings.

The battle cruisers trailed them in hot pursuit, but their enormous size made their acceleration sluggish as they fought against Nyctan's gravity.

Some green disrupter blasts whisked by the *Skywend*'s port side, but they were nowhere near enough to be of concern. The *Skywend* was far enough away that the deflectors easily bent the blasts away from the ship. They'd have to be much closer before the laser blasts would do any serious damage, and that wasn't likely at this point.

Not wanting to risk them getting close enough to threaten the ship, Raven kept the throttle on max burn. At least this way they'd maintain a safe distance.

It looked like it would be smooth sailing until they got to the ice belt around the moon, but before they could make it halfway, the *Subjugator* jumped into high

Nyctan orbit and cut them off from their destination.

"Holy shit balls!" Kregor barked, his voice filled with shock by the sudden and wholly unexpected appearance.

Almost instantly, Dakroth began firing on the Nyctan cruisers. It seemed that he wanted the *Skywend* all to himself and wasn't about to let anyone else have Jegra.

Jegra grabbed the back of Raven's chair and leaned forward, looking out at the ships blasting away at one another.

"That idiot just gave us the out we needed," Raven said, a large smile forming on her lips.

The comm chimed and Gyllek came onto the speaker. "FTL is back up and running, captain. Ready to kick this bucket right in her shiny little ass."

"Excellent," replied Raven. "And just in time, too." Looking over her shoulder at Jegra, she asked, "Where to, your majesty?"

"We're back to that, are we?" Jegra laughed.

"You are the Empress of the Galaxy."

That gave Jegra an idea, and a wide grin came across her face as the perfect destination came to mind. "We're going to go to the last place in the entire galaxy he'd expect."

35

The Imperial Palace on Dagon Prime was grander than the Taj Mahal and three times the size of the Taj Palace hotel in Mumbai. It had very similar features to Arabian architecture on Earth and was just as ornate in its beauty.

Golden Persian domed spires rose up on four turrets which surrounded a fifth, much larger, domed tower. A long stretch of the royal pool ran about a hundred meters right up to the main, back entrance.

The grand entrance overlooked the Dagon metropolis from its hilltop perch. There was no easy direct access from below to the palace grounds, as the hill was too steep and also fortified.

The *Skywend*'s landing thrusters kicked dust and leaves up as the ship, a six-hundred-foot-long vessel – the size of the largest megayachts back on Earth – came down on the back lawn of the palace grounds. Its landing skiffs deployed, and with a compressed hiss of the hydraulics, it set down.

As the landing ramp began to open, Jegra was already descending to greet the small security force that raced towards them.

The palace security detail of two dozen private security guards, who were well-armed, trained their weapons on the ship. One got on his helmet-mounted loudspeaker and said, "This is the Imperial Palace, you are trespassing. Prepare to surrender yourselves and hand over your vessel. I repeat, you are trespassing."

"I think not," Jegra said, stepping off the ramp as she looked at the stunned faces of the Dagon security force. She was wearing her chainmail gladiatrix bikini, along with her full array of trophies and trinkets, so as to be the most recognizable version of her celebrity self. That way, there'd be no mistaking who she was nor what authority she had.

Shocked and awed, all the guards picked their mouths up off the palace lawn and lowered their weapons. "Your majesty," the chief security officer said, kneeling. As soon as he had knelt, the other guards, in one simultaneous display of allegiance, all knelt as well. "My apologies, we had no idea. It was believed you were dead."

"The rumors of my death were exaggerated. Even my wayward husband, the emperor, still thinks that I'm dead. Please notify me when he arrives. Until then, grant my friends full access to the imperial grounds and palace."

The guard nodded his head, stood up, and then swiveled a finger in the air. This gesture immediately dissipated the rest of the security detail, which went back to their posts.

"Your majesty, my name is Meleh'kendar, and I'm chief of palace security. May I see your wrist, please."

Jegra shot him a sharp glance, yet, upon realizing he meant her no ill will, she extended her arm. He took it and then pulled out a scanner from a pouch on his security belt. It scanned her invisible barcode, making sure she was who she appeared to be, and not an assassin in disguise.

Satisfied it was really her, Meleh'kendar then reprogrammed her designation as that of the Empress of Dagon, giving her full authority over the palace. And until her warmongering husband returned from wreaking havoc on the galaxy, she supposed she was in charge. Of everything.

Raven Nightguard emerged behind Jegra, and the Empress turned and introduced her. "Meleh'kendar, this is Captain Raven Nightguard. She has full authority here. Anything that can be said in front of me can be said in front of her. Do I make myself clear?"

"Yes, your grace," Meleh'kendar replied, bowing his head.

"Good. Now, alert the staff of my arrival. My guests have had a long, wearisome journey. I owe my life to each and every one of them and they deserve the finest hospitality we have to offer."

"As you wish, your grace." Meleh'kendar bowed reverently then spun on his heels and, without wasting a moment, marched off to carry out Jegra's requests, speaking into his wireless earpiece as he barked orders at the staff to make things ready. The empress had returned.

Jegra turned to Raven and shrugged.

"You know," Raven said nonchalantly, "They very well could have had orders to fire on sight."

Jegra laughed. "It was a risk I was willing to take. Besides, with the emperor's gallivanting around like a madman, I highly doubt he's had the time. As far as the people are concerned, we're happily married." Placing her hand on her hip, she waved her hand across the vista behind her of the royal palace lingering over her shoulder. "Shall we?"

Raven laughed in return and then headed back up the ramp of her ship. "I'll alert the others that it's safe to come out." She smiled the rarest of smiles and then disappeared inside. Just as she entered, Danica appeared at the top of the ramp.

Stunned that Jegra's plan had actually worked, Danica looked around the grounds, thinking it might be a trick, but then came to the conclusion that it must be exactly as it appeared; they were honored guests of the royal palace.

Overjoyed by the prospect of Jegra actually being accepted by the Dagon people as their empress, she raced down the ramp and leapt up into Jegra's arms.

Again, Danica's sudden display of affection caught Jegra by surprise and she barely had time to catch her. The two women crashed together and, absorbing her momentum, Jegra hoisted Danica up and spun her around and laughed at the unexpectedness of it.

She wrapped her arms tightly around Danica's waist, bringing Danica comfortably into her ample bosom, and squeezed. Jegra arched her chin upward while Danica bent down to meet her lips.

Danica placed one hand on Jegra's shoulder, the other on her neck, and pointed her toes outward as they kissed like she'd seen the women in the romantic televid shows. "I was so worried," she admitted.

"It's all right," Jegra insisted. "We're safe now, at least until my darling husband gets home," she laughed.

She set Danica back down and they gazed into one another's eyes, their arms still hanging on the gradual curve of the other's hips. Danica's face grew serious and she shook her head in a solemn manner.

"No, Jegra. It's not safe. It will never be safe as long as you are with him. The sooner you realize this the sooner you can prepare yourself for the inevitable."

"Inevitable?" Jegra asked.

"The day that Emperor Dakroth decides to kill you. Because, heed my words, luv. That day is fast approaching."

"Then what are we waiting for?" Jegra said, determined not to let her psychopath of a husband manipulate her any longer. "Let's get ready."

Danica smiled and nodded in agreement. It was time to stop running and make a stand. And with the support of the Dagon people behind her, Jegra might just pull it off.

Three weeks went by and Jegra finally got news that the emperor was giving up his search for her and would be returning to Dagon.

After the servants dressed her in the finest silk gown, replete with shoulder epaulettes and a flowing white cape with golden interior, she spun around and marched out of her room and into the hallway.

Naturally, the outfit had a plunge neckline that maximized her cleavage. The dress itself was pearl white with gold embroidery and an intricate rosemaling of traditional Dagon floral patterns trailed off to lace fringes which gave the dress an almost feather-like appearance.

Although the dress was long and trailing, there was a solitary slit running from her hip all the way down the side of the dress, accentuating her shapely leg yet allowing her complete mobility.

The empress, according to Danica, also had the secondary role of being the emperor's body guard. Which meant her outfit was designed as much for fighting as it was elegance.

Elaborate details were etched neatly into the pearl-like metal of the shoulder armor that glimmered iridescently in the beams of sunshine that shined through the towering windows of the corridor and, split by the window frames, spread themselves across the room like the folds of a luminous oriental fan.

Jegra marched across the empty marble floors of the throne room and up the dais to the throne, which sat overlooking the main chamber. Since there was only one seat, due partly to the fact that the emperor had planned to be rid of her, she took it and sat down.

Her hands gripped the ends of the chair's arms and she crossed her legs. Her tan leg escaped the white dress and she moved the slit skirt aside, making sure the maximum amount of skin was exposed and held her sexy pose.

Meleh'kendar rushed into the throne room and, huffing to try to catch his breath, he announced. "The emperor is transporting down now, your grace."

"Thank you, Meleh'kendar," Jegra said. "You may be excused."

As soon as he had exited the large standing doors, a yellow beam of light appeared in the middle of the throne room. A few seconds later Emperor Dakroth materialized.

The look on his face was priceless. Upon seeing Jegra, decked out in the clothes of the one true empress, sitting upon his throne, his jaw dropped to the floor.

A sinister grin came across his face. He tossed his long platinum hair over his shoulder and laughed. "But, of course, you're here! Why didn't I think of it sooner?"

"Because, darling," Jegra sneered, playing up her false politeness for added measure, "You have a simplistic, one-track mind."

Displeased with her brazen disrespect, he frowned and then scratched his chin. "Yes, I suppose I do." Raising his glowing finger, he pointed it at her and grinned. "But if you knew me so well, then you should have also known it would be unwise to meet me here alone where nobody could witness your demise."

He let loose a laser blast and it flew across the room. Mere centimeters before hitting Jegra's face, it deflected off of an invisible shield and then blew a hole in the wall of the palace.

An energy field of blue flickered around Jegra as she stood up. Her eyes held Dakroth's gaze and the calm, cool look in them disturbed him greatly. It was as though she had anticipated his every treacherous move.

"I don't know how you did that," he growled, "but you won't be so lucky the next time."

She started down the stairs toward him which caused him to grow tense and panic began to fill his chest. Fumbling back, he shot off several more blasts in a desperate attempt to stop her before she reached him. But they, too, deflected away from Jegra. Small explosions erupted where the ratcheted laser blasts impacted.

"How are you doing this?" he roared, staggering back to try to keep his distance. But soon enough, she was upon him.

Jegra glided across the distance that separated them, grabbed Dakroth by his throat, and hoisted him into the air. She held him up; her eyes remained serene as she strangled him. She wanted him to know he meant nothing to her, and that, if she wanted to, she could squash him like a bug.

The emperor wheezed through his crushed windpipes, "Wait! *ack* We can...*ack*...come to some kind of...*ack*...agreement!"

Jegra clamped down even harder and watched him struggle to pry her fingers away from his throat. His legs kicked uselessly in the air as he squirmed to escape her grasp.

She held him there until his eyelids began to flutter and he was about to black out. Finally, she relinquished her grasp and let him crumpled to the floor.

Hacking and coughing, he sucked in as much air as he could, his lungs rattling as he fought his way back to consciousness.

"My dear Rhadamanthus, don't you know who I am?"

"You are Jegra," he replied. "Gladiatrix of the Galaxy."

She immediately clutched him by his throat and hoisted him off his feet again. "I asked: Do you know who I am?" she growled.

This time her eyes were smoldering, like dark coals that were still hot enough to ignite anything they might touch. And she was sure to make him feel her fire and fury.

"*Ack!* You're...*ack*...the Empress!"

She dropped him to the ground. "There. That wasn't so hard to admit, was it, my dear husband?"

Emperor Dakroth rubbed his throat and looked up at her. She climbed back up the stairs and, once again, helped herself to his seat. Impressed by her cunning, he smiled.

"What is it you want, my dear wife?"

"I want you to understand something, sweetheart. I'm no longer yours to toy with. Imperial Law dictates that I have equal authority with you over the empire. I am your *equal* by law, though I think you might agree I'm slightly superior in every other way. If you continue to play these little mind games, I'll outmatch you at every turn. Because, unlike you, my dear, I have friends."

Danica stepped out from behind the throne, a blue shimmer of shielding flickering all around her and Jegra. Her eyes glowed hot yellow with radiant energy.

At the same time, from behind the pillars, emerged Raven Nightguard and her crew of top-notch mercenaries, all of them decked out in the finest armor

Dagon credits could buy. Each of them was also notably equipped with the latest weaponry and tech.

Even the new Bre'lal girl, whom Jegra learned was called Raphine, was with them. If that wasn't impressive enough, both Estriel and Sanakar joined them. Sanakar sported a new, bio-metal arm and flexed it, showing off, as they took Jegra's side.

Dakroth scanned all their resolute faces and then, after a pause, laughed out loud. "You are a cunning one, my dear! It seems I chose wisely when I made you Empress of Dagon."

Jegra stood up again and marched down the stairs. Nervous as to what she might do, Dakroth scuttled back. But she stopped twenty feet from him.

"There is a Nyctan saying you should heed, my love: 'An eye for an eye. A heart for a heart. An oath for an oath.'"

"I am well aware of this expression," Dakroth said. But his dismissiveness was gone. Now, she had his full attention.

"Thessalonica is mine. My palace is finishing completion as we speak. But don't think for a minute that because I choose to live there, away from you, that I don't have eyes and ears everywhere. I've had three weeks to plan and I've made powerful allies in that short time. So, I'm not going anywhere. But if you come at me again with these Machiavellian schemes to dominate me, then I'll take that saying literally and I'll rip out your eyes and your heart with my bare hands. That is my solemn oath."

Finished, Jegra spun and left the throne room. Her elite troupe of warriors following her out in tight succession.

The last to leave was Kregor. As he passed the emperor he deliberately nudged Dakroth's shoulder.

"Watch where you're going, lizard!"

Kregor stopped and spun around. "Did you say something to me, blue-skin?" he hissed.

Dakroth was about to lose his cool when he realized that the Dragonian wore a class-7 series shield modulator. Not only was Jegra shielded from his laser blasts, so was her entire group of bodyguards.

Dakroth backed off. "No," he grumbled.

Kregor snorted. "That's what I thought."

With that he turned and stormed out of the room.

Dakroth, still stunned by everything that had just transpired, slowly climbed the stairs and went over to his throne. Planting himself in the chair, he noted it was still warm, and despite himself, he was aroused thinking of Jegra's beautiful body and unmatched prowess. He gazed out across the empty room, his mind deep in thought.

After a long, drawn out silence, he kicked his head back and began to bellow with laughter. Slumping down in his chair he rested his chin on his fist and stared out of the windows at Dagon and chuckled. Damn. he had chosen well. She'd played him. And played him good.

36

Arena City bustled with the sounds of construction. The new gladiatorial arena was beign built and repairs to the rest of the city were nearing completion. Not only that, but Jegra's palace was finished.

Jegra stood on her twelfth-story balcony, which overlooked the city, and scanned every inch of the activity going on below. Emerging from her personal chambers came Danica, wearing a see-through, deep purple lace lingerie which complimented her violet skin. Tossing her turquoise-purple ombre hair across her bare shoulder, she said, "I think you may have rattled him. It's been three weeks and there hasn't been a peep from Emperor Dakroth."

Jegra turned around. Her dress was a translucent tangerine color which went with her bronzed, sunbaked skin. She wore her hair up and now had on a lot of makeup. Jewels adorned her neck and she wore elegant bracelets that coiled up her forearms like gilded serpents.

It was no secret–everyone had taken notice. She no longer looked the part of a slave. But the gladiator in her could still be seen in the finely sculpted ripples of her muscle tone, in the deep cut of her calves, and in the raw strength of her broad shoulders.

"He keeps sending me jewels," she laughed, brushing her fingers along the opaline necklace she wore.

"He's probably horny," Danica teased. "He wants to win some favor back with you, so he's showering you with gifts. He'll probably invite you down to the royal palace for some wining and dining followed by a drunken and desperate attempt to seduce you."

Jegra chortled. Danica's description of Dakroth was spot on. "I'm afraid

Dakroth's sex privileges have been permanently revoked. Attempted murder has a way of turning off a girl's romantic desires."

"I hope they're not completely shut down," Danica said, sauntering across the balcony, her hips swiveling seductively. Meeting Jegra, she threw her arms around her hips and pressed her pelvis into Jegra's thigh. Looking up into her partner's eyes, she smiled. "Because I have something to confess."

"A confession?" Jegra said, raising an eyebrow. "Do tell."

"More of a question, really. I helped Dakroth hurt you in unimaginable ways, yet you found it in your heart to forgive me. And even after you found out about my terrible sins regarding the slaughter of countless innocent Nyctan lives, you still found room in your heart to love me. Why?"

"Because I saw the good in you, Danica. It's always been there. But, like everyone else, you were afraid of the emperor. It's why you blindly carried out his orders. In the end, we're all just human."

Danica balked and then made a sour face. "No need to be insulting." She made sure Jegra knew it was all in jest. She used to be prejudiced against Jegra for what she viewed as an inferior genetic code.

As it turns out, Jegra's genetic code may be the very key to unlocking the galaxy and uniting all the races and species within. In fact, it was Danica's opinion that Jegra was far more valuable than any one realized. The only thing was, her research was incomplete.

Even with Jegra's genome mapped, it was still unclear how her DNA could override that of other species'. But as soon as she solved the puzzle, she'd share her findings with Jegra.

Jegra turned her head and looked out at the arena. "The first fights will be in my honor," she said. Her voice was neither sad nor hopeful. She was just stating a fact.

Stuck in their embrace, Danica turned her gaze to the arena as well. "How does that make you feel?"

"I don't know how to feel. But Raven was right. I hear the whispers. The people across four quadrants and seven star systems are hailing me as their savior."

"It was always part of the plan to make you into a legend."

"In that much Dakroth succeeded. I just don't feel like any great hero. I haven't done anything deserving of their faith in me."

"But you have. It's not just silencing the emperor, Jegra. You have given them hope. Hope that they might rise beyond the harsh conditions of their miserable lives perchance to become great, just like you. And, maybe, this hope is enough to give rise to a better world."

"Or a better galaxy," added Jegra.

"Or that," Danica laughed.

A sudden sandstorm erupted out of nowhere and the two women shielded their eyes. Squinting through the fine particles of sand, Jegra saw Dakroth's shuttle decloak as it landed in the courtyard below.

To Jegra's surprise, however, the only person to step off the shuttle was Meleh'kendar. He looked up at her from the courtyard twelve stories down and then rushed inside the palace.

Jegra shot Danica a confounded look. She shrugged as if to say she had no clue as to what was going on.

"Come on," Jegra said, "We best go see what he wants."

"Should I even be attending these meetings?" Danica asked as she slipped out of her evening clothes. "People might begin to suspect I'm influencing the choices of the Empress."

"That's why I'm officially promoting you to the title and rank of *Premiere dame d'honneur.*"

"What language is that?" Danica asked. The universal translator had failed to translate the French, apparently, they had said it best and the idiom stuck.

"It's an old Earth language called French."

"It sounds so beautiful. What does it mean?"

"The *dame d'honneur* was an office of the royal courts on ancient Earth. She was tasked with assisting the queen in anything and everything she might need. Do you feel up to the job?"

Danica smiled. "It sure beats pretending to be your consort everywhere we go."

"I thought you liked being my consort?" Jegra teased, slipping into some day clothes.

She put on a rust colored, floor length, Kaleigh gown with crisscross halter top that was adorably chic while Danica slipped into a stylish, knee-length teal one-piece with a frill hemline. Not only did it accentuate her lovely curves and show off her stunning legs, but it also looked lovely in contrast with her purple skin.

"I much prefer to be your consort after sundown."

"Oh, you do...do you?" Jegra laughed. Danica winked at her playfully doing little to hide the innuendo.

Dressed, the two women turned to one another. Danica wrapped her arms around Jegra and replied, "I'd be honored to serve you in any way you see fit."

"Good," replied Jegra, giving her girlfriend a peck on the lips. "Now, let's get going. The sooner we appear, the sooner we can have our palace back to ourselves. We've kept everyone waiting long enough."

Several minutes later Jegra stepped into the meeting room where Raven, Raphine, and Meleh'kendar sat chatting as they waited for her arrival. Everybody was situated around an enormous, round, stone table, just like the one of renowned Arthurian legend.

"What's going on?" she asked, sitting herself down directly across from them. Danica quickly joined her, sitting on her right.

"It's finally happened," Meleh'kendar informed. But Jegra had no clue as to what he was on about.

"The Nephilim have returned."

"Who?" Jegra asked.

"The Nephilim are an ancient warrior race, the sworn enemies of the Nyctan empire," Danica informed.

"They're not too fond of Dagons either," Raven added.

"But weren't they thought to be extinct?"

Meleh'kendar frowned. "The Nyctans had hunted them to near extinction, believing them to be the winged demons of light warned about in the Enchiridion, which prophesied that they would go to war with Hastur in an attempt to wrangle control of the universe."

"The last Nephilim ships escaped around three hundred years ago," Danica continued. "The Knights had warred with them for so long that a Nyctan victory seemed inevitable. But then, unexpectedly, the Nephilim just up and disappeared, vanishing from every known star system in charted space. Nobody had heard an utterance regarding them or seen a trace of them, until now."

"They must have been recouping their losses all these centuries," Raven said. "Three hundred years is certainly sufficient to rebuild a fleet and an army. Their forces must be tremendous."

"Indeed, the outpost on Riverion reported at least six-hundred battle cruisers and at least a thousand other ships before the feed was cut out," Meleh'kendar informed them.

"What of the Emperor?" Jegra asked.

"That's what I'm here to see you about, your majesty. The emperor immediately responded to Riverion's blackout as a military threat and a potential invasion and took the *Subjugator* along with five new Tetra class battle cruisers and went to intercept the fleet." Meleh'kendar slid a holovid module to the center of the table and them brought up a three-dimensional holographic scene of burning wreckage. "This is all that is left of our armada."

Jegra gasped. The *Subjugator*, the most powerful ship in the galaxy, lay in ruins along with five other state of the art battle cruisers.

"What could do this level of damage in such a short time?" Danica asked.

Meleh'kendar flicked his wrist and swiped to the left. The scene panned across the debris and the stars until it settled on three glowing objects. They were giant space-squids, made of light.

"For fuck's sake!" Jegra balked, seeing the *squidies* again. "Just one of those things took out half a Nyctan and Dagon armada. Now there's three of them?!"

"That's not the worst part," Meleh'kendar replied.

"No?" Jegra asked, her curiosity piqued as to what could be worse than a family of starship-gobbling-space-squids. She was now certain they were secret, Nephilim bio-weapons of mass destruction. Engineered to cripple both the Nyctans and the Dagons and use their very technology against them.

"The emperor has gone missing."

"Not dead?" Danica asked.

"No," he replied in earnest.

"That *is* bad news," Jegra replied.

Danica and Raven both snickered.

Meleh'kendar smiled and glanced around the room at their faces, not understanding what was so funny, before continuing on with his debriefing.

"None of the *Subjugator*'s crew survived, but initial long-range scans show that the emperor's emergency captain's yacht was launched prior to the explosion that crippled the ship."

Meleh'kendar pulled his hand back from the hologram and it zoomed out. Stars and nebulae whisked by until a bright-green glowing dot appeared. He then zoomed in to the image, honing in on the dot. The emperor's emergency escape yacht soon appeared in the middle of the room and as the image zoomed into maximum capacity the hologram flickered. The elongated pod had scorch marks from what appeared to be disruptor fire and was badly damaged. The emperor was adrift in space and, by the looks of it, his emergency life support was on the brink of failing.

"We spotted the emperor's yacht this morning, but he was nowhere to be found. However, there was a message."

Jegra motioned for him to play it.

The hologram flickered and the emperor's face materialized before her. He had a gash in his forehead and was bleeding badly. Sparks rained down from the ceiling and the automated fire extinguishers on the ship hissed as they shot white puffs of dry chemical spray to douse the fires.

Dakroth turned toward the camera and said, "If anybody out there is receiving this, please send word to the Empress. The empire is under attack. Jegra, you're the galaxy's only hope."

Suddenly, there was a flash and a large explosion. The emperor turned to look off-camera and then mumbled some panicked obscenities before the feed cut out completely.

Meleh'kendar gazed at Jegra with a worried look. "Majesty, you are now the Regnant Imperatrix of the Galaxy."

Jegra stood up and paced the room as she took in all the information.

"The people need to hear your reassuring voice," Danica said. "You must address your subjects."

Jegra stopped pacing and looked at everyone.

Meleh'kendar, worry lines creasing his forehead, cleared his throat. "My grace, what are your orders?"

"Let the Nephilim come," she said, after a long pause. "And we will show them the combined might of Nyctan and Dagon." Turning her attention toward

Meleh'kendar, she said, "Get me the Administratrix, Anaïs Nin, on the comm. We have some things to discuss. Also, get me a status update on my new personal battle cruiser, she needs to be ready for deployment before the Nephilim fleet arrives."

Meleh'kendar stood up, crossed his right arm over his chest and took a deep bow. Having his orders, he rose back up, spun on his heels, and then raced off to complete his tasks.

Raven slowly rose from her seat. "I'll debrief the crew on what's happening and prep the *Skywend* for departure. Just give us the word when you're ready."

Jegra nodded and Raven returned the gesture, acknowledging her duty, then turned and left the room.

Danica put her hand on Jegra's arm. "I'll go prepare the royal briefing room so you can address the people."

Jegra smiled at her and then watched her leave.

Slowly rising to her feet, Jegra exited the rear doors of the palace, doors that rose all the way to the ceiling, and stepped out by the glorious pool. Marble benches, in sets of two, ran along the entire one hundred meters of the glistening blue pool. The pool, which was just deep enough to allow Jegra her morning swim regimen, stretched all the way to the edge of a lush, green lawn.

The greenery of the palace grounds continued on for about another hundred meters where it came to an abrupt edge. A small perimeter forcefield kept the sand at bay, creating an epic landscape where the green sward and the golden sands of Thessalonica met. A perfectly clean line existing between them, neither spilling out onto the other. Everything was kept confined to its own particular region, a not so subtle metaphor for Jegra's relationship with Dakroth.

Jegra walked the full stretch of lawn and then kicked off her low-stacked heels before stepping out onto the hot desert sands. Letting the sand burn her feet, she climbed to the top of a nearby sand dune, her rust-colored dress flapping elegantly in the warm desert breeze. To her, it felt like a hot summer day back on Earth, and for the first time since she arrived on Thessalonica, she felt as though it was her home.

Above her, hanging in the sky like a glorious, blue and green opal, was

Dagon Prime. She looked up and smiled. Never in a million years would she have guessed she'd be the ruler of a whole planet, let alone an entire star system.

Even when she had accepted that unlikely role, she hadn't remotely anticipated that the moment she found a quantum of solace she'd be pulled into yet another war. And with an alien race she knew nothing about. An alien race which seemed to have superior fire power and was just as zealous in their religious beliefs as were the Nyctans.

As a gust of hot air kicked up her flowing brown hair and fluttered her dress, Jegra smiled and made two fists. If only the Nephilim knew what they were in for, of whom they had picked a fight with, they would never have dared intrude on *her* empire. After all, she was Jegra the Magnificent, Imperatrix of the Galaxy.

BOOK 1
EPILOGUE

It had been approximately three weeks since Raphine Agnar had taken up with the Empress Jegra Alakandra and the crew of the *Skywend*. She was the youngest sister of Abethca, however, she hadn't told anyone her true identity.

She had been given her own suite at Jegra's Imperial Palace on Thessalonica and mostly kept to herself. She figured the less interaction she had with the others, the fewer chances there were she'd be found out. Everyone just assumed she was shy.

But it wasn't her identity she feared discovering. It was the item, a thing of utmost value that she needed to keep secret at all costs.

Her sister, Te'Legra Onelle Agnar, one of the wealthiest people in the Commonwealth, owned seven moons and sixteen ore mining facilities, and had amassed a fortune rivaling that of all of Dagon Prime's gross capital combined. And, as it so happened, Te'Legra had paid nearly two billion credits for the item currently in Raphine's possession.

The item was so important, in fact, that her sister would entrust the safe delivery of the item to nobody but Raphine.

Originally, the plan was to have Abethca obtain the item, but, sadly, Abethca had mysteriously vanished from the Commonwealth. Raphine still didn't have all the details, but she knew she had been with Jegra the week of her disappearance. And if Abethca was still alive, Raphine would find her. If not, Raphine vowed to track down those responsible for her death.

Of course, she hadn't found the right time or way of broaching the subject with the empress, and so thought best to continue her investigation in private until she had more information.

Raphine brushed her short, purple hair back and strode confidently across the elaborate and finely embroidered Thessalonican carpet in her room. She stopped in front of a large writing desk which was mainly empty, all but for a singular item.

On the desk sat a claret box with gilded leaves and spiraling vines adorning it. The box itself was a perfect square, no bigger than a half a loaf of bread.

Cautiously, she glanced around the room to ensure nobody, no servants, no guards, or any prying eyes were present, and then cautiously unlatched the box. She slowly opened the lid and looked inside and smiled. Golden light streamed out and lit up her face.

"How are you doing little fella?" she asked, dabbing her pinky finger inside the box.

Tiny golden tentacles, seemingly made of light, reached out of the box and wrapped themselves around her hand, almost as if they were greeting her. She wasn't the least bit scared. She knew the creature well enough to know he was harmless in this infant state.

"I brought you something to eat," she said, pulling a fully-charged battery out of her back pocket.

Patient, she held out the battery and waited for the little squid arms to unwrap themselves from her fingers and slide themselves over the battery. The moment the creature had the packet of energy, it began to feed.

As it absorbed the energy, its tentacles pulsed with little beads of light. Once it had finished syphoning the last ounce of power from the battery, and there was no more juice to be had, the tentacles let go of the dead battery.

The battery dropped to the floor with a clunk, and Raphine promptly slid it under the desk with the edge of her foot. The battery rolled against a pile of similar packs, all of them drained of their energy.

Being as gentle with the creature as one would be with a newborn kitten, she tucked the baby space-squid's tentacles back into the box. Naturally, he tried to reach out again but, again, she tucked him in so as not to pinch him when she shut the lid.

"That's all for today, I'm afraid," she said, shutting the top of the box and sealing in the glowing creature.

Raphine closed the latch and locked the box up tight, ensuring the little rascal wouldn't escape. Satisfied he was secure, she turned and exited her room.

BOOK ONE
FINIS

THE CHRONICLES OF

JEGRA

IMPERATRIX OF THE GALAXY

1

Emperor Dakroth's escape pod spun uncontrollably through a star spackled percheron-black expanse. Distant stars blurred as the chaotically whirling craft spiraled into the infinite blackness. And the cold of space offered little comfort to those lost in its vast, inhospitable domain.

Unconscious, Dakroth slumped over in his cockpit, the safety harness of his seat keeping him firmly strapped, amid the crackle of sparks that hissed and fizzed from dislocated paneling that sprouted wires like stiff copper hairs. The structural integrity alarm blared noisily throughout, as though the ship was crying out in agony. The escape yacht twisted counterclockwise in a shambolic summersault, cutting its way through empty space. Behind it floated a sparkling trail of debris that glinted in the light of a distant star like the glittering tail of a comet.

As the escape yacht tumbled unsteadily, a looming shadow fell across the hull of the battered vehicle and a loud clunking sound, the sound of mechanical jowls opening wide, rang above the alarm. All of a sudden, the spacecraft lurched to a halt. The abrupt jolt aroused Dakroth to consciousness.

Groggy, Dakroth rubbed his aching head and squinted through bloodshot eyes as he looked out the front view portal to see a giant scavenger perched above him, its magnetic grappling hook tethered to his hull. Another jolt kicked him back in his seat and soon his disabled vessel was being reeled into the cavernous bay area of the mammoth ship above him.

As he came into view of the ship's insignia, he let out a sigh from the corner of his mouth and grumbled, "Bloody space pirates."

With a bout of frustration, he slammed his fist on the control panel and killed the alarm. Its winding down sounded like a slow-motion video going off the reel and then the main control panel blew. Sparks shot up in a brief, excited display and then faded away again just in time to be replaced by a haze of white electrical smoke.

Dakroth raised an eyebrow at the fussiness of his luxury pod and then ignored the commotion. The fire-dampening shields were already busy working on putting out the burning console.

Once fully inside the pirate vessel, heavy bay doors clanked shut behind the escape yacht and the artificial grav-plating kicked on. The pod crashed to the deck of the cargo bay with a resounding *clang* and then tilted onto its edge, rocking back gently until it came to a standstill.

Dakroth undid his harness and slid out of his seat. Stumbling to the floor of the pod, which was set at an awkward angle due to the haphazard landing, he staggered to his feet and made his way to the rear hatch.

As if on cue, when he reached the exit, a rugged voice from outside hollered a customary warning in anticipation of making first contact. "You in there, come out and surrender your vehicle to us. You and your vessel are now the property of Novac Tamoran, King of the Space Pirates!"

Dakroth slapped the panel on the door, but it bleated at him curtly as if to say "don't bother me." Raising an orange glowing index finger, Dakroth aimed at the control panel next to the hatch and released a powerful blast of energy. The door blew off its hinges and flew into the center of the cargo bay where it crashed to the ground and skidded ten meters, kicking up a spray of hot white sparks before screeching to a halt.

"I wish to register a complaint," Dakroth said, stepping out of the damaged pod with as much regal pomp and circumstance as he could muster, given his condition.

"Stay where you are!" a menial pirate ordered, holding up a blaster. A quick peripheral glance made him aware of the fact that there were three others in the room, all with disruptor pistols trained on him, but Dakroth ignored them as though they were unimportant, not worth his time or energy, and casually continued striding toward the cargo bay doors.

The first man stepped into Dakroth's path and puffed up his chest. Still holding the blaster in his right hand, he raised his left, gestured for Dakroth to halt, then reissued the order. "Stop where you are, or I'll shoot."

Dakroth rolled his eyes, held up his luminous finger, and shot the man dead with a red laser beam. His finger then cooled again, returning to its normal, cobalt blue hue.

The pirate collapsed to the ground, a shocked look frozen on his face. A small hole smoldered in the center of his forehead. Dakroth paused long enough to scan the terrified faces of the pirate crew and then asked, "Anyone else want to order me to do their bidding?"

The other pirates withdrew their weapons and stepped back, making way for Emperor Dakroth, who grinned at his own supremacy.

"That's what I thought." Letting out a sigh of inconvenience, he stepped over the dead body and came to the double standing doors that led out of the cargo hold and into the main body of the ship. He tapped the panel to open them and they whisked apart.

Before he could step across the threshold, he looked up to find a pair of black boots standing in his way. A familiar bald head with an elegant, red face, and a series of black tribal tattoos and two golden eyes glared back at him with the cold, unfeeling detachment that he knew so well.

"Ishtar Bantu?" he said, perplexed by the presence of his personal assassin.

"What can I say?" she answered, a malicious grin spreading across her thin, burgundy lips. "Work has been hard to come by these days." Ishtar jammed a taser-rod into Dakroth's ribs, zapping him with enough volts to render him little more than a spastic blue tangle of limbs on the floor before her.

"Red-skinned-bitch," Dakroth barked through a clenched jaw and gritted teeth.

Ishtar brushed off his insult and then kicked him in his nut sack just to remind him who held the upper hand.

Dakroth groaned with what might be taken for pleasure and then looked up at her with a lecherous grin. "I didn't know you liked to play so rough," he taunted. "Best be careful; you're getting me hard."

She grinned superficially at him again, her white teeth shining lustrously as she dialed the taser-rod up to one-hundred and fifty miliamps and fried him again, jamming the taser-rod right into his lower gut.

He stiffened and groaned as the volts of electricity surged through his body. Once she let up on the switch, Dakroth twitched on the floor plates like a fish on dry land, gasping for air.

Enraged, Dakroth spat out another threat. "When I get my hands on that taser-rod, I'm going to ram it right up your two-timing c—"

Fed up with his slew of meaningless insults, the crack of her boot quickly rendered him unconscious. "There. Much better," she said, looking down at the unconscious Dagon. With that, she bent over, grabbed Dakroth's left ankle, and dragged him into the ship and up the corridor and then disappeared from view.

As the cargo bay doors automatically slid shut, the remaining pirates glanced around at one another to confirm that was who they thought it was, and then, with one simultaneous shrug, they went to work dismantling the small shuttle as they broke it down for spare parts.

When Dakroth finally roused back to consciousness, he found himself sitting in a state-of-the-art holding cell wearing nothing but a loincloth. Looking up, he saw Ishtar Bantu standing in front of his cell alongside Novac Tamoran.

Dakroth rose to his feet and walked over to the energy field that prevented him from escaping and, with a gesture of his hands that drew attention to his naked form, growled, "Where are my clothes?"

"Nice to see you again, my dear Rhadamanthus," Novac said, ignoring Dakroth's previous inquiry.

"That's Emperor Dakroth to you, Tamoran."

"That's King Tamoran to you, my dear emperor." Tamoran smiled at him, as if to say *checkmate*, which aggravated Dakroth's already agitated state. He had little patience for such trivial chitchat.

Insulted by Tamoran's posturing, Dakroth raised his finger and tried to blast through the energy shield of his cell, but to his surprise, nothing happened. He examined his blue finger with a perplexed look.

Tamoran cleared his throat. "Dampening field," the pirate informed him. "As long as you are in there," he said, nodding his head at Dakroth's cell, "your powers are rendered useless."

Dakroth lowered his finger and shot Tamoran a cold glance. He wanted nothing more than to wipe the smirk off the infernal pirate's mouth. But Tamoran had the upper hand, and Dakroth decided it best not to test the so-called pirate king's resolve.

"What do you want, Tamoran? I mean," he paused, mulling over how best to rephrase it, "how may I serve you oh mighty King Tamoran of the noble and illustrious pirates?" Dakroth didn't even try to hide his glibness.

Tamoran's grin turned up into a cruel snarl and he laughed softly to himself. Even if Dakroth didn't actually mean it, he'd still said it. *King of the pirates.* And that was victory enough, in his estimation. "I have it on good authority that you've chosen a new empress."

Dakroth raised an eyebrow. "Should that be such a surprise? I've had many wives."

"None that have survived your psychotic tendencies," Ishtar chimed in.

Dakroth shot her a stern glance and then relaxed. "That's why I've never married you, my dear. I enjoy your company too much."

She grinned back at him with what seemed like genuine amusement, but it quickly melted from her face. After all, she was still nursing a grudge against the empress, Jegra Alakandra, for besting her at the Cove. And Ishtar swore that if their paths ever crossed again, it would be Jegra who paid the ultimate price.

Perhaps worse was the fact that she felt scorned by Dakroth for choosing Jegra over her as his companion. That pissed her off to no end, because she was secretly in love with him. Well, if she couldn't have him, then no one could. Which is why she had struck a deal with Novac Tamoran, the pirate king, in the first place.

First, she'd use Dakroth to lure Jegra to her. Then, as the unsuspecting mouse entered her trap, she'd kill her rival and win Dakroth's affection back. He always did prefer violent women most of all. Far be it from her to disappoint her emperor.

Meanwhile, it was almost certain that Dakroth would pay Novac Tamoran whatever he wanted in exchange for his freedom, which is why Ishtar had convinced the pirate king to ask for his own personal battlecruiser. This would solidify Tamoran's sovereignty in the sector, crowning him the one true king of the pirates. At the same time, it would obligate him to her in a way which ensured he couldn't ever betray her. Not without invoking her ire and risk losing everything she had helped him attain.

After all, if she was willing to go through such extremes to kill the Empress of the Galaxy, she would be more than willing to dispatch a lowly space pirate who had delusions of grandeur.

"It's a pity you didn't invite me to the wedding," Tamoran said, his grin fading into a reprimanding scowl.

"Save your scolding for someone who cares," Dakroth balked, waving his hand in front of his face as though he were shooing away a pesky housefly.

"Regardless, I shall meet her soon enough. In fact, I'm rather quite looking forward to meeting the new Empress of the Dagon Empire," Tamoran said, linking his hands behind his back in a sage-like stance.

"Wait, what? Meet her?" Dakroth looked to Ishtar for clues, but she merely smiled at him again, which was no help at all. Scanning back to Tamoran, Dakroth clamped his slack jaw shut. "Jegra is coming here? Why in Dagon would she do that?"

"Is it not the empress's job to ensure the safety of the emperor at all costs?"

"Yes, but I doubt she'd come looking for me. We aren't exactly on speaking terms at the moment. She's been deliberately neglecting me for months."

"Be that as it may," Tamoran said, rubbing his chin in thoughtful contemplation, "something tells me she'll make an exception this time." With that said, Tamoran cleared his throat and turned to leave. "It was a pleasure chatting with you, my dear emperor."

"Likewise, my dear king."

Novac Tamoran glanced over his shoulder and flashed one last trumped-up grin before leaving the brig. Once the outside doors hissed shut behind him, Dakroth snapped his gaze to Ishtar and scowled.

"What's the meaning of all this? What was he on about? Jegra is coming here? What are you two planning?" He demanded answers, but to his surprise, Ishtar merely let down the forcefield and stepped into the cell with him.

This unexpected intrusion startled him and he took a step back. To his relief, she didn't assault him. However, she did strip off all of her clothes and step boldly towards him.

Ishtar pushed Dakroth up against the wall and pressed her athletic body into him, kissing him vigorously on his mouth.

Ishtar appeared like a she-devil, her skin a smooth, blood-red but for the black lines that ran down her neck and body like aboriginal tattoos–custom mods which were more than decoration. They enhanced her abilities, including her strength and stamina.

As an elite assassin, she was twice as cunning and a hundred times deadlier than any woman in the galaxy. She also despised Jegra with every ounce of her being. It was Jegra who had survived an incurable poison. It was Jegra who had bested her at the Cove and made a fool out of her. It was Jegra who'd stolen Rhadamanthus's heart from her. And it was Jegra who was now sitting on the throne instead of her. Ever since their last encounter, Ishtar had done nothing but plot her revenge.

Ishtar pushed away slightly, and slid her dainty red breasts across Dakroth's chest, brushing her maroon nipples tantalizingly over Dakroth's Prussian blue ones with a delicateness that was as soft as down feathers. With her black polished nails, she gently stroked Dakroth's chest, ran her hands up to his broad shoulders, and squeezing him tightly, she leaned in and kissed him more tenderly on his full, deep blue lips.

Momentarily taken aback by the unexpected passion, he drew his head back and looked at her with a reasonable suspicion. "I don't understand what's going on here," he said, perplexed by her sudden sexual advances.

"You don't have to," she replied, tilting her hips as she slid out of his arms and lay down on the cot. With a curling of her finger she beckoned him to join her, and with lecherous desire in his eyes, he complied.

While she kept Dakroth occupied with sex, Ishtar carefully reached under the cot and slid her fingers along the cold metal frame until they found the miniature transmitting device she'd planted there earlier, along with a mobile vid cam. Tapping the screen, she began broadcasting their tryst via Dakroth's personal emergency signal.

As the device secretly recorded them, she tilted her head back and craned her neck. As Dakroth dappled the slender expanse with feather light kisses, she looked directly up into the camera lens. A vindictive smile curled onto her tight lips and her golden eyes flashed with a smoldering rage just beneath their lustrous veneer as she gazed unflinchingly at her audience.

She lingered a while; the recipient of the video would see her fiery eyes staring back at her from across the empty room as though she were standing there in person, watching it all unfold. Staring, so that she'd know beyond doubt, that every single debauched act, every single salacious moan that slipped passed Ishtar's lips as she rode the emperor to his climax, was all deliberately orchestrated for her viewing pleasure.

2

A tangerine sun settled across the sands of Thessalonica as the turbines of the white shuttle pod perched on the palace lawn spooled up to a high-pitched whine. Jegra Alakandra, newly crowned Empress of Dagon, threw open the palace doors to her personal terrace that overlooked Arena City–the metropolis where she'd first learned of life beyond the stars. Here, she had begun a new life as a slave and had risen to prominence as an undefeated gladiatrix–until fate intervened. Now she gazed out as empress of an entire galactic empire.

As she descended the stairs and stepped out into the garden, a hot blast of desert air swiftly tangled the long tresses of her hair that danced on the currents undulating from the pulsating turbines. She tugged up her copper colored dress as she made her way to the shuttle and swiftly ducked under the clamshell wing door of the elegant craft and climbed aboard.

It was no secret that Jegra preferred traveling by shuttle over teleportation. Although teleporting was considered perfectly safe for low orbit transports, its safety diminished with range. Eight hundred meters beyond the recommended range of the goldilocks radius and you'd come out the other side a scrambled egg. That didn't sit well with her, which is why she preferred to get off world the old-fashioned way.

Jegra settled into the plush white Targarian leather seat and looked out the window as the automated clamshell doors shut. She collected her hair back over her shoulders and brushed down her dress, chasing out the pleated folds as the shuttle rose up into the blue sky and slowly pivoted in mid-air as it found its course. It gracefully climbed away from the palace, its engines spitting out blue-tipped torches of high yield plasma as the thrusters ignited.

As the craft darted up toward the atmosphere, she glanced down and watched her glorious palace shrink away till it was the size of a toy model. As Jegra broke through the atmosphere, the halo of Dagon's star burst over the arc of the planet Dagon Prime; it hung in the distance like a majestic blue and green opal. Between her moon and the planet hovered a silver shard, a sliver of reflective light hanging in space. It was her personal battlecruiser, which idled in low orbit like an ever-vigilant guardian angel.

Newly commissioned and fresh out of space dock, the Dagon cruiser was sleek. A costly coat of chromatic thermal paint made the slender vessel look like a heavenly teardrop floating in space.

It was roughly the shape of a Helianthus seed, and the length of a large ocean liner; approximately four hundred sixty meters long. It had eighteen decks and could hold up to four thousand passengers and two thousand active crew. Although the vessel had only one shuttle bay, it made up for it with three supersized cargo bays and eight docking ports. Each cargo bay was large enough to fit an entire six-passenger shuttle and also acted as emergency storage for transporting survivors or refugees. One of Jegra's goals was to crack down on poaching in the empire and prevent the illegal trafficking of aliens from off world.

Naturally, Jegra had personally seen to the designs and specifications of this new vessel. It was more than a statement of her supremacy in the empire; it was the first vessel in the Dagon fleet capable of slip-stream travel through hyperspace. Also, it was the first Dagon vessel to use a hybrid system of state-of-the-art Cordovan engine technology, Nyctan shield technology, and Dagon structural engineering. There was nothing like it in all seven systems of the empire. It was, simply put, iconic.

The sleek vessel was powered by a 7-simplex hyperborean fusion drive. Cutting edge stuff. The slipstream drive was an experimental prototype of a dark energy transfusion drive. Once the hyperborean drive got the ship into hyperspace, the slip-stream transfusion drive would take over and the vessel would enter a kind of accelerated current that ran between the edge of hyperspace and the existence of dark energy.

During slipstream travel, the ship's ram scoops would open up in the slipstream and pull in dark energy directly from the interstellar medium, thereby effecting a *virtual* perpetual motion propulsion. The only thing preventing it from being a *true* perpetual motion machine, was basic physics and the inevitable superheating that threatened, over vast distances, to quite literally melt the engines.

Eventually the ram scoop engines would grow so hot, they'd automatically shut down. But it took hours to get them that hot, and at slipstream speeds, it only took two to three hours to traverse each system–a mere sixteen hours to traverse all seven systems. That beat the six-month journey it took any other, more traditionally configured vessels.

Subsequently, this new engine technology made the ship faster than any vehicle ever created and gave Jegra a galactic reach far beyond even the emperor's. Moreover, she could hop from one end of the empire to the other in a matter of hours versus days, weeks, or even months.

One downside to running such high-power through the ship's systems, however, was that it meant there had to be sacrifices. A weapons system was out of the question due to the feedback it caused. During test flights of the prototype, whenever they activated the weapons systems, the complex physics of running two separate engine technologies in one hybrid system caused a huge power feedback that destroyed the ship. Jegra lost a test crew of two-hundred Dagon souls. As such, she ordered the engineering team to leave the weapons out of the equation, an order that raised a lot of eyebrows, but she had made her point quite clear: any further loss of life was simply unacceptable.

Which meant her ship was without fangs; although, not entirely defenseless.

Because of the high energy output of the vessel, Jegra had three times the number of shield modulators built into the ship, meaning its shields were therefore three times more powerful than anything in the system. She didn't need weapons when she could use the ship like a molten hot needle to literally cut through any enemy vessel simply by ramming it. Which is why she'd named her beautiful glistening flagship the *Shard*.

[*Approaching the* Shard, *Your Grace*], a computer voice chirped as the shuttle pulled up alongside the long, gleaming cruiser that shone iridescently like a freshly polished ocean pearl.

The small white shuttle pulled up next to a portion of the *Shard* which wavered briefly and then, as if the hull had turned molten and melted away, an entire section of the ship opened up to reveal a shuttle bay. Jegra leaned back in her chair as her craft passed through the shield barrier, the blue shimmer wavering as the ship's energy shields mingled with the shuttle bay's.

Reverse thrusters fired off in spurts and the shuttle slowly landed inside the markings of a yellow rectangle painted on a section of the floor.

As the landing prongs of the pod met the korridium deck of the landing bay with a resounding *clank*, the shuttle bay doors shifted and then, like liquid aluminum, meshed back together and solidified. It was as if the ship had miraculously healed itself from a gaping wound.

Jegra rose and walked over to the rear hatch of the shuttle and waited for it to depressurize. There were a few spurts of compressed air as the shuttle matched the air pressure of the bay and then the hatch rolled to the side to allow Jegra out.

She exited the shuttle and shuffled down the ramp that extended out from beneath the clamshell wing of the door, then confidently strode across the walkway, her dress hugging her feminine form like liquid copper.

Although the cruiser's artificial gravity generators mimicked terrestrial gravity, there was a strange sensation, like a stickiness, that took some getting used to every time she stepped onboard a space vessel. But it always passed after several minutes. She didn't know if it was a trick of imagination or if the body simply needed to acclimate to its environment like it would when stepping off an airplane into the dense humidity of a tropical climate. There was the initial shock of the change, but after a brief stint in the new environment, you hardly noticed it anymore.

At the other end of the shuttle bay stood Danica, waiting to greet her partner. Her hair was a turquoise and purple ombre, cut shoulder length and permed so it was wavy at the tips. The shade complimented her lavender skin tone; she wore a white jumpsuit with a narrow yellow band running full length down either side. As usual, her jumpsuit was unzipped just the right amount to allow her ample bust to spill out generously in all the right places.

"Dani?" Jegra asked, greeting her girlfriend with a quick peck on the lips. She was curious as to why she'd met her all the way down here rather than aboard the bridge. "What's so urgent that it couldn't wait?"

Danica held up a transparent touch-pad device. "You've got an encrypted call from Emperor Dakroth."

"So, you located him, then?"

"More like he located us," she replied, handing over the device. "It came across on his emergency broadcast signal."

Jegra took it in her hand, but felt tension on it and looked up with a curious expression when Danica didn't relinquish the device to her.

"I should warn you," Danica said in a somber tone.

"Warn me about what?"

"Never mind. See for yourself." She let go and Jegra tapped the display and replayed the transmission.

Jegra watched for a moment and then smirked and raised a curious eyebrow. After having seen enough, she swiped right on the touch-screen and the video shrank away and disappeared. She looked up at Dani's amber eyes and gave her an obligatory smile–the smile of an empress who's been slighted but who keeps her composure, providing an example of womanly strength and grace.

"Don't say I didn't warn you," Danica said, shooting Jegra an apologetic look. Even though she had nothing to be sorry for, she genuinely felt sympathy for Jegra and the awkward position she'd been put in.

"It's fine," Jegra said, returning the touchpad.

"It is?" Danica asked, puzzled.

"Yeah," Jegra said with a subtle smile. "It's not like I'm going to sleep with him ever again. And besides, he's the emperor. He can do what he likes. Even if it is with that blood crazed thunder cunt."

"Ah," Dani said, smiling at Jegra spryly.

"What?"

"So you are mad, then?"

Jegra squinted at Dani crossly and then started up the corridor. "More like disappointed."

Danica followed after Jegra and they climbed into an elevator at the end of the corridor. Jegra hit the button on the wall, the elevator chimed, and the doors slid shut. There was a light undulation as the lift began to rise. While they rode, Jegra let out a sigh.

Danica just watched her, gauging how best to console her partner. The elevator doors opened with a hiss and they made their way down another corridor and to the bridge. Once they passed through the sliding doors, the bridge crew greeted them, and Danica turned to her. "Will you be all right?" she whispered, keeping her voice down so nobody would overhear.

"Yes," Jegra replied without so much as a second's hesitation. After a brief pause, she laughed softly to herself. When she noticed Danica giving her that inquisitive look, she shared what was on her mind. "They really are a match made in heaven." She laughed again. "Can you imagine what their children would be like?"

"Honestly," Danica sighed, "I don't want to imagine it. It's too terrifying to even think about."

"Purple fang-toothed psychopaths in metal diapers is what would fall out of that woman's cunt," Jegra intoned.

Danica and Jegra shared a brief sideways glance and then burst out laughing. They leaned into one another, bumping their shoulders lightly, and shook their heads until the awkward vision of Dakroth's illegitimate love demons faded and the present once again resumed its rightful place.

"All kidding aside," Jegra said, getting back to the task at hand. "The emperor is still being held captive by the assassin, Ishtar Bantu, and I intend to fulfill my duty as empress and protector of the throne." She turned to the officers on her bridge crew and continued in a more commanding tone, "We will not rest until the emperor has been secured and returned safely to the empire. For Dagon! For the Empire!" She made a fist and extended it out in front of her.

The crew echoed her words back to her, "For Dagon! For the Empire!" and mirrored her gesture. They held their fists out until she lowered hers, and then returned to their duties.

"Ensign," Jegra said, placing her hand on the shoulder of a young Dagon girl in an immaculate, white uniform. Her long white hair was tied up in a ponytail and she glanced up at Jegra with orange eyes that sparkled like Citrine gemstones. "Input the coordinates of that emergency broadcast and punch it."

The girl gave Jegra a confounded look.

Danica leaned in and whispered into Jegra's ear. "She doesn't know what 'punch it' means."

A sheepish grin came over her and she laughed apologetically. "Reminds me of someone I know," she said, shooting Danica a familiar glance. Dani blushed and looked away. Returning her attention to the young ensign, Jegra clarified, "Just take us to those coordinates. Maximum speed."

"Yes, ma'am," the girl said. Her fingers danced across the touch-display of her console as she inputted the coordinates and then she paused. "Maximum speed, ma'am?" she asked, uncertain whether Jegra wanted the top cruising speed or the full slipstream drive.

"Maximum cruising speed," she clarified.

"Right," the girl said, embarrassed by her mistake. "Sorry."

"Sorry, *Your Majesty*," Danica corrected, giving the ensign a sharp look. She had not patience for insubordination, rookie or not.

The girl gulped. "Y...yes, Your Majesty," she echoed, heeding Danica's prompt to address the empress properly.

"It's quite all right," Jegra said, giving the ensign's shoulder a reassuring squeeze. "We all make mistakes. Just don't let it happen again."

Jegra turned and marched off the bridge. The girl looked up at Danica with a worried expression only to find the intimidating Dagon staring at her with an unforgiving gaze.

"Get it together, ensign," she ordered, then swiveled on her heel and double-timed-it to catch up to Jegra.

Danica matched Jegra's brisk pace in the corridor and said, "You shouldn't be so lenient with the crew members. It sets the wrong example. Dagons pride themselves on discipline. The girl was undisciplined and would benefit from a stern reprimanding."

"And what example would that set?" Jegra asked, raising an eyebrow. "That I'm to be feared?"

"You're the Empress of Dagon now. Whether you like it or not, you're married to the most imposing figure in seven systems. If you show any sign of weakness, then your enemies will use that opportunity to exploit you."

"Empathy and compassion are not weaknesses, Dani. One can be firm yet fair. And without fairness, all you have is tyranny. I set my course apart from Dakroth's, and if that means an adjustment period for the officers, then, so be it."

"You're treating them like children."

Jegra stopped mid-corridor and spun to face Danica. "Is not the Empress often referred to as the 'Mother of Dagon'?"

Danica smacked her teeth in annoyance. "Yes, but—"

"But nothing," Jegra said, cutting Danica off. Brushing her bangs out of her eyes, she smiled at Danica to let her know she wasn't upset with her. "They are my children and it is my duty to watch out for them."

"Just… be careful. You may be the empress of all Dagon now, but there are those who don't recognize your authority."

"You're speaking of the rebel faction."

"Yes. The Harbingers of Truth have grown emboldened as of recent. They are even going as far as to make public declarations against you."

"I thought they were just a fringe cult."

"They're a growing cult with dangerous allegiances in the underground. And their whole platform hinges on not recognizing your authority. You will always be an outsider, Jegra. They do not accept you as the rightful heir to the throne. In their minds they believe that Jennica is still technically the Supreme Empress of the Galaxy, as she never abdicated the throne, and Dakroth never issued a death certificate. They're using her as a martyr to rally around. They are calling you the Illegitimate Imperatrix."

"Jennica is dead," Jegra answered with a scowl. "Nothing will change that." She looked down at her hands with a profound sadness in her eyes. Jennica's blood would be forever on her hands and it ate her up inside.

Danica reached up and touched Jegra's arm. "He gave you no choice," she said in a soothing tone.

"There's always a choice," Jegra replied.

"She would have killed you. The throne meant everything to her. And, believe me Jegra, she was just as vicious and power-hungry as he is. It was only a matter of time before the one turned on the other like a couple of Zalakian piranhas."

"Maybe that would have been for the better," Jegra replied. She wasn't in the habit of throwing pity parties for herself, but this was one of her biggest regrets. She'd bashed Jennica's brains in and splattered her skull across half the wall. It hadn't been an honorable or even merciful death. It had come of pure brutality fueled by fear and rage.

In the back of her mind, she constantly chastised herself. She should have found another way out of Dakroth's morbid death-trap, even if it had meant stealing away with Jennica and going on the lam, spending the rest of their lives playing a galactic game of cat and mouse with the emperor.

It was just as likely that Jennica would have slit Jegra's throat in her sleep and returned to Dagon a hero, having harrowingly escaped her captor. But whichever way she spun it, at least her hands wouldn't be stained with the blood of an innocent woman's life.

Jegra turned and continued up the corridor without saying another word. Danica followed close behind, practically treading on her heels.

It pained Danica to see Jegra taking it so hard, but she too remembered the grisly scene like it was yesterday. She recalled unlocking the doors and seeing the blood and gore so thick it dripped down the walls like gruel. And the vision haunted her even now. Still, she couldn't imagine how much more difficult it must be for Jegra.

After taking Jegra's side, Danica huffed out a frustrated sigh and said, "You're wrong. The empire is far better off with you in charge, regardless of what anyone might say. Especially that zealot Dimeris Ferison and his cult of purist fanatics."

"I appreciate your confidence in me," Jegra said, walking under the arch of the door and into her quarters. Danica followed her in and let the door close behind them.

Once inside, Jegra stopped and turned to face Danica once more. "It means the world to me that you're by my side. I don't know what I'd do without you. You've made my life bearable in this inhospitable and cruel galaxy." She reached up and touched Danica's face and smiled. Her warm touch drew a pink blush from Danica in return and Jegra slowly leaned in to kiss her partner's lips.

After a long kiss, Jegra drew away and turned her back to Danica. Pushing back her shoulders so her shoulder blades nearly met in the middle, she craned her neck and looked back at Danica with a harried look. "Help me out of this dress, please."

Danica nodded and reached up with her lavender fingers and pastel pink nails, unhooked the elegant rust-colored dress at the top, and watched the back spread open as she ran the zipper down to the small of Jegra's back.

Jegra loved this gown's metallic shimmer and the fact that it clung to her body like silken mud. It sparked fond memories of the non-lethal mud bouts in the Arena, where the games were about the exploitation of the female combatants and the gratification of the audience. It still may have been demeaning, in a sense, but at least nobody had to die.

Jegra relaxed her shoulders and let the dress slip to the floor. It puddled beneath her and she elegantly arched her feet, pointing her toes downward so as not to snag them on the delicate fabric, and gracefully stepped out of the discarded garments as though she were stepping out of a cool lake after a scandalous yet refreshing dip.

With soft steps like that of a panther, she stalked across the bedroom floor and slipped into her satin sheets. "I'm beat," she mumbled into a pillow. "Wake me when we get there."

Danica nodded. "Is there anything else? Do you need me to draw you a bath?" But Danica's question was met with the soft sound of snoring. She fetched the edge of the bedspread and folded the triangle end across so that it covered Jegra's naked form as she tucked her into bed.

A gradual smile formed on Danica's lips and she bent down and kissed the side of Jegra's cheek. "Sleep well, my empress. I will love you, forever and always."

After scanning the room once, she determined it was secure and dimmed the lights, then exited Jegra's quarters and headed back to the bridge.

In the dark of Jegra's quarters, underneath a hand carved cherry oak desk, a small box with elaborate rosemaling sat. After a brief moment, the lid rattled and then cracked open; a golden tentacle made of light slipped out.

3

Commander Lianica Blackstar greeted Danica with a formal salute across the left breast then relinquished the command chair. "Vice Admiral," she said, gesturing for Danica to take the seat.

She was one of the few who knew of Danica's former identity and had no problems mentioning it freely among close company. Danica knew Lianica did it simply to rub in her loss of station and to point out that she was no longer a pure blood but now a loathsome mod.

And even though becoming a mod was viewed as shameful in her culture, Danica had to do it under royal decree so as to change her biometric readout and keep a low profile. It would, at the very least, make it more difficult for bounty hunters to track her and she could easily pass through any space port using fake I.D.s with her new face.

It may not have been the path she had imagined her life taking, but Danica understood that Jegra had ordered her to do it because it would save her life. But for how long, she didn't know. Emperor Dakroth was not the forgiving type. Surely, he'd sentence Danica to death for her failure at the battle of Sector B-13. He would brand her a deserter and a traitor and that'd be the end of it.

Even though she was no traitor, she knew that this passable fabrication would merely serve as a cover for the real reason he wanted her dead: Danica had stolen Jegra's heart right out from under him and made a cuckold of him. Undeniably, this was an unforgivable offense, particularly to a man with such massive pride that it was in danger of collapsing in on itself and forming a black hole. Bringing such dishonor to her emperor could mean only one thing–public execution.

Not that she had any choice in the matter. Being extracted mid-battle by a Knight of Caelum wasn't exactly something she could have anticipated, let alone defended against. Not in the middle of a ship to ship disruptor exchange. It was a bold move and had the signature stamp of Jegra all over it. Impetuous. Reckless. Fearless. All the things that made Jegra a force to be reckoned with.

Perhaps the only good to come out of the whole debacle was that the Dagon Imperial High Command had given Danica an honorable discharge, post mortem, assuming she'd been killed in battle. But even so, Lianica was resentful, and all she could see in Danica was a monumental failure, a disgrace to the very meaning of what it meant to be Dagon.

Commander Lianica Blackstar was headstrong and on a mission to make a name for herself. And one thing was clear: she wanted desperately to please the empress. But no amount of ambition could compete with the Vice Admiral's thirty-six-years' experience under Lord Dakroth.

Danica smiled tersely at Commander Blackstar and sat down in the captain's chair. Aboard the empress's ship, according to Imperial Law, the empress held the rank of Admiral of the Fleet, whereas the emperor held the rank of Lord and Commander of all militaries.

Annoyed by Lianica's passive aggressiveness, Danica leaned back in her chair, crossed her legs, and looked straight ahead at a swath of purple nebulae that was spread across a starry dappled expanse. Beyond the bow of the ship, she watched two distant battlecruisers cutting across the cosmic vista as if in slow motion.

Danica put Lianica's risky remarks out of her mind, and said, "Report."

Her back to the vice admiral, Lianica stood beside the command chair and stared out at the same nebulae that had Danica mesmerized. Without taking her eyes off the vista, she replied, "We will arrive at Dakroth's last known coordinates in about three hours. But we could get there in one, if we activated the slip-stream drive."

"That won't be necessary," Danica said, waving her hand as though she were brushing away the suggestion.

"As you wish, Vice Admiral," Blackstar answered. The commander's voice tightened slightly, revealing a hint of priggishness tucked into her tone. She smiled at Danica in a strained fashion that did little to hide her contempt.

Danica smiled back in an equally strained fashion that betrayed the fact that she had let Blackstar's vitriol get under her skin. "You will refer to me as Danica Vallencia of Thessalonica, Head of the Royal Guard and Personal Bodyguard to her majesty, the Empress of Dagon. Now, if there's anything else you wish to say to me, commander, there's no better time to get it off your chest."

Lianica Blackstar looked sideways at Danica out of the corner of her eye and then swiveled to face her. "Permission to speak freely, ma'am?"

"By all means," Danica said amusedly. She steepled her fingers and leaned forward to listen.

"Your fall from grace is well known throughout the empire. And now you sit here as though nothing has happened."

Danica's eyes narrowed. She uncrossed her legs and then re-crossed them. "Go on, commander. Don't let rank and protocol hold you back. Speak your mind."

"Very well. If you're not going to maintain your previous rank of Vice Admiral, I do believe ship protocol requires you to relinquish the command chair to your superior officer. Which would be me."

By now, the rest of the bridge crew was watching them with a vested interest in how this little power struggle would pan out, and the sudden absorption in their catty exchange didn't go unnoticed. Feeling that all eyes were on her, rather than Lianica, Danica vacated the seat and motioned for Lianica to resume command.

"I serve at the pleasure of the empress," Danica stated in a regal fashion as she stepped aside. "And it is you, Commander Blackstar, whom she has seen fit to place in command of this vessel."

"Some people are just better suited for the job," Lianica said smugly, rubbing it in.

After an intense stretch of silence, Danica decided on diplomacy to save face. She cautiously edged up to Lianica and leaned in to whisper, as she didn't think the rest of the crew needed to hear the rest of their private conversation. "Commander Blackstar, I serve the empress in another capacity now. Since I no longer hold an official rank, I acknowledge you are the commander of this vessel. I apologize if I overstepped."

"Don't mention it," the commander replied, a subdued smile curling onto one corner of her mouth. "We all make mistakes. Some more than others."

The extra dig merely added insult to injury, but Danica let it go. Of course, she wanted to slap the smug grin right off Lianica's pretty little mouth, but there was nothing more to be said on the matter and dragging it out further would just reflect badly on her. All she could do now was roll with the punches.

Danica sent the curious faces of the crew a sharp glance which informed them to mind their own business and they quickly snapped back to work, pretending as though nothing of interest had transpired. Even the ones who didn't have anything particularly pressing to do found busy-work to hold their attention.

"The bridge is yours, commander," Danica said with an air of artificial nicety, and she stormed out into the corridor.

Lianica watched Danica go and the small curl at the corner of her mouth widened into a haughty grin.

Once Danica made it to the lift, safely out of sight, she smashed the button angrily. The doors slid shut and, in that moment of solitude, she found a volcanic rage bubbling up inside of her and she was unable to hold back her emotions. Letting out a roar, she smashed a fist against the elevator wall and then mumbled a flurry of obscenities. After her flare up, she took a deep breath and tried to compose herself best she could, but it wasn't enough to hold back the torrent of tears that suddenly burst from her as though a deep well had overflowed.

The sudden switch in emotions caused her to giggle without intending to, and soon she stood laughing and sobbing simultaneously like a crazy person. With tears streaking her cheeks, she sniffled and wiped her nose on the back of her hand and then brushed down her uniform, soothing herself deliberately until she finally calmed down enough to regain some semblance of sanity.

It was clear to her that Jegra's DNA had somehow impacted her with its ability to rewrite other species' genetic information. It did so through the CRISPR gene altering technology that was built into her genetic code. Prolonged contact with Jegra's skin, such as during sessions of coitus, meant one's own DNA would slowly be rewritten. Altered to become more human.

Consequently, one of many peculiar side-effects of the genetic imprinting was that one developed the human characteristic of empathy–something entirely foreign to the Dagon way of life–and it was currently wreaking havoc on Danica's ability to keep her emotions in check.

Everything seemed to have been thrown out of sync. Where she used to be decisive, she kept questioning herself. And, as was Dakroth's greatest fear, this hesitancy made her weak. It made her question her motives. And it contradicted years of evolutionary theory that taught that only the strong survive—an adage no Dagon would ever deny being true.

It was the preeminent Dagon belief that through following one's self-serving nature, one could become stronger. Only the most selfish and opportunistic can thrive, the weak get taken advantage of, and this had been the Dagon way as long as she could remember. To question this meant her entire worldview was being called into question. All because of the fact that, in so following her selfish desires, she chose to get involved with the only woman who had any true power over her.

While in the throes of her little breakdown, the lift had gradually slowed and stopped. To her dismay, the doors had spread open to reveal two officers standing before the entrance. They stared at her with profound looks of discomfort.

The two male Dagon officers had witnessed the back end of her little meltdown and were obviously horrified. She caught herself mid-mumble and gave them the evil eye, letting the silence linger until they both squirmed in their military-issue boots.

"What?!" she snapped angrily.

Not wanting to cause a row, they dutifully stepped aside, one of them mumbling, "Nothing ma'am," and they let her storm past them without saying so much as another word.

As soon as they boarded the lift and the elevator doors clamped shut, they would almost certainly gossip about her. After all, it was the Dagon way; be polite to one's face then talk behind their backs the first chance you got. Make yourself strong by belittling others. But she couldn't blame them. After all, she'd been acting like a lunatic all bloody morning.

When she finally arrived at her personal quarters, she caught a glimpse of the black mascara melting down her lavender face like tribalistic war-paint in her reflection on the window that looked out at space. Letting out a rather depressed sigh, she headed to the food synthesizer to order something that might help her relax after having had such a rotten day. Tapping on the panel, she input her order. "Dagon herbal tea, hot, and one nutrient bar with dehydrated fruit blend."

The panel on the wall lit up as the food synthesizer unit hummed. A few seconds later, the light died down and she opened the panel and pulled out her food. The tea steamed, and its sweet aroma filled the room.

She took her things to a circular glass table and sat down in a navy-blue armchair. Having set her tea to the side, she crossed her legs and began to nibble on the nutrient bar as she stared vacantly out at the middle of the floor. She let out another pent-up sigh then reached for the tea when, without warning, Blackstar's voice came across the ship's comm. She pulled her hand back, letting it hover just above the cup's handle, and waited to hear the full message.

"Blackstar to all hands, prepare to slipstream acceleration."

Danica let out another sigh and frowned angrily. The commander had blatantly disregarded her orders. Obviously, she was trying to push her buttons even after she'd relinquished the battle. If she reacted, it would only compound things and make her situation worse. As such, she decided to let it go. She curled her finger around the glass teacup's handle, brought it to her lips, and took a sip.

As she was setting her tea back down, everything in the room blurred. There was a low murmur that could be heard throughout the ship, like the pulsing of some vital organ, and everything, including the ship's hull itself, slowly stretched out as time dilated. Once the brain adjusted to the time dilation, everything snapped back into its proper order and time resumed its normal pace.

The glass cup of steaming tea clinked down onto the glass table and Danica stood up and headed for the lavatory; if the tea couldn't calm her, then maybe a nice, cleansing sonic shower would.

She shed her clothes at the foot of the shower stall, simply a ceiling high cylindrical glass tube with a metallic strip around the center of it that did little to conceal the person's nudity within.

Still, it was an elegant design and took up minimal space. She preferred function over comfort anyway, and stepped inside, letting the glass door slide shut behind her. Once she was inside the stall, the glass went from transparent to a frosted white, and the metal band, which wrapped completely around the inside of the stall, began to hum, sending out pleasant vibrations that rippled across her skin.

The vibrations tickled the skin at first, but as they grew in strength and frequency it felt like being in the path of a massive bass speaker; the stimulation intensified until becoming a full-body massage, only with sound waves.

Gradually, the frequency increased and the vibrations tightened to the point where they could no longer be felt. Little by little, in patches all across her body, the inorganic particles and dead cells on the surface of her skin began to break apart and flake off.

White flecks of debris rose off her lavender colored body and hovered in the air briefly, then the tiny vacuum nozzles turned on inside the floor and ceiling of the shower and the organic waste was quickly sucked up into a small vacuum chamber where it was disposed of.

A moisturizing spray spritzed her from head to toe as the final stage of the shower cycle completed its cleansing procedure.

Danica pressed her forehead against the glass panel as the stall filled with steam. She remained troubled by her previous interaction with Lianica. It came as no surprise that Commander Lianica Blackstar Van Scarion reminded Danica of her former self. Headstrong. Obsessed with honor and duty and by making a name for herself in the Imperial Guard. She could see why Jegra had picked her as the one to command the *Shard*.

Danica sighed and waited as the shower ran through its final cleanse cycle. As the doors opened, another brief spritz of a finishing body perfume atomized in front of her. She walked through the cloud, which smelled like the ocean breeze, emerged from the tidy space and headed to her closet.

The moisture on her body cooled to a nice chill and caused her purple nipples to stand erect. She rummaged through her clothes, looking for the right outfit before settling on the white, leotard-styled dress. Skin-tight top and flowing skirt with a slit on either side to reveal her long, slender legs.

She threw on a wide, designer belt made from gold medallions which hung across her hips, forming themselves to her figure's natural sway and tilt.

Danica found white leather strap sandals to go with the dress and slipped them on. Sitting on the edge of her bed, she did up the straps and then went over to a large chest at the edge of her room. Opening it, she lifted a dagger and sheath and strapped it to the inside of her thigh. She then pulled out two golden armbands that resembled coiled serpents.

She grabbed the serpent's head, squeezed, and then snapped her wrist forward, extending her entire arm as though she was thrusting with a fencing sword. The snap of her wrist caused the serpent armband to uncoil and extend itself to form a long shank. Once she released her thumb from the head, the bracelet recoiled and returned to its previous form.

Satisfied with her selection, she slipped a serpent over each bicep and secured them on her upper arms.

Finally, she selected a carved golden cuff. She fitted it to her right wrist and then twisted it. A red laser beam flicked on and, aiming across the room, she deftly cut a leafy protrusion from her bedroom plant, a type of majestic fern, then quickly flicked off the beam again. She watched as the giant leaf fluttered to the floor and landed without so much as a sound.

"Makeup," she said, and turned to face the wall mirror that hung on the inside of her door. She closed her eyes and a series of pinpoint blue and green lasers danced around her face, painting her flesh with a coat of semi-permanent makeup. She held perfectly still as the lasers tattooed the color right into her flesh. Of course, it was completely reversible; when she grew tired of her look she would merely have the lasers erase the colors in a reverse process.

The only thing the lasers couldn't do permanently was eyelashes and brows; these were too fragile and transient. If one desired that dark, smoldering look, one still needed to use good old-fashioned mascara and eye liner. Danica opened her eyes and smiled at the glammed-up version of herself staring back at her.

She was about to go wake Jegra and run through some strategies for when they caught up with Dakroth's captors when, unexpectedly, the ship's red alert echoed throughout every compartment of the vessel.

Commander Blackstar's voice came onto the comm. "Intruder alert," she said. "An unknown entity has breached the bio-filters and we're—"

When her voice cut out, Danica knew it wasn't good news. Her first priority was the empress; securing the ship would have to wait.

4

A mysterious pink glow flooded the main corridor. Danica couldn't make out where the light energy was coming from, though it just seemed to saturate the entire ship.

On her way to Jegra's quarters, Danica swung by the observation deck. It was the one room where she might be able to look outside the ship and see what was going on.

Racing into the room, she skidded to a halt. The pink light filled the room; she ran to the tinted ports and frowned at some kind of gelatinous goo that had smeared itself across the outside hull of the ship. That, however, wasn't the strangest part.

In the middle of the observation deck, laid strewn about on the floor, was a ring of discarded uniforms including the undergarments of the officers. But not a body in sight. The officers themselves appeared to have disappeared without a trace, as though they'd vanished into thin air.

Danica rushed back out into the hallway and was halfway to Jegra's quarters when she practically ran into a female officer who was stuck to the wall as though she were a fly stuck to flypaper. Hanging at an awkward horizontal angel, she was writhing about with a sticky, restrained motion and moaning incoherently.

"Lieutenant Brei'Alas, are you all right?" Danica asked, approaching the science officer. When she grew nearer, she discovered the woman's eyes were rolled back in her head so that only the whites showed. "Lieutenant Brei'Alas!" she hollered in a reprimanding tone, hoping to jolt the woman out of the bizarre trance. But it was no use.

Slowly, she extended her hand to touch the woman's shoulder and try to pry her off from the wall when from behind her a voice rang out.

"Is she in pain?"

Startled, Danica withdrew her hand and quickly spun around to find the empress standing a few meters from her, gazing at the woman on the wall with the same level of concern.

"Thank the Gilded One you're safe," Danica said as she and Jegra met in the middle of the corridor. Jegra had on a burnt orange satin nightgown that had a sharp v-cut down the center. Merely a gossamer veil, the garment hugged her womanly form like a silk glove and molded itself to her voluptuous curves. "As for whether or not she's in pain," continued Danica, "I don't know. But, if you ask me, judging by the sounds of her moaning, I'd say she's in a state of ecstasy."

Jegra jutted a thumb over her shoulder and gestured at the empty corridor. "There are two more back that way. Same condition. What could be causing this?"

"My guess is that it has something to do with that pink aura that's saturating the ship. But we'll know more once we get to the bridge and run some scans of the anomaly," Danica said.

"Agreed," Jegra responded, and moving in unison, they marched up a branching corridor of the ship and made their way to the bridge.

The lights flickered in the command center as though something was draining the ship's power, and Jegra stepped into the dimly lit room and let out a shocked gasp at what she saw. Danica, having followed Jegra in, drew back away from the grotesque form almost as soon as she could process what it was. It wasn't like anything they'd ever seen before.

"What in Dagon is going on?" Danica asked in a hushed tone. Jegra shot her a baffled look and shrugged. Together, they cautiously took a step toward the undulating mass of flesh.

A flood of salacious moans washed over them and they stood before a tower of writhing blue bodies made up of the crew, and stared in dumbfounded awe. It was like a living sculpture, a mass of at least thirty bodies high, and certainly as dense, that ran from the floor to the ceiling. It looked like a Vorean caterpillar trying to balance upright; its worm body wriggling to find the right balance, its myriad legs probing the air to help counterbalance its unstable body.

The pile of intertwined flesh seemed as though each person was glued to the next, but in such a way that their blue Dagon bodies held at impossible angles and inclinations and which defied natural law. Odder still, perhaps, was the vigorous and lewd exhalations that escaped their lips, even though not a single one of them seemed to be consciously aware of the erotic acts they were performing. It was as if they they'd become a hive-mind and they were all drones merely satisfying the lustful needs of their lubricious queen.

Both Danica and Jegra simultaneously gasped when they saw who sat upon the hive. At the top of the heap of tangled bodies was Lianica. She leaned back in a reclined position, the extremities of her fellow crew, their arms and legs, forming a kind of organic throne just for her. But her eyes remained eerily vacant as she stared out at nothingness.

As if by instinct, she slowly slid her hand down her cobalt blue body and gently reached down between her smoldering thighs with roving fingers. Her face altered slightly, an expression of shock almost, and then she bit her bottom lip and moaned out loud, the proof of the gratifying tactile engagement manifesting in the form of thick beads of sweat which added to the sheen of her already glistening chest.

The orgasm she experienced rippled through the tangle of bodies like a wave. When she moaned a second time, everyone in the orgy joined her in a chorus of orgasmic professions that rang throughout the corridors of the ship.

"What could be causing this?" Jegra wondered aloud.

"It must have something to do with that pink substance engulfing the ship," Danica replied.

"What substance?" Jegra asked, turning to Danica.

"It's like nothing I've ever seen before. Some kind of buildup of slime. Algae, maybe. I won't know until I retrieve some physical samples and run tests."

"In hyperspace?" Jegra asked. "Is that even possible?"

"Not that I'm aware of," Danica replied. "Which is why we have to bring the ship to a stop and get to the bottom of this before we succumb to the effects as well…." Her voice trailed off as she got swept away by her thoughts.

"What is it?" Jegra asked, urging Danica to finish her thought.

"Nothing, I was just…thinking."

Lianica screamed out as she orgasmed again atop the heap, interrupting the two women's discussion and distracting them. They glanced up in time to watch as the orgasm trickled down among all the members stuck in the entanglement, and Jegra couldn't help but raise an eyebrow.

Danica rushed over to a control panel that ran along the far wall and started digging through the ship's systems.

"That's weird," she said.

"What is?" Jegra asked, gradually sauntering over to Danica and edging up beside her. She looked down at the display, which had glowing graphs and charts and all kinds of readouts she couldn't make heads or tails of.

"All systems are nominal," Danica answered. "There's no indication of anything out of the ordinary. And the slipstream anti-matter drive is functioning well within recommended parameters. The main fusion reactor seems to be running a little hot, but nothing that should raise any concerns."

"Scan for alien lifeforms," Jegra said.

"I already have," Danica answered.

"And?"

"Nothing registers. So, at least, we know it's not sentient." Danica raised her eyes until they locked with Jegra's, a perplexed look plastered across her face.

Another orgasm rippled throughout the living sculpture of Dagon bodies.

Jegra turned and looked at the heaving, gasping, and fluid-secreting tangle of people and thought to herself for a moment. No more than a handful of seconds had passed when the shrill wail of a warning alarm went off. As it blared noisily, Jegra looked to Danica. "That doesn't sound good."

Danica checked the control panel again and then mumbled, "No, no, no." She slammed her palms down against the glass display of the control panel, the lights flickered briefly, their colors dimming then coming back to full.

"That *really* doesn't sound good," Jegra repeated, placing a hand on her hip and tilting her head curiously at Danica as she waited to be brought up to speed.

"It says the hyperborean quad fusion core is now overheating."

"I thought you said—"

"I know what I said," Danica snapped, growing frustrated with this whole situation.

Jegra left it alone. She knew Danica was freaking out as much as she was so she kept her voice calm and controlled. After all, it's what a queen would do. "I thought there were redundancies to prevent that from ever happening."

"There are," Danica replied. "The slime must be clogging up the slipstream dark energy ram scoops and causing the coolant system to feedback on itself."

"How do we fix it?" Jegra asked.

As if on cue, the moment the question was aired, Lianica moaned out again, her prurient breath passing over her Prussian blue lips. "*Ahhh...*"

"Oh, shut up," Danica snapped, irritated by the lewd interruptions. Turning back to Jegra, she stroked her chin and thought for a moment. "We're going to need to head down to engineering and shut down the hyperborean drive manually."

"I see," Jegra said.

Danica brought up a cut-away map of the ship's internal layout. Her finger landed on a red glowing section at the mid-aft area of the ship and she frowned. "But we won't be able to do that until we syphon off the heat from the engines; the excess heat has spilled into main engineering."

"We could wear the EV suits," Jegra suggested.

Danica shook her head in a way that seemed like she was warning Jegra that was a bad idea. "The doors are sealed. The only way in is to get the coolant system back online. Until then, it's a nuclear death trap."

"What if we just jettison the core then send out an SOS and wait for a pick up?"

"I'd only recommend that as a last resort. Being stuck in hyperspace–there's no telling what will happen to the core once it passes through the electromagnetic barrier of the shield. It could detonate the moment it makes contact with the normal space and create a black hole."

Jegra snapped her fingers and looked right at Danica. "I have an idea," she extolled optimistically. It didn't seem to fit with the direness of their situation, which caused Danica to grow curious.

Jegra pivoted back toward the exit, headed off the bridge, and stepped into the corridor. "Follow me," she beckoned with the wave of her hand.

Danica shrugged and followed after Jegra. Now she was really curious. What did Jegra know that she didn't?

After a few minutes of racing through the empty corridors, they arrived at Jegra's quarters.

"Why are we back at your quarters?"

As the doors parted and let them in, Jegra glanced over her shoulder at

Danica. "Can you keep a secret?"

"Yes."

In the far corner of the room, Jegra pulled the wooden box out from under the fancy antique writing desk and set it on top of the desk. She gave Danica a stern look, as if to say *this stays between us,* then slowly opened the lid.

5

Danica's eyes lit up with terrified revelation as she peered into the antique box. Golden light streamed across her face and a tiny space squid rose out from the container and began hovering before them.

"It's…it's…" Her voice faltered as she stumbled over the myriad of frantic thoughts that rushed through her mind. And she had questions. Questions like: *why in the seven systems would Jegra have one of these monstrosities?* and: *how in the galaxy did she acquire it?*

The DSC, or Dagon Science Council, had been trying to capture one of these things for decades with no luck. They were as elusive as they were destructive. Yet, here was one, riding along as Jegra's pet.

"Where in the bleedin' galaxy did you get that monstrosity?"

Jegra shot Danica a harsh look. "This little *monstrosity* is going to save our lives," she confidently informed Danica. "And his name is La'Garren."

"La'Garren?" Danica inquired. "You named *it* after the most famous gladiator to have ever lived?"

"Seemed fitting. A most powerful name for a most powerful being."

Danica rolled her eyes and spoke out of the corner of her mouth. "All right, then."

Jegra held up her hand and made a fist, leaving only her pinky finger stretched out. The glowing squid hovered close and wrapped a radiant tendril around her finger.

"What are you doing?" Danica asked in a worried voice. She stepped forward and took a grappling posture just in case she needed to wrangle Jegra away from the creature. Jegra merely raised her hand and gestured for her to hold back.

"It's how he communicates. Although he's just an infant, he already understands basic mental commands; they speak using images—a kind of telepathy."

The baby space squid let go of Jegra's finger and wafted about in the air for a moment, as though it were processing some kind of command code.

"What did you tell it?" Danica asked.

"I told him he could have a nice meal by heading down to the engine room."

They were about to turn to leave when the emergency alarm for a core meltdown began to blare.

"In that case, I sure hope he's hungry," Danica said, leading the way out of the room and to main engineering, "because things just got serious."

The baby space squid trailed after both women as if he were a helium balloon tethered to them by a string, pulling up the rear. By the time they'd made it through the winding corridors to engineering, steam was coming out from under the doors, and both women looked down.

"I sure hope nobody was trapped in there," Jegra said.

Danica tried to open the doors by hitting the panel, but it was no use. She manually opened the access panel to the wiring to see if she could hotwire a door release, but that was no use either. The wiring was melted into a nonfunctioning mess that smelled of copper and burnt plastic.

"I guess we'll just have to do it the old-fashioned way," Jegra said. She reached out and jammed her fingers into the space where the sliding doors met and gripped down. The metal door crumbled beneath her grip and her hands began to smoke and sizzle. Jegra screamed out in pain as she pried the doors apart with burning hands.

Intense energy pierced the opening and Danica had to shield her eyes and look away. Jegra stepped aside once the opening was big enough for the baby space squid to slip through, and as he flew by she whispered, "Bon appetite."

The space squid flew through the opening and into the glowing hot room.

Danica rushed over to Jegra, gripped her by the wrists, and flipped her hands over so they faced palms up. Her flesh looked like seared hamburger. "Are you insane?"

"Got singed pretty good," Jegra grunted, trying to suppress the pain. "But I'll live."

"You're bleeding," Danica said.

"I don't have time to bleed," Jegra quipped, drawing her wrists back.

Danica let her go, but not before giving her a concerned look.

"I'm fine. Really. I am. Now, all we need to do is get back to the bridge and make sure that when La'Garren cools down the engines, we don't drop out of hyperspace and crash into a moon or get sucked into a black hole."

Without warning, Jegra charged up in the middle of the corridor, collapsed to her knees, and groaned. Danica rushed to her side and knelt down, placing a gentle hand on Jegra's shoulder.

"Unngh," she groaned, as if in pain.

"What's the matter?" asked Danica, her hand stroking Jegra's back in a soothing manner. She felt Jegra's muscles tense up at her slightest tough as if she were fighting with all her strength against some invisible foe and Danica knew instantly that something was terribly wrong.

"I can't hold back any longer."

"Hold what back?"

"Ever since you touched me," she relayed through a clinched jaw, "I've been going out of my mind with the desire to rip your clothes off and take you here and now."

Jegra's right hand reached out to grab Danica, but she caught it with her left. "I don't know how much longer I can hold back these carnal urges, but it seems that you're the only one that's immune," Jegra managed to say with some effort.

"Because I'm a mod," Danica said, only half certain.

"There's not time to discuss the details. We've...got...ngh...to..." Jegra grunted even louder and collapsed to her side, then, after straining against her own body–which was acting as though it were possessed by some kind of demon– fell onto her side and curled up into a fetal position.

Her face turned beet red, as she fought off the pure sensation of lust and the urge to force herself on Danica. That's when the intensity of it hit her. It was so powerful, she had to fight just to stay conscious.

"I can hear them," Jegra muttered.

"Who? Who can you hear?" Danica asked.

"My mind...it's...ngh...somehow linked with the others. It's...ngh...overwhelming."

"How is this even possible?"

"I don't know," she answered with great effort, fighting off the flood of voices that penetrated her consciousness. "But it feels like I'm losing my mind. Go!" she shouted. "Hurry."

Danica, reluctant to leave the empress's side, did as ordered and slowly turned away. As difficult as it was leaving her like that, she had her orders: Save the ship.

Back on the bridge, Danica's fingers danced across the controls of the navigation station as she frantically charted a clean exit point. Once she got the coordinates inputted, all she had to do was watch the fusion core temperature levels. Once they dropped back down to optimal range, she'd hit the button and bring the ship full stop.

"Danica," a voice whispered.

She looked up to find Lianica Blackstar, perched on top of the heap of bodies like a sex goddess, staring down at her. Danica was about to turn away and ignore her when, all of a sudden, Lianica began to slide down the tangle of bodies. Arms helped guide her down and gently set her on the floor as if she were royalty.

Her dainty toes met the cold floor and she stepped away from the living sculpture. Even as she broke with the strange entity, her mind remained connected by whatever strange force was at play.

Lianica's body glistened with her own sweat and the residue of sixty other participants. She took a step forward, her feet flattening under the weight of her hourglass figure, her perfectly rounded hips causing her to walk with a seductive gait, her hips swiveling side to side as she drew nearer and nearer. "Please, join us. We want you…"

"Stay back!" Danica warned.

Lianica ran her fingers down her own body, touching her collarbone and gliding them down her torso, around the cusp of her breasts, and to the soft patch of snow-white hair nestled between her thighs. "We need you here," she said in a sultry voice. "We need you inside us."

Danica watched with a disinterested gaze as Lianica brought her glistening fingers to her lips and slowly opened her mouth.

There was a strange shuddering throughout the ship and without warning the main power cut out. Danica brought up auxiliary power and slammed her fist down onto the controls, bringing the ship abruptly out of hyperspace. The ship's engines went cold and time dilated as the ship re-entered normal space, everything slowing down.

With the ship having dropped out of hyperspace, the *Shard* began to drift aimlessly in the vacuum of space. The pink slime that coated every part of the ship quickly hardened in the near absolute zero temperature and began to break away in chunks as if it were a frozen Jell-O, a strange Earth food that Jegra had dared Danica to eat one drunken night and which still caused her to have nightmarish flashbacks of the hideous sensation of it as it wriggled and slid around in her mouth like a gelatinous alien life form.

Once the strange pink gel began to break off from the ship, the glow dissipated and the pile of Dagons slid to the floor. Bodies smacked wetly against the cold deck of the bridge, and people lay strewn about groaning from the pain of their physical exertion and complaining of splitting headaches.

Lianica awakened from her spell and looked down in mortified shock at her blue-skinned nudity and then up at Danica. Quickly covering herself up best she could, she asked, "What the Helios happened? Why am I bare?"

Just then the bridge doors opened and La'Garren flew into the room and pulled up next to Danica as though it were the most natural thing for him to do.

Lianica looked at the space squid with a startled look, then back at Danica, and before she could piece together what in the world was going on, she passed out and collapsed to the floor.

"Good work, little fella," Danica said, staring down at an incapacitated Lianica with a smug smile on her face.

The baby squid pulsed with yellow light, getting paler and dimmer like a Dagon firefly on a warm summer's night.

Lianica awoke to find herself in her own bed. Sitting up a little too abruptly, she clasped her head and moaned in agony as a throbbing headache pounded her skull relentlessly. Then she reached between her legs and groaned as another painful throbbing manifested itself. As the dim recollection of what had transpired gradually came back to her, she groaned again out of the indignity of it all.

"Good, you're awake," a voice said.

Lianica startled and swiveled in the direction the voice had come from. Sitting in the corner of her room and looking up from a book was Danica.

"What are you doing in my private quarters?" Lianica sneered at her sworn rival. She didn't mean to sound as menacing as she had, but she didn't take kindly to the intrusion. She was a rather private individual and having an uninvited guest lounging in her quarters while she was sleeping made her feel wary.

"Only to make sure you were recovering all right. Sickbay is filled to capacity with crew members. And since I'm the only one unaffected by the strange anomaly, which, after running some scans, I now think was a kind of algae that, miraculously enough, grew exponentially in the hyperspace displacency, I volunteered to monitor you until you found yourself well enough to return to active duty."

"Volunteer? But why would you do that?" Lianica asked, her face squinting in bewilderment at the selfless act. "We're not exactly friends."

"Because," Danica replied, her voice growing serious. "This ship needs its commanding officer. And, the last time I checked, that is still you."

"Oh," Lianica replied, relinquishing her tough-girl façade, "I see." For one second, she let slip the slightest of smiles. Something genuine. Something heartfelt.

Lianica groggily climbed out of bed and looked down at the dark purple, two-piece nighty she had on. The top was a satin camisole and the bottoms consisted of barely a triangular patch. Lianica found the nighty both sexy and in good taste.

"You pick this out?" she asked.

"I felt it suited you," Danica replied.

"It's nice." Another smile formed on her face as she continued to examine the fabric, running it through her fingers.

Danica nodded approvingly.

"Can I get you something to drink? Some tea perhaps?" Lianica offered, thumbing over her shoulder at the food synthesizer. She wasn't sure what else she could offer in way of showing her gratitude, but she was grateful for Danica's taking care of her and wanted to offer the slighted token of thanks in return.

"Tea would be perfect," Danica replied.

Lianica fetched them both a nice cup of Dagon herbal tea and sat down across from her.

They sat sipping their tea, not saying anything for the longest time and then, finally, they both spoke up simultaneously. Interrupting each other, they stopped, shared and awkward glance and chortled softly at their bad timing.

"You go ahead," Danica said.

"No, you go. I insist."

"Alright." Danica sighed and set her tea down on the small glass coffee table between the two reading chairs in which they sat, and looked across the divide at Lianica. She blinked her golden eyes contemplatively and then took a deep breath. Finally, she got up the nerve to ask what she'd been dying to ask ever since she had come aboard the *Shard.* "Why do you hate me so much?"

"I don't hate you. I envy you," Lianica answered. "All my life I aspired to be like you. More than that; I wanted to *be you.*"

"That doesn't explain why you've been so cold toward me. Or why you constantly run me down every chance you get."

"I know there's no excuse for my behavior. All I can offer is an explanation. You see, I had to watch my heroine fall from grace and take the job of a common slave. I hated that you compromised. I hated that you gave up and let it happen without so much as a fight. I hated the weakness I saw in you. It infuriated me and pushed me to do better. Pushed me to never show an ounce of weakness."

"Surely, you realize I had no choice in the matter. The emperor wants me dead, and Jegra, your empress, is merely protecting me the only way she knows how."

"By concealing you among the commoners. I know. It's just that…it's not fair."

"On that we can both agree."

They shared another exchange of hushed smiles and then Lianica continued on with her explanation regarding her actions. She figured that she owed Danica at least that much.

"I thought that if it happened to you then it could happen to anybody. Even me. And I swore I wouldn't let it befall me. I swore to be stronger than you. Tougher than you."

"Bitchier than me," Danica added.

Lianica grinned. "Yes, and that." She let out a small laugh, then cleared her throat and looked at Danica. "Then, when I found out you were coming aboard, all that rage and insecurity came flooding back. And I took it out on you. In retrospect, I believe I could have handled it better than I did. My overreaction, I'm ashamed to admit, was an act of weakness."

Danica stood up abruptly and Lianica grew tense, not knowing what she was about to do. Closing the distance between them, Danica put her hand on Lianica's head and drew her into her abdomen so that her cheek was pressed against her warm belly. "You're not weak, Lianica. You're one of the strongest women I know. And, for what it's worth, I forgive you."

Lianica wrapped her arms around Danica's waist and squeezed tight, letting her know she was grateful for her forgiveness and understanding. She kissed Danica just below her bellybutton and then hugged her again.

Danica held Lianica's face to her soft stomach until their combined heat, spurred on by their racing hearts, made the burning desire welling up inside her unbearable and she let go. Withdrawing from the embrace, she turned to leave when, unexpectedly, she felt Lianica's hand grasp her by the wrist and halt her.

"Please, stay."

Danica looked back and smiled. "You know I can't," she replied.

Lianica looked away and Danica could sense that she felt rejected. Reaching over, she grabbed Lianica's chin and drew it back so they were facing one another again. Danica slowly leaned in and kissed Lianica on her deep blue lips.

It was a long, sultry kiss that neither of them could have anticipated, and afterward, they shared another lingering gaze as they tried to process what it all meant. Danica shook her head, as if to say *no, this could never be*, and turned to leave. "I'm sorry," she said as she scurried out of the room. "I have to go."

Once outside of the commander's quarters, Danica strode across the corridor and leaned against the wall, trying her best to calm her racing heart. Throwing her head back in frustration, she slammed the back of her head against the wall. Then she did it again. And again. "What the hell were you thinking, Danica?" she said to herself, staring up at the ceiling. "Get a hold of yourself. You're acting like an insane person."

Just then the two Dagon officers she'd met earlier at the lift came around the corner of the corridor. They stopped in their tracks when they saw her bashing her head into the side of the wall repeatedly and speaking to herself.

Uncomfortable, they lowered their gazes and passed by without saying a single word. As they sulked by, she merely glowered at them with a wild-eyed gaze that dared them to say something. Anything. Just so she could tear them a new one.

But to her relief they were smart and kept their eyes down and their words to themselves. Regardless of what a couple of low-level crewmen might think, she was pretty certain that half of the crew thought she was completely insane.

A few minutes later she stormed into Jegra's quarters and began pacing in the middle of the room. Jegra was feeding La'Garren an energy pellet she'd synthesized and he was curled up on her bosom, tucked snuggly into her cleavage like a small kitten.

Noticing that Danica was in a nervous kerfuffle, Jegra raised a finger and was about to ask what the matter was when Danica blurted out, "I kissed Lianica."

Jegra closed her hand and calmly withdrew it. She looked at Danica's flustered face and smiled. "That's wonderful news. So, when's the wedding?"

"Har, har. Very funny. But it's killing me inside. I feel like I've cheated on you."

"Because you kissed a woman and liked it?"

"No, because I kissed a woman who wasn't you."

"Danica," Jegra said, letting out a long sigh. "You know me well enough to know I'm not built like that. As long as I have the smallest piece of your heart, I'm satisfied. The way I see it, there is more love inside you than can be contained. If you want to share that love, then, for the life of me, I cannot see how that would make the world a lesser place. So, love who you wish. You can be with whoever you please, and whoever pleases you in return, because in that union you'll find happiness. And my love for you is bigger than that; I only ever care about your well-being and happiness."

Danica threw up her arms. "I know! It's just that…"

"Let me guess, you surprised yourself and don't know why you like her so much, is that it?"

"Yeah. How'd you guess?"

"Trust me, you're getting yourself worked up over nothing."

"We were practically biting each other's heads off this morning. Then some weird space algae that somehow exists in the folds of hyperspace plastered us with its psychedelic love goop and, the next thing you know, Lianica and I are trying to tear each other's clothes off. Not under the influence of the lust inducing algae, mind you, but because of some strange attraction that, apparently, secretly existed between us all along."

"You know what it would be like though, right? It would kind of be like fucking yourself," teased Jegra.

"Because we're so much alike? Or because we're both royal bitches?"

"Now you're getting it!" Jegra added with a snap of her fingers.

"Ha, ha. You're full of wisecracks today, a real comedian. But I wouldn't quit my day job if I were you" Danica put her hands on her hips to let Jegra know how *unfunny* her joking around was. After pacing the floor a bit more, she stopped and looked into Jegra's brown eyes. "Please, Jegra, be serious. This isn't any laughing matter. *I kissed Lianica.*"

Jegra nodded patiently, as if to let Danica know she'd already said as much, and gently placed the sleeping squid baby, made of radiant energy, back in his box and closed the lid as though she were tucking in a newborn. She strode over to Danica and placed her hands over her blue shoulders, looked deep into her amber eyes, and gave a reassuring squeeze.

"As your empress, I order you to go back to Lianica's quarters and tell her how you really feel."

"But..."

"No buts, Dani. Just be honest with her. Be honest with yourself. And come what may, at least you had the courage to be true to who you are."

"Are you sure?" she asked, brushing her ombre hair away from her golden eyes and looking into Jegra's brown ones.

"If I need you, I'll know where to find you."

Jegra's warm smile elicited the same from Danica and she slowly withdrew from the room. Sending a hesitant look across her shoulder, Jegra met her gaze and with a shooing gesture of her hand, motioned for her to stop diddle-daddling and just go.

Several minutes later, Danica was standing beneath the archway of Lianica's open door with Lianica staring at her, a mystified expression on her face. "You came back."

Danica's chest heaved as she took in a deep breath to try and calm herself. Then, without saying so much as a word, Danica reached out, clasped Lianica by the nape of her neck, and reeled her in. Their lips crashed together and they shared a deep, satisfying kiss. The second in just as many hours.

Lianica's eyes lit up with excitement and the women stumbled back into the room together. "Are you sure?" she asked between the soft smacking noise of wet kisses.

"I'm sure," Danica whispered.

As the doors shut behind them, out in the hallway the two officers, returning from their rounds, looked at each other and shrugged. Without speaking of what they had just witnessed, they continued on down the corridor as though nothing was out of place. Just another ordinary day on the *Shard*.

6

"**Dropping out of** hyperspace, now," informed Commander Lianica Blackstar. The empress stood next to the commander and watched eagerly as Novac Tamoran's vessel appeared on the wall-sized vid-monitor which filled the ship's front view portal.

"Right where we expected them to be."

"Rather convenient," Danica said. "It looks like a trap, if you ask me."

"Oh, it's most definitely a trap," Jegra said, folding her arms across her chest as she frowned at the enemy vessel.

Lianica looked over at Danica and they shared a confidential smile between them as the satisfying recollections of last night impressed upon them both. Turning to Jegra, Commander Blackstar tugged at her white military jacket, straightening the sharp shoulder pads and golden tassels and cleared her throat. "What are my orders, Your Majesty?"

Jegra rubbed her chin and ran through her options.

The *Shard* didn't have powerful disruptor cannons, just pulse beams for breaking up asteroids, so, she couldn't fire a warning blast. Although the two class nine Dagon fighters parked in the shuttle bay were equipped with heavy disruptors. Flying in with an escort would send a message.

She could also beam aboard wearing her Knights of Caelum armor. Although, she felt that might be a bit over dramatic. Yet another option would be to take the diplomatic approach and go as herself; as Empress of the Dagon Empire.

"Send them a message that I'm coming aboard. I'll need a couple of escorts as my personal shuttle doesn't have any firepower. Danica, you take one fighter and find a second pilot for the other."

"I'll fly it," Commander Blackstar said.

Jegra looked at her and then nodded. Although it wasn't protocol, there weren't any rules against it. And she strongly doubted Blackstar would take no for an answer.

"All right then, you're both with me."

Jegra turned and began making her way to the shuttle bay. Blackstar raised her hand and motioned to the comms officers to relay the message with a quick gesture.

Out in the corridor, Danica stood waiting for Lianica near the entrance. Once they were in the corridor together, Lianica said in a hushed tone. "I hope I didn't cause any trouble between you and the empress."

"It's quite all right," Danica said. "We talked it through and surprisingly, she was a little more than supportive. I think she's beginning to think more and more like a Dagon woman every day. Promiscuity before romance, and all that."

"So promiscuity isn't a problem for her? But I thought her species was mainly monogamous."

"They are. But, as you are certainly aware, Jegra's no ordinary woman."

"Well, in that case, it's lucky she got stuck with us rather than the Nyctans. They'd have her swearing off sex for the rest of her life."

"Not Jegra," Danica laughed. "She'd probably turn them into a sex cult before they managed to convert her."

Both women laughed in unison as they came around the bend to find Jegra standing there waiting for them.

With a toss of her long brown hair, she smiled at them both and asked, "What's so funny?"

Both Danica and Lianica looked at each other and blushed. Lianica was the first to respond. "Nothing of importance, Your Grace."

Jegra squinted at them both then let it go. "Right." Turning on her heels, she beckoned them to keep up with her. "This way, ladies, if you'd be so kind."

The entrance to the shuttle bay parted and Jegra strode across the flight deck to her shuttle craft. Both Lianica and Danica climbed into the strange, five-point light fighters, which looked like skewed stars drawn by a child rather than combat spacecraft.

As strange as they appeared aesthetically, however, being Dagon fighters meant they were armed to the teeth with far more firepower than any other vessel their size. Jegra knew that having them as an escort would send Novac Tamoran a clear message not to mess with her.

Jegra climbed into her shuttle, settled into her seat, and looked out her view portal at Dani and Lianica, who were settling into their cockpits. Tapping her controls, she shut the clamshell doors and then brought the main engines online. The ship's system hummed to life and the blue repulsor beam droned with a deep pulse that sounded like a washing machine undulating a rinse cycle, but instead of tossing around clothes, it tossed around particles and created a blue static-bubble which enabled the ship to lift off the flight deck.

Her fingers danced across a various assortment of colored buttons, red, yellow, orange and green, all of the blinking in response to her touch. The maneuvering thrusters ignited with small two-second bursts, and the shuttle gradually turned toward the inner wall of the ship's hull.

Using a new technology they'd acquired, the ship's hull melted away, as if made of liquid metal, and revealed the open expanse of space to her. Jegra tapped the controls again, her shuttle's primary thrusters came on, and the small white vessel shot out of the hangar and into open space.

Both fighters, distinctive in their five-pronged design, trailed closely behind the empress's shuttle. Once they were fully away, both fighters took the typical escort flight pattern and buzzed Tamoran's clunky freighter that hung before them like a massive, angular, deformed shark.

Accompanying either side of Jegra's shuttle, her wingmen let off a few warning blasts at the giant pirate ship. Green bolts of energy streaked across Tamoran's bow, practically singeing it, alerting him to their presence, and to the fact that the Empress wasn't arriving unarmed.

The energy bolts flew past Novac Tamoran's ship, nearly scorching his paint off, they passed so close, and then continued off into the blackness of space. Eventually their energy would dissipate as entropy sucked the life out of the plasma bolts, but that's why disruptors only really worked in close combat. Laser canons worked a little better at long distances; their controlled beams were continuously fed power from the ship. But only battle cruisers had enough power to charge super massive lasers required to do any serious damage. And, of course, there were high yield missiles for those medium range attacks where disruptors weren't enough but super lasers were overkill.

Jegra received a communications hail from Tamoran's vessel and brought up the audio. "This is the Empress of Dagon," she started, not giving the caller a chance to speak first. "I'm en route to your ship. You will permit me to board or be destroyed."

"Why of course, your grace," Tamoran's voice replied in a glib tone, the comm crackled softly, signifying the fact that his technology was rather dated. "I welcome you aboard with open arms."

Jegra tapped the button and cut the chatter and then sent out an encoded message to both fighters. It simply read, "Keep company until mission complete.'" Two WILCOs came across the monitor in reply.

Jegra slowed her craft to docking speed and hovered in front of the pirate vessel's large hangar doors, which opened with a clunky, aggravating slowness. Their heavier-than-usual weight meant that Tamoran had reinforced the entire ship's hull with extra plating to shield it from disruptor fire. She imagined it could take a heavy beating, if need be.

Once the hangar doors were fully retracted, she brought her ship inside and looked for a place to set down. Unlike her brand new, clinically clean vessel, Tamoran's landing bay looked like a veritable salvage dump of spare parts and random junk. Finding a place to set down proved to be a bigger challenge than she had anticipated.

As the hangar doors began to close again, she saw both fighters streak past the gradually narrowing opening as they ran circles around Tamoran's vessel. Buzzing around the ship like a couple of menacing wasps, the fighters acted as a quaint reminder that should he try anything disreputable, he'd be shot out of the sky and turned into the same type of space debris that littered his landing bay floor.

Eventually, she found an opening large enough to accommodate her craft and set the shuttle down on the landing pad. The retractable landing arms of the craft unfolded just in time, and the ship landed with a soft clank. The hydraulic limbs whined with resistance as the ship sank down then was pushed upright again as the ship automatically steadied itself. After locking into position, the hydraulics decompressed, letting out a hiss of air, and no sooner had the air settled than the clamshell doors swooped open and Jegra stepped out.

She did a quick scan of the hangar, searching for hidden threats, but found it was empty. Not so much as a greeting party to meet her; she wasn't sure if that was a good or a bad sign.

She shrugged and pinched the form-fitting dress at her hips, giving it a firm jerk to stretch out any wrinkles that may have formed when she crouched under the clamshell door, and stepped down on the three retractable stairs as she came onto Tamoran's ship. Straightening her posture, she pushed out her chest and glanced around the room one more time just to be on the safe side.

She imagined Tamoran was playing it safe. He knew what she wanted, and he wasn't going to get in her way. Then again, with a man as unscrupulous as Novac Tamoran, it was sometimes hard to tell when he was being cunning or when his cowardice simply compelled him to act in his best interests. He could, after all, simply be biding his time, waiting for the opportune moment to strike.

She headed to the entrance and stepped through the large sliding doors that led out into the corridor. Once inside the long, branching veins of the ship's anatomy, she tapped the bracelet on her wrist and brought up a holographic display of the ship's technical blueprints; the display itself also happened to be blue.

With her free hand, she stuck her fingers into the projection and spread them wide. Cutaways of the ship's interior decks incrementally spread apart and hung suspended in midair. She briefly studied the layout of the ship and then reached in and pinched one of the sections as though she were reaching into a dealer's deck to pull out a card. As she brought the selected layer to the top, the remaining layers folded back up and vanished from the projection. The main cut-out contained a blinking red dot that signified the location of Emperor Dakroth.

[*Genetic signature identified*] the computer voice chirped from her smart-bracelet. She double tapped the blinking red dot and then a thin green line traced its way through the blueprints of the corridors, highlighting for her the quickest path to the emperor's location.

"I'm coming, darling dearest," she said in a dry and scathing tone. She still hadn't forgiven him for the death of Abethca, and for what he'd done to Dani. If anything, he was lucky she wasn't coming here to finish him off. And even though he deserved a less than merciful death for his crimes, she wasn't a cold-blooded killer like him. Although, there was no denying the fact that she was a killer.

But, even as life in the arena had hardened her and taught her to survive, it had also taught her honor. Something Dakroth knew little of. Of all the alien life she'd encountered, with all their various customs and cultures, Dakroth was, by far, the least honorable man she knew. And although he'd likely take that as a compliment, she wasn't here to set him straight. She was here to fulfill her duty as Empress and Protector of the Lord Emperor. Once she had fulfilled her obligation, however, as far as anyone was concerned, she was through with him.

Jegra navigated her way through the corridors, following the projection until she arrived at the brig. Standing in front of the doors, she twisted her bracelet and the hologram flicked briefly and then cut out. She took in a deep breath, puffed up her chest, and said to herself in a hushed tone, "Here goes nothing."

The doors slid apart to reveal Dakroth lounging on his cot behind a light blue, glowing security forcefield. He had his cheek perched on one palm of a bent arm, propping his head up as though he was expecting her. If not her, then someone else; a concubine, perhaps. Or that red-headed cunt, Ishtar Bantu.

"It took you long enough, my dear," he said with a less than appreciative smile. It slid off his face as easily as it had slid on, and she merely glowered at him.

"Be glad I came at all."

Dakroth pushed himself up and swung his legs over the edge of the cot. Steepling his fingers in front of him, his elbows planted on his knees, he leaned forward and pressed his fingertips against his chin in contemplation. His eyes lingered on her and then another grin appeared, harder to read this time, but what she assumed could only be amusement settled onto his pursed lips. "And yet here you are."

Miffed at his nonchalance and lack of gratitude for her coming to rescue him, Jegra stormed up to the control panel on the wall and smashed her fist against it so hard the metal plating of the panel caved in and sparks shot out irritably as the circuitry hissed with great protestation at its mistreatment.

The damage done, the containment cell's energy shield flicked indiscriminately and then fell away.

"Where are your clothes?" Jegra asked, eyeing Dakroth's mostly naked blue body from head to toe. He only had on a loincloth made from a Candorian cotton mesh, which was just translucent enough to reveal the outline and contour of Dakroth's groin.

Catching her eyeing his junk, he walked past her and said, "Come along, wife. We don't have time for any lovemaking."

Disgusted at the mere thought, Jegra scoffed and turned to protest. "I wasn't thinking about…I was merely….Gah! You're infuriating." She threw up her hands and gave up, feeling the very attempt to correct him was a futile endeavor, and then turned and followed Dakroth from the brig and out into the corridor.

With vigor in his steps, he strode confidently down the corridor in the wrong direction. Jegra cleared her throat and poked a thumb over her shoulder. "This way, Your Majesty."

"Right," Dakroth replied, quickly came about, and marched on in the correct direction, once again taking the lead.

"By all means, after you," Jegra said with a full helping of sarcasm. She even gestured for him to go on even though he was already well ahead of her.

After a few moments, they returned to the hangar and the doors slid open. They entered the shuttle bay to find Novac Tamoran waiting for them along with Ishtar Bantu and an entire security contingent armed with blasters.

"Now, now, my dear. You didn't really think you could just welcome yourself aboard, break out my prisoner, and take off without paying a price, now, did you?"

"And what price would that be?" Jegra asked, raising one eyebrow yet keeping her voice calm and steady.

"What is the Lord of the Galaxy worth to you?" Tamoran asked with a sneer. He could full well sense the tension between her and Lord Dakroth and plucked her strings like a master manipulator testing to see which one might snap. After a long pause, he added, "I'm perfectly happy to let you both go, of course. But I believe Emperor Dakroth and I have an agreement. Isn't that right, Your Majesty?"

Jegra looked at Dakroth, who shrugged. "What's he talking about?" she demanded to know.

"As payment for handing me safely over to you, he wants his own battlecruiser."

"And let me guess…to save your own skin you promised it to him."

Dakroth waved his hands about defensively. "At the time I really didn't have much of a choice. How was I supposed to know you'd come for me? For an entire year you've ignored my calls and dodged my advances."

Jegra balked. "Well, whose fault is that?!"

"Come, darling. Let's not be so emotional."

Slowly, Jegra clenched her fist. Her whitened knuckles automatically popped from the strain of her own strength. "I'll show you emotional," she growled through gritted teeth. This gesture caused Dakroth to bite his tongue and take a cautious step away from her.

Eyeing him once more to make sure he stayed in his place, Jegra turned and marched up to Tamoran. The security detail raised their weapons and trained them on her, but Tamoran simply raised a hand, gesturing to them that it was unnecessary, and they lowered them again.

Stepping up to him so that they were nose to nose, Jegra said, "Fine. You'll get your battlecruiser. Anything else you want to run by me before we get off this filthy rust-bucket?"

He took a deep breath and brushed down his flowing, leather jacket. "My associate here," he added, nodding his head at Ishtar Bantu, "would like something in return as well. And seeing as I'm indebted to her for saving my life on more than one occasion, I promised her she could have anything she wanted. *Anything*."

It was the final "anything," with the stressed inflection, that unnerved Jegra. She turned and glared at Ishtar Bantu, who merely grinned at her, the ends of her mouth curled up maliciously.

"And what would that be, precisely?" Jegra asked, not breaking eye-contact with her sworn enemy–the woman who had killed Abethca, Ellia, and who had left Jegra bleeding out on the hangar deck of the Nyctan battle cruiser after a vicious attack on her life.

"She wants a rematch with you. Mano a mano, no holds barred. To the death!" Tamoran announced in a gleeful manner. She could picture him rubbing his hands together in excited anticipation of the prospect of an all-female death match.

"Is that all?" Jegra asked, turning the question to Ishtar.

"No," the red-skinned woman replied. Looking down she slid the palm of her hand across her stomach and let it rest on the lower abdomen. "I also want you to let me keep our baby."

"Our baby?" Jegra squinted at Ishtar as she tried to decipher her meaning. "Whose baby?" That's when it dawned on her. The videogram she'd received aboard the *Shard*. The way Ishtar looked into the camera as though she were looking into Jegra's eyes just to spite her.

She did a double take between Dakroth and Ishtar and then huffed, "You've got to be kidding me." Jegra spun around and shot Dakroth a furious look. "I'm sure you and your deranged mistress will be happy together raising the perfect little sociopath."

"It's not what you think. She seduced me and…"

"And you couldn't keep it in your pants. Oh, I know all too well about your womanizing ways, dear husband."

"You sound jealous," Ishtar remarked, the sneer on her face tightening with malicious delight as she watched the sting of the news prick at Jegra's emotional heartstrings.

"No," Jegra answered. "Just disappointed that he'd stick his dick in that festering radioactive garbage heap that is your cunt."

The insult did little to wipe the smile off Ishtar's face, which peeved Jegra even more.

Although her relationship with Dakroth was a strained love-hate kind of affair, she had assumed that he had at least the same amount of feeling for her as she had for him. But, apparently, she was mistaken.

She shot Ishtar a cold, hard gaze. "You do realize, Red, the emperor cannot allow an illegitimate heir to the throne. Which means that abomination you call a child is as good as dead."

Ishtar chuckled from deep inside her throat and the sound came out her nose in a nasally, almost mocking sort of way. "Oh, my dear Jegra. You really are clueless, aren't you?"

Jegra didn't know what she meant by that, but noticed the atmosphere in the room shift to something more hostile. A tensing in body language. A change in posture. A cold calm fell over everyone, the kind of calm you experience in sporting competitions as you wait for the gun to go off or the whistle to sound. Everything slows incrementally and then one's focus becomes razor sharp. It was like that.

She took a step back from the red-skinned woman and scanned the faces in the room, feeling in her gut something was about to go down. Finally, she settled on Dakroth, who slowly drew away from her as though she were marked by the plague.

"My dear Jegra," Dakroth said with a sinister grin. "I'm afraid our relationship has been what one might call bittersweet. But Ishtar has talked some sense into me."

Jegra laughed out loud. She caught herself mid chuckle and forced herself back to seriousness and the quietude that accompanied it.

"You're a loose cannon," he went on. "Unpredictable. Emotional. Volatile. And I can't have you being a thorn in my backside for the rest of, well, whatever this is," he said, wagging a finger between the two of them. "Which is why I regret to inform you, my dear, I am requesting a separation."

"A separation? Why not just divorce me if I'm such a pain in your backside?"

"Because," Dakroth growled through a clamped jaw and a strained grin, "an emperor must sign off on a divorce. But a separation? Well, that's all on you."

"So, you need a scapegoat. Someone to blame for it not working out, other than yourself."

"You guessed it in one."

"Typical," she replied with sunken eyes that flamed red hot with the rage of a woman scorned.

Ishtar let out an annoyingly perfectly timed laugh and redirected Jegra's attention back to her. She brushed her lip with her thumb as though she had just finished eating a delectable, creamy desert and grinned coyly at Jegra.

"What's so funny?" Jegra leered at Ishtar, waiting for her to explain herself.

"Oh, nothing," she said dismissively. Then, pulling out a blade from behind her back, she held it out and pointed it at Jegra. "Now, Your Majesty, how about we finish what we started at The Cove when you sucker-punched me and threw me off that ledge. Just you and me. Here and now."

Jegra grinned sardonically. "I think not."

"Actually," Ishtar sneered, "you don't really have a choice in the matter."

"Oh, there's always a choice." Jegra reached over and grabbed Tamoran by his collar and reeled him in to her. Holding his head in a deathlike grip, ready to snap his neck at the slightest misstep, she slowly backed away from the group.

The security personnel all raised their blasters again. This prompted Novac

Tamoran to finally speak up.

"Hold your fire!" he wheezed. "There's no need for senseless violence."

"And here I thought you couldn't be reasoned with, Tamoran," Jegra said. She then shoved Tamoran into Ishtar, lunged across the room, and caught a fleeing Dakroth by his wrist. She then flung him into the group of guards, toppling them over like bowling pins.

Ishtar, jumping into action, retrieved a flash grenade from her belt and threw it at Jegra. The device exploded just next to Jegra's face.

Disoriented and blinded by the blast, Jegra stumbled over to the wall. Leaning against the cold metal plating, she felt her way toward the exit when out of the bleariness, the stiff muzzle of a blaster pressed against her forehead.

"That's far enough, Queen of Thessalonica!" Tamoran barked angrily. Waving the gun, he gestured to her to return to the center of the room. She complied.

"You can't blame a girl for trying," Jegra said.

"Bind her," Tamoran said, looking at Ishtar.

Ishtar shot him a hard look but he ignored it.

"There'll be time for your fun another day. For now, secure the prisoner."

She grumbled as she fetched the magnetic shackles, the same shackles that Jegra had worn when she was first abducted by aliens and sold to the Intergalactic Gladiatorial Syndicate.

Jegra held out her wrists for Ishtar to shackle her, but the magnetic binders simply slipped through Jegra's arms.

"What's this?" Ishtar gasped.

Jegra grinned. "It's called being one step ahead, sweetheart."

Just then, the empress's ship, along with the transmitted facsimile of her, disappeared. At the other end of the deck, a pile of cargo containers phased away to reveal Jegra's real ship. Safely inside the cockpit, she had already initiated the takeoff protocols.

"But how?" Dakroth asked.

"When the flash grenade went off," Tamoran said. "She must have evaded our detection."

Ishtar threw the shackles onto the deck and roared out in anger. She glared at Jegra, who looked at her from the cockpit of her shuttle and shot her a mocking wink.

The vessel's turbines whined to full throttle and Jegra's ship rose off the flight deck. Turning the ship about, she brought its nose in line with the hangar doors.

"Wait!" Dakroth cried out, raising a hand. "You can't just leave me here."

"I'm sorry, but I thought you said we were separated," Jegra replied through the ship's comm. Her voice echoed in the shuttle bay as though addressing an anxious crowd.

"There's no escaping," Ishtar Bantu hollered above the whine of the shuttle's turbines. She jutted a finger out toward the shuttle bay doors, which were sealed shut.

Jegra hit the comm and broadcast wide. "Ladies, if you'd be so kind."

A sudden explosion blasted right through the shuttle bay doors, opening up a giant, gaping hole. Novac Tamoran, Ishtar Bantu, and Dakroth all flew back from the force of the blast and tumbled to the unforgiving metal floor. Then, as atmosphere began to vent, they scrambled to grab onto something latched down. A few of Tamoran's thugs were sucked out into the vacuum of space.

Once the shuttle bay doors' energy barrier came online and the atmosphere stabilized, Ishtar Bantu was the first to get back onto her feet and she whipped out a pistol. Firing a flurry of shots at Jegra's shuttle as it made its escape proved futile. The small blaster didn't even singe the paint of the glossy white ship. Nonetheless, she continued pulling the trigger until the blaster overheated and automatically shut off, steam rising from its muzzle.

Novac Tamoran turned his head sharply toward Dakroth and scowled. "You do realize that if she escapes you'll have lost your only leverage. Then all bets are off."

Dakroth grinned. "I underestimated you, Tamoran. You are as ruthless as I am." Raising a red-tipped glowing finger, Dakroth took careful aim at the fleeing shuttle, which had already safely exited the ship's hull and was making ready to break away from Tamoran's freighter. As the charge grew bright pink with a buildup of plasma energy, Dakroth let go and launched the bolt of energy. It streaked out of the ship and impacted Jegra's shuttle.

There was a minor explosion and the shuttle jolted violently to the side as the right engine blew out. Spinning off into space, a tail of smoke coiled around

Jegra's shuttle as it tumbled away into deep space.

Dakroth began a second charge. His long, silvery hair whipped around in the breeze of the coolant leak somewhere overhead, and he stepped up to the cusp of the gaping hole and looked out into space at the hapless shuttle. "A pity it has to end like this, my dear," he said in a hushed tone.

Inside the shuttle, Jegra tried to get on the comm and send out a mayday, but the explosion had killed that system, too. The thrusters were also shot, and she couldn't get the ship under control.

Jegra slammed her fists down on the console in frustration and screamed.

Dakroth steadied his hand and grinned. "Goodbye, my luv," he whispered, and then fired off a second blast.

This time it was a direct hit. The shuttle sparked and flamed as the laser blast cut through its hull.

Back inside the cockpit, Jegra watched as half of the back of the ship tore away and flew off into space. Her hair violently whipped about as the oxygen was sucked out and she gripped her chair tightly, thinking this might be the end.

[*Hull breach detected,*] the computer voice said. [*Initializing emergency shields.*] Immediately, a blue veil spread like liquid glass across the gaping opening at the back of the ship and the atmosphere inside the shuttle returned to normal.

Jegra sighed in relief that she'd narrowly avoided getting sucked into the infinite blackness. Just then, a flap to a cubby in the mid-section of the ship rattled and fell open. She looked over to find golden light pouring from the opening. Surprised by the unexpected visitor, Jegra watched the baby space squid slide out from his cozy sleeping area.

"You're not supposed to be here," she said in a chastising yet affectionate manner. Getting up and rushing over to the squid, she quickly took the creature's glowing body in her arms and cradled him like her own infant. Without warning, another blast hit the ship and Jegra screamed out as a field of debris exploded all around her. For some reason, however, it all seemed to slow incrementally until the motion had completely ceased. She was able to move, but everything around her seemed as though it were frozen in time.

That's when she noticed something even more peculiar. All of space seemed to be folding in all around her. Flowing into a central point, like the lip of a waterfall streaming away into an abyss, the closer you approached. And, at the center of this attraction, was little squidy, La'Garren. He was glowing so bright that he looked like a roman candle lit in the middle of a vast, dark void. Fearsome though it was, his light did not burn her.

Soon he was glowing so hot that she feared he'd explode. Jegra reached out to touch him, and just as her fingers brushed one of his tentacles, there was a bright flash of light.

Jegra opened her eyes to find herself in the middle of a freefall, plummeting toward an unknown planet. A green and gray sky stretched all around her as bits and pieces of flaming debris went streaking by at a forty-five-degree angle toward the drab rocky surface below.

She squinted against the force of cool air and searched for the baby squid, but couldn't find him. She cut through thin wisps of cirrus clouds, entering a whirling freefall. After an intense moment that seemed as though she'd never regain control, she finally managed to stabilize herself. Looking down, she saw the jagged rock formations rising up fast to meet her and clenched her jaw.

This is gonna hurt, she thought to herself, bracing for impact. It was going to be a rough landing.

Jegra tightened into a ball, gripping her knees, and closed her eyes. From a distance, there was a great clap of thunder. But it wasn't thunder.

The impact of her crash was so fierce it kicked up a massive cloud and an explosion of rock and earth that sounded as though a bunker penetrator bomb had gone off. As the dust dissipated, Jegra lay at the center of a gigantic crater, approximately twenty feet deep and sixty feet around. She stared up at the muted green sky. In the distance, a bird, or birdlike creature, screeched like a roving hawk and Jegra blinked.

7

Commander Blackstar and Danica Valencia watched helplessly as the flash of radiant light and energy engulfed Jegra's shuttle. Throttling their thrusters to full, they raced toward her position in a desperate rescue attempt.

"What the hell was that?" Lianica said, shielding her eyes with her gloved hand. When she looked again, the ship, along with the strange light anomaly, was gone. It had vanished along with all the surrounding debris, and the only thing remaining was an empty pocket of space.

"I'm not getting any readings," Danica said, her voice fluxing with panic. "No life signs. No ship responder. Nothing."

Lianica brought her split-wing fighter up alongside Danica and looked out of the canopy to find Danica gazing back at her with a dismayed look. Bringing her attention back to her scanner readouts, she studied the display, looking for a clue as to what had just happened. But there wasn't anything in the database she could identify. At least, not in the known realm of physics. The anomaly was just that…an anomaly. "It's as if they simply—"

A fiery bolt of pink energy scorched Lianica's bow and she pulled hard to starboard, then brought the ship around to see Lord Dakroth standing at the edge of a sparking bulkhead, framed in the fractured opening where their missiles had blasted through, aiming a hot, glowing pink finger at her.

The escaping atmosphere from inside the ship whipped Dakroth's hair wildly as he stood poised, his finger slowly tracking the trajectory of the fighter. A subtle grin formed on Dakroth's lips and she imagined she could almost see him mouth the word, "Farewell."

A roaring scream filled the comm and Lianica snapped her head around just in time to see Danica's fighter streak by at a reckless speed, all blasters firing on the pirate vessel.

"Pull back, Dani!" Lianica shouted. "You're closing in too fast. You're not gonna be able to pull out in time!" But her warning was drowned out by the primal scream blaring over the comm.

Thrusters burning hot, Danica plowed her way through the opening of the pirate ship and crashed her vessel onto the deck of the freighter in an attempt to take Dakroth out kamikaze style. Sparks erupted from the collision as metal scraped metal and the small, split-wing fighter hit the deck with a hard screech and scraped across the hangar floor. A trail of flaming sparks shot up behind the vessel as it gouged the hangar deck with its reinforced korridium wings.

Dakroth leapt out of the way of the fighter and rolled to a stop, watching it crash into the aft wall of the hangar deck. He was busy pushing himself up off the floor when he caught the pirate king, Novac Tamoran, and the double-dealing Ishtar Bantu, exiting the hangar with haste. Almost as soon as they disappeared out the sliding doors, a massive section of the bulkhead crashed down from above, sealing off the entrance, and blocking off any potential escape route. Dakroth was trapped on the hangar deck.

Just then, a panel flew off from the wrecked fighter and clanged against the floor, rattling to a halt when a violet skinned beauty, her flight suit in tatters, landed on top of it.

Danica crouched beneath the battered and flaming hull of her fighter and honed in on Dakroth. Her eyes were filled with a rage Dakroth recognized all too well. A rage he'd seen a thousand times in the faces of his countless victims. The rage of a someone who'd witnessed a cherished loved one cut down before them. A face with the desire for vengeance etched upon every angry crease in its brow.

"Dakroth!" Danica shouted across the hangar, her eyes burning with rage as they locked onto him like heat-seeking missiles.

He raised his hands, giving a notably mendacious apology, and then cautiously backed away. With the doors to the hangar entrance clamped shut and blocked by debris, Dakroth raised his finger and blasted a hole in the wall next to him. Nodding at Danica, as if to bid her adieu, he quickly dashed through the smoldering exit and disappeared into a thick haze of dark gray smoke.

Danica ran toward the exit but was tossed into the air by a sudden explosion.

More paneling came down, a massive sheet of korridium blocked the hole and prevented her from following after the emperor. She slammed a fist onto it and screamed, "Coward!" Banging her fists against the plating, she screamed from frustration and rage.

Her voice raw from all her screaming, Danica's vocal protest faded into sobs and she collapsed to her knees with an overwhelming sense of defeat. Resting her head against the cold surface of the metal plate, she took a deep breath and exhaled again, letting out the last of her pent-up rage.

Numb from the shock of losing Jegra, and exhausted from the adrenaline spike that was now quickly fading, she slid back against the metal sheet and slumped to the ground. Staring despondently out across the burning hangar deck, she replayed the terrible incident in her mind, each time with the same conclusion: Jegra was gone.

Another explosion sounded in the bowels of the ship and the artificial grav-generators gave out. Danica felt herself become weightless and slowly float into the air. Feet rising off the ground, she began to tilt backward, as though she were doing a slow-motion backflip, and summersaulted toward the ragged hull breach in the side of the ship.

Caught up in the current of escaping gases, she was pulled toward the gaping hole, unable to slow herself. Drifting past a broken pipe, she reached out and tried to take hold, but she was already passing too quickly and her fingers merely slipped away from the pipe as she was dragged out of reach.

Without anything else to latch on to, she looked up in time to see the breach looming above her like a giant yawning mouth. Passing through, she was swallowed up by the breach and, her body spinning out of control, she was spat into the vacuum of outer space.

Ice crystals began to form on her face from the absolute cold, their crystalline trails tracing the bulging veins that ran across her marbling skin. She exhaled everything in her lungs, as the force of the depressurization threatened to burst them, and fought off the terrible urge to inhale.

A vast, glittering sky opened up before her and Danica watched with a deep sense of awe as she waited to lose consciousness. Her vision began to blur when, all of a sudden, a small fighter pulled up alongside her. The fighter's thrusters spurted as it moved into position above her, and just before she blacked out, she saw the canopy open.

Commander Lianica Blackstar, wearing her flight spacesuit, stood up and extended a hand toward Danica. Her fingers brushed Danica's fingers in a close pass, but she missed. Hopping up onto the edge of her craft, one hand gripping the edge of the canopy, she tried again. This time her hand clutched Danica's with full force and she pulled her back down into the ship.

Relieved, Lianica took a deep breath and exhaled again, trying to refocus her mind on the task at hand. Stowing Danica's unconscious body in the copilot's seat, she strapped her in and quickly closed the canopy.

Once the cockpit re-pressurized, Lianica took off her helmet and let out a pent-up sigh. As a shadow crawled across her cockpit, blotting out the starry sky above her, she looked up in time to see Novac Tamoran's vessel pulling away, aft thruster flaring bright as the ship accelerated away from her.

"Oh, no you don't," Lianica snarled under her breath. She flipped up the trigger guard on her joystick and activated the hyper-sonic, mag-guided Viper missiles.

With a press of the red button, two angry Viper missiles launched off the tips of her wings and sped toward Tamoran's ship. Their after burn looked like a couple of volcanic flares streaking through the night sky as they honed in on the bulky freighter. But before the warheads could hit their mark, three massive Dagon Imperial battlecruisers jumped into the system.

The first cruiser absorbed the blast of the two missiles, their detonations flaring bright yellow against the vessel's hull and then dissipating just as swiftly.

Barely a scorch mark was left on the korridium alloy plating of the Dagon battlecruiser. Even so, the powerful blast certainly caught their attention. Before Lianica knew it, the battlecruiser's side-mounted disruptor cannons swiveled around and targeted her small, split-wing fighter.

"Oh, shit," Lianica yelled, pulling back on the throttle and hitting full reverse on all thrusters.

The battlecruiser's cannons erupted with red plasma bolts that streaked across the black void and lit up the surrounding ships with a menacing red glow. The first few shots missed, but the cannons quickly auto-corrected. With a brilliant explosion, the disruptor blast tore through her wing and sent the small fighter into a whirling tailspin.

She fought to regain control and finally, corrected the zero-G rotation. Just then, another blast bombarded her forward shielding and subsequently knocked out all main power. One more hit and she'd be a goner.

Lianica looked up to see the battlecruiser come full about, all cannons trained on her. She gulped hard, realizing this might be the end of the line for her and Danica.

She flinched when a blinding flash of silver light engulfed her ship. To her surprise, however, it wasn't an attack. It was the *Shard*. The streamlined vessel manifested directly in front of her, its silver hull deflecting the battlecruiser's cannon blasts like a mirror redirecting a laser. Disruptor fire glanced off its reflective hull in every direction and lit up the dark like a laser-light show.

"Cutting it a little close, don't you think?" she spoke aloud to herself, the question being rhetorical in nature. Bringing the ship about, she set her down on the landing bay hangar, the liquid metal door reforming behind her and blending seamlessly into the sleek hull of the ship.

Her landing skiffs clanked down onto the hangar deck with a harsh clangor, and she quickly threw open the canopy. Jumping up, she yelled down at the first personnel officer she saw. "Get a medic up here ASAP!"

The officer, a young man with a white pony tail and a tan engineering uniform with a red stripe that ran across the shoulders and down the length of the pants, nodded his head and raced over to a wall panel. He pressed his hand against the touch-screen and quickly called for a medical team. Once he'd finished that task, he ran back and helped Lianica get Danica out of the cockpit.

Once they had gotten her safely out, Lianica set her on the hangar bay floor and began administering CPR. The med team arrived just as Lianica got Danica breathing again, and whisked her away to sickbay.

As hard as it was to watch Danica being rushed off in such an uncertain condition, Lianica had bigger concerns at the moment, like not getting everyone killed in a firefight against two Imperial destroyers. Easing up to the comm, she tapped the console and said, "Commander Blackstar to the bridge…get us out of here. Right goddamn now!"

She smashed the palm of her fist against the control panel, fracturing the glass, and cut the comm feed. Pressing her head against the cool glass of the display, she finally let her body relax. The tension melted out of her and, for the first time since she climbed into that cockpit, she felt safe. Exhausted, but safe.

Back from the brink of death, Danica awoke to find herself in her own quarters, in her own bed. She sat up, slowly, and winced from the pain of a throbbing skull. She pressed her palms against her head and moaned, but it did little to help ease the splitting headache.

"Good, you're awake," a voice said.

Danica started, covering herself with the sheet, since she wasn't wearing any clothes, or underwear, for that matter, and looked over to see Lianica sitting in bed next to her. This time, it was Lianica who was reading a book. She had on reading lenses and slowly pulled them off as she looked over at Danica.

"Lianica? What are you doing here?"

"What? I can't take care of my girlfriend and nurse her back to health?"

"The G-word? So soon?" Danica said, a coy grin spreading across her lips. Danica shook her head and replied, "What I was going to say was, I didn't expect to find you in my bed."

"Oh," Lianica said, brushing a stray lock of white hair behind her ear. She looked down at the pearl white nightgown she wore. "I guess I just wanted to be close to you. After all, you would do the same for me."

A shiver running through her, Danica looked down at her cleavage as she wrapped her arms around herself and rubbed her skin for warmth. "Out of curiosity, why am I naked?"

Lianica sighed. "Yeah, about that. You've been asleep for four days. And, like every other day, I had just given you a sponge bath and dried you off when I was called to the bridge. So, I tucked you in and went and took care of things upstairs. When I got back you were sleeping so peacefully. I didn't want to disturb you."

Danica stretched her arms out and wrapped herself around Lianica in a warm embrace. Lianica's eyes widened momentarily, a bit surprised by the sudden show of heartfelt affection, but then hugged Dani back. "You're safe now."

"And what of the empress?" she asked in a feeble voice.

There was a brief silence, then Lianica spoke. "I'm afraid we haven't been able to locate her. Don't worry," she added, watching the anxiety spread onto Danica's face, "we'll keep looking until we find her. You have my word."

"I'm going to hold you to it," Danica said in a drowsy voice. Then she fell asleep, her head resting on Lianica's lap.

Stroking Danica's turquoise hair, Lianica looked down at the perfect lavender face of her sleeping beauty and replied, "I have no doubt you will, luv. Now, rest. Tomorrow is a new day."

8

Jagged rock formations protruded from the terrain like tilted Gothic cathedrals all bowing before some mighty ancient god. Their tapered summits pressed down to slanted points stuck out at forty-five-degree angles as they pierced a sickly green sky.

Jegra woke herself with a harsh bout of coughing that caused her entire chest to ache and her throat to burn. She spat up excess blood that had flooded into her mouth as internal organs had obviously ruptured in the fierce impact, but also because the air was thick with carbon monoxide, which made it very difficult to stay conscious. Luckily, however, there was just enough oxygen in the atmosphere to keep her alive.

Even so, it was like breathing in the worst levels of pollution back on Earth, and she couldn't help but cough some more. And more blood came up. When she tried to sit up, fragments of shattered bone ground against one another and she screamed out in agony and fell back onto the dirt. As she lay panting, every breath became painful.

She waited for what seemed like hours, allowing her enhanced healing factor to gradually repair her wounds, but every wheezing breath and arbitrary cough racked her body with such immense agony that she felt as though she'd pass out from the pain.

The periodic spurts of asthma and the subsequent jolts of acute pain, like a thousand hot needles slowly creeping out of her from the inside of her gut to the outer edge of her flesh, only sought to remind her of how bad her condition really was. She coughed up more blood and groaned out loud as she shifted her body to try and find a more comfortable position. But no matter what she tried, the droning pain wouldn't abate. It was torture.

Another three hours crawled by and with a bit of effort, Jegra finally managed to sit up. When she did, her copper satin dress practically slid off her body. Catching it with one hand, she pressed it to her chest and strained to look over her bare shoulder. A sudden surge of pain prevented her from much further movement and she fell back onto the slope of the crater, panting.

Her flesh was stained with dirt, burn marks, and smears of her own blood. She looked worse than after the most brutal pummeling she'd ever taken in the arena, but she was determined not to give up. She still had enough fight in her to kick this planet's ass, if need be.

After catching her breath, she managed to sit up again. Still holding onto the dress, she realized that the impact of her fall had shredded the back of the garment to nothing. As such, she began to tear off pieces of it and tie them around her. It took two pieces fitted together to stretch around her chest, and the remaining large piece she tied off at her hips and made a loincloth. Of course, she hadn't any underwear on, which made it a bit drafty. But at least she wasn't entirely naked.

It wasn't quite a two-piece bikini, but it would do. She grunted in satisfaction and slowly shifted her body weight onto her knees then finished tying off the piece at her waist. Looking around, Jegra searched for something she could fashion into a crutch and eventually settled on a metal rod, a piece of debris from the shuttle. She bent the top into a "Y" shape and then pulled herself up. Placing the crutch under her left armpit, she propped herself up and for the first time since the crash, stood on her own two feet.

With the makeshift crutch firmly under arm, she took a deep breath of the smoggy air and grudgingly trudged up the inner wall of the crater. Arriving at the cusp, she looked back at the debris field that tarnished the mountainside and let out a defeated sigh.

There wasn't a salvageable piece of the ship anywhere. If anything had survived, it would be the black box, but since she didn't even know where she was, that wouldn't be of any use to her. Besides, she was in no condition to search for it. Right now, her priority was finding shelter and water.

She shambled down the small mound that encircled the lip of the crater and staggered through more wreckage. Her foot hit something that rattled hollow and she looked down to see what it was. Her eyes widened when she saw it was the shuttle's first aid kit and, what's more, it was still in one piece.

A surprised gasp escaped her lips and Jegra fell to her knees. Tossing the crutch aside, she dug at the dirt with her bare hands and freed the first aid kit. She fumbled excitedly at the latches of the tin box before finally managing to open it. Rummaging through its contents, she found a NeedleAir jet-injector and set the pain-killer setting to maximum. Pressing the jet-injector to her neck, she mashed the button with her thumb and let a hiss of compressed air discharge. She sighed out in relief as a dose of painkillers mixed with antibiotics flooded her system.

Before the effects had even fully taken hold, she jammed the jet-injector into her inner thigh and shot herself with another dose, then repeated the procedure on her other thigh. Still, it was barely enough to mask the thrumming pain that ran through every inch of her battered body.

Jegra sat in a daze as the drugs surged through her system. She was riding a high and didn't feel like doing anything, lest it interrupt the bliss she was feeling. It wasn't till the clap of thunder interrupted her nirvana that she decided to get moving again.

In the distance, Jegra heard the faint cry of an animal. From her position, it sounded the like the call of a hawk, but much bigger. Soon after the creature's cry had abated, the green sky cracked with a discharge of electricity. This was odd since there weren't any rain clouds–just a general green altostratus that stretched on in every direction with uniform consistency. A perpetual storm.

Another spark of lighting sent her scrambling to gather up her supplies. Tucking the kit under her left arm, she fished for her metal crutch and then rose back up onto her feet. The pain killers were obviously working because she didn't feel but the slightest twinge of pain.

As the lightening began to flash with more regularity, Jegra knew she needed to get off this rocky bluff and find adequate shelter. Being fried by a lightning storm wasn't her idea of a good time. As static bursts exploded pockets of terrain wherever the lightning struck, Jegra double timed it down the side of the mountain. That's when she noticed the cliff's edge.

She planted her foot hard and began to skid to a halt. But before she could stop her forward momentum entirely, she heard a loud crack. Not the crack of thunder, but a bone shattering crack.

Her ankle snapped underneath her as a loose rock rolled away and she toppled to the ground. Tumbling head over heel, she rolled down the remainder of the slope and spilled over the ledge, arms flailing desperately as she tried to grab onto something.

Barely managing to grab the rocky edge as she went, she caught herself and pulled her body tight against the cliff face. She looked down the six-hundred-foot drop as her makeshift crutch and first aid kit shrank away into the distance.

"Balls," she muttered to herself as her painkillers fell away with the sudden jolt and ensuing adrenaline. With a grunt, Jegra pulled herself back up onto the ledge of the cliff and flopped onto her back. As her knees hung over the ledge, her feet dangling in mid-air, she took a deep breath and then slid herself the rest of the way back onto the cliff. "That was cutting it rather close, hon," she said aloud, addressing herself.

Without her crutches or painkillers to assist her, she slowly pushed off from her knees and stood up. Even then, she could only manage a hunched posture as the pain was already beginning to overtake her senses.

She was about to head back up the rockface when a sharp blast of wind hit her. She threw up her hands and shielded her eyes just in time to see what appeared to be a massive flying pteranodon with a thirty-foot wingspan, a giant beak, and leathery skin, land directly in front of her. Unlike the toothless dinosaur of the Cretaceous period back on Earth, however, this creature had dual rows of needle like teeth.

She thought it odd that a dinosaur should be so far from home, but, then again, she'd read of convergent evolution. And why not? Why couldn't dinosaurs, which were just giant lizards, when you thought about it, evolve on other worlds?

The giant beast squawked at her and flapped its wings aggressively. Jegra made a hard right turn and tried to hobble along the cliff's edge, but before she could even get more than a few feet she felt the creature's mighty talons clutch her by the waist and hoist her into the air.

As the pteranodon's wings beat around her, they climbed high into the murkiness of the primordial green sky, electric discharges flashing all around them.

"Balls!" she grunted, trying to pry herself out of the creature's fierce grip. But her strength hadn't returned yet and without clean air to breathe, her athleticism was hobbled by short asthmatic wheezing that didn't allow her to fully recharge her oxygen content. Her body was drained and she was in no condition to fight, let alone fend off a gigantic meat-eating dinosaur.

After flying several kilometers, the creature swooped down and grazed the jagged branches of an outcropping of dead trees. Trees which had dried and withered to a vein like branching of thick hard protrusions, mere skeletal forms of their once fertile selves. And like everything else on this godforsaken planet, the slow decay of death had already consumed the last ounce of life force from them.

The creature came dangerously close to impaling Jegra on some of the branches, forcing her to take a chance to clasp one of the thicker limbs. She managed to snag a branch; it snapped off in her hand and she brought it up to inspect it. About the size of a longsword, she looked up and, holding the shard of dead wood in her hand like a javelin, she thrust it into the neck of the flying beast.

A squirt of blood shot out and splattered across the left side of her face and the beast screeched out in pain.

Not feeling that its prey was worth the trouble, the flying lizard relinquished its grip on Jegra and dropped her from about two hundred feet up. She fell away, branches snapping around her as she plummeted down through the deadwood forest. She watched the beast shake the splinter from its neck and flap away in an erratic pattern, more like that of a bat rather than a bird of prey.

The splintering of a rather large branch against Jegra's back caused her to turn her head just in time to see a nasty tangle of thorny branches spread out beneath her. She gritted her teeth as she plowed through the fanning array of dead growth, most of it thick as elephant tusks and twice as sharp.

Each spear-like branch snapped under her weight until, finally, she hit a thick enough stalk that it halted her fall. The only problem was, one of its many protrusions had skewered her left thigh.

The branch was sticking straight up out of the center of her leg. Gripping it with both hands, she snapped the stem and freed her leg. Without the branch anchoring her to the tree, she slid off on her own crimson slick, and crashed through several more ligneous appendages before meeting the cracked surface of the hardened ground. It was about as forgiving as asphalt.

Winded, all Jegra could do was let her blood-laced saliva dribble from the corners of her half-open mouth as she waited for her body to register the pain of having broken all her ribs along with the gaping hole in her left thigh. As her breath came back to her, she screamed out in a dry, raspy voice and then fell onto her back and stared up at the murky green sky.

"What the fuck is wrong with this planet?" she groaned as she lay on her back, looking up through the hole she'd left in the needle-like skeletons of the dead timber.

Jegra clasped her ribs like an invalid and sucked the sulfuric tasting air through her teeth as she rose to her feet for the umpteenth time today. Hobbling a few steps, she fell against the trunk of one of the trees and rested for a bit.

The high-pitch screech of the dino-bird cut through the air and prompted her to get moving again. He was obviously building up the courage for a second attempt at making her his dinner and she didn't want to waste any more time out in the open. Although the dead trees could provide enough cover to keep her safe from aerial predation, they'd be pretty useless against one of those electrical storms.

She winced from the pain as she pushed her tired body off the tree trunk and limped along a downward slope. It wasn't long until she found a greenish pool of liquid.

"Water," she whispered through parched lips and knelt down beside the small pool that bubbled up from below the cracked surface of earth.

Sun baked and barren without a sign of life in any direction for as far as the eye could see, the terrain in this region reminded her of the salt flats outside of Salt Lake City back on Earth. Only, this particular valley had an endless forest of dead wood and numerous green puddles.

Jegra looked down at her reflection in the green pool which mirrored her battered and bruised image back up at her. She cringed at the sight of how broken she looked. As she stared at herself, she thought: *I won't be winning any beauty pageants any time soon, that's for sure.*

She cupped her hands and was about to dip them into the pool when she accidentally knocked a piece of deadwood into the pool. It sizzled and caught fire before sinking into the undrinkable spring of acid.

"Balls," Jegra said out of the corner of her mouth as she drew her hands back away from the pond of death.

Sitting on her knees, Jegra slumped back on her heels, her arms hanging limply at her sides as though they were boneless bags of meat. Slowly scanning the horizon, she looked around for something she could use as shelter. But everywhere she looked she saw nothing but a wasteland. She knew if there was life enough to support a giant winged dinosaur, there must be drinkable water somewhere; she just had to keep pushing onward until she found it.

Jegra rose to her feet and snapped off a sharp branch. She balanced it in her palm, testing its weight and felt satisfied it was sturdy enough to use against the leathery skin of the reptile. Using the makeshift weapon as a walking-stick, she began to limp off in the direction the pteranodon had flown.

If it had a nest or den, there may be eggs. And eggs meant dinner. Sustenance. More importantly, it would mean there's water nearby.

9

Pacing back and forth with worry, Danica unclasped her hands from behind her back and looked toward the sonic shower where Lianica was running through the cleanse cycles before heading out for her morning shift. She looked away and then muttered, "I'm perfectly fine."

There was a touch of resentment tucked into her voice, due mostly to Lianica ordering her to take the day off and rest, something she was positive she couldn't do. Not with the empress missing. Not with all the work that needed to be done.

"I know you're strong, but you've been through a serious trauma," Lianica said, stepping out of the shower. The steamy mist dripped down the curvature of her naked blue body as she had skipped the air-drying cycle. The cool air of the open room caused her dark purple nipples to stand erect and she placed her hands on her hips and shifted her stance which, unintentionally, gave her a seductive appeal.

Danica paused to admire Lianica's youthful body thinking it odd how the younger generation chose to shave all their hair, but she quickly turned away again, having realized she was gawking, and resumed her pacing. "I'm bound to go mad if all I can do is wear a groove in the decking and lust after you."

Lianica rolled her eyes and went over to her closet. Tapping a wall panel, it slid to the side and a rack of uniforms slid out. She picked one from the series of identical white and gray uniforms and began dressing.

"Look, I only ask you take it easy because I care about you. But if that's too much to ask, then, feel free to disregard my overbearing protectiveness and do what you need to do."

Danica stopped in her tracks and spun around to find Lianica perched on the arm of a lounger as she struggled to get her knee-high black patent boots on. "You mean that?"

"Yeah, I do," Lianica replied. Having finally zipped the boot over her right calf, she began the struggle with the other one. After finishing that boot, she stood up and made eye contact with Danica only to realize Danica was staring at her, mouth slightly open and with a partial smile frozen on her face. "What?"

"Nothing," Danica replied.

Lianica squinted suspiciously and then laughed. "All right, sweetie. Whatever you say. But, if you're coming," she added, waving a finger up and down Danica's mostly exposed figure, "you'd better change out of that. You may give the crew the wrong idea."

Danica looked down to discover that her nightgown had slipped open just enough to expose both areolas and more than enough breast to be on the scandalous side. She quickly wrapped back up and then sauntered over to the sonic shower.

Lianica fastened the golden shoulder tassels to her uniform along with the chain that connected them, her pins and stripes, and her various medals and commendations. It was the Dagon way to always present your accomplishments boldly at all times. Clasping the last ornament over her left breast, she made her way to the door, tossed her hair, and looked back over her shoulder. "Meet me in the astrometrics lab when you're ready."

With that she exited her quarters and left Danica alone in the shower.

The lingering silence was louder than the hum of the sonic shower, and Danica couldn't help but resent herself for being unable to protect the empress, to protect Jegra. When a faint series of tonal chirps broke her nagging conscience and interrupted her cleansing, she checked the holographic vidcom to see who was calling. The incoming signature only read *Unknown Caller*. The computer's voice informed [*Encoded communique for Danica Valencia. Will you accept the call?*]

"I'll accept," she replied, surprised that anyone had her private I.D. tag. Very few people even knew it, so whoever it was, she assumed it must be important.

Raven Nightguard's indigo face appeared on the digital display on the curved inside of the glass shower stall. She brushed aside the white tuft of hair that blended into a purple ombre and smiled. There was a brief silence between them and then Raven asked, "Is it a bad time?"

"I'm just taking a shower," Danica answered. Seeing the embarrassed look on Raven's face, she quickly added, "But if you're calling me, you must have heard the news."

"Is it true?"

"I'm afraid so. The empress is gone."

"Do you have any leads?"

Danica raised her gaze again. "It's true she was blasted out of the sky, but her actual disappearance seemed to be caused by one of those celestial squid entities. Otherwise, I'm at a loss."

There was a long pause as Raven mulled over the best course of action. "All right. You keep searching for her on your end. I'll put out some feelers and see if anyone in the Commonwealth has heard anything along the smuggling routes and the merchant hubs. At the moment, I'm afraid that's the best I can do."

"Every little bit helps," Danica replied. Raven nodded.

As Raven leaned over to disconnect the call, Danica's voice called out, "Wait." She stopped her hand and looked back into the cam-recorder.

"I appreciate you doing this," Danica said. "I know we haven't always seen eye to eye, you and me, but this…just know it means a lot to me."

Raven gave a subtle nod and then cut the feed.

Danica broke down in the shower and sobbed her eyes out. Once she'd gotten it all out of her system, she finished showering, dressed, and then headed to astrometrics.

When Danica strode into the room, Lianica practically choked on her own gulp. "That's almost worse than the nightgown," she teased.

Danica looked down at the banded top made of semi-translucent, white cloth which revealed almost everything, only slightly subdued by its wedding veil-like opacity. Not only that, but the various layers were cut in revealing ways. Violet bikini bottoms that practically matched her skin tone were only overshadowed by the garter that held chap-styled leggings. The leggings, of course, were skin-tight polyurethane, white, with a series of circular cutouts down the sides that spiraled in such a fashion that they formed a rather hypnotic pattern.

To complete the ensemble, she had bright red buckle strap ankle boots that fit perfectly over the white leggings and added a garish splash of color.

She looked back up and threw one hand on her hip. "You don't like it?"

"I didn't say that," Lianica replied. The outfit was distracting to say the least, and now it was Lianica who found herself gawking.

After having stared for a bit too long, she looked away and began reading some star charts. Unable to help herself, though, she snuck another peek as Danica went over to the table and leaned over to pick up a holovid tablet.

Loosely clenched fist to her mouth, the commander cleared her throat and said, "Getting back to the task at hand, I've plotted the least number of slipstream jumps it would take to cover the entire Commonwealth and the Outer Rim worlds."

"How many?"

"If we can manage eight different jumps a week, it will take us roughly thirty-seven odd years to cover every inch of charted space."

Danica tilted her head slightly and looked up from her charts. Rubbing her chin contemplatively, she asked, "What if we just covered the Outer Rim planets and deep space ports first?"

Lianica looked down at her holovid pad and did a few quick calculations. "Assuming we find her out there, it would take about five years."

"All right, let's assume we get lucky within the first couple of those. Is that something you think this crew would be willing to undertake?"

"It doesn't matter," Lianica replied, her eyelids half lowered, her face deadly serious. "I am willing to undertake it. And this crew will obey my orders or get a free spacewalk courtesy of airlock eight."

Danica knew that airlock eight was the airlock that jettisoned its refuge directly aft of the ship. In your last wheezing breath, as your lungs began to freeze shut and your heart grew so swollen that it's about to burst in your chest, you see garbage floating around you and the ship sailing away from you. You die without hope. Without dignity. Without honor.

It's a death reserved for traitors. And if Lianica was willing to threaten the crew with such a shameful demise, then Danica knew what she said was genuine.

However long it took—no matter what obstacles they ran into—the *Shard* would search every quadrant of the Commonwealth and beyond and would not stop until it found its empress, Jegra Alakandra of Thessalonica, Empress of

Dagon.

It wasn't until several minutes later that Lianica noticed a series of yellow dots show up on the astrometric holographic display of the Commonwealth. She looked over Danica's shoulder to see what she was doing.

"What are these?" She pointed at the sporadic appearance of golden dots that hovered in a disordered cluster all around the system.

"I'm plotting all known sightings of the celestial squid entities. If there's a pattern to their movement, then maybe we can use that as a springboard for launching the search for the empress."

"Now, why didn't I think of that?"

"You would have. Eventually," Danica reassured.

Lianica smiled. "I guess it's true what they say: There's no substitute for years of experience."

As more dots appeared, Danica squinted at the coordinates and then gasped. She looked at Lianica with a pleased expression, eyes wide with the excitement of the revelation.

"What is it?"

"There is a pattern. Look," she said, pointing out the series of dots, tracing them down the curvature of an arc. Each of the dots followed a similar arc, and all the arms of each arcing branch met at a centralized point. "Here, here, and here."

"It's a spiral?"

"That's what I thought at first, too. But take a look at this." With a pinch, Danica shrank down the spiral then opened her fingers again and a duplicate spiral popped up. Moving the copy over the star chart, she repeated the process five more times. Each time she overlaid the outer stars over the mid-point stars of the previous map. "You see?"

"It's a fractal."

"Yes," Danica said. "And if they travel in fractal patterns, large and small, we should be able to extrapolate their jump points."

"Let's increase their range by a factor of thirty. That way we can see all the jump points beyond the Outer Rim but that are within the creature's reach. After all, we have them ranked at the same energy reading as the Dreadnaught class warships. So, assuming they're folding hyperspace for instantaneous jumps along these coordinates, starting with where the empress disappeared…"

"We should be able to chart the squid's possible jump points." Danica snapped her fingers and then tapped the hologram of the fringe area just beyond charted space a few times. A series of yellow dots just beyond the Outer Rim turned orange and she said, "Here. These points are possible jump points of the creature, assuming babies can jump just as far as the adults."

"That's still roughly three-thousand light years we need to cover."

"It beats thirty-thousand."

"Even with the slipstream drive working around the clock, that's still roughly five years."

"Four point seven, to be exact," Danica added, being her meticulous self.

"Yes," Lianica smiled. Her smile was infectious as it spread to Danica.

"What is it?" Danica asked.

"Do you realize you just single handedly gave this mission a directive, a direction, and a detailed map all in one morning in the astrometric lab. I heard your genius was legendary on the battlefield. The way you devise strategies is studied at the academy. But I just never thought I'd see you working your magic up close and in person. It's…well, it's impressive."

"Be careful, commander, if I didn't know you any better, I'd say you were fishing to become teacher's little pet."

"How could I not?" Lianica replied.

Danica looked around the room. The dozen or so hours they'd worked had left them the only two people remaining in the astrometrics lab. Meaning they had the space all to themselves.

Danica started undressing and Lianica swallowed hard and looked around. "I'll lock the door," she said.

"No," Danica replied, reaching out and grabbing Lianica's wrist and stopping her. "It's more exciting if there's a risk of getting caught."

"Oh, you're naughty." Lianica grinned and bit her bottom lip as she watched Danica reach behind her back and unfasten her bra.

Lianica only had time to unfasten her belt by the time Danica scooped her up and set her down on the projection table. The hologram of space danced around the shadows their bodies made as they lay back on the table.

Danica leaned in and kissed Lianica's full lips and had reached down to help peel off her tight-fitting dress pants when, unexpectedly, the ship rattled with the concussive force of a blast.

"What in Helios was that?" Lianica said, sliding out from under Danica and getting dressed again.

Danica was doing the same; both women were dressed faster than it had taken to undress, an ability that years of service lent them in times just like this one.

Lianica went over and tapped the wall comm. "Report."

"It's the emperor, Commander. He's found us."

"Blast that man," Danica mumbled off to the side.

Lianica shot her a sharp glance and then leaned into the comm. "Tell him he has got my attention and that I'll take his call in my personal ready room."

"Um…" the voice on the other end said hesitantly.

"Well, spit it out," Lianica ordered.

"The emperor is on his way here."

"He's coming here, personally?"

"Yes, Commander. What are your orders?"

Lianica thought for a moment and then said, "We'd best greet His Majesty as he expects. Have everyone wearing their dress whites and we'll convene in the hangar landing bay."

A half hour later, the hull of the ship dissolved and Emperor Dakroth's personal shuttle appeared. "Attention!" the XO shouted above the din of whispers and everyone snapped to attention as a fast silence settled across the crew.

Of course, the only one not in attendance was Danica, for obvious reasons. She couldn't show her face–not after her little stunt back aboard Tamoran's vessel.

The menacing black shuttle, with its folding wings, landed on the deck. Its wings, like the venomous flesh-eating butterflies of Skallek, rose up vertically and a hatch on the underbelly of the ship opened, revealing a massive loading elevator. The lift descended from the ship's underbelly along with a spray of steam from the atmospheric regulators and then clanked onto the metal hangar deck with a resounding shudder that could be felt in the boots of all the crew who stood at attention as they awaited the emperor's arrival.

As the steam cleared, Commander Lianica Blackstar took several steps forward and stopped halfway between the crew and the shuttle. Emperor Dakroth and the red-skinned woman, Ishtar Bantu, manifested out of the steam, as if they were specters, and met her in the middle of the flight deck. They stood sharing intense glances in silence and then, Lianica cavalierly clapped the heels of her boots and saluted.

"Lord Emperor Dakroth," Commander Blackstar said, crossing her fist over her heart and taking a deep, ninety-degree bow. Rising back up, she added, "As ship's commander, it is my great pleasure to welcome you aboard Her Majesty's royal battle cruiser, the *Shard*."

10

Sweat glazed Jegra's soiled skin as she stood panting under a hot, red sun. She wiped her neck with her hand, her fingers plowing through the grime and leaving trails of freshly exposed skin, and sighed, plucking out the wooden spear she'd fashioned from the deadwood. The head of the pteranodon hit the dirt with a resounding thud and a splatter of blood spurted out of the creature's gaping neck wound.

A sharp pain surged through her and leaning on the spear for support, Jegra moaned and then checked her side. "Balls," she said, running her fingers along three large gashes in her torso where the reptile's taloned foot had clawed her.

Her foot on the creature's neck, she took ahold of its beak and, giving a hefty, twisting jerk, tore it off. Hobbling over to the acid pool, she dipped the beak in. Everything sizzled away except for the bone, and she drew up a small portion of the acid and splashed some of it on her wound.

Her subsequent scream cut into the night as deeply as the claw marks cut into her side. Her wound sizzled and smoked as her flesh burned away from the acid, and Jegra screamed again and then crashed to her knees. Hunched over, she gripped her side and whimpered from the pain. But at least the wound was disinfected now and sealed shut. Her healing factor, albeit slowed by this planet's harsh conditions, would handle the rest.

A couple of hours later, Jegra sat perched in front of a giant spit she'd fashioned from the dead wood and roasted the giant pteranodon. The crackle of the fire was the only sound that filled the night, as there wasn't much life on this barren world. What life she had come across was currently becoming her feast, its flesh sizzling tantalizingly.

The dinosaur-like bird, glazed in its own offspring's yoke, looked like a giant, succulent chicken, the size of an Earth cow. Reaching across her lap, she fetched a half cracked eggshell the size of a beach volleyball, reached in, and pulled out the wet goop of the yoke and albumin left inside. Tossing the contents onto the pteranodon meat and smearing it around with her hand, she slowly spun the shaft of the spit until the dino-goose was golden brown.

Although the past couple of days had been a living hell, getting a fire going was easier than expected. All she did was dip a branch into the acid water and wait for it to catch on fire. Then she quickly reeled it out, walked over to her firepit, and ignited her bonfire. There was enough deadwood to keep it going indefinitely.

Once she cooked the meat to perfection. She picked up the branches she'd twiddled down into chopsticks using a jagged rock, and plucked a piece of sizzling meat off the bird's body, blowing on it a few times before tossing it into her mouth.

"Hot, hot," she said, chewing with her mouth open and sucking in as much air as possible to help cool the scalding, yet succulent meat. Even as it burned her tongue, the meat's juices dribbled down her chin and, overwrought with the savory deliciousness of it, tears welled up in her eyes.

It dawned on her that this was the first reprieve she'd been granted since she'd set foot on this savage alien world. And for now, this was enough to give her the slightest shred of hope that she might survive being stranded in this godforsaken place long enough for a rescue mission to find her. But that could take days. Weeks. Months even. So she had to find water and shelter and prepare for the long haul.

Although she hadn't very much survival training, she had read more than a fair share of prepper books during her globe-trotting daydream phase when she was all about backpacking across Europe, India, and other far-off exotic destinations. As a quaint librarian back on Earth, who wanted nothing more than to get away from her dusty collection of books and see the world, she had a fairly good idea of the survival basics. The rest would have to be relegated to guesswork and trial and error.

When she was still Jessica Hemsworth of Omaha, Nebraska, she'd dreamed of seeing Paris, Madrid, Rome, and Ankara. But her former self wasn't the type of woman to simply uproot and boldly set out to chase her dreams. She had been timid, shy, and predisposed to worry more often than not. So, books were her only escape. They were wondrous, but above all, they were safe.

Of course, she had the annual camping trips with her father in which he'd taught her the basics of starting a camp fire using only sticks and dry moss for kindling, along with things such as how to gut a fish and skin a rabbit. But their camping excursions came to an abrupt end when her father ran out on her and her mother after her thirteenth birthday. She only saw him once, at her high school graduation, before he disappeared from her life for good. She carried a deep-seated resentment for him ever since.

She understood that sometimes people fell out of love. In fact, it didn't bother her that he'd wanted distance from her mother, who could be overbearing at times. Nevertheless, what hurt her more than anything was that he had brushed her aside, too. She knew it wasn't her fault, but he had merely discarded her as though she was somehow part of the problem, a source of his unhappiness. And this crushed her.

Jegra shook her head and took a deep breath of the evening air. Surprisingly, this planet cooled far more than she had expected. Even after having acclimated to the drastic desert temperature swings on Thessalonica, which could get as hot as one-forty during the day and drop up to around forty at night, she was starting to shiver. But that could also be due to her level of exhaustion and that fact that she hardly wore any clothes.

As she was about to take another helping of meat, a fierce roar cut through the night air and Jegra tensed up. It sounded like a mix between a lion and a howler monkey, but several decibels lower and much, much more vicious.

"That can't be good," Jegra said to herself as she scanned the perimeter of visible area before the firelight's illumination was devoured by the darkness. It was that dim area, just on the cusp of her visibility, where she peered with bated breath, watching for any signs of movement. Something was out there. And it sounded hungry.

Slowly, she reached over and grabbed a long stick she had sharpened into a spear and which she had intended to use as a kabob skewer for the dino-bird's dense thighs. Now, however, it was her only means of defense against whatever was breathing heavily in the seclusion of the shadows.

She could make out the beast's breath rattling in its nostrils more clearly now as the sound grew incrementally nearer to her little barbecue. Obviously attracted by the scent of her cooking, Jegra kept crouched and slowly slunk back into the darkness and away from the glowing halo of the fire. Gripping her spear tightly as she gradually sunk away into the shadows, she squatted low and waited.

The soft, prowling footsteps picked up and erupted into a rumbling charge. Out of the darkness thundered a tyrannosaurus rex. Or, what appeared to be every bit as identical as the long extinct terrestrial dinosaur of her home world.

"What is this place, The Lost World?" she muttered under her breath as the T-Rex burst into view. Now she was beginning to think convergent evolution was a bit of a stretch. One winged creature, maybe. But two identical species? The odds were astronomical. Now, it seemed that she was stuck on some kind of preserve; maybe some alien zoo-keeper's exotic, prehistoric menagerie.

After all, if poachers had picked her up and sold her off to the Intergalactic Gladiatorial Syndicate, it wasn't that far of a stretch to imagine poachers having collected dinosaurs off Earth and sold them off as pets, spectacles, and perhaps even food to upper class patrons willing to dole out their credits for a chance to sample exotic wonders from other worlds.

The dinosaur whipped its tail around and arched, snout up, and roared at the moon. Then, without so much as a care for whose meal it was, it trampled her campfire, and gobbled up her only food. Snatching the pteranodon meat, it shook the dead bird just for good measure and, then, tossed it up into the air before gulping it down with three, jaw chomping bites.

Satisfied, its belly full, the tyrannosaurus huffed out from its nostrils and then stalked off into the night.

Jegra let out a pent-up breath, one she had been holding so as to avoid detection, and then walked over to the smoldering fire. A disappointed look came across her face when she realized there wasn't a scrap of food left. And the three eggs she'd tried to preserved lay trampled, their contents mashed into the dirt.

She fiddled with her stick, stirring the broken egg yolk into the earth and making a mess when, all of a sudden, she got a phenomenal idea. Setting her mind to the task at hand, she used the mud to make molds of her breasts, shoulders, shins and forearms.

After mixing a batch of yoke laced mud, she set it out carefully and lay down close to the smoldering fire pit, and slept uneasily until day break.

The morning sun was subdued behind the dun colored sky and looked like a yellow faded stain on a brown carpet. Jegra couldn't help but grin at the ugliness of this planet. It was the first world she'd been on in which the sunrise was as repulsive as the rest of the godforsaken wasteland. The only redeeming quality was that it had a breathable atmosphere. At least, breathable enough for her to stay alive. And that gave her hope that if she could tough it out long enough, help would come.

After stretching out her cold, aching muscles, she headed over to her molds and checked them. Once they were finished, she gathered together every bit of scrap metal she had collected on the long hike to find the pteranodon and with the aid of a rock, she hammered it all with a smooth rock fastened to the end of a thigh bone till each and every piece of plating fit the molds.

Not letting what little remained of the creature go to waste, she tore out some of the finer teeth from the beak, the ones which were thin enough and sharp enough to fashion into needles, and used her own hair to thread the armor plating to the cloth of the leather bikini that she'd cut from a small piece of hide left from the quarter section of the dino-bird's severed tail. Although only a bony morsel ignored by the tyrannosaur, it suited her needs perfectly.

Of course, she'd busted the first needle-tooth on the metal before realizing she needed to use the acid to etch holes into the metal plates. Dipping the end of the sewing needle into the acid, she then applied it to the metal. The tip of the acid-coated tooth burned its way through the metal plating. Although an agonizingly slow process, she had all the time in the world.

As for the strength of the thread, like the rest of her, her hair had been made ridiculously strong by the super-serum. It hung down her back to her butt, and though lightweight, the brown strands of hair had the tensile strength of slender steel wire. Plucking out a few strands, she whimpered slightly and then held up the fistful of hair above her. The strands crisscrossed against the dim dawn's light and she whispered, "This'll do."

That afternoon, Jegra stretched what remained of the pteranodon's hide over several branches, crafting a modest awning to keep the sun at bay while she added the finishing touches to her armor.

With a metal bikini, shoulder plates, and bracers for her shins and forearms, she had at least minimal protection against whatever else might be stalking her. She slipped on her newly fashioned body armor and tested it by karate chopping a nearby rock in half.

If that wasn't enough, the long, forty-one-hour days of this strange world gave her more than enough time to fashion a crude blade, using the acid pool to temper and sharpen one of the ship's ore cutter blades intended for asteroid mining. She'd discovered the piece of debris a few clicks west of the encampment when she was looking for a water source. After all, she knew the dinosaurs had to be getting their water from somewhere. But, still no sign of it. Not a spring. Not a creek. Just desert and deadwood as far as the eye could see in every direction.

Although extremely heavy, the ore cutter being about as long as a two-handed longsword and twice as thick, she'd managed to give it a bone handle and a Tsukamaki leather wrap, the same style that ancient Japanese samurai swords used.

She briefly inspected her work, then, satisfied it was the best she could do with what she had, tucked the blade under her leather sash. She then tied it off leaving enough length on the ends to use for making strips should she need to sew anything together using the needle tooth of the pteranodon in the future.

She fastened her armor plating to herself with thin strands of leather that she'd shredded, and by the end of the day, she looked like a barbarian woman with a gladiatrix pedigree. Even so, she was starting to feel like her old self again. A powerful warrioress, not just a survivor stranded on an alien world.

Jegra didn't dare sleep that evening, for as tired as she was, she couldn't shake the distinct feeling that the T-Rex was still out there, circling her for when it grew hungry enough to pay her a return visit.

Dehydrated and a bit delirious from the long day's heat, she licked her chapped lips and then laughed out loud at nothing. Curling up next to the fire, she clutched the blade to her chest like a teddy bear, and gazed wearily into the flames. Their hypnotic dancing had brought her to the verge of slumber when she heard the roar off in the distance and sat upright. Eyes wide open, she held her blade at the ready and peered into the darkness.

After a few minutes of nail-biting anticipation, every muscle in her body wound tighter than bridge cable as a pair of them came into view. One male, one female, lumbering along the cracked landscape, dry branches snapping underfoot, as they bared down on her.

"Balls," she muttered as she realized she was out matched by the tyrannosaur team.

11

Emperor Dakroth Rhadamanthus returned Commander Blackstar's salute and set her at ease. "Please, my dear, this visit is merely an informality. You see, I too saw the empress's shuttle destroyed after that terrible pirate, Novac Tamoran, shamelessly attacked her." Dakroth spat at the floor to make his ire known to all the crew.

Lianica nodded at her XO and she blew her whistle, calling everyone to attention. The entire deck clicked their heels, straightened into a formal posture, and saluted. Dakroth returned their salutes as he passed the long line of officers.

"This way, if you please, Your Grace." Lianica motioned to the open doors of the shuttle bay and the emperor nodded.

They passed the rows of crew members, and every person lowered their salute once the emperor had passed.

In the corridor, Lianica turned and nodded at the XO, who waited for the doors to shut and then blew his digital whistle and shouted, "Dismissed."

"Your Excellency," Commander Blackstar began, "We have it on good authority that the empress's ship was not destroyed, but rather transported out of the system."

"Really? That's excellent news," he lied. "What system?"

"Well, it's a bit complicated, you see—"

Emperor Dakroth raised a hand and stopped her. "Let me stop you there, commander. Either you know where she is or you don't."

Lianica looked at the red-skinned woman who stood in silence just behind the emperor and then back at Dakroth. She lowered her gaze. "I'm afraid we don't know. Not with any certainty."

"Then you agree with me," he stated as they resumed strolling along up the corridor, "that until we have definitive proof of life, we must assume the worst."

"Rescue operation protocols dictate that we—"

The emperor shot her a sharp glance. "What rescue operation? I wasn't aware I had issued any such orders."

"No, Your Excellency. I took it upon myself to issue the orders on your behalf. After all, I know how much the empress means to you. I know you'd want us doing our best to ensure the safe retrieval of—"

He raised his hand again, cutting her off for the third time in a row, something she was beginning to find more than a little bit aggravating. She clenched her jaw in annoyance at the constant interruptions and complete dismissal of her position but kept any further signs of protest to herself.

"Yes, and that's all fine. We must search high and low for the empress. But there is a slightly more pressing matter I need you to help me with."

They came around the bend to Blackstar's personal ready room and she showed them in. Making himself at home, the emperor deliberately sat in her chair to remind her of his position over her.

"Would you like some tea?" she offered, motioning to the pot she had made before rushing down to the hangar deck to greet the Lord Emperor. He shook his head, declining her offer.

She took her seat across from him in one of two reception chairs and glanced behind herself, finding Ishtar Bantu standing just over her shoulder like an intimidating centurion.

"With all due respect, your excellency, what could be more pressing than retrieving the empress?"

Dakroth leaned back in her chair, steepled his fingers beneath his chin, and grinned. "In the coming days, Nyctan will declare war against the Dagon Empire," he informed her. "My best intelligence officers say the Nyctans are already amassing their fleet along the border. I am promoting you to Captain and want you to lead the blockade, Commander Blackstar."

"Me?" Lianica gasped. At once she felt under qualified, but at the same time had dreamed of this opportunity for so long that she couldn't say no. Such chances only came once in a blue moon. She'd be a fool to decline the emperor's offer.

"Is that a problem?" Dakroth asked, raising an eyebrow.

"No," she said, a smile spreading across her face. "I'd be honored, Your Majesty."

"Excellent!" Dakroth chirped. He waved his hand, a subtle gesture to Ishtar to back off, and she took a couple of steps back.

Lianica looked over her shoulder at the red-skinned woman, acknowledging that she was there to ensure Blackstar fell in line with the emperor's wishes, one way or another.

The Lord Emperor pulled out a small wooden box made of beautiful Dagon cherry wood, and slid it across the table. "Open it," he said, his grin holding firm on his mauve lips.

Lianica opened the box to find bars the rank of Captain. Pulling out the small brass pins, she admired them and began to fasten them to her uniform.

Dakroth stood up and walked around the table. Even though it was completely unnecessary, he helped her fasten the bars, and said, "I'll expect your plan of attack in two weeks."

Captain Lianica Blackstar stood up and turned toward him. She bowed her head reverently.

"Seeing as this is the most advanced ship in the fleet, I am giving you full command of the *Shard*." The emperor turned to leave, but pausing in front of the door, he snapped his fingers as a thought occurred to him. "Oh, there's one more thing. Whether you know it or not, you're harboring a traitor aboard this ship."

Lianica gulped and looked at Ishtar then back to Dakroth. Although he didn't know that she was the one who had piloted the other fighter, he definitely knew Danica had been at the helm of one. She'd gone off the rails and tried to kill him herself, something Dakroth wasn't likely to forgive anytime soon.

"A traitor?" she gasped, acting as though she had no clue. "Aboard the empress's vessel?"

"Indeed," Dakroth grinned viciously. "A woman by the name of Vice Admiral Cassera Van Danica Amelorak. Of course, she now goes by Danica Valencia."

"The servant of the empress?!" Lianica balked, feigning surprise. "But she looks nothing like the vice admiral."

"She's had modifications. A fair warning, though, Captain, she's ruthless and cunning and may be the most dangerous fugitive in the galaxy." He pulled out a holovid tablet and held it out. Tapping it with his thumb, a picture of Danica, as she appeared now, popped up. "This image was recorded on Novac Tamoran's vessel. The woman attacking me is the so-called servant you speak of. Now, I trust you will resolve the matter and help me apprehend this fugitive."

"Yes, my lord," Lianica said. Even as she said it, she could feel her heart pounding inside. Her mind raced as she tried to figure out how she could warn Danica. But it didn't seem like there was any way out of this.

"Lead the way, Captain, my Captain," Dakroth said with a wave of his hand, gesturing her to go on ahead of him.

Both the red-skinned woman and Emperor Dakroth accompanied Lianica to the astrometrics lab where they happened upon Danica.

Caught up in her work, Danica didn't even notice them come in. When she looked up from the star charts, a shocked expression came over her, one which quickly faded into one of profound disappointment. When her eyes fell onto Lianica's, she noticed the shiny new bars signifying the rank of Captain. Lianica, realizing she'd betrayed Danica in the most unforgivable way, looked away in shame.

The truth was, she hadn't planned for it to go down like this. But the emperor had swooped in and pressed the matter. She was caught off guard and had no good plan in place. Now, all she could do was offer up Danica as a scapegoat.

"Vice Admiral," Emperor Dakroth sneered, the right-side of his lip knotting tightly in disgust. "It's been too long."

Before Danica could react, Ishtar raised a slender black stun-gun with a burnt chrome finish. "Please, don't."

Danica paused, looking between Lianica and Dakroth's faces. She lunged at the emperor; there was a blast, and Ishtar zapped Danica, preventing her from laying hands on the Lord Emperor.

The stun bolt solicited a grunt and Danica crumpled to the ground and spasmed as the electric shock dropped her like a lead weight. Lingering tendrils of blue electricity crawled through her muscle sinews and caused her body to twitch uncontrollably.

Prostrate before the Lord Emperor, his assassin, and her back-stabbing ex-girlfriend, who all stood above her with condescending looks, silently judging her, caused Danica to feel a burning rage ignite inside her. Unable to move, though, all she could do was scream out in frustration.

"Excellent work, Captain Blackstar Van Scarion," Dakroth said, clearly pleased. He nodded at Ishtar, who took the stun-gun from Lianica and stowed it. Smirking, Ishtar helped Lianica pick Danica up by her arms and dragged her limp body out of the lab, down the corridor, and back to Dakroth's shuttle.

Lianica had never felt more conflicted in her life. Although it was true that she and Danica had started off as rivals, she liked to think they'd moved passed that. Over the course of the past couple of weeks, she'd gotten to know Danica well enough to know that this level of betrayal wasn't something she'd likely forgive. And yet, if Lianica didn't do it, it wouldn't take a clairvoyant to know what Dakroth would do if she went against the Lord Emperor's wishes.

Once they had finished boarding, Lianica turned to leave when Dakroth's blue hand landed upon her chest, stopping her. She was startled by the sudden contact; surprise became trepidation when he didn't remove his hand, but let it linger there.

"I'm glad to have such a loyal officer as you on my side, Lianica. But, if I should ever find you harboring an enemy of the Empire aboard this ship again, I won't be so forgiving the next time. Are we clear?"

Lianica gulped. She could already feel him projecting his fear-based telepathy her way. She tried to ignore it; it wasn't the first time she had experienced his little mind games. But it was still unnerving. "Yes, my lord," she answered timidly, her voice cracking.

His hand slowly slid inside the flap of her uniform and crept down her left breast until he was cupping it firmly in his palm. Giving her a gentle squeeze, his thumb massaging her nipple, he leaned in to her so that his lips hovered dangerously close to hers. "Do we have an understanding, Lianica?"

Lianica grabbed Dakroth by his neck and reeled him in. Their lips crashed together and she kissed him long and hard. At the same time, she grabbed his probing hand with hers and forced him to squeeze her breast even tighter. She had to make her submission look genuine, which meant she needed to hold back her gag reflex long enough to convince him she wanted his grubby hands all over her. This was the only way to ensure him of her sincerity. Her loyalty.

Finally, she relinquished her grip and, taking a deep breath, answered, "We have an understanding, your excellency."

"Good," he said, a crooked grin betraying the fact that he was secretly delighted by her acquiescence.

It was almost as though he'd expected her to resist him. *But why?* she wondered. *Was it a test of loyalty?* Lianica swallowed hard. Could he somehow know that she was part of the Pe'tharell, an ancient order devoted to the protection of the empress above all else? Could he possibly suspect that she'd die for the empress, even if it meant going against him?

In the end, she hadn't any other choice. If she hadn't given Danica up, Dakroth would have suspected something. He would have dug into her past until he uncovered the fact that she was a Pe'tharell, and he would have imprisoned her, or worse. At least for now, she had convinced him she was on his side. Even if it had meant destroying an ally's trust, a person who she cared for a great deal.

With their business concluded, Lord Emperor Dakroth beamed at her with his trademark debonair grin and watched her stroll down the shuttle's loading ramp. He admired the way her hips swiveled and how tight her ass looked in the white uniform. Perhaps the kiss had excited him more than he'd anticipated. Licking his lips, taking in her lingering flavor, he smiled and turned back into the shuttle.

Not knowing what else to do, Lianica found herself back in the astrometrics lab. Without warning, she began to hyperventilate and collapsed to the floor. Her hands trembling, she clutched the edge of the holographic display table, the same table she'd almost had Danica on earlier. She bowed her head between her arms and began sobbing.

"What have I done?" she whispered between gasps of air. Sniffling, a steady stream of tears ran down both her violet cheeks. Shaking her head, she rose to her feet and slamming her fists on the holographic display table, she let out a gut-wrenching scream. Even if, by some miracle, Danica could one day come to forgive her, the fact was Lianica wouldn't ever be able to forgive herself.

Angered by her own lack of resolve, her betrayal of Danica, and her utter failure to protect her girlfriend, Lianica tore the brass bars off her uniform and threw them across the room. They pinged off the surface of the wall and fell to the floor. Leaving them, she stormed out of the astrometrics lab and headed to the recreational lounge to hit up the bar and have a few drinks.

Maybe if I get drunk enough, she thought, she could forget about this terrible, horrible, no good, very bad day.

12

Back aboard his private shuttle, Emperor Dakroth shackled Danica's arms above her head, fastening them to the rear bulkhead with magnetic clamps. Opening a vial of smelling salts, he wafted its potent scent beneath her nose and revived her.

Danica snapped awake, the inside of her nose burning, and found herself shackled to the back of the emperor's shuttle transport with unbreakable korridium alloy restraints. The same restraints used for transporting slave labor to the Outer Rim mining asteroids and for the extraterrestrial chattel bought and sold by the Intergalactic Gladiatorial Syndicate.

"Dani, is it?" Dakroth said in an amused tone. A slight smile formed on his Prussian lips as he eyed his former Vice Admiral up and down, taking in her new, augmented appearance.

"Only Jegra calls me that," she snapped defensively. Her words had a sharper edge than she had intended, but her new name and persona was part and parcel of her attempt to redefine herself. To distance herself from the emperor and become something different. Something better.

Even so, it seemed her abrupt tone caught his attention because his eyes widened and his grin grew strained, as if the ire was bubbling up inside him but, then, he quickly forced it back again and found composure.

"I think I preferred Cassera, actually." He locked his hands behind his back and smiled again. This time, his gaze drifted off to the side as though some nostalgic reminiscence from their past caught his attention.

"Cassera is dead," she replied.

"Good," Dakroth replied. "Because Cassera Van Danica Amelorak is a traitor to the empire. And as you well know, there's only one fate for traitors."

Danica merely gazed back at him with a blasé look that seemed to say she'd heard it all before. Nothing he could say would shock her. She knew him too well; she could tell exactly how all this would pan out.

But, if she was being completely honest, being called a traitor to her face did sting. She was many things, but a traitor wasn't one of them.

Ever since she was a young girl all she wanted to do was serve a greater purpose. The greater purpose she'd found was expanding the empire, securing the future, and making Dagon great again. That's why she joined the Imperial Navy. She wanted to be a part of something bigger than herself. She wanted to make a difference.

Then, one day, the Lord Emperor took notice of her and for reasons unfathomable to her, decided to prime her for admiralship. And he took her under his wing and began her training. The unimaginable had happened, and she was caught up in the great expanse of the Dagon Empire. He was her noble leader and she his dutiful servant. Fulfilling the Emperor's every command was her sole purpose in life.

Dakroth's vision of a unified galaxy became her vision. And it consumed her. In her blind devotion, she did terrible things, despicable things, at his bequest. And never once did she question any of his orders. Not even when he ordered her to bomb countless colonies and decimate entire cities to get them to surrender to the will of the Lord Emperor.

In her zealotry, she did not question. She only obeyed. And it was because of this single-mindedness to serve her emperor at the cost of all else, that she had risen through the ranks faster than any Dagon officer before her.

She had been ruthless. Fearless. And she would have gladly continued to be so if it weren't for the small fact that the most unexpected thing happened. She fell in love.

What's more, she fell in love with a common slave. And although it wasn't unheard of for nobles to raise slaves to the status of permanent courtesans or sometimes even wives, it was completely another to have to share the love of your life with the cruelest dictator the galaxy had ever known.

It was the events that transpired on the moon Cordova that had caused Danica to doubt Dakroth's greatness. Dakroth's betrayal of Jegra, their run-in with the Knight of Caelum, and the little fact that he had shot her to prevent her from saving Jegra, had shaken her faith.

In that moment, Dakroth had revealed his true colors. And the illusion of the great warrior emperor came tumbling down like a stack of Vorteshian playing cards.

It was when he ordered her to hunt Jegra down and kill her that Danica's disillusionment was finally complete. Dakroth's obsession with Jegra's genome, his desire to weaponize her, and his single-minded drive to achieve galactic domination at any cost revealed a power-hungry madman willing to burn the whole bleeding galaxy to dust and ash just so long as he could continue to rule over its charred remains.

No matter how big or how powerful the empire became, no matter how many star systems folded under Dagon military might, the Lord Emperor was always thirsty for more.

Now, with the recent losses at the hands of the Nyctans, the Dagon Imperial Armada was stretched dangerously thin across every sector. The emperor's lust for power was becoming detrimental to the wellbeing of the empire. Meanwhile, power struggles amongst the senatorial committee threatened to bring the Dagon Empire imploding in on itself. If that happened, the military heads would take sides and Dagon would collapse into all out civil war.

It was now Danica's opinion that if things continued on this way, Emperor Dakroth would drag the Dagon Empire down along with him into his descent into madness. For too long had a tyrant reigned. And no longer could her métier of serving the empire go hand in hand with serving her emperor. In the end, she could only serve one. And the truth was, the empire was greater than just one man.

What Dagon direly needed was a change from war to diplomacy. And that was a skillset Dakroth sorely lacked.

Jegra, on the other hand, had caught the imagination of the people. Every sector of the empire knew her name. Her gladiatorial fights were that of legend. Her battle with a Knight of Caelum in hand to hand combat was a tale for the ages. And her ability to out maneuver even Dakroth himself made her the perfect candidate for leading the Dagon empire out of an age of war and into an age of peace and prosperity.

But if Danica was going to help Jegra usher in a new era of change for the empire, she'd first have to survive Dakroth's anger and whatever twisted form of punishment he had in mind for her.

"Danica, then," Dakroth said, nonchalantly waving off her acrimonious response. He rubbed his chin and gazed at her from half-sunken eyelids that suggested that he was no longer in the mood for sardonic banter. "It seems you and I have come to an impasse," he continued, his voice shifting in tone from affable to hostile. "If I kill you, I make a martyr of you, enhancing your already legendary status throughout the system. The great war heroine turned traitor, turned rebel, turned hero again. No. I'm afraid I must permit you to live...for the time being. You see, I'm in somewhat of a bind; I have no choice but to grant you your miserable, traitorous life."

She eyed him stiffly and then quipped, "How merciful of you." As expected, he merely ignored her retort and continued on with his little tirade.

"Humiliation and torture are what you have to look forward to, Vice Admiral. And then, once I break you, and you *will* break, I will take your dignity by selling your worthless, impure flesh to whichever loathsome slaver will take you. Only then will you be free of me."

"This little speech of yours is torture enough," she said, sarcasm dripping off her every word like corrosive acid. "So feel free to consider us squared up and sell me to the next slave ship that comes our way."

Unamused, his red eyes flared with rage. Pink wisps of Dagon energy seeped out like ethereal vapor. He pulled a knife from the back of his belt and held it to her throat. Leaning in, the knife drawing a dab of blood, he snarled, "You will learn your place, banjax!"

In the Dagoni language, the term "banjax" meant the lowest of the low. It was worse than slave, worse than whore, and the searing label was not used lightly. It meant "the defiled," and if the emperor branded you such, it was a veritable curse.

Nobody would associate with a banjax. They were viewed as a black stain on society. They were impure, and they had to go, had to be eliminated. There was a threat of contamination by association, which no one dare risk. Therefore, anyone deemed a banjax was forthwith banished or killed.

Dakroth gripped Danica's garments tightly in his left fist and began hacking at them with the blade in his right. He cut away her clothes piece by piece until she was naked before him, helpless to do anything but watch.

Once he'd finished stripping her bare, he spat on her body and returned to the front of the shuttle.

As his spittle dribbled down her chest and between her breasts, Danica's rage swelled within her. "Defile me all you want. Hurt me. Dismiss me. Kill me, for all I care. Just know that there's one woman you'll never hold power over. And when she learns of what you've done to me, she'll come for you. Do you hear me?!" Danica was practically shouting across the cabin at Dakroth, but he continued to ignore her. "Heed my words, oh great emperor. Jegra will have your head. And there's nothing you can do about it."

Ishtar looked over her shoulder and glowered at Danica. "Does she ever shut up?"

Dakroth lowered himself into the pilot's seat and let out a heavy sigh. After a short pause, he said, "You may begin."

Ishtar's scowl melted away and a malevolent grin spread across her burgundy lips. She slowly rose up and sauntered over to Danica. There was a light spring in her step, her demeanor almost child-like in its giddiness.

Pulling out a slender vial from the inside of her uniform, she held it up in front of Danica's face. Inside was what appeared to be a ferocious looking centipede. It had a black armored body with hundreds of thorny red legs and giant mandibles that looked like they could bite through a korridium hull.

"Do you know what this is? It's a Dagon demon-worm. They live only on the southern continent of Krylon; they are subterranean. Their contact with the Dagon species has been limited, but they have evolved in a way that has given them a most unique property."

Danica looked at the worm and then at Ishtar's black tattooed face. Defiant, she said nothing.

Noting Danica's reticence, Ishtar smiled and continued. "You see, they have an affinity for burrowing under the flesh, and they make their way to the lower abdomen. There, they coil around the nerves of your umbilical cord, just beneath your belly button," she informed Danica, touching her stomach and running her red finger along the radius of Danica's navel.

"They pierce a feeding needle into your gut and then begin to feast on your reproductive organs, a delicacy, in their view. Once they've wreaked havoc on your insides, they proceed to lay their eggs. Three weeks later you give birth to a host of their offspring which burst from your abdomen. Dagon males, I'm afraid, die an excruciatingly painful death. But, luckily, a Dagon female will typically survive. You see, the creatures end up filling her uterus; this female attribute prevents her death in about half the reported cases–assuming she can get the medical attention she requires, that is."

"Did anyone ever tell you that you talk too much?" Danica hissed in her most sarcastic tone.

Enraged, Ishtar sucker punched Danica in the gut. Unable to defend herself, she took the brunt of the blow like a punching bag and spat up blood.

Ishtar unscrewed the lid of the jaw and dumped the centipede onto Danica's shoulder. It crawled around in figure eights, searching for an entrance point but couldn't find one. As it slithered across her chest, Ishtar sucker punched Danica again.

"Gah!" Danica gasped for air and the creature climbed into her mouth. As it made its way down her throat, she began coughing and heaving. Then the heaving turned to screaming and she jerked and thrashed against her shackles as the creature burrowed its way deep into her body.

"Did I forget to mention that each slender leg of the creature releases a prick of venom as it bears down on your flesh? Venom which burns like acid as it scorches you from the inside out? Yeah, I think I forgot to mention that."

Through gritted teeth, Danica snarled, "Go to hell, you duplicitous psycho-hag."

"That's the Cassera Van Danica I remember so fondly!" Dakroth said from the shuttle's forward cabin.

Ishtar glanced down to see the rounded outline of the creature already coiling around Danica's umbilical cord. Another punch to the gut, just above the creature's nesting area, sent unfathomable pain throughout Danica's entire body.

Ishtar, a wicked smile spreading clear across her face, was winding up to hit Danica again when Dakroth intervened. "That's enough, my dear. We don't want to spoil her before we get her home."

Ishtar grabbed Danica by the chin and raised it. Looking into her golden eyes with her green ones, Ishtar leaned in and French kissed Danica. As she pulled away, her spittle stretched from her bottom lip to Danica's. Once the strand of saliva broke, Ishtar shoved Danica's face away, mumbling "Banjax," and then let go of her.

Danica's head slumped down in defeat and Ishtar laughed and returned to the co-pilot's seat next to Dakroth, as commanded. *The dutiful little assassin*, Danica thought, *like a dog. Always willing to do anything to please the master.*

Danica's head hung between her shoulders and it took everything she had not to scream out in agony as the poisonous creature burrowed into her tender flesh. She couldn't let Dakroth win. No matter what he did to her. She had to stay strong.

As she struggled for composure, her thoughts sought out Jegra. As much as she had enjoyed her time with Lianica, it was Jegra that was her true love. Her soulmate. And it would be the thought of being reunited with her that would keep her going. No matter what Dakroth threw at her. At least she had the hope of being with Jegra again.

A sudden prick inside her pelvis caused her to scream out in agony. The burning sensation was so intense, she wanted to die. Then the creature drilled down into her ovaries and the real pain began. Hot, searing, unbearable pain. Then, only blackness.

When Danica came too, she felt an insatiable burning in her gut. It felt like the time when she was a little girl and had wandered into a fire-ant's nest. She'd been stung so badly she thought she was going to die. It felt like that, but on the inside.

She raised her head, grunting from the effects of the venom which coursed through her entire body, even her neck, and looked around. She was no longer aboard the shuttle but found that she was tied to some kind of stone slab inside a large chamber.

A table just beyond her held a litany of surgical devices, some of them crude and ancient, some illegal, all meant for the gratification of her torturer.

Just beyond the shadows, Danica could make out a familiar figure. Stepping into view, the figure, dressed only in a white ceremonial loincloth and nothing else, stepped into the light. It was the empress. It was Jegra.

"Impossible," Danica muttered.

"There's no time," Jegra said, grabbing a scalpel from the table. She ran over to Danica and began cutting the leather straps that bound her to the table. "I have to get you out of here before he finds out."

"Dakroth?" Danica asked, her voice too weak to say any more. The creature's venom had practically paralyzed her. When she did try to move, all she could feel was a searing pain coursing through every muscle fiber.

The leather strap snapped and Danica, using every ounce of strength she had left, began to undo the other wrist strap. Jegra knelt and freed Danica's ankles and then helped her down off the table.

With Danica's arm draped across Jegra's shoulder, they began hobbling toward the exit. "I snuck away from the ceremony of consummation while the emperor was busy burning his face in the cunt of some Bre'lal servant girl. But he'll know I've stepped out soon enough."

"How?" Danica asked. "How'd you know where to find me?"

"Lianica told me that Dakroth had taken you," Jegra answered hastily.

"It's a miracle she found you at all." Danica smiled. At least Lianica hadn't let her down on that front.

"Tsk, tsk, ladies," a voice said from beyond the open entrance. Dakroth stepped into view, his finger already glowing. "And here I thought the time for traitorous back-stabbing was over. I must admit, I'm very disappointed in both of you."

"Back off, dear husband," Jegra growled.

"I'm afraid that's not possible," Dakroth replied, aiming his glowing finger at them. "You see, you've both been very naughty and one of you must be punished."

Before either of them could respond, Dakroth let the laser beam go and it hit Jegra right between the eyes. Danica watched in horror as Jegra's head exploded, her blood and gray matter splattering all over her body.

"Nooo!" Danica screamed. The demon-worm's venom surged with the added excitement and caused her to crumple to her knees. Jegra's body fell to the ground next to her, the gaping neck wound bleeding out before her. And all she could do was watch.

Danica looked up in time to see the emperor standing over her. She growled, "I'll kill you. If it's the last thing I do in this life. I swear by the Gilded Master, I'll kill you."

"Sorry, my dear Vice Admiral, but you're in no position to be making such threats. Empty as they are."

With the bottom of his boot, Dakroth kicked Danica in the temple, knocking her unconscious.

A few hours later, Danica groaned and opened her eyes. She found herself back on the stone table again, her arms and legs bound. It was as though she'd never made it off the bloody slab in the first place.

She scanned the room and when her eyes settled upon the crimson pool of blood gelling in the corner of the chamber near the arch of the exit, she began to sob. Her sobbing sent searing pain coursing through her veins, but she fought through it. Jegra was dead and she was back where she started. Almost. Now she had a very singular-minded mission. Avenge Jegra by killing Dakroth.

13

Massive jowls filled with razor sharp teeth encircled Jegra. Saliva dripped from between the four-inch teeth of both tyrannosaurs as they eyed their prey hungrily.

"Don't you even think about it," Jegra growled, clutching her blade in her left hand and the spear in her right. She shifted her feet and spun to maintain a steady eye contact with the female, glancing ever so slightly every so often to remind the male that she hadn't forgotten about him either.

One of the dinos warbled in a deep, throaty manner that caused Jegra to tense up.

"I feel I ought to inform you," she began, addressing the creatures, "that I've had myself a rotten two days and I'm not in any kind of mood to play around. So, let's get this tango over with, shall we?"

She tossed the spear straight up into the air, got under it, caught it again, and, taking a javelin thrower's stance, wound the weapon back as far as her arm would go. Just as she was about to launch the spear, however, she caught, like a flash out of the corner of her peripheral vision, the female's leathery tail slicing through the air like a bullwhip.

It happened so fast that Jegra hardly had time to process it. The tail slapped so hard it sent her tumbling to the ground. She rolled four times and skidded to a halt in the dirt. In the summersault, she'd lost her spear but managed to hold on to her blade. She raised it up in front of her and sighed disappointedly when it came up bent at a ninety-degree angle.

"Balls," she hissed, and tossed the useless piece of scrap metal aside. All that work for nothing.

The male T-Rex roared, asserting his dominance, but kept his distance. At the same time, the female, being the huntress, darted in for the kill. But Jegra was onto her; she took a lunging step forward and caught the beast by its upper and lower lips mid chomp. Jegra halted its snapping jaws and skidded backward in the hardened sand, the sunbaked ground beneath her feet flaking away like fish scales from a chef's knife.

As she plowed backward through the cracked earth, she dug in her heels and brought the female T-Rex to a standstill. Its tongue slithered out of its mouth and licked her forearm; Jegra made a disgusted face as she watched the dinosaur's drool ooze down her arm and drip off her elbow.

The great lizard almost seemed surprised that such a tiny creature as Jegra exhibited such great strength and wriggled her head free of Jegra's grasp, sauntering back a few steps as she re-adjudicated her best course of action.

Jegra scooped up a rock roughly the size of a basketball and threw it at the female. It shattered against her side, but was enough of a hit to startle the beast. She hurried back, putting distance between herself and Jegra; it was unusual for dinner to fight back so. The male, on the other hand, grew bolder.

The male huffed impatiently and the female snapped at him in protest—a curt reprimand that conveyed the sentiment that this particular prey was proving harder to catch than it should be. He snorted again, to stress his impatience with how long this affair seemed to be taking, and they both began circling her again.

"You two are dizzying," she said. Then, taking the initiative, she dug her toe into the ground and kicked up a blinding spray of sand. It must have stung, too, because the she-rex yowled and drew back.

Using what strength she could muster, Jegra charged the male T-Rex and slammed into him with her shoulder. He, too, wasn't prepared for her impressive strength; his footing went out from under him and he toppled onto his side. Kicking and squirming to get up, he rolled across his back and, with a flick of his tail, sprang back up onto his hind quarters.

Both tyrannosaurs withdrew a safe distance away from Jegra who squatted, hands on knees, huffing rapidly to catch her breath. Seeing that the pair were about to come at her again, she struck a fierce pose to deter them, if not give them pause. She threw out her firsts and screamed at them with everything she had.

This seemed to do the trick, as it scared them off. They galloped heavily off into the thick of the dead forest, leaving the feisty hominid for another day.

Jegra, exhausted and days without sleep, collapsed to her knees and let out yet another sigh. Although she wanted desperately to hold onto consciousness, she could no longer resist the Sandman's calling. Fatigue had set in and she collapsed onto her back and let the peaceful nothingness of deep sleep overtake her.

When Jegra awoke it was twilight, and she gazed up at the twin moons slowly rising from the east.

She spat dirt out past her chapped and peeling lips and pushed herself up off the ground. Once back on her feet, she tottered there for a bit, feeling lightheaded and knew that she needed to find water. And soon.

It had already been three days, and although she'd found some replenishment with the Pteranodon egg she had drunk right from the shell, it was the only sustenance she'd had since landing. Another day like this, and she feared she wouldn't make it.

But, in all this, she had noticed one thing. The dinosaurs kept retreating to the southwest, which gave her an inkling of hope that she'd find water in that direction. So, she followed the trail of the tracks of the tyrannosaurs, confident that they must know exactly where to find water.

She stalked the beasts for fifteen kilometers from her camp when she finally came upon an oasis of fertile greenery. The verdant jungle growth, including ferns and vines and coconut-like trees, came right up to the edge of the dead forest. It was as though there, at that precise line, the desert of scorched earth met the Garden of Eden.

Jegra found an alien coconut and cracked it open on a rock. Although its juice was sour and tasted nothing like the tropical fruit she'd loved as a child, it was the only liquid she'd had since she crashed. She gulped it down thirstily, choking on its potent juices a couple of times. Then she wiped her mouth with the back of her hand and continued into the lush jungle foliage.

After hiking for what felt like another five or six kilometers into the jungle, she felt the humidity spike. She also made out the distant sound of running water.

"A waterfall!" she said out loud, practically startling herself with the sound of her own voice.

Her pace quickened and she rushed the last four kilometers to a clearing where she found a waterfall feeding into a crystal-clear pool with two streams winding away from it into a fern covered bank. She scanned the trees to make sure the fang-toothed couple weren't lurking about and then rushed to the water's edge. She looked around again to spy an albino opossum-kind of creature on the other side of the lake taking a long drink and realized it was safe.

Jegra slid down onto her belly and dipped her whole face into the water, practically inhaling the liquid.

She drank until she choked herself and sat up hacking and coughing. Then she cupped her hands and brought up several more water-filled palms to her parched and cracked lips and drank until every ounce of thirst was quenched.

Finally satisfied, she let out a refreshed sigh and slumped her shoulders. Inside the forest, the air was rich with oxygen and didn't stink like out in the sulfuric haze of the blistering desert.

A light breeze picked up and she caught a whiff of her own putrid stench, of sweat, blood, and dinosaur drool, and almost gagged. Dipping her right foot into the water, she wriggled her toes and then slowly waded out into the cool water until she was waist deep in the lagoon. Leaning back, she slipped down and let the water consume her. Coming up for air, she took a deep breath and wiped the water from her face.

The only light came from the twin moons above her as Jegra climbed out of the water and lay across a spring-side boulder and basked in the moonlight. The cool water and forest breeze felt like a soothing balm against her sunburned skin.

Jegra did her best to rub the soreness out of her weary muscles and bruised bones, but it wasn't enough. Sliding off the boulder, she slipped back into the water and waded over to the water fall. She moved under the crushing shower, letting it cascade down her neck and back and moaned in pleasure as the pounding force massaged her body. That's when she heard the rattling snort of the T-Rex just beyond the cluster of trees.

The foliage directly opposite her rustled with excited movement and Jegra watched in dead silence as the beast appeared out of the thicket. It was only the male. Alone. He hadn't yet caught scent of her; he bent down and began to drink without so much as a care in the world.

Cautiously, Jegra slowly eased back into the waterfall, letting the curtain of water close around her. She slowly receded, slipping into a small alcove formed in the cliff face. Here she was safely hidden and out of sight.

She waited for several minutes, giving the giant lizard plenty of time to drink, and then slowly edged around the bend of the inlet and pressed her face into the veil of waterfall. As she poked her nose out, her face mashed up against something leathery. She opened her eyes to find the T-Rex's nose pressed directly upon hers.

"Balls," she muttered to herself.

The dinosaur snorted, sending a spray of water and foul smelling breathe into her face.

"Behave," she said in a steady voice, throwing up a hand and easing her way out of the waterfall. The T-Rex slowly moved back, matching her stride for stride, and playfully wagged its tail. She raised an eyebrow as it backed up onto the shoreline. Somehow, it seemed smaller than the previous two she'd encountered, and much more playful and energetic. That's when she realized she was dealing with an entirely new dinosaur.

Uncertain as to the creature's intentions, she cautiously backed away and, with both hands raised defensively, she said, "Good boy. Now, just stay put while I slowly inch away."

But as soon as she'd put a safe distance between herself and the creature, he bounded forward and landed directly in front of her. His eyes sparkled and he let out a playful snort.

"Oh, you're just a pup, aren't you?" she said, realizing she was dealing with a youngling. He wagged his tail and snorted excitedly again, then turned in a circle.

Jegra looked around for a boulder or something she could use as a weapon, but there was nothing in sight. So, she continued her backward retreat until she noticed another giant snout appear directly to her right. Her eyes widened as she gazed into the nostril of another T-Rex. It was the female. Mom.

Slowly, Jegra turned to find the female staring right at her with what Jegra could imagine was a concerned expression, and then she roared, letting Jegra know that she was treading on thin ice.

The female's roar excited the young male and it reared up on its hind legs, mimicking its mother, roaring even louder than she had.

The female had obviously had enough of her males for one day and nipped at the pup's neck. This irritated him, and he rammed into her, shoving her back in a show of dominance. As she stumbled blindly, Jegra had no recourse but to leap out of the way.

The ground smashed hard into Jegra's side, but she rolled with the fall and sprang back up to her feet. She quickly darted away from the tussle and jumped over a tail, which whipped by at such a ferocious velocity it cut down two trees, leaving only splintered stumps in its wake.

"You two should seriously consider counseling," Jegra yelled above their mutual grunts of disdain for one another. Before she could clear out of their radius, however, the male's tail inadvertently clipped her and sent her skipping across the water. She sank into the lagoon and came up choking on a mouthful of fresh water kelp.

Swimming to the opposite shoreline, she crawled out and panted for a bit as she tried to catch her breath. Just then, a deafening roar shook the trees and Jegra felt the very ground shudder beneath her as mammoth footsteps stormed up to the shoreline.

The two smaller dinosaurs looked up in time to see dad appear, who let forth a displeased roar. He was, after all, the king of the lizards here. The youngling scampered off into the trees, not wanting to face the wrath of its parent. The mother roared back, as if she were scolding him, and then stalked to the other end of the lagoon.

Jegra stared in awe at the giant T-Rex, who was easily three times bigger than the largest specimen ever found on Earth. "My God," she said in a hushed tone. "You're one big mother fu—"

"Get down!" a voice called out. Jegra whirled around in time to see two blue plasma bolts scorch past her.

She lunged to the side, crashed into a fern, and rolled out of the way of the disruptor blasts.

The two blasts hit the giant T-Rex in his rib cage and the monster roared out in agony and then retreated into the foliage. Startled, the female scampered off, too, and soon enough all the tyrannosaurs had hightailed it out of there.

Jegra looked up to see a cloaked figure standing on top of a large boulder at the crest of the waterfall, her plasma rifle held at her side in a non-threatening manner. She squinted to try and make out the figure's face, but it was concealed by a navy-blue wrap that matched the rest of the shawl. *Probably to help combat the smog and the sweltering desert sun*, she surmised.

Only a narrow slit allowed for two gorgeous emerald eyes to peer down at her from behind the muffler. Jegra's mysterious savior's eyes sparkled in the dim light cast by the twin moons and, after a brief silence, her rescuer spoke. "It's best we clear out. They'll be back soon." The woman took out a canteen and, kneeling down next to the rushing water, filled it. She then stood up and tossed Jegra the canteen of water. "Here, you'll need this. The walk through the jungle is a long one."

Jegra slung the canteen's strap over her shoulder and looked back the way the dinosaurs had fled and then back at the woman who was already turning to leave. Given her options, she'd rather join this stranger than get stomped into the ground by some pea-brained lizard with only food on its mind.

Plasma rifle clutched in both hands, the mysterious woman paused and looked over her shoulder. "Well? You coming or not?"

Jegra nodded in compliance and began scaling the slope of the rockface that wound its way up the waterfall. Once she'd made it to the top, she found the woman waiting for her at the edge of the tree line. Seeing that she'd made it, the figure stepped into the forest and Jegra quickly followed after her.

They hiked along a trail for the better half of an hour and then came out of the oasis to a bluff that overlooked a lush valley. Just beyond the valley was a mountain range peaked by jagged rock formations.

"There," the woman said, aiming a finger at the mountains. "That's home."

"That is far," Jegra sighed disappointedly.

"When I saw your shuttle crash, I set out right away. It took me three days to get to you."

"Three days?" Jegra asked. "Is that all?"

The woman's eyes flickered as they scanned Jegra's face. Then she set out without so much as another word.

"All right, then," Jegra said aloud. "Nice talk."

Fifty-six hours later, they'd come to the foothills at the far end of the valley. Jegra finished the remainder of water in her canteen then tipped it back and tapped the side trying to get every last drop. Realizing it was no use, she huffed disappointedly and then twisted the lid back on.

"We're here," her travel companion finally said, as she stopped before a steep rockface.

Vines and moss clung to the rockface and climbed almost to the top. That's when Jegra noticed it. At the very pinnacle were two giant rock faces that formed a narrow passage. And wedged in-between the mammoth cliff sides was a spaceship.

It wasn't a big ship. Most likely a freighter or commercial hauler of some kind. But it was a ship, none-the-less. Completely intact. Apart from it being wedged three hundred feet above the ground, it looked salvageable.

"Is that yours?" Jegra asked the cloaked figure.

The emerald green eyes settled onto Jegra's brown ones and then, without uttering a word, the woman slung her rifle over her shoulder and began scaling the vines that tendrilled their way up to the where the ship was.

Jegra shrugged, the sunburn on her shoulders stinging slightly as she did so. Without seeing any option but to place her trust in this complete stranger, she grabbed ahold of a thick vine and followed her up.

14

A headless Jegra, straddled the emperor's thighs and ground her pelvis into his. He reached up and squeezed her oversized breasts and groaned loudly as he coupled with her. After a few minutes, he climaxed and then let out a deep, breath-laden sigh. A twisted smile remained on his face as he looked up at the decapitated corpse that was settling into him, soaking him all up.

"It's been three days of this morbid roleplaying fantasy, Rhadamanthus, and you still haven't gotten sick of it?" the corpse asked in a dour tone.

"Don't talk," Dakroth said, "It ruins the illusion."

Jegra's hands reached up to her gaping neck wound and fumbled for an invisible pull. Unzipping the holographic suit, Ishtar peeled the garment down to her waist and looked at Dakroth.

"Maybe you're not tired of fucking your dead ex, but I sure as hell am tired of pretending to be her just so you can get off."

"Oh, quit your bellyaching," Dakroth griped. "You were certainly into it the first several times."

"Yeah, because it's twisted as fuck. But doing it night after night...it kind of loses its morbid charm."

"Fine then," he grumbled, roughly pushing her off of him as if she were a common prostitute. "I was finished with you anyway."

He clapped his hands and two green-skinned Bre'lal courtesans entered his bed chamber. He rose to his knees and wrapped his arms around their waists as they stood by his bed dressed in nothing but the translucent gossamer skirts and nothing else. Looking over at Ishtar with a mocking grin, he said, "Is there anything else I can help you with?"

Ishtar shot him a sharp glance then stormed out of the emperor's personal chambers. *If he wants to fuck green-skins,* she thought bitterly, *then he can fuck green-skins. If he wants to fuck blue-skins, then, by all means, fuck blue-skins.* But if he thought he could fuck her over like this without consequences, he was dead wrong. She'd see to it that he remembered the exact moment the red-skin fucked him in return.

Angry, she tore at the damn holographic suit, its fake Jegra breasts jiggling as she peeled it off her body and discarded it in the hallway. Leaving the wrinkled husk in the middle of the floor, she marched past some maidservants who quickly scattered out of the way as she rushed past them. The black tribal tattoos running down her red, naked body, dripped with the residue of her lustful encounter with Dakroth. She marched into a lift and then hit the button for the fourteenth level basement. The doors slid shut and she tilted her hips and tapped her foot impatiently as she waited for the lift to sink deep beneath the royal palace.

When the doors opened again, Ishtar wasted no time and cut across the large chamber to the far end. The stone floor and walls hinted at the fact that it was an ancient part of the palace; the original stone slabs that made up the foundation were still intact after a thousand years.

Massive Doric styled marble columns, about twenty in all, supported the ceiling, which stood thirty feet tall. Candles, rather than lights, provided illumination to the sprawling chamber, giving it an ancient mystique, an almost temple-like quality.

Ishtar went over to a clothes rack set up along the back wall and found some black leather strips with a series of interlocking buckles hanging on them. She fiddled with the various strands of leather for a bit and then pieced together a dominatrix outfit. Slipping into the leather attire, she strode over to a large marble slab that stood upright at the center of the broad chamber. Bound to it by her wrists, waist, and ankles was Danica, fast asleep. Even at the vertical angle, she managed to sleep soundly. Even with the threat of parasitic life growing within her swollen abdomen.

Ishtar gently leaned in and kissed a sleeping Danica on the lips, urging her awake. "Rise and shine, my pet," she whispered in a faintly melodic, singsong voice like that of a mother waking a sleeping child.

Ishtar ran her fingers along the bloated and bulbous abdomen of Danica, now ripe with the eggs of the demon worms. Danica's belly was so swollen it looked as though she were eighteen weeks pregnant. Her purple veins could be seen under her thinly stretched blue skin; Ishtar's fingers followed the branching vessels; it looked as though the slightest amount of extra pressure would cause her belly to burst, spilling demon worm eggs all over the place.

Danica slowly opened her eyes and looked up at the grinning red face staring back at her. Waking up from one nightmare into another caused her chest to seize with fear and she began hyperventilating.

For the past three weeks, she'd had plenty of time to become intimately familiar with the kinds of depravity Ishtar Bantu was willing to stoop to just to get that small hit of perverse gratification that only her twisted little mind could conjure up.

"What's the matter, my pet? Aren't you happy to see me?" Her voice was all cutesy, as though she were talking to a baby, which made it all the more disturbing.

Ishtar rubbed her hand over her bald head, her fingers tracing the lines of her tattoos, a kind of ceremonial war paint unique to her people. Caught in a moment of ecstasy, Ishtar's eyelids fluttered and her eyes rolled back into her head so only the whites showed. It was like she was experiencing an orgasm, even though she'd only just arrived.

Danica's eyes welled up with tears. If Ishtar was this excited before she'd actually begun her depraved session of playing doctor, she obviously had something truly twisted in mind.

Ishtar took a deep breath to calm herself and her face returned to normal. Her gaze hardened and settled on Danica; the corners of her mouth curled upward with a twisted sort of preoccupation.

"Shall we begin today's session?"

Tears trickled from the corners of Danica's eyes and slid down her cheeks, but she dared not respond. Any response, positive or negative, was only ever met with just one thing. Torture. If she didn't respond, sometimes Ishtar would grow bored and leave her alone. Sometimes.

Ishtar went over to one of the pillars in the room and found a control panel. She flipped a switch and the table lowered and tilted back. It locked into place with a loud *clunk* and Danica raised her head and watched Ishtar make her way to a pristine white machine that looked like a high-end mobile medical lab unit.

The machine had a series of robotic arms, three on each side which, disturbingly enough, gave it a crab-like appearance. Each arm was fully automated and capable of performing multiple intricate surgeries simultaneously.

Ishtar wheeled the robotic device over and positioned it at the head of the marble slab. Danica strained against her restraints and thrashed her head in protest, but it was of little use. Ishtar locked the machine down and activated it.

Clamps rose up from under the stone table and pinched Danica's head in a vice grip, holding it firmly in place. With a menacing mechanical whine, three of the machine's arms swiveled around and curled downward. Blades at the end of each arm gleamed in the dim light and they came into position above Danica's face. The blades retracted and were quickly replaced by a series of syringes. Each needle dripped with a reconditioning serum designed to make Danica submit to anything Ishtar wanted to do to her.

Ishtar tapped on the control pad and the needles slowly bore down onto Danica's forehead and temples.

"*Please*," Danica whispered. "Please...don't."

"Don't?!" she snarled, her eyes wide with menacing rage. "How dare you tell me what to do." She jammed her thumb onto the control pad and the needles penetrated Danica's flesh and bone. She screamed out in agony, the tendons in her neck tensing so tightly they bulged under the skin as thick as piano wire.

"No, please, stop," Danica pleaded in a barely audible voice. "Please, I can't take it anymore." Tears trickled out of the sides of her eyes.

Ishtar looked down at Danica and grinned. Again, it was that strange, child-like glee that Danica found so disturbing. Ishtar was a true psychopath. Other's suffering caused her great pleasure. There was no way she would ever stop. A deep sadistic urge compelled her to go through with it till the end. Whether Danica would survive remained uncertain.

The only thing that could stop Danica's suffering now would be to give up and just let herself fade away. Let herself die. But some nagging voice in the back of her mind told her not to give Ishtar the satisfaction.

"I'm afraid we're just beginning, my dear *Vice Admiral*." A vicious grin spreading across her face, Ishtar tapped another sequence of commands and the syringes hissed as they injected Danica with their mind-altering drugs.

At the same time, the remaining three robotic arms came alive. One was equipped with a scalpel, another with a bone cutter, and the third with a white-hot sealing torch. The servos whirred inside the retracted arms and they slowly extend toward Danica's body.

"They say one of these machines can piece a body back together as quickly as it can tear it apart."

The arms all repositioned themselves directly above Danica's legs and then the cutting, searing, scorching pain of the automated arms simultaneously bit into her and she cried out in agony.

As the stress grew and the pain intensified, the narcotic serum kept her conscious. She began to bleed from her eyes and ears. But all she could do was watch as the terrible robotic limbs dismantled her body piece by piece from the feet up. At the same time, the very same device began mending her. Even so, without the proper anesthesia, it was enough violent trauma to cause even the soundest of minds to go mad.

Not even halfway through the procedure, Danica's nervous system shut down and she passed out from the excoriating pain. In her mind, she was certain she had died, except, for some reason, her consciousness was still very much aware of her condition. She realized that she'd retreated so far into herself that she was observing everything going on as though she were an outside observer. A kind of out of body experience. Then, slowly, everything grew even more distant. The terrible sound of the mechanical arms, Ishtar's voice urging her to wake up again, all slowly faded to a distant white noise.

She didn't remember the exact moment she'd blacked out. All she remembered was waking up again and hearing unfamiliar voice.

"In here!" a man shouted.

His voice was filled with panic and dismay and for a brief moment Danica thought she had dreamed it. Slowly, she came back into her own body and opened her eyes. Awakening from the paranormal experience, she winced at the bright lights all around her. She blinked several times, giving them time to adjust, and then opened them again. Blurry faces wrapped in white medical masks swarmed her and she fought through hazy vision to try to make out what was going on.

She heard the faint sound of the same man's voice speak again, but this time it drew nearer. She heard other murmured whispers and, then, the first voice gasped out in horror filled dismay. "Oh my Gilded Lord."

Danica opened her eyes to see a doctor and several medics standing over her. She lay in some kind of warm muck, but was uncertain as to what it was. Slowly, she looked down to see her entrails sprawled out across the floor. Demon worm eggs mixed in with her blood and guts. Apparently, the machine had malfunctioned when it got to the worm larva in her body, not knowing how to deal with the foreign entity.

When the worm brood had exploded, so had most of her abdomen. And the worm's lethal venom would have most certainly killed her if it wasn't for the fact that it had literally all spilled out of her faster than it could affect her systems.

Ironically, being so near to death is precisely what prevented her from dying.

"Get her onto the gurney. We need to get her to the OR immediately if we're going to have any chance of saving her," the doctor shouted. The medics complied and reached under Danica's arms and hoisted her onto the gurney. The hover coils hummed as they set her down onto the stretcher.

As they hauled what remained of her bloody body out of the chamber, one of the medics slipped an oxygen mask over her face. She turned her head to the side as she breathed in the cool flow of air and glimpsed Dakroth standing off to the side, his arms clasped behind his back, radiant pink energy streaming out of both eyes. A sign he was beyond enraged.

In the corner of the room cowered Ishtar. One of her arms had been completely vaporized, the nub of what remained smoldering white wisps of smoke that curled upward in the dimness. She clutched her side and looked absolutely pathetic, groveling at the emperor's feet. She had gone too far and would certainly be punished for it.

As the medics ushered her out and rushed her to the operating room, Danica felt her heart stop inside her chest. As she flatlined, a smile settled onto her face. At last now, she thought, the pain has finally come to an end.

15

High above the sprawling canopy of the jungle, Jegra looked out the ship's view portal at the alien landscape below. It seemed that the dense patch of vegetation that enclosed them now was only the size of a small city. Beyond it only lay the dead forest ruins and a never-ending desert.

The stranger gradually unwrapped her shawl and revealed herself to be a Bre'lal woman who bared a striking similarity to that of one deceased Abethca Agnar, except that she had a beauty mark, was about four inches taller, and had slightly less muscle definition.

"Abethca?" Jegra gasped, thinking she was in the presence of a ghost.

"No, I'm her sister. Onelle Te'Legra Agnar."

Jegra rushed over and snatched Onelle up in her arms and gave her a great big hug. Onelle laughed at the unexpectedness of it and Jegra gently set her back down again.

"Does the empress of Dagon greet all her subjects that way?" Onelle asked.

Jegra smiled but understood the question was rhetorical. "I knew your sister. I knew Abethca," Jegra informed Onelle.

"Then you must know who killed her," Onelle said. Her tone was cold and vicious and contained a menacing quality that hinted at the fact that Onelle was out to get revenge for her sister's murder.

Jegra nodded solemnly.

Onelle's voice came out rough and hard, the voice of a warrior on the battlefield, one who knew he was headed into a battle he couldn't possibly win but who had been in a hundred other such battles and, miraculously, lived to tell about it. "Tell me," she said. "Tell me who killed Abby."

"An assassin named Ishtar Bantu killed her. I had left Abethca alone to bathe herself after a bout in the arena. If I had only returned sooner, I could have..." Jegra's voice seized up and she choked on the sadness that the painful memory of Abethca's death, her first great loss in or out of the arena, drudged up.

"Who hired this assassin?" Onelle followed up as she slowly removed the rifle from her back. She held it in her hands in a ready posture in case she needed to use it, but Jegra merely looked away.

"Emperor Dakroth," she murmured under her breath. "He was getting back at me for having taken a liking to Abethca. Apparently, he isn't too fond of competition."

Onelle threw the disruptor rifle down onto a table with some other junk. It all rattled about and, without a care of how it ended up, she stalked off to a nearby control panel. She reached out and let her fingers glide across the surface as she looked over some technical schematics.

"How long have you been stranded here?" Jegra asked.

The Bre'lal woman brushed a lock of green hair out of her eyes and stared at the charts without responding for the longest time. Jegra almost thought she'd been so deep in concentration she hadn't heard her, but then she spoke. "Three months, two weeks, and seven days." Looking back up, she glanced out the main view portal at the valley below. "Luckily I crashed here. It seems this is the only spot that the nuclear winds don't reach."

"Nuclear winds?" Jegra asked in a startled voice.

"This valley is all that remains of a nuclear holocaust."

"But I only saw dinosaurs down there. Are you saying there were other beings too?"

"There are some ruins about seventy kilometers northeast of here. But I didn't dare seek them out as it's far too dangerous. Once I got the ship's scanners back online, I did a preliminary survey of the topography of this place. Outside the reach of the oasis, it's chaos. Nothing much survives for very long. Lucky for you that you crashed on the adjacent mountain range. If you had wandered off the back side, however, you would have seen a radiation spike and then nothing for days. Eventually, the radiation poisoning would have killed you. That's why I was racing toward you. I needed to get to you before anything else did, including radiation sickness."

"I appreciate that. I do." Jegra looked over at Onelle's green face and smiled.

"With your help, I can finally get this shuttle's engines running again. And once we free this ship, we'll be able to get off this hellish rock."

"If you get me off of this rock," Jegra added, "I'll use my position as empress to see to it that you'll never need for anything again." She started unfastening the heavier parts of her armor and set it on a nearby console. Being as high as they were, with no way in or out except for the ship's hatch, she knew they were safe.

"That's not necessary," Onelle, said, waving her hand as if to decline the offer. "Besides, I'm richer than you are."

Jegra raised an eyebrow as she bent down and slid off her shin guards. "You're kidding me?"

"No, I own two whole mining sectors and all the entertainment zones on Arkadia and Kree'alek. And unlike Dakroth's tight-knit little empire, my trade is open to both Nyctans and Correlians alike."

"Impressive," Jegra said, eyeing Onelle Te'Legra Agnar up and down. She liked other strong women; their confidence allowed them to be unpretentious and straightforward, yet there was always more to them than met the eye. It was only the shallow ones, with their superficial aspirations, who pretended to be more than they were, yet they hoped for pathetically small rewards.

Jegra played with the ends of her hair and glanced down at the schematics that held Onelle's attention. "What is it you need me to do?" she asked.

Onelle smiled. "The work can begin tomorrow. Tonight we eat and drink."

Onelle walked over to the satchel she'd tossed to the side and opened the flap. Reaching in, she pulled out a teal, smooth-skinned lizard the size of a turkey and, holding it by its tail, plopped it down on a nearby console. On the same console was a portable gas stove, similar to those used for camping and outdoor barbecues.

A flint sparked and Onelle lit the gas stove. Reaching down, she withdrew a knife from the leather sheath on her thigh and twirled it in her hand, then began carving the animal. "I'm afraid it's not much," she said, pausing briefly to look over at Jegra, "but it beats starving to death."

Half an hour later, the lizard meat was sizzling in a cast iron skillet with onion sauce and a side order of what seemed to be green-colored yams. "Here," she said in a proud voice, handing Jegra a platter of the meal she'd prepared.

Jegra raised an eyebrow as she took the sizzling platter of lizard steak from Onelle. "Looks perfect. I'm famished."

"Yeah. Me too." Onelle looked at Jegra as though nothing were out of the ordinary, but seconds later she closed her eyes, pinched the bridge of her nose, and sighed.

"Is something wrong?" Jegra asked.

"No. It's just..." Onelle paused and waved her hand around the room as though she were trying to swat down a deviant fly. "This place. I can't really explain it. It's like being held under water and then brought up just long enough to catch your first breath, but not enough to replenish you. You know?"

"What doesn't kill you only makes you stronger," Jegra recited. A mantra she lived by when she was taking her licks as a rookie in the arena.

Onelle smiled. "I can see why my sister was so fascinated by you. You have an unwavering optimism about you. Some people might call it naïveté."

"And which are you? Naive, or optimistic?"

Onelle squinted at Jegra, having gotten cornered by her own carelessness. She chose to ignore the question and changed the subject. "Did you know that she'd become so obsessed with you that she rejoined the IGS? The very organization she'd spent a decade trying to get away from. But for you, she freely signed herself up for a champion's bout." She held a piece of steak up on the end of her fork, bit down on it, and smiled at Jegra as she chewed.

"She was pretty intense, I'll give you that much."

"My entire family line is intense," Onelle shared openly. She crossed her legs and looked at Jegra with a long, deliberate gaze, studying her every detail, then took another bite.

"Answer me this," Jegra said, using her royal language to get a response out of Onelle, "what kind of woman, a woman who owns half of the trade route in the Commonwealth and is wealthier than the Empress of the Dagon Empire, ends up being a courtesan on the side?"

"The Dagons aren't the only promiscuous species in the galaxy. Most species cannot afford to be as selective as yours. The harsh conditions they evolved under on their own worlds prohibits anything like monogamous marriage or partnership. My species fucks first and then decides later if they're compatible with the other."

"It seems you know an awful lot about my species," Jegra said, stroking her chin suspiciously.

"After I got wind of Abethca's death, I suspected you might be involved somehow. So, I did my research."

"Makes sense," Jegra answered, taking it all in.

Onelle continued with her story about how she became to be the titan of two seemingly unrelated industries. "At first, being a courtesan was more lucrative than my trading business, but then I bought my first abandoned asteroid mine, hoping to transform it into a luxury resort and casino. We accidentally tapped a new vein of korridium during the refit, however, and I instantly made several billion credits. Subsequently, I bought every derelict mine on the market to try and replicate my success."

"Did it work?" Jegra asked, having grown fully invested in Onelle Te'Legra Agnar's story.

"Sometimes. When we could mine, we mined. When we couldn't we converted the asteroids into luxury resorts and floating casinos all up and down the golden trade route. And business has been booming ever since. But somewhere down the line I felt that I'd spent all this time building an empire and had nothing to show for it but a fat bank account. My longing for companionship, something so ingrained in my species, never subsided. So, I decided to throw the gala of the century and invited my best clientele. I really don't know what I was thinking at the time; perhaps that I'd meet that one elusive person; more likely I just thought that if I couldn't be happy, perhaps I could make others happy. The party was a sensational success; one thing led to another and now, here I am. Entrepreneur, titan of industry, and head courtesan and mistress to the most successful entertainment and gambling venture this side of the Commonwealth."

"So how exactly did you cross paths with Dakroth?"

"After I began investigating you, learning everything there was to know about you, I only turned up dead ends. I couldn't understand why until I began investigating your husband. That's when I hit the jackpot. I uncovered all kinds of secretive deals and projects, shady ventures he didn't want anybody shedding light on. He sent his red-skinned assassin after me."

"Ishtar," Jegra growled as though her name was a dirty curse word.

"She ambushed me as I was returning to Arkadia. My shuttle had come under heavy fire when, out of nowhere, a whole fleet of those squids jumped into the sector. I nearly collided with one of them. It seemed perhaps our disruptor exchange startled them in return, for they jumped out of the system almost as quickly as they'd jumped in."

"And they took you along with them."

She nodded. "The next thing I know, my systems have shorted and I'm barreling down toward this cliff face. I've been marooned here ever since."

"You're lucky you survived the crash and in one piece." Jegra took a seat at one of the science stations and used the darkened console as a makeshift table. Slowly cutting a chunk of steak off, she examined the meat, then took it with her teeth and began chewing, her mind still grappling with the fact that there was actually another survivor on this barren world.

Onelle settled in beside her, taking a seat on a cargo crate, and resumed eating, too.

They ate in silence, sharing a sideways glance now and again, assessing the other just to be sure they were in good company. Once they'd finished their food, Jegra let out a loud belch. The sound pierced the silence as it echoed up and down the length of the ship's corridor.

Embarrassed, she instantly covered her mouth, and excused herself. "Pardon me, I'm so sorry," She said into a closed fist which she held to her mouth just in case another burp tried to escape. Her cheeks flushed rosy pink as she looked over at Onelle apologetically.

"It's quite all right," Onelle replied. "It's only natural." She then let out an equally loud burp and both women looked at each other in a moment of shared shock and then began laughing. It was a nice way to break up the tension.

"I am feeling rather bushwhacked, so I think I'll turn in for the evening," Jegra said, looking around the ship's bridge for a place to recline and sleep.

"The only available bed is in my personal quarters," Onelle informed her guest. "But you're the empress, so feel free to take it if you wish. I'll be fine out here." Onelle threw her feet up on the console and leaned back on the crate so her back pressed against the ship's bulkhead, and locking her hands behind her head she closed her eyes.

"Nonsense," Jegra said. "I'll have you know I'm no prude. I'd be more than happy to share a bed with you."

"Are you sure?" Onelle asked.

"Perfectly," Jegra replied.

"All right then," Onelle said, rising to her feet. "Bedroom's this way."

The sleeping quarters were no bigger than a bathroom. A sonic shower, a small folding cot to one side, and a shelf with some old books on the wall opposite the cot filled the tight space. The two women both squeezed through the doorway together, and laughed as their bodies pressed tightly against one another, causing them to get wedged in the doorway. They laughed, finally tumbling into the confined space.

Jegra reclined on the bed, and Onelle climbed under one of Jegra's raised legs and settled in on the opposite side of the cot.

"Comfortable?" Onelle asked, her legs tangling up with Jegra's in a surprisingly intimate position that seemed more comfortable than it did weird.

"Surprisingly, yes," Jegra laughed.

This solicited another round of laughter and they quickly looked away from one another when it became clear there was an undeniable physical attraction between them.

"Is this how you seduce all your clients? You bring them to a bedroom so small they have no choice but to mash themselves against you? Are you a masher, Mistress Onelle?" inquired Jegra with a dubious grin.

She laughed. "Let's just say with the ship's power supplying essential and emergency systems only, at least we won't freeze to death." She sat down on the bed and gestured for Jegra to get comfortable next to her. Jegra sat down beside her and Onelle reached around Jegra and, with some effort, slid the door shut. The room dimmed to near darkness except for the small emergency lamp above the door and Onelle leaned back into the bed. "Can I ask you something?" Onelle finally inquired.

"Sure, go ahead," Jegra said, snuggling up against the Bre'lal woman. They spooned quite comfortably in the cramped quarters. "I'm an open book."

"Do you love him? The emperor, I mean."

"I used to think so, briefly. But what I saw in him as a glimmer of kindness was merely his attempt to manipulate me into sleeping with him. As embarrassing as it is to admit, I fell for it. And, now, because of his treachery and scheming, here I am."

"So, you'd have no qualms if, say, a powerful woman like me decided to take Dakroth's head and place it on a pike for all the Commonwealth to see?" Her voice grew cold and vicious. Almost sinister.

"Not only wouldn't I have any qualms, I'd gladly help you do it."

Onelle pulled Jegra's arm down and wrapped it around her and squeezed it affectionately. "You know something, I just might be madly in love with you right now."

Jegra laughed. "I'm literally speechless."

It was Onelle's turn to laugh, and she did so as if by habit. Talking to Jegra felt like talking to a long-lost sister, and she was a little surprised at how well they clicked. "Now, get some rest, Empress," Onelle replied drowsily, "Tomorrow will be another long day. One of many to come."

"Sweet dreams, Onelle Te'Legra Agnar," Jegra said, relieved to have found someone she could trust in the back waters of an uncharted and overtly hostile planet.

Jegra chuckled lightly and then let herself drift off to sleep. Onelle studied the empress's face, dwelling on her features for a while and, then, for the first time in what seemed like ages, fell asleep with the comfort of a warm body next to her.

16

A luminous flash erupted instantaneously out of nothingness. In the blink of an eye, the *Shard* had manifested in the Galliforn system, home to the mighty Galliforn. This ancient race of highly advanced satyr beings had ventured into the stars and colonized three worlds: Qu'Mar, Veridion, and their homeworld, Galliforn.

These majestic worlds, along with their seven inhabitable moons, although not a part of the Commonwealth alliance, comprised the strongest independent united planetary system in charted space.

Unlike the Seyferrans, Nyctans, and Dagons, however, the satyr people of Galliforn kept primarily to themselves. Much like the Dragonian lizard race, they were highly wary of outsiders. Unlike the Dragonians, however, Emperor Dakroth's father, Loki'Alloran Rhadamanthus Dakroth the Third, had failed in his attempt to conquer their noble race.

A never-ending sore spot for Dagon pride, the satyrs proved too cunning in their military strategy and too advanced in their technology to be so easily conquered.

Even so, the previous emperor's campaigns had forced the satyr race to retreat from the territories of the Commonwealth, most of which was under the control of the Dagon Empire. And in the aftermath of the Loki'Alloran Dakroth's unlawful campaigns against Galliforn, the satyrs took extra measures to safeguard their worlds from future attack, creating a vast orbital defense grid.

All three planets were protected by automated orbital platforms equipped with high-power laser cannons capable of shooting down most vessels that dared to intrude upon their system without welcome. If you didn't have the proper authorization or access codes, the platforms would open fire and blow you clean out of the system.

Captain Lianica Blackstar clasped both hands behind her back and looked out at the painterly swaths of orange and green nebulae that made up much of the system. An orange alert chimed and began flashing on all visible monitors and view portals.

"Report," she said, her voice rough from another long night of binge-drinking.

One of her bridge officers turned toward his captain with a nervous look and informed her, "Ma'am, the Galliforn Space Defense Front is requesting orbital access codes. We have three minutes and thirty seconds to comply or the orbital defense grid will open fire."

There was a long silence in which the crew grew rather tense and shared uncertain looks as Lianica contemplated her best course of action. "Hold position," she finally said.

"Ma'am, at current we are not armed with any offensive capabilities, nor are we in possession of the access codes. The orbital defense platforms will open fire on us in two minutes and sixty-eight seconds."

"This ship is designed to deflect a heavy laser canon from a Dreadnaught class Dagon battlecruiser. Those orbital defense platforms only yield a fraction of that kind of power. Unless they have hyper-sonic Viper class missiles, they're no threat to us. Their lasers will simply deflect off this ship like rain gliding off treated glass."

"Yes, ma'am," the officer replied in a hesitant tone. Not wanting to cause any further trouble, he acquiesced and followed her orders regardless of how reckless they seemed.

In the middle of explaining herself, the bridge doors whisked open and shut again, briefly distracting the captain and making her irritated. Lieutenant Brei'Alas, keeping her head down and eyes to the floor, scuttled up to her post.

Without so much as looking over at the girl, Captain Blackstar chastised her in a low tone. "You're late, Lieutenant Brei'Alas. Don't let it happen again."

The young woman clicked her heels together and stood at attention. "It won't, ma'am." In her zest, she had practically yelled the words without meaning to. Taking a quieter approach, she humbly added, "You have my word."

Lianica gave the girl a judgmental look, the dark rings under her eyes adding to the ominous nature of her gaze, and then said in a cool voice, "I should hope so."

With a wave of her hand, Lianica gestured for the lieutenant to return to her post manning the science monitoring station. As science officer, Brei'Alas would be vital in giving her a minute by minute update on what was transpiring outside.

The young lieutenant let out a deep sigh when she was let off the hook so easily and, not wasting another moment, rushed to her post as ordered. Catching herself up on the events currently in progress, she glanced at the monitors and, then, looked up in alarm.

"Ma'am," she said, clearing her throat, "seven orbital defense platforms have come online and are training their laser cannons on the *Shard*."

"Thank you, lieutenant," Lianica answered curtly. "I'm well aware of the situation."

"Yes. Of course, ma'am. Apologies." Brei'Alas tried to choke down her embarrassment and went back to monitoring the orbital platforms as ordered.

Right on time, as the countdown hit zero, the orbital defense platforms all opened fire. The cannons flashed with brief pulses of red laser discharges. Each blast lasted no more than two or three seconds. Once the cannons had all fired their initial volley, they gradually cooled and began to recharge.

Although the ship had barely shuddered at the blasts, deflected by the *Shard's* hyper-polished korridium alloy hull that glistened like a silver tear drop, Lianica demanded a damage report, nonetheless. It was always better to be safe than to be sorry.

"Zero damage to the hull, ma'am," Brei'Alas said, swiping through the readout of her console's green glowing holographic display panel. "Structural integrity is holding at maximum. Magnetic shielding within normal parameters. All fusion cores are online and remain unaffected by the low-yield lasers."

"Good," Lianica answered calmly. "Let them fire another round, and once the orbital platforms begin their recharging sequence, take us in past the defense network."

"But Captain," Brei'Alas began, genuinely confused, "that would take us into the Galliforn atmosphere," she said, shooting the captain a timid glance.

"That's right," Captain Blackstar replied without any further explanation on her part. She wasn't in the habit of publicly announcing every little detail of her strategy to the whole crew.

"Yes, ma'am," Lieutenant Brei'Alas replied. Diverting her eyes and looking out the forward portal, she watched the green and blue planet come onto the main viewscreen. A marbled overlay of white clouds slowly wafted over the greenish-brown continents of the fertile planet while a typhoon was forming in the lower southwestern hemisphere.

After a moment of intense silence, Lianica let out a disgruntled sigh. "I can practically hear you thinking, lieutenant," she said, puffing out a blast of air that jostled a few strands of her hair that had escaped her extremely tight ponytail. "Do you have something to add?"

"Permission to speak freely, ma'am."

"By all means," Lianica said, waving her hand impatiently as if to say get on with it.

"The Galliforns will consider this an invasive act by the Dagon Empire. It seems an unnecessary way of provoking their attention. One that may potentially cause more harm than good."

"Do you have a better idea, lieutenant?"

"Instead of adding fuel to the fire, why don't we just contact them?"

"As you are well aware, Lieutenant Brei'Alas, the Galliforn people do not respond to uninvited guests. Our hails will only land on deaf ears."

"I didn't mean we…" her voice trailed off as she cut her words short in order to reformulate what she wanted to communicate. "What I meant to say is, instead of hailing them directly, we make them come to us."

Lianica raised an eyebrow. "How so?"

"We issue a distress call and ask for their help. After all, that's actually why we're here in the first place, is it not? To solicit the Galliforn people's assistance in locating Empress Alakandra?"

"Indeed, it is. We need access to their long-distance hyperspace relay network to secure all possible jump coordinates in this system if we're going to have any chance of rescuing the empress."

Lieutenant Commander Barrion, a physically fit Dagon officer with a chiseled jawline who'd remained quiet until now, interjected, "But the moment they realize we're not in any true need of assistance, they'll consider it a trap."

"Not if we're up front with our intentions," Brei'Alas quickly added, making sure to tack on a deferential, "ma'am," at the end.

Captain Lianica Blackstar looked to Barrion, sending him an appreciative nod for pitching in and then turned back to Brei'Alas and gave the girl a contemplative look. Lianica turned back toward the view portal and looked out at the planet coming into view. Galliforn.

She wasn't wrong. Stoking the flames of the already unbearable tension between the Dagon Empire and Galliforn was a risky gambit. No doubt a gentler touch was required.

And Lieutenant Brei'Alas's plan might just be the best way to establish a dialogue without all the puffed-up chests and unnecessary genital wagging that inevitably follows such aggressive stances, Lianica thought.

"All right, lieutenant. Have it your way. Issue an S.O.S. But if this plan should fail, I will hold you personally responsible and dole out the fifty lashes myself."

"Yes, ma'am!" Brei'Alas said, an unabashed smile spreading across her Prussian blue lips. She stole a quick glance at Lt. Commander Barrion and stuck out her pink tongue at him. He just grinned and swiveled around in his chair, ignoring her schoolgirl antics.

Not that her little flirtatious jest was much of a snub, since Barrion and she were currently enjoying a secret tryst. She'd be sure to let him ravish her later. Right now, though, she merely wanted to make her captain proud.

"Are we good, lieutenant?"

As an amber alert echoed throughout the ship, she turned to Captain Lianica Blackstar, her grin still plastered on her youthful face. "Emergency distress call sent, ma'am."

Lianica sat back in the captain's chair and looked back out across the glowing vista of distant nebula and the swirling white and blue orb that cut in front of it. She crossed her legs loosely, balancing her right calf on her left knee, and waited for the next orbital defense platform circling high above the planet to come into view.

Fully recharged, the defense platforms trained their laser cannons on the *Shard*, readying for a second volley.

The glistening hull of the vessel hung in low orbit. A seemingly innocuous spec of white light hanging in the shadow of a lush and thriving planet. A planet that didn't take kindly to interlopers.

"Now we wait and see," Lianica whispered to herself.

17

It was twilight when Danica awoke to the distant sounds of cheering. Still groggy and uncertain as to where she was, she slowly sat up in a concrete cell and looked around. It appeared she was in some kind of holding cell. But why, or for what purpose, she couldn't guess. Glancing down, she discovered that she had on a tan leather bikini top and matching loincloth and nothing else. A slave's outfit.

To her surprise, her terrible wounds were completely mended, suggesting she'd been out for quite a while. Days, if not longer. In fact, the laser suture had barely left a scar across her lower abdomen where she'd been welded back together.

She ran her fingers over the scar, reflecting on the fact that it was a stark reminder of what she had endured. That it wasn't all just a figment of her imagination, but rather it had happened. All of it.

"Good. You're awake," a soothing voice said.

"Who's there?" Danica asked, scanning the small room. Of course, she was alone. Her eyes fixed themselves on the barred entrance to her cell. She tensed when she saw the outline of a dark figure standing just beyond the light of her room. A figure keeping to the shadows.

Slowly stepping into the light was a curled-horned satyr distinguished only by his burgundy waistcoat and the fancy antique pocket watch which he checked and then neatly tucked back into his breast pocket.

"Do I know you?" Danica asked, swinging her legs over the edge of the concrete slab that was her bed and eyeing the satyr suspiciously.

"No, my dear. But I know everything about you. The Great Vice Admiral Cassera Van Danica Amelorak. High ranking officer turned traitor turned freedom fighter."

"That was by necessity…not choice," she added sternly, making sure the satyr knew she was not entirely without honor. She rose to her feet, groaning from the pain, as her stiff body ached and creaked from the left-over effects of her violent trauma.

"I'm sure it was." He grinned at her amusedly, his slatted eyes scanning her up and down.

His undivided attention caused her to grow slightly self-conscious; she wrapped her arms around her mostly naked body.

"How long?"

"How long for what?" he asked, stroking his white beard contemplatively as he tried to guess her meaning.

"How long was I asleep?"

"Ah, yes. Let me see…" He looked up and to the left as he mulled over the amount of time she'd been indisposed. "The Medica on Dagon Prime held you for three months."

Danica gasped. "Three months?"

"Yes, well, I hear they needed to induce a coma. The amount of damage your body had sustained was quite extensive, you see. But the Lord Emperor Dakroth ordered his best doctors to mend you and repair your condition so that you were as good as new."

Unconsciously, Danica ran her finger along the scar where the medical laser had mended her.

"Well, almost as good as new," he added, correcting his prior statement as he watched her trace out the evidence of her old wounds.

"Why am I here?" she asked after a long silence. She gestured at the cell, which looked as though it were part of an ancient dungeon right out of Dagon antiquity.

He cleared his throat and gave her a solemn look. "Because I bought you." He tugged at the bottom of his burgundy vest and waited for her inevitable follow up question.

"Sold, then?"

"Into the gladiatorial games, yes," he said, a sparkle in his bovine eye. "I got an excellent deal too, as nobody wanted a worthless *banjax.*"

"Dakroth," she growled. "That scheming, double-crossing, no good—"

"Let me stop you right there, Danica Valencia," Grendok said, treating her with a certain amount of dignity by calling her by her new name. He glanced to either side cautiously and then slowly turned to face her. "The walls have ears in this place, so I suggest you bite your tongue lest the emperor's spies hear your treasonous slanders."

"I don't care if they hear me," she replied obstinately. She spat at the floor in disgust. "The emperor can burn in Helios for all I care."

"Suit yourself," he said, taking another step closer to the bars. His face was now practically wedged between them as he talked to her.

"Let me ask you something," Danica said, walking up to the bars of her cell and looking down at the short creature. "How much did I go for?"

"Two hundred thousand credits," the satyr answered. His voice was proud. "I won out in a bidding war to acquire the famed insurrectionist."

"Lucky me," she quipped dryly. But she supposed being sold into the gladiatorial games was better than ending up in a brothel for some loathsome space pirates.

"The other one went for much less."

"What other one?" she inquired.

"The red-skin," he answered.

Danica took a step back and began breathing faster. Her heart raced through her chest as it tried to catch up with her thoughts.

"Red skin?" she echoed, her breathing already dangerously shallow and rapid.

"Yes," Grendok grinned. This time he bared his yellow goat teeth and the face he made was downright sinister. "The one they call The Assassin."

"Ishtar Bantu?" Danica whispered to herself. She suddenly found herself petrified. She didn't know how to respond to such information. She was the property of the satyr now, but apparently so was her sworn enemy and torturer. "Why?" she asked, her heart pounding so furiously she was certain it would leap up out of her throat. "Why would you buy us both?"

"My dear Vice Admiral," the satyr said, his mannerisms concise and his tone controlled, "The answer is simple. People will pay good credits to see a revenge bout. The fallen hero versus her vicious rival and tormentor. Two titans of the

Dagon Empire facing off in the arena…it'll be legendary. I'll have you know, tickets have completely sold out since going online just yesterday. Until the event, however, get some rest. You'll need it."

With that he turned and disappeared back into the shadows.

"Wait!" Danica called out, slamming her body into the bars and gripping the metal rungs tightly in her hands. "I beg of you, put me in the arena with anyone else but her. Please!"

But her words faded into the empty tunnel, for the satyr had already left the holding facility.

Danica sank to her knees and tried to catch her breath. Her panic had caused her to grow sickeningly lightheaded and now she sat on the cold concrete, the fearful revelation lingering in her mind.

Another half hour passed when a large Dragonian in leather armor replete with steel-tipped spikes, stepped up to her cage. Pulling out a jangling set of keys, he fished for the right one and then slid it into the keyhole. With a click, Danica's cell door unlocked and slowly swung open.

"It's time," the Dragonian enforcer announced.

Dragonian security was standard throughout the Commonwealth. They were rough, tough, and they loved a good rumble. Most security outfits sought them out and placed them as enforcers, guards, and hired muscle throughout the seven systems. In fact, the common folk had a saying: The only thing more certain than the treachery of the Dagon Empire was the likelihood of finding a Dragonian fork-tongue at a security checkpoint.

"Get up!" the Dragonian hissed impatiently, entering Danica's cell and scooping her up by her right arm.

"Unhand me, fork-tongue!" she growled, eyeing the lizard with contempt. He ignored her sharp looks and shoved her out of the cell and into the dimly lit corridor. "Do you know who I am?" she said, intending it more of a statement about her race's class than who she was personally. Neither seemed to impress the Dragonians much.

"Yeah, I do," he said, a faint smile forming on his narrow lips. "You're a blue skin slave about to die in the arena." He smiled at her then gave her a fearsome shove forward.

Danica stumbled toward the entrance and then swatted his hands away from her, which had been slowly easing up to give her another push.

"Move it," he grumbled. His voice was course, like the crunch of gravel under heavy footsteps. Of course, his commands were met with a sharp glance over the shoulder and a scowl from Danica, but it did little to deter him and he gave her another strong push forward.

"Fine!" she said, raising her hands. "I'm going."

Stepping up to the opening that led into the arena, the Dragonian placed his massive clawed hand on her shoulder. She looked up, ready to chastise him for mishandling a Dagon woman of high pedigree, when she noticed a strange calm settle over his features. When he spoke, he wasn't even looking at her. His voice was smooth and calm and his eyes were transfixed on the center of the arena sands.

"Good luck, Vice Admiral. There are many of us rooting for you."

Whatever she was about to say, along with the rage that quickly boiled to the surface, swiftly evaporated away. She bit her lower lip in deliberation. She wasn't quite sure of what else to say, but she knew her situation was more complicated than it had first appeared. "Thanks," she finally added as he gave her a gentle nudge forward, letting her know it was time.

Danica looked back over her shoulder at him as she stepped out into the sunbaked sands of the amphitheater. He merely nodded, as if to impart a vote of confidence in her.

The roar of the audience erupted all around her as she emerged from the corridor and into the stadium. At the same time, the announcer's voice acknowledged her arrival and several televid drones swooped down, their red, insectoid eyes zooming in and out as they focused in on her.

Danica raised her hand, blotting out the brilliant sun above. First, the throng came into view and then the giant blue and green orb hanging over her. Dagon.

There was no doubt about it, she was on Thessalonica. Arena City, no less. The same city Jegra had risen to fame in and had become the empress of. Now, she was destined to fight as a gladiatrix in the very same arena that Jegra had. And, for the first time in a long while, she felt a newfound respect for Jegra. Because the truth was, Danica was terrified. Whereas, Jegra, it had seemed, reveled in the glory of each bout.

A young Dagon lad wearing only a toga and leather sandals raced out onto the field carrying a wooden shield and a spear. He handed it off to Danica and then raced back off the field just as fast as he'd come onto it.

Danica, holding the tools in either hand, looked up at the emperor's personal viewing booth only to find it empty. *Typical*, she thought. She wasn't even important enough to him for him to come watch her death.

And even though she was expecting it, she still seized with fear when she heard the announcer speak that hideous name.

"Ladies and germs from all corners of the Commonwealth! I am pleased to announce the Vice Admiral's one and only foe–the vicious, blood lusting, red-skinned assassin…Ishtar Bantu!"

The crowd erupted with applause and screams of elation. One woman's squeal was so piercing it cut through the white noise and made it to Danica's ears, causing her to cringe. She looked over in time to see a topless Bre'lal woman swoon and faint. Nobody seemed to care though, as they let her fall at their feet while they all continued cheering for Ishtar Bantu.

Danica spun around, gazing at the exit she'd just come out of, only to find two Dragonian lizard guards, wearing their trademark red and black IGS armor, watching her from afar. She frowned, realizing she wouldn't be getting out of this any time soon, and then turned back again only to find Ishtar Bantu standing fifty meters off, staring at her with a sinister look on her face.

Her left arm was a slightly paler red than the rest of her body, suggesting she had it replaced with a synthetic. A thin, purplish scar, where her shoulder met her sternum, was evidence of the procedure. As the new skin of the synthetic arm grew thicker, it would eventually darken to match the surrounding color, since synthetic parts were always grown from one's own stem cells.

The young boy raced out and handed Ishtar two scimitar blades and then disappeared again. Once he was gone, she held the swords high above her and crossed them over her head. The crowd went wild.

Ishtar was wearing an armor-plated leather bikini, not so dissimilar from the kind Jegra was fond of wearing. She sauntered over to where Danica stood.

"Did you miss me?" Ishtar asked, shooting Danica a wink and a taunting kiss.

Danica realized she was trembling and her nostrils flaring with rage, gripped her shield and spear tightly in her hands, clamping down on her jittery nerves.

"Spare me the small talk, assassin. Let's just get this over with."

Ishtar smiled and then cracked her neck. She hopped a few times, pumping blood into her meaty thighs, and then rotated her shoulders and stretched each arm behind her back as she limbered herself up.

Danica just stood poised, trying her best to hold it together. In her current condition, she was no match for Ishtar. In fact, she was positive the woman would make quick work of her. Most likely carve her up like one of Jegra's famed roasted beef turkey things she was so fond of reminiscing about.

Before the bout could begin, though, the announcer unexpectedly made a surprise announcement.

"Ladies and gentlemen, this just in. Today's revenge bout has been changed."

A flurry of boos and hisses made their way down the rows of the disappointed throng.

"Hear me out!" the announcer cried out over the din. "This revenge battle has turned into a survival match. In order to live to fight another day, mortal enemies must team up to face a powerful enemy."

"Wait, what?" Ishtar said, lowering her blades as she turned to the announcer's booth, a look of bewilderment settling across her face.

"You're shitting on me," Danica said, trying to use one of Jegra's phrases she'd heard her say a thousand times before but feeling, somehow, she hadn't quite gotten it right. She shrugged it off and looked up at the televid drone that buzzed noisily above their heads. Its myriad of cameras zoomed in on their terrified faces, plastering their dread across millions of televid monitors in every system from here to the Outer Rim of the Empire.

Ishtar shot Danica a disgusted and slightly perplexed look out of the corner of her eye, but for the most part did her best to ignore her.

The thunderous clank and rumble of the heavy gate being ratcheted upward filled their ears and they turned, along with several televid drones, toward the monster's pen. They watched in silence as the steel toothed portcullis slowly climbed upward revealing a dark, gaping hole filled with unfathomable terrors.

Emerging from the dark holding cell came a massive insect-like machine with six legs, and a full battery of weapons, including a saw blade arm attachment, and a shoulder mounted laser canon. Alongside this armament was a Heliosfire missiles mount, each containing five hundred micro-darts equipped with high yield explosives. Upon recognizing the machine, the pits of their stomachs sank;

a sense of dread slowly coiled around each of them, making their chests grow tight and their breathing difficult as it seized them.

It was a Seyferrian Centurion. A deadly war robot designed to kill any living thing standing in its path. A war machine that had long since been outlawed, and which was banned and ordered dismantled after the joint peace treaty between the Seyferrian Republic and the Dagon Empire was signed.

"I thought those things had all been destroyed," Ishtar said under her breath.

"Apparently, not," Danica muttered in response.

They hadn't ever faced off against one of the machines themselves, seeing as they'd been decommissioned more than six hundred years ago, but they'd both seen the war footage during their school and military training. Entire battalions of Dagon soldiers, the fiercest warriors in the galaxy, single-handedly obliterated by just one of these machines. It was because of this advanced and undefeatable technology that Emperor Loki'Alloran Dakroth had agreed to the peace accords. The ferocity of this machine had given rise to the Commonwealth, and led to an era of never before seen peace among the alien worlds brought into the fold by two great warring empires.

And although tensions continued to run high, and there was a general distrust amongst most species of anything outside their own race, it was the first time in history that the galaxy had grown stable.

It was the Seyfferian Republic, which held independent treaties with both Nyctan and Dagon Prime, that provided the basis for the Commonwealth and the great trade route. Although three independently governed empires, each realm agreed not to encroach upon the other's territory. Any territorial disputes were to be taken up by the High Council, which resided at Correll, the only neutral planet in the entire Commonwealth.

The war machine buzzed and hummed as it scuttled onto the field. It flared its metal plating and showed off its menacing weaponry, a display that sent the throng of spectators into a frenzy. Its three red eyes, contained beneath an insect-like hood, swiveled around and locked onto the two women standing mere meters away. Its whining buzz grew louder and louder until the sound became unbearable.

Without warning, the painful sound ceased and the war machine reared up on its hind legs and let out a mechanical growl, its chainsaw buzzing wildly and its metal pinchers opening and clamping shut with bone-crushing force.

Rattled by the startling appearance of a Centurion war machine, both women glanced at each other and then gulped nervously. And as much as they despised one another, the announcer hadn't been wrong. There was no way either of them could single handedly take down a Centurion. Even with all the luck in the world, it was still going to be an uphill battle every step of the way. And that's assuming they figured out how to put their grudges aside and join forces.

If they wanted to come out of this with their tits intact, they'd have to learn how to work together–and fast–or they would both surely pay the ultimate price.

18

"**Take my hand!**" Onelle Te'Legra shouted as she lunged for Jegra. A split second later, she would have missed her chance to rescue the empress completely.

Jegra's fingers brushed Onelle's but came up empty. She quickly flattened her palms and flipped herself onto her back, the soles of her boots scraping as she dug her heels in.

Unable to get a good foothold, slowing down wasn't exactly easy, and as she skidded down the side of the vessel's hull, the edge was careening toward her fast. Beyond that, there was nothing but a thousand foot drop all the way down to the bottom of a very rocky crag.

Time running out, she quickly gauged whether she could leap across the divide and latch on to the distant cliff face, but it was seemingly impossible. This side of the ship was the end that jutted out into open air, and the cliff's edges were too far away to make it in one jump. She'd only end up plummeting to her death.

"Gradack!" Jegra grumbled as she came quickly up to the cusp of the ship. Nearly out of time, she noticed a sharp groove at the edge of the ship that faded into the hull further up. The sharpness of the edge stuck out just enough for her to grip a split second before she slipped over the edge.

Onelle's heart pounded in her chest as she witnessed Jegra disappear over the edge of the ship. Quickly, she loosened her harness and rappelled down to where she saw Jegra go over. Easing up to the ledge, she looked over, dreading the sight of Jegra's body crushed to pulp against the jagged rocks below.

"Just figured I'd hang out here for a while," Jegra jested, looking up at Onelle's panicked face as she hung onto the edge of the ship by one arm. Onelle let out a huge sigh of relief and then bent down and clasped Jegra's forearm with both hands and began to hoist her up.

"Thank the Gilded One you're all right!"

As Onelle pulled her up, Jegra looked down at the unfathomably long drop and the narrowly escaped fate of having to relive another terrible plummet. The first one she had experienced, crashing on the far mountain range, had caused her more than enough pain. Even with her hyper-active healing factor, it had taken her three agonizing days to mend–something she wasn't looking forward to experiencing again anytime soon.

A green sky stretched into the distance above the canopy of rainforest down below. According to the ship's scanners, there were only five oases left on the entire planet. Everything else had burned up in a nuclear fallout roughly a thousand years ago.

With nowhere to go, it was imperative that they got the ship up and running again. And it had taken a little over three months of working together to get it to the point where it could run under its own power. Now, all they had to do was free it from the crevice that it was currently wedged within, which was proving easier said than done.

"You need to be more careful!" Onelle chastised, her heart still racing in her chest and her face turning dark green with frustration.

She wasn't wrong, of course. It was a stupid mistake and one Jegra didn't intend to make again.

Reaching out, Jegra reeled Onelle into her arms and squeezed her tight, picking her up off the ground in the process. "Thanks," she said, "I owe you one."

Barely able to breathe, Onelle wheezed, *"No problem."*

Jegra finally let go of the Bre'lal woman and gently set her back on her feet. Then, she glanced one more time over the edge and shook her head in disbelief at the thought of how narrow her escape had truly been. Turning around, she followed Onelle back up to a more secure section of the ship's outer hull and then raced forward when she saw Onelle sink to her knees.

"Onelle!" Jegra shouted. She raced over to the woman and knelt down beside her, one hand on her shoulder. "Are you all right?"

Out of breath, Onelle fanned herself to keep cool. "After all this excitement, I think maybe we should take a break. Besides, we've been working non-stop since dawn." She then slid off her heels and sat down on the ship. Throwing out an arm, she leaned back and unzipped her yellow laborer's coveralls with the orange-red stripe down the side, exposing her green cleavage.

The cool breeze lapped at her glistening chest, and she took in a deep breath and slowly exhaled. The thought of losing Jegra and being alone again, stranded on this nightmare world, was too much to bear.

"Nice idea," Jegra said, taking a seat next to her. She, too, wore coveralls, but hers were army green with a gray stripe. Copying Onelle's methods of free air conditioning, she, too, unzipped her jumpsuit, but the zipper got jammed up less than halfway as it reached the bulge of her giant chest. "Not again," she lamented, puffing out a blast of air disappointedly.

"Happens a lot does it?" Onelle asked, a thin black eyebrow rising to the top of her forehead. She watched with great amusement as Jegra struggled to get the zipper free.

"More than you could possibly imagine," Jegra lamented, fiddling with the zipper, but it wouldn't budge.

"I can imagine it happens quite a lot, actually."

"Every damn time," Jegra immediately responded.

"Here..." Onelle said, reaching over and taking the zipper in between her index finger and thumb. "Let me try." She gave a vigorous jiggle, then, another. But it was no use. The zipper was beyond stuck. "Maybe if I..." she tried another strategy and gripped the opening near Jegra's neck with one hand and pressed against Jegra's right breast with the palm of her other hand, trying to squeeze the massive boob back into the outfit, perchance to free up some room.

Jegra looked down and just watched Onelle grope and squeeze her in multiple ways as she struggled epically against physics to try and help fix the wardrobe malfunction. Unable to get it to budge, Onelle paused, her hands mid-squeeze, her tongue sticking out of the corner of her mouth in deep concentration, as she weighed an alternative course of action.

In the midst of deliberating on the situation, however, she suddenly realized what her hands were doing. Her cheeks flushing with embarrassment, she quickly withdrew her hands and apologized. "I'm so sorry," she said, abruptly looking away. All of a sudden, she felt flustered. "I didn't realize I was..."

"Here," Jegra said, grabbing the neckline and tearing it apart as though she were Supergirl ripping open a pristine blouse top in a back alleyway somewhere.

The metal zipper pull flew off from the work clothes and shot out into the air. It pinged vigorously off the hull of the ship and then deflected overboard. Just before it vanished out of sight, it glinted in the dimming sunlight as if winking goodbye, and then it was gone.

Jegra stood up and tied the coveralls around her waist, her bikini clad top finally free of its oppressive confinement.

She reached down and offered a hand to Onelle who smiled up at her and took it. Helping her to her feet, Jegra said, "I'll finish fastening the vines and then we can hoist the ship onto the grooves we carved into the rockface."

"I'll double check the rollers we welded to the hull to make sure they're all in working order. With any luck, we'll get off this sorry excuse for a planet sometime tomorrow afternoon."

A series of faint pops sounded as Jegra arched her back and cracked her spine. She then turned, hands on her hips, and looked out at the setting sun. Even though this barren planet was a veritable death trap, it sure did present a beautiful sunset.

Onelle drew up beside Jegra and watched it along with her. After another moment, she finally said, "Come, we'd better finish up before we lose the light."

Jegra nodded then fetched the nearest vine and began threading it through a series of already linked vines which she then proceeded to tie off. At the same time, Onelle ran her final checks on the rollers which would, if their measurements were correct, allow the hull to settle onto the grooves they'd carved into the cliff. Momentum would then drop the ship at a forty-five-degree angle before curving back up and launching the vessel into the air at the precise trajectory then all they had to do was ignite a thruster burn and hightail it off this accursed rock.

Of course, the ship only had enough thruster fuel to get one pass at it. So, should they be off by even one micron in their calculations, they'd be doomed to die and rot on this miserable planet.

"There," Jegra said, dusting off her hands and standing upright. She'd completed tying the harness to the shuttle and fastened it to the pulley system that they'd rigged up. They used giant bamboo stalks, as thick as her body, and massive vines to hold everything together.

The shuttle craft was about the size of a large fishing trawler, eighty feet long and half as wide. The vines were thick enough and strong enough to lift twice that weight. And the alien stalk was like bamboo on steroids. Back on earth, bamboo bridges had been known to take the weight of fully loaded lorry trucks. So, really, what it came down to was their engineering skills; success hinged on them.

Jegra hopped off the shuttle and onto the cliff's edge, a length of vine tied around her waist. She then scaled the wall for about thirty feet and pulled herself up onto the bluff. Heading over to a massive boulder on the top of the cliff, she undid the vine and then secured it to the rock.

The vine was tethered to a larger strand of woven vines which formed a kind of knitted elastic. This elastic quality was vital in ensuring the vines didn't just snap with the weight or force of the tension. They only had one boulder to use, after all, and there was no other way to hoist a rock that size up to the top of a thousand-foot cliff.

It just happened to be serendipity that Onelle, having trained as a professional courtesan, knew how to weave as well as she did. With Jegra's help, they'd spent the nights weaving and talking and getting to know one another. And over the course of three months, their friendship had blossomed. Which was why when she heard Onelle's footsteps approaching from behind, she was utterly shocked to turn and find a blaster pointed at her.

"I'm afraid this is where we part ways, empress," Onelle said, her eyelids hanging heavy as she gazed at Jegra with nothing but malice.

Jegra laughed, thinking Onelle was having her on, then grew deathly silent when it became clear to her that it was no joke. "Et tu, Brute?" Jegra said, her face growing stern.

Onelle raised an eyebrow. "I don't know that language," she informed.

"It's an ancient saying from my world. There's a story about a great leader who was betrayed by one of his most trusted friends and advisers. After being stabbed in the back by a lethal dagger, he turns to find the one he had trusted most had murdered him."

Onelle shrugged. "The problem is, Your Majesty," she snarled. "It was because of you my sister threw away her life. It was because of you she got tangled up in the emperor's twisted scheming. And it was because of your inability to rein in your emotional feelings for her that in his jealousy, Dakroth sent his assassin to slay Abethca. I'm afraid, Jegra Alakandra, this is goodbye. Who knows?" she shrugged before continuing on. "Maybe in a decade or two I'll come check on you. See how you're doing."

"Revenge, then? That's it?"

"What?" Onelle scoffed. "Were you expecting a more civil send off? Sorry, to disappoint, empress. But I got from you want I needed. Your brawn and strength. Too bad you're not half as smart as you are strong."

Jegra had to think about that last insult for a moment. Then she shook her head. "It is too bad."

"What is?" Onelle asked, confused by the vagueness of Jegra's response.

"I was going to help you kill Lord Emperor Dakroth. Now, you're all on your own."

"Oh, I guarantee you I'm not alone. Who do you think hired those bounty hunters that caught up with you at Mardok?"

"But..." Jegra announced, confused, "they said that the Nyctans had hired them."

"I instructed them to say as much. As long as Dakroth thought that the Nyctans were actively hunting him, then he'd react just the way I expected he would. By using you to save his neck and then lead me right to his secret shipyard."

"Let me guess," Jegra said, taking a cautious step toward Onelle. "You didn't cross paths with Ishtar Bantu on a mundane return trip home. You stuck your nose where it didn't belong and he sicked his dog on you."

"Very good, Your Majesty," she quipped sarcastically.

"I found where he was building his fleet and I decided to cripple him. I was midway through planting the explosives when his pet assassin found me."

"You're lucky to still be alive."

"I'm not as innocent as I look. A stun grenade took her down and I made it out alive. However, I only managed to destroy a small section of the facility at Cordova. But, you know, you count your blessings."

"This whole time you were playing his mistrust of the Nyctans against him."

"Of course, I was. Dakroth is a fool. All he cares about is power and prestige. And the might of the Nyctan Empire threatens that. Once I'm off this rock, I'll be able to finish what I started."

"That's all fine and well," Jegra said, rubbing her chin inquisitively. "But aren't you forgetting something?"

"Like what?"

"Like who's going to push this rock off the cliff." She eyed Onelle's petite frame as if to suggest it wasn't likely that the compact Bre'lal woman had the necessary strength to accomplish the feat.

Onelle grinned and pulled out a small remote control. She then aimed it toward an unassuming patch of smooth rock on the top of the bluff and hit the button. The air wavered like a mirage, and suddenly a large container appeared.

"On one of our salvage hunts, I found this." She tapped the button again and with a few flashing lights and a mechanical click, the crate automatically opened. Inside was Jegra's Knight armor.

"That's my power armor," Jegra said, taking another step closer.

Onelle stiffened and trained the blaster on Jegra and shot her a look that warned her not even to try it. "I think you mean *my* power armor," she corrected. "I decided it was probably best to keep my discovery a secret until I had a use for it. Now, as you can clearly see, I have a use for it. What I no longer have a use for is you, empress."

The blaster fixed on Jegra, Onelle began to squeeze down on the trigger.

Jegra's fighting demeanor came on and took her over as if by instinct. She dug her toe into the rough dirt and shot a spray of sand and pebbles into the air, momentarily blinding Onelle.

Without pausing for Onelle to react, Jegra made a mad dash toward the edge of the cliff. Some of the rigging extended beyond the cliff's edge and she took a desperate leap, reaching out for a loose vine.

The instant she leapt into the air, a blast scorched her right shoulder. She screamed out as she felt her flesh sizzle and blacken just as her hands made contact with the vine. Gripping tight, she swung out and back around. A second blast severed the vine and she began to plummet towards the cliff's edge. Luckily, her momentum flung her across the gulf.

Jegra clenched her jaw as she smashed into the rockface about fifty feet below the bluff's edge. Gripping tight to the contours, she stuck the landing. But her impact was forceful; pieces of rock broke off and she began to fall, skidding roughly down the surface. About another fifty feet, she managed to clasp onto a large fragment of rock jutting out from the side of the cliff.

Dangling in the air, she clutched the overhang by one arm and looked up to see Onelle peering over the ledge at her. The green skinned woman aimed her blaster downward and let off several shots.

Jegra cringed, her eyes squinting shut, as she fully expected the laser bolts to hit her. Being under the overhang, however, provided enough protection to safeguard her from the blasts. A couple of shots impacted the rock but did little damage while several other shots just buzzed by her.

Opening her eyes, Jegra looked around and let out a big sigh of relief when she realized the shots had missed their mark. She reached up with her other arm, gripped the overhang with both hands, and then started to swing. Once she had her momentum going, she swung her feet up toward a fissure in the rockface.

Although it was difficult, she managed to wedge her left foot into a crack in the cliffside. With a grunt, she pulled herself toward the wall and rested there for a moment.

There was no way that Jegra would be able to climb the hundred odd feet back up to the top of the cliff before Onelle suited up and kicked the boulder free. Looking down, Jegra ran through every possible action; none of them ended with her getting off this rock.

Stuck on the side of a cliff, betrayed by someone she thought was her friend, she let out an annoyed huff. That's when she heard the cry of the pteranodon and looked down to see the winged dinosaur circling about a hundred feet below.

"Not you again," she lamented. But even as she gazed apprehensively down at the winged lizard, an idea came to her. An idea that might just allow her to get off this godforsaken rock after all.

19

The fighters of the Galliforn Space Defense Front thronged the *Shard* like a swarm of killer bees. The long cylindrical vessels had ram-shaped bows; their curling horns wrapping around and flowing into the robust architecture of the vessels gave them a distinctly phallic appearance.

Aboard the command deck of the *Shard*, Captain Lianica Blackstar tensed, arms clasped tightly behind her back, as she waited for a response from the Galliforn fleet leader. After what seemed an unnecessarily long time, the comm system crackled and the communiqué came through.

"You're in restricted space," a gruff voice came from the other end. "You have precisely sixty seconds to explain yourself."

"This is Empress Alakandra's personal cruiser and we are in need of your assistance."

The other end went silent for a moment and Lianica watched from over Lieutenant Brei'Alas's shoulder as the numbers of the digital clockface on the lieutenant's console incrementally ticked down.

When it came down to the last five seconds, Brei'Alas looked up at the captain and shot her a panicked look. If this didn't work, it'd be her head on a platter. Then the clock struck zero. A hush fell over the bridge, and after another few moments of uncertainty, the comm crackled, startling Brei'Alas.

The same gruff voice as before grumbled, "What seems to be the problem?"

Brei'Alas let out a pent-up sigh and whispered, "See, I told you it'd work."

Lianica nodded approvingly, and then shook her arms and wiggled her fingers to loosen up and help relieve the tension she'd built in anticipation. Once she got her blood flowing again, she replied to the leader of the Galliforn fighter squad. "I feel it's my duty to be up front with the Galliforn High Command. Although our ship is in working condition, we're a bit rudderless at the moment, so to speak."

Another long paused seemed to signify he was relaying orders directly to his superiors before responding. But, eventually, the disgruntled voice returned. "Explain what you mean."

"We're headed to the rift that verges on the Outer Rim, an area known only as Dark Space. I'm afraid we do not have an up to date navigation chart for this region, and since we're on a rescue mission and we are in desperate need of your noble assistance, I thought maybe, if you would be so inclined, you might—"

"Denied," the voice abruptly replied, cutting her off before she had finished making the request.

Shocked by the abrupt dismissal, Lianica looked out across the faces of the bridge crew and then back at the display of fighters taking formation outside. "Then, may we at least—"

"No," the voice barked before she had even finished the question. Then there was a static crackle as the comm was cut and all communications were promptly severed.

Lianica huffed in annoyance but reined in her temper. She opened her mouth to try another approach when a warning shot flashed and the ship rattled.

The comm channel opened up again and the lead fighter announced, "You have exactly one hour to make your repairs and leave the system. If you do not leave Galliforn space once the allotted time is up, we will destroy your vessel."

With that, the small swarm of ships pulled back, giving the *Shard* some breathing room.

"So much for diplomacy," Lianica mumbled to herself.

"Captain," Brei'Alas finally spoke, taking a little bit longer than usual to build up her nerve to address the captain. "What are your orders, ma'am?"

Lianica thought about it for several moments and then said, "Spool up the slipstream drive. They may deny us access to their hyperspace navigation charts, but I guarantee you they don't have a ship in their fleet faster than this one."

"Ma'am, if we cut through their system blind, we could risk colliding with a cargo vessel, a heavy cruiser, or an asteroid field in hyperspace transit. The *Shard* is tough, but not tough enough to survive a head on collision with objects of that density," Lt. Commander Barrion informed his captain. Lianica nodded and paced the floor as she mulled over the new information.

As the highest-ranking officer on the bridge after the captain, it was his duty to provide the captain with alternative options. He looked over at Brei'Alas who seemed to have garnered the confidence of the captain with her quick thinking and quirky, albeit enduring, personality.

Never mind her tepid demeanor and diminutive voice, a trait not so common among the Dagon people, who prided themselves in posturing and word games, demonstrating their dominance in any given occasion. Brei'Alas was different.

But Lt. Commander Barrion knew one thing, her way wasn't to be confused with weakness. She was anything but weak. She was bold and assertive herself, even if it took her a few minutes to build up to it. And she never gave up. That was what made him so attracted to her.

"That's a risk I'm willing to take," Lianica finally said, stopping in her tracks. Noticing the expressions on the faces of the crew, she cleared her throat and added, "Need I remind you that the empress's life is at stake?"

Brei'Alas shook her head. "No, ma'am," she replied almost by habit. "We're with you. One-hundred percent. Besides, the odds of a collision are astronomical. Right?" She turned to Barrion for support.

He cleared his throat. "Uh, right. Astronomical."

Brei'Alas's reassurance did little to assuage the hesitancy of the crew making a blind jump through Galliforn space. But when she caught the captain smiling at her and giving her a single nod of gratitude, her entire soul filled to the brim with happiness.

They had two options. Make many short jumps, using long-range scanners to map the sector themselves, always knowing that the Galliforn armada would be hunting them, or they could just take the risk of traveling blind.

Neither option was optimal, but Lianica knew the sector was desolate enough that long range scans hadn't shown any signs of star-faring species. As such, flying blind should, technically, be no problem.

At the same time, however, there was the off chance that they could bounce into an asteroid belt or get too close to a super-nova, and that'd end their trip real quick.

"Set course to the Outer Rim," Lianica ordered, finally having made up her mind. "Maximum speed."

"Yes, ma'am," the navigations officer called out, and he carried out his order. Once he typed in the coordinates, he let the computer crunch the numbers and then nodded, giving her the okay.

"Engage slipstream drive."

A loud reverberation sounded, like a massive hydro-electric coil running down, and then the ship gradually stretched and time slowed. The silver vessel went from the shape of an elongated raindrop to the shape of a needle and, then, in a flash of light it vanished from space.

The sudden disappearance of the gleaming vessel sent the Galliforn fighters scrambling about as they took evasive action, half expecting a new cloaking technology or some other classified weapon. By the time they realized what had happened, it was too late.

The *Shard* was not only gone, but was tearing through Galliforn space at three times the speed of light. And it was, most certainly, faster than any ship currently in the Commonwealth could go. All but for, perhaps, the *Skywend,* of which the specs were classified.

Although the faint possibility of a collision weighed on her mind, it wasn't enough to deter her from the mission.

Lianica knew from her training at the Academy that if a ship collided with something in hyperspace, it would merely result in falling out of hyperspace as a collection of fiery wreckage.

But traveling through the Stream, as they called it, was like becoming a supercharged particle in a particle accelerator. A collision in the Stream with something traveling at roughly the same speed and energy, or that had an immense density, would ultimately yield enough explosive energy to collapse space and form a black hole. Not exactly an ideal way to go out, albeit painless, but, also so unlikely as to be virtually impossible. At least, that was the gamble, at any rate.

Anything else that got in their path, small fragments, rogue meteors, derelict ships and the like would be vaporized with minimal damage to the vessel. With the new self-healing microphase korridium hull, the *Shard* could quite literally brush up against a small moon and come out the other side unscathed.

The moon, however, would be pulverized. It'd be like firing a rail gun through a watermelon. There'd be very little left except a sticky pink residue creating one massive mess.

The interesting thing about slipstream technology was that it was so aptly named. The Stream naturally flowed around high-density objects, so, planets, stars, black holes and yes, even large moons could be easily avoided. Any massive gravity wells were automatically diverted.

It was like water slipping past a large rock in a creek. As such, colliding with any heavy celestial bodies was highly unlikely. And colliding with large asteroids or ships was even less likely still, simply due to the vast distances in space.

If the *Shard* really were the size of a needle, it would be like flying the needle through the whole of the ocean without hitting a single plankton. Meanwhile, large fish like sharks, giant squids, and whales were avoided simply by their mass.

Everything else could potentially get in their way. But then again, they weren't traversing the whole of the intergalactic medium. They were merely navigating a small part of it, making it even more unlikely that they'd collide with anything at all.

In the end, Lianica figured if she steered clear of any of Galliforn's main worlds and populated moons, they'd be safe. If she was wrong, then so be it. But whenever her gut instinct and statistical data aligned, she knew the risk was nominal. And what she knew now was that they would make it to the Outer Rim in just a matter of hours. Jegra's life depended on it.

Three hours later, as Brei'Alas finished her shift for the day, she waited in the lift for Barrion. When the captain stepped in instead of her lover, her giddiness immediately faded and she stepped to the side. "Captain."

"Lieutenant."

As the lift started, they tried not to look at each other but eventually caved in and gave one another glances. Catching a look simultaneously, they both looked away again, embarrassed.

"I just wanted to say, good work today," Captain Blackstar said.

Brei'Alas smiled. "Thank you, ma'am."

The awkward silence returned and they rode in tense quiet until the lift finally lurched to a halt and the doors opened.

"Well, this is me," Brei'Alas informed Lianica.

Lianica merely nodded and made room for Brei'Alas to step off comfortably. Just as the doors began to shut, Brei'Alas turned to say something, but it was too late.

"Never mind," she murmured to herself as the doors clamped shut before her.

Turning back around, she headed to the rec-lounge where she found Barrion waiting for her. He had already ordered dinner and drinks. Blue Targadian Lobster boiled in saltwater and then saturated with butter, a tossed salad with a nice red wine vinaigrette dressing, and a side of Dagoni honey spread for a basket of freshly baked rolls.

"You remembered!" Brei'Alas said, leaping up into Barrion's arms and kissing him. They quickly pulled away and glanced around the room to see if anyone had seen their little display of affection. Safe, he turned back to her and said, "You bet. Happy Birthday, Brei."

Unable to wait, she sat down and began digging into her meal. Every bite was accompanied by a moan of pleasure. It got to the point that Barrion was forced to put down his utensils and laugh.

"Are you all right?" he asked with a chuckle.

"I'm more than all right. Why do you ask?"

"Because every mouthful sounds like an orgasm," he laughed.

"It's just sooo good," Brei'Alas said, her mouth full of lobster meat.

Desert was chocolate cake with chocolate frosting and Brei'Alas could hardly move. Seeing that she had a smidgeon of frosting on the corner of her mouth, Barrion leaned in and brushed it off onto his thumb. Sucking it off, he smiled at her as she gazed dreamily into his eyes.

"You wanna go back to my room or yours?" she asked.

"Are you sure you want to have sex right now?" he asked. "With the amount you just ate…"

Brei laughed. "What are you afraid of?"

"I'm afraid that cake might pop back out of you in a different configuration."

She laughed. Then, reaching across the table she took his hand, stood up, and towed him behind her. "I guess there's just one way to find out."

As they were leaving the lounge, the doors slid open and Captain Lianica Blackstar entered, went over to the bar, and took a stool.

"This is the third week she's been coming here after her shift."

"So what?" Barrion said. "The captain likes her liquor."

"It's not that. It's just…ever since she handed Danica over to the emperor, she's been wallowing in misery. It's not healthy."

"The captain's a big girl. She can handle it."

"That's the thing," Lianica said, turning back to Barrion. "I don't think she can."

He shrugged, and then, throwing his arm across her shoulder, he walked with her back to her quarters, leaving the captain to be alone at the barstool so she could drown her sorrows in yet another Dragonian ale.

20

Heliosfire missiles exploded in a daisy chain of fiery orange plumes overhead. Extending her hands above her, Danica deflected the barrage with a blue umbrella-shaped energy shield. The rapid succession of explosions was too much for her, though, and the shield quickly faltered under the brunt of the relentless volley. A rush of hot air came swooping into the dissolving energy bubble, picked Danica up off the ground, and tossed her back twenty feet.

The air rushed out of her lungs as she hit the ground hard and tumbled to a stop in the coarse sand. Ignoring the sting of fresh scrapes, she looked up in time to see Ishtar Bantu dart past a weapons rack in time to snatch a korridium spear off it.

A series of miniature missiles exploded behind the red-skinned assassin as she evaded each micro-explosion by running up the side of the arena wall.

Explosions ignited at her heels, and with a vociferous grunt, she kicked off and did a back flip over the series of fiery orange plumes. She landed in a squatting position as debris, including smoldering concrete chunks of the wall, rained down around her. Glancing over her shoulder, she quickly located the Centurion which had shifted its attention onto her.

The machine chased after Ishtar, scuttling across the sands like a menacing scorpion, and quickly pinned her into the corner of the stadium, just beneath the senatorial booth. Her back to the arena wall, she took a defensive position as the scorpion-like machine brought its whirring saw blade down, the buzzing cutter crying out for a taste of her blood.

Almost reflexively, Ishtar managed to block the Centurion's attack with the korridium spear. The machine's saw blade grated into the korridium alloy shaft with an ear ringing squeal, sending up a spray of hot white sparks in the process.

But with her back pinned against the arena wall, and all six of the machine's armored legs dug into the ground for traction, there was no easy way out. And if the blistering spray of white-hot sparks cascading down her body was any indication, unless her rival-cum-teammate, Danica, found a way to get her out of this mess, the Centurion would make quick work of her.

Across the battlefield, Danica bristled at the thought of having to help her captor and tormentor, a woman who had literally put her through a living hell. A woman who didn't deserve the spit from Danica's mouth. But, at the same time, she knew that if she was going to get out of this mess alive, she needed to check her emotions and suck it up.

And as much as she despised Ishtar Bantu, as much as her skin crawled every time she was near her, in this instant, they needed each other. Because, the truth was, Danica wouldn't stand a chance alone against that thing. Let alone whatever else the GGS could think up to throw at her. Hate it or love it, they were stuck together. And that's something she'd just have to live with.

"Gradack!" Danica growled as she pushed herself to her feet. Charging the robot, she formed a half shield, the bulb glowing bright blue as the edges that wrapped part way around her remained jagged, like a cracked egg. Doubling the shield's forward strength for ramming speed, she roared out her most fearsome battle cry and charged full speed ahead.

The machine's triangular head, with three menacing red eyes, swiveled around at the sound of the oncoming threat. Even as it honed in on her, it didn't have time to react. She had gotten the jump on it and smashed into the machine with the full force of her weight.

Upon colliding with it, she instantly expanded her energy bubble so that it expanded outward, like a rapidly rising cake, and along with her forward momentum, forced the robot up onto its hind quarters. It teetered in the air, trying its best to balance itself, and was only overturned when Danica let down her forcefield and slammed into its underbelly with her shoulder.

The robotic scorpion toppled onto its backside, its legs groping aimlessly at the air, its metal body squirming as it tried to flip itself upright and regain its footing.

"Thanks," Ishtar grumbled somewhat reluctantly.

Danica shot her a stern look, as if to reprimand her for her recklessness, and then asked, "Can you fight?"

Ishtar nodded in the affirmative and twirled her staff.

"Good," Danica said, turning back toward the machine which was now jerking like a fish out of water as it tried to flip itself back onto its feet. "Because we're going to need to hit that thing with everything we've got if we're going to have any hope of defeating it."

Almost as soon as she'd finished her little pep talk, the Centurion managed to right itself using its scorpion tail. It scuttled back briefly, re-evaluating the level of threat its opponents posed, fanned its legs, crouching slightly, then reared back up and roared out like a razorback lion of Scallios Prime.

"I'll take out its eyes," Ishtar said, ducking a swipe of the Centurion's protracted saw blade.

At the same time, Danica leapt to the right, curling into a ball mid-air, and then rolled beyond the reach of the pincer arm that came crashing down on her previous position. The metal prongs of the pincers clanked down behind her as she sprang back to her feet. Not waiting for it to lock onto her, she quickly circled around to the back of the hideous machine, keeping it preoccupied with her evasive dance long enough to give Ishtar a chance to mount her offensive.

"I'll try to keep him off balance long enough for you to do that." Danica threw out her palms and released what appeared to be a bunch of small bubbles. Each bubble, was, of course, a small energy sphere piling up like sea foam.

The machine got caught in the stickiness of the multiplying energy bubbles. And even as it helped slow the Centurion down, it wasn't enough to stop it entirely. But Danica didn't need to stop it. Just prevent it from striking them down before they could decommission its sensors.

Ishtar tucked, ducked, and rolled between the machine's front legs and then sprang up directly beneath its chest plating. Thrusting her spear upward with full force, she jammed the pointed tip straight into the red lens of one of the Centurion's eyes.

A crunching of glass fracturing from the blow was heard and Ishtar sprang away, retreating to a safe distance. The Centurion's primary eye exploded with a hiss of sparks, and fragments of red glass crumbled away to reveal the mangled censors inside. The crowd erupted with elated cheers as the machine backed away from Ishtar who, not wanting to lose the offensive, swung her spear wide and raced in for another attack.

The two women continued to dance around the machine, taking turns attacking it, never staying in one place long enough for it to get a good fix on them.

The dizzying pirouette continued until, at last, a window of opportunity presented itself. Striking fast, Danica and Ishtar successfully knocked out another eye in tag-team fashion. Again, the throng of spectators erupted with cheers for the underdogs. But by the third round, the Centurion had analyzed their strategy and, instead of evading, it growled and bull-rushed Ishtar.

With bone crushing force, Ishtar rebounded off the Centurion's metal chassis and crashed onto her back. Stunned, she didn't have time to scurry out of its way before it was already bearing down on top of her. Pinchers clanging, saw blade arm buzzing, it pinned her down with its front legs and growled at her like a wounded beast.

Ishtar threw up her left arm to attempt to block its attack, but screamed out as the jagged metal teeth of the saw blade bit into her flesh.

Thick dabs of dark purple blood along with shreds of red flesh splattered her face and chest as her arm, mid-bicep, flew away from her body.

Ishtar's scream pierced the uproarious cheers of the crowd which grew into an excited frenzy at the sight of freshly spilt blood. The red-skinned assassin, the only one who had consistently seemed to be able to hold her own in a fight, was badly wounded. This would make the remaining bout all the more exciting and the crowd let the contestants know it with their renewed zeal.

Violet blood gushed from her severed limb and, fighting through the shock, she rolled out of the way just in time to avoid another swipe of the saw blade. The teeth dug into the sand, missing their mark, but the machine quickly tore the blade out again and searched for its prey.

The moment she had made it into the clear, her nemesis was right there again—on top of her, blade buzzing, pinchers clanking viciously as it came for her. She screamed out in pain-laced frustration, "Gahhh!" Scurrying backward, her bloody stump gushing blood, she looked up and prepared herself for the impending deathblow of the buzzing saw.

This time the bloodthirsty war machine aimed for Ishtar's neck, hoping to sever her head. And it would have surely decapitated her, too, if it wasn't for the energy shield that abruptly formed around her.

Blue energy rippled as it absorbed the brunt of the attack. The saw blade stopped mere centimeters away from Ishtar's face. She scrambled backward to get away from the threatening robot.

"Leave...her...alone!" Danica roared. Her voice rattled with fury. Then, with all the strength she could muster, she erected a giant energy wall that plowed into the distracted Centurion.

Her energy sphere expanded forcefully so that it propelled the death machine straight into the concrete wall of the arena. There was a loud crunch as the wall fractured and the robot was embedded part way into it, the forcefield crumpling its legs like empty beer cans.

Still shaking with adrenaline, Danica screamed out even louder, her cries rising above those of the roaring crowd. She expanded the energy bubble again, smashing the Centurion further into the wall. The machine's servos groaned against the compressive force of the energy shield, but even so, the machine proved relentless and began clawing at the concrete wall with its mangled limbs, trying to pull itself free.

"No you don't," Danica growled, and with a wave of her hands, the energy bubble popped, an assortment of patchwork fragments hanging in the air momentarily as if caught in slow motion. The tiny fragments solidified into a myriad of raindrop sized energy balls and, with the speed of a machine gun, they shot into the Centurion. Sparks flew as the energy projectiles, as powerful as disruptor blasts, tore into the armored beast.

If that wasn't enough to destroy the Centurion, each of the individual energy pellets, now imbedded inside the machine, dissolved again and began to mend themselves back together like liquid mercury, spreading across the surface of the Centurion, filling in every seam and coating the machine with a uniform glaze of blue glowing energy. Danica held up her open hand and growled, "DIE!"

In a last-minute hail Mary attempt to put the machine out of commission, she used every ounce of remaining energy, clasped her hands into tight fists, and gritted her teeth. The energy bubble instantly contracted, constricting the machine with it, causing it to crumple inward from the added force.

The Centurion squealed like a pig being taken to slaughter and tried to break free, but Danica held on tight. By now her entire body was shaking with adrenaline; the veins in her neck bulged from the physical stress exerted on herself. She screamed one last time and a deafening boom rang out as the machine imploded under the weight of the forcefield.

A flash of blinding light dazed the onlookers and the vid-drones pulled back to avoid the backdraft of the explosion as the Centurion's main power cells ignited. This time an even larger blast followed, blowing everyone's hair back with a rush of hot wind, and smoke flooded the arena floor, engulfing everything in a black haze.

Moments later, emerging from the billowing strands of smoke was a bowling ball sized chunk of metal. The metal ball sparked briefly and then went silent.

A hush fell over the stunned faces of the stadium patrons as events took an unexpected left turn. Even the two-headed serpentine announcer watched on in stunned silence as he grappled with what had just happened.

Never before in the history of the arena had anyone gone up against a Centurion war robot and won. But they'd done it. Ishtar and Danica had actually done it.

It was just as Grendok had foretold. In their moment of peril, two mortal enemies had come together and survived. It was a match for the ages.

An eerie silence permeated the amphitheater as the smoke settled. Barely able to stand, Danica staggered back a step. Her arms limp at her sides, she did her best to gather herself and stand poised. She stood looking up at the countless faces looking down at her, both sharing an equal dismay for the outcome of this bout.

Before the announcer could declare the women as the triumphant victors, however, Danica's eyes rolled back in her head and she collapsed to the ground.

A few feet off to the side of where Danica lay, amid a scattering of carbon fiber and steel wreckage, was the Centurion's last remaining eye. Cables dangled behind the red device, which miraculously survived the implosion. It pulsed with one final angry red flare then faded to black.

Barely able to believe her eyes and still reeling with shock, Ishtar Bantu struggled to her knees and let out a heavy sigh, her head slumping between her shoulders.

Numb from it all, she clutched her bloody appendage and stared out across the hot arena sands at Danica's unconscious body. For the life of her, she couldn't figure out why this woman–a woman whom she had tortured to within an inch of her life, whom she had violated, and who had every reason to despise her–had, against all odds, fought with all her strength to save her life.

Maybe, Ishtar thought, she had misjudged Danica. Maybe beneath that pale blue skin was the makings of a real warrior. Not just a soldier who took orders. But a woman who could defeat any enemy and emerge victorious.

21

The setting sun cast a sickly lime green light across the primordial valley. The lush basin was the only strip of fertile land as far as the eye could see in any direction from Jegra's rocky perch of the eastern cliff face. Everything beyond the small patch of green was a barren wasteland, burnt and decaying.

The harsh electrical storms which came out of the thick green stratus that engulfed the planet never seemed to touch down on the oasis. Jegra guessed it had something to do with the electromagnetic atmosphere of the planet. A naturally occurring protective barrier that gave shelter to the small amount of life that endured on this unforgiving surface.

But, as she had quickly learned after having arrived in this hellhole, natural selection had guaranteed that everything that had endured down here was the fiercest and most dangerous of its kind. Only the fittest could survive the harsh conditions of this inhospitable planet. Everything else was relegated to the food chain for the predators that thrived and preyed on the weaker animals. Which was precisely why she wanted off this rock.

High up on the cliff, far above the green canopy, the wind snarled like a beast and the gathering of charcoal gray stratus that hung so low it seemed as if she could reach up and touch it, crackled with blue tendrils of electricity that curled down from the dark gray clouds like the throbbing veins of some invisible monstrosity. As the cloud front slowly rolled in, she knew the electrical storm would cause too much interference for the shuttle's navigation system and any attempt at takeoff would be compromised.

Thankfully, this approaching storm front worked in Jegra's favor. This way, Onelle would be grounded long enough for Jegra to either talk some sense into her or pound it into her. Either way, she wasn't about to be left behind on this godforsaken rock all alone.

A hot flash of blue lightning seared the nearby rockface, brining all of Jegra's senses into the present. Still clutching the side of the cliff, she turned her face to avoid the spray of sparks that blew her way and looked down to find the pteranodon still circling below.

She only had one chance at this. If she missed, she'd be back to square one and without a ride off this rock. But, if she timed it just right, she would have a fighting chance.

Determined not to be marooned on this hostile world, she took in a deep breath and then, without any further hesitation, kicked off the side of the cliff and entered into a freefall.

Vaporous wisps of fog rushed passed her as she plummeted past the blurred rockface. Cutting through another thin layer of white, the green, scaly back of a pteranodon abruptly manifested beneath her and she crashed landed on its back. Startled by the sudden interloper, the dino-bird squawked noisily and frantically flapped its wings about as it zigged and zagged in a random pattern of course changes. Yet no matter how hard it tried to lose the uninvited rider clinging to its back, it could not shake her.

Jegra held on tight, settling onto the dino-bird like a cowboy settles onto a bucking bronco. "Calm...the frack...down!" she yelled, bringing a pointed elbow down onto the creature's backbone. The dinosaur's spine cracked as her elbow drilled into it hard and the beast reluctantly conceded the struggle and began a more normal rhythm of flight.

"That's more like it," Jegra whispered with a victorious smile curling onto her mouth.

For as much trouble as this bird had been for her from the moment she'd set foot on this barren world, she had decided it could make it all up to her. All it needed to do was get her back to the top of the cliff before Onelle initiated the launch sequence.

Her hands found the elongated crest of the bird's skull and she jerked its head back. It squawked in protest and ignored her tug as it kept to its holding pattern around the cliff. When she did it again, it seemed to catch the hint and rose up a few meters. Jegra repeated this until they broke the cloud cover that hung just off the cliff's edge.

Together, they flew up and over the shuttlecraft wedged between its rocky walls and slowly circled overhead. "Thanks for the lift," Jegra said, scooting up to the edge of the monster's neck.

As they rose higher and higher into the sky, she gauged her trajectory and waited for the precise moment to jump. Deciding it was now or never, she leapt off, falling away like a skydiver entering a freefall.

The beast, finally free of its burden, flapped frantically away as fast as its leathery wings could carry it, putting as much distance between itself and the savage rider as possible. It squawked loudly and shook its bone plated head as it shrank away into the distance.

Onelle was running through the final launch sequence check when out of the blue a shadow blanketed her console. She looked up in time to see a large object crash onto her windshield. She barely had time to flinch; she screamed and drew back as a stress fracture grew out from the impact point on the glass. Looking up, she saw a series of fracture lines leading back to the foreign object that had struck her windshield. Jegra's knee.

"Are you insane?!" she screamed when she realized what had happened. "If you break the glass then neither of us will be getting off this rock!"

"Don't you fucking dare..." Jegra snarled with a flair of her nostrils. She pulled her fist back and smashed the glass. The stress fractures grew a few centimeters more, threatening to crumble under the unrelenting strength of the gladiatrix.

"Stop!" Onelle insisted, throwing up her hands.

"I'll stop when you let me in." Jegra's fist cracked against the glass again. And again the small cobweb-like array of fractures grew outward, inching their way to the furthest ends of the shuttle's windshield.

In the near distance there was a clap of thunder followed by the crackle of the approaching lightning storm. It would be upon them in a matter of minutes. All Jegra needed to do was keep hammering away at the windshield until it either caved in or until Onelle did, forced to give up and let her in.

Jegra slowly raised her fist, ready to strike again, and held it in the air long enough to gaze at Onelle with wild eyes. She smiled, letting Onelle know she wouldn't stop till she got her way and brought down her fist with a final, glass shattering force.

"Wait!" Onelle shrieked at the last possible instant and threw up her hands in surrender.

Jegra's fist stopped a fraction of a centimeter away from the glass and hovered there, every muscle strand in her arm rippling with tension. Glowering at Onelle through the fractured glass, she waited for her response.

"Wait! Just wait a second. I'll let you in," she grudgingly said, flipping a switch and popping the hatch on the roof of the ship.

The hiss of the shuttle's emergency hatch decompressing sounded above her and Jegra looked up to see the square hatch rise up automatically. Looking back down at the woman behind the glass, she slowly rose to her feet and placed both hands on her hips. Although her knuckles were bloodied from smashing them on virtually indestructible glass, she ignored the pain. "That's better," she said.

She strolled up to the opening and looked back over her shoulder at the electrical storm. The dark clouds slowly engulfed the ship; flashes of blue light lit up the dark vapor like giant angry blue fireflies. It was finally here.

Not wasting any more time topside, Jegra quickly slipped through the opening and into the ship. She scrambled down the ladder and pulled the hatch closed behind her. *Just in time, too, by the sounds of it,* she thought. The sound of static discharges crackling and popping as lighting struck the shuttle's hull could be heard up and down the length of the hull. There was no way they were capable of taking off now. Not in this.

"I can explain," Onelle squeaked as Jegra stepped onto the bridge. The Bre'lal woman had on a form-fitting white jumpsuit and was cowering in the corner of the cockpit when Jegra arrived. Hands raised defensively, she could barely force herself to make eye contact. "Just hear me out," she pleaded, stealing a quick glimpse at Jegra to be sure she wasn't going to attack her.

Hands on her hips, Jegra paused in the center of the bridge and growled, "You have thirty seconds to explain yourself or I punch you in your self-serving little cunt so hard that your future children will be born disabled."

Onelle Te'Legra Agnar gulped nervously. "The truth is, there's only enough fuel to get only one of us off this rock. With our combined weight, we'll never break free of this planet's gravity."

"So, your grand idea was to ditch me here and leave me to die? I thought we were becoming friends."

"Let's make one thing clear," Onelle said, straightening up. "You're the woman who got my baby sister killed. And there's no forgiving that."

"I'm not asking you to forgive me," Jegra sighed out in frustration. She strode up to where Onelle stood, wedged between the seat and the console panel. "I'm just asking you give me a chance."

When Jegra reached out toward her, she flinched and cried out in a panicked voice, "What are you going to do?"

The wrenching of steel caused her to open her eyes in time to see Jegra rip the co-pilot's chair right off the floor. The bolts snapped like dry pretzels.

"Exactly what it looks like. I'm going to lighten the load," she answered. Turning around, Jegra went over to the aft of the ship and opened the main loading platform. A gust of wind crashed into her and she staggered back a step. Regaining her footing, she edged up to the lip and looked out at the black wash of clouds that encircled the entire ship.

With a grunt, she tossed the chair out into the violently swirling air and watched it twirl away as though it were sucked up into a cyclone. A streak of lighting followed after it, trailing it down into the cloud cover and Jegra watched as a subdued glow, like a dim lamp, lit up and then faded again, like a firefly flaring briefly before disappearing back into a shroud of darkness.

The loading bay open behind her, Jegra turned around to face Onelle as blue arcs of electricity danced outside like those inside a plasma globe. Jegra's smoldering brown eyes locked onto the Bre'lal woman and her brow grew heavy and sank into a scowl.

"Look, I'm leaving with you whether you like it or not. So you can either just stand there doing nothing or you can help me. Your choice."

Onelle quickly looked around and then found a large crate wedged into a corner. She went over and picked it up, grunting from the unexpected weight of it. Trudging over to the opening, she dropped the crate and watched as its corner nicked the edge of the ship and then spiraled away, spare parts spilling out into the open.

"See, that wasn't so hard," Jegra said, drawing close to Onelle's ear. Onelle pulled back in surprise and gave Jegra a wary look.

"You're not going to throw me out too, are you?'

"It would serve you right," she said, drawing even closer, her brow furrowed as she stared disparagingly at the duplicitous woman. Jegra was beginning to understand Onelle's way of thinking. When it came to revenge, there was no moral high ground. It was a dark and dirty business. And she'd done what she felt had to be done to right a perceived wrong. Only, in Jegra's estimation, Onelle had blamed the wrong woman for her sister's murder.

It wasn't Jegra, after all, who'd killed Abethca. That dishonor fell upon Ishtar Bantu's shoulders. Of course, Onelle wasn't entirely wrong, either. It was Jegra's actions that had somehow made Abethca obsessed with her. But, how was she supposed to have predicted Abethca's unhealthy preoccupation with her and what the consequences of that passion would be? That was entirely out of her control, and it was less than fair for Onelle to hold that against her.

Onelle took a step sideways to avoid stepping out of the opening of the ship and then glanced back up at Jegra's eyes, looking for any sign that she might show mercy.

Jegra's fist came up and smashed the control panel and the cargo bay doors slowly clamped shut. "Now, what do you say we put the past in the past and focus on working together to get off this rock?"

"We'll have to wait till the storm passes before we can..." Onelle stopped when she noticed Jegra still inching closer to her, the empress's arm boxing her into the corner of the rear cargo hold. Her back up against the wall, she stiffened, growing incrementally nervous. "What are you doing?" she asked, her voice wavering with unease.

Practically nose to nose, Onelle had to look away lest their lips unintentionally come together. Or, maybe, it was intentional? Maybe, that's what made it so exciting. The danger of it. Of being intimate with someone who was inexplicably attractive but, at the same time, undeniably dangerous. How could these feelings even exist? Were they worth exploring, or should she ignore them and exercise caution? It was a tough call. All she knew was that after months of being stranded on this ridiculous planet, a vigorous fuck would do her good.

She tensed up even more when she felt Jegra's breath pass gently across her right ear. A tingle ran down her spine and she could feel the heat intensify between her already warm thighs.

"I have half a mind to punish you right here and now for your crimes," Jegra whispered.

Onelle closed her eyes and swallowed. Hard. Without warning, Jegra's other hand reached up and brushed Onelle's forest green hair out of her eyes in a sensuous fashion. "Punish me how?" she asked, glancing down as she watched the empresses slide her thick, tanned thigh between her slender green ones. Their bodies came together in the tight space and Jegra leaned in, her massive breasts entrapping Onelle.

Without expecting it, Onelle's heart began fluttering inside her chest and she felt a yearning ignite deep within her. She'd underestimated Jegra's resolve, and now the Empress of the Dagon Empire breathed down her neck, contemplating whether to snap it or dapple it with kisses.

Onelle bit her bottom lip and let the empress brush her nose against her cheek. A strange sexual energy; hate mingled with raw attraction, surged between them. If anything were to happen, it would be rough, wet, and painful in all the right sorts of ways.

But, to Onelle's surprise, Jegra took a deep breath and pulled away. In their excitement, they found themselves staring at each other, both caught off guard by the unexpectedness and depth of their attraction for one another.

The women shared a look of astonishment as they tried to quell the abrupt swell of lustful desire that had, unexpectedly, risen up between them.

"I apologize," Jegra said, shifting her gaze and taking a step back.

No longer trapped against the wall, Onelle moved to the center of the shuttle and took a deep breath to try and calm her racing heart. "I admit," she said with a wave of her hand, "I acted rather impetuously. I guess my resentment toward you went deeper than I had realized and I took it out on you in the worst, most selfish way possible. And having had a moment to reflect on it, I realize that wasn't fair. I was out of line."

Unfair was one way of putting it. Jegra much preferred the more accurate terms of arrogant and imprudent. But she didn't want to get into another row, not after it seemed like she was about to mend things with Onelle.

She looked over at the Bre'lal woman but held her tongue. Even though she was dying to lash out at Onelle for her petty act of selfishness and set her straight, she knew that what Onelle needed the most was resolution for her sister's death. And biting her head off now with a strict reprimand wouldn't help ease matters between them, nor would it lift the shuttle from the planet. So, she went with the softer touch, listening to the woman instead.

"I don't know if I'll ever be able to forget your role in my sister's death," she finally said, "but given enough time, perhaps I can learn to forgive you. Regardless of my personal feelings, I shouldn't have tried to abandon you here on this planet. That was beyond cruel." She turned toward Jegra and looked her straight in the eyes. "For what it's worth, I'm sorry."

"Apology accepted," replied Jegra. After a long pause, she added a whimsical, "Just don't let it happen again."

Onelle chortled lightly then cleared her throat. "I won't. I mean...you know..."

Jegra folded her arms and gave the green skinned woman a droll look. "No. I don't know."

"*You know...*" Onelle insisted, cocking her slightly head and biting her bottom lip. She took another small step toward the empress, making sure her swagger had that extra hint of seduction to it.

Jegra shook her head and forced herself to suppress a grin. Onelle took another step forward and batted her baby-blue eyes at Jegra. Her arms locked behind her back, she swiveled her hips and leaned into the empress, letting her breasts gently brush Jegra's arm.

Jegra grinned as Onelle playfully swayed next to her as though she were about to give her an erotic lap dance.

CRACK! Jegra moved so fast that Onelle didn't even have time to see it coming. Onelle's head jerked back from the brunt of Jegra's headbutt and suddenly everything went dark.

Onelle went out like a light and collapsed to the ground, landing in a heap at the empress's feet. The stun gun she had been concealing behind her back tumbled out of her hand and skidded across the floor before scraping to a halt next to Jegra's feet.

A disappointed look settled across Jegra's face as she bent down and picked up the device. She would have preferred to have been the other way, with her sprawled out on her back with Onelle's head between her thighs. As nice as the thought was, it wasn't like she hadn't seen it coming. Onelle had proved herself to be a compulsive liar and a duplicitous snake. And the moment she'd gone from fearful of Jegra to practically throwing herself at her, Jegra knew something was up.

Jegra hung her head and sighed. "Nice try, bitch," she said to the unconscious woman. "But you're dealing with the Empress of the Dagon Empire, not some slave girl who was born yesterday.

22

"**Evasive maneuvers,**" Lianica shouted above the noise of the collision alarm. She leaned forward in her seat and stared out the main viewscreen as the *Shard* came out of hyperspace only to emerge in the middle of a massive debris field. Taking evasive action, the ship arced and then dipped again, narrowly avoiding a large spiraling section of a derelict cruiser's hull. The *Shard* shuddered as another massive piece of debris collided and scraped along its hull. The grating metal sounded as if a giant can opener was busy trying to wrench the hull in two.

The ship corrected course only to suffer a violent jolt that shook the bridge crew and almost sent Lianica tumbling out of her seat. Lurching forward, she gripped tightly to both arms of the command chair with white knuckled tension. As she gazed out the viewscreen in jaw-gaping shock, the wreckage of numerous vessels drifted in the dead of space directly in front of her. It was a ship graveyard.

Another vessel sized piece of flotsam appeared above the *Shard's* bow, jostled loose, no doubt, from the pinball like effect of the *Shard's* having agitated the dormant debris field. The collision alarm, which had died down briefly, began to wail again and Lianica gripped tight and leaned back as the ship dove down and veered right, its hull rotating counter-clockwise as it narrowly avoided the massive saucer section of an ancient warship that spiraled in a clockwise fashion. NCC17-something-or-other was written in bold navy-blue letters across the top of the saucer, but the final letters were too battered and worn off from relentless collisions to make out.

Long after they were clear of the larger pieces, smaller fragments bounced and pinged off the vessel's hull. It sounded as though they were traveling through a rogue meteor storm. Emerging from the thick of it, the *Shard* slowly course corrected and came back to its original trajectory.

Pitted with dents and dings, the slender silver teardrop hull of the *Shard* looked blistered with boils and pock marks. But the liquid-hull technology quickly went to work healing the ship's surface. Soon enough, there wasn't a single hint of damage anywhere across the surface of the ship's hull.

"Structural integrity report," Lianica barked.

An ensign off to her left swiveled around in his chair and said, "Structural integrity ninety-eight percent and holding."

"Good," she replied. "Keep me updated on the damage reports for each deck as they come in."

The ensign nodded and then turned back around and brought up a cut-away view of the *Shard's* eighteen decks and began checking the damage reports for each level.

"What's a ship graveyard doing way out here?" asked Brei'Alas, looking over at Captain Blackstar with a perplexed expression on her face.

"Good question, lieutenant," Lianica replied. Then, turning toward the crew, she glanced toward a young male Dagon officer of lavender complexion and said, "Ensign Dree'alek, scan for any distress signals or emergency beacons."

He ran the scan as ordered and then shook his head. "It seems that whatever battle this was, it happened a long time ago, ma'am. It's dead silent out there."

"Scan the hull signatures. I want to know who it was that fought out here."

"That's odd," Dree'alek said. The captain shot him an inquisitive look, urging him to come out with it. "They read Galliforn and Dagon in origin."

"I wasn't aware that Galliforn and Dagon Prime were ever at war with one another," Brei'Alas said, looking out of the view portal at the debris.

"They weren't," Lianica said, rising to her feet. She had a bad feeling about all this, but if her intuition was correct, this wreckage might just be the key they needed to finding Jegra. "If you need me, I'll be in my ready room."

Lianica turned and left the bridge, leaving Dree'alek and Brei'Alas to give each other a confused look.

Once in her personal office, Lianica sat down at her desk and brought up the holographic console.

"Computer," she said, "Locate and bring up file 8472."

<<*There is a video file attached. Would you like me to play it?*>>

"Yes," Lianica replied. A blue line traced out the edge of a viewing screen. Soon the blue rectangle filled in with high definition color. A disheveled Dagon captain appeared on the monitor and he looked into the camera.

"This is Captain Regnarwald of the Enmity. We were responding to a border infraction by the Galliforns when both fleets encountered a strange celestial entity. I don't know how to explain it except to be in awe of its destructive power. These glowing, squid-like creatures the size of starships have already destroyed half the Galliforn fleet and are now approaching our position."

The captain glanced off screen for a moment, as though he was analyzing a chart, and then looked back again. "It seems they are protecting some kind of spatial anomaly. A rift between dimensions. Our readings are inconclusive, but it appears as though a pocket universe has formed. For whatever reason, these celestial entities are determined to protect this location at all costs. I don't believe they..."

A sudden spray of sparks along with several electrical explosions erupted in the background. An officer's voice came from somewhere in the background and frantically relayed, "Sir, they're attaching themselves to the hull of the ship."

The captain looked back at the camera and static interference caused the image to distort and flicker. His worried expression came back into view for just a moment and then the video feed cut out.

Lianica leaned back in her chair and steepled her fingers under her chin as she thought. She had vaguely remembered hearing stories of the first encounter with the squidies, but she hadn't thought to make anything of it until now. With the reappearance of the celestial entities, she knew that something was coming. Something big.

If the squids could jump through hyperspace, they might be able to jump into other-dimensional space, too. If so, it was possible that Jegra had been taken to the Dark Zone, the mysterious rift that Captain Regnarwald spoke of. Every attempt to send a probe in had been met with silence. It was as though the region were a black hole, but without the destructive forces of a singularity. It was just a tear in space that swallowed unsuspecting ships whole.

If Jegra was stuck inside the rift, there'd be no way to get her out except to use the *Shard's* slipstream technology. Theoretically, the vessel could pierce multi-dimensional space. And it was the only vessel that could do so. Even if Jegra wasn't stuck in the void of multidimensional nothingness, Lianica could at least gather some intel. Maybe even chart the other dimension. Something nobody else had managed to do in three hundred years, and not for a lack of trying.

The bustle on the bridge died to a calm murmur as Lianica strode back in. "Lieutenant Brei'Alas, scan for any spatial anomalies that coincide with the rift."

"Ma'am?"

"I have a gut instinct that Jegra is somewhere on the other side of that rift." She pointed at the starry backdrop on the viewscreen. Only a faint shimmer of gravitational lensing denoted anything out of the ordinary.

"It's my duty to inform the captain that every attempt to penetrate and retrieve information from the rift has failed. No ships have ever returned from it. And there's no guarantee anything can survive what's on the other side."

"I understand the risks, lieutenant," Lianica said, her voice controlled and calm. "But it's a risk I'm willing to take, if it means rescuing the empress."

"With all due respect, ma'am, what makes you so sure that Empress Alakandra is stuck on the other side of the rift?" Dree'alek asked.

The captain shot him a fierce look that made him cast his eyes downward. She then eased up and replied, "Like I said, it's only a hunch. But this ship is the only vessel in the Commonwealth capable of piercing the alternate dimensional fold. And if my intuition is correct, we'll find the empress on the other side."

"And if we don't?" Brei'Alas asked.

"Then we take readings, gather data, and use the slipstream drive to re-enter normal space."

"That is, if we survive the initial trip," Dree'alek replied. This time when she shot him a disapproving stare, he didn't look away.

Lianica scanned the faces of the bridge crew and took note of their worried expressions. "Look, I understand what I'm asking you to do is dangerous. But I wouldn't be asking you to do this if I wasn't so certain."

"You yourself said it was just a feeling," Brei'Alas reminded her. "So, explain to us why we should risk our lives on a mere feeling?"

"Have you ever been in love?" Lianica asked, gazing right at the lieutenant.

"Not that I can say, sir."

"Well, when you do fall in love, you'll know it. There'll be no explanation for it, but the feeling will be unmistakable. Undeniable. It will consume you. And that's how you'll know it's real. It's a lot like that."

Brei'Alas looked over at the other officers who merely nodded in agreement. She then turned back to Captain Lianica Blackstar and smiled. "We're with you, captain. No matter what."

"Good," she replied. Slowly, she removed her hand from the blaster that sat in its holster at her hip. She was afraid she'd have to make an example of someone if things took a wrong turn.

"Ensign, the moment you have the heading, set a course into the rift. Hyperstream velocity."

"Yes, sir," Dree'alek replied as he swiveled in his chair and began typing the coordinates into his console.

The *Shard* slowly eased toward the wavelike ripple marked by the gravitational lensing that denoted the edge of the anomaly. Gradually, the ship stretched and distorted and then, in a flash, it leapt into the rift.

Lieutenant Brei'Alas awoke in her quarters. Not realizing how she'd got there, she slowly sat up. She was in bed. She had on her finest Kreelack needle spider silk pajamas and the korridium bracelet her mother had given her after she graduated from the academy.

She slipped out of bed and slowly rose to her feet. She steadied herself as an intense wave of vertigo washed across her. Once it passed, she looked toward the portal of her room and saw a frightening backdrop. It appeared as though space itself was on fire.

It didn't make any sense. In order for flames to exist there had to be atmosphere. Gases to ignite. And although she'd heard of nebulas that burned, she'd never seen anything quite like this before.

She crept up to the window and reached up with an open hand. She was afraid it might be hot, but when she touched the glass, she found it cold. As cold as the dead of outer space.

In the lower right corner of her view she could make out a green and brown swirling sphere. *A planet,* she thought. *An ugly planet, but a planet, nonetheless.*

An abrupt flare shot up from the planet and Brei'Alas startled. When she looked again, she saw what appeared to be a shuttle launch. Her eyes followed the white trail of exhaust through the atmosphere until the tiny object broke into orbit. Eyes fixed on the glimmering object, she heard the comm in her room chime.

"Lieutenant Brei'Alas, you're exactly thirty-eight minutes late for duty. Please report to the bridge, ASAP."

Late? Brei thought. *But I just woke up.*

That was assuming a lot, considering she didn't remember going to sleep. Or, for that matter, returning to her quarters after her shift. "Computer, what is the date and time?"

[**It is 8:38 in the morning, currently the 48th revolution of the seventeenth era, Dagon standard time.*]

Forty-eighth revolution? She'd lost more than a whole day. *But how?* And had anyone else experienced the strange time lapse?

By the time she arrived on the bridge, there was an energy and excitement uncommon to the usually calm and collected Dagon crew.

"Glad you could finally join us," Captain Blackstar said.

"Has anyone else been experiencing strange time warps?" she asked, looking around at the blank faces. Only Dree'alek responded. "No. I mean, I don't think so." He glanced around to see several nodding faces confirming his answer. "Why? What kind of time distortion?"

"Never mind," she replied, pinning it for a more appropriate time. Returning her attention to the task at hand, she went and sat down at her station.

"Report," the captain said, a touch of impatience tucked into her voice.

Brei'Alas scoured her console, studying multiple readouts all at once. "It appears to be a mid-sized transport. It has just broken into a decaying orbit and is now requesting emergency assistance."

"Put it on screen," Lianica said, motioning for her to play the emergency broadcast.

"I'm afraid there's only audio."

"Then play it," Lianica said, shooting her lieutenant a sharp look.

"Yes, ma'am. Right away, ma'am."

There was a static crackle and pop and then a voice came through. "This is Empress Jegra Alakandra of the Dagon Empire requesting an immediate pickup. I repeat, our vessel is in distress and our scanners are down. If you are receiving this, we are in need of immediate assistance."

"It's her!" Dree'alek said.

Lianica rose out of her command chair and walked up to the view portal. "Lieutenant, get us within grappling distance of that ship."

"Yes, ma'am," Brei replied, her voice filled with the first bit of optimism since they'd taken this mission.

The *Shard* moved in over the small vessel and the shuttle bay wall melted away. Magnetic grappling hooks shot out and latched onto the vessel and began reeling it in.

Without warning, Brei'Alas felt lightheaded. There was a strange distortion and everything and everyone on the bridge began to wobble and distort. She felt extremely woozy, as though she'd been out drinking all night, and had to fight to prevent herself from keeling over and vomiting.

"Don't move!" a Bre'lal woman said, holding a blaster to Empress Jegra Alakandra's head.

The woman had on knight's armor and used the empress as a body shield.

Brei'Alas crouched behind a large crate and looked over at Captain Blackstar who held her abdomen. She'd been shot with a low yield disrupter blast and was lying on her side, writhing with pain.

Looking down, Brei'Alas realized she had a blaster of her own in her hands. Without even thinking it through, she abruptly stood up and, raising her hands in surrender, held out her gun which dangled on her pinky finger. "Don't shoot. I surrender."

"Throw the blaster on the ground and kick it to me," the green-skinned woman ordered.

Brei'Alas complied with the demands and kicked the blaster to the woman. She made sure that it skidded to a stop just beyond her reach, though. When the woman saw this, she rolled her eyes. "Do you think I'm stupid?" she barked angrily.

"No, I don't think that…what I mean is…I wouldn't ever dream of accusing you of…it's just that…" As the lieutenant stalled by playing it dumb, she glanced over at the captain and then to the empress.

If she could get close enough to the Bre'lal, she could use herself as a battering ram and smash into the armored aggressor and break her hold on Jegra. That would give the empress time to fetch her discarded blaster and then use it on the crazed woman.

Relying on the element of surprise, Brei'Alas screamed out and lunged at the woman. Before she had made it even half the distance she heard the shot of the blaster and stopped dead in her tracks.

She suddenly found it difficult to breath and looked down at the wound only to cringe at the sight of a gaping hole in her abdomen. She looked back up in time to meet the empress's eyes and tottered on her feet. She mouthed the words "I'm sorry," and swaying gently to the left then the right, she collapsed under her own weight and fell in a heap on the floor.

As she felt herself bleeding out, time began to distort again.

Lieutenant Brei'Alas awoke in her quarters. Not realizing how she'd got there, she slowly sat up and slipped out of bed. Fetching a fine silk gown, she wrapped herself up and tied the sash loosely around her slender waist and headed over to the view portal of her room.

She stood before the large oval window and peered out at a frightening backdrop. It appeared as though space itself was on fire.

Although she'd heard of nebulas that burned, this was something different. This was primordial, like the infinite plasma at the dawn of time. She shook her head and pinched the bridge of her nose as an overwhelming sense of déjà vu came over her. "What in the world?"

That's when she remembered the ship rising up from the green planet's atmosphere. She peered out the window at the swirling globe of khaki and sage green. She sighed out in relief when there was no sign of the shuttle. Just then, her morning alarm went off, startling her.

She hurried and got dressed, made herself a cup of coffee from the food synthesizer, took only a couple of sips of it before setting it back down, and then rushed to the bridge to report for duty.

As she arrived at the bridge, there was an excited commotion atypical of Dagon officers. "What's going on?" she asked.

"A ship just launched off the planet," Dree'alek informed her.

She looked at the viewscreen and, sure enough, it was the exact same ship as before.

She slowly settled into her station, not once taking her eyes off the vessel.

"Lieutenant?" Lianica barked, her voice filled with concern. "Is everything all right?"

Brei'Alas put it out of her mind and replied, "It's nothing, ma'am."

Captain Blackstar nodded and then said, "Report."

Lieutenant Brei'Alas checked her console, reading each graph and readout that scrolled past her display. "It appears to be a mid-sized transport vessel. Badly damaged. And we're getting an audio only distress call."

Again, the overwhelming sense of déjà vu came over her, but she quickly shook it off.

"Play it," the captain ordered.

The lieutenant did as told and brought the message onto the ship's comm. After the static crackle died down, a voice said,

"This is Empress Jegra Alakandra of the Dagon Empire requesting an immediate pickup. I repeat, our vessel is in distress and our scanners are down. If you are receiving this, we are in need of immediate assistance."

"It's her!" Dree'alek chirped excitedly.

Lianica rose out of her command chair and walked up to the view portal. "Lieutenant, get us within grappling distance of that ship."

"Yes, ma'am," Brei replied, her voice filled with the first bit of optimism since they'd taken this mission.

The *Shard* moved in over the small vessel and the shuttle bay wall melted away. Magnetic grappling hooks shot out and latched onto the vessel and began reeling it in.

"Ensign, you're with me," the captain said, as she turned to head to the shuttle bay to meet the empress.

"With all due respect, ma'am," Brei'Alas interjected. "Maybe I should accompany you two. After all, we don't know what condition she is in and she may need immediate medical assistance."

Lianica nodded and then said, "Grab a med-kit and meet us down there."

Brei'Alas hopped to her feet and quickly followed the captain and the ensign off the bridge as they all three made their way to the shuttle bay landing pad.

Due to the fact that Brei'Alas stopped off at the med lab to grab a medical kit, she arrived a few minutes after the others. When she arrived on the scene, she found the captain lying on the floor behind some containers and Dree'alek lying in the very same spot she somehow remembered dying in herself, just before the second time jump.

The Bre'lal woman, who once again held the empress hostage, trained her blaster on Brei'Alas when she entered the room. Brei'Alas froze in her spot and held up the med-kit. "Don't shoot!"

"Stop right there!" the green-skin growled, brandishing her weapon and motioning for Brei'Alas to set the case on the floor. "Just set the case down and slowly back away."

Instead of doing as requested, however, she boldly charged forward, using the metal case of the first-aid kit as a shield. The green-skin pulled the trigger and let off a blast, but Brei'Alas managed to deflect the shot with the med-kit. Its polished surface was heat resistant, and the plasma bolt deflected off of it and ricocheted across the room. It hit a light fixture above the empress and the Bre'lal woman and sent down a smattering of sparks and fine glass.

This caused the Bre'lal woman to flinch and duck out of the way of the debris, giving Brei'Alas the chance to strike. Bringing the med-kit down across the woman's temple, she clocked her as hard as she could.

With a skull fracturing crack, the green-skin crumpled to one knee and, dazed, tried to push herself back up. That's when a second, even more devastating blow hit her in the exact same spot as before.

Out cold, the green-skin hit the metal deck plating, face first. The blaster flew out of her grasp and skidded across the floor where it scraped to a halt several feet away.

When Brei'Alas turned to Jegra, she noticed that she had an immobilizer fastened to her back. It kept a steady electrical charge running through a prisoner's body, seizing up their motor functions and freezing their muscles. Reaching up, she plucked it off, a small static discharge popping as she tore it from the empress's back.

Brei'Alas dropped the device to the floor and immediately got under Jegra's arm to help steady her. Using her boot, she squashed the immobilizer and it crackled and sparked under duress then fizzled out.

"I've got you, Your Majesty," Brei'Alas said, hefting the empress back to her feet.

"Thank you," Jegra said. Then, looking down at the Bre'lal woman, she added, "That woman is relentless. You can't turn your back on her for an instant."

Brei simply nodded and glanced over at the unconscious Bre'lal woman.

Standing up straight, Jegra held Brei's shoulder with one hand and got her bearings. Once she was oriented, she thanked the lieutenant. "I'm fine, now. Thanks to you."

The empress hurried over to where Lianica lay on the floor curled into a tight ball, clutching her singed abdomen. Jegra glanced back to ask for the med-kit but Brei'Alas was already standing beside her, offering it to her.

She smiled and took the med-kit and set it down next to Lianica. "Hang on, my friend," she said opening the box. "You saved me, now let me save you."

Lianica grinned painfully through gritted teeth. "I'm not dead yet," she said.

"That's the Dagon spirit," Jegra said, smiling as she worked to mend Lianica's wounds.

While the empress attended to the commander, Brei wandered over to where Dree'alek lay. She crouched down and checked for any signs of a pulse. Nothing. She gently ran her fingers across his face and closed his eyes. "I'm so sorry, my friend," she whispered.

A single tear trickled down the side of her face as she realized it was her fault he was dead. She had put him in this position, suspecting what was about to happen; even if she hadn't known for certain, the vague recollection of events, a kind of premonition if you will, made her aware enough to strategically sidestep her own death.

If it hadn't been for the strange time jump, she would have been the one lying dead on the floor. Instead, ensign Dree'alek paid the ultimate price while Brei had narrowly escaped, and saved the empress.

She didn't know how or why she was the only one experiencing the strange time shifts, just that she was. Regardless, she decided to keep it to herself until such information absolutely needed to be conveyed.

23

In the dark barracks beneath the arena, a mysterious figure crept through the shadows and stepped cautiously between the piles of sleeping gladiators all sprawled about the shared communal room. Creeping daintily across the sandstone floor with bare feet, moving as stealthily as a Lafor'allenthal indigo panther, the prowling shadow came to a standstill above the sleeping red-skin, Ishtar Bantu, who lay sound asleep on a cement shelf against the farthest back wall.

A pair of hands reached down and carefully coiled their way around Ishtar's throat, slowly tightening like the giant boa constrictor of Thermicron 5–the moon of the Snake King, Niddak Najara. Delicate hands squeezed tighter and tighter, clamping down with white-knuckled determination. Almost instantaneously, Ishtar's golden eyes snapped wide open and her hands flew to the wrists of her attacker.

When she saw Danica's hate-filled eyes staring down at her, she mustered a hoarse growl from her clamped air pipes. "Do it," she wheezed. To test Danica's resolve, she let go of her wrists and gave no further protest.

Danica's amber eyes glowed hot with rage and her clasp tightened, her slender blue fingers sinking into the red flesh of Ishtar's neck. On the battlefield, she'd killed lots of enemy soldiers. This would be no different, she told herself.

"Kill…me…" Ishtar managed to say with whatever remaining breath she had left, then, unable to get her breath back, her eyelids began to flutter and her eyes rolled back in her head.

Just to be sure the deceitful wench wasn't playing tricks on her, Danica leaned forward, applying her full weight on Ishtar's throat, and snarled, "Die you unholy succubus."

From behind her, a vicious shock hit Danica between the shoulder blades and she stiffened into a board and motor functions completely frozen by the immobilizing bite of raw electricity, she tottered to one side and fell to the floor beside Ishtar's unconscious body.

The blue sparking tip of the stun-rod crackled and hissed like an angry electric knifefish from the sulfuric swamps of Skallek. It hovered above her menacingly, warning her to stay still. When she tried to move, the stun-rod rammed her squarely in the lower back, directly above her right kidney, hitting her a second time with another paralyzing volt. She groaned from the burning, pain-laced current that surged through her and convulsed on the floor.

"Save it for the arena, sweetheart," a large Dragonian said, his forked tongue flicking on the air as he gauged her resolve to continue on with this misconduct.

Danica rolled onto her side and gazed up at the guard who held the flickering baton at his side. She recognized the lizard man as the same one who'd given her a vote of confidence before ushering her out onto the battlefield early yesterday.

"Don't you ever sleep?" she grunted through the pain. The sharp twinge of clamped muscles now began to burn as though scorched by fire. Electrocution sucked.

"Double shift," he said with a friendly nod. "Now am I going to have to tase you again and drag your sorry ass to a detention cell, or are you going to behave?"

Danica nodded. "I'll behave," she grumbled defiantly. The Dragonian grinned at her and then sauntered off, twirling the stun-baton as he went.

Every muscle ached and Danica let out a heavy groan as she sat up. She rolled her neck across her stiff shoulders and tried to loosen up. But it was like trying to bend planks of oak. Groaning again, she gave up and just lay back on the cool cement wall.

"You should have slit my throat with a knife," Ishtar said, her voice rougher than gravel. She reached up and massaged her bruised neck. "It would have been quicker and quieter."

Danica scowled at Ishtar, her hate still burning intensely behind the veil of her amber eyes. "I didn't have a knife," she informed acerbically. "Otherwise I would have."

Ishtar stared at her for a moment and then let out a quaint chuckle.

"What?" Danica snapped.

"We make a good team, you and I," Ishtar finally said with a raspy voice, and gave Danica a half smile.

Danica shot her a disgusted look and smacked her teeth in annoyance at even the mere suggestion. Then, refusing even to entertain the idea, she rose to her feet and stalked off.

Ishtar couldn't help but smile to herself. Reaching down to her loincloth, she slid her hand across her left thigh and the brought up a small shank she'd crafted from some twine and a piece of broken glass from one of the beer bottles she had found at the dining hall earlier. It was curved like an eagle's talon and gleamed in the dim rays of light that came from the edges of the room.

She twirled the makeshift blade in her hands and then lay back down. Sure, she could have taken Danica out at any moment. But she was more than a little bit curious to see if the blue-skin had what it took to kill her. More importantly, however, she knew that tomorrow's match would be even tougher than the one they had faced today. And that meant she would have to rely on the banjax for a little while longer, whether she liked it or not.

When Danica returned to her quarters, she found an unfamiliar green-skin sleeping on her cot. The woman's avocado colored leg hung limply off the bed, poking out from a heather brown cotton blanket, as she snored lightly.

Danica nudge the woman's leg with her foot to jostle her awake, but she was a sound sleeper. So, Danica kicked her. Hard.

"Ow!" the woman yelped, recoiling her leg and sitting up. She rubbed her bleary eyes and let out a tired yawn, which she proceeded to speak through groggily. "What was that for?"

"Because…you're in my space, stranger," Danica informed the squatter.

"Then how come you ain't sleepin' in it?"

"I had some affairs to settle." Danica stopped herself as she realized she didn't owe this woman an explanation. Growing terse, she barked, "It's none of your business. Now move it, sister."

The Bre'lal woman sat up and threw off the blanket and stretched her arms behind her head, locking her elbows and staring back at Danica with a seductive smile. "You sure? After all, nights are cold in this Helios hole."

Diverting her gaze, Danica looked away. "My Gilded God, you're not wearing any clothes."

"I never do when I sleep," said the girl as if sleeping in the nude was a requisite for a good slumber. "Except, you know, when there's a dozen raunchy gladiators who'd gladly take advantage of you while you slept. But sometimes a girl just needs a break from it all, you know?"

Danica slowly craned her neck back around and met the girl's gaze. "So, let me guess, you're the hired comfort woman."

"One of about a dozen full-time sex workers who work in the hypogeum under the amphitheater. Mostly we attend to the victors' needs, and are paid handsomely for it. But sometimes we will steal away to other contestants…the ones who catch our fancy…if you get my meaning."

She winked and tossed her wavy forest green hair over her avocado colored shoulder and then leaned back onto the cool wall of the cell. Her dark green nipples stood erect on her ample breasts and her teal eyes seemed to have an unnatural depth to them.

"You seem uncommonly comfortable for a slave girl," Danica said, putting one hand on her tilted hip as she studied the Bre'lal woman.

The girl laughed and sat up. Leaning forward she gave Danica a peculiar look, one eye squinting at her with scrutiny. "I'm no slave. This is my profession. Like all sex workers, I'm contracted by IGS to work the arenas. The better you do your job, the better the arena you're assigned. Unlike you, however, *gladiatrix*, I can come and go as I please."

All of a sudden Danica's interest piqued and she took a step closer. If what the green-skin was saying was true, then she might just have her key out of this place.

The Bre'lal girl smiled, batted her teal eyes, and spread her bare legs apart, inviting Danica to come closer.

"I know this is a lot to ask, but can you get a message out for me? I'll pay you handsomely, of course."

"Well, that sort of depends," she replied, cocking her chin as she looked vacantly up at the corner of the room mulling it over. "I might be able to help you…under one condition."

"Anything. Just name it," Danica said, her eyes wide with anticipation. For the first time in what seemed like ages, she felt things were going her way. If she could get a message to Lianica, she'd be saved.

The green-skin slid to the edge of the cot and arched her pelvis forward. At the same time, she grabbed her knees and pulled them apart even more, spreading her nether regions as far as she could as she put herself on full display. Sliding her hand across her thigh, she reached between her legs and spread the tender folds of her labia to show Danica how wet she already was.

Danica had heard that Bre'lal women had exceptional control over their libido. Not only could they turn it on and off at will, but they could dial it up to eleven in less time than it took for a crooked senator to get it up. Which made them the perfect species to monopolize the sex trade in the galaxy. Which they did. There wasn't a planet, moon, or backwater asteroid mining belt that didn't employ Bre'lal women. And they weren't just a part of the empire, they were a necessary part of it.

Without their services, violence and chaos would run rampant. They served a vital function in society, and although some condemned them as wanton whores and unclean harlots, Danica knew there was more to them than that. Like her, they were people. And like her, they were just doing what they needed to get by in this harsh end of the galaxy.

"You get me to orgasm and I'll gladly help you out," she answered, a faint smile forming on her lips. "But, if you don't get me off, then I'm afraid the deal will also be off."

Danica raised an eyebrow. "Let me get this straight. All you want is to have an orgasm?"

"Look, lady," the Bre'lal woman said in an exasperated tone, she clamped her legs shut and raised a finger as though she were making an important point, "I work all day and sometimes all night long and it's all the same thing. Wham, bam, thank you ma'am. It's fun, sure. Rough and tumble. Sometimes even pleasurable. But I can't even remember the last time I came. So, help me to help you. I think that's only fair, don't you?"

Danica didn't need to think twice. She got down on her knees and scooted up to the edge. Resting her hands on the Bre'lal woman's soft thighs, she got into position. "You have yourself a deal," Danica mumbled.

The Bre'lal woman smiled and then reached down and grabbed the back of Danica's head and guided the Dagon's blue lips to her labia. She moaned as she felt the spongey softness of Danica's pink tongue slip inside her and slide up through the folds of her labia until it found the small nub of her clitoris.

"By the way," the green skinned woman said in a haughty voice, "my name is Algaia Octavia Zhan."

Danica attempted to pull away to introduce herself, as awkward as the timing was, but Algaia merely reeled her back in and forced her to keep going down on her.

"No, don't stop," she said between pants. "Everyone...knows...who...you are."

Danica ran two fingers up under her moist chin and then shoved them into Algaia with extreme force. She let out a surprised chirp and clamped her thighs together tightly around Danica's face. Massaging with both her fingers and tongue, Danica licked and fingered her partner for several minutes. Unable to it hold back any longer, Algaia gasped loudly and orgasmed.

"Don't...stop..." she said, her chest heaving as her heart pounded with ecstasy. This invigorated Danica and she doubled down on pleasing the green-skin whose legs were currently wrapped around her head.

The fact remained, she needed Algaia's help. And even though her jaw felt like cramping, she wasn't going to quit until the girl had made good on her promise.

It was only another minute or so before Algaia covered her mouth and screamed a muffled cry into her cupped hands. At the same time, a spray of ejaculation erupted from her and soaked Danica quite thoroughly, but she did not shy away from the thick, sweet scented shower. Rather, she realized that she, too, had grown rather excited in the carnal act and wanted to keep going until both participants were completely satisfied.

"Thanks," Algaia huffed, gently stroking her own skin in a euphoric daze. She allowed her fingers to fondle her nipples, as though they had a mind of their own, and then glide across her sweat dappled chest from one breast to another. "I needed that more than you'll ever know."

"I think I can imagine," Danica replied. As she rose to her feet, her carnal excitement growing inside her, she began undressing. Letting her soaked rags fall to a heap on the floor, she stood before Algaia; her male organ having unfurled from its hidden pouch from within her vagina, it now stood fully erect on her feminine body. Its engorged purple tip bobbed softly in the cool air, as if presenting itself for the green-skin to with as she pleased.

"It appears I'm not the only one in need of relief."

Embarrassed by how vulnerable she felt revealing her true nature to a complete stranger, Danica blushed and covered her penis with both hands and looked away. "It's been a rough few weeks, to say the least. I'd rather not—"

Before Danica could even finish her sentence Algaia had her lips around Danica's cock and began giving her the best blowjob she had ever experienced. No more than three minutes had passed when Danica groaned out in pleasure and came inside Algaia's mouth.

"Oh my Gilded Lord!" Danica cried out as she came. It was a complete shock to her that she ejaculated at all since the penis of all Dagon women, intersex by nature, was merely a vestigial leftover in their specie's evolutionary history. It wasn't supposed to be capable of producing sperm. But in rare cases, something would activate the dormant gonads and the woman's penis could work.

She suspected that the doctors had repaired her body more thoroughly than she'd had originally estimated. Running her finger along the scar that stretched cross her lower abdomen, she realized that her male organ was now fully functional. She didn't know quite what to think about that in this moment, so she pinned the thought for later.

Out of breath and reeling with Bacchic delight, she pushed Algaia back onto the bed and rested her blue face on her sweaty, avocado colored breasts. As they lay there, panting softly, Danica swirled her blue finger around the Bre'lal woman's forest green nipple and sighed out a satisfactory breath.

"That was…"

"Amazing," Algaia answered, finishing Danica's sentence for her. Curling up on the bed, Algaia wrapped her legs and arms around Danica and held her. She had a million things she wanted to talk about and about twice as many questions, but Danica was already passed out in her arms and had fallen into a deep sleep. She smiled and then let herself drift off to sleep, too.

In the morning Danica was pleased to find that Algaia had not slunk off in the middle of the night and left her abandoned with but a fading memory of their prior entanglement. She stayed. She lay on the bed beside her, gazing into Danica's yellow eyes with her teal ones.

"You stayed," she said in a surprised voice.

"Good morning to you too," Algaia said. She batted her green eyelashes and leaned in and kissed Danica on her dark purple lips.

Danica pulled back, taken aback by the candid nature of the Bre'lal woman. Last night was one thing, but acting as though they were old lovers, like it wasn't just a one-night stand, was, well, she didn't want Algaia getting the wrong idea.

They had given each other what they had needed. What their bodies craved. But beyond the physical attraction, the green-skin had nothing to offer her. This wasn't love. This was just raw, uninhibited, sex. No attachments. No drama.

"What's the matter?" Algaia asked.

"Nothing…it's just that…"

"Well, spit it out," she goaded, trying to get Danica to get whatever was bothering her off her chest.

"I don't usually bed prostitutes."

Algaia sat up and then wrapped her arms around her bare chest. "That's how you view me? A common hooker?"

"But last night you said…I mean, well? Isn't that what your people do best? Sex and seduction? I just thought—"

"Thought what, exactly? That I was good for a one-night stand?"

"Well, yeah," Danica replied, feeling rather self-conscious. "Don't Bre'lal women run the largest sex trade in the Commonwealth? You yourself said that's why you're here. You're working."

Algaia laughed and shot Danica a credulous look. "Yes, but we're far more than harlots and streetwalkers. Or don't you think I'm worthy of your superior Dagon anatomy? Is that it? I'm just a servant and you're the master race. That's what your people believe isn't it?"

Danica bit her lip in shame and looked away. She hadn't intended to start a row. She actually didn't mind Algaia's company. She just didn't think they had anything in common beyond the excellent sex. "I'm sorry," Danica said, pinching the bridge of her nose and shaking her head as she tried to force back the headache she already felt coming on. "I just meant that…"

"Oh, I think I know what you meant," Algaia said, raising her voice.

Without waiting for Danica's response, she slid out of bed, grabbed her things, and slipped on her clothes. Marching over to the door of Danica's holding cell, she reached out to hit the biometric scanner and open the door.

"Wait!" Danica called out, forcing the Bre'lal girl to pause. "What about your promise to help me?"

"Help you do what?" Algaia snapped, twirling around and giving Danica the evil eye.

"Help me get a message to my friends."

"It sounds complicated. I doubt a lowly prostitute could help someone like you." She scowled at Danica, who looked down at her feet in unease and tried to figure out another way of asking. She'd beg if necessary. Anything to have Algaia relay her message for her.

What Algaia wasn't expecting was to find Danica's eyes brimming with fresh tears. She felt a sudden twinge of regret for how she had gone off the rails. It wasn't like her to be defensive of her chosen profession. She'd never reacted this way with anyone else; she usually shrugged off their insensitivity, knowing it to stem from their ignorance.

She understood that for many species, sex was a personal act. A private act. Something they wanted to shelter away from the world and keep like a precious pearl. Other species, like the Dagons, used sex for pleasure and leisure, treating it more like a sport than a reproductive act. And still other species simply dismissed it as a banal act that was more of a base necessity than anything else.

But for the Bre'lal, sex was all this and more. And as a race, they had mastered the skills and techniques required to please more than a hundred alien species. This was what they did. Green-skins were universally known as pleasure makers.

"Look, I may have overacted. I just was really into you and wasn't expecting the sudden judgmental, holier than thou attitude."

"No, it's I who should be apologizing to you. You are right. I have no excuse for my rudeness. I hope you can forgive me for being such a bitch just now."

Algaia squinted at Danica and gauged her sincerity. Deciding Danica was being honest, she let out a sigh and composed herself. Her voice softening, she added, "Look, I can't make any promises, but I'll see what I can do."

Danica sprang to her feet, her breasts jiggling as she hopped up. She raced into Algaia's arms. "Thank you so much!" she said, squeezing the surprised Bre'lal woman in a strong and wholly unexpected embrace.

Algaia smiled at her and reached up and tucked a strand of Danica's white hair behind her ear for her. "Just hold out until I can get back to you either tonight or tomorrow night."

"I'll be here," Danica replied.

Then, palming the scanner and unlocking the door, Algaia turned to step into the hall. "*Hurk!*" Algaia's hands rushed up to her neck and pressed tight against the gash in her throat. But the blood poured out like a red waterfall.

Horrified, she turned back toward Danica and tried to let out a plea for help, but only the sound of garbled words sputtered out, along with flecks of blood.

As the thick red fluid gushed out of her throat in spurts, Algaia tottered briefly, becoming lightheaded from too much blood loss, and then fell forward into Danica's arms.

Danica caught Algaia under her arms and cried out in shock as the young woman's blood spilled out onto Danica's naked body. Sinking to the floor, she cradled the girl in her arms, and murmured under her breath, "No, no, no."

Algaia tried to speak one more time, but only bubbles came up through the thick blood pooling into her mouth. Her eyes looked up at Danica, full of fear and Danica brushed her hair back and whispered, "I have you, Algaia. I'm here."

Not that it mattered, since by the time she'd finished consoling the dying girl her teal eyes had gone blank and Danica could see their life force fade. She stared up at Danica with a haunting look that seemed to ask, "Why didn't you help me?"

Danica, still naked from the night before, stood and turned toward the entrance to her cell. She ignored the smears of blood, which she wore like body paint, and took a fighting stance. She wanted to enact revenge on whoever it was that stood on the other side of the shadow. "Show yourself!" she snarled, her nails biting into her palms with penetrating force.

When Ishtar Bantu stepped out from the shadows brandishing a shard of glass soaked in Algaia's blood, Danica growled angrily, "You murderous hag! I swear, I will kill you if it's the last thing I ever do."

Ishtar shrugged and let out a vexed sigh. She gazed at Danica with eyelids half open, and after a long pause she finally replied, "I can't have you ditching out on me. I intend to survive these humiliation bouts, and I need you with me in order to do that. So don't think for an instant that I'm going to let you sneak an SOS out of here so that your little girlfriend comes to your rescue."

"I swear by the Gilded Master I'll…"

"You'll what? You kill me and you doom yourself. Like it or not, we're stuck together." Ishtar smiled a cruel grin and then winked.

Before turning to leave, she eyed Danica up and down one last time and licked her lips as though she were thinking of something delectable, then turned and vanished back into the dark corridor from which she came.

Danica raced over to Algaia's side and wept silent tears for the girl. She may have been hired to serve, but she didn't deserve this.

"I'm so sorry," Danica wept, sobbing lightly as she slouched over the dead girl. Reaching up, she gently touched Algaia's face and ran her fingers along her soft cheek. One of her own tears dripped from her nose and landed on Algaia's cheek and Danica gently rubbed it away with her thumb.

She had to be more careful next time. Ishtar was keeping a close eye on her. But she had a plan.

Next time they were in the arena fighting for their lives, she'd help Ishtar just enough to keep her alive. She'd let her get mangled badly enough that she would need medical treatment. That would buy Danica enough time to find another Bre'lal woman and convince her to be her courier. It was the only way she was ever going to get out of this mess alive.

24

Droplets of water glistened on Jegra's bronze skin like sparkling diamonds as she dried herself off with a soft, organic cotton towel. Lianica diverted her gaze away from the empress's nudity out of deference. It had been so long since she'd been in Jegra's company that she had nearly forgotten the brazenness for which the empress was famous.

"No need to be shy," Jegra laughed, noticing the captain glance away and fix her eyes on a potted plant off to the corner of the room. "Your gaze won't offend me."

"It's not that, Your Majesty. Your beauty is uncontested throughout the Empire…it's just that you're not…with all due respect, your grace…you're simply not my type," Lianica replied. She tried to keep a polite tone, but it came off more harshly than she'd had intended. It almost sounded as though she were criticizing the empress for being the wrong species. For not being Dagon. "What I mean, Your Majesty, is that…"

Under the impression she had royally messed up, Lianica's shoulders slumped and she smacked her forehead and muttered a strict reprimand to herself. *"You idiot."*

Jegra laughed again and held up her hand, motioning Lianica to stop talking. "It's fine. You like members of your own species. I get it. But after several weeks on that tiresome planet, I am in desperate need of a good massage. I have a rather nasty kink in my neck," she informed Lianica, rotating her shoulder and stretching her neck to the side. "Do you mind?"

Lianica nodded submissively and followed Jegra into a side room where a massage table was already set up. Scented candles had been lit and Brei'Alas was waiting for them.

"I just finished setting up, as you asked, your grace," the lieutenant said, bowing reverently. She too was shocked by Jegra's stark nakedness but felt it would be rude to look away, so she studied the fine contours and lines in Jegra's muscular form as a way to distract from her nudity.

"Thank you," Jegra said, touching the girl's shoulder. With a thrust of her chin she dismissed the Brei'Alas, who, keeping her head bowed, scurried out of the room and headed off to resume her regular duties.

Lianica shot Jegra a curious look.

"Why do you look at me like that, Lianica?" Jegra asked without looking back over her shoulder.

"It's just that…Your Majesty does realize we can assign her some personal servants at any time, right?"

"I won't have slaves working under me," Jegra replied. "I prefer to have people I can trust."

"What about paid labor?" Captain Blackstar asked. "I could vet a few Dagon officers and find some suitable to your tastes."

Jegra rubbed her chin as she thought it over and then replied, "I'm intrigued by this suggestion. I suppose as long as they are willing and they are getting paid, I'd have no problem with attending servants. I'll send you a list of my requirements."

Lianica nodded. Then, after a long pause, she added, "If you don't mind me saying so, I believe you've grown more powerful since we last saw one another. Physically, I mean. Your muscles are much more defined and you seem… harder, somehow. Like you have an edge about you."

"In that case, this massage will be a workout for you."

Lianica chortled lightly to herself and then motioned for Jegra to lie down on the massage table. Walking over to the carefully prepared shelf, she selected some essential oils and poured them into the palms of her hands. "I'm sure it's nothing I can't handle," she replied, lathering her hands together to warm up the oils.

Ready to begin, she pressed her greased palms into Jegra's lower back, just above the dimples over her buttocks, and began to run her hands up along the gentle curve of the empress's spine, spreading the oil across each rippling muscle.

Lianica repeated this several times, working the oils in as she went up and down the length of Jegra's backside.

When Lianica's fingers came down to Jegra's thighs, she let her fingers gently slip down between her legs and then she rubbed downward to the back of Jegra's knees and calf muscles. Again, she repeated this motion until she was satisfied Jegra was well coated in the oil.

After adding some more oil to her palm, she worked her way down to Jegra's ankles, taking ahold of the empress's right foot. Using both hands, Lianica jabbed her thumbs into the palm of each of Jegra's feet. With small but firm force, she kneaded out any knots. Finally, working her way back up to the toes, she fingered deftly, letting each digit slip between her fingers, and then gripping tightly she stretched Jegra's toes back as far as they would go.

"Oh, that feels amazing," Jegra sighed.

"There's something—"

"I think we should—"

Both women spoke simultaneously and stopped almost as soon as they had begun, realizing they'd interrupted one another.

"You first, Your Majesty," Lianica insisted.

"No, you go. Everyone always stops when I speak, as if my words were golden, somehow. They're not. I can assure you, whatever I had to say isn't as important as something you need to get off your chest."

"It's not proper for me to speak before my empress has said her piece of mind. I'll tell you after you tell me." She began working her way back up Jegra's legs and to her lower back where she paused to work on a tight spot.

A soft moan slipped out of Jegra's mouth as Lianica worked the knot out of lower her back just above the dimple of her right buttock.

"Mmmph. I was merely going to say we need to track down that back-stabbing husband of mine if we're going to find and rescue Danica. I have more than a few words to share with him, especially since he knows how much she means to me. I will never forgive him if anything happens to her."

Lianica nodded. "Once we're back into regular space, I'll have Lieutenant Brei'Alas run a trace on all known sightings of both the Lord Emperor and Danica Valencia."

Another heavy moan escaped Jegra's lips as Lianica worked her magic.

"Right there," Jegra said. "That's perfect. Now, what was it you wanted to say to me?"

Lianica wanted to confess her betrayal of Danica, of how she'd handed her over without putting up a fight, but she was now having second thoughts. She wasn't sure the empress would take it well, given what she'd just said. And after such a harrowing ordeal, she didn't want to burden Jegra with any unnecessary stress.

"It's nothing," Lianica lied. "It can wait."

She wasn't sure about that second part. For all she knew, Emperor Dakroth was torturing Danica as they spoke. But she kept it to herself and simply focused her attention on the task at hand.

Jegra let out another pleasure-filled groan and rolled over onto her side. Lianica took a step back and froze. "Was it not good?"

"No, it's good. Excellent, in fact. It's just that, I know it wasn't easy for you."

Lianica cocked her head and raised a curious eyebrow.

"Making the decision to come after me instead of going after Danica when she was taken."

"You know about that?"

"Brei'Alas briefed me."

Lianica lowered her eyes in shame. "So, then, you know what I did. You know that I betrayed you."

"There was no easy path there, Lianica. You could have left me to die on that planet or you could leave Danica to suffer at the hands of a madman. But for what it's worth, I fully back your decision. Danica is a big girl. She can take care of herself. On the other hand, if you hadn't found me when you did, I'd be a frozen space corpse drifting in an infinite vacuum right now."

Lianica looked up, her pale-yellow eyes meeting the empress's deep brown ones. There was a dampness to them she wasn't accustomed to. This was the first time anyone had forgiven her instead of raking her over the coals. "Your faith in me will not be in vain," she informed, trying to hold the urge to smile at bay. This was no time to get overly emotional.

Jegra had just lain back down on the table and stretched out when the door to her chambers chimed. "Enter," she said, resting her face across her forearms.

Two brawny Dagon men, both the most muscular men Lianica had ever seen, stepped into the empress's quarters. Both men had light blue towels draped over their left arms and they bowed reverently after having entered.

"These men will relieve you, captain," Jegra said, craning her neck and looking up at Lianica.

Lianica stiffened and saluted, crossing her fist over her breast, as was custom. She then marched over toward the door, only glancing back briefly to glance at the two men taking over her masseuse duties. Except, they were obviously there to do more than a bit of physical therapy, considering one of them already had his face buried between Jegra's thighs and the other had his tongue swirling around the empress's nipples. The empress moaned in a slightly different tone as Lianica stepped into the corridor.

The doors swooshed shut behind her with a pneumatic hiss of air and Lianica let out a deep breath. She probably shouldn't have looked back, she thought. But she quickly chased the image out of her mind. Even as she tried to calm herself with a deep breath, her heart pounded inside her chest from the strain of having held in her dark secret for so long. As the stress drained from her in the form of a mild panic attack, she whispered to herself, *"Get your shit together, Lianica."* Tugging at the waist of her uniform jacket, she straightened out the creases and then made her way to the bridge.

Lianica was about to step into the lift that would take her to the bridge when she heard a peculiar noise. It sounded like soft weeping coming from behind the wall. But it wasn't like Dagons to reveal such emotion, especially in public. As such, her curiosity got the better of her and she followed the muffled sound to its source.

Rounding a bend, she found Brei'Alas standing in the nook of a nearby maintenance closet, quietly sobbing to herself. When the lieutenant saw the captain appear from around the corner, she immediately wiped her tears away and ceased her sniveling.

"Lieutenant Brei'Alas…are you crying?"

"It's nothing," Brei'Alas reassured her. "I'll return to my duties immediately," she said, and then attempted a bold bypass of her captain.

Lianica's hand stopped Brei'Alas from escaping and she gave her officer a sympathetic look. "Then, why do I get the feeling it's not nothing?"

Brei'Alas looked at the captain with a fearful gaze. "If I tell you, you'll likely confine me to my quarters for the rest of all time."

"Don't be so melodramatic," Lianica said with a laugh. "If the safety of the ship is at stake, then I order you to tell me; if not, I ask you to."

Brei looked into the commander's eyes and took a deep breath. "I killed ensign Dree'alek."

Lianica laughed, thinking it was some kind of bad joke. "What in the galaxy are you talking about? I was there. I saw Onelle gun him down in cold blood. I can assure you, lieutenant, it wasn't your fault." She put her hand on Brei'Alas's shoulder to let her know she was fine. She'd be fine.

"That's not what I meant. What I mean is…I don't know…none of this makes any sense. But you have to believe me. I was the one that died that day, not Dree'alek."

"You're not making any sense," Lianica said. "Try taking a deep breath, lieutenant. That's an order."

Brei'Alas did as asked, inhaled, and then slowly let out the air. "The prisoner, Onelle," she relayed, "shot me when I tried to rescue the empress. I know it doesn't make sense, but I remember it all as clear as day. I'm the one who bled out on that landing bay floor. Not Dree'alek."

"Brei," she said, dropping the formal labels in order to try and connect with the girl, "are you even listening to yourself? If you're the one who died, then how could you have possibly killed Dree'alek?"

"Because, the time anomaly reset everything."

"What time anomaly?" ask Lianica.

"That's what I'm trying to tell you. The ship experienced a time anomaly, or, well, I did, anyway. The day reset, three times I think, maybe more. And for some reason, I was the only one who knew anything about it!"

"And you didn't think to report this?"

"At the time, it was clear what was happening. And then, once it had passed, it was like nothing had happened at all. Except, I was alive and Dree'alek was dead."

Captain Lianica Blackstar reached out and took Brei'Alas by her shoulders and squeezed her firmly. "I think you may be experiencing survivors' remorse, lieutenant. Anomaly or not, the green-skin killed Dree'alek in cold blood. Not you."

"Still," Brei'Alas said, rubbing her chin, "if I had done something differently. Chosen a different course of action, he might not be dead right now."

"If you need to talk about it more, I can meet you when my shift is over in the lounge. I'll be there having a few drinks. In the meantime, let's keep this under wraps for now. If anything like this time anomaly should happen again, you tell me immediately. Do you understand?"

Brei'Alas simply nodded her head, relaying that she understood the captain's orders.

Captain Lianica Blackstar smiled and put a hand on the lieutenant's shoulder. "Just take a deep breath and," Lianica began, "and clear your head. We still have work to do. And I need you at your best, lieutenant."

"Yes, ma'am," Brei'Alas said.

"Good," Lianica said, stepping aside and letting the lieutenant out of the closet. As they made their way to the lift together, Lianica continued speaking as though this little breakdown in the middle of the corridor had never even happened. "First, I need you to do a long-range scan of all ship activity and track down the Lord Emperor. Check every ship's log from here to Cordova if you have to. But find him. The empress wants to have a word with him."

"Yes, ma'am," Lieutenant Brei'Alas replied, feeling renewed after having cleared her conscience. Lianica turned to Brei'Alas and motioned for the lieutenant to go on ahead of her. They boarded the lift together and rode in silence up to the bridge. As the numbers on the deck readout ticked down, Brei'Alas stole a glimpse at the captain.

Although she hadn't noticed it till now, it was Brei'Alas's opinion that the captain was looking a bit withered. She had dark rings under her eyes, probably from too many late nights of binge drinking. Her hair, although pulled back tight in a ponytail, had some rogue strands sticking out that she had neglected to fix. And although she still had beautiful, smooth skin, the first sign of creases from the stress of the job could be seen winding their way into her complexion.

Lianica looked over at Brei'Alas, who smiled gently and then looked away again. She smiled in return and then tapped her foot anxiously for the elevator ride to be over.

The doors opened and Lianica let out an audible sigh. To cover up the fact that she was coping with enough stress of her own and didn't need the burden of Brei'Alas's additional anxiety, something she could never admit to without appearing weak, she quickly stated, "After you, lieutenant," and motioned for Brei'Alas to go on ahead of her.

The lieutenant gave a courteous nod and stepped off the lift. Captain Lianica Blackstar brushed down her uniform one last time and readied herself to tackle another trying day. Before stepping off the lift, however, she muttered to herself, "What I wouldn't give for a drink right about now."

25

Lord Emperor Dakroth strutted across the smoky marble floor of the assembly room and looked up at the senatorial committee, which sat behind eight-foot-tall podiums and looked down on him with stern gazes.

Emperor Dakroth put a fist to his mouth and cleared his throat, but before he could speak, the head chairman spoke first.

"We cannot, in good conscience, agree to send a quarter of the fleet in search of the empress."

"Chairman, if only you'd hear me out on this matter, I can assure you that—"

"Your assurances mean little these days, Lord Emperor," another senator interjected.

Dakroth snapped his head to the ancient woman who spoke down to him. He scowled up at her pale-yellow eyes; she seemed little threatened by his sharp glare.

"You assured us that you could defeat the Nyctan fleet and instead you returned to Dagon Prime, tail tucked between your legs, licking your wounds."

"You lost half the fleet in an unnecessary border skirmish," another senator added. "And now you want to take half of what's left on a rescue mission?"

Dakroth brushed his elegant, white naval suit down, minding the numerous pins and medals that plastered his right breast, and took a deep breath.

"If the senate would just hear me out. I know I could persuade—"

"I'm afraid," the chairman interrupted, "I cannot allow you to weaken the already limited defense of Dagon Prime on the off-chance the empress survived. Your request is denied." He slammed the wooden gavel down and offered that as the final period to his remark.

Dakroth managed a smile from behind a clenched jaw and then bowed reverently.

Without saying another word, Dakroth spun on his heels and stormed out of the assembly chambers.

Halfway down the open corridor, lined with a long row of ornate columns, ten meters high, replete with curling scrolls and decorative acanthus leaves carved into them, he met a servant boy who waited for him.

The boy bowed reverently and then informed the Emperor, "You have an incoming subspace hypercast, sire."

"Patch it through to my shuttle."

"Yes, sire." The servant boy bowed again and then scurried off ahead of the Emperor to make the necessary preparations.

Once the boy had disappeared from the atrium, Dakroth's eyes flickered to the shadows cast by a couple of pillars and scowled.

"I thought we agreed not to meet in public."

A figure stepped out from behind one of the columns but kept to the shadows. In a gruff voice, which sounded as though it were filtered through a mask, the figure answered, "We have a problem."

"I pay you handsomely to avoid any inconveniences," Dakroth growled.

"The Empress's ship has been sighted in Galliforn space. My spies say she is aboard, safe and well."

Dakroth mulled over the information and clasped his hands together behind his back. He turned toward the fountain in the atrium, his eyes watching the spouts of water cascade down the petals of a lotus flower as an effigy of a naked nymph from ancient lore rose up from the center of the blossoming flower, and grinned. "It seems that fate has acted in our favor and done all the work for us."

"What would you have me do, Lord Emperor?" The figure stepped out of the shadows to reveal a green skinned woman. She had on body armor, a purple cape, and a mask with a narrow visor that concealed her face. Only the hint of piercing teal eyes peeked through the narrow opening.

"See to it that her ship doesn't make it back to Dagon space. If, for some reason, she evades you–track her down and deal with her personally."

The mysterious woman bowed and then slowly withdrew into the shadows, disappearing as though she was never there.

Dakroth tugged at the waist of his uniform, pulling it tight, and cleared his throat. Without so much as stealing a backwards glance, he promptly exited the courtyard and strolled past the towering pillars of the senatorial assembly hall and down the grand steps. Arriving at the base of the staircase, he stepped onto a luxurious green lawn and cut across to the small, egg-shaped shuttle that waited for him in front of the senate.

Unlike Jegra's pearl white shuttle, Dakroth's shuttle was coated in a dark chrome that seemed to reflect more shadow than light. As he approached the vehicle, it cracked open and two doors rose up on either side, giving the strange vehicle the appearance of an egg with wings.

Dakroth ducked under the uplifted door and sat down on the luxurious, suede leather seats. Brushing down his uniform, he tapped a display panel and brought up a holovid screen with the Imperial seal on it and hit the "answer call" button.

Soon enough, a familiar face was staring back at his. A forbidding grin slid across his blue lips as he looked at the dark, smoldering eyes that stared back at him.

With faux excitement, he grinned even wider, and said, "My dear, you're alive! I'm so glad to see you're safe and well."

"I'm sorry I can't say the same of you, my love," Jegra replied, glaring at her traitorous husband. She brushed a clump of hair out of her eyes and tucked it behind her ear as they both shared forced smiles that were as hollow as their love for each other.

"To what do I owe the pleasure of this call?" Dakroth asked, ignoring her previous affront to his honor.

"I hear you've been looking for me."

"It's true, I've been *so* worried—"

"Spare me your lies," she said, her voice full of disdain. "We both know you were secretly hoping I'd quietly disappeared."

"My dear Jegra, it pains me to learn that you think so little of me. But, believe me, my luv, there are no hard feelings. It's simply politics. I played you, you played me, and now here we are, ready to begin round two of this cat and mouse game which so perfectly defines who we are as a couple. Two titans locked in an internal battle of wits and cunning."

Jegra did all she could not to involuntarily groan out of exasperation. She'd rather not be the counterpoint to a conniving madman. She didn't need the stress. But as aggravating as her conniving husband was, he wasn't entirely wrong about them.

It did seem that they were fated to be stuck in a never-ending chess match whereby the only end to the game was for one of them to completely destroy the other. Knowing Dakroth's brand of treachery, Jegra realized that in order to defeat him, she either needed to be just as ruthless as he was or rely on something that Dakroth didn't have the luxury of. Friends.

That's how she would beat him. She'd create a vast network of alliances so unshakeable that Dakroth wouldn't ever be able to touch her. She'd unite the warring empires and create the first ever cosmic alliance. It would be in this allegiance that she'd find a strength that Dakroth could only dream about.

"I just wanted to let you know, my darling," she said, her jaw flexing with tension, "there's no need for you to come looking for me. Because I'm coming for you." Jegra kept her voice low and steady, but there was no denying it was infused by forty-eight months of pure rage which was on the verge of boiling over.

Dakroth smiled. "Wonderful!" he chirped, rubbing his hands together. "I can't wait to see you. Till we meet again, my luv."

"Be seeing you real soon, Dagie-poo," she said, playfully making a mockery of his name. She could see this annoyed him and his grin grew taut, as if he were forcing every muscle in his face to hold it for no other reason than his own ingrained sense of regal formality.

Jegra began to raise her hand as though she were going to wave goodbye to him, but quickly twisted it around and flipped Dakroth the bird instead.

Dakroth swiped the holovid away and the screen disappeared. He rolled his eyes and let out a disgruntled sigh and muttered under his breath, "That woman will be the death of me."

As the egg-like shuttle pierced the upper atmosphere and climbed toward the massive Dagon destroyer hanging in orbit, Emperor Dakroth reclined in his chair and brought up the gladiator games on the holovid display.

On the screen, two female gladiators made their way toward the center of the arena. They were surrounded by three gigantic eight-foot tall gorilla creatures with ice-blue fur and shaggy white manes.

Dakroth tapped the display and zoomed in on the two contestants. As the camera of the televid drone focused on Danica's face, he chortled lightly in an amused tone and watched as she and Ishtar came back-to-back, their fists at the ready as they began their seventh consecutive match this week.

With nowhere to run, they had no choice but to engage the snarling, chest-thumping apes from the icy plains of the planet Riverion.

Ishtar was the first to advance. Shoving one of the large apes out of the way, she kicked the back of its leg and brought it to its knees. One of the other apes took off after her and she led it away.

The largest of the three apes puffed up its chest and beat on its pecks with massive leathery hands, roaring out to let Danica know it was the dominant combatant on the field.

Cautiously, Danica eased away from the beast, but when she moved, it grew agitated and swiped at her with its meaty hands. She leapt back, her skin avoiding its filed nails, but her garments were ripped off in the process.

Annoyed, Danica sighed, letting out her stress as her boobs flopped out for all the millions of viewers to see.

Humiliation bouts weren't like your normal, everyday bouts. Gladiators weren't permitted protective armor or even heavy weapons during the fight. But it was a grueling death match. Here, all contestants fought until one was crowned the victor or until all were lying dead in a heap upon the blood-soaked sands of the arena.

Amid an eruption of cheers, the monstrous beast brought Danica's bikini top to its nostrils and sniffed it. Uninterested in the flimsy clothing, it tossed her things aside and then thumped its chest one more time as it roared up at the rows of cheering spectators.

She rolled her eyes when, out of the blue, a flash of something metallic beneath the sands of the arena caught her eye. It was a discarded spearhead, left over from a previous bout, no doubt.

Thanking her luck, she slowly bent down and ran her fingers through the sand, and when she rose back up, she had a spear clutched firmly in her right hand.

As the beast pandered to the audience with its hammed-up ferocity, Danica clutched the spear tightly and raced toward the creature, breasts flopping as she ran.

The blue ape turned just in time to see the topless violet-skinned woman leap into the air. It roared menacingly, but it was too late. Danica ran the tip of the spear right through the beast's throat.

It tried to growl out in protest, but the only sounds that came from its mouth quickly turned into a wretched gagging, an animal choking on its own blood.

Danica used her forward momentum and, holding firm to the shaft of the spear, she kicked out her legs and swung around, twisting the ape's neck along with her. As Danica swung across the backside of the beast, there was a hideous crack and the ape's neck broke just as she relinquished her grip. The ice-blue gorilla swayed drunkenly on its feet, its tongue hanging out of the side of its stunned faced, and then it toppled to the ground.

The ground shook as the eight-foot tall behemoth hit with a resounding thud and the violet-skinned warrioress landed in a crouching position a meter to its side.

Danica rose to her feet and pressing a foot to the lifeless ape's collar bone, plucked her spear out and flicked cornflower blue blood from its tip.

Halfway across the arena, Ishtar held off two additional apes. Unable to match their strength or weight, she used mainly defensive moves to evade or throw the large animals. This only seemed to provoke them all the more and one of them charged her, ramming into her at full speed and sending her tumbling to the ground.

With a grunt, Danica launched her spear. It flew across the arena and struck the ape which had sent Ishtar to the ground straight through the center of his sternum.

A loud roar echoed throughout the arena as the wounded beast snapped the shaft of the spear off and threw it to the ground.

Sidetracked by Danica's surprise attack, the wild-eyed ape reeled around and trained its sights on Danica. It snorted and then started lumbering toward her on its massive fists. Approaching fast, it leapt up into the air and raised its mighty fists above its head like two leathery hammers.

Danica leaped out of the way and rolled three times, barely dodging the pummeling attack. Springing back to her feet, she whipped around just in time to find the ape already bearing down upon her. She stumbled back, frightened by its abrupt speed, but wasn't able to escape its giant arms.

The monstrosity scooped Danica up in its massive arms, clutching her by the waist, and began squeezing her with all its strength. She arched her back and pushed against the ape's burly chest with all her might, but it wasn't enough. She couldn't break free of the gorilla's vice-like grip.

"Fine," she growled, as televid drones swooped down to get a close up of her, zooming in on her breasts. The crowd went wild as the titillating fan service wetted their licentious appetites. "You asked for it."

A blue energy bubble surged out from Danica and the ape's arms tore off from its body. Danica dropped to her feet and quickly threw up another half-bubble, like a tortoise shell, and prevented the ape's heavy body from crushing her.

Across the battlefield, Ishtar had managed to climb onto the third ape's back and was hacking at its thick neck with frenzied chops with the shank she had used to kill Algaia.

It wasn't expert or precise, but Ishtar wasn't one to play nice when it came to a chance to amplify the amount of gore. The crowd got off on the brutality of the sport and she had quickly risen through the rankings to become a fan-favorite. And although Ishtar could have easily dispatched the creature with a single, clinical swipe to its jugular, she gave it five additional lacerations before finally taking off its head.

Ishtar rode the beast to the ground and leaped off just as its body met the ground. Landing on her feet, she trotted out to the center of the arena, riding out the momentum. She posed dramatically, looking over toward the eastern wall to see Danica crouched underneath half an energy shell, the dead body of the final ape draped across her.

"A little help here?" she grumbled, noticing Ishtar just standing there watching her. She strained against the creature's immense weight. Needless to say, she wouldn't be able to hold the energy field much longer and was already beginning to feel rather drained.

Ishtar waited another moment before heading over to assist Danica when, halfway there, the energy bubble burst and the large ape collapsed directly on top of her.

There was a loud *oomph* and Danica disappeared beneath her furry blue opponent. Ishtar stopped in her tracks and the crowd fell silent, waiting with bated breath to see what had become of the popular Dagon warrior.

Just as the tension grew to unbearable heights, a lavender arm shot out from beneath the dead ape. Violet fingernails dug into the sand of the arena and Danica clawed her way out from under the beast's heavy body.

Once again, the televid drones swooped down to zoom in on Danica's bare chest, which heaved with every deep breath she took. Rising to her feet, she clutched her bruised ribs with one arm, her other arm hanging limply at her side from exhaustion.

"Thanks for nothing," Danica groaned, eyeing Ishtar with an icy stare.

Ishtar shrugged. "It looked as though you had things under control."

The two women sidled up to one another and looked up toward the emperor's booth. Without warning, a giant hologram of Emperor Dakroth's face appeared, causing both women to tense, and his voice boomed over the speaker system. "Well done, ladies! Well done, indeed!"

The crowd roared out with applause and then quickly died down again. The image of the emperor panned out to show his upper half and he held out his fist. Jutting a thumb out, he waited till the sounds of the arena died down to a murmur, and then turned up his thumb.

"They will live to fight another day!" he announced.

After an eruption of applause, he raised his hand and gestured for them to simmer down. "Hear me, my loyal subjects! I have a very special announcement. In the next match, our valiant gladiators will face none other than the champion herself. The Empress, Jegra Alakandra, Jegra the Merciless, the reigning supreme champion!"

The arena went wild. The cheers were so loud it sounded like the rumble of an avalanche.

Danica's face went numb at the news while Ishtar grinned excitedly next to her. If they were really to go up against Jegra, she knew it would be a death match. Last one standing gets to live.

Naturally, Danica would never deliberately harm the one woman she loved with all her heart. But even if she chose to fight, there was no way she and Ishtar, not even with their combined strength, could defeat Jegra. It was impossible. And

Dakroth knew it.

Dakroth swiped away the holovid display of Danica and Ishtar standing amid the roar of the crowd and leaned forward in his seat. Placing his chin on steepled fingers, he grinned to himself, pleased by his own cunning.

Not only would he force Jegra to fight a title bout, but he'd kill two birds with one stone, as his lovely wife would be obliged to take out two royal pains in his neck. As for the empress, he'd keep her around a bit longer. After all, he still had the Nyctans to worry about and he needed her as a bargaining chip. The other two, however, were dead weight. At least he'd get some good ratings to close out the season.

26

Avocado colored breasts and olive-green nipples flashed Jegra as Onelle Agnar changed her clothes behind the glass wall of her state-of-the-art cell aboard the *Shard*. Jegra didn't feign to look away but merely kept her gaze focused on the Bre'lal woman. Given their history, Jegra didn't trust her for an instant.

For reasons unclear to Jegra, Onelle blamed her for Abethca Agnar's death. Somewhere along the line, in her quest to track Jegra down and avenge her sister, she'd ended up marooned on the same alien world that Jegra crash-landed on months later. It was a bit much and though she couldn't put all the pieces together, Jegra didn't think it was all simply a coincidence.

Although there was no way to have known the squid entity would transport her there, it still seemed like all the dominoes fell into perfect formation, as if someone had orchestrated it all.

But who could arrange so many seemingly random events in such a way as to ensure two people were destined to meet in no other way but the way they did? That's when Jegra remember the Nyctan oracle.

Surely, if anyone, Sanakar must know. She was the only person Jegra had met who could see glimpses into the future. Even if she hadn't planned it herself, chances are, she would know who had.

"I know I'm the last person you want to see right now," Jegra said, watching Onelle change out of her clothes and into an orange prison-issue jumpsuit, "but, I need you to hear the truth. Whether you accept it or not, whether you can find it in your heart to forgive me or not, that's up to you. But, here it is. The truth is I tried to save her. I couldn't. That regret will forever be in the back of my mind, nagging at me. Reminding me of my greatest failure."

Onelle slowly looked up at Jegra and gently touched the welt on her head from where Jegra had headbutted her. There was a long silence before she chose to answer.

"I suppose I owe you an apology. After all, you've watched over my youngest sister, Raphine, for several months now. Kept her safe. And for that I'm grateful."

Jegra nodded. "It's the least I could do for Abby's little sister. Please, if there's anything you need, do not hesitate to ask."

Onelle brushed down her bright orange prison-issue jumpsuit and grinned devilishly. "I could use better clothes."

Jegra laughed and stepped closer to the glass, her eyes meeting Onelle's. Her teal eyes were like the ocean, and she still couldn't believe how much Onelle resembled Abethca. If it wasn't for Onelle's more chiseled form, thanks in no small part to the harsh conditions of that terrible planet, Jegra was certain the two sisters would look virtually identical.

And she couldn't help but sense old feelings stirring. She had to remind herself that this was a different woman. That the woman she'd loved and known was gone now.

"I'll see what I can do, but I'm not making any promises. Captain Blackstar runs a tight ship and she's not likely willing to budge on regulation or protocol."

Onelle ran her finger down the edge of her jumpsuit's V-neck and tugged at it and fanned herself. Beads of sweat ran down her forehead and she wiped them away. "Does it feel hot in here or is it just me?"

"Now that's something I can help you with. What temperature would you like?"

Onelle shrugged. She wasn't sure. In fact, she was having trouble thinking clearly. Her head was spinning and she felt as though a fever were coming on. But she didn't feel sick; that was the weird part.

"Well, if you make up your mind, just tell the guard. I'll personally instruct them to assist you and change the temperature if need be." Jegra slowly turned to leave and began to move toward the door when Onelle called out to her.

"Wait! I need to tell you something."

Jegra turned to hear what Onelle had to say.

"I just wanted you to know that..." she paused briefly, her dizziness abruptly spiking into a migraine. She cringed and pinched the bridge of her nose, trying to push back against the searing pain in her head. Then, without provocation, her face went blank and a cruel smile incrementally formed on her Brunswick green lips. "When I get out of here, I will hunt you down and gut you like an Angorian king fish."

Jegra took a step back, raised an eyebrow, then shook her head disappointedly. She had given Onelle a second chance, but she was as two-faced as ever. It seemed like someone had literally flicked a switch in her mind and caused her to go from pleasant to psychotic in a split-second.

"For crying out loud! And to think that I was trying to give you the benefit of the doubt. But, apparently, you're bat-shit insane. So, enjoy your stay in the brig, sweetheart." Jegra turned, her arms at her sides, fists balled up in aggravation, and began to march toward the exit.

Just then, Captain Lianica Blackstar and a security team burst into the brig, almost crashing into Jegra. Whatever business it was about, it seemed urgent.

"Apologies, your grace," Lianica said, "but we just picked up a strange transmission coming from this room."

"Transmission?" Jegra asked. "What sort of transmission? Onelle and I have been talking for the past five minutes, uninterrupted."

Onelle stood behind the glass staring at both women with a blank face. It was as if she was in a trance of some kind. Meanwhile, one of the security officers pulled out a device and began scanning the entire room, searching for the mysterious signal.

"Captain, the signal…it's coming from…her."

Everyone turned their gazes toward Onelle, who was now grinning at them. But her smile was too big, too forced, to be genuine. To their surprise, her smile disappeared from her face leaving only the deadpan glare once again.

Onelle opened her mouth and a voice not her own came out. "Feed me," it said, gurgling. "Feed me!"

"Shit!" Lianica shouted. "It's a mind-control worm!"

She raced over to a security panel on the wall, opened a cubby, and pulled out a handheld device roughly the size of an electric razor. Without hesitating, she unlocked Onelle's cell and entered.

"What's that?" Jegra asked, eyeing the device in the commander's hands.

"It's a multi-purpose medical wand."

Rushing up to Onelle, who seemed to be frozen in a trance, she began running the wand up and down Onelle's neck and ears, scanning for any signs of the mind-control device. When the device in Lianica's hands chimed, its LED lights blinking wildly, she sighed. "Found it."

Lianica pulled out what looked like a small pitch fork and jammed it into Onelle's left ear. Jegra cringed at the sight. But what came next was far worse.

The captain twisted the fork and carefully drew it back out of Onelle's head. Skewered on the end of it was a translucent slug with pulsating internals that glowed dimly then faded again. It looked part organic and part mechanical, a mesh of bioengineered technology. A personally tailored parasite.

"These things can take over a person's entire nervous system, giving the hacker access to one's brain, muscles, and body functions. You basically become a living puppet."

Lianica flicked the fork and threw the slug on to the floor. Raising her boot, she promptly stamped it out of existence. There was a grotesque sounding *squish* and then the commander turned to her men, "Get this woman to sickbay. Have the doctor run a full neuro-scan to see how bad the damage is."

Onelle, who looked comatose, was ushered out of the room by the two guards, leaving only Jegra and the commander to stare at each other in silence.

"If that thing was controlling her," Jegra finally said, nodding down at the remains of the worm on the prison floor, "then her actions weren't her own."

"She was a sleeper assassin. It seems that whoever infected her with the parasite wanted to use her to get to you."

"I'll give you one guess who it likely was."

Lianica nodded then stroked her chin in contemplation. "Your assumption may be true, but let's not get ahead of ourselves. As bold a move as this was, it's not the emperor's style. He likes a certain amount of theatrics. Big space battles. Half-naked assassins. A no holds barred match in the arena. That sort of thing. Using biologically engineered parasites doesn't fit his modus operandi."

"In that case, I'm going to need you to find out who implanted her with the parasite and make sure it doesn't happen again."

Lianica crossed her right fist over her heart and bowed deeply. "Yes, Your Majesty."

"I'm thankful you found it in time. But how did you know she was infected?

Aren't those things designed to be undetectable?"

"Under normal circumstances, yes. Unless you know what it is you're supposed to be looking for, they don't show up on any scans. However, because these holding cells scramble all communication frequencies, it needed to amplify its signal to maximum, putting too much strain on its host. Whoever is controlling it wanted very badly to cut through the interference. I suppose they had hoped to get to you before getting found out. Luckily we were running a ship-wide scan at just the right time and caught it."

Jegra and Lianica entered the corridor together and slowly made their way to the bridge. "I appreciate the catch. Keep me updated on her condition. I want to know the moment she's able to answer questions."

"As you wish, Your Maj—"

Jegra raised her hand and stopped Lianica in the middle of her sentence. "Please, just call me Jegra. That's an order."

"Yes, Your Majes–I mean–yes, Jegra."

Jegra smiled and reached over to Lianica and gave her shoulder a gentle squeeze. Lianica smiled back.

"Now, where are we on locating Danica?"

Lianica tilted her head ever so slightly and gave the empress a puzzled look. "I thought you knew."

Jegra shook her head slightly, confirming she wasn't clear about what Lianica was referring to.

Lianica walked over to a wall display and brought up a holovid. She tapped a few buttons and tuned it to the gladiatorial games on Arena City. In the picture, Danica and Ishtar stood back-to-back as they fended off three enormous apes with ice-blue fur. Jegra recognized the creatures. They were Korgons from the ice world Riverion. Although no more intelligent than a silverback gorilla back on Earth, they were extremely brutal in the arena and liked to tear the arms and legs off their opponents.

"That bastard," Jegra said under her breath. "He sold her into the games."

"It's the seventh match in the humiliation bout. She's being forced to fight alongside her interrogator, the one they call the red-skinned assassin. Rumors are the tenth game will end with a Bull and Swan bout."

Jegra knew that a "bull and swan bout" was merely slang for an anything goes styled match, where the token warrior must go up against a gang of combatants, all with the single-minded goal of humiliating the defender by any means necessary. This included lewd acts of sexual assault, unthinkable violence, defecation, and even defilement after death—should it come to that.

It was a match reserved for the worst offenders of the law, as well as anyone the Emperor deemed particularly worthy for the role of the swan. Jegra had had to fight her bout after her escape attempt. "No bad deed goes unpunished," Dakroth had informed her the night before her match. Needless to say, she won the competition, but it wasn't something she'd wish on anyone.

Very few ever survived the ordeal. But if they did, they were rewarded with a temporary reprieve. Two months furlough to visit any loved ones, travel destinations, or just recuperate. Of course, many tried to escape during their furlough, but IGS always sent their bounty hunters to collect their prized gladiators. Something which Jegra had found out the hard way.

Even though Jegra knew the awful direness of Danica's situation, she couldn't help but smile to herself as the memory of her own humiliation bout entered her head. She may have been the only gladiator in the entire history of the games to have successfully defended off every attacker in her Bull and Swan bout. At the end of her match, she remembered the sands being so saturated with the blood of her enemies that it was like wading through sticky mud after a rainstorm.

That was the match in which she had inadvertently caught Emperor Dakroth's eye and in which he had taken a fond interest in her. That very same night, he met her in her personal chambers, underneath the arena, for a moonlight tryst.

He continued to meet with her every night for two weeks before being distracted by the political concerns of an empire embroiled in a trade war with the Nyctans. She didn't see him again until his battlecruiser jumped into orbit above Thessalonica, the very same day she had met Abethca.

The rest, as they say, is history.

"What are your orders, Mistress Jegra?" Captain Blackstar shifted uncomfortably on her feet as she tried to get accustomed to using the empress's actual name rather than any formal designation. Still, she applied the honorary title of mistress before it just to be safe.

"First, I want you to track down that signal and find whoever it is that's controlling Onelle. They obviously want me dead, and I want to know who and why. After that, we'll figure out how to break Danica out of Arena City."

Lianica bowed reverently. After straightening up again, she enthusiastically clicked her heels together, crossed her right fist over her heart, and then turned and headed up the corridor, leaving Jegra to be alone with her thoughts.

Jegra turned and stared out of a nearby portal and watched the stars. They were in Galliforn space and she had been out of commission for several months. As she began hatching a plan, there was a flash of light off the starboard bow and the *Skywend* suddenly appeared.

Without even realizing it, Jegra smiled faintly. Raven Nightguard wasn't only her greatest ally in the fight against Dakroth's corruption, but she was the most morally grounded person Jegra had ever met. And Jegra knew that she was in desperate need of Raven's expert counsel. If anyone knew what the next step should be, it would be her.

27

Liquid silver tendrils stretched out from the hull of the *Shard* and reached out toward the *Skywend*. In the blink of an eye, the numerous tendrils twisted, spiraled, and tightened around each other forming a cylindrical conduit. The lip of the silver tube rippled, as though it were composed of molten steel, and then, like the mouth of a vacuum, it wrapped its quivering lips around the docking port of the *Skywend* and latched on.

A loud clank sounded, signifying that the seemingly liquid metal docking arm was inexplicably solid again.

Jegra waited anxiously in front of the airlock, hopping up and down with excitement. When the airlock door melted away on her end, she could see the *Skywend's* circular door roll away. Raven stepped through and smiled when she saw the empress waiting for her personally.

Raven, wearing a sleeveless white jumpsuit with teal sash, sauntered down the corridor, running her hand along the inside of the docking arm, admiring the smooth metallic surface of the state of the art korridium alloy called microphase korridium—a metal which was able to, via the use of specially designed nanostructures, change between a solid and molten form with just the addition of electrical signals.

Raven ducked under the archway of the airlock and stopped in front of Jegra, pleased by her white body suit, its low, straight cropped neckline barely able to hold in her cleavage. Both women smiled, then, unable to hold her giddiness back, Jegra, scooped Raven up into her arms and gave her a massive squeeze.

"I missed you so much!" she gushed.

Speechless, Raven merely patted the top of Jegra's head. Unable to catch a full breath, she wheezed, "It's nice…to see you again…too, Your Majesty."

Jegra set Raven back on her feet and rolled her eyes. "Not you too?"

"Did I say something to offend? I didn't mean…"

"No, it's not that," Jegra cut in. "It's just that, you're my close friend. And I don't want my friends keeping me at an arm's length simply because of some archaic rules about titles and formalities and all that nonsense. Just call me Jegra. That's an order."

"Empress!" a cheerful voice chimed and Skuld peeked out into the corridor.

Jegra buried her face in her palms and let out a long sigh. She couldn't escape her title even if she tried. Slowly looking back up, she smiled warmly and waved at the always impossibly optimistic fish-man. There he was, approaching quickly, wearing his special breathing suit which looked like the perfect blend of a diving suit and an astronaut's EV suit.

The giant, bowl-shaped helmet he wore as part of his environmental suit amplified his features, including the catfish-like tendrils that hung down either side of his mouth and made it look as though he had a long Fu Manchu mustache on his aquatic face.

"Mistress Alakandra," Raven said, side-stepping her orders to call her by her first name, "In our search for you I happened across some vital intel that I think you'll be quite interested in seeing."

"Right," Jegra said, realizing the family reunion was over. "In that case, follow me to my personal chambers."

Just as Jegra turned and sauntered off, her hips swiveling seductively as she strode away, Skuld appeared next to Raven and nudged her elbow.

She ignored the dopey look on his face as he ogled the empress's backside and then followed after Jegra with haste.

Once the three of them arrived at her quarters, she motioned for them to go on in ahead of her. Closing the chamber doors behind her, Jegra headed past the classic burgundy leather furniture arranged atop a luxurious claret carpet woven with a kaleidoscope of golden floral patterns. Matching gold tassels lined the edges of the plush carpet, and Jegra kicked off her shoes and walked barefoot across the splendid rug.

In the corner of her chambers, she approached a solid wall and waved her hand across it. The wall melted away to reveal a doorway and beyond, a room that glowed with the blue light of holovid computer displays.

Inside the room was a large semi-circle shaped desk. A large computer chair sat behind the desk which was surrounded by floating holovids. There were about seven displays open in all, each one tracking people of interest. On one of the displays, Danica and Ishtar fought in Arena City. On another of the displays, one of the Grendok clones was brokering an arms deal.

Jegra spun to face Raven and stuck a hand on her hip. "I'm all ears. What is it you wanted to talk about?"

Skuld watched in fascination as the doorway solidified behind him. "Amazing," he said, genuinely impressed. He reached out with a webbed hand and touched the wall. It was completely solid. If you didn't know where to look, you would never even know there was a secret chamber.

Raven unzipped her tactical suit, her lavender breasts swelling up to bulge over the tight edges of the restrictive apparel. Slipping her fingers in between her breasts, she fished out an orange glowing data stick and handed it to Jegra. "Everything is on this."

"What is it?" Jegra asked, inspecting the data stick. It was made of a translucent orange glass with circuitry that glowed bright yellow beneath the smooth surface. Jegra placed the data stick on her desk and the golden veins seeped out of the device and extended into the desk itself, like the roots of a tree. Bringing up a new display, Jegra motioned her hand to enlarge the holographic image that hung in the air before them.

A schematic of the planet Jegra had been marooned on appeared. As the video played, it showed that the planet was in the middle of a massive wormhole. Their part of space was marked with a green glowing dot. Past the planet labeled as Planet X and beyond the long stretch of the wormhole's spout that exited onto an uncharted sector of space, was a red dot. This dot signaled an unknown frontier. A place where nothing had ever returned from. The dreaded "dead space" beyond the rift, as it was known.

"We're here," Raven said, placing her finger over the green glowing dot. "And this is the planet you were marooned on."

"Yeah, what is that place?" Jegra asked, eyeballing the planet with resentment. Needless to say, it wasn't the loveliest place she'd ever been.

"It's a fulcrum station," Skuld answered.

Jegra turned and gave him a blank stare and smiled. "What in the galaxy is that?"

"Wormholes are highly unstable. Even naturally occurring ones often collapse in on themselves, reform elsewhere, and open up again at a different location. The Commonwealth gave up experimenting with wormhole travel long ago because they were impossible to traverse safely. A fulcrum station is a kind of pillar. A massive support beam that not only holds the wormhole in place but provides one with a reliable shortcut to the other side of the galaxy."

"Is that where it exits?" Jegra asked. "The other side of our galaxy."

"That's just the thing," Skuld relayed, waving his slender, webbed fingers across the holovid display and panning out. "It exits in a different galaxy entirely. And not just any galaxy, one that is halfway across the known universe."

"Obviously the technology is beyond anything we have ever seen," Raven said.

"But what's so important, beyond finding a stable wormhole, that you had to rush to find me?"

"When we couldn't locate your emergency tracker, Skuld had the idea to develop a method for tracking the squid entities. He managed to hone in on their particular radiation, which leaves a residual footprint, and found this."

Raven swiped up and a transparent overlay flew up and then bonded with the holovid. Golden traces, like time-lapse photography of taillights, stretched from her end of space all the way toward the other end of the wormhole. Every single line, for every squid's passage, either originated in or returned to the mouth of the wormhole opposite them.

"They're coming from the other galaxy."

"Correct," Raven replied. "Every squid's route traces right back to here." Her finger landed on the red dot that marked the coordinates of the uncharted galaxy.

"I'm not one to be an alarmist, but the space-squids pose a very real threat to our sector of space. They've been trickling over in a small, exploratory, capacity. First there was one sighting. Then a couple more. Now we're hearing of sightings every day."

"They're foraging," Jegra said.

"Exactly!" Skuld said, snapping his fingers as if a lightbulb went on in his head. "Like ants and other wingless insects. They're searching for food."

"And they found some," Raven said. Swiping off the display, she turned to Jegra with a stern gaze. "I fear that in the coming months, more of those entities will breach into our space. And as you already know, they're a bitch to kill."

"You fear a full-on invasion."

"Our fusion engines supply them with the energy they need to reproduce," Skuld interjected. "Chances are, they have gotten a taste of our technology, which means more will be coming any day now."

"I thought you should know," Raven said, touching Jegra's arm. "Because you, of all the galaxy's leaders, are probably the only one who cares enough about others to do something about it."

Jegra glanced down at Raven's hand on her arm and smiled. Looking back up, her eyes met Raven's enhanced purple ones, and they held one another's gaze until Raven grew overly self-conscious regarding their brief intimacy and looked away.

"I'll debrief the captain and figure out a plan. I appreciate your bringing this information to my attention."

Raven crossed her right fist over her chest and Jegra did the same. She needn't salute the empress, but it was habit from when she'd served in the military. And Jegra was, after all, the Empress of the Dagon Empire.

"Skuld," Jegra said, looking over at the fish-man. "You're dismissed. Feel free to tell the others to come aboard and help themselves to the mess hall and any recreational activities they may desire."

"Roger that, Your Majesty."

Jegra clinched her jaw and smiled through the annoyance she felt for such meaningless trivialities.

Skuld waved his hand in front of the wall and a small patch dissolved, revealing the exit. "Amazing! Just like the tesseract."

"Tesseract?" Jegra inquired, shooting Raven a peculiar look.

"It's a long story," Raven said.

Skuld swung his lanky arms as he strode out into the empress's personal chambers. The two women watched him cut across her room and then leave.

"I heard about Danica. You need to talk?"

"You read my mind," Jegra answered, offering the chair behind her desk to Raven.

Raven dipped her chin in gratitude and took her seat. Leaning back, Jegra sat on the edge of the desk and crossed one leg over the other. "I know Dakroth expects me to go in guns blazing. He wants the Senate to think I'm a liability so that they'll turn against me. So, that's clearly not an option. Another strategy is I sneak in and mount a covert rescue operation. But he'll likely be ready for that, too. Everything I do is likely being tracked. And even aboard my own ship I don't know who is and who isn't a spy."

"*Ah*, I see," Raven said, leaning back and resting her chin on her palm. "You need me to carry out the rescue mission while you distract the emperor."

"Exactly."

Raven smiled. "I think we can handle that."

Jegra leaned forward, sitting straight up with excitement. "Really?"

"Anything for you, Your Majes..." Raven trailed off and gave Jegra an apologetic look.

"It's fine," Jegra said, waving away the slip up.

Raven rose to her feet and stood directly before Jegra. "Listen, Jegra, I'm always here for you. You know that."

Unable to keep her emotions in check, Jegra threw her arms around Raven and gave her another impossibly strong squeeze.

Raven fell into Jegra, her head nestling into Jegra's shoulder as they embraced one another. Slowly, she raised her hands, hesitating briefly before wrapping them around Jegra's waist. Returning displays of affection wasn't exactly her strong suit, but she felt a surprisingly close bond to the empress. She imagined that they'd be friends for a long, long time to come. And that suited her just fine.

After what seemed to be an abnormally long stretch of time, Raven finally said, "You can stop hugging me now."

"Yep," Jegra said, embarrassed that she may have overdone it, burdening Raven with all kinds of affection she probably didn't want. She relinquished Raven and drew back, only to find Raven grinning pleasantly at her. She couldn't help but laugh when she saw that Raven wasn't upset with her. Quite the opposite, in fact.

"As I was saying, if there's ever anything you need, don't hesitate to call on me." Raven turned to go and walked out of the secret room and into Jegra's main chambers.

Jegra followed her out, the invisible door conveniently materializing behind her, and she cleared her throat, stopping her friend in her tracks.

Raven glanced over her shoulder and smiled. "Was there something else?"

"Nothing of importance. I was just sort of wondering if…" Jegra ran her fingers nervously through her hair and looked up at Raven, "you'd like to get a couple's massage with me and then take a rejuvenating mud bath?"

Jegra bit her bottom lip as she waited for Raven's reply. She felt surprisingly close to this woman even though they barely knew each other. But every time they'd had a chance to talk, it was always like talking to a friend she hadn't seen in years.

"I appreciate the offer," Raven said, brushing her purple hair out of her eyes, "but I need to run a full spectrum diagnostic scan of the ship before we head off."

"Let my people do that for you," Jegra said without thinking.

Raven raised an eyebrow and shot her a stern look. "You know I don't let anyone touch my baby," she replied.

"Right," Jegra said, kicking herself. "What was I thinking?"

Seeing that Jegra felt let down by her rejection, Raven took a step toward the empress. Waving her hand to the side, she said, "Look, maybe once the diagnostic scan is complete, if there's still time, we can do some mud wrestling, if you'd like."

Jegra held back a laugh. "Not mud wrestling," she informed Raven, a half grin curling onto her face as she gently corrected her friend's mistake. "A mud *bath*. Mud wrestling is where we tear each other's clothes off and smear mud over each other's bare-naked bodies for no reason."

"Sparring in such conditions is an excellent way to improve one's skills," Raven answered. Without skipping a beat, she added, "It teaches you how to grapple at a disadvantage, where adapting is the key to overcoming your opponent, and where you must rely on strategy and skill rather than brute strength." Raven held her gaze, and then smiled and winked at Jegra.

Jegra nudged Raven's shoulder. "You're messing with me!"

Raven smiled. "No, I'm not. I'll take you down so fast your head will be spinning."

"Oh?" Jegra chuckled. "I'd like to see you try it."

Both women laughed at the absurdity of agreeing to an impromptu mud wrestling match between them. But a deal was a deal and Jegra was going to hold her to it. And Raven knew she would.

Raven looked into Jegra's eyes one last time, as if to test the limits of their platonic bond, and then bowed politely and took her leave.

Jegra stood there and watched her step out into the corridor. She raised her hand to motion for Raven to hold up, but whatever question she'd been about to ask quickly dissipated from her thoughts.

She pulled her hand back and found her cheeks were flush with a rosy tinge. Touching her face, she smiled and watched Raven glance back one last time before disappearing around the corner of the corridor.

Jegra leaned against the door frame of her entrance and smiled to herself. *That woman never ceases to amaze*, she thought. No sooner had she entered her room, her chamber doors sliding shut behind her, when the doorbell chimed.

She stopped mid-stride and turned back toward the door. She gazed at it curiously, and thinking it might be Raven returning, she quickly said, "Come in."

The door remained shut, but chimed again.

"I said, enter," she said in a more formal tone.

Still, the door did not open. Letting out a sigh, she rolled her eyes and then reached out and touched the touch control panel on the wall and the doors whispered open.

Jegra looked up and, as the shock sank in, she gasped. "It's you."

28

The teal ocean which ran up to the foot of the royal palace on Dagon Prime rippled with the disturbance of Dakroth's royal battlecruiser as the landing thrusters revved up to full. Greenish-blue waves swirled into white froth as the ship lowered into docking position. A docking ramp extend from the seaward facing terrace and met the cruiser's lower hatch and locked into place with a loud *clank*. The minimalist, stealth-like angles of the maroon ship stood in stark contrast to the elaborate Gothic-styled aesthetic of the royal palace.

With a mechanical whine, the ship's hatch opened and Dakroth, wearing his all-white military dress uniform, replete with a flowing cape and golden lining, his silver hair tied back in a ponytail, marched across the ramp toward the terrace. Waiting for him there was a security team of about half a dozen royal guards. They had on their burgundy armor, helmets that sported a shark fin on top, and long, flowing, purple capes that concealed a rifle-sword, basically a double-bladed sword with a gun barrel running the length between them—the signature weapon of the royal guard.

The six guards stood in tight formation around a red-skinned woman who, in turn, stood glaring at Dakroth as he approached. Her wrists and ankles were shackled with heavy korridium restraints, and she wore only the black Targarian stingray leather bikini she'd been allowed to take from one of the dead contestants she'd defeated earlier that day. Right after the match, she was summoned to her chambers where she'd found the royal guard waiting for her.

"My dear Ishtar," Dakroth said as he approached the scowling woman. "It seems there's been a change in plans. I have it on good authority that the empress herself is planning to attend the final humiliation bout."

Ishtar's face swiftly changed from angry to worried. This turn of events complicated her mission. "But if she finds out Danica is fighting, she'll likely put a stop to it. Ratings will plummet and your plans will be…"

"You let me worry about Jegra," the emperor interrupted. "You just take care of the vice admiral, as per our arrangement. I'll handle the rest."

The devious grin on Dakroth's face alerted Ishtar to the fact that he already had a plan in motion. Still, she knew what it would mean if she failed. Her head.

"All the same, my lord, if something should go wrong?"

"That's why you're there. To ensure that it doesn't." Dakroth walked right up to Ishtar and locked his hands behind his back as he looked down into the woman's yellow-green eyes with his red ones. "Keep her alive until the Bull and Swan bout. Her humiliation bout won't end until she is ravished and defiled and left for dead on the battlefield."

"You know the empress won't allow her lover to be raped on live televid for all the Commonwealth to see."

"As I said. You let me worry about Jegra. You just make sure the woman you're fighting with lives long enough to enjoy her ultimate humiliation. If she dies before that time, I will personally see to it that you do not walk off that field alive."

Ishtar frowned and looked away. Then, begrudgingly, she answered, "Your wish is my command, my lord."

Dakroth brushed past Ishtar, nudging her aside as he went. She gritted her teeth in anger and watched him out of the narrow corner of her eye.

"Oh, and one more thing," he said, pausing briefly without so much as looking back, "after you fulfill your contract, our relationship is over. We never even met, you and I. Am I clear?"

"Crystal," Ishtar growled.

Dakroth grinned and then walked off, disappearing through the tall glass doors of the palace's southwest entrance.

"Move it," one of the guards said, shoving Ishtar from behind with his stun-baton.

She glanced back at him, her eyes hard and cold, but he merely shoved her toward the ramp a second time. She staggered forward and began making her way across the ramp toward the ship. It would take her back to the moon hanging above them. Back to Arena City.

Half way out, Ishtar looked up at the creamy yellow orb hanging in the sky. Although Thessalonica was a desert moon, it had several small oceans with green halos where life thrived. Around these green borders were the cities. The density of the cities acted like a protective barrier that allowed the fertile land between the towns and the oceans to thrive. It seemed as though a giant Elder God had clawed the moon only to reveal green flesh underneath the sand-worn scab-like surface.

"Get moving," the guard grumbled, and gave Ishtar another shove.

"Touch me again, and I'll snap your neck like a twig."

The guard looked at his comrades and they all shared a chuckle. Then, as predicted, he doubled down on his show of authority and shoved her even harder. "You're not the one in charge here, princess. So, why don't you shut that pretty mouth of yours and get moving."

When he went to shove her with the stun-baton again, she stepped to the side, grabbed his wrist, and then in one fluid motion of gymnastic expertise, swung up and around his arm. Wrapping her thighs around his neck, she brought him to the ground in an armbar, her thighs wrapped around his face. The guard squirmed to get away, but Ishtar squeezed her thighs and tugged his arm so hard that his neck snapped between her legs.

She laughed and let go of his arm. "Warned you," she said, grinning.

A flurry of crackling batons came down on her all at once as the remaining five guards all took turns shocking her into submission. As soon as she fell limp, they dragged their friend away and then began another round of shocking her.

One of the guards kicked her in her side and growled, "You think that's funny, red-skinned bitch?"

Two of the guards reached down and hoisted Ishtar up by her arms. As they did, the angry guard got in her face and said in a low and menacing voice. "You just killed my buddy. Give me one reason I shouldn't end you right here and now."

Ishtar snapped her head forward and headbutted the guard right across the bridge of his nose. The crack was so loud the other guards tensed when they heard it.

"Ow!" the guard screamed, reeling back. He grabbed his shattered nose, blood gushed down his face and dribbled off his chin. "You broke my nose, you stupid cunt!"

Reaching around his back, the guard retrieved his riffle and shouldering it, he jammed the muzzle against Ishtar's forehead. Hand on the trigger, he trembled with rage and adrenaline.

"Be careful, lover boy. You're getting me all kinds of wet," Ishtar said, grinning at the wild-eyed, blood-soaked guard.

One of the other guards reached up and put a hand on his shoulder. "Lord Dakroth ordered us to return her to Arena City in one piece. I suggest you stow that weapon, comrade, and complete the task lest the emperor finds out you disobeyed a direct order."

Reluctant to let it go, the guard pressed the muzzle of his gun even harder into Ishtar's head. Then, after a brief moment of weighing the pros and cons, he huffed out in frustration and reluctantly lowered his weapon.

The two guards holding Ishtar by her arms began to drag her away. "That's right," she called out, taunting the guard she'd mangled. "You walk away…just like the little bitch you are."

The guard growled with rage and turned to come at her but was quickly restrained by the remaining two men. They held him back long enough for Ishtar to be taken safely aboard the cruiser.

As her two escorts dragged her down the long corridor toward the brig, she glanced at one and then the other and cleared her throat. "I wasn't kidding," she said, a salacious smile forming on her black painted lips. "I'm riper than a Targarian peach right now. So, if you boys want to take a slight detour, I could make it worth your while."

They ignored her, their eyes and shark fin helmets fixed straight ahead. Without slowing, their boots clanked along the metal corridor with urgency. Before she knew it, they'd ushered her into a small room with a back cell cordoned off by four-inch nano-mesh glass. The very same glass that starship windows were made of. It was so strong that it could deflect a micro-meteorite shower and come out unscathed. Creating prison cells out of the stuff was smart, because it was nearly impervious yet allowed perfect visibility of the prisoner.

The guard on Ishtar's right took her by the arm and guided her into the cell, entering with her. Meanwhile, the second guard remained outside the cell where he could keep eyes on her if she tried anything.

The first guard shoved Ishtar hard and she stumbled forward. Laughing, she slowly turned around, her hand sliding down her taut stomach, round hips, and, finally, beneath her loincloth. The guard raised an eyebrow when she pulled her hand back out to reveal two glistening fingers. She reached over and wiped her essence on the guard's top lip and then laughed again. "I told you."

There was a pounding on the glass and the other guard yelled, "Stop messing around and get on with it."

"Turn around and face the wall," the guard in the cell with her barked, waving his stun-baton at her to compel her to knock off the games and get back to being an obedient prisoner.

"Fine," Ishtar grumbled. "Your loss."

She did as asked and faced the wall and placed both palms flat against it, forehead pressed to the wall, spreading her legs to the appropriate distance marked on the floor with a yellow line. This was the posture all maximum-security prisoners were required to take whenever a visitor entered or exited the cell. Ishtar glanced over her shoulder when the guard didn't leave only to see the glowing blue arc of his stun-rod kiss the back of her neck with a menacing crackle.

There was a loud zap and a painful surge of electricity that froze every sinew in her body. The invisible tendrils wound their way into her like crabgrass and seized her tight and Ishtar, stiff as a board, dropped to the ground. Landing awkwardly across her right arm, she moaned with half-pleasure, half-pain. She'd be lying if she said she didn't enjoy it. The moment the guard let off the trigger, she gasped out in near ecstasy.

The guard kicked Ishtar in her side and rolled her over onto her back. Still unable to regain motor control, her yellow eyes flitted toward the guard's sneering grin as he stepped over her and looked down at her with a twisted yearning.

Ishtar strained with all her strength and lifted her head off the cold metal floor, but the guard merely growled, "Stay down," and jabbed the rod into the soft part of her abdomen for good measure. She stiffened again, as more sizzling volts penetrated her. Standing over her, the guard stowed his stun-baton and began unfastening his belt. "Now be a good girl and smile for me, because I'm about to give you a nice treat."

With haste, he dropped his pants to his ankles and then got down on all fours, roughly spreading Ishtar's legs apart and sliding off her black panties. His carnal excitement growing in anticipation, he licked his lips lecherously, and reached down and took his erect blue penis in his hand. Slowly, he guided its purple tip toward the lips of Ishtar's vagina–the very same one she offered him moments earlier.

Granted, what she had in mind went beyond merely treading the line between rape and sex. It was no secret that she liked the illicit and debauched forms of sex, so this kind of violation was right up her alley. Usually, however, she was on the giving end, not on the receiving end of the assault, but, for whatever reason, this time she felt herself getting excited by the mere thought of being forced. The loss of power. The fact that the guard knew exactly what he wanted.

Of course, she went along with it and pretended that she couldn't stop it. That way the vileness of it would titillate her. Dwelling on the fact she could trigger her internal biochem-regulators at any moment, flood her system with adrenaline at a mere thought, then, rise up and snap this fool's neck, would make it less satisfying somehow, so she allowed him to continue to think he was the one in power.

The guard groaned as he entered her with surprising ease and after a few slow pumps to test the waters, so to speak, he began pounding furiously.

Ishtar felt as though she was being humped by a horny teenager who hadn't the skill or control to make it worth her while, but, then again, very few men could meet her particular sort of depraved needs.

The guard finished with a stereotypical grunt and pulled out. Looking over his shoulder at his friend, he offered her as the spoiled prize she was. "You want a turn?"

The guard standing outside the cell simply shook his head no. It's not that he didn't enjoy having a slave girl. He just wasn't sure about defiling a red-skin. It seemed so unsavory in his mind. Interspecies relations. It grossed him out.

"You sure, man? She wasn't lying. She's riper than a Targarian peach. The juices are literally flowing out of her. Come on, give it a shot. You'll thank me later."

"I'm good," the stoic guard replied, not budging on his discriminatory policy on interspecies relations.

Ishtar rolled her eyes and then mumbled, "Damn, and I was hoping to get some satisfaction, not this two-pump chump."

"What did you say?" the guard asked, turning his attention back toward the woman sprawled out on the floor before him. He held her gaze, not intimidated by her in the least, and then bent down and took her by the neck in a show of dominance and squeezed.

"Was there something you wanted to say to me?" When she didn't offer a snide quip in response, he grinned wide and said, "That's what I thought, bitch."

Ishtar's hands moved so fast the guard didn't even have time to react. Even with the heavy restraints binding her wrists, she managed to grab the back of his skull and his chin in either hand and twist. There was a loud, sickening crack and the guard's face spiraled around, his head backwards on his shoulders, gazing at his friend on the other side of the glass.

The other guard watched in horror as Ishtar snapped his friend's neck with such speed that he had to blink a couple of times as it took a moment for him to register what had happened.

Ishtar started laughing and she pushed the guard off of her. He slid away and fell to the side, his body landing with a *thump*, his backward head still staring across the room at his partner. Sitting up, she locked eyes with the outside guard and shot him a morbid grin. She chewed on her lip seductively, licked her teeth and smiled up at him.

"Care to come inside and play?" she asked, her grin growing even wider. She kept her eyes fixed on him the entire time, licking her lips with a passionate display of her unadulterated lust. "I'm so ripe. Riper than a Targarian peach," she taunted, using his partner's exact same words to try and goad him into coming into the room.

The guard slammed his hand down on the door panel and secured the door. It slammed shut with a sturdy *thud* and the locking mechanism clanked into place. Ishtar glanced at the door and then back at the guard. "You're no fun," she huffed disappointedly.

Ishtar rose to her feet, pulled up her panties, and readjusted her loincloth. Once everything was back in its proper place, she walked up to the glass and stared into the guard's eyes. "I promise I'll play nice," she said, her crooked grin spreading into a full smile as she couldn't even take her own lie seriously.

"Step away from the glass," the guard said, not wanting to take any more chances with this psychopath.

Ishtar held his nervous gaze with her composed one, and then blew him a kiss. She could tell it bothered him, which is exactly why she had done it.

Just then, the room filled with the sound of the ship's engines humming to life and, then with the sudden momentum of the ship taking off. It felt exactly like riding in a high-speed elevator up to the top of a skyscraper as the ship ascended into space. Once the momentum had stopped, the grav-paneling came online to counteract the zero-gravity environment.

Ishtar slapped her palms on the glass, startling the guard. Then, she licked the glass, making it seem as though she were licking his face.

"I warned you," the guard growled, and then he slammed his hand down on the blue lightning bolt symbol on the control pad next to the door.

The metal floor beneath Ishtar's feet surged with five thousand volts and dropped Ishtar on her back like a lead weight. Once the guard stopped the electricity, Ishtar coughed as she took in air and rolled onto her back and stared up at the ceiling. Her cough quickly turned into a bout of laughter and gradually, her laughter grew until the guard pounded on the glass and yelled at her to: "Shut up!"

For her, this was all rather quite fun. She thrived on the pain and anguish of others. Fear excited her, sexually. Pain aroused her most libidinous desires. Together, pain and fear got her so worked up the only way she could deal with it was to unleash her dark nature on others. And there was a reason she was the galaxy's deadliest assassin. Killing, for her, was pure unadulterated joy. If she could kill someone during sex, well, that was just the cherry on top.

Ishtar let out a long, heavy sigh, chortled quietly to herself as she replayed the day's carnage in her mind. Feeling good, she closed her eyes and relaxed the rest of the way to Thessalonica and Arena City.

Back at the Imperial Palace, Dakroth pushed open the ceiling-high doors and strode into the main throne room where a pale skinned woman in an exotic black dress that seemed to be made of strange rubber-like micro-fiber mesh, stood waiting for him.

"Sorry to have kept you waiting, Administratrix," he said, taking an apologetic bow.

Anaïs Nin slowly turned around and gazed upon the Lord Emperor with a less than amused sort of look. Her large dark eyes peered at him with a reserved kind of revulsion. It was clear she disliked him greatly, but what wasn't clear was why. Full well knowing the feeling was mutual, he had invited her all the way to Dagon Prime.

"What's so important that you had to use a royal pardon to get me here, Lord Emperor Dakroth?"

"It's true, I called in every remaining favor I had with the council to get you that pardon. But I wouldn't have done it if it hadn't been absolutely vital."

Anaïs Nin raised a hairless eyebrow. The wrinkle in her brow, however, gave away the surprise on her face. "Well, I'm here now. So, if you don't mind dispensing with the formalities and getting down to it, I have other engagements I need to keep."

"Just hear me out," Dakroth said, raising his hands in a gesture of polite surrender. "It's about the prophesy."

This seemed to catch her attention; her head perked up and her posture straightened. Dakroth grinned. The Nyctans were so easy to manipulate. Bring up religion and you had their undivided attention.

"I'm listening," she said, clasping her fingers together as she waited to hear what Dakroth had to say.

29

Jegra's fingers curled tightly around the pillow, squeezing it with all her strength. The tendons in her neck drew taut and she groaned out in pleasure, "Don't ever stop fucking me!"

Kregor arched his back and wrapping his green, talon-like fingers around Jegra's meaty thighs, he drew her hips into himself and began tapping her even faster. Double-timing it, he sped up and forced another moan from Jegra's lips.

"Eventually," he huffed, "I'm going to...have to..."

"Don't you dare!" Jegra shouted. The pillow tore in half and feathers exploded across the bed. One landed on Jegra's mouth and she spat it aside. "Don't you dare stop now."

Kregor was so close, but he held back for as long as he possibly could. He didn't want to disappoint the empress, but she had a warrior's stamina and was pushing him to his limits.

"As empress, I command you not to come yet,"

"That's...not...fair!" he groaned, maintaining his impossible jack-hammer-level of pounding.

Kregor's bulbous, lizard eyes grew overly large, his pupil's dilated, and then, after a silent pause, his tongue flickered.

"Did you just do what I think you did?"

"No?" Kregor replied timorously, his voice sounding more like a question than a definitive answer.

"It's fine," Jegra laughed, grabbing the brawny Dragonian's shoulders and pulling him into her massive chest.

She kissed him on the mouth and then smiled at him.

"I have been dying to finish what we started ever since..."

"Ever since Cordova," he answered.

"It was nice not having any interruptions this time," Jegra said. Kregor nodded when, as if on cue, the doorbell chimed.

Jegra and Kregor looked at the door to her quarters then back at each other. Letting out a sigh, Jegra said, "It appears I may have spoken too soon."

Jegra took ahold of her sheet and slipped out of the covers. Wrapping the sheet around her like a toga, she went to the door and leaning in to block the angle of her bed, she opened it.

"Sorry to bother you, Your Majesty" a youthful voice said, "But the captain was wondering if you've seen Kregor by any chance?"

"Gyllek!" Jegra said loudly enough for Kregor to hear all the way across the room behind her. "What a pleasant surprise."

Gyllek brushed her bright orange hair out of her eyes and looked Jegra up and down suspiciously. "Sure," she said in her droll monotone voice that never seemed to betray an ounce of excitement. She wasn't the sentimental type. The only affection she had was for gadgets and strange tech. Leaning over, Gyllek tried to peek into Jegra's chambers, but the empress leaned to the side along with her and blocked her view. The tacky grin on her face suggested she was definitely hiding something. And although Gyllek could guess exactly what, or more precisely–who it was–she didn't want to know the details.

"I'll tell you what, if I see him I'll be sure to tell him Raven is looking for him."

"Right," Gyllek said, a touch of sarcasm tucked into her reply. "You do that." Gyllek turned to leave but paused and turned back again. This caused Jegra to put both arms up along the door frame and pretend to stretch. Tossing her hair, she smiled at Gyllek and waited for the girl to come out with whatever it was she had on her mind. Pointing at Jegra's sheet, she said, "FYI, I can totally see your nipples through that."

As Gyllek turned and hurried up the hall as though nothing had happened, Jegra looked down at her chest only to discover it was true. The artificial lighting in the hallway somehow made her white sheets practically translucent. Embarrassed, she gulped loudly and then stealthily drew back into her chambers.

When Jegra turned around she found Kregor already pulling up his boxer-briefs. "I guess I'd better get going. Duty calls."

"Did I say you were dismissed?" Jegra asked.

Kregor stopped dressing and looked up. When he shot her a puzzled look Jegra let go of the sheet and let it slip to the floor. Striking a seductive pose, she said, "Now, strip and get back into bed, big guy. I'm not finished with you yet."

"Yes, Your Majesty," he replied, taking a reverent bow.

Once he'd finished doing as she asked, Jegra leapt forward and tackled him onto the bed. They both tumbled into the covers, laughing as they began round two of their midnight rendezvous.

Lianica Blackstar kicked her leg up on the edge of the tub and ran the laser-shaver over her calf. The bristles of each small hair crackled as they were singed away to nothing and the smell of singed hair was counteracted by the dozen scented candles she'd placed about the entire room and along the edge of the bath.

After finishing with the other leg too, she stood up and reached for the sash of her bathrobe when, all of a sudden, the ship's emergency alarm went off. Spinning around, Lianica marched over to the door and hit the com-link. "This is Captain Blackstar. What's going on up there?"

"A small scout vessel has fired warning shots across the bow and has demanded we let them board."

"They are demanding to board her majesty's royal cruiser?" Lianica laughed. "Tell them 'request denied.'"

Lianica slapped the com off and went back to her steaming hot bath. She reached down to unwrap herself when the ship received a startling jolt from what felt like a plasma blast.

"Grah!" she roared out in frustration, kicking her head back to let it all out. Turning back to the door, she hit the com again and said, "Return fire. And I want whoever that idiot is towed into shuttle bay two and then marched straight to the brig. Do I make myself clear?"

"Yes, ma'am," the voice on the other end replied.

Lianica looked back down at her bath one more time and then sighed. Her relaxing night off was going to have to wait.

Several minutes later, she stepped onto the bridge. Brei'Alas greeted her and then, discretely, pointed at her own collar, signaling to the captain that something was wrong with hers. Lianica reached down and found that she'd missed the last hook on her mandarin collar and quickly fastened it. It seemed, maybe, her drinking was finally taking its toll on her. She quickly put it out of her mind and got back to more pressing concerns.

"Report," she said, looking out at the vessel being reeled in by the magnetic grappling hooks.

"It's a class nine series scout of Galliforn design," the tactical officer said. He was an older Dagon with a hoary goatee, a chiseled physique, and a tight ponytail. "Extremely fast and agile but, usually equipped with minimal armaments. This ship, however, seems to have been heavily modified and is carrying type seven plasma disrupters."

"Type seven?" Lianica asked. "But a ship that size doesn't even have a fusion drive to power such a weapon."

"This one does, apparently," the lieutenant answered, bringing up the scans of the ship onto the main display.

After giving the scans a cursory glance, Lianica swiped her hand right and waved the schematics off the main display. The holovid flickered and the outside view of the ship being towed into shuttle bay two reappeared.

"I want two security teams down there when that ship arrives." Turning to Brei'Alas, Lianica said, "Lieutenant, Sub Commander Kolivan Dan Koreth, you're with me."

The older Dagon officer and Brei'Alas both followed the captain off the bridge and to the grav-lift.

"Shouldn't we inform the empress?" asked Brei'Alas, her voice as meek as ever.

"I don't want to burden the empress unless it's absolutely necessary. She's been through enough as of late."

Brei'Alas nodded. Kolivan, meanwhile, was the strong silent type and simply rode the lift in stoic silence.

When the trio arrived at shuttle bay two, both security teams were already in position around the small craft that sat on the middle of the platform. The *Shard's* outer hull was slowly reforming as the tendrils of the microphase korridium reached out for one another like grasping fingers.

The metallic fingers locked together, forming a tight mesh, and then the air gaps quickly disappeared as the liquid metal smoothed itself out and became solid again.

Captain Lianica motioned both security teams to train their weapons on the entrance. Five of her men were taking up positions along the second story balcony railing as overwatch, and about half the security team on the main deck took cover behind crates and equipment.

Lianica wasn't going to take any chances with security. Not this time. Not after Ishtar Bantu infiltrated Jegra's ship at the battle for Sector B-13 and certainly not after the debacle with Onelle Agnar who had, unfortunately, killed ensign Dree'alek on this very same hangar deck.

After taking their positions, Lianica Blackstar stepped out onto the hangar floor and peered at the ship. Its reflective glass prevented her from seeing inside the small scout ship.

"You are in violation of the Intergalactic Peace Accord which grants safe travel to all ships within the Commonwealth. You will surrender yourself and your vessel to us and be prosecuted. Failure to comply will result in the forceful seizure of your vessel. You have thirty seconds to surrender yourself."

There was a hiss of air as the ship's canopy popped open and a heavily armored individual clambered out. Landing on the floor with a metallic *clunk*, the figure slowly rose up and turned a masked visor toward Commander Blackstar.

Slowly reaching up, the figure unfastened its headgear and pulled off the helmet to reveal a beautiful green-skin.

"You're Bre'lal," Lieutenant Brei'Alas gasped.

"My name is Angellyk Adronis of Arkadia, and I've come with a message for Empress Alakandra. 'He's coming.'"

"Who's coming?" Lianica asked.

"Zira Ha'ppek."

"Zira Ha'ppek?" Brei'Alas asked, unfamiliar with the name. "Who's that?"

"He's nobody," Captain Blackstar replied almost as soon as the lieutenant had asked the question. She cleared her throat and narrowed her eyes at their guest. "Because he doesn't exist."

"Oh, I can assure you," Angellyk replied, matching the commander's intense gaze with one of her own. "He's most certainly real. And he's on his way here."

"Who are you again?" Brei'Alas asked, pointing at the woman in heavy combat armor.

"I'm just a messenger. But I was tasked to deliver this communication to the empress personally." Angellyk took a step forward, testing the room. She heard the shuffle of shoulders and the clicking of plasma riffles being cocked.

Lianica raised her hand and gestured for Angellyk to stop where she was. "I'm afraid the only way I'll allow you to be in proximity of the empress is if you're behind nano-mesh glass in a holding cell.

The green-skinned woman scanned the room of soldiers, all their weapons trained on her, waiting for Lianica's signal to intervene should she try anything. Cautiously, Angellyk raised her hands, showing her bare wrists to Lianica, and answered, "Then, you'd better arrest me."

Lieutenant Brei'Alas pulled out some magnetic restraints from behind her back and walked hesitantly toward the Bre'lal woman. She was surprisingly tall for a green-skin. But even with her more athletic build, like all Bre'lal, she maintained a level of beauty that made her people renowned throughout the galaxy.

Brei'Alas looked over her shoulder to confirm and was met with a silent nod from the captain urging her to proceed.

Just as Brei'Alas was turning back around to cuff Angellyk, a gloved hand wrapped itself around her mouth and reeled her back. Her back hit the metal chest plating of Angellyk's body armor with a *thud* and the woman's forearm slowly constricted around her neck like a python. In her other hand was a small dagger which was pressed firmly to the lieutenant's neck.

"Hold your fire," Lianica shouted, raising her fist in the air and gesturing for her men to exercise restraint.

"I don't think you understand. My mission," Angellyk snarled through her clenched teeth, "is to personally relay my message to her Majesty, Jegra Alakandra. And I intend to do just that."

"Unless the information you have pertains to Dagon galactic security, I'm afraid you'll wait in the cell until the time I deem you're no longer a threat to my crew or this ship, or until the empress orders me to do otherwise."

"You're making a mistake," Angellyk growled.

Unexpectedly, Angellyk's arm twisted about in such an unnatural way that she immediately relinquished her hold on the knife. Another wrenching of her arm and her shoulder dislocated from its socket. Angellyk let out a scream as she shoved Brei'Alas out of the way and spun around, taking a wild swing at the air.

"I know you're out there!" she hollered at the thin air. Her arm limp at her side, she ignored the fleet of soldiers all around her who trained their laser-scopes on her.

Another invisible *thump*, which sounded like a heavy boot slamming into Angellyk's breast plate, sent her staggering back. She lunged forward only to have her feet go out from under her. Flying up, she came down on her back, hard.

The air shimmered above her momentarily, and then the invisibility cloak of the steel armor dissolved to reveal Raven Nightguard standing before the green-skin.

"I can't say I'm surprised to see you, Raven," Angellyk said. "After all, it's just like a Dagon to crawl into bed with whomever offers them the sweetest deal."

Raven ignored the woman's words and reached down and pulled her to her feet. "I don't make deals with snakes," Raven said. It was true, she wasn't one to ally herself with Dagon interests, seeing as they'd exiled her family when she was little on the accusation of being insurrectionists. But Raven was loyal to Jegra, which is why she intervened.

Lieutenant Brei'Alas held out the restraints and handed them to Raven. "Maybe you should handle this."

"Yes," Angellyk said, a coy grin curling onto her forest green lips. "You'd best handle me."

"Enough, Angie," Raven finally said, letting out a sigh. "Just do as they say and things will go smoothly."

"Smoothly?" Angellyk balked. "Like when you dissolved our marriage contract over the fact that I stole your stupid necklace? Because I've never seen anyone slide right out of a marriage for something as trivial as that."

"I don't know how many times I have to repeat myself to you, Angie. It wasn't a bloody necklace! It was a hyperborean crystal. I needed it to power my ship. You pawned it off so you could pay back that debt collector you owed and, thanks to you, I was left stranded in unfriendly space only to be picked up by pirates and sold into slave labor where I was augmented against my will." She exhaled loudly. "That's why I divorced you."

"Wait," Brei'Alas interrupted, unable to help herself. "She's your ex-wife?" Glancing over at the commander, she was met with a stern look. "What?" she asked defensively, "We were all thinking it."

"She's right," Mr. Kolivan said, finally breaking his siege on words and ending his long silence. "I was thinking it."

Brei'Alas smiled, and motioned to Kolivan. "See?"

"Yes," Lianica said, eyeing Kolivan suspiciously, as though he might speak again at any moment, "I see. But that doesn't change the fact that, I'm sure, these two have a lot of catching up to do." Turning back toward Raven, she nodded down at the restraints that Brei'Alas had handed to her. "If you'd be so kind as to do the honors."

"The pleasure is all mine," Raven answered briskly. Then, smiling at Angellyk, she slapped the restraints onto her wrists with a vicious snap.

"Ow!" Angellyk grumbled. "That hurt."

"Serves you right," Raven replied without a hint of remorse. Giving Angellyk a firm shove, she added, "This way, sweetheart."

Raven left the shuttle bay with a full squad of guards trailing after her as she escorted Angellyk to the brig. Once they'd cleared the bay doors, Brei'Alas turned to Captain Blackstar with an astonished look.

"Is it just me or is there never a dull moment on this ship?"

"It's definitely not you, lieutenant."

"Good, because for a moment I thought it might be me."

Lianica nodded politely and then motioned for all the remaining officers and guards to return to their regular duties.

"Lieutenant," Lianica added at the last possible instant. "I want you and Kolivan to stay behind and scour this ship from top to bottom for anything out of the ordinary."

"Yes, ma'am," Brei'Alas replied, throwing her hands onto her hips and turning toward the vessel to examine it.

As Lianica took her leave, Kolivan sauntered up beside Brei'Alas and studied the ship with her. "Well, let's get to it," she said, holding her elbow and stretching her bent arm over her head in preparation for the work that lay ahead of them.

30

Carcosan virgins attended to the ritualistic garments of Anaïs Nin. They dressed her in a Nyctan styled kimono layered with intricately woven silk that was harvested from a genetically enhanced form of Angorian weaving spider engineered to produce the finest golden thread. The gold kimono with white satin lining represented the protective cloak of the shared Nyctan and Dagon god, the Keeper of the Yellow Sign, and enemy to the Outer Gods, H'aaztre–or in the common tongue of the lay people, Hastur.

Once the administratrix was fully clothed in the golden kimono, one of the Carcosan virgins, a bald-headed girl of no more than eighteen, with milky white skin and clad from neck to toe in the traditional red and gold-trimmed hakama-styled dress of her order, approached Anaïs Nin with a golden bowl filled with red powder.

A second, ashen-skinned virgin, just as pale as the first and wearing the same ceremonial garb as her sister, brought over a crystalline chalice and sidled up next to her virgin sister. She brought the bowl to her forehead in a display of thanks and then carefully poured the shimmering water from the chalice into the bowl. Having added the perfect amount, she dipped her fingers into the mixture and stirred the water into the red powder until it made a fine paste. Removing her fingers, she drew a red dot on her forehead, then on her sister's, and, finally, she turned toward the administratrix and drew a line down the center of Anaïs Nin's forehead. The girl added a dab of red to her mistress's chin before taking the bowl and disappearing back the way she'd come.

The other Carcosan virgin remained behind for a few moments and then bowed reverently, holding herself mid-bow, only to slowly draw back into the shadows just beyond the soft, wavering glow of candlelight.

The administratrix turned around and holding her posture stiffly, paced in small steps across the red carpet that was laid out before her. The carpet stretched across the larger room all the way to a wide bed that sat at the end. The bedspread itself was of black satin, and it glimmered, like oil, in the dancing light. At the foot of the bed waited Dakroth, his arms locked behind his back. He, too, wore a gold and white trimmed ceremonial hakama and had three red lines painted down his face. The outside lines ran from the top of his forehead down either cheek. Likewise, the central line extended down past his nose and over his lips and chin.

Never in a million years did he imagine that he would be in this position. Standing before the Nyctan's holy religious leader, the Administratrix, Anaïs Nin, ready to strip down to nothing and engage in a ceremonial task of *coitus clavis aurea.*

The literal translation of "the golden key through sex" made little sense, but the implied meaning of unlocking the secret of the Gilded Master through a ceremonial fornication, was what the ritual was all about. It was also referred to as the ritual of the Chosen One.

For the sacred text read, *"The High Priestess and the Lord of the Enemy realm shall, together, produce an offspring that, being not of one land or the other, shall inherit both lands and usher in a thousand years' peace. But, should the child's blood be spilled in the blood sacrifice to He who creates and destroys, the all-powerful H'aaztre, then this blood sacrifice will end in three signs—the final sign being the sign of the Yellow King, and every plague and calamity known throughout the lands will descend on both houses and bring forth the second coming of H'aaztre."*

Anaïs Nin glided up to Dakroth and he held out his hand. She took it in hers and curtseyed, as was the custom when engaging in the ceremony of the Gilded Master.

"If you are right, the child made of our union will either be a vessel for our Lord or, if the High Priestess deems it, be sacrificed and herald the coming of calamity, by bringing the Lord of Life and Destruction's wrath upon us. In so doing, set the gears in motion to vanquish all those who oppose the Gilded Master, including the infernal Outer Gods who recklessly play with time and space against H'aaztre's wishes. It is only H'aaztre who can bring stillness to time's infinite march and rebuild the universe in his hallowed image."

"If you will have my seed," Dakroth said, quoting the lines of the Enchiridion by heart, "We shall bring forth the hybrid child as foretold in the Book of Eternal Light and the Gospel of Aldebaran, whose blood sacrifice will set in motion the final revelation of the prophet Haruk Ereshva, and bring about the return of our lord, the King in Yellow, Lord H'aaztre."

Anaïs Nin bowed her chin, affirming Dakroth's words with a slow nod. When she looked back up, their eyes locked, and without surrendering her gaze, her hands gracefully peeled off the layers of her ceremonial kimono, shedding each piece until she stood before the Emperor with her bare-naked flesh exposed.

He studied her porcelain white skin which practically lit up in the glow of candlelight. Her orchid pink nipples stood erect on her white breasts and her vagina, which was stapled shut with brass rings, glinted in the flickering light.

Dakroth shed his robes too, and revealed his double pronged penis standing erect on his naked blue body. Taking the porcelain-skinned woman in his arms, he ran his hands down Anaïs Nin's shoulder's and then her bare breasts, as he admired the contours of her womanly form. Finally, he knelt down on both knees and kissed her taut abdomen, working his way lower and lower until his Prussian lips came to the first brass ring.

Her white flesh bristled with goosebumps and her ass tightened with both nervousness and excitement as the Lord Emperor's wet, hot kisses quickly cooled on her flesh in the open air of the ceremonial chamber.

The fulfillment of a most ancient prophesy–the coupling of the Nyctan Empress and Dagon Emperor–and the half-breed offspring which was foretold in the pages of the Enchiridion was all coming to a head right here, in this very room. Both her people and his would write hymns to commemorate this day. The day they put aside their petty differences and came together to fulfill the prophecy.

Brushing the series of brass rings with his finger, Dakroth enticed a sultry moan from Anaïs Nin's champagne colored lips. As he continued to tease and titillate her, she reached down and ran her long fingers through his silver hair.

In the Nyctan culture, sex was forbidden except for reproduction and ceremonial purposes. This qualified as the latter. But the amount of self-control required for the administratrix to remain true to her position, meant that even the slightest touch would trigger an orgasm. And no matter how hard she wanted to resist, she knew she had to give in to the ritual. If she didn't give herself fully over to the act, it was her fear that the prophesy would not be fulfilled as promised.

The Lord Emperor's left finger lit up bright red, then hot pink, but instead of using it as a laser weapon, he used it as cutter to slice through the rings, taking extra precaution not to singe the administratrix in the process.

One by one the rings fell away and the chastity belt that was sewn into her flesh from the time she was a child fell off and rattled on the floor.

After the last ring had been removed. Dakroth rose back up and scooped the administratrix up in his arms and moved her over to the bed. Laying her down, he slowly climbed on top and then began kissing her neck.

She closed her eyes and moaned, her hips thrusting upward into his with carnal anticipation. It was the first touch she'd received from a man in her entire life, and the raw feeling of pure lust surged through her and drove her into a fit of ecstasy. She reached down and helped guide him to his intended destination. As he penetrated the curtains of her sacred temple, she gasped out with libidinous delight.

Pleasure and pain flooded every square centimeter of her body and she chirped with sexual gratification as Dakroth revealed to her the true reason why he was considered the most virile man of the Dagon people.

Three hours later, they fell back onto the bed panting, both drenched in the residue of their sex laden encounter. Filled to the brim with the ecstasy of the illicit act they'd just performed, Anaïs Nin started laughing. It was overwhelming. Although Dakroth was a veteran when it came to sex, this was her first time. Because the sacred law was clear. As High Priestess, she was forbidden to have sex unless it was in the service of H'aaztre. As such, her loins trembled from the flurry of small orgasms that cascaded down her body, from the back of her skull to the very tip of her toes.

A strange noise rang out and Dakroth startled. When he opened his eyes, he found all seven Carcosan Virgins standing around their bed, hands raised in the air as though they were giving praise to their deity. They had shed their ceremonial robes and were all naked, apart for the gold paint they wore and the red markings on their bald heads that gave them an almost aboriginal quality. With their hands held up high, they stood in a circle, chanting the sacred hymns of H'aaztre.

Surprisingly, their womanly voices dropped several octaves, taking on the baser tones of the male vocal range, making their chants seem otherworldly as a consequence. Without warning, Anaïs Nin jolted and screamed out in labor pains.

Her primal grunts and groans seemed to entice a greater magic from within the Carcosan Virgins and as they continued to chant, their hands and eyes lit up with golden white light. The more the administratrix suffered, the greater the energy grew, until, finally, the entire room was basking in the radiance of their strange magic.

Light streaming out of them like a ruptured plasma conduit, their chanting became even deeper and more alien. Dakroth tensed with nervousness at the unfamiliarity of the ritual, but sat watching, in astonishment, as Anaïs Nin's belly began to swell with the life he had impregnated her with.

As the chanting continued, they spoke in the ancient tongue of the Oracle, and Anaïs Nin's abdomen grew plump and round with child. The fetus's growth, accelerated by the séance of magic, quickly grew to maturity in its mother's womb. Before Dakroth knew it, Anaïs Nin looked as though she'd burst at the seams. Her screams, along with her agony, only intensified as the child came to term.

In span of ten minutes, Anaïs Nin was ready to give birth. She screamed out with labor pains and the tight wrenching cramps of relentless contractions that made her delirious with fear and laughter. It seemed she was going to lose her mind if the pain continued, but all Dakroth could do was sit off to the side and watch in astonishment as life grew inside Anaïs Nin's body.

Finally, a midwife, dressed in the same red robes that the Carcosan Virgins wore but with the addition of a golden sash around her waist, approached the end of the bed and began to attend Anaïs Nin.

The stout woman with sturdy arms helped the administratrix to the edge of the bed and assisted by taking hold of her knees and spreading her legs as the baby's head crowned.

"Push, now!" the midwife shouted above the din of Anaïs Nin's grunting and screaming. "Push," she growled with a kind of urgency suggesting that if they didn't get the baby out soon the mother's abdomen would literally burst.

Dakroth slowly rose to his knees. He watched in jaw-dropping bewilderment as he bore witness to the strange mysticism happening before him. He'd never seen anything like it. And the light of the séance kept every gory detail in plain sight. Stranger still, the virgins' naked bodies started swaying as they looked up at the ceiling, towards the heavens, their voices continuing the chants.

Blood gushed from Anaïs Nin and she grunted and groaned, fighting to push out the child. The midwife pushed her hand deep into Anaïs Nin's vaginal canal and cupped the baby's head, giving it a firm tug. The baby slid out into her arms along with a flood of blood-laced amniotic fluid.

The virgins all screamed out simultaneously in orgiastic delight and Dakroth startled. Looking at them, he noticed blood streaming from between their legs, running down the insides of their thighs, painting their porcelain legs in a glossy crimson of forking menstrual rivers.

The midwife slapped the infant's back and brought air into its lungs. The small thing, silent a moment earlier, began to shriek with the pangs of being torn from its warm, dark home and brought into the coldness of an indifferent and hostile world. Holding the wailing infant in her arms, the midwife turned to Emperor Dakroth and held the child out to him. "It's a boy," she intoned with awe at the glory she beheld.

Dakroth received the child and, cradling it in his arms, couldn't help but feel amazed at the sight of his progeny. And, for one split nano-second, he regretted what he had to do next.

One of the Carcosan Virgins approached him and, taking his hand in hers, she gently placed a ceremonial dagger in his palm. His eyes widened with terrible revelation as he looked down at the hot white blade and the golden hilt with elaborate etchings which displayed an ancient spell related to the blood sacrifice.

"You know what you must do," whispered Anaïs Nin in a weary voice. "You must complete the ritual."

Dakroth gazed down at the infant he cradled in one arm and in that moment, when father and son's eyes met, the wretched thing stopped crying. Its large, dark, Nyctan eyes blinked twice and then it smiled.

Dakroth, still numb from the shock of the experience, examined the small bundle in his arms, noting the baby's flesh was the same color as his when he was born, a soft cornflower blue. In that moment, the baby cooed up at his father and Dakroth felt that infernal pull of compassion well up inside him.

"Could he not be a vessel instead?" Dakroth asked, gazing into the eyes of his newborn.

"If he were to be the vessel, I would know it." Of course, Anaïs Nin lied. She somehow knew this child would be strong and make the perfect vessel for her

Lord, but because he was the offspring of the Lord Emperor, the man she reviled more than anything in the galaxy, she couldn't bear to force herself to raise *his* child. Instead, she deemed the infant unworthy. Which, in her estimation, was the right of the High Priestess. "I know it is difficult, but the child is unworthy. You know what you must do, Rhadamanthus." Anaïs Nin smiled faintly, looking at him with her dark, alien eyes. Eyes that urged him to follow through with it, lest the prophecy remain unfulfilled.

There was no avoiding it. If he betrayed her now, he'd lose everything. He'd lose the peace he'd brokered with the Nyctans, he'd lose his throne to the child, and he'd lose his dignity for having fucked his enemy for nothing–a woman he despised but whom he needed in order to get to the next step in his plan.

Dakroth slowly raised the blade in his right hand, never breaking eye contact with the child for an instant, and readied for a swift strike. He'd make sure it was as painless as possible. After all, it was his son and he didn't want his own flesh and blood to suffer needlessly.

This ritual–this sacrifice–was necessary; he knew that.

But, for reasons beyond his comprehension, he found himself struggling to go through with it. He'd taken thousands of innocent lives from more than two dozen worlds. He conquered entire civilizations, took their queens as his concubines, and slit the throats of their husband kings before their cowering, weeping eyes. Why should this be any different?

The emperor knew exactly who was to blame for his indecisiveness. His infuriating empress, Jegra. It was her DNA's strange ability to rewire his own that had made him so weak. This alien ability to feel compassion, which she deemed a strength in her species, was only a hinderance in his. It made him question his actions. It made him second guess himself. Pathetic.

He shook off the emotion and quickly put all thoughts of sparing the child out of his mind. Saving an innocent life was what his darkling wife was good at. This wasn't the time to grow a conscience. He had bigger plans. Plans that entailed more than just the fulfillment of an ancient prophesy. More importantly, plans that required a greater sacrifice than the mere blood of a half-breed child.

With his mind cleared of all inhibitions, he closed his eyes, took a deep breath, and brought the knife down. The infant's cooing went silent and the only sounds to fill the room were Anaïs Nin's awful moaning and the low murmuring sounds of the Carcosan Virgins' voices as they hummed the final few bars of their haunting chant.

Once the deed was done, the midwife took the lifeless bundle from Dakroth's bloody hands and whisked it away to god knows where. At the same time, one of the Carcosan Virgins brought him his robe and slipped it over his shoulders for him. The other six women gathered around Anaïs Nin and placed their hands firmly over various points across her body and transferred the glowing energy back into her.

Anaïs Nin's eyes shot wide-awake and she gulped in a huge breath. Sitting up with the help of her team of virgins, she sat in the bed, panting.

She made eye contact with Dakroth but didn't say anything. Instead, she slipped out of bed and put on her robes.

The procession of virgins guided her out of the ceremonial chamber and left Dakroth standing alone.

As he stood there, his mind racing, he felt sticky as the blood of his murdered son dripped from his fingers and dappled the floor with warm, gooey drops of crimson. "The tears of sacrifice lead to a father's remorse," Anaïs Nin had said to him as she had explained every detail of the ritual during their long conversation back in the throne room hours earlier. "But you will forget the child. For it is merely the first step in unlocking the mysteries of the Ancient Ones and in bringing back the God of life and destruction, H'aaztre."

In the back of his mind, he couldn't help but think *what have you done, Rhadamanthus? What in God's name have you done?* But his old self swiftly retook control and he growled, "No!" Getting a hold of himself, he added, "What was done is done. There was no other way." He fought back the urge to let loose a torrent of sobs with every difficult breath and repeated, as if still trying to convince himself of the inevitable nature of the morbid ritual. "It is over. The prophesy has been fulfilled."

31

Dirt and rust colored blood-stained Danica's lavender skin. She stood upon the field panting heavily, a droplet of sweat running down her forehead and then dripping off the tip of her nose. Thessalonica's languorous sun was steadily setting outside the arena. Its shafts of golden light streamed down through the open roof and pillars of the stadium and cut through the dusty haze, spreading out like the folds of an oriental fan.

Exhausted, Danica staggered forward, her legs trembling with fatigue as she fought to remain upright. Her fight wasn't over yet. One contestant still remained. Across the heaps of slain bodies that littered the blood-soaked sand stood a beast unlike anything she had ever seen before.

It had four mandibles resembling the legs of a crab, which stretched open to reveal an inner jowl with jagged incisors. Its beady yellow eyes gazed out from behind an intimidating brow that seamlessly rose into a ridged cranium. It sported thick, dreadlocked hair that was more akin to tentacles than actual hair. And it wore the modified shell of a dead beetle-like creature over a fishnet mesh hauberk, obviously the spoils of victory that it had adapted into its warrior outfit.

More intimidating than its menacing appearance, however, was the fact that it stood eleven feet tall, give or take a few centimeters for the thick, metal-toed boots it wore. Its veins wove themselves visibly through every strand of the taut sinews of its dense musculature, and through thick arms and legs like those of a body builder amped up on body-enhancing steroids.

Ishtar sidled up to Danica, tightening the straps on the bracers on her forearms, and looked up to see what it was that Danica was staring so intently at. When she eyed the beast, she groaned in protest. "Graddack. Not one of *them*."

"You're familiar with that thing?"

"It's a Bakktu Danav," she said, her tone instantly settling into a cold and controlled voice that Danica knew all too well. The voice of someone for whom killing came naturally. But for the first time since they'd been forced to fight together, it didn't fill her with dread. Because, against *that* thing, she would need a killer by her side.

Danica knew that if Ishtar was already psyching herself up to fight the monster, then she meant business. Which meant this thing was dangerous. Really dangerous. If the creature could rile up the most vicious killer this side of the galaxy, then they had a tough fight ahead of them.

"The Bakktu are a rare warrior-like species that love to hunt inferior beings. Or, at least, what they consider inferior beings. They're big, powerful, and most of all dangerous." Danica shot Ishtar a sideways glance. "Anything weaker than them is on the menu. Nobody knows where they come from. Some say a distant galaxy. Others say they are nomads that just hunt whatever prey they come across. Regardless, the last time I went up against one it nearly took my life."

"Bakktu Danav means *Terrible Demon* in the ancient tongue," said Danica, making the statement as more of an aside to bide the time before the announcer gave the go ahead for the gladiatorial bout to begin.

The televid drones swooped down and buzzed both women and then moved over to get a closer look at the new monster. One of the drones flew too close though, and the Bakktu reached out its massive clawed fingers, caught it in mid-air, palmed it like a child's ball, and then crushed it. Sparks flew everywhere as the drone crumpled in his clenched fist and smoke rose up from the spaces between his fingers.

The crowd cheered and the alien beast threw the smoldering husk of the drone onto the ground and then threw out its arms, flared its mandibles, and roared up at the audience.

"I have a bad feeling about this," Danica said as the weapons racks rose up from the ground. Arming themselves, Danica noticed Ishtar do something she'd never done since their time in the gladiatorial arena. She reached over and grabbed a shield from the weapons rack.

"Make sure you get a couple of those smoke bombs," Ishtar said, nodding at the clay smoke bombs. The round clay ball had an igniter tab that, much like a more complex grenade, would spark a small flame to set off the smoke bomb.

Danica didn't question Ishtar's advice. She grabbed three of the clay balls which were roughly the size of Dagonian oranges. Dropping them into a small satchel she had fixed to her belt, she turned and picked a couple of the sharpest looking blades off the rack. With her powers, she had a natural shield, so arming herself more heavily than Ishtar gave her a slight offensive advantage. She turned in time to see the Bakktu's entire body dissolve into thin air. Danica gulped.

"It turned invisible."

"Get ready," Ishtar said, sword and shield at the ready.

The announcer's two snake heads hissed into the shared mic simultaneously. "Let the *gamessss* begin!"

A series of loud alpenhorns blew from the tops of the portico of the arena, letting the combatants know it was time, and the crowd rose to their feet with cheers of elation as the penultimate match of this season's humiliation bout got started.

Danica knew that if they survived this match, the next one in three days would be the Bull and Swan bout. The grand finale of her and Ishtar's little drama playing out before a live audience. What would happen to her after that, she couldn't guess.

Ishtar shouted, "Down!" and shoved Danica out of the way. A spear, seemingly coming out of nowhere, lodged itself in the dirt where she'd just been standing.

"Thanks," she said, glancing at the spear and then back at Ishtar. Her partner merely nodded in reply.

"Use all the smoke bombs," she said in a low voice, "and I'll take the creature head on. You flank it from the left and use your forcefield power to knock it off its feet. If we time this right, we'll be able to take it out in one go."

"If we don't?" Danica asked.

"Let's just say failure isn't an option."

Danica nodded. It wasn't the news she'd hoped for, but after several weeks of fighting, she'd begun to see the appeal Jegra found in the gladiator matches. There was a simplicity to them. A kind of unspoken understanding between warriors that if you fought with honor, you would die with honor. It wasn't the kind of thing Danica ever expected she'd grow to understand, let alone enjoy, but here she was. Finding herself excited for the challenge.

"Go! Now!" Ishtar yelled.

Danica tossed two of the smoke bombs, making sure they landed roughly thirty feet apart. Then she began running. She glanced back to see Ishtar running toward the red and blue smoke that streamed out of the small balls and gradually filled the arena with a purple haze.

The arena wall to the east provided Danica with some shade. Keeping to the shadows, she ran along the circumference, making sure to keep just out of sight. In the distance she heard Ishtar engage with the creature whose purplish silhouette, like a giant translucent shadow, could be seen in the smoke.

She turned back in time to see the air waver before her, like a heat mirage, and she dropped and slid, narrowly avoiding the blade that flew over her head. Grinding to a halt in the sand, she quickly rose up, fist full of dirt, and threw the sand out at whatever was standing before her.

The fine desert sand rained down onto a second form, revealing the outline of another Bakktu.

"Fuck me," Danica said. She turned to warn Ishtar and screamed out, "There's two of them. Ishtar, we need to—"

Her warning was prematurely cut off when something gripped her neck and choked her throat shut. To her dismay, she felt her feet leave the ground as her body was hoisted into the air. Dropping her two blades, she gripped the wrists of the invisible hands choking her.

With wild kicks, Danica thrashed and squirmed, but she couldn't break free. Her eyes turned to see Ishtar impaled with a spear right through her torso. Ishtar shot up into the air, like a skewered fish on the end of a spear fisherman's harpoon, and the Bakktu's invisibility cloak gradually dissolved and it reappeared. Hoisting Ishtar high above it, it began laughing in a guttural, throaty voice.

Almost as soon as the first Bakktu had turned off its invisibility cloak, so too did the one gripping her by the neck. She was a little bit shocked to find a female Bakktu holding her, but there was no doubt about it, it was just as strong and ugly as its male counterpart, but with massive breasts wrapped up in fishnet and armor plating.

Instead of shells for a bikini top, however, the female wore skulls over her breasts, and instead of armored underwear, like her male counterpart, she wore a leather loincloth with teeth woven all along the seams, which gave it a jagged and formidable appearance. Strapped to her bracers were two blades that extended outward roughly thirty-five centimeters. If a swipe of her clawed hands didn't do you in, then her blades certainly would.

"Let…me…down!" Danica growled, barely able to get the words out. Even though she pried on the Bakktu's arms, trying to free herself, it was no use. The monster was too strong.

The female Bakktu just cocked its head, then snorted once and flung her into the arena wall as if she weighed nothing more than a ragdoll. Before crashing into the cement, however, she managed to throw up an energy shield to protect herself. Still, the force of the impact fractured the wall behind her, sending a cobweb-like series of cracks off in every direction.

She collapsed to the ground, coughing. Even with her energy shield up, the blow was enough to knock the wind out of her and she fell to her hands and knees gasping for air.

The female Bakktu tossed her dreads and then strolled toward Danica with a more or less feminine gait, the swivel of her hips setting her apart from the male. Other than her walk, her slightly longer tentacle-hair, which ran down to her buttocks, and the massive breasts she had, there was not much else to distinguish her from the male.

Danica spit out some blood and then rose to her feet. Shaken by the blow, she knew she couldn't wait for the Bakktu to make its next move, not without taking another bad hit. So, she made sure to get the jump on it. Throwing up another energy shield, she raced forward and rammed into the creature's thigh. It braced itself and Danica rebounded off of it as though she'd just crashed into the korridium bulkhead of a starship.

Her ass hit the dirt with a *thump* and she yelped. Not having the luxury of time to process the pain, she quickly scrambled back on all fours as the Bakktu bore down upon her and took a swing with its double-pronged blades.

She stretched her neck as far as she could, leaning backward as the blade barely missed slicing through the bridge of her nose. She watched as several strands of loose purple hair fell away, severed by the blade. Scrambling to her feet, she managed to throw up another forcefield in time to block the Bakktu's follow-up attack.

Irritated by the interference of the energy shields, the Bakktu roared out in protest and then, leaning back, it kicked her shield with all its strength. Danica flew up into the air as though she were a child's kick-ball, and toppled to the ground again with another bone bruising thud.

This time she coughed up sand and spit up blood-laced with sand. Wiping her mouth with the back of her right hand, she looked up to see both Bakktu laughing and jeering. They were enjoying this brutality more than any creature should.

Danica rolled onto her side and glanced over at Ishtar. The male Bakktu swung the spear with Ishtar dangling off the end like a croquet mallet and, tearing the spear out at the height of its pendulum arc, flung her off the end. She hit the wall with wind-stealing force and a splatter of her own blood and crashed to the ground. Groaning from the pain, she forced herself to roll over onto her back and clutched the wound left in her abdomen to try and ease the bleeding.

"Fucking helios," she cursed as she lay staring up at the open sky above the arena. It was blue and clear and there was only a trace of white cirrus high in the distance.

With both Bakktu barreling toward her, Danica used what remaining strength she had to throw up two energy bubbles–one around each Bakktu's head.

The audience instantly began booing when they realized she was simply going to suffocate both creatures and end the match. But, to her dismay, the female Bakktu reached up and tore the energy bubble in half, as though it were little more than bubblegum.

Danica gasped. "Impossible." That's when she noticed the korridium plating on their sharp talonesque nails. They had literally welded sharp metal plating to their fingernails so they could cause more damage. *They are every bit deserving of their infamous moniker, terrible demons*, she thought.

Both Bakktu were nearly upon her when a spear pierced the male Bakktu's shoulder. It let out a furious roar that seemed to startle its companion. It tore the spear out and then, in a fit of rage, snapped it in two across its thigh and tossed both pieces to the ground. Turning around, it saw the red-skin woman struggling to stand upright as she clutched her bleeding gut.

With a roar the male Bakktu leaped up into the air and flew across the arena in a single bound. It landed in front of Ishtar with a startling force, slowly rose up, and flared its mandibles and roared at her. She slowly craned her neck upward and grinned at it with a bloody-toothed smile.

"Over here, you ugly bitch!" she shouted, drawing the female's attention back toward her. Waving her arms in the air, she added, "Yeah, you heard me. Ugly. Biya—"

The female moved so fast that Danica barely even saw it coming. All she knew was that the Bakktu's fist had embedded itself in her gut and she heard several of her ribs snap.

A scream rose from the back of her throat but a follow-up punch by the creature's calloused fist fractured her jaw and sent her straight down into the dirt.

The female Bakktu raised its foot high and Danica rolled over just in time to see the foot come down on her. She groaned as more ribs fractured inside her chest.

Desperate to not get stomped into mush, she grabbed the Bakktu's foot and refused to let go, even as it tried to shake her off. But Danica knew that if she let go, she was done for. All her ribs were broken and another sharp blow could send bone fragments into her lungs and heart.

Saliva and foul breath flew from the male Bakktu's mouth and plastered Ishtar's chest and face. Ignoring her gag reflex, she flooded her system with biochems. A mixture of adrenaline, painkillers, and antibiotics surged into her system. The male Bakktu snorted and then threw a punch. Ishtar caught his fist with her bionic arm, and to their surprise, she stopped it mid-punch.

As the servos inside her artificial arm whined, Ishtar smiled and then growled through her clenched teeth, "My turn, asshole."

Trained in over half a dozen forms of martial arts, Ishtar used the beast's immense body weight to her advantage and tossed him over her shoulder. He landed with a *thud* and, without skipping a beat, she leaped into the air. As she came down, her bionic arm crackled with energy and fluidly transformed itself into a blade. With a wet sounding *thwack*, she buried the blade into the Bakktu's chest. It howled with pain and flung Ishtar off.

The male's pain-filled cry momentarily distracted the female, who glanced back at her companion to see what the matter was. This gave Danica the opening she needed. Reaching down into her satchel, she retrieved the last smoke bomb. Using her remaining strength, she smashed it into the female Bakktu's foot. It ignited with a hiss and smoke began streaming out of the clay ball that was now plastered to the creature's foot.

The Bakktu hopped about, trying to shake off the clay bomb, but only managed to disperse blue smoke even further and in a much bigger radius. Using this diversion to her advantage, Danica drew back into the blue haze and unsheathed the swords that were strapped to her back.

By the time the Bakktu had finally stamped out the smoke bomb, it had lost sight of her. Angry, it roared menacingly at the wall of smoke.

A flash of silver cut through the blue smoke and a spiraling sword imbedded itself in the female Bakktu's sternum. Screaming out in pain, the Bakktu reeled back and tore the small blade from her chest. Hot neon-green blood spurted out and the Bakktu flung the blade aside and then, with its clawed hands, began taking wild swipes at the blue smog, hoping to cut down its troublesome opponent.

Keeping low, she raced around to the side and flanked the Bakktu. As she dashed out into the open, smoke trails curled behind her as she flew into view. The monster barely had time to turn when Danica rammed into the back of its legs with a plow shaped forcefield.

Both contestants tumbled to the ground. As she hit the dirt alongside the Bakktu, she saw the creature's twin blades snap under her weight as she threw out her arm to break her fall. Danica knew that her small size and speed were the only things giving her the edge now, and she sprang to her feet as fast as she could.

While the Bakktu struggled to roll over and push herself up, Danica thrust both of her blades into its back.

As the creature howled in pain, she bent down and picked up one of the broken blades. The weapon felt massive in her hands and she could barely hoist it up above her head, especially with her broken ribs. But somehow, she managed it. However, just as she got the blade to where she wanted it, her strength failed her, and the weight of the heavy blade became too much for her, and she let the tip fall back to the ground.

"Gah!" she growled, clutching her busted ribcage with one hand. With a deep grunt, she gave it another go. But, again, the heavy blade crashed back to the ground. "Come on!" she screamed, seeing the Bakktu pushing itself to its feet, her swords sticking out of its back.

With both hands resting on its knees, the female demon raised its head and looked right at her with those yellow, beady eyes. It flexed its freckled mandible and seemed to grin before letting out a hideous roar.

"Let me help you with that," a voice said.

She looked over to see a bloody Ishtar standing beside her. The red-skinned assassin reached down and, fitting her hands between Danica's, took up the broken blade. Together, they raised the weapon high, just in time to ram it through the chest of the Bakktu, right between her skull crested breasts.

The Bakktu gasped in shock as the massive blade passed through her, surprised by the fact that the two insignificant creatures had managed to run it through. Then, staggering back, it gave them a look that was both one of bewilderment and, at the same time, slightly amused. With a blood gurgling chuckle, it spit up neon-green slime and then crashed onto its knees again. Still laughing at its own fate, it fell to the side and landed on the ground with a harsh *thud* that sent up a swirl of dust.

Ishtar kicked it in its ribcage just to be sure it was dead. Satisfied, she turned to Danica and nodded.

That's when the most stomach-churning, spine-tingling scream they'd ever heard rang out.

Both women turned to see the male, gripping its wounded chest, standing in the clearing smoke only to see its beloved companion lying dead at the two women's feet.

"Move back," Ishtar said. "I've got this."

Danica did as asked and watched in awe as Ishtar's bionic arm crackled and then transformed into an arm mounted blaster-canon.

The large Bakktu raced over to its fallen companion and knelt down beside her. Putting its hand on her forehead, it wept and let out another deep, bone-chilling wail. A cry of pure misery compounded by heart wrenching sadness.

"Don't worry, you'll be reunited with her soon enough," Ishtar said, placing her plasma canon against the creature's ridged forehead.

It ignored her presence and just sat there, devastated, its heart broken.

Without hesitating, Ishtar fired a shot through the creature's thick skull. The plasma blast punched through the Bakktu's impossibly thick cranial plating and shot out the other side. Grey matter splattered across the arena sands and the male Bakktu slumped forward, a glowing hole piercing its forehead. Thin wisps of white smoke curled up into the air from the smoldering wound and the irritating televid drones swooped down to get a close-up of the grisly scene.

Ishtar raised her boot and, with a sturdy kick, knocked the Bakktu onto its back so that it could lay down beside its deceased lover, blade protruding from her sternum.

"May you be reunited in the afterlife," she said stoically, as the televid drones swiveled around to capture the exhausted faces of the defending champions.

Still clutching her side, Ishtar looked back at Danica and then started to limp back to the exit.

Danica looked down at her badly bruised ribs and realizing she'd broken more than a few, let out a painful sigh. Her breath caught prematurely in her chest, a spike of pain cutting every breath short, and she grunted out the remaining air. Turning slowly, she glanced back one time at the fallen Bakktu and then, realizing she'd just defeated a couple of demons, turned back and limped after Ishtar.

In three days, she'd either die in the arena fighting for her survival or face a fate worse than death. Because even with her and Ishtar's powers and abilities, the two of them alone weren't going to be enough to fend off twelve of the Intergalactic Gladiatorial Syndicate's best warriors in the Bull and Swan bout. She wasn't impossibly strong like Jegra. And even with Ishtar's rage and bloodthirst, they wouldn't be at their best. The odds were stacked against them, and all she could do was try to mentally fortify herself for what was to come.

Despite several weeks of grueling matches, she still felt green around the edges. She walked away from every match with more bruises and broken bones than she had the previous one and it was always an uphill battle. Now she understood what it truly meant to be a warrior. It wasn't issuing orders from the bridge of some fortified starship high in orbit. It was getting your hands dirty. It was fighting for something you believed in. Fighting for your very survival.

She just wasn't sure about how much more of it she could endure. Even if, by some miracle, she made it out of the Bull and Swan bout unscathed and alive, what next? What would it take to regain her freedom?

32

"**I hear you've** been looking for me," Jegra said, eyeing the prisoner from behind the nano-mesh glass of the security cell. "Well, you found me."

Teal eyes gazed back at her and the green-skinned woman stood up and scanned Jegra from head to foot. "You're taller than I imagined you'd be."

"I get that a lot, actually. Most people aren't accustomed to seeing a six-foot-three female." Jegra tossed her long brown hair over her shoulder, threw her hand on her hip, and carefully studied the woman who studied her in return.

The inevitable "*sizing up,*" as she so aptly referred to it. It was an unspoken greeting among warriors. Gauging one's opponents' skills, capabilities, and motives with a simple glance wasn't a talent that just anyone possessed. It took practice and the right sort of conditioning so one would know precisely what to look for. But if two and a half years in the arena had taught her anything, it was how to read an opponent.

"One-hundred and ninety-one centimeters? Impressive. I am about one-eighty-six. What are you, two-hundred-twenty pounds?"

"Two-fifty, actually," Jegra replied, brushing her hair out of her eyes.

"One-ninety," Angellyk answered, brushing her wavy forest-green hair from her eyes.

Both women stared at each other in silence for a bit and then Jegra spoke. "I hear you're Raven's ex-wife."

"News gets around fast on this ship."

"I'm the Empress," Jegra said in a stately tone. "If there's something to know aboard this ship, you'd better bet I'm going to be sure to know it."

"Speaking of which, that's precisely why I'm here. I have a message for you."

"Right," Jegra interjected, waving her hand in the air nonchalantly. "Something about Hastur invading the Commonwealth and me being the only one who can stop him."

"It's more complicated than that," Angellyk said, her eyes growing serious. "It's about the prophesy. It's about your husband, the Emperor, Lord Dakroth."

"What about the Lord Emperor?" Jegra stopped fiddling with her hair and quickly matched Angellyk's level of intensity. Squinting suspiciously, Jegra put her fist to her mouth and cleared her throat. "What aren't you telling me?"

"The emperor hired me to intercept you. I'm to stop you from returning to Thessalonica at all cost. Even if it means I must kill you."

"But..." Jegra said, connecting all the clues to the mystery, "you're not going to do that."

"No. Because what the emperor doesn't know is that I'm part of an ancient order. I'm a Voroxian Priestess."

"Voroxian Priestess?" Jegra echoed. She hadn't heard of them.

"It is said, in the prophesy, that H'aaztre has three harbingers of light that will precede his coming. Each one will take the form of one of the Gilded Master's traits. You'll have the Warrior which represents his power. The Priestess which represents his devotion. And the Destroyer which represents his vision. It is their mission to open the breach from their universe into ours. The Order of Vorox intends to keep that portal shut at all costs."

"How come I've never heard of your order...of Vorox...until now?"

"Because, we are considered a heretical order by the Nyctans. We are the female Knights of Caelum. The first of us being Lady Vorox Amadeen. And it was Lady Amadeen's belief that the Nyctans had misinterpreted the sacred texts. She felt the ancient scribes had mistranslated certain passages in the Enchiridion more than seven thousand years ago and believed Hastur wasn't a benevolent being who'd destroy and rebuild the world in his image, but was merely a being of pure destruction. For this she was martyred. Burned at the stake in a barbaric display for all to see what happened to heretics."

"The Knights allow women now. I should know, they inducted me into their ranks."

"Not precisely," Angellyk said, rubbing her chin. "They promoted you to the position of head emissary. It's the only position, beside the oracle, that a female can hold within the Knighthood. Then they just bent a few of their own rules, given that you were an outsider and an alien. But, as the saying goes, the enemy of my enemy..."

"What's any of this have to do with Dakroth?"

"Dakroth intends to help the administratrix bring the prophecy to fruition. As we speak, they are undertaking the sacred ritual of *coitus clavis aurea*, also known as the ritual of the Chosen One."

"Wait a nano-second, does coitus in this context mean what I think it means?"

"Yes," Angellyk replied in all seriousness. "They are creating a half-breed. If deemed worthy by the Carcosan virgins, he will be prepared as the vessel for the coming God. If not, the offspring will be sacrificed to Hastur, as an offering. And then the priestess will have to wait another hundred years before trying again. If this sacrifice happens, though, the breach will open and the first of the emissaries will come into our universe."

"Then what?" Jegra asked, rubbing her chin as she mulled over the shocking details that Angellyk had shared with her.

"Then we go to war. For the fate of the galaxy."

"How do I know I can trust anything you say? You've already admitted that you came here under false pretenses. Now you just want me to accept everything you have to say?"

"I don't expect you to believe me or even trust me, for that matter. But I know of someone whom you'd believe and trust implicitly."

"Raven," Jegra whispered, having guessed the answer.

"Precisely. And Raven will be the first to tell you; I cannot lie. I suffered a brain injury, an old battle wound from a long time ago, that scarred my brain in such a way that telling falsehoods is impossible for me. I am only able to tell the brutal truth."

"How do I know you didn't have yourself modded so as to fix the problem?"

"Because," she said with a slight grin, "Raven was there when I was diagnosed. The amount of surgery required to chip me was too invasive, life threatening. I could have taken that risk, but I'd much rather live with a small inconvenience than lose my life simply to be chipped."

Jegra stood taking it all in and then nodded silently to herself. After another moment, she finally said, "Naturally, I'll have to confirm all this. Until then, just chill out here."

Angellyk backed away from the glass and gestured with a shrug that seemed to say "you gotta do what you gotta do." She took a seat on the bench in her cell and crossed her legs, bopping her leg up and down on one knee.

Jegra quickly exited the brig and stormed up the corridor. She marched all the way to the airlock and quickly stepped into the connecting bridge between her ship and the *Skywend*.

The door to the *Skywend* was open with a dozen or so cables and various assortment of cords running from the *Shard*, down the corridor, into the docking arm, and over the lip of the *Skywend's* airlock and then down various corridors inside the ship.

Jegra ducked under the bulkhead and took a hard right toward the engine room where she knew Raven would be. Entering the engineering room, she scanned the interior for the captain and found her under a large, partially dismantled, conduit. She had on a welding helmet and was sending sparks everywhere with a bright plasma torch.

"Need a hand?" Jegra asked.

Raven finished welding whatever it was she was welding and then slid out from under the conduit. Flipping up the visor of her welding helmet she looked up at Jegra.

"I'm good. But by the expression on your face…"

"I just had a talk with your ex."

"That bad, huh?"

"Actually, she wouldn't shut up about the prophesy and some secret order called the Voroxians. She says she's a High Priestess of the Voroxian Order and a Knight of Caelum. She sounds outright delusional, but then swears up and down that she can't tell a lie. So, which is it? Is she telling the truth or is your ex-wife batshit insane?"

"Although I'd love to claim the latter, the truth is," Raven let out a deep sigh, "she's telling the truth. It's one of the reasons we didn't work out so well. She was caught up in her religious faith and I just wasn't all that religious. Still, we had our moment. Brief though it was."

"That's what I thought." Jegra turned to the side and gazed off at some blinking lights on a control panel and got lost in thought.

Raven stowed the torch, slipped off the welding helmet, and stood up. She had dirt and grease stains all over her and wore a medium gray tank top that sported sweat stains.

"If you want I could go have a talk with her and handle the situation. Maybe try to reason with her."

"No," Jegra said in a soft tone, still deep in thought. "I don't want to cause any unnecessary friction between you two. I'll deal with Angellyk when the time is right. There are more pressing matters at the moment that may need our attention. Danica is going to be in for the fight of her life in three days and I intend to intervene before anything bad happens to her."

"Ah, I see," Raven said, letting out a disappointed huff.

"I'm afraid that waiting for you to make all the necessary repairs will take too long. I want to be on our way by O-seven hundred."

"That only gives me about ten hours to get her up and running."

"Can you do it in that amount of time?"

Raven mulled it over for a moment, grabbing her elbow with one hand and her chin with her other. "If I keep my crew working around the clock and I borrow two from your team, then, yes. It's doable."

"Great," Jegra said, smiling. "I'll have Captain Blackstar send over two of our best engineers."

"Just one thing," Raven added at the last minute just as Jegra was about to leave. "I'm afraid I'll need to take a raincheck on our wrestling match."

"Oh, you were serious about that? I thought we were just…"

"Thought we were *what*, exactly?" Raven batted her eyes at Jegra, deliberately giving her an inquisitive look that imitated the innocence of a small child.

"I thought we were flirting. Kinda." Growing self-conscious, she hemmed and hawed, swaying nervously as she held one arm and shot Raven a guilty look. "I mean, I thought you were just teasing me about that. You already know I'm as much into women as I am men and that I like to mess around more than your average girl."

"Oh, I know," Raven said, smiling affectionately. "And if you weren't the empress, I'd be inclined to maybe ask you out for a drink."

Jegra grew even more self-conscious, which was out of character for her, but around Raven, she simply didn't know how to conduct herself. "Why am I so nervous right now?" Jegra asked out loud. Raven shrugged, still smiling at her. Feeling that it was awfully hot in the room, Jegra bent her arms and raised her elbows and checked her armpits. "And I'm sweating."

Raven laughed. "Just relax. We're friends first. That'll never change. But I know what you mean. It's like flirting with someone you've had a secret crush on for ages but then, once you get the chance to be alone together, it feels like…"

"It feels like making sexual advances toward your sister," Jegra added, finishing Raven's sentence for her.

"Right," she replied. "That's exactly what it's like. It would be like hitting on your own sister. Not me, though. I'm not a big perv like you." Raven held her serious face as long as she could but then, unable to hold it back any longer, cracked a smile.

"Oh, *you little…*" Jegra replied with a laugh. "If we weren't such good friends," she said, waving a playful finger at Raven, "I'd totally slap you right now."

"Be careful," Raven teased back, "I might like that."

Jegra gulped. "Seriously, what's gotten into you?"

Raven laughed again. "I have no idea. It's just been ages since I have felt this comfortable around someone." Looking into Jegra's eyes, she added, "But I'm glad it's with you."

"Me too," Jegra answered. After an awkward pause, she thumbed over her shoulder, and said, "Alright. I best be getting back to it. I'll send over those engineers asap."

"I'll be right here," Raven said, returning to her stripped-down power conduit and picking up her welding torch. As she bent down, she thrust her hips out in such a way that Jegra couldn't be sure she wasn't doing it on purpose or if Jegra was recognizing for the first time how beautiful Raven truly was. Admittedly, she'd been so preoccupied by other matters that she'd never paused to take a good look at the woman. Raven was just sort of the friend who came and went at her leisure, and that had always suited Jegra just fine. Now, she seemed to occupy a special place in Jegra's mind.

Jegra looked back one last time, hoping maybe Raven would glance back over her shoulder too, but instead of loitering about like a love-struck vole, she decided to shelve it for later and hurried out of the engineering bay and back up the corridor to the airlock that conjoined their two ships.

"Empress!" Skuld's voice chirped as she rushed past an open door that led to the mess hall.

"Can't talk now, Skuld. Got important business."

"Righteo!" he shouted back, seeing as she was already out of sight.

She felt bad for ditching him like that. Skuld was one of the few friends she knew she could trust with her life. But time was of the essence and as much as she'd like to catch up with him, they were working against the clock.

It only took her a few minutes to make her way to the bridge, and ducking under the bulkhead she stepped onto the command deck of the *Shard*.

"Her Royal Eminence on deck!" an officer shouted.

Lianica looked up and turned to see Jegra. Standing to greet the empress, she asked, "What is it?"

"We've got a lot of work to do," Jegra answered. "And not enough time to do it in."

Back in the prison cell aboard the *Shard*, Angellyk hummed a hymn she'd learned as a child, when a voice called out, "So, what do you think? Is she the savior the holy texts speak of? Is she the Daughter of Sol?"

Angellyk stopped mid-hum and slowly rose to her feet. "Who's there?" Walking up to the glass, she cupped her hands and peered out into the room and scanned the adjoining prison cells. Finally, she saw another like her–a Bre'lal woman. But unlike her, she was quite fetching. She had super-model looks and eyes that burned with a deep-seated passion that Angellyk instantly recognized.

"Onelle? Onelle Agnar? What in the bleedin' galaxy are you doing here?"

"It's a long story. But, to summarize, I tried to kill the empress."

"What?! Why would you do that?"

"I had a parasite. Or so they tell me. But just to be sure it was the parasite talking and wasn't me, I'm back here. Waiting for the test results of my neuro-scan." She motioned to her cell as if she were giving a grand tour of the place.

"Makes sense. You can't just go around assassinating the Empress of the Dagon Empire and not expect to find yourself in prison."

"So I've learned. But enough about me. What brings you here, Angie?"

Angellyk snorted as she laughed. Hardly anyone but Raven and her mother called her Angie. "Oh, I was ordered to kill the empress. But I decided to warn her instead. After all, I think my ex has a thing for her. And if I killed her Raven would never forgive me. So, here I am. Talking to you."

"That's funny," Onelle said, a soft nasally sounding chortle rising up from her throat.

"Why's that funny?"

"We're both in here for essentially the same crime."

"I guess we are," Angellyk answered.

"So, what do you think she'll do with us?"

"You mean other than collecting enough green skins to start her own brothel?"

Onelle smiled amusedly. Her species prided themselves of their monopoly on the sex trade. Angellyk's implication was that Jegra was honorable, and therefore would let them continue in a profession they both honored and respected.

But, at the same time, it implied Jegra would have some small degree of power over them. Maybe not as slaves, per se, but as business associates. Not that it would necessarily be a bad thing to get in bed with the empress. Onelle could think of two dozen ways that allying herself with the Empress of the Dagon Empire could greatly benefit her and her enterprise.

"Yes, other than that," she replied with a laugh.

"I have no idea. But if I had to venture a guess..." Angellyk paused and then shook it out of her mind. "Nah."

Angellyk looked at Onelle across the room and smiled. She waited patiently as Onelle formed her thoughts into words.

"It's just that Jegra always does the unexpected. I can never get a read on her. And believe me, I've tried. Now, I'm beginning to see what my sister, Abby, actually saw in her. She's virtually a goddess. Something our people worship with great reverence. To be in her presence is to be..."

"Is to be reminded of our mission in life. To uphold the principles of the Goddess, to never surrender our will to man, and to love the world as Mother Nature, in her great wisdom, so loved the world."

"Yes," Onelle replied, taking a seat on her cot. "But I'm afraid the damage is done. If I'm lucky, she'll leave me on some junk heap of an asteroid mining facility and be done with me."

"Oh, I don't know," Angellyk said, tossing her hair. "The empress seems to be the most compassionate ruler to have ever sat on the throne. If you make amends for your crimes, she will most likely forgive and forget."

"And if she doesn't?"

"Be content knowing that you at least tried to be a good person."

"You sound like Raven," she said, narrowing her eyes at Angellyk.

"I'll take that as a compliment," she retorted.

Onelle nodded and then sat back and lost herself in her thoughts. Across the room, Angellyk sprawled out on her cot and threw her arm over her brow, using it to block out the bright lights of the holding cell and maybe get a little shut eye.

"See you in the morning," Angellyk said, her arm still covering her eyes to block out the light.

"Yup," Onelle said. She too stretched out across her cot and, almost as soon as her head had hit the strangely comfortable bean-pillow, the lights dimmed to sleep mode. Yawing, she added, "See you in the morning."

33

Dakroth raised his arms toward the upper echelons of the stadium and, standing in place, slowly turned in a half-circle as he scanned the myriad of cheering faces gazing down at him from high up in the stands. The golden epaulettes on his white uniform, along with the floral embroidered cuffs on his sleeves, glinted in the light and he motioned for the throng to quiet down so that he might announce the start of the final, and much awaited, match of the three-week long humiliation bout.

The stadium was teeming with aliens from all across the Commonwealth. Species who'd traversed half the galaxy to come watch the fight of the century as the televid previews had described it. After a moment, a hush fell over the crowd and Dakroth lowered his hands and stepped up to the edge of his royal balcony.

"Ladies and gentlemen," Dakroth announced from his private booth, which overlooked the sands of the arena, "the moment you've been waiting for has finally arrived. Three long days since we last saw our harrowing vixens, who fought with valor and spilled blood, both their own and that of their rivals, on this very field. Well, tonight, I present to you the ultimate in humiliation battle royals–the Bull and Swan bout!"

The entire amphitheater shook with the uproarious cheers of the masses. Dakroth raised his hands again and basked in the euphoric energy of the crowd. Smiling up at the televid drones to show that he wasn't above the celebratory saturnalia of the people, he waited for the throng to simmer down to a steady murmur, like the rushing sound of a river, and then cleared his throat and continued with his speech.

Glancing up at the sky, he saw two flashes and knew exactly what it meant.

The *Shard* and the *Skywend* had arrived. The empress had returned home. And just in time to watch her beloved girlfriend, Danica Valencia, be torn to shreds by the most bloodthirsty brutes he could find this side of the galaxy. A crooked grin spread across his blue face, and he slowly turned his attention back to the opening ceremony of the games.

"Hear me! Hear me! Ladies, gentlemen, and species from every corner of the Commonwealth, I have a special surprise in store for you this fine day. But first, let's introduce our contestants!"

Loud cheers drowned him out and he gestured for the crowd to simmer down before continuing.

"Twelve of the top ranked gladiators from all across the Commonwealth will face off with the infamous traitor, Cassera Van Danica Amelorak," Dakroth informed the crowed, pausing as the stadium erupted with upset jeers, hisses, and booing. Speaking more loudly to compensate for the added noise, he continued, "And fighting to regain her honor after a most terrible disgrace, the blood-thirsty assassin of a thousand stars, Ishtar Bantu!"

Unlike Danica, Ishtar's name was met with a mix of praise and condemnation, but nothing nearly as damning as Danica had received.

And while Danica was universally despised, due to the narrative that Dakroth had expertly woven, which painted her as a wretched traitor, it wasn't clear if the naysayers were booing Ishtar because of her relationship to Danica or for some other reason. Regardless, the Emperor had the plebeians eating out of his hand and was quite confident he'd break all previous ratings records with this year's humiliation bout.

The Lord Emperor smiled wide and raised his hands, motioning for the crowd to settle down again. Once they complied, he fanned his hand across the arena and gestured toward the large southern gate, drawing the audience's attention to the entrance and location of the soon to be arriving gladiators.

A loud *clunk* followed by a rattling of chains filled the arena as the massive portcullis to the south gate began to rise. The gate led to an antechamber where the chariots and larger beasts would be prepped and stored until it was time to enter the main bout. But this time, only a small group of twelve, battle-worn and fearsome warriors ambled out of the shadows and onto the blistering orange sands.

As the group of warriors made their way toward the center of the arena, the faint sound of music came on the stadium's speaker system and then gradually began to swell into a rousingly heroic anthem that heralded the mighty gladiators.

Deep down, in his bones, the Lord Emperor knew this was truly going to be the fight of the century. It was his genius that so expertly turned Danica's betrayal of him into a betrayal of the empire. In his desire to see her destroyed, he'd figured out a way to bring the masses onto his side and unite them in their hate against the traitor.

And it was, he, the great Rhadamanthus Dakroth, reigning Emperor Supreme, who would go down in history as the emperor who gave the galaxy the best gladiator spectacle in the entire seven-hundred-year history of the games.

On the field, twelve warriors, all of varying species, strode out to the central location as one massive group and stopped to bow before the emperor. They looked more like an eccentric mix of elite swords for hire, than simple gladiators, but that's because they were armed to the teeth with every imaginable weapon that wasn't a blaster.

There were the incestuous Twins of Regolus, Apex and Pallis, glamorous Bre'lal brother and sister who made inappropriate and lascivious displays of affection toward one another during their matches. Not only that, but they boldly promoted the fact and had even released a top-selling smut video, proving themselves as debauched as the rumors had claimed.

Both were lean, with muscles as tight as rope that wove through their tall, wiry frames. Both green-skins had korridium scimitars and long, flowing forest green hair that floated about their shoulders as they danced about like acrobats, twirling their blades in a fanciful manner that seemed to mesmerize the audience.

After the twins came the Dragonian lizard man, Kegon the Fearsome, who was notorious for sinking his serrated teeth into the flesh of his victims as he tore their meat from their limbs. He always shredded the right shoulder off first, a signature move that maimed his opponents so badly they usually needed to amputate their mutilated limb; occasionally replacing it with a robotic prothesis. Assuming they survived the vicious mauling at all, that is.

Four battle droids equipped with various attachments; massive chain saws, heavy-duty bolt pistols, and electric prongs, marched in formation to the cheers of the spectators. Of all the contestants, they seemed the most out of place since they barely had a blemish anywhere between them. They were the top of the line X4 battle droids, courtesy of the Intergalactic Gladiatorial Syndicate, and looked as though they had come right off the assembly line.

If their software was up to date, they could prove more than effective on the battlefield, giving even the most veteran fighter a run for his money. Not much could slow these battle droids down, even if they were relegated to using the simple tools of bludgeoning.

As if on cue, two Salamandarian women strutted to the center of the arena, one a reddish-orange skin and the other green with azure markings running along the length of both sides of her body. Each of them wore thick leather armor and had countless straps with blades, battle axes, and swords fastened to their voluptuous bodies. One girl had a large shield across her back with a small crescent shape at the bottom that allowed room for her tail to poke out, whereas the green-blue Salamandarian girl had only half a tail, due to battle damage, but had fixed a spiked ball, like a morning star, to the end of it to compensate.

Next in the procession was a rather peculiar duo that stood out among all the rest. One large rock-man of unknown origin and his side-kick, a small Galliforn satyr of black and brown markings and only one horn, the other filed down to nothing, who went by the name Angor.

Angor only had one good eye, the right eye. An eyepatch covered the other, but had a laser sight built into it, which, given his choice of weapon, a crossbow and quiver of arrows slung across his back, made all the more sense. His rock-man companion, meanwhile, was threadbare, covering only enough of his body to maintain his modesty; his stone body was armor enough for anything that could be thrown at him in the arena.

Finally, standing at a massive twelve feet tall, was a colossal Bakktu with scars threading nearly every aspect of his body. This particular Bakktu was the current reigning champion, Niktor Ektan, and he flared his four crab-leg-esque mandibles and chomped at the open air with a menacing second jaw of filed teeth underneath.

His beady yellow eyes flitted left and then right as he swung his tentacle-like dreadlocks from side to side. He threw out his powerful clawed hands and roared. Saliva flew out of his mouth as he let loose a resounding battle cry. Raising his double-sided battle-axe above his head, a weapon that would be impossible for anything weaker than the towering brute to pick up, let alone wield skillfully, he paraded about the center of the arena. The other members of the group made way for him as he paraded about, and the crowd chanted *Ektan! Ektan! Ektan!*

The emperor knew that any one of these warriors would be a challenge for Jegra, let alone a lesser warrior like Danica, which is why he had hand selected them. But more importantly, perhaps, was their sociopathic tendencies and penchant for violence. After all, Dakroth wanted cold-blooded killers, barbarians, and thugs, not morally righteous heroes.

Turning around slowly, the Lord Emperor put his hands behind his back and looked down at the group of warriors from his high perch in the stands. They all knelt before him, bowing their heads reverently in humble submission, even the formidable Bakktu, Niktor Ektan.

"Rise my fearsome warriors!" Dakroth said, motioning for them to rise up and prepare themselves for battle with a wave of his hand.

As he turned around, he shot Ishtar a look that said, *you know what to do,* and then, waving to the audience one last time, he bid them adieu just as a yellow beam came down from the sky and transported him to his ship.

"Dagie-poo," an overly sweet-sounding voice said as soon as Dakroth had fully materialized aboard his ship. He turned to find Jegra standing off to the side of the transporter platform smirking at him with that obstinate grin of hers. She wore her Knights of Caelum armor and cracked her knuckles.

"What are you doing here?" he asked brusquely, confounded as to why she'd visit him here and now, while the match was under way down below in Arena City.

Jegra moved so fast that Dakroth didn't even have time to defend himself. Her fist impacted the side of his jaw with a loud *crack* and the emperor crumpled to the ground, completely unconscious. A perfect K.O.

"That was for Danica," she said, stepping over the Emperor's unconscious body. Reaching over the console, she quickly typed in the transport coordinates. Hitting the delay timer, she hurried over to the center of the transport platform and took in a deep breath. She still wasn't certain dematerialization and matter reassembly was perfectly safe and it gave her butterflies in her stomach every time she did it, which is why she avoided it as much as humanly possible.

In a flash of yellow light, Jegra materialized on the battlefield to see Danica and Ishtar fighting valiantly to fend off a fleet of attackers. They kept themselves moving, never stopping long enough for any one fighter to get the upper hand on them, but at this rate they were bound to wear themselves out before any of their opponents were taken out of commission.

If she exhausted herself before the real fight began, then there would be no avoiding the hungry wolves that descended upon her, all of them just as bloodthirsty as the next. Knowing Dakroth, she knew he had likely seen to it that Danica wouldn't make it out of this match alive, no matter how well she fought. As such, she needed to act, and fast. After all, she wasn't simply going to stand idly by and let her best friend in the whole galaxy be raped and murdered for spectacle. Not on her watch. Not while she was the empress of the whole goddamned mother-fucking galaxy.

Drawing out her plasma sword, she ignited it. The blade hummed to life and glowed bright orange and then, gradually grew hotter and hotter until, finally, it became a blinding hot white.

The resonant hum of its plasma core drew the attention of the other combatants as well as the crowd. When they all saw who the unannounced contestant was standing on the opposite end of the field, a reverent silence settled across the arena.

The two-headed serpentine announcer from Thermicron 5, the snake-planet, cleared his throats and, then, with the excitement of a fanboy who, like the rest of the audience, was taken entirely off-guard by the empress's surprise appearance, hollered a most feverish declaration into the mic. "Ladies and gentlemen! We have ourselves a surprise entry. I present to you, her royal majesty, Jegra the Merciless! Jegra the Undefeated!! The Imperatrix of the Galaxy!!!"

She looked over at her lambskin bikini-clad girlfriend and saw a profound sense of relief on Danica's face when their gazes met. Jegra merely nodded, as if to say, *I've got your back,* and the stadium erupted with such adoration that they shook the rafters.

Beyond the city gates, the sand dunes rippled with small waves caused by the uproarious sounds of cheering that emanated from the stadium. The noise-induced undulations caused the thirty-foot-long sand worms, the girth of anacondas, which usually drifted about the outskirts of the city where the sand was soft and where prey was easiest to catch, to be sent into a frenzied writhing.

"Was this part of the deal?" Angor asked, raising an eyebrow as he glanced curiously at the others. But he was only met with uncertain shrugs.

Nobody knew whether Jegra's arrival had been planned all along or not but, either way, he wasn't going to let that distract from his mission of killing the traitor and reaping the rewards. Getting the chance to defeat the former reigning champion was just a bonus. Shrugging, he raised his crossbow and took aim.

The korridium tipped, armor-piercing arrow whistled through the air as it flew across the empty space between him and Jegra. But to his astonishment, she reached out and caught the arrow in her hand without so much as batting an eyelid and then, with a resounding crunch, snapped it like a dry twig.

"Fine," the satyr said in a disgruntled tone, "You take her down, instead." He thrust his chin in the direction of the empress, and his companion, the rock monster, threw up his arms and bellowed out with a voice so tremendous everyone winced from the sheer volume of it.

The ground shook as the rock monster stormed across the arena, lumbering along on his fists and front arms like a gorilla. Leaping up into the air several meters before his target, the beast brought his massive stone fists down onto Jegra with bone crushing force. The blow was so powerful it sent out a kickback of dust and sand that engulfed both warriors.

Another silence came across the arena as the fate of the empress was uncertain. The audience waited with bated breath for the cloud of dust to settle while the other warriors cautiously circled about, keeping their eyes fixed on the plume of dust. As the haze finally thinned to reveal Jegra, holding the rock-man's fists at bay with the flat part of her plasma sword, the whole stadium erupted into cheers.

[*Suit fully charged,*] a female voice cooed. The rock creature looked down at Jegra and cocked its head in a curious sideways manner. Jegra merely grinned up at him and then winked.

Her gauntleted fist punched straight through her opponent's chest with the piercing force of a rail-gun. Debris exploded out of his back and sprayed the other contestants, forcing them to throw up their hands and deflect the incoming fragments of rock and pebble. The monstrosity yowled in pain as Jegra tore her fist back out of its torso, leaving only a gaping hole. Through the hole in the rock-man's chest, Jegra could see the shocked face of his partner, Angor, whose mouth hung open in dumbfounded awe.

The rock monster sank to its knees, clutching its chest-wound and gradually looked up at Jegra with the pathetic expression of a creature not accustomed to being the underdog. Unable to feel sorry for it, she thrust an armored boot right into its torso. The monster toppled to the ground and reached up with one hand as if to plead for mercy. Igniting her plasma blade, Jegra ignored it and with a bit of showmanship, spun around once, flaming sword crackling through the air, and then drove her blade clean through the creature's head and down through its sternum, cleaving him in two.

Jegra turned back to face the group of warriors and motioned with a wave of her hand for them to come at her. "My dance card is all freed up. Who's next?"

The battle droids all turned in formation, and fanned out, forming a perimeter around the empress and then began to slowly close in. Flanking her from all sides, they each took cheap shots at her, hoping to throw off her defense. Luckily, Jegra's armor protected her from the brunt of their attacks and, not waiting for one of the bots to get off a lucky shot, she twirled around, her plasma blade sparking and buzzing as it cut through armor plated bodies like a row of sushi.

A thin orange line spread across the chest-plating of all four robots. Jegra, poised in a crouch, sword extended like a samurai, looked over her shoulder at the robots to find each of them glancing down at the thin molten line stretching across their expurgated torsos. As if on cue, each battle droid abruptly exploded in a daisy chain of fiery destruction.

One after another went up in smoke and, one after another, their scorched and burning armor collapsed to the ground. A subtle yet distinctly satisfied grin spread across Jegra's lips and, after a twirl of her blade, she swiveled around and faced the remaining gladiators, shooting them a rather unimpressed look.

"I missed you!" Danica shouted above the din of the fighting and the chaos.

"I missed you too," Jegra shouted back, to the enthusiastic cheers of the audience.

"Why don't you two get a room," Ishtar grumbled, rolling her eyes at the public pronouncements of affection.

The two Salamandarian women, not particularly interested in taking on the undefeated champion of the arena, quickly turned their attention to Danica and Ishtar. The large Dragonian, Kegon, joined them in their attack. As the battle split into two groups, this opened up a window for the Twins of Regolus and the giant Bakktu, Niktor Ektan, to charge Jegra.

Not wasting a second, Jegra raced to meet them head on. As they darted across the hot sand, she glimpsed out of the corner of her eye the satyr, Angor. He dropped to his knees beside his slain friend and began weeping.

The twins, being lean and quick, were the first to reach Jegra. To their surprise, she leaped over them, tucked into a ball, and hit the ground rolling. Crashing into the legs of the giant Bakktu, she pummeled into him like a bowling ball crashing into pins. The Bakktu flipped head over heels and then bit the dirt. Hard.

Before it could even push its bulky mass all the way back to its feet, Jegra manifested behind it with startling speed, and raised her armor-plated boot. The Bakktu slowly turned its head just in time to eat a face full of Jegra's metal-clad foot and collapsed back to the ground. Coughing up sand, it tried getting back up.

Ektan was clumsy on the ground, and Jegra knew that if she let him get back onto his feet he'd tear her limb from limb, so the trick was to keep knocking him off balance. And it was working. As he rose to his hands and knees, she twisted about with a low, spinning sweep kick and took him down again. Ektan roared out in frustration and pounded his fists on the ground. Realizing he wasn't getting anywhere fast, he started to roll away, the first defensive tactic he'd had to use the entire time he'd been champion.

"Oh, no you don't," Jegra said in a hushed tone as she watched Ektan roll away from her. Leaping into the air, she calculated her trajectory and thrust out her right leg. Coming down like a missile, she stomped Ektan's head into the ground, his skull crushing under her boot and instantly turning to mush.

Ektan's brains squished under the weight of Jegra's foot like a juicy cockroach, the gory contents splattering everywhere. A communal "Eww" rose through the crowd and quickly turned into an enthralled "Ooh."

The minute the televid drones swooped down to get a close-up of the gory aftermath to throw up onto the giant stadium monitors, more cheers erupted, celebrating Jegra's swift victory over the current reigning champion.

"Jegra! We love you!" one of the green-skinned women shouted from the stands. She jumped up and down excitedly, her supple breasts bouncing in defiance of gravity, and blew a kiss at Jegra.

A drone swooped down and zoomed in on Jegra to catch her response, starting with the glistening lines of sweat trickling down the bulge of her breasts and into her cleavage, then slowly panning up to reveal the confident grin on her full lips.

She made a "V" with her fingers, spreading them wide, and then licked at the gap, performing a mock cunnilingus in response to the woman's shouts of admiration. She then pointed her finger up at the woman, singling her out of the crowd as the lucky recipient of her affection.

The young woman screamed out, barely able to believe that the great Jegra Alakandra, the Empress herself, had recognized her at all. In her excitement, she pulled up her ragged shirt and flashed her large breasts at the empress.

In the old days, Jegra would have likely invited that girl down to her personal chambers after the match to make good on her promise. But even though the times had changed, Jegra still knew how to keep the audience eating out of her palm.

It was all part of the show, after all. The show that Dakroth had rigged to make himself popular by association to the champions he groomed. And when they no longer served his purpose, he got rid of them. Replaced them with something new. Something fresh. And he only ever brought back old champions if he was certain it would garner him ratings.

If fact, it was clear to her now, that the only reason Abethca had entered her life was because Dakroth had willed it. But when Jegra's affections shifted to Abethca and not Dakroth, he had handled the situation like he always handled an unfavorable situation—by killing whatever or whoever was standing in his way.

And, now, the simple-minded asshat was trying to pull the same old shit with Danica. Something which infuriated Jegra to her very core and filled her with a burning rage she didn't know she possessed.

"No," she muttered under her breath, slowly turning to face the remaining combatants. "You won't beat me." *Not again. Not this time.*

With Ektan out of the picture, it was anyone's game. Fame and fortune favored the brave. At least, anyone brave enough to try and take on Jegra.

The opportunity presenting itself, the twins charged forward, weapons drawn. They leaped, twirled, and flipped about with such acrobatic frenzy that Jegra had a hard time keeping track of them. Out of nowhere a foot kicked Jegra's sword from her hands and the blade lodged itself into the sand a safe distance from their current position.

The plasma melted the sand to glass around it before the automated shutoff engaged. As it cooled and solidified, however, it became impossible for Jegra to tear it out without getting a firm hold on it and putting her back into it. It would have to wait. Giving up on the blade for now, she turned her attention back to the female twin who raced toward her with a bloodthirsty glint in her eye.

Not holding back, Jegra threw back her arm, her fist locking just behind her head, and held it. At the right instant, she let loose. Her fist cut through the air with the force of a cannonball, but the green girl skidded to a halt and, reversing direction at the last possible second, and did a back handspring out of the way, narrowly avoiding Jegra's attack.

Astonished that the girl could evade her so easily, not something many could do, Jegra lunged forward with a spinning back hand swipe. But, again, the agile girl bounced out of the way, effortlessly evading Jegra's follow-up attack. At the same time, the girl's brother joined the tango they had going on, and flanked Jegra from the side. She pivoted and threw out another spinning backhand. But he too cartwheeled out of the way as though he were as light as a feather.

"Would you two damn pixies hold still!" Jegra barked, annoyed by their prancing about like a couple of woodland fairies. She was accustomed to brawlers. Not ballet dancers.

"You weren't a part of the deal," the male Bre'lal said accusingly, pointing his blade at Jegra. He and his sister circled her, never stopping long enough for Jegra to get a good fix on them.

Confused, Jegra lowered her fists and asked, "What deal? What are you talking about?"

"The deal…" the female twin replied from behind Jegra's shoulder, "was to help the red one kill the traitor."

"You mean Danica?"

"But you're obviously here to prevent us from doing that. The Lord Emperor won't be very pleased with you."

"The Lord Emperor only cares about his precious ratings," Jegra answered, glaring at the young man. "You'd best remember that, because he'll flip on you the moment a more attractive offer presents itself."

"In that case, you just gave him a win in that department, sister," the female twin snarled.

There was a long stare-down between the two of them and then Jegra snickered. "The fight isn't over yet," Jegra replied, her subtle sneer widening into a full-sized grin.

Both women charged one another while letting loose their best battle cries. Jegra thrust a flat palm forward, her fingers stiffer than a board as they cut through the air. She hit the green-skin squarely in her abdomen, and the girl folded like paper and crumpled to the ground.

Momentarily stunned, and wheezing as the wind rushed out of her lungs, the Bre'lal girl barely had time to roll out of the way to avoid Jegra's follow-up knee attack.

As she rolled away, her brother leapt up over her and did a spinning roundhouse kick right into Jegra's bulky armor. Thrown off balance, Jegra fell backward and sent up a small dust cloud as her heavily armored body crashed to the arena floor.

In the blink of an eye, the green-skin girl flipped back up onto her feet and with a fanciful twirling of her blades, signaled to the empress that she was already ready for round two.

Jegra now found herself in a similar situation to Ektan before she'd stomped him out of existence, and felt a bit like an overturned tortoise in her heavy battle armor.

The bulky Knights of Caelum armor was only weighing her down now and made her movements sluggish and predictable. Besides, it had served its purpose of taking down the heavy hitters. Now, she needed to match the speed and finesse of the two spinning, twirling terpsichoreans or risk getting cut to ribbons.

The clock ticking down, Jegra slapped the emergency release function and the armor decompressed with a pneumatic hiss of air. A series of interlocking panels unfurled and flipped open, allowing Jegra to climb out of the suit. Gradually, she rose out of the armor and shed the metal husk like a butterfly shedding its cocoon.

The green-skins regrouped and circled back around, hesitant about how to proceed now that Jegra had ditched her armor. She wouldn't be held back any longer and this meant they'd need to be extra cautious when engaging her.

When the female sister caught her brother eyeing Jegra's stunning and sweat dappled body, she slapped him in the arm. "Hey! Stay focused."

Once she'd fully exited the armor, Jegra stretched and then cracked her neck side to side. She sported her trademark metal bikini, minus all the traditional trappings, trophies, and décor she usually wore–all but for the thick, silver bracelets she had on. Bracelets made out of microphase korridium alloy.

Out of the blue an arrow came streaking toward Jegra. Sensing it, she spun to try and deflected it away with her bracelet, but she was too slow and the arrow embedded itself into her left shoulder. She groaned in pain and looked at the feathered shaft jutting out of her flesh. "Goddamn it," she muttered in frustration.

Fearful of removing the korridium arrowhead and causing damage to her muscle tissue, she decided to leave it in for the time being. Turning to face the new threat, she glared at the satyr from across the field who was busy readying his crossbow with another bolt. Her brow creased into a sharp scowl and she shot him a look that said *don't even think about it, buster.*

But he simply ignored her glowering and went about making ready for a second attack. After all, she'd killed his best friend, something which he wouldn't likely forget anytime soon. Besides, the satyrs were a stubborn, loyal race. He'd simply keep on coming at her until he succeeded in avenging his partner's death or until she put him out of his misery.

Distracted by the satyr's antics, Jegra felt a lacerating pain across her back. Before she knew it, the female twin had sliced and "X" across her shoulder blades, cackling like a witch as she pranced off, proud of her handy work.

Jegra yelled out in pain laced frustration and staggered forward, shaking her fists and mumbling obscenities under her breath as she tried to shake off the sting. "You assholes!"

The twins laughed in reply to Jegra's complaining, finding pleasure in their small victory.

Her ears caught the sound of another blade slicing through the air and, crossing her wrists above her head, Jegra blocked the incoming swipe just above her head. The blade sparked against her metal bracelets and, with a grunt, she thrust her powerful arms upward and threw off her attacker.

Spinning around, she saw the male twin leap backward, tuck into a ball, and roll out of range. The moment he shrank away, his sister leaped over him and landed a sturdy flying jump kick right into Jegra's abdomen.

Both women toppled to the ground and began scrambling to their feet. Jegra quickly did a crouching roundhouse and knocked the girl back onto her ass. Quickly getting to her feet ahead of her opponent, she narrowly dodged another arrow that whispered past her head.

Without even looking, Jegra reached out and caught the shaft of the arrow, mere inches away from her right ear. Breaking it over her knee, she tossed both pieces to the ground and then ran full speed toward the arena wall.

Everyone paused and watched her, not understanding why she was heading away from the fight. Of course, Jegra's tactics weren't always conventional, so even Ishtar and Danica's fight with the Dragonian lizard man and the two Salamandarian girls slowed to a standstill as everyone stopped to see what Jegra was doing.

In a single bound, Jegra jumped up to the top of the arena wall. Spectators screamed with elation and reached out to touch their heroine, but she kicked off before probing hands could clasp her and flew across the arena like one of the satyr's arrows. Drilling into the Bre'lal brother, she knocked him clear across the battlefield with such force he hit the wall on the opposite side.

A wet cough came from his red-stained mouth and, slumping to his knees, he spit blood onto the sands. Wiping his lips with the back of his hand he examined the color, pushed himself off the wall, slowly raised his head, and let out a fearsome shout. But it was cut short when his sister's body slammed into him, knocking him back into the wall again.

The twins fell into a heap on top of one another, both rendered unconscious. In the distance, Jegra dusted her hands off as if to say *good riddance*, the first arrow still protruding out of her left shoulder.

While the twins were out for the count, she turned her attention to Angor, the satyr. When he spotted her stomping across the sand toward him clearly determined to break him over her knee like one of his arrows, he quickly plucked a fresh bolt from his quiver and began loading his crossbow.

"Oh, no you don't!" Jegra growled as she approached. Reaching out she tried to grab onto the creature's one good long-horn. The other seemed to have broken off a long time ago and had been filed down to prevent splintering. But the satyr simply fell away from her, evading her grasp, and launched his arrow behind him.

It sailed through the air and embedded itself into the back of Danica's left thigh. She yelped at the sharp pain and looked down at the back of her leg to find a long arrow shaft sticking out. The Dragonian, Kegon, came rearing up behind her with a battle axe, ready to chop her in half. Danica flinched, realizing she wouldn't be able to hobble away fast enough to evade the lethal swipe of his blade.

Her every muscle tensed and she cringed, waiting for a swift death, but when the attack never came she slowly opened one eye and peeked at the giant lizard man standing over her shoulder. Something was off; a peculiar look of astonishment was etched into his face and he wasn't moving. It was as if he'd been frozen in time. That's when Danica noticed the thin red line open up along his throat.

Kegon sunk to his knees and then fell to the side. When his left shoulder hit the ground his severed head rolled off his shoulders and across the dirt. It only stopped when it rolled against the sole of a boot.

Danica looked up to see Ishtar resting her foot on Kegon's head as though it were a Galactic League soccer ball. She flicked the green blood from her blade and nodded at Danica who nodded back at her in gratitude.

Frustrated by Angor's little ruse, Jegra reached down, and with an annoyed huff, grabbed the creature by his chest plate and hoisted him into the air with one arm.

His armor crumbled beneath Jegra's powerful grip as though it were tinfoil and with an angry puff, she flung the goat halfway across the arena. Angor crashed into the blue Salamandarian girl and, together, they toppled to the ground.

The red Salamandarian girl scrambled to help her friend up and then met Ishtar head on. Ishtar was fast, though, and used the momentary snafu to launch a blitzkrieg attack on the two lizard women.

Meanwhile, Danica felt a sudden onset of vertigo, as though she were drunk with alcohol, and stumbled forward. Throwing out her hands, she tried to steady herself, but the dizziness only grew worse. When she tried to speak, her words came out garbled.

"Wuh, fuh-dah-em did ah-vis."

"What did you say?" Ishtar asked, glancing back momentarily as sparks flew off her sword.

"Dani! Are you all right?" Jegra called out in a loud enough voice that Danica would hear.

"Iffel abbett woozy…" she said, her voice growing extremely weak.

Angor pushed himself back up to his hooves and began laughing in Vaudevillian fashion. "Poison tipped arrow," he informed Jegra with a chuckle.

Through gritted teeth, Jegra said, "You have exactly three nano-seconds to hand over the antidote or I tear your head off your shoulders and shove it up your ass."

The satyr stroked his beard and let out a bleat that was part amused laugh, part cough. "It's not that kind of poison," he answered. Turning toward Jegra, his eyes went cold and, after a deep breath, he addressed Danica. In a most chilling voice, he commanded, "Kill the empress. Kill Jegra."

"Hey!" Ishtar shouted, looking over her shoulder at Danica. "Snap out of it." But it was no use. The poison had already taken effect.

Danica stood inert in the middle of the arena, the blank expression on her face unmoving. She seemed stuck in an emotionless stupor, staring at some unremarkable patch of dirt in the distance. But, like a robot programmed for a very specific mission, she blinked twice, looked up, and then promptly reached down and tore the arrow out of her leg without so much as a whimper.

Blood spurted as the arrow tore free of her blue flesh, but the pain didn't seem to register. Unfazed, she merely turned to face Jegra, her eyes somehow entirely vacant. Her sunken eyelids and detached gaze were evidence enough that the toxin surging through her system had altered her in some terrible way. It seemed as though her soul had been swallowed up by a great dark void along with any compassion she might have once had. All that remained was a stone-cold viciousness.

With the arrow clutched in her hand, she charged forward with a single-minded goal. *Kill the empress. Kill Jegra.*

34

Raw, throbbing pain swept through every inch of Dakroth's body. Jegra's sucker punch not only fractured his jaw but left his entire body in shock. His whole body felt as though it had just survived a stampede of Angorian bison. "She'll pay for this," he grumbled, rubbing his jaw.

"Try not to speak," a nurse said as she administered a painkiller using a hyper-air-spray-injector called a NeedleAir injector. She mashed the device into the side of his neck and it went off with a hiss. Dakroth groaned and clutched the nurse by her slender, indigo arm. She flinched from the pain of his grip. But as Dakroth's eyes glossed over with the soothing balm of the drugs, he slowly relinquished his hold.

As the nurse packed her first-aid kit, Dakroth's roving eyes followed her indigo legs up to the white miniskirt she wore. Of course, she was dressed according to how he liked his medical staff to dress. Both the women and men nurses wore short tops and miniskirts. Perhaps a little sexist, but he felt that as long as the dress code was gender mutual, there wasn't any inequality going on. So what if there was an occasion nip-slip or a bit of plum-peekaboo?

He also couldn't help but admire her darker indigo skin. Like many species, Dagons were made up of a variety of races. There were fair skinned lineages, who had lavender skin or baby blue skin, and there were those who had deep rich blue tones of indigo and cobalt to their skin. In his estimation, this nurse was a real beauty. One of the prettiest he'd seen in months. Her dark indigo skin and full, black painted lips drove him wild with lust and he knew that he had to have her, right here and now.

After she finished putting away her things, the exotic-looking nurse put the strap of the first-aid kit over her shoulder and helped Emperor Dakroth to his feet. Bracing him up, she threw his arm over her shoulder and helped steady him. "Let's get you to your quarters so you can rest a bit."

"You read my mind," he said in a slurred, yet distinctly orgiastic manner. "And I can think of ten ways right now on how you can help me rest." He leaned in to her and whispered something into her ear which prompted her eyes to widen as her cheeks flushed with shock.

"My lord," the nurse gasped, taken aback by his brazenness. "With all due respect, it wouldn't be proper."

"Proper?" he laughed drunkenly, "I wouldn't dream of it. I simply want you to try and relax."

"Relax?" she asked in a seductive voice, playing along with him as was expected. "Tell me, my lord, how do you want me to relax?"

Dakroth paused and eyed the nurse up and down, admiring her cleavage. "You know. Just let down your hair, relax, be open with me. Let's get to know each other better."

"Be open with you?" she teased. "How open?"

"I want you to be as open with me as you can be," he said in a salacious tone. She smiled at him, ignoring his lewd innuendo, and bit her bottom lip in a flirtatious manner. "What's your name?" he asked, rubbing his hand along her arm, letting his fingers dance across her indigo skin.

"Callestra Van Morgan," she replied.

"You wouldn't happen to be related to Targon Van Morgan by any chance, would you?"

"Yes," she said, her eyes lighting up. "Senator Targon is my father. How'd you know?"

"The aquiline nose gave it away," he said suavely, rubbing the arc of her nose and then playfully bopping it with his finger. A trait all Morgans shared. He winked at her and then added, "A truer sign of pedigree there's none."

Callestra blushed and looked away when, all of a sudden, the emperor pressed her firmly into the wall. Leaning up against her, he reached down and felt up her skirt. "Ah," he said with a pleased, smile, "Just the way I like it. Ready and willing."

Callestra let the first-aid kit slip off her shoulder and fall to the metal floor plating. As it landed with a *clink*, she clutched Dakroth's wrist, holding his hand in place, right between her thighs. Then, swiveling her hips, she slid down onto his fingers and back up. "I always want to be open with you," she said, throwing his same innuendo back at him.

There was a brief pause as they stared at each other with a burning intensity, and then, as if the start of a race had sounded, Callestra threw her leg up for Dakroth to catch and she clutched the emperor by the nape of his neck and drew him into her.

As their lips came together hungrily and their tongues danced a sultry tango between each other's open mouths, they shared a sensual moan. Hands ran up and down one another's bodies as they quickly began undressing each other in a lust driven haste. The quicker they could get down to business, the better.

Once Dakroth had stripped off Callestra's white nurse's uniform only to reveal a classy set of mango colored lingerie that complimented her indigo skin, he buried his face in between her breasts, dabbling them with hot kisses, and running his fingers up the curve of her back, he paused midway to unfasten her bra. His fingers fumbled to unhook the brassiere and his face buried in the soft mounds of her breasts, he never even saw the second NeedleAir jet injector spray she drew up.

A loud, menacing hiss stung Dakroth's arm and he shot a sharp glance to where the pain came from, only to find Callestra jamming the medical device into his shoulder. Dakroth winced from the pain and looked back at the dark painted eyes gazing at him with a gleeful kind of rebelliousness. He wasn't certain if this was some kind of kinky foreplay or something else. But, either way, he didn't much care for unexpected surprises.

"*Hey, what did you do that for?*" Barely able to finish the sentence before blacking out, he buckled under the heavy weight of the drugs and slumped to the ground.

Not wanting to harm the emperor visibly, Callestra caught him under his arms and set him down gently.

After dressing, she reached up and touched her ear. A faint digital tone chimed and her entire visage rippled with a digital distortion and then the holographic image turned off revealing Raven Nightguard, wearing only a skimpy nurse's uniform.

"Jegra warned me you were all hands," she said, in a disgusted tone. Shuddering as she made a sour face, she knew she'd need to take a long hot shower in order to get the Dakroth off her. Tucking the medical injector into a side pocket on her tight-fitting, white vest, she turned and scooped Dakroth up in her arms and hauled him back over to the transportation pad.

She quickly proceeded to fold his arms across his chest and then rearranged the rest of him into a fetal position. Once she'd finished placing him in the exact position she needed, she marched back over to the control panel and typed in a set of coordinates.

The computer chimed, signaling the coordinates were imputed, and she rushed back to the transportation pad. climbing on, Raven knelt down by the sleeping emperor and waited as the transportation pad hummed to life. A few seconds later they were both engulfed in a yellow light.

Gradually, their very matter began to dissolve into tiny hexagonal packets of light, the particles swirling about in a counterclockwise fashion and then rising into the ceiling only to be projected to some distant location where they'd be reassembled again.

No sooner had they transported away when the doors slid open with a whisper. A cute, petite nurse wearing the same skimpy nurse's outfit that Raven had worn earlier stepped into the room. She looked around only to find an abandoned first-aid kit sitting in the middle of the floor by itself.

"That's odd," she said, scratching her chin as she scanned the room for the emperor. Assuming he must have gotten tired of waiting and left, she shrugged, picked up the extra first-aid kit, and left to return to her regular duties.

Part of her was glad the emperor wasn't there, because she knew his penchant for having his way with cute nurses and although she'd never admit it publicly, she didn't really like the emperor. He was a womanizing brute and a power-hungry dictator. Among the Dagon citizenry, there were just about as many people fed up with Dakroth's arrogance and failed policies as those who still supported him. But with the rise of Jegra, it seemed a new dawn was approaching.

Still, the empress, not being of pure Dagon blood, faced a lot of opposition. Although she may have secured the people's confidence, her political sway was minimal at best. In fact, the entire senate was only lukewarm when it came to their appreciation of their new imperatrix and what she represented. And she still had a lot to prove. Most of all to Senator Targon Van Morgan, who was the longest sitting senator on the Dagon council and who closely allied himself with Dakroth's political interests. He was Jegra's most vocal detractor.

Nearly all his televid tirades were admonitions against the empress. She could never do any right in his eyes. Which was funny, considering that Dakroth was the one who had made her Imperatrix in the first place.

The nurse cleared her mind as she walked along the ship's corridor back to sickbay. As she passed a portal, she glanced out at the beautiful starscape. Dagon Prime hung in the sky like a blue and green opal, while Thessalonica glowed hot orange as its orbit brought it into the evening eclipse behind the glorious planet.

There was a brief glimmer just beyond the window and for an instant, she thought she had seen the form of a ship. But the moment she blinked it was gone again. She blinked a couple more times for good measure, just to be sure her eyes weren't playing tricks on her. This was her first time stationed aboard a starship, let alone a battlecruiser, so she was still all nerves. But she took a deep breath and calmed herself. *It was nothing*, she assured herself.

"Amora Van Gogh!" a voice called out.

She spun to find Doctor Darius Ebbedon waving to her from the four-way junction up ahead. She smiled and waved back as she continued along at her brisk pace.

"I heard you treated the Lord Emperor. How was your first time?" the doctor asked, pulling up alongside her and matching her brisk pace.

There was a subtle implication that she didn't appreciate, but she felt she had a responsibility to relay the truth. Pausing in the middle of the corridor, she turned to the doctor and relayed her account of what had transpired. "That's the thing. You see, I went to treat the emperor," she said timidly, "but when I arrived on the scene he was simply gone."

"But the emergency medical call came from the Lord Emperor personally," Dr. Ebbedon said, scowling at Amora. "As his attending physician, he is your responsibility."

Amora turned her head and looked back over her shoulder the way she'd come. "I'm sorry, doctor. I can go back if—"

"No, that won't be necessary, Amora," Dr. Ebbedon reassured her. If the emperor really had gone missing, he'd be as much at fault as she was. And he didn't want to be the one to incur Dakroth's wrath, so he promptly went over to the glossy black wall panel and touched it with the palm of his hand. A sudden flurry of activity lit up around the pane where his hand was pressed, showing all kinds of displays related to the activity of the ship. "Computer, locate the Lord Emperor for me."

[*The Lord Emperor is not currently on board,*] replied the ship's computer.

Dr. Ebbedon shot Amora a confused look. Keeping his hand on the touch-panel display, he frowned, and said, "Explain."

[*The Lord Emperor is logged as transporting off the ship seven minutes ago.*]

"That's a couple minutes before I arrived," Amora informed the doctor.

He nodded, taking in Amora's information, and then formulated a new question for the computer. "Computer, what was the Emperor's destination?"

The was a brief pause, unusual for a state-of-the-art quantum computer and fully functional A.I. Then, the female Dagon voice of the ship's computer replied, [*Unknown.*]

Upset, Dr. Ebbedon pinched the bridge of his nose and closed his eyes for a moment as he gathered himself. Opening them again, he turned to the black panel on the wall and said, "Computer, playback the last known video footage of Lord Emperor Dakroth.

A digital televid box lit up on the screen and Amora and the doctor watched as Dakroth finger-banged an incredibly sexy, yet unfamiliar nurse.

"Do you recognize this nurse?" asked Amora.

"No, I haven't seen a nurse with legs like that," Ebbedon said in all seriousness. Amora shot him a curt look but he didn't seem to notice.

"Maybe she's new."

"You're the newest member on staff that I'm aware of," Dr. Ebbedon relayed. They both watched as Dakroth and the sexy nurse sank out of view of the digital camera. Although there wasn't any further footage, the transporter log registered two bodies. Dr. Ebbedon didn't need to have a medical degree to know what likely happened next. Dakroth had beamed his little plaything to a secret love den somewhere. In fact, the Imperial code had been used to encrypt the transport site, meaning only another member of the Imperial family could decode it.

Amora and Dr. Ebbedon turned toward each other with confounded looks.

"I know the emperor is famous for his sexual prowess, but logging an official medical request to bang the first nurse he came across seems a little suspect. Doesn't it?"

"I don't know," Dr. Ebbedon replied, his tone gravely serious. And, the truth was, he honestly didn't know. It seemed like something Dakroth might do, but it didn't seem to be the way he'd go about doing it, especially since the emperor was injured. Also, there was the issue of the mysterious nurse that neither he, the attending, or Amora, another nurse, could recognize. The ship was big, and this sleek and mysterious vixen could be part of the medical staff. But until he was absolutely certain, he didn't want to risk making any premature assumptions. After thinking it over, he finally sighed and said, "I suppose I'm going to have to report this."

"Will you have to report me, too?" Amora asked, a twinge of fear in her voice.

"No, no," Dr. Ebbedon chuckled, waving his hand as though he were shooing away an absurd suggestion. "I'm sure we can work out some other arrangement so that I don't have to write up a formal reprimand."

When she caught him eyeing her figure, she rolled her eyes. Of course, by other arrangement, he meant sex. That's all most Dagon people could think about. Duty, honor, and sex.

Ever since she was a little girl, though, she'd felt different somehow. The lubricious and promiscuous inclination of her species never seemed to interest her much. Sex was not only uninteresting to her but seemed completely unnecessary. If she had to, she'd go through with it. But she'd rather not, if it could be helped. She was rare among the Dagon people, being a virgin and all, especially since virgins were virtually unheard of in this day and age. But her personal life was none of anyone's business but her own. If she decided to have sex, it would be on her own terms.

"Uh…yes," she finally replied. "Whatever you think is a fitting punishment for me given the fact I failed to carry out my duties."

"All right," the doctor replied in a pleased tone. "We'll talk more about this later." With that said, Dr. Ebbedon and she hastily turned and retreated up the corridor. As he hurried along, he glanced off to the side, his eyes fixing themselves on Amora, and added, "I'll need to take this news to the Sub-Commander. In the meantime, return to your duties."

"Yes, doctor," Amora replied, bowing cordially as Dr. Ebbedon disappeared around the bend of the corridor a short distance ahead.

Once he was out of sight she straightened back up and let out a pent-up sigh. At least she wouldn't need to resort to appeasing her superior's sexual lust just to get out of a minor incident that wasn't even her fault. Hopefully by the time he'd finished figuring out where the Lord Emperor had disappeared to, he'd have forgotten all about her role in the matter.

Groggy, Emperor Dakroth tried to sit up, but found himself firmly secured to what appeared to be an automated dental hygiene chair. Even his wrists were strapped down, so he couldn't very well use his laser finger ability to break free. Which meant, whoever had abducted him knew exactly what they were doing.

Still unable to focus, he scanned the room and examined the blinking lights of a computer console and the faint glow of some red backlighting over the exit. The rest of the room was shrouded in darkness.

With barely enough light to see anything at all, he squinted as he peered into the dimly lit crevices of the chamber. Once his eyes had adjusted enough to see more clearly, he was able to make out the outline of a darkened figure standing off in a corner of the room. It watched him in silence and he felt a small twinge of dread building in the pit of his stomach.

"Who's there?" he asked in his most authoritative tone which came off sounding more like a demand than an inquiry. The one thing Dakroth couldn't afford was to appear weak. At the last minute, he added, "I order you to show yourself."

The mysterious figure slowly stepped forward and into the light to reveal none other than the famous bounty hunter and smuggler, Raven Nightguard.

"So, it was you!"

Raven didn't reply. She merely looked down at him feeling nothing but disgust. This was the man who'd had her parents killed and who had made her life a living hell.

But even as she wanted nothing more than to reach down and rip off his pruney little ball sack and shove it so far up his ass he would choke on it, she knew that exacting revenge on him now would defeat her cause. A cause she believed in with all her heart and soul. A cause to unite the Commonwealth under a banner of peace rather than war.

Although she had to eat a big serving of humble-pie, she pushed down her feelings of rage and calmed herself with the appeasing knowledge that the time was fast approaching when he'd get precisely what was coming to him.

"Is there nothing you wouldn't do for her?" he scoffed, imperiousness saturating his every word.

By *her* she knew he meant Jegra. But he'd asked the question with such disdain she had to fight the urge to chew him a new one. She couldn't let his negativity get under her skin. If she did, then he'd use it against her. That's what Dakroth did. He manipulated you until he turned you against yourself.

"Unlike you, Lord Emperor," Raven said in a straight forward tone, "Jegra wins people over with love, not fear. You could learn a thing or two by following her example."

Dakroth balked at the suggestion. Annoyed by her self-righteousness, and not wanting to get into a moral debate with her, he promptly changed the subject. "You realize, don't you, that abducting me constitutes treason?"

"As I recall," Raven said with a sly grin, "You were the one who absconded with me. Remember?"

Dakroth looked away. "I'm sure I don't know what you're talking about."

Raven held up a small holovid projector in the palm of her hand and an image of Dakroth seducing her in the transportation room lit up in 3D, filling the space between them. "Maybe this will help jog your memory."

"What's this?" Dakroth growled, noticing that the disguise Raven had tricked him with didn't show up on the video. It was just him and her, as she appeared to him now.

"Isn't it obvious? It's you seducing me, right before running off with me."

And by the evidence playing on the video, it really did appear as though it was he who had seduced her. Conveniently enough, the two of them slipped off camera before it could show her dosing him. Then the image was filled by the golden flicker of the transportation beam dancing about the room. It all fit his modus operandi so well that he knew she was right. Nobody would believe him.

Still, he couldn't let her know she'd beaten him.

"Nobody will fall for that fabricated nonsense!"

"Maybe. Then again, maybe not. But if anyone is tempted to look for you, they'll quickly discover this holovid feed and will know exactly what happened. You seduced me and then whisked me away to your secret bedchamber for a more discrete liaison. And the wonderful thing about it is, nobody will think twice about it. They'll merely say to themselves, there goes Lord Dakroth again, on another one of his many dalliances."

Dakroth frowned, but managed to squeeze out a smile. "Well played, Ms. Nightguard, well played indeed." Raven bowed her head, accepting his compliment and then turned as though she were going to leave. "Just one question," Dakroth said, stopping her and bringing her attention back around to him. "How in the galaxy did you tap into my ship's video feed, anyway? Military encryption is impossible to break."

Raven smiled yet did not respond. She brushed the white tuft of hair back between the layers of her purple ombre and tucked it behind her ear. Then, taking out the hyper-air-spray from the side pocket of her vest, she looked down at Emperor Dakroth and said, "I'll wake you again when I need you."

"No, wait!" Dakroth pleaded, but it was too late. The hiss of the medical spray shooting into his leg silenced his protest. His eyelids fluttered and then, with one last heavy breath, he fell into a drug induced sleep.

"Now, to get out of these ridiculous clothes and take that hot shower," she said, looking down in disgust at the skimpy nurse's outfit she was still wearing. Tucking the hyper-air spray back into her pocket, she looked back at the lightly snoring emperor one last time and, then, turned to leave, the doors whisking open before her.

Once she was out in the corridor, she turned and secured the doors behind her. Pressing her purple finger onto the biometric scanner, the circuitry under her skin in her forearm lit up bright pink as she input an asymmetric encryption key that not even Skuld or Gyllek could crack.

Because, the truth of the matter was, if her and Jegra's plan was going to work, she couldn't risk anybody learning that she was holding the emperor captive aboard the *Skywend*. Not even her own crew.

35

A clear blue sky hung over the gladiatorial stadium in Arena City like a soothing blanket. Thorn birds, the only indigenous bird on the desert moon, flew across the sky and the steady buzz of Angorian cicada could be heard in the distance. From down in the arena, however, rose a cry so tortured that it ruined the peaceful scene with its dreadful shriek.

When Danica reached Jegra's position she leapt into the air, roared out in rage, and thrust the arrow forward with all her strength.

In her mind she screamed for herself to stop, yet her body would not listen to her mind. It was as though she were possessed by some terrible force, and all it wanted to do was kill Jegra.

"Danica, stop!" Jegra said, leaping out of the way. "This isn't you. It's the poison. It's poisoning your mind."

Jegra's pleas fell on deaf ears, however, and Danica merely took another swipe, aiming for Jegra's neck. Jegra leaned back and then sidestepped Danica and slapped her on the ass, hard.

Danica stumbled forward, surprised by the familiar swat. Although it had nearly sent her toppling to the ground, she caught herself and spun around to face her opponent.

"I don't want to have to hurt you, babe," Jegra said, her hands raised defensively as she slowly eased away from Danica.

In the distance, Angor bleated and cackled as if he'd just heard the world's funniest joke. Annoyed, Jegra shot him a menacing look over her shoulder and growled, "I'll deal with you next!"

"Fine, fine," he laughed, slapping his leg.

The twins began to rouse and sat up to see the red-skin woman, Ishtar, pinned against the far wall by both Salamandarians, the satyr rolling around in the dirt laughing hysterically, and the blue-skin, who was the empress's best friend, fiercely attacking the empress. Helping his sister up, Apex asked, "What is going on here?"

"I have no idea," Pallis answered, a slight frown settling onto her face as she tried to follow the chaos tearing up the battlefield. "Do you think we should intervene?" Pallis finally asked, turning toward her brother for confirmation.

Apex shook his head and then replied, "No, we'd best sit this one out until there's a clear winner."

Almost as soon as he finished saying it, he locked eyes with Angor. "Don't even think about it!" he shouted, as the satyr snatched up his crossbow.

Apex began dashing straight for the goat, hoping to intercept him before he could get a shot off. But he was a few seconds too late. The arrow flew from the flight groove and streaked through the air. Apex raised his hand defensively, the arrow piercing his hand. Yelping from the pain, he stopped in his tracks, clutching his wrist. "You backstabbing little prick," growled Apex. "We're supposed to be on the same side!"

Angor simply kicked back his head and laughed. It was clear he'd lost his mind. Probably the trauma of losing his longtime companion. Either way, sane or not, Apex didn't have time for games. But he suddenly felt weary.

"W-what is happening?" he asked, his vision beginning to blur.

"Same mind-control serum that I hit the blue-skin with."

"But I'm already trying to kill the empress..." he said, staggering sideways, as if he lost his footing, before catching himself.

"I don't want you to kill the empress," Angor said placidly, a sinister grin curling onto his goat face. "I want you to fuck and kill your sister. Strangulation sounds nice. Who knows, knowing you two, she might even enjoy it."

A horrified look came over Pallis's face as her brother tore the arrow out of his hand and turned toward her with that hungry look in his eyes.

"No, Apex. Don't!" she pleaded.

But Apex moved so fast she barely had time to react. He pounced on her and they tumbled to the ground. She scrambled back, trying to get out from under him, but he threw himself on top of her and prevented her from getting away.

Soon enough, one hand clutched her throat and at the same time, she felt his other hand pull away her loincloth.

"*Apex, no,*" she wheezed, clutching his forearm to prevent him from crushing her larynx. But even though she struggled against her brother's grip, his hand squeezed her neck so tightly she couldn't breathe.

If fighting to breathe wasn't difficult enough, Pallis cringed when she felt a different pain. She groaned out loud when her brother forced himself inside of her. It wasn't the first time they'd made love, but it was the first time it was done in such a humiliating fashion. Still, she let him do it. There was no point in resisting. Not now.

She looked over at Jegra, a fleeting glance that almost seemed apologetic in nature, then, grasping her brother's other hand, she brought it up to her neck and helped him place it around her throat.

"Do it," she whispered, her voice coming out raspy through a strained larynx. If it had to be this way, then she was glad it was him.

Angor began laughing even more as he watched the madness he had sewn. Reloading the crossbow, he turned toward the Salamandarian girls and, without so much as a moment's hesitation, shot the red one in the back of the head.

The blue girl cried out in shock, seeing her sister go down. She turned to see who had shot her teammate but took an arrow in the neck before she could turn all the way around.

Stunned, she reached up and tried to catch the torrent of blood gushing out of her neck wound in her hands, but it just flowed between her fingers like a sticky crimson waterfall. Gurgling, she tried to speak, but her words were inaudible.

Ishtar watched her fall face first into the dirt next to her partner and almost laughed at the stupid look frozen on the girl's face. Refocusing her attention on the chaos happening around her, she looked up in time to see an arrow arcing through the air for her. She reflexively leaned to the side and watched it impregnate the wall with its poisoned tip.

Ishtar bent down and slid the spiked morning star tail-guard off the dead combatant at her feet and fixed it to her right hand. "I'll be taking this, if you don't mind." Swiveling around, she eyed the satyr with a ravenous look and licked her lips.

Startled by the wild look in her eyes, Angor reached back to pluck another arrow from his quiver but came up empty. "Graddack!" Not waiting for Ishtar to bash his skull in, he turned and loped away.

Ishtar ignored the satyr, who was already racing toward the weapons rack to fetch himself something to fight with, and ran straight up to the weak-minded green-skin asshole raping his own sister.

She unfastened the spiked ball from the fixture in the gauntlet and let the chain rattle out until it stopped just above the ground. Slowly, Ishtar began to swing her arm in steady arcs until the morning star picked up momentum and began spinning in full circles. Getting her hips into the act, Ishtar gyrated and tilted with the spiked ball as she swung it in a wide arc, spinning with it like a pirouetting ballet dancer. And with a powerful swing of the spiked ball she whipped it around so fast that if anyone blinked, they would have missed it. A tortured sounding scream rose from the back of her throat and she dug in her feet, took the chain in both hands, and drove a four-inch spike right into Apex's temple.

The young man's eyes widened with astonishment, the thought of what had just transpired not seeming to register due to the amount of damage done. A gurgle escaped his lips and then he slowly slumped to the side, falling off his sister.

Pallis scurried to her knees and then crawled over to her dead brother, ignoring the trauma he'd just inflicted on her. Gore oozed from the hole in his head and began to puddle at his sister's green knees.

"Nooo!" she screamed in a hoarse voice. Then, her head hanging between her shoulders, she began sobbing deep, painful sobs. As a torrent of tears streamed down both cheeks, she sniffled and said in a meager voice, "Don't leave me, brother. Not like this."

As she wept for her dead brother, the spiked morning star landed directly on top of her head with a bone fracturing *crack*. Her eyes rolled back as it tore out of her skull and, losing the back of her skull in the process, she fell across her brother's chest. A final embrace before their souls were ushered into the afterlife.

Ishtar brought the red dripping ball to her mouth and licked off Pallis's blood. Grinning, her white teeth mottled with crimson, she turned toward the remaining contestants. Noticing Angor pick up a spear, Ishtar leaped over the twins and sprinted for the goat.

Angor turned in time to see the wild-eyed red-skin racing toward him. Launching the spear, he grinned as it grazed her left arm. But she ignored the scrape and continued for him, full speed ahead.

"Shit," he grumbled, scouring the weapons rack to try and find something else he could use before the psychopath could pick him off. Fetching a dagger from off the rack, he spun back around just in time to take a mouthful of spiked ball.

Angor flew up into the air, teeth and blood exploding out of his face. His tiny goat body crashed to the ground with a *thud*, and he fought off the blurriness best he could. All manner of shapes and colors came in and out of focus, until, finally, he looked up to find Ishtar standing over him. An excited grin pulling her thin lips tight across her blood-soaked teeth as she stared down at him. She wasn't a warrior. She was a rabid animal. Chuckling, he spat at her feet and then hissed through his remaining teeth, "Go ahead, you insane cunt."

Ishtar's already impossibly tight grin tightened even more. "My pleasure," she growled in a disturbingly deep voice.

A wet *crunch* sounded as she brought the morning star down on Angor's face. The crowd let loose a round of cheers for the gruesome deathblow.

Four down and two to go, Ishtar turned and flung the morning star to the ground. Looking up, she watched Jegra put Danica in a choke hold.

Danica kicked her legs and scratched behind her head in a desperate attempt to try and break free of Jegra's sleeper hold, but it was no use. Jegra both outweighed and out powered her. Soon enough, her body grew lethargic and she felt herself gradually slipping away.

"Sorry, my love," Jegra whispered, gently laying Danica's limp body onto the arena sands. Putting her ear to Danica's chest, she checked to see if she was still with her. The sound of a heartbeat and soft breathing confirmed the good news and Jegra let out a sigh of relief.

"Now it's just me and you," Ishtar said, pointing her finger at Jegra as though she were issuing a challenge.

Jegra slowly stood up, holding Ishtar's gaze the whole time, and watched as the televid drones swooped in to get a closeup of the inevitable showdown between the two most vicious warriors the arena had ever seen.

"If you'll recall," Jegra said, "the last time we faced off, I handed you your ass."

Ishtar laughed. "Last time, I didn't have this." Throwing out her arm, Ishtar's bio-organic limb changed shapes and transformed into a long sword. Whipping her arm back, the sword separated into a series of segmented blades all strung to a chord. Swinging her giant razor whip about in a figure eight, she let it go with a crack so loud it sounded like thunder.

With no time to react, Jegra leaped out of the way and tumbled to the ground. When she looked up again, she saw the series of blades grating through the sand as Ishtar reeled them back in.

Worried about Danica's safety, Jegra pushed up and charged Ishtar. She arrived within striking distance at the same time Ishtar had fully retracted her blade. The sword changed forms and a battle-axe appeared on the end of Ishtar's forearm.

Barely skidding to a stop in time, Jegra leapt back just as Ishtar swung her axe-hand. Ishtar moved too quickly though, and Jegra yelped as a deep gouge opened up along her abdomen.

"Ha!" Ishtar laughed. "Whose ass is getting handed to them now?"

The empress looked down at her bleeding gut and pressed her hands against the wound. Removing her hands a few seconds later, revealed that the wound was already beginning to mend. "You'll have to do better if you want to best me," Jegra taunted.

Ishtar laughed. Then, through gritted teeth she answered, "Challenge accepted."

Not wanting the royal pain in her ass to get the upper hand, Ishtar launched a series of relentless attacks. But for every move, Jegra had a counter-move. After several minutes of lacerating blows, she began to tire. Jegra was just too fast and too strong to take down with brute force.

Ishtar had never seen anything like it. The empress was maddeningly difficult to kill. Growing frustrated, she threw out her arm and it transformed into a crossbow. A series of red arrows launched in rapid succession.

At close range, Jegra wasn't able to avoid the arrows, so she used her forearm to catch them all like a pin-cushion. "*Ahhg!*" she cried out in agony, as five arrows jutted out of her arm like porcupine quills.

All of sudden the arrows exploded one-by-one. Jegra screamed and turned her face away as her flesh sheared from bone in a terrible blast of fire and smoke. By the time the smoke dissipated on the breeze, from the elbow up, only her skeletal limb remained.

Unable to fire any more explosive tipped arrows, and unable to change her arm again due to the fact that each arrow used up a portion of the mass of her prosthetic, Ishtar reached up and twisted her fake arm just below the shoulder. It unhinged with a *click* and she dropped it to the ground.

Stunned by the injurious blast, the blistered and scorched skin on Jegra's face slowly began to heal, the burns erasing themselves as her hyperactive healing factor mended her wounds in real time.

Both women stood across from each other. Both women with an arm missing or mangled beyond repair.

"You know something," Jegra said, her voice full of disdain. "I've had it up to here with you." She raised her good hand to her chin gesturing how full up she was with Ishtar's nonsense.

Ishtar laughed. "The feeling's mutual, bitch."

"Well, you better say your prayers, little girl, because I'm about to spank you so hard your long-lost ancestors will feel it."

"Very amusing, Jegra. You always have some smart-ass quip in your quiver of come-backs."

"Why, thank you," Jegra said, taking it as a compliment. She smiled subtly, simply to annoy Ishtar, and then sighed and looked across the carnage they'd wreaked. "Well, it seems that we've both played right into his hands."

"What are you talking about?" Ishtar snarled.

"The Lord Emperor. Clearly, he wanted it to end like this. The two most lethal women in the galaxy fighting to the death. If you win, he gains his pawn back and is rid of his pain-in-the-ass wife. If I win, he loses this round but will have the ratings he so desperately chases after. Either way, he wins and we lose. Surely, you can see that by now."

"You think I do this for him? I don't do it for him," Ishtar sneered. "I do it because before you, he didn't care about anybody or anything. He was everything I wanted in a man. Unfeeling. Powerful. Full of ambition. But then you came along and Dakroth lost sight of his true self. He became corrupted by you. The only man I'd ever known to be like me, became weaker the moment he became involved with you. You ruined the once great Emperor Dakroth, made him into something I despise. And for that, I can never forgive you."

"What in the galaxy is wrong with you? Dakroth never changed. He's the same old vicious, power-hungry, war-mongering cock-wart he's always been. The only difference is he stopped slumming it with you and graduated to a real woman. One who could fulfill *all* his needs."

"You lie!" Ishtar screamed, and she charged Jegra, her eyes full of a fiery rage.

Their hands locked in a grapple and they leaned into one another. Nose to nose, Ishtar spat at Jegra's eye but missed and hit her cheek instead. It dribbled down her face and gathered at the corner of the empress's mouth.

Jegra ran her tongue across her lips, catching some of Ishtar's saliva on her tongue, and licked herself clean. "*Mmm,*" Jegra said, a spiteful grin curling onto her lips, "Tastes like grade-A, one-hundred percent bitch."

Crack! Jegra staggered back as Ishtar headbutted her. Disoriented slightly, she looked down to find Ishtar's fingers still interwoven with hers. Feeling a tug on her arm, she lurched forward only to get rammed again with another powerful headbutt.

"I'll show you what a bitch I can be, your highness!"

"It's…" Jegra began, rearing back and launching a headbutt of her own, "Your Majesty!"

CRA-KOW!!!

The two combatants stumbled backward, both befuddled by the string of unyielding blows they'd administered to one another's skulls.

Light-headed, Jegra fell onto her ass with a thump, and sat in the sand trying her best not to black out.

Ishtar, meanwhile, staggered forward in a haphazard zigzag pattern, but was too dizzy to attack. Instead, she crashed face first into the dirt beside Jegra. Rolling onto her side, she pushed herself back up, and spat out a wad of sand. "I'm going to kill you, if it's the last thing I do," she growled, refusing to give up. Even though she could barely get her arms and legs to move, she fought through the exhaustion and began crawling toward Jegra at a snail's pace.

"Oh, for Pete's sake," Jegra griped, throwing up her hand and catching Ishtar by her face, holding her at bay like a big sibling fending off a zealous smaller sibling. "Let it go already."

"Not till you're dead," Ishtar growled.

Unable to shove the persistent wench off of her, Jegra fell onto her side. Still persisting, Ishtar climbed on and straddled Jegra's waist. Picking up a large rock with one hand, she raised it high above her. "Die already!"

The first blow struck Jegra's forehead so hard the whole world went out of focus. Sensing another one coming, she instinctively raised her bony appendage to block it. She heard the crack of her bones breaking under the weight of the rock, but was too out of it to do much about it.

Ishtar raised the rock again and screamed, "Why won't you die? I just want you to die!" Again, the rock came down. And, again, it struck Jegra's forearm. On the follow-up blow, Jegra's radius snapped at the joint.

Ishtar raised the rock a third time. With Jegra's skeleton hand fractured beyond repair, another couple of blows would finish her. The red-skinned assassin stretched her arm as high as it would go, her chest pushing out as her back arched.

"DIE!" she screamed with the biggest breath she could muster.

Before Ishtar could bring the rock down on the empress, however, Jegra reached over to her mangled arm, tore her radius out with a terrible blood-curdling *snap*, and using the sharp end of her own bone as a shank, stabbed Ishtar through her neck.

Jegra's enhanced, lightning quick reflexes allowed her to move so fast that Ishtar hadn't even had the chance to react. All she could do was murmur the word, "*Impossible*," as a stream of blood poured from her mouth and ran down her chin.

Jegra twisted the bone and then tore it out of Ishtar's neck. "I'm sorry," Jegra apologized, knowing what she had to do. She didn't like killing. But Ishtar was too dangerous to let live. And it wasn't like Jegra was going to win any Nobel Peace Prizes any time soon. She was a gladiatrix. But, more than this, she was the empress. And she needed to make a statement.

Sluggishly, Jegra forced herself to sit up and took Ishtar by the back of her neck and drew her into her, locking into an embrace. As she hugged the woman, she stabbed her repeatedly in the torso, twelve times. Twenty times. Possibly more. She lost count. All she knew was that she literally had bathed herself in her opponent's blood.

As Ishtar's mutilated body fell next to her on the sand. Jegra's face and chest stained red with gore, the empress finally relinquished her blood-soaked bone and dropped it into the sand. Soaked in bright red, Jegra's entire body glistened with glossy red from the neck down. Injured, she struggled to breathe, her lungs wheezing as she raised her eyes to the crowd of spectators looking back at her from the stands with equally shocked expressions.

A hush fell across the stadium. Poetically enough, at the same moment, Ishtar's head fell to the side, her entire body becoming limp like a child's discarded rag doll and the life gradually drained from her eyes. Eyes that were once a fierce, sparkling topaz, were now pale and depleted. And her vibrant red skin turned to ashen pink.

Exhausted, Jegra slumped back onto the sand, and took a moment to rest on her heels. She panted heavily as she scanned the agape expressions of the various alien species that made up the crowd. Her mangled arm dangling limply by her side, she saw something she had never seen during her entire tenure as a gladiator. Awestruck admiration.

No jeers were made. No lewd catcalls. No shrill whistles. No booing. No shouts for more blood. No unwanted propositions. No complaints or gripes of any kinds. Just a suffusing silence that nobody wanted to break for fear of ruining a near perfect moment.

Finally, after what seemed a near eternity of silence, somewhere in the distance, a lone voice screamed out, "Long live the Empress!" There was a pause, then another voice shouted the same. And then another. And another.

Voices continued to join the chorus until the entire stadium was chanting those rejuvenating words. They filled Jegra with a newfound confidence and the realization that Dakroth was just one man who ruled but one world. She, on the other hand, had the entire galaxy behind her.

At long last, the sign she'd been waiting for had arrived. A unification of all the alien races, under one common cause, their faith placed in someone who'd fight on their behalf and never for selfish ambitions. Jegra smiled. This was just the beginning of a much bigger revolution. A revolution against Dakroth's tyranny. A revolution she'd see through to the end.

36

"**Unacceptable!**" **Senator Targon** Van Morgan barked as Captain Lianica Blackstar stood before the Council, her nerves tighter than freshly tuned guitar strings as she conveyed the bad news. "What do you mean the emperor's missing, again? Am I mistaken, or didn't your team just recover him less than a month ago?"

"You're not mistaken, your excellency. But this seems to be a new, different matter." Captain Blackstar paused, glanced around at the stern faces of the senators sitting up on their lofty bench, and then added, "He has a penchant for getting himself into trouble."

"Then attend to it!" Targon shouted, throwing his hand in the air and then slamming an angry fist down on his podium, which stood at the center of a long bench seating all twelve senators representing the twelve provinces of Dagon Prime.

"Yes, sir. As the senate wishes." Captain Blackstar crossed her heart with her right fist and bowed humbly. Then, returning to her rigid posture, she clicked her heels, spun, and marched out of the senatorial chamber.

Senator Mykos leaned over and whispered into Targon's ear, "Dakroth is becoming increasingly unreliable."

Targon frowned, the corners of his mouth pulling downward and his fingers rapping at his podium. "I hate to say it," he finally agreed, "but perhaps it's time."

A pleased grin spread across Senator Mykos's face as he leaned back in his chair. The other senators all looked to Senator Targon to clarify himself.

Senator Targon ran his fingers through his short, spiky tufts of white hair and, then, clearing his throat, he addressed the Council. "My fellow council members, as you well know, the emperor's behavior has been growing increasingly erratic ever since the human female's arrival. And although not all of you agree with me that Jegra is the root cause of this questionable behavior, the fact remains that the Lord Emperor's judgement has been compromised."

"What are you suggesting?" Senator Tivian, a young but ambitious and extremely loyal Dagon woman, asked.

"A vote of no confidence!" Mykos blurted.

Targon lowered his eyes. It wasn't shame so much as disappointment. The young Rhadamanthus Dakroth had been the leader he'd always hoped for. But the recent Dakroth was becoming something of a threat to the stability of the Empire.

"I'm afraid Senator Mykos is correct. We have no recourse but to take a vote of no confidence."

"But won't that mean the human will become the reigning sovereign over all of Dagon Prime?" Tivian asked, a frown forming on her face. "Like many Dagons," she added, "I too am a purist. Allowing an outsider full reign of the Empire, let alone our homeworld, is unthinkable."

"Here, here!" another senator chimed in, praising Tivian's devotion to Dagon heredity.

"Which is why, in addition to a vote of no confidence, I am going to issue a decree of martial law. The Imperial forces will fall under the command of our newly instated fleet admiral, Admiral Callestra Van Morgan," informed Senator Targon, clasping his hands behind his back as he scanned the surprised reactions of the senate council.

"Your daughter?" one of the young senators at the far end of the council bench asked, raising a curious eyebrow.

"We will be in good hands, then," Tivian interjected, reassuring the senate of her confidence in Callestra's capabilities. Seeing that not everyone was convinced, however, she quickly added, "I, for one, will sleep well knowing we have a Morgan as the guiding force of justice in the Empire."

"And justice we shall have," Mykos added, his crow's feet wrinkling around the corners of his graying eyes as he smiled at Tivian and then nodded reassuringly for the rest of the council.

"But martial law can only be declared if there is an imminent threat to the Empire and the emperor is deemed unfit to continue to lead the Empire. What threat, pray tell, my esteemed senators, do you suggest we tell the people is the justification for this extreme shakeup?"

All faces turned toward Senator Proxima Cortana, a full figured, if not stout, Dagon woman with a tight ponytail and dark painted eyebrows that gave her a permanently critical appearance.

"Maybe I can be of some help answering that," a voice said, reverberating from down the chamber corridor. The faces which had been locked on Senator Cortana now quickly turned themselves to the entrance.

Gasps rang out when the dark silhouette of a woman stepped into the light streaming down from the glass domed ceiling. Senator Targon, the only one not taken by surprise, smiled and slowly rose to his feet.

"Respected members of the Dagon Council," Targon proceeded, "allow me to present to you, her Eminence, the Administratrix of Nyctan, Anaïs Nin!" He fanned his hand across the room and gestured for them all to behold the tall, pale figure with elongated skull and black eyes sauntering up the isle toward the council bench.

Hushed whispers broke across the council and even Tivian, who was on Targon's side, gave him an astounded look. It was one thing to think up a valid excuse to declare martial law, but to invite the Empire's longest enemy was a different matter entirely. "What is she doing here?" Tivian asked.

Anaïs Nin, composed and regal, addressed the chambers. "What I am about to reveal to you, many will find shocking. I swear upon the Enchiridion of H'aaztre that my words are true; believe me or not, it makes no difference. It was your Lord Emperor, Rhadamanthus Dakroth, who lured me here, to Dagon Prime, under false pretenses."

"What are you trying to say, Madam Administratrix?" Senator Cortana asked in a sympathetic, almost motherly tone.

Anaïs Nin looked away from the curious faces gazing down at her from their high perch upon the Council bench and stared down at the floor, appearing to feel ashamed or embarrassed about something. "Emperor Dakroth convinced me to perform the Ceremony of the Chosen One with him. But, I see now, his intentions were less than honorable."

"Just to set the record straight, are you saying that the emperor tricked you so as to lure you into his bed?" Tivian asked, her scowl tightening. "Before you answer that, let me remind the administratrix the serious nature of these accusations."

"Yes," Anaïs Nin answered. "That is correct. Emperor Dakroth raped me." Her answer was followed by an eruption of astonished gasps and an exchange of concerned whispers.

"A criminal offense if there ever was one," Senator Targon said. He tried to hide his smirk, as his plan was unfolding exactly as he'd hoped. Inviting the administratrix to convince the council that Dakroth has not only committed a heinous crime but had also put the Empire in danger meant he could wrangle power away with a vote of no confidence.

The only thing he hadn't anticipated, however, was how willing Anaïs Nin was to perjure herself. She really must, he mused, hate the Lord Emperor with every fiber of her being.

"The defilement of the royal head of a neighboring empire is nothing to take lightly. We cannot overlook this grave offense," Senator Mykos added, piggybacking on Targon's point.

"What is it you suggest the Council do, Senator Targon?" Tivian asked, scanning the faces of the other senators who were all thinking the same thing.

"I believe I can answer that," Anaïs Nin replied. "If Nyctan and Dagon Prime go to war over my defilement, a war to regain my honor, then not only will a vote of censure be most reasonable, it allows you the justification you need to declare martial law."

"It is settled then!" Targon said, slamming a wooden mallet on his bench. "We shall take a vote. All those in favor of removing Emperor Dakroth from sovereign reign, thus issuing a vote of no confidence, say 'aye.' Those not in favor, say 'nay'"

The ayes were unanimous. Senator Targon grinned and slammed the mallet twice then held his hand up to silence the murmurs filling the room. "Now, those in favor of declaring martial law and handing gubernatorial power over to Admiral Callestra Van Morgan, say 'aye;' those not in favor say 'nay.'"

Again, the ayes won by a large majority. With a whack of the hammer, Senator Targon announced, "The 'ayes' have it!"

Anaïs Nin bowed reverently, and Senator Targon returned the gesture in kind. Having no more pressing business on Dagon Prime, she turned and stormed out of the council chambers. Her first issue of business–return to Nyctan and make a declaration of war against the Dagon Empire.

Senator Targon convened the Council and dismissed the council members, himself leaving the senatorial hall with the rest. On his way back to his chambers, however, he heard a voice call out his name and turned to see Senator Tivian hurrying toward him.

"Senator Targon," she repeated, panting lightly as she tried to catch her breath, "may I have a word with you?"

The senator paused briefly and looked up and down the long passageway to see if there were any eavesdroppers. Confident they were alone, he turned back to Tivian. "Why, yes, of course," he said in his rigid, senatorial, voice. "Anything for a fellow senator."

"In private," she said, grabbing Targon by the elbow and pulling him into the ladies' restroom with her.

The moment they disappeared into the women's bathroom, Targon and Tivian's lips mashed together and they fell into the tiled wall, clawing at each other's clothes with carnal desire.

"I've wanted you so badly since the Council convened this morning. I could barely contain myself."

"I felt the same way," Tivian said, letting Targon slip off her panties from under her black miniskirt. Grabbing his hand, she guided it back up between her glistening thighs. "See?" she said in a seductive voice, letting him feel her for himself.

He kissed her mouth again and then pulled away. "As much as I'd love to finish this, I'm afraid another matter has come up."

Upset by his sudden rejection of her, Senator Tivian reached down and pulled her underpants back up. "More important than us? What could be so urgent?" she asked.

"It seems the empress has a mole in the senate. Someone has been feeding her inside information."

"In that case, we shall root them out together," Tivian said. Leaning in, she stood on her tiptoes and kissed Targon on the lips. Then, taking his face in her hands, she said, "Let me handle this. I'll discover the traitor and take care of them. You have my word."

Senator Targon smiled. Tivian smiled back, then spun on her heels and, still buttoning her blouse back up, started heading toward the exit.

All of a sudden, a pink laser blast flashed from behind and the sound of a plasma bolt scorching the wall stopped Tivian in her tracks. Her eyes went wide with shock as she saw the scorch mark on the bathroom door directly in front of her. Then, her eyes rolled back in her head and she collapsed to the floor. Dead.

"Consider it taken care of," Senator Targon said in a contemptuous tone. He looked down at Tivian's lifeless body with disgust and stepped over her, exiting the women's restroom. Outside he brushed down his uniform and took a deep breath to compose himself.

He would never have believed it could possibly have been Tivian, if it hadn't been for the bug that Senator Mykos had planted in her personal transport shuttle. Sure enough, she'd been feeding Jegra Alakandra inside information ever since Jegra had become imperatrix.

In the end, Senator Tivian's puritan line was just an act. She, like many who followed the empress, wanted change. Wanted a revolution. But Senator Targon had other plans.

At least now, Tivian's double-dealing and playing both sides was over. Now, Senator Targon had complete control of the senate and his daughter, Admiral Callestra Van Morgan, had control of the military. Together, they'd usher in a new era of prominence for the Empire.

37

The EKG monitor chirped with the steady pulse of Jegra and Danica's heartbeats. With an aching groan, Jegra sat up in bed, finding herself in a medical suite next to Danica. The suite, she recognized, was on the third floor of her palace on Thessalonica. A cute Dagon doctor attended them both.

"Who are you?" asked Jegra, yawning at the same time.

The physician rushed over to her bedside and gently pressed upon her shoulder, easing her back down onto the double layer of soft pillows. "My name is Amora Van Gogh," she said, smiling softly. "I'm part of the Imperial medical staff and have been personally assigned to you."

"What did you do to mess up?" Jegra smiled, giving Amora a knowing look.

It was Dakroth's twisted rule that if you royally screwed up serving him, you were reassigned to the empress's personal detail. It was partly a punishment, as serving someone other than a Dagon was seen as a kind of humiliation, but because Jegra was the imperatrix, technically, there was no shame, though everyone knew the emperor's backhanded slams. They still were obliged by both custom and law to fulfill their duties; it was merely a snub to be assigned to Jegra. So, if someone new showed up on her staff, she knew they'd likely messed up.

"I sort of failed to treat the emperor."

"Oh, did something happen to dear Rhadamanthus?" Jegra asked wryly. Of course, she knew exactly what had happened. She'd cold-cocked the scheming bastard and then had Raven handle all the messy cleanup. But she wasn't going to share all that just yet.

"It wasn't my fault, I promise. I just—"

Jegra laughed, cutting off the hesitant girl before she could finish what she was saying. "It's no problem, I assure you. Rhadamanthus has a way of blaming everyone but himself for the trouble he raises. But that's neither here nor there, my dear."

Jegra groaned and sat up again. She looked down are her arm which was perfectly mended. It wasn't a prosthetic, she could tell. Somehow, her enhanced healing factor combined with cutting edge medical science gave her her arm back. She sighed with relief but the sigh quickly turned into another aching groan.

When Amora saw her struggling against the pain, she reached over to gently nudge her back down, but the empress's hand flew up and caught hers, stopping her.

"I'll be fine," Jegra responded.

"I'm sorry," Amora said. "I didn't mean to…" She trailed off when she realized Jegra was still holding her hand. Looking back up at the empress, she saw a hard gaze like nothing she'd ever encountered before and felt as if she'd wither away to nothing beneath the weight of the hard stare.

"When you serve me, you serve only me. If you betray me, I'll deal with you personally. Do I make myself clear?"

Amora gulped. "Yes, Your Majesty," she said, looking down at her feet and curtseying.

"If you abide by my rules, then you'll be safe here. Even from the emperor."

"Yes, Your Maj—"

"Now," Jegra said, changing the subject, "How is she doing?"

Amora followed Jegra's gaze and saw that she was looking at Danica. "She's been through a lot. Not only that, but apparently her entire bottom half was severed and then genetically rebuilt."

"What are you saying?" Jegra asked.

"I'm not sure. If I had to guess, I'd say someone removed her legs, pelvis, and lower part of her internal organs then, for whatever reason, made genetic copies and pieced her back together."

Jegra swung her legs over the edge of her bed and slid out. Her feet slapped softly against the cool, tile floor of the medlab, and she strolled over to Danica. Taking Danica's hand in hers, she squeezed softly and whispered, "What did he do to you?" After brushing a rogue tear away from her eye, she turned to Amora. "Will she be all right?"

"She's recuperating well and, with the accelerated healing process, should be healed up in another day or two. We'll have to keep her in an induced coma until then, but otherwise, she should make a full recovery."

"Thank you," Jegra said, keeping her eyes fixed on Danica's lavender face. Reaching down, she gently stroked Danica's cheek and then bent down and kissed her on the forehead.

Unexpectedly, the door chimed and Jegra called out, "Enter."

Whispering apart, the doors opened to reveal Raphine Agnar standing in the entrance. Stepping into the room, she said, "Someone wanted to see you."

The baby squid entity came floating in behind her and then wafted forward and wrapped its little tentacles around Jegra's hand.

Amora screamed and drew back, bumping into a medical cart. "What is that thing?!"

"This is La'Garren," Raphine said, smiling ear to ear.

"Where have you been, little fella?" Jegra asked, letting the squid feel her energy pulses. Pulling him into her bosom and squeezing him so tightly that he got comfortably wedged between her breasts, she said, "I owe you one for saving my life."

"But it—it's a s-su-squid monster."

"Just a baby one," Jegra said, breaking into baby-talk. She stroked the little glowing squid creature until it finally broke free of her embrace and floated back over to Raphine.

Raphine raised her fingers and snapped. A couple of Bre'lal servant girls rushed in and brought the empress two selections of clothes. Jegra mixed and matched them, picking a copper wrap skirt and a black see-through lace halter top with a Queen Anne style neckline.

Immodest and completely comfortable with her perfectly formed body, Jegra stripped off her medical gown in front of everyone. Standing before all four women naked, discounting Danica, who slept, Jegra handed the extra clothes back to the servant girls and dismissed them. They bowed and quickly took their leave. Raphine, meanwhile, just smiled and watched Jegra as though this were a common occurrence, but Amora blushed, her cheeks turning a deep purple.

"Don't worry, you get used to it," Raphine said with a soft chuckle. "The empress isn't exactly shy."

"That's good to know," Amora said, glancing at Jegra's naked form out of the corner of her eye. She still couldn't bring herself to make direct eye-contact with the nude empress.

"She has a way of upsetting one's expectations," Raphine informed the doctor. "By shocking people's sensibilities, she can get a better read on you. Figure out what your true intentions are."

"I see," Amora said, finally managing to look up. When she did, she saw Jegra reaching under her lace shirt with her hands and taking a handful of boob, adjusting everything so it would settle into place with just the perfect balance.

"Raphine is right," Jegra said. "Even now, I was able to get a read on you."

"Really?" Amora asked. She was genuinely terrified of what Jegra might have discovered about her. But at the same time, her curiosity overwhelmed her timidity. "What did you learn?"

"I learned you're not like other Dagon women. You're not a trans; you are fully female. You're bashful around anything sexual. You glanced away from my naked body where most Dagons would literally be trying to figure out how best to win my favor so they could fuck me."

"How'd you know I was fully female?" Amora asked. "Nobody knows that but the doctor who birthed me."

Jegra twisted the waist of her dress around so the slit between the two folds appeared in front, revealing the tan flesh of her inner thighs. Then, looking up at Amora, she tapped her right ear. "I can hear the pulse of your heartbeat. In most Dagon women, there is a loud, throbbing pulse that emanates from their vestigial member when they get excited. But not you. I don't hear anything. Which would indicate you're without the vestigial organ. And since surgery would make you a mod, yet you are not shunned as a mod, I'm assuming it's a natural consequence of your birth."

"See," Raphine said, smiling at Amora. "She got all that from your lack of a dick-heartbeat."

Amora laughed out loud and then covered her mouth and stopped herself.

"And this one," Jegra said, throwing her arm around Raphine and getting her into a playful headlock, "Says whatever thing pops into her pretty little head." Making a fist, Jegra gave Raphine a noogie, messing up her hair.

"Ah, come on!" Raphine protested, struggling to break way. "You know I hate it when you do that."

Jegra laughed and relinquished her hold on the poor girl who quickly went about trying to straighten her disheveled hair.

Amora giggled as she watched Jegra play and jest with Raphine as though she were her own sister. And, in a way, she was. Jegra was virtually alone in this part of the galaxy. Her species hadn't made it this far out yet, and so all the family she had was adopted. She made her own family wherever she was.

Raphine stuck her tongue out at Jegra then turned to Amora. Sticking out her hand, she said, "It was nice to meet you, Amora."

"Likewise," Amora said, shaking Raphine's hand. With that, Raphine turned and departed the medlab. The small squid creature followed after her as though it were a balloon tethered to a small child.

"You two seem close," Amora said.

There was a long silence as Jegra stared at the door through which Raphine had exited. "I killed her sister," Jegra finally confessed.

"Oh," Amora answered, not knowing what else to say.

"I feel I owe her so much. Yet she never makes any demands of me. But, as long as I draw breath, that girl will be under my protection and care."

"And what about the squid entity?"

"His name is La'Garren," Jegra stated, turning toward Amora with a stern look on her face.

"Isn't it…I mean…is La'Garren dangerous?"

"Probably," Jegra answered. She then shrugged. "But that little guy has already saved my life on more than one occasion, and until I can repay that debt I'll protect him with my life."

Amora gazed admiringly at the empress. She'd never met anyone so noble and just before. And more than that, it seemed like Empress Jegra Alakandra genuinely cared about her subjects. The Lord Emperor cared about no one but himself. So, it was refreshing to see how Jegra could still maintain her integrity as a fearsome warrior and retain her obvious abundance of compassion. A strange combination if there ever was one.

"And I'll do my best to take care of your friend here," Amora said, turning toward Danica and picking up her chart off the end of the bed.

"She's more than my friend," Jegra said, her smile growing bright. "She's my love and my best friend. If anything should happen to her…" Stopping, Jegra took a breath. "I don't know what I'd do."

"And that's why I'll give her my utmost attention and care," Amora said, putting the chart back after making some small notations.

"I appreciate that," Jegra replied. Then, turning to leave, she added, "If you'll excuse me, I have other business to take care of. But if there are any updates, any updates at all…"

"You'll be the first to know, Your Majesty."

Jegra smiled once more at Amora, and then exited the medical lab. Once out in the hall, she gripped her ribcage and groaned. Although not yet back to a hundred percent, she couldn't waste any more time lounging in bed.

After returning to her quarters, Jegra locked her door and opened a secure channel to Senator Tivian on the holovid. But there was no answer. Feeling it odd she wouldn't answer her encrypted channel, she called the senator's office, since she sometimes stayed after hours.

Senator Targon Van Morgan's face appeared on the holovid in 3D and answered, "This is Senator Tivian's office, who is this?"

"This is the Empress Jegra Alakandra," Jegra said in her most regal sounding voice. "What is going on? Where is Senator Tivian?"

"I'm afraid the senator has had a terrible accident."

"Accident?" Jegra repeated, not believing the words. Senator Tivian was careful. Accidents didn't just happen to overly cautious types like her. "What kind of accident?"

"I'm afraid," Senator Targon added, shaking his head remorsefully, "it was a suicide."

It was Senator Tivian who'd approached Jegra in confidence and asked for her help. It had been Senator Tivian's plan to clamp down on the corruption of the senate, enlisting Jegra's help. It was highly suspect that she'd abandon all hope and kill herself. That just wasn't like her. It was more likely she had been murdered and framed.

"That's a shame," Jegra replied, keeping a stately composure.

"Yes," Targon answered. "She will be missed." His words rang hollow and Jegra eyed him suspiciously. Noticing Jegra's skepticism, Targon asked, "Is there anything that I can help you with, Your Majesty?"

"Maybe another time, perhaps," Jegra said, smiling artificially.

"Well, then, until we speak again. Sorry about the bad news."

"Yes, please send her family my deepest condolences."

"Of course," Targon said, still grinning like a fool.

Jegra cut the feed and shivered. Something was seriously wrong with that man. All she ever got from Targon was bile and hate, but amid the scandal of Senator Tivian's mysterious suicide, he was nothing but roses and kindness to her. It almost seemed as if he were hiding something.

Her gut told her he was likely the one who sniffed out the alliance between Tivian and Jegra and then had Tivian killed. But how could she prove it? Without any allies among the Council, she was facing an uphill battle that she didn't believe she'd win. Politics weren't exactly her thing.

Worse still, Dagon politicians loved nothing more than to get embroiled in meandering displays of maddening rhetoric where they talked in circles, slinging insult after insult at one another, trying to see who could make the biggest mockery of the other. If she came at him with unfounded accusations, he'd eat her alive and spit her out.

"Dammit," she cursed, slamming her fist down on the console at her desk. The console sparked and then fizzled in protest to the abuse and died. Jegra frowned at the wisps of white smoke curling into the air and then let out a pent-up sigh.

The cry of a thorn bird just outside her balcony caught her attention and she swiveled around in her chair, crossed her long, bronze legs, and peered outside.

The blue sky was unexpectedly disrupted by a flock of thorn birds taking flight, their murmuration so dense it blotted out the sun and cast a shadow across the entire palace. Jegra slowly rose to her feet and, throwing open the tall glass doors, stepped out onto her balcony.

Whatever it was, the birds weren't the only ones reacting peculiarly. The sand worms were cutting through the sands at random angles and zagging back and forth as though they were trying to escape some terrible calamity.

In the distance, Jegra heard the sandstorm alarm blaring on the palace comm system and she turned toward the west to see the largest, darkest sand front she'd ever seen.

Burnt orange sand plumes merged into dark purple pockets. In the darkest part, lightning flickered and the rolling sandstorm was heading right for them.

Something was wrong. She could feel it in her bones. And it wasn't just the last few days. It was the whole year. It seemed the very moment she'd taken care of one problem ten more arose in its place. And now, with Senator Tivian's suspicious death, here she was, met with the worst sandstorm she'd ever experienced during her entire time on Thessalonica. It was too much to be coincidental.

Jegra hopped up onto her balcony, and crouching down, she leapt high into the air. The empress sailed across the pond and gardens below and landed on the very edge of her property. Rising back to her full six-foot-five height, she stood firm as she stared down the sandstorm. She watched it with great intensity, trying to spot anything out of the ordinary as it raced toward her.

A sand plume thirty stories high smashed into the energy shields inches away from Jegra's nose. She didn't even flinch as the sand blast crackled along the energy field that protected the palace. Blue flickering swirls formed all across the dome, giving the palace a kind of snow globe effect, and Jegra turned and, tossing her long brunette hair, began her march back toward the palace.

Meleh'Kendar, her chief of security, met her at the main entrance of the palace.

"What is it?" she asked, realizing that Meleh'Kendar wouldn't burden her with anything unless it was absolutely vital.

"The senate has just voted in favor of a vote of no confidence regarding Emperor Dakroth. Also, Senator Targon has just declared martial law and instated his daughter, Callestra, as Admiral of the Fleet. He has effectively taken control of all of Dagon Prime."

"A coup then?"

"A coup to arrest power away from you, your grace. Without the Lord Emperor to contest the ruling, the reign of the empire falls to you."

"Suspicious, I'd say, that the Lord Emperor goes missing just before a coup."

"Indeed. But that's not the worst of it." Jegra raised an eyebrow as Meleh'Kendar briefed her on the shocking details. "They're saying the Nyctans have made a declaration of war for Dakroth performing the Ceremony of the Chosen One under false pretenses."

"The Ceremony of the Chosen One..." Jegra repeated, rubbing her chin in contemplation. "But that means Dakroth would have had to impregnate the administratrix with his seed."

"You are familiar with the ritual, then?"

"I'm familiar, but I never dreamed he'd actually go through with it. Anaïs Nin is everything he despises. Self-righteous. Hyper religious. Tight lipped and even tighter legs that open for no man."

"She is claiming he lied to her about his reasons and impregnated her. The ritual ended in the termination of her fetus. Because of this violation and crushing loss, she blames Dakroth and has sworn to get her vengeance on him."

"It's a ruse," Jegra said, clutching her fist. "It has to be."

A static discharge as loud as a clap of thunder sounded and Meleh'Kendar and Jegra startled in fright and glanced up at the sandstorm raging against the energy shield. Putting his hand on the small of Jegra's back, he ushered the empress toward the entrance. "Come Your Majesty, we'll be safer inside."

Once inside the palace, Meleh'Kendar touched a wall panel and said, "Computer, secure the palace."

A loud clanking could be heard as the blast shutters all rattled into place. As the grand hall darkened, the automated lighting kicked on.

After giving it some thought, Jegra looked at her chief of security and said, "Find out everything you can about this coup. In the meantime, let's weather out this storm."

What she left out, however, was that she had a bad feeling about all of this. Not just the storm, but the bad omen it represented. The likely assassination of a senator; a coup from two fronts. The Empire was being destabilized from the inside out. But to what end? Was it just a power grab by Targon and his acolytes? Or was something more sinister going on here?

Determined get to the bottom of it, however, she swore she wouldn't rest until she had the truth. Even if it meant defying the senate and going against the expected customs of Dagon traditions, the main one being never give up power at any cost. She was willing to let her enemies think they had the hand up on her. Meanwhile, she'd sow the seeds of rebellion. Show them a thing or two about good old-fashioned grass-roots resistance and perseverance.

38

Stormbreaker, the flagship of the Galliforn Space Defense Fleet, GSDF, jumped into the system at the coordinates of the anomaly simply known as "The Rift." The rift contained a dark space, a gravity well that often sucked unsuspecting ships in. Ships that were never seen again. It was a place that was to be avoided at all costs. And yet, one had escaped it. And ever since Empress Alakandra's harrowing escape from this theoretically inescapable void, there had been a mysterious signal emanating from the rift. A signal that Captain Lodbrok was tasked with investigating.

Captain Lodbrok stroked his coarse black beard and leaned forward in his chair. "Hold her steady here, Quartermaster Oddgrim."

The massive ship slowed to a stop, the giant horns of a bighorn sheep curled elegantly around the head of the ship and subtly blended back into the architecture of the bovine face that made up the bow of the vessel.

The hull of the ship, which looked like a massive sledge hammer, had an elongated tail-wing that, like a whale fin, fanned out horizontally, extending away from the ship's eight aft thrusters situated both above and beneath.

All along the hull of the ship were interwoven patterns, mostly the geometric shapes of bones and rams, etched in a Nordic jelling style that spanned from bow to stern.

"Aye, sir," Oddgrim shouted with robust enthusiasm. Although the chocolate colored satyr was the oldest officer aboard the ship, he approached his job with the energy of a faun half his age.

Oddgrim, it turned out, also happened to be blind. But his whitewashed eyes didn't detract from his performance as ship's navigator, since he had most of the star charts devoted to memory. And navigating a warship like the *Stormbreaker* had more to do with calculating speeds, trajectories, and inputting the correct coordinates than it did the agile by-the-seat-of-your-pants piloting of something like a split-wing fighter.

A starfighter, the ship was not. Whereas smaller vessels may need to navigate delicate paths through asteroid fields, the *Stormbreaker* smashed through anything in its way. Including, but not limited to, asteroid belts. It was a battering ram in space, after all.

In a way, having a blind helmsman was sort of fitting. It reflected the Galliforn philosophy of life: *Strength in the face of weakness. Honor over cowardice. Kindness in lieu of selfishness. Practice the old ways over the new. And always honor the Moon Goddess, Selene.*

"Sir, we're picking up strange readings," ensign Phobos informed the captain.

Captain Lodbrok stood up and clasped his hands behind his back. His classic naval uniform looked more like that of an ancient mariner than the captain of a state-of-the-art starship, but it all went back to the adage about practicing the old way over the new. If it wasn't broken, then there was no reason to fix it. The Galliforn people prided themselves in honoring the ancient while, simultaneously, embracing the new. As such, everything new, though incorporating the most progressive technology, had an almost antique aesthetic about it.

"Precisely what kind of readings are we picking up, ensign?" Lodbrok asked.

"There seems to be an energy surge building up on the other side of the rift, captain."

That didn't make any sense. After all, the gravity well should swallow up anything that was there. *Unless...* the captain thought, *something that registered high energy readings is gathering inside the gravity well. But, then, that would mean...*

Lodbrok's eyes grew wide as the revelation of what was about to happen set in. "Quickly now, open an emergency channel to our sister ship, the *Chiron*."

Up on the viewscreen the aged face of the most infamous satyr in the Commonwealth appeared, Grendok of Galliforn.

"Ah, Captain Lodbrok, what an unexpected surprise. I pray all is well with you and your lovely family."

"Apologies, old friend, but I must dispense with the pleasantries as this call is regarding a matter of utmost importance."

Grendok raised a hoary eyebrow and stroked his fleece beard pensively, pulling it into a long funnel and twisting it before repeating the process all over again. "A security issue then?"

"I'm afraid it's worse than that, even. I'm issuing the *De Defectu Oraculorum* protocol."

A heavy silence fell across the bridge crew and everyone turned to their captain with stunned faces. The *De Defectu Oraculorum* was the name of the ancient text of death, the final chapter in the Enchiridion. It prophesied the end times of Galliforn. Not just Galliforn, though, but the entire galaxy.

"So, it begins," Grendok said in a solemn tone.

"Please," Lodbrok beseeched of his fellow countryman, "I need you to—"

A burst of static interrupted the captain's words and one of his officers began shouting that the rift was opening up. More static was followed by the garbled shouts of the crew and, finally, Captain Lodbrok could be heard barking orders.

The video feed came back on and revealed the captain's fear-stricken face. A strange, ethereal golden light of unknown origin cast itself over the entire bridge of the ship.

"They're already here!" shouted Captain Lodbrok. Turning back to the vidcom, he leaned in, his bovine snout and slatted eyes taking up the entire frame. "You must warn her, Grendok. You must warn Empress Jegra Alakandra. The—"

Another burst of static interrupted his speech. In the background, the mysterious golden light intensified. It continued to do so until Grendok could no longer make out any of the details. A nano-second later, the crew began screaming out in agony as the brilliant light grew so intense that Grendok was forced to look away from his vidscreen.

Amid the crew's screams, Lodbrok's panicked voice broke through. "I repeat," he intoned with utmost urgency, "the invasion has begun! The invasion has begun."

Just then the televid feed cut out. Saddened by what it meant, Grendok lowered his head in a moment of silence. The *Stormbreaker*, along with his friend, had been destroyed.

Nevertheless, Captain Lodbrok had not died in vain. Far from it. It was because of his dying message that Grendok would be able to get word to Empress

Alakandra in time.

With any luck, she would be able to use both the combined might of the Dagon Imperial Navy as well as the Knights of Caelum to mount a defensive. In the meantime, he'd have to round up every remaining Galliforn warrior he could find as well as call in a few favors of some unruly space pirates.

"You there," Grendok hollered, pointing at a younger clone of himself who was busy tidying up an ornate office decorated with the finest artifacts from every corner of the Commonwealth. Prized among his treasure was a bronze statue of Jegra's naked body standing upon a pile of defeated warriors.

"Yes, sir?" the young Grendok replied.

"Prep the ship for immediate launch. We have much to do and very little time to do it in."

"As you wish, sir. Any particular destination?"

"Thessalonica," Grendok said. Before the young faun could prance off to do his elder's bidding, the graying Grendok shook his head, as if he'd changed his mind, and called out, "No, wait. I'll send the message personally. You get dressed and take command. Make haste for Galliforn."

"Yes, sir," the satyr replied.

"And get me Raven Nightguard on the comm. I'm going to need all hands on deck for this. And be quick about it my boy! The very fate of the galaxy is at stake."

The young satyr nodded and quickly skipped away. Grendok turned back toward his desk and fixed his gaze on the battle-axe hanging on his wall above it. It was his from the campaigns and the war against Loki'Alloran Rhadamanthus Dakroth. One which Galliforn had narrowly won.

But if Grendok's hunch was right, this battle would take the entire Commonwealth of planets working together to win. If not, they'd most certainly be doomed.

Grendok typed a few keys on the touch display surface of his desk and a computer's voice chimed on. [*Satellite coming into range now.*]

"Show me a visual," Grendok said.

Up on the wall, a large televid lit up with the image of sparking debris. By the patterning of the shards floating through space, Grendok knew it was what remained of the *Stormbreaker*.

"Zoom out," he said, eyeing the image suspiciously, waiting to catch a glimpse of whoever, or whatever, was capable of destroying the galaxy's toughest warship. Suddenly, a golden tentacle whipped by. "Zoom out seventy percent," he added.

The satellite image zoomed out, capturing a wide panoramic view. The horizon came into view and a long slender tear in space, emitting golden light, filled the viewscreen. Also pouring out of the rift were thousands of cosmic squid entities, of all different sizes.

Some of the creatures were as massive as small moons. Others were the size of large starships, while many more were the size of shuttles and smaller transports.

He stared at the squid invasion for a long time and then narrowed his eyes. "Zoom in on the entities of light," he said.

The computer complied. In the spaces between the squid creatures' massive bodies were warships unlike anything he'd ever seen before. They seemed to be made out of the same glowing, radiant material as the bodies of the squids. But there was no mistaking them. They were ships of war.

The warships, the size of dreadnaught class battlecruisers, had elongated frames and barbed, spear-like, tendrils that extended past the bow of every ship like thorny sea urchins. The sterns of the ships were no less intimidating since trailing behind them were tentacles of a mechanized nature.

Attached to the end of each of the robot tentacles were massive laser cannons more powerful than anything in the Galliforn fleet. The tentacles coiled around huge thrusters that guided the destroyers toward their final destination. And, it just so happened, Grendok had an idea of where that would be.

As bad as things seemed, luckily enough, Grendok knew a thing or two about thwarting invaders. That said, this time they weren't going up against blue-skins. They were dealing with an entirely different kind of monster. Something ancient. Something sinister.

Determined not to give in to his fears, Grendok cleared his throat and, then, with the swipe of a finger, flicked off the monitor. Turning to leave, he paused, turned back again, and retrieved his battle-axe from off the wall.

"It seems we'll be back in the fray very soon, ole chap," he said, kissing the axe on its head.

39

"**At long last**, there she is," Angellyk said with a smile, looking up to find Raven enter the brig. Angellyk eyed her up and down, admiring her figure complimenting outfit—a tight, charcoal gray tank top that hugged her figure so tightly that her nipples budded underneath the fabric. She also wore black jeans with tears in them that showed off patches of indigo skin. Her belt was tactical in nature but had an elegant salmon colored, single-plate buckle that added a bit of flash to her otherwise drab attire. Rounding off her ensemble were her patent black military issue boots, which she kept her pant legs tucked into at all times.

"Apologies," Raven said, "things have been so hectic lately I haven't had the time to work through whatever…well, whatever this is." She pointed at Angellyk and then to herself.

Not waiting for a response, Raven's heavy, black leather boots clomped across the metal floor as she marched over to the locking mechanism on the outside of Angellyk's cell and, leaning over the retina scanner, input her biometrics.

"Stunning as always," Angellyk said warmly, leaning against the glass barrier as she let her eyes linger on Raven's ass long enough for Raven to shoot her a scornful look. She shrugged it off and smiled coyly, still impressed by how the tight-fitting denim really did hug her every curve on Raven's perfectly sculpted figure like a second skin.

Finished at the console, she stood up just as the red light above the door flickered to green and the glass plate slid open. Raven stepped aside, gesturing with a casual nod for Angellyk to pass through the opening unobstructed.

Angellyk stepped out of her cell, tossed her forest green hair across her avocado colored shoulder, and faced Raven. "For a while there I thought maybe you had forgotten about us."

"I've been busy," Raven replied. "I take it Skuld has taken good care of you, though?"

"He has," replied Angellyk.

"Good. That's good," Raven said. She shot her ex-wife a quick but fleeting smile and then turned to leave.

"Wait a nano-second," her ex said, stopping Raven with a hand on her shoulder. "Is that all? Just, 'you're free to go' and then goodbye?"

Raven paused. "It's not like that. It's just…I'm a bit preoccupied. I have other things on my mind."

"Maybe I can help?"

Raven looked back at Angellyk and took her hand in hers. "I wish that were possible. But this is something I must do alone. You understand, right?"

Angellyk's teal eyes held Raven's purple eyed gaze for a long time and then she nodded silently, motioning that she understood. She understood Raven was a lone wolf and would rather struggle in vain than ask anyone for help. "Same old Raven," Angellyk laughed. "You haven't changed a bit."

"Hey, as much as I love to see a good old-fashioned reunion," came the disgruntled voice of Onelle Agnar, who stood glaring at them from behind the glass of her enclosure, opposite the one Angellyk had occupied. "Do you think you could, maybe, wrap this up sometime in the next century and let me out of this place? I have places to be too, you know."

"And yet nobody has even bothered to wonder where you disappeared to," Raven said coldly. "If I were you," she added, "I'd see to it about getting myself some new friends."

Onelle had been missing for months and not a single person had come looking for her. In fact, Raven had a hunch that everyone in her life was properly celebrating the insufferable woman's disappearance. But until the empress decided on what to do with her, Onelle was her problem.

Irritated that nobody would listen to her, Onelle went over to the corner of her cell to sulk. Sitting on her cot, she put her leg up on the edge and smacked the back of her teeth, looking away from the two love birds with disgust.

Angellyk and Raven's eyes locked. "It's about Jegra, isn't it?" asked Angellyk.

But she was fairly certain she already knew the answer to her question.

"What is about Jegra?"

"The thing that has you so tight lipped."

"You were always good at reading people, Angie," Raven replied. "But I'd rather not talk about it, given our current company."

Both women slowly turned and looked over at Onelle and stared at her with blank faces. Onelle caught their judgmental expressions and she scoffed, folded her arms, and turned away.

"No, it's not just Princess Pleasantries over there…it's a sensitive matter. I'm sorry, that's all I'm at liberty to say."

"You love her, don't you?"

"What?!" Raven laughed. "Onelle?"

"No, silly. Jegra," Angellyk replied.

Raven laughed again. It sounded so absurd. But the look on Angie's face suggested she was being sincere. "Oh," she said, her tone softening, "you're serious."

She was fond of Jegra and would go to the ends of the galaxy and back to make sure she was safe, but it wasn't *love*. At least, she didn't think so.

"I wouldn't joke about your love life, hon. There's nothing funny about it. In fact, it's pretty dang sad, if you ask me."

"Ha-ha," Raven replied, narrowing her eyes at her. "But Jegra's my empress. We're friends. That's all."

"*Mmm-hmmm*," Angellyk said skeptically, folding her arms over her chest. "Just friends."

Raven blushed. "That's right. Just friends."

"I'm not the one blushing," Angellyk teased.

Raven's cheeks darkened even more, but this time with a hint of anger. "I forgot how frustrating you can be sometimes," she said, storming out of the brig.

Angellyk raced out after her. "Don't be like that! I didn't mean anything by it. Just that…"

Raven stopped in the middle of the corridor. "Just…what?

"It's just that you've not let many people in close to you. But I see you and Jegra are very close. I guess what I'm trying to say is, I don't want to see you get hurt."

"I appreciate that," Raven said, reaching out and brushing Angellyk's face with the back of her hand. "But, like I said, we're just friends."

"In that case," Angellyk said, throwing her arms around Raven's waist and reeling her in. "I've been dying to do this since I came aboard."

Her lips crashed into Raven's and they shared a hot, mouth-watering kiss. Midway through their make out session, the doors parted and they quickly pulled apart, trying their best to pretend nothing had happened.

Skuld was standing in the entrance holding a tray of food for the remaining prisoner, Onelle. "Sorry to interrupt, but I have to…" he nodded down at the chow and then glanced nervously back up at the two women, "you know."

"Uh, yeah," Raven said, motioning for him to continue on with his duties. "We're done here anyway."

Not waiting around long enough for Angellyk to try and talk her into something she'd likely regret, she scurried up the corridor and disappeared out of sight.

"Apologies," Skuld said, glancing timidly at the sad looking green-skinned woman standing before him.

"No, it wasn't you. I was, perhaps, a little too forward." Angellyk smiled at Skuld and then turned to go roam about the ship, clear her head, and maybe take a cold shower.

Raven entered the bridge to find Kregor and Gyllek both busy on the comm. "Do you read me?" Kregor asked. "I repeat, this is the *Skywend* responding to the *Chiron* distress call, do you read me?"

"What's going on?" Raven asked.

"It's the *Chiron*, ma'am, they issued a system wide distress call."

"Where's the call coming from?"

"Galliforn, Captain," Kregor replied. He looked at her, awaiting her orders. His nictitating eyelids blinking twice as he watched her mull over their next course of action.

"Set course for Galliforn, maximum speed," Raven informed. Turning to leave, she glimpsed Gyllek and Kregor both giving her a curious look. She knew they had questions, but until she knew more, it was best just to keep her assumptions to herself. "I'll be in my quarters sending an encoded communiqué to Empress Alakandra. If this is what I think it is, we're all in a pot of boiling water and the only way out is going to be by jumping into the fire."

After Raven exited the bridge, Gyllek turned in her chair and looked at Kregor with a confused expression on her face. "What in the galaxy was the captain on about? Pots of water and jumping into fires?"

"Bad news, I'm afraid, kid. Just your average all around bad news." Settling into his seat, Kregor leaned forward, flipped on several switches, and dialed up the ship's FTL drive.

"That's what I thought," Gyllek replied.

"Strap in, kid," he said, pushing the throttle all the way up to maximum. Outside the main view portal, the stars all around them began to stretch into a kaleidoscope of different colors, "and settle in for the long haul. B'cuz this adventure is just getting started."

"Aye, aye, sir," Gyllek replied in her cutesy voice. Giving Kregor a playful salute, she winked and then sat back and buckled in for the ride.

40

The *Chiron* **passed** through the stream at maximum speed making its way toward the satyr homeworld, Galliforn. Outside the window of Grendok's quarters, a rainbow kaleidoscope of colors whisked by. The colors, like a psychedelic light show, danced along the hull in a hypnotizing blur. It was beautiful, but staring at it too long could give you a headache. Or a bad case of vertigo.

A sense of lightheadedness overcoming him, Grendok turned away from the hyperspace vista to face the mirror and stared at his solid reflection. Having put on his admiral's uniform, he finished fastening his collar and then tugged at his sleeves, popping them out so he could clip on his cufflinks.

Lost to his thoughts, the time had come, he felt, to utilize every asset he'd been building for the past one hundred and forty years. Arms dealer, black market trader, illegal clone provider, renowned war hero, all of it had come to a head.

Before exiting his room, he fetched his battle-axe and slung it across his back. The magnetic clamps locked it into place and, taking a deep breath, he strolled out into the corridor.

The short walk from his quarters to the bridge only took a few minutes but he used the time to clear his head. He'd need a clear head to think through the next step of this shit storm. Not only had a coup been executed on Dagon Prime, but Senator Targon's daughter, Callestra, now led the Dagon Imperial fleet. And for some strange reason, they were holding on the Southern Rim of the Empire, as if they were waiting for something.

But that position held no strategic value and it left Dagon Prime wide open to attack by the Nyctans. What did Callestra know that he didn't? Not being privy to such information got his goat, but he already had an idea about how to obtain such sensitive information.

Upon arriving on the bridge, Sub Commander Tabitha looked at him, straightened up, and announced his arrival. "Admiral on deck!" she hollered. The bridge crew all stopped what they were doing and rose to their feet and saluted, holding their salutes until their captain returned them with one of his own.

Grendok saluted and said, "Everyone, at ease."

His crew turned back to their stations, returning to their duties. He skipped up to Tabitha, who stood before the large monitor.

"Coming out of hyperspace now," the navigations officer informed. This prompted the crew to look up at the forward viewscreen.

The rainbow kaleidoscope of paper-thin light strands shrank into pin-points of stellar light. The blue streaks snapped into closer stars, the red into far away stars, the yellow into system stars, the green faded into invisible dark matter, and the purple, well, the few purple streaks signified black holes.

THUNK! The ship jolted as something struck the *Chiron's* outer hull. "Take evasive maneuvers!" Grendok barked.

With a heavy groan, the massive ship swooped down, narrowly avoiding another, much larger, asteroid, half the ship's own mass. More rocky debris *clanked* and *pinged* against the ship's korridium hull and the ride through the debris became exceptionally bumpy.

Tabitha watched the thick debris outside the viewscreen crashing, ricocheting, and spinning off in every direction. It was chaos. "There shouldn't be an asteroid belt here."

"It's not an asteroid belt," answered the admiral in his grimmest tone. He raised a finger as the ship emerged from the thick of it only to reveal their homeworld, Galliforn, cracked in half like an egg, floating lifeless in the sky.

There was no grid of city lights lighting up the surface. No transports going to and fro as with most bustling space ports. No signs of life of any kind. Just the hot orange of a molten core bleeding out of a green world that had been cleaved in two. As the molten core cooled in the frigidness of space, it hardened, forming a metallic strand, like the severed umbilical cord of an aborted fetus that dangled lifelessly in the dark abyss.

As the terrible, horrible realization set in, the crew all gasped as one, their hearts instantly breaking. Many broke down into sobs. But Grendok said nothing. It took everything he had not to break too.

The Galliforn Space Defense Front, their flag battleship *Stormbreaker*, and every single one of the orbital laser platforms had been destroyed. There wasn't a ship or laser platform remaining between their homeworld and The Rift. Just an endless string of destruction and debris. The skeletal husks of destroyed vessels and the rocky remains of the planet were all that was left of the once mighty Galliforn. Whatever it was that had hit the planet had utterly decimated it. The Good Ole Girl was gone.

"What in the galaxy could do something like this?" Tabitha asked, wiping tears from the corners of her eyes.

"Not what, but who, my dear."

Tabitha looked over at Grendok, a frown forming on her face. "What do you mean? Do you know who's responsible for this, admiral?"

"It's an omen," Grendok said.

"An omen for what?"

"That all worlds will fall."

"Fall? Fall to whom?"

Grendok turned to Tabitha and, speaking in a hushed yet equally gruff tone, his voice betraying the first signs of trepidation, he answered, "He has returned."

"Who?" Tabitha asked. "Who has returned? What aren't you telling me?"

"The one I cannot name. The one drawn back from countless eons and inconceivable dimensions. He who instills dread in the fiercest warriors and compels the most ruthless knaves to cower and hide. He who carries with him the Yellow Sign. A golden light delineated by a single and incontrovertible trait; everything it touches is laid to ruin. My dear Tabitha, you ask who has returned? But isn't it already clear?" Grendok paused, turning back toward the viewscreen to take in the destruction of his fallen homeworld. Taking a moment to let the direness of his words take root in the minds of the men and women of his crew, he finally answered, "The Yellow King."

BOOK 2
EPILOGUE

Administratrix Anaïs Nin entered the throne room to find all of the court assembled. Even her political and military advisors had convened. She felt rage growing within herself as the crowds parted, all of them eyeing her with startled faces. It was only when the throng parted to reveal the gleaming backside of a figure she recognized all too well that she understood their edginess wasn't because they feared her, but because they feared Him.

A beautiful Nyctan man with silver flowing hair, skin as soft and pure as the finest ivory, and sunken eyelids gazed over his shoulder at her with sanguine eyes. It seemed as if he recognized her at first glance, but for some reason unbeknownst to her, he seemed sorry to see her.

Brilliant golden armor with what seemed to be enormous, gilded eagles' feathers hung from his back. The gold-plated feathers swayed as he slowly turned to greet her.

"My dear daughter," he said, his arms clasped behind his back. "I have been waiting for this day for more than seven millennia."

The Gilded Master swept back his wings as though he were sweeping back a cape and, catching the air, they fanned out and then promptly curled back into pleats, each feathery fold falling back into place.

With slow deliberate movements, he smiled down at the administratrix with hypnotic black eyes. Eyes blacker than obsidian; all but for a golden halo that ran around the circumference of his irises which gave him an otherworldly appearance.

Anaïs Nin could hardly believe her eyes. Was this real? Had her God returned?

Was it really him? What about the prophecy? What about the emissaries? If it really was her God, she needed to know.

She wanted to pinch herself just to be sure she wasn't dreaming, but then he smiled upon her. And she knew. She knew because instead of feeling warmth or love, she felt nothing but dread and despair echoing throughout a cold and infinite void. She felt her stomach sink and a crippling sense of hopelessness come her. *It must be Him*, she thought. She was sure of it.

"My Lord," Anaïs Nin said, kneeling before the feet of the Gilded Master, H'aaztre. She trembled in fear but clamped down on her nerves and hid her spine-tingling feelings deep down inside her.

"Rise," H'aaztre said, reaching down and guiding the administratrix to her feet with a gesture.

"I too have waited for this day," she said, taking his hand and kissing it, "my lord."

The Supreme Lord H'aaztre raised an eyebrow. "Is this so?" he asked in a skeptical tone.

"Yes, my lord," Anaïs Nin replied truthfully. "I would not lie to you. I swear it on my life."

"Then why are the preparations not complete?"

"My lord?" she asked, confused by the question.

"The Ceremony of the Chosen One," he answered. "Where is my chosen vessel?"

"I'm afraid a suitable vessel could not be discovered in time." She bowed her head apologetically.

The Gilded Master reached down and gently raised her chin. "Are you barren?" he asked.

"No, my lord," Anaïs Nin replied, her eyes watering with remorse for the awful guilt she felt for disappointing him. "It's just that..." she trailed off. There were no excuses. She had deemed the child unworthy and sacrificed it, knowing very well the repercussions. She had failed in her sole mission as High Priestess to provide her Lord with a suitable vessel. "My lord, I am not worthy. I have failed you. I have failed my sacred duty as High Priestess and I deserve to be punished."

Never in a million years had she expected that H'aaztre would return but a handful of days after the ritual. Yet, she got the distinct feeling that He saw right through her weakness. He knew she was a whore who had let herself be overcome with the carnal desires she'd felt for so long. He knew of Dakroth's sickening seed being impregnated in her, and she knew that He saw through her—that she ignored all the signs of His divine return.

Unable to bear the weight of her abysmal failures any further, an unforgivable sin in her eyes, she fell to her knees before her Lord, prostrate, and burst into tears. Clutching his feet, she kissed his golden boots and begged for his forgiveness.

"Oh, my child, do not weep," H'aaztre said, pulling Anaïs Nin back to her feet. Guiding her gently into him, he placed her head against his metal-plated chest. He hushed her like a loving mother would a weeping babe and, stroking her hair softly, said, "There, there, my child. Everything will be all right. You shall see. Soon, it will all become perfectly clear to you."

Her face pressed to her Lord's bosom, she felt her heart racing in her chest, the fear, the guilt, her penitence, the reverence, the excitement…all of it churning inside her like a building storm. She allowed herself to let loose, and pressing her cheek into his warm embrace, threw her arms around him and held him as he held her.

That's when she felt the terrible agony of H'aaztre's hand tearing through cloth and flesh as he reached into her back and tore out her spinal column. A viscous sounding splatter was the last thing she heard before the infernal darkness seized her.

The administratrix's body crumpled to the ground and landed in a disfigured mess along with an excess of her sticky green blood. Her flayed back looked like the toothed opening of a zipper, as small bone fragments protruded from the gory wound.

Clutched in the Gilded Master's bloody hand was the spinal column and head of the administratrix. Her dead eyes peered out across the court with a look of utter terror frozen on her face. And as though some part of Anaïs Nin was still inside somewhere, a single tear trickled down her forehead.

Not a single gasp or murmur was made. The distinguished guests of the court were beyond petrified. They dared not react in any other way than that which showed the utmost veneration of their Lord. An ancient supreme being which many of them had only heard about in the scholarly texts, but who walked among them now. A God whose namesake a large majority still prayed to daily. A God they would not question, for their faith drove them to blind obedience and servitude. For that is what the phrase "Nyctos etd've H'aaztre," meant. *The Slaves of Hastur.*

If their God wanted their queen dead, then he must have his reasons. How could a God be wrong?

"You there," H'aaztre said to one of the Carcosan Virgins that cowered off to the side like a frightened animal. She reluctantly stepped forward. Placing the gory skull and backbone into her hands, green globs of gore dripping from them, he commanded, "Dispose of this."

"Yes, my lord," she said, taking the remains of her queen and scurrying back.

Sir Lance Bishop, one of the top-ranking Knights of Caelum, stepped forward. His gauntleted fists clenched. And a rage burned inside him as he grappled with the death of his beloved queen. He wanted nothing more than to have his vengeance, God or not. But he was abruptly halted in his tracks with one sharp glance from the Gilded Master.

"Is there something you wish to say, Sir Knight?"

"No, my lord," Sir Bishop answered, easing back into line.

Yolkai Estan, the current oracle, brushed back her red and gold trim robes and placed her hand over the knight to let him know it was all right.

This was neither the time nor place to mount a protest. But she understood the knight's deep-seated urge to protect the queen at all costs. It was literally programmed into his DNA. All the Knights were genetically enhanced in such a fashion. And now, the queen was dead. Slaughtered before her loyal servants as a symbol of H'aaztre's terrible might as well as what would happen to those who dared to defy him.

"Most Excellent," H'aaztre said, a satisfied grin spreading across his beautiful lips. Turning to the throne, he sauntered over, his wings swaying behind him, and took his rightful place.

The Gilded Master leaned back into the golden and ivory chair and gazed out across the sea of faces of his people. One by one they knelt down and lowered their wretched gazes, making themselves prostrate before their new ruler. Even the headstrong order of Knights submitted to H'aaztre's authority, and seeing their leader acquiesce so too did the rest of the knights. The people of Nyctan and their planet were now his. And soon, the whole galaxy.

BOOK TWO
FINIS

BOOK 3

741

THE CHRONICLES OF

JEGRA

DESTROYER OF GALAXIES

1

Black stars filled the white phosphorus sky. Only, they weren't stars. They were the pinpricks of empty space that existed between the flood of celestial squid entities that illuminated the firmament with their atomic radiance. Their heavenly glow was both beautiful and terrifying as they spilled out of the jagged tear in space known to deep space travelers as The Rift.

Behind the giant celestial cephalopods that, like other dimensional refugees, streamed into the borders of the Commonwealth, a cosmic alliance encompassing seven star systems with multiple inhabitable planets and moons, was an armada of unknown origin. An invasion force from beyond the other side of The Rift. A strange enemy from a realm existing somewhere at the farthest reaches of the universe.

The scribes of the Enchiridion surmised that at the end of the universe lies an unfathomable place where the very edge of all existence meets the infinite void. A place where time and space have no meaning, and the laws of physics do not abide. A place wherein, they say, lurk ancient beings so terrible that to fathom their primordial essence would cause the greatest minds alive to fracture with madness.

The *Chiron*, Admiral Grendok's flagship and the only remaining vessel in the sector that hadn't been completely wiped out by the energy-sucking celestial squids, hung in space suspended like an ancient monolith. The massive starship, designed as a ram's head, kept a safe distance from the advancing armada and celestial entities.

"I want a full scan of that armada. I want to know armaments, shielding output, what kind of engines they're using. And by Pan's beard, I want it yesterday!" the satyr growled as he clutched the arms of his command chair with such intensity that his nails left shallow scratch marks.

"Sir," Sub Commander Tabitha Almathea said looking up from her station. "We can't seem to breach the interference caused by the CSE's energy output. They're scrambling all our readings with their radioactivity."

"How close to the Celestial Squid Entities would we need to be to cut through the interference and get a read on those ships?"

"Technically speaking?" Tabitha scratched behind her twitching goat's ear and then turned toward the admiral. "We'd need to be on the other side of the entire wall of CSEs to get a solid read. But that would, of course, leave us open to attack, flanked on all sides. And since those ships managed to destroy most of our fleet, it's a good bet that they'd make scrap out of us too."

"Ready a probe," he said, standing up as he gazed out the view portal at the yellow sparkling sky, filled with giant monsters. The smallest of them were the size of the largest sea-faring whales on the ocean world of Kree'alek; the largest of the creatures rivaled even the *Chiron* in size.

What the CSEs were known for, however, was their voracious appetites. They feasted on atomic power and would drain any starship using fusion propulsion.

And to make matters worse, they absorbed almost all energy-based weapons too, including laser and disruptor blasts, and could defang any war ship. Their crustacean shells looked like a mix between a marine squid and a king prawn, and made the creatures that much harder to kill. Only missiles did any actual damage to their spiny plating, but the damage was always mitigated by the creature's natural ability to absorb the energy of the blasts.

A chime from one of the officer's consoles sounded and the ensign looked up toward the viewscreen. "Probe launched, sir," he informed the admiral.

The bridge crew watched in silent anticipation as the probe flew toward an opening between a cluster of the CSEs. It looked hopeful, too, as though it would pass through uninterrupted when, all of a sudden, the probe's power drained away and the cylindrical device died halfway to its target. Its thrusters unable to fire, it drifted at an uneven keel until crashing into one of the squids and rebounding off only to continue its spinning cartwheel out into deep space.

"Report!" Grendok growled, annoyed by the probe's failure. He'd been certain it would work, considering that the older model probes still used combustion technology.

"It appears the squids drained the electrical system before the thrusters could fire. Once the batteries were out of juice, the navigation system shut down and the engines, not having any coordinates, simply cut out."

"Blast it all to Helios!"

"Sir," Tabitha said, swiveling in her chair and eyeing the captain from across the command bridge. "We could try blasting a hole in the cluster of CSEs using the missiles. It might give us a chance to send in another probe through the opening we make."

"Do it," Grendok said.

"Lock onto target and fire the first missile on my command," Almathea instructed the crew. "Wait twenty seconds then fire a second missile at the first, and a third at the second. We'll detonate them after the first one loses power; that way, by the time the second reaches the blast zone, we will trigger a chain reaction that will take the first one with it and blow those creatures into calamari."

"Yes, ma'am," the ensign replied with a nod.

Tabitha pointed through the view portal at the glowing wall of celestial bodies and gave the order. "And fire!"

The *Chiron's* missile canopies opened and the first Python class missile raced away from the war vessel at remarkable speeds. In a blink, it twinkled away, its bright thrusters burning like blue-tipped Roman candles as they shrank into the distance. The moment it could no longer be tracked visually, the second missile launched.

The approaching missile neared the first one's position when, as predicted, its thrusters also died down. All its power was already being syphoned off by its proximity to the energy-sucking creatures.

The third Python missile came in hot, and just before it could be shut down, it detonated behind the others.

One by one the remaining missiles exploded, the energy of the first igniting the subsequent one following it, creating an explosive daisy chain that, at last, reached the first missile. Luckily, it was well within the cluster of the celestial bodies.

The missile flashed bright, like a mini nova, and five of the nearest squid entities were incinerated in its fiery wake. A couple smaller CSEs, close enough to be injured but not destroyed, rapidly dimmed, their blue luminescent bodies cooling to a dull gray.

The sub commander's tactical ploy had worked, and the bridge crew of the *Chiron* erupted with cheers. It was a small victory, but important nonetheless.

Tabitha puffed up her chest, her furry, white cleavage filling her v-cut, leather uniform quite nicely, and smiled to herself. Her gambit had paid off. She hadn't been sure it would, but it did. Now they had a chance to get a probe through the enemy fleet's defenses.

Although the CSEs seemed to absorb most forms of energy, including nuclear energy, she'd suspected that releasing high-yield neutron missiles would create a spike in energy so extreme that the CSEs wouldn't be able to absorb it all fast enough. Basically, she forced them to overdose on their favorite drug.

Admiral Grendok nodded in approval and Sub Commander Tabitha Almathea smiled at him and returned his gesture with a slight bow.

He had picked her as his first officer when he discovered that she was something of a tactical genius. Back in the academy, she had beat an "impossible to beat" war simulation called *Meka Kakon*, when she tricked the computer into perceiving itself as the enemy. In the simulation, the enemy ships turned on one another, but the program couldn't handle the error and shorted. She was put on probation for the destruction of the school's property, but it didn't matter. She had not only won the simulation but helped reveal a critical weakness in the military security programming.

This alone was enough to catch his eye when hand picking his bridge officers. And that's why he put her in command of his ship.

"Launch the probe now," he ordered, and another probe shot from the missile tube and tore away from the *Chiron* at full throttle as it headed into the dark pocket left by the previous explosion.

When the torpedo-shaped device sailed through the opening in the squid armada's barrier, there were small shouts of joy and audible sighs of relief.

Without taking her eyes off the viewscreen, Tabitha relayed the good news. "The probe has broken through successfully, sir."

Admiral Grendok clasped his hands behind his back and stood and watched with a keen interest in what would happen next. "Well done, Sub Commander," he said, praising her success.

"Sir," the ensign said in a nervous voice, looking up at the admiral with worried eyes that almost seemed to water at the very thought of having to share bad news. "The probe is having trouble getting any readings. It seems the enemy fleet is jamming it somehow."

"Is it the radiation spikes?" the sub commander asked.

"I don't think so. It seems to be something else, commander."

"Can you get me a tally of those ships? At the very least, I want to know the size of the invasion force we're dealing with here."

"Pinging the ships now." There was a brief pause as the sound of a sonar emitter echoed through the command center. The young satyr gulped nervously as he gazed down at his display panel. "Um…"

Tabitha leaned over the ensign's shoulder and glanced at the readout. "Eight hundred and ninety-seven vessels and roughly the same number of CSEs."

"By Pan's beard," Grendok said, stroking his own beard unconsciously. "That's the exact number of war capable vessels in the entire Commonwealth."

"They intend to match our galactic defenses with a one to one ratio. But, surely, their firepower is superior to over half of the rundown ships available for immediate deployment. And that's not even including the number of ships stuck in space docks for repairs and retrofits."

"Sub Commander, give me an assessment of how many of those vessels we could take out if we made a hyper-jump straight into the center of their armada."

"Sir?"

"Just the raw estimates, Tabitha," he reiterated, using her name to soften the terribleness of his request.

She fetched a small glass touch-display from a side pocket and began imputing some rough estimates. After a moment, she looked up. Her expression was unresponsive. More bad news.

He could sense she was hesitating. "Just spit it out," he said after another second. He tried not to sound harsh; he knew that was how he came across much of the time.

"We would barely penetrate the CSE defense perimeter."

"Maybe we could try another barrage of Python missiles?" the tactical officer suggested.

"No," Tabitha said, pointing out the view portal at the cluster of celestial squids. "They're already repositioning themselves to neutralize any head-on attacks. I'm afraid our luck this time around was a one-off event."

"In that case, we have no choice but to withdraw from this engagement," Grendok stated. Although, it was more of an order than an observation. If there was a chance they could win it, even with a glorious sacrifice, then they'd need to regroup and rethink things.

Sub Commander Almathea looked at Grendok. In three centuries, no Galliforn vessel had ever retreated from a battle. But nobody had ever encountered a force like this before, either. Even though it was unprecedented, they may very well be the last of their kind, and to go down fighting wasn't the answer. It was suicide.

"Full reverse," Grendok said.

"Full reverse," Almathea echoed.

"Set course to…" he paused, then, against his better judgement, said, "Dagon Prime."

Sub Commander Almathea didn't even question the order. As strange as it was to show up on your enemies' doorstep, if they were going to stand a chance against this invasion force, they'd need the might of the Dagon Empire behind them. And the might of the newly crowned empress, Jegra Alakandra.

Without the empress to back their cause, there would be no way of brokering a deal between Galliforn and Dagon. But as an intermediary, she might be able to make a plea on their behalf. At the moment, it was their best shot.

After all, they had just watched an unknown enemy force lay waste to their homeworld, and if any Dagon had an ounce of common sense, they would realize that doing nothing merely meant they'd be next on the chopping block.

Even as sympathy was lacking among the Dagon people, Grendok had a hunch that even the most corrupt politicians of the Dagon High Council had enough common sense to protect their self-interests both at home and abroad. They wouldn't dare risk sitting idly by while their precious empire crumbled all around them and a foreign power stripped them of their vitality.

In the end, the old adage was true—the enemy of your enemy is your friend. It wasn't the perfect plan, but right now it was all they had.

In a flash, a halo of light engulfed the *Chiron* and it disappeared into the hyperspace stream. As the rainbow kaleidoscope of psychedelic light stretched away into an infinite funnel before them, Grendok looked away from the forward view screen and settled into the command chair.

Sub Commander Almathea swiveled around in her chair and gazed at him from across the bridge. He glanced up and they shared a moment. Neither of them could muster a smile, but given the circumstances and the great loss they had just experienced, it was enough that they could maintain their composure at all.

Grendok leaned back and crossed his hoofed foot over his knee. After giving his uniform a tug at the waistline to draw out the wrinkles, he leaned onto the arm of his chair with a heavy elbow and planted his chin on his fist. He soon found himself lost to his thoughts, his mind dedicated to one and only one thing: finding a weakness in this seemingly invincible and terrible new force…and exploiting it.

2

It had been three days since Danica had awakened from her coma, for which Jegra was extremely relieved. But her body was so severely fatigued that she needed to be bedridden for another few days. Per the doctor's orders, she was confined to their quarters and was only allowed to get up and move around on crutches to use the bathroom and to do her physical therapy.

"This sucks," Danica lamented, sitting up in bed next to Jegra, who sat beside her in a chair, reading *Moby Dick*.

"What does?" Jegra asked, placing the book down. She scooted over to her lover and took her hand.

"I need to pee," she answered. Before she could get out of bed, however, a shocked look settled onto her face and her cheeks flushed bright pink. Looking down at the bed, she let out a disappointed sigh.

"What is it?" asked Jegra, worried for her best friend.

"I just pissed myself," Danica replied, her face glowing with embarrassment.

"It's fine," Jegra said, touching Danica's shoulder. "I'll clean it up." Jegra rose from her chair, stretched, and headed over to grab a towel and some cleaning supplies.

"You do realize you literally have nurses, servants, and an entire cleaning staff to do this sort of stuff for you, right?"

Danica watched as Jegra nodded, bending down to open a pantry in the bathroom. "I know."

"Yeah, but I don't want you to suffer the humility and indignation of…well…you know. You'll have to touch my sopping sheets full of urine. It's not dignified."

"If I was afraid of a little bit of piss, I wouldn't have had my face down there for two hours last night." Jegra nodded at Danica's crotch.

Still embarrassed, she covered herself and the wetness soaking through the bedspread. "Admittedly, that was wonderful!" Danica said, a subtle smile edging onto her lips and then disappearing again. "But you don't have to do this. Really."

Jegra laughed, turning around to confront Danica, a towel draped over her arm. "Stop being a big crybaby and let me do this for you."

"You know, once upon a time I found you completely repulsive because you did stuff like this."

"What? Piss the bed? That was one time! And I was sloshed."

Danica shrugged. "I think it was more than just one time."

Jegra shrugged and they both laughed. She returned to the bedside and, kneeling down, took Dani's hand in hers. "I know," she said, smiling ruefully. "But the temptation was too much for you. You just had to have me."

"Is that so?" Danica batted her eyes, brushed a strand of hair out of her face, and stared into Jegra's eyes.

"After all," Jegra whispered, her lips getting dangerously close to Dani's, "the forbidden fruit tastes so much sweeter when nobody is watching."

"Oh, hush! I didn't fall in love with you because you were easy. I fell in love with you because you did something…something I could never muster up the courage to do. You stood up to Dakroth. Right then and there, I knew you were a woman to be reckoned with. And *that* was more attractive to me than all your faults combined."

"You flatter me!" Jegra said, batting away the compliment with a gentle wave of the hand.

"Do you think I've changed?" asked Danica, after a moment's thought.

"I know you have, Dani. And for the better," Jegra squeezed Dani's hand and then began gathering the bedding up in her arms.

With a grunt, Danica tried to climb out of bed but Jegra stopped her with a gentle touch. "Don't worry, my love. I'll handle it."

"You sure? You'll smell like piss afterward."

"According to you, when don't I?"

"Oh, stop it! I was only teasing about that."

"I know," Jegra replied. "And I love you too, so, of course, I'm going to take care of you. At the end of the day, it's just you and me, babe."

Danica slid to the side to allow Jegra to pull the bedding out from under her. As she sat there, she turned and gazed out the window of their bedroom. "It's just that…"

"You've basically turned into me? Yeah, I know. Apparently, my DNA has that effect on people."

"Don't get me wrong. I'm happy to be more like you. But sometimes I miss the old me. I miss Cassera."

"That bitch?" Jegra said, squinting her nose and giving Danica a sour look. "The one with the stick so far up her ass that smiling made her butt hurt?"

Both women laughed out loud and Jegra finished collecting the linens and tossed them into a pile in the corner of her room. She'd finish with them later. Then, using her best fake British accent, she asked, "Fancy a bath, m'dear?"

"Will you be joining me?" Danica asked with a coy grin.

"Why, my dear Dani," she waved her hand dramatically and stuck out her hips, striking a pose, "are you hitting on me?"

"And what if I am?" Dani, reached for her crutches but Jegra intervened and scooped her up in her arms as though she were a bride on their honeymoon.

Surprised by the sudden maneuver on Jegra's part, Danica threw her arms around Jegra's neck and leaned in and gave her a peck on her cheek. "You do know you're the most important thing to me in the whole bleedin' galaxy, right?"

"Ditto," Jegra said as she gently set Dani into the piping hot bath, which had been set to fill on an automated timer.

"My robes," Danica laughed, looking down at her garments soaking into the hot water. Jegra ignored it and climbed in with her satin robes on as well.

"At least we'll save on the dry cleaning bill."

Dani laughed and leaned in and kissed Jegra on the lips.

Jegra pulled back, slightly, "Oh, hon," she said, waving her hand in front of her face to signify a putrid smell, "my morning breath is practically lethal right now."

"Don't worry. I've sort of gotten used to all your foul odors over the past year and a half."

"Oh, you have, have you?" Jegra shot Dani a devious look. Danica nodded politely but Jegra didn't relinquish her firm gaze. It was only then the bubbles rose to the surface and made small *plip-plip* sounds as they expelled a most hideous odor. An odor so foul that Danica's nostrils virtually screamed out in terror before she pinched them shut.

"Oh, my Gilded Lord!" Danica said, her face turning green. "You're downright nasty, girl."

"You know you love me," Jegra said, squinting up her face and acting all cutesy. One final bubble blipped on the surface and Jegra smiled.

Unable to deny it, Danica smiled too and slid over to her partner, her open robe floating on the surface of the water like angelic wings. Softly, she pressed her warm body up against Jegra's. "I do love you. And to prove it beyond a shadow of a doubt, I shall now kiss you, stank breath, fart-water and all."

The two women laughed and then locked lips. Slowly, they slid beneath the water in a romantic embrace; the bath overflowed onto the granite floor.

After their little morning tryst, both women rinsed themselves off and reclined in opposite ends of the ample tub.

"I could stay in here forever," Danica said, throwing one leg up over the edge of the tub and another over Jegra's, which was already hanging over the edge of the tub.

"Me too," Jegra said, exhaling a long, drawn out breath as she closed her eyes and just let herself feel at home for once. She couldn't remember the last time she'd truly felt at home. It was a feeling she didn't want to take for granted.

Before they could get too comfortable, however, the palace comm system chimed, signaling an incoming message.

"Answer," Jegra said, sitting up in the tub. Hovering before them, a holovid screen came to life, its blue light projecting its image onto Jegra's bare skin. Reaching out, she pinched the holographic projection as though it were a layer of acrylic body paint and peeled it off her. The holovid responded to her gestures and acted like a real kind of film, even falling limp in her fingers like a loose sheet of paper.

She whipped out her hand and tossed the glowing display out into the open room. It flew up onto the wall, revealing the well chiseled jawline and hooked nose of her favorite Dagon officer.

"Sorry to bother you, Your Majesty," said her chief of security, Meleh'Kendar. Although he was short for a Dagon male, he was built as sturdy as they came.

He was six-foot-even, barrel chested, and appeared as though he could take on a Kalaxian rhino single handedly. The perfect man to head her security detail.

"What is it, chief?"

"My contact has informed me that a shipment of Nividium will be arriving at the port in Arena City at zero seven hundred hours."

Kalax also happened to be in the province Meleh'Kendar was from, one that had been ravaged by civil unrest for over a century. It was the last place on Dagon Prime where outlaw activity still existed.

Needless to say, Jegra had surprised Dakroth when she requested Meleh'Kendar become her head of security on Thessalonica. Dakroth had merely hired him for his black-market connections in Kalax, but the emperor, being the fickle man that he was, had since grown bored with that business venture. Thereby allowing Jegra to attain Meleh'Kendar's services.

And Jegra put him to good use, too. He was her eyes and ears among the people. He employed "whisperers," the Dagon term for spies, in every province on the planet and had an information network that would get you dirt on any high ranking official that you liked.

Over the course of the past year, Jegra had rummaged up the juiciest and most scandalous details about everyone she could possibly think to hold leverage over. Danica had helped create profiles for Jegra's worst potential enemies, ranking them from highest threat level to the lowest.

Naturally, Senator Targon Van Morgan topped the list. And his daughter, Callestra Van Morgan, came in at fourth place, after a couple of other corrupt politicians and one loyalist Drug Lord and business tycoon named Gerard Van Zallek.

Although the sale of recreational drugs at dispensaries for personal use wasn't outlawed on Dagon Prime, the unlawful distribution of them was explicitly illegal. Which meant all drugs, including the current favorite, Nividium, needed to go through proper channels.

Zallek, who had inherited his father's import and export business, was the first to realize the potential for a drug trade, whereby he owned an entire network of distributers and vendors. That's why Zallek's drug empire was so vast. He was the first to capitalize on commercial drug sales, turning what had been a small venture into a veritable empire.

Nowadays, he produced and manufactured his own narcotic commodities, and his drug Nividium was all the rage throughout the Commonwealth.

But even as he was a legitimate businessman, there was a recent surge in unlawful distribution of the drug that was getting onto the streets of nearly every major city across the sector—including Arena City. Jegra had suspected for several weeks now that it was Zallek himself who was leaking the drugs as a way to entice new customers to his dispensaries. And if it was, she was determined to shut him down.

Jegra rose out of the bath, her sodden robes sliding off her graceful figure and falling across the edge of the tub. Meleh'Kendar diverted his eyes from her naked body as she grabbed a cotton bathrobe off a nearby hook.

"I appreciate the update," she said, cinching up her sash and fastening it around her waist with a loose knot. "Inform Raphine I'll be needing her particular expertise this morning."

"Yes, Your Majesty," Meleh'Kendar replied, and with that, the holovid screen flicked and then disappeared into thin air.

A grunt escaped Danica's lips as she forced herself out of the tub and Jegra spun around in shock. "What do you think you're doing?"

"What does it look like?" Danica asked, her voice defensive. "I'm going with you."

"Like Helios you are!" Jegra took a step forward only to be stopped by Danica throwing up a firm hand.

"I've been useless to you for longer than anyone would care to acknowledge and I'm going out of my mind being cooped up in this place! Please, don't make me beg you. I need this."

"I thought you liked it here."

"I like being with you. But when you're gone, this place feels like a mausoleum. I need to get out and do something. Breathe the fresh air. Feel alive again."

Jegra hurried over and knelt by the tub. Taking Dani's hands in hers, she managed to calm her down and have her settle back into the bath. "I had no idea you felt that way."

Danica took a deep breath and folded her arms across her chest. "Yeah, well sharing my feelings isn't exactly my strong suit."

"Dani, look at me." She waited for Dani's beautiful amber eyes to fix on her brown ones. "Whatever it takes, we'll get through this together. And, I know, believe me, *I know* you didn't ask for my help or my sympathy. But you have it anyway. Just put that Dagon pride of yours away for two minutes and hear me out on this."

Danica reached up and moved a wad of wet hair that clung awkwardly to the side of her face, tucking it behind her ear. "I'm listening," she said, restlessly tapping her foot.

"I beg you. Please, let your body recover. We have all the time in the world to be together. To go on adventures. To get neck deep in trouble. Your people live hundreds of years and I hardly age at all now that I've been modified into..." she gestured at her Amazonian physique and continued, "this."

"I hate to admit it, but when you're right, you're right," Danica said after a long pause. She smiled and Jegra leaned in and kissed her forehead.

Danica unfolded her arms and smiled as she watched Jegra leave the room to prep for her secret mission. Before leaving her completely, though, Jegra paused in the doorway, looked over her shoulder, and blew Danica a kiss.

Dani pretended to catch it and smiled warmly. Jegra smiled back and then disappeared out the exit. After Jegra was gone, she waited as the large chamber doors latched shut and then, with a bit of effort, she clambered out of the tub. Her legs wobbled beneath her slender blue frame, and she hobbled over to where her crutches leaned against the wall, next to the robe Jegra had laid out for her.

Making haste, she threw on the robe without even bothering to tie it off. Swinging on her crutches, she raced across the room as quickly as she could and came to the oak dressers.

Danica tossed the crutches aside, not caring where they fell, and slumped down to her knees. Her fingers were already trembling as she rummaged hastily through her bottom drawer until she finally found the small inhaler of Nividium that she'd stashed there.

She promptly drew it out and put it to her lips. Inhaling deeply, she held it in and then gasped out. The effects of the drug took hold almost immediately and she fell onto her back, caught up in a state of pure euphoria.

Nividium was about the only thing that helped ease the pain of her recovery, the pain of her trauma, and provided a recreational outlet while she wasted away in this palace tower like some kind of barred princess.

Sprawled out across the cool black marble floor, replete with floral arabesque patterns and interlaced with fine silver throughout, she lay staring up vacantly at the mustard painted ceiling. Her pupils dilated and her thoughts became dream-like.

Danica shifted her hips to a more comfortable position, her white bathrobe slipping open allowing the pleated folds of the robe to frame her naked, indigo body like a pair of angel wings. Her eyes rolled back in her head, her back slowly arched, and her nipples stood erect on her supple breasts. Unable to hold back the euphoric sensation of what felt like an orgasm, she gasped, and a shiver of ecstasy shot up and down her entire body.

3

Rainbow colored light danced across the metallic hull of the *Chiron* as it traversed the stream. Inside the command center, Admiral Grendok was so deep in thought, he barely caught a glimpse of his first in command, Sub Commander Almathea, peering at him with her doe eyes.

Another time, another life, he may have very well asked her out on a date. But he was old and weary and the threat of a new war weighed him down. He was no longer the strapping young faun he'd once been, and didn't have time for such luxuries.

The admiral let out a sigh and closed his eyes. Opening them again, he gradually raised his gaze to find Almathea still staring at him. He tried to muster a smile, but found his lips frozen on his face.

"Is there something I can do for you, Sub Commander?" he finally asked, realizing she wasn't looking away.

"You look tired, sir. And it will be at least eight hours before we reach Dagon space. If the admiral would like to retire, I can hold down the fort until we arrive."

"I prefer to remain on the bridge, my dear," he replied. "I do my best thinking when I can gaze upon the heavenly beauties."

She blushed when he did not look away from her face. Not only did she blush, but she found her heart racing inside her chest as well. And although she'd nurtured a crush on the admiral for years, she'd never had the courage to reveal her true feelings for him. But now, in their time of great mourning, it seemed as though he could see right into her soul.

"As the admiral wishes," she said, smiling gently. Turning back toward the view portal, she crossed her arms behind her back and gazed out with him at rainbow swirl of stars. He wasn't wrong; it was hypnotic and somehow eased one's mind. The thoughts came easily and she ran through a thousand and one scenarios of how she might express her admiration and love of him that didn't involve her immediate dismissal.

No, Tabitha, she thought, reprimanding herself in her own mind. *There are more important things to concern yourself with now than whether or not the admiral wants to bone you.* Like the entire fate of the galaxy, for one. And for another, Grendok was never the kind of faun-folk to engage in dalliances with crew members. Thank the Bearded One. He is a gentleman, through and through. A noble satyr.

Eight and a half hours later, they dropped out of hyperspace and settled into a geosynchronous orbit over Dagon Prime, just behind the moon Thessalonica. It was Sub Commander Almathea's idea, however, that they jump into a stationary orbit behind Thessalonica to mask their presence from the Dagon security forces long enough for them to contact the empress. After all, they weren't entirely sure the emperor or the High Council would even hear them out. But Jegra would. It was in her nature to want to help. A strange trait of her species, he supposed.

"Approaching Thessalonica, sir. Should I hail the empress?"

"No, that won't be necessary. Just signal her that the Galliforn fleet commander wants to meet with her and that it's a matter of utmost urgency."

Grendok signed morning reports on his way to the shuttle bay. Leaving the *Chiron* in the care of Tabitha was easy. There was no one better suited to the job than she, and she was the best.

As he climbed aboard his shuttle, he handed the last glass touch-pad to the ensign trailing him and then looked for Tabitha. She was standing just a meter behind him and smiled when he looked upon her. "I take it you'll take good care of my ship?"

"As if she were my own," Tabitha replied with a small curtsy.

Grendok smiled, brushed down his uniform, and then turned and boarded his shuttle.

Sub Commander Tabitha Almathea watched the shuttle–shaped like a wooly sheep, in her estimation–rise up and slowly ease toward the opening bay doors. Once the doors were fully open, the shuttle penetrated the energy shields that kept the hull pressurized but allowed objects to pass through. The technology was based on negative mass liquid.

In a nutshell, such shield technology was built on a kind of dark-matter field that maintained its tension the same way dark matter keeps spinning galaxies sticking together, preventing them from falling apart by creating a kind of cohesion that, at the same time, has surface tension which can maintain pressure.

The easiest way to imagine it was to think of a bubble. If you were careful enough, you could pass through the film of a bubble without actually rupturing it. This was the same thing, but with more advanced physics.

And with the shield regulators helping make the negative mass liquid more static, it prevented the ship's pressure from evacuating into the vacuum of space whenever the bay doors were open.

A blue static ring engulfed the shuttle as it passed through the shields and then it was safely out the other side. As Grendok altered course, he looked out the view portal and saw Tabitha standing on the landing bay deck looking up at him. He nodded stoically and then turned his attention back to the controls.

He cleared the bow of the *Chiron* to find the orange, dusty ball of the moon, Thessalonica, glowing bright against the green and purple swirls of Dagon Prime.

Dagons, as a species, were rather large. The males were about six-feet three inches on average; the females were six-feet one. The satyrs of Galliforn, however, averaged around four-feet eleven inches in height, the tallest of them being around five-feet two. But Grendok had modified his clones with Dagon DNA in such a way that allowed them to grow to gigantic proportions. Jegra had bested one such clone in the arena three years ago.

The impossible feat had caught his attention and prompted him to keep close tabs on Jegra, the Gladiatrix of the Galaxy. It was just over a year ago that he'd decided to meet with her at Mardok, outside of the local pub, Scarback's, and had acquired the services of Raven Nightguard for the purpose of arranging the meet up.

Back then, he'd lied to Jegra about being a clone. But he could never be too careful revealing his true self or his motives for doing what he did. He found that a certain amount of anonymity went a long way in easing the tensions of those who assumed having certain allegiances meant having certain agendas. Not an entirely wrong summation, but if one didn't know of your allegiances, then they would be more willing to deal with you when it came to your personal agendas.

The control panel lit up letting him know that they'd breached the lower atmosphere and were now en route to Jegra's personal palace, which sat on the bluff overlooking Arena City.

For all intents and purposes, Arena City was *her* city. All commerce was related to the gladiatorial games, her reputation, and the fact that ever since she'd become empress, Arena City had grown substantially in both population and size.

Many new businesses wanting to exploit Jegra's fame had opened up; everything from travel agencies to new hotels, restaurants, and entertainment establishments wanted to profit from her image.

Of the new establishments, perhaps the most outlandish and bizarre was one called Mardok's Delight. It was a night club that hired Jegra lookalikes from both Dagon and Bre'lal species, spray painted the women bronze to look like Jegra, and then had them dance and strip for the patrons. Although, Grendok felt the bronze paint and poorly done wigs only caused them to look like cheap imitations, which, of course, they were.

Still, Mardok's Delight had attracted a certain amount of business, which is why, a year ago, he had bought it.

Through owning a business on Thessalonica, he was able to have eyes and ears where he needed it the most—right at the source of all the galactic excitement. This is how he kept such a close eye on the empress and her goings on. Even so, spying wasn't his intention. He just wanted enough information to be able to decide whether she was an ally or a threat. As it turned out, Jegra was the best ally to the people they could have ever hoped for. Not only was she compassionate toward all the races, but she didn't back down or cower from the emperor, which was seen as a huge boon throughout the galaxy. That meant there was now a gatekeeper that could keep the Lord Emperor's empire building in check.

And, truth be told, she'd done just that. The battle at Sector B-13 proved she could stand up to him. Now, with the emperor missing and the Dagon council declaring martial law, Jegra was perhaps the only ally they had left.

The sheep-like shuttle pod, with is bulbous body and slender, protruding cockpit, sank down out of the blue sky and maneuvered into position over the palace lawn.

The green grass and trees waved in the wake of his thrusters, but he set her down gently and then unbuckled the moment he felt the landing gear make contact with the ground.

Grendok wasted no time and rushed to the back of the ship where the landing ramp was already lowering. He paused and tapped his hoof impatiently as the ramp lowered the rest of the way. Once the ramp had opened completely, there was a hydraulic hiss and Grendok stepped out of the shuttle.

Scampering down the ramp, he looked out across the sward to find Jegra and her chief of security standing at the center of the lawn, waiting for him. She had on a burnt orange satin dress with a slit up the side that ran all the way up her hip and revealed her muscular thigh. Her chief of security was wearing a standard Thessalonica tan security uniform and a matching hat with a glossy, patent black rim.

He skipped up to them and then took a deep and reverent bow. When he rose up, he was shocked to find Jegra scowling at him with an almost disdainful look in her eye.

"Why you grubby, double-crossing, no-good swindler. You've got a lot of nerve coming here, after what you pulled."

Confused, Grendok cleared his throat and said, "Your Majesty, I can explain."

To his surprise, Jegra's stern face melted away into a mischievous grin and she laughed out loud. "I'm just messing with you, you old goat!"

Grendok sighed out in relief and watched as her chief of security subtly tipped his hat and then, without so much as uttering a word, took his leave.

"Come here you," Jegra said, scooping Grendok up in her arms and squeezing him tightly into her bosom as though he were a prized stuffed animal.

Grendok bleated softly as the air was literally squeezed out of him. Jegra held him to her cleavage longer than he'd have liked, but he tolerated it. After all, he'd been in far more unpleasant situations than this.

"If you don't mind, Your Majesty, I have urgent matters to discuss," he said in a muffled fashion as he spoke into the crevice between her breasts.

"Oh, yes, please," she said, putting him down. "It's been ages since I saw you last.

"Scarback's," Grendok said.

"Oh, then that was you?! Wonderful!"

"I'm afraid the news I bring is anything but wonderful, Your Majesty."

Jegra motioned for him to walk with her, and they leisurely strolled across the lawn together as he relayed the terrible news of recent events. Once they reached the palace pond, Jegra sat on a marble bench and offered him a seat beside her.

"I'm so sorry to hear about your people's loss. *Your* loss. I couldn't imagine losing my homeworld." She reached down and took his hand in hers. He looked down at her embrace and then back up at her eyes.

"You're too kind, my empress. I just thought you should know, war is coming. You should be ready for it when it arrives."

"Oh, I will be. But, perhaps..." she trailed off and looked up at the palace window in one of the upper floors of the five-story palace. She shook her head, as though she were shaking a thought from her mind and then looked back at him. "What do you know about Nividium?"

"Nividium?" he said, stroking his hoary beard. "It's a highly addictive recreational drug. It eases pain but also causes a feeling of ecstasy. It can cause hallucinations too. And in high doses, it is quite lethal. The Nividius flower, from which it is refined, is one of the most toxic plants in the galaxy. But Nividium can be quite soothing when using a vape stick that regulates its intake and prevents any threat of overdose."

Jegra smiled. "I meant, more along the lines of the business end of things."

"Oh, yes. That makes more sense," Grendok chuckled. "In that case, the Nividium trade is quite profitable. I dabble a bit in selling to the asteroid mining colonies, but anything within Dagon space is controlled by Gerard Van Zallek, a most unscrupulous fellow."

"I'm thinking of hi-jacking his operation. I've already ordered raids on today's shipments."

"Why in the galaxy would you want to do that?"

"Because, my dear noble satyr, without Dakroth's mad bloodthirst to keep the vultures at bay, every corrupt politician, noble person, and criminal entrepreneur is vying for power. As you are well aware, the coupe has left me powerless to do anything about it. So, I intend to outplay them at their own game."

"By becoming a drug kingpin?" Grendok asked curiously.

"It's not the drugs I care about. It's the trade empire he's built."

"And you intend to steal it out from under him?"

"On the contrary, Admiral, I intend for him to give it to me."

Grendok chuckled. "I'd love to see that. Which is why I've decided to help you, Your Excellency." Grendok bowed his head and then looked up to find her staring at him with a sheepish grin on her face.

"What is it?"

"How come I get the sneaking suspicion you already knew all about my plans? Plans which only three people were privy to."

"Your Majesty," he said, hopping off the marble bench and turning toward the empress. "It's my job to know everything. Down to the color of the underwear you chose to wear today. Which, by the way, is a nice tropical indigo."

"So, you have been spying on me?"

"Let's just say I excel at hearing the whispers."

"Indeed. But, be careful my dear Grendok," she said, slowly rising to her feet, "because even whisperers can sometimes get it wrong." She turned, the fine fabric hugging her perfectly formed ass like a second skin, and glanced over her shoulder at him. Smiling, she added, "I'm not wearing any underwear."

It was the same mischievous grin as before, which told him she was telling the truth. "My sincerest apologies, Your—"

"Call me Majesty one more time and I'll sock you in the mouth. My friends call me Jegra. And you'll do the same."

Grendok's furry muzzle spread apart with a wide grin. He hadn't quite been sure what she considered him to be to her: foe, ally, or pain in the ass. Now, he was confident that their allegiance would be the exact thing he needed to prepare for the coming war.

"Join me inside," Jegra said, nodding toward the palace doors, which overlooked the garden and led into the foyer. "We have much to discuss…in private."

"Yes, my…Jegra." He bowed again and then skipped after her, hopping stride for stride alongside her shadow.

4

Callestra Van Morgan's magenta eyes flashed hot pink with rage, wisps of energy seeping out of them like smoke. "What do you mean the invasion forces have crossed the neutral zone and entered into Dagon space?"

The officer stammered but was too nervous to spit it out. Impatient, she reached out and clenched her fist around the officer's collar, yanked him close and then shoved him out of the way as if he were no good to her.

"If H'aaztre thinks he can overstep his bounds with me, by using the Dagon Empire, then he's sorely mistaken."

"Admiral Morgan," the officer said, gulping nervously for fear of any further reprisal. "H'aaztre is viewed as a god to so many. If the people hear about his return, we'll face opposition from the religious sects."

"That's why my father declared martial law, you pleb. To ensure the people wouldn't find out about this imposter's claim to be the divine H'aaztre. Until then, let's humor him, shall we?"

Callestra spun in her heeled boots and locked her hands behind her back. After giving it a moment's thought, she added, "Send thirty ships to the border to intercept the invasion fleet. We'll hold them there until we can figure out H'aaztre's plans."

"Yes, ma'am," replied the bridge officer, avoiding eye contact with the admiral. He then scurried off like a dog with his tail tucked between his legs.

Callestra's outfit was unconventional for a Dagon commander. She didn't like the drabness of the formal uniform and instead had something a little more revealing custom made to suit her tastes. Far more revealing, in fact. Her "uniform" was basically shoulder pads, a white strap across her chest, a white strap across her groin, and some additional straps to hold those straps in place.

It wasn't a dominatrix's outfit per se, but it was made in a similar fashion, cut from the finest white leather, and it could hardly contain her dark indigo skin.

Her heels clacked on the korridium alloy floor as she cut across the command center. Looking up at the view portal, she watched the glowing orange sand ball called Thessalonica hanging in the distance.

The brief glint of something hiding in the shadow of the moon caught her eye and she immediately issued orders. "Condition red. There's a bloody ship out there. How did we miss that? Somebody had better get me a damn scan of the dark side of that moon, or there will be hell to pay!"

There was increased chatter as the lights flickered to a soft, pulsating red glow and the sound of the red alert issued up and down the corridors of the ship. Someone was hiding on the far side of Thessalonica, and she was going to find out who it was.

"Ma'am, you're not going to believe this, but it's the *Chiron*."

"What's the flagship of the Galliforn people doing here?"

"Convening with the empress, perhaps."

"I highly doubt that," Callestra balked. She couldn't bring herself to believe that a satyr would risk starting a war by coming to Dagon Prime. No, something else was up. She was sure of it. "Bring us around, full thrusters. I want a visual on that ship ASAP."

Just as her ship, the *Verlag*, swiveled into position, there was a mysterious distortion off their front bow. A mirage-like ripple bent and wobbled in an empty patch of space and, out of thin air, the *Shard* manifested before them.

"This is Thessalonica space, territory of the Imperatrix of the Dagon Empire, you have sixty seconds to turn around or be destroyed."

Infernal Nyctan cloaking technology, Callestra thought to herself. Why they ever let Jegra keep that technology was beyond her. *It is cowardly to hide in the shadows like a would-be assassin,* she felt. "This is Admiral Callestra Van Morgan of the Imperial Fleet. You will desist with this meaningless posturing and let us pass. In the name of the Empire's security, you will comply." Secretly, she dared them to test her resolve.

The holovid screen aboard Callestra's ship, the *Verlag,* flickered to life and the face of one Captain Lianica Blackstar appeared.

Callestra smiled with strained politeness. "Captain, nice to see you again."

Lianica matched Callestra's strained smile with one of her own. "Indeed. It's been ages since we were at the academy together. By the way, congratulations on your promotion. Unexpected yet pleasant news, to be sure."

"Not so unexpected when you look at my service record, I should think. Anyway," Callestra said, waving her hand and brushing the topic aside for another time, "to what do I owe the honor of your little call?"

"I'm afraid I'm under explicit orders to prevent any ships from leaving or entering Thessalonica, Admiral. The empress has erected a blockade to crack down on illegal drug smuggling."

"Even one of your own ships?" Callestra clicked her tongue in annoyance at the mere suggestion.

"As you know, even friendly ships are banned when an imperial blockade order has been issued," Lianica said without batting an eye. "Apologies. But as admiral of the fleet, you wouldn't want us breaking protocol, now, would you?"

"Right," Callestra replied tersely. She smiled at Lianica, who had out maneuvered her. "But I want you to send me an updated report ASAP."

"As you wish, Vice Admiral," Lianica replied. She returned Callestra's smile and then the glowing screen vanished and everything went dark.

"That bitch!" Callestra growled in a low voice.

"Ma'am, shall I hail your father?"

"My father?" Callestra asked, turning to the officer who'd suggested it. She scowled at him till he broke eye contact. "My father is busy with overseeing the state of emergency down on the surface. Up here, my command is supreme." Scanning all the faces of the crew with wild eyes that suggested a hint of mental instability, she screamed, "Do I fucking make myself clear?"

"Yes, ma'am," a chorus of voices responded.

She paced the floor in her boots and then stopped and let out a sigh. "Ease back to a safe distance and hold position just outside of the Thessalonica defense perimeter."

"Yes, ma'am." After following orders, the same officer timidly asked, "What do we do now?"

"We wait and see what all this is about. Or, more accurately, you wait and see what all this is about and report to me if anything happens. I'll be in my quarters, if anyone should need me."

When Callestra returned to her quarters, she found a handsome Dagon man waiting for her. Naked. In bed.

She laughed and flung herself onto the bed and into his arms. After kissing his lips, she said in a sultry voice, "My dear Zallek, what brings you to my bed chamber?"

"Why, the privilege of fucking the galaxy's most elegant noblewoman, of course."

"Oh," she said, somewhat surprised, pulling away from one of his attempted kisses. "You think you can just show up uninvited, rattle off a few compliments, and get lucky?"

"Depends," he said, reaching down between her sweaty thighs and sliding his hand into her pants. "How thirsty is the vice admiral of the fleet?"

"How can I be thirsty when I'm already soaking wet?" she laughed, letting him feel between her legs.

Gerard Van Zallek raised his glistening fingers back to his face and examined the residue. "Indeed," he replied with a smile.

Callestra took his hand in hers and proceeded to suck off her own nectar from his fingers.

Before she could even finish, he took her firmly in his arms and began kissing her neck, adding several small bites to tantalize her all the more.

"You're so tense," Zallek said, rubbing his light blue fingers across her dark blue neck. "What has you so wound up?"

"Just work, my luv. Nothing you need to concern yourself with."

"If you say so. But, just know, I'm good for more than just an occasional fling. I can also listen, should you ever want to talk."

Callestra laughed. "Don't act like you care, my dear Zallek. We both know you merely seek insider knowledge into military patrols so that you can continue your smuggling operations. You could care less about my little ole feelings."

Zallek shrugged. "Perhaps. But, right now, what I want more than any of that is your perfectly formed body on top of mine."

Callestra laughed at the bad line and sat up in bed. Straddling his waist, she tossed her hair over her shoulder and then reached back with her hands to unfasten her one-piece dominatrix outfit.

The whole thing slid off her body with ease, liberating a taut abdomen and revealing dark blue nipples that stood erect on her melon sized breasts. "Tell me, Zallek. Do you have any on you?"

"Why, my luv, I thought you'd never ask." Stretching to the small bedside drawer next to them, he opened it, reached inside, and pulled out a Nividium vape stick.

Callestra leaned down and took a hit, inhaling deeply. Zallek followed her lead, taking a hit from the same vape stick, and leaned back in bed with her.

As they grew high together, they sank beneath the covers of the bed and began to make love. It wasn't real love, but it felt glorious nonetheless. Especially with the Nividium amplifying everything tenfold.

In fact, each orgasm she experienced felt as though she'd entered a whole new dimension of space and time. The drug was that good.

The sex was a bit short for her taste, but she felt satisfied and drifted into a peaceful, drug laden sleep. As soon as she'd slipped off, however, Zallek carefully slipped out of bed. Trying not to make a sound, he fetched his things and put on his clothes.

From his pocket, he fished out a data stick and then went over to the admiral's holovid console. Lighting it up, he placed the stick onto the machine's surface and the circuitry began to glow, pulsing like living veins made of energy.

The translucent blue screen showed the incrementally expanding green bar of a file upload in progress. If this program worked, it would feed him the coordinates of the entire imperial fleet in real time. That way he could avoid any and all patrols, random checkpoints, and cargo searches.

"Zallek," a blithe voice called from over his shoulder. "Come back to bed. I need you."

He glanced over in time to see Callestra fall back onto the bed, unaware that she'd even called out to him. Ignoring her supplication, he turned his attention back to the file upload. Finally, the computer chimed. He quickly swept the data stick up in his hand and slipped it back into his shirt pocket.

Gerard Van Zallek stood over Callestra's bed admiring how stunning she truly was. He would have liked to stay and play a while longer, but he had other urgent matters to attend to.

A fresh shipment of Nividium was going out today and with the trade routes on high alert due to the rumored invasion, he didn't know when another transport would be coming in. Which made this shipment his highest priority.

Of course, fucking Targon Van Morgan's daughter just to stick it to the old man could wait for another day. After all, she was right. He didn't love her. He was merely using her for sex and for revenge. After all, it was Senator Targon's bill to make distribution of Nividium illegal that put a damper on his business. But it was a minor obstacle. Now, with this data mining worm uploaded to Callestra's computer, he could avoid getting caught altogether.

With a smug grin, he turned and fetched his jacket off a nearby leather armchair, threw it on, and then exited Callestra's bedroom. As he stepped out into the white light of the corridor, he made sure nobody was around so as not to draw any unnecessary attention to himself.

After slipping out of Callestra's bedroom, he headed to the teleportation room and set the coordinates to transport down to his warehouse on Dagon Prime. "Be seeing you again, sweetheart," he said as the teleport began and yellow light engulfed him.

A shiver caused Callestra to stir and, half awake, she lethargically reached over to where Zallek should be only to find cool, empty sheets. She forced her eyes open and looked over to discover he was no longer there.

Callestra sat up in bed and looked around the room. He wasn't anywhere. "Prick," she said through a yawn, stretching her arms above her head.

She didn't like being taken advantage of. She wasn't just some booty call he could come hit any time he was in the mood.

The light from the computer monitor caught her attention. She slowly rose from bed and went over to it. After all, it should have automatically gone back to sleep mode after being used. But it was still on for some reason.

She tapped the screen and an upload bar appeared with a dialog box that said: upload complete.

"That asshole!" Callestra muttered angrily.

Zallek had uploaded a malicious file into her computer and now she would need to purge her system. Luckily, there was no accessing the ship's main systems without proper security clearance, so the only things Zallek had access to were standard reports.

She opened up the coding to see what the program was reading and discovered it was merely relaying ship deployments.

"Ah, smart," she said, impressed that he'd thought of it. "Trying to avoid being caught. That makes me wonder though, what's so important that you're trying to hide it, Zallek?"

She manually shut down her system and then turned to look out her tall view portal. Thessalonica hung in the distance, the *Chiron* and the *Shard* flying in formation next to one another.

She was getting fed up not knowing what was going on around her. First, she was denied access to Thessalonica, and now Zallek was messing about on her ship.

If anyone was going to lose control of the situation, it wasn't going to be her.

But the more she thought about not having a hold on the situation, the dizzier she seemed to get. Her breathing became shallow and the room began to spin. Her heart pounded in her chest so hard she could hear it in her ears and, before she knew it, she was having a full-on panic attack.

"Fuck!" she screamed out, balling up her fists. Her eyes flashed magenta and then bright pink and wisps of energy began to seep out of the corners of her eyes like smoke. Even the Dygra crystal inside her chest pulsed red, lighting up her indigo skin.

She quickly got ahold of herself and took a deep breath. She couldn't afford to go off the rails now. Not at this critical moment.

After getting dressed, she grabbed her workout clothes and started out the door to the training room. She needed to work out her stress there; that was the only thing that seemed to help when she got like this.

But something came to mind as she entered the doorway, and she paused. Zallek had made a big mistake betraying her trust. If he only would have asked her to help him, she may have considered it–for a small cut. But instead he went behind her back and comprised her security and her trust. For that, he'd need to be punished. She smiled deviously and then turned and went back into her room, tossed the duffle bag of gym clothes on the floor, and sat down at the computer console.

Although she hated the new empress, she knew that Jegra didn't much appreciate the drug trade happening under her nose on Thessalonica. That's why, to teach Zallek a lesson, Cassera went ahead and typed in the coordinates of where Zallek was making the pickup in Arena City. Just an anonymous tip alerting the empress as to Zallek's illegal activities. She smiled to herself as she hit send. It was the precise amount of trouble he deserved for his betrayal.

774

5

Glinting silver against the backdrop of a dusty moon, the *Shard* maintained its position in defiance of the *Verlag* and Callestra's bold attempt to enter sovereign space in violation of Dagon security protocol. According to military law, whenever there was a blockade, even Imperial ships needed authorized clearance to enter the no-fly zones.

Additionally, Thessalonica belonged to the empress. Its territory remained as an independent sovereign nation within Dagon Prime's jurisdiction. As such, it was off-limits to any military and political proceedings, without the empress's explicit approval.

Jegra had once likened Thessalonica to the Vatican, a sovereign nation within a nation back on her homeworld. But Lianica hadn't really understood the reference. Regardless, by christening it an independent territory, she was able to create her own laws.

The first official law she had written was to make Thessalonica into a safe haven for mods. For any Dagon who was deemed impure or modified, either because of a medical condition, an injury, or because of deliberate defiance of state law, Thessalonica would act as a home. These Dagons were viewed as tainted, impure, or unfit for acceptance into normal Dagon society.

It was the boldest move Jegra had made insofar as her political standing was concerned, but to everyone's surprise, there was zero opposition to the law on the homeworld. It seemed that even the Dagon High Council wanted to see it passed. Not only did it make them look good in the eye of the people by allowing the empress this charitable act, but it gave them the perfect excuse to relocate the deplorables. A win-win in everybody's book, so to speak.

Now, several months after the bill had passed, Jegra was accepting the last of the refugees with open arms. Not only had they brought new business and industry onto the dusty moon, but because there were so many migrants, one million and counting, Thessalonica had grown exponentially in a matter of months.

Even the desert town Mardok, known for its ore mining and being a hub for black market trade and smuggling, doubled in size almost overnight. The only other oasis town, on the dark side of the moon, simply known as Sabi, which meant "lonely" in Dagoni, expanded by several thousand. Meanwhile, Arena City had nearly tripled in size.

Currently, down on the moon, construction had commenced building a high-speed maglev train to connect the three cities. The one from Sabi space port to Arena City was the first on the docket with another line from Sabi to Mardok and back to Arena City by the end of the cycle.

Lianica had thought Jegra's suggestion of building public transport was genius. Not only did it supply plenty of jobs for the new refugees, but it would strengthen the overall economies of the otherwise three most backwater cities in the galaxy.

It was also the reason that Jegra had ordered Lianica to monitor the borders. Anything illegal could disrupt the already delicate balance of the Thessalonican economy. And she couldn't risk a civil uprising or race riots or black-market allegiances that would offset the fine-tuned equilibrium of the moon.

Moons, unlike planets, had limited resources. And most of those resources needed to be mined out of the ground. The influx of refugees had brought new workers onto the moon to do the dirty grunt work, yet most of the miners still held old fashioned, somewhat racially charged, views on outsiders joining their labor unions.

At a time like this, when tension was at the highest, Jegra needed everyone to work together peacefully. Which is why the empress frequently had her imperial enforcers run weekly inspections and quality checks on all Thessalonican industry. She even accompanied some of the checks, just to make her presence known.

Lianica could see that Jegra regretted the fact that such overreach was necessary. It was slightly authoritarian, but no more so than strictly managed corporations on any other world.

The fact remained, however, Jegra had inherited the role, so she needed to play the part or risk losing control. And if the empress let things degrade into civil chaos, people would revolt, tap the gas lines, steal gas right out of the pipes, or set fire to the whole enterprise. That was not acceptable.

So far, the empress remained popular with her people. The citizens of Thessalonica didn't mind her butting into their affairs and showing up in the streets from time to time to greet fans and converse with the locals. For them, it was refreshing to have a leader interested in their daily lives. It made them feel a connection with her that many other leaders throughout the Commonwealth lacked.

"Captain, we are receiving a level-three encrypted communiqué from the palace. It's the empress," Lieutenant Brei'Alas informed her, the lieutenant's voice snapping Lianica out of her contemplative state.

"I'll take the message in my ready room," Lianica said, rising from her command chair and briskly cutting across the bridge with long strides.

The doors to the room parted and accepted Lianica inside then quickly slid shut again behind her. Taking a seat at her desk, she flicked on the holovid then leaned back in her chair and crossed her legs.

The blue hologram flicked on, rising up from the glossy black glass surface of her desk, and Jegra was standing beside Admiral Grendok, looking at her. Lianica had heard rumors of the infamous satyr, but she'd never met him personally.

"Admiral," Lianica said, nodding reverently. "I'm sorry to hear about your people's unfathomable loss."

"I appreciate the sentiment, Captain, but I'm afraid now is not the time for mourning. You see, an invasion fleet has just breeched Dagon space. And if they're planning to do to your world what they did to ours, then we must be ready for them."

"Why wasn't I informed of this?"

"You're being informed now," Jegra said. "Admiral Callestra Van Moran has dispatched a third of the fleet to head off the invading army, but it will likely do little good."

Grendok brushed down his uniform and cleared his throat. "We're dealing with a military force unlike anything we've ever encountered before, Captain. They destroyed Galliforn, our entire defense grid, and nearly eighty percent of our fleet before I could make the hyperjump back to my planet. This invasion force doesn't care about resources or power. It only cares about one thing: your utter and total destruction."

"Understood. And you believe we're next?"

"Enemies like this don't often take no for an answer, Captain. As far as I'm concerned, our hands are tied in the matter. We have no choice but to make ourselves ready so that the rest of the galaxy doesn't face the same tragic fate as Galliforn."

Jegra nodded her head. "The admiral is confident they will attempt to knock out Dagon Prime next, as it is the dominant superpower in this part of the galaxy. Once Dagon Prime falls, the rest of the galaxy will be ripe for the taking."

"If Dagon Prime falls, there'll be nothing to stand in the way of their military forces," Brei'Alas said, letting out a startled gasp.

"That's right," Jegra replied, nodding at the lieutenant. "If they are anything like other conquerors, their first tactic will be to break the will of the people. They will pillage, burn, and destroy with abandon. Those that survive will be left destitute, without technology, and will wither and die or turn to the warm embrace of the enemy, exchanging their loyalty for scraps, and ally themselves with an evil power that will effectively diminish our chances of a successful overthrow. This is a doomsday scenario, Lianica, and I want you and Grendok to spearhead the resistance."

"What of Vice Admiral Morgan? Should we not at least confer with her regarding our plans?"

"You let me deal with Callestra. Right now, I want you and the admiral to set up a war room here, at the palace. The *Chiron* will act as the flagship in this operation seeing as the *Shard* lacks any offensive capabilities to lead the charge."

"Yes, ma'am," Lianica said. "Just..." she paused, looking out the window at the stars, then turned back to the holovid projection, "how are we going to build a fleet big enough to defend against an armada capable of wiping out entire civilizations?"

"We're already working on that. I'll fill you in on the details when you arrive. For now, just get down here."

"One more thing, Your Grace…how is she?" Lianica's voice was soft and contrite. She didn't want to overstep her bounds, but at the same time she was scared out of her mind to have to face the woman she had betrayed.

Jegra could see the remorseful look in Lianica's eyes. "If I'm being truthful, I haven't told her yet. It has nothing to do with the mission. Until we can wrap our heads around what's going on right here and now, I'm going to ask that you shelve that issue for a later date."

"Is that an order, Your Grace?"

Jegra shot her a sharp look. "Damn straight it's an order."

"Yes, ma'am," Lianica said, crossing her right fist over her left breast and bowing slightly in a customary salute.

Jegra folded her arms and held Lianica's gaze until the image of the empress and the admiral cut out. Lianica swiveled in her chair and let out a sigh. She wasn't looking forward to having to face Danica. Not after what she'd done. As she gazed out at the stars, contemplating her sins, she lost herself in their distant glow.

"You did what?!" Danica could hardly catch her breath, since she was so irate. The pacing back and forth didn't help matters, but it was all she could do so that her hands wouldn't tremble with rage as a surge of adrenaline kept her revving past the red line.

"I know it's hard to hear, but I wanted you to hear it from me first instead of finding out later and then resenting me for not having said anything. I'm setting up the war room here," Jegra said, fanning her hand behind her and motioning at the whole of the palace. "You knew this."

"Yeah, but I didn't know you'd invite *her* into our home. That two-faced bitch handed me over to Dakroth to be tortured, abused, and manipulated in the worst imaginable ways. I almost died! More than once! And you just welcome her into our home, arms wide open?"

"Dani, please. It's not like that. This is strictly business. And, if you're feeling up to it, you can hash it out with her when she arrives. Or not. It's entirely up to you."

"She'll be lucky if I don't claw out her eyes and tear off that pretty little head of hers." Danica shook her hands and continued to paced the floor in a tizzy, trying to talk herself down from the sudden flood of anxiety, but it was doing little good.

"I'd rather you not," Jegra said in all seriousness. "We need her."

"No. *You* need her," Danica hissed, wagging her finger in Jegra's face. "I can live without her. Trust me."

"All right. But I just thought you deserved to know. I'll be sure to mention it to her that she ought to steer clear."

"You do that." Danica folded her arms in a sign of protest. "Because if I so much as cross paths with *that snake* I'm going to skin her alive and feed her to the sandworms."

"Message received, loud and clear," Jegra said, raising her hands defensively and surrendering to Danica's will.

Unable to calm down, Danica puffed out a disgruntled gasp of air, and then stormed out of the foyer where Jegra had ambushed her with the dreadful news. She limped down the long corridor, slammed the door at the end, and didn't bother looking back.

At least Jegra was smart enough to give her a bit of space. But she was having a hard time as it was. Her recovery was taking longer than expected and she still couldn't get a solid night's sleep. Not without seeing that dreadful red face in her nightmares. The face of her tormentor, Ishtar Bantu.

To make matters worse, her hip and leg were already throbbing with pain and she couldn't seem to get her emotions in check. Which only made her feel that much worse as her Dagon pride constantly berated her for an emotional instability that bordered on mental illness, in her mind.

After roaming the palace halls, Danica found a dark, unfinished room which only had a lonely sofa with a sheet on it. The sofa sat in front of a fireplace and the drapes to the room were drawn, so the light was subdued. Danica plopped down onto the sofa without removing the sheet and drawing out her vape stick, she examined it for a moment. Putting it to her lips, she hit the button and inhaled deeply.

The Nividium flooded into her lungs, making her feel a thousand times better. She leaned back onto the sofa, exhaled, and then let the soothing high of the drug bring her down, slowly, like a feather wafting back and forth upon a gentle summer breeze.

After another drag on the vape stick, the euphoric effect of the Nividium truly began to work its magic and her body became so relaxed that even if she were being tortured, she wouldn't be able to feel it. In fact, she wished she had had the stuff when Ishtar Bantu was cutting her open and turning her inside out for the thrill of it. At least then the agony would have been somewhat bearable.

Right now, though, Nividium was the only thing that helped her escape the terrible pain-filled memories that haunted her. It gave her reprieve from the torture she'd endured, and the betrayal she'd experienced at the hands of a man she'd devoted her whole life to. The drugs helped wash away all that trauma, all the pain, and all the unpleasant memories and replaced them with a sensation of pure ecstasy.

At last, her breathing returned to its standard rhythm and her heart no longer raced so hard that it felt as though it would tear out of her chest. The aching in her body gave way to waves of pleasure that trickled through her extremities, causing her to gasp out loud as she rode the high as far as it would take her.

She ran her fingers down her neck and breast, letting the amplified sensation send tantalizing tingles down through every nerve ending on her skin. Her fingertip stopped at her erect nipple, and its hardness signaled her to the fact that she, all of a sudden, had the deepest urge to fuck someone.

With nobody around to appease her, however, she let out a disappointed groan and took another hit of Nividium. "Oh, my Gilded Lord," she said as she exhaled. *It was glorious.*

She now understood why Nividium was banned in the military. The soldiers would never keep to their duties, they'd all be off someplace getting high all day long. It was really quite that good. All your troubles just seemed to melt away, leaving only the feeling of ecstasy, pleasure, and contentment.

When she went to take yet another hit, the vape pen beeped at her, sending the warning that she had exceeded her limit. Having an automatic failsafe like this ensured that people didn't overdose, as high concentrations of Nividium could be fatally toxic.

"You bloody infernal mechanized piece of shit," Danica grumbled, letting the vape pen slip from her limp hand. Reaching down her shirt with her other arm, she dug around in between her cleavage and drew out a brand new Nividium vape stick.

This one, however, had been hacked so that it would think her biosignature was that of someone else, thereby allowing her to keep imbibing the drug. Although high concentrations of the drug could prove lethal, two sticks wouldn't be *too* risky. At least, that's what she told herself as she took another drag on the new vape pen.

Danica lay back onto the sofa and tried to hold it in. But this time it was more difficult and burned her lungs some. She coughed on it and tried to mask her cough with a laugh, because she was too high to care whether or not her body was attempting to reject the drug.

She examined the vape stick in her hand as though she was seeing it for the first time and then laughed again before taking one final hit. Smoke wafted from her open mouth as she lay back and allowed herself to slip into a psychoactive stupor. She stared with half sunken eyelids up at the dancing shadows on the ceiling and pondered their philosophical significance.

6

"**I still don't** understand what we're doing out here," Angellyk said, griping about their current job. Kregor spun in his co-pilot's chair and shot her a sharp look then turned to Raven, who manned the flight controls of the *Skywend*.

"Seriously, what's she doing here again?"

Raven laughed softly. "Don't worry, she can be trusted. I'll vouch for her."

"Yeah, don't get your panties up in a bunch, big guy," Angellyk said, leaning forward and placing her hand on Kregor's bulky shoulder, giving him a firm squeeze. "I'm perfectly harmless."

Kregor swiveled back around in his seat, breaking free of her irritating touch, and let out a disgruntled puff of air. "Look, lady, I'm sure you mean well and all, but until you prove yourself to me and this crew, I'll be watching you."

"You do what you gotta, big guy," Angellyk said, drawing her hand back defensively. "But like it or not, I'm here to stay." She dusted her hands off, as if to say she was done arguing with him.

Raven merely glanced at Kregor with a controlled smile. Ever since inviting her ex to be part of their crew, Kregor had been keenly suspicious of the woman. Looking back over her shoulder at Angie, she shrugged. Angellyk puffed up her cheeks and then leaned back in her chair to pout. She folded her arms and crossed her legs as she gazed out the portal window.

From the corridor there was a loud clangor, a rattling, the sound of an electrical pop, and a string of disgruntled cussing.

"Graddack ben de'kek vak mortigrak!" Gyllek's voice grumbled in fluent Dagoni.

"You all right out there?" Raven asked without looking away from her console. She knew that whenever Gyllek began cursing in Dagoni, things weren't going too well. As Gyllek had often reminded her, she only ever liked to curse in the royal tongue because it seemingly had a way of making one's foul-mouthed profanities come off sounding sweeter than silk candy.

"Fine, Captain. Nothing I can't handle."

"You sure? With Skuld taking some shore leave back on his homeworld, I thought maybe you'd be a bit short handed. Feel free to use Angellyk as you see fit."

Angellyk sat straight up, eyes wide, and shook her head in a slow, but definite, *no thank you*. Although the hulking Dragonian was gruff with her, that quirky girl downright scared her. For all her training as a Voroxian priestess, learning how to read and manipulate people so as to serve the greater purpose, Gyllek was the one person she could never get a read on.

"I appreciate the offer, but I'm sure she'd just mess things up worse, Captain."

Raven turned toward Angellyk to see her face turning a pale shade of green in nervous anticipation. "Go help the kid. Please."

"All right. But you're making it up to me later. Dinner. My place."

Raven did her best not to roll her eyes and turned back to navigating the ship. Although the computer handled the bulk of the calculations, she liked to tap in with her neuro interface and find short-cuts that the computer neglected due to safety protocols programmed in by overly cautious engineers who had never traveled outside of their labs let alone traversed the stream. But she relied on first-hand experience and knew every micron of space between Dagon Prime, the Cove, and Nyctan. And with her bio-electronic and neurochemical enhancements, she could calculate her way through an asteroid field in real time, if she wanted.

Angellyk stepped into the junction of the corridor outside the bridge to find several of the wall panels and one ceiling panel removed and stacked neatly along the edge of the corridor. Even though there were tools strewn about and a lot of candy wrappers littering the floor, there was no sign of Gyllek anywhere.

"Hey, twerp, where'd you go?"

Unexpectedly, a head popped down from overhead, manifesting in the open ceiling area. Upside down, with neon-green hair that dangled about like an inside-out umbrella, a teenage girl's face stared at her from behind reflective soldering goggles.

Without saying a word, the young girl huffed in annoyance and withdrew back into the shaft overhead.

Angellyk stepped up to the opening and brushed past a series of wires and cables that were dangling out as if she were pushing through a thick grove of vines deep within an electrical jungle. "What is it you're doing, again?"

A voice echoed down the maintenance duct, and said, "I'm installing a microphase neurocognitive interface."

"A micro-what-phaser?" Angellyk asked, rubbing her chin and cocking her head in a mystified manner. She wasn't stupid, but when it came to technical stuff, she was at a loss.

"A device so that the *Skywend* can be navigated mentally. That means by using one's thoughts and mind," Gyllek replied, the last part sounding a tad patronizing. "Assuming the person has the proper modding," she added, "theoretically, they could control every aspect of the ship at the speed of thought."

"Is that even possible? I mean, wouldn't the feedback from the ship's quantum computer overload a mental interface?"

"Under normal circumstances, yes," replied Gyllek. "But I've installed eight cyclic buffers and a static noise filter to prevent any feedback from overloading a neuro-link. But the operator would need some pretty advanced neuro-interfacing technology to even handle such a system."

"I think we both know someone with the hardware to take on such a challenge." Angellyk looked back over her shoulder toward the bridge, her thoughts settling on Raven.

When she turned around, the face was back. This time, right in front of her. She would have startled, except for the fact that Gyllek was so peculiar you instinctively froze to take in whatever it was you were looking at. Of course, Gyllek was harmless. Unless you were going up against her online in the Digital Silk, what the techies called the cyberverse.

"On second thought, maybe you could be of some use to me after all. Hand me that plasma welding pen…if you don't mind."

The reflective pause before the "if you don't mind" part suggested Gyllek had to will herself to tack on the nicety, but at least she was trying.

"Is this it?" asked Angellyk, picking up a pen-like object.

"Lucky guess," Gyllek said, holding out her gloved hand.

Tight leather work gloves with the fingers cut out hugged each of Gyllek's dainty hands snuggly. She received the welding pen and disappeared back up into the maintenance duct. Angellyk doubted anyone else but the petite girl would fit in the confined spaces of the ship's maintenance access ducts; certainly not her own wide, green ass.

"Out of curiosity, how old are you, Gyllek? If you don't mind my asking."

"I don't mind," the girl called back. "I'm eighteen, three months, seven days, and twenty-two hours old. I could give you the minutes and the seconds too, but the captain has informed me that it's a bit of an overkill."

"I see. And what of your species? You seem, almost feline to me. But apart from hyper-intelligent Vorgothian cats, I don't know any species like you in the entire commonwealth."

"My people, the cat folk of Baast, come from a primitive world called Valandra Prime, just beyond the Outer Rim. Like Jegra, I too was abducted by slavers when I was young. But instead of being sold into the gladiatorial fights, I was sold into mining labor on the asteroid colony Brexis. As it turned out, however, I was a fast study when it came to their outdated computer systems and figured out how to hack the security protocols. Of course, I was caught, but instead of being jettisoned out the airlock, they gave me a job as their chief digital security consultant. Raven found me several months later and recruited me. And, well, the rest is history."

"Sounds like you've led an interesting life."

"Not really. Until I met the captain, I was stuck behind a dusty old desk surrounded by outmoded tech in a dingy old room on a smelly mining asteroid. It wasn't exactly the life I dreamed of. Which is why I took Raven up on her offer. And with the parts she lent me, I was able to automate the station's security and just left."

"You simply up and left?"

"Yup. Just walked right out the doors. Nobody ever said anything. In fact, the dimwits that ran that station probably still think I'm showing up to my shift every day."

Angellyk chuckled. "Well, you are an interesting one, Gyllek. I'll give you that."

The cat-like girl dropped from the ceiling and landed on the floor beside Angellyk, her metal grav boots clapping against the plating with a heavy *clank*. Gyllek gradually rose up and dusted off her hands. "There, that ought to do it."

"You're finished? So soon?"

"Yeah. Why?"

"I was just having fun getting to know you."

"Oh." Gyllek turned and started gathering her things without saying so much as another word. After she'd put everything back in the tool box, she looked at the loose wires and the dislodged plating. "You mind helping put all this back? I have to make a routine check of the engines. Normally Skuld would do it, but since he's not here, the responsibility has fallen to me."

"Sure, I'll take care of it. No problem," Angellyk answered, smiling at Gyllek who still had on her reflective goggles. Gyllek handed her the toolbox and then turned and pranced away, disappearing around the bend at the end of the corridor. "Well, that's gratitude for you."

Angellyk turned and looked at the tangle of wires, cords, and loose cables and let out a long drawn out sigh.

"I just don't like her. No offense, Captain. She's so..."

"Permission to speak freely, Lieutenant Commander."

"Green."

"She's Bre'lal. Of course, she's green."

"But all they ever want to do is have sex."

"I'm sure that's just a stereotype."

"I'm just worried about ship's morale is all."

"Is that so?" Raven asked, looking at Kregor with a suspicious, yet slightly amused squint.

"It's true. With a woman like that roaming about, I'm worried that some of the crew will become distracted."

"You don't need to worry about me. Angellyk and I broke up over very clearly defined differences of opinion. Something that hasn't likely changed in the years we've been apart."

"I didn't mean you, Captain," Kregor said apologetically.

"Surely you didn't mean Gyllek?" Raven asked, perplexed by who else would be distracted by her ex. Then it dawned on her. He meant himself. She laughed. This caused him to raise a scaly green eyebrow. "Oh, I see."

"What?"

"You have a little crush on her, don't you?"

"Me? Don't be ridiculous. Not in a million cycles. It wouldn't be appropriate," Kregor said in his typically gruff manner. His nictitating eyelids flashed across his reptilian eyes as he shot the captain a surprised look.

"You have my permission to bang my ex-wife," Raven said half-jokingly. Although she was only teasing him, she really didn't think it was any of her business who Angellyk chose to sleep with. But Kregor was so honor-bound that he wouldn't likely make a move, especially if he thought she disapproved. So, it was better to bring her feelings on the matter to bear rather than keep them to herself.

Besides, the poor man never took shore leave. He was cooped up on this ship twenty-four seven. Apart from landing missions, he never had a chance to stretch his legs and get a bit of R&R. Besides his little fling with Jegra, (she'd gotten the full disclosure from Skuld, who was extremely fond of discussing interspecies relations), the poor guy hadn't been laid in ages. Not that it was any of her business. But as ship's captain, she did worry about morale.

"I was simply thinking of asking her out for some drinks. I wasn't going to...I mean, I would never..."

Raven laughed. "It's quite all right, Kregor. I know how you can't resist strong women."

"I, uh..." Kregor clammed up. He really had nothing more to add and he felt overly self-conscious as it was. Romantical stuff wasn't his wheelhouse. And he felt somewhat exposed confessing his fondness of the captain's ex, so, he opted to bite his tongue for now.

Raven smiled puckishly, keeping any further comments to herself, and then turned back to her controls. "Ah," she said excitedly as she glanced down at the console. "We're here." Reaching up, she clutched the throttle and pulled back, bringing the ship out of hyperspace.

An icy dwarf planet hung in the sky before them. Kregor looked down at his monitor. "This is the Lagrange point between Gamidon and Nyctan." A nervous look came across his face and he turned to the captain. "As second in command, it's my duty to inform the captain that we are now officially in Disputed Space."

"Precisely. And this is why Dakroth chose to hide it here."

"Hide what here?" Kregor looked out the view portal at the dead, icy world hanging before them like a frosted pearl in a black and purple expanse.

"This icy dwarf is known as Kelipsis. Unimportant. No precious metals or gases. An outer crust of methane infused ice, but not enough to bother mining the water out of. Just a useless ball of frozen dirt. The perfect place to hide a secret ship yard."

"Are you saying this is a space dock?"

"There's only one way to find out," Raven said, a spry grin forming on her purple painted lips. With a flick of her wrists, she typed some code into the key panel and then broadcast a security clearance signal to the moon.

Both of them waited for something to happen, but after a minute, Raven inputted the command again.

"Is something supposed to happen?"

"Grendok gave me these codes personally. They should work."

"Unless his intel is wrong."

"His intel is never wrong," Raven replied, her brow settling into a frown on her forehead.

"Maybe there's too much ice."

"I knew it!" Raven exclaimed. And with the tap of a button she shot a Python missile at the dwarf planet.

An explosion lit up the surface of Kelipsis and particles of ice floated into space, forming a crystalline cloud.

Gradually, as the smaller particles dissipated, boiling away in the vacuum of space, and the larger chunks of ice simply floated gently back down to the surface, two large hangar doors appeared.

Excited by the reveal, Raven typed in the code again and the door's running lights lit up and the doors cracked open and slowly pulled apart. A space opened up large enough to accommodate the *Skywend*, a corvette class battlecruiser of unknown origin. Although, Raven was pretty confident they were about to find out where she was made. The *Skywend* represented a prototype for a new high-power, high-speed vessel in the Dagon fleet that would replenish all the old ships.

Dakroth had made everyone believe the secret shipyard was at Sector B-13, adjacent the black hole. It made sense to use the radiation of the singularity to mask any secret bases or shipyards. However, he'd only used it as a decoy. A point to ambush Jegra with the super destroyer he'd built.

If the CSEs hadn't intervened at the battle of Sector B-13, the outcome could have very well been quite different. As it was, however, the Nyctans and the Dagons both ended up retreating from a battle gone completely sideways and returned home to lick their wounds. The embarrassment of the battle was too much for either side to report to their superiors, so it went largely unreported. Missing ships were chalked up to increased pirate activity in the sector. After all, when one was hellbent on covering their tracks, the easiest way was to offer up a scapegoat.

Dakroth, after his run in with the notorious space pirate Novac Tamoran, had pinned the blame on him. Which is why he wanted Dakroth to suffer. Only, Ishtar Bantu had inserted herself into the little drama and convinced Tamoran to use Dakroth as bait to lure Jegra to them. Then, once she had what she wanted, she convinced Dakroth to give Tamoran his own state of the art Dagon battlecruiser in exchange for his freedom.

Now, there was a dangerous pirate out there with enough firepower to destroy a small moon. But that was neither here nor there. And right now, Raven had more important concerns to occupy her time.

"Take us in, slow and smooth," she said.

Kregor nodded and took the controls. Guiding the ship into the gaping mouth of the hangar, they slowly sank into the blackness inside.

Raven flicked a switch and the ship's running lights came on, illuminating a path in front of them. Luckily, the cavity of the hidden base was large enough to house a hundred ships the size of the *Skywend*.

No sooner had they made it inside the space dock than the doors behind them began to close again. The dim light from the distant Nyctan star slowly shrank into a sliver and then, with a resounding *clunk*, the light was snuffed out and the hangar doors sealed shut again.

"Now what?" Kregor asked.

"Let me see if I can activate the facility's automated docking procedures." She tapped the keys on her touch panel display and sure enough, there was a loud *clunk* followed by a *pop*, as if somewhere, a generator fired up.

Incrementally, the lights in the hangar turned on, giant halogen floodlights meant for brightening up the entire space dock. As they came on, row after row of incomplete ships, just like the *Skywend*, appeared. By the time the lights had warmed to full radiance, revealed were more than two hundred vessels lining the inside wall of the massive cavern.

Every ship sat securely in a cradle of sorts. The cradles had robotic arms along with access tubes for workers to move about the ships as they were being constructed. For whatever reason though, the facility had been prematurely shut down.

Raven's best guess was that Dakroth had ordered a pause on construction to speed up the completion of his dreadnought destroyer. But once that was destroyed in the battle with the Nyctan fleet, he didn't have the money or resources to complete two hundred new ships.

This suggested that the state of the empire was much worse than she had initially thought. If Dakroth had put a hold on expanding his military might, it meant the empire was floundering. From the propaganda, however, one could be forgiven for thinking it was as strong as ever.

Of course, this revelation didn't bode well. If Grendok's report was correct, they'd need the full might of the Dagon Empire to fend off this new invasion force. The Nephilim, as the satyrs referred to them, was an old Galliforn word for angel.

Without touching anything, the *Skywend's* thrusters spurted and it began its automatic docking procedure.

"Over there," Raven said, pointing out the window at a series of green flashing running lights that led to a pressurized docking port.

"So, let me see if I have this all straight. We're supposed to get the automated systems back online so they can finish building Dakroth's armada. Then, we hijack the ships and use them for the war against the Nephilim?"

"Something like that. These ships will be part of Jegra's personal defense force. It will make her the eminent superpower in this part of the galaxy."

"I doubt the emperor will be very pleased about that."

"If the emperor even knows about it. Right now, nobody has seen hide nor hair of his holier than thou self." Raven lied, of course. If Kregor found out that she was keeping the emperor prisoner on this very vessel, he'd blow his gasket and chew her a new one.

But, the fact remained, they might need Dakroth to activate the facility fully. Until she was certain they didn't absolutely need him, she was happy to follow Jegra's orders and keep him sedated for as long as possible. Besides, the long rest would do him good. The emperor always seemed a little stressed out, in her estimation.

As the ship locked into the cradle on the upper left section of the space dock, Raven stretched out of her seat and yawned. "All right, let's notify the others that we have arrived at our destination and have a bit of exploring to do."

"I don't know, Captain. The last time you went exploring—"

"I'm well aware, K," she said, cutting him off. She'd rather not have to dredge up the memories of finding H'aaztre's homeworld, a ring world known as Aldebaran. It was a place that existed in perpetual transit, allowing the golden entity to live eons longer than the rest of time and space, which simply flowed around him.

In fact, she wished she'd never stepped foot on that terrible place. And although Kregor didn't join her ragtag crew until shortly after, he'd heard all about it from Skuld, who seemed to be infinitely fascinated by the discovery.

She used his nickname to soften her response and let him know her somber tone wasn't meant to be critical. She just wanted to focus on this mission.

"Yes, Captain. Sorry, Captain."

"It's quite alright. Let's just get this over with. The sooner we complete our mission, the sooner we can rejoin the others back on Thessalonica."

7

Prime Minister Boyega of the Seyfferian Republic, an allegiance that consisted of Correll, Galliforn, Qu'Mar, and Veridion, all of which were free worlds and stood apart from the Commonwealth, gently tossed back his folded robes and strolled up to the strange golden ship that had landed in front of parliament.

"Sir," the premier's aide said, clutching him nervously by his sleeve. "I suggest you wait until security arrives."

"Son," he said, brushing back his long, braided hair and withdrawing his arm from the young man, "if I believed security to be worth a damn, I'd have let them handle it. But if this is who I think it is, security is worth about as much as my slagon's dung droppings."

"Very vivid imagery, sir," the aide replied, reluctantly relinquishing the premier's robes.

Boyega descended the stone stairs with dainty, fast steps, so smooth it almost seemed as though he were gliding on the air. As he emerged from the stately columns of the capitol building, he held his long braids draped over his forearm, hurried across the promenade, and stood before the alien vessel.

Easing up behind him with cautious steps, his aide whispered timidly, "I have a bad feeling about this."

"You're not the only one, son. But let me assure you, the Seyfferian Republic has no wish to get involved with the disputes of the warring empires. If this is the supreme being of the Nyctan and Dagon peoples, we will let them hash it out over which species is his favorite. Until then, you just let me do the talking."

A loud pneumatic hiss startled them as steam shot out either side of the ship's landing ramp. The ramp began to lower from under the vessel's belly until, finally, it clanked down on the cement of the courtyard in front of the parliament.

The sound of a single pair of armored boots echoing down a metal ramp could be heard, and both men peered anxiously into the white haze of steam curling out of the ship's rich internal atmosphere, spreading across the grounds like a low rolling fog.

The prime minister twisted his braided hair nervously in his hands and squinted into the billowing steam, as a much more humid atmosphere seeped out of the ship. Then, to his surprise, an elegant Nyctan woman with a porcelain complexion and dressed in a skin-tight leotard of what seemed to be organic body armor, appeared to them.

Not only was she beautiful, but she sported knee-high armored boots, matching shoulder plating that wove itself seamlessly into the uniform, and a golden cape with a claret lining which fluttered elegantly on the breeze.

He rubbed his eyes in disbelief and did a double take just to be sure. He recognized the woman. She was someone he'd known well a long time ago. "Azra'il Nun?" he said, perplexed by her arrival. His face drooped in disbelief as he stared at her. "But I heard that you died at the battle of Sector B-13."

"The reports were, perhaps, premature. My ship was teleported by the squids to another galaxy. Don't ask me how they can jump across the interstellar medium, beyond the void, to entirely different galaxies. Our best scientists haven't been able to crack that code yet. Believe me, if we had, H'aaztre would have conquered half the universe by now."

"H-h-hastur?" the aide asked, his voice quivering with fear.

"Yes, my scrumptious delight," Azra'il Nun said, raising her gauntleted hand, taking a golden claw and running it along the soft part underneath young man's chin. She forced his eyes up to meet hers and studied his coppery skin. "My Lord sends his tidings."

"If your Lord wishes to convene the council, all he need do is file a request with the—"

"My lord," she stopped him, "doesn't wish anything of you. As the Voice of his Holiness, I speak with full authority. H'aaztre will spare Correll and the rest of the Republic's planets if you refrain from intervening in his affairs. Should you, however, decide to take sides in the coming war, you will be given one and only one chance to surrender to His authority. Failure to do so will result in your world's immediate destruction. Do I make myself clear?"

Boyega tossed his braids over his shoulder and bowed reverently, his metallic brown forehead shining in the glow of Azra'il's radiant ship. He didn't speak, for words weren't necessary. Just the acknowledgement of the agreement, of which he would most certainly keep–by any means necessary.

"Good, it is settled then," she said, smiling at him with her extremely pleasant expression. It was almost *too* pleasant, as if it had been rehearsed so as to hide something much more perilous beneath its highly polished veneer.

"You have my word," he assured her, rising back up to look her squarely in the eyes. "We will refrain from any involvement in this conflict."

"Then you may want to tell that to your pet goat, Admiral Grendok," she snarled, her disposition shifting to one of deep-seated indignation.

Her porcelain skin seemed to pulse with a yellow surge of energy just beneath the surface, which coursed through her veins when she grew angry.

Boyega grew frightened, not having known about Grendok's insolence. "What has he done this time?"

"He's allied himself with the Imperatrix of Dagon, Jegra Alakandra."

"That fool!" Boyega said, shocked by the news. "I don't know what he was thinking, but I can assure you tha—"

"With all due respect, ma'am," the aide intervened, seeing that the premier was floundering, "but Grendok's people's world was unjustly destroyed. It's only natural that he—"

"Hush!" Boyega barked, eyeballing the young man with his harshest glare. "The satyr is an outlaw. And we will have no further discussion on this point." As a politician, he did his best to try and disarm Azra'il's temper and assured her that Grendok wouldn't pose any threat to them.

"But—" the aide tried to protest, but was cut off again.

"You heard your master, little man. The goat is an outlaw."

"Yes, ma'am," the young man said in a reticent voice as he looked down at his feet. Although it wasn't fair, he knew that the Republic would disavow any loyalty to the admiral if it meant protecting what they had left.

"You are wise beyond your years, Prime Minister. I anticipate a long and healthy relationship between our two peoples."

Boyega nodded graciously and then bowed once again.

Azra'il smiled and then turned around to return to her ship, but paused midstride and looked over her shoulder at the young man who watched her with a hard gaze that told her everything she needed to know about his moral character. "Tell me boy, have you ever made love to a Nyctan before?"

"I beg your pardon, Mistress Azra'il Nun, but I cannot say I've had that pleasure. From what I understand, sex is unlawful on your world."

"On my world, perhaps. But we're not on my world, are we?" She reached out and extended her slender white hand for him to take. He was reluctant at first, but then took her hand in his. She smiled and then addressed the prime minister. "I hope you don't mind if I borrow your servant for an hour?"

Prime Minister Boyega waved his hand as if to say, *do whatever you want* and then turned to head back up the stairs. *Besides*, he thought to himself, *it's not my place to tell an emissary of a God what to do.* He looked back one last time to see Azra'il tow the young man onto her ship, his feet stumbling like a novice behind him.

Before boarding the ship, the young man gulped nervously and glanced back over his shoulder to catch one last glimpse of the prime minister, who was watching him. Just then, their tense look was interrupted by another blast of steam and the shuttle bay ramp began to retract back into the underbelly of the radiant vessel.

Once inside, Azra'il held out a finger to his chest, forcing him to stop and look at her. "Take off your clothes," she demanded.

The young man obediently complied and began stripping. Once he was completely bare, his copper colored skin rippling with goosebumps from his extreme nervousness, he looked to her for her approval. She merely looked him up and down and nodded, as if inspecting a nice cut of meat rather than a young man.

"Aren't you going to undress?" he asked.

"Heaven's no!" Azra'il laughed. "I don't want to have sex with you."

"Then what you said was...a lie?"

Azra'il's eyes flashed with rage and then, almost as soon as she'd tensed up, she relinquished her anger by exhaling and taking a deep breath. And then, closing her eyes, she smiled calmly. "No, I would never lie. As the mouthpiece of our lord, I am not permitted to speak untruths." She opened her eyes again and gazed upon the young man. But her gaze seemed distant somehow. "I merely asked if you had ever made love to a Nyctan; I didn't say Nyctan woman." She let out a laugh, looked at the shocked expression on the boy's face, and laughed again.

"My most humble apologies, mistress, but I'm confused."

The main doors slid open and a large Nyctan man dressed, in heavy battle armor topped by a gilded helmet, entered the room. His muscles rippled and flexed with tension as he eyed the young man up and down and smiled in a peculiarly dissolute manner.

"This is Gordack. He has never made love to anyone in his life and, as a present for his loyal service, I promised him a good time here on your world. You wouldn't mind showing my loyal soldier a good time, would you?"

The young man, covering himself best he could, gulped down the frog-sized lump in his throat. "I'm not...what I mean to say is...he's, uh, not my type," he whispered.

"What was that?" Azra'il asked, cupping her hand around her ear and leaning in to try and hear him better.

He repeated himself. "I'm just not into other guys. Sorry."

"Oh, that's a pity. Gordack was so looking forward to it." Turning to the beast of a man, she said in a most apologetic voice, "Maybe some other time, my pet."

Gordack huffed in disappointment and then disappeared out of the room, his broad shoulders barely fitting through the doorway, which he had to slump under so as not to hit his helmeted head on the archway.

"Mistress, um, the Voice, may I go then?"

"What?" Azra'il said, snapping out of her daydream. She looked down at the trembling boy. "I'm sorry, I didn't catch that."

"Am I free to go, ma'am?"

"Oh, my sincerest apologies," she said, her face filling with genuine remorse. "I just thought that...never mind what I thought." She laughed to herself and then straightened up. "Fetch your clothes and come with me."

He did as asked, quickly pulling on his underwear and then struggling to keep up with the Nyctan woman as she strode down the corridor at a brisk pace, he scurried behind her like a pup following its mother.

They arrived at the aft of the ship, and she guided him into a small room with a kennel. Inside the kennel was a hideous looking dog creature with sharp spikes, thorny ridged, pangolin-like armor, and a menacing look in its eyes. Black eyes with a golden halo gave the creature a truly otherworldly look.

"What is that thing?" he asked in a startled voice.

"That's a Nephilim wolfhound. They make great pets and even greater hunters. But they do have voracious appetites."

The beast snarled and snorted, causing the young man to fearfully draw back. To his surprise, he accidentally bumped into something soft and turned around to see he'd inadvertently knocked into Azra'il Nun's chest.

Never having touched a woman's breasts before, he grew extremely nervous. "I'm very sorry, ma'am. I didn't mean to…I uh…think I should be going." He slowly backed away and jutted a thumb over his shoulder. "Lots of paperwork to file and what not. You know how it is. Busy, busy, busy." He laughed nervously, hoping his little fib would be enough to get himself excused.

Seeing as she wasn't answering but merely staring at him with an unsettling look, he tried to move past her, but she caught him by his neck with a grip so intense it made him wince.

"Please, mistress, you're hurting me."

"No, I'm feeding you…to him." She turned and waved her hand. The kennel door slid open and the dog snarled and paced excitedly about in its kennel.

"No! Please! I'm begging you!"

Azra'il ignored the young man's pleading and shoved him into the kennel with such force he dropped his bundle of clothing from his arms.

The young man startled as the kennel doors clanked shut behind him. He ran to the bars and rattled them to no avail and then, slowly, turned back around to see the dog still pacing, its eyes locked onto him. The young man inched his way into the back corner and sank down, clutching his knees to his chest and sobbing.

Azra'il watched with intense interest and then said, "*Etzah.*"

The feral beast lunged forward, pouncing on the young man who let out a terrible scream. Its carnivorous growls filled the room along with the young man's shrieks of agony as he was torn apart, limb from limb.

Azra'il watched the carnage with a sick and twisted grin forming on her thin lips. Blood splattered onto her white skin, as some dribbled down her neck and into her cleavage. She wiped it up with her index finger and brought the gooey red gore to her lips. Sucking her finger dry, she moaned in what could be mistaken for ecstasy, and then smiled as more splatter dappled her neck and face.

From out on the promenade, Prime Minister Boyega convened with some officials who'd gathered around him to inspect the curious spacecraft parked on their capitol's doorstep. When he heard his aide's cries coming from within the vessel, he assumed they were cries of delight and chose to ignore them. After all, it wasn't his place to tell the emissary of a God how to enjoy herself when visiting his world. He turned back to the discussion at hand.

"Is that who I think it is?" a black woman wearing the official robes of a high official asked, nodding her head at the spacecraft parked before them.

"An emissary, at least," Boyega replied. He then turned toward the small gathering and announced, "My fellow colleagues, it seems we must decide on what to do with Admiral Grendok's hasty allegiance."

"Grendok has always made things difficult for us," the young black woman said. "I vote we renounce him. The satyr elders will stand firm with us, rather than risk going to war against an unknown foe on their own."

"Still," Boyega said, "we'll need to handle this carefully. At the moment, Grendok has his people's pain to rally them to his cause. We need to help alleviate that pain in order to weaken his stance against H'aaztre. The more he appears to be a raving madman hellbent on revenge, the more we can ween his people from his influence."

"And how do you expect we go about doing that, precisely?" an older gentleman, equal to Boyega in age, asked.

The premier smiled at the man and locked his hands behind his back. "We shall reveal his cloning operation to the authorities and issue a warrant for his arrest. That alone will discredit him among even his most staunch supporters. After that, we reveal to the empress that he was the one who concocted that little serum that made her into a hulking beast of a monster. Once she knows the truth about how he played her, he'll have lost allies on both fronts."

"Very well, then," the woman said. "Although I don't like this backhanded business, it appears we are left with little choice in the matter. Our hands are tied." She glanced over at the ship and noted that it had become deathly quiet. Only the chirp of some distant birds wafted on the warm breeze that brushed against their skin.

"There's one more thing," the gentleman began, "the empress. If she takes the news poorly and retaliates against the Seyfferian Republic, and not just Grendok, how will we respond?"

Boyega looked up at the blue sky, took in a deep breath, and then exhaled. "Leave that up to me, my friend. I'll worry about the dirty little details. You just make sure that every news outlet and televid across the Commonwealth knows about Grendok's criminal activity by this evening."

The man nodded and scampered off. The woman hesitated a bit, and then took her leave as well. Boyega took another deep breath and then began to make his way back up the stairs of the capitol building. Before he was even halfway up, Azra'il Nun's ship began to take off. He paused in the middle of the staircase and watched the ship disappear up into the atmosphere. That's when it dawned on him that he'd have to find a new aide.

8

The war room bustled with activity. A fleet of satyr officers moved in and out setting up equipment. One of Jegra's aides whispered something into her ear and she turned and flicked on the large televid monitor that took up an entire wall. On it was Admiral Grendok's face. The scrolling text at the bottom mentioned something about his criminal activity. "Are you seeing this?" Jegra asked without looking back at the satyr.

"A smear campaign to undermine my authority, no doubt," Grendok said in a less than amused tone.

Jegra spun around and faced him. "Why now, though?"

"It seems that our enemy is more cunning than I had initially anticipated. If he can sour my people's trust in me, then there will be no one to rally together and stand up to him. Everything between here and Nyctan will be ripe for the taking. And Dagon will be the last remaining stronghold."

A frown settled across Jegra's brow as she thought about it for a moment and then, aiming the remote control at the televid, she flicked it off. The screen's light shrank down to a pinprick, like a star collapsing in on itself, and then went dark.

"If a blue warrant goes out for your arrest, every bounty hunter in the system will descend upon us."

"Don't worry about that. I'll have my clones running interference. Just let them sweep the palace with their scanners. They won't be able to detect me." He patted his breast pocket as if to suggest he had a concealed device that would mask his bio-signature.

Jegra nodded, giving him the benefit of the doubt. After all, the satyr had never steered her wrong. Not even when they'd first met and she'd had to face off with one of Grendok's enhanced clones in her very first gladiatorial fight. Even then, he was giving her advice on how to survive. For this reason, she felt an uncommon bond with the satyr. And she trusted him implicitly.

"Ma'am, Captain Lianica Blackstar is teleporting down with one of her officers," Meleh'Kendar informed her. "Shall I lower the security grid?"

Jegra motioned with her fingers for him to turn it off and he swiveled around in his chair and typed in the codes to temporarily drop the palace's energy shields which, if left on, would scramble the insides of whoever was trying to come through like Chidiyan goose eggs.

A yellow beam of light appeared in the center of Jegra's war room and then it split into two bars. Particles of light fluttered about the golden shafts like lightning bugs flickering in and out of existence. After another few nanoseconds, two figures materialized.

The translucent visages of Captain Lianica Blackstar and Lieutenant Brei'Alas Kusagara solidified into tangible people and they both took in a big breath. In a panic, Brei'Alas ran her hands up and down her body, feeling herself to check if everything was intact. Letting out a deep sigh, she finally said, "I really hate teleporting."

Lianica looked around, spotting both Jegra and Admiral Grendok to her right. She crossed her left breast with her fist and saluted them. She held it until Brei'Alas, slow to catch on, did the same. They returned her salute and she went over to them.

"I have the *Shard* jamming all scans of Thessalonica. If anyone wants to eavesdrop, they'll need to be less than a kilometer from here with some very heavy-duty equipment."

"Which we'd detect," Meleh'Kendar added without looking over his shoulder. Then, at the last moment, he said, "Palace security grid going live in three, two, one...now." He hit the button and then turned his attention to a report left on the side of his desk by one of Grendok's officers.

The empress cleared her throat. "All right, folks. All non-essential personnel, please return to your normal duties. All officers, report to my conference room."

Everyone not meeting Jegra's list of essential personnel looked up from what they were doing and leaving it for later, got up and left the room as fluidly as if they were running a fire drill.

As Jegra's group entered her conference room, Brei'Alas, who was admiring the lavish curtains, bumped into Jegra's chest. Practically bouncing off, she spun around only to realize she'd crashed into the empress herself and then began to apologize quite profusely.

"Your Majesty, I'm so terribly sorry. I didn't mean to...of course, I'd never...that is to say I hold you in the highest regard and would never dream of..."

"It's quite all right Lieutenant Kusagara, no harm, no foul as they say."

A puzzled look came over Brei'Alas's face, and without even thinking about it, she asked, "Who says that?"

A throat clearing sternly alerted Brei'Alas to the fact that she was, once again, overstepping her bounds. She drew back, bowing reverently and apologized again. Captain Blackstar sidled up next to Jegra and apologized once more on the girl's behalf.

"I'm terribly sorry about her; she's aloof as they come. But she's a damn fine science officer, and I thought we could use her expertise."

"It's fine," Jegra said without so much as thinking twice about it. "Captain, tell me. I've been wondering this since I first met you...is Blackstar really your family name?"

Lianica laughed. "Yes, but in Dagoni it's a little hard to pronounce. Which is why I only ever introduced myself to you in your native tongue."

"If you don't mind telling me now, I'd like to know your true name."

"It's Khatri'LaGharia, which, in Dagoni, literally translates to 'black star.'"

"It's beautiful," Jegra said, smiling at Lianica.

Lianica smiled but maintained her professionalism. She took a slight bow and then followed after Brei, who was now fiddling with the height adjustment of her chair and bouncing up and down like a child. One look from Lianica's stern glare, however, stopped Brei'Alas in her spot which was several notches lower than she'd have liked.

"Lieutenant, get your act together. That's an order."

"Yes, ma'am," Brei said, feeling embarrassed.

When Jegra sat down, directly across from Brei'Alas, the remaining officers followed suit. Brei turned her attention to Jegra, fascinated by how she'd so elegantly slipped her hand under the slit of her dress, pulled the long satin folds aside, and draped them over her chair so she could be seated comfortably. The way the folds hung over the edge of the chair, along with the burnt orange color, reminded Brei of the tail of a Númenorian red fox.

The round glass table is a nice touch too, Brei thought to herself, admiring how you could see everyone equally. Not only that, but nobody would be able to conceal any weapons. At least nothing obvious, as one would be able to see them right through the table. It was quite ingenious, actually.

That's when the empress crossed her legs and Brei practically screamed out loud upon discovering that Jegra wasn't wearing any underwear. In her shock, however, she couldn't look away. Something about those long bronze legs that seemed to go on forever and then, when you were least expecting it, you glimpsed *Vyraj*–the great paradise at the center of all things.

Her dainty blue hands clamped her own mouth shut and she muted her shriek of astonishment. Everyone turned to the young lieutenant to see what the matter was; it sounded as though she'd been bitten by an Angorian weaving spider.

"Are you all right, Lieutenant?" Admiral Grendok asked in his usual gruff voice. He whipped out an e-cigarette that looked like a classic hand-carved wooden smoking pipe, and lit it up. The delicate vapor emanating from the pipe smelled of Talakian mangos and seemed to soothe everyone in the room.

Jegra shifted in her chair and recrossed her legs again. This time Brei bit her lip in anticipation of getting flashed, seeing as she had a direct view right up the empress's slit. Her eyes widened upon seeing it all over again and she quickly began fiddling with her chair, raising herself to a normal height so she wouldn't be staring directly at...it.

The lieutenant let out a sigh and turned to find the captain glaring at her with icy daggers for eyes. The big tubular vein on her temple was acting up again too; it throbbed with each hot pulse of her heartbeat. Brei knew she was in trouble any time the captain's vein appeared. And it only seemed to appear whenever she was being particularly wearisome. She smiled sheepishly back at the captain, as if to apologize for her inappropriate behavior.

"Are you quite finished making a spectacle of yourself, Lieutenant?"

"Yes, ma'am." Brei looked around and met Grendok's face again. The satyr, holding his pipe like a wise old sage, winked at her. Taken aback by the gesture, she had to do a double take, not fully knowing what he meant by it. She clasped her hands together on the table in front of her and took a deep breath, trying her best to act casual.

Jegra stood up to address the group when the doors opened and Danica appeared. She stepped into the room and apologized for being late then took her seat next to the empress. As she sat down, her eyes locked with Lianica's across the table and she stared until Lianica, obviously upset, looked away out of shame.

Meleh'Kendar fanned his hand across the table and a hologram rose up from the glass to show Thessalonica, the *Chiron*, and the *Verlag* locked in orbit. He waved his hand more broadly, and the image shrank away to reveal Dagon Prime. Thessalonica, now the size of a tennis ball, orbited the giant blue and green orb that took up the entire table. The security chief zoomed out again, then again, until a large swath of space sat before them.

"According to Admiral Grendok's intelligence, the enemy fleet is holding position here." Meleh'Kendar tapped the area of space and a yellow dot appeared. He fanned his hand in a downward motion and the map followed him. A few parsecs later, he tapped the hologram again and a red dot appeared. "Currently, Callestra has ordered the Dagon fleet to hold position here."

"That's standard protocol," Lianica informed everyone. "You create a perimeter and meet the unknown force upon the field. At that point, communications will be opened and a dialog will be permitted. Once each side has expressed their intent, the ships will either engage one another in combat or continue on their way peacefully–with an escort."

"It's no peace mission," Grendok grumbled. "We have reports from our base of operations on Cordova that the enemy fleet is taking up position here, just beyond Gamidon."

"They'll likely use the gas giant to mask their numbers," Danica added.

"Precisely," Grendok replied. "Also, they'll probably have a small contingent of ships hiding here in the asteroid belt near the Cove. That way they'll be able to flank us when we meet for the...'peaceful dialog.'"

Jegra straightened up in her chair, her chin resting on her fingers. Slowly, she raised her brown eyes and scanned the faces of everyone in the room. "I agree. By all appearances, it seems like an ambush. Which is why I'll only be sending one ship to rendezvous with their envoy."

Lianica laughed. "Callestra would never allow it. She'd intervene and take control of the whole operation."

"The girl is fearsome, I'll give her that much," Grendok said. "But she has squat for strategic brains."

Brei'Alas chuckled and then stopped herself when she drew the attention of the others.

"What do you think, Lieutenant?" Jegra asked, singling Brei out.

"Me?" the girl asked timidly. "You want to know what I think?"

"This is a round table discussion. Everyone's opinion holds equal weight at this table."

"I agree. It's definitely a trap. But..." she trailed off and looked over at her captain, who nodded at her, gently urging her to continue sharing her thoughts, "...but I think sending even one ship shows we're trying to do things by the book. They'll likely tell us what we want to hear and then thrust the dagger into our...backside the moment we turn our backs to them."

"I agree with the lieutenant; it's too risky."

"Lieutenant Kusagara," Jegra said, smiling gently, "so far you've merely repeated what everyone else here has said. I want to know what you genuinely think."

"What I think?" Brei gulped, the pressure coming on hot and heavy. She began sweating in places she didn't know she could sweat and squirmed in her seat.

All eyes on her, she turned to the star map glowing in the center of the table and peered into it. The deeper she gazed, the more it all seemed to make sense.

"We need to be the ones to stab them in the back."

"And how do you suppose we go about doing that? What leverage do we have?" Danica asked.

"They want Dagon Prime...so, we surrender it to them."

"Ah-ha!" Grendok chuckled in his jovial fashion. "We lure them into a false sense of superiority and then crush them."

"Yes. Something like that," Brei said. She sat back in her chair and let out a sigh of relief.

Danica turned toward Jegra. "That might actually work. And it will buy us the necessary time we need to—"

"To make our preparations," Lianica chimed in, cutting Danica off unintentionally.

An awkward silence followed. Finally, Meleh'Kendar cleared his throat and asked, "But what about Callestra? She's sure to go in guns blazing."

"We use her as part of the ruse," Jegra said, leaning back in her chair. "She'll put on her fiercest face and charge headfirst into the front line and likely get decimated. But that little sacrifice will make the surrender all the more convincing. It will appear as though we're fracturing from the might of their invasion force. Then, we lure them into Dagon's defense grid and flank them from all sides with the combined forces of the Dagon and Galliforn armadas." Jegra swiped her hand across the hologram and turned it off.

"There's just one problem," Lianica said, her voice sounding rather worried. "We don't currently have enough ships to engage a fleet of that size."

Jegra turned to Grendok and smiled.

"Leave that up to me," the empress said. "In the meantime, the rest of you put your heads together and come up with every possible battle simulation you can think of. I want to be twenty steps ahead of our new friends at every turn."

"Yes, Your Majesty," the room said all at once.

With that, Jegra rose up. Everyone stood with her. "I have other matters to attend to, so I hereby conclude this meeting. We'll meet again in twenty-four hours."

Everyone saluted and she turned and headed toward the exit. Danica got up, shot an icy look at Lianica, and then followed Jegra out into the hallway.

"I told you, Raphine and I can handle this."

"Please, don't turn me away," Danica pleaded. "I'm losing my mind in here. I need to see some action. Something to spike my adrenaline. Something to make me feel alive again."

Jegra stopped in the middle of the hall and turned to face Dani. "Look, I know you're going stir crazy. But the doctor's orders are for you to rest another week. Once you're fully healed, I promise to stop mothering you."

She could see Danica fuming, but stood firm on her stance. Danica was too stubborn to allow herself to heal, and it was up to Jegra to order her to do it. If not, then she'd be in store for a life of chronic pain and misery.

"Yes, *Your Majesty*," Danica said, her words had an icy chill to them that gave Jegra pause.

It was the coldest response Jegra had ever received from Danica, and she tried her best to brush it off and smile, even though Dani was testing her patience right now.

"The others could really use your tactical know-how, Dani. You'll serve me better here than down in the slums of the city."

"Oh…hell…no," Danica said throwing her arm back and pointing at the war room. "I'm not going back in there. Not while that back-stabbing, fang-toothed, queen of the cunts is there."

Unable to remain patient any longer, Jegra threw her arms up. "Fine! I give up. You win. Come if you want. Stay if you want. It doesn't make any difference to me. It's your life. Your choice."

Danica's eyes lit up. "You really mean it?"

"Look. I'm tired of fighting with you, Dani. And it's clear you're not happy here. So, yeah, I'm fairly certain I mean it."

Danica leapt into Jegra's arms and began planting her with so many hot, wet kisses that Jegra began to laugh.

"If we had the time, I'd bathe your entire body in kisses."

"There'll be plenty of time for that later," Jegra said, with a laugh. She blushed when Danica slipped her hand into the slit of her dress and reached up and ran her fingers along the soft skin of her inner thighs.

"Dani, seriously. We don't have time to…ah…" Jegra's breath caught in her throat; she bit her lip and tried not to let a scandalous moan slip out as Danica's fingers met her flesh and began to work their magic.

Jegra reached down and grabbed Dani's wrist, stopping her. Dani's eye's flared white hot as she stared Jegra down. A sly grin forming on her lips, Jegra brought Dani's hand firmly into her crotch, forcing her to feel the heat radiating from her. "Is this what you want?" Jegra asked, her voice low and sultry.

"I thought you'd never ask," Dani replied, her mouth opening wide as she accepted Jegra's penetrating kiss.

Forty-five minutes later, both women lay on their backs looking up at the domed ceiling of the palace library, their bare bodies glistening in the afternoon sun that streamed in from the ceiling-high day windows which ran the length of the eastern-facing wall.

Her chest heaving, Jegra took in a deep breath and turned to Danica. "That was…"

"Amazing? Yeah, I know," Danica said, complimenting herself in typical self-centered Dagon fashion. Jegra smiled.

"I'm glad to see you have your strength back."

Danica sat up and tossed her ombre turquoise and purple hair across her indigo shoulder. "I told you, I've been going out of my mind. Everyday I've felt like a rat trapped in a lab experiment. And you've been so busy lately that you haven't…" she paused mid-sentence and then smiled.

"Haven't what?" Jegra asked.

"Had any time for me."

"Oh, babe, I'll always make time for you." Jegra took Dani's face in her hands and pulled her onto her. Danica lay across Jegra's chest and looked down at her. Jegra raised her soft pink lips and kissed Danica's Prussian blue ones.

"You'd better," Danica warned. "*Or else.*"

"Or else?" Jegra laughed, tossing her hair out of her eyes.

"You don't even want to know of the sorts of punishments I have in mind should you neglect me ever again."

Jegra laughed. "I can only imagine."

Danica leaned down and dappled Jegra's neck with soft, feathery kisses. Jegra relaxed into it and just let the euphoric sensation flood over her.

Without warning, Jegra's personal comm device chirped and she rolled onto her side and stretched out to reach it. As she did, Danica's arms slipped around her waist. Danica pressed her blue cheek against Jegra's warm back and held her. Basking in the essence of her lover, Danica took in a deep breath and let the scent of Jegra, who smelled of cactus blossoms, fill her with a contentment she never even thought possible.

Jegra lounged on her side, Danica spooning her from behind, her bronze skin and Dani's blue skin mingling in a union of their perfectly sculpted bodies. Danica traced the contours of a scar on Jegra's shoulder with a delicate finger. Smiling over her shoulder at Dani, Jegra tossed her hair and put the small earpiece inside her ear. "This is Jegra."

"Hey, where are you?" Raphine's voice came through the small speaker. "I've been waiting at the back gate for over forty-minutes now."

"I'm sorry," Jegra said, feeling terrible for delaying so long. She had told Raphine to be there at one thirty, and it was already fifteen past two. "The meeting went a little longer than expected," she told her. Although, that was merely a half truth. Still, she doubted Raphine wanted to know the details of her sex life. "Just hold tight, I'm on my way now."

"All right. I'll be here. Waiting."

"Oh, and Danica will be joining us."

Danica raised her head and said, "Damn right I'll be joining you both."

"Hear that?" Jegra asked Raphine.

"Loud and clear," she replied.

Jegra tapped the earpiece, hanging up the call, and then sat up. Her long strands of brown hair slid down her shoulder and back like a silken waterfall. Danica rose up with her, threw her arms around Jegra's neck, and kissed her on the cheek. Jegra laughed.

"What was that for?"

"For being you. For being kind to me. For sticking by me and loving me even though I can be a total bitch sometimes."

"I like bitchy Danica. She's strong. Feisty. And great in the sack."

Danica laughed. "See, that's what I'm talking about." Running her finger down the bridge of Jegra's nose, she let it rest on the soft perch of Jegra's lower lip. "You're too nice to me."

Jegra feigned biting Danica's finger and Danica jerked it away and laughed.

"Not too nice, I hope."

"I know I haven't always been the best of friends to you. But I'm convinced now more than ever that you are my soulmate."

Jegra's mouth widened into a full-on sparking smile. She hadn't felt this in love with anyone before and knew Dani and she were a perfect match. A match made in blood and war, but a match made, nonetheless. She was head over heels for the blue skinned woman, so in love with Dani that she thought she might explode. A serious look hardening in her deep brown eyes, she turned to Danica and, on an impulse, said, "Marry me."

Danica drew back, sitting on her heels, her face frozen in shock. It was unexpected. In fact, it was the first time Jegra had officially proposed to her. "What?"

"I said…marry me."

Danica laughed. "We've been over this. I can't marry you when you're still married to Dakroth. He'd never allow it."

"I'm allowed as many consorts as he has."

"Yes," Danica replied, "but he'll never forgive me for my betrayal. That asshole literally demoted me to the status of a slave. This," Danica said pointing at the scar that ran across her taught abdomen, "is because of him. He'll never let us be together because it would mean, for once in my life, I'd actually be happy."

"Then we'll elope and get married in secret."

Danica smiled. "Do you really mean it? You want to be with me that badly that you'd risk the emperor's wrath?"

"I am with him in decree only. I am with you always, in every way," Jegra replied, earnestly. She placed her hand on Dani's left breast, and Dani cupped her hand over Jegra's. They leaned in, their lips meeting in the middle, and kissed once more. "What I'm asking you is…do you want to be with me?"

"Always and forever!" Danica's eyes overfilled with a torrent of tears and she instantly began to cry. Embarrassed by her sudden outburst, she laughed and sniffled, wiping the tears away even as more came rolling down her cheeks. "Yes. And yes! I will marry you, Jegra Alakandra."

Both women embraced one another and wept together. Amid rows of towering shelves filled with dusty old books, they sat naked. For the first time in what seemed forever, they put their guard down and allowed themselves to be completely vulnerable in the presence of the other because they trusted so completely in one another.

It wasn't the greatest love story ever told. But it was *their* love story. And that's what counted.

Just then, Jegra's communicator began chirping again.

"Shit," she said, leaping up and grabbing her clothes. "Raphine is going to have a cow."

Danica jumped up and grabbed her things, too. Her clothes bundled in her arms, she watched Jegra race by. "Oh, we're going like this?"

"No, time to dress, undress, and redress," Jegra said as she cracked the library door and peeked out.

"Right," Danica said, following Jegra's lead.

Finding the coast clear, Jegra nodded for Danica to follow her and, together, they streaked up the hallway.

Meleh'Kendar opened the conference room door and, standing in the doorway, turned back toward the group. "I'm going to get some coffee. Anybody want anything?"

"I'll have a coffee," Grendok said without looking up from some star charts he was busy studying.

Lianica shook her head. "No, thank you. I'm fine."

Lieutenant Brei'Alas looked up and said, "I'll have a tea. Whatever is available." Just as she'd finished her order, she saw the empress and Danica Valencia streak by the open doorway, completely naked. "Seriously?!" she screamed out.

Everyone startled and looked over at the girl.

"What is wrong with you?" Lianica asked, unable to maintain her patience with the girl any longer.

Pointing at the doorway, Brei asked, "None of you saw that? Are you kidding me?"

Meleh'Kendar looked over his shoulder, not seeing anything out of the ordinary, and then he looked back to the lieutenant and shrugged. "Why? What did you see?"

A disappointed frown settling on her face, Brei folded her arms and threw herself back in her chair and huffed. "Nothing. It was nothing. Never mind."

9

Novac Tamoran's battlecruiser took heavy fire. Green plasma blasts scorched the hull of the dark gray vessel, leaving charred streaks in their wake. The two fighters, which resembled armored crustaceans, shot past the bow of the newly christened *Avarice*. The ship, which the self-proclaimed pirate king had received from Dakroth in exchange for the emperor's freedom, delivered, as promised.

"Where did they come from?" growled the pirate. Captain Tamoran slowly rose to his feet, adjusted his leather tricorne pirate hat and glowered out of the viewing portal at the swift moving ships made of radiant light. They seemed to flicker and glint as they zipped past the bow of his Dagon dreadnought class battleship.

"Unknown, sir. They just…appeared out of nowhere," a young crewman said.

"Well, what are you all waiting for? A promotion? Return fire, already!"

"Yes, sir," a surly looking pirate said. The large man's buccaneer coat had no sleeves, which allowed his massive biceps and strong arms to flex as he quickly moved over the weapons controls and mashed the button that launched the Helios Python missiles. Eight missiles, the blue torches of their afterburners flaming brightly, streaked away from the ship in pursuit of the enemy vessels. Locking onto their targets, they exploded on the hulls of the tiny vessels and sent them spinning off into space.

The enemy ships twirled about aimlessly, as though they were shaking off the blast, and then, just as they had seemingly got their bearings, the two small fighters quickly flashed out of sight as they made the jump into hyperspace.

"Who the hell were those guys?" the young officer asked.

"Scouts," the burly pirate said.

"It appears we've been made," Tamoran snarled, looking out at the blank stares of his bridge crew. Tossing the folds of his black leather buccaneer coat back, he re-adjusted the brim of his hat and then stroked his thick, black beard as he contemplated his best course of action.

"What are your orders, Captain?" asked a slender Dagon woman with an eye patch and dark purple hair that was tied up into an elegant bun. She had on fishnet stockings, knee-high brown leather boots, and a velvet coat with green brocade and a plum satin lining.

The elegant jacket she wore had black lace accents which matched the stylish underblouse with deep cut V-neck and cascading ruffled folds. She adjusted her oversized cuffs, which had brass-toned buttons, and turned to face Novac Tamoran.

She gazed at him loyally with her one good eye. It shone cerise pink in the dim redness of the emergency lighting and changed colors with a kind of pleochroic iridescence, shifting from a saturated pink to an almost purple, depending on what angle the light touched it.

"Resume our original heading to the rendezvous point, Sub Commander Ladgara. It seems our little friends have lost interest in us for now. But if you so much as catch a whiff of one of those vessels, I want you to blast them right out of the bloody sky."

Ladgara smiled and nodded silently, as the rest of the pirate crew all shouted at once, giving a robust, "Aye, aye, Cap'in!"

Callestra Van Morgan sat alone at her dinner table. A couple of lit candles were set out on the table and flickered gently, their light dancing across the walls of her quiet room. She picked up her napkin, unfolded it, set it on her lap, and then brushed it flat.

Before her sat a *Magdalorian* chicken salad with a nice balsamic vinegar dressing and a pair of silver chopsticks. She delicately gathered up her chopsticks and began to fastidiously pick at the salad piece by piece until there was nothing left.

Finished with her meal, she set her chopsticks back in their proper position on the simple jade resting stone, picked up her napkin, and dabbed the corners of her mouth, then gathered up her dishes and dismissed herself from the table.

She placed her dirty dishes into the automated sonic dishwasher and then sauntered over to the corner of her room, her hips swiveling seductively as she walked. Two large windows running from the ceiling to floor looked out at a red and orange nebula beyond the southern constellation of Alabaster.

She paused to take in the view and then began unbuttoning her uniform. Piece by piece, she stripped away each layer until she was standing in her black lingerie, her double d-cup gossamer and lace bra doing little to conceal her maroon nipples, her lace thong disappearing into the crevice of her perfectly sculpted butt cheeks. The cool of the room washed over her and made her skin bristle with goosebumps. But she didn't mind. It felt invigorating.

Slowly, she took in a deep breath and then settled down on the floor in front of the window, crossing her legs to meditate. Callestra placed her feet on her inner thighs in a standard lotus position and slowed her breathing to better clear her mind.

After she calmed her center, she placed her hands on the floor and gradually raised herself up on just her finger tips, holding her lotus position. She maintained the pose, her fingers accustomed to the daily routine so that there wasn't even the slightest tremble in her taught muscles.

From any outside observer, it would appear as though she was hovering ten centimeters above the floor, like the venerable Dagon yogis of Gardonia, the ancient land remembered for its illustrious gardens. Closing her eyes, she slipped effortlessly into her nightly ritual meditation. It was the only thing that seemed to calm her. Without it, she would have likely had a psychotic break a long time ago and have gone on a murderous rampage.

This is why she admired Emperor Dakroth so much. He wasn't afraid to live according to his passions. Her father, Targon Van Morgan, on the other hand, was a cold and calculating man. And although she respected her father, she didn't admire him in the same way she admired Dakroth.

In truth, she would gladly side with Dakroth over her father if it meant becoming his right-hand woman. She wanted to be what Cassera Van Danica Amelorak was to him before her fall from grace. Before she betrayed him and became a *disgusting banjax*, that is.

As her mind unfurled, her thoughts shedding from her consciousness like sheets of water shedding from a waterfall, she could sense herself receding into her own subconscious.

It had taken her many years to learn how to meditate properly. At first, she struggled to focus on not thinking. But the more she fought it, the more she couldn't help but give in and let the deluge of thoughts overwhelm her. Once she realized the key was to simply allow the thoughts to work themselves out on their own, then she was able to find a kind of Zen state where she could think of everything and nothing all at once.

A distant sounding voice called to her, urging her back to consciousness. She often lost track of time when she meditated, which is why it was her personal assistant's duty to fetch her when it was time to finish.

"Are you coming to bed?" the young man asked, his satin robe slipping from his blue shoulder as he waited for Callestra to join him in her after meditation sex. Another duty of his which he gladly performed, seeing as Callestra was the most gorgeous Dagon woman of the last century. If she hadn't gone into the military at her father's behest, he felt she would have made a stunning super model.

Callestra cracked an eyelid and glowered at him from over her shoulder. He shivered, pulling up his robe, and returned to bed on his own volition. Relaxing back into her optimal position, she let herself find her center again and basked in the unfathomable darkness that waited for her there.

The darkness. That's where she felt most at ease.

It was peace. It was serenity. A place empty of all thought and emotion. It was where she could disappear to find a quantum of solace just for herself and not be burdened by the constant pressures of her station, her job, and most of all, her father.

A blinding flash outside her window followed by the entire ship shuddering so violently she thought the glass would fracture and burst and suck her out into the vacuum of space drew her attention to the massive object that had manifested beside the *Verlag*. The collision alarm drowned out the panicked voices coming over the comm—all of them asking for her.

Callestra let out the longest, most drawn out breath of air of her life and then gradually opened her eyes. A dreadnought class battlecruiser had jumped out of hyperspace directly beside them and hung outside her bedroom window, quite an intimidating specter. It was but a stone's throw away, and she rolled her eyes and sighed loudly when she saw the garish red letters painted on its side. The *Avarice*.

"J'axen, will you please have someone tell that asshole to kindly learn how to fucking navigate."

"Yes, ma'am," her assistant said. Tying his robe as he slipped out of bed, he swiftly exited her room and headed to a comm station in her personal office to relay her message.

Incrementally lowering herself back down, she shook her hands loose and then rolled her head across both shoulders as she stretched her neck. Instead of simply getting back up, she gradually stretched her arms and legs, sliding her hips up, pointing her ass in the air. Keeping both palms of her hands planted firmly on the floor with her back straight, she formed a perfect reverse downward dog pose.

After relaxing, she sat back on her heels and reset her core. Slowly, she stood up and switched into a one-legged tree pose. Arms and hands steepled above her head, she slowly raised her left leg, balancing on the right, and maintained her pose for another thirty seconds.

Once she counted down to zero, she extended her folded leg outward like a ballerina, pointed her toes straight, and twirled around on her planted foot. Then, in one fluid motion, she leaned forward, allowing the momentum to carry her, and quickly took a step. Callestra effortlessly fell back into her standard cadence, and walked around the bed and headed into her bathroom.

Upon entering the bathroom, she grabbed a face towel from off a rack and holding just the corner, let it unfurl. She dabbed her neck, chest, and underarms where a delicate glaze of perspiration had formed and then tossed the towel into an auto-wash bin. She tapped the display next to the automated closet. Its panel slid open and a freshly pressed uniform glided out on a hanger.

As she caught a glimpse of herself in the full body mirror on the wall, she paused to scrutinize every inch of her skin as she scoured herself for imperfections. Turning her hips slightly to the left, she slipped her thumbs under the lace waistband of her thong and gave it a gentle tug, making sure the delicate strip that covered her bottom disappeared entirely into the wedge of her buttocks.

Still peering into the mirror at her backside; she clenched her ass as tightly as she could to make sure the bottom curve formed a perfectly round shape and nothing lopsided. Anything less than perfection was unacceptable. Unclenching, she smiled at herself, satisfied that everything passed inspection. It almost seemed as though her own reflection was complimenting her, and though she acknowledged her narcissism, as it was, it still made her feel good. Finished in the bathroom, she took the uniform off the rack and headed back out into the bedroom to change.

She had barely gotten her shirt on when the holovid call came through. Although she hadn't even had time to button it up yet, she accepted the call nonetheless. Novac Tamoran's ugly mug appeared on the holovid projection and she shot him a sharp look. Upon seeing her in her underwear, he let out a crude catcall.

"You look as stunning as ever, Callestra."

"That's Admiral Morgan, to you, pirate. Now, are you going to stand there ogling my tits all day or are you going to tell me what's so urgent that it couldn't wait?"

"The only thing that couldn't wait is my desire for you, my sweetness." He gave her a sly grin and looked her up and down. She smiled back at him, albeit it superficially, but he didn't mind. She was stunning to behold regardless of whether she smiled or not.

Callestra endured the pirate's shameless gaze as she was more than accustomed to getting hit on by every guy this side of the quadrant. And maybe under different circumstances, she might be able to stomach being with Novac Tamoran for one night, seeing as he had a rugged, bad-boy charm about him that wasn't completely revolting.

Even so, his rudderless nature and his extreme infidelity to anything that breathed meant that he couldn't be trusted on the best of days. And on the worst of days he wasn't an enemy you'd want to face off with. Which is why she entertained him just enough to hold his interest and keep his allegiance to her.

"Get to the point," she grumbled, reaching up to end the call, "or are we done here?"

"No, wait," Tamoran said, his voice flooding with a sense of urgency. "It's the Nephilim. We encountered a scouting party just outside the Cove."

"And did you do as I asked?"

"Yes. We collected the readings you wanted. But I don't think you're going to like them very much."

"I'll be the judge of that. Just transmit the data to me and I'll get back to you once I have a better grasp of what we're dealing with here."

"Not so fast, Admiral," Tamoran said, an unscrupulous smile curling onto one side of his overly wide mouth. "I'll relinquish the data in exchange for the thing we talked about. After all, Admiral, the deal was I scratch your back and you scratch mine."

"Out of the question. I'm not going to tolerate you over a romantic candlelit dinner, completely naked, Tamoran."

"Not *that* thing…" he whispered in a low, raspy voice. "The *other* thing."

"Oh…right. *That.*" She rolled her eyes and folded her arms across her chest in a show of disgust but, whether she liked it or not, he was right. A deal was a deal. "Fine," she acquiesced, surrendering to his demands. "I'll hand them over. But I don't see what you could possibly want with them."

Callestra slipped out of the view of the holovid monitor for a moment and then popped back up. Hanging on the crevice of her thumb were the straps of her lace thong that she'd slipped off. She looked slightly perturbed, though she let her black lace underwear dangle for him to see. "I'll have them sent to you right away. Unwashed and untampered with, if I remember your terms correctly."

A depraved look slithered onto Tamoran's face and he nodded quietly. "And you shall have your precious data the moment I have them hung on my wall."

Novac Tamoran stepped out of view to reveal a back wall full of panties from all kinds of women from various specious from all over the Commonwealth. He even had a pair of Ishtar Bantu's underwear. The rainbow assortment of lingerie really added to the drab gray of his personal quarters.

Now, he'd have the underwear of the most powerful woman in the Dagon fleet right up there beside the original loincloth that Jegra had worn during her first ever match in the arena. That particular item had cost him more than he'd ever admit to spending on a woman's undergarment, but it was his prized possession. Admiral Callestra Van Morgan's thong would complement the rest of his collection perfectly.

"You do realize you're a sick man, right?" Callestra asked as she gazed in revulsion at the wall of filth which he revealed to her.

"We all have our vices, Admiral. I suspect even you have dark desires that you keep repressed. I simply choose to express mine. Keeping it all bottled up isn't healthy, you know."

"I really wish it had stayed in the bottle, Captain," Callestra said, already lamenting her decision. "Really."

Novac Tamoran's hologram reformed in front of her and she frowned, feeling disgusted by him. Even so, he remained endlessly fascinating to her. He had that bad boy buccaneer charm that absolutely slayed her. More than this, though, there was something in his manner with her—the way he treated her like a normal girl and nothing special when nearly every other man doted on her and danced around her in their pathetic mating rituals all trying to win her affection. But not him. And that attracted her to him.

Yes, he was revolting. Yes, his strange quirks sickened her. And as repulsed by him as she was, she was equally attracted to him. She couldn't quite explain it.

"I'll be expecting your package shortly," he said tersely, seeing as their conversation had run its course. With a wave of his hand, he flicked off the holovid and was gone.

Callestra breathed deeply and then blew a loose clump of hair out of her face in annoyance at his sudden dismissal of her. She'd been in the middle of trying to figure out her strange feelings when he so rudely hung up on her. *Typical man. Ducking out the moment he got what he wanted.*

All she was to him was another trophy on his wall of menstrual stained cloth. A shiver of disgust shot down her spine and she had to shake the thought of him and his dirty little hobby out of her mind.

After dressing, she was about to leave when J'axen returned to her room. Slapping her unwashed panties into his hands, she said, "See to it that Novac Tamoran gets these. Oh, and gift wrap them for me."

The shocked look on the young man's face was priceless and Callestra smiled at him as he tried to figure out what any of it meant only to shrug it all off and accept it for what it was—an order from his commanding officer.

J'axen watched as Callestra marched past him, leaving him to stand there awkwardly holding her panties. She dashed out the door without so much as looking back. J'axen stared down at the lacy undergarments and let out a discouraged sounding sigh.

Still, orders were orders. So, he went to the desk and got out the finest gift wrap he could find, some ribbon, and a bit of tape. Gently folding Callestra's delicates, he placed the flimsy fabric onto a layer of tissue paper and then gently put it into a small box.

Five minutes later he took a step back and admired his handy work. The pearly white wrapping paper that adorned the box gleamed in the soft lighting and the maroon lace ribbon bundled it all so nicely, pulling the ensemble together. Dusting off his hands with satisfaction, he nodded proudly and then rushed the package off to deliver it, as commanded.

10

A red laser drilled into the wall above Raven's head, creating a smoldering hole and white wisps of smoke. She had barely enough time to duck the blast and shouted, "Will somebody please turn off that damned laser turret!"

"I'm on it!" Gyllek announced, and the girl raced toward the weapon that was firing off wild shots left and right. Although they'd blinded its camera with reflective spray paint, the damned thing somehow activated and began guessing where its targets were. Which meant it probably had an infrared heat sensor which wasn't working properly due to the utter cold of the station and the inability to penetrate the thermal suits they wore beneath their armor.

As the turret turned toward the sprinting girl, she instantly dropped to her knees and slid under a red bolt that nearly grazed her scalp and scorched the korridium deck plating behind her. The sweltering hiss of the *zap* drew everyone's attention as Gyllek slid up to the wall directly beneath the gun turret.

Yanking a compact tool kit off her magnetic belt, she opened it, pulled out a pen-sized automated screwdriver, and began unscrewing the access panel beneath the gun turret.

As another scorching laser blast shot passed Raven's head, she shouted, "Any day now, Gyllek!"

"I'm going as fast as I can, Captain," the girl replied. Placing the screwdriver in her mouth, she gripped the panel and rattled it until she was able to tear it off the wall. A tangle of electrical wires revealed themselves to her and, tossing the metal plate on the floor, she mumbled something to herself as the laser turret overhead fired another series of aimless shots in quick succession.

"Just one more moment…" Gyllek said, studying the layout. The clock ticked down and, drawing out a set of wire cutters, she hemmed and hawed as she tried to determine which wire was the correct one to cut. "Ah!" she said, finding the proper wire. But before she could cut it, she heard a booming battle cry and looked overhead to see Kregor leaping over her with a giant war hammer.

He swung with all his might and a loud clangor rang out as Kregor knocked the laser turret right off its mount on the wall. The metal turret crashed to the deck, rattling and screeching to a halt a couple meters away. Meanwhile, frayed wires dangled out of the wall where the turret had been and intermittently spat sparks, which rained down on Gyllek's head. She pursed her lips in frustration as she sat staring at the wire. "I had it," she grumbled.

Kregor's serpentine lips curled into a slight smile as he threw the long shaft of the giant hammer across his shoulders and shrugged. "Apologies. I thought it best to end the threat quickly by whatever means possible. I have full confidence in your abilities, Gyllek. But I couldn't risk you or the captain's life."

"Hey, what about my life?" asked Angellyk, throwing up her arms in dismay. She was standing right there with them, but nobody had so much as acknowledged her presence.

"Oh, yes," Kregor said almost as if it were an afterthought. "And your life too."

Angellyk glared at him menacingly and threw her hands on her hips. She wanted to give him a piece of her mind, but held back. After all, they were on a mission and Raven wouldn't appreciate it very much if she started picking a fight with her crew.

"All right, that's enough everyone," Raven cut in, preemptively putting an end to their little quarrel. "We've got work to do."

Unwilling to let it go, Gyllek cut the wire anyway and then placed her things back in their proper place, closed the tool kit, and attached it to the magnetic panel on her belt.

Angellyk offered a hand to help Gyllek up but the girl ignored it and hopped to her feet then made her way back up the corridor as though the offer had never been given.

"Don't take it personally," Raven said, sidling up to Angellyk. "She's a bit of a lone wolf."

"That's amusing," Angellyk said. "The cat-girl that wants to be a wolf."

"And what are you?" Kregor asked, deliberately brushing Angellyk's shoulder as he walked passed. "An avocado that wants to be a comedian?"

"First of all," Angellyk said, her cheeks flushing red as she got defensive, "that doesn't make any sense. And secondly, you're green too! So, if I'm an avocado then…you're a…" Unable to think of anything to say, she trailed off without finishing her retort.

Kregor looked back over his shoulder at her and asked, "I'm a what?"

"You're a big stupid head!"

"Ha!" he laughed. "Takes one to know one."

"Guys!" Raven shouted, growing angry. "Stop acting like a couple of adolescents and get back to the task at hand. That's an order."

Kregor and Angellyk stared each other down with glowers so hot and fierce that it made the heat of the laser gun turrets pale in comparison.

Finally, Kregor let out a deep breath and followed after Gyllek.

When Raven passed Angellyk, she leaned in and whispered, "It's cute, really."

"What is cute?" Angellyk asked snootily.

"How badly you two want each other but are both too stubborn to admit it."

Caught completely off guard by Raven's comment, Angellyk balked but couldn't think of anything to say. Raven left her behind to mull it over and continued walking up the hall. "Wait. What are you trying to say? Does Kregor like me?"

"Think about it," Raven said from over her shoulder. She tapped the side of her temple, giving Angellyk a sly sideways glance and instantly had to hold back from laughing out loud at the sight of the astonished look on the girl's face as she pieced it together.

"You're kidding me, right?" she asked, catching up to Raven.

"Nope. He has the hots for you. And bad. But you didn't hear it from me."

"Okay, I get it," Angellyk said, nudging Raven's shoulder. "But I'm still going to have a little fun with him."

Raven smiled at Angellyk's tenacity. "Just, be nice. He's a good person."

Angellyk nodded silently, taking Raven's advice to heart. A few moments later, she fixed her eyes on Kregor's muscular frame and let her gaze gently settle onto his tight ass. Biting her lower lip, she said, "Mmm-hmmm. I bet he can quench a girl's thirst."

Raven shot a sideways glance at Angellyk, prompting the Bre'lal woman to laugh. "I wouldn't know anything about that."

"Don't tell me you've never once thought about it."

"Give me a break. *You* hadn't even thought about it until thirty seconds ago when I told you that he liked you."

"Yeah, but…"

"No buts, Angie. I don't think of him in that way. He's like my little brother. Just…you know…*big* little brother."

"I'm sure he is big in all the right places," Angellyk said, measuring the length of her forearm and trying to estimate the centimeters, a sly grin spreading across her face as she teased out the probable length of Kregor's *anatomy.*

"If you want to know that sort of thing, you can always just ask Jegra about it."

"He slept with the empress?!" Angellyk asked, sounding both surprised and impressed.

"Twice," Raven informed, throwing up two fingers.

"That stud!"

Angellyk paused in the middle of the corridor, her hand stroking her chin contemplatively, her other hand holding her elbow. She thought about how maybe she'd misjudged Raven's crew. Maybe it was like Raven had warned her when she decided to join, and they really were just taking a while to warm up to her. Now, however, she was certain that she was starting to warm up to them.

"Hey, K! Wait up," Angellyk said, racing up to Kregor.

"What do you want?" he said in a disgruntled fashion, shooting her a sideways glance. Although he secretly nurtured a crush on her, he still wasn't entirely comfortable with her being on this mission. Which is probably why he was being a bigger hard ass than he needed to be.

Angellyk raised both hands in polite surrender. "Look, big guy. I think we may have gotten off on the wrong foot back there. What do you say we start over?" She stopped and held out her hand.

Kregor paused and turned to face her. Wondering suspiciously why she'd had sudden change of heart, he looked down at her hand and mulled it over for a moment. Maybe she actually had a big heart like Raven had suggested, and if she was willing to try then so was he. He smiled at her and took her hand in his, his massive fist practically engulfing hers.

"Oh, wow, you have such a firm grip," she said, giggling flirtatiously. In the distance she caught a glimpse of Raven shaking her head in amusement for what she knew to be par for the course of Angellyk's seduction game. She just ignored Raven and tossed her hair and gently touched Kregor's arm.

Kregor smiled and then continued on his way, looking over in surprise when Angellyk started walking alongside him.

"I hear you've met the empress," Angellyk said after a moment.

"Yes," Kregor said, smiling down at her.

"That's amazing. Tell me, what is she like?"

"I thought you had met her," he said, giving her a curious look.

"She visited me while I was being detained. We had a brief five-minute chat where she interrogated me and that was it. It really wasn't a social visit. But I was impressed by her."

"Understandable," he said, nodding his head. "She's an impressive woman."

"Tell me about her," Angellyk said.

After another moment, Kregor began to extol all of Jegra's virtues to the green skinned woman as they made their way toward the station's command center.

Raven, hanging back, listened amusedly as two of her favorite friends became closer. Like Jegra, Raven had lost her parents at a young age. She had gone her entire life without belonging to anywhere or anything. For her, too, her friends were her family. And she'd do anything to see that they were happy.

Jegra, of course, went one further and tried to ensure all her friends stayed safe. But Raven wasn't an ideologue like the empress. In her line of work, feeling secure wasn't in the job description. She took dangerous jobs with even more dangerous clients. She knew the risk. And so did her crew. But she admired Jegra for caring that deeply for her friends.

In fact, over the past couple of weeks, Raven had been feeling lonely and all she wanted to do was call Jegra on the holovid and have a woman to woman talk. What they'd talk about was beyond her, but it seemed that any time they were in a room together they always found something of interest to discuss.

That's one of the things that made it so easy to feel close to Jegra. She listened to you. She engaged with you. She felt what you were feeling, sympathized with your problems, and rejoiced along with you in your accomplishments. She was exactly as Kregor had explained, wonderful in almost every way.

"Over here!" Gyllek's voice came echoing down the hall.

The team gathered around a couple of large doors.

"The control center for the whole base is behind these doors," Gyllek informed them. She tapped a code into the wall panel and it flashed red and buzzed rudely at her as if to say, *it's not going to happen.* She quickly fetched a small black box from her utility belt and slapped it onto the surface of the control panel. It stuck with a magnetic *clack* and she flipped a switch on its side and activated it.

"What's that?" Kregor asked, nodding his chin at the device.

"It's a code breaker. It should have the doors open in just a nanosecond."

Unexpectedly, two heavy blast doors slid shut and crashed together with a metal *clank*, cutting them off from the room with an added layer of protection.

"Is that supposed to happen?" Angellyk asked, jutting a thumb over her shoulder toward the doors.

"No," Gyllek grumbled, a frown settling on her brow as she watched the black box crackle and fizz as it burned itself out. "It seems they have a five-tier firewall rather than the standard three tiers. I can hack it, but I'll need to go back to the ship and get my things. It'll take some time."

"How much time?" Kregor asked.

Gyllek counted her fingers and ran the numbers through her head. Settling on a rough estimate, she replied, "About eight hours."

"Eight hours?" Angellyk echoed, not amused by the prospect of sitting around on her thumbs for eight hours doing nothing.

"Here," Raven said, stepping forward. "Let me try." She plucked the small device off the panel, handed it off to Gyllek, and then placed her hand over the wall panel. After a moment, delicate, vein-like circuitry just beneath her skin began to glow bright pink. Her eyes, too, lit up with Dagon energy as she hacked into the station's security system.

After another moment, the blast doors reopened. Then the main doors.

"That'a girl!" Angellyk said, relieved she didn't have to suffer eight hours of boredom. "I knew you could do it." Turning to Kregor, she smiled. "I knew she could do it."

He simply nodded in agreement. The captain, after all, was as resourceful as they came.

"Uh…guys…" Gyllek's voice said meagerly.

"Even if she hadn't gotten the doors open," Kregor said, addressing Angie, "I have a plasma cutter back on the ship. One way or another, we'd have gotten through. It was just a matter of time."

"Guys…" Gyllek hissed, finally getting their attention.

They turned to look at the girl; she was pointing into the room. Her hand trembled with fear and she cautiously eased away from the entrance as though something terrible lurked in the darkness beyond.

"What is it, Gyllek?" Kregor asked.

Raven quickly drew her blaster and dropped to one knee. Just then the room's lights automatically flickered on and, standing in the middle of the room, was a Seyferrian Centurion. A massive, six-legged war machine that was a cross between a Correllian scorpion and a Kree'alekkian armored crayfish. It was armed to the teeth, and it wasn't the type of thing that could be taken out with just a simple disruptor blast. You either needed some serious firepower or an EMP grenade. Of which they were fresh out.

Activated when the doors opened, the machine reared up on its legs, its three front mounted eyes glowing a menacing red.

<<Intruders>> it intoned in a most intimidating voice.

"Just perfect," Kregor said, gripping his battle hammer in both hands and holding it in front of him.

Gyllek slowly retreated behind the Dragonian and cowered. "I think, maybe, opening this door was a huge mistake," she whispered fretfully.

Angellyk pulled out dual blasters from twin holsters on her thighs and trained them on the war machine. "Why did it have to be a Centurion? Why couldn't the emperor be a cheapskate like every other monarch in the galaxy and just buy a damn X4 battle android like everyone else? At least their heads make a satisfying *pop* when you blast them. These things are just…mean."

The Centurion's dual mounted gun turrets, which were essentially mini-gun plasma blasters, began spinning as they wound up.

A red bolt of energy shot across the room, followed by another, and another, in rapid succession. As the machine warmed up, the blasts were firing off at an astonishing seven thousand rounds per minute. Both guns blazing, Gyllek screamed and threw her hands up defensively, believing this was the end.

After a moment, however, she realized she hadn't been vaporized and peeked between her fingers to find Raven holding the laser blasts at bay with a blue energy shield she'd erected from her hands using the Dagonian energy she carried inside of her.

The blue shield, which took up the entire entrance way, flickered with each blast. "Everyone, get back to the ship," Raven shouted. "I won't be able to hold it for long," she said with a fatigued groan. Stopping that much firepower was a serious drain on her, but even though it took all her strength to keep the energy barrier up, it sure as hell beat the alternative. "I can give you all enough time to get clear of it," she said through gritted teeth and a clenched jaw.

"We're not going anywhere," Kregor said, taking a step forward and tightening his grip on the handle of his war hammer.

"Damn right we're not," Angellyk said, sidling up to Raven, her blasters still trained on the Centurion. "No one is getting left behind. Not today. We face this thing together."

Gyllek sighed, and then joined the others under the archway of the entrance. Drawing out a min-blaster from her back waistband, she said, "Fine. Let's get this over with."

Even as they were facing their imminent demise, Raven couldn't be prouder of her crew. They weren't just loyal, they were family. *If*, she thought to herself, she was going to die this day, then, she was glad that it would be standing on her feet next to them.

11

A brilliant orange sun beat down on the stucco and mud structures of Arena City, baking it and everyone inside of it until, like a red clay pottery that had been left out in the sun for too long, everything was dried and cracked.

The summer heatwave caused water shortages and the weathered faces of those who made the city their home looked for reprieve under outdoor tents and solar paneled awnings that ran the length of the old dusty streets. Raphine, Jegra, and Danica kept to the shadows as they crept along the side streets of the bustling city. Dressed in the desert garb of muted tans and browns so as not to draw unwanted attention to themselves, they jostled through the crowd as they made their way to the heart of the marketplace.

In addition to their everyday apparel, Jegra had dyed herself blue and had prosthetic ears put on to better blend in with the Dagon patrons and so as not to be recognized in the city where she was most famous. Raphine signaled for them to hold up, and they ducked into the seclusion of an unimportant alleyway. Checking her scanner to make sure they had the right coordinates, she pointed at the open street ahead of them, bustling with street vendors of all kinds, and said, "Up ahead is the drop point."

"Good. You head up and scout the area, Raphine. We'll wait here for a few minutes then we'll sweep both sides of the street before rejoining you," Jegra said.

Raphine nodded and strode off, determined to carry on the mission. As she disappeared around the corner and entered the bustling market, Danica turned toward Jegra with a sly grin on her Prussian blue lips.

"What?" Jegra asked, feeling self-conscious. She examined her blue arms and hands to see if something might be wrong. "Is something off with my coloring?"

"No. Not at all," Danica said, still smiling at her.

Jegra laughed. "Seriously, why are you looking at me like that."

"Because I didn't think I could love you any more than I already did, but this color on you…it's…absolutely splendid."

"And here I thought you loved me for me," Jegra teased.

Danica's grin widened. "I didn't think I'd react this way, but even I have to admit you make one fine Dagon woman, my empress."

"Why, thank you, milady," Jegra said playfully, bowing with exaggerated regality.

Danica laughed.

"Did you dye your whole body or just the parts that are exposed?" Danica asked, reaching up and curling her finger around the low-cut neckline of Jegra's tan shirt. Pulling it down to reveal more skin, she leaned in and peered down into the depths of Jegra's cleavage. "Oh, wow! You did!"

Jegra laughed again. "It wouldn't be a convincing disguise if I didn't go all out…what if I lose my clothing out here? Anyway, right now, we'd better keep our minds focused on the task at hand."

"Right," Danica said. She'd felt fidgety all afternoon. She desperately wanted to steal away and take a hit of Nividium. But if she let Jegra down now, she would only confirm Jegra's concerns that she wasn't ready for active duty. No, she pushed down the urge to dose herself and followed Jegra's lead.

The two of them stepped out of the alley together and entered the noise and bustle of the market. Vendors were shouting out verbal advertisements for their products, saying practically anything to turn your head, and customers haggled for better deals up and down the boulevard.

"You sweep that side of the street and take position over there," Jegra said, pointing up the street toward a row of canopy styled tents where some vendors were selling faux, brand name bags and cheap jewelry guaranteed to be "the real thing." "Act casual, and pretend to do some shopping. Maybe even buy something, just to make it convincing."

Danica nodded and casually slipped into the lively throng of shoppers, merchants, and passers-by and disappeared.

Jegra turned and spotted Raphine's position up the street and thrust her chin, acknowledging her. The girl gave a subtle nod in return and then pretended to peruse a rack of delicate gossamer scarves in an assorted rainbow of colors and traditional Dagon floral designs.

Masterfully weaving in and out of the crowd, Jegra moved up the street. All walks of alien life roamed the busy marketplace, including Bre'lal, Dagon, Skyllakkian, Salamandarian, and numerous other strange and exotic species. There was even a Bakktu examining blades at a blacksmith's shop facing a narrow side street.

Two Dragonian women batted their double eyelids at Jegra and looked back at her as she passed. They giggled and locking arms, whispered some snide remarks to one another at Jegra's expense which sparked a fit of the giggles. She ignored them and continued up the street.

Another block away, she came across a brothel and saw a small Nyctan child standing in front of it with a shock collar around her neck. The girl stood, looking down at her feet, between two common street women. Although Jegra had no qualms with the profession itself, she couldn't tolerate them selling underage flesh.

"Who runs this establishment?" she demanded to know.

Her intimidating stature and blue-skin prompted the two women to become extremely accommodating. Dagons were the dominant species in the galaxy, and apart from the infrequent sideways glances and occasional patronizing remark, nobody wanted to cross a Dagon.

"Madam Elowiin is out at the moment, but I'm sure we can find someone to suit your needs."

"This Nyctan girl. How long has she been working here?"

"Ah," the first whore said, a lascivious grin forming on her lips. "If the small ones are what you like, this girl is guaranteed to satisfy you."

Jegra knelt down, making herself accessible to the child. "Are they treating you well?"

"Yes, ma'am." The girl didn't make eye contact and her response was so quick that Jegra thought it likely rehearsed.

"If you don't want to do this kind of work, you can come with me," she said.

The two sex workers looked at each other, confused as to whether or not they should intervene. After all, it wasn't wise to cross a Dagon, but they weren't certain that this girl was up for sale.

"Mistress Dagoni," one of the women said, "I do not believe this girl is for sale. But I can inquire on your behalf should you have your mind set on her. Our madam is fair and, if the price is right, I'm sure she'd be willing to part with the child."

Jegra stood back up, towering over the two women. "I am Empress Jegra Alakandra's envoy. Tell your madam that child prostitution is forbidden on this world and that the empress shall be sending inspectors to ensure the girl is well treated, well taken care of, and not on offer. If Madam Elowiin should disregard the empress's wishes, she'll find herself and her business relocated to Brexis, the farthest asteroid mining colony beyond the Outer Rim. Do I make myself clear?"

Jegra was practically fuming, but she redirected her ire into a fiery gaze that caused both women to lower their eyes in submission and take a step back.

"We shall relay the message, Your Elegance."

"And take that shock collar off of her, too," Jegra added.

The smaller Bre'lal woman on the left complied and unbolted the collar. Once the girl was free of the device, she looked up at Jegra with her black, Nyctan eyes and held her gaze. After a moment, the short woman ushered the little girl back up the steps and into the brothel.

"Apologies your elegance," the remaining Bre'lal said, and then she too scurried up the stairs and disappeared inside the ornate twin doors of *Madam Elowiin's Sanctuary.*

Although Jegra desperately wanted to liberate the girl, Thessalonica wasn't exactly the most lawful place in the universe. There was still all manner of crime and the black market thrived here. If she killed it dead, the moon's economy would die along with it, which is why, at the moment, she could only regulate it.

"They're here." Raphine's voice came through Jegra's earpiece.

Jegra turned and looked up the street to see two large brutes, one a Rhinoptrus, resembling a humanoid rhino with four sets of arms, and the other a copper skinned Jacquardian, an islander race of humanoids from the tropical region of the moon Riverion. Jegra had always suspected that Ishtar Bantu had hailed from Riverion as well, except for Ishtar's striking Dagon features, which made her specific species nearly impossible to identify.

The copper skinned man, who had ethnic tattooing from head to foot, had a duffle bag slung over his shoulder. He'd stopped two blocks up the busy street and looked back, pausing to check if they were being followed. The Rhinoptrus flexed his four massive arms and joined his partner in taking one last look at the crowd before the two of them ducked down a small side street.

"We need to keep an eye on them," Jegra said, finger pressed to her earpiece.

"I'm on it," Raphine's voice came back.

"Me too," Danica said.

"Negative, Dani. Hang back and wait for me to rejoin you."

"Too late," Dani replied. "I'm already—" *skrrrr...*

Danica's comm signal abruptly cut out and Jegra, panic filling her voice, called out, "Dani? Danica? Can you hear me?"

By talking to herself in public, she was starting to draw too much attention to herself and decided to continue up the street. As she took quick strides to catch up with them, she called Raphine. "Raphine, do you have eyes on Danica?"

"No. But I have eyes on our mark."

"Zallek? He's here?"

"It looks like it's going down now. He's got a land rover parked a klick up the road."

"Don't engage until I get there," Jegra said.

Jegra picked up her pace and broke into a jog. Shooting around a bend and down another winding side street, she nearly crashed into Raphine, who was hanging back. Sidling up to the girl, she asked, "What did I miss?"

"They teleported four large crates down and loaded them onto the truck."

"They must have a ship already on the planet somewhere since there's no way through the blockade. The *Shard* would have already identified them and alerted me."

"And a location to location teleport would merely seem like normal traffic. What I don't get," Raphine said, "is why Zallek doesn't just beam the drugs directly to his base of operations."

"Because unlike starships, which change locations so frequently that the teleport signatures dissipate over time and distance, a fixed location with frequent teleports would leave too big of a residual ionized particle trail and could be traced."

"You sound like my big sister," Raphine said, laughing about how the blue-skinned Jegra was rattling off the technical babble like a seasoned pro. "She's tech savvy too."

Jegra almost said *I know*, but cut herself short. She still hadn't revealed to Raphine the fact that she had not only run into her sister Onelle Te'Legra, but that she was currently being held aboard the *Skywend* on charges of attempting to assassinate the empress. Instead, Jegra merely replied, "I read a lot and like to keep myself abreast of things. You never know when the information might come in handy."

"'Aye miss," a thick Jacquardian accent said, and they both turned to see the copper skinned man approaching them. "May I speak with you for a moment, girlie?" The man placed his hand on Raphine's waist and ushered her to the edge of the street.

"Hey, don't touch her," Jegra growled, but the bulky frame of the Rhinoptrus stepped out in front of her, effectively cutting her off from Raphine and preventing her from intervening. Ruffled, Jegra drew back a step, scowled at the hired muscle, and tightened her fists. "You're making a big mistake."

Unintimidated by the blue-skin, the Rhino just puffed out a blast of snot-infused air from his nostrils and folded both sets of arms across his burly chest. He eyeballed her from across his two horns with a stern gaze that cautioned her not to try anything heroic.

"Hands off!" Raphine shouted, slapping the brute's arms away. He approached her again, this time more forcefully, grabbed her by the scruff of her neck and slammed her face-first into the wall of the nearby building.

The brute smashed her into the stucco so hard that she thought her cheek would split open. At the same time, he twisted her other arm behind her back. "Ow!" she yelped.

"The boss don't like ye' girlies snooping. It be time for you to get along now. Savvy?"

Not one to stand around and watch a friend be abused, Jegra's eyes went wide with rage. In the distance, she caught a glimpse of Zallek. He paused, as though he sensed someone watching him, and slowly turned around. Their eyes met and he smiled condescendingly at her. She wanted to wash that smug grin off his face with her fists, but that would have to wait. Right now, Raphine needed her help.

With a two-finger salute, as if to bid her adieu, Zallek turned back toward his vehicle and disappeared around the back end, the crates of Nividium stacked neatly in the rear cargo bed.

Displeased that she had to let the big fish go, Jegra looked back at the Rhino and, raising a fist, flexed her jaw angrily. "Like I said," she snarled, "big mistake!"

ZAP!

Jegra's muscles seized up and she collapsed to the ground like a sack of bricks. The stun-rod had hit her from behind, and due to the way in which she fell, she couldn't get a clear look at her attacker. All she could do is watch the shocked look on Raphine's face as she seemingly recognized the identity of the one who had snuck up on them.

"You?" Raphine asked, staring with mouth agape at the person holding the stun-rod that had so fortuitously gotten the jump on them.

"I really wish you hadn't seen that, girlie," the copper skin said, and then smashed Raphine's head into the wall so forcefully she was rendered unconscious. Her body collapsed to the ground next to Jegra's, her green forearm falling across her waist.

Anger and adrenaline surged through Jegra and she tried desperately to get her muscles to respond so that she could push herself up and take these assholes out. But a second zap of the stun-rod prevented her from doing so.

"Dagon or not, I think you should stay down, Your Elegance," a woman's voice said.

Even though it took everything she had just to roll over and face her attacker, she somehow managed it. Flopping onto her back, Jegra looked up to find none other than the madam of the brothel herself, Madam Elowiin, standing over her.

The madam's narrow eyebrows condensed at the center ridge of her brow and her low hanging eyelids, painted green, brought out the color of her icy blue eyes. She wore an oriental silk kimono with an elegant swan brocade stitched into the black, white, and gold floral-styled dress. The only thing that Jegra wasn't expecting was for Madam Elowiin to be Seyferrian.

"The boss appreciates the assist, Madam Elowiin," the copper skin said, and handed over a data stick. A large sum of universal credits for her troubles. After passing along the money, he turned back around, stepping over Jegra's paralyzed body, and slapped the back of his partner's shoulder in a jovial fashion. "Let's get out of here before security arrives."

The two men jostled their way back into the crowd and disappeared into the daily grind of the marketplace. Madam Elowiin, meanwhile, looked down at the blue-skinned imposter and with a knowing look in her eye, said, "Now, what are we going to do about you, Empress Alakandra?"

Gerrard Van Zallek opened the driver's side door of his SUV to find an attractive Dagon woman sitting in the passenger seat, dosing herself with Nividium.

The glovebox was open and his sample kit of the new batch lay sprawled out on the seat beside her. She sighed out in euphoric bliss and then let her head fall to the side, her half-hung eyelids struggling to stay open as she studied his face.

"And who might you be, luv?"

"I'm just a girl, enjoying a little taste of your newest product."

"I sure hope you can pay for it, my dear. Because if not…"

"I'm good for it," she said in a lackadaisical voice that faded away as she drifted in and out of her blissful state. She smiled and let her head rock back on her shoulders. "This new stuff is heavenly," she said. She wasn't about to stop just because she'd gotten caught red handed. She had needed this hit all bloody afternoon.

In the distance the sirens of local security could be heard and Zallek looked over her shoulder and frowned.

"I'm afraid I'll have to collect another time. Right now, I'm in a bit of a rush. So, my luv, I'll need you to skedaddle." He jutted a thumb over his shoulder, showing her where she could take herself and her troubles to get lost. She merely smiled at him again, no longer fully aware of her surroundings.

Annoyed, he tried to yank her out by her arm but she was as limp as a rag doll and wouldn't budge.

"I didn't want to have to do this," Zallek said, reaching behind his back and pulling out a blaster. Placing the gun against the temple of her head, his finger incrementally slid toward the trigger.

Danica began unbuttoning her shirt, revealing her cleavage to him, teasing him with her breasts. If she played it right, he'd simply think she was an addict doing whatever it took to get a fix.

"What are you doing?"

"You think I'm a scag, don't you??" she asked. Scags were drug addicts who hung around drug dealers like Skallakian cockroaches. If she turned out just to be another junkie, he probably wouldn't hesitate to shoot her and leave her body in the alley.

Given this, she knew that she had to convince him, and fast, that she was of some value to him. Her body was her only leverage at the moment and, truthfully, she didn't have any better plan. "I ain't no scag," she said as seriously as she could muster in her drug induced rapture. "And I ain't no vid-skinner. Check me for a vid-collar if you want." Her finger trailed down to the first button of her tan shirt and she flipped it open. Then another. And another.

Zallek's eyebrow raised on his forehead as she undid her shirt and pulled it open for him to see that she wasn't lying. Not a scag. And definitely not a vid-skinner—that is, an undercover drug enforcer who used holovid screens to mask their identity and infiltrate a drug dealer's operations. Although, there wasn't much worry of this on Thessalonica, it never hurt to be careful since the risk was never worth it. But this time it was different, because she was telling the truth. No vid-collar. Not a skinner. The bare neckline and ample, soft curving breasts proved that much.

Sirens, growing even closer, forced him to refrain from offing her and he looked over his shoulder again. "Graddack," he grumbled and pulled the gun away.

At least by the time he got back to the base, she'd be so high he could do whatever he wanted to her. That would be her payment for stealing his drugs.

Zallek climbed into the vehicle and shut the door behind him. "Very well then, you'll be riding with me," he said, settling into the driver's seat. He placed his blaster on the dashboard, and then hit the start button. The electric engine turned on with a deep whine that gradually grew higher in pitch, then he shifted the car into drive.

Ready to roll out, he glanced once more over at Danica, and then hit the accelerator. The oversized all-terrain wheels bit down on the dusty street and made purchase. With a jolt, the vehicle launched out into the street and tore down the crowded streets of Arena City. Dodging bystanders and labor droids left and right, a dust cloud rose up from the rear of the speeding vehicle.

Danica fell back into her seat, her shirt slipping fully open. She didn't care to bother dressing herself at the moment. Right now, she just wanted to enjoy the extreme high she was having.

This new stuff was far more potent than standard Nividium. And maybe, if she was lucky, Zallek would not only take her to his secret base of operations, but he might sell her the first official batch. The high was, in her estimation, the best she'd ever had.

12

Three Nephilim fighters streaked by the bow of the mid-sized freighter. The captain of the cargo vessel, Abdul Akkar Kalim, jammed the throttle forward and tried to engage the hyperdrive. But instead of jumping into hyperspace, all he heard was a loud and ominous *clunk.*

"Graddack!" Kalim muttered to himself. "The hyperdrive is busted. Again. Bloody, useless, piece of junk!" He rose out of the pilot's seat and gave the console a swift kick with the thick sole of his boot. If only his griping were enough to get the ship working again, then that really would be something.

But the engines were only part of his worries. The other was the nature of his cargo. It was of the highest priority. An order issued directly from the emperor himself. And it came with strict instructions. No matter what, he couldn't let his cargo land in the hands of this new enemy. If it looked like the enemy was going to get ahold of it, he was to destroy it.

The console lights began to flicker spastically and he gave it another good kick. The lights froze into place, seemingly fixed, and he dusted off his hands proudly. Quickly exiting the small cabin of the freighter's two seat cockpit, he entered into the adjoining corridor, hooked a right, and set out for the engine room.

"Anna!" he shouted, hollering up the corridor for his first mate. "Anna, where are you? We've got company and these engines aren't going to start themselves."

"I'm here, boss," a slender Bre'lal woman in overalls and covered in grease said, joining him in the junction way.

She had on flight goggles and had a utility belt that rattled with the various tools used for keeping this old bucket up and running. From plasma welders to foil duct tape for the heating conduits, it was all there. And if Anna was good at anything, it was keeping this ship up and running.

"The hyperdrive broke down again," Kalim informed her as she walked with him down the narrow confines of the corridor.

The drab gray paint of the ship's interior was peeling off the walls in patches and the ship had that well-worn look from years of service and not enough money to make all the necessary repairs. Regardless, the old hauler still got her cargo to its destination on time. Every time. Something Kalim prided himself on.

"I know, I heard it *conk* out from all the way in the cargo hold."

Kalim slowed up and looked over at the girl. Although she was only half his age and about five-foot four, she was the prettiest little thing he'd ever set his eyes upon. But romance wasn't on his list of skills when it came to people, so he'd spent the past few years admiring her from afar.

Besides, he didn't want to risk losing her by pulling some stupid sexist stunt. She was the hardest working crewman he'd ever had the pleasure of teaming with and he couldn't afford to lose her or her expertise.

If he was being honest, he had always hoped that the small crush he nurtured was mutual. But their relationship had always been Platonic. Even after three years of living in tight quarters together. They simply fell into a rhythm of doing things that worked for them. And that's how he liked it.

"And how's our precious cargo faring?"

"The cryostasis unit is functioning well within the specified parameters and suspended vitals check out as normal."

"That's excellent. Because I promised we'd get this unit to Emperor Dakroth no matter what. If we don't, it will be both our heads."

"And what about those vultures out there?" she asked, pointing a finger past a bulkhead toward the outer hull. "What if the Nephilim decide to board us and take the cargo for themselves? Then what?"

A grim look settled across Kalim's face. "I'll self-destruct the ship before I let this cargo fall into the hands of the enemy, Anna. If it comes to that, I want you to take the only remaining escape pod and save yourself."

"But Kalim—" she began in protest, but he quickly raised a hand and silenced her. She looked away, saddened by the thought of losing him. He was a good man.

An honorable man. And that was a rare thing to find in the backwaters of interstellar space.

"But nothing. I'm the captain of this ship, and a captain always goes down with his ship. That's an order, Anna."

"You're a good man, Kalim. Don't let anybody ever tell you otherwise." She placed a hand on his chest, paused and then smiled at him.

A pleasant smile formed on his lips, too, and he placed his hand on hers, winked to let her know there was nothing to worry about. Once their moment was over, they both turned and entered the engine room together. The heavy doors groaned in protest as they slid open to admit them inside.

It only took half an hour to get the hyperdrive's plasma infusion matrix patched and the power coupling replaced. Once they'd repaired the barely functioning fusion drive, Kalim wiped his hands with an already dirty rag and then headed back to the bridge to check on the status of their uninvited guests buzzing around the ship like agitated bees.

When he stepped into the cabin of the cockpit, one of the fighters was hanging directly in front of the front view portal and startled him. He froze in the archway of the cabin's entrance and waited as it ran a deep scan of the ship. A red laser grid washed over the captain as he stood in place.

"Bloody aliens," he said. Even though literally everyone was an alien from another world these days, the only aliens he hated more than space pirates were those that wanted to cause trouble for everyone. The vicious war mongers and conquerors that always felt they could lay claim to an infinite expanse. He sometimes wondered if they even understood the concept of cosmic inflation.

Up till now, the reports were coming in from all over the Commonwealth regarding these new aliens, and none of it was good news. First, there was communiqué that these assholes had destroyed Galliforn and that cargo vessels should steer clear. Then came whispers that they had invaded Nyctan and laid siege to the world, preventing anything from entering or leaving the planet.

By all accounts, it seemed as though this new race had come through The Rift from another galaxy and were slowly taking over the Commonwealth one system at a time. And rumors were, they had their greedy tentacles set on Dagon Prime next.

Which is precisely why Kalim needed to get his cargo to Dakroth. Kalim wanted to secure his last big payment before he and Anna made themselves scarce and laid low until this whole thing blew over. He had a nice little apartment he rented on The Cove where they could blend in and live comfortably for a few months, or even years, if need be.

Sure, it wasn't ideal. But it was better than getting picked off by some overzealous, trigger happy war mongers.

Naturally, Anna was free to do whatever she liked. He just assumed that she'd prefer to continue on with their partnership, since they worked so well together. It was extremely hard to find trustworthy crew members nowadays and he dreaded the thought of having to try and vet a new crew from scratch.

Also, he treated her well, paid her an equal split of their earnings, and never yelled or took advantage of her. That had to count for something.

The cargo they carried was so important to the Lord Emperor that he had classified it as top-secret. To even access the pod required a military-issue security passcode. If his ship *did* get boarded by pirates or a random border patrol, they'd need Imperial access codes to even enter the cargo bay, which only Kalim had.

Upon pain of death, Kalim was not to open the doors to the cargo bay under any circumstances. The only exception was if the ship was in imminent danger of being destroyed. In which case, he was supposed to safeguard the cargo and erase all record of it from the ship's data banks.

The glowing ship's scan ceased and then a husky voice, which sounded eerily like an A.I. but somehow wasn't, came over the comm system. "You are carrying an unmarked cargo container with a masked signature. Prepare to be boarded for inspection."

"Graddack," he said under his breath. The situation just went from bad to a whole lot worse.

Upset by the turn of events, he smashed a button on the nearby wall panel, flicked on the comm, and issued a response. "This is the cargo ship *Hermes.* We are a Commonwealth deep space freighter and do not recognize your authority in this sector. If you can give us the proper access codes, we'll gladly let you board for inspection. If not, we will have to report your illegal activity, along with your ship's I.D. tags, to the Trade Commission." He flicked off the comm and ignored their responder signal. Swiveling in his chair, he opened a line down to the engine room. "Anna, how are things looking down there?"

"We can make one last jump into hyperspace. But I don't know how long the patch will hold. It will need to be short if we want to keep the engines from going critical."

"Understood. It's going to have to do, for now, because we've got company up here, and they're demanding a free tour of the place."

"Screw that!" Anna practically shouted.

"You spoke my mind. But they're currently blocking our flight path and we don't have time to slow down and reverse our course. Not in this old bucket. So, hold on to your seat; things are about to get a little bit rough."

She knew exactly what he was planning. After years of working together, it was as though they could read each other's minds. "Are you sure that's such a good idea, Captain?"

"Sure? Not in the least. But I'm confident this ole girl will hold together long enough to get us out of here." *Please hold together,* he said as an aside, addressing the ship directly as he reached up and touched a nearby bulkhead for good luck.

"Aye, aye, boss. You're the captain."

The comm went silent and Kalim plopped down into the well-worn command chair, the leather cracking so badly in places you could see the faded yellow foam padding beneath. He quickly began flicking one switch after another as he ran through the hyperdrive start-up sequence and the ships FTL engines came online, grumbling and whining as they always did.

Just one last jump, ole girl, he whispered again, talking to his ship as though it were a pet and giving her encouragement. "Making the jump in 3…2…1…" At the zero mark he jammed the hyper drive throttle full forward and watched as the pinpricks of distant stars stretched into thin, spaghetti-like strands of multi-colored light.

A sudden flash, followed by what sounded like the hull of the ship screaming in agony rang throughout every part of the ship. Every bulkhead from head to stern whined as though it were going to tear apart. They crashed into one of the enemy vessels entering hyperspace, which meant their trip would be short lived as well.

The tunnel of hyperspace they'd entered only lasted a few moments before a deep rumble in the bowels of the ship followed by an explosion, forced them to drop out again.

A flaming mess, pieces of Kalim's cargo ship were breaking apart all around him. "Anna!" he called over the comm. "Anna, can you hear me?"

He knew the power coupling had blown and that it was only a matter of minutes before the power cycle caused the engines to overheat. And in their condition, it was almost certain that the fusion drive would go into meltdown. Worried for Anna's safety, he turned in his seat, bound to find her before the ship went up in a nuclear explosion when she appeared in the doorway...panting.

"That was a close one, boss."

"You're tellin' me," he said, relieved to see her uninjured.

The enemy ship they'd collided with had come out of nowhere, the wreckage likely being towed in their wake, which explained the delay. Fragments smashed into the view portal of the ship and then rebounded away. The collision was so loud that it startled them both and Anna screamed out with a high pitch shriek, clutching onto Kalim's arm and digging her fingernails into him.

"We're breaking up here," Kalim said. "You'd better get to the escape pod while you can, Anna."

"I'm sorry, boss, but I can't."

"I told you, Anna," he said, placing his hands on her shoulder. "You don't have to go down in flames with me. We've been through thick and thin, but I'm calling it. This is the end of the line."

"That's not what I meant, boss," she said, placing her hand on his. "I reallocated our cargo to the escape pod."

Kalim smiled at her, wishing he would have thought of it. "In that case, it's been a pleasure serving with you, Anna Evaria."

"The feeling is mutual, Kalim," she said, leaning into him as he wrapped his arm around her shoulder drew her close. Together, they stood on the bridge, keeping each other company in their final minutes and watched as the ship fell apart all around them.

In the distance hung a small moon. It might be Cordova, Kalim thought, since they'd been rounding Gamidon when they crashed the ship. But, without the ship's nav-computer, it could be anywhere, really. All he knew was that it had an atmosphere and their cargo would survive.

Wherever they were, they were back in Dagon space now and so their cargo at least had a chance of getting picked up by the good guys. Those enemy fighters would have to be pretty damn bold, not to mention stupid, to take on the Dagon Empire.

"Computer, this is Captain Abdul Akkar Kalim. Initiate self-destruct sequence and jettison the escape pod on my command. Three, two, one…execute!"

The sound of the escape pod launching signaled them to look out the view portal and, still embracing one another, they watched it rocket away from the ship, its thrusters flaring blue as it shrunk into the distant starscape, heading for the lonely moon in the distance.

Kalim turned toward the green-skinned woman and running his thumb across her cheek, he wiped away a grease stain. "I've been waiting for three long years to do this."

He simultaneously raised her chin and leaned in to kiss her. She closed her eyes, waiting for his tender lips to meet hers and, then, in a bright flash of fiery light they went up together in a grand explosion as the fusion reactor blew.

The escape pod streaked away from the exploding cargo ship. Behind it, a towering plume of orange and yellow bubbly flames expanded outward from the ship. As the gasses burned up and the fuel dwindled away to nothing, the large fire-bubble shrank back in on itself and fizzled out.

Small fragments of the cargo ship, like confetti, trailed after the escape pod, catching the light of a distant star and lighting up like the tail of a comet.

The escape pod's emergency beacon activated and its thrusters died down. Now all it needed to do was let the moon's gravity reel it in.

A few minutes later, the escape pod heated up as it entered the moon's atmosphere. As the belly of the craft grew dangerously hot, flames ignited from the drag and the small craft's automated thrusters fired, rolling it over so that the heat shielding absorbed the brunt of the friction.

Once through the atmosphere, the vehicle's triple parachutes deployed and slowed the pod to a safe speed. The white, egg-shaped pod floated down toward a desert landscape, its red parachutes appearing like three colorful parasols above it.

Inside the pod, the collision alarm rang and a blue hand flew up to the glass as two eyes that sparkled like pink sapphires, darted around with panic.

13

The space pirate Novac Tamoran's ship, the *Avarice*, jumped away leaving Vice Admiral Callestra Van Morgan watching from the observation deck, hands locked behind her back. She now had to analyze the data Tamoran had supplied her and find a weakness in the enemy fleet's defenses.

The alien technology they'd encountered was unlike anything she'd ever seen before. It would take several days to crunch all the relevant data and the clock was counting down to the inevitable confrontation between her fleet and theirs. Still, she was prepared to do whatever was necessary to protect Dagon Prime. As admiral of the Imperial fleet, she couldn't afford to be soft. Not as the threat of all-out war loomed on the horizon.

After Tamoran's ship jumped away in a bright flash reminiscent of a lightning strike, she turned her attention to her planet's moon, Thessalonica, rounding the planet on its orbit.

The bulge of the orange, sandy world crested over the curving arc of the blue and green planet that was her home. She couldn't understand why the Lord Emperor had allowed a non-citizen to become empress, let alone gift her their precious moon. It didn't make any sense to favor her in such a way. She wasn't even a pure blood.

Apparently, though, she had the emperor by his ball sack, because he was acting like a lovestruck pup rather than the leader of an entire galactic empire that spanned seven full star systems.

But Jegra was a problem for another time. As long as she no longer had political sway, she was toothless in this fight. Callestra's coup had worked, and all Jegra could do was take it bending over backwards. Right now, though, the only thing that worried Callestra was securing the safety of the empire.

She turned her back to the vista of the moon growing large over the cusp of Dagon Prime's horizon and exited the empty observation area. In a few hours, people would be getting off their shifts and coming up here to unwind. But Callestra preferred to keep a low profile during the busy hours. It was the middle of the morning, when it was a place of quiet and solitude. A place where she did her best thinking, staring out at the stars, and losing herself in their grandeur.

When the exit doors parted, Callestra was shocked to find her father standing in the corridor, already on his way to see her. She stood frozen in the open doorway, not knowing what to make of it.

He never visited her up here. And she wasn't exaggerating, either. She couldn't remember a single time he'd come up to the ship. He had always preferred to televid conference with her.

She'd always assumed it was because he was such a busy man and rarely could find time for her. He barely managed to make time for their weekly televid calls, let alone make house visits, but here he was. Aboard her ship, standing before her, looking at her with an affectionate grin.

"What's the matter, father? Is something wrong?" she asked, perplexed by the sudden, unannounced visit.

"Why does something need to be wrong," he asked, "for a loving father to visit his only daughter?"

It felt as though she were a schoolgirl again and he was waiting for her at home so he could scold her for getting less than a perfect score on some exam or other. She felt her hands grow balmy and her chest tensed up with a sudden bout of nervousness. She took a breath and mustered up a smile, and this helped calm her jittery nerves.

Senator Targon Van Morgan smiled and opened his arms to accept Callestra's embrace. Resting her hands on his chest, she leaned and rose up on her toes and kissed him on his lips—a customary family greeting in her culture. Their exchange completed, she drew back and regained her formal composure. "Do I need an excuse to see my beautiful daughter?"

"No, father. I'm glad you came. Really. But it's so unlike you. I can't help but worry. Is everything well?"

"If by 'well' you mean besides the fact the emperor is missing, a new enemy threatens our borders, and war seems to be imminent, then, yes, all is well."

Callestra merely nodded in agreement but didn't reply. She simply was fishing for answers; if he didn't want to tell her, he wouldn't. So, she let it be.

She gestured for him to join her as she made her way up the corridor and he nodded and joined her, matching her stride as she went.

Her father cleared his throat and then, after a pause, gave her a tender look. A look he only used when he was begging for her forgiveness for some misdeed or when he wanted something from her.

"I hear you have intercepted some classified information that might give us the edge in the upcoming confrontation with the Nephilim."

Needless to say, Callestra was surprised to find he had already learned about the information she'd gotten from Tamoran. After all, she had only received it a half an hour ago.

It was doubtful that Novac Tamoran would have betrayed her trust in such a way, seeing as the embarrassing leverage she had over him would make him a laughing stock from one corner of the galaxy to the next. What's more, Tamoran had nothing to gain by giving up her trust and everything to gain by keeping it. Which meant her father had spies aboard her ship.

That revelation pissed her off to no end. It wasn't that he was keeping tabs on her to watch over and protect her. He was doing it to have power over her, like he always did, and it infuriated her.

He still treated her like a child who couldn't tie her own shoelaces, so instead of teaching her and letting her fumble through it, he swooped in and did it for her. Always expecting thanks afterwards for having to do everything for her. As though she were ungrateful. She wasn't, but that's how he always made it seem.

"News travels fast," she said with a slight sardonic tinge, forcing a polite smile onto her purple lips to mask her irritation.

Her father smiled back, his narrow grin seeming just as forced as hers. She pushed down her feelings of anger and informed her father, "You'll be pleased to know that I have my team working on deciphering the data as we speak. When I know, you'll know."

"Excellent," Senator Targon said, his grin spreading out in genuine fashion this time. He placed his hands behind his back and rejoined his daughter as they made their way through the long, crisscrossing corridor.

After a momentary silence, Targon hummed contemplatively, letting out a long drawn out "Hmmm."

Callestra fought the urge to roll her eyes, seeing as this was her father's way of forcing others to ask him what was on his mind. He usually proceeded to not only tell you what he was thinking, but also would be sure to explain why you should be thinking it was well.

"There's one more matter I want to discuss with you regarding the empress. I have it on good authority that Jegra Alakandra has found the location of Dakroth's secret shipbuilding facility. If this is true, she'll not only have access to ships and weapons of her own, but she'll be able to build more ships and increase her own fleet. We need to prevent her from getting her hands on that facility before we do. The council has voted. You are to find its location, lock it down, and ensure the empress keeps her nose out of it. If she should give you any trouble, just tell her it's a matter of national security and that in a time of martial law, your authority overrides hers."

"If she should still resist?"

"If the empress should disregard Dagon law, then you will treat her as any other common criminal. Arrest her and take the facility by force. As admiral of the most powerful fleet in the galaxy, it is your responsibility to remind her who holds all the power."

Callestra smiled, threw her fist over her left breast, and bowed as a gesture of familial reverence. Although she found her father to be a difficult man, he was also wise. He would not lead her astray, and so, she decided it best to comply with his wishes. For now.

"As you wish, father."

Senator Targon paused in a junction, and looked over at Callestra. His warm fatherly persona melted away leaving only the hardened senator. Even his sky-blue eyes seemed to change to an icy cold and his mouth turned downward in a disapproving manner that made his every look seem exceptionally stern.

"I'm afraid I cannot stay to visit, my dear. Important matters call me back to the senate. The Council is convening to discuss contingency plans should we, heaven forbid, fail in our mission to defend our world and need to issue a planet wide evacuation."

"Emperor Dakroth would never allow such a thing," Callestra said. It was more of a reflection than a statement, but her words obviously upset her father because he shot her a displeased look and grabbed her by her arm just above her elbow. His grip was overly firm and she felt the inclination to pull away. But she clenched her jaw and bore the discomfort as he lectured her.

"Dakroth is a bloody fool," he growled. Seeing that he had startled her, he let go of her arm and then softened his voice. "My child, there is still a lot for you to learn. Dakroth was blinded by ambition and delusions of grandeur. But wars are never won with brute strength alone. You need planning. A strong defense to match your offense. And, most of all, patience."

Callestra smiled and nodded as though she'd been taught a profound lesson. Of course, she knew all of this already and didn't appreciate being talked down to like a child, but there was nothing she could say that would convince her father that she was more than capable. She decided to let it go. Now wasn't the time to start yet another row with the old man.

"In that case, I wish you a safe return, father."

They kissed again and then parted ways at a junction. Callestra frowned once her father had disappeared around the bend of the corridor on his way to the teleportation room. There was a spy in her ranks and she had a good idea who it was.

She found J'axen waiting for her on the bridge. When he turned to greet her with the Dagon salute, he held his position until she saluted back.

He smiled and then started to approach her. On his way to her, he realized something wasn't quite right. The look in her eyes was all wrong. Before he could even ask what was bothering her, however, she drew a knife on him.

Callestra thrust the korridium blade into J'axen's throat in a merciless surprise attack. With one fluid swipe of the blade, she slit his throat. As the red line opened wide and burgundy blood began to ooze from the gaping wound, the whole bridge crew grew silent.

J'axen's body hit the deck of the command center with a thump, landing face down. His blood pooled around his head, gradually expanding outward as the circumference of the puddle grew.

The bloody knife clutched firmly in her hand, Callestra scanned the shocked faces of everyone and then snarled, "If anyone else here is a spy, just know this is what happens to traitors who betray my trust."

Finished with her little speech, she looked down in disgust at J'axen's lifeless body. "Set a course for Cordova, maximum speed. And, will somebody please get this piece of trash off my ship."

"Ma'am?" one of her officers asked.

"Dump him out the airlock for all I care."

"But he's an Imperial officer ma'am. Shouldn't we at least—"

Callestra's eyes flashed hot pink with Dagon energy and pierced the soul of the officer like a pair of glowing hot daggers. The officer gulped nervously, realizing his mistake in questioning the orders of the admiral. Falling into rank, he let out a meager, "Yes, ma'am. Right away, ma'am" and scurried away to do as commanded.

With that small unpleasantry out of the way, Callestra puffed out a hot breath of air, jostling a few loose strands of hair out of her eyes. She composed herself and then turned on her heels in a rigid, military fashion, and stormed off the bridge.

As soon as the admiral was off the bridge, the first officer, a young man named Orsek Van Tavaris, took the command chair. Inclined on the padded arm of the raised seat, he stared out of the view portal into the depths of space and said, "You all heard the admiral. Full speed to Cordova." He raised a finger, pointing at a distant cluster of stars and, leaning forward in his chair, said, "Engage."

The combat training center aboard the *Verlag* was where Callestra liked to blow off steam. She stood at the center of the large cubical room and began unfastening the button on her uniform.

The training center was laid out in an equilateral grid pattern. Every square meter was divided into six smaller squares. Each of these inner squares was in turn broken into another set of six, smaller squares. This densely packed series of slender rods could rise and fall like a pin impression mold, creating a real-time topography on all six surfaces of the room.

Overlaid onto this intricately shifting grid was a holographic projection that recreated high definition visuals of famous battle sites recorded for posterity throughout Dagon's illustrious history of empire building. Here is where a soldier could train and learn in real combat simulations. They could run through classic battle scenarios or set the computer to offer entirely new ones where the AI was programmed to outsmart the user.

Callestra set the simulation to level ten, the highest setting, and then stripped off her formal white admiral's uniform, leaving only her light gray sports bra and matching cotton underwear on. She folded her white slacks and set them down next to her jacket and then slowly rose and turned to face the opposite wall.

"Run simulation *Jegra Four.*" She raised her blue arms above her head as she waited for the program to load and began stretching.

A few seconds later, the computer chirped and an image of Empress Jegra Alakandra incrementally pieced together in front of her. The hologram flickered briefly, revealing the robot dummy beneath the translucent skin. When the details of Jegra finished loading onto the combat android, the skin solidified and the empress came to life with a breath.

As they stood in the senatorial chambers on Dagon Prime, Callestra cleared her throat. "Empress Alakandra," she said in a commanding voice, "in the name of the Empire, by the authority of the War Council, I hereby place you under arrest."

"For what?" Jegra asked, crossing her arms under her chest in uneasiness and shifting in place. She gave Callestra an apprehensive look. A look that said she wasn't going to come easily.

"For crimes against the Empire," she answered. Callestra pulled out a set of magnetic shackles and dangled them in front of her for the empress to see. "Let's not make a scene here. Come peacefully, and we'll get this all sorted out."

"I'm afraid you're mistaken, Admiral. I've committed no crimes. And until my lawyer gets here, there's no way I'm going with you. If you insist on arresting me, you'll have to subdue me. Then we'll have all the hot wet sex."

Callestra rolled her eyes and made a mental note to have the computer try to create a more apposite dialog for the training exercise. Although the empress was renowned for her assorted dalliances, the simulation shouldn't be bringing it up during a battle scenario. Probably some programmer's idea of an amusing joke.

"The hot wet sex will have to wait, Your Eminence. Right now, I'm taking you into custody." Callestra reached out with the handcuffs to clasp them around Jegra's wrists when, without warning, the empress twisted around and extending her leg, planted a roundhouse kick squarely into Callestra's gut.

Callestra felt the wind rush out of her as she flew backwards into a marble pillar. Pushing herself up, she looked up to see Jegra flexing her enormous biceps and kissing them in a display of self-aggrandizement. Although she'd never seen the real Jegra act in such a manner, she wouldn't put it past her. If the empress had anything in common with the emperor, it was that she thought extremely highly of herself. At least, that was Callestra's impression.

The Jegra robot was set to eighty percent the strength of the real-life empress. Not because it was too dangerous to go higher, but because the robot simply couldn't handle the strain of Jegra's upper strength limit in battle simulations. It either tore itself apart or ended up crippling the trainees. Often permanently.

But even at eighty percent strength, the simulation of the gladiatrix was no laughing matter. She could still snap Callestra's neck, if the safety protocols were turned off. Which is what made the simulation so arousing.

With a lightening quick kick up, Callestra sprang to her feet. Fists at the ready, she charged the gladiatrix. The two combatants danced about, Callestra launching a rabid offensive of left and right hooks. The dummy blocked each blow while retreating to the corner of the room. Once cornered, Jegra turned and ran up the wall.

Callestra cursed under her breath and said, "Graddack," when she realized she'd fallen for a simple but effective trap.

Jegra landed behind her and kicked her between the shoulder blades. Before Callestra could even react, she found herself pressed up against the wall, the fake Jegra wailing on her kidneys as though they were bongo drums.

A sudden blow to the back of her head, her skull smacked into the wall, causing red to encroach upon her vision from all sides.

She sensed another headshot and caught Jegra's wrist. Seizing the opportunity, she ran up the wall, retaining her hold on the empress's wrist. With a fluid backflip off the wall, she landed behind the empress, twisting her arm, and bringing her to the ground.

Jegra rose up only to get a mouthful of Callestra's knee. She fell to the side and the vice admiral landed a boot to her gut. Jegra coughed and rolled away, narrowly avoiding a devastating stomp.

Her sides bruised with purple and yellow markings, Callestra ignored the pain and bull-rushed the gladiatrix. Jegra stood up in time to catch Callestra's fist in her hand and slowly began to squeeze. "Fuck you!" Callestra screamed, holding her wrist with her other hand as she tried to break free. But it was no use. Jegra's grip wasn't letting up. That's when she heard the crunch of her bones and screamed out.

Jegra let go of the admiral's mangled hand and Callestra sank to her feet. "Do you give up, Vice Admiral Van Morgan?"

"Give up?" balked Callestra. "What kind of Dagon woman do you take me for?"

"One that enjoys all the hot wet sex," the Jegra dummy replied.

"God, I hate you," Callestra growled. Slowly, she staggered to her feet and, still holding her wrist, roared out her fiercest battle cry.

Even with one arm, Callestra showed a tenacity that would have made the real Jegra proud. A jab, followed by a flying knee, then another punch, a backward sweep, another knee, and finally a hard right cross that landed on Jegra's temple.

The Jegra-bot went down, its holographic skin flickering briefly before snapping back into focus.

"Oh, no you don't!" shouted Callestra as Jegra began to push herself back to her hands and knees. She came down on it with a leaping downward hook that landed in the back of the empress's skull.

Sparks exploded from the back of the bot's head and Callestra began a no holds barred bashing of the dummy. Taking out all her rage, she pounded the fake Jegra relentlessly. Eventually she noticed blood and stopped, wondering how in the galaxy a robot could bleed. That's when she realized it was her own blood.

Her fists bloodied and battered, she inspected her hands. Both looked the worse for wear. Just then, Jegra's hand came up and grabbed onto Callestra's sports bra. Jegra slowly began pulling the bra down until Callestra's breasts threatened to fall out.

"That's quite enough," the admiral said, grabbing Jegra's hands and twisting so as to break her hold on her top. Maintaining her grip on Jegra's wrist, she raised her boot and, with one final kick, took off Jegra's head.

The moment the dummy's head ripped from its body, the holographic skin dissolved revealing only a drab gray training bot. The unit toppled to the ground, sparking, as its head, still sporting Jegra's face, rolled into the far wall.

Callestra looked down to see her maroon areola peeking out from her disheveled sports bra. Adjusting her top, she tucked her breasts back into their rightful place and then limped over to her uniform.

Her body was badly bruised. Her sides, her ribs, her back, her neck, her face and her forehead. It looked as though Callestra had been made a punching bag. But it was her weekly ritual to pick a day to go all out against a simulation of Jegra. It was the only way she'd ever be prepared to face the woman in real life–should it ever come to that.

"Bloody helios," Callestra said as she tried bending over to pick up her things. Blood dripping from her battered fist, she picked up her clothes and groaned out in agony. "This one's going to hurt like a bitch after a gangbang in the morning."

"End simulation," she said as she headed out the exit. The holographic overlay cut out and the room jostled a bit and then snapped back to its standard grid pattern layout.

Upon entering the corridor, Callestra drew looks from the passing crew members. She ignored their shocked expressions and carried herself up the passageway on her way to the medical bay, one bloody bootstep at a time—a line of red footprints trailing after her.

14

Smoke filled the asteroid command center. Raven looked over her shoulder to find Gyllek taking cover behind an upturned desk. Behind her, Kregor rose up, as if in slow motion, and launched his hammer like a javelin. It flew through the air and smashed into the scorpion-like Centurion's face with devastating force. Sparks flew out and the machine staggered backward as it fought to regain its footing.

A figure wielding dual blasters appeared out of the swirling smoke, both guns blazing. Angellyk stepped up to Raven, reached down, and grabbed her by the collar of her body armor that had saved her from a direct disruptor blast.

After dragging her back to safety behind a bulkhead, Angie crouched down alongside Raven and let loose another flurry of disruptor blasts, all of them striking their target and unleashing an explosion of fiery sparks.

"Are you out of your mind?" Angellyk said, shooting Raven a displeased look. "That was the stupidest, most heroic, thing I've ever seen."

"You're welcome," Raven grunted.

"Shut up," Angellyk said. Grabbing Raven's armor, Angellyk pulled her in and kissed her squarely on the lips.

Raven smiled but didn't say anything. It was just a romantic gesture, one made in the heat of the moment. After things settled down, it would be forgotten about. But it was nice, nonetheless.

Angellyk rose up and provided cover fire as Kregor pulled out a device from the holster on his leg. It unfolded into a laser crossbow and he took aim at the Centurion. Retrieving a high yield explosive bolt from his other leg holster, he loaded it into the slide mechanism mounted on the stock and then pulled back the bolt until it locked into place.

Kregor looked over at Gyllek, a giddy grin on his face, and winked at her. Rising up from behind his stronghold, he shouted, "Hey you! Yeah, you, ye ugly good for nothing over complicated toaster oven!" Once the Centurion locked onto him with its laser sites, he smiled and pulled the trigger.

The bolt flashed across the room like a streak of lightning heralded by the gods of old and drilled into the Centurion's central chassis. A massive explosion sent Kregor diving for cover.

Angellyk reared back and slid over next to Raven, their backs against the bulkhead. A flash of heat forced her to turn her face away and she mouthed the words, "*What the hell?*"

The Dragonian crashed onto the floor next to Gyllek and rolled onto his back. Smiling up at her, he grinned sheepishly and kissed the stock of his weapon.

"What in the galaxy is that thing?" Gyllek asked.

"This here is Bodacious."

"Bodacious?" Gyllek asked. "Is that an Earth name or something?"

"Jegra says it was the name of the strongest beast to ever walk the lands of her home world. It was called a 'bull.'"

"What's a bull?" Gyllek asked.

Kregor shrugged. "Apparently, they were mammalian grazing beasts the size of buildings and tasted delicious, according to Jegra, that is."

"Why would anyone eat such a peaceful creature?" Gyllek wondered aloud to herself. Kregor overhead her and offered his best guess.

"Apparently humans like to eat everything they come into contact with," he informed her.

Raven unfastened the ruined armor chest plate and tossed it to the floor. Looking down, she examined the scorch mark in her black environmental suit. The disruptor had burned through that too, exposing a large patch of violet skin in the middle of her chest.

She touched her skin, making sure it wasn't singed, and then tugged at her suit, letting the cool air flood in. The chill reinvigorated her and she pushed herself to her feet.

"Is everyone all right?" Raven asked, taking a mental head count.

"We're fine," Kregor said, waving at them from behind the desk he and Gyllek used for cover.

Angellyk was standing halfway out into the open room, both blasters trained on the Centurion. It twitched, as if it still had some fight left in it and she let off a merciless volley of shots. Gyllek startled, half expecting the machine to rear up again. When it didn't, she let out a sigh of relief.

Once the machine stopped twitching, Angellyk let off the trigger. "I'm fine...now," she said, answering Raven's previous question. The vents of her overheated disrupter pistols glowed red-orange and radiated steam. With a soft breath from her forest green lips, she blew the steam from her pistol like a gunslinger of old.

Gradually, everyone emerged from the shadows and stepped into the center of the room. Angellyk nudged one of the Centurion's crab legs with her boot just to be safe, but it didn't budge. She let out a sigh of relief and everyone relaxed along with her.

"That was a close one," Gyllek said, her heart still racing. She turned to Raven, who dusted herself and added, "Thanks, boss, for stepping out in front of me like that."

Raven smiled at the girl. "I'm just glad the armor was able to absorb a shot like that in close quarters."

Kregor raised his crossbow and rested it on his shoulder, glancing at everyone, making a mental check of their condition, and then scanning their surroundings.

"I'm going to do a sweep of this level to make sure more of those things aren't lurking about," he said, holstering his crossbow and fetching his hammer.

"I'll join you," Angellyk said, following after him. She, too, holstered her blasters and shot Raven a sly look. Before exiting the room, she turned back to face her ex; she rolled her tongue inside her mouth and gently bit down on it, a little trick she did whenever she was thinking about getting lucky.

Raven rolled her eyes and replied, "Gyllek and I will try to crack the station's security systems. Once we're in, we'll bring all the systems online."

Angellyk merely gave a two-finger salute and then spun back around and raced to catch up to Kregor—a bounce in her step that hadn't been there before.

"That poor man," Gyllek said, shaking her head solemnly.

Raven cocked her head and gave her a curious look.

"She's going to eat him alive."

Raven laughed—not a small, subdued laugh, but one that rose up from her belly and filled the whole room. Gyllek startled, unaccustomed to bursts of emotion from the captain, and she began to laugh too.

"That she will," Raven confirmed. "That she will."

Not wasting another minute on frivolous banter, Gyllek settled into the seat behind the one of the many computer consoles and began opening up systems files, looking for a back door to the security programming.

Raven went over to a wall station and gave the paneling a strong boot. The panel caved in, small screws snapping as the corners pulled out. She bent down and tore off the loose panel and tossed it aside. Getting down on the floor, she reached into the small rectangular crevice, rummaged around and then pulled out a handful of wires.

It only took her a minute to locate the bio-interface module. She unclasped it and drew out the cord with what appeared to be a surgical needle on the end. Then, finding a vein on the inside of her forearm, she jammed it in.

Raven's amethyst eyes lit up with electric purple energy as a carousel of code flashed across her vision.

"I'm in," Raven said.

"That was fast," Gyllek answered, her fingers working furiously on the keyboard.

"Make sure I'm not being tagged by tracker bots. And shut down all second-tier security measures while you're at it. We don't want to accidentally trigger any alarms by breaching some random protocol."

"On it!" Gyllek said, one corner of her mouth forming a half-grin. Hacking was her passion, and after the captain, there was nobody better at it than her.

The only access point that wasn't locked down at the moment was a discrete maintenance closet, but it was good enough for their needs.

Angellyk and Kregor stumbled into the narrow room, bumping into a mop and an assortment of other supplies. There was a cluttered workbench off to the side with toilet paper, cleansers, and other cleaning supplies.

Kregor shoved the supplies onto the floor hastily and then took a seat on the bench, looking up in time to see Angellyk unzip her EV suit and peel it off like a second skin. Letting it fall around her waist so that the top half hung over her curvaceous hips, she wasted no time pulling her black tank top over her head.

"Is this really happening?" Kregor asked, still unable to believe his luck.

Angellyk settled onto his lap, straddling him, tossed her forest green hair over her bare shoulder, and began kissing his mouth.

As they made out, she hastily helped him peel off his environmental suit. Her dainty green hands slid up under his shirt and pinched his nipples.

Kregor, growing excited, reached around and grabbed Angellyk's ass. He squeezed it firmly and hoisted her up, her legs locking around his waist. Angellyk let out a moan when her back slammed into the wall, his thick chest mashing into her soft green breasts.

Finally getting his shirt off for him, she threw it to the floor and then grabbed his neck, their mouths still entwined in a sultry tango.

Between exchanges of hot, wet kisses, Angellyk said, "I've never been with a Dragonian man before."

Kregor stopped and looked down at her. "I've never been with a Bre'lal woman, either."

They stared at each other momentarily then thrust themselves back into another heated round of making out. His forked tongue swirled around with her soft pink one and they slowly shifted back to the bench.

Angellyk reclined on the bench and raising her pelvis, began to unfasten her belt. Kregor, who was kneeling on the bench on one knee, also worked quickly to unfasten his pants. Angellyk had her pants down around her thighs when, without warning, an alarm blared up and down the station.

They stopped what they were doing and gave one another a look that showed no interest in responding to the alarm.

"It's nothing," Angellyk breathed.

"Yeah," Kregor replied. "It's nothing."

<<Self-destruct sequence initiated. T minus 30 minutes and counting,>> the female computer chimed over the station comm system.

Angellyk and Kregor shot each other a worried glance.

"I just can't seem to win," Kregor said, disappointedly.

"Rain check?" Angellyk asked.

"You'd better believe it!" he replied.

She smiled at him and sat up, pulling her pants back on in one swift motion. Rising up, she gave him a peck on the cheek and then went to collect her things.

"What did you hit?" Raven asked.

"Nothing!" Gyllek cried out. "I swear!"

Raven, still plugged into the mainframe, began running a check to see what had triggered the station's self-destruct sequence. "Bloody hell," she said, disappointed in herself. "That's what I was afraid of."

"What is it?" Gyllek asked.

"Bleedin' second level security protocols. Basically, when I brought the station's systems online, the *Skywend* didn't have the correct access codes. The station thinks the ship is a security breach. It's reading it as a hostile element."

"Will undocking do anything? Because I can send a prompt to the *Skywend's* computer to begin automated decoupling."

"I doubt it will help at this point. Besides, if we can't get this auto-destruct turned off, we'll need to get back onboard the ship and get out of here ASAP."

"Maybe I can bypass the docking protocol by tricking the computer into thinking that the ship never left drydock."

"Do that," Raven said, pointing a finger at Gyllek. "In the meantime, I'm going to try to turn off the auto-destruct one line of code at a time."

"What in the galaxy is going on?" Angellyk asked as both she and Kregor rounded the corner and jogged into the command station. They seemed to be rather out of breath for the amount of time they were gone, and Gyllek shot Raven a wry look.

"We accidentally triggered a security protocol when we docked. Gyllek and I are working on it now. But I want you two to get back to the ship and prepare for departure. If we can't get this locked down, we'll be needing the ship's engine warmed up and ready to get out of here lickety-split like."

"Hey, big guy," Gyllek said, nodding at Kregor's half-zipped environmental suit. "Your undershirt is on backward."

Kregor blushed and quickly zipped up his EV suit the rest of the way. "Right, Captain," he said, ignoring Gyllek's astute observation. "We'll be waiting for you both aboard the ship."

Kregor tapped Angellyk on the shoulder, a show of affection that had been lacking earlier this morning. He nodded at her to follow him and she smiled. They dashed out of the command center almost as quickly as they'd come in, brushing shoulders as they squeezed through the entrance together.

Raven and Gyllek shared one more sideways glance and both giggled.

<<T minus 25 minutes until automated self-destruct sequence is initiated,>> the computer reminded them.

"There!" Raven announced triumphantly after another minute of intense silence with nothing but the computer counting down the minutes. "I got it."

The computer's voice became garbled, as if a glitch had infected her. After another moment, the voice came back on again, seemingly healed of her ailment. <<T minus 10 minutes until automated self-destruct sequence is initiated.>>

"No!" Raven shouted, slamming her fists down on the console. The touch display's image scrambled briefly as it absorbed the brunt of Raven's disappointment, then flickered back to its normal settings.

Raven turned to Gyllek and gave her a worried look. But, at the same time, it was a reassuring look. They still had enough time to get back to the ship…but they'd lose the shipyard and the empress's secret armada.

"You've done all that you can, Captain. You go on ahead without me. I'll finish things up here," Gyllek said, her eyes not looking away from the monitor as she flew through the station's security code.

"I won't leave you behind, Gyllek," Raven said, placing a hand on Gyllek's shoulder.

"I know, and that's why I already initiated the ship's automated decoupling."

"You did what?!" Raven gasped.

"I believe you're needed aboard your ship, Captain." Gyllek turned to Raven and smiled. Her look said it all.

Unexpectedly, tears filled to the brim of Raven's eyelids and she blinked, wiping a rogue tear from her cheek.

"I've got this," Gyllek said, reassuring Raven that she could complete her mission.

Raven bent down, kissed the girl on the head, and then turned and raced back toward the ship.

<<T minus 7 minutes until automated self-destruct sequence is initiated.>>

"Oh, do shut up!" Gyllek said, letting out an agitated sigh expressing the displeasure she felt with the computer's droning on and on about how it was so eager to blow them all to back into the stardust from which they came.

15

Danica awoke to find herself sprawled out on a luxurious bed with gold satin sheets and translucent white curtains that filtered the bright light coming in from the open doors on the terrace.

Strangely enough, even though she was in an unfamiliar place, she had slept like a baby. Sitting up in bed, the satin sheets slipped down her naked body and she raised her arms above her head, stretched, and then let out a long, drawn out yawn.

A warm breeze coming in from the open doors, which led out to a balcony that overlooked the city street, lapped at her violet skin and warmed her. She scooted up to the edge of the bed and cautiously poked her head out from the princess curtains draped along the hanging rod from one bed post to another and peered out into the comfortable bedroom to take a look around.

She found herself in a small apartment loft, decked out in mostly white. It was almost completely spartan except for a white leather love sofa, a small, rectangular table in front of the kitchen island, and an efficiency kitchen with refrigerator, food synthesizer, and a double bowl sink made from black granite and surrounded by matching black granite counter tops that contrasted nicely against the white-washed apartment.

On a spacious wall opposite the bed hung a glorious piece of artwork done in a splatter of vibrant paints. The canvas consisted of an assortment of energetic swirling colors including purple, pink, teal, electric blue and streaks of yellow. This spiraling galaxy of colors was speckled with red flecks of crimson that resembled an asteroid belt cutting diagonally across the dynamic image.

Off to the left of the kitchen was a small hallway which led to a bathroom and what appeared to be a set of bifold doors concealing a storage closet. Seeing that the room was virtually empty all but for herself, Danica slipped out of bed and stepped onto the plush white carpet. Her toes sank deep into the fuzz and she stretched again as she let her body be warmed by a shaft of morning light that cascaded over her shoulders and breasts.

It was a little hard to believe she'd slept all through the night and till midday the next day, but by the angle of the sun she knew it must be sometime in the afternoon. She could only imagine how worried Jegra was for her. But she'd practically forced Jegra into bringing her on the mission, and if she didn't feel like she couldn't handle it, she wouldn't have pushed so hard to be included on this mission. Besides, she was a big girl and could take care of herself. Surely, her luv knew that by now.

Danica stepped out into the center of the room and looked around for some clothes but couldn't find any. Hers were mysteriously gone.

On the edge of the sofa, though, was a short, satin robe laid out for her. She quickly fetched it up and slipped it on. Her hands fumbled around for the sash, but when she looked down, there wasn't one to be found. Unable to tie her robe to keep it closed, she gripped it at the waist with a tight fist and held it in place.

Danica strode over to the balcony, a casual sensuality in her walk, her hips swaying with a kind of insouciance only a high-class woman brimming with confidence could pull off. She was feeling particularly rejuvenated and, apart from having been abducted by a well-known drug kingpin, she felt the best she had in ages.

When she emerged from the apartment loft and stepped out onto the balcony, she found herself on the fifth story of an old apartment building downtown. Vendors haggling with shoppers could be heard in the streets below and she realized that she was only about half a dozen blocks from where she'd been taken.

That's why we couldn't locate him, she thought. *Zallek was hiding in plain sight— right under their noses. Right in the middle of Arena City.*

"You're awake," a surprised sounding voice said unexpectedly.

The immediate sound of another person startled her and she spun around to find Zallek in a dapper white suit, sitting off to the corner of the balcony. He lounged about on some patio furniture and was drinking what appeared to be a

Dagon iced-tea perched on a glass table. The beverage filled a tall glass with a lemon wedge balancing on its lip. Beads of perspiration rolled down its glistening sides and soaked into a cork coaster. Next to the tea was a bowl of fruit with a particularly enticing red apple that made Danica's mouth water.

Zallek looked Danica up and down and noted her interest in the food and drink and smiled at her. "Care to join me?" he asked, gesturing to the open seat next to him.

"Where are my clothes?" she asked sternly, fanning her hand across the robes and shooting him a distrusting look.

Zallek raised his hands defensively and replied, "No worries, my dear, nothing nefarious has transpired. I took the liberty to see that your clothes be cleaned and pressed. They'll be returned to you shortly, fresh and neat."

"I suppose you're the one who undressed me," she said, letting the robe slip open ever so slightly, allowing him to catch another glimpse of her flesh. It wasn't as though it mattered, since he'd already seen everything already. Including the glorious scar that ran across her abdomen.

He motioned again for her to have a seat.

Strolling over to the chair he'd offered her moments earlier, her open robe fluttering on the gentle breeze, she took a seat opposite him. Without even waiting for him to pour her a drink, she leaned over and took his tea, and drank it down as if it was her own. Then, grabbing the apple hastily from the bowl, she bit into it hungrily. Her teeth pierced the fruit's skin with a satisfying crunch and apple juices flooded into her mouth; some escaped the corners and dribbled down her chin. She reached up and wiped the excess juices away with the back of her hand and let out a satisfied sigh.

Zallek raised an amused eyebrow. "You are a curious one, Danica Valencia. I'll give you that much."

She almost choked on another bite of apple when he'd unexpectedly used her real name. She gulped it down and looked up at him. He merely laughed off her sudden astonishment, reclined in his seat, and crossed his left leg over his right knee.

"Yes, I know who you are, Danica. Personal servant to the empress. Once the right-hand woman to the emperor himself. You sure do get around, don't you, my dear?"

"If you know who I am, then why am I still alive?"

"You mean, why haven't I had you killed and tossed in a dumpster out back?" Zallek balked and waved his hand in front of his face, brushing the ugly notion aside. "I'm not a barbarian, Danica. Just a drug dealer."

"A womanizer, perhaps then," she said, pulling the robe closed so her breasts wouldn't spill out when she leaned over the table to refill her tea from the pitcher. She shot him a snide grin and then raised her glass as if to say cheers for the hospitality.

He smiled and looked away.

"I'm surprised you didn't just have your way with me when you had the chance."

An offended look settled across Zallek's face. "Like I said, I'm not a barbarian, Danica. And you're no common scag, either."

Danica's cheeks flushed with a mixture of embarrassment and suppressed outrage. *She wasn't a scag.* But she was willing to admit she might have a small problem when it came to dosing on her drug of choice. The cravings for Nividium were growing by the day and now she could hardly go more than a single hour without needing to take a hit.

"I'm good for the drugs, if you're worried."

"I know you are, my dear," he said smiling at her. This made her feel self-conscious and she pulled her robe shut even more tightly. What had begun as a confident form of posturing was now turning into a self-conscious examination of her very real insecurities. *I'm not a scag*, she repeated in her mind.

"If you don't want me for my body, or my money, then what do you want me for?"

He shot her an amused glance and then, after a short pause, steepled his fingers underneath his chin and said, "I want to know why the empress is sticking her nose into my business where it doesn't belong. Tell me that, and I think we can call ourselves even."

"Ah," Danica said in a revelatory tone. "A tit for tat sort of thing." She folded her arms and looked out across the street, losing herself to her thoughts, of which there were plenty.

Zallek watched her for a while, enjoying the sunshine and the beautiful woman next to him. When she finally turned back to him, he smiled again, letting her know that he was no threat. "As long as you're my guest here, no harm will come to you. That's a promise. In the meantime," he said with a gesture of his hand. "What's mine is yours, so feel free to help yourself to anything."

"I'm assuming I'll be your guest indefinitely, then?"

"At least until you decide to cooperate and divulge what you know about the empress's vested interest in me and my operations. Yes. But, until then, there's no reason you can't enjoy your time here and get a bit of rest and relaxation." Reaching into his white suit pocket, he pulled out a cartridge of the newly processed Nividium and set it on the table along with a vape stick.

"Just so we're clear, I think you're in for a long wait since I'd never willingly betray my empress."

"Yes," Zallek said, slowly rising to his feet. "I thought as much. But, then again, we shall see what we shall see." He smiled at her with a debonair grin, pulled out a pair of dark sunglasses from his inside pocket, slipped them on, and turned to take his leave.

Just as he was leaving the apartment, Danica caught a glimpse of two armed soldiers standing guard outside her door. She guessed there were probably more guarding the stairwell and the entrance of the building downstairs. Maybe even the rooftop. So, escaping wasn't likely an option.

Not that she was planning her great escape or anything. She still wanted to try and gather as much intel on Zallek and his drug operation as possible. In the meantime, she had a nice loft and all the Nividium she could want. It wasn't all bad.

"It was a pleasure making your acquaintance," Zallek said, glancing back at her over his shoulder from the doorway. He adjusted the lapel of his white suit, nodded at Danica, and then disappeared out the door.

The click of the door automatically latching shut snapped her out of her pensive gaze and she looked back over at the cartridge of Nividium sitting on the table before her. It beckoned to her to take it. After a moment or two of trying to resist the temptation, she gave in and said, "Fuck it."

Her hands trembling, she picked up the vape stick, slapped in the cartridge, and brought the mouthpiece to her lips. Inhaling deeply, she sat back in her seat, her entire body growing lax as the drug's tranquil effect took hold of her.

As a feeling of bliss settled over her like a soothing blanket, her robe slipped open again, but she didn't care to fix it. She simply wanted to enjoy the high while letting the hot Thessalonica sun beat down on her glistening chest.

Danica let out a sigh of ecstasy from deep inside her as the feeling of bliss seeped into her inner self and slowly filled her. She felt so happy she could almost cry. And if she could stay this way forever, she would. And, to be truthful, that was the appeal of Nividium. It was an escape from the pain and suffering of everyday life. It gave you reprieve from a relentless world and allowed you ten minutes of bliss.

Who in their right mind wouldn't want that?

Maybe she was just making excuses to keep taking a drug she knew was bad for her. Maybe her life really had gotten so out of control that the only way to stop from being miserable was to take Nividium. Either way, whether it was an excuse to get high or a deeper seated need to self-medicate, it didn't matter anymore. All that mattered was enjoying the rush.

She put the vape stick to her lips once more and breathed in. A gradual smile spread across her lips and she felt as though her entire body was caught up in rapture so powerful that everything else just faded away.

Danica's arm fell limp and flopped over the edge of the chair. Her hand popped open and the vape stick fell out and hit the ground.

That's when she began to realize something didn't feel right. This shot of Nividium was far more potent than anything she'd ever used before. It wasn't regular Nividium. This was something else. Something new.

For starters, the high wasn't wearing off. After seven minutes, her body started shaking as though she were having an epileptic fit. But it was actually her body shuddering from the intense waves of pleasure that coursed through her.

She slipped out of her chair and sank to her knees then fell to the side and landed with a thud on the floor of the white, cement rendered balcony.

She writhed with pleasure, rubbing her hands up and down her body. Without warning she felt herself orgasm and she screamed out with a sigh of ecstasy. Tears started streaming out of her eyes because as good as it felt, it was too much. She wanted it to stop, but the waves of pleasure kept washing over her in relentless torrents and what had begun as the best high ever quickly turned into a torturous marathon of overwhelming sensations.

Danica rolled over onto her side and vomited. At the same time, she unintentionally pissed herself. But even those sensations, the release of it all, was amplified by the drug and she screamed out in agony, wrenching her hair in her fists as the intense bout of pleasure refused to subside.

Gradually, she could feel her sanity beginning to fracture. And just when she felt that she couldn't take it anymore and her psyche would burst into a thousand discordant shards, the high stopped.

She began panting heavily, her entire body soaked in sweat, piss, and vomit. She slowly pushed herself up but slipped in her own mess and crashed to the plaster floor again. Panting heavily, she rolled onto her back and stared up at a serene blue sky.

And even though she knew it in her bones that she had come to the brink of death just now, for whatever reason, she inexplicably felt the urge to do it all over again.

16

Raphine stumbled up the alley in a state of delirium. Her vision was blurry and her forehead had a nasty gash in it from where her head had smashed into the wall. Even her legs felt wobbly beneath each staggering step. "Ow," she murmured, touching her forehead lightly as she faltered and propped herself against the corner of a building that looked out onto a busy market street abuzz with the daily grind.

Even though she had lost track of time and, perhaps worse, she'd lost both the empress and Danica, she had at least one thing going for her. Reaching into her back pocket, she fished out the security key of the Jacquardian who'd roughed her up. She'd lifted it off him when he was knocking her about.

With the card clutched tightly in her hand, she stumbled into the hectic crowd and disappeared from sight.

A blue Dagon woman with a striking resemblance to the empress sat on a chair in the middle of a luxurious bedroom. Her hands cuffed behind her back with magnetic shackles, her feet tied to the legs of the chair so she wouldn't escape, Jegra glared over at Madam Elowiin who stood in the open doorway, smiling at her.

"My dear empress, believe me, this is for your own good. If Zallek thinks I've gotten soft, he'll try to take over my territory. And if he thinks you're still hunting him, your friend's life will be in danger."

"So, you're just going to leave me here? Tied to a chair? That's your grand masterplan?"

"I like to think ahead before making my next move. Once I've figured out the best course of action, I'll be back. Until then, enjoy the girls."

Two women entered the room, one Bre'lal and one Dagon woman with a scar on her throat. She appeared to be a banjax, usually a child born destitute or discarded by parents that didn't want it and sold into slavery. If a girl was fair, the brothels snatched her up. If they were homely, they were either sent to the asteroid mines or, a small percentage, found their way into the gladiatorial fights.

The women surrounded Jegra and began rubbing their hands all over her body. Gliding over her clothes, teasing out every delicate curve, the Bre'lal whispered in her ear, "Just relax. We'll take care of you."

"I'll leave you to it, then," Madam Elowiin said, bowing slightly. With that, she took her leave and withdrew from the room as quietly as a specter, her long kimono flowing behind her.

"How'd you get the scar?" Jegra asked, as the Dagon woman leaned in and licked Jegra's lips.

"A jealous ex-lover cut my throat when I refused to let him buy me for a pittance. Madam Elowiin found me and nursed me back to health."

"I'm sorry."

"For what?" the Dagon woman asked, her lips hovering dangerously close to Jegra's. "It helped make me the woman I am today."

Still curious, Jegra was about to ask another question when the Dagon woman silenced her with a sultry kiss. Her tongue slid down into Jegra's mouth and they began a heated pirouette of delicate tongue-play.

At the same time, the Bre'lal woman was squatting behind Jegra's chair in a seductive pose. She reached around with her hands and began unfastening the buttons on Jegra's clothes. Peeling off the empress's shirt, she flung it to the floor and then began working on Jegra's khaki safari pants.

With Jegra's pants unbuttoned, the Bre'lal's delicate fingers unzipped Jegra's pants, then slowly slipped under the waistband of her panties.

"Although I appreciate all you're doing for me, I'm going to have to take a raincheck on this little tryst," Jegra said. Both women shared an amused glance and ignored her, continuing on with their act of seduction. "Don't say I didn't warn you," Jegra said.

Kra-Crack!

Both women's heads snapped back from the lightning quick double headbutt Jegra had dealt them. Whipping her head back, she took out the Bre'lal woman behind her first, then, snapping her head forward, she headbutted the Dagon woman. Both women collapsed into a heap of scantily clad flesh on the floor.

Snap! Jegra easily broke from of the ropes tied around her ankles. Lose strands of rope coiled around her feet, she stood up and took a deep breath, arched her shoulders, and then with a grunt broke the magnetic shackles. A metal crunch sounded as the shackles snapped into pieces and clattered to the floor. Jegra wasn't wasting a moment, as she didn't have any time to play games. She needed to get back out there and find her friends.

She tossed the busted shackles onto the ground and then zipped her pants back up. "Sorry, ladies. As much as I'd love to stay and play, I have other matters to attend to first." She fetched her shirt and slipped it on. Heading to the windows, she peeked outside, buttoning up her shirt as she glanced at the busy street below. That's when she saw Raphine jostling her way through the crowd.

Raphine was passing by Madam Elowiin's Sanctuary when a sixth story window exploded and a chair crashed to the sidewalk in front of her. She stopped and looked up only to see a blue body leap from the window. She scurried back, to make room for the large object plummeting toward her.

The concrete crunched under the weight of the muscular frame of the empress, who landed on one knee in a superhero pose. Raphine smiled when the recognition of who it was set in.

Jegra rose up to her full six-foot-three height and looked at the girl. "Are you all right?" she asked, a worried look lingering in her eyes.

"I could ask the same thing about you. You just leapt out of a sixth story window."

"A bit hard on the knees, but I've survived worse." Jegra winked at Raphine and then looked up when she heard voices above them. Madam Elowiin's head popped out of the broken window and scowled down at the empress. Jegra ignored the woman and then ushered Raphine ahead of her. "Let's go. We've already drawn too much attention to ourselves."

They jogged down the street together, not looking back at the scary woman hanging out the window and screaming obscenities at them in a dialect of Seyfferian neither of them recognized.

"What's got her in such a tizzy?" Raphine asked jutting a thumb over her shoulder at the screaming woman.

"I may have knocked a couple of her girls unconscious. In my defense, they had me tied up and were about to stick their tongues in places they didn't belong."

"Doesn't sound all bad," Raphine said. Jegra raised an eyebrow and shot her a sideways glance.

"You're eighteen. Just a child on my world. It would be weird taking you to a brothel with me."

"You do know that my people train to be courtesans from eight years old, right?"

"Yeah, that's no less weird. It only makes it weirder for me."

Raphine gave Jegra a sour look. "I thought you knew."

"Knew what?" asked Jegra, shooting the girl a confused look.

"I'm sexually active. I have been since I was fifteen. Meleh'Kendar and I have…"

"Let me stop you right there…" Jegra said, her face now tightening into a sour look. She was having a hard time processing the visual of Meleh'Kendar and Raphine as a couple.

"It's not like we're dating," Raphine said. "More like friends with benefits."

"I'm sure it's none of my business." Jegra looked away and then, realizing that she had been following Raphine's lead, slowed up. "Where are we going?"

They stopped in front of the glass doors of a fancy hotel. It was a little old, but it was refurbished. And recently, too, by the looks of it.

"Here," Raphine said, pulling out the security pass.

"What's that?" Jegra eyeballed the translucent green keycard.

"I took it off the brute who attacked me. It's a security pass for a bedroom suite at the Blue Royale." She nodded at the entrance of the hotel.

"You think Zallek is hiding out here?"

"Maybe. It could just be a front. Or a safe house. I guess we're about to find out."

Jegra smiled. This is precisely why she had invited Raphine on the mission. The girl was resourceful.

They were about to head into the lobby when a block up the street an explosion rang out. The thunderous boom caused them to cover their ears and duck down in the entrance way.

"What was that?" Raphine asked.

Jegra looked up the street to hear a lot of commotion. More than was to be expected, even after a terrorist attack. Without warning, a disruptor fire exchange could be heard and wounded were already stumbling into their street.

"We can't just wait here," Jegra said. "We have to help."

Jegra reached out and pulled one of the dazed survivors aside. "What happened?"

"It's the Harbingers of Truth!" the man lamented.

Startled, Jegra let go of his arm and he continued on up the street.

"The Harbingers of Truth?" asked Raphine. "Isn't that Demeris Ferrison's group?"

"The one and only. Apparently, he's growing emboldened enough to attack my territory directly. Until now, however, he's only sponsored protests on the homeworld."

"If you want," Raphine began, gently touching Jegra's arm, "I can infiltrate the Harbingers of Truth for you and gather intel."

"As much as I appreciate the offer, the Harbingers are a close-knit boy's club. They don't allow women."

"Why would they do that?"

"Because they're a bunch of incels."

"An incel? What's that?"

"It's an Earth term for a man who desperately wants to have sex with a woman but denies himself the pleasure because he is so terrified of the brain attached to the vagina that he'd rather hide in his room and write hate mail about how women are oppressing him than learn how to respect women for individuals worth more than the value of their genitals."

"That's messed up."

"You have no idea," Jegra replied with a solemn look.

The crackle of static interrupted their girl talk and Meleh'Kendar's voice came over the comm. Jegra touched her earpiece to focus on his voice above the pandemonium of people flooding into the street to get away from the chaos a block away.

"We've detected a massive explosion. Are you guys all right?"

"We're fine. But the Harbingers of Truth have decided to make a statement by blowing up the cultural center up the street."

"I'm sending a security team right—"

"That won't be necessary," Jegra said, cutting her security chief off. "Just send me my armor and some weapons. I'll handle this personally."

A shaft of yellow light touched down in the center of the street and all of Jegra's items appeared as requested.

Raphine dashed up to the weapons rack and began offloading blasters and blades.

"What are you doing?" Jegra asked, peeling off layers of her clothes and just leaving them in the street.

"What does it look like?" Raphine asked, although the question was rhetorical. "I'm coming with you."

Jegra slipped on her metal bikini top and fastened it, keeping one eye on Raphine. "Fine," she said, after giving it some thought. "I like to get up close and personal, if you know what I mean. So, hang back and provide some cover fire."

Raphine nodded.

Jegra pulled down her pants and kicked them aside with her foot. She swiftly pulled on the leather skirt, its pteruges fitted with brass studs, and then strapped on her armored shin guards, replete with knee plating. Finally, she pulled on her fitted metal bracers, the same ones she'd used since her first day in the arena, and grabbed her battle-axe, a shield, and a disruptor pistol.

Almost as soon as she'd finished gearing up, a couple of News Corps televid drones streaked by overhead. Jegra watched them pass by as they headed toward the carnage.

Armed to the teeth, both women jogged up the street. "Meleh'Kendar," Jegra said over the comm. "Can you do something about this skin color?"

"If I teleport you, I can filter out the blue pigment in your skin and return you back to normal."

"Do it," she said.

A golden shaft of light came down from the *Shard*, picked her up, and then relocated her to the site of all the destruction. Her body, carried away on light packets, began to reassemble. Once the teleportation was complete, she took a deep breath and then looked down at her hands and arms. She was back to her proper sunbaked self, deep tan and all.

"It's her!" one of the Harbingers cried out. Jegra looked up just in time to see a man wearing desert-styled military attire, including a *shemagh* that covered all of his face but for the fierce, yellow eyes staring down at her.

He was positioned on a heap of rubble from the building that they'd blown up. He drew his blaster and trained it on her. In the sky, the televid drones buzzed around noisily, recording the skirmish in real-time.

Two blasts rang out and Jegra tensed, but the man went down. His body rolled off the cement slab and crashed to the ground, disruptor scorch marks burned into his chest.

Jegra looked back up to see Raphine shouldering a plasma riffle. She smiled and nodded at the empress and Jegra turned and rushed up the same cement slab the man had been standing on. When she arrived at the top, she started taking heavy disruptor fire from several Harbingers dug in behind a pile of rubble.

She managed to deflected most of the blasts with her korridium shield, but one shot scorched her right arm, singeing her good. She groaned and looked down at the smoldering skin and the blackened scorch mark left behind.

Irritated, she kicked a chunk of concrete like a soccer ball and sent it whirling through the air. It crashed into the torso of the Harbinger who'd shot her and he flew back into one of the few remaining concrete walls that hadn't gone down with the rest of the building.

Both the man and the concrete chunk rebounded off the cement wall and crashed to the ground. The man groaned out in pain as every rib in his torso had snapped like a dry twig.

Three other men surrounded their friend and began providing cover fire for him. Luckily, Raphine had flanked them and took one of them down with a precise headshot.

Raphine's sneak-attack distracted the second soldier, who turned to deal with her, leaving the remaining man to leave his crippled friend behind and take on the gladiatrix herself.

The Harbinger drew a blade and bull rushed Jegra. *A rookie mistake.* As a veteran soldier, Jegra didn't even need to think about how to counter his attack.

She merely acted. Dropping her shoulder, she got down low and blocked his blade with her axe, then used her shoulder to ram him. He flew up into the air, flailing helplessly as he tried to grab ahold of something—anything.

Jegra whipped her axe around and swatted him back down with the flat side as though he were a pesky horsefly. He hit the ground so hard it sent up a dust cloud. A televid drone swooped down to get a close up of the soldier's battered face.

With him out of commission, Jegra returned to help Raphine who was firing periodically, keeping her target pinned behind a stone pillar. Jegra recognized the pillar as part of the cultural center's central lobby. *These bastards would pay for the people they killed today.*

Before she could reach him, however, two more Harbingers appeared from around a section of broken wall. Jegra threw her shield and took out the one to the right and then leapt into the air, her eyes fixed on the man standing on the left.

Disruptor blasts followed her into the air and she hurled her axe like a tomahawk. It spiraled through the air and then, with a wet sounding *thwack*, lodged itself in the man's chest. He fell to his knees and looked over at his friend, who had a shield embedded in his shoulder. His eyes widened as he realized it was too late for him and then toppled over onto his side.

Wasting no time, Jegra landed between the two men. Her breathing steady, her mind clear on her objective, she tore her shield out of the man's shoulder and heard the crunch of his clavicle. The Harbinger gripped his crippled shoulder and howled in pain.

"I'm going to kill you, you stupid Earth bitch!" he growled.

Ignoring his insult, Jegra merely ripped her axe out of his friend's chest and flicked the blood off, making sure it splattered across the remaining Harbinger's face. The second televid drone swung around to catch it all on bloody live television.

"You dirty cunt!" the man shouted. "You'll pay for that! The Harbingers of Truth will show the world how unfit you are to be ruler. You and your filthy mods have no place in Dagon society!"

Tired of his inane drivel, she gave him a mouthful of her boot and his head snapped back with such force his neck broke.

Slowly, Jegra turned to the televid drone. It slowly hovered into place to get a closeup of the empress. "This is the Mother of Dagon, Empress Jegra Alakandra and rightful ruler of the Dagon Empire. If the Harbingers of Truth think they can kill innocent Dagon civilians and brand me as unfit to rule, then they have another think coming to them. From this moment on, anyone brandishing the symbol of the Harbingers will be arrested on sight. Anyone caught in terrorist plots against the empire will be put on trial for treason. And anyone who kills my people will have to deal with me."

"Long live the Empress!" Raphine shouted. Several more bystanders shouted out the same. One by one others joined in the rallying chant praising the empress for her heroism. Praising the famed Gladiatrix who took it upon herself to put her life in danger so as to ensure the safety of her people. Praising that heroine whom the Harbingers so despised because she was an outsider and not of pure Dagon blood; rubbing it in their collective noses. And all of it caught on live televid so that everyone from Thessalonica to Dagon Prime would know exactly what had transpired that day.

The hero of the arena had become the hero of the people, and fighting off a legend like that was nearly impossible. The Harbingers of Truth were fools for even trying. But they didn't care about ratings like Dakroth did. They only cared about sowing mayhem and destabilizing Jegra's regime enough to hurt her. But she wasn't having any of it.

Jegra reached out and grasped the televid drone and pulled it close, its rotary propellers groaning in defiance of being manhandled.

"Listen up. I have a message for that asshole Demeris Ferrison. You try to turn the people against me through tactics of fear and violence. You blow up cultural centers and murder innocent people because you see them as less worthy than you. And for what? To prove I'm not Dagon? To prove I'm not of noble, pureblood lineage? To prove I'm not worthy of ruling as empress? Look, jerk-off, I didn't ask to be here. Your people's custom of poaching aliens from other worlds and forcing them to fight in your gladiator games is what brought me here. And I fought until I gained my freedom. I fought using your rules. I fought for the honor of Dagon. And as fate should have it, I won an even more difficult feat. I won your emperor's heart. Like it or not, that's a fact. So, here's the deal, ass-face. I'm coming for you. Run. Hide. It makes no difference. I will find you. And I will catch you.

Then, when I finally have you in my grasp, I'll give you what you've always wanted. A chance to kill me. A no holds barred match in the arena. To the death."

If Jegra had learned anything from watching Dakroth, it was that he always persuaded the people to take his side by offering them what they wanted. Who wouldn't want to see the empress, the undefeated gladiatrix of the galaxy, take on a known terrorist in a death match? Even though it would appeal to the fans, Demeris was cunning. He was playing a long-term game. His was about disrupting the system. Of breaking the rules and creating anarchy. But as long as the people were on her side and not his, she'd win out in the end. And her trash-talking him across the entire Commonwealth would mean that wherever he went, whoever he met with would look at him and judge him for being a coward for refusing to face her.

Maybe he was prepared to live with such humiliation. Maybe he didn't care about the games or popularity contests. Maybe, at the end of the day, he was just a cold-blooded killer with an axe to grind. So be it, but she couldn't let herself be intimidated by such a scumbag. She couldn't appear to be weak. Not at a time like this. Not when the government was overtaken by a power-hungry senator and the army taken over by his daughter. This was no time to be merciful. It was time to live up to her moniker—*Jegra the Merciless.*

The last remaining Harbinger had ducked down behind some rubble and was dug in tight. Raphine couldn't get a clear line of sight and Jegra wouldn't be able to reach him. So, instead, she leapt into the air and swinging her axe in a large arc, came down on the rubble with a powerful strike that sent a spray of debris in either direction. It was as though she were parting the Red Sea, but instead of water, it was dirt and rubble.

A path opened up, revealing the final Harbinger. His eyes locked onto the empress's, who marched toward him, her armor boots clanking menacingly. He grinned as she approached and he pulled out a proton-grenade.

Jegra's eyes widened and she skidded to a stop. "Everyone get back!" she shouted, waving her hand at the growing crowd of curious onlookers and then locking eyes with Raphine.

The moment Jegra's brown eyes locked onto Raphine's blue ones, the Bre'lal girl slung her rifle over her shoulder and made a mad dash away from the blast site. If a proton-grenade went off, it would obliterate everything for a full city block.

Smiling a crooked grin, the Harbinger flicked off the safety and mashed the detonator. There were only four seconds till detonation.

Jegra dashed forward, her every muscle sinew tightening into iron-like cords. The man's eyes flashed with astonishment as Jegra clasped her hand around his; he screamed out as she crushed every bone. With a swipe of her axe, she severed his hand at the wrist and then spun and, using every ounce of strength she had, launched the grenade straight into the air.

It flew up like a missile and three seconds later, it detonated.

A giant explosion flared a hundred and twenty odd feet above the city. A massive shockwave grew out of the epicenter, and spread across the city. Windows for a radius of three city blocks shattered as the blast of sweltering air from the explosion shook Arena City and acted as a violent reminder of what the Harbingers were capable of.

After the heat dissipated and people began poking their heads out of darkened windows and doorways, Jegra finally let out a sigh of relief.

"Did I ever tell you that I've always felt you were a little bit nuts?" a voice said.

Jegra turned to see Raphine sauntering toward her, a subdued smile on her face. It was one of both relief and appreciation.

"I couldn't let more people be killed for a madman's bloodlust."

"And that's where the Harbingers of Truth get you all wrong. You may not be the empress we would have chosen, but you're certainly the empress we need right now. And the more people who can see that truth, the more will be able to see Demeris Ferrison for what he is. A charlatan."

The televid drones pulled back as the first responders arrived. Jegra waved them over to her position. "I want you to sweep the area for any survivors. Attend to the wounded. And let's get this place cleaned up."

Raphine rolled up her sleeves and walked over to a large slab of concrete. Hoisting it up, she turned around and faced Jegra. "Where do you want it?"

Jegra smiled and then pointed at an undisturbed area where they could pile the larger chunks of rubble. "Over there."

When others saw the Bre'lal girl joining to help, more came over and began pitching in. Soon enough, the crowd of onlookers that had stayed back became volunteers in the cleanup effort.

17

The escape pod's thrusters ignited as it came plunging out of the atmosphere like a meteor. As the vessel slowed, an internal alarm bleated with such maddening sounds of distress that the occupant slowly opened her weary eyes. Seeing that she was trapped inside a coffin-sized shell plummeting toward the surface of a barren desert landscape, panic set in and she started hyperventilating. Her hands flew up to the glass and she braced herself for a crash landing.

Under the scorching heat of a midday sun, a Thorvian camel with three humps grazed at a small watering hole under a grove of palm trees. There were no other watering holes for kilometers in any direction. His mid-day drink was interrupted by a loud impact explosion, and he reared his head up in time to see a sand dune erupt into the air as though a landmine had gone off. Startled, the beast took off running.

There was a pneumatic hiss and the escape pod decompressed. Almost as soon as the air had fizzled out, the glass hatch flew off. A beautiful, blue-skinned Dagon girl dragged herself out of the pod, slumped over the edge, and fell to the ground. The soft sand broke the barely conscious girl's fall and she slowly sat up.

Half delirious, still trying to shake off the after effects of stasis, she shook her head and opened her eyes wide, blinked, and stretched her face by doing some facial exercise. Doing this always seemed to help her wake up.

She dusted off her white body suit, a skin-tight outfit made of elastane that clung to her young, nubile form and left little to the imagination. Although she had no memory of who she was or where she was from, she did have one overwhelming sense of purpose. To find the Lord Emperor. Emperor Dakroth.

The girl spotted a distant oasis and what appeared to be a Thorvian camel galloping away from it. She didn't know why she knew it was Thorvian, or a camel, but the information just seemed to be already in her memory. And if she could remember something as obscure as a Thorvian camel, she was pretty sure the rest of her memory was intact, too. But, for whatever reason, she couldn't access it.

Parched, she stumbled to her feet and then worked her way down the side of the sand dune she had crashed into.

Skid marks dragged behind each footstep as she gradually made her way down to the basin. Upon reaching the bottom, she stumbled, tripping on her own feet, and took a tumble. Eating dirt, she slowly pushed herself up and spat out a wad of wet sand. Then, crawling on all fours, she scrambled up to the spring. Dunking her whole face into the water, she drank. She drank until she choked herself of the refreshing liquid.

Drenched and coughing, the girl reared back and plopped down on her ass. Water dripping from her dark purple hair, she leaned forward and studied her face, hoping her reflection might jog her memory. She was Dagon, and only about sixteen years old. *At least I'm pretty*, she thought. That had to count for something.

She touched her face, lingering on her lips, then aquiline nose, and finally taking in her own striking, crystal rose colored eyes. Her skin was dark blue, like that of royalty. Of pure stock. But her features were otherworldly. She looked exotic. Not quite Dagon, but somehow fully Dagon.

"Who are you?" she asked of her own reflection. But it merely echoed her words back to her, knowing little more than she did. "More importantly, perhaps, where am I?"

The girl scooted back into the shade of the palm trees. The midday sun was sweltering hot and the arid climate was already draining her strength. And although she couldn't remember much, somehow, she knew this was the first time she'd ever stepped foot on a desert world.

After drinking and taking some time to acclimate to her new environment, she staggered to her feet and began following the camel's tracks. After all, it had to be going somewhere. It wouldn't just run out into the middle of the desert to die.

Three hours later, the scorching sun beating down on her dark blue flesh, she found the camel, dead from dehydration and lying in the middle of an endless sea of sand dunes that stretched all the way into the horizon.

"Jikto-belrag, ekt-ta-gamut daggon!" she cursed. It was Dagoni and literally meant, "Goddamn stupid fucking camel."

She made a mental note to herself that Thorvian camels were fucking brain-dead and licked her chapped lips. Shielding her eyes with her palm, she looked up at the clear blue sky. The sky seemed so serene. So peaceful. And if she didn't find shelter, she knew it would probably be the last thing she saw before she withered away into a shriveled corpse.

Heat aches setting in, she collapsed to her knees beside the carcass of the beast and stared out at the shimmering air that drifted over the sands like a barely visible ocean. In the distance, amid the rippling heat waves, she could make out a dark figure wrapped in a brown and tan checkered *shemagh* and wearing tinted sun goggles to keep out the intense light.

Slung across his chest was a burgundy Bohemian shoulder bag with gold zigzag patterns woven into the knitted fabric. She didn't know if the person was a mirage or not, but she reached out a hand and, in a hoarse voice raw with the dryness of the desert air, whispered, "*Help.*"

Then, heat exhaustion settling in, she collapsed beside the camel.

A metal whine, like the old hinges of an iron door grinding against one another, roused her from her bout of heatstroke. The cool shade of a dwelling sent a chill through every inch of her overheated body and caused her skin to bristle with goosebumps.

"You're lucky to be alive," a raspy voice said. It was masculine and she sat up on the pile of blankets she rested on and looked over at the figure who sat in the corner of the room, but her eyes were still not accustomed to the dimness and she could only make out a dark gray blur.

"Who are you?" she asked, her voice equally coarse.

"Who I am doesn't matter. Right now, you need to drink."

She felt the mouthpiece of a leather canteen brush against her lips and she reached out and clutched the bag and squeezed. A refreshing stream of water shot into her mouth and wetted her dry, aching tongue with a blast of refreshing liquid.

She sloshed the water around in her mouth, making every drop count, and then swallowed. Taking another thirsty gulp, she choked, coughing up some water which ran over her Prussian blue lips. Once her thirst was quenched, she wiped the edge of her mouth with the back of her hand and looked around the room.

It was stark except for a single bed off to the side, a coarse rug that looked handmade strewn across a dusty cement floor, and a small lamp that stood on a bedside table fashioned crudely from a coarse wood.

The man unwrapped his shawl to reveal the bovine face of an old goat. His eyes were gray with age and he looked the worse for wear.

"Who are you?"

"Just an old desert hermit," he replied.

"You're from Galliforn aren't you?"

"Yes," he said, shuffling over to a small fire pit in the center of his floor. Stirring the coals with a stick, he stared into the softly glowing embers. "But I'm afraid I'm no longer welcome on my homeworld. This is my home now."

"Not welcome? Why not?"

The satyr stroked his beard and then looked over at the young girl and smiled. "I betrayed my people. You see, during the wars, I allied myself with the Lord Emperor Dakroth. I fed him intel that would help end the war. At the time, I believed it was the right thing to do. I thought I could save countless people's lives by giving Dakroth a swift victory. But when my people turned the tide and won the war, I was exiled for my crimes."

Excited, the girl rose up to her knees, still clutching the canteen in both hands. "You know the emperor? You know Dakroth?"

"Yes, we fought together in the campaigns that forged the very foundation of the Commonwealth. But, these days, he keeps a low profile. I haven't spoken to him in many cycles."

"I need to find him," the girl said, an unforeseen urgency weighing her words down. "I may not be able to recall my name, or where I'm from, or even how I came to find myself on this barren world. But I do know one thing...I *must* find Emperor Dakroth."

"What could a girl as young as yourself possibly want to discuss with the emperor?"

The young Dagon woman looked into the fire and the satyr followed her gaze, both of them honing in on a single unimportant point.

"I…don't know. Just that I have to find him."

"Well, like I said. He's rather scarce these days. He's left the well-being of the empire in the care of the empress. She handles most of the day to day affairs. The Council handles all the rest."

"Then I will find her and convince her to take me to the emperor."

"I'm sure she'd get a kick out of you. The empress, is, well, rather eccentric. And, in my estimation, you seem precisely like the kind of person that she'd be interested in."

"You make her sound as though she isn't Dagon," the girl said with a light chuckle.

"She's not. Dakroth married a human woman."

"A human? What in the galaxy is that?"

"They're a species of hairless ape from a distant world called Earth."

"Hairless ape? Dakroth married a hairless ape?" gasped the girl. She sounded downright repulsed by the notion of it, proving to the satyr that she was, indeed, of Dagoni lineage.

"She's no stranger than any other hairless beast, I'd reckon."

"They all weird me out. Whether it's a hairless cat, a naked mole rat, or a nude wombat, they're all a little unsettling. I can't imagine what a naked ape would look like."

"For the most part, she looks Dagon. But instead of blue skin she has pink. And she lacks pointed ears. And the women of her species aren't intersexual, like yours are. But other than that, she's genetically compatible. Which is why Dakroth took an interest in her in the first place. He always did have a soft-spot for beautiful women from other worlds."

"I supposed that's his prerogative as emperor. Personally, I wouldn't touch a hairless ape with a ten-foot pole even if my life depended on it." The girl made a sour face as she tried to shake the image of the beautiful emperor making love to a giant, gorilla-like creature with watermelon-sized breasts that flopped about like droopy beanbag chairs. A beast that made far too many grunting noises during passionate bouts of love making and, for that matter, in daily life, too.

"She's not too hard on the eyes, even if I do say so myself. More of an acquired taste, actually. But I can assure you, her personality more than makes up for her strange appearance. She's quite…fascinating."

"Well, you sound completely enamored with her." The goat smiled sheepishly and turned away from the girl. After another long stint of staring into the fire, she asked, "How do I find her?"

"You're in luck, child. She makes her home on this very moon."

The girl gave the satyr a perplexed look. "Moon…the empress…you mean…she's here?"

"Naturally, my dear. You're on Thessalonica."

The girl let out an audible sigh of relief and sank to the ground. Lying face down, arms outstretched, she hugged the dirt and whispered, "After all this time, I'm finally home."

Before the satyr could inquire further, there was a loud rumbling sound. The entire compound shuddered. Outside the walls they could hear the deafening sounds of large turbo thrusters reversing. The satyr and the girl shared a startled look.

The old goat rose to his feet and hollered above the noise of the screaming engines, but his words were in vain as he was drowned out by high-pitched whine of the turbines. After a few moments, the blare of the engines died down and a heavy thud shook the ground as the ship set down outside.

"Are you expecting company?" the girl asked.

"No," the satyr replied, shooting her a concerned look. With that, he fetched his walking stick and headed for the bunker door.

She followed the satyr to the entrance and watched as he pushed open the heavy metal door and stepped out into the brilliant sunlight and arid desert air. In the distance, a large transport had set down and the landing ramp was already halfway open by the time their pupils had acclimated to the intensity of the scorching desert afternoon.

Together they waited outside his abode beneath the handmade awning that he had built over the entrance of his doorway. They watched with unease as the ramp lowered all the way and, finally, three shadowy figures emerged from the bowels of the ship.

Three heavily armed mercenaries sauntered down the ramp, shouldering military assault rifles, and wearing Dagon special ops body armor which was a matte black with glossy shoulder and chest plating. The white skull of some kind of elk-like beast adorned their chest armor and their glossy black helmets with built-in eye gear gave them an uncanny resemblance to Valusian beetles, the girl thought. The menacing kind.

"Who goes there?" asked the satyr in his hoarse, displeased, old-timer voice.

Of the three large mercs, the middle soldier stepped forward. The other two held back, providing eyes and cover for their envoy.

"We don't want any trouble," he said, his voice masked by a synthesizer to make him sound more diabolic and frightening than he already was. "We're here for the girl. Hand her over and we'll be out of your hair, old man."

The old goat glanced at the girl only to catch her shaking her head fearfully, letting him know that she wasn't with them. She didn't know them. And she certainly didn't have any intentions of returning with them, either.

"I'm sorry, but this young lady is my guest. If you'd care to join us, perhaps we can all get better acquainted over a cup of chilled green tea."

Ignoring the satyr's invitation, the soldier held up a portable biometric scanner and scanned the satyr and his little bunker. Checking the readout, he let out a throaty chuckle. "Ural Bazhov of Galliforn. The infamous traitor of the Galliforn Empire."

Unexpectedly, the soldier raised his riffled and shot off a single blast. Bazhov dropped to the ground, clutching his left shoulder which smoldered from the low-level disruptor blast. The scent of burnt fur lingered in the air.

"That was the low setting," said the soldier. He dialed up his blaster to full power and then trained the gun onto the girl. "The next shot will be set to kill. As such, I recommend you stay out of this, goat. It's none of your concern."

"You just made it my concern," the old goat growled. Reaching his fingers up to his lips, Bazhov let loose a shrill whistle. Almost as soon as he had given the signal, the sand all around them erupted in fountains that shot six feet into the air as though they were sand geysers.

As sand rained down, the air thinned to reveal four X4 battle androids standing on the sand. The soldiers instantly began exchanging fire with the robotic security detail and, finding themselves outnumbered, slowly drew back into the safety of their ship.

In full retreat, the three mercs managed to take out one of the robots. The remaining three androids grouped together in a triangle pattern, the rear two dropping behind their point man, and pressed forward. The lead droid took a lot of fire but its unit still managed to push the mercs back toward their ship.

The drop ship's thrusters ignited and the black ship, with the same animal skull painted in white across both sides of its outer hull, gradually began to rise into the air. The three mercs managed to take down the lead android, leaving the final two. One of the droids still in commission bent down and took his comrade's weapon and, with double blasters, returned fire on the drop ship as it rose into the air.

The lead soldier stood on the edge of the ramp watching the goat with an unnerving gaze while his compatriots provided cover, continuing their fire exchange with the battle droids. One of the droids got off a lucky shot and hit the second merc directly in his chest armor. He yelped out in pain as he went down and his comrade, rushing to his aid, quickly dragged him back into the ship and out of the line of fire.

Unfazed by the firefight, the leader stood poised, watching the girl and the goat, as disruptor blasts pinged off the ship's hull and danced all around him like a lethal laser light show.

Bazhov had a hunch that whatever or whoever was behind that mask, they were dangerous. He could feel it in his old goat bones.

The ship rose into the sky and the rear hatch shut with a clangor. Pivoting in place, its afterburners ignited and the drop ship raced off in the direction of the desert town Mardok. A dive for all manner of scum and villainy and a way stop and fueling station for galactic wayfarers. The only outpost on the hot side of the moon beyond the borders of the cool oasis metropolis of Arena City.

"Who were those guys?" the girl asked.

"I don't know. But they'll likely be back. And with reinforcements." Bazhov turned back toward the girl, his slatted goat eyes hard and grim. Breaking his somber look, he smiled at her with a row of yellow teeth. "Until then, however, we shall enjoy a cup of cool, refreshing green tea. After all, I don't get many visitors this far into the scorched lands."

"I'd love some," the girl said cheerfully, returning into the confines of the satyr's abode to join him for a cup of tea. Before shutting the door, however, she glanced behind her shoulder one last time just to make sure they were truly gone.

18

A soft beeping aroused Callestra Van Morgan from her slumber. The regeneration cycle was complete and she opened her eyes and gazed through the glass shell of the regeneration chamber as physicians and nurses wearing light green scrubs raced about as they attended to patients. It wasn't long before someone came over to her capsule and unlocked it for her. "How do we feel?" the doctor asked.

Doctor Darius Ebbedon's name tag dangled in front of her as he leaned over the open capsule and touched the soft part of Callestra's neck, checking her pulse. After a moment, he jotted something down on a touch panel display.

She was a bit foggy coming out of the anesthetic. She had been in the regeneration chamber for ten hours. Everything from tissue regrowth to bone reconstruction could be done inside the state-of-the-art medical compartment.

Regeneration pods, as they were called, were mini-hospitals in a compact tube, so to speak. They could be packed up and taken almost anywhere you needed to go. More importantly, they were vital in the new age of healthcare.

A wounded soldier could be patched up and sent back out onto the battlefield in a matter of hours. A sick patient could have their illness diagnosed and be given a treatment for whatever ailment they'd been stricken with in the very same day. Even surgeries could be performed with the right robotic attachments. The regeneration pods were a miracle of modern medicine. At least, Callestra thought so.

"Wait," Callestra called out, beckoning for the doctor to hang back for a moment. "Do I know you from somewhere?"

Doctor Ebbedon paused and then looked up at her and smiled. "Perhaps you do. I'm the Lord Emperor's personal physician. But, as our dear great leader has taken a leave of absence, I have been reassigned to the *Verlag* by your father."

He didn't sound too awfully pleased about it, though he didn't let his bitterness towards her father's toiling get in the way of his professional care of her. She appreciated that.

Callestra nodded and slowly sat up. As she raised up, so too did the pod. The bed folded into a chair as it tilted forward and then lowered down like a dentist's chair. A pneumatic hiss sounded once it stopped and the bottom portion of the pod's shell whisked open. Panels folded and slid out of the way, allowing Callestra to step out with ease.

She climbed out and stood in the middle of the room, the cool air of the ship cascading across her bare skin and causing it to bristle with goosebumps. Medical staff in white coats and aquamarine scrubs busily rushed up to her and took blood samples, analyzed her blood pressure, and did a number of other minor medical checks on her. A couple of minutes later, Doctor Ebbedon returned with a nurse by his side.

"You check out fine," he said, giving her a clean bill of health. He nodded at the nurse standing next to him, who held a freshly folded uniform in her arms. "Here's a fresh set of clothes synthesized to your exact measurements."

The nurse stepped forward and handed the bundle to her. Callestra received it graciously and watched as the nurse scurried off to return to her regular duties.

She quickly put on her uniform and cinched her belt tight and buckled it. Brushing her white jacket down, she chased out any lingering creases and turned to the mirror on the far side of the wall to do a final quality check.

Up to code, she popped her cufflinks in and followed up with a tug on her mandarin collar. "That's better," she whispered, speaking to herself.

Prim and proper and ready for duty, she turned her attention back toward Doctor Ebbedon and waited for him to look up. She met his gaze and nodded, her way of showing gratitude. He nodded in return and, swiveling on her left heel, she marched out into the corridor of the ship.

On her way to the lift, she raised both hands then opened and closed them, inspecting them as if they were brand new. And to a large extent, they were; reconstructed from an entire cloth of living organic nanofiber created from her own stem cells.

Dagon medical technology had come a long way in recent years. The regeneration pods were essentially portable medical labs. The robotic arms, equipped with every conceivable tool, could weave organic material back together in minutes. They could generate plates and create fresh cartilage, bone, and muscle sinews that were then sprayed with an oily substance and bombarded with ultraviolet light to initiate skin growth. A few hours of enhanced regeneration and a person's damaged flesh, broken bones, even a full hand, arm, or leg could be replaced and made whole again.

This cutting-edge technology had allowed the doctors to rebuild Callestra in a matter of hours verses days or even weeks; weaving DNA back together, new cells replacing damaged ones in real-time. Of course, the technology was only available to the most privileged among society.

Over the past few weeks, Callestra had been relying on her regeneration capsule more and more. She always pushed herself to her limits and then, maybe because she wanted to prove to herself that she was the best there was, she deliberately stepped across that line.

In her mind, she had to do it. Having physical limits was a challenge necessary for growth. One had to push through those limits, shatter that glass ceiling so to speak, and eliminate the very boundaries that held one back. If you were ever going to overcome your limitations, perchance to become something more than you were born, you couldn't afford to stop when things got hard. You had to keep pushing. Keep fighting. Death was the only end to the battle.

She couldn't afford to be weak. That simply wasn't an option. Not for her. And, sure, she'd always been an overachiever. That went without saying. But perhaps more than this, having an overbearing father and an absentee mother made it so that she always was trying to please her old man, Senator Targon.

As long as she could remember, everything she did was in an attempt to get into his good graces, perchance to win even just one ounce of affection and admiration. But nothing she ever did, no matter how fearless or successful, ever seemed good enough to please him past the moment.

Her mother, on the other hand, had been a high-level attorney, but she'd become addicted to Nividium when it had first hit the streets.

At first it was just to take the edge off her high stress job, her mom had told her. But it quickly became clear that she had developed a real problem. This was before the days of vape regulators, before the shocking statistics of death by lethal dose. Once, Callestra's mother had overdosed on Nividium and had survived.

Not many do. But she had. She was a fighter.

After a full rehabilitation, everything seemed fine. And for a time, their family life fell back into its normal rhythm. Her mom even began doing legal work again. Then, on the day of Callestra's graduation from the Imperial Academy, her mother hadn't shown up. In fact, afterward, she couldn't find her mother anywhere.

So she marched to the slums of Imperial City in her cadet's uniform where, after tracing some leads, she found her mother scagged unconscious, sprawled out on the floor of some drug den.

She was so blazed out of her mind, in fact, that she didn't even recognize her own daughter standing there before her. Perhaps worse than this, though, was that she looked like a used-up sex doll, having turned favors for just one more hit of Nividium. That's the day Callestra realized how weak her mother actually was. She was nothing but a deplorable scag.

Sickened by her mother's feebleness, Callestra left her there on the dirty scum-stained mattress and headed back to her dorm on the base. That night she cried for the loss of her mother, who was as good as dead to her. She never saw her again after that.

Meanwhile, her father continued to support her ambitions as she climbed steadily through the ranks of the Imperial Fleet. Always doing her best to please him, Callestra never got anything more than a congratulatory nod.

A year ago, two things happened that changed Callestra's life forever. She met a charming man named Gerrard Van Zallek. A drug dealer, as ironic as it was, with whom she began a relationship. During that same time, Callestra was serving onboard the *Zorveth*, Dakroth's newly commissioned battlecruiser–the same ship he lost to Jegra at the battle of Sector B-13 in the Zargora system.

She was one of the few crew members to make it to the escape pods after the Lord Emperor had abandoned ship. And after a commendation for her service and her bravery, she accepted a Sub Commander position, though she'd quickly been promoted to full Commander after her ship had died terribly on an away mission to an asteroid simply designated as Dark Six.

Dark Six was an asteroid that floated so far off from the main belt that it had initially been thought to be a dwarf planet. But strange readings emanating from the rock demanded a more thorough investigation. What they found there was beyond horrifying. It was inhabited by a species of glowing, tapeworm-like creatures that could sear through your suit. Once inside, they wrapped themselves around your skin and slowly burned through your flesh until they got inside your body. That's when the real damage began.

Callestra had nuked the asteroid. New life form or not, she didn't dare let such a hideously vile creature exist.

During that time, she was getting commendations and praise for her service, and the empress had somehow gotten back into Dakroth's good graces. She didn't know how or why, but it had happened. Dakroth pardoned Jegra for her war crimes. The news of his granting her a full pardon had shocked the empire.

It was so suspect, in fact, that her father had commissioned an inquiry into the emperor's mental state, assuming that Jegra could have mind-control powers they were unaware of. They didn't find anything.

As it turned out, the emperor was just so enamored with the stupid hairless ape that, according to her father, he couldn't be trusted to make the best decisions for the empire. He had been blinded by the insipid poison of love.

Ever since that dreadful realization, her father had worked diligently to subvert Dakroth's power, an emperor whom Senator Targon viewed as impotent, erratic, and dangerous. It was only the success of the recent gladiatorial games and Dakroth's little ploy to make Jegra into the idol of the people that stalled her father's plans of taking over the government and issuing martial law.

"Stalled" being the key word. Because, now, here she was. Vice Admiral of the fleet. Second in military command only to the emperor himself.

So, while her father's coup had worked to a point, and with the emperor out of the way, Senator Targon oversaw the government proceedings while she managed the military's affairs. But the stress of directing the entire Imperial fleet was more than she could have imagined, and she had called upon the support of Zallek, and his wonder drug, more times than she would have liked.

The past few days, as stressful as they'd been, had left her more determined than ever to make her father proud.

And, as a proud Dagon officer, she knew that it was because of Jegra that she had almost died a year ago at Zargora. It was because of Jegra that the grotesque mods got their equality. And it was because of her that the empire had been tainted by alien blood.

In fact, she was glad for her father's coup. Because, at least now, they could start to work together to make Dagon great again.

Although she didn't agree with the terrorist tactics of Demeris Ferrison, she understood his point of view. If Dagon simply allowed any alien to become ruler, the greatest empire the galaxy had ever known would grow so saturated with impure bloods and foreign cultures that it would no longer be recognizable as Dagon. It would become something else. Something faceless. Something tarnished. Something false.

She didn't want to see that happen. Which is why she agreed to the plan when her father expressed taking back their beloved empire from Dakroth. Even if it meant starting a civil war.

"Admiral on the bridge!" an officer cried out as Callestra stepped onto the command deck.

"As ease," she said, scanning all the faces that paused to look at her. She smiled and locked her hands behind her back. "Set course for the Viridian asteroid belt at the Cove."

"Aye, aye, ma'am," said the navigation officer. He typed in the coordinates and spooled up the hyperdrive.

Callestra turned to look out the main view portal at the stars. One moment, they were tiny pinpricks of light. In the next moment, they were spaghetti thin strands of brilliant color that stretched infinitely into the distance.

"Arrival in six hours."

"I'll be in my personal chambers," she said.

Callestra grew exceedingly excited as she made her way to her quarters. She was meeting Zallek for an after-work booty call, as was their habit whenever her ship was in orbit, and was desperate for the release, a marathon evening of good sex would bring her. As usual, the plan was for him to teleport aboard and meet her after her shift.

Unclasping the collar of her uniform, she hastily began unbuttoning it before she had even arrived at her door. She wanted nothing more to do than tear off her clothes and get down to business and she wasn't going to take no for an answer.

Her chamber doors slid apart and she sauntered into the room as seductively as she could manage. Throwing her jacket to the floor, she turned to the bed with a smile on her face. The smile vanished, however, when she found her bed chambers empty. There was no sign of Zallek. He'd stood her up.

"Computer, scan ship for Gerard Van Zallek's bio-signature."

<<There is currently no Gerard Van Zallek aboard the *Verlag.*>>

"You son of a bitch," she growled, an angry scowl settling onto her face.

She wasn't the kind of girl accustomed to being stood up. And, like any woman, she had her insecurities and doubts. She couldn't help but wonder what it was that had kept him away from her. Had he grown so tired of her already? Did he have pressing business he couldn't tear himself away from? Another tryst, perhaps? What? What in the whole galaxy could possibly be more enticing than spending an erotic evening with her?

19

"**Lock teleporter onto** Gyllek's location," Raven said, sliding into the pilot's seat beside Kregor. "I want her out of there the moment I give the say so."

"On it," Kregor said, his fingers dancing across the controls.

"What do you need me to do?" Angellyk asked.

Without looking back, Raven said, "Get down to the engine room. If anything goes wrong, I'll need you to take care of it."

"I don't know anything about engines."

Raven shot her a look of confidence from over her shoulder. "Don't worry, I'll walk you through it."

"While you handle everything else?"

"The captain's kind of awesome like that," Kregor said, smiling to himself.

"All right, you don't need to twist my arm. See you both later, I guess."

She stepped forward, stopped, hesitated for a bit, then kissed Kregor on the cheek. With that, she turned and rushed out of the room.

"Is it weird?" Kregor asked.

"Is what weird?" Raven responded.

"I mean, she's your ex-wife and all that."

A rather obnoxious and needlessly noisy alarm went off in the cabin and the ship shuddered violently. "Pay attention to the mooring clamps!" snapped Raven.

"Right. Sorry." Kregor remedied the situation and got the ship back on track. His brow creased in contemplation as he focused on not making any more mistakes.

"Easy," Raven said, pulling back on the joystick as she guided the corvette class ship away from the docking arms. "Easy does it."

Kregor flicked the comm on. "How are you holding up in there, kid?"

"It's going to be close..." Gyllek said.

"We've got a teleport lock on you, so when that countdown hits one minute, we're beaming you out of there."

"Roger that," Gyllek responded.

Kregor turned in his seat and looked at Raven with somber eyes full of worry for his friend and crewmate. "How much time has she got?"

Raven leaned over and glanced at the in-dash digital clock. Under the regular star date, it had bright orange numbers running through the countdown in real-time. "Five minutes," Raven answered.

"Some days I really miss that happy-go-lucky fish," Kregor said. "His wealth of optimism never runs dry."

"Skuld!" Raven chirped excitedly.

"Yes, I know his name. I was just saying—"

"No! Skuld would know how to bypass the interface. His people's technology is aquatic based. So, their circuitry is organic."

"I'm not following you..."

"Gyllek," Raven said, jumping onto the comm. "The system is using Skallekian encryption. You need to input a..."

"A DNA sequence to fool the computer's organic checkpoints," Gyllek said over the comm, finishing the captain's sentence for her. "I'm on it."

Kregor pinched the bridge of his nose. "Would somebody mind translating that into something a lizard brain could comprehend?"

"The reason Gyllek and I couldn't crack the encryption is because we're approaching it like a straight up digital interface. But it keeps locking us out at every turn because it's looking for a biological signature. Without that DNA reading, it won't let us past the security protocols."

"So, you're saying it's a hybrid system?"

"Very ingenious, actually."

"So, what DNA sequence does it want?"

Raven looked at Kregor and then sprang from her seat. "I'll be right back."

"Right back? Wait...what?"

"Just don't crash the ship!"

Raven ran through the corridors of the *Skywend*, her boots clanking noisily on the metal flooring. Arriving at the small room where she kept the automated dental hygiene chair, she pressed her thumb on the security scanner and leaned in to let it take a retina scan.

The doors swooshed open and Dakroth, hands bound so he couldn't cut himself free with his laser finger, looked up and smiled.

"Miss me?" he asked in a suave voice.

Raven ignored him and stepped into the room. Shutting the door behind her, she went over to a steel counter and picked up a syringe. "I need some of your blood," she said, prepping the needle.

"Out of the question!" Dakroth replied.

"Good thing I wasn't asking one," Raven said. With a roguish grin she pricked him with the needle and he almost fainted. "Don't tell me the great Rhadamanthus Dakroth is afraid of something as innocuous as a tiny little needle?"

Practically green around the gills, Dakroth gulped down his nerves and tried to put on a strong face. "It's nothing. I'm fine. Really."

"Mmm-hmm," Raven said, drawing out the syringe and placing the cap back on it.

"Thanks for the help."

Dakroth could only nod.

"Now, you've had a busy day, so please rest," Raven added, pulling out a NeedleAir injector with sedative.

"No, wait," Dakroth pleaded, "I can't go to sleep again. All this sleeping is driving me nuts. I want do get out and stretch my…"

The hiss of the injection drowned out his complaint and he looked down at his leg then up at Raven. His startled expression quickly drained away into a tranquil, sleepy look and he nodded off.

Raven tucked the syringe into a breast pocket on the sleeveless vest she wore over her environmental suit. Not having had the time to change, it still sported the burned opening that revealed her chest.

Raven went over to a wall console and typed in an emergency teleport code and then turned and stood prim and proper as a golden beam of light washed over her. Little by little it broke her apart into hexagonal light packets that flew up along the sparkling shaft of the beam.

A few moments later, Raven reformed next to Gyllek. The girl paused and looked up with a perplexed look. "Captain?"

"Here," Raven said, drawing out the syringe with Dakroth's blood. "You're going to need this."

"What's this?" Gyllek asked, taking the blood sample form her.

"It's the key to shutting this down." Raven nodded at the large monitor in front of them, the countdown reaching T minus 2 minutes.

Gyllek hurried over to the biometric scanner and placed a single drop on the hand sensor. Looking up, it was T minus 1 minute 30 seconds. "I hope this works."

As they waited, Kregor's voice came over the comm. "Captain, do you have her?"

"Yes."

"I'm pulling you both out."

"No, wait," Gyllek said. "Just one more second."

"We don't have one more second," Kregor replied. "We don't even have one more nanosecond."

There was an intense silence. And although it only lasted a second or two, to Gyllek it seemed like an eternity.

<<Automated self-destruct sequence is now deactivated,>> the female computer's voice announced.

Gyllek shot a relieved looked at Raven and she too let out a sigh of relief.

"Whatever you two did down there," Kregor's voice shouted over the comm, "I'm glad it worked." He let out a sigh and then the comm flicked off.

Raven tapped the console in front of her and said, "Bring the *Skywend* back to the docking port, and meet us back down at the command center."

"Aye, aye, Captain," Kregor replied.

Raven turned to see Gyllek staring at her with a suspicious look. Her arms were folded across her chest. "Captain?" she said, urging the captain to come out with the truth that she was obviously hiding. "Do I even need to ask?"

Raven sighed and let her rigid posture melt into an apologetic slump. "I suppose it was only a matter of time before you found out. But I'm keeping Emperor Dakroth aboard the ship."

"The Lord Emperor is on our ship?!" Gyllek practically shouted it and Raven motioned with her hands for Gyllek to bring it down a notch.

"I've been keeping him prisoner since Jegra's appearance in the arena."

"That was over a two weeks ago!" she blurted out. Still in shock, Gyllek paced up and down the floor.

"Please don't tell the others. Not just yet."

"I don't know if I can keep such a big secret," Gyllek said.

"And it's not your burden to bear. Just let me find the right time to tell them. That's all I ask."

Gyllek trusted Raven Nightguard more than she trusted anyone else in the galaxy, so she agreed to let the captain have her time. She nodded and then stood in the middle of the room, not knowing what to do with herself.

"Until then," Raven said, nodding for Gyllek to come help her. "What do you say we get this facility up and running?"

"Sounds good to me," Gyllek agreed, sidling up next to the captain. "Besides, it'll help me take my mind off of…you know what."

Raven nodded and then they both delved into the command stations console and began bringing each system online, one at a time.

The *Skywend* locked back into place, the mooring clamps holding. Kregor put the ship into standby mode and then rose from his chair, stretched, and headed for the airlock.

Halfway there, he ran into Angellyk who'd apparently had the same idea. "Going my way, stranger?" she asked in a playful tone.

They stared into each other's eyes for a few moments then, as if pulled together by some unseen force, their lips were mashed up against one another and their hot, wet kisses resumed with a renewed vigor.

They fell into a doorway that was usually locked, but for some reason hadn't closed all the way. The door slid open and they stumbled into the small room, tearing off each other's clothes as they went.

Angellyk had her shirt and bra off in no time and was helping Kregor remove his when her back pressed up against something.

Kregor began kissing her neck when there was a loud moan. "Mmm…"

He reached around and grabbed her ass and moaned in response. But she pushed him back.

"What is it?"

"That wasn't me."

"What wasn't you?"

The "Mmm…" she repeated, making the same moaning sound as before, but in her own voice.

"If not you then who?"

Angellyk turned, taking a step back so she'd be next to Kregor, when they both saw the Lord Emperor, strapped to a chair, in the room with them. Angellyk screamed and covered her bare breasts.

"What in the galaxy?" Kregor mumbled under his breath.

"Is that…"

"The Lord Emperor," Kregor said, finishing her question for her.

Both stood with astonished looks on their faces, totally caught off guard by this unexpected twist of events. Mouths agape, they turned to one another and said, simultaneously: "Dakroth."

"It makes so much sense now!" Angellyk said, fetching her shirt.

"What does?" he asked.

"The reason why Raven has been so guarded lately. I thought maybe it was because of us," she gestured, pointing at herself and then him. "But, now, I see it was because she had a secret…a big one."

"Why would she be keeping the Lord Emperor captive aboard the *Skywend*?" Kregor asked, scratching his chin as he tried to figure out what Raven's agenda might be.

"Not her…" Angellyk said. "She's obviously doing it for the empress."

"For Jegra?"

"Think about it," she said, tapping her temple. "Raven is too smart to try something so risky. But if she was ordered to do it…"

"Then she'd have no choice."

"Exactly."

Kregor crossed his arms and turned to look at the emperor, passed out in the dental chair before them. "But what's her game?"

"She needed him out of commission so she could save Danica. Dakroth wouldn't have let that match end the way it did. Which means he was likely taken out of commission prior to the bout."

"Or during it," Kregor said.

Angellyk shot him a curious look.

"There were a few teleport logs that didn't make sense. Raven teleported over to the *Verlag* and then back. But it was only for about five minutes, give or take. Far too short for anything other than…"

"Abducting the emperor."

"Right."

"And you never questioned her about it?"

"I never had any reason to. Sometimes she does things that aren't by the book. It's what makes her such a cunning strategist. She can think outside the box. And, besides, she's never let us down. Not once."

After a long pause, Angellyk asked, "What do we do now?"

"We pretend we never stumbled into this room and keep it to ourselves. The captain will divulge everything when she's ready. There's no reason to mention it now."

Angellyk nodded. She wasn't sure if that was the wisest choice, but if she was being honest, Kregor had spent more time with Raven than she had over the past several years and probably had a better read on her. As such, she decided to go with his suggestion. For now.

"Right, then," Angellyk said, opening the door and exiting the room. Kregor joined her shortly. Together, they shut the door and made sure it locked this time.

"Come on, the boss will start to wonder what we're up to if we're gone for too long."

Angellyk spanked Kregor on the ass with a loud smack. "I know what we would have been up to had we not run into unforeseen circumstances."

Kregor checked his watch. "There's still time," he said.

Angellyk strode up the corridor and ducked into the airlock, looking back and smiling coyly. "Maybe next time, stud."

Kregor watched her disappear into the airlock and then let out a frustrated sigh. Shrugging, he pulled on his shirt and then followed after her.

Dakroth's eyelids cracked just enough to see the soft glow of the yellow exit lamp. The room's inset lighting was set to its lowest setting and gave everything a sleepy glow.

He had a bad itch on his nose that desperately needed scratching and jerked his hand. To his surprise, the wrist clamp jostled. Looking down, he found that the latch had somehow been unfastened. Tearing his hand out, he stretched his nose and let out a deep sigh of relief.

"So much better he said."

A sly smile spreading onto his lips. He raised a glowing finger, hot pink light filling the room as his energy surged into his fingertip. Once it was hot enough, he reached over and began to cut the other restraint with a hot laser that sprang from his finger tip.

In just a moment he'd be free again. And Raven and her merry crew of marauders would pay dearly for their crimes. He'd make sure of it.

20

Blue fingers clasped the sheets and Danica let out a lust drenched moan. Zallek thrust his hips harder and faster, as their bodies rocked with the throes of passion. "Don't ever stop fucking me," Danica cried.

Zallek reached down and ran his blue thumb across her lips. She opened wide and wrapped her lips around his pointer finger, performing a mock fellatio on it and enticing him to play longer.

"I knew you'd come around," Zallek said, smiling down at Danica with a superior grin.

Danica forced a smile. She'd rather not be fucking some guy she hardly even knew, but she desperately needed another hit of Nividium. And after the scare she'd had three days ago with the explosion and all, she felt that she could get two birds with one stone. Relieve some tension while securing some more Nividium.

It was a win-win for them both, she told herself. She got what she wanted and he got what he wanted. The sex was just that…a means to an end.

At least, that's what she convinced herself. Because that was better than the alternative of admitting that she was now officially a bleedin' drug addict—a scag.

Zallek finished, pulled out, and then walked over to the standing bar and poured himself a drink.

Danica lay on the bed, starring up at the ceiling, and trying not to think about anything but her next dose of Nividium. "Do you have it?" she asked. She rose up on one elbow and Zallek turned, sipping his tonic, and smiled.

Reaching over to a drawer on the counter, he opened it and pulled out a cartridge and tossed it to her. She scrambled to catch it, but missed. It fell to the bed with a soft touch and she hastily scooped it up. Scrambling over to the bedside table, she fetched her e-stick and slapped the cartridge in.

Although this new stuff worked phenomenally, the high lasted twice at long, which meant whenever she doubled the amount she could keep feeling it for whole swaths of time rather than a handful of minutes. Danica put the electronic stick to her lips and inhaled. The dose of Nividium filled her lungs and the drug began to work almost instantly.

She fell back onto the bed again, her eyes glossing over as the effects of the drug took her away. She barely noticed Zallek climb back on top of her. He raised his fingers to his lips to hush her, and then she felt him enter her.

Under normal circumstances, she would have said "no thanks" to a second round. But she was feeling too good to care. He could have his way with her as long as he left a few cartridges by her bed.

Five hours later, Danica shot awake. She rolled over and found three Nividium cartridges sitting on her bedside table. Letting out a sigh of relief, she rolled over again and stared at the ceiling. As doubt started to creep in as to what she was doing, she shook her head and tried to cleanse her mind of the thoughts.

"No," she said to herself. *This is necessary.*

Danica climbed out of bed and got dressed. Although the guards wouldn't let her leave the loft, she could do anything else she pleased. And in-between her sessions of Nividium, she liked to paint. She'd never been much of an artist, but while she was being held captive, she thought she'd try her hand at it.

If splattering paint on a canvas could be considered art, she thought, what the hell. The truth was, however, that it was far harder than it looked. Every piece she'd attempted had been lopsided, or the colors didn't mesh, or the paint bled and mixed into muddy lines that looked like a hooker's mascara-stained face after finding out she had an incurable STD. Basically, her art sucked.

With a fresh pallet, a new canvas, and a brush in her hands, Danica stared down the canvas. She had a feeling today was the day she'd finally get it right. After a week of trying—it was finally time to prove to herself she had a spark of talent or else give up in shame.

"Pssst!"

Danica looked over her shoulder to see Raphine slinking across the balcony.

Excited to see Raphine, she put down her things and rushed over to her. They hugged in the doorway and laughed.

"What are you doing here?" Raphine asked.

"Teaching myself to paint," Danica said, thumbing over her shoulder at the myriad of canvases propped up against the walls of the apartment.

"I can see that. But it's been three days since we last saw you. And you never even checked in. Jegra is losing her mind and I've been scouring the streets day and night looking for traces of you."

"I'm sorry, but I decided that going deep undercover was the best way to infiltrate Zallek's drug ring."

Raphine looked over at the ruffled-up bed spread and the phrase "deep undercover" gained a whole new meaning. But she kept her mouth shut. "Still, you should have at least shared your plans with Jegra first."

"Well, now you can tell her I'm fine. No harm, no foul." Danica turned and went back to the center of the room and picked her paints back up. Balancing her pallet on her forearm she eyeballed the canvas.

"So, what is your plan, exactly?" Raphine asked, slinking into the room.

"Finish this painting for starters," joked Danica. "And then I was thinking of offering up a scapegoat to prove my loyalty. Maybe gain greater access to Zallek's operation."

"A scapegoat?" Raphine echoed. "Where are you going to find…" Her voice trailed off as she realized Danica meant her. "You're kidding me, right?"

Danica turned back to Raphine. "I need to do something. Zallek won't let me out of this room. Not until I give him what he wants."

Raphine looked back at the bed. "And what would that be, exactly?"

"He wants to know what Jegra is planning. But until I give him some concrete reason to trust me, I'm a prisoner here."

"So, your big plan is to turn me over to a known drug dealer and killer?"

"Actually, he doesn't like to kill," Danica informed her friend, "but that's neither here nor there." She shook her head as if she were shaking out the irrelevant thought. "Anyway, if I hand you over, he'll trust me."

"And what happens to me?"

"You become his prisoner, like I am, I suppose." Danica shrugged. She actually didn't know how Zallek would respond, but she didn't think he'd hurt the girl. She was only eighteen years old, after all.

"Fine," Raphine finally agreed. "But I don't like keeping Jegra in the dark."

"When you go missing, she'll comb every inch of this city looking for us. It will only be a matter of time."

Danica put her things down again and began hopping up and down.

"What are you doing?" Raphine asked.

"I need you to hit me."

"What?"

"You know, rough me up. Make it look like I tried to defend myself before wimping out and calling for help."

"Gladly," Raphine said, and she sucker punched Danica right in the gut and dropped her to her hands and knees.

Coughing up a spatter of saliva, Danica grumbled, "No, not my stomach. My face."

"I know," Raphine said with a mischievous grin. "That one was for you using me. And this one is for cheating on Jegra."

Confused, Danica looked up just in time to see Raphine's fist. She felt the strike across her cheek and fell to the ground. Pushing herself up, she laughed. "Good."

Before she could continue on, Raphine struck her again, breaking her skin just above her left eyebrow.

Danica touched her brow and examined the dappling of blood on her fingertips. "I think that's good enough."

"On my world," Raphine said, "when you are engaged to someone, you postpone your other sexual liaisons until after the wedding."

"I beg your pardon?" Danica looked up, a mystified look on her face. Jegra must have told Raphine the news about their engagement. Either that or she'd severely underestimated the girl and Raphine was a better spy than she had initially estimated.

Another strike of Raphine's fist knocked her back down. Raphine reached down and hoisted Danica up by her arms.

"Seriously, what are you doing?" Danica asked.

"Making it look good," Raphine replied.

Raphine tugged on Dani's arms and thrust a knee into her gut.

Danica nearly barfed on the floor and coughing and hacking, she reared back. Once she caught her breath, she cried out for help. "Guards!"

Raphine smiled and dashed forward. As the door opened and the guards rushed in, Raphine tackled Danica. Scrambling for the top position, she began wailing on Danica relentlessly. That is, until the shock of a stun-rod immobilized her.

"Thanks," Danica said, wiping a bloody lip. "I'm pretty sure she's crazy."

"Do you know this woman?" the guard asked.

"It's one of the Empress Jegra Alakandra's spies. She's trained well, so be extra careful with her." She got up and stood over the green-skin lying on the floor. Danica looked down at Raphine with an emotionless gaze. "And tell your boss that I have a present for him."

As the guards hoisted Raphine to her feet and dragged her out of the room, Danica turned toward the mess they'd made when they'd toppled over the paints and canvas. The mess had left a nice splatter effect and a body imprint of her female form that was both fetching and colorful.

Not bad, she thought. *It's one way to do it.*

Exhausted from the day she'd had, Danica had barely finished cleaning up the mess from her tussle with Raphine when the door opened. She turned to find Zallek standing in the frame, his dark shades fixed on her.

There was a long, uncomfortable silence when, finally, he cleared his throat and said, "Get your things and come with me."

"I should change first." Danica gesture at her paint stained clothes. He nodded but didn't remove himself from the doorway.

She felt nervous as he watched her undress. It was the first time she didn't truly know what he was thinking. She found a nice, white, one-piece strapless dress and slipped it on.

The super soft stretchy fabric hugged her body so tight that you could even see the folds in her skin. Although she was in shape, she wasn't as thin or taught as she once was. But Zallek seemed to appreciate her womanly curves, and for whatever reason, having a man's approval of her body felt nice. It wasn't necessary, but she enjoyed the fact that he couldn't take his eyes off of her.

She slowly pulled the dress up her bod, wiggling into it, then reached into the deep V-neck and adjusted her breasts. When she turned around to grab her vape stick and additional cartridges, she let him gaze at the low backline which added to the elegance, and shot him a sly glance from over her shoulder.

She tucked the vape stick and the additional cartridge into her cleavage and walked over to him. As she cut across the room, a seductive sashay in her step, she said, "You wouldn't believe the day I've been having."

He reached out and accepted her slim waist with his hand. She leaned in and kissed his cheek, trying to be as affectionate as possible. After all, as long as he believed he had her in his little pocket, she'd be free of his suspicions.

"Come, my dear," he said. "We have important matters to discuss."

They climbed into the elevator lift at the end of the corridor and he hit the button for the basement. Instead of moving down, however, the small enclosure filled with two radiant beams of golden light. A couple of teleport beams.

Danica turned to ask where they were going but the teleportation process had already begun dismantling their organic forms and carrying their genetic information away on light packets. A few moments later, the light packets reassembled their bodies in a secret, underground, facility.

Danica blinked a few times as her eyes adjusted to the low level of lighting. She stepped off the teleportation pad and looked through the glass doors that, in turn, looked out onto an entire manufacturing plant.

"Welcome to my empire," he said, motioning for her to accompany him out the doors and into the facility. "One in which borders don't exist and everyone, every species, is united by one thing and one thing only."

"Nividium," Danica said, sidling up to the balcony railing. They looked down at workers in white lab coats and white medical masks, checking samples of Nividium which slid down a chute and onto a conveyor belt where more inspectors checked the product, separating the faulty batches form the good batches.

"The Lord Emperor wastes too much time and energy trying to break cultures. People resist him because he represents everything they despise. Power run amuck. Cruelty. Corruption. But I offer them unity. I offer them bliss. I offer them my hand, and they shall take it willingly as they kiss the brass ring of the hand that feeds them."

"You want to use Nividium to create unity through dependence."

"Some will call it dependence, I prefer to call it loyalty. And as long as I'm the only one in the galaxy offering them Nividium, I will grow greater and more powerful than the Lord Emperor could have ever hoped to be. I will be heralded as the person who unified the races and set Dagon on a new path of peace and prosperity."

"By making it impure," Danica said.

Zallek turned to her, a shocked look on his face. He pulled off his sunglasses and tucked them back into his inside jacket pocket. "I thought you, of all people, would understand. You, Danica Valencia, are a mod. You, yourself, are impure. Besides," he continued, turning back to the railing and resting his palms on it, "getting dirty can be such good fun."

Without looking to gauge her response, Zallek reached into his jacket pocket and pulled out a pristine cartridge.

"What's that?" Danica asked.

"I call it Nividium 3. It's three times more powerful, three times more pleasurable, and three times more expensive than normal Nividium. When people get a taste of this, regular old Nividium will taste like swill. Care to try it?"

Danica didn't even hesitate. Her hands snatched the cartridge out of Zallek's and she fished for her vape stick. Slapping the cartridge in, she put the device to her lips and inhaled.

"Holy fuck," she said, her legs buckling. She leaned on the railing and let wave after wave of euphoria wash over her.

"How do you feel?" Zallek asked, smiling at her.

"I think I'm having an orgasm. No, multiple orgasms all at once," she said.

Suddenly, Danica broke out in a sweat. Her whole body dripped with perspiration and her pupils dilated. Slowly, she sank down onto the grated plating of the balcony and lay down. Her white dress, growing damp with perspiration, became see-through.

Her limbs twitched and her back arched, as if she were having the best orgasm of all time. "I want you," Danica said, reaching up and tugging at Zallek's sleeve. "I want you right here and now."

"I know you do," he said, unfastening his neck tie.

Even as a fleet of factory workers toiled away at their various jobs, Zallek and Danica made love for all to see.

The drug did, in fact, replicate the sensation of pure euphoria. As a consequence, it triggered a body-wide orgasm that lasted for minutes. In fact, several of the lab mice had died of heart attacks because of how excited it made them. But the ones that survived were addicted for life.

And now Zallek had Danica Valencia, the empress's right-hand woman and girlfriend, right where he wanted her. Dependent on him and his product. Now, all he had to do was begin phase two of his master-plan and release her back into the empress's hands.

Once she was in, she'd act as a mole for him, feeding him vital intel which he could use to his benefit. If she didn't comply with his wishes, he'd simply stop the flow of Nividium 3. For good.

Of course, there was one more thing that Zallek kept to himself: the more problematic side effect of this new strain of Nividium. As it so happened, all those who remain addicted to Nividium 3 for an extended period of time eventually lost their minds. *And not in a good kind of way*, he often thought. No, this was more the "reality is shattering like a fractured mirror" kind of way where one is trapped inside their own nightmares.

Until then, however, he had a double agent working for him. And that's what mattered. And if she resisted his offer, he'd merely threaten to kill the green-skin. Either way, she'd signed her soul over the moment she had stolen from him.

The only way out now was to do precisely as he wanted.

21

JEGRA strapped on the breastplate to her mechanized battle-suit. She was going in to find Danica and Raphine and get them back. She snapped the chest plate into the socket; it a made a satisfying click as it locked into place. It was a snug fit, given the fact that her chest filled it completely, but it wasn't uncomfortable. The power-suit was a necessary persuasion as she suspected she might have to go up against Centurion war machines and didn't want to waste time waltzing around with them. She wanted to come down hard, like her battle-axe, and crush them in one fell blow.

After the explosion downtown, Jegra and Raphine had helped the first responders and volunteers clear the rubble left in the wake of the Harbingers of Truth's terrorist attack.

The terrorists had chosen the cultural center as their target since, in their twisted minds, allowing multiple cultures to thrive somehow meant diminishing Dagon's greatness. She didn't understand the logic, though. Even back on Earth, such racism never made sense to her. How could one person's rise to prominence make another prominent and proud culture less important? Less relevant? Less meaningful. It couldn't. Which is why such an attack reeked of small-minded cowardice.

The hardest part of the clean-up, however, had been digging up the dead bodies. There was a total of sixteen casualties. Three of them children. Something she could never forgive the Harbingers of Truth for. Their "truth" meant nothing to her, because it was as corrupt as their entire ideology. Their truth was simply a lie they chose to believe because they were too scared to look beyond the lies, perchance the real truth threaten to destroy their worldview and strip them of the power they'd gained through heinous and vile acts of violence.

If Demeris Ferrison thought he could intimidate her by killing innocent lives—many of them his own people, he had another think coming. She'd hunt him down and drag him to the arena where she'd beat him to a pulp and make a public mockery of him. She'd be the non-Dagon "hairless ape" who beat him. Of course, she'd spare his life. After all, she didn't want to make a martyr of him. But she certainly wanted to force him to live with the shame and humiliation of a public defeat.

Jegra locked her boot down and the suit came alive with an automated hum. Blue LEDs lit up in various places all along the pale gray armor. Blue lines and utility markings added a little style to the otherwise drab suit.

"Are we ready?" she asked, walking over to the hull of the drop ship and taking down her trusty battle-axe.

Meleh'Kendar's voice shouted from the front cockpit over the blare of the reverse thrusters. "I'm bringing you down right on top of Raphine's last known coordinates."

Jegra slapped the button next to the bulkhead that let down the loading ramp. They were flying above a fancy apartment building. Up the street was ground zero of yesterday's attack. That's when she realized that this was the same building she and Raphine had been planning to investigate before the bombing incident.

"Dammit. We were so close."

"What was that, ma'am?" Meleh'Kendar asked, not making out what Jegra had said. "Nothing. Bring me over the balcony."

The drop ship lowered itself down into the street, barely fitting between the rows of buildings. Jegra leaped off the loading ramp and dropped twenty feet onto the balcony with a resounding *thud*.

She turned and waved at Meleh'Kendar, letting him know he was good to go. She watched briefly as the drop ship rose back up and Meleh'Kendar bugged out.

"Hey, you! This is private property!"

Jegra turned to see two guards rush into the room armed with fully automatic disruptor guns.

"Do you know who I am?"

"Y-you're the empress," one of the guards answered. He seemed shocked to find it was the empress herself coming to see them.

"My friends. Two women. A blue and a green. They were here. I want them back."

"I'm afraid they're with the boss, Your Majesty."

"Boss?"

"Zallek—ow…hey!"

The other guard hit his friend in the arm. "Shut up! She don't need to know any of this."

"Oh, but I'm afraid I do," Jegra said, tightening her grip on her battle-axe and taking a confident step forward.

Zallek's more loyal henchman raised his blaster. "I'm afraid we have our orders—so, don't come any closer or I'll be forced to shoot."

"You're not actually gonna shoot the empress, are you?" the first guard asked.

"I'm just doing my job."

"Maybe we should notify the boss first."

"Notify the boss?" The man shot a sharp look at his friend. "Our orders were to shoot any trespassers on sight. That includes her." He nodded his head at the empress and then turned to find her standing directly in front of him. She'd moved so swiftly and quietly he hadn't even heard her. Even her battle-axe was stowed on the magnetic clasp fitted on her back.

Jegra snatched his weapon out from his hands and snapped it in two as though it were a twig. She tossed the pieces aside and then glared at him. His Adam's apple bobbed as he gulped down the nervous lump in his throat.

Thwack! Jegra's headbutt was so fast that the first guard had to blink twice before he realized his partner had dropped out of view. He looked back at Jegra, dropped his own weapon to the ground, and raised two trembling hands. "Look, I'm loyal to you, Your Majesty. I don't want no trouble."

"You're fine," Jegra said. She winked at him then brushed past as she made her way into the hallway. "Which way?" she asked, glancing back over her shoulder. He motioned toward the elevator. She nodded at him in a gesture of gratitude.

It felt weird standing in front of an elevator, all geared up. She tapped her metal boot impatiently and waited for the elevator doors to spread apart.

Once on the lift she looked over at the control panel and found the basement button. She suspected that Zallek must be keeping Danica and Raphine there, seeing as scans of the building didn't reveal anything out of the ordinary. But the basement was shielded, leading her to believe that his base of operations was below ground.

She mashed the button three times, impatiently, and waited some more as the doors slid shut and the elevator music played a song that was eerily similar to *The Girl From Ipanema.*

After about another minute and a half, the elevator doors parted again and she was not disappointed. Standing in the middle of a long corridor was a class three Centurion war machine. The scorpion kind–impossibly hard to kill.

Jegra stepped out of the elevator and into the hallway and unslung her battle-axe. The droid reared up to meet her and locked its blasters on her. Instead of bull-rushing it, however, she slipped out an EMP grenade from the various ammunition around her waist and lobbed it down the hall.

The grenade skidded along the floor until it came to a halt directly beneath the war machine. Its little red-light incrementally pulsed faster and faster as the device powered up. Once fully charged, a massive electrical shock bubble, like a plasma lamp, erupted all around the device. Blue and purple tendrils of electricity crawled along the floor and up the walls. More tendrils latched onto the Centurion and pulled it down. Its menacing, red, insect-like eyes flickering as it fought to stay alive. Then everything went dark and the machine slumped down, its servos whining against the dead weight of its bulky, armored body.

Jegra gripped her battle axe with both hands and rushed forward. With a single swipe she cut off the beast's head. But that wasn't enough to take down a Centurion, so she took another swing, her axe embedding itself into the machine's torso. Sparks shot out like a fountain as she ruptured its power core. Tearing her axe back out, she shoved the machine aside and it toppled to the ground. Dead.

At the end of the hallway was a junction. Jegra poked her head out and checked to see if the coast was clear. It was. Stepping into the junction triggered three panels to open and three automated gun turrets lowered from the ceiling on all sides. Jegra grabbed another grenade-like device and stuck it to the wall. A forcefield lit up around her just as the automated laser cannons began firing on her position.

Her suit's built-in shield generator read seventy percent and she then tapped the little ball-like shell on the wall. Legs abruptly sprouted from the device and it scuttled off like a crab, its pointed claws clacking along the metal surface as it went.

Once it passed through her shields, the device split into three separate entities, and each new section sprouted even more legs. The little robots made their way to the turrets and attached themselves. A nanosecond later, three explosions rendered the laser turrets a smoking pile of scrap metal.

"Smoke on that," Jegra said out loud. She glanced down both corridors and decided to go left.

Several meters down the hall she came to a fortified door. It seemed to have a heavy-duty, vault-style locking system. Nothing was getting through this door short of a tank. Luckily for her, she happened to be wearing one.

Her armor's motors whined as she ran forward and launched a solid kick into the center of the door. The massive door blew off its hinges, folding in half. Hitting the floor, it skidded to a halt several meters into the darkened room.

Cautiously, Jegra held her battle-axe in front of her and eased into what appeared to be a storage room. As her eyes adjusted, she saw the figure of someone tied to a chair, sitting at the far end of the room. She squinted until the person's face came into focus. It was Danica.

Unfortunately, Danica was bound tightly and gagged. She had on dull gray sweatpants and a sweatshirt, but otherwise looked unharmed. When she saw Jegra standing in the entrance, she mumbled something, but the white cloth in her mouth prevented Jegra from figuring out what she was trying to say.

"Hold on," she said moving toward her, "I'll get you out of here in a—"
BOOM!

A massive explosion rocked Jegra and sent her flying into the wall. Danica was knocked over in her chair by the blast as well and grunted as she hit the floor and smacked her head on the metal plating.

Jegra scrambled to her feet but noticed her battle-axe had landed on the far side of the room. From above, a metal pincer swiped at her head and she ducked, only to get rammed into by a Centurion.

She went with the momentum and slid across the floor, clasping the end of her axe just in time to roll onto her back and use the staff to block another snapping pincer.

"Where the hell did you come from?" she asked, shoving the machine off her.

The strength of her power suit surged as it revved up and she caught one of the crab legs of the mechanical beast and swung it around. Smashing into the wall, it collapsed under the weight of some debris.

Rising back up, it turned to lock its micro-missiles onto Jegra, but she did a roundhouse kick and launched it the rest of the way through the wall. It crashed into the hallway, through the next wall, and into a separate room.

Sparks sprang up from the metal floor as Jegra charged forward, dragging her battle-axe behind her. Getting the proper momentum, she leapt into the air and came down onto the machine. With one slash of the axe blade, she severed three of the Centurion's legs and losing its balance, it toppled over onto its side.

Jegra brought her axe down on it, cutting it into two, and then booted the battle robot, sending both pieces spiraling away. One portion of the robot crashed into the far wall while the other scraped to a halt in the middle of the large room.

The fight won, Jegra turned and ran back to Danica and helped her untie the bonds. She unfastened her gag and then cupped her hands around Dani's face and kissed her.

"I was so worried about you," she finally said, taking a pause in between kisses to express her feelings.

"I'm fine. I'm here," Danica said. "I'm here."

They touched foreheads and took in the moment. After a few seconds, Jegra looked around. "Where's Raphine?"

"Zallek has her," Danica informed her.

"God dammit!" Jegra growled, pushing away from Danica and trying to walk off her rage. "Do you know where he took her?"

"There's a production facility. A warehouse where Zallek processes and manufactures the Nividium. If she's anywhere, she'll be there."

"Where is it?"

"I don't actually know. We teleported into it. It seemed to be underground. There were no windows. That's about all I can say. He only took me there just the once, and it wasn't like I got the grand tour."

Jegra paced back and forth for a minute and then settled on the small victory she'd made. She may have lost Raphine, but she got Danica back.

"We'll keep looking. But first, let's get you back to the palace and get you checked out."

"I'm fine," Danica said, placing a hand on Jegra's shoulder.

"I'm sure you are, but I'd certainly feel better if the doc gave you a once over. You know, just to ease my mind."

Danica nodded and then smiled, threw her arms around Jegra's neck and standing on her tippy-toes, kissed her pink lips.

"What was that for?" asked Jegra, smiling coquettishly.

"For being my heroine," Danica replied.

Holding Danica's hand, Jegra turned and headed back out the basement the way she'd come. "Let's get out of the place."

Both women squeezed into the small elevator, or at least it seemed small with Jegra's bulky armor. Danica hit the button and together, they waited for the doors to close.

As they waited for the doors to close, a florescent light in the hall crashed to the ground from the damage Jegra had wrought. It exploded, the metal casing rattling about on the floor agitatedly before, finally, settling down. Jegra looked over at Danica and shrugged and they both grinned at one another as elevator doors slid shut.

22

"GIRL," **Ural Bazhov** said loudly enough to arouse the sleeping young woman, but not loud enough to startle her. The old desert hermit gently shook the girl awake and gazed down at her with slatted goat eyes. "It's time to go," he informed her in a soft voice.

He handed her a type of poncho, for the desert grew cold after dark, and together they made their way out of his small bunker and into the cool night air.

The satyr had on a poncho similar to hers, except it was extra-long and dragged behind him, obscuring his footprints in the sand. At the same time, he carried a gnarly, old walking stick. The staff seemed to be well taken care of; he had given it a nice dark varnish to preserve it. It appeared as though it was fashioned from driftwood, but there were no beaches nearby. At least, none that she was aware of.

They walked for several hours, the stars twinkling overhead in the clear night sky. Neither said a word between them, but it was a comfortable silence. A hermit and a girl without memory alone in the middle of a vast desert landscape...there wasn't much to talk about and besides, they were each the type of person that enjoyed the quietude.

The horizon began to turn a deep shade of cerulean and a few moments later, a sliver of hot pink spread across the landscape, basking the dunes in dawn's early morning light.

"The sun will be up soon," the goat said. "We will rest for now. It's still half a day's hike to Arena City."

"Arena City?" the girl asked, excitedly. "So, you're going to take me to see the empress?"

"I have to do something. It didn't appear to me that those thugs were going to take no for an answer. Besides, I'd rather play it safe than sorry. You're the first guest I've had in nearly seven years. I'd be a terrible host if I let you get killed on my watch. Not on my watch, girly," he said wagging a finger. "Not on my watch."

He drew a cloth-bound food satchel from the inside of his cloak and unwrapped it. Inside was some flat bread and he broke off a piece for her. She graciously accepted and ate it. It was hard and stale like a biscuit, but she didn't complain. After everything Bazhov had done for her it wouldn't be polite to complain about his cooking.

Grateful for his hospitality, she smiled at him and then gulped down the lump of dry bread.

The satyr smiled back at her and then handed her his leather canteen. She took several big gulps of water and then let out a refreshed sigh, wiped her mouth, and placed the cap back on.

"Thanks," she said, handing back the canteen.

"You're most welcome," he said, his smile showing off his yellow teeth again.

She eyed him inquiringly for a moment and then asked, "Why are you being so kind to me?"

"Can't an old man be nice to a beautiful young woman?"

"I have nothing to give you," she pointed out, feeling ashamed that she wouldn't be able to repay his hospitality with anything of value.

"Nonsense!" he bleated, surprising her. "Your pleasant company is reward enough for an old hermit like me. Being a recluse has its benefits, but at the same time it can be a lonely sort of affair. Having you brighten my doorstep, even if just for a couple of days, has been a great pleasure. Don't think otherwise."

"I just wish I could do something for you. For finding me and saving my life. For being so gracious."

He took her hand in his and patted it. Then he chuckled and grabbed his walking stick. "Come. We'd best get going. The sun is rising fast and the day will only grow hotter from now on. And the journey is just getting started."

She nodded and then walked along beside him as they reached the crest of the dune. More dunes, all just as large as the mammoth mound of sand they stood upon, stretched out as far as the eye could see. It was a never-ending desert.

The girl gulped, her throat feeling dry at the mere thought of trying to traverse such a barren and unforgiving landscape. "We're going to cross that?"

"I'm afraid we have no choice my dear."

"Why can't we just head back to your place and wait there for another day?"

"Because," he said drawing out a small, silver device with a red flashing light at its center, "my home has been compromised." It beeped softly, a kind of alarm.

She shot him a perplexed look.

"Those men. The ones who were after you, they have returned, obviously."

"Oh," she said, looking over her shoulder. They'd come a long distance but if those men caught up to them, there was no telling what they'd do.

Bazhov pressed the flashing light on the device and in the far distance a loud explosion went off. The girl startled and she looked in the direction of the satyr's home only to see a large sand plume shooting into the air and mingling with a dark gray smoke.

"That ought to slow them down," he said, giggling at the thought of their surprise as his entire home exploded all around them. Traps were such fun.

"What about your home?" she asked him, upset that he'd given up his home for her.

"Oh, there'll always be another home. Home is where you make it, my dear. That was just a place. A cold, dank, and dusty ole hole in the ground. Right now, my home is right here, with you."

She squinted at him playfully. "You never told me you were such a romantic."

He laughed, his laughter turning into a bleat, and then he shook his head in an amused manner and continued on without saying another word.

The girl looked back one more time, still shocked by the fact that he'd sacrificed his home just to protect her. A stranger that fell from the sky.

After a while, she said, "I'm sorry you lost your hole in the ground."

"I'm sorry you lost your memories." Bazhov glanced over and winked at her. This solicited a smile from her blue lips. "There!" he said, excitedly. "There's the smile I knew you had hidden inside."

She smiled all the more. "If you weren't so charming, I'd half expect you were flirting with me."

"Bah!" he balked, waving his hand and shooing away the very idea of an old goat like him hitting on a beautiful young woman like her. Stopping, he turned to her. "I assure you, my dear, my skirt-chasing days are long behind me. Besides, a nubile young woman such as yourself has better things to concern herself with than an old goat like me."

She smiled at him and leaned forward as though she were going to kiss him on his lips. She paused, letting the tension build, and then kissed him on his cheek instead. "You're only as old as you imagine yourself to be," she said, still smiling fondly at the old satyr.

"I suppose that's true," he chuckled. He took her hand again and patted it. Then they continued along with their journey.

Five hours later, a drop ship buzzed them.

"They've found us!" the girl shouted above the roaring noise of the ship's screaming turbines.

The drop ship swooped low, then arced high, coming back around. As it did, its rotary turbines rotated into landing mode and the rear facing landing ramp opened. Several large figures dropped to the ground ahead of the four-man team waiting for the ship to set them down gently. Bazhov recognized the two imposing figures rising up out of the sand as Bakktu.

"Run, girl! Run! I'll hold these brutes off."

Bazhov threw off his poncho and raised his cane. To her surprise, the gnarled and tangled wood seemed to come alive. It uncoiled, like a snake, and straightened into a fighting staff. The old satyr twirled the staff and widened his stance. He was old, but he obviously had some fight left in him yet.

The girl hesitated. She was scared, but she couldn't just abandon her friend.

The two male Bakktu, geared up in their ritualistic hunting armor, pulled out two large, curving, antler shaped scimitars. The crescent moon-shaped blades twirled about as the hulking Bakktu circled the satyr and his traveling companion.

"I'm warning you, leave the girl alone or there will be hell to pay."

"The only person who will be seeing hell today is you, goat," the large Bakktu said.

"Don't say I didn't warn you," Bazhov replied. With that, he chucked the staff at the Bakktu like a javelin. The Bakktu blocked the staff with his blade, but to his surprise, the staff coiled around the blade then slithered down it to his arm.

"What's this?!" the Bakktu cried, shaking his arm as the serpentine staff slithered up his arm, across his chest, and to his neck. Once it reached his neck, it coiled tightly around his throat and began to constrict.

The Bakktu dropped his blade and fell to his knees, clasping at the metal snake around his throat.

"*Grah!*" the second Bakktu roared as he brought down his blade.

Bazhov merely closed his eyes stood tall and proud, chin up as the blade came slashing down. When the lacerating sting of the blade didn't come, however, he opened his eyes again to see a forcefield erected in front of him.

The girl grunted and he looked over to see her hands raised, fingers spread with tension as she held her energy shield in place.

"I don't know how much longer I can keep it up," she said.

"That girl is wanted alive," the Bakktu said. "But you're just excess baggage, old goat."

"I won't let you harm him!" the girl shouted.

Her shield bubble flared, expanding briefly and throwing the Bakktu to the ground. He landed with a thump and looked over to find the severed head of his partner.

The large beast scrambled to his feet, startled by the snake-like object slithering toward him in the sand. Bringing down his blade, he cut Bazhov's staff in two. The snake sparked and twitched and then, after flopping about aimlessly, came to a standstill.

As the automated cane died, it turned back into the appearance of driftwood.

"That was my favorite walking stick," lamented Bazhov, eyeing his broken staff sadly.

"I'll get you a new one," the girl said.

"I'll hold you to it."

By the time the remaining Bakktu had collected his nerve, his fellow mercenaries had taken up positions all around them and were slowly closing in.

Bazhov raised his hands in surrender and nodded at the girl to do the same. But she shook her head and refused.

"Don't be foolish, girly. Just do as they say and you won't be harmed."

"I'm not worried about me," she said. "I'm worried about you."

"And old goat like me doesn't deserve your kindness, child. But I'd be lying if I said I didn't appreciate it all the same."

"Don't move," one of the masked soldiers ordered.

Bazhov looked over at the girl and smiled. "The past couple of days have been an honor," he said. Then, turning a full circle, he scanned the faces of the mercenaries. "Do you know who I am?" he asked.

"Silence!" the lead merc growled.

"I'm Ural Bazhov. The traitor of Galliforn! And the bounty on my head is far more substantial than this nameless girl."

"I said silence!" the merc cocked his blaster, the gun whining with a menacing high-pitch drone as it charged. He fixed its laser sight on the satyr's chest, the red little dot marking its target.

Bazhov merely brushed the dot on his chest as if he were brushing away a pesky housefly. Of course, it didn't move, but it was the gesture that was important. It was the gesture of a gladiator who brushes away the sign of surrender before he kills his opponent.

The soldiers ignored the gesture and tightened their perimeter. Bazhov looked around once more.

"I don't think you gentlemen understand who you are dealing with. Perhaps a history lesson is in order."

"Quiet, goat. You'll be put out of your misery soon enough."

"The name isn't Goat," growled Bazhov, finally voicing his disdain for their disrespect. As he spoke, his voice lowered to a menacing roar and his body began to grow. And it continued growing until he had doubled and then tripled in size. The girl stepped back, startled by the sudden transformation. "The name is Bazhov the Shunned!"

The satyr grew to twenty feet tall and then brought down his fist on the giant Bakktu, squashing the monster like a bug.

Startled by the Galliforn's sudden transformation into a colossus, the remaining mercs opened fire.

"No!" screamed the girl.

She threw out her hand to plead with one of the mercenaries to spare Bazhov's life, when, out of the blue, a bright laser blast tore from her fingertip and pierced the soldier's helmet right between his eyes. A glowing hole in his head, he dropped to the ground. Shocked by her unexpected release of energy, she looked down at her glowing finger.

Perhaps stranger still, her entire chest pulsed with pink light as the Dygra crystal insider her flared with powerful energy. It was as though it was calling out to her. Trying to tell her who she was—what she was.

Even the look on Bazhov's face seemed to exhibit a profound surprise by the sudden blast of energy. And, in that moment, somehow, she could recall things she didn't remember studying. She recalled how all Dagons had such crystals as part of their anatomy. She recalled that it had something to do with how their heart splits in two when they are still a fetus in their mother's womb, and how one piece grows into the organ, and the other piece solidifies into a powerful crystal.

Somehow, she also knew that only the strongest Dagons could tame and wield the energy. And even then, it took years of training with masters. The fact that she could already control her powers at such a young age suggested she was special somehow. At least, that's the feeling she had.

But what did it all mean? Was this the reason these mercenaries were after her? Was she indeed special?

Bazhov swiped his giant arm and knocked two of the soldiers onto their asses. The third soldier, he snatched up and tore in half. Tossing the severed pieces to the ground, the satyr turned around to see the two remaining mercs stagger to their feet and race back toward the drop ship.

Out of the blue, a red flash of a high-power laser blast streaked past them and blew up the drop ship. The blast sent the mercs flying into the air only to come crashing down again. They landed in the sand with a harsh *thud* and both scrambled to their feet.

Bazhov, weakened by the disruptor blasts, fell to one knee. His breathing was strained and he had a score of burn marks all across his fury body.

The lead merc pulled out a grenade but the girl, aiming a pink finger at him, said, "I wouldn't do that if I were you."

Cautiously, the merc replaced his grenade and lowered his gun. "I don't want any trouble. I'm only here to collect you."

"So, you know who I am?"

"I do. If you come with me, I can tell you. I can tell you everything." He reached out his hand. This made his compatriot uneasy and he looked over at his boss.

"Our orders are to secure the girl at all costs. It says nothing about sitting her down and telling her fairy stories."

"Screw our orders!" the head merc snarled. "Our orders didn't say anything about a twenty-foot tall monster satyr either."

Bazhov's hand came down and squashed the leader. His partner raised his gun and fired a blast straight into the goat's chest, point-blank. Bazhov yelped and toppled onto his side. The entire ground shook as his giant body came crashing down.

The girl turned to the soldier at the same time he trained his gun on her. "Put the hand down, miss. I don't want to hurt you."

"I'm not the one who's going to get hurt. Now, lower your gun before I'm forced to vaporize you."

The soldier raised the rifle, showing her that he was going to surrendering the weapon. At the same time, she caught him subtly reaching behind his back. Almost as soon as he drew out the knife, she let off a power discharge.

The knife flew through the air and sliced her shoulder. Luckily, however, her shot had hit him squarely in his chest. The mercenary dropped to his knees, then tottered briefly before crashing onto his side, a gaping melon-sized hole in his chest.

"Bazhov!" the girl screamed running over to where the satyr lay, curled into a ball.

His body shrank back to normal before her very eyes and as she approached him, his breathing grew erratic. Severe burns covered most of his body and the smell of singed fur filled the air.

She dropped to her knees and reached out to touch him but stopped her hands short, not wanting to add to his pain.

Bazhov coughed. "Did we win?"

"Yes. We did. You were magnificent," she said, her voice cracking as tears filled her eyes.

"Head west," he said, another violent cough erupting from his blood-stained lips. "That is where you'll find her."

"Find who?" the girl asked.

"Your mother."

"Mother?" she echoed. "What are you saying? Do you know who I am? Who's my mother?"

But her questions were in vain, because the noble Bazhov was already dead. His slatted eyes stared out at the carnage they'd wreaked.

The girl fell across Bazhov's torso and began sobbing. He was the only friend she had. The only person that had ever been kind to her and wasn't trying to kill or capture her.

"I'll never forget you, my friend," she said, pressing her cheek against his chest and sobbing gently. After she calmed down, she sniffled, wiped her eyes and then collected the canteen of water and stood. She raised her palm to the sky, blocked the radiant yellow sun, and checked the shadows on the ground to determine which way the sun was setting. That would be west.

23

Brobdingnagian and deformed asteroids hung in a massive cluster arching from one end of the sector to the other. The Cove was in the middle of the Viridian asteroid belt, a large sprawling series of asteroids stretching between the gas giant Gamidon and the planet Arkadia, home to the Bre'lal.

The asteroid belt was treacherous to navigate, which is why most ships opted to chart courses around. Because of the natural divide the Viridian asteroid belt provided, however, Nyctan had remained the most secluded planet in the system.

Because of their seclusion, their empire had grown strong independently of the Dagon empire and the Seyfferian Republic, which consisted of the planets Correll, Galliforn, Qu'Mar, and the dwarf planet Veridion—the only dwarf planet in the sector with a stable atmosphere. Even so, Vice Admiral Callestra Van Morgan was concerned with one and only one thing—using the asteroid belt to her benefit.

She stood on the observation deck of her ship, the *Verlag*, as was her habit, and stared out at the string of rocks cutting across a vast red and green mixed nebula.

Soon enough, several flashes appeared outside her window as other ships of the Dagon fleet began entering the sector. She, of course, had arrived two hours prior to calling the fleet to her position. She wanted the military presence to be known and to give the space pirates and galactic traders time to get out of her way.

Her beef wasn't with the illegal activity in this sector. It was with the fact that the Nephilim forces had been hiding behind the asteroid belt while they continued to send in scouts to gather intel on the Dagon side of space. These illegal infractions could no longer be tolerated and she was here to make a statement.

Callestra knew that if she brought the entire enemy fleet to the Viridian asteroid belt, the Nephilim would send out their patrols to investigate. Now, it was just a waiting game.

Out of the view portal, three more flashes occurred as the Dagon armada convened at the specified coordinates.

"Vice Admiral," Sub Commander Orsek Van Tavaris, her first in command, called out to her from behind.

She admired Tavaris for his always cool and collected demeanor. Even under the most stressful circumstances, he stayed composed. He was the perfect counter balance to her more volatile nature. And though she was cold and cunning, she did have a temper; something that had always been a somewhat embarrassing feature of hers.

Most Dagons preferred to be catty about their displays of anger, often making snide comments or exchanging mean-spirited remarks in what amounted to condescending speech and offensive belittling. But she often raged. Not a total loss of control, because she always pulled back, but just enough to remain unpredictable. Dangerous.

"What is it?" Callestra asked without looking back.

"The remaining ships have arrived and the commanders are awaiting your order to begin sending down landing teams."

"Good," Callestra said, her eyes fixed on the wash of colors that made up the nebula outside her window. "Start sending teams immediately. I want three hundred installations up by tomorrow."

"Ma'am?" Tavaris asked, making sure that number was correct. "Three hundred?"

"Is there a problem?" Callestra asked, craning her neck and glancing over her shoulder at him with an icy gaze.

"No problem, ma'am. We'll get it done."

Tavaris saluted, gave a dutiful nod, and then took his leave.

Callestra returned to her meditation. She knew that it would take nearly three thousand officers working twelve-hour rotations to get it done. But for her plan to succeed, they needed to work fast. The Nephilim would be sending scout ships any day.

It was likely they'd pick them up on long range scans, then wait ten hours to see if more ships joined the barricade. They'd probably send the first scout ships after twenty hours. They'd be here in twenty-four.

After several minutes, the doors to the observation deck opened and Tavaris returned. A startled look on his face—it was as if he'd seen a ghost.

Callestra raised an eyebrow out of curiosity.

"Ma'am, a long-range transmission is coming from Cordova."

"And?" she asked, anxiously tapping her foot.

"It's…it's the Lord Emperor ma'am. He wants to talk to you personally."

"Dakroth?" she gasped.

"Yes, ma'am." Sub Commander Tavaris saluted again and held it until she returned the gesture.

"Put the holovid call through here," she said. "Oh, and you're dismissed." He bowed again, tapped the holovid projector on the way out, and disappeared from the room.

A flickering image of Emperor Dakroth appeared before her and she knelt on one knee and bowed her head reverently. "My lord."

"No need for formalities, Vice Admiral Van Morgan."

"Yes, my lord," she replied. Callestra rose back up and met his gaze. Not knowing what to do with herself, she felt her chest tighten and her breathing grew laborious as she found herself both flustered and simultaneously thrilled to be recognized by the Lord Emperor.

"I see your father has been busy in my absence. Congratulations on your promotion. I know you will serve me well." Dakroth stressed the *me* part, seeing as he had not personally recommended Callestra for the position of Vice Admiral of the fleet and wanted to remind her where her loyalties lay.

He suspected this bit of nepotism on her father's part was some sort of long game power grab. After all, the senator liked to play things close to his chest. Better to stack the deck in one's favor than risk everyone turning on you at the eleventh hour. Whatever Targon's plans were, though, Dakroth had bigger fish to fry at the moment. He rubbed his wrists again, massaging away the soreness left by weeks of being shackled to a dental chair.

"Thank you, my lord. I will not disappoint you." She watched him; he kept rubbing his wrists. Also, she couldn't help but notice that his appearance seemed rather unkempt, as though he'd slept in his clothes and was, for whatever reason, rudely awakened. He also sported a 4 AM shadow of silver on his face. She was extremely curious as to what all this was about, but didn't dare question the emperor.

"I have some business to finish up here on Kelipsis before I join you. After that, I look forward to your debriefing."

"You'll be joining us, then?" Callestra asked. Although she wasn't opposed to the emperor's arrival, the announcement of his visit did catch her by surprise.

"Yes," he laughed in an amused fashion. "Imagine my surprise when the station's long-range sensors picked up the entire Dagon fleet gathered at the other end of the system."

She looked up at him as he studied her face for any clues as to what she was up to. But she knew that he knew that whatever it was, they couldn't talk about it over an unencrypted holovid call. It was too risky.

Dakroth raised his fist to his mouth and cleared his throat. "I'll look forward to you filling me in when I arrive. Oh, and be a dear and send a shuttle to fetch me. The ship I arrived on won't be of much use to me when I'm through here."

"Yes, of course, my lord. As you wish."

Dakroth gave her a long, unsettling look, as though he was still uncertain about her and then broke into a wide, pearly grin. She felt a sudden wave of relief come over her and she gave the Dagon salute. He nodded and then the holovid cut out.

Callestra shook her hands and used the air to dry her palms. The entire time she'd been talking to the Lord Emperor her anxiety had been compounding. At first, she thought it was just the nerves of the mission. Then she thought maybe it was because of how hard she'd been pushing herself. But by the end of the call, when he'd hung up and the connection between them was severed, the flood of relief was instantaneous. That's how she knew he'd been using his psychic powers on her.

But she didn't feel he was targeting her specifically. It seemed like whatever he was embroiled in at Kelipsis, he had his telepathic fear-projection dialed up to full. As a friend and an ally, it seeped into her as a form of deeply rooted anxiety. The thing she feared the most: not performing at her utmost—of being a failure.

She shook off the lingering feeling of anxiety and then turned her attention back to the starscape and the reds and greens of the nebula that hung before her like an oil painting from the Dagon Renaissance.

Two bright flashes of light caught Callestra's attention and a couple of enemy craft appeared just off the bow of her ship. The code red alarm echoed up and down the corridors.

<<Enemy vessels detected,>> the prosodic voice of the computer said over the blare of the alarm.

The lights of the entire vessel had dimmed and the red alert lights flashed, bathing everything in a wash of crimson.

"Actual, this is Vice Admiral Callestra Van Morgan…jam those ship's sensors and intercept them before they jump out of the system and warn their friends."

The *Verlag's* bulkheads groaned as the massive engine roared to life. The behemoth ship's thrusters ignited to full, shooting out blue-tipped arcs the size of the tallest mountains on Dagon Prime. The ship slowly rose up above the asteroid belt and quickly approached the glowing crustacean-like scout ships. The two fighters turned tail sharply and began making their way toward the asteroid belt, hoping to lose the giant ship in the dense outcrop of rocky asteroids.

Callestra broke into a run and burst onto the command deck. Skidding to a stop, she turned toward the viewscreen and examined the various real-time displays, studying the events as they unfolded. "Do we have any installations set up?"

"Not yet," Tavaris informed her. "They got the drop on us. They must have already been in the system."

If that were the case, she thought, *then these were probably the same fighters that Novac Tamoran had encountered.* Which meant they were running patrols throughout the whole system. Monitoring the border. But for what? What were they looking for? Were they waiting for her to show her hand, or was it something else?

"I want those ships shot down before they enter the asteroid belt. We can't afford to lose them in there. Do I make myself understood?"

"Fire disruptor canons," Tavaris ordered. "Full volley."

"Sir," an officer said, shooting a nervous glance back at the Sub Commander, "if we fire a full volley, we may risk harming our own men working on the surface of those asteroids.

"I know the risks, Lieutenant. Just follow the orders."

"Yes, sir," the officer replied.

A volley of green plasma blasts lit up the black of outer space and painted it in green hues. Many asteroids began breaking up in a series of fiery explosions. The internal gases of each rock were released and burned up as hot plasma drilled into them.

The enemy scout ships swooped down, dodged, and did tailspins to avoid the blasts. They were fast. Agile.

"What's the matter?" Tavaris snapped, upset that all they were hitting were random space rocks. "Why aren't we hitting them?"

"Automated targeting systems are being jammed. We're having a hard time locking onto the enemy vessels, sir."

"Try manual targeting," Tavaris ordered.

Numerous officers reached over and took ahold of some joystick controls and began manning the gun turrets manually.

"The scopes are reading them, but there seems to be some kind of interference. A strange kind of residual echo. They're somehow ghosting our targeting systems and evading our canons."

"Arm Python missiles," Callestra said. "All tubes."

"Missiles armed," the lieutenant replied. This time he didn't hesitate, knowing that if he questioned his superior's orders again, he'd be lashed for insubordination.

Sixty-eight missiles chased after the enemy fighters. In a matter of seconds, massive explosions erupted all around. After the last of the missiles had detonated, a large cavity, the size of a small planet, was all that was left in the massive asteroid field.

"Two confirmed kills," the lieutenant said victoriously.

A round of cheers erupted on the bridge and Callestra shot everyone a cold look. This shut them up tighter than a giant Kree'alekkian sea clam.

"How many of our landing missions got caught in the crossfire?" she asked.

Sub Commander Tavaris leaned over and peeked around the shoulder of the lieutenant, checking his console, and then turned to the vice admiral. A grim looking settling over his face, he answered, "Three teams were killed in the fire exchange, ma'am."

"Thirty Dagon souls," she said, her voice growing quiet. They had died on her orders. And although she was furious at herself for putting her own people into harm's way in the first place, she was more furious at these invaders who had no place coming across her borders and entering her people's territory.

She managed to hold back her temper though and put on her "admiral's face." Locking her arms behind her back, she took a step forward, cleared her throat, and scanned the faces of her crew.

"Listen up and listen good. The enemy will send more ships, looking for the ones they lost. We'll deal with them too. But don't think it will be an easy victory. More will come. They won't quit coming until we are conquered or until we destroy them all. Let us not forget the brave souls who died today because an enemy force with sights on sacking our great empire illegally crossed our borders and forced our hand. Do not let your brothers' and sisters' deaths be in vain. I promise you, we'll secure this border even if it means killing every last one of these mother-fucking invaders."

More cheers erupted and Callestra felt justified in taking the actions she had. Even so, the war was just beginning. The enemy was already on their front doorstep and she had made the first move. Now the invaders would make theirs.

24

Raven and Gyllek turned to greet Kregor and Angellyk when they arrived at the command center. They all exchanged hugs and gave each other the same look; they were all thankful to still be alive.

That's when the comm came online and a familiar, yet terrifying voice came across the speaker system.

"My dear Raven Nightguard. It seems you've become a greater thorn in my side than I had initially anticipated. Don't worry, my luv, tis' but a minor inconvenience. And one I shall remedy shortly."

"Dakroth?" Angellyk asked, sounding surprised. "What's he doing here?"

"It's a long story," Raven said.

"Care to enlighten us?" Kregor asked, folding his arms and giving the captain a stern look.

"Later. Right now, he's coming for us and I doubt he's in a forgiving mood. We need to be ready for him when he gets here. This isn't some Centurion war machine or a complex computer algorithm we're going up against here, people. This is an unstoppable force. A man who has, quite literally, won entire wars singlehandedly."

"So, what do you suggest?" Gyllek asked, supporting the captain's decision.

"He's going to play with your minds. He's going to make you see your worst nightmares. But you have to be strong. You have to overcome them. Because if you don't, you're as good as dead."

"How does Jegra put up with him?" asked Angellyk.

"Jegra is immune to his mind control. Something about her superior genetic makeup. It's one of the reasons Dakroth is so obsessed with her. She's basically the counterweight to his evil. She represents goodness that he cannot corrupt. Justice he cannot escape. And she has a strength that rivals his own."

"A match made in heaven," Gyllek added sarcastically.

"What about you?" Angellyk said, addressing Raven.

"I'm going to confront him, and buy you guys time to hide."

"Are you sure that's a good idea?" Kregor asked, growing fidgety and looking over his shoulder at the entrance of the command center.

"I've modded myself so his thought projections won't affect me. Believe me, after encountering it even just once, you don't ever want to experience it again."

"I take it this isn't your first run in with the emperor." Angellyk placed her hands on her hips and gave Raven a prodding look.

"Let's just say when my parents defected to the Seyfferian Republic, the emperor didn't take things lightly and sent his son, the young Rhadamanthus, after us."

"That's when he destroyed your ship."

"Yes," Raven said in a sad voice. "He boarded our vessel and shot my mother and executed my dad. He then sensed me cowering under the console and looked inside my mind. Whatever he did gave me nightmares. Nightmares I had for years. That's why I modded myself in the first place. To lessen the damage he'd caused when tinkering inside my head."

"I'm sorry," Angellyk said, reaching out and gently taking Raven's hand. "You never told me any of this."

"It's not a memory I like to relive. I only share it now because I want you to understand what it is you're going up again. If he wouldn't hesitate to kill a child's parents in cold blood right in front of her and then turn on the child and mess with her mind so that she spends half her life believing she has a mental illness. Imagine what he'll do to you. Don't be fooled, you're not dealing with a man. You're dealing with a monster."

The Lord Emperor sauntered down the retractable docking passage and up the platform that led into the confines of the station. The station was built in tiers right into the inner rockface of the asteroid. At least fourteen levels, each platform having numerous docking ports for ships, both finished and unfinished.

"It seems you found my little secret," Dakroth said, rubbing his hand along the railing as he looked out at the rows of unfinished ships. "To bad none of you will live to tell anyone about it."

He smiled and turned to the heavy, sliding doors that led into the main facility. When he approached, the doors bleated at him defiantly and the light above the entrance flashed read.

<<Unknown contaminant detected,>> the computer's voice said in her stereotypical transatlantic accent.

"Smart," he said to himself. "You issued a quarantine protocol to trick-out the computer and keep me locked out. Oh, and don't think for a moment that the joke is lost on me. I'm a dangerous contaminant. All very amusing." His words dripped with sarcasm, but that was to be expected. He didn't like being toyed with, and he was at his wit's end.

"Glad you like a woman with a sense of humor," Raven's voice came back across the comm.

"I do. I do," he replied in a jovial fashion.

"Then, you're going to love this. You beloved empress is the one who ordered me to take you out of commission. In fact, it was her idea and hers alone. But, if you're going to be angry with anyone, it should be me. Do you know why?"

"Why?"

"Because I'm the one who convinced her to marry your sorry ass. On the way to Cordova, Jegra was having doubts. She wanted to back out. But then where would we be? She'd be a retired gladiator. You'd still be gallivanting about the galaxy, sticking your dick in anything with a pulse. And I'd be back at it, arresting low level bonds. Instead, here we all are—making sure justice prevails and your tyranny ends. Not with some epic grandstanding, but with a whimper, as you slowly fade into obscurity and your wife—the amazing Jegra Alakandra—reigns supreme."

There was a long silence before Dakroth responded and Raven could practically picture the steam coming out of his ears.

"Yes. I suspected Jegra was behind it, all things considered. And you'll have to forgive me for not being more gracious for your divulging that tidbit to me. But, you see, I've had a rather rough few weeks. Be that as it may, if it's any consolation, just know that I still miss the taste of your lips, my dear Raven," he said in a cynical tone.

"Please, don't remind me."

"I've never felt such passion come from such a deep and repressed place before. It was enthralling, to say the least."

"Honestly, I can't believe I ever let you lay your hands on me. It makes me sick to my stomach just thinking about it."

"All just part of the job…" he quipped, grinning at her slyly. "You, the noble peacekeeper. The woman who'd do anything to see me usurped and stripped of all my power. But, my dear Raven, can't you see? We are the same!"

Raven balked at the notion. Dakroth ignored her little interruption and continued on with his self-aggrandizing speech.

"The galaxy *needs* me. Without me it would devolve into chaos and bloodshed. Piracy would run rampant. Entire worlds would be ransacked and burned for their resources while other worlds starved because they lack the skills and technology that could save them. And the suffering would compound until, up from the ashes, rose an even crueler and fiercer dictator than I. My dear Raven, search your feelings and ask yourself, is that really what you want?"

"Don't," she said with a scowl. "This isn't about me or what I want. It's about you. It's about you losing to Jegra. It's about you losing to Jegra everything single time you go up against her. It's about her becoming the ruler you could never be. And so far, she's proving herself more than suited to the job."

"Perhaps," he said in a disinterested tone. Growing bored of their idle chit-chat, he raised his right arm and pointed a glowing finger at the large doors keeping him out of the main station. "Then again, perhaps all this is just a distraction."

Drawing energy from the Dygra crystal inside his chest, he let it charge for an extra few moments and then let the energy beam rip. In a matter of seconds, it melted a man-sized hole in the door. "Come what may, one thing is certain," he said, ducking under the glowing hot edges of the doorway he'd just carved out.

"And what would that be?" asked Raven.

"By the end of this day, your friends will lie dead at your feet, and you will kneel before me, take my hand, and kiss the royal ring. Should you refuse to surrender yourself to me fully, I will rip out your traitorous heart and bathe myself in your blood."

"In your dreams, Dakroth." Raven took a deep breath then asked, "Do you want to know the difference between us?"

"Not especially, but I have a feeling you're going to tell me anyway."

"I do what I must to see justice served. You do what you must to see that *you* are served. But never forget, Dakroth, at the end of the day, you're just a man. Eventually, your reign of terror will come to an end. And all that will be left then, is to serve justice."

Pleasantly amused, Dakroth raised an eyebrow. "Spoken like a true fanatic."

"Is it so wrong to put one's faith in loftier principles?" she asked.

"Perhaps that's the other difference, between us, my luv. You're a dreamer. And I'm but a humble pragmatist. But don't kid yourself about my intentions. I fully intend to track you down, force you to your knees, and make you beg for your life."

Several meters up the corridor, Raven stepped into view, appearing before his very eyes. "Let's not and say we did," she said in her forthright, matter-of-fact tone.

Clasped in her arms was a hefty, plasma-bolt crossbow. Although slow and notoriously difficult to load, they were extremely powerful. One bolt had enough destructive power to topple a small building or take down a shuttle craft.

Rebel insurgents were known to take down fighters with thunderbolt crossbows not so different from the one Raven held. It was not a weapon to be trifled with, that was for certain.

"Shit," Dakroth grumbled as he watched Raven squeeze down on the trigger. The sly grin forming on her face annoyed him to no end. He knew precisely what she was thinking. She was thinking that she was better, smarter, and more cunning than he.

Then again, he mused, *it really wouldn't be a victory worth talking about if it wasn't also a worthy challenge.* And Raven was as worthy an opponent as they came. A true warrior. And that brought a smile to his face, subdued though it may be. More of a smirk, really.

A quick glance around showed that he was stuck between a rock and a hard place. There was no time to turn and run, nowhere to duck out of the way, no way out from the length of the long corridor that separated him from Raven, and their ultimate fate.

Before he could think on it any further, a hot fiery bolt of tungsten, equipped with explosive tip, flew toward him at a furious rate.

Though barely able to get a blast off with his energy shot, the bolt exploded in the middle of the corridor. The concussive blast sent Dakroth flying back out of the hole he'd made and he smashed into the railing of the external platform.

The railing buckled under his weight as the nuts and bolts tore away from their anchors, leaving bare steel divots in their wake. Flying over the ledge, Dakroth reached up and clasped the falling section of railing.

Lucky for him, it caught on the next section, which held long enough for him to get a firm hold. Then, suddenly, that section gave way as more bolts snapped. Obviously, the heat of the blast, coupled with his weight, made the entire thing unstable, but as he dangled over the edge, he felt glad to be alive and not some scorch mark left on the side of the wall.

The more railing that tore off, the more it began to resemble a rope ladder. Finally, after another section broke free, the entire section of railing caught. This time it held firm. Dakroth slammed into the wall and grunted, his ribs taking the brunt of the impact.

His heart racing, he looked down to see a vast cavern open up beneath him. It was like looking into the mouth of a giant beast opening up to swallow him whole.

Below him there were a series of crosswalks and docking arms that held unfinished battle ships in place. The drop was a perilous one and would either suck him back into the jagged rock wall of the cavern or, if he got caught in the zero-gravity pocket, would pull him farther out into the center of the large cavity with no way to make it back to the station. Basically, he'd float out there until somebody rescued him. But nobody was coming for him. That much he was certain.

Slowly, Dakroth began to climb up the newly formed rungs of the railing. Once he reached the top, he pulled himself over the ledge and rolled onto his back, panting heavily, as he tried to catch his breath.

"My dear Raven," he said, still fighting to catch his breath, "when I find you…and I will find you…I'm going to have a bit of fun with you first. After all, you've had your fun. Now it's my turn."

Dakroth rolled over and pushed himself up to his feet. Looking down the corridor, all he saw where scorched walls and some sparking cables where some of the ceiling paneling had come down and was now bleeding red and blue wires.

He stepped up to the hole in the doors and the doors cracked open. They ground apart, the molten edges splitting as the powerful motor pulled the heavy doors back. Halfway open, however, the motor burned out, grinding to a halt, leaving only a waft of gray smoke that seeped out from the inside wall.

Dakroth paused, waiting for the doors to finally settle down, and then passed through the entrance. Resuming his hunt, he called out, "Come out, come out, wherever you are. I want to play." His voice dripped with menace as he strolled up the long passageway.

It would only be a matter of time before he found them. And one-by-one he'd do to them what he did to Raven's parents.

Of course, he toyed with the idea of keeping her alive. Allowing her to suffer the nightmare all over again. Then again, he also wanted to ravish her and punish her for her misdeeds. Then, as he clutched her throat, he'd end her at the same point he climaxed. But either way, he'd have his fun.

Dakroth turned a corner to see a glowing light at the end. Creeping up to the area where the light was coming from, he spotted a small access panel that had been opened. He peered inside to see the petite, frail, cat-girl.

A vicious smile curled onto his lips and Dakroth reached into the access area and said, "Peekaboo, I see you!"

He let off a blast; it passed right through the girl and scorched the wall opposite her.

"*Shhh*," she said, hushing the emperor without looking back. "I'm busy."

Irritated by the little ruse, he fired off another blast, causing the hologram to flicker. It snapped back into form and the girl turned and raised a finger to hush him.

"Ah, yes. Very clever," he said. Turning back into the main room, he lost his cool and roared out with rage. "*Ahrg!*" he shouted, kicking the wall.

They weren't going to make it easy on him. He realized that now. And instead of continuing on with his little tantrum, he took a deep breath and calmed himself.

"The fun is only just beginning," he murmured to himself, a malicious smile curling onto the edges of his mouth.

25

The white walls of the Arena Palace, as Jegra had so aptly named it, loomed in the distance. Meleh'Kendar brought the drop ship over the walls and landed it on the meticulously kept palace lawn at the back end of a grand terrace with a hundred-meter-long rectangular pool. The thrusters jostled the plants and flowers in the garden and sent ripples across the surface of the crystal blue water of the pool.

The cargo ramp at the back of the ship immediately lowered and Danica clambered down and stepped onto the virescent lawn. Jegra, pausing in the open mouth of the exit, looked back over her shoulder and shot Meleh'Kendar a nod of gratitude for getting them back safely.

He nodded in return and then watched her follow Danica out of the ship.

With her feet firmly back on familiar ground, Danica stretched her arms over her head and took in a deep breath of fresh air. The vegetation in the palace garden gave off a cool, leafy scent with just a lightest touch of sweet fragrance from a variety of blooming flowers and trees. "I can't wait to take a long hot bath and just sleep for the rest of the week."

Jegra chortled lightly as she stopped beside Danica. "Don't sleep too much. We need your expertise in the War Room."

"Ah, yes, almost forgot about that."

"Forgot that we were at war?" Jegra laughed.

"It all seems like a distant dream," replied Danica.

"Understandable," said Jegra, walking alongside Dani as they made their way along the length of the pond back toward the palace's rear entrance. "These past couple of weeks have been an utter whirlwind."

When they arrived at the back patio, Jegra slapped a button on her armor and the mechanized body suit opened up. She was wearing only a skin-tight, semi-translucent, smart suit. If it weren't for the seams of the suit, she would almost appear to be nude.

Jegra climbed out, leaving the suit parked on the patio, and then accompanied Danica inside.

"I know you've been through a lot in the past few days, but after your bath, I need to debrief you on everything you know about Zallek and his operation and how we might go about getting Raphine back."

Danica nodded and placed her hand on Jegra's arm. "I swear to you. If he harms even a single hair on her head, I'll…"

"I know," Jegra said, placing a hand on Danica's shoulder. "I feel the exact same way. She's like our little sister."

Danica squeezed Jegra's hand and gave her a peck on the cheek. Then she turned and headed for their shared bedroom. The bath there was the most luxurious in the whole palace. And she couldn't wait to soak her aching limbs and neck in a hot, scented bubble bath and just lie back with a bottle of her favorite champagne, letting her troubles melt away.

A few minutes later, Jegra stepped into the War Room to the bustle and noise of everyone diligently working on multiple problems all at once. Upon realizing the empress was watching over them, the whole room simmered down. "Your Grace," Lianica said at last. "You're back."

Jegra nodded. "Don't stop what you're doing on account of me," she said, gesturing with a wave of her hand for everybody to return to as they were before she'd interrupted them.

The noise and the chatter started back up again and Jegra headed over to where Lianica and Grendok sat examining a wide, flat screen monitor. The monitor contained a series of blue-colored dots showing the Dagon fleet position. Gold dots represented the Nephilim and Nyctan fleet. And the dots moved around in real time as they relayed the exact position over every ship down to the nanometer.

"I've moved several satellites into range and am monitoring fleet activities live," Grendok informed her. "There is a thirteen-minute lag, however, due to the immense distance."

"And what about our contact down on Dagon Prime?" She turned to Lianica for the answer. Lianica raised her hand and waved Brei'Alas over to them.

"Nice to see you again, Lieutenant," Jegra said, smiling at the awkward young woman.

"I saw you naked," Brei'Alas blurted. Lianica shot her a stern look but she didn't seem to notice. "I just wanted to get that off my chest." She sighed out of relief and then looked at all the stunned faces. "What?" she asked. "And I did."

"It's quite all right," Jegra said placing an arm on the girl's shoulder, drawing her attention back to more pressing concerns. "What about my contact? Any word?"

"The senate has convened as scheduled. Senator Targon is prepped to give a televid speech later today regarding the disappearance of the emperor. There's no word on Demeris Ferrison or the Harbingers of Truth. After your little confrontation in Arena City, they've been laying low."

"Good work, Brei'Alas," Jegra said. She then turned and walked over to the broad, standing windows and peered out at the garden. Meleh'Kendar and a team of gear-heads were working on the drop ship, getting it ready again in case they needed it.

"There is one more thing, ma'am," Brei'Alas said, speaking up slightly so that Jegra would hear her from where she was standing.

Jegra turned her head slightly and acknowledged her.

"A rather large explosion went off outside of Mardok. Although, there's been no word about who or what caused it."

"I see. Thanks. And keep me posted on anything you might learn." The empress, still peering out the window, clasped her hands behind her back and lost herself to her thoughts.

"Good work," Lianica said to Brei.

"Thank you, Captain," Brei replied. She then hurried back to her post to resume her regular duties.

Lianica noticed a distant look on Grendok's face and leaned over the desk and whispered to him. "Is everything all right, Admiral?"

"Wha…what? Oh, yes, yes. I was just thinking about something," he replied. More specifically, he was thinking about some*one*. But she was busy running his ship in his absence.

Another several minutes rolled by when all of a sudden, the entire palace shook with the violence of a level six temblor.

"That was no quake," Grendok said, rising out of his chair. He shot a look at Lianica.

"It was a missile blast," she said.

Jegra didn't move from the window but stared out at the blue hexagonal shielding that lit up all around the palace, protecting it like the dome of a snow globe.

Fiery plumes ignited on the surface of the shielding as more missiles hit the palace's defense barrier.

Meleh'Kendar's voice came over the comm. "Your Majesty, we're under attack."

"It's a diversion," Jegra said.

"A diversion for what?" Brei'Alas asked, looking up from her station.

"I don't know," Jegra said, turning back to the group. "But a direct assault on the palace as retaliation for what occurred in the city isn't Demeris Ferrison's style. He's not the revenge type. Everything he does carries a political agenda. We just have to figure out what that agenda entails."

"Another call is incoming, Your Grace," Brei'Alas informed everyone. "It's Senator Targon."

"Put him on the holovid," Jegra said, turning to the round table at the center of the room. Soon enough, Targon's overly concerned face appeared as a hologram.

"Is everything all right, Your Majesty? We've detected a missile attack on the palace."

"I appreciate your concern, senator. But we have everything under control here. Thank you."

Targon nodded stoically. "If there's anything you need, don't hesitate to call on the help of the Senate."

She bowed slightly and then waved her hand for Brei to cut the feed.

Once the holovid call cut out, Jegra turned to Brei'Alas. "Replay that message. And enhance the reflection in the glass of the book cabinet behind the senator."

"What is it?" Lianica asked, shooting Jegra a puzzled look.

"I thought I saw something. Or more likely…someone in the background."

Brei nodded and did as asked. The holo-image of the call replayed in high speed and she paused it on the cabinet behind Senator Targon. In the unenhanced image, there was a dark figure standing off to the side.

"Who's that?" asked Grendok.

"Enhancing now,"

The pixilated hologram looked like an old video game graphic before the jagged edges tightened into a smoother, more focused image. The shadow solidified into a person. And the person had a face.

"No way," Brei'Alas said, completely taken aback by what she saw.

"It's as I thought," Jegra said.

"That's Demeris Ferrison, in the flesh," Brei'Alas observed, still in shock.

"You were right," Lianica said. "This attack is a diversion."

"But why would the senator be in league with a known terrorist?"

"Because," Jegra said, smiling, "they both have a common enemy."

Brei looked around at the others but wasn't quite sure if she understood.

"Me," Jegra informed the girl. "Targon Van Morgan would love nothing more than to see me out of power. Demeris Ferrison would like nothing more than to see me dead. If they've formed a temporary alliance, then that means they have a plan to remove me from power."

"So, what do you propose we do?" asked Grendok.

"Right now, I want you to order your ship to drop a tungsten rod on those missile batteries. Then, we wait and see what their next move is and try to figure out a pattern to the madness, so to speak."

Grendok nodded and then turned and put on an ear piece. "This is Admiral Grendok to the *Chiron*. Sub Commander Almathea, there's something I need you to do."

A couple of minutes later, a massive explosion went off in the distance and a one-kilometer geyser of sand shot into the air.

Grendok turned around with a smile on his face. "Targets obliterated."

"Yes!" Brei'Alas said, doing a subtle fist-pump in celebration of the victory.

"Don't celebrate just yet," Lianica warned. "Things are bound to get worse before they get better."

Brei gulped down the nervous lump that formed in the back of her throat. "Get worse?"

"I'm afraid so," Lianica answered.

Jegra cleared her throat and addressed her senior staff. "Until then, we need to be ready for whatever they throw at us. Grendok, you know Thessalonica probably better than anybody through your intelligence agents. I'm going to make you head of land operations for now. Lianica, you continue to monitor the fleet and keep me apprised as to what Callestra is doing. Brei'Alas, I now have a feeling that whatever that unknown explosion was at Mardok might have something to do with all this. I want you to delve into that and get me any information you can find."

"Yes, ma'am," they all simultaneously replied. They saluted and held their salute until the empress left the room.

Sometimes the best thing she could do to clear her own head was roam the halls of the palace. It helped her to think. Before long, Jegra found herself back in the library, the same place she had made love to Danica and proposed just days earlier. It seemed like an eternity ago.

And speaking of Danica, she was starting to become worried about her. It had already been an hour since they'd arrived back at the palace, and she hadn't heard a peep out of her. Deciding to check on her friend, she returned to their bedroom.

"Dani?" Jegra said, entering the room. She reached behind her back and tried to get the zipper for the smart-suit, but it was too high up for her to reach and she gave up.

When there was no reply, Jegra called out again, "Dani? You here?" Her feet squished into the carpet, and she looked down. The entire floor was sopping wet. "What in the world?" She looked over at the bathroom and saw water streaming out from underneath the door.

That's when it dawned on her something was terribly wrong.

She hurried over and threw open the bathroom doors where, to her dismay, she found Danica's unconscious body lying on the floor beside and overflowing tub. A stream of sickly yellow foam dribbled out of her mouth. In her open palm was a Nividium inhaler.

Flashbacks of Abethca lying dead next to the tub in her chamber beneath the arena came back to her. The horror she felt then, the rage of being powerless to save her, and the deep remorse she'd felt ever since was all just as painfully raw as it had been back then. And, to make matters worse, it seemed it was happening all over again.

"No, no, no," Jegra said dropping to her knees and scooping Danica up into her arms. She checked for her pulse and then let out a relieved sigh when Danica's weak heartbeat came through.

Jegra cradled Danica in her arms and sobbed. "Why, baby, why? I knew you were dosing, but I didn't know it had gotten this bad."

She wiped a sniffle away with the back of her hand and then tapped the wristband on her smart suit and called for the medic. "Jegra to Doctor Amora Van Gogh, I have an emergency."

"This is Amora," the calm, professional voice came back. "What seems to be the problem."

"Dani's overdosed on Nividium. I need an emergency teleport straight to the med-lab, ASAP."

Still clutching Dani close to her chest, two beams of yellow light whisked them away to the sick bay. In shock, she watched as a team of nurses took Danica out of her arms and rushed her over to a med table. Everything seemed to move in slow motion as she watched them administer first aid. A warm hand on her shoulder brought her back to the present and she looked over to see Amora standing next to her.

"It will be okay," Amora assured her. "Nividium can be lethal, but if you catch an overdose early enough, recovery is just about guaranteed."

Numb from the shock of Danica's overdose, all Jegra could do was nod. At the same time, she watched the medics do everything in their power to resuscitate her fiancé.

26

"**Get the fuck** off of me!" the girl screamed as she pried the mouth of the sandworm from her leg. It had attached itself to the calf of her right leg and was viciously clamped on. Not only did it smell like rotten slop, the thing was hideous looking too. It was the size of a household cat, had several rows of lacerated teeth, and a bloated, fleshy body that looked like the wrinkled and shriveled-up skin of a flaccid penis.

She finally managed to pry the worm off her leg and then tossed it as far away as she could. It squirmed about for a bit and then burrowed back into the soft sand and disappeared from sight. Although the pest wasn't poisonous, the sandworms could pose a serious risk to desert travelers. If you were caught in the desert dehydrated and happened to fall unconscious, a swarm of them could devour your body in a matter of minutes.

Luckily, she still had plenty of water and enough fight in her to kick any one of these sandworm's overgrown asses. But the bite wound on her leg needed to be cleaned and bandaged lest she risk infection. Using a small amount of water from her canteen, which she poured onto a cloth, she dabbed away the muddy colored blood around the wound, revealing a circular pattern of perforated bite marks circling the muscle of her dark blue calf.

The only cloth long enough to use as a wrap was her *shemagh*. Quickly, she unwrapped the head scarf, tore off a segment, and then tied it around her injured leg, making sure it was extra tight.

Once she had finished bandaging her wound, she took a gulp of cool water and then put the cap back onto the canteen. With a grunt, the girl rose up onto her feet, being extra cautious to put just the right amount of pressure onto her hurt leg. It was painful, but it wasn't so bad that it would prevent her from making the long trek. It would, however, make it a quite miserable journey.

Another worm slithered nearby, barely cresting above the sand, and she kicked at it. "Get out of here you *va'pa'mashtaq*!"

She didn't know if it was a different worm or the same one, but regardless, yelling at it and using the vulgar slang for *cocksucker* in Dagoni seemed to help ease her pain.

The girl followed the windswept crest of the dunes, always heading west, as instructed. She had traveled non-stop for seven and a half hours and was beginning to feel like the desert would never end. It just kept going on and on and on. Needless to say, it made her a little disoriented and slightly anxious.

A few kilometers after the worm attack, however, she heard a loud series of explosions going off in the distance. Excited that there was something going on beyond the dunes, she scrambled up to the top of the highest one, reached around her back, and fetched the military issue binoculars she'd taken off one of the dead soldiers. Placing the binocs to her eyes, she panned across the desert landscape in the direction of the thunderous explosions.

She almost missed it at first, as it was so far away, but zooming up by forty-five percent revealed a giant palace that sat on the outmost territory of a vast oasis.

The oasis had a large lake at the center and three rivers that supplied water to every section of a sprawling city. At the center of the city was a massive gladiatorial arena; that's when she knew precisely where she was.

"Arena City," she said in a soft voice.

It wasn't far. The binoculars read thirty-two kilometers. She could make that in a few hours.

The girl sighed out in relief. The finish line was in sight and all she needed to do was get to that palace. There, she'd be sure to find the empress. And, with any luck, the empress would help her locate Emperor Dakroth.

The only thing that troubled her, however, was Bazhov's final words to her. "Find your mother," she whispered, recalling the bombshell revelation that he'd dropped on her.

Mother? Did she have a mother? Was she on Thessalonica, in Arena City? She didn't remember having a mother. In fact, she didn't remember anything about her life prior to finding herself on this sandblasted moon.

But, Bazhov knew something she didn't. And, the noble satyr had died to help her get this far. Why would he lie about her having a mother? Or, for that matter, her mother being here, on Thessalonica?

The girl wrapped her *shemagh* back up and covered her face. Determined to make it to the palace, and with a newfound urgency, she limped toward Arena City.

Before she could get even twenty meters down the back of the sand dune, however, a low-flying ship buzzed her. It shot over the dune and kicked up a whirl of sand, forcing her to shield her eyes. It was another military drop ship and it landed no more than fifteen meters in front of her and deliberately blocked her path.

"I'm not in the mood," she said, raising a pink, glowing finger.

The ramp to the rear of the drop ship came down and a bronzed skin woman in a tight-fitting metal bikini emerged. She tossed her long brown hair and looked out across the wind-swept sand at the girl. "Quickly, now," she said in an urgent tone, "get onboard."

"Who are you?" asked the girl, lowering her glowing finger and letting it cool. She pulled her *shemagh* down around her neck, revealing her young, curious eyes, and cocked her head to the side as she adjudicated whether this strangely dressed woman was a threat or not.

"I'm the empress, Jegra Alakandra. You'll be safe with me. But we must go, now. It's not safe here."

The girl squinted at the woman, thinking it might be a trap. "The empress?" She was having a hard time believing it. What kind of royalty would parade around all day in a metal bikini? It was ridiculous.

"Listen, believe me or not, but our long-range scanners have picked up several enemy drop ships heading our way. It's not safe here and we need to evacuate this area, right now."

The girl shrugged and began to make her way to the ship. As she headed up the ramp, she paused next to the empress. "Why are you wearing that?" the girl asked, pointing at the bikini.

"It's comfortable," Jegra replied, ushering her into the cargo bay.

"You look like a prostitute," said the girl, not waiting for Jegra to respond to her critical remarks. She went over to the bench style seats that ran along the wall and sat down. Kicking her head back, she closed her eyes and let the cool droplets of sweat run down her face.

Jegra rolled her eyes. "Nice to meet you too."

"Ma'am, I hate to cut the introductions short, but they're approaching fast."

"All right. Get us the hell out of here," she said to Meleh'Kendar, who was piloting the ship.

"Yes, ma'am."

The drop ship rapidly rose into the sky and raced back toward the palace. Almost as soon as it had left, five additional drop ships—all of them painted black with white skulls and crossbones on the sides–came roaring over the sand dunes.

"Strap in," Jegra said to the girl, pointing at the bench seat harness. She continued up to the cockpit. Leaning over Meleh'Kendar's shoulder so she could get a better view out the cockpit window, she asked, "What's the news on our friends back there?"

"Not good, ma'am," Meleh'Kendar replied. "Those ships are equipped with Python missiles. The palace, as you well know, uses an electrical generator to power the shields, not a fusion reactor like a starship. They could easily knock the shields out with one shot. Destroy the palace with another."

"What are our options?"

"I recommend you contact the *Shard* and deploy the fighters."

Jegra reached over Meleh'Kendar's shoulder and flipped the communications switch on the dash. The comm crackled and Jegra leaned forward and spoke. "Captain Blackstar, I need you to make a call to the *Shard* and scramble the fighters. We have some bad company out here, and these black wasp ships look extra mean."

"Will do, Your Majesty," Lianica replied over the radio. With that, the comm cut out.

Before anything could be done, however, several bright green plasma blasts streaked past the nose of Jegra's drop ship.

"Hang on to your hats," Meleh'Kendar said. He pulled back on the joystick and the ship entered into a steep climb.

Jegra held onto the back of his chair and braced herself when she heard the girl scream out. She looked down to see the young woman sliding down toward the open hatch.

Meleh'Kendar leveled out the craft just before the girl toppled out of the back of the ship. Rising to her feet, she dusted herself off and then laughed. That was a close one.

Before she had time to get back to her seat, however, a disruptor blast struck the hull of the ship, jolting everyone inside. The girl lost her footing and screamed as she tumbled out the back. Jegra yelled out for her to hang on and raced to the back of the open ramp where she found the girl hanging onto the edge for dear life.

"A little help would be appreciated," the girl said in a snootier tone than Jegra was accustomed to.

What it is with teenagers? Jegra reached down and hoisted the girl back up into the ship and set her back down squarely on both feet. "This time…" she chastised.

"Strap in. I know, I know." The girl sat down and buckled herself in. She shot Jegra a sharp look as if to say, *"See, I did it. Happy now?"*

Whoever this girl was, she was full of herself, that much was sure. Jegra just ignored the conceited look and headed up to the cockpit of the ship.

"Do you find there's something familiar about her?" she asked her chief of security.

Meleh'Kendar looked up into the rearview mirror at the girl and studied her features for a moment. When the girl caught him staring at her, he looked away.

"With all due respect, ma'am, she looks a little bit like you. If you don't mind me saying so."

"It's quite all right," Jegra said, glancing back at the girl. "But I can assure you, she's nothing like I was at that age."

"What?" the girl snapped, annoyed by their whispering and gawking. "Take a holoscan if you want. It will last longer."

"Are you always this much of a pain in the ass?" Jegra asked.

"Only to uncouth strangers who keep staring at me for no fucking reason," the girl fired back.

"We're just talking about how beautiful you are," Jegra said, trying to assuage the girl's ego and maybe soften her brusqueness. She made an effort to smile past her irritation with the girl, hoping a friendly face might help. The girl didn't seem to be impressed.

Even though she was headstrong and a total pain, she also happened to be quite stunning for a Dagon. At the same time, thought, she didn't look *fully* Dagon. There was something exotic about her. Something different.

"Do you make it a habit to pick up young girls wearing that hooker outfit?" the girl replied, a snide grin forming on her lips.

Jegra looked down at her metal bikini. "It's a part of me. A part of my history. A part of my identity, I guess I just haven't felt the need to toss it out yet."

The girl shrugged. "Suit yourself, Your Highness."

"Actually, it's *Your Majesty*. But I don't really care for formal titles. Just call me Jegra."

"Jegra," she said, raising her eyebrows. "Sounds like a hooker's name."

"Right," Jegra said, trying to laugh off the girl's constant digs. "Speaking of names," Jegra said, placing a hand on her hip as she stood in the entrance to the cockpit. "What's yours?"

The girl looked down, as if she were ashamed. "I don't know. I mean…I'm sure I have one. I just…you know…can't remember."

"You can't remember?"

"Look, I don't know. I woke up in an escape pod that had crashed on this butthole of a moon. I don't know what ship I came from or why it was evacuated. All I know is, something deep inside of me is telling me I'm supposed to find you."

"Find me?" Jegra asked, surprised by this sudden revelation.

"Well, not *you*, specifically. I need to find Emperor Dakroth."

"The emperor? What do you need him for?"

"I think it's part of my mission or something. But I don't…"

"Remember," Jegra said, finishing the girl's sentence for her.

She nodded.

"Well, let's get you back to the palace and cleaned up and fed for now. Then we'll talk about this mission of yours."

"Really?" the girl asked excitedly. "You mean it?"

"My word is my bond," Jegra answered.

"Thank you!" she said, happy to finally be getting somewhere. "I'll be the perfect guest. I won't even make a…"

The girl's eyes rolled back in her sockets and her head jerked back violently. All of a sudden, she began convulsing in her seat.

"Shit!" Jegra shouted, rushing to the girl's side. Steadying her head so she wouldn't bang it on a bulkhead, she shouted up to Meleh'Kendar. "She's having a seizure."

"It's probably the dehydration," Meleh'Kendar said. "She's been rationing too little water for too long. We need to get her on a saline drip and rehydrated as soon as possible."

"Then what are you waiting for, Chief? Get us back home," Jegra said, her voice growing firm.

"Yes, ma'am." Meleh'Kendar jammed the throttle to full and tore away from the ships chasing them. Sure, he'd burn the engines out again, but such was a day in the life in the service of the empress. Never a dull moment.

The craft tore across the stretch of sand that led up to the palace walls. A three-foot-high Kelvin wake of sand rippled behind them as the heat of the thrusters stirred the dunes into a swirling frenzy.

Almost home free, Jegra unhitched the girl and scooped her up into her arms. "I've got you," she said. The girl had stopped seizing but remained unresponsive.

The blue forcefield dissolved as they came over the palace walls and set down on the palace lawn. A team of medics were already waiting for them when they arrived. Jegra hurried out of the back, leaping to the ground, and handed the girl off to two medics who placed her on a hover-gurney and whisked her away.

Jegra turned toward the enemy ships that were in hot pursuit. They were almost to the barrier when two of the ships began firing their disruptor canons before the palace shields could be fully raised. Several shots tore through the palace walls. A few more shots missed their mark but left burn marks on her lawn.

As the blue hexagons lit up, each energy segment linking together, the blue dome of the shields fit back into a protective field.

With the shields back up, the enemy drop ships pulled away just in time, avoiding a near collision. Circling around, they started their approach for another pass. An alarm back in her own drop ship started ringing and Meleh'Kendar's voice shouted out, "They have a missile lock."

Horror filled the pit of her stomach as Jegra watched a lone Python missile wind its way through the air and explode against the shields.

The boom was deafening and the whole of the palace grounds shook.

Luckily, the medics had gotten the girl inside to safety before the blast, but they wouldn't be safe for long if those shields went down. Turning back to the point of attack, Jegra watched as the thing she dreaded occurred. The blue dome of the palace shields flickered and then faltered.

Gradually, each hexagonal segment shorted and turned off. One by one, the shields dissolved until there was nothing left standing between them and the five enemy ships.

With the shields down, the drop ships circled back around and came in for another attack. They'd be here in less than a minute.

Jegra tightened her fists, preparing herself for the worst, when, out of the blue, six forked-wing fighters swooped down from the sky and began blasting the hell out of the black drop ships.

One of the black ship's turbines blew out and the ship spiraled downward wildly, like a drill bit that had come off its mount. It crashed into the side of a dune and exploded. A fire ball rose up into the air followed by a trail of black smoke. The other ships broke away, tucked tail and ran.

"It seems the cavalry has arrived," Meleh'Kendar said, sidling up next to the empress, his blaster drawn.

"That it does," Jegra said with a smile. With the threat diverted, she took a deep breath and let her shoulders relax. The tension melted away and she turned to the chief and smiled. "Now, let's see about getting those shield generators back online."

"Yes, ma'am," he said, following after her as she raced to the palace's power station, which sat just beyond the garden shed.

With any luck, they'd only need to flip the breakers. If the damage overloaded and blew the generators out completely, it might take a couple hours before they got them fixed and up and running again. But the chief's engineering crews were more than capable of repairing the generators. That wasn't what she was worried about.

What she was worried about was the mysterious girl they'd picked up. Jegra made a mental note to check on her first thing after they got the palace secured.

In the meantime, they'd remain on high alert. After all, there's no telling when those black ships would be back.

27

Radiant golden ships made of light-infused armor dropped out of hyperspace. The Nephilim fleet consisted of ten large battlecruisers and a throng of roughly two hundred fighters. A formidable force, to be sure.

Almost as soon as they'd appeared, the fighters swarmed the Dagon cruisers and a fire exchange broke out. *It was inevitable*, thought Callestra as she stood on the bridge watching the green and red disruptor fire crisscross between the massive ships. War always was.

The Dagon flagship, *Verlag,* held back as the remaining twelve Dagon battlecruisers engaged the enemy ships. The main fleet needed to hold the line for as long as possible in order for her plan to succeed. Callestra also held back on deploying the Dagon Ravenclaw fighters, too. Instead, she relied on the disruptor cannons to try and take down as many enemy fighters as possible.

Sure, they'd take a beating. And their ships would come out burnt and ugly. But that was a small sacrifice to pay for a much bigger reward. *Patience*, she told herself. *You must exercise patience.*

Her military training had taught her that the catalyst of most wars boiled down to one of three things. Land, natural resources, or lust for power. Religious wars fit somewhere on the spectrum too, but she suspected that it was much more primal than that, even.

Every species in the galaxy had to start from single-cell organisms and then evolve against all odds—always facing a hopelessly daunting, uphill battle—always having to engage in the cruel game of survival of the fittest. This desire for fighting, even when it didn't make a lick of sense, was, she felt, programmed into nearly every living thing. The moment they crawled out of the primordial muck they began fighting for scraps of dry land.

The irony of it was that so many advanced species should throw away millions of years of progress by seeking to send themselves and others back to oblivion over things as trivial as territory or whether or not you believed in the right set of superstitions. Entire races and civilizations came to the brink of extinction because they'd rather kill each other off and pronounce themselves King of the Hill than learn to solve problems together. It was disgraceful.

"We need to draw those Nephilim destroyers in closer," she said, speaking out loud to herself. She slouched back in her chair, which sat at the center of command actual, and crossed a long, elegant leg over her knee. Bridge officers manned their stations all around her as the firefight raged on outside the main view portal.

She knew that if she pulled back, they'd just form a perimeter and send more fighters. If she closed in, their destroyers would open fire and, if worse came to worse, they'd call upon the squids to take down as many heavy cruisers as possible. Right now, however, they merely kept their distance.

Enemy fighters burst all around the massive Dagon ships. They exploded with such frequency it looked like corn popping all around. Each fiery plume bubbled out then disappeared again as the flames consumed the gases and then went dark.

It is a little bit surprising that their ships don't have escape pods, Callestra thought. The pilots either succeeded or went down with their fighters. Even so, they had more than enough to defeat her armada twice over, which is why brute strength wasn't going to win this battle. She needed to rely on her cunning and good strategy.

After several minutes of letting things play out, Callestra raised a hand and all eyes turned to her. "Signal the asteroid crews to bring all heavy disruptor batteries online, now."

"Disruptor canons online, ma'am," tactical replied.

"Fire!" she said, clinching her fist.

Three hundred disruptor batteries stationed on the surface of the asteroids opened fire on the enemy fleet all at once. Red plasma bolts filled the darkness and looked like a thousand-million hot, angry needles streaking through the night.

As Callestra had predicted, the enemy fleet was unprepared for the attack and had neglected to supply adequate power to their aft shields. In no time, the Nephilim cruisers began losing engines left and right and began drifting toward a wall of Dagon battlecruisers.

Flanked by the asteroid field to one side and the Dagon armada to the other, Callestra uncrossed her legs and rose out of the command chair. She paused in front of the main view portal as an enemy Nephilim fighter tried a kamikaze attack but rebounded off of the deflector shields and spiraled away before exploding somewhere out of sight.

"Open all comms." She gestured her hand for the comms officer to comply. "This is the vice admiral of the fleet. All cruisers, move in. Scramble all fighters. I want those overgrown glow sticks to burn!"

"Scrambling all fighters," the comms officer relayed.

An alarm raged deep in the bowels of the ship and soon enough, Ravenclaw fighters poured out of the bay doors that opened beneath the large destroyers. They matched the two hundred fighters of the enemy and with the added power of the asteroid installations, the enemy fleet quickly began to dwindle in size. No sooner had Callestra ordered the Python missiles loaded than three giant squids jumped into the sector.

Starship killers.

"I want all Python missiles trained on those cephalopods," she said. "If they latch on to any of our ships with their tentacles, there's no escape."

"Missiles armed," the gunner's mate said.

"Lock onto targets."

"Targets locked," confirmed the officer.

"Fire!" Callestra shouted, shaking her fist excitedly as the first salvo of Python missiles launched.

Eighty Python class missiles raced toward their targets. One by one the barrage ignited on the surface of the celestial squid entities. Each CSE lurched under the pressure of each concussive blast.

Of the three squids, one of them faltered. Its shell was fractured with an array of thin, glowing veins that spread out like a cobweb. It looked as though it was about to fall apart or bleed out. Instead, its death was rather anticlimactic. The creature's inner light source faded then flickered like a spent neon bulb, before going out completely. Lost, adrift, a trio of Dagon fighters closed in and blasted the squid into space dust.

The other two squids latched onto a battle worn cruiser. They obviously sensed the higher radiation output of the older fusion cores. Old ships like those had to vent excess radiation directly into space just to keep the engines cool. And for the CSEs, that was like dangling engorged milky tits in front of a baby. Nevertheless, Callestra had anticipated this and, before the battle had even begun, had ordered the oldest cruisers be complimented with only a skeleton crew and a ton of bombs.

"*Verlag* to the *Scalaggoth*, abandon ship and prepare for operation No Mercy."

A few minutes later, her comms officer gave her the signal. "Fire on that ship on my command." She paused, took in a breath, and thought about how they'd stockpiled the *Scalaggoth* with enough neutron bombs to crippled a gas giant. "Now!"

The *Scalaggoth* ignited in a massive explosion that vaporized the two squids as though they were made of rice paper. The squids burned up, along with nearly two dozen of the enemy's fighters…and about a half dozen of her own.

"Absorb that," she snarled. Turning back to the main view portal, she ordered, "Recall our fighters and focus all remaining firepower on those destroyers."

Although the Nephilim destroyers had better shielding, just like the Nyctan ships from which they undoubtedly had borrowed the technology, the Dagon fleet had amped up its shield output as well. By nearly tenfold. Enough, at least, to hold their own in a ship-to-ship cannon exchange.

Not only this, but the Dagon fleet had amped up its disruptor power, too, nearly doubling the output of the Nephilim vessels. But it wasn't the Nephilim destroyers that worried her. It was more of those CSEs. If more squidies descended upon them, they'd be in for a real fight; worrying, as they'd already spent eighty percent of their missile reserve and depleted every neutron bomb they had.

"The enemy fleet is retreating!" an officer shouted jubilantly.

"Yes…tuck tail and run, little Nephilim. This is the Dagon Empire you're messing with."

It was almost guaranteed that today would go down in the history as a great win for the empire. Be that as it may, the admiral knew that wars were won one battle at a time, and not by grand heroics, but by manpower and perseverance.

Callestra let out a deep sigh. Her battle strategy had worked. The day was won. But this was no time to celebrate. The Nephilim would be back. That was all but guaranteed. And next time with more ships. That's why she needed to be ready. Ready for whatever they threw at her.

That evening, Callestra couldn't get to sleep. No matter how hard she tried, she merely tossed and turned in bed. This agitated state continued until she grew fed up with her inability to calm her mind that she threw off her satin sheets and sat straight up in bed.

Her chest shimmered in the dim light of her room with a gossamer sheen of perspiration. She slipped out of bed and walked over to the windows where she liked to practice yoga and stared out at the fleet hanging in the distance.

The ships moved gradually, like giant mechanized space whales. It was peaceful. And she lost herself in the deep of outer space.

A moment later, a chill crawled through her body and her bare skin bristled with goosebumps, but she ignored it. The cool air felt good on her damp skin. Deciding she wasn't going to get any sleep, she headed for the shower, pausing briefly in front of her mirror to check her body–a bad habit she'd developed ever since her father had asked if she'd put on weight shortly after she'd turned eighteen.

She hadn't, of course, but his words had bothered her deeply. From that moment on, she began dieting, even though she hadn't needed too. Also, she started wearing makeup to try and make herself appear more mature, since mature women rarely got asked such questions. Not without giving everyone a piece of their mind, in any case.

That was ten years ago but, somehow, it felt like yesterday. For the life of her, she just couldn't shake the feeling of inadequacy that constantly loomed over her head like a perpetual raincloud. It was vexing, to say the least.

She wasn't overly vain, though. At least, she didn't think so. But she'd been blessed with good looks and figured she'd best not let them go to waste.

People who were given natural advantages in life but wasted them disgusted her. They did so either from cowardice or weakness, and she found both traits revolting. Which is why she worked so hard to keep herself together and in good shape. She wasn't about to waste her good fortune like so many others seemed to do.

In her spare time, she was either in the training facility or in her quarters doing yoga. Every other moment was spent either working or recuperating in the regeneration pods.

But in a time of war like this, she didn't think taking up leisure activities was appropriate. She didn't want to allow herself to be distracted by non-essential matters. She needed to keep herself grounded, in the present. Her mind focused on the mission.

Callestra climbed into the sonic shower and turned it on. A gentle vibration rippled across her skin. The tingle felt good, but at the same time she wanted more than just a sonic cleanse. She wanted heat and steam and the soothing feeling of water cascading down her neck and back. She took the shower head and turned on the water spray.

She adjusted the flow, setting it to pulsating mode and let it massage the soreness from her neck. Then, she slid it off the hook and brought it down her between her thighs. She held it to herself for the longest time, closing her eyes and enjoying the warm waves of pleasure that flowed through her body. She squealed when it got too intense for her, but like everything in her life, she pushed herself. She kept the spray right where it was and held it there until her breathing was indistinguishable from panting. Reaching out with her other hand, she slapped the glass shower wall, palm open, fingers spread wide, and moaned loudly.

The jet of water undulated between soft and firm as she used it to mash her clitoris into heavenly bliss. Another second later and she couldn't hold it back any longer. She gasped loudly as an orgasm erupted from deep inside of her. She squirted all over the side of the shower stall, thighs quivering so fiercely that she could scarcely stand. But like everything else, she didn't stop there. She pushed herself to her limits and kept masturbating. Even after it began to hurt. And beyond that was a new kind of pleasure.

After coming three more times, she switched the shower mode to sonic cleanse and watched as the droplets of water danced across her blue skin like raindrops across a tin roof. Turning up the dial, the water rose off of her in a mist and hung in a delicate balance in mid-air. The water droplets sparkled all around her like a crystalline aura. As the shower cycle finished, the air vents sucked away the water, leaving her clean and dry.

She missed the company of a strong man to be with, but there weren't many who could satisfy her carnal desires. Zallek sure didn't.

Finished showering, she stepped out of the stall and stepped onto the white plush carpet and let her feet sink into it. She wriggled her toes inside the fuzzy carpet, a most delightful sensation, and then went over to her closet, her hips swaying with a sexy, pendulum swing. Picking out today's uniform, she laid it out on her bed and just stood in the open room staring at it.

Eight minutes later she was fully dressed and standing on the observation deck gazing out the windows at the fleet hanging against the paint like smears of a green and yellow nebula. She was still horny as hell, but that would have to wait. She needed to prepare for the next encounter with the Nephilim. And with the Lord Emperor coming, she wanted to make a good impression.

She didn't try to hide her feelings. She'd harbored a major crush on the emperor ever since she was a teenage girl. And although he was about twelve years her senior, she had always fantasized about meeting him one day.

If his reputation was at all accurate, she knew that she might even have a chance with him, seeing as he always insisted on having the most beautiful woman in the room. And that excited her.

Not only would it make her father furious, a win in her book, but just by being with him it put her into the company of an elite sisterhood. From Jennica, to Cassera, to Jegra herself. The emperor only bedded the strongest, most impressive women. And if he chose her, well, she'd gladly accept the honor.

Callestra suppressed an arbitrary yawn and then turned away from the observation window. She was about to head back to command when a bright flash drew her attention back to the vista outside. Approximately three hundred Nephilim battlecruisers and two dozen squid entities appeared off the bow of the *Verlag.*

"Fuck me," she said. It was overkill by any definition. But, apparently, this phony pretender calling himself "H'aaztre" was all about showing his might. *Obviously, compensating for something,* she smiled to herself.

The only problem now, Callestra realized, was that it was her fleet that was grossly outnumbered and outgunned. And without any backup coming, this wasn't a fight she was likely going to win. Be that as it may, she'd go down fighting. For the glory of the Empire.

28

Onelle Te'Legra Agnar called out from her cell. "Hello? Anybody there?" But there was no answer. In fact, nobody had come to see her in over twenty-four hours and she was beginning to worry.

Being locked up on trumped up charges was one thing, but being neglected and starved out was entirely another. Then there was the ordeal regarding the ship. It had docked, left an hour later, and redocked again shortly after that.

Each time it had happened she could hear the docking clamps engage and disengage as the ship came and went, but where the hell were they? What was that self-righteous do-gooder Raven Nightguard up to?

About ten minutes earlier, a deafening explosion had rattled the entire ship. And by the sounds of it, the blast had come from somewhere within the depths of whatever space port they were docked at. Just her luck, however, it had been violent enough to cause a brief power outage. She had seized the opportunity to pry open the door to her cell with her dinner tray. By the time the power came back on, she had it a good fifteen centimeters open.

Even though the security breach alarm went off, nobody came to throw her back into her cell. The very fact that nobody had come started to make her a little bit nervous.

"Come on," she grunted, using her thigh as a fulcrum to gain leverage on the aluminum tray, and leaning into it with her full weight managed to force the door open more.

She knew that if she pulled too hard, the tray would fold in on itself. So, taking extra precaution to be as gentle as possible, she applied just enough pressure to get it to act as a lever. A few seconds later, the door hissed open.

"It's about time," she said, tossing the tray to the floor. It hit the metal floor of her cell and rattled to a standstill. She ignored it and went over to a console and shut off the alarm.

Not wasting another minute, she rummaged through the lockers for some clothes other than the beige prison jumpsuit she wore. She found nothing. Upset, she slammed the locker and mumbled a few obscenities under her breath. That's when she got a bright idea.

Onelle headed back to the main console and brought up a floor plan of the *Skywend's* internal layout. "Computer, show me the fastest route to Captain Raven Nightguard's quarters."

A red pulsating line appeared on the floor plan and guided her to the captain's quarters. *Good,* she thought, the captain and she were about the same size.

Excited to do a bit of shoplifting, she rushed out of the brig and up the corridors and made her way to the captain's cabin.

Raven dropped down from the ventilation shaft, landed on the floor stealthier than a cat, and quickly scanned her surroundings.

Emperor Dakroth was on a rampage, but she was keeping him busy while the others made their way to the far end of the station. Gyllek had located an active shuttle and it was their plan to get to it and take it back to the *Skywend.* Raven would hang back and distract Dakroth and then teleport back to the ship once they were ready.

She wasn't worried about Dakroth getting control of the station anymore because Gyllek had already rewritten the security protocols and buried them behind the five-tier encryption of a multi-phase quantum firewall.

The clangor of footsteps coming up the hall drew her attention back to the task at hand, and she quickly slid up against a bulkhead and disappeared into the shadows.

Almost as soon as she'd concealed herself, Dakroth came around the corner of the corridor. He hummed a little ditty to himself as he twirled a blaster on his hand. Not that he needed it. But the emperor was smart. He'd conserve his energy for when nothing else was at hand.

Raven held her breath and slowed her heart rate. The mods in her body allowed her to inject neurochemicals that gave her more control over her brain functions and thereby, more control over her body. Her eyes were also enhanced so she could see perfectly in low light, whereas Dakroth could not.

She blinked once and switched into the ultraviolet spectrum and the emperor stopped and paused just in front of her. His violet glowing form sparked in the ultraviolet spectrum, and he looked around as though he had heard something. She calmed herself even more; he looked away and carried on with his little ditty.

Once he disappeared around the turn up at the top of the junction, she took a long, deep breath and sighed out in relief. A smile crept onto her face as she followed after him. Now, she'd stalk him for a while. She peeked around the corridor and, seeing that it was safe, she stealthily made her way up the passage in pursuit of her prey.

Raven continued up the long corridor, oblivious to the fact that Emperor Dakroth had stepped out behind her from one of the bulkheads. He had copied her move and had done it better. Even with her enhancements, she hadn't detected him.

Slowly, he raised the blaster, a malicious grin spreading ear to ear. He squeezed down on the trigger and fired off a blast.

The visage of Raven flickered and Dakroth threw his arms and griped. "Is everyone around her a freaking hologram?"

From out of the shadows, the muzzle of a blaster pressed firmly into the right side of his head.

"Not everyone," Raven said, stepping into view.

Dakroth let the blaster go limp in his hand and smiled. "Well played, my dear. There aren't many who can get the jump on me."

"Even when you're paying compliments you somehow manage to make it about yourself."

"What can I say? I have an enigmatic personality."

"More like self-absorbed," Raven replied. "Now, drop the gun." She jammed the muzzle forcefully into his temple to let him know she meant business and he complied.

"Alright, alright, no need to get physical." He tossed the gun to the floor and

Raven kicked it away with her foot. The blaster scraped to a stop a few feet away and Raven grabbed Dakroth and spun him around then slammed him into the wall.

"You know, I like a woman who likes it rough," he said, eyeing her out of the corner of his eye with a less than wholesome gaze. "Should we talk safe words or...?"

"Don't test my patience, Your Excellency," Raven whispered into his ear. "Because unlike your beloved wife, I'm not so forgiving."

"Ah, yes. Ever the compassionate one, she is. A small imperfection, but one I'm willing to overlook. After all, the sex is to die for."

"You're wrong," Raven said in a low and angry voice. "You mistake compassion for weakness. It's not. It's her greatest strength. And it's what will save the whole bleeding galaxy from tyrants like you."

"A tyrant, am I?"

"Why? What would you call yourself?"

"An ideologue, perhaps. A lover. A jack of all trades."

"Right," Raven said, sounding unimpressed.

"I unified seven-star systems. I brought order to a chaotic universe. And I brokered a new era of peace. You may not agree with my heavy-handed methods, but they work."

"Peace?" Raven balked. "You killed countless men, women, and children in the name of glory. You didn't bring peace. You crippled entire planets and cultures so that they couldn't rise up. Then you fed them false hope and empty promises by filling their heads with the idea that they could aspire to the same prominence as a Dagon, if they served you. And you continued this lie in order to exploit them for their talents and resources.

"You don't get peaceful empires by sitting everyone down and telling them to talk through their difficulties, my dear. Most of the species we encounter are too primitive to even comprehend a better version of themselves let alone a universe in which they can set aside their petty differences. No, there needs to be someone to lead them to that understanding."

"And let me guess...you're just the man to do it?"

"Do you see anyone else ruling the universe?"

Raven gave up trying to reason with him. It was clear that he nurtured delusions of grandeur and was unwilling to accept responsibility for the terrible things he had done in the name of his empire building.

"All right, enough chit-chat. Let's get moving." Raven shoved him hard and directed him back down the way they'd come. Her plan was to get him back to the *Skywend* and lock him up in the brig.

They turned the bend and almost ran right into Onelle Te'Legra Agnar. She stood in frozen in her tracks, shocked to see them. "Shit."

"What are you doing out of your cell?" Raven demanded to know. "More importantly, are those my clothes?"

Onelle merely grinned sheepishly in return.

Dakroth glanced between the two women and, finding them rather preoccupied with the other, he lunged forward and shoved Onelle into Raven.

Both women stumbled back as Dakroth dashed away.

"He's getting away!" Raven shouted. She angrily shoved Onelle out of the way and she fell to the ground.

"Ow!" Onelle complained, scraping her elbow on the floor. She sat up to examine her arm but Raven was already storming after Dakroth, her boot clomping away down the corridor at a brisk pace.

Gyllek, Angellyk, and Kregor arrived at the southern docking station and searched for the docking platform with a shuttle.

"This way," Gyllek said, reading a handheld scanner.

They passed through a corridor and stepped out onto a large platform. It appeared empty.

"I don't get it," she said. "It should be here. It says it should be here."

"Maybe it's cloaked," Angellyk said, slowly making her way to the center of the landing platform, waving her hands about like a blindfolded child searching for a piñata.

"If it was cloaked, we wouldn't be reading it on the scanners," Gyllek said. She shot Kregor an exasperated look—as if to say they weren't dealing with the brightest bulb in the pack. He merely shrugged.

Angellyk threw her hands on her hips and turned back toward them. "Maybe someone took it?"

"There aren't any life signs in this whole entire facility other than ours, the captain, and Emperor Dakroth.

"That's only five people."

"Yes," Gyllek said in a mystified tone. "Your point being?"

"Okay, smarty-pants. Then, answer me this. Why are there six glowing dots on your scanner?" She pointed over at the scanner in Gyllek's hands.

Gyllek looked down and, sure enough, there were six bio-signatures. "Bloody Helios!" she said, dismayed to find that Angellyk was right.

"What is it?" Kregor asked.

"She right. There's an additional bio-signature."

"Can you identify who it is?"

"No. But, the fact remains, we're not alone on this station."

Before she could look away from the monitor of her scanner, a seventh bio-signature appeared. "Give me a break!" she said, smacking the scanner.

"What now?" Kregor asked.

Gyllek held up the scanner. "Now it's telling us there are seven bio-signatures on board."

The comm crackled and Raven's winded voice cut through the staticky interference of the frequency.

"I'm in hot pursuit of Dakroth. Also, Onelle has escaped and is somewhere onboard."

"Onelle?" Angellyk repeated, sharing a surprised look with the others.

"Captain," Gyllek said. "We're not the only ones aboard the station."

The static interference caused her reply to be interrupted and she wasn't sure she'd gotten through. The captain's reply came back, but it was too garbled to make out a single word. Then the comm link cut out.

"Dammit!" Gyllek said. "I lost her."

"Where's the seventh life form right now?" asked Kregor. He drew out his war hammer and turned to face the station behind them.

Gyllek looked back down at the scanner. She studied it for a bit then turned it 180 degrees. Then she rotated it back around to its original orientation.

"What's the matter?" Angellyk asked. She drew out her twin blasters just to be on the safe side.

"The dot just jumped across the screen. It was near Raven's position but now it's on this side of the station."

"But it took us nearly thirty minutes to get here."

"Maybe it teleported," surmised Kregor.

"The scanner would have read a teleportation signal. There wasn't one."

"Maybe the scanner is broken," Angellyk suggested. She turned to see Gyllek and Kregor looking at her. "I mean, it said there was a ship here too. But there's clearly no ship. And now it thinks there's another bio-signature. What if it's just broken? That would explain all the anomalous readings."

"Don't move a muscle," Gyllek whispered out of the corner of her mouth. Kregor's face, too, was frozen in a state of shock.

"Why? Is there something on my face?"

"Not exactly," Gyllek replied.

The air behind Angellyk wavered like a mirage on the desert and then two yellow eyes flashed. The eyes disappeared back into thin air and Gyllek drew out her blaster and fired.

Angellyk jumped forward as something reached out for her. Narrowly escaping the invisible talons that reached for Angellyk, Kregor rushed forward, battle hammer in hand.

"Hold up!" a voice cried out. "I mean you no harm."

Kregor held back as Angellyk scrambled on her hands and knees to get behind the large Dragonian. Gyllek helped her up and they trained their blasters on the translucent specter wavering before them.

A flicker of light followed by some electrical discharge flashed before their eyes, then the shimmer slowly melted away to reveal a solid form. All three watched in complete astonishment when an unexpected face revealed itself to them.

29

Grendok of the once noble world Galliforn, stood at the foot of the girl's bed. The girl with no memory and no identity. A strange twist in an otherwise typical week. But, regardless of the circumstances that had brought her here to the palace, there was something that had caught his attention. Something she had said as the medics whisked her away to the infirmary. And among the words she had spoken in her state of delirium, she had said a name. A name she couldn't possibly have known.

Jegra, covered in grease from working with Meleh'Kendar getting the shield generators working again, sidled up next to Grendok and shot him a curious glance before turning her attention to the sleeping girl. "You, of all people, are the last person I would have expected to find standing here."

Grendok let out a throaty chuckle. "I suppose I'm turning into a sentimental old goat." He fell back into a comfortable silence for a while then added. "The girl was mumbling something in her sleep. She spoke a name I hadn't heard in ages."

"A name?" Jegra asked, glancing from the girl to the goat and back again.

"Bazhov," he said.

"A Gallifornian name."

"Indeed."

"Why does that name sound so familiar?"

"Ural Bazhov was known as the 'Traitor of Galliforn.'"

"The satyr who aided and abetted Dakroth's father in the campaigns? I remember reading about him."

"Yes, well, he was banished after the war."

"Where to?"

Grendok shot Jegra a wry grin. "Why here, of course. To Thessalonica."

"Here? The traitor of Galliforn has been living out his days on my moon?"

"As you are aware, in his shame, it was impossible for him to return to Galliforn, seeing as the punishment for high treason is death. And Dagon ultimately lost the war and needed…well…a scapegoat to pin the blame on."

"I see," Jegra said, turning her attention back to Grendok. "So, then, the question becomes how does this mysterious girl without a memory or a name come to speak of the most infamous war this side of the galaxy?"

"Yes. That is the question." Grendok turned and smiled at the empress, his hands locking behind his back. "I've taken up enough of your time, Your Majesty. There's still much work to do, so I'll leave you to it." He bowed recently and then excused himself from the recovery room.

Jegra turned and folded her arms across her chest. "Who are you?" she wondered aloud as she gazed upon the young woman's face.

There was something so familiar about her, but *what* escaped her. It was as if Jegra knew the girl from somewhere even though she was quite certain they'd never crossed paths before. It felt like those times when you had the name of someone on the tip of your tongue but just couldn't remember it.

"How are we doing today?" asked Doctor Amora Van Gogh.

Jegra turned and smiled at the doctor, who had on her trademark white medical coat and was holding the patient's charts. "I'm fine doc, just came to check *uuughah!*"

Without warning, Jegra released a stream of vomit which splattered all across Amora's torso. She managed to hit nearly every part of her.

Embarrassed beyond belief, Jegra wiped her mouth and did her best to apologize. "Oh my god, I'm so, so sorry."

Amora raised a hand to prevent her from trying to help clean the sick up and instead just shed her coat and let it fall to a heap in the puddle of vomit on the floor. Two nurses instantly manifested beside them, one carrying cleaning supplies, and began attending to the mess.

Amora took Jegra by the elbow and ushered her over to a bed. "Have you been feeling ill recently?"

"I don't even feel ill now. It just came out of nowhere. Again, I deeply and sincerely…"

Amora sat her down and held up her hand again. "It's nothing. Really. If I was bothered by a little puke then I picked the wrong profession to be in. Luckily for you, I'm damn good at my job. But I'm going to run a few tests just to be on the safe side."

Jegra nodded in agreement as Amora drew out a medial scanner and began scanning Jegra's vitals. She pressed a NeedleAir injector against her neck and drew out a blood sample. Inserting the vial from the injector into the slot on the medical scanner brought up a string of data, including a fully mapped genome sequence.

A second genome sequence appeared in faint orange under the red helix on the display, and Amora raised an eyebrow.

"What's the diagnoses, doc?" asked Jegra, a worried tone in her voice. "Am I dying?" Of course, she was only joking. But, if she was being completely honest with herself, the sudden onset puke-storm did have her a little bit worried.

"You're fine. More than fine, actually."

"I don't get it?" she said, perplexed by how getting sick was somehow an indicator of her being more than fine.

"Don't get me wrong," Amora said with a warm smile. "You'll be having a lot more of these bouts of morning sickness over the next few months. But, it's nothing to worry about. It's perfectly normal for expecting mothers to have a little bit of morning sickness."

"Expecting mothers?" Jegra face went pale. "Are you saying…?"

"Yes," Amora said, taking Jegra's hands in hers and squeezing firmly. "You're pregnant."

"I—I mean, how? How is this even possible?"

"Well," the doctor said, "When two people love each other very much, sometimes…"

"No, that's not what I meant," Jegra said rolling her eyes. "I know about the birds and the bees. But the only person I've had sex with recently is Dani."

Amora smiled and checked her chart. "Yes, Danica's DNA is a match."

"But her vestigial organ isn't supposed to be…I mean, she's not supposed to be able to make babies."

"As you know, in rare cases, Dagon women have been known to have working gonads. It's all part of being an intersexual species. My guess is, after her trauma, the medics repaired her and made her 'better than new.' It appears that Danica is fully functional in every way."

"That's…that's wonderful," Jegra said, still beside herself as she grappled with the news. She was glad she wasn't sick. But a baby? She didn't know what to do with a baby! She didn't even know how to process the news.

"I suppose you'll want to tell her yourself?" Amora asked, gesturing with a nod toward Danica's bed.

Jegra looked over at her sleeping fiancé and she immediately felt anger well up inside of her. She took a deep breath and tried to calm herself. As furious as she was with Danica for overdosing on Nividium, the fact remained, she was still the mother of their child and deserved to know.

Jegra slowly got up and went over to Danica's bed and sat down beside it. Amora returned to her duties but paused long enough to squeeze Jegra's shoulder and whisper into her ear. "You'll make a fine mother, Your Majesty."

Jegra smiled and watched the doc head off to attend to her other duties. One of them being mending Meleh'Kendar's hand, which he'd cut pretty badly on some sharp paneling while they were replacing the circuits on the shield generator.

"Hey you," a sleepy voice said, drawing Jegra's attention back to Danica. Danica smiled lazily and reached out with her hand to take Jegra's.

Hesitant to take Dani's hand, Jegra finally gave in. The warmth of her touch melted her and all the emotions, the anger, the love, the sense of betrayal, came welling up inside and she couldn't help but begin to shed tears.

"What's the matter?" Dani asked. "Why are you crying?"

"I thought I'd lost you. Just like I'd lost everyone else I've ever felt close to."

"I'm not going anywhere," replied Danica in a stern tone. She squeezed Jegra's hand with all her strength to let her know it was going to be all right.

"You'd better not go anywhere," Jegra said. She looked down and touched her belly with her free hand. "Because I need all the help, I can get raising this baby."

Danica slowly sat up in bed. "What?"

Jegra's eyes rose back up and met Dani's. "I'm pregnant," she said, her voice barely audible.

"Oh my god," Danica said. She covered her mouth, afraid she might scream out with joy. Jegra threw her arms around Dani's neck and nearly toppled into bed with her.

"We're going to be mothers," Jegra said, smiling.

Danica kissed Jegra's lips and Jegra slid onto the medical bed with her. Brushing her luv's hair out of her eyes, Danica made a solemn promise.

"I'll never use again. I swear. I'll get my act cleaned up. In fact, the doc has me on a detox cleanse already. But…she says the next few days are going to be extremely rough."

"I have faith in you, Dani," Jegra said, wrapping her arms around Dani's waist.

After a long silence of getting lost inside one another's gazes, Danica finally broke the silence. A concerned look falling across her face, she asked, "What word have you of Raphine? You know, Zallek threatened to kill her if I didn't betray you and give up vital information to your plans. Which I'd never do, mind you."

"Raphine?" Jegra said with a light laugh. "Raphine can more than take care of herself."

Danica let out a relieved sigh and pressed her forehead against Jegra's. After another short pause, she whispered, "We're going to have a baby. It's so…surreal."

"Yeah, it is," Jegra agreed. And both women laughed softly as they held each other. Their entire future had changed. It was frightening, but at the same time, exhilarating.

Grendok had briefly returned to the *Chiron* to run the blood sample he'd taken from the sleeping girl. The girl with no name.

For a moment he thought the empress had caught him red handed, quite literally speaking. But, to his great relief, she proved unaware of his misconduct. And although he knew it was highly unethical to take an unconscious girl's blood without consent, there was something that deeply troubled him about their guest. Something he couldn't shake.

Almathea entered his ready room and stood at attention in front of his desk. "At ease, Sub Commander," the admiral said.

"Yes, sir." She shifted her feet a bit and clasped her hands behind her back. Otherwise her posture was nearly the same as before with, perhaps, a little less tension in her shoulders.

"I want to be up front with you. I've done something that could cost me my position here and, if it should get out, the command of the *Chiron* will fall to you."

"Understood, sir."

Grendok raised an eyebrow. He was surprised that Almathea would so easily entertain his recklessness.

"I know you must have had your reasons, sir. You always do."

Grendok smiled. A more loyal officer there was none.

The vial practically glowed blue in the dim lighting as he held it up for her to see.

"What is that?"

"It's Dagon blood."

"Whose?"

"That's precisely what I intend to find out."

He placed the vial into the receptacle on his desk. The blood drained out and the computer began to unravel the genome. About thirty seconds later, his desk chimed, signaling that the task has been completed.

With a swipe of a hand, he threw up the double helix strand onto the wall display. Almathea turned to look at the data with him.

"Computer," Grendok said, rising to his feet. "Give me a breakdown of what we're looking at here."

<<Customized genome detected.>>

"A full mod?" Almathea said, a little bit surprised. Dagons outlawed genetic modification because of their purity beliefs. To find a person fully modded from conception, sometimes while still in the womb even, was not only rare, it was highly illegal. The very existence of such a person was viewed as an abomination.

Grendok scratched his hoary chin and then mumbled something to himself. Clearing his throat, he repeated his thoughts. "Computer, is this a unique genome or are we looking at a variation?"

<<Three genome strands identified.>>

"Show me," he said.

The large double helix unraveled. Various branches of gene sequences lit up red, some blue, and others yellow. Each of the three independent genomes seemed to be a part of three separate individual's DNA. After another moment, Emperor Dakroth's face appeared over the red portion of DNA. Next, Jegra's face appeared over the blue. And, finally, over the yellow...

"By the beard of Pan," Almathea gasped. She could scarcely believe her eyes.

It shouldn't even be possible. Yet, here she was staring at it with her own eyes.

"This is what I was afraid of," Grendok said.

"But how is it even possible? The celestial squid entities aren't even remotely compatible with Dagon DNA."

"It appears Dakroth's scientists have been working overtime to weaponize Jegra's DNA. What better way than to combine hers with that of the most powerful creatures the empire has ever faced off against?"

"If the Dagon High Council finds out Dagon has created a monster, they will kill her."

A grim look came over Grendok's face. Almathea knew he was worried, but she didn't know how he'd react to the news.

"If doctor Van Gogh runs a DNA scan of the girl, that information will automatically get locked into the royal database on Dagon Prime."

"Has she?"

"I don't think so. She seems preoccupied with the other patients. And the girl was merely suffering a bit of dehydration. An easy remedy. No need to concern themselves with a full DNA analysis."

"Unless the patient wakes up and requests one to discover who she is."

"That's just the thing," Grendok said, turning to Almathea, "she's a chimera. She's the first of her kind. A biological weapon unlike anything we've ever seen before."

"What should we do?"

"I'll return to the surface and make sure the empress is briefed on our findings. If, however, things go south, I'm going to need to ask you a favor...and you're not going to like it."

"Name it," Almathea said.

"I'm going to need you to get a missile lock on the palace."

"You're right," Almathea replied, "I don't like it." With that, she turned and stormed out of the ready room and returned to her duties on the bridge. She'd do it as a last resort, of course. But she, like everyone else onboard, was hoping it wouldn't come to that.

Grendok went over to his chair and slumped down into it. "Dismissed," he said, long after she was gone. He knew that he was asking a lot of Almathea and he knew she'd carry out her orders. But he hated the fact that she'd lost faith in him.

That was the problem with seeing everything in terms of strategic possibilities. There was never a third choice. In war, there was no room for such naïve optimism. There was only winning strategy and losing strategy.

In this case, the best strategy was to ensure that the girl's identity didn't go beyond his or the empress's knowledge. Anything else would be very bad for the girl, not to mention the whole of the empire.

If found out, her very existence would cause riots and Emperor Dakroth would be cast out as a criminal king. And Jegra would, by default, loose her position as empress. Nothing good would come of this news, which is why he had to keep it a secret at all costs.

30

A sharp spray of frigid water pelted Raphine's skin. It felt like a thousand needles pricking her skin all at once, if the needles were made of ice. The sting of it caused her to cry out as she held her arms and sobbed in the shower stall in the dingy basement holding cell.

"Any further witticisms, my dear?" Zallek asked, shutting off the fire hose.

"No," Raphine grumbled, her teeth chattering in her mouth as she stood against the back wall and wrapped her arms around her torso to try and fend off the cold.

It didn't help either that she had a fresh smattering of bruises from the previous day's interrogation. And the one before that. *Zallek must be getting desperate*, she thought, *if he's willing to resort to torture tactics.*

In an attempt to add insult to injury and humiliate her, Zallek had forced her to strip down. The good news was that he'd let her keep her underwear on. Hopefully, that meant he wouldn't find the micro-grenade she was carrying. Of course, even if he had forced her to strip naked, he still probably wouldn't have found it, due to where she had it stashed.

"W-what d-do y-you want?" she finally asked through her clacking teeth.

"Want?" Zallek looked at the girl with a surprised expression and balked. "What I want doesn't matter. It's what you want that matters. So, the question is, my dear. What is it you want?"

"I want to rip out that forked tongue of yours and shove it right up your ass so you'll learn exactly how full of shit you really are." She smiled and raised her eyebrows at him as if to say, *smoke on that, ass-face.* Of course, her mouthing off was met with another icy spray and she screamed out as the water shrapnel tore across her skin like jagged icicles.

"I can do this all day," Zallek shouted above the blast of water.

"So can I," Raphine replied. This was a lie. She didn't know how much more of it she could take. But she didn't want to give him the satisfaction of appearing weak before him.

Zallek pulled back on the valve and slowed the water to a drizzle. Cupping his hand over his left ear, he asked, "What was that, luv? I didn't quite catch that."

"So can I," Raphine said loudly. Her lips were blue and her teeth chattered in her skull like a bag of marbles, but she was determined not to give in to this *va'pa'mashtaq.*

"Are you sure?" A cruel grin spread across Zallek's lips as he unleashed the water, full stream. It tore out of the nozzle with a vengeance and bit into Raphine's skin causing her to shriek out all over again. She found herself wishing she'd have thrown in the towel. But it was too late for that. She had pressed her luck and now all that was left was to endure the torment.

Pressed up against the wall, Raphine sank to her knees and curled into a ball. She sobbed as the water stabbed at her with each painful prick.

Finally, Zallek stopped the water. Her caving in was the sign he needed to know she was at her breaking point. "I guess you're not as strong as you thought you were," he sneered. "Pity."

His smug grin never faded as he coiled the firehose back up and then motioned for one of his henchmen to take over for him. Zallek turned back to Raphine, shivering in the corner, and smacked his teeth in disappointment.

"You stay here and think about your options. You can either enjoy more of this or tell me what I want to know. It's a simple choice, really. No pressure, though. Take your time." He turned to leave and waved over his shoulder, "See you in the morning."

The thug finished gathering the fire hose and glanced back at Raphine to catch a glimpse of her mostly naked green body. She scowled at him threateningly, and he merely grinned in return.

"Don'tcha worry, miss," he said. "It won't last long. You'll break like 'dem all does. Them's always break."

Raphine flipped him off with the bird and he chuckled to himself as he left the room. She heard the door bolt behind him and once her hosts were gone, she started sobbing.

She didn't bother wiping away her salty tears as they mingled with the drops of water trailing down her shivering body; they felt warm by comparison. Reaching up, she clutched her forest green hair in both hands and wrung out as much water as she could.

The excess water drizzled onto the floor and she slowly rose to her feet, body numb from the cold. In the desert climate, she rarely ever felt cold. Truly cold. But right now, she'd give almost anything to be back under that relentless, scorching hot sun.

Raphine jumped up and down and rubbed her arms for several minutes. She knew that if she didn't combat the cold, she'd likely experience hypothermia and then she'd be in real trouble.

She was starting to wish she'd never made that deal with Danica. But lately Danica seemed distant. Ever since her humiliation bout in the arena, there was a hard shell around her and she wouldn't let anyone in. Only Jegra seemed to be able to get through to her, but she'd been extremely stand-offish and uninterested in the affairs of the empire. Which was totally unlike her.

Raphine finally got her heart rate up high enough that her body temperature slowly returned to normal. More importantly, she'd warmed up enough that she could see steam coming off her avocado colored skin.

First things were first. She needed to get out of this dive and get some dry clothes. Zallek was gravely mistaken if he thought he could keep her there the whole night—freezing to death.

She took a deep breath, tightened her stomach, and then slid her hand down the front of her panties. After fishing around for a bit, she brought up a capsule no bigger than a vitamin supplement. One tip flashed red and she held it up under the florescent lighting and grinned.

Not wasting any more time, she went up to the heavy iron door and placed the capsule in the keyhole. Even if the door was reinforced, she could still blow out the locking mechanism with this micro-explosive. But then she'd have to deal with the guard. That's when an idea came to her.

Since she was being held in a standard room of what appeared to be a basement somewhere, there were no amenities. And no toilet. Pulling her panties down to her ankles, she squatted in the middle of the floor and shouted for the guard. "Hey! Hey, you in there!"

After a moment she saw the face of the man who'd gathered up the fire hose peering through the slot on the door at her. "What do you want?" he grumbled in an agitated tone.

"I need something to wipe with," she said.

"Use your hand!" he replied with a snide laugh.

"That's unsanitary. Not to mention uncivil. Please?"

"You have your options, girly. Right or left. Now, if you'll excuse me, I have a game of solitaire to get back to."

As his face turned away, Raphine's heart raced as she tried to think of a way to keep his attention. "Wait!" she called out.

His face reappeared and she let out a small sigh. "What now?"

"I'll…um…let you wipe me."

"What?"

"Bring me some tissue paper and you can have the honor of cleaning me off. That's a fair trade off, don't you think?"

Although the thought of having his grubby fingers touch her grossed her out, the bait was set. Now, all he had to do was bite.

The guard looked behind him, checking if the coast was clear, and then she heard the key enter the keyhole. *Yes,* she thought. *He took the bait, hook line and sinker.*

She swiftly pulled her panties up then dashed to the corner of the room and curled into a tight ball. There was a loud explosion and when she turned around, the door swung open to reveal a gory bloodstain dripping down the opposite side of the door and the hallway walls.

Raphine leaped to her feet and sprinted out of the room, cautious not to slip on the crimson oil-slick left in the wake of her little explosive trick.

She ran up the hallway, her bare feet slapping along the cold concrete of whatever underground facility she was in. She knew it had to be underground because it was far too cold, to dank, for it to be above ground.

Voices echoed up the corridor and Raphine slowed to a stop in the middle of the long corridor. She looked around for an escape but there was only a small utility closet. It would have to do.

She ducked into the closet and carefully shut the door behind her, doing her best not to make any unnecessary noise. Once inside, she turned around to see a fresh janitorial uniform neatly hung in a locker that was missing its door. The was even an extra pair of worker's boots sitting beneath a tool belt.

"Lucky," she whispered. Quickly, she put on the drab gray uniform, boots, and leather tool belt along with a matching cap. *Whoever this uniform belongs to must be skinny*, she thought, because it fit her nicely.

She adjusted the brim of her cap to cover her eyes and then grabbed a bucket and mop. Pretending that she worked at the place, she began whistling a generic tune she'd made up off the top of her head, opened the door, and casually stepped out of the maintenance closet and into the hall.

Sure enough, the moment she stepped out, two Dagon guards were approaching her from the other end of the corridor. Raphine took a breath and kept herself calm. In fact, she was willing to bet they wouldn't think anything of a Bre'lal janitor. After all, her people usually only took low end service jobs, anyway.

"You there!" one of the guards said. His eyes fixed themselves to her and she kept her head down. "You hear anything strange? Like an explosion."

"No, sir. Just gonna clean this corridor like Mr. Zallek ordered, sir."

"Yeah?" the guard said, walking up to her. "When you're done cleaning these pipes," he said, gesturing at the perspiring pipes that glistened with beaded droplets of moisture, "then why don't you give my pipes a good cleaning." He grabbed her hand and pulled it into his crotch and snickered. His partner snickered along with him at the lewd invitation.

"You like that, Bre'lal whore? Because there's more where that came from. A whole lot more."

She pulled her hand away and tried to look even more bashful than she was already pretending to be. Before the guards headed down the hall any further, though, the first guard turned and slapped her ass.

"I'll be seeing you shortly, sweet-tits," he said, eyeing her body up and down, never once looking her in the eyes.

She bit her tongue and held back a dozen scathing retorts. Instead of getting herself into trouble, she stewed quietly, trying to stay as low key as possible. Her diminutive approach must have worked, too, because, to her surprise, both guards burst into bawdy laughter and continued along their way.

Once they turned the bend at the end of the junction, Raphine looked up.

Ditching the bucket and mop in the middle of the hallway, she raced away as fast as her feet would carry her.

When she made it to the end of the hall, she came to a door with a security pad. It needed a key-card to get through. "Graddack," she cursed under her breath. Just then, the security alarm went off–no doubt due to the mess she'd left back there. The two guards must have stumbled across her handiwork.

Raphine looked around, her chest heaving as she panted heavily. There was literally nowhere to go except back to the maintenance closet. But she knew the guards would be back to question her. So that was out of the question.

Just then, the door clicked and opened wide. Two guards rushed into the hallway, one of them brushing up against her. "Make way," he said. She kept her eyes down.

Holding the door for them, she looked up as they cleared the bend at the end of the junction; she looked around the open door, there was a stairwell leading up.

She smiled. This was her way out.

She let the door close behind her and paused briefly. She knew they'd loop back for her once they found that she'd escaped. So, she took the wrench from her utility belt and raised it high then brought it down on the security access panel on the wall next to the door.

The panel tore off the wall with a sparking hiss and the mechanism shorted, locking into place. It would take a real maintenance crew to get the door in working order again. *That ought to hold them*, she thought.

Several flights of stairs later, she came out the top of the stairwell only to find herself in some vaulted, indoor greenhouse. She let the door swing shut behind her and then cautiously walked along the main concourse as she searched for an exit.

Numerous plants grew under the red glow of special heat lamps. She recognized the species; the plant's nectar was milked and processed to make Nividium–that much she knew already. But that's where her knowledge on the subject of drug production ended.

At that moment, Danica's words popped into her mind. *When trapped behind enemy lines, do as the enemy does. Blend in. Then disappear. Sound advice*, she thought. *Especially now.*

Raphine casually strode the rest of the way up the passage as if she belonged there. She passed people in white lab coasts and even a couple more guards. Nobody asked her for her badge or I.D. Nobody tried flirting with her. They simply ignored her. She was too far below their station to even matter.

A couple more guards raced toward her and she gingerly stepped out of their way. They passed without so much as a glance and she smiled again. It was almost too easy.

"Hey you!" a gruff voice called out.

She froze in her tracks then slowly turned to see a stout Dagon with a white mustache approaching her. He too was wearing the brown janitorial jumpsuit, but unlike hers, his had two chevron bars on the shoulders, signifying a management rank of some kind.

"Yes, sir?" she said.

"Didn't you get the memo?" he asked sarcastically. "There's a mess to clean up in section C-8."

That was the section she had just come from. The letters had been painted on the walls. But if one thing was certain, it was that she had no intention of going back there any time soon.

"Uh, yes, sir. I just need to visit the lady's room first, if you know what I mean?"

"Why? You can't hold it?" he asked tersely.

"I've been holding all day," she informed him. "In fact, I think a little has spilled out already. My underwear is all damp and I'm starting to itch. I might be developing a rash. I can show you if you want proof."

"No, that won't be necessary," he grumbled. "Just hurry it up. This ain't no paid holiday."

"Yes, sir. I'll be quick, sir." She raced off, hooking a right at the end of the corridor. A stern clearing of the throat halted her, however, and she looked back.

"The restrooms are that way," the manager said sternly.

"Right, sir. Sorry, sir. Won't happen again."

Raphine quickly turned on her heel and raced off in the other direction. She could hear the custodial manager mumbling, "Goddamn foreigners," behind her as she went.

No sooner had she rounded the corner at the end of the hall than she stumbled upon the lady's restroom. She quickly ducked inside and, finding it empty, let out a huge sigh of relief. She placed both hands on the sink and stared at her face in the mirror. She looked terrible, but she was alive.

However, that could change at any minute. Especially now that they knew she'd escaped. Now there'd be a manhunt to catch her. Just finding her way out of the facility would be problematic, to say the least.

The melodic tweet of a bird caught her attention. She looked over to the bathroom window to see that it was cracked open, barely big enough to squeeze through, though. She grabbed the trash can and flipped it over. Using it as a stool, she climbed up and peered outside.

Could it really be this easy? Or was it a trap? She was staring outside, and there wasn't a person in sight.

Raphine pulled herself up and wriggled out through the window. She dropped to the ground on the other side with a *thud*, landing somewhat awkwardly, but shook it off and quickly got back onto her feet.

Now all she needed to do was find a café or someplace she could make a holovid call and then contact Jegra.

When Raphine turned to leave Zallek's compound, she came smack dab face to face with a lush, green tropical forest.

Now, Raphine knew two things. First, there was no forest on Thessalonica and, therefore, she wasn't on Thessalonica. She was Dagon Prime.

"You've got to be shitting me," she said, looking around.

From within the bathroom she heard the door smash in. "This way!" a guard's voice shouted.

Raphine whipped her head around. They'd be onto her in no time if she stood around twiddling her thumbs. Not wishing to get caught, she turned and ran into the forest.

Like a first-class athlete, she hurdled giant roots of mossy trees and ducked beneath the leafy canopies of mammoth ferns. Her tool belt jingled and jangled as she ran and she quickly began unfastening it. Before she tossed it, however, she plucked out the boxcutter knife and then ditched the tool belt.

The sound of an alarm filled the jungle behind her and she knew that they'd be coming after her. All she could do was keep running. Keep heading deeper into the forest where she could lose them. She'd work on figuring out how to get back to Jegra and Thessalonica later. Right now, she just had to stay alive.

31

Nephilim ships took formation, spreading out across the breadth of the opposing fleet in a five-point grid pattern. When lit up, the armada resembled a giant net. The kind a fisherman would use.

"Don't get too close to those tentacles," Callestra warned. The navigation officer nodded in confirmation.

"What are our orders, Vice Admiral?" asked Sub Commander Orsek Van Tavaris.

"We know the enemy fleet's weakness. But in order to take out those destroyers, we're going to need to sacrifice the *Verlag*."

Sub Commander Tavaris shot her a startled look. "Ma'am?"

Callestra waved a finger at the viewscreen. "That grid pattern may be their strength. But it is also their greatest weakness."

"Ma'am?" Tavaris asked, raising a curious eyebrow.

"It's a simple matter of physics. All we need to do is locate the chink in their armor, so to speak, and then hit it with everything we've got. And this ship's Duodeca-plex fusion reactor is the most powerful ever built. It's basically a giant fusion bomb multiplied by twelve. If we cause a core breach right at their weakest point, we can trigger a cascade effect, thereby allowing their fleet to cannibalize itself."

"Is that even possible? How would we even find their weakest link?"

Callestra stared up at the viewscreen and then pointed at a section of the enemy ship deployments. "There."

Sub Commander Tavaris zoomed in on the area she was looking at and magnified by sixty-eight percent. "Is that...?"

The object was massive. It dwarfed the *Verlag* by at least three times. "A squid," Callestra said, stating the obvious. "A damn big one, by the looks of it."

The celestial squid's shell had all kinds of damage markings. Scrapes, gouges, burn marks, pock-marks from missile blasts, but the creature had survived everything thrown at it. And it had placed itself directly in front of the Nephilim flag ship.

"Even if we do get up close and personal with the thing," Tavaris began, "how can we defend against that destroyer?"

"Have you ever seen a ship hyper jump directly into another ship?" Callestra asked, turning to reveal a devious smile on her face.

"No," Tavaris replied.

"Me neither. But we're about to find out."

"Yes, ma'am," Tavaris said, a small amount of hope taking the form of a grin.

"Get the ship commanders on the holovid and secure the channel."

The lighting on the bridge dimmed and then one by one the ship's commanders all appeared in a ghostly blue light. All of them sitting in their chairs.

Callestra returned to her chair and then addressed the gathering of holograms.

"I have a plan, but the sacrifice will be great. We will lose most of our fleet, but so will the enemy."

"Are you sure this is wise, Vice Admiral? With all due respect, the fleet is the last defense against the invaders."

"I'm well aware of that, Commander Hoag. But it's time to face the music, and the music is grim. We are no longer the dominant force in the galaxy. As of now, all you need to do is look out your view portal to see that we're outnumbered and outgunned." Callestra rose from her chair and pointed at her own view portal. "Look! That's what we're up against."

There was a long silence. Callestra calmed herself and then sat back down. Brushing down her uniform, she cleared her throat then looked up at the holographic faces starring back at her.

"We have one, and only one, chance at this. There are enough celestial squid entities out there for every one of our starships. The moment we engage, those things will descend upon us and drain our power until we're nothing but lifeless husks floating in the dead of space. The enemy fleet will be free to march onward, unhindered, to their victory over Dagon. Is that what you want?"

"No, ma'am," Hoag said, looking away in frustration.

The rest of the commanders echoed his sentiment with the same grim tone.

"All right then. Here's what we need to do…" she briefed them, holding up her touch pad and swiping a blue finger across it. Her encrypted battle plans detailing everything from ship formations to the cascade attack uploaded to all command ships in the fleet. After a few seconds, the commanders nodded in confirmation, having received the data and their orders. "Good," Callestra said, rising to her feet. "We're all on the same page. For the Empire!"

"For the Empire!" the commanders all shouted in unison.

One by one the blue holovid faces of the other fleet commanders flickered and then turned off. Once they had all returned to their duties, Callestra turned and gazed out the wide glass view portal in front of her and watched the battle unfold.

The Dagon fleet settled into an arrowhead formation ahead of the wall of Nephilim ships. The thirty-eight remaining heavy cruisers of the Dagon forces were all that was left standing between H'aaztre's army and their homeworld. If they failed, Dagon Prime fell.

"More bogies inbound, ma'am," informed Tavaris.

The *Verlag's* forward canons blazed. Nephilim ships began exploding as soon as they met the destroyer's heavy guns. The other destroyers in the formation opened fire too. They convened all their firepower at the central point just beyond the bow of the *Verlag,* creating a hot glowing wedge of fire and destruction. Slowly, the armada advanced.

"Steady," Callestra said, choosing to stand rather than sit during this intense exchange. "Steady as she goes."

"Load all remaining missile batteries and fire when ready," she ordered.

The gunner's mate nodded and after inputting the coordinates, said, "Firing, now."

Sixty missiles all screamed toward the mammoth CSE. Just before they reached their target, however, two other squids jumped into the path of the incoming missile volley and took the hit.

"They're protecting it," Tavaris said, pointing out the obvious.

"Yes, but those two squids opened up vital areas." Callestra turned and snapped her fingers to get the comms officer's attention. "Signal all ships. I want anyone who has any missiles remaining to fire on that giant CSE."

The comms officer nodded and relayed her message. Soon enough, a couple hundred missiles all raced forward, honing in on the massive squid.

As expected, the smaller CSEs moved into the path of the missiles to protect the larger one. That's when the Nephilim destroyers opened fire.

"Shields at seventy-two percent!" shouted the tactical officer.

"We won't be able to hold out for long. Not with this level of fire power," Sub Commander Tavaris relayed.

Callestra merely nodded and turned back toward the view portal to watch as the net of enemy ships began to encroach on their position.

One by one, the ships on the outer ends of the arrowhead formation began to lose their shields. Explosions lit up as both the right and left corners of the battle formation went up in flames.

"We've lost the *Vortex* and the *Razkor*," Tavaris said.

Callestra remained clam. Losses were inevitable. They were bound to lose many more before the day was done.

Finally, the vice admiral spoke. "Send the destruct code to all asteroid batteries."

The asteroid batteries, which had helped in the first battle with the Nephilim, were too far out of range to do any serious damage to the current enemy fleet. But by obliterating the asteroid belt, they could create a massive wall of debris, and the subsequent destruction of hundreds of asteroids in the belt would trigger tons of rock and ice to be expelled into deep space. Some of it, hopefully, would tear through the enemy fleet and cripple their vessels.

On Callestra's orders, the batteries on the surface of the asteroids self-destructed, and a daisy chain of massive explosions ignited all along the Veridion asteroid belt. A whirlwind of rock and debris smashed together and chunks of rock escaped their gravitational tethers and raced toward the enemy fleet.

The entire crew of the *Verlag* watched with bated breath as the jagged rocks spread out and headed toward the enemy fleet. Unfortunately, the plan was a dud. The distance was just too vast. Most of the rocks flew past their intended targets without so much as making a dent. Any damage done to the enemy fleet was minimal at best.

As disappointed as she was that her little ploy had fizzled out, Callestra knew that not having tried—simply throwing in the towel and giving up without a fight—would have been a much bigger personal failure. One she couldn't have lived with.

In every war, battles were won by taking the small victories wherever you could find them. It might be something as simple as securing a resupply mission for food rations for your troops. It could be something as trivial as securing a bridge before the enemy gets a chance to blow it up. It might be something as unpredictable as finding a sympathizer inside the enemy ranks. But it was never just one thing that won wars. It was an entire series of events which cascaded into an all-out victory.

"Continue with the mission objective. I want that main squid taken out."

"We've lost three more ships, ma'am," Tavaris said, keeping her updated.

She looked at him and then scanned the faces of her crew.

"I'm not going to pretend that we can survive this. I'm a realist. This is a suicide mission. Which is why I'm giving the order to evacuate."

"With all due respect ma'am," Tavaris said, speaking on behalf of everyone there. "We're in it with you till the very end."

Callestra smiled and then turned back to the view portal. "Good."

She raised her hand and gave the signal. Two of the Dagon cruisers pulled away from the fleet and jumped to faster than light travel. Like two swords slashing, a large X-shaped beam lit up the darkness. The massive squid flickered, lost its light and then went dark. The crew erupted with cheers.

"We're not done yet," Callestra hollered above the premature celebrating. "Make for ramming speed. Ahead full."

The *Verlag* lurched forward, pulling away from the remaining fleet. Dagon cruisers exploded one by one as their flag ship broke formation.

This is it, thought Callestra. *This is the end.*

The destruction of the super squid had left a gaping ring of debris around the Nephilim flagship. This ring of destruction absorbed much of the disruptor blasts coming from the bigger cruisers and gave the *Verlag* a straight path to the heart of the enemy fleet.

Callestra Van Morgan stood proud, arms linked behind her back as she watched them draw near. She'd use the *Verlag* to destroy that ship and take out the Nephilim fleet. Victory was all but assured.

Out of thin air, a yellow beam of light appeared on the bridge.

"Unauthorized teleport," Tavaris shouted, warning her of the security breach. His head turned toward Callestra as he reached for his blaster.

Suddenly, a woman dressed from head to toe in golden armor materialized at the center of the bridge and stood next to Callestra. She slowly turned her head and glanced at the stunned faces of the bridge crew as she stood before them. She was Nyctan...and looked awfully familiar.

"All but for Callestra," she said in a cold and commanding voice, "place your guns to your heads and take your own lives."

Callestra watched in despair as her entire bridge crew drew their blasters and shot themselves in a mass suicide. Even her loyal first officer, Sub Commander Orsek Van Tavaris placed his gun to his head, hand trembling as he fought against the spellbinding suggestion with every fiber of his being. But the woman's words couldn't be disobeyed. For whatever reason, they had complete and utmost power over them all.

"Callestra," Tavaris said, his voice calling out to her as though she could help him. As though she could stop it. His eyes locked onto hers, tears welling up, one rogue tear escaping and running down his face. Then, a muzzle flash; he pulled the trigger and ended his own life. Just as the woman in gold had commanded.

"No!" Callestra screamed.

What could be this powerful? she thought frantically. *What could compel a man to kill himself as though it were the most natural thing in the world to do...with but a mere suggestion?*

The Nyctan woman turned and locked gazes with her. Black eyes with a golden ring around the circumference of where the iris should be stared back at her almost apologetically.

"The famous Callestra Van Morgan. Your rise to prominence has been much talked about even among the Nephilim security council. You know, when H'aaztre first informed me that you were special, I didn't believe him. But, now, I can see it too. I can see what he saw in you that first time he watched you smiling as you laid waste to our fleet."

"I recognize you now," Callestra said, trying to hold her rage back and keep it from overwhelming her. "You're Azra'il Nun. I thought you were dead."

"Yes. You're not mistaken, my dear. The Azra'il Nun you knew is dead." The woman in gold waved her hand across her body and continued, "I am the Voice of his Glory. The Voice of H'aaztre."

"Voice of H'aaztre?"

"I am but a humble servant. A representative, you might say. I represent His word. And His word is His will. And His will be done as spoken to his acolytes, whispered in our ears by the Gilded Master himself, that we may heed his wishes and carry them out so that others may see the truth and be brought into obedience of him."

"You killed my people," Callestra said, her words colder and sharper than shards of ice.

Azra'il shrugged. "They were all going to die anyway. I simply saved them from an inevitable suffering. And I can spare your life, too. All you must do is kneel before me and pledge yourself to H'aaztre and his might."

"Never," Callestra snarled. She drew up her disrupter pistol with lightening quick speed and said, "Now, kindly remove yourself from my bridge or I will."

Azra'il kicked her head back and laughed. "I admire your spunk."

Callestra began to pull the trigger when Azra'il's eyes widened. "Stop," she ordered.

Callestra grunted, trying her best to pull the trigger, but she couldn't. Her own body was fighting her. She reached up with her other hand, hoping to force herself to pull the trigger, but it too disobeyed her mind. She hung, helpless, like a puppet on a string, and the voice whispering in her ear was the puppet master's.

"I was so hoping this would have gone a different way. But I will give you Dagons one thing, you are a resilient species. Perhaps the most resilient I've ever come across. No matter. In the end, all species succumb to His might."

"Why don't you spare me the proselytizing and stick your head up your own cunt and choke to death."

"Quaint," Azra'il replied, looking less than amused. "Maybe, instead, you should put that gun to your own head."

Without intending to, Callestra placed the muzzle of the gun against her own temple. Her arms and fingers, her entire body, defied her thoughts—all of them screaming for her not to listen. Not to listen to the voice telling her to commit such a terrible atrocity.

"Better yet," Azra'il said with a smile, "why don't you put the gun down and go over to that console over there and turn your canons on what remains of your own fleet and finish the job for me?" She nodded at the console and, before Callestra knew it, her legs were already moving.

"No...please, I...beg you. Don't...do this."

But it was too late. Callestra looked down and watched her own hand type in the command for the *Verlag's* canons to lock onto her fellow ships. Then she watched herself press "fire."

She spun and looked up at the view portal to witness the *Verlag* mercilessly destroy the remainder of her own fleet. Tears streamed down her face as she watched the unthinkable.

"No need to be sad, my luv. They will be remembered as heroes."

"These aren't tears of sadness," Callestra said, slowly swiveling back around to face Azra'il. "They're tears of rage."

Callestra screamed out and lunged at the woman in gold. But she merely whispered, "Halt."

Callestra, leaning forward with all her might, screamed in Azra'il's face.

"Are you quite finished?" Azra'il asked, not amused.

"I'm going to pry apart those smug lips of yours, reach down that throat, and tear out your tongue. Then I'm going to send it to your beloved god with a note telling him exactly where he can shove it."

"Blasphemer!" Azra'il shouted, and with a powerful backhand, she smacked Callestra across her left cheek and jaw.

Callestra flew across the bridge like a rag doll and crashed into a console. It crumpled under her weight and a spray of sparks shot up in the wake of the damage she'd wrought.

With a grunt, she forced herself to get up. One rib was broken for sure. The others were bruised and her shoulder dangled limply in its socket.

"Apologies," Azra'il said, brushing her hair behind her ear. "I let my emotions get the best of me."

Callestra reached up and grabbing her sagging arm, snapped it back into place. She screamed out at the sharp pain but quickly put it out of her mind. With smoldering eyes and a determined grimace, she gradually turned toward Azra'il once more.

Determined not to remain a victim of this mad psycho-bitch, she reached up and slapped her own ears so hard she burst both of her eardrums. Blood trickled down from her ears canals and she smiled.

"Stay back!" Azra'il's lips mouthed the words, but her words went unheard.

Callestra reached down into her boot and drew out a korridium blade. Then, still grinning, almost manically, she dashed forward and plunged the dagger into Azra'il's gut, where her armor was weakest.

Just then a flash outside the view portal caught both their attention. It was Novac Tamoran's warship, the *Avarice*.

A yellow beam of light came down, but this time it surrounded Callestra. "No!" she screamed out. "I have her at my mercy!" But it was too late. She was already being whisked away.

Azra'il smiled and then sank to her knees. She watched as the giant battle cruiser jumped away.

"I'll be seeing you again, Callestra Van Morgan," she said as a golden light came down to fetch her too.

Every squid entity in the Nephilim armada descended upon the *Verlag* and attached themselves to it. They syphoned off the ship's power before it could self-destruct. As the ship fell dark, the celestial squid entities used their tendrils to rip it into a thousand pieces.

32

"**Skuld?" Gyllek said,** astonished to see her crewmate standing before them. "I thought you were on vacation?"

"I was," he replied, "until the captain sent me an encoded message saying she needed my expertise on getting this place up and running again."

Angellyk lowered her blaster and took a step forward, raised her hand and greeted the fish man beneath the environmental suit that kept him alive on dry land. "It's good to see you again, Gilly."

"Gilly?" Kregor asked, raising an eyebrow.

"Why, mademoiselle," Skuld said, taking her green hand in his scaly fish hand, his long, slender, webbed fingers holding it tenderly, "the pleasure is all mine." Since he couldn't kiss her hand through the glass of his EV suit, he merely bowed slightly.

Angellyk, leaving her hand in his, smiled demurely and curtseyed just as expected of a lady when greeting a true gentleman.

"I must be missing something here," Kregor said, shaking his head in a confused manner. "Since when do you let anyone call you Gilly? And how come you're so friendly with one another?"

Gyllek laughed and then turned and slapped Kregor's meaty arm. "Relax, big guy. They're friends from before. When Jegra and Angellyk were...you know."

"Also, my time in the brig allowed us to get reacquainted."

"Ah, yes. I understand now."

Skuld glanced between Kregor and Angellyk, who shared a long glance, and he smiled. "Ah-ha! You two have hooked up!"

"What?" Kregor said, taken aback. But he couldn't deny the accusation. It was, after all, a hundred percent true.

"A gentleman doesn't ask a lady her personal affairs and a lady doesn't tell," she said, smiling coyly, her eyes still locked with Kregor's.

"Yes, well, your increased heart rates tell me quite enough."

Angellyk covered her left breast and gasped. "Why Mr. Skuld, are you undressing me with your eyes?"

"Only down to your heart, madam. And I'm proud to inform you it's one hundred and ten percent full of love."

This time she curtseyed. "Why thank you, my good sir."

"Is this normal?" Kregor asked, turning to Gyllek and thumbing over his shoulder at the two thespians. "Because this doesn't seem normal to me."

"It's normal for them. Trust me."

"All fun and games aside, I've noticed we're one captain short. Where is she?"

"Somewhere back there?" Gyllek said. "Facing off with Emperor Dakroth."

"Dakroth?!" Skuld gasped. "Dakroth is here?"

"Yes," Gyllek, said. "And that's not the worst part. He's more than pissed and is on the warpath."

"In that case, there's no time to waste. We must help the captain." Skuld turned and waved at them to accompany him. "Come, my shuttle is this way. We'll loop around and get back on board the *Skywend*."

"Hopefully we get to her in time," Gyllek said, biting her finger nails out of nervous habit.

"Don't worry, we will," Angellyk said, placing a reassuring hand on the girl's shoulder.

Gyllek smiled at her and then trailed after Skuld.

Kregor motioned for Angellyk to go on ahead of him, and she smiled and playfully nudged him as she walked past. He smiled and followed after her, his eyes incrementally sinking down to her perfectly sculpted ass.

She smiled without looking back, knowing exactly where his eyes were fixed. As they came to the corridor, she didn't even bother warning him about the low hanging bulkhead. When she heard the loud *clank* followed by his grumbling, she smiled even more.

Emperor Dakroth ran along the upper most level of the station's maintenance platform, releasing energy shots behind him without looking back.

The high energy lasers deflected off Raven's shields, which she threw up in time to deflect Dakroth's energy blasts.

Raven slowed to a walk when Dakroth came to the end of the line. Reaching the end of the walkway, he stopped and turned to face her.

"It seems we've come to an impasse."

Raven shrugged.

"Now, now, my dear Nightguard. No need to hold a grudge. Let's take the diplomatic approach and talk about this."

"There's nothing to talk about," she replied. "You tried to kill my crew. And now, I'm going to arrest you and throw you behind bars in a Correllian prison, where you will await your sentencing for criminal conduct."

"Criminal conduct?" he balked. "What criminal conduct?"

"The one that has a Blue Warrant out for your arrest. The sexual assault of a royal sovereign from another system."

She threw up the holovid display of the warrant issued by Anais Nin, declaring that Dakroth had entrapped and raped her.

"That's a blatant fabrication and you know it!"

"I'm afraid I don't know it. But I will be the one taking you in."

Dakroth scowled at Raven and then held up a glowing finger. The Dygra crystal inside his chest lit up under his blue skin and glowed bright pink.

"I'd stay back if I were you, peace keeper. I have no inclination of letting you take me down for bogus charges, and this energy bolt will tear through your shielding."

"A chance I'm willing to take," Raven said, taking one cautious step forward.

Dakroth's arm stiffened. "I'm warning you!"

Raven boldly took another step forward. Before she could press him any further, however, two yellow beams of light appeared behind her. She drew her blaster and held it fixed.

Vice Admiral Callestra Van Morgan and Sub Commander Ladgara of the *Avarice* materialized behind Raven by about ten feet. They quickly drew their blasters and trained them on the smuggler.

"Drop your weapon," Callestra demanded.

Raven scowled at her. "You drop yours."

Callestra smirked. "Look, we don't have any grievance with you. We're only here to collect the emperor."

"Raven," Ladgara said, her one good eye fixed on Raven. "Pleasure to see you again."

"I wish I could say the same, Ladgara, but it seems you're keeping some bad company."

Ladgara shrugged. "A girl has to make a living."

"And so you'd climb into bed with these snakes?"

"If they pay me well enough, I'd be willing to crawl into bed with anybody."

"That's the difference between you and me, Ladgara. I have standards."

Ladgara laughed. "Yes, I suppose you do. But remember, my little birdie, that moral compass of yours gets you into trouble more often than not."

"Step aside, Raven," Callestra said in a stern voice, her finger tightening around the trigger. "I'm not going to ask you a second time."

"Ladies! Ladies!" Dakroth said, raising his hands in a gesture of surrender. "I hand myself over to the custody of Ladgara and ask for parlay."

"Parlay?" Raven asked, her head swiveling back around. She stared at Dakroth with a dumbfounded look. "Parlay hasn't been invoked in over eight hundred years."

"Yes, well, I'm invoking it now."

"By article 15 of the Commonwealth Charter," Ladgara stated, "I accept the Lord Emperor's surrender into my custody."

Raven let out an agitated sigh and then stepped back, making room for Dakroth to pass her unaccosted.

As he walked by, he grinned at her and winked.

"I'll be seeing you again," Raven growled in a low voice.

"Is that a promise?" Dakroth asked, pausing to glance over his shoulder at her. It tickled him to see her so miffed.

"You can bet your last credit it is," she replied.

"Excellent," he said. Once he was standing beside Callestra, he gave her a thankful nod. Turning around, he smiled at Raven.

Three beams of yellow light engulfed the trio and their bodies began to dissolve, their physical essence being converted to photons and whisked away to be reassembled aboard the *Avarice*.

"Asshole," Raven muttered to herself.

Boots clamoring up the platform opposite Raven drew her attention. She turned to see who it was and spotted Onelle Te'Legra dashing toward one of the shuttles docked at the end of a long walkway.

"You there," Raven shouted, pointing her blaster at the escaped convict. "Halt!"

Onelle paused, turned to see Raven aiming a blaster at her and instead of obeying Raven's warning, she responded by flipping her the bird. Then she turned and made a mad-dash to the shuttle.

Raven let off a couple of warning shots, but Onelle ignored them. The Bre'lal woman boarded the shuttle and quickly shut the hatch. A moment later, she pulled away from the docking platform.

"Why you little…" Raven steadied her blaster across her forearm and fired off two more shots.

The disruptor's blasts scorched the small shuttle's bow as a more serious warning, but the ship didn't slow down. It merely wore the scorch marks as a badge of honor and then raced toward the open mouth of the asteroid doors at full speed.

Raven squawked with frustration and holstered her gun. Not only had she lost the emperor, but she had also lost the woman who'd tried to assassinate Jegra.

It was very rare that she ever let things get this out of hand. For whatever reason, it seemed the Fates were working against her.

No sooner had Emperor Dakroth returned to the *Avarice* with two beautiful and powerful women than he propositioned them, promising a night they wouldn't soon forget.

Jegra had once explained to him how Dagon promiscuity was much like the casual sexual encounters among the Icelandic people of her world. According to her recollection, and a brief mention about something called a one-night stand in Reykjavík, Icelanders didn't engage in prolonged bouts of courtship, but rather preferred to find their partners by having frequent casual sex and whittling down those who were the most compatible versus those who weren't.

It was no surprise to him, then, that it was mainly the Icelandic women who initiated the sexual advances. It was the same in Dagon culture. The women there were the most sexually liberated in the galaxy.

That said, being emperor did afford one big advantage: women almost never turned him down.

His arms wrapped around Callestra's slender waist as she rode him, rocking with the ebb and flow of his motion. She chirped excitedly, inviting him into her depths, and his hands ran down the rolling curves of her form until they came to rest on her thighs. He dug his fingers into her soft blue flesh and held on as though he never wanted to let go of this heavenly creature.

At the same time, Dakroth had his face buried deep inside Ladgara's groin. Ladgara closed her eye and moaned loudly, rocking her hips and rubbing her nectar all over the emperor's wagging tongue and face.

She didn't care if he couldn't breathe because even the mere thought of him smothering himself to heavenly bliss between her thighs made her excited. She had the emperor of the entire friggin' galaxy at her mercy, and that alone was enough to make her gush. And gush she did, letting her wetness pour out of her and into his parted lips.

Both women faced each other and leaned forward and kissed. Their soft, pink, forked-tongues flicked and danced as a kind of handshake between strangers as they got to know one another intimately. That was the tantalizing part of threesomes, though. You were allowed to taste-test the sample platter, choosing the treats most to your liking.

But even though they felt a natural attraction drawing them deeper into each sultry kiss, they couldn't be more different in appearance. Ladgara was covered head to foot in tattoos, whereas Callestra's flesh didn't have a mark on it. Ladgara's body was further exemplified by its series of battle scars, including her missing eye, all of which she wore as badges of honor. Callestra, meanwhile, appeared to be the pristine virgin—not yet fully touched by the cruel fist of experience. Yet appearances could be deceiving. Because although their looks were polar opposites in almost every way, they were kindred spirits at heart.

Ladgara's hand slid up Callestra's side, up to her chest, where she squeezed her rounded breasts, letting their softness slowly gather between her splayed and clasping hands like kneaded dough gathering between the fingers of a baker's firm hands.

A powerful sensation built up inside of Callestra. It was like the hot excitement of a primordial plasma gathering at the beginning of all space and time. It was the crest of a wave breaking and crashing in on itself. It was the heavy rains saturating the fertile soil that gave rise to a new beginning. It was in this pregnant moment, where everything crescendos and the swelling can no longer be contained, the instant before the explosion, that Callestra teetered.

She felt it growing deep down inside her. And then, suddenly it was everywhere and she couldn't contain it.

Overwhelmed by the sensation engulfing her, her entire body tensed as a tremendous orgasm surged through her flesh. Callestra broke away from Ladgara's embrace and gasped loudly. Unexpectedly, she rose off Dakroth's hips as if the goddess of love herself had possessed her. At the same time, she spontaneously squirted all over his abdomen, drenching him in her milky nectar. If he was the dark void at the beginning of it all, she was singularity that spewed out of it; the light that birthed the entire universe.

"Shit, shit, shit," she said, sliding off him, embarrassed by her tempestuous and sudden loss of control. She had no idea how overwhelming her passions could be, and they had accumulated into a perfect storm of ecstasy that not even she had been ready for.

"Quite impressive, actually," Dakroth said, reaching around her waist and pulling her close to him. She stretched out beside him, panting heavily and letting the final orgasmic ripples work their way through her body. She moaned as his fingers slipped between her legs and began teasing her newfound sensitivity with probing touches and playful petting—pushing her beyond her climax and into uncharted territory. She absolutely loved it.

Ladgara slid down on Dakroth's right side and ran her fingers along his taught abs. She scooped up Callestra's essence and licked the young woman's nectar off her experienced fingers. She smacked noisily at Callestra's juices, delighting in their natural sweetness.

"My father will never forgive me for this," Callestra said, letting her words escape her lips without thought of the present company.

"Your father?" Ladgara asked. "What does he have to do with anything?" She nibbled on her finger and smiled at Callestra with a sultry yet inquisitive look.

A shocked look came over her face and, realizing what she had said, she looked away in embarrassment. "Never mind. It's nothing."

Dakroth laughed. "Yes, well, I'm sure your father has better things to worry about than who you desire to sleep with."

Callestra blushed, diverted her eyes, and didn't dare say another word. It was bad form to bring up your dad in the middle of a three-way orgy. *What the hell was she thinking?*

Ladgara rose up and then climbed onto Dakroth, taking the position that Callestra had been in moments earlier. "My turn," she said gleefully as she reached down and fished for Dakroth's shaft. Once she found it, she guided him past the petals of her garden path, each fold parting with a natural ease at his coming.

Dakroth let out a pleasurable groan as Ladgara sank down onto him and gradually began rocking her hips. Dakroth grabbed her blue, pear-shaped hips with both hands and rocked with her, matching her motion with carefully timed thrusts.

"Don't ever stop fucking me," Ladgara said.

Taking a breath, Dakroth informed her, "I can go all night, my luv. The only question is, can the both of you?"

Callestra repositioned herself, taking Ladgara's previous position, and straddling Dakroth's face she reached down and guided his chin toward her slit. "Less talking, Your Excellency. More licking."

With a newfound enthusiasm, he gladly obliged.

An incoming call chimed and a holovid display of Novac Tamoran's giant face appeared at the foot of their bed. His blue glowing holographic head swiveled around to find all three entwined in a hot, wet orgy of physical delight. He raised an eyebrow, partly impressed with how fast Dakroth had gotten the two women into bed with him. But, also impressed by Callestra's angelican form. He'd never seen a more heavenly creature than her.

The glow of his blue hologram bathed the trio in azure highlights and cerulean undertones, alerting them to the fact that they weren't quite alone and they all paused what they were doing and looked over at the giant floating head.

As much fun as his voyeuristic peeping was, there were more important matters that took priority. He cleared his throat before speaking. "Sub Commander Ladgara," he said in his deep throaty voice; the one he typically reserved for intimidating milksops and lily-livers. He took his pirate hat off and rubbed his hand through his woolly salt and pepper hair. "Your presence is needed on the bridge."

"Give me ten more minutes," she said.

"You have five," Tamoran replied, placing his hat back on his head and adjusting it. He glanced one more time at Callestra's naked body and then the holovid flickered and the giant head disappeared.

All three participants paused and shared amused glances.

"Awkward," Callestra said in a sing-song voice.

Spontaneously, they all burst out laughing as though they'd been caught by their parents doing something they shouldn't be doing.

Dakroth slapped Ladgara's ass. "You'd better hurry it up, my luv. After all, you're under a direct order to satisfy me in five minutes."

"Is that a challenge?" she said, smiling down at him, her tourmaline pink eye sparking in the dim light that seeped up behind the bed via the subtle backlighting and silhouetted her form.

"I sure hope so," Dakroth replied with a suave grin.

Ladgara tossed her wavy purple hair over her shoulder and, thrusting out her chest and arching her back, started riding Dakroth cowgirl style with as much vigor as a bull rider. Dakroth lay back, rested his head in Callestra's lap, and watched Ladgara go to town on him like a seasoned pro.

As she worked her magic, he studied the numerous tattoos on her body and found one he especially liked. It was the great Cthylla, numerous tentacles reaching out as if they were latching onto Ladgara's own flesh. Her demonic wings spread wide and her numerous nautiloid eyes all seemingly fixed on those who gazed upon her, reminding them that if they stared too long her terrible and zealous wrath would befall them too.

Just then Ladgara screamed out as she climaxed but didn't slow down for a moment. She pushed her stamina and tested his with each thrust of the pelvis and each clap of their flesh.

Dakroth grunted as he lost himself inside of her. The great Cthylla had drained another victim. She began to climb off when Dakroth stopped her. "Don't go," he insisted.

"Apologies, my liege, but duty calls," she replied apologetically. She fetched her clothes and began dressing, letting him watch her as she did and secretly enjoying the attention.

Dakroth waved his hand and dismissed her from her obligation to be with him. As far as he was concerned, she'd done a satisfactory job. And besides, he'd have her again this evening after her shift. When she was tired, needing to relieve the day's stress, and a little bit salty.

"Remind me," Dakroth asked, Callestra's head resting on his chest as she lay in bed with him, "why in the galaxy I ever fell for that lumbering barbarian woman when Dagon women this fine can satisfy me like no other?"

"How about I help you forget her instead?" Callestra said, a sly grin on her face. Dakroth smiled and leaned over to accept her sumptuous lips. They shared a long kiss and, as they pulled away, she found herself wanting to kiss him all over again.

"You two crazy kids have fun," Ladgara called out to them. She grabbed her leather buccaneer coat off the hanger and slipped it on over her uniform.

Before exiting the room, she stretched her head around and blew them both a kiss from over her shoulder. Her crooked smiled stayed on her face as she departed and the doors slid shut behind her.

Dakroth let out a long sigh and quietly said, "I think I love you."

"What?" Callestra asked, batting her eyes at him.

There was a long pause as they stared at one another for longer than seemed normal, trying to gauge whether this strange attraction they felt between them was just the hormone saturated sex talking…or something more.

"That's ridiculous," Callestra said. "You don't even know me."

"But I feel like we've known each other for a lifetime."

She laughed, and brushed her hair out of her eyes. "Does that line actually work on women?"

"I'm serious," he said. "I have never met a more perfect specimen than you."

In the Dagoni culture, that was the highest compliment. But Callestra didn't know if he really meant it. After all, Jegra was the textbook definition of a perfect specimen. "What about your beloved barbarian woman? Isn't she perfect in every way?"

"Don't compare yourself to her. You are Dagon. She is but a mere ape masquerading as something more."

"But you don't deny her perfection."

"Would you have me to lie to you?"

"No," Callestra answered, without hesitation. "Be honest with me. Always."

"In that case, yes, some part of me is irresistibly attracted to her. But we aren't compatible here," he said, reaching out and touching Callestra's heart. "Or here," he added, touching her temple.

"And we are?" she asked, reaching up and taking his hand in hers. She was genuinely curious, because although she'd loved him from the time she began to notice boys all the way up to this moment, she could scarcely believe he felt the same for her in return.

"If you're not convinced, perhaps we should explore these feelings further?" he asked, having used his telepathy to read her mind. She felt him probing her thoughts, but didn't force him out. That kind of acceptance felt good. It felt like going home. There were no walls or barriers between them, and that made all the difference in the galaxy to him. And to her.

"I think I might like that," she answered.

Dakroth reeled Callestra in, pressing his lips to her. Rolling on top of her, their sultry kisses grew wet and hot as they melted into one another, searching each other's mind, body, and soul for that thing they'd been missing their whole lives; unprejudiced, unlimited, love. A love that wasn't bound by rules or regulations. A love that didn't need to appease the impossible expectations of overbearing fathers or cater to the whims of a capricious society. Just a love that was free to be completely open and exist as its own thing apart from what the world or anyone else thought of it.

Raven found her crew waiting for her on the *Skywend*. She looked over to find Skuld manning the science station on the bridge and she smiled at him. "Glad you could join us, old friend."

"Apparently the battle against the Nephilim has taken a turn for the worse."

"I thought as much. I just saw Vice Admiral Callestra Van Morgan."

"Van Morgan?" Kregor said, looking at her. "The vice admiral of the fleet was here?"

"Yes," Raven said. "Which doesn't bode well. She came to collect the emperor."

"That means the Dagon fleet has fallen," Angellyk said in a stunned voice.

"What will we do?" asked Gyllek.

"We do exactly what Jegra ordered us to do. We get this station operational and start building ships again."

Everyone shared an understanding look and then, without even being ordered to, returned to their duties. They had a lot of work to do and very little time to do it in.

33

Sweat glazed Danica's forehead as Jegra sat beside her bed and dabbed her face with a damp cloth. "Hang in there, babe," Jegra said. "The doctor said with this strain of Nividium, withdrawals will feel ten times worse, but that you'll survive."

"How would the doc like to survive my foot up her ass?" Danica asked agitatedly.

Off to the corner of the medical lab, Amora raised an eyebrow and shot Jegra a worried look. Jegra smiled at her as if to say that Danica was only joking and then looked away.

"It's not Amora's fault that you're in this mess," Jegra said as clemently as possible. "You did this to yourself. So be nice."

"I know," Danica mumbled apologetically. Through agonizing grunts and groans she managed to add, "It's just…right now…this…totally sucks. My entire body aches. And I'd do anything…literally anything…to get another hit."

"I know," Jegra replied. "That's why you're confined to the med-bay until doctor Amora gives you the okay to leave."

"You know something?" Danica chuckled through another groan. "Sometimes you can be a royal pain in my ass."

"What?" Jegra asked, reaching under Dani's covers. "This ass?"

She pinched Danica. Hard. Dani let out a yelp and then slapped Jegra's hand away.

"Exactly like that! That's exactly what I'm talking about."

"But your mind is off your other pain now, right?"

Danica leaned back and did a self-check. "Holy shit, you're right," she chirped excitedly. Rolling onto her side, Danica threw off her covers and pulled aside her medical gown, revealing a perfectly round butt cheek with a dark blueish-blackish bruise. "My lord, Jegra. Did you have to pinch me so hard? That's going to be there for weeks."

Reaching up inside Danica's gown, Jegra grabbed a soft bit of tissue near Danica's belly. "I'm just getting started," teased Jegra.

"Don't you dare," Danica said, prying Jegra's hand loose and shoving it back toward her. "Don't even dare think about it!"

Both women laughed and Jegra leaned over Dani's bed and touched her forehead to hers. They closed their eyes and then shared a soft kiss.

"No, don't! Please!" a voice cried out in terror from across the room.

Jegra leapt to her feet and spun around only to find Admiral Grendok standing at the foot of the strange girl's bed with a blaster drawn. The girl squirmed to try and get away, her back up against the wall.

"What's the meaning of this?" Jegra demanded to know.

"I was about to ask the same thing," doctor Amora said, a deep crease forming at the bridge of her nose as she frowned in displeasure.

"Admiral!" Jegra said, raising her voice. "You will answer me."

"She's not supposed to be here," Grendok said, holding the blaster firm and keeping it trained on the girl.

"What do you mean she's not supposed to be here? Where else would she be?"

"No. You don't understand," informed the satyr. "She's not supposed to exist at all."

"W-what are you saying?" the girl asked, her eyes wide.

Jegra could tell she wanted answers just as badly as the rest of them. And it seemed the only one who had any was currently out of his bleedin' goat mind.

"Dammit!" Grendok growled. He lowered the gun and everyone let out a collective sigh of relief. "The truth is, this girl is a genetically modified clone."

"A designer mod?" Amora asked, drawing up a scanning device.

"Not just any clone, either," Grendok said, turning toward the empress. "She's *your* clone."

"*My clone?*" Jegra laughed. "But she's Dagon."

"Dakroth used his DNA as well when he designed her. But, essentially, her genome is a 99.9% match to yours."

"I'm afraid he's telling the truth," Amora said. "I didn't get around to analyzing the blood sample I took earlier. But it's showing a tri-weave genome."

Jegra shot her a confused look.

"It means there are three separate DNA strands woven together to form a completely original life form. Think of her more as a daughter."

"A daughter?" Jegra echoed, still not able to belief her ears.

"I'm not a clone," the girl said, slipping out of bed and backing into the corner of the room. She reached up and put her finger to her temple. "I have memories. From before."

"*Designer memories*, I'm afraid," Amora said. "Programmed in like computer code. Those memories, experiences, all of it, are just simulacrum."

"But I have a family. I have…parents. I may not be able to picture them up here," she said, pointing to her head again. "But I can feel them in here." She covered her heart with her hand.

"Look," Amora said, "we'll get to the bottom of this. But I'm going to need to run more tests."

The girl looked over at Jegra and in that instant she realized everything the doctor had told her was true. She broke down crying and Jegra opened her arms to her.

"Oh, honey, it'll be okay." The girl rushed into her arms and they embraced. Jegra turned her eyes to Grendok and in a cold and hard voice, as sharp as her battle-axe, she said, "Nobody will harm you here. That's a promise."

Grendok holstered his blaster and looked away.

"We have to keep this to ourselves," Danica said. "This news cannot leave this room. If word gets out that Dakroth has made a designer clone, it will create civil unrest. Not only that, there would be those who would seek to harm the girl. Maybe even take her life."

The girl buried her face into Jegra's chest and began to sob.

"Dani," Jegra said. "You and Dakroth were studying my genome quite extensively, correct?"

Danica nodded. "That's right. Like I told you, Dakroth wanted to weaponize you. At first, I thought he merely wanted to make an army of clones to do his bidding. Never in a million years did I think he'd actually create a chimera."

"All I see is a very lovely, scared, young woman," Jegra said, lowering her eyes and smiling upon the girl.

The girl wiped her eyes with the back of her hand and took a step back. She scanned all the faces turned toward her and fought off the urge to start crying all over again.

"Well," Grendok grumbled, "what are we going to call you? We need to call you something other than 'girl.'"

"I want to be called Lycia," the girl finally said after giving it some thought.

"Lycia?" Jegra asked, raising an eyebrow.

"Yes. After the homeland of the first chimera."

"How do you know about that?" Jegra asked. "That's ancient Earth mythology."

"I don't know," the girl replied. "I just know."

Jegra turned to Danica to search her face for answers, but she was just as baffled as everyone else.

"It's possible she has your memories too," Amora answered, looking at the girl and then Jegra.

"My memories?" Jegra echoed. "Including Dakroth?"

"Dakroth," the girl whispered.

Visions of flesh rubbing up against flesh, moaning, and the sensation of pure ecstasy came over her. Her knees grew weak and she began to sink. Jegra caught her in her arms and asked, "Is everything all right?"

"I'm fine," the girl said, trying to shake the erotic visions from her mind. "It's nothing."

"Fine, then," Grendok said. "Lycia it is. Lycia Alakandra, daughter to Jegra Alakandra, and heir to the royal lineage of Dagon."

With that Grendok grunted and stormed out of the room.

"What's got his goat?" Lycia asked, thumbing over her shoulder. She turned to see all three women staring at her with wide eyes and open jaws.

"You're so totally my daughter!" Jegra exclaimed. Delighted, she reached out and embraced Lycia, drawing her back to her bosom.

"I'm not going to call you mom," Lycia mumbled, her face mashed into Jegra's breast.

"What was that, dear?" Jegra squeezed her even more.

"I'm seriouth…I campt breathd in hrmmm."

"I didn't quite catch that," Jegra said, not relinquishing her bear-hug.

Lycia rolled her eyes and surrendered. "Mom…!" she gasped, pulling back with all her might and taking in a big gulp of air. "I can't breathe with your tits mashed up in my face."

"*Ahhh,*" Jegra said, finally letting go of the girl, "isn't she sweet?"

"Why are my lips so salty?" the girl asked, puckering and licking her lips as she sampled the strange seasoning lingering on her lips.

"Sorry," Jegra said, fanning herself. "Today's been a hot one."

"Oh," Lycia said, making a sour face. "That's so gross."

"Oh, you'll get used to it," Jegra said, waving her hand and brushing Lycia's negativity away.

"Not likely," she said, using her medical gown to wipe her lips off.

"Suit yourself," Jegra said with a shrug. "But your father never complained."

Lycia cringed as more explicit visions of Dakroth flooded into her mind. This time he was kissing Jegra's sternum, dappling her chest with a thousand feathery kissed. Then his blue lips found her ping areolas, his forked tongue swirling around her nipples. His teeth grazed Jegra's nipples and Lycia shuddered as she felt every sensation.

"What's the matter?" Amora asked.

"Nothing," Lycia lied. "Just a headache. And he's not my father," she said sternly, shooting Jegra the evil eye. "He's no better than that Frankenstein person. And I'm just his creation."

Jegra turned to Dani and looked for some support, but Dani was at a loss. "Don't look at me, she's your kid. Not mine."

"Lycia," Jegra said, motioning for her daughter to accompany her. "Let's get you out of those medical threads and into some real clothes."

"Uh, Your Majesty, I'm not quite finished running tests yet."

"I think we've had enough excitement for one day," Jegra said. "What she needs now is a good meal and a nice night's sleep. You may finish your tests in the morning."

Amora nodded and let the women leave.

Halfway down the corridor, Lycia cleared her throat and caught Jegra's attention. "You're not really going to make me call you mom in public, are you?"

"I was thinking about it," Jegra said with an impish smile.

"You do realize I have all your memories, right?"

Jegra stood still and looked over at the girl.

"So, maybe you can understand that I recall his every little touch. How his tongue tasted inside my mouth. What he felt like when he slid himself inside of me and how my legs trembled with each thrust of his—"

"Okay!" Jegra said, throwing up her hands in surrender. "Point taken. It's a little bit weird." She paused for a bit and rested her hand on her hip as she eyed the girl up and down.

"What?" Lycia asked in a churlish tone.

"Well, what would you like to call me?"

Now it was Lycia's turn to place her hand on her hips and eye Jegra up and down. "I suppose Jumbo-Tron is off the table? You know, because you have massively huge tits."

Jegra smiled. "Ha-ha. Very funny."

"What about...My Milky Pleasure?"

"Are all of these going to be boob jokes?" Jegra asked.

"I'm just getting warmed up," Lycia said.

"Wonderful!" Jegra laughed softly and then turned and continued up the hall. Lycia followed after her rattling off other potential, and unsurprisingly derogatory, nicknames.

"What about Funbags Jegra, or better yet, Queen of Silicone? No, wait, J-Lo Love Pillows! Or L.L. Cool J.J.! Lady Loves me some Cool Jegra Jugs."

"How about you pick something that doesn't involve my breasts or we'll just go back to 'mom.'"

Lycia cringed. "Fine, have it your way."

"I'm listening," Jegra said, glancing over her shoulder at the girl. She wasn't exaggerating, either. She was genuinely curious as what the girl was going to decide to call her.

"How about...just...Jegra?"

Jegra paused at the end of the hallway and placed her hand to her chin and pretended to give it ample consideration. "You know what?" she said, "I like it."

"You do realize it's just your name, right?" Lycia winked at Jegra and then sauntered up the hall, leaving Jegra there having to bite her own tongue so as not to give in to her desire to chastise the smart-ass version of herself.

"I was never that mouthy as a teenager," she said to herself watching Lycia's backside hang out of the completely open medical gown.

Jegra smiled fondly and watched the girl head up the hall without so much as telling her that her ass was hanging out. Soon enough she caught up to the girl and showed her to her room.

As they entered the room and crossed a standing mirror, Lycia caught a glimpse of her backside and then turned and glowered at Jegra. She had let her pass all those staff members, from maids to butlers to some security staff with her butt on full display. "Could you be more of a bitch!?" Lycia asked, still fuming at the slight.

Jegra shrugged. "Takes one to know one, my dear."

Lycia gave up trying to one-up the empress. It seemed that they were equal sparring partners and the sniping was getting a little out of control. "Truce?" Lycia asked.

"Truce," Jegra confirmed.

The girl smiled and then stripped her gown off and picked a set of clothes from the wardrobe. She was surprised when they fit her so perfectly. "Whose clothes are these?" she asked.

"These are Raphine's. You'll meet her soon enough."

"Where is she now?" Lycia asked, her curiosity ever piqued.

"She's on a very important mission for me. I'll tell you about it at a more suitable time. Right now, let's just get you dressed and then get you something to eat."

Lycia nodded, finding Jegra's suggestion quite agreeable. Besides, she was famished. Once she finished dressing, she asked, "Will I be staying here with her? With Raphine?"

"Until we can have your own room set up. Will that be a problem?"

"No. In fact, it will be nice to have someone to talk to."

"Good. I'll see to it then. And since you're about the same age, you'll join her in taking lessons with Danica."

"You mean, like school?"

"Also, martial arts training. War strategy. Things like that. I think you'll find Danica a quite excellent teacher." Jegra pointed her finger at the girl at the last minute and added, "But no hitting on her. She's mine."

"I wouldn't dream of it!" Lycia said, drawing back away from Jegra. "Besides, you two make such a lovely geriatric couple."

A shocked gasp escaped Jegra's lips. "Now that was some low hanging fruit right there."

"Sorry," Lycia replied. "I just wanted you to know that I'm not into grandmas. I'd rather find someone my own age."

"Grandma now, is it?" Jegra asked, both hands firmly on her hips as she eyed the girl with a suspicious look.

"I wouldn't sweat it," Lycia replied. "You look good for your age." She slapped Jegra's ass and then headed toward the kitchen.

"Hey," Jegra called out to her. Lycia held up and turned. "How do you know where the kitchen is?"

"I guess that's been programmed in, too," she said with a shrug.

"Yeah, I guess so," Jegra whispered as she watched the girl make her own way to the kitchen.

Jegra couldn't help but wonder how recent the girl's memories were. Lycia didn't seem to recall anything before Dakroth's mysterious disappearance. Because if she did, she'd be looking for Raven.

The girl paused under the archway of the hallway door and turned to Jegra. Her face was serious and, for a moment, Jegra thought she'd been found out.

"Hey," Lycia inquired, "what's for dinner anyway?"

A huge wave of relief came over Jegra and she laughed away her needless worrying. "I'm pretty sure they can whip you up anything from scratch. If not, there's always the food synthesizers."

"*Bleck!*" Lycia said, pointing a finger at the back of her open mouth and pretending to gag. "I hate synthesized food. It always has that artificial after-taste that's just not satisfying. No matter how much you eat, it never feels like you've eaten anything."

"I know what you mean," Jegra replied. She laughed again to try and mask the fact that her first laugh was covering up her jittery nerves. The girl probably just thought she was a flake or something. But better that than have the truth revealed.

"Lycia," Jegra called from the doorway of Raphine's bedroom. "You go on ahead of me. I'll join you shortly."

Lycia waved nonchalantly and carried on her merry way. She hadn't had a full meal in days and was dying of hunger. At least, that's the way her stomach told it every time it gurgled and growled as though it were in its death throes.

Once Lycia was out of sight, Jegra turned and slipped back into the room. Heading over to Raphine's writing desk, she opened the box tucked underneath. Glowing light spilled out along with a bunch of glowing tentacles.

"It's time, my friend. Let's go and get our girl back," Jegra said. She reached down and let the tentacles coil around her hand and up her arm. She then drew out La'Garren, the squid entity that Raphine was keeping as a pet.

34

A stitch began to form in Raphine's side as she ran. She'd been running non-stop for two and a half hours now and needed to take a short break. She slowed to a jog. She looked around as she caught her breath and her bearings. But other than running due east, she didn't have the foggiest clue as to which jungle she was in or on which continent. All she knew was that it wasn't populated and that it was in the thick of Dagon's rainforest.

Her only comfort in all this was that when she looked up, she could see Thessalonica hanging above her like a glorious iridescent pearl. And just knowing that Jegra and her friends were up there gave her some small semblance of comfort.

Raphine grabbed her aching side and leaned up against one of the thick tree trunks. The cool, moss-caked bark felt good against her hot, sweaty skin as she stood panting. After another few deliberate breaths, she pushed off the tree and started jogging again. The ache in her side hadn't gone away but she did her best to push it out of her mind.

A couple of kilometers later she collapsed mid-stride and crashed to the dirt. Exhausted, overheated, and almost certainly dehydrated, she had nothing left to give. Her limbs were like rubber and she felt so dizzy that even if she could get back up, she'd have just walked in circles until she collapsed again.

She groaned and rolled onto her back, twisting her head and spitting up muck infused with leaves. Her heaving chest expanded and contracted as she took deep gulps of humid air to try and take in enough oxygen to cool her. She couldn't afford to black out. Not now. *Blacking out would be bad,* she told herself.

Raphine sat up and unzipped the jumpsuit partially, letting what little breeze there was slip into her sweat saturated garments and help cool her a few degrees. A few degrees was all it took to make a difference between getting up again or passing out from heat exhaustion. Luckily, she was able to get a handle on the throbbing in her temples, shake off the lightheadedness, and get back onto her feet.

If she put enough distance between herself and the search party, she could afford an hour or two of downtime. But she wasn't going to let her time go to waste. Looking around, she found a plump vine and went over to it. Using her boxcutter, she sliced the vine and pulled it to her mouth like a hose. Fresh water from the canopy above her dribbled out of the vine and into her mouth. After she'd thoroughly drained the vine, she wiped her moist chin with the back of her hand and let out a refreshed sigh.

Until now, Raphine hadn't known how Zallek was getting his product off world with the blockade up, since teleportation was impossible without being detected. But the fact that she was on *terra firma* only sought to confirm her suspicions. Zallek was using cloaked cargo ships to transport Nividium undetected.

In all likelihood the raw product was grown and harvested here on Dagon Prime. Then it was taken to Thessalonica where it was processed into its current form before being shipped to every far-spanning corner of the galaxy.

Before Jegra's arrival, Nividium sales were doing okay. It wasn't popular enough to be all the rage. But the drug seemed to rise in popularity along with Jegra's rise in fame. More and more spectators went to the games to have a good time and get high. And with no regulations or checks on recreational drugs in Arena City, a Nividium boom was bound to happen. She just didn't expect to get caught up in any of it.

A buzzing noise came from the trees; Raphine froze in place and slowly turned and scanned the canopy of trees. The jostling of branches above her drew her attention to a patch of the canopy. A drone abruptly shot out of the thicket and began scanning the area with red lasers that reached out like the spindly tendrils of a sea anemone. She ducked behind an old, twisting and knotted root of a tree and pulled some nearby ferns over her for added camouflage.

The drone buzzed around a bit, scanning random areas in its search for her, but, not finding anything, it quickly flew off to scan a different section of forest.

She let out a deep sigh once it had cleared the area and she slowly rose back up through the foliage. She looked around for signs of additional surveillance but was relieved when she didn't find any.

Still, she knew the drone would be back. They always tracked back. And if it caught her, the security detail would know precisely where she was right down to the millimeter.

The way she saw it, she had two options. Continue running and hope to find civilization before civilization found her, or stay right where she was and mount a defense.

It was a no brainer. It was time to stop being the prey and become the hunter.

Raphine began collecting dry branches in her arms and carried them over to a log. She sat and carved sharp points into the ends of each and every stick. She also made snares with vines and set up trip wires throughout the forest, covering everything with mulch and leaves.

Almost two hours later, with the sun beginning to set through the trees, Raphine managed to get a fire going. Next to the fire was a mud pit she'd fashioned, using vine water to fill it. Bending down, she smeared mud onto her face and chest, darkening her bright green skin and making it blend into the rest of the jungle.

After applying a liberal coat of mud to help camouflage herself, she rose back up and took a thicker branch, one end tightly wrapped with dry vines, and held it to the fire. The end lit up and burned like a torch. She slowly turned and raised the burning torch high above her and waved it in the air. "Come and get me!" she shouted, drawing the drone back to her position. "I'm right here!"

After a minute, the buzzing sound returned and the insect-like eyes of the drone zoomed in on her. She waved the flaming stick some more, allowing its motion sensors to detect the movement. It scanned her with its red lasers, mapping her features. It registered she was the target and an orange flashing beacon turned on.

The drone flew upward, piercing the canopy overhead, its beacon pulsating to help mark her exact location. Then it began to blare an emergency siren, startling the sleeping birds in the surrounding tree canopy and sending up a flurry of squawking birds.

"I found it," a voice called out. "The beacon. It's over here."

They were already here.

Slowly slinking back into the shadows, Raphine tossed the stick onto the fire. A whimsical dance of hot sparks erupted from the disturbance and then settled back down, leaving only incandescent coals smoldering softly on a bed of white ash.

With a long, thin strand of resilient vine wrapped around both fists like makeshift boxing gloves, she secured the cutter to her right, fastening it to her palm so that even if she lost her grip the blade would stay with her. A trick she had seen Jegra do in the arena once after having fought to the point of exhaustion.

Voices approached and she quickly crouched down out of sight next to a large tree with upturned roots, fading into the shadows as though she were one herself.

Two guards stalked past her position but they didn't notice her, not even as the whites of her eyes peered out at them from behind the gnarled roots. After they'd passed, she reached over and grabbed one of the spears she'd made and placed in strategic locations throughout the area. Without knowing where they were or what to look for, each spear blended seamlessly into the rest of the layers of the jungle.

Not making a sound, she stepped into the clearing and launched the spear. It sailed through the air and pierced the guard on the right. He yelped out in pain and shock and then looked down and clutched the sharp stick protruding from his chest. He glanced once at his partner and then fell to the ground. Dead.

The second hunter spun around, disruptor rifle raised, and shouted, "Show yourself, girl!"

"Right here," Raphine whispered into his ear from behind. His eyes widened as she dragged the razor-sharp blade across his neck, opening him up as though she were gutting a fish.

The man grasped at his neck wound and Raphine shoved him out of the way. He toppled over his friend and crashed to the ground beside him.

Raphine stared down at her handiwork and felt sick to her stomach. She hadn't ever killed anybody before and her hands trembled uncontrollably. Without warning, she felt the vomit rise into the back of her throat and she bent over the log of a dead tree and hurled. That's when a blaster shot rang out and a scorching burn tore across her right thigh.

She screamed out in agony and looked down. Luckily, it was just a flesh wound. She looked back up to find that the drone had returned and it was equipped with a laser gun. Snatching up a large rock, she yelled as she launched the projectile.

The stone smacked the drone's central eye, shattering it. Unable to see, the drone over-corrected and then lost control of itself and spiraled out of control. Rebounding off a tree, it came back toward her, buzzing and whining like an angry insect. To her surprise, it began firing laser blasts haphazardly in every direction. One of the shots came dangerously close to her and she decided to put the thing out of its misery.

Raphine ducked down, picked up a large stick in both hands, and inched toward it. When it was in range, she wound back and then swung with all her strength. A resounding *crack* rang out and the drone twirled violently away, crashed into a tree trunk, and fell to the dirt, its rotary fans hopelessly stuck in the mud.

Its little motors whined in protest as if begging for mercy as it tried to free itself from the sticky black muck, but the more it struggled, the more it seemed to get itself deeper into trouble. A grin came across her face as she stood over it.

"None of you understand," she said, raising the stick high above her head. "I'm not trapped out here with you. You're trapped out here with me." The crunch of the heavy branch squashing the drone added a final period to her sentence and made it feel, somehow, more definitive.

She bashed it again just for good measure, letting out a scream as the machine's internals sparked and hissed one last time before fading away for good. She didn't care if they heard her. They already knew she was out here. Might was well lay down the welcome mat for them.

The burn on her thigh throbbed terribly. Tearing off the sleeves of her jumpsuit, she tied them together and wrapped her wound. It wasn't a perfect bandage, but it would suffice. As least it would keep the burn from getting any more infected than it already was, and would prevent the frighteningly large jungle mosquitos from making a meal out of her.

No sooner had she finished tying off her leg than several more voices rang out. The crunch of branches and footsteps fast encroaching upon her position from three sides sent her into heightened alert. Raphine closed her eyes. She took in a deep breath and calmed her racing heart. She needed to focus.

Almost as soon as she had gotten a hold of herself, a torch light settled onto her exact position. But all it landed on was an empty patch of jungle turf. She'd successfully ghosted.

One thing nearly all Bre'lal people could do was "ghost." She remembered Jegra talking about how her sister Abethca had ghosted her in the arena. Jegra had referred to it as invisibility, but it wasn't turning invisible so much as it was the unique property of their skin and its inexplicable ability to refract light.

The only problem was that in order to do it for prolonged periods of time, you had to have pristine focus and excellent muscle control. It was like flexing every muscle in your body at the same time and holding it until you felt as though you'd cramp. It wasn't pleasant at all.

And although she wasn't as hardy as her older sister had been, nor as skilled when it came to fighting, she was able to do it for short stints. Long enough, she hoped, to finish what she started.

"I think I found something," a voice called out. A man stood over the smoking remains of the drone and waved over two more men. "She was here. And quite recently by the looks of it."

"What should we do, boss?"

"Fan out," a stout man said, waving his burly arms across the jungle backdrop. "She's out here somewhere."

"And when we find her?"

The leader smiled ominously. "Kill her."

The third man, who stood several feet away, looked over at the other two with a startled expression on his face. "Um…guys. I think I've found Rothgal and Xorthan."

He looked down at the remains lying at his feet. The other two came over to inspect whatever it was he was looking at.

"At least, what's left of them," the third guard observed, glancing down at the mutilated bodies of their friends.

"It's just scare-tactics!" the leader growled. "Don't let her get inside your heads. She's all alone out here. And there's three of us."

Without warning, a vine snapped and a large log came swinging down from between two trees. The log knocked all three men onto their backs.

Raphine, unable to hold her natural invisibility any longer, appeared standing over the middle guard with a raised spear.

"No!" the man screamed out, his eyes widening with terror. Throwing up a hand just as she plunged the spear deep into his chest, his face contorted as the pain pulled and twisted at his nerves, and then the life drained from his bulging eyes, leaving only the terrible contortions. His hand fell back to the ground with a padded thump.

The other two guards looked at her then at each other. "Get her!" the leaded shouted and they scrambled to their feet.

She was already sprinting for the shelter of the jungle when proton blasts streaked by her head, scorching tree trunks ahead of her and burning away foliage left and right.

Quick on her toes, she zigged and zagged so as to make herself harder hit. Moving targets always were. Not wanting to press her luck, she ducked behind a large tree trunk and heard the blaster pelting the other side mercilessly with hot energy discharges.

Pumping herself up, Raphine waited till one of the guards was practically breathing down her neck and then stepped out from her hiding spot and screamed like a wild banshee. She leapt onto the man, and jammed her thumbs into his eye sockets.

A loud squish, like grapes popping, sounded and he yowled in pain and staggered back. His foot snagged on a vine, causing him to trip and they went down together, her landing on top of him.

She pulled her thumbs out of his bleeding eye holes, gore and stringy eyeball sticking to them, and gripping her blade, she plunged her knife into his chest.

"*Arrrrgh!*" he shouted out in pain. Before she could stab at him again, he groped at her chest, trying to locate her center mass. He raised his blaster to shoot her in the side. She quickly rolled off him and out of the way as his shot flew straight up into the sky, missing its mark.

Almost as soon as she'd removed herself from the equation, another energy blast found the exact spot she'd been standing moments earlier. Instead of hitting her, however, it hit the man's hand and he screamed out again as his entire hand and forearm dissolved into thin air. Vaporized.

"You idiot!" he shouted, clutching his bloodied and smoldering stump.

"Sorry, boss!"

"I'll show you sorry," the man growled as he struggled to get onto his feet.

"Listen," his lackey said, cautiously drawing back, hands raised defensively, "it was an accident. She's fast."

"Damn right I'm fast," Raphine said, manifesting as if out of nowhere.

The man's head darted to the right to see the blur of a green skinned woman flash by. She flew by at such a quick pace that he barely felt the lacerating sting of the blade. Clasping his middle, the guard looked down to see his guts spilling wetly from his abdomen.

He reached down to add pressure to his fatal injury but it was already too late. He slowly sank to his knees, tottered briefly, then toppled onto his side. His face landed with a wet smack in the middle of a coil of his own intestines and insides. Blood continued to gush out of him in waves, slowly soaking into the fertile ground beneath him.

"I don't need eyes to find you, bitch," the blind man said, staggering about, his one good hand probing the air in search for her. "Heed my words, I'll make you pay for what you've done!" he shouted.

"I don't want to have to kill you too," Raphine said from a distance.

The guard spun in the direction of her voice and scowled, squinting into the darkness with bleeding eye sockets.

Calmly, Raphine stepped into the light. The sun's light was almost gone now and the forest cast deep shadows across every part of her except her turquoise eyes. Her eyes sparkled in the dusk like that of the jade python of Thermicron 5. Hypnotic. Deadly.

Although he couldn't see her standing directly in front of him, his men's blood dripping from her hands, he sensed an eerie calm settle over the forest and froze in place. Disarmed, blinded, and unable to defend himself, he cowered before her. Raphine could barely hold back her smile when she noticed him pissing himself in fear as he stood before her.

"Wait," he said, finally changing his tact. "Let's talk about this. Maybe I...return and...say you got away." He gestured at his gory face. "Obviously they'd believe me."

"But then they'll think I'm weak," she whispered.

Without warning, a spear lodged itself in his chest. He gulped, hands finding the shaft, and sank down to his knees. He tore the pole out and dropped it beside himself.

"Bitch," he murmured one last time then fell to his side. His breaths grew rapid, shallow, and his own blood gurgled from his mouth like a crimson babbling brook. His breathing stopped and his chest deflated with one last breath—a final death rattle.

In the heat of battle, it had been as though a completely different woman had taken her over. She wasn't even fully aware of what she was doing until she had done it. Perhaps it was her personal training with Danica taking root. Perhaps it was studying Jegra's battles in detail that had lent her the edge. Whatever it was, she had found a survival instinct inside her she hadn't even realized she'd possessed. And whatever it was, it had kept her alive. That's what counted.

Unfortunately, Gerard Van Zallek wasn't the kind of man who'd take kindly to her killing his men and running away with his secrets. She knew that when his men didn't return with her in tow, Zallek would send more to retrieve her. Maybe even a security android or two. And she wasn't equipped for that kind of an escalation.

One thing was certain. If she got caught, things would get a whole lot worse before they got better. But she couldn't think about any of that now. Right now, she needed to get back on her feet and get out of this damn jungle.

So, she did the only thing she could do. She turned and ran as fast as her weary body would allow and didn't dare look back.

35

Arkadia hung in the sky like a giant blue sapphire. Its twin habitable moons, Rivelon and Riverion, hung in the distance like studded diamonds. When the three heavenly bodies lined up just right, they appeared as a gem encrusted wedding ring and, in so doing, garnered Arkadia the nickname *Ourania Oceanus*, which meant the *heavenly river.*

Arkadia was predominantly a water-based planet with a meager sixty-nine islands boasting numerous extravagant beach resorts which the Bre'lal exclusively ran and controlled. As a luxury resort world, where the predominant attractions were the brothels and the casinos, Arkadia acted as a refuge for wealthy merchants, ship captains, and politicians, and those with enough credits to burn through and who needed a break from the daily grind of their stress-filled lives amid the frigid emptiness and unnatural isolation of space.

Space could get awful lonely sometimes. And that's precisely why such a pleasure oriented world existed it the first place.

It was a place where all your bodily desires and needs could be fulfilled. Whether it be food and women that you craved or simply some alone time basking in the warmth of the sun on your own private beach, on Arkadia your every dream could be fulfilled.

That was the pitch anyway. The one Onelle Te'Legra had written when she'd purchased the majority of the resorts and made Bre'lal women the marquee comfort providers in the galaxy. In return, she grew more prosperous and powerful than she could have ever dreamt. And yet, even with all her amassed wealth and power, she still felt empty inside. It was as if at the center of her being was a black hole that swallowed up any happiness she might experience and crushed her every attempt at a normal, sane life. A dark void that constantly threatened to plunge her into the depths of dreadful insanity. The only thing holding her back was her sheer strength to carry on.

Onelle Te'Legra dropped her shuttle out of hyperspace just above Arkadia, its engines dying down to ion thrusters only, and brought it into geosynchronous orbit above the planet.

In the distance the rotating space station and casino resort known as *Providence* came into view.

The space station sparkled in the light of Arkadia's star and resembled a cluster of massive icicles clinging to the spokes of a massive spinning wheel. *Providence* wasn't just a space station, though, it was also a port of entry as well as a luxury resort. It was a place where travelers could pass through immigration and be processed before being issued temporary travel visas where they'd be shuttled down to the planet's surface. It was also a humble pit-stop where wary travelers, who couldn't afford the fancy ocean perched villas down on the planet, could rest for a night or two above it, enjoy a burlesque show with a heavenly backdrop, and play the slot machines before heading on their way.

The space station also acted as the main space port and trading hub in the Arkadian sector. Officials there ensured that the politics of the Commonwealth stayed in space where they belonged and never darkened the doorstep of the lovely, beach mottled world. If anyone attempted to bring the drama of politics down to the homeworld, they were exiled off world and banned from *Providence* for life.

And Onelle owned it. She owned nearly every inch of property on it—she owned as much as any one person could own of a planet, that is. All but for one-tenth, which was split between the Lord Emperor and Grendok of Galliforn.

She leased her land to casinos, restaurants, and hotels on the planet and increased her earnings by leaps and bounds. *Providence,* however, was all hers. Every bolt and bulk head paid for in full. And she ruled over her self-made empire like a sovereign queen.

"Home sweet home," she said, smiling to herself as she gazed out the view portal at the crystalline space station that grew ever closer to her.

After all this time, she'd finally found her way back home. Now, she would put her great fortune to good use and stock pile every essential supply and product she could think of. From water and food rations to ship parts; from baby food to medical supplies. All of it would become indispensable in the coming months. And all of it more valuable than a dozen new starships or an asteroid belt rich with korridium.

And when the Nephilim and Nyctan empires came to take their resources—and they would come—and the people were left with nothing, desperate for someone to liberate them from their great suffering—she'd be there. She'd be there, arms wide open, bestowing them gifts to keep them going in their time of need. All for a pretty credit, of course.

Won't Raphine be surprised to see me, she thought, her mind wondering back to more menial things. She hadn't thought about her little sister in a long time. But now that she had returned home, she was looking forward to seeing how much her sibling had grown and matured. In fact, she'd be eighteen years old by now. A proper woman.

"*Providence,*" Onelle said, opening a comm link to her floating palace, "place me into contact with Raphine Agnar."

<<Raphine Agnar no longer resides in this jurisdiction. Would you care to leave a video message at her new place of residence?>>

"New place of residence?" Onelle repeated to herself, confused as to why Raphine would up and leave *Providence,* the only home she'd ever known. Here she had everything. Servants waiting on her every beck and call. Unlimited credits. And anything else she desired. "Where would that be, precisely?"

<<Raphine Agnar currently resides in the Royal Palace at Arena City on the desert moon Thessalonica and is under the guardianship of her eminence, Empress Jegra Alakandra.>>

"The empress? Jegra?!" Onelle muttered in a displeased tone. "That bitch has my sister?"

"Unidentified craft, you do not have permission to access Providence's comm systems. We ask you to send your identity number and digital permits or we will be force to confiscate your ship and detain you under order of her eminence, Onelle Te'Legra Agnar of Arkadia."

Onelle flipped on the holovid. "It's me, you idiots."

"Apologies, ma'am," the security officer replied. "I had no idea you would be back."

"Well, I am. Now, get me a landing port ASAP and have my personal security escort waiting for me when I arrive. I have an important mission that I need to see through."

"Yes, ma'am. Right away."

The comm cut out and her console flashed with docking coordinates. She smiled and sat back in her seat as the autopilot guided her into the station.

An entire entourage of servants and security guards greeted her at the airlock and she stepped out to cheers and applause. A Bre'lal woman wearing a low-cut purple dress that was translucent around the waist stepped forward. Her face was loaded with piercings, the silver metal playing off her white lipstick and eyeliner. She bowed reverently. Onelle's most trusted attendant. "Your eminence, we thought that we'd lost you."

"A lot has happened, Anna'Sek. But right now, I need a new set of clothes and my personal yacht prepped and ready to go within the hour."

"Go where?" Anna'Sek asked, sidling up to Onelle and matching her pace as she stormed up the corridor toward the lift.

When they arrived, Anna'Sek raised her hand and motioned for all the additional staff to stay behind. Only Onelle and Anna'Sek boarded the lift. As soon as the doors clasped shut, Onelle threw her arms around Anna'Sek's neck and began weeping.

Her hot tears poured onto Anna'Sek's shoulder and the woman stroked her hair. "It's all right, O. You're home now," she whispered.

Onelle pulled away, sniffled, and wiped her nose with the back of her hand. "Nobody has called me O in so long. I almost forgot how happy it makes me to have someone as close to me as you." She smiled at Anna'Sek and watched as her ever faithful custodian drew a see-through handkerchief from her cleavage and handed it to her.

Onelle took it and dabbed her running nose and wet eyes and then handed it back. Anna'Sek merely tucked it back in-between her breasts again where, eventually, it disappeared between the green valley of her womanly form.

"I've missed you more than words can express," Onelle said.

"Likewise, Your Eminence. Will we be departing immediately or should the mistress require some refreshment and relaxation first?"

Onelle leaned against the padded railing in the lift and let out a long sigh.

"What did you have in mind?"

"A hot meal and, if you are so inclined, and even hotter man to massage out the tension in that neck and shoulders of yours." Anna'Sek smiled and waited for Onelle to respond.

"I supposed that would be nice. A lot has happened and I need to take a breather and collect my thoughts."

Anna'Sek bowed. "As my mistress wishes."

The elevator came to a halt at the appropriate floor and the doors slid open. Onelle stepped out and looked back at her trusted attendant, an understated smile forming on her lips. "You had better make it two men."

"Yes, your eminence. As you wish." Anna'Sek bowed again and waited for the doors to close.

Once the elevator doors had clamped shut again, Onelle found herself unable to move. She merely stood in silence and looked out one of the view portals. As she watched the stars in the distance, she couldn't help it; being back felt surreal. None of it felt *real*. She sighed and then headed to the large oak doors at the end of the corridor that marked her personal quarters aboard *Providence*.

Made of real wood, she pushed them open and entered into the luxury suite that was her home.

Almost as soon as she'd finished taking her bath, her doorbell chimed. Onelle, quickly dried her naked body with the softest towel she'd ever felt and slipped it around herself.

"Come in," she said, and two strapping Bre'lal men in tight uniforms sauntered in. One carried a masseuse table under his arm and the other carried a bucket of ice with two bottles of her favorite wine. Anna'Sek knew her too well. She reached for the wine first and, biting the cork and yanking it up with her teeth she spat it out and then took a long swig of the red cabernet sauvignon.

After the first man had finished setting up the table, he placed a soft towel upon it and brushed the creases out. The other man patted the table and offered her his hand. She flicked the fold of her towel and let it unfurl and fall to her feet. Standing before them naked, she took another drink of wine right from the spout and went over and lay down on the table.

Three hours later, and after several more bottles of wine, she struggled to dress herself. Managing to get into an elegant turquoise dress that glimmered like liquid metal and clung silkily to her voluptuous form, Onelle sauntered drunkenly over to the bucket of ice which was now little more than a bucket of lukewarm water. "I thought there was another bottle," she said.

"You're holding it, your eminence," one of the men said.

"Oh, yeah." She smiled and, staggering on her inebriated legs, she took another drink.

Her doorbell chimed again; she looked at the faces of the two servants. She snapped her fingers at them and gestured for them to get out of her bed and then turned to the door and, straightening her messy hair with little success, opened it.

Standing in the entrance was a person she hadn't expected to see. "Zallek?" she said, hiccupping softly across purple grape-stained lips. "What are you…hic…doing here?"

"We need to talk," he said in an urgent tone.

She reached into the air and snapped her fingers. Right on cue, two hunky green men, completely naked, scurried out of the room. Zallek diverted his eyes away from their massive cocks which swung between their legs as they rushed out.

"Pardon me," one green man said.

"Apologies," the other said as they raced by.

Zallek stole a glance of them streaking up the hall, a few tourists giggling as the naked green-skins passed them by, their perfectly formed butts disappearing around the bend at the end of the corridor.

Onelle turned and sauntered back into her room as seductively as she could muster on tipsy legs. It appeared as though she was having trouble walking. And not just because she was drunk, either. Her gait was somewhat peculiar, almost as though she were sore in all the right places.

Zallek rolled his eyes when she neglected to invite him in and stepped inside.

"You and I need to discuss securing our resources. The Dagon fleet has fallen and rumors are there is going to be an occupation."

"My resources are secure," Onelle said.

"Mine aren't," growled Zallek.

"What's your point?" she asked, showing no interest in his business woes. She took another sip of wine and stared at him waiting for his reply.

"I need your help."

"And why would I do that?"

"In exchange, I'll give you a ten percent cut of my earnings."

"Make it twenty and you have yourself a deal."

"Twenty is a bit steep, don't you think?"

In fact, she didn't think so. Instead of replying, she just glared at him. "If you don't want my help," she said in a sleepy voice. She yawned, making a show of it to express how bored she was with their conversation.

"Fine," Zallek relented. He held out his hand. She took it. Bowing down, he kissed her hand and then let her go.

There was a momentary silence between them and then she waved her hand as though she were shooing away a bug. "Well, don't linger about. There's work to do."

He managed to dredge up a smile, although it wasn't easy. Then, with a bow, he excused himself from her personal quarters.

"What an ass," she said to herself.

She didn't need his twenty-percent. She was rich enough as it was. But having access to his contacts might prove useful down the line. And he was right. There was bound to be an occupation.

It was always "by the book" with conquering races. They marched in, took what they wanted, exploited resources and people, and then either left the place in ruin or, after a decade or two, things calmed down and they acclimated. The cultures mingled, blended, fused together in some instances, until one day everything returned to normal.

It was an endless cycle. The proverbial snake eating its own tail. The powerful always preyed on the weak. And on and on it went. That's just the way of things. It was life.

Which is why Onelle Te'Legra Agnar insulated herself with wealth and power. And she easily allied herself with the master races, because, she thought, *if you can't beat them, join them.* It was a philosophy that had kept her at the top of every dwindling food chain for ages. And she intended to stay at the top–no matter the cost.

The door chimed again and she let out a disgruntled huff. "Now what?" she said.

The door chimed again and she rolled her eyes.

"It's open," she grumbled.

The door slid away to reveal Anna'Sek standing in the opening, backlit by the light in the hallway.

"Oh, it's you," Onelle said, smiling. "Is the ship ready?" When she didn't respond right away, Onelle laughed. "What's the matter, dear Anna? Cat got your tongue?"

Anna'Sek stumbled into the room and then tripped and fell to the ground. She landed with a bone fracturing thud and Onelle tensed up, startled by the unexpected happenstance. When Onelle noticed the blood pooling around her most trusted servant's body, she dropped her glass of wine and screamed.

"Quiet," a voice whispered and Onelle inexplicably felt *compelled* to stop screaming. And so, she did.

When she raised her eyes, an elegant Nyctan woman with black eyes stared at her from the spot where Anna'Sek had been standing moments earlier. "W-who are you?"

"I am the Voice of his Holiness, the Keeper of the Yellow Sign, and the one true God, our every lasting Lord H'aaztre."

Azra'il Nun strolled into Onelle's quarters and looked around as though she were searching for something.

"What do you want?" asked Onelle. She glanced down at Anna'Sek out of the corner of her eye but the woman didn't move.

"It's not about what I want, my luv. It's what you want. Tell me, Mistress Onelle Agnar, what is it that you desire most in the world?"

"I want Jegra Alakandra to suffer as I've suffered," she blurted without intending to. Shocked that she'd said anything at all, Onelle covered her mouth, eyes wide with horror. If anyone knew her intentions, they'd have her arrested for treason.

Yes, it wasn't so long ago that she'd had a slug controlling her mind, courtesy of the Lord Emperor, who wanted to exploit her hate for Jegra when Ishtar Bantu had failed to apprehend her at the Cove. Initially she'd told him to take a hike and that she didn't want to get involved in a lover's spat. But his technique of persuasion had proved quite impossible to turn down.

Besides, she had relished in the thought of killing Jegra, ever since she'd murdered her sister, Abethca. The video footage Dakroth had given her cut through the lies and had shown the truth. Jegra had fired upon her sister while she slept, vaporizing her without mercy or remorse. A cold blooded murder, which she had gotten away with. And Onelle would make sure she paid with her life.

Of course, she hadn't expected a squid to attack her ship and maroon her on an alien world. Imagine her stunned surprise when she found Jegra there too. Things hadn't turned out the way she'd wanted. But now, she was beginning to see that another chance presented itself.

"Good," Azra'il Nun said, smiling back at Onelle. The woman stepped close and reached out her slender white hand, her talon like fingernails blending seamlessly in with the flesh of her fingers. Gently, she stroked Onelle's green cheek with the backside of her hand as one would stroke a pet. "I'm pleased to hear you say that. Very pleased, indeed."

36

Viridescent jungle foliage spread apart and Raphine's green face emerged. The overalls she'd been wearing were caked in blood and dirt and were torn to ribbons from her fight with the security detail. The good news was that they were no longer tracking her. At least for the time being.

Raphine had hiked through jungle for the past eighteen hours and was dying of thirst. Earlier, she had climbed a tall tree and watched the birds, to see where they circled before they landed. If they weren't carrion birds, they were setting down for food and water. She had followed a large flock several kilometers to the south west.

A nearby squawk of one of the birds caused Raphine to take pause. She listened intently and then heard something else. The sound of running water.

"Finally," she said in a parched and raspy voice. She licked her chapped lips and pushed through the branches and giant leafy ferns until she emerged in a clearing. There was a wide lake with a waterfall.

It wasn't a large waterfall. But just big enough to send up a refreshing spray of misty water to cool her and sooth her aching muscles. She dropped to her knees at the edge of the shore and dipped her face in and drank. The water was pure, refreshing, and clean and she drank until she choked herself and came up gasping for air.

That was the nice thing about Dagon Prime. It was mostly oceans and jungles. And all but for the major cities, much of it was a vast wilderness too dense for tourism, and so went untouched.

She looked around for signs of people, a small village or perhaps a park ranger or a random hiker, but didn't find signs that anyone had even been here.

Which meant it was equally as unlikely that anyone would be, any time soon.

She quickly slipped off her boots and then unzipped her overalls. Her underwear was tattered and muddy and so she peeled them off and discarded it too, then waded out into the middle of the blue lagoon. Like a forest nymph, she scooped up handfuls of water and bathed her body. Brown layers of mud thinned and then washed away as she repeated the process, scrubbing every inch of herself with the calloused palm of her hand.

Raphine went and stood under the waterfall for a long while and let it beat against her tired neck and sore back. Its powerful spray washed away any remaining grime that was plastered to her avocado colored skin and soon enough she was sparkling clean and fully refreshed.

She held in a groan when her skin felt raw and the blast of water became too much to bear any more. Finished bathing, she turned and slowly began to wade back toward the shoreline.

Before she could make it even half of the way back, there was a large flash of light just beyond the trees. Golden rays streamed out from the spaces between the branches and probed in every direction like wayward spotlights then quickly dissipated again.

Raphine froze. She wasn't sure if it was a teleport or something else. Startled and caught completely off guard, she wrapped her arms around herself, her hands cupping her bare breasts and looked in every direction she could think of for a place to duck and hide.

The lake was so crystal clear that even if she dove under the surface and held her breath it wouldn't do much to help conceal her.

She glanced over at the waterfall, wondering if she had enough time to make it back and use the white spray of mist as a natural screen, but before she could react the sound of rustling leaves caused her to whip her head back around. She tensed up, knowing that something was coming through the tree line.

Her eyes locked onto her boots and the handmade spear that lay next to them. If only she could get there in time.

"Raphine!" a familiar voice called out. "Raphine Agnar!"

"I'm here!" Raphine shouted, relieved that someone had finally found her.

She turned in the direction of the voice and began to wade toward the shoreline when, unexpectedly, La'Garren flew out of the thicket of trees and came to her, just as a loyal pet would its master.

"La'Garren!" she shouted, happy to see her pet squid. He was getting so big and was now the size of a large cat rather than the cute hamster-sized pet he had been. He came to her and began coiling his tentacles around her naked body, overjoyed to see her.

She laughed and gave him a big hug and basked in the warmth of his radiant body.

Someone cleared their throat and Raphine looked up to see Jegra standing at the side of the bank of the lagoon, hands on her hips, as she watched her and La'Garren get tangled up. "Perhaps I'll leave you two alone," Jegra teased, raising an eyebrow.

"It's nothing like that!" Raphine assured her. "Also…" she added, stepping out of the water, "that's so gross."

Jegra squinted up her face and smiled mischievously and said, "I worried about you, you know?"

"I know," Raphine replied. The women embraced, giving La'Garren just enough time to escape getting squashed between them. Holding onto Raphine's waist with one hand, Jegra slipped out a communicator from a satchel strapped to her hip and said, "Get your clothes and we'll get the heck out of here."

Raphine nodded over at a piled of muddy, blood soaked, overalls that looked as though they'd be regurgitated by a Skallekian sea slug. "You mean those?"

"Ah," Jegra answered, aware of Raphine's predicament. "You're pretty much without." She raised the small handheld communicator, which resembled a brushed metal egg, to her lips and said, "This is Empress Jegra Alakandra. Three for an emergency teleport to my personal chambers."

"This is the Imperial Palace on Dagon Prime, responding. It's good to have you back, Your Majesty." The voice was friendly and welcoming. But, for some reason, there was something quite familiar and off-putting about it. Although she couldn't quite put her finger on it.

Two beams of light came down and spirited the women away. Moments later, they materialized on the wrong side of seven-centimeter thick glass of an Imperial holding cell.

Raphine immediately covered herself up, clutched onto La'Garren, and scurried behind Jegra to try and hide her nudity.

Jegra turned to see Senator Targon standing on the other side of the glass divider, smiling at them both. His white hair was slicked back and he had on his senatorial robes. It looked as though he'd just come from a council meeting. He locked his hands behind his back and smiled. "Welcome back, Your Majesty."

Jegra folder her arms across her chest and scowled down at the man standing on the other side of the glass, who was several centimeters shorter than her. "What's the meaning of this?"

"Just a precaution," he informed her. She eyed him hesitantly and he smiled again. "I know we haven't seen eye to eye but, right now, there are more important things to discuss. As the Defender of the Realm, it's your duty to go to Nyctan and attempt to broker a peace deal with the Nephilim and this so-called Gilded Master everyone is talking about before it's too late."

Jegra raised an eyebrow. "So, you lost the fleet?"

"My daughter lost the fleet," he corrected. "But the fact remains, Dagon is defenseless and the enemy armada is *en route* to our system. Your ship can get to Nyctan before they get to us. That gives us a narrow window of opportunity."

"Agreed," Jegra said, after giving it some thought. "But I wouldn't recommend pulling a stunt like this again," she added, gesturing at her current surroundings. "Next time you redirect one of my personal teleports I'll rip out your tongue through your asshole and then feed it to the palace guard dogs. Do I make myself clear?"

"You always have had a way with words," Targon said, running his hand back along his already slick hair.

Jegra maintained a fixed gaze, never once looking away from Targon's smug face. "La'Garren, get us out of here."

There was a flash of golden light and Jegra, Raphine, and La'Garren disappeared. Not a teleport, but a faster than light dimensional jump.

It was the same technique La'Garren had used to save Jegra when Dakroth had blown her shuttle out of the sky after rendezvousing with the space pirate Novac Tamoran.

Raphine had been working with La'Garren on jumping short distances. At first, it was just from the palace to the end of the palace lawn. Then from the palace to Arena City. Then to neighboring cities. Then from the moon to the homeworld. Each time he successfully hit his target.

"So," Senator Targon said contemplatively, after they had disappeared. He rubbed his chin and a subtle yet conniving smile formed on his thin blue lips. "You have a pet celestial squid. Interesting."

Moments later, Jegra was back in her quarters aboard the *Shard*. She was surprised that La'Garren had transported them there. He could have placed them back in the main hall of the royal palace on Dagon Prime, or back at her home on Thessalonica, but it almost seemed as though he'd understood her and Targon's discussion and knew she needed to be here. *Maybe*, she wondered, *the squids communicated via a form of telepathy?*

Raphine was in the corner of the room slipping into a freshly synthesized uniform. It was navy blue and looked fetching with her green skin. Jegra turned just in time to see Raphine tuck her breasts into the stretch fabric and then zip up the central zipper all the way to the mandarin collar.

"You look nice," Jegra said, smiling at Raphine.

"You do too," she said, returning the compliment.

"I've been wearing this gladiator getup ever sense I went to rescue Lycia. I guess I'm just most comfortable in what I know."

"It's my favorite outfit of yours," Raphine said.

"You don't think it's too slutty?" asked Jegra.

"It's totally slutty. But it suits you."

Jegra stuck her tongue out at Raphine and they both laughed. Turning her attention back to the task at hand, she called out for the holovid display.

"Holovid on," she said and, almost immediately, a blue light came down from the ceiling and scanned her features. Once it had finished, a three-dimensional hologram of her likeness flickered into being and it stood in the middle of a glowing blue grid hovering waist high in the middle of the room. "Transmit this message directly to my security council," she said.

The computer chimed and then Jegra proceeded with her message.

"I must go at once to Nyctan and attempt to broker peace. As it is likely a trap, I will only take the most essential personnel with me. That includes Danica, Lianica, and Brei'Alas. You three will return to the *Shard* immediately. Admiral Grendok, you will remain behind with the *Chiron* and defend Thessalonica in my absence."

The security council sat at the glass roundtable in the war room on Thessalonica. Grendok stood up and cleared his throat. "You can count on me, Your Excellency."

Lianica and Brei'Alas stood up. Two golden beams of light touched down and recalled them to the *Shard* in an emergency teleport. Their bodies broke apart in little packets of hexagonal light and were quickly whisked away in a whirlwind of spiraling energy.

Doctor Amora, who normally didn't sit in on war meetings but was requested this time around, shifted nervously in her chain, cleared her throat, and stood up. Facing the miniaturized blue glowing hologram of Jegra situated at the center of the table, she said, "I would recommend against taking Danica. Her recovery isn't finished yet and this is a critical time in her detox program. Cutting it short is risky."

"I understand the risk, doctor, but I need all key players by my side for this one. Especially Danica. Right now, I want you to see to it about getting Lycia situated and make sure she's well taken care of in my absence. Work with Grendok on figuring out just who she is, where she came from, and why she showed up now. I'll except a full report when I get back."

Amora nodded and then sat back down in her chair.

"Meleh'Kendar," Jegra said, turning to her chief of security. "The palace is under your care. I trust you shall keep everything in order until I return."

"You have my word," Meleh'Kendar answered. He crossed his fist over his heart in the Dagon salute and bowed his head.

The tiny blue Jegra returned the salute and then the hologram feed flickered and cut out.

Sleek and silver, the *Shard* tore away from Thessalonica and Dagon Prime. It broke orbit and, with a flash, stretched out of view as it entered faster than light travel.

"Prepare for slipstream," Captain Lianica Blackstar said.

"Yes, ma'am," Brei'Alas replied and she tapped the code into the console and activated the slip stream drive.

Raving past stars that stretched into spaghetti-thin strands of light, the ship wavered and then phased out of hyperspace and into the slipstream. Everything outside the windows turned to golden light, the same light that the squid entities seemed to be made of.

Brei'Alas wondered if this particular dimension of sub-space, just beneath the surface of regular spacetime, was where the celestial squid entities came from. *Could it be their natural habitat?*

Her thoughts were interrupted when the regular navigation officer came on duty. She relinquished the seat to him and removed herself from the navcom station before returning to her own post at the science station.

"Three hours and fifteen minutes till arrival," the navigation officer said after taking his seat.

"What is the current ETA of the enemy fleet's arrival to Dagon Prime?" asked Lianica. She crossed her legs and leaned back in her command chair.

"Approximately three days, seven and a half hours."

"Let's assume they're pushing their engines to full in order to surprise us. That gives us two days' advantage. Hopefully, the empress can broker a peace treaty in that time. Otherwise the war is only just beginning."

Everyone nodded solemnly. As Dagon people, they were a proud bunch. Nobody wanted to admit they were losing a war that most back on the homeworld didn't even know they were fighting.

Part of the problem was the Nephilim had descended upon the empire so quickly, taking out strategic points before anyone could react. And whoever this Gilded Master was, he was extremely keen on strategy. Callestra had lost to him, and she was currently the best strategist, next to Danica, the Dagon fleet had.

But maybe Danica could figure out something that Callestra had not. Lianica would normally pray to her god to watch over them, but it seemed it was her god that was attacking her people. These days, she placed her faith on the back burner and focused on what was important. Her job. Her duty. And her friends.

Two hours and forty-nine minutes later Lianica called Jegra to the bridge. A handful of minutes later, Jegra, along with Raphine and Danica, arrived on the bridge.

Raphine and Danica wore navy blue jumpsuits with gold trim. The stretch fabric hugged their feminine curves and made them look both official and officially sexy all at the same time.

Jegra had on her gladiatrix battle bikini along with her royal purple cloak. A silver helmet of a Roman pretorian adorned her head, replete with a synthetic horsehair plume dyed to match her cloak. In one arm she carried a korridium shield with the Dagon hawk logo emblazoned on it, and in the other arm was her trusted battle axe. She swung the axe around and over her back. It wavered in the air over the magnetic sheath, reverberating with an electronic hum and then clamped down with a resounding *clank*.

Lianica stood at attention and the rest of the crew followed. "Her Royal Excellency, Jegra Alakandra, Defender of the Realm and the Mother of Dagon on the bridge!"

Everyone's fists thumping their chests in a simultaneous salute resounded throughout the command center. Jegra returned the salute. "At ease, ladies and gentlemen."

"Return to your stations," Lianica ordered. Everyone returned to their stations and Lianica looked over at Jegra. "Dressed to make an impression, I see."

Jegra smiled but didn't reply. She merely kept her eyes fixed on the horizon. Just then the ship dropped out of the slipstream and entered normal space. The yellow and red planet of Nyctan filled the view portal and Jegra took a slow, deliberate breath.

"The last time we were here they threw us in their prison for winning a war for them," Danica said. "I wonder what they'll think of us returning without invitation."

"I could care less what anyone thinks. They've declared war on my people and my empire. Unjustly, I might add. All I want is to look eye to eye with this H'aaztre and see if he's what everyone says he is or if he's just a poser."

"Set us down in their Mid-Atlantic Ocean," Jegra said, pointing at the planet.

"You want the whole starship to land on their planet?"

"The *Shard* is designed for it. It will make a bigger impression and it will afford us a base of operations. And a safe haven, if things take a turn for the worse."

Captain Lianica Blackstar shouted, "You heard the lady! Prepare for atmospheric entry. We're landing this big girl."

"Yes, ma'am!" the entire bridge crew shouted in return.

Jegra looked over at Brei'Alas. "Lieutenant, if you'll be so kind to accompany me."

Brei pointed at herself as if to ask, *who me?* Jegra merely motioned with a finger for her to come over.

Hesitant, Brei'Alas complied and then fiddled nervously beside Jegra. "You want me to go with you?"

"We may need your…special abilities," replied Jegra, looking fondly at Brei'Alas.

"Oh, you know about that." Jegra nodded in response. "I just want you to know, Your Grace, I don't have control over it yet. If anything should happen, I can't—"

"It's quite alright Lieutenant," Jegra said, cutting her off. She didn't need doubt right now. She needed an officer. She gave her a reassuring look, letting the girl know everything would be okay. Of course, she didn't know that for certain. But Brei was the kind of girl who responded to positive feedback. "I know that if push comes to shove, you can hold your own. You're not as timid as you let on, Lieutenant Brei'Alas. There's a fierce goddess beneath that façade of a meager young officer."

Brei'Alas blushed. "Oh, I don't know about that."

Jegra scanned all the faces of her crew. "Alright people," she said authoritatively. "This is it."

37

The *Avarice* dropped out of hyperspace at the far end of the galaxy. A thin asteroid belt and the glowing lights of a mining cluster strung out along dozens of asteroids alerted him to the fact that they'd arrived at Brexis mining colony, just as planned.

"It's too bad you'll be leaving us so soon," Novac Tamoran said in an insincerely.

Dakroth ignored his less than flattering tone and smiled curtly. "Yes, well, apparently the wretched wench Anaïs Nin wrote me off as a war criminal. Now, everyone will be looking to turn me in to the Nyctan security forces. It's best if I lay low for a while."

Novac Tamoran nodded and then turned to Callestra. Taking her hand, he bowed reverently and kissed it. Dakroth rolled his eyes at the gesture. "My dear, are you sure you won't change your mind and stay with us? There's no need to get embroiled in this man's drama."

"This man is my emperor," Callestra said, smiling at Dakroth, nothing but affection in her eyes.

"Yes, but if you should ever change your mind, my luv, my ship's docking ports will always be open to you."

"I appreciate that," Callestra said, turning back to Tamoran. She let him hold her hand longer than was necessary, but he had been the perfect host during their two-day journey to the Outer Rim.

Dakroth turned and found Ladgara at her station. She winked and blew him a kiss provoking a subtle smile from him.

"All right, then. That settles it. We'll leave you here and then be back to pick you up in six months, as planned."

"Things should be calmer by then," Callestra said. But, in all honesty, she wasn't sure things would settle down that quickly.

Six months is the amount of time it took a fully automated ship yard to construct the hull of a ship. It took another six months for crews to fit the insides and get everything up to spec. With a limited crew with limited hands, it would take years, maybe even a decade, just to get three or four ships built and working.

Dakroth reached out his hand and beckoned Callestra over to him. "Come, my dear. It's time."

She took his hand and they walked over to the center of the room. "We're ready when you are," Callestra informed.

Novac Tamoran raised his hand and then swiped the air in a chopping motion giving Ladgara the signal.

Ladgara looked down at her console with her one good eye and then ran her fingers along the teleportation controls.

A golden swirl of light descended and wrapped itself around the Lord Emperor and Vice Admiral Callestra Van Morgan. Their bodies broke apart in packets of light and were whisked away in the blink of an eye.

"I can't say I won't miss them," Ladgara said. "They fuck like gods."

Novac Tamoran groaned and turned toward the view portal. He could care less about any of that. Right now, he wanted to put as much distance between them and this infernal, backwater mining colony as he could. "Get us out of here," he commanded.

"Yes, sir," Ladgara replied.

The *Avarice* slowly turned away from the asteroid colony and then, in a flash, jumped away.

On Brexis, several workers were disrupted when two rods of golden light touched down in the middle of their excavation. When the emperor and a high-ranking officer appeared before them, they looked at each other confused.

"Can we help you, sir?"

"It's Sire," Callestra said angrily, taking a step forward.

Dakroth threw out hand and stopped her. "It's best if we don't draw any unnecessary attention to ourselves," he said. "These men were just doing their duty."

"Yes," Callestra said, backing off. "My apologies. Carry on."

The men shared one more glance between themselves and then shrugged and went back to chipping away at the inside of the rock tunnel.

"Which way is the exit?" Dakroth asked.

One of the miners jutted a thumb over his shoulder. "Back dat'away."

"Thanks," Dakroth said, drawing out an imperial coin. He flipped the coin to the miner for a tip and sauntered off with the pretty blue girl in tow.

The miner looked down at the coin in his hand and chuckled. "I would have preferred a few additional credits instead."

His friend laughed and, pocketing the coin, he got back to work.

After coming to the end of a long meandering tunnel, Dakroth and Callestra emerged at a work check-in. They drew curious looks and Dakroth motioned for Callestra to follow him.

"I know the praefectus of this colony. He'll be able to find us accommodations and get us some new clothes. Something less…auspicious."

Callestra nodded and followed after Dakroth, who seemed to be familiar with the layout of the facility.

They made their way through numerous corridors and junctions until they came to a large concourse with a bustling promenade that cut down the center. Lining both sides of the promenade were shops and restaurants and all manner of entertainment establishments. Bre'lal women wearing translucent clothing that did little to hide their flesh beneath, littered the nooks and crannies propositioning customers and offering their services for creds.

And although the place was worn looking, run down, with steaming and leaking pipes strewn all over the place making it thick with humidity, there was something comforting, Callestra felt, about being able to get lost in a sea of strangers.

"How do we know we can trust any of these people?" Callestra asked nervously. She kept close to Dakroth as they made their way into the crowd.

"Because, as tempting as turning us in for the hefty price on our heads is, it's not worth losing your life over."

After weaving through the crowded central path of the promenade for several minutes, Dakroth pointed up at the glass windows of an office that jutted out of one of the rock walls and overlooked the entire promenade. "That's the praefectus's office. We'll get what we need there."

"Are you sure he'll be accommodating? What's to say he won't turn us in?"

"We go way back, the praefectus and I. Don't worry," Dakroth reassured Callestra. "It'll be like a reunion with a dear old friend. You'll see."

The only problem, Callestra thought, was that he didn't seem convinced of his own words. There was an uncertainty in his voice that made her all the more nervous.

A winding staircase carved directly into the rock led up to the office. When they arrived at the top of the stairs, they found a guard posted outside.

"What do you want?" he said, eyeing them both suspiciously.

The guard was a mammoth Dragonian. *Even I would have a hard time taking him on,* Callestra thought.

"We want to see your boss," Dakroth said.

"The praefectus is busy. Come again in an hour."

"Do you know who I am?" Dakroth said, stepping up to face the guard. Craning his neck back, Dakroth scowled up at the lizard man.

The Dragonian looked away. "I know who you are. That don't change nothin'. The boss ain't taking no visitors."

"Doesn't change *anything* and isn't taking *any* visitors," Callestra corrected.

Both men shot her a perturbed glance. She raised her hands defensively and shrugged. Her father had always been a stickler for her to act and speak properly. It was a hard habit to shake even though, admittedly, it sort of made her into a tight-ass.

Shifting her tone and tact, she put her hands on her hips and addressed the big lug standing in their way. "Look, you big dumb leather neck, we don't have time to argue," Callestra said in a much harsher tone, her magenta eyes flaring up with energy. "Either you let us through or you'll face charges for disobeying your emperor."

"First off, that's racist, and I'd appreciate it if you didn't call my people 'leather necks.' The boss wouldn't like that. Secondly, Gamagor is busy," the guard reiterated, not budging. He crossed his arms over his chest and doubled down on his refusal to move out of the way. "So, make like a couple of Muscoid flies, and scram."

"Gamagor?" Callestra inquired, finding the name strange if not a little intimidating. *Who in their right mind goes by Gamagor?*

The hulking Dragonian was finished debating the subject with them and only responded with a grunt.

Moments later, the doors swung open and Callestra pinned the large Dragonian guard's arm behind his back and shoved him against the wall, allowing Dakroth to march unimpeded into Gamagor's office.

Callestra reached up and slammed her palm against the back of the guard's head and smashed his face into the rock wall. "Thanks for your cooperation," she snarled. Finally, she let go and trailed into the room after the Lord Emperor.

The guard, rubbing the back of his head and brandishing a fresh welt on his cheek, sulked as he brought up the rear. "Sorry, ma'am, they insisted."

"Gam, baby," Dakroth said in his most pleasant voice and on best manners. He stopped halfway into the room and made a sour face.

Callestra looked up to see what had made him turn green around the gills. She saw a large Dragonian woman, one leg up on the desk, another leg on the shoulder of a servant, her dress stretched so wide it appeared as though it would tear, while a nurse pulled on something that seemed to be stuck between her legs. More accurately, it seemed to be latched onto her private area.

At first glance, Callestra thought the woman was giving birth, but when Callestra realized it was a space leech, she grimaced and then, holding back a gag reflex, tried not to vomit into her mouth. The leech was the size of a Dagoni python. She couldn't remember seeing a more hideous sight than this in a long time. If ever.

"Ah, the Lord Emperor himself," Gamagor said in a less than amused tone. She grunted as her nursed tugged on the leech, hanging on with both hands and not letting go for fear of the thing coiling back up inside its host. "Doesn't privacy mean anything to your royal assholiness? The least you could have done was knock first."

Fed up with the creature's stubbornness, the nurse pulled out a taser. With a crackle of blue electricity, she jammed it into the side of the worm. Gamagor screamed out in pain as the nurse relentlessly zapped the parasite with a taser, the electricity traveling up the length of the creature and into her groin. Finally, the leech let go and the nurse drew it out as quickly as she could.

It slipped out of her hands and flopped onto the floor with a sticky sounding *plop*. Gamagor reached down between her legs and pulled out a long, sticky strand of mucus and flicked her hand, sending the mucus flying off her finger tips.

The sticky goop landed on the parasite. Gamagor reached over and grabbed a handful of tissues that sat on the end of the table and cleaned her nether regions then tossed the wadded-up tissues into a waste bin next to her desk.

Standing up, Gamagor went over to the squirming body of the leech, drew out a blaster, pointed the barrel of the disruptor gun at it, and fired several rounds.

The creature writhed in agony and Gamagor fired off two more shots. Once the thing was smoking, she stopped firing and, standing over it, raised her boot and brought it down with a resounding splat.

"I think I'm going to be sick to my stomach," Callestra said, covering her mouth with her hand.

"The larvae get into the food sometimes," explained Gamagor. "There's a pill to help flush them out once every three or four months, but every now and again a resilient one grows inside you until you need to tear it out. They're usually not this big," she laughed, nodding at the dead leech with an impressed look. "But I have a voracious appetite." Gam strode up to them and leaned in and whispered into Callestra's ear, "As I'm certain Dakroth has told you already." She licked her lips and then snapped her teeth at Callestra in a feral, almost vicious way that caused her to reflexively tense up.

Callestra took a step back from the formidable woman and bowed her head cordially. Although she was a *leather neck*, she did have a pretty enough face.

She still looked feminine, that was, even though she was quite bulky. At least she had enough fat on her body to look wholesome while not offsetting the muscle tone of her domineering physique. It was clear that she had once been a gladiatrix and for whatever reason, had retired to Brexis.

"Gam!" Dakroth said excitedly, throwing his arms into the air with a newfound interest in the woman. He embraced her and kissed her long and hard on the mouth.

When he pulled away, her long, slender, forked tongue retracted from his mouth like a slithering snake. She glanced over at Callestra with a sly look and smiled.

Gamagor returned to her desk and rested on the corner. She brushed the wrinkles out of her dress, which was a size too small, and gestured for them to take a seat across from her in the luxurious, red-dyed leather chairs. The whole while, she ignored the nurse and the guard cleaning up the mess off to the side.

They acquiesced, lowering themselves into their seats simultaneously.

"So, Dakroth, what brings you to my humble station in the leech infested boondocks of the outer most reaches of space?"

"By now, I'm sure you have heard that we're fighting a war with an unfamiliar enemy. Someone claiming to be a god."

"More like losing a war, but do go on, dear," Gam said, impolitely interrupting Dakroth.

He ignored her insult, smiled, and continued. Callestra was still sore about her defeat at the Viridian asteroid belt near the Cove; she merely folder her arms and looked away.

"I need to collect on my debt. I'm asking for safe haven," he said.

She frowned. Her ridged brow settled across her serpentine eyes. She blinked twice with nictitating eyelids and then smiled. Her teeth were extremely white and perfectly formed. When she smiled, her face lit up and her beauty magnified by ten, it seemed.

Even with the perfect smile, Callestra still had a hard time imagining Dakroth willfully choosing to be with a woman like that. Especially after the leech incident.

"Of course!" she finally answered. "You shall have it."

She reached into the top drawer of her desk and drew out two orange key cards. "This is the newlywed suite," she said, grinning at Callestra. "It's the second largest suite on the station and it will draw less attention to you two than the Imperial Palace suite would. Oh, and it comes with a complimentary wedding gift…two hundred thousand credits, on the house."

"Excellent," Dakroth said, placing his hand on the key cards. Before he could take them, Gam's hand was plastered onto his, pushing down firmly. She stared him straight in the eyes.

"I don't want any funny business. As long as you are in my house, you follow my rules. I don't care if you're the emperor of the entire galaxy or a flea on my backside. If you so much as make an ounce of trouble for me I'll squash you. Dearie."

She let go of his hand and he drew it back.

"You won't even know we're here."

"Good," Gam said. Then, waving them away, she said, "Now get the Helios out of my office."

On the way back down the flight of stairs leading to the office, Callestra grabbed Dakroth's sleeve. He paused in the stairwell and gave her a surprised look.

"Why do you let her talk that way to you?"

"Gam earned her freedom in the Arena. She's free to address me anyway she sees fit."

"Yes, but doesn't her lack of respect bother you? Anyone else would be dealt a punishment."

"It's true, she's rough around the edges and can be a bit catty at times, but she was the most glorious fighter. In her prime, there was no one like her."

"Not even your beloved empress?" Callestra asked in a snooty tone.

Dakroth raised an eyebrow. "Why, my dear Callestra, is that a tinge of jealousy I detect?"

Callestra let go of his arm and folded her arms. Smacking her teeth, she let out a disgusted grunt. "Of Jegra? Never."

"Of Gam, I mean."

"Please don't tell me you slept with her?" Callestra said, glancing back up the stairs. "She literally had a giant leech stuck up her twat!"

"It was before the leeches, my dear," Dakroth reassured her. He, too, glanced back up the stairs, a pleasant grin spreading across his face as he relived happier memories.

Callestra shivered. "I can't get the image out of my mind."

"Be sure to remind me to pick up enough of those worm meds for our sojourn here," Dakroth said. "Lest we suffer the parasites too."

"Heaven forbid!" she laughed, linking her arm through Dakroth's as though she were his and he was hers.

He smiled upon her and allowed her the display of affection. After all, she was the prettiest Dagon woman he'd set eyes upon in ages.

When they returned to the promenade and entered the bustling crowd of the marketplace it seemed as though they drew even more looks than before. Callestra glanced up to see Gamagor watching them from her window office high above things. When their eyes met, Gamagor gave a self-satisfied look and withdrew from the window. Honestly, she wasn't sure what to make of it.

As they continued up the street, the chattering gossip of speculation broke out among the regulars of the side street noodle shops and tattoo parlors, the local food markets and black market trading posts, all of them wondering who these two displaced Dagons were and what they were doing in such a dump as Brexis. More eyes turned toward them and followed them up the crowded path that stretched up and down the promenade.

"I don't like this," Callestra whispered into his ear, divulging her discomfort with the amount of attention they were drawing to themselves. It seemed more than should be considered normal and she worried about how they were going to keep a low profile when everyone had a vested interest in learning who they were.

He patted her hand, which rested on his forearm. "It'll be fine. Things will die down in a few days when we are no longer a couple of new faces to gossip about."

After making it halfway up the street, Dakroth nudged Callestra's elbow and said, "This way." He nodded his chin at a hotel up the street, as that was where they'd be staying. But before they could get even a couple more steps in its direction, an inquisitive voice called out to them.

"Aye, you blue skins look awfully familiar. Wait, wait! I knows…yeah. Ain't you the Lord Emperor? Yeah, yeah. I do knows yeah. You're Rhadamanthus Dakroth, Emperor of the Dagon Empire!"

"Sorry, you must be mistaken." Dakroth grabbed Callestra's elbow and ushered her along more quickly. He was beginning to think she was right. There was something off about all of this.

"Hey, Yer Majesty, who is that fine fox of a lady with ye?"

Dakroth, fed up with the twenty questions, turned to see a toad-like fellow dressed in gold, balancing on one hand on the edge of a vendor's cart. He wasn't more than four-feet eleven inches tall, yet displayed an uncanny dexterity and impressive set of acrobatic skills. In one swift motion, he switched hands, his body never moving as he maintained a perfect balance.

"Look, friend, we're in a bit of a hurry and we really must be getting on our way. Apologies." Dakroth bowed his head cordially, then, towing Callestra along behind him, he switched directions and headed back the way they'd come.

"Friends, are we?" the little toad-like creature asked. He cartwheeled off the stand and landed on the ground with a flourish. Taking a bow when a slight round of applause broke out, he quickly hopped along until he caught up with them.

Dakroth rolled his eyes out of exasperation. Stopping, he turned to face the creature. "Look, what do you want? Money? An autograph? Name your price and maybe we can come to an agreement."

The toad raised a long, slender finger with a bulbous fingertip and pointed it at Callestra. "I want one night with her."

"Out of the question," Callestra snarled, her face turning dark purple as she fumed with rage.

The toad raised his hands in alarm. "No, no, no. Nothing like that. I merely want to pick your brain."

"Really?" Callestra said, raising an eyebrow and folding her arms. "And what, pray tell, would you pick my brains about?"

"About how the Voice overwhelmed your crew. How she forced you to watch them take their own lives. About how that made you feel."

"What is he talking about?" Dakroth asked.

Callestra's heart raced. Nobody could possibly know about that. Nobody was there except for… "We need to go, now," she said, tugging Dakroth's arm. But Dakroth resisted.

"Where can we go?" he said. "We're stuck here."

"Indeed, you are," said the toad.

Dakroth turned and glared at the creature. "Who are you again?" he asked impatiently.

"Oh me, oh my! Where are my manners?" The toad stuck out his webbed hand. "The name's Giddion. Bearer of Signs."

"Bearer of signs?" Dakroth asked in a confounded tone.

"No, no, no. This isn't good," Callestra warned him. But he pushed her aside and squared off with the creature.

"I come bearing only one sign," said Giddion. He waved his hand and all the commotion of the promenade slowed to a crawl. It was as if everyone was caught in an old-fashioned movie reel that had been wound down to its slowest setting. Everything and everyone moved at a glacial pace, even a nearby buzzing fly seemed to slow down to a rate equal to that of running molasses.

"I see," Dakroth said. "You're one of *them*."

Giddion shrugged. "I'm but a servant. A humble avatar, if you will. The

Gilded Master uses us as he pleases, and we are happy to oblige."

"So, who sold us out? Was it Gamagor? Novac Tamoran? Or someone else?"

"Perhaps, all of the above," replied Giddion, a wide yet undeniably malicious smile forming on his amphibian lips. "You know, you really should see about getting better quality friends. Not a single one was willing to stand up for you. Instead, they all lay down like a deck of cards and pointed the way to you."

Giddion clapped his hands twice and time snapped back to normal.

Dakroth and Callestra looked around. Many of the curious onlookers had returned to their business and weren't as interested in them anymore.

"I suppose you'll be wanting us to accompany you, then?" asked Dakroth.

"Indeed, friend," Giddion answered, hopping up and down joyfully, his eyes widening to manic proportions. "This way. This way! Follow me." He did a cartwheel and then skip-hopped away.

"You're not serious," Callestra said, eyeing Dakroth with a hard look that expressed the fact that she had absolutely no desire to go with one of H'aaztre's lackeys. The last time she'd faced off with one, things didn't go so well. She ended up losing her entire fleet and almost her life.

"I don't see we have any other choice," Dakroth said, following the peculiar creature. "Besides, it's about time I faced this H'aaztre personally and had a face to face with him."

Callestra watched as Dakroth followed after the strange toad creature and then, reluctantly, followed after them. She had a bad feeling about this.

So far, these avatars, along with their signs and omens, had been nothing but manipulative. Malicious. And each time she was in their presence, she couldn't escape this strange feeling that made her skin crawl. It was as if she were in the presence of something truly evil.

If she had to describe the feeling, it was as though a great malevolent force was lingering over them. And all its hate redirected to you the moment you came into its purview. And then it smiled upon you, offering false pleasantries and artificial niceties as it tore your beating heart out of your chest and dragged your soul to whatever hell you believed in.

38

Meleh'Kendar sounded the alarm and dashed across the garden path to the shield generators. The repairs he and Jegra had made were holding. Another explosion rattled the protective dome erected around the palace and he turned to see the black ships hovering in formation as they swarmed the perimeter. They had returned. This time there were more. A lot more. *A dozen or more,* he estimated.

"Meleh'Kendar!" a voice shouted. He turned to see Doctor Amora Van Gogh racing toward him, her white lab coat flapping in the breeze. "The girl! Have you seen her?"

"No," he said, "I can't say that I have."

"Nobody has," Amora answered, resting her hands on her knees and panting as she tried to catch her breath.

"What do you mean 'nobody has seen her?'"

"The kitchen crew was the last to have seen her. After that, she dropped off the radar."

"She must be around here somewhere. I'll have search teams—"

"Admiral Grendok already has a full contingent of his own people scouring the palace. Still no sign of her. And there's one more thing."

Meleh'Kendar raised an eyebrow. "Well, are you planning on keeping me in suspense or are you going to spit it out?"

"Sorry," Amora said. "I'm not used to running so much." She took a deep breath and then cleared her throat. "One of the empress's hover bikes is missing."

"Dammit," Meleh'Kendar said. Now was not the time to be dashing off and getting into even more trouble. But he would have to worry about that another time. Right now, he needed to keep the palace secure and the shields up and running.

Another loud explosion startled them both. They looked up at the blue flickering dome above them and watched in fright as it faltered briefly. Luckily, however, the wavering shield strength was short lived and the energy dome snapped back into solid form, prompting both Meleh'Kendar and Doctor Amora to let out a great big sigh of relief.

"Will that thing hold?" Amora asked, gazing up at the blue energy dome high above them.

"For now. But if they keep firing at it like that, we may have to fight sooner rather than later." He turned to her and eyed her up and down. "Are you well versed in hand-to-hand combat and self-defense techniques?"

"I'm afraid not."

"In that case, if they breach our defenses, you return to the medical lab and barricade yourself and your staff inside. Admiral Grendok and my forces will handle the dirty work down here."

Amora nodded and turned back toward the palace. Another loud boom shook the grounds like an earthquake and she cringed as she ran back along the garden path to the palace.

Amora did as Meleh'Kendar had instructed and gathered her full staff in the medical wing and barricaded themselves inside. "Listen up people, if those mercs break through the palace defenses and manage to get inside the grounds, we're to hold up here."

"What about casualties, ma'am?"

"We'll wait till the smoke settles and begin bringing in the wounded. Until we can safely leave, we'll rely on the teleporter to bring us the wounded."

Her staff all nodded and she dismissed them. When she turned toward the hallway, she saw Grendok standing outside. He had a peculiar expression on his face. It was as if he were trying to hold back a smile because he'd thought of something funny.

"Is everything all right?" asked Amora. It was a peculiar emotion to be having at a time like this, but she couldn't help but ask if he was doing okay.

"Perfectly fine, miss," he said, still smiling to himself. "Everything will turn out fine."

She nodded and then turned away from him. As she returned to preparing for wounded, she glanced back at the satyr and made a mental note to keep an eye on him. He seemed…unstable, somehow.

Thirty klicks to the west, a hoverbike toured across the scorched desert surface, kicking up a billowing sand plume in its wake.

Lycia Alakandra, wrapped in desert garb, her face wrapped up tight to keep the sand out, and wearing biker goggles, revved the throttle. Then, jamming on the brake at the same time she gunned the throttle, the reverse thrusters fired and she entered a broad tail slide, cutting a large crescent shape in the flat sands. Letting off the gas, she brought the bike to a stop and kicked out her leg to balance the heavy vehicle as she let the engine idle.

Although the bike ran on an electrical system, its turbines still made a deafening sound. Killing the engines, she put the bike in park, unwrapped the shemagh from around her face, and left it sitting as she strolled over to Bazhov's bunker.

If she was correct, it would still be here.

Before she even reached the entrance of his house, the sands jostled and a battle android rose up to greet her. It held a forearm blaster trained on her. "Halt. This is private property," it said in a standard, factory issued robotic voice.

She stopped, raised her hands in surrender, and slowly drew back. "Do you know who I am?"

The X-5 series android coked its head. "Voice recognition authenticated. Bazhov's last command was to protect the girl. Are you the girl?"

"I am the girl," Lycia said. "My name is Lycia. Lycia Alakandra."

"Inputting designation." There was a brief pause as the robot input the data then it lowered its arm and stood at attention. "How may I serve the Lycia?"

"I need your protection," she said.

The android didn't reply. It just stared at her. Then, after another moment, it answered, "Guardian mode activated."

She nodded, a faint smile settling across her lips. "Come with me," she said, and turned back toward the hoverbike. The android waited for her to take the lead and then complied and trailed after her.

After climbing onto the hoverbike, she patted the passenger seat behind her and motioned with her chin for the robot to join her. It paused and stared at the seat, as though it were deliberating on whether it was safe or not, and then climbed on board.

"Hold on to my waist," she said, reaching back and helping to guide its metal hands to her mid-section. Soon its metal hands gently, yet firmly, gripped onto her. She pulled down her goggles and smiled. "Now, hold on to your hat."

The X-5 battle android began to respond, "I don't have a ha—" when its voice was drowned out by the revving of the bike's engine and the blare of the turbines as the thrusters came online.

Lycia kicked in the clutch and slammed the throttle hard. The bike's thrusters opened wide and two elongated blue torches shot out the back like giant Roman candles.

The robot's head snapped back as they tore away from the bunker at breakneck speed, going from zero to sixty miles per hour in two point three seconds.

Thrilled by the adrenaline rush that came with the power and the speed, Lycia shouted, "WooHoo!" as they shot across the desert like a silver bullet.

Her next stop would be the space port in Mardok. It was risky heading into a busy city, but she had transferred some imperial credit to her name before she left. Grendok had graciously set her up with her own bank account and funded her quite handsomely. She didn't know why the satyr was being so nice to her, but whatever the reason, she was grateful.

The blast of a lucky missile strike finally took down the blue dome and the palace was left vulnerable. The twelve drop ships wasted no time, quickly setting down all around the palace. Soldiers in black armor poured out of the ships, all of them heavily armed and equipped with the latest tech and weaponry.

"Who are these guys?" Grendok asked, hiding behind a pillar in the main entrance, his high-power disruptor riffle drawn.

"I don't know," Meleh'Kendar answered, "but they really seem to want this girl of yours."

"Yes, well they're shit out of luck, then," he informed the chief security officer. Meleh'Kendar shot him a puzzled look. Grendok smiled at him with his yellow goat teeth. "What I meant to say is, it's probably a good thing the girl is gone, wouldn't you agree?"

"How come I get the feeling that there's something you're not telling me?"

Grendok smiled again, but kept his mouth shut. He didn't tell Meleh'Kendar about how he'd helped Lycia escape or how he'd given her enough credits to get off world. It really didn't matter anyway. If they knew what he knew, they'd have done the same.

It was his cloning facility that had made her and it was his responsibility to keep her alive in the absence of the empress to safeguard her. And if nobody knew where she was, not even him, then she'd be safe. Which is why he had given her explicit instructions to find a ship with clearance to leave, buy her way onto it, and then disappear for a while.

"You ready for this?" Meleh'Kendar asked the goat. He drew out dual blasters and shot Grendok a courageous look.

"Ready as I'll ever be."

They shared one last look and then, together, stepped out into the open and began firing their blasters at the men in black who'd descended upon them.

Meleh'Kendar managed to take out three mercs and Grendok had wounded five more and managed to shoot a sticky grenade at one of the transports. Ducking back behind the pillars, Grendok motioned for his soldiers to advance. A troop of twenty Galliforn soldiers, decked out in heavy armor, leapt into the fray and began laying down extreme cover fire.

Just then a grenade landed on the floor and skidded to a stop between them. "Grenade!" Meleh'Kendar shouted, and he threw himself onto it.

"No!" Grendok shouted. But he couldn't do anything about it. The grenade went off, vaporizing Meleh'Kendar in the blink of an eye. The subsequent blast picked Grendok up off the ground and sent him flying backward into the pillar. He hit with a harsh crack, a sound like bones breaking, and fell to the ground.

Grendok struggled to his knees, realizing his shoulder and an entire set of ribs were fractured, and looked up to see flakes of ash fluttering down to the ground like gently falling snow. "Rest in peace, brave soul," Grendok said in a low voice. "Your sacrifice will not be forgotten."

Red encroached upon his vision and he fought to stay conscious. One of his men raced over to his side. "Sir, are you okay?"

Grendok couldn't respond. His head was ringing and he was still too much in shock to say anything. Mustering up everything he had, he growled, "Hold the line!"

"Yes, sir!" the soldier cried.

Grendok staggered, the soldier catching him with outstretched arms, and then with a smile, the old goat's slatted eyes rolled back into his head and he passed out.

Forty-five minutes from Bazhov's home, Lycia and her X-5 battle android pulled into Mardok space port. It was the landing and takeoff site on the far Western side of the moon.

She pulled up next to a dingy looking pub called Scarback's and parked her bike next to a row of other bikes. Sitting outside on the deck that led right up to the dirt street was a burley looking biker with a cowboy hat resting his boots on the table as he sat under a parasol and rolled himself a paper cigarette.

A Lafor'allenthal indigo panther was chained to his side and sat in the shade of the table, gnawing on the femur of some large animal. The man was a Coxian, an ethnicity of Dagon which had pale blueish-gray skin and dark hair. He wore an open leather vest, black war paint on his face, and sported tribal markings and tattoos that littered his body. His long hair was tied in various braided strands that gave him the appearance of having dreadlocks, and was pulled to the back of his head and tied off with a hairband, leaving the rest free to dangle behind him like a dozen furry tails.

He raised a curious eyebrow and looked over at the girl with red eyes, his hands never stopping as he worked tobacco into the paper and rolled it so effortlessly it seemed as though he'd done it a thousand times before. "I like your bike," he said, his voice as rough as gravel.

"I like your cat" she said, eyeing the indigo panther.

The man looked down at the cat then back up at the girl. A grin spreading across his face. "I purchased it from a space captain who rescued it from an animal fighting ring. Thought it would make me look fierce, but all it does is eat and shit. Fancy a trade?"

Lycia plucked the keys out of the ignition of her bike, tossed them into the air, and caught them again. She turned to the man and eyed him, one hand on her hip as she gauged his sincerity. Her X-5 droid climbed off the bike and stood behind her like a personal bodyguard. After giving it some thought, she finally said, "It's a deal." She tossed the biker her keys and he handed over the leash.

Lycia bent down and started rubbing the cat's ears and talking to it, "You're a good boy, aren't you? Yes, you are."

The cat began purring and rubbing up against her. The full-sized panther, enthusiastically affectionate, nearly knocked her onto her ass. She laughed out loud when it licked her with its sandpaper-like tongue.

"I think he likes you," the biker said.

"He got a name?" asked Lycia, pushing the affection starved cat off of her.

The Coxian rose to his feet, towering over Lycia by thirty centimeters if not more, then grinned at her one last time, tipped his hat, and turned to enter the pub. Just before disappearing inside, he replied, "He goes by Allie. Short for Allikandra."

Allikandra was the local dialect of the name Alakandra, which meant the cat was named after the empress, and which also meant, to Lycia, that she had found her kin in the form of a Lafor'allenthal panther.

She squatted down, took the leash off the cat, and rubbed him behind his soft velvety ears. "So, you're royalty too, eh?"

"It is imperative," her battle droid informed her, "that the Lycia know there are two armed guards heading our way."

Lycia looked up and saw two of the mercs patrolling the street. She recognized their glossy black armor and their advanced tech. Also, the strange tusk elk skull insignia they wore gave them away.

It didn't seem as though they'd spotted her yet, however, so, she quickly wrapped the *shemagh* around her face and, taking the panther's leash in her hand, said, "Come along, Allie. We best get going."

In a bold move, she walked toward the guards, instead of away. When she passed one of them, she deliberately bumped his shoulder. "Hey, watch it!" she shouted, feigning outrage at the small incident and acting like a belligerent drunk. Seeing as she was coming from the direction of the pub, they'd probably not even think twice about it.

"You watch it," the guard fired back, standing his ground. He shoved her aside and she held out her hand to steady herself as she continued to act tipsy.

Allie growled and she gave a tug on the leash. "No, Allie. He's not worth it." She balked and waved her hand at him as if to suggest they weren't worth the trouble and then continued on her way.

The second guard looked over at the X-5 robot with a puzzled look on his face as he mulled over where he'd seen on like that before. "Hey, wait a minute, isn't that the droid from…"

X-5 leaped into action, ramming the first guard with its shoulder, sending the him into the ground. At the same time, it clasped the other one by his chest armor and pulled him close, put its fist under the second guard's chin, and fired of a blast with its forearm disruptor.

The energy blast shot through the soft underside of the guard's jaw and he collapsed to the round, a smoldering hole exiting the top of his helmet.

The first guard, still sprawled out on the ground, scrambled back on his hands and feet, eyes wide with fear as he glimpsed his dead comrade's lifeless face staring back at him. His hands fumbled desperately for his gun and, getting a firm hold of it, he drew it up and fired several shots off with his blaster.

The plasma bolts ricocheted off the robot's korridium plated body, catching the machine's attention. It turned toward him and, marching forward like the lethal automaton it was, aimed its smoking forearm barrels at the mercenary. "No loose ends," the robot said in its mechanical voice.

"Wait!" the man shouted.

The machine let off two intense blasts. The first one blew the man's hand into a spray of red mist that splattered his face. The second blast drilled him right between the eyes.

"All threats neutralized," X-5 stated as he turned back and rejoined Lycia and Allie.

"Right. Thanks…for that," the girl said, eyeing the carnage with a sour look on her face. She slapped the battle android's arm and said, "Let's get out of here before more of them show up."

Lycia and her two companions traipsed up the dusty street till they came to the landing pads at the space port. There were several small, one-person, cargo ships, a Galliforn fighter, and a light freighter readying for takeoff. "That one," Lycia said, pointing at the freighter.

"May I inquiry as to why the Lycia has picked that particular vessel?" X-5 asked.

"See that?" she said, her fingering sliding over to the captain, a tall, slender, Seyferrian woman with copper colored skin, light brown eyes, and a black jumpsuit that seemed to be ex-military. "A woman captain."

"I shall interrogate her and access her threat level," X-5 said, marching forward on a self-imposed mission.

"That won't be necessary," Lycia said with a chuckle. It seemed that guardian mode might be too much for the droid to handle. His processor speeds weren't up to task to thinking ahead. She'd have to upgrade his core RAM speed the first opportunity she had.

"As the Lycia wishes." X-5 stopped in his tracks and waited for further instructions. She passed him by and like a lost puppy, he followed after her when it was clear she wasn't going to be coming back for him.

Lycia strode up to the woman who was loading power cells into the cargo hold of her ship. Her jumpsuit was zipped down part way so that when she bent over to pick up the power cells, Lycia got a full glimpse of her cleavage.

A random rush of attraction surged through her and Lycia realized that, not only was she Jegra and Dakroth's hybrid clone, but she'd inherited their preoccupation with carnal desires and bisexual promiscuity. But more than that, she also had modified pheromone glands that could trigger the same sexual urges in others…which could come in handy when she needed to be persuasive.

The woman looked up when she saw the peculiar and unlikely trio approaching her.

"I'm not taking any bookings," she said.

"I can pay. Handsomely," Lycia informed the woman.

She stared at the group for a moment. Something about the girl oozed sex appeal and although she was a little young for her tastes, she couldn't help but be captivated by her. "How handsomely?"

"Five million credits now, and fifteen million more when we get to our destination."

"So, let me get this straight," the woman laughed. "You expect me to believe that a young kid like you has a spare twenty million creds just lying around?" She folded her arms under her chest and gave the girl a doubtful look.

Lycia held up her hand and nodded at the glowing implant in her wrist. The woman came over to her, raised her own wrist, and touched her glowing patch of skin to Lycia's.

The captain looked down at her wrist and sure enough, it read fifteen million credits in bold blue numbers. All of it successfully transferred into her account. She raised an eyebrow and then looked back up at the girl. Extending her hand, she smiled and said, "Welcome aboard!"

Lycia took the captain's hand and instead of shaking it, she kissed it the way Dakroth always did when he met a new love interest. "The name's Lycia. Lycia Alakandra."

The woman raised an eyebrow and, a pleasant grin forming on her mouth, asked, "How old are you, Lycia? If you don't mind my asking."

"Eighteen cycles," she said. Although that was simply her apparent age, since she was matured artificially in a test tube. She actually didn't know her *real* age, that is, when she was created or how long she'd been traveling in stasis. But, none of that mattered.

Frankly, the captain didn't need to know her complete origin story to take her on as a passenger on her ship. In fact, the less the captain knew about Lycia's past, the better off she'd be. There was no reason to drag her into her drama, too.

As they boarded the ship, Lycia said, "I didn't catch your name."

"The name's Deunan Atiyah. And this freighter," she added, running her hand along one of the inner bulkheads, "is the *Lycia Alakandra*."

"What?" Lycia paused, looking at the captain as though she were joking.

"I just named her, in your honor."

"Are you messing with me?" Lycia said, squinting at Deunan suspiciously.

Deunan stared at Lycia with a hurt look on her face. "What? You don't like it?"

"I mean, it's a little bit unexpected, if not sudden," Lycia said, brushing a clump of hair behind her ear and looking away.

All of a sudden Deunan bent over with laughter. "Oh, you should have seen your face!" She yowled so loudly that Lycia looked out the back of the ship to see if they'd drawn any unnecessary attention to themselves.

"Ha-ha," Lycia replied, a nervous smile on her face. "You got me."

"Come on, kiddo, you'll need to do better than a pheromone mod if you want to seduce me."

"Seduce you?" Lycia asked, taken aback.

The woman's left eye lit up as she scanned Lycia's vitals. "You're oozing pheromones like you want to mate right here on the dock. And as tempted as I am to tear those dirty rags off your body, you're just not my type. I'd rather give you a bath than a night you'd never forget."

"I don't know whether to be flattered or insulted," Lycia said.

"As a mother of five, I know all about dealing with hormone saturated teenagers."

"You're a mother?" Lycia asked, shocked by Deunan's admission. In all honesty, she didn't look much older than Jegra, perhaps her early thirties.

"Seyfferians age less rapidly than other species. And we're modded from infancy, so out bodies always have the precise amounts of nutrients growing up, making everyone as perfectly fit as their genetic makeup will allow for."

Her glowing eye scanned Lycia one more time and Deunan raised an eyebrow. "Interesting."

"What?" Lycia said, feeling a bit self-conscious as Deunan studied her in depth.

"I'm not reading any mods. So, either you have extreme control over your pheromone glands or you're—"

"Just horny," Lycia replied. She smiled and threw her hand onto her hip. "What can I say? I'm a hormone saturated teenager. You know how it is."

Deunan laughed. "Right. Just don't get any ideas. I'm not sleeping with you."

"I wouldn't dream of it!" Lycia said, throwing up her hands in surrender.

Deunan squinted at her and then nodded for her and her companions to come the rest of the way onto the ship.

Once they were fully boarded, Deunan closed the loading ramp and offered the co-pilot's seat next to her to Lycia.

"I'm afraid there's no place for your friends to sit," she said, looking back into the main cargo hold at the robot and the cat.

"That should be no problem," Lycia replied. Then, turning around, she pointed her finger and said, "X-5, go stand in the corner over there and power down till I wake you."

"Yes," he responded, "as the Lycia wishes."

The cat leapt up onto a couple of crates, turned in a circle, twice, then stretched out and made itself comfortable.

"See?" Lycia said, "No problem."

Deunan flipped some switched and then ignited the ship's thrusters. "Hold onto your hat, kid," she said. "We're bugging out of here."

The freighter gradually rose up off the landing platform, kicking out a blast of sand in every direction. Five black-armored mercenaries stood over the remains of their dead comrades and slowly turned their heads and watched as the ship rose into the sky.

"Is that her and her infernal war toy?" the head merc asked.

A second soldier raised a device and scanned the ship for the tracker that their recon team had embedded into the war robot when they'd arrived back at Bazhov's bunker the first time.

Although they lost that unit in the explosion after they'd accidentally set off the satyr's booby trap, they had already completed their secondary mission in placing a long-range tracking bug inside the robot, just in case the satyr or the girl decided to come back for it.

By the look on his officer's face as viewed through his glass visor, it was clear that their little gambit had paid off.

"Yes, Captain Xarthon," the soldier replied, "it's them."

"Excellent," Xarthon replied. "Log that freighter's serial number and send word to Demeris Ferrison that we have the mark tagged and will be pursuing her."

"Yes, sir," the officer replied. He saluted and then started back to the black drop ship that waited for them.

Xarthon slowly looked back up at the sky. The freighter was but a pinprick now, but its thrusters blared bright. "We'll be seeing each other again real soon. You can count on it."

39

The *Shard* **drifted** off the coast of Nyctan's capitol city, Vallorium, in the aquamarine bay just outside the city. Jegra stood on the shoreline, alone, her purple cape flowing in the breeze, her korridium bikini glinting in the warm sun, as fine, sandy beaches stretched into the distant horizon, disappearing where the blue sky kissed the white sands.

A troop of seven Knights of Caelum marched up to her position and, with a rattle of heavy armor, they all formed a perimeter, clanked their metal boots together, and blocked her route to the palace.

The lead knight, holding center position, stepped forward and spoke. "Emissary, we were not expecting you."

"I demand an audience with the Administratrix, Anaïs Nin," Jegra said. There was an audible silence and Jegra could feel in her bones that something was wrong. Her cape fluttered and a distant seagull cried out, its voice dissipating as it was carried along by the salty ocean breeze.

The knight reached up and touched his helmet. The helmet came apart like a living jigsaw puzzle, opening up and then folding into the back of the suit, revealing a familiar face.

"Sir Lance Bishop?" Jegra said, smiling at him. His demeanor remained stiff, cold even. "It's so good to see you."

"I wish I could say the same. But, I regret to inform you, Emissary, that the Administratrix is dead."

"What?" Jegra gasped. "How?"

"It no longer matters," he said. "But if you'll kindly follow us, we shall escort you to the imperial strong hold. Nodengoth wishes to converse with you."

Even hearing the name of one of H'aaztre's acolytes made her shudder. She nodded and looked back at her ship floating upon the gently rolling waves of the bluest sea she'd seen this side of Earth. She knew her people were monitoring her from the ship and that they'd be ready to intervene at the earliest signs of trouble.

"Yes, that would be acceptable," she replied and turned and accompanied the knights back to the palace.

The large palace doors drew open automatically and revealed the royal hall. The knights stopped on the steps and raised their swords then, crossing their tips, created an archway for Jegra to pass beneath.

She paused at the end and looked at Lance Bishop's face. He didn't register any emotion but merely gestured with his hand for her to go on inside, alone.

Jegra reached out to touch him, feeling sorry for him, then stopped herself. Nyctans weren't accustomed to displays of affection and it might send the wrong message. She nodded graciously and then turned to go inside.

Then entire throne room was empty all but for a sleek, black, grand piano sitting at the very center of the room.

"Oh, my god!" Jegra blurted. "A piano!"

She made her way to it at a brisk pace. She couldn't believe a musical instrument from Earth was sitting here in the palace of Nyctan. But she didn't care. Brushing back her cloak as she pulled out the bench, she sat down and began to play.

As her fingers touched down on the keys and the glorious sound rose out from the vibrating strings, Jegra had to hold back her tears. Taking a deep breath, she calmed herself and then started to play *Nuvole Bianche* by Ludovico Einaudi.

Her head bobbed and her body swayed with the rhythm and flow of the music as her fingers glided across the ivory and glossy black keys. As the music filled the throne room, she let its glorious melodies enrapture her.

"Such a beautiful piece of music," a voice said, halfway through her private concert. Jegra stopped playing and looked up to see a Nyctan man dressed in golden armor smiling at her from across the room.

They shared a long, silent gaze and she slowly rose to her feet, the bench screeching along the floor as she got up.

"No need to get up," the man said, motioning to her that it was all right to continue playing. "I was rather enjoying listening to you play. Such a joyous melody.”

“I appreciate the compliment,” Jegra replied. “But, as we both know, I’m not here to perform for you.”

“I suppose not,” he said, his smile still holding strong as he looked at her. After a moment, he laughed and said, “You know something, you’re not at all what I expected.”

“And what did you expect?”

He pursed his lips and looked her up and down. “I anticipated a more barbarian aspect,” he answered, pressing a finger to his chin as he studied her figure. “I hadn’t expected a sophisticated mind to be in control of the brute strength.”

“I think you’ll find I’m full of surprises,” Jegra replied.

“Oh, I sure do hope so,” Nodengoth replied.

Jegra stared at the angelic creature for the longest time then said, “Obviously you need me for something, otherwise you would have had me killed the moment I set foot on Nyctan.”

“And smart too,” he said, his smile widening.

Jegra crossed her arms under her chest, her cleavage pushing up as she shifted her hips and waited for him to spill it.

“You see, this body is but an avatar, my final form has yet to come. My power is too great to contain in any one form at present, which is why I need three avatars. My high priestess failed in her duty to find me a suitable body, and paid dearly for her failure.”

“And what does any of that have to do with me?” asked Jegra.

“A single body cannot contain my power, unless it comes from an exceptional lineage and pedigree. I am guessing that you have the right DNA to contain my essence.”

“You want to use me as your vessel?”

“Not exactly.” He smiled at her in a way that was unnerving. “I am almost certain you can supply me with the vessel I need for my permanent form.”

“You want me to have your child?” She raised an eyebrow. “Why would I want to do that?”

He paused and looked at her curiously, as though he didn’t quite understand the question. “No, none of us are suited to give you the divine seed. But, as I understand it, it won't be necessary. You are with child already, are you not?"

Jegra covered her abdomen and took a cautious step back. "How did you know about that?"

"I can hear the life growing inside you."

"Since you're such a good listener," Jegra said, smiling at him in a strained manner. "Maybe you can hear my plea. A long and bothersome occupation doesn't suit either of our causes. I'm here to extend an olive branch in the name of peace. Allow Dagon Prime to remain an independent entity in the empire you're building, and I promise you that my people will not get in the way of your plans."

"My plans?" he said, his grin fading. "I think you mean H'aaztre's plans."

"I'm confused, am I talking with Nodengoth or H'aaztre?"

"Both," he sneered. "And what do you know of my plans anyway, human? Can you comprehend the mind of a god?!"

Jegra shrugged. "Be it man or god, it doesn't make any difference to me. You types are all alike. You only crave one thing…power. Tell me I'm wrong."

Nodengoth's arm flew out faster than she could react and clutched her by her throat. Hoisting her up, he hissed, "How dare you liken the Gilded Master to a common mortal. Do not think for an instant your puny mind can comprehend the magnificence of H'aaztre! He is beyond your reasoning. Compared to him, you are but an insect, an insignificant spec. Know your place." He dropped her to the ground and turned away, taking a moment to calm himself.

"I beg your pardon," Jegra said, rubbing her sore neck and watching him carefully as her hand slowly brushed her cape back, and inched closer to her battle axe. "I misspoke."

H'aaztre calmed himself and his readily available smile reappeared with ease. "Yes. I suppose you did. But…all is forgiven."

Jegra nodded in thanks. Although, she was growing a little tired of this prick, and quickly, she bet dimes to dollars she could take him with one hand tied behind her back.

"Do you think so?" Nodengoth asked out loud.

"Excuse me?" Jegra asked, confused by the question. "I didn't say anything."

"You mentioned something about taking me in a fight with one arm tied behind your back."

Shocked that he could read her mind, she smiled politely. "It was a fleeting thought. Nothing but a vagary of the human mind which, as you are probably well aware, is insect-like and filled with unimportant thoughts."

"Yet, you entertained the thought long enough for me to see it. Do you believe this random notion?"

He strolled up to her, verging on her personal boundaries. She felt the urge to draw back. Instead of showing weakness, however, she held her ground.

A dark aura clung to his gilded frame and she squinted and looked into his black eyes. Eyes encircled with a gold ring that flared bright in the dimness of the large hall. That's how she knew she was talking to H'aaztre, and not Nodengoth. When H'aaztre was present, so were the golden rings around the irises of his eyes.

"If it was a matter of brute strength, yes. I'm certain I could beat your physical form. But somehow, I doubt you're the kind to limit yourself to physical strength alone. You would fight with everything you have and, apparently, that includes reading minds. In which case, I'd be foolish to try and take you on."

"Yes," he chuckled, taking a step back. "I suppose you would need to be rather foolish to entertain such a fleeting thought. It would be virtually impossible to win a battle with one who could see your every move before you made it."

His words seemed to linger in the air, as if they were more of a warning than an observation.

Jegra nodded and tilted her hips, resting her hand on the inlet of her hourglass shaped curve as she contemplated what came next. "What is it you want?" she asked.

"I want you to submit to my will. Not just you," he corrected, "everyone. Everything. Everything that is, ever was, or that will ever come to be."

"And, if I may be so bold as to inquire, why would I do that? Why should any of us bend the knee to your authority?"

"Because I am God," he said with a certitude that, although deadly serious, couldn't help but seem completely and utterly ludicrous.

Jegra had to squelch a laugh before it erupted out of her. "I think you'll find that free people don't take kindly to tyrants with delusions of grandeur."

"Is that what you think of me?" he asked.

"Maybe you are a god," she said, waving her hand dismissively at the mere thought of it. "Or maybe you've simply never been put in your proper place. Either way, I could care less. Regardless of whether you are what you say you are—I see right through you."

H'aaztre threw back his head and bellowed with laughter. It was a hearty laugh that rose up straight from his gut. Wiping his eyes, he said, "I think I may like you, Jegra Alakandra. You are noble and true. It's a pity, then, that I must destroy you and everything you hold dear if I am to bring dominion over your rebellious little empire."

Jegra smiled. "In that case, I wish you the best of luck. You are going to need it."

She spun on her heel, throwing out her cape, and stormed back toward the main doors.

"It was a pleasant chat," H'aaztre said bitingly. He wasn't accustomed to being walked out on, but he held back his temper. "Let's do it again sometime."

Jegra paused and looked over her shoulder. "I don't know what you are, but I will find a way to defeat you. On that you have my solemn oath."

When she turned to leave again, H'aaztre called out to her.

"Wait." She paused and glanced back at him. "I have a counteroffer. Give me the life growing inside you and I will agree to your terms. Your people will not be harmed. Your empire will experience peace. And I will avoid interfering in your affairs. A fair trade, if you think about it."

Offended, Jegra spun on her heels and glared at the angel-like being standing before her. "Never," she said, placing both hands across her belly in a protective manner. "I'll never let you have my child."

H'aaztre cocked his head again and then shrugged. "That's too bad," he said at last. Stepping aside, he gestured for her to go on, their conversation had run its course. "You're free to go, Empress Jegra Alakandra."

She bowed her head respectfully and then stormed out of the palace and down the stairs. The Knights of Caelum snapped to attention and saluted her as she passed.

As Emissary, and with the Administratrix dead, she now held the rank of Commander of the Order. A little-known fact that even H'aaztre didn't seem to realize. And, not only this, but once she was aware of his ability to read minds, she started masking hers. A little trick she had learned after discovering how to block Dakroth's mental influences.

When Jegra returned to the wharf, the Nephilim military was there waiting for her. A number of Nyctan men and women had been conscripted into the Nephilim army and Jegra stood poised, scanning all their faces.

"What is the meaning of this?"

The general of the Nephilim stepped forward. "I apologize, Empress Alakandra, but we're under strict orders not to let you leave Nyctan."

"Under whose authority?"

"Under H'aaztre's authority," he replied.

Jegra grew furious inside as the Gilded Asshat double crossed her, allowing her to walk into his trap. But she wasn't having it. She squinted at the man with cold, hard eyes. "I'm going to ask you once and only once. Step aside or face the consequences."

The general, ever the faithful soldier to his golden god sitting upon the hill, did not budge. Jegra glanced back at the knight, who flanked her and would easily tear through her if she tried to take them on in a fight. She turned back and did a quick head count of the Nephilim forces. There were roughly sixty of them to one of her and seven Knights.

She sighed out a lengthy breath that was both sad and a little bit exhausted from all the drama. Perhaps more than this, it was simply an unfair fight. For them.

"Knights!" she shouted. "To arms!"

She knew that, like her, Sir Lance Bishop viewed H'aaztre as an imposter to the real God they all worshipped. And although most of Nyctan had been brainwashed by this powerful new poser, the fact remained that the knights were genetically programmed to serve a commander. That commander had been Anaïs Nin. But she was dead. Now, their loyalty fell to Jegra.

"Slay the heathens of the false god!" Sir Lance Bishop shouted, taking Jegra's side and drawing out his plasma blade. The blade glowed orange hot and hummed and crackled on the cool seaside air.

The Nephilim general drew his sword and lunged at Sir Bishop. But Bishop blocked his blow.

"You're making a grave mistake, Sir Knight," the general said.

"The Knights of Caelum don't follow false gods," Bishop growled.

The clash initiated, the Nephilim soldier charged forward, disruptor guns blasting away at the knights, swords drawn and screaming out *"Deus hoc vult!"*

Jegra looked around at the carnage and the chaos as the knights encircled her, protecting her. She had failed to broker peace. Now all that was left was to fight. "I'll see you soon, my friends," she said as the golden light came down to retrieve her.

"Don't worry about us, ma'am," Sir Lance Bishop said. "These fools don't know who they're dealing with."

Jegra replied with a subtle nod and then she was gone.

Back at the Nyctan palace, the decadent golden spires rising high into the sky like those of an ancient cathedral, the cherry trees waved in the warm autumn breeze that cut through the courtyard and H'aaztre peered up into the sky and watched intently the small silver spec flying away.

Empress Jegra Alakandra's ship, the *Shard*, was swiftly climbing into the atmosphere as it made its hasty retreat. As it shrank away, there was a flash as the ship made the jump to hyperspace.

He smiled up at the blue sky, the sound of a battle raging in the distance. "Run as fast and far as you like, my child," he said, speaking out loud to himself, vitriol filling his every word, "but there is no hiding from me. I will find you. And when I do, I promise you, I will gut you like the insignificant ape you are and tear that child out of your womb with my bare hands and make it my own."

"Gruesome," a gleeful voice said. H'aaztre smiled and turned around. Standing at the other end of the courtyard were his siblings, Giddion and Azra'il Nun. Both smiled at him and he smiled back at them.

Giddion did a back flip and fidgeted, hopping from one foot to another. At the same time, Azra'il checked her fingernails, making sure the metallic gold nail polish hadn't chipped.

"Brother, sister," he said cheerfully as he greeted them. "What news do you bring me?"

"Everything is falling in line with the prophecy," Giddion said.

"What about the woman?" H'aaztre asked, turning his attention to Azra'il.

"She posed no problem at all. In fact, you may say we lucked out in finding a zealot."

H'aaztre smiled even more broadly. Linking his hands behind his back, his golden armor gleaming in the light of the courtyard, he replied, "No, not luck. Providence, my dear."

The three shared a glance and then all together broke out into a fit of laughter. As they laughed, the cherry trees withered in their presence until they were beyond saving.

"What would you have us do now?" Azra'il asked.

"Now, we occupy the system. I want every planet, every moon, and every hyperspace route monitored and regulated. Dispatch the fleet to every sector. Set up check points. Limit cargo and trade routes to special clearance personnel only."

"What of the emperor and his woman?" Giddion asked.

"Oh," H'aaztre said, the corners of his mouth tightening into a malicious grin. "I have something special in mind for those two."

Giddion hopped up and down excitedly. He rubbed his hands together and said, "Goody, goody! Can I watch?"

H'aaztre nodded. This seemed to excited the toad creature even more.

"Yippy!" Giddion said, cartwheeling around the other two with the excitement and energy of a small child.

"Brother," Azra'il said, placing her hand on H'aaztre's arm, "if there is anything else I can do for you, I beseech you, give me the honor of fulfilling your deepest desires."

H'aaztre moved closer, her thigh slipping in between his. He reached around her, grabbing the small of her back with one hand and gently brushing her hair out of her face with the other.

Gradually, he stroked her shoulder and ran his hand down her feminine figure, pausing at the bulging curve of her breast.

He squeezed tightly, causing a small moan from Azra'il and then drew her into him. She reached up with her hands and placed them around his face and drew his lips down to hers.

Whispering, he spoke softly, his hot breath passing from his lips and sticking to hers. She licked her lips and waited for him to do something. Anything.

"The depths of my desires know no bounds. Can you say the same, dear sister?"

"No, but I live to serve."

"Oh, what fun!" Giddion clapped his hands again and then hopped onto a nearby bench to watch and see whether the two love birds would tear each other's clothes off and make love to each other right there and now.

Without warning, all three bodies froze in place. Their heads and arms fell limp on stiff bodies, giving them the appearance of sleeping marionettes. Their golden armor dimmed as the radiant energy faded and, in their darkened state, they stood there, staring at random corners of the courtyard. Not a single thought ran through their heads and, for all intents and purposes, they were dead.

Several minutes went by until, at last, all three drew in large gaping breaths as though they had just resurfaced from a deep dive in the placid waters off the coast of Vallorium. The light in their golden armor returned with full luminosity and they glanced around at one another's placid faces.

Reactivated, the avatars turned, as if programmed with new orders, and exited the courtyard without so much as saying a friendly goodbye.

40

Debris and people flew out of the gaping wound in the side of the empress's battle cruiser, the *Shard*. Screams rang out as people were torn away from whatever they were doing and sucked into the vacuum of space along with a clutter of debris and all the items of a lived-in ship. Everything from personal belongings to tools and supplies stripped right out of storage and jettisoned into space.

Four entire decks were now exposed to the frigid elements of space, and the glittering trail of carnage left in the wake of the ship-to-ship collision looked as though this might be the end of the *Shard*. With such a massive gash in the side, the self-healing membrane of the ship's hull couldn't regenerate. At the same time, the kamikaze styled attack had left the enemy ship even worse off.

Amid the chaos swirling about the medical bay, Jegra screamed out as her contractions clenched down on her. Outside the med bay windows, people flew past, their arms and hands flailing as they reached out to clasp anything that they could to try and prevent themselves from being sucked into the vacuum of space.

The hull breach was severe enough that where there was once a normal corridor, and behind that a room, and behind that room several layers of piping and power conduits, wiring, and bulkheads, was now a star dappled expanse. Even the ship's liquid skin had been peeled away to show a full host of glowing enemy vessels with their radiant energy and heavily armored crustacean designs.

A blue wavering sheath of energy blanketed the open wound. The emergency dark-energy shields kicked on and a shimmer of blue congealed into a translucent veil. However, this was a Band-Aid at best; the ship's hull was severely compromised. With such a large swatch of the bulkheads gone, structural integrity became a main concern for Lianica, who manned things from the bridge.

The entire ship creaked and moaned, the bulkheads threatening to buckle under the weight of the upper decks and collapse in on themselves, filling the gaping cavity left across the port side of the gutted hull.

"It's time," said doctor Amora Van Gogh from the foot of the birthing bed. "The baby is coming."

She gently placed Jegra's feet into the stirrups of the bed to raise her legs and then carefully spread her knees apart. The empress let out another grunt and tried to resist the contraction. With super-strength came super contractions. If she was a hundred times stronger than a regular Earth woman, her contractions, she assumed, were a hundred times more painful.

The agony was too much to bear. Her hand reached out and she grabbed the sleeve of Danica's teal scrubs. Tugging hard, she drew Danica close and grumbled, "Painkillers! Now!"

She screamed out again, the veins bulging in her taught neck, and Amora nodded, agreeing with Jegra's request, and handed Dani a NeedleAir injector. "Give her this," she said.

Danica did as asked and injected the empress with the painkillers. Jegra lay back down on the bed and took a full breath–the first she was able to take since the contractions had started.

Jegra lay back on the bed; a puddle of sweat had already pooled below her lower back, but she didn't care. Rather, the coolness of the soaked sheets helped to soothe the sore hotness of her lower back.

"You've gotta get this baby out of me, Doc. That's an order!"

"That's the general idea," Amora quipped.

Danica shook her head as if to say joking wasn't such a good idea right now. With Jegra unable to control her strength, the pain-fueled surges of adrenaline and her general irritableness were a deadly combination.

"Don't worry, Dani. She'll be alright. All mothers feel an equivalent pain."

Jegra's hand flew out and grabbed Dani's scrubs again. She pulled her near and whispered something in her ear.

Danica nodded sympathetically and dabbed Jegra's head with a cool wet cloth which she had prepared earlier. "Don't worry, my luv. Everything will be all right."

"The head is crowning!" Amora announced, reaching in between Jegra's thighs to take the baby's head and help guide it out of the vaginal canal.

As she tugged on the infant's head, a space opened up slightly below the baby's neck and let out a deluge of amniotic fluid, which poured out of its mother like a bucket of water being dumped onto the floor.

"A little further," Amora said. She added a motivational, "Push!" when Jegra's contraction came.

"I AM PUSHING!" she screamed along with the contraction.

"Harder!" Amora shouted.

"I AM!!!"

"Keep pushing!"

"AIEEE!" Jegra screamed at the top of her lungs.

A violent jerk shook the ship and everything in the med bay slid to the left of the room. Amora dropped to her knees and scooped up the baby into her arms, catching it as it slipped out.

Without even hesitating, Danica threw up her hand and erected a forcefield, preventing them all from crashing into the far wall. Outside the medical bay windows, fighters streaked by, green proton blasts firing, and explosions lighting up the dark expanse. The battle did not seem to be going well. But, at least, Lianica was doing her best to keep them all alive.

"I gotcha, little one," Amora said, rising back to her feet.

"Oh my god!" Danica cried out, clasping her hands over her mouth. "He's so beautiful!"

"He?" Jegra asked. "It's a boy?"

Amora snipped the umbilical cord and wrapped the baby up in a soft white towel. She quickly flipped him over and slapped him on his lavender back. Startled, the infant began whaling. The sounds of newborn life filled the medlab.

She handed the bundle to Jegra, who took him in her arms and looked down at her beautiful son. "He's gorgeous," she said.

Danica leaned in and pulled the blanket down so she could get a better look at her son's face.

"We made that..." she said, still stunned by it all. Stunned by the fact that their DNA was compatible, by the fact that her male organs were functioning, and that they now had a baby in their life. She didn't know what to do with a baby.

She wasn't the mother type. And she was desperately hoping that Jegra's primate instincts would kick in, for both their sakes. After all, primates were among the most nurturing species found on any planet.

Just then the little babe reached up with tiny lavender fingers and grabbed Danica's pinky-finger. She let out a sigh as her heart melted and she turned to Jegra and kissed her on the lips.

Jegra pulled the bed sheet down and the little one nestled into her bosom. Finding her nipple, he began suckling.

"That's good," Amora said. "He's strong. Most babies take a few attempts before they figure out how to breastfeed, but this little one is a natural."

"That he is," Danica said, brushing her son's dark hair on his light purple head.

"The good news is, you are both producing breastmilk. So, you'll each be able to take turns feeding him and enjoy bonding with him in your own way."

"He's definitely going to grow up to be a breast man," Jegra joked. Danica laughed.

"Doc, do you think—" Danica looked over at Doctor Amora's wide eyes and saw the blood dribbling down her mouth and chin. She screamed.

Jegra craned her neck to see what the matter was and clutched her baby tight at the horror that stood before them.

The yellow glowing blade withdrew from Amora's torso and disappeared out of view. The doc dropped to her knees, a stunned look on her face, and then fell forward onto the floor with a harsh smack—the side of her face splashing in Jegra's fluids, now mingled with Amora's blood.

H'aaztre stood grinning at them. His awful black eyes fell onto the newborn and Danica stepped into his line of sight, blocking him from looking at her son.

"Don't you dare look at him," she snarled.

H'aaztre didn't even shift his gaze, as he was still fixated on the child. His future vessel. Raising a hand, he shot off a blast of radiant energy that smashed into Danica with a force so powerful it swept her off her feet. She was instantly picked up and flung across the room like a rag doll.

Danica hit the back wall with a bone shattering crunch, her spine fracturing and her head getting a terrible concussion in the process. She collapsed to the floor and struggled to push herself up. She desperately wanted to help shield her baby, but a relentless bout of vertigo crippled her and made her nauseous.

Perhaps worse than this, when she tried to reach over with her left arm to prop herself up, she realized it was missing. Looking down, all she found was a bloody stump for a shoulder. Nothing else remained of her arm. That was the last grim realization she had before passing out from the severity of her trauma.

Jegra's head snapped to Danica then back around to H'aaztre. "Stay away from us!" she warned. Clutching her child tightly in her arms, she reached up and grabbed his head. "I'd sooner crush his skull and save him from you than let you get your bloody hooks in him."

"You'd do that?" H'aaztre asked in an inquisitive tone. His eyes finally flitting to her. The gold halo that ran around the circumference of his pupils seemed to glow with excitement. "You'd sacrifice the life your own flesh and blood, of your own child, to keep him from me?"

She gently began to squeeze down on the crying infants head. Harder and harder. H'aaztre took a cautious step closer. She screamed, fighting against her own instinctual urge to save the baby from the monster standing before them and, at the same time, knowing that she must kill him in order to save him.

No baby should have to suffer. And certainly no mother should have to kill her own child. There had to be another way. There had to be. Unable to find a way out that didn't end in her doing something she'd regret for all eternity, she relinquished her grip on the wailing infant and kissed him on his head instead.

H'aaztre gently took the baby from her arms and Jegra began weeping. She was too exhausted to resist. Too tired to put up a fight. She could barely sit up in bed, let alone stay conscious.

"At long last, my final form has arrived," the golden king said, smiling down at the infant cradled in his arms. "Now, together, we will rule the galaxy as prophesied."

"Please," Jegra pleaded. "I beg of you. Don't take him. Take me instead."

H'aaztre gave her a surprised look. "You?" he said, in a disgusted tone. "What good are you to me? You lay there in your own filth, a weak and pitiful woman. You cannot even protect your own child. Why would I ever want you?"

"Please," she begged, a desperation filling her voice. He merely ignored her pleas and, cradling the baby in his arms, fanned his wings, turned, and walked back to the other side of the room.

Jegra threw off her covers and, letting out a painful grunt, swung her legs over the edge of her bed. Her feet touched down on the cold floor and she slowly, agonizingly, slid out of bed.

H'aaztre looked back in time to see her collapse under her own weight and then tapped the chest plate of his golden armor. The spot he had touched glowed with the residual heat of his fingertips and then a comm link opened. "I have the child," he said. "Bring us back to the ship."

A golden teleport beam came down and whisked both the Gilded Master and Jegra's child away with it.

The sparkling light faded even as Jegra crawled through her own blood and muck crying out for her son. She reached out to him, letting out one last scream, but slipped and fell onto the doctor's lifeless corpse. She sobbed into Amora's back, feeling numb as the swirling chaos of her emotions matched the swirling chaos outside the medical bay. That's when she remembered Dani was sitting in the corner of the room, bleeding to death.

"Dani!" she hollered. Finding the strength in her to try and get to her love, she turned when an abrupt jolt shook the ship. Another layer of the ship's hull and the decks above them tore away.

Jegra was knocked onto her side and everything in the room slid to the port side of the ship. She crashed into the wall. The artificial gravity cut out and everything began to float.

Jegra strained her neck as she looked for Danica. Just then, shrieks of terror rang out as more crew members were ripped out of the ship by the clutches of the invading blackness. At the same time, concussive explosions occurred in succession several decks below and several above. The ship was breaking up.

The artificial gravity kicked back in and everything slammed back down to the floor. Jegra hit so hard she spat up on herself. Wiping a string of saliva away from her mouth, she continued crawling toward Danica, who lay slumped in the corner of the room, head resting against the far wall.

Lianica's voice came across the ship-wide comm system. "This is Captain Lianica Blackstar. All hands to the emergency escape pods. I repeat, all hands to emergency escape pods. Abandon ship."

The medical bay window flashed with a wash of fiery plasma bursts as a power conduit a deck above blew out. Luckily, the medical bay's reinforced design held against the blast. But the fact remained, in a matter of minutes there would be no more ship. No more shields. Nothing protecting them from the cold vacuum of space. If Jegra couldn't reach Danica in time, they'd be doomed to meet the same ghastly fate as all the rest.

"Danica!" Jegra called out, crawling toward her lover. Her partner. Her best friend. "Wake up, babe. We have to go."

Red encroached around her vision as the trauma began to take its toll. But she fought through it and pushed forward. *Don't give up,* she said to herself. *Just a little bit further.*

The pressure in her head intensified and flashed red-hot, then incrementally began to seep out into a layer of blackness. *No, she told herself. You can't pass out. Not yet.* She was almost there. Almost to where Dani sat, leaning against the wall, hunched over.

Nearly there, Jegra reached her hand out toward Danica, who wasn't responsive. Tunnel vision took hold of her, and Danica retreated from Jegra's grasp. "No!" she shouted. *Don't quit on me. Not fucking yet!*

Danica's image faded until it was but a pinprick of light. Jegra held on to that light as long as she possibly could. But, even with all her strength, she was still mortal. Eventually, the cold cruel reality of it all came crashing down around her and the light was extinguished.

41

A blast of blast of white-hot sparks rained down from the ceiling of the medical bay. As the embers fluttered to the floor, cooling on the polished gray surface, two bars of light lit up in the center of the room.

Materializing in the center of the medlab was Captain Lianica Blackstar and Lieutenant Brei'Alas Kusagara. Once the teleport process finished and the two women's ghostly visages solidified into tangible people; they each took in a deep breath and scanned the room for survivors.

"Over here," Brei'Alas shouted above the series of explosions ringing out all around them. The ship was going up in flames and the Nephilim fleet continued to bombard them without any remorse. If it kept up, the *Shard* wouldn't last for very much longer. "It's the empress."

"I found Doctor Amora," Lianica said, rushing over and checking for a pulse. A deeply troubling sense of disappointment came over her when she felt the coldness of Amora's skin and the lack of any cardiac rhythm whatsoever. She looked up at Brei and shook her head solemnly.

A moan from the corner of the room drew both their attention and Blackstar leapt over Amora's lifeless body and pried a medical table out from the corner of the medical bay. Pinned beneath it was Danica. And by the looks of it, she was in extremely bad shape. Her right arm was missing and she had hit her head so hard that she couldn't form any words, but mumbled incoherent sounds instead.

"Don't speak," Lianica said, scooping Danica up in her arms. "You've experienced a severe head trauma." She looked up to see Brei struggling to get under Jegra's much larger body. Just then another violent blast shook the ship.

<<Core breach imminent,>> warned the computer.

"That's not good," Brei said, redoubling her efforts to try and rescue the empress.

"No," answered Lianica, "no it's not."

She placed Danica gently back onto the floor and leaned her against the far wall and then rushed over to the main entrance. The main doors had sealed shut due to the fact that the hull breach had torn half the ship out into space and it was venting atmosphere.

Next to the doors was a wall panel which she smashed in with her elbow, grabbed ahold of the jutting corners and pried the metal plate off. She tossed it to the floor, where it rattled about before dying down.

"What are you doing?" asked Brei.

"The medical labs on military vessels double as lifeboats. If the ship goes down, it's the safest place to be. I'm going to manually override the release clamps and jettison us into space."

"But won't the Nephilim see us and shoot us down on sight?"

"We're just going to have to risk it. Hopefully the debris will provide enough cover to buy us some time. But it's now or never," Lianica reached inside the opening and pulled down on a red handle. There was a loud *clunk* followed by an even louder pneumatic *hiss* which was, in turn, followed by a pressurized *pop*.

The medlab abruptly jolted and then pulled away from the main ship. Gas bursts pushed it out of the debris field and to a safe distance from the ensuing battle.

As they pulled away, Brei and Lianica both looked out the medical bay windows at the *Shard*. The gorgeous sleek ship was broken, its liquid metal hull faltering and unable to mend itself. The bulkheads of the ship beneath appearing like a skeletal frame and fires and explosions igniting all across the circumference of the ship.

A flurry of escape pods jettisoned out into space. Two dozen broke away from the ship as it went critical.

Out of nowhere, four giant squid entities jumped into the field of view and wrapped themselves around the dying vessel. The core exploded just as the final squid locked itself into place and to both Brei and Captain Blackstar's surprise, the celestial squid entities absorbed the entirety of the blast.

"Holy smokes," Brei gasped, her jaw falling open with complete and utter astonishment. "Did you see that?"

"I saw it," Blackstar said.

As they wafted lifelessly amid the remaining debris, the Nephilim fighters began using negative field tractor-beams to collects the escape pods. No doubt to apprehend the survivors.

Blackstar had to wonder why they'd taken prisoners at all. Why not just destroy the enemy? But she imagined they had much more nefarious reasons for taking the prisoners alive.

"They're collecting the survivors, captain," Brei observed, pointing out the obvious. She turned to Lianica with a frightened look. "What do we do if they come for us?"

"We fight," Lianica said. Brei shot her a timid look. "That's an order, Lieutenant. Under no circumstances can we let them take the empress."

Shards of scrap metal pinged off the hull of the medical lab. Lianica knew it was only a matter of time before the Nephilim's censors picked up their life signatures. And almost as soon as she'd had the thought, the lime-green glow of a tractor beam washed over them.

The medlab lurched to a halt, its weightless spiraling out into space prematurely stopped. Brei looked out the starboard windows and saw a giant cruiser lingering above them like an olden time air balloon-ship from the clockwork and steam days of ancient Dagon.

"I think we're about to have company," Brei said, her tone flexing with the precariousness of their situation.

Captain Blackstar drew her blaster and set it to maximum yield. If they board us, start firing and don't stop until you're out of coolant cartridges. Then use your hand-to-hand combat skills.

Brei'Alas gulped down the nervous lump in her throat. She didn't want to kill anyone let alone have to fight tooth and nail for her survival. Yet, here she was. And the empress's life depended on her.

Captain Blackstar took a breath and then fixed her gaze on Brei'Alas. "Brei," she said in a soft voice, "you've got this."

"I've got this," Brei echoed, repeating the captain's words to herself as a form of motivation.

Out of nowhere explosions ignited all across the hull of the large Nephilim battlecruiser.

"Who's firing?" Lianica asked.

Brei merely shook her head. She couldn't get a clear look. In fact, she didn't see anything out there. No ships. Just sudden explosions.

Both women peered out the medlab windows when, all of a sudden, a large piece of wreckage smashed into the glass, startling them both. Worse, however, was the fifteen-centimeter crack that it left behind.

A jagged vein opened up and then slowly started to expand in both directions. The internal pressure pushing against the vacuum of space, the crack grew, splintered off into several new directions, then cobwebbed.

"It's been a pleasure serving with you, Captain," Brei said as she watched the cracks in the window grow almost exponentially.

"Likewise, Lieutenant Brei'Alas Kusagara."

A wavering patch of space rippled and warped as if it were bending around something. Then, to their astonishment, a ship decloaked right off their bow—or what would be considered their bow if they'd been in a ship and not a lifeboat.

"It's the *Skywend*!" Brei squealed, elation filling her voice as she realized they were saved.

The comm in the medlab crackled and Raven's voice came over the airway. "Looks like you gals could use a lift."

"Your timing couldn't be better," Lianica replied, glancing nervously over at the fracture window. She turned back toward Brei'Alas just as golden beams lit up around all four remaining women. An overwhelming sense of relief washed over her as they teleported off failing lifeboat and to safety.

When they rematerialized, they found themselves on the bridge of the *Skywend*. Raven did a quick head check to make sure they had retrieved the empress and then snapped her fingers at Kregor, who was manning the teleporter controls.

"Get her to the medical bay," Raven said to him as she slipped down into the pilot's seat of her ship.

Kregor rose up from his station and Gyllek effortlessly slipped in after him and took over for him.

"I'll need your help," Kregor said, nodding at Angellyk as he scooped Jegra up into his massive arms.

Angellyk, who was watching with interest from the side wings, went over to Danica and scooped her up into her arms as well, and followed after the large Dragonian.

"I'm coming with you," Brei'Alas said trailing after them both.

Kregor glanced back and nodded at the small, but determined woman, and together the rescue team rushed their wounded companions to the medical bay.

"Apologies, Captain Blackstar," Raven said, her hands dancing across the controls as she manually inputted their exit strategy into the navcom. "Under normal circumstances I would have greeted a fellow captain more formally. But as you can see..."

"You're busy. Don't fret it," Lianica said. "I am a little curious as to how you found us though. Communications blew out in the initial attack. For all intents and purposes, we were sitting ducks."

"We were in the area, so to speak," Gyllek informed her without looking up from the controls. "We were monitoring the *Shard* on Nyctan via long range scanners. After your hasty withdrawal, we tagged three enemy vessels in hot pursuit. The captain felt they were probably ordered to intercept you. So, we intercepted them first."

"I appreciate that," Lianica said, glancing over at Raven. But she was too busy to respond.

The peculiar, almost cat-like girl swiveled around in the co-pilot's chair, brushed her purple hair out of her eyes, and squinted inquisitively at Lianica. "How are you at firing plasma cannons?" asked Gyllek after a moment of consideration.

"Why?" Lianica shot her a puzzled look. The computer's automated guidance systems could handle the disruptor canons just fine. Only in the case of a catastrophic system failure would the gun turrets need be manned the old-fashioned way, with a bit of muscle and some elbow grease. "Did something happen to your weapon's targeting and guidance systems?"

"Our dang cloak overloaded the whole friggin' thing and fried the entire deck. I'll need to replace the entire weapons system, motherboard and all, but until then we could use someone on those guns. Because, right now, those guys out there aren't going to hold back for nothin'." She pointed out the window at the formation of enemy fighters coming into range. In another minute they'd be within firing distance.

Lianica nodded. "I'm on it," she replied, springing into action. She promptly found the cupola hatch on the floor in the center of the bridge and knelt down and opened it. It led down a small gangway that opened up into a confined space with a seat, a joystick, and weapons controls. She gracefully lowered herself down inside and settled into her seat. Strapping herself in, she flipped on the weapons systems and manually took control.

The small cockpit lit up with an array of blinking lights and she breathed in deeply as she grabbed the controls. Outside the view portal of the turret she could make out three Nephilim fighters fast approaching. "We've got bogies at twelve o'clock," she shouted up the gangway from inside her cockpit.

"I see them," Raven replied. "Just give me another thirty seconds to make the calculations to FTL. Just thirty seconds."

"Is that all?" Lianica mumbled to herself. She flicked off the safety and then said in a determined voice, "Weapons hot!"

She smashed down on the triggers and massive bolts of plasma erupted from the disruptor cannons. They streaked across space like tracers from old anti-aircraft machine guns she'd seen in history videos of Dagon's numerous wars in the times before advanced weaponry.

More exciting than the bright green bolts that tore through the Nephilim fighters as though they were made of paper was the massive concussive sound the canons' recoil made as a new plasma bolt was loaded into the firing chamber and ignited.

The sound of it igniting was like a giant buzzing hum, so she knew it was hot. Then, as it shot out it made a whooshing hiss, its energy crackling briefly when the hot plasma met the coldness of space. It sounded like the crackle of lighting before the thunder.

A smile formed on her lips. And she brought the thunder.

The *Skywend* pulled away from the Nephilim fleet as a host of glowing ships began their pursuit. Down below, Lianica roared with a scream that rose from her gut as she blasted away at the enemy fleet.

"All right," Raven said, placing her hand on the throttle of the FTL drive. "Here goes nothing."

She jammed the throttle fully forward and took in a breath. As she breathed in, the stars all around them stretched into thin white lines which began to pulsate in a myriad of random colors that danced across the light spectrum.

Gyllek let out a pent-up sigh and looked over at Raven.

Raven opened the comm to engineering. "Skuld, how are things looking down there?"

"She's in tip-top shape, Captain," he replied. "Not so much as a scratch and the engines are purring like a kitten."

"Excellent. Keep me posted on how the engines are doing. We may be traveling for a while and I can't afford to have them overheating on us."

Gyllek raised an eyebrow. "So we're officially on the run?"

"The Nephilim have just destroyed the Dagon fleet and attacked the empress's vessel. They will likely invade every system from here to the Outer Rim. So, the only way we're going to outlast them is to out run them."

"In that case, I'm glad we have the fastest ship in the fleet."

"The *Shard* was the fastest ship in the fleet," a voice said from behind them.

They both spun around to see Lianica climbing out of the hatch. She closed it behind her.

Raven stood up and went over and extended her hand.

Lianica looked down at Raven's hand and then, after a brief pause, she took it.

"Glad to have you aboard, Captain Blackstar."

"And I'm glad to be aboard, Captain Nightguard."

The two captains held their handshake and their gaze for longer than necessary then finally let go.

Lianica turned toward the front view portal and looked out at the kaleidoscope of lights. "Do you have any plans on where we might be going?"

"There's an old space station beyond the Outer Rim that only a handful of people know about. An old friend of mine runs it."

"Can he be trusted?" asked Lianica, shooting Raven a skeptical look.

"No," Raven replied with a sigh. "But he has no love for the Nyctans and certainly won't have anything to do with the occupation."

"How can you be so sure?"

"Because," Raven said, "he's Galliforn. And the Nephilim just blew up his homeworld."

Lianica nodded. She understood now. She even had a good hunch on who they were going to see. They were going to see the most notorious criminal in the entire galaxy. Grendok of Galliforn.

Not the admiral. Not any one of his numerous clones which he used as smoke screens and red herrings. No, they were cutting through the nebulous decoys and going straight to the man himself. The one man in the entire galaxy who could help them.

"Are you sure he'll help us?" Lianica asked. "It's a lot to ask."

"He'd better," Raven said sternly. "After all, he owes me. Big time for saving his hide a few years back. Oh, and, there's one more thing I neglected to mention."

"What's that?"

"He sort of stole Aldebaran from H'aaztre."

"He what?"

"As it turns out, Aldebaran is a ring world that can traverse hyperspace."

"So, when you said it was a space station...?"

"I lied. It's more than that. It's a planet. A man-made planet, but a planet nonetheless."

"It's spooky is what it is," Gyllek interjected, the hairs on her arm standing up at the mere thought of that dreadful place.

"You've actually been there?" Lianica asked, scanning their faces for any signs that they were pulling her leg. But their sincerity checked out. She could scarcely believe it. If they had the location of Aldebaran, then they could use it to locate H'aaztre's true form and hopefully figure out a way to kill him.

"I wasn't planning on going back anytime soon, but it's our best chance of evading the Nephilim."

"So, the old goat is the real deal. He really is the galaxy's best criminal."

Raven gave a one shoulder shrug. She couldn't deny it even if she wanted to. Only the most cunning criminal in the galaxy would even dare stealing a throne from a king. "It would appear that way."

"To Aldebaran then?"

Raven nodded and gestured for Lianica to take a seat. She did, and Raven returned to her pilot's chair.

After settling into her seat, she reached out and put a hand on Gyllek's shoulder.

Gyllek looked at her, but it wasn't a look of relief, or even of reprieve. They weren't out of the woods yet. The Nephilim would be searching for them. Hunting them. And that didn't sit well with her.

A reassuring squeeze on her shoulder elicited the slightest smile, and Gyllek turned back and did one last check on the auto-pilot. "Everything checks out here, Captain. Now, if you don't mind, I think I'll go help Skuld down in engineering."

Raven nodded and dismissed her. After she left, Lianica took her seat beside Raven. She glanced over her shoulder once, just to be sure Gyllek had left the bridge and then turned and gazed at Raven long and hard.

"It's been a long time…big sis."

"I told you never to call me that," Raven said tersely without looking over at her little sister. "You stopped being family the moment you betrayed mom and dad."

"For heaven's sake, Ray, we've been over this a thousand times. Mom and dad made their choice and I made mine."

Raven swiveled in her seat and glared at her little sister with a pent-up rage that she could barely contain.

"You gave them up to the imperial forces and they were killed because of it. You did that. And here you are, acting like I should just forgive you?"

"What? You don't think I feel bad about it? I feel absolutely terrible. Devastated!" Tears welled up in her eyes, and they grew glossy with the overwhelming remorse she felt. "I didn't know Dakroth would go through such extremes to make an example of them. If I could go back and change things I would. But I can't."

"Just be thankful I didn't leave you back there for the Nephilim and make an example of those who betray their family."

Disturbed by Lianica's dredging up old, painful memories, Raven got up and stormed away.

Lianica reached out toward her big sister. "Ray, wait." But her pleas of forgiveness fell on deaf ears.

Raven left the bridge and let Lianica stay behind to reflect on what she had done. Lianica lowered her hand, realizing she still needed to prove to Raven how truly sorry she was. It wasn't like she was expecting a warm embrace or anything. But she had hoped after thirteen years they could at least sit down and talk about it like two adults.

Losing herself to her thoughts, she stared at the rainbow tunnel of hyperspace swirling about outside the window. She didn't blame Raven for not being able to find it within herself to forgive her. After all, she couldn't even forgive herself.

Lianica wiped a stray tear away with the back of her hand and slumped down in her seat, letting her mind be drawn into the psychedelic light show happening outside of the ship.

In her estimation, it all boiled down to a game of hide and go seek. The ultimate game, because if they were found out, they'd most certainly be killed. Which is precisely why she swore that she'd keep Jegra alive until the very end. If the empress fell, then so too did the galaxy.

As long as Jegra lived, hope lived. And that was a more powerful thing than any amount of madness or chaos a tyrant god could sow.

And maybe, just maybe, if she saw this thing through to the very end, Raven would see how she had changed for the better. Maybe then, her big sister might finally forgive her.

42

A distant shriek roused Callestra from her slumber. When she sat up, she found herself virtually naked with only a burlap loincloth covering her. She was trapped in a dank cell in what appeared to be a dungeon. Her body ached from the cold, and she wrapped her arms around herself and began to rub them to fend off a sudden shiver.

A buzzer startled her and the bars to her cell mysteriously swung open. She slowly got up, covering her blue, naked body the best she could, and slowly crept up to the entrance. She peered out into the dimly lit hallway but didn't see anybody. Stepping out, she glanced up and down, still trying to find clues as to where she was and what she was doing there.

The sound of another buzzer caught her attention and she spun around to see another barred gate swing open. To her great relief, a familiar face stepped out.

"Dakroth?" she said in a pleasantly surprised voice.

The Lord Emperor was also without clothes but for a similar, equally scant, loincloth. He turned to her and eyed her up and down. "Where are we?"

"I don't know. I just woke up," she replied.

He nodded. He too didn't remember anything before waking up here.

A thunderous clank at the end of the corridor resounded and they both spun around to see a heavy metal door rising up. Blinding light came flooding into the holding cell and they averted their eyes.

Once the door had fully opened, Callestra shot Dakroth a deferential look. He took the hint and made his way toward the exit, Callestra treading his heels as they crept toward the radiant mouth at the end of the tunnel. Callestra gently reached up and put her arm on his shoulder. He glanced back and acknowledged her presence but was otherwise unresponsive.

Slowly, both captives stepped into the light. As their eyes adjusted, they found themselves in a massive arena. But that wasn't the strange part. The strange part was that it was empty. Not a soul was seated in the stands. Not even the sound of a bloody cricket could be heard.

"Where are we?" Callestra asked.

"I haven't the foggiest, luv," Dakroth answered.

Their bashfulness wore off, as they were the only ones around. They strode confidently out to the center of the sands of the arena and scanned the empty stadium.

"Do you think this is some sort of deranged payback? Do you think the empress is toying with us?"

"It doesn't seem to be her style. She's not manipulative, like a Dagon. She's rather brunt. If Dagons are akin to a poison that kills you slowly over time, she is a wrecking hammer that smashes your knees out."

"And you actually love her?" Callestra asked, eyeing Dakroth. He smiled at her.

"I have loved many women in my lifetime. She is just another delicacy among a vast platter of lovely appetizers I have whetted my appetite with."

"And how is your appetite now?" Callestra asked him, taking a step forward and placing her hand on his bare chest.

The two of them stared into one another's eyes for the longest time and them came together in a passionate embrace. Their kisses were hungry and their flesh willing. Callestra moaned out as Dakroth reached around and squeezed her bare ass.

Impatient, she threw her arms around his neck and looked up into his ruby red eyes with her sparkling purple ones. "I've waited so long for this," she confessed, her breath hot and savory on his lips.

A blast of hot wind tossed her hair about and they both stopped what they were doing and stepped back to take a breather. Looking over in the direction of where the hot rush of air had come, they saw a young Dagon man with long golden robes, standing several meters off.

The boy, who couldn't have been more than fifteen or sixteen, watched them with curious red eyes that sparkled like rubellites. He didn't greet them or try to approach them, but kept his distance as an observer.

Dakroth felt his temper well up inside of him, but not knowing who this was or what the hell was going on, he decided to take a diplomatic approach instead of killing the insolent kid outright.

"May we help you with something?" he grumbled in irritation.

The young man didn't reply right away. Instead, he watched them for a while longer than blinked a few times. "It's always the same with you two isn't it?"

Callestra quickly shrank behind the emperor to better conceal her nudity from the young man. She wasn't particularly bashful, but there was something about this kid that unnerved her.

"Who are you?" Dakroth demanded to know.

"Don't you recognize me?" the young man asked.

Dakroth squinted. "I've never seen you before in my life. I'd know if I had because I never forget a face."

"And you, Callestra Van Morgan? Do you not recognize me?"

She shook her head. "I've never seen you before." It weirded her out that he knew her name. Not just that, but the way he spoke it. As if she was familiar to him. Like an old friend. The only difference being, when he said her name, her gut clenched with a penetrating and crippling fear.

"I wasn't going to reveal myself to you both just yet, but I couldn't resist. You see, today is a special occasion," the young man said, pacing about as he examined his arms and hands as though her were testing out a new prosthetic.

"What is?" Dakroth demanded to know.

The young man turned and looked at him. His face was serious but then he smiled. "Today marks the day of the Final Tribulation. The day I take what is rightfully mine."

The boy noticed Callestra had drifted away from the conversation and followed her gaze to see what she was looking at. When he realized what it was, he laughed. "Do you like it? I built it to train the best gladiators in the galaxy. After all, the best gladiators make the best warriors, do they not?" He glanced over at Dakroth, who seemed to be mildly amused.

"Where are our clothes?" Callestra asked, feeling self-conscious standing naked in front of what appeared to be a fifteen-year-old boy. If that's even what he was.

"Oh, yes. Don't worry about that," he said, eyeing her up and down and smiling at her with an almost licentious grin. "You won't be needing those. They merely represent the decadence of a fallen empire."

"Fallen empire? What are you talking about? Who are you, really?" Dakroth asked, stepping into the boy's line of sight and preventing him from gawking at Callestra longer than necessary.

"I think you already know the answer to that, Rhadamanthus," the boy said, calling the emperor by his first name just to flaunt the power he held over him. A subtle smile formed on the young man's thin, Prussian blue lips and, in a blink, his eyes changed from ruby red to black with a golden halo that flashed around his dark pupils.

The sudden appearance of those ghastly eyes caused Dakroth to take a step back. "H'aaztre, I presume."

The young man bowed. "In the flesh."

"What do you want with us?" asked Callestra. When the young man's eyes fell on her she moved again, using Dakroth as a human shield to evade his unnerving gaze.

"I want you to fight one another. To the gruesome end. The winner gets to join my army of legionnaires. The loser, I'm afraid, will face a fate worse than death.

"And if we refuse to fight?"

The boy sighed in a disappointed fashion and turned to face Dakroth. "Do you honestly believe you can refuse me?"

Dakroth bit his tongue. Truthfully, he didn't know if he could take this overpowered kid. Regardless, something about this young man was familiar to him. But he couldn't quite put his finger on it.

"So, what?" Callestra asked, clearly irritated. "We're just supposed to wrestle around naked for your pleasure?"

"And why not?" H'aaztre asked. "You've done it hundreds of times for me already."

"What do you mean?"

H'aaztre laughed. "So full of curiosity." Without answering their questions, however, he turned and began to walk toward the massive wooden doors that marked the exit to the arena.

"How many times?" Callestra called out. It was the only question that was on her mind. How many times had she and Dakroth faced off simply to appease some bratty kid?

The young man looked back and smiled at her. "Three hundred and sixty-five, to be exact."

Dakroth and Callestra looked at each other. In that moment, they knew they couldn't let this asshole dictate the conditions of their life. Or their deaths, for that matter.

Simultaneously, Dakroth and Callestra pressed their own glowing fingers to their temples. A nanosecond later, they both discharged their energy blasts and took their own lives.

H'aaztre glanced back at the two dead Dagons lying in the middle of his arena and let out a disappointed sigh. "Well, that was rather unexpected. Perhaps, they're not quite ready."

With that, he turned and walked off the field, leaving the corpses behind.

A distant shriek roused Callestra from her slumber. When she sat up, she found herself virtually naked with only a burlap loincloth covering her. She was trapped in a dank cell in what appeared to be a dungeon. Her body ached from the cold, and she wrapped her arms around herself and began to rub them to fend off a sudden shiver.

A buzzer startled her and the bars to her cell mysteriously swung open. She crept up to the entrance and peered out into the dimly lit hallway. It was empty. Stepping out, she glanced up and down the hallway when another buzzer sounded. She twisted around to see another barred gate swing open. To her great relief, a familiar face stepped out.

"Dakroth?" she said in a pleasantly surprised voice.

The Lord Emperor was also without clothes, all but for a loincloth, as scant as hers. He turned to her and eyed her up and down. "Where are we?"

"I don't know. I just woke up."

"Me too," she said.

Dakroth paused momentarily, a strange sensation seizing him. Apparently Callestra noticed it too, because she placed her hand on his arm.

"What is it?" Callestra asked.

"I don't know…But I just had a sudden feeling of déjà vu. It's as though…"

"We've been here before," she said, finishing his sentence.

They shared a grave look. Something was seriously off about this place. They both could feel it.

An abrupt clank at the end of the corridor resounded and they both spun around to discover a heavy metal door rising up. Blinding light came flooding into the holding cell and they averted their eyes.

Once the door had fully opened, Callestra shot Dakroth a deferential look. He took the hint and made his way toward the exit, Callestra treading his heels as they crept toward the radiant mouth at the end of the tunnel. Callestra gently reached up and put her arm on his shoulder. He glanced back and acknowledged her presence but was otherwise unresponsive.

Slowly, they stepped into the light. As their eyes adjusted, they found themselves in a massive arena. It was all so familiar.

"Where are we?" Callestra asked.

"I haven't the foggiest, luv," Dakroth answered. "But for some reason, I know we've been here before. I'm sure of it."

She nodded in agreement with him as they made their way out to the center of the arena and scanned the empty stadium.

Callestra reached over and took Dakroth's hand in hers. "All of a sudden I'm feeling sick to my stomach."

"Chin up, my dear. We'll get through this. I promise." Dakroth smiled at her and she smiled back.

Whatever nightmare they were in, at least they didn't have to go through it alone. That's when the visions seized them.

Terrible visions of violence and brutality flashed before Callestra's eyes. Gruesome images of Dakroth's bloodied corpse. Every image that reeled past her vision consisted of him dying a slightly different, yet equally grisly death. Gore and blood, disembowelment, evisceration, flesh and bone.

She saw herself slice him open with a blade, reach into his abdomen, and tear out his insides. She laughed hysterically the whole time she disemboweled him. Unable to stop her, he merely screamed horrifically.

As the visions increased in frequency so too did the mental anguish. She screamed out when it all became overwhelming for her. Dropping to her knees, she clutched her temples and mumbled for the visions to go away.

"What is it?" Dakroth asked. Then the same happened to him. Seized by awful visions, he too dropped to his knees.

His visions were of Callestra's demise. Her broken and deformed body laying at his feet. A burned corpse. Then him tearing her heart out and, holding it high above him, squeezing the last of its contents out onto his face as he laughed hysterically.

"W-what's happening to us?" Callestra asked.

"I don't know," Dakroth said through gritted teeth.

All at once, the intense visions stopped and both Dakroth and Callestra took deep breaths and collapsed to the ground. They lay on the sands of the arena panting, their bodies glazed in the balmy sweat left by crippling fear and anxiety.

Before they could fully catch their breath, however, the visions started up again. But this time they were magnitudes worse.

Callestra's back arched and she screamed out as loud as she could. It felt as though her vocal cords would tear right out of her throat. She felt Dakroth's hands at her throat and she tried to fight him off. She wasn't sure if it was real or just another one of the visions, but soon enough, her worst fears were confirmed.

Her eyes rolled back in her head, only the whites showing, and her eyelids fluttered spastically before everything went dark.

A distant shriek roused Callestra from her slumber. When she woke up, she found herself naked and trapped in a dank cell in what appeared to be a dungeon. Sensing a shiver come on, she wrapped her arms around herself and began to rub her arms.

"What is happening to me?" she whispered. Something was dreadfully wrong. She could feel it in her bones. And whatever it was, somehow, she knew she'd been here. And she knew she'd be here again.

But the worst part of it all was, she didn't know how to escape it. Not the paralyzing bouts of déjà vu. Not the weight of dread that hung over her like a malevolent specter. Whatever was keeping her here, it wouldn't let her go. She was, quite literally, trapped inside a living hell.

BOOK 3
EPILOGUE

Dark and dusty skies hung over the New York City skyline like an old gray blanket. The clouds were so pregnant with rain that they were ready to burst any minute and a cool breeze rolled in from the east. Yellow taxis honked noisily up and down the bustling patchwork of city blocks and streets, all the way from Wall Street to Times Square.

A flash of golden light above the Empire State Building sent out a shockwave that blew the rainclouds away, blasting them into billows of steam. A massive alien ship that pulsated with a strange golden energy had manifested out of nowhere, causing a commotion in the streets below.

Cars crashed into one another, people stopped checking their cell phones and began holding them up to the sky to take pictures of the alien vessel. A baby's wailing could be heard in the distance along with the ruckus of neighborhood dogs barking in every corner of the city.

Every neighborhood and borough, from the Bronx to Central Park, to Greenwich village all the way down to Wall Street and Hudson River Park, from Staten Island to Long Island, everywhere was abuzz with the arrival of visitors form another world.

Meanwhile, the Statue of Liberty watched on from Liberty Island with her customary sunken gaze, looking on as three beams of light touched down in the center of Manhattan.

Times Square bustled with people who paused their typical busy chatter and ceaseless motion to watch as three beings of radiant golden light miraculously appeared to them.

There was a woman, a toad like creature, and a man with wings. They were massive, nearly ten feet tall and dressed in decadent armor that glowed and pulsed with an otherworldly energy.

"So," Nodengoth said, fanning his wings as he slowly turned and looked out at all the stunned faces and gaping jaws that stared back at him, "this is the Empress's homeworld."

"It doesn't look like much," Azra'il replied.

"Should be ripe for the picking, yep, ripe for the picking," Giddion said, restraining his urge to jump around.

"Excuse me," an elderly man said. He held a thick black book with gilded pages and clasped a golden necklace in his hands, nervously twiddling the X-shaped jewelry between his bony fingers. He had on a black suit of some kind with a white collar. "Are you Him? Are you our Lord and Savior?"

All three avatars of H'aaztre smiled down at the man. With a gentle hand, Nodengoth reached out and touched the small Earthling's head. "Why, yes. Yes, I am your Lord and Savior."

The man dropped to his knees and, raising the crucifix high into the air, shouted out, "Hallelujah! Praise be to Jesus Christ! For He has returned!"

H'aaztre glanced at his siblings and then back to the man, a perplexed look on his face. "I'm sorry, my dear servant. But I think you have mistaken me for someone else."

The man looked up in shock and trembled as H'aaztre placed his massive palm on the top of the man's head. "I am your Lord. No others. Certainly not this...Jesus you speak of."

"But...I thought..."

"Shhh," Nodengoth said, hushing the man to silence.

In a flash, the man turned to ashes, vaporized before everyone's eyes, including the nearby news crew, who broadcast the proceedings all across the world.

"Is this some kind of act?" a tourist asked, flashing a photo of the three golden beings.

"Oh, I assure you, my darlings, it's no act," the Voice said. She raised her hand and a pulse of radiant energy wavered. The tourist instantly disintegrated to ash, just as the man had.

"Ooh, what fun! What fun, indeed!" Giddion chirped excitedly. He hopped around vaporizing people left and right.

"That's quite enough," Nodengoth said, after Giddion had taken out seven people.

Pandemonium broke out in the streets as the revelation dawned on the people that this wasn't an act. This was real.

H'aaztre looked around as everyone scurried about like screaming cockroaches when his eyes settled on the news crew. Turning to the cameras, he addressed the world.

"I am the Gilded Master, bearer of the Yellow Sign. I represent the Body of the One True God, H'aaztre. She is the Voice, she represents H'aaztre's divine will. And our little friend here is H'aaztre's Ears and Eyes."

The streets were starting to empty just as sirens could be heard as the NYPD made their way to Times Square.

Nodengoth raised his hands high into the sky in a dramatic yet undeniably pious gesture. "All we ask of you, people of Earth, is to surrender yourself to him. Allow him to show you the light."

Azra'il Nun continued where Nodengoth left off and said, "Honor him with your humble obedience, kneel before us and promise us your everlasting devotion."

Giddion hopped up onto a nearby car, and raised his hands to the sky, "Promise your life to the Lord Et'vat H'aaztre, and rejoice."

"Or," Nodengoth added, the ominous proselytizing coming back around to him. "Watch your world burn for its insolent defiance! The choice is yours. Please, my brethren, choose wisely. The very fate of your world depends upon it."

BOOK THREE
FINIS

Tristan Vick is a multi-genre author who specializes in sci-fi, fantasy, and horror and has dabbled in mystery and suspense as well. He graduated from Montana State University with degrees in English Literature and Asian Cultural Studies and speaks fluent Japanese. He lives with his wife and three children in Japan. When he's not commuting on the train or teaching English, he spends his time reading, writing, blogging, binge-watching his favorite television shows, and eating sara-udon. In addition to being traditionally published, Tristan Vick continues to self-publish under his own imprint, Regolith Publications. You can learn more about him and his works on his official author webpage at:

Visit Tristan Vick's official author website at:

www.tristanvick.com